Funeral Nights

Kynpham
Sing Nongkynrih

SHEFFIELD – LONDON – NEW YORK

First published in the UK and USA in 2024 by And Other Stories
Sheffield – London – New York
www.andotherstories.org

Originally published in India in 2021.
Copyright © Kynpham Sing Nongkynrih, 2021

1 3 5 7 9 8 6 4 2

ISBN: 9781913505967
eBook ISBN: 9781913505974

Series Cover Design: Elisa von Randow, Alles Blau Studio, Brazil, after a
concept by And Other Stories; Author Photo: Miss Marbiang Khongwir.

And Other Stories books are printed and bound by CPI in the UK on FSC-certified paper.
The covers are of G . F Smith 270gsm Colorplan card, which is sustainably manufactured at
the James Cropper paper mill in the Lake District, and are stamped with biodegradable foil.

A catalogue record for this book is available from the British Library.

And Other Stories gratefully acknowledge that our work is
supported using public funding by Arts Council England.

Supported using public funding by
**ARTS COUNCIL
ENGLAND**

MIX
Paper | Supporting
responsible forestry
FSC® C171272

To
All Khasis—
Khynriam, U Pnar, U Bhoi, U War,
Maram, Lyngngam, Nongtrai-Muliang.

'Literature that is not the breath of contemporary society, that dares not transmit the pains and fears of that society, that does not warn in time against threatening moral and social dangers—such literature does not deserve the name of literature; it is only a facade.'

—Alexander Solzhenitsyn

Contents

Acknowledgements

Most of the action in *Funeral Nights* takes place in the jungle village of Nongshyrkon. My gratitude, therefore, is especially due to the people who helped me during my journey to that village. Among them were Denzel Nongkynrih, Yondalin Nongkynrih, Dhoi Nongkynrih, and members of the family that conducted the elaborate rites of Ka Phor Sorat, the feast of the dead, many years ago. Chandra Shyrkon, Werly Shyrkon and one of their cousins (who does not wish to be identified) were the most resourceful of all my guides. They have been transformed, with their permission, into the characters of Chirag, Perly and Victor. The novel's other major characters are entirely fictional, though, as Horace suggests, I did 'look to life and morals' for my real models, and I did try to 'draw thence, a language true to life'.

I am also deeply grateful to my late mother, Perisibon Nongkynrih; to my late uncle, Mama Hores; to my elder brother, Khaiñsing Nongkynrih; and to my friends, Kamailang Nongmalieh, Robin Singh Ngangom, Ever E.F. Sancley, Mebanker Lapang and Sukalpa Bhattacharjee, for sharing their stories with me over the years.

Others who helped me in one way or another, consciously or unconsciously, include Rimi Nath, Raphael Warjri, Lostin Lawrence Kharbani, Kanchan Verma, Vivek Menezes, Mridula Nath Chakraborty, Justman Synrem, Christene Nongbet, Shongdor Diengdoh, Tarun Bhartiya, Constantine Jaraiñ, Gavett R. Rumnong, Samuel Jyrwa, Mona Zote, A. Blah, Ires Rynjah, Praiñ Syiemlieh, Ravikant Kshetrimayum, K. M. Deb, Suranjana Choudhury, S. F. Rynjah, Willie Gordon Suting, the late August Bang, and members of my family, Lyngksiar, Marbiang and Ruby. I thankfully acknowledge their contributions.

My super-efficient editors, Karthika V.K., Ajitha G.S. and Dipanjali Chadha, trimmed the rough edges of the novel with a very sharp knife; Saurabh Garge and Lyngksiar designed a stunning cover, and my poet friend, Michael Scharf, assisted me in all sorts of ways. I am forever in your debt.

My special thanks to the kind well-wisher who helped with the production of this book. Your wish to remain anonymous is all the more appreciated. Additionally, my gratitude is due to the following journals, magazines and anthologies, where some of the sections included here first appeared:

Planet: The Welsh Internationalist, Wasafiri, India Today Travel Plus, Down to Earth, Indian Literature, The Oxford Anthology of Writings from North-East India, Pilgrim's India, Fresh Fictions, Earth Songs, Where the Sun Rises When Shadows Fall, Day's End Stories, Talk of the Town, GPlus, Raiot, Café Dissensus, The Hindu Business Line, 100 Great Indian Poems, The Indian Quarterly, Ka Thwet Jingstad and *Ka Thiar ki Nongthoh*.

1

MY NAME IS
AP JUTANG

'In all my writing, I tell the story
of my life over and over again.'

—Isaac Bashevis Singer

My name is Ap Jutang, a rare and beautiful name (even if I say so myself), perhaps the rarest and most beautiful of all Khasi names, meaning 'keeper of the covenant'. And what is more, unlike many Khasi names, it is not a big tongue-twister. Even non-Khasis manage to pronounce it properly. I know this for sure, because many of my non-Khasi friends say it exactly as it should be—/ap ju:taŋ/, that is how it should be said.

But I don't know if that's how I should begin. Perhaps I should first clarify that, when I speak of Khasis, I mean the Khasi people of Meghalaya in northeastern India. The mainlanders used to call us Khasia because Khasi sounds too much like *khasi–sardi*, cough-and-cold, and taking a cue from them, the British began calling us Cossia or Cassia. But we are 'Ki Khasi', the Khasis, scions of the Hynñiew Trep people, the seven sub-tribes. Among these sub-tribes are the Khynriams of Ri Khynriam, East Khasi Hills; the Pnars of Ri Pnar, Jaiñtia Hills; the Bhois of Ri Bhoi district; the Wars of the Ri War areas bordering Bangladesh; the Marams of Ri Maram, West Khasi Hills; the Lyngngams of Ri Lyngngam, West Khasi Hills; and the now-never-heard-of Dikos, whom many believe to be instead the still existing Nongtrais and Muliangs also of West Khasi Hills. Khasis also live in many parts of Assam and the Sylhet district of Bangladesh.

Now that's out of the way, I can return to my introduction. Khasi names are, as a rule, exotic to non-Khasi ears, more exotic still when mouthed by non-Khasi tongues. My friend is called Kynpham—among our more easily pronounceable names, but the best that many non-Khasis can do with it is 'Kingpam'. Or Kimpan, Kingpin, Fiang Fiang and so on. The worst distortion was by Douglas Smith, an Englishman who visited the Khasi Hills in 1995. Smith's friends used to call him Doug, but Khasis, because they could not manage that properly, called him, out of respect, 'Mr Dog'. But proving himself as bad as the Khasis, Mr Dog called Kynpham 'Flimflam'. No such embarrassment, however, has ever come my way. I am truly grateful to my mother for giving such careful thought to my name and what might happen to it.

Mostly, though, I'm not even called Ap Jutang. Some people call me *Bah Ap*, which means 'elder brother Ap', or roughly, 'Mr Ap'. This is a peculiar

Khasi practice. If you are Ap Jutang, people will call you 'Bah Ap'; and if you are Risa, they will call you '*Kong* Ri', 'elder sister Ri', or 'Miss Ri' or 'Ms Ri'. I suppose it's a way of simultaneously expressing closeness and respect, or perhaps even a way of reducing one's linguistic burden. Friends and my immediate family call me Ap, but all my relatives call me Bahduh since I am the youngest in the family. This is another odd Khasi practice: the persistent use of kinship terms. If you are the eldest son, relatives will call you Bahbah or Bahheh, which means 'eldest brother'; if you are next to the eldest, they will call you either Bahdeng, 'middle brother', or Bahrit or Hep or Bahhep (signifying an indeterminate 'younger brother'); if you are the youngest, they will call you Bahduh. The same thing goes for girls: the eldest are Kongkong or Kongheh, the middle ones are Kongdeng or Kongrit, and those at the end of the line are Duhduh. Sometimes, daughters between the first and the last will be called Kongnah or Konghep (signifying an indeterminate 'younger sister'), or even Kongieit, 'beloved sister'.

But there's more. There's Hephep, Heprit, Heplung, Hepieit and so on for sons (sometimes for daughters as well) and Theiheh, Theirit, Theilung, Theiieit and so on for daughters. We apply the same principle to uncles and aunts, so your eldest uncle may be a Mabah—sorry, Mabah is 'granduncle'—a Maheh or a Marangbah; your middle uncle a Madeng or a Marit or a Makhynnah; your youngest uncle, a Maduh. In the same way, your eldest aunt may be a Meiheh or a Meirangbah or a Meisan; your middle aunt a Meideng or a Meirit or a Meikhynnah; your youngest aunt, a Meiduh.

Confused? Not to worry: we are too. In fact, Khasi militants, in their heyday between 1993 and 2001, realised the tactical value of these terms and took to calling each other Marangbah, Maheh, Marit and so on. The heads of the state police, many of whom were non-Khasis, were in a spin trying to sort out who was who.

With parents, it gets worse. We are truly teknonymous with them. Near relatives, for instance, would rather call my mother Mother of Ap than by her real name or even her pet name, Kongrit. The consequence of all this is that most names fall into desuetude. Take the following conversation, for instance:

'Do you know what Hep did yesterday?'

'Which Hep?'

'U Hep, *mə*, who lives in Block 6?'

'But which one? There are many Heps in Block 6!'

'The one who drives a taxi.'

'But there are many Heps who drive taxis! Which one?'

'The bow-legged one.'

'Oh, you mean U Hep Bracket! Why didn't you say so?'

Or this:

'What is the name of Bahbah?'

'What Bahbah?'

'Bahbah, mə, Meiduh's son!'

'Meiduh of Khliehshnong or Pdengshnong?'

A quick side note: 'mə' (pronounced /mə/ as in 'huh') is a crude way of addressing close male acquaintances. So 'Bahbah, mə' would roughly correspond to 'Bahbah, man'. The equivalent of this for women is 'pha'. A more courteous way to address both men and women is 'phi', like the French 'vous'. 'U' (pronounced /u/ not /juː/) is also a masculine marker used before the name of a male. For a female, we use 'ka', but if we want to be nice, we use 'I' (pronounced /iː/ as in 'we') for both men and women. I'm sure I'll be using a lot of these expressions, so you may as well be told about them now.

But to return to pet names: when newspapers publish obituary notices, they always mention the names of the dead with their pet names within brackets. So, for instance, Mr Pimpdoris Lyngdoh will be followed by 'Bahhep Pimp' within brackets. (More on names such as this a little later—in Chapter IV, to be precise.)

❧

Sohra is my birthplace, where my ancestral home is, and though only tenants live in it now, two rooms have been left vacant so we can use them whenever we visit. I usually spend my winters there because it's slightly warmer than here in Shillong. But that's just something I used to say to myself; the truth is that I love everything about Sohra, for it was there, to use the words of Welsh writer John Owen of Morfa Nefyn about Anglesey, 'that [I] was born and raised, it was there that [my] mother taught [me] to talk, it was there that the paths were which [I] had walked as a child'.

I'd like to tell you a few things about Sohra. I do believe that, in telling you about it, I will reveal myself, for everything that I am has been shaped and moulded by my hometown—not only by the customs and manners of Sohra's people but also by the silent influence of the hills, rivers and woods that surround it and surround me still.

This book is not about Sohra or me. It is, as the title suggests, about the unique funeral traditions of the Khasis—especially the funeral nights that are so full of tales and stimulating talk. I only introduced myself because I thought you might also want to know a little about me—the narrator—and my friends, the other characters, before you spend time with us.

So, to continue, the name Sohra is a strange one. Not many people know what it means, not even the people who live there. I do, though, because I know many things Khasi. I'm not bragging. That's the last thing I'd like people to think of me. You could describe me as a practitioner of the community's faith and customs, which, in turn, has made me a curious and interested seeker of all things Khasi—even though I'm not an enthusiastic believer when it comes to religion. And there lies the difference between many of my compatriots and me.

Sohra was founded by the people of Khatar Shnong, a province of twelve Ri War villages to the north and east of Sohra, and by those of Khathynriew Shnong, a province of sixteen Ri War villages to the south and west. Their villages were situated on precipitous jungled slopes or deep at the bottom of even more thickly jungled gorges. The only approach to them was in the form of uneven steps roughly cut into sheer cliff faces, which made it difficult for the villagers to meet, trade and barter daily. The two provinces, therefore, came together and created a central marketplace on a level field, which was in those days simply called Madan Umleng or Ïewrim. Situated on a vast mountaintop tableland, it commanded a sweeping view of the villages below, those on the slopes and in the gorges. The market was held twice a week, on Ïewbah, or big-market day, and on Ïewpohïa, or small-market day. There was a gap of four days between the two and a gap of eight days between one big-market day and the next. The four-day gap is known as *ka ïa*, or the half-week, and the eight-day gap is known as *ka taïew*, or the week. It is from this practice that Khasis evolved the eight-day week, which, incidentally, makes the Beatles' *Eight Days a Week* not so charmingly far-fetched after all.

From establishing the market, it was but a tiny step to settlement: some people, rather than make the gruelling journey back and forth every market day, chose to build homes near the marketplace, earning their livelihood by providing services to the market-goers and traders. The settlement grew quickly in size, and soon it was the biggest, most flourishing community in the area. As is the custom with Khasis, the founding clans of the town became the *bakhraws*, that is, the nobles or the ruling clans. Among them (just to give you an idea of Khasi clan names) were the Nongrum, Khongwir, Shrieh, Myrboh, Tham, Nongtraw, Majaw, Umdor, Dohling, Mawdkhap, Sohkhia and Diengdoh clans. The Myrbohs and Sohkhias were later replaced by the

Kharngapkynta and Nongtariang clans. That said, I must also point out that clans considered as the Sohra nobility may be just ordinary clans elsewhere. And even in Sohra, they are nobles only in terms of administrative functions. In the social set-up, which is casteless and classless, they are neither above nor below any other clan.

Over time, the new settlement grew in influence, rapidly becoming the focal point for all the outlying villages, including the original twelve in the north-east and the sixteen in the south-west. In short, it became the capital of the surrounding territory.

At around this time, there was a fierce dispute between the people of Mawphu from the Khathynriew Shnong province and the people of Laitïam, in the south-east. The people of Laitïam were backed by two other villages, Ryngud and Sohbar. Both claimed ownership of a large tract of land bordering the heavily wooded River Umïong that extended up to another river called Risaw, north of Umïong. Soon, a protracted war broke out. The Mawphus killed the warrior leader of the Laitïams, called U Dei, near a place known as Nongsawlia; however, the Laitïams retaliated and killed the Mawphus' warrior leader, called U Sohmen, not too far from where Dei had fallen. These places came to be known as Pomudei and Pomsohmen, that is, the hacking-of-Dei and the hacking-of-Sohmen. At this juncture, the founding clans of the new settlement of Sohra intervened. They talked to both parties about how futile and destructive the war had already been, and offered the idea of merging all their villages into a single *hima*, or state, comprising the provinces of Khatar Shnong, Khathynriew Shnong and Ki Lai Shnong—the three villages of Laitïam, Ryngud and Sohbar. The warring parties readily agreed, and a new state was born out of the war.

The founding clans now began to look for a *syiem*, a king, who would be wholly responsible for the day-to-day administration. But nobody wanted a king from one of the other clans. They did not want to grant that kind of power and prominence to one who was not their own. It was when they were sitting in an open *dorbar* (council), trying to find a ruler, that a gentlewoman of divine grace mysteriously appeared out of nowhere and declared in front of the founding clans that her children would be the kings of the new state. When asked for her name, she said, 'Sohra', and when asked for her purpose, she said, 'My purpose is to teach grace and good manners to the people.'

From that time, the new settlement was known as Sohra (for the settlement itself), Hima Sohra (for the state of Sohra) and Ri Sohra (for the country of

Sohra). The names were given in honour of the mysterious woman, who, true to her word, tutored the people in the ways of civilised living and refined manners. It is for this reason that the community regards Sohra as the birthplace of Khasi etiquette and good conduct—'ka akor Sohra', a kind of savoir-vivre.

But though the woman was accepted as divine, or at least as an agent of divine intervention, nobody thought of asking her what her name meant. It was only much later that people realised that she had chosen a name to reflect the most typical feature of the Sohra landscape. Since it is the wettest place on earth (I am sticking to this assertion because, although Mawsynram, the other East Khasi Hills village, has recorded higher precipitation now and then, the matter is far from settled—rain being a notoriously whimsical thing) and has a gently sloping tableland overlooking the plains of Bangladesh, Sohra has no topsoil. All of its topsoil has been washed away, either to the fertile and heavily forested gorges at the foot of the tableland, known as Ri War (where the War people live in their bountiful jungle farms), or to the plains of Sylhet, which are transformed every summer by the pelting rain of Sohra into a gigantic inland ocean. It follows then that Sohra is a place where nothing grows. And that is the meaning of Sohra: fruitless. In a way, the name completely justifies the description of the place as the wettest desert on earth.

There is another version too about the founding of Sohra, but this, I believe, is the authentic version. I may tell you the other one later.

And yet, to say that Sohra is a wet desert is not the whole truth either, for it is encircled by law kyntangs (sacred forests), law adong (prohibited forests), law shnong (community forests) and law kur (clan forests), which grow in ravines, low-lying valleys, hill slopes and catchment areas within the tableland itself. I will tell you more about them, or at least about our sacred forests, by and by.

Or perhaps I will only speak of them if there is a suitable occasion. What's the point in talking about anything if you cannot make it enjoyable? That's what I always say and that's something I keep in mind during my lectures. Oh yes, I do a lot of lecturing, though that's not my primary job. In fact, I do not have a job. I've just resigned from my position as a university lecturer to become a full-time writer. My mother calls me a fool, and when she shouts at me in anger and bitterness, I am often reminded of the plight of a friend, a poor Nepali farmer, who writes poetry in Khasi. His wife, a termagant Bhoi peasant, harangues him daily: 'You lazy good-for-nothing! Can you dig potatoes with poetry; can you buy dried fish with it?' This woman always raises my hackles: it is as if she were indicting me too, you know? Otherwise, I love women. Many women have inspired me. I do not know if I could write at all without their inspiration. That I am not married already is because I find it more exciting to live in this state of perpetual possibilities. If you do not understand what I mean, consider this poem:

…[that] electric sparkle,
that silent laughter in their eyes,
inviting, daring, mocking …
Those eyes that lifted to him unexpectedly,
the opening of petals, the parting of dawn,
the day that begins with a new zest—
eyes …
haven't we known those eyes
that danced naughtily seeing your eyes?
Weavers of romances and dark fantasies!
Each one had been such a possibility,
a love, a joy, a celebration …

It is precisely like that with me. Every nice woman I meet is a hope, a promise and an inspiration. But that is not the whole truth. Should the opportunity arise, I'll tell you more about my love life and my beloved Saia.

Anyway, this is what I do nowadays; my mother may not think much of me, but who knows, I may yet make it big, my books may yet become textbooks—the hope of every Khasi writer, since Khasis do not read books except in school—and I may yet earn a lot of money. Not from writing, of course. There's no money in writing books unless you become a bestselling author, and there's no hope of that if you write in Khasi. My mother knows it too, which is why she calls me a fool. What I mean to say is that I have a little side-business in real estate: that may flourish in time. But I am not ambitious that way. I do not desire riches. I am happily well-off from the income I get from my two houses here in the city. (Most Khasis fondly call Shillong a city, although a fierce debate still rages as to whether it is a town or a city.) No, I am not ambitious in that way at all. My hope is simply this: that my name should make itself heard like the sound of the wind and the rain blowing and pouring according to the season. It is in that hope that I have started writing in English, for whatever you may say about this language, cannibalistic or not, it is still the key to a wider world.

The lecturing I do is mainly due to my reputation as an authority on Khasi culture. I am invited to deliver talks by this or that organisation, but primarily by units of Seng Khasi. This organisation describes itself as the custodian of *Niam Khasi*, the indigenous Khasi religion, and of Khasi culture. It organises many *seng pyni*, or instructive gatherings, for the benefit of the faithful. I am often called to these gatherings as a resource person. That does not mean I am a religious fanatic. No Khasi–Khasi ever is, since his religion recognises the same God, not only for every human being, but also for every creature on earth.

Khasi–Khasi is a playful name we give to a Khasi who, like me, adheres to the indigenous faith. (I, of course, adhere only in name. I am more interested in my people as a race and in their cultural wisdom. In fact, though I know a great deal about the Khasi religion, I am not even remotely religious. I quarrel a lot with God. But that does not really mean anything, does it? I mean, being irreligious and quarrelling with God is surely not the same as being wicked, is it?) In the same manner, a Khasi convert is called Khasi-Presbyterian, Khasi-Catholic, Khasi-Hindu or Khasi-Muslim, though there are not too many in the last two categories.

The British, whom we call *phareng* (from 'feringhee') or *ki dohlieh* (white meat) or *ki sahep Bilat* (the sahibs of Britain), came to Sohra in 1828 when David Scott (the Governor-General's Agent to the Northeast Frontier of Bengal) built his house on the plateau, having obtained permission from the king in exchange for land in the plains of Sylhet. After the Anglo–Khasi War (or the Khasi War of Freedom, as we would rather call it) came to an end in 1833, the saheps established Sohra as the first capital of the Khasi–Jaiñtia Hills, and then as the capital of the united province of Assam. But when they first arrived, they found it hard to pronounce the name of the place and called it Cherra, and later, Cherrapunjee. As with everything British in India, this mispronunciation quickly and effectively tossed the rightful name into local and partisan usage.

☙

In the 1990s, I found myself in Delhi for the first time. It was also the first time I came face to face with the naked truth about how the rest of India treats its citizens from the hills of the Northeast. During that trip, I suffered from a deep sense of alienation. People thought I was from Japan or China or Korea, and at the hotel where I stayed, the rude fellow at the desk actually asked for my passport. I was just too different. I didn't look like the rest of them; I didn't speak like them; I didn't act like them. Had they known me, they would have learnt that I didn't eat like them.

Nobody knew about our state (carved out of Assam in 1972) or about the beautiful city of Shillong where I lived. When I told people that I came from Meghalaya, they asked me, 'Where's that?' And when I told them of Shillong, they responded, 'Ceylon? You're from Ceylon?' To make things worse, the Hindi they spoke was almost incomprehensible to me since I knew only the bazaar Hindi of Shillong. It was in sheer frustration, therefore, that I replied to a rickshaw wallah: 'I'm from Cherrapunjee. Do you know Cherrapunjee?'

To my utter surprise, he replied, '*Wahan to bahut zyada barish hai.*' ('They have a lot of rain over there.')

I was so moved that I took hold of that *mama*, that uncle, and embraced him like a brother. Cherrapunjee had saved the day for me, and I said to myself, 'So, they do know about us after all. Thank you, Sohra.'

After that, of course, I used the name of Cherrapunjee everywhere. Regardless of its origin, it brought me lots of smiles.

I love everything about Sohra, including things that many of my friends find extremely unpleasant. And as it is the birthplace of education in the hills, I am also very proud of it. Formal Western education in Northeast India originated in Sohra, where the first schools were established by the Welsh Methodist missionaries a little after 1842. Since then, Sohra has produced many great (relatively speaking, obviously) writers and scholars. Among them were the pioneering writers who broke the missionaries' monopoly over cultural and literary matters towards the end of the nineteenth century. Sohra remains a significant centre of learning even now and continues to draw inspiration from its famous sons, such as Rabon Singh Kharsuka, the first Khasi to ever write a book, and Soso Tham, the Khasi bard.

But most of all, I love the pure, wild rain of Sohra, which has baptised me over and over in its holy waters, linking my soul forever with its cloud-tending wind and its cherubic mists floating among, and hanging from, verdant summer trees in sanctified woods. As the rain of Chile was to Neruda, the rain of Sohra is to me 'an unforgettable presence'. I never tire of reading poems and writings on the Sohra rain:

This is the famed rain,
making a fool of sorry umbrellas!

Zooming in like swarms of fighter planes!
Bouncing back metres high to the sky!
Now it sprints with the wind!
Now it turns waltzing round!
Now it's a million whips
for the gale to lash at pretty legs!
And now, it's a violent downpour
to whitewash the ditches and the roads
till at last, the fog comes cloaking all.

It is because of this multifariousness and its divergent nature that Khasis have so many names for the rain: *Slap* (rain), *lapbah* (heavy rain), *lapsan* (immense rain), *lap-theh-ktang* (pouring-from-bamboo-tube rain), *lap-lai-miet* (three-night rain), *lap-hynriew-miet* (six-night rain), *lap-khyndai-miet* (nine-night rain), *lapphria* (hail rain), *lap-erïong* (dark-wind rain/ black storm), *u kyllang* (stormy rain), *lapiwtung* (smelly rain, because it continues for many days, causing clothes to stink), *lappraw* (light rain), *lap-boi-ksi* (louse-swarming rain, because it looks like lice and nits when it settles on hair and clothes), *lap-ñiup-ñiup* (soft, flaky rain, very light drizzle), *lapshiliang* (partial rain), *laplynnong* (rain confined to certain locales), *lapkynriang* (slanting rain), *lapmynsaw* (rain of danger, which has both literal and metaphorical meanings) and *lap-bam-briew* (human-devouring rain, because it does not stop until some human has fallen victim to a rain-triggered disaster).

If you read the statistical handbooks, you will know that Sohra gets an average of more than 12,000 mm of rain per year, and often as much as 450 mm in a single day. On 19 August 2015, for instance, it shattered a ten-year-old record when it received as much rain as 471.7 mm in twenty-four hours. However, the 1964 record of 853 mm within the same period, which also made Sohra the wettest place on earth, still stands. The highest recorded total annual rainfall was 24,555 mm in 1974. And, typically, all this rain falls within a period of six months, from April to September, although it can continue right up to October and even into the first two weeks of November. But again, this is hardly the complete picture. The fact is, we often get the first rain of the year as early as January or February. This early rain, however, is intermittent and does not become fierce and big and heavy and incessant till about April. From this you can easily see how silly the claim is that the rain in India is born in Kerala. While Kerala gets its first rain in June, we get it in January or February.

The rain, coming from the hills and driving with fury through the land, used to scare people out of their wits. Those with tin roofs used to spend sleepless nights intoning mantras and saying, 'Mab Blei, mab Blei' ('God forgive, God forgive'). There was no saying when the rain would suddenly switch to the terrible Sohra *erïong*, the dark tempest. When the erïong came, corrugated sheets flapped like wings, making deafening sounds the whole night through—sometimes they flew right off. Forests spun around and swung violently from side to side in a mad rhythm; trees collapsed; hills growled; overhanging rocks tumbled down precipices as the rain poured into roaring waterfalls to wreak even greater havoc in the plains of River Surma in Bangladesh. This is the kind of rain that poets have described as the season of continuous darkness, when:

> The sun too is not there that rises or sets;
> Only now and then would it peep from the cloud that is dense,
> At the sea frothing white and the gleeful waterfalls.

Many of my friends do not share my enthusiasm for a Sohra that is all water, wind, cloud, darkness and terrorising tempests. Why, they wonder, would I experience a *hiraeth*, a heartrending longing, for such a land? And why should I take so much pride in the relentless rain? Had it not—according to well-known Welsh writer Nigel Jenkins, author of *Through the Green Doors: Travels Among the Khasis*—dismayed even the 'web-footed Welsh' missionaries and driven 'many a demented Company wallah to suicide'? But how will people who fear to get their feet wet understand that we used to jump for joy when it rained, that with cries of 'Yahoo!' we would tear off our clothes and rush out with bars of soap to bathe naked in the downpour? And bathing we would sing:

> *Ther, ther lapbah lapsan,*
> *Ban dup pait ka maw ka dieng,*
> *Ban dup tat u kba u khaw,*
> *Ther, ther lapbah lapsan.*

> (Strike, strike big rain, great rain,
> That the stone the wood would break,
> That the rice the grain would be cheap
> Strike, strike big rain, great rain.)

Or this song:

Ah, ah, ah, ba la ther u lap Sohra!
Syngit ki jaiñ ngi pynjyndong,
Shong kali kulai tom tom.

(Ah, ah, ah, that the rain of Sohra is pelting!
We tighten our clothes and make them short,
We ride on horse-drawn carriages.)

We had never seen horse-drawn carriages of course, for the British who drove them were long gone, but we sang about them all the same.

Sometimes, we dashed naked to the playground near our house, where rainwater gathered in deep pools among the tall grasses, to roll on the ground and engage in fierce fights of *kynshait um*, water-splashing. This is one of the most enjoyable games I have ever played, one with no losers and, thus, no hard feelings. When we were tired of the game, we used to take out our *knups*, which are carapace-like rain shields made from bamboo and leaves, and get into the fast-running water, to create waterfalls with split bamboo poles and large leaves. Or we would float our paper boats among the pools and play with the tadpoles that were spawning everywhere. Our parents never chided us since the water was always clean (there is no mud in Sohra, only sand and pebbles), and the rains were considered therapeutic. Even now, it is said, '*U slap Sohra u long dawai*', the Sohra rain is medicine. I do not know if this is a fact, but our frolicking never made us ill.

Rain time in Sohra was also story time. Mother used to say, 'The perfect time to tell a tale is a rainy night.' And so, she would choose one of those dark pre-monsoon nights during the black month of April to tell us about all the famous places in Sohra, behind every one of which is a tragic tale. As blinding flashes of lightning and ear-splitting crashes of thunder tore the dark sky asunder, as the wind shrieked with mad fury, lashing the houses with rain and hail, she told us about Likai and how her horrible fate had endowed the waterfall with its unhappy name, Kshaid Noh Ka Likai (the plunge of Ka Likai Falls). It was also in this way that I learnt about Kshaid Daiñthlen (Daiñthlen Falls), where Thlen, the legendary man-eating serpent, was killed. And about Ramhah, the giant who terrorised the people of Sohra so cruelly that they were forced to kill him by feeding him *jadoh*, a local delicacy, mixed with powdered iron filings. I learnt, too, about Kshaid Noh Sngithiang (the plunge of Ka Sngithiang Falls) and Sngithiang, who committed suicide because her parents did not approve of the man who loved her. And Ka Lyngknot U Ïar, the stool of Ïar, the man who married an infant-eating nymph and was killed by his brother-in-law for protesting against her inhuman habit. I learnt about U Suidtynjang, the deformed demon who abducts people and puts them on ledges in the middle of a precipice if they cannot scratch his sore-covered body without pause. If it had not been for the rain, I doubt if Mother would have had the time or the inclination to tell us all those stories.

It is the fog which is a real nuisance, not the rain. After each violent downpour, it creeps out of crevices and chasms, cloaking everything, so that all of Sohra seems to be wiping itself dry with an immense white towel after being drenched by the rain. It is thus also known as *lyoh khyndew*, land-cloud, creeping and crawling over the earth and spreading across the sky:

> land-clouds seeping
> through tall trees—
> a will-o'-the-wisp.

It seeps into homes through chinks and cracks in doors and windows, making everything wet and damp and stinking. It fills spider webs with minuscule diamonds, clings to people's hair and eyebrows and seeks to lay claim to everything:

> monsoon mist—
> my sister's eyebrows
> dotted with crystals.

The fog is a blinding white gloom, and when it floats up from the ravines, you can see nothing. Cars on the road, with their lights glowing eerily, crawl like caterpillars, following a thin black thread and blaring their horns at regular intervals:

> wind, rain and fog—
> my car crawls
> to a Cherra welcome.

Sometimes it is so dense that you can barely see your hand in front of your face. On the streets, you bump into people; you watch their ghostly silhouettes and listen to their voices as if they were disembodied souls:

> foggy afternoon:
> my sister nearby,
> a bodiless soul.

The dense fog was a big hit with us children. We loved playing hide-and-seek in it, and the denser it got, the happier we were. When I grew older, the fog was even more wonderful: I could kiss a girl right under her friends' noses. Most adults, however, dislike it because of the physical discomfort it causes, and associate it with evil. Perhaps because it encourages a sort of dangerous freedom.

The fog in Sohra is probably most spectacular when the rain has stopped, the sky has cleared, but the ravines are still choked with the pure, impregnating land-cloud. The deep gorges that yawn like fiendish mouths suddenly vanish and the tableland becomes one gigantic expanse of rolling green-and-white. This spectacular vista, almost a seascape, has an enchanted quality. It makes you feel like you would 'float on rapture's charmed carpet', as someone put it, if you jumped into that enormous mass of whiteness. Perhaps that was what Jiei, a Pnar from Ri Pnar, had also felt a long, long time ago.

According to the story, Jiei, who was visiting Sohra for the first time as a carrier of his king's tidings, found himself beset by the rain and could not leave for many days. He stayed on as a guest of the Sohra king, but he turned out to be a vainglorious, loutish sort of man who bragged about his adventures and the power and glory of his king. His king was richer and mightier than Sohra's. His state was bigger; it extended to the plains of Sylhet. His nation's women were more beautiful and gracious than anyone he had seen in Sohra. His people were taller and stronger. Like him, they were also more skilful and more capable, be it in the art of war or the art of peace. Since he had lived in the lowlands of Sylhet, he could do anything that a plainsman could, and better. He could do things that hill people could not even dream of. He had swum in big rivers, even in the ocean. He could swim anywhere; he could do anything.

The people of Sohra, who were generally polite and gracious to others, did not like the boorish ingratitude of the fellow, who ran them down at every opportunity even as he enjoyed their hospitality. One of the elders, who had suffered his arrogance and condescension in silence for many days, decided to teach him a lesson. He took Jiei to the edge of a vast ravine, which at the time was filled with land-cloud, and said, 'Look at it! You said you could swim anywhere and that you have swum in big rivers and even in the ocean, which we have not even seen. Can you swim here?'

'What is this?'

'A river of land-clouds. Can you swim here? It's at least a thousand feet thick, so it should support you easily.'

Jiei, who had never seen such a thing before, replied right away, 'A thousand feet! Why, haven't I told you I have swum in oceans thousands of feet deep? This is nothing! Of course I can swim here! Are you mocking me?'

With that, he threw himself into the white emptiness and became a legend.

Taken aback, the Sohra elder exclaimed, 'Waa, *khun ka mrad*! Son of an animal! She jumped! I was only playing a prank, and she really jumped!'

When Khasis are angry or in shock, they have this tendency to address a man as a woman. As the story spread, a new ridicule was born. Anyone who behaves arrogantly is now simply dismissed as *U Jiei jngi lyoh*, the cloud-swimming Jiei. Even I have been called that once or twice, not because I am arrogant, but because my father, who died when I was still in the womb, happened to be a Pnar from a village called Nangbah.

If, however, I were to analyse my fondness for the Sohra of water, wind, cloud, darkness and terrorising tempests, I would say, as I have said before, that it is because I was born and brought up there. It was there that my mother taught me to talk; it was there that the paths were, which I walked as a child. The years of growing up among the sacred woods, panoramic hills and clear streams of Sohra, among warm and compassionate neighbours, were the best part of my life, despite our poverty back then. And though we left for a better life in Shillong, I find myself going back to that time again and again. My roots are still buried deep in the soil of Sohra; my trunk and branches still draw sustenance from its rugged terrain; my love for it extends to everything else that is in it. That is why my only hiraeth now is for Sohra, for I still consider myself a true son of the wettest place on earth, baptised by its wind-driven rain and its impregnating fog. Do you wonder then that I fondly call it the land of time-warped legends, the rain, the fog and the poets? It is only my mother—who wants to live here in Shillong, to be close to my two brothers and sister and her other relatives—who is keeping me from my Innisfree now.

I must add that there is more to Sohra than water, wind, cloud, darkness and terrorising tempests. A high plateau, about 4,200 feet above sea level, it is surrounded by the deep and thickly wooded gorges of Ri War. In the dry months of late autumn and winter, the scene is breathtaking—criss-crossing streams, luxuriant sacred forests and yellowing hilltops with spectacular views of Bangladesh's watery plains in the shimmering distance. During these months, one can enjoy leisurely strolls in the hills and outdoor picnics on the edge of a cliff. Or pick fruits and gather flowers, wild plants and herbs in the forest, collect wild honey from crevice hives, swim in the hill streams, or fish with rods or bamboo cones and suchlike contraptions.

Despite all that Sohra makes readily available, my uncle, whose name was Krokar but whom we call Madeng, used to tell me, 'When in Sohra, never be content with the surface of it, like superficial tourists. He who hasn't trodden the rock bottom of these precipices can never claim he knows his land.' And so, we would go down to the deep forests in the gorges to catch fish or birds, or simply to explore. Of all my boyhood activities, the bird-catching expeditions are the most deeply etched on my mind.

We used to leave home at the first cockcrow, lighting our way with flickering flambeaus. We would hurry through hills and valleys dark with the lingering night so we could reach certain waterholes or shrinking streamlets much before the birds arrived to bathe and drink at sunrise.

(It is said that birds do not come to wash when there is plenty of water and the current is strong. For that reason, bird-catching is carried out only in winter, when the water in the streams and waterholes has almost dried up. But I think that in the rainy months, since water is plentiful, birds do not need to flock to a waterhole to drink and bathe. Also, rainwater weakens the tackiness of the birdlime, made from jackfruit or rubber tree gum, and so, whether people go to the waterholes or simply lay their snares on some fruit trees favoured by birds, they always do it in winter.)

At the waterholes, we first took out our cane sticks—which we had swathed in birdlime paste, except for their sharpened ends—and planted them in the soft ground just inches above the trickling water. Any wet ground that the cane sticks did not cover was taken over by very thin bamboo splits, smeared with birdlime and laid haphazardly on both sides of the waterholes. All this had to be done before dawn broke, in the light of flambeaus, so as to not frighten the bathers away. Once we had arranged everything, we would retire to a secluded spot, some distance from the waterholes, to wait and watch.

I could see everything from our hiding place. How exquisitely lovely those colourful crowds were as they sang soulfully, danced and hopped about, took their ritual dips in the pools and played and preened in the sun. There were birds of all shapes and sizes and colours, from the dullest grey and brown to such a riot of colours I cannot even begin to describe now! All I can say is that the rainbow itself seemed to me like a very dull sight when compared with the multicoloured splendour of those gorgeous creatures. And what strange hairdos some of them had! Any punk would drool with envy, looking at the flamboyant black-crested bulbuls and fancily crested finchbills. Some birds, like the hoopoe, even seemed to be wearing crowns.

My favourites were the sunbirds, close cousins of the hummingbird and known locally as *ki pohkait*. They have long, down-curved bills with brush-tipped tongues, which they use mainly to drink nectar from flowers, their staple diet. These birds always came in large colourful swarms, but though they belonged to the same family, they never resembled one another very closely, except for the females. That was what always struck me as wonderful. There were many among them who were olive above and yellowish below, from the chest to the belly, quite attractive, but drab when compared with the others in their group with their vivid colours and iridescent plumage, vibrant beyond belief. Some were a luminous purple-blue from head to tail; others had maroon breast-bands that extended to the sides of the head, glowing green crowns, bright purple throats and yellow underparts bordered with white; and yet others had dazzling yellow flanks, red throats, bright blue wings and velvety purple crowns. One time, I saw a bird, one only, who was entirely red, flaming red, as red as the embers in a smithy. Madeng told me he was their syiem, their king. (Please note that I'm not using the neuter gender when referring to animals, birds or even insects, in keeping with the Khasi tradition.)

He also said that the more drab-looking ones, the ones with the olive-green over-parts, were female, while all the handsome ones were male. I thought he was kidding, but it turned out to be true. He also told me about how they were monogamous, like most humans, and lived in nests suspended from slender tree branches, constructed in the shape of a gourd from grass and other vegetation and bound together with strands of spider's web. I never saw their nests and never closely observed the way they lived, but I fell in love with them when I heard about their marvellous customs.

Another favourite of mine was a bird we called *sim pyrem*, bird of spring, who was draped in deep sky-blue from head to tail. He was a very rare bird, seen only in the deep woods. Watching the birds from our hidden retreat was always the best part of these expeditions. But soon, the birds were flapping their wings pitifully on our cane stalks or floundering helplessly across the soggy ground, entangled in the bamboo splits. What terrible destruction we wrought upon those magnificent and delicate creatures that never did anyone any harm! The little pools, serene until then, bathed in the day's first rosy rays and resonating with a medley of sweet melodies, became a veritable killing field. Hundreds, thousands of them were caught, and while we boys laughed and patted each other on the back with each new catch, the men quickly strangled them, robbing the birds of life and colour. What a dreadful shame it was to strip them of all that loveliness and roughly toss their naked, wretched bodies into gaping gunnysacks! Amidst all the excitement, I felt a weighty sorrow. I used to ask my uncle, 'Madeng, do these birds have children? What will happen to their children now?' But Madeng would only say, 'Het, mə! You're a pest! Stop pestering!'

On our way home, the men bragged about the birds they had caught or lamented the ones they had missed. And the thought of the chicks waiting in their nests, waiting to be fed by mothers who would soon be sizzling in our frying pans, troubled me for hours.

There were two kinds of birds that we loved catching because they flew in vast swarms. One was a dull brown migratory bird of the quail family, called *mrit*, and the other was the steely blue drongo. To catch the mrits, we went early in the morning to the sacred woods to lay our birdlime traps on their favourite fruit trees. For the drongos, because they were insect catchers, all we had to do was to identify their favourite perching trees and lay our traps there. We used to catch hundreds of them in a day and either had them for dinner or sold them. The drongos were ferocious, biting and tearing at our hands with their claws. To neutralise their resistance, we carried small round sticks with which to beat them on the head.

Sometimes, when we laid our snares on a tree, we used a songbird as bait. When the songbird—caged and hidden amidst the foliage—sang, other birds, especially his own kind, flocked to the tree and got entangled in the birdlime. Sometimes the cage itself became the snare when it was made in such a way that birds could get in but not out. Another method of snaring birds was with a spring bow made of bamboo. The snare, customarily laid on the ground in marshy places, was used mostly to catch snipes and woodcocks.

All these years later, when I look back at what we did, I find it distasteful and distressing. I no longer shoot birds with catapults; I no longer trap them with birdlime; I no longer eat bird meat, and if it were not so difficult, living among the rampantly carnivorous Khasis, I would have long ago stopped eating other kinds of meat too.

In fact, I find birds so colourful and lovely and mesmerising that I have spent thousands of rupees on digital SLRs and video cameras, recording their visits to my garden. I am so fond of them that I have planted fruit trees like plums, peaches, pears, mulberries, cherries and other local varieties specifically for their sustenance. My relatives call me miserly when I do not allow them to pluck fruits from my trees, and they laugh when I explain that they are meant for the birds, and ask, why this sudden love for them? Well, I tell them, you can buy your fruits from the market. Where will my visitors get their daily meals? My greatest friends now are the red-bottomed bulbuls living in a nearby bamboo grove: they wake me up at dawn with their raucous feeding.

My mother once told me the tale of why bulbuls have red bottoms. There was an extraordinary man who lived long ago, somewhere in Ri Bhoi, to the north of Ri Hynñiew Trep, the original name of Ri Khasi or Khasi Land, which the British called the Khasi-Jaiñtia Hills. He could communicate with all living beings on earth. But he was also an unfortunate man, for he was all alone in the world. A plague had wiped out his entire clan. This is why he was called Raitong the Poor by everyone, even though he was, in fact, a very rich man, the sole inheritor of his clan's immense wealth and property. But his riches, instead of bringing him power and influence, only brought him into conflict with the king: Syiem Sait Mokkhiew. The king and his ministers, knowing that he had no one to defend him, took away everything he owned and left him with only a little hut and a plot of land which he could farm to eke out a meagre living.

Realising that he could not seek justice from a council of fellow men, Raitong tried to seek it from a council of diverse creatures, which he convened on a hill called Lum Soh Raishan. At the council, all the animals, birds and little creatures railed against the greed and cruelty of the king, except for the bulbul, Ka Paitpuraw, who lived in the king's orchard and depended on the fruits growing there for her survival. As the others were discussing the matter and denouncing the king one by one, Paitpuraw tried her best to obstruct the proceedings. She flew in front of every speaker and said, '*Paij, paij, kum ïa mə une!*' which could be rendered as: 'Kiss my arse, kiss my arse for such a one as you!'

Raitong was so enraged by this obstructionist behaviour that he spat a mouthful of scarlet betel nut juice at her. (Khasi mouths are always full of betel nut juice, although there are exceptions.) He aimed at her eye but missed and hit her bottom instead, as she was turning it towards him. The whole gathering erupted in thunderous laughter. Ashamed, Paitpuraw rushed out of there as fast as she could. It was from that time that her bottom became red and the stain was passed on as a badge of dishonour to all her descendants. The democratic Khasis (I shall explain this later, through other stories) believe that a council is always *ka dorbar* Blei, a God-given council. Since Paitpuraw had behaved in an unpardonable manner at a council, she had to be cursed for all time to come.

The story would have been funny, except that it took a tragic turn. For organising the council and passing judgement against the king, Raitong was condemned to death as a common criminal and had his neck crushed between two logs.

This story is singular in Khasi lore—it presents the king as a greedy and cruel tyrant, something he is not usually allowed to be. A king is merely a titular head and enjoys only limited powers, those powers granted to him by the *dorbar hima*, the council of state. The little bulbul too comes off quite badly in it, but I cannot help loving her because she now seems to me not merely a bird but a mythical creature.

Now that I have resigned from my job, I will revive my childhood expeditions, and with my cousin, who feels and thinks like me, I will go back to the waterholes in the jungle, before the crack of dawn, to chronicle the daily lives of the birds with my camcorder. What would the world be like if part of its loveliness was lost forever?

The gorges of Sohra are truly bountiful places, rich in fruits, crops and the produce of the dense jungle, which reverberates with the calls of wild animals and birds. But they are also places of incredible hardship, and your knees tremble as you negotiate the slopes. I remember going to one of those deep villages with friends on some official business. We had to travel for hours (more than five, I think) and when we finally reached the village, situated thousands of feet down the gorge, right at the bottom, beside a boulder-choked river, we found that we simply could not stand still on our feet. Our knees (even mine, for city living had made me soft) trembled so much that we had to conduct our business sitting cross-legged on the spacious veranda of the headman's hut.

Later, when we finished our job, the villagers, in all innocence, produced half a dozen jackfruits for us to carry home. We stared at them, and then at each other, and burst out laughing. If we'd had so much difficulty coming down, what would it be like going up? Nevertheless, so rich and mouth-wateringly delicious did the jackfruits look that one of our companions wanted to carry at least one of them home with him. We shouted him down, naturally, and it was lucky that we did, for halfway up the steep slope, we had to hire a local carrier to haul that very man out of the precipice and up to level ground. He was carried in a specially designed bamboo basket called *khoh kit briew* (human-carrying bamboo cone, or conical palanquin).

I can never speak about Sohra without feeling the hills beckoning me or hearing the autumn songs floating on the fragile wings of a *ñiangkongwieng*, the festive cicada. I can never think of it without recalling the sunny streams, naked and splashing with childhood. I remember the afternoon bonfires and the sweet, burning smoke filling my lungs, seeping into the very marrow of my bones and rising above the woods warbling with winter. I remember the deep deciduous gorges, animated and soaring with migratory birds looking for ripening fruits in sanctified woods. I feel a burning desire, a terrible hiraeth, and my soul's lament for Sohra, my place of repose, will not be silenced. One day I shall return to stay, for Sohra, though still stunningly beautiful, has been ravaged everywhere by coal mines, stone quarries and lime kilns. I shall return to revitalise its wounded earth so that its hills, grinning like rat-bitten potatoes and gaping with the hideous maws of depredation, may become green again with proud foliage. And when my *sai hukum*, the thread of divine dispensation, the thread of life, breaks at last, may I be rested on the highest peak of the land so I can watch over my home.

Strangely, Shillong, the so-called Queen of Hill Stations and Scotland of the East, has inspired in me neither love nor admiration; it has given me neither happiness nor a sense of belonging. Panegyrics in prose and poetry have been sung to this beautiful city, established by the British in 1864, when they finally had to flee the hard and relentless rain of Sohra. Named after Shillong Peak, it is a place that fills visitors and inhabitants alike with a quiet longing. While strangers yearn to revisit the place with 'rolling downs on all sides, picturesque waterfalls, rows of fragrant pine trees', older residents pine for 'the Shillong of twenty or thirty years ago'. Ungratefully though, despite having lived more than half my life in Shillong, my only hiraeth is for Sohra, whose memories fill the inhospitable ravines of my soul with the fluffiness of land-clouds.

Of the Shillong of my childhood, I can only recall the squalor of its wretched tenements; the harsh and ignoble life of a ragged rustic; the mocking of rich girls giggling on the road and that of loud boys on bicycles.

And though I wrote my first poem amidst that misery, it was only of ugly things that I wrote. The cold, hard indifference that drives students to the streets and boys to the therapy of the gun; the rottenness that would sell our holy mountain for a car and a few concubines; the blood and the riots; the terror, the fake and genuine encounters: these were my themes.

It is only occasionally, when the cool deciduous breeze whispers a welcome, as I approach the meandering road to Shillong on my way back from the heat and dust of the flatlands, that I feel something of a homecoming.

I am not the only one enamoured of Ri Sohra, the Sohra country. Robert Lindsay, resident and collector of Sylhet in 1778 or thereabouts, was smitten by the spectacular magnificence of the Sohra mountain ranges. Viewing them from Pandua in the Bangla plains, and contrasting the air of the Khasi foothills with 'the close and pestilential atmosphere of the putrid plain', he felt 'transplanted into one of the regions of paradise'. The inhabitants of 'this Garden of Eden' were a different matter altogether. Deeply lamenting the oversight of his God, he felt 'it certainly deserved a different style of inhabitants from those wild-looking demons then dancing on the banks before me'.

The 'wild-looking demons' were, obviously, my ancestors, the old Khasis. But I am not foaming at the mouth with anger as I read this incredibly discourteous description. In fact, I understand why Lindsay said that. I really cannot help chuckling to myself. But more about that later. For now, I am happy to have given you a picture of Sohra, a picture of me, Ap Jutang, an inhabitant of 'one of the regions of paradise'. Whether I and all Khasis are merely wild-looking demons dancing on a riverbank—that is for you to determine as we go along.

When I set out to write, my intention was to introduce myself as briefly as possible. But I find myself lost in my love for Sohra: there seems to be so much to say, and as you know, when there is so much to say, everything seems interesting.

I have always wanted to write about us, Khasis, as a people. Who are we? What are our roots, spiritual and sociological? What is our culture? What does it teach? What can it teach? Where are we going? Why do we seem to lose ourselves, like 'bees without a queen'? As you have seen, outsiders can misunderstand us as 'wild-looking demons'. And the misinterpretation and calumny continue. Vivek Ghosal wrote an article about us, which he called 'Mom's the Word', published in the 1 May 1997 edition of *Femina* magazine. Listen to this: '[Khasi] Men are good for nothing. While women earn for the family, men just eat and drink. They are parasites.' Am I a good-for-nothing then? A parasite? Are we all?

And there is more. Thomas Laird and Paul Andrews, writing in an Australian magazine, headlined their piece thus: 'Where Women Rule and Men Are Used As Breeding Bulls'. They even quoted a Khasi youth who supposedly said, 'If I marry, then I am under my wife's control. I am just a servant.' Are Khasi men mere 'breeding bulls'? Will I, Ap Jutang, a respected writer (sorry about this self-aggrandisement, but it is true, I am quite well-known among the Khasis) come 'under my wife's control' and become a mere 'servant' when I get married, if I ever do?

And what about the Welsh evangelist, William Jenkins? Jenkins took a photograph of a Khasi priest performing a ritual, way back in 1897, and wrote this caption for it: 'Heathen priest consulting the demons before breaking the egg.' I cannot help laughing at the daftness of these assertions, but at the same time, I cannot help thinking what a disservice they have done us over the years. Sometimes, too, I feel a sense of frustration, of helplessness and uselessness, when strangers come here and say whatever they like about us and get away with it. Among us, we have a word, *jemdaw* or *jemrngiew*, which means a souring of one's luck, enfeeblement of one's essence, destruction of one's personality. That is how I sometimes feel when I come across such oppressive statements.

But even more appalling is the ignorance of my own people. We may have a literacy rate of about 60 per cent, and many of us may be highly educated, but we know hardly anything about ourselves. We seek illumination from around the world but are blissfully unaware of our own histories. And worse still, we care nothing about such self-knowledge. We have only contempt for our own customs, our myths, our inheritances, as if these are all merely things of the past that can offer us no sustenance or useful lessons. As S.K. Bhuyan, the distinguished Assamese scholar, said in the late nineteenth century, Khasis 'never perceive that there is [any] good in their own …'

And when we do take an interest in our own culture, we generally speak out of turn, with no understanding and with only a tiny bit of knowledge. Some of us even describe our traditional democratic system, for instance, as something that resembles the Taliban way of life. I am tempted to summarily dismiss such allegations as a demonstration of shameful ignorance and repulsive disdain for all things Khasi. However, on second thought, I realise they are too serious and complicated for me to reject out of hand.

Instead, I would like to engage with them through stories about diverting incidents and characters, stories, long and short, that have clung to me since childhood. I have nursed them over many, many years with tender care in the flower pots of memory. Others have been gathered from life's varied experiences, carefully picked like mushrooms from the dark floor of a lush pine forest.

You do see the point of my desire to speak about my people, don't you? When Hamlet was dying, he said to Horatio:

> O good Horatio, what a wounded name,
> Things standing thus unknown, shall live behind me!
> If thou didst ever hold me in thy heart,
> Absent thee from felicity awhile,
> And in this harsh world draw thy breath in pain,
> To tell my story.

It is very much in the spirit of Hamlet that I would like to tell you the story of my people—to clear their 'wounded name'. And yet, my objective is not to glorify or defend them at all costs, against all charges. I have spoken with fierce resentment about the allegations of Lindsay, Ghosal, Laird, Andrews, Jenkins and my Khasi compatriots. But truth be told—though many people may not like it, though I may not like it—there is some basis to what they say.

There is much in Khasi society to which we could sing paeans. But there is much we could laugh at too, and much that should be criticised without equivocation. A writer may have his failings, but hypocrisy should not be one of them.

I have been thinking long and hard about this. I have been asking myself: 'How do I speak about my people's contemporary circumstances? How do I speak about aspects of their culture—their world view, their religious beliefs, their social, political and economic practices—without sounding like one of those wearying pedants whom I dislike so much and from whom I ran away in such a hurry?' And that was how I began to think about our funeral nights.

We Khasis have a unique funeral tradition. We keep our dead for at least two nights, in some cases longer, before they are buried or consigned to flames, depending on whether the family is Khasi-Christian or Khasi-Khasi. I refer to these divisions only because they represent the largest rift in our society. There are also a few Khasi-Hindus and Khasi-Muslims among us. During the two-night wake, relatives from far and near, friends, neighbours and residents of the locality or village, where the family lives, come in hordes to condole and support. Many of them stay late into the night, quite a few for the whole night, playing cards, carrom, word games and so on, or simply chatting and telling stories.

Now, if I attempted to capture these stories and discussions, would it not make for a terrific collection? After all, have not the Khasi wakes been called 'temples of wisdom'? Just as I was thinking along these lines, a few friends and I came to know of *Ka Phor Sorat*, the feast of the dead, a strange (even for us) six-day-long traditional funeral ceremony of the Lyngngam sub-tribe. The ceremony—involving the sacrifice of as many as fifty bulls—was to be performed in connection with the cremation of Ka We Shyrkon, whose body had been kept in a tree house for *nine months*. By mistake, however, we travelled to the jungle hamlet of Nongshyrkon seven days before the beginning of the ceremony—the last one that would ever be performed. Stuck in the hamlet for eleven days (eleven, because we could not stay back till the end, only till after the cremation), we spent our nights around a fire in the middle of a spacious hut (built especially for us), debating issues and sharing stories in what turned out to be a journey of discovery for all of us.

Let me then tell you the story of my people through an account of that journey: the grave and funny things we talked about, the light-hearted self-examination we indulged in, the illumination we sought, and most of all, the stories we exchanged. *Funeral Nights* is an attempt to capture those stories, not of a morbid or macabre character, as one might imagine, and not even so much about death, though death did feature prominently. These are stories about life—past, present and future, rural and urban, high and low; about admirable men and women, raconteurs and pranksters, lovers and fools, politicians and conmen, drunks and taxi drivers; about culture and history, religion and God. There are, among them, anecdotes in poetry and prose, tragic tales and funny tales, myths and true stories so strange that they sound like tall tales. And all of them, without exception, are Khasi, native to the soil, nurtured by the sun and rain of home, and reveal not only their specific qualities, but also their humanity and universality.

In the end, despite the jocular tone and the playful posturing that often marked our nightly sittings, we travelled further than the Lyngngam jungle, where we had gathered to witness the feast of the dead. As elaborate rites steered the soul of the departed to its eternal place of rest, I believe we were able to discover where the soul of our race lies.

2

THE
JOURNEY

As you set out for Ithaka,
hope the voyage is a long one,
full of adventure, full of discovery.

...

Keep Ithaka always in your mind.
Arriving there is what you are destined for.
But do not hurry the journey at all.
Better if it lasts for years,
so you are old by the time you reach the island,
wealthy with all you have gained on the way,
not expecting Ithaka to make you rich.

...

—C.P. Cavafy
translated by Edmund Keeley

It was Raji Manai who first told us about Ka Phor Sorat.

One night, some of us, friends and acquaintances, found ourselves sitting together in the drawing room of a death house somewhere in Shillong, talking about strange deaths and strange ways of disposing of the dead. We spoke of the sky burial of the Tibetans, the Parsi towers of silence, space burial, and new ways of treating human corpses. As we marvelled at the uniqueness of each, Bah Kynsai interrupted us to say, 'I think, of all the strange ways of disposing of the dead, na, the Torajans' is the strangest.'

Bah Kynsai used the word 'na' as many people in the Khasi Hills would use the word 'em', or 'no', as in this sentence: 'Kane ka jong phi, em?' ('This is yours, no?') Obviously, this is something a native English speaker would not say, but among the Khasis, 'em' is liberally used at the end of sentences, sometimes even in the middle.

Bah Kynsai's full name is Kynsai Marmaduke Nongbri. Kynsai means 'of the best kind' and Nongbri is his surname or clan's name. His middle name is the result of a Khasi penchant for foreign tags. Most of us have English given names, but even those with Khasi names often have something English-sounding in the middle.

Bah Kynsai does not look like your typical Khasi. He has a dark, round face, but with a sharp nose and a head of thick, curly black hair that never seems to be out of place even when the wind blows hard and fast—people suspect it is a wig, though no one has dared say it out loud. He is huge, too, for a Khasi, about five feet ten and weighing about 85 kg. He is the exact opposite of me, for instance: I am fair-complexioned and stand at about five feet four inches in my socks—the average height of Khasi men—and weigh only 55 kg. Most of us call him Bah Kynsai because he is much older than us and out of respect for his profession. He teaches geography at the university.

'The Torajans,' he continued in response to our queries, 'are a mountain tribe living in the south of Indonesia. Like us, they have a population of more than a million, and like us, most of them have converted to Christianity, though some still practise the old animistic religion, which they call *Aluk To Dolo*, or the way of the ancestors. They have a very elaborate and costly funeral ceremony that can last for several days. But the strangest thing, na, is that this ceremony takes place only weeks or months or even years after a person has died!'

'What? What?' almost everyone asked incredulously. One of us even laughed out loud and said, 'I don't believe you, Bah Kynsai.'

People tend not to take Bah Kynsai seriously since he is always pulling their leg with tall tales. But, for all his jesting, he is a well-read, knowledgeable man.

'*Bew, liah, tdong!*' Bah Kynsai cursed the laughing doubter. 'You don't believe me? Ask Ap! Ask Ham! We watched the documentary together, man!'

'Tdong' means arse, but 'bew, liah' are among the worst Khasi expletives, so I will not even try to translate them. If you're wondering why Bah Kynsai was cursing in a death house, it was because we had the room to ourselves.

Ham is Hamkom Dkhar, a college professor and historian. He is deeply interested in exploring the history of what he calls the 'Jaiñtias'. These are, in fact, Pnars, as I told you earlier, living in Ri Pnar or Jaiñtia Hills district. Sometimes they are also derogatorily called Syntengs. But many Pnars today prefer to call themselves Jaiñtias, and even refuse to accept that they are part of the Khasi family. But more of that later. Dkhar, as you might have guessed, is his clan's name, and the word Hamkom is from the Pnar dialect. I don't know what it means, and Hamkom has never offered an explanation. But Bah Kynsai said it could mean the same as the Hindi movie *Hum Kisise Kum Naheen* (*We Are No Less Than Anyone*), or in the case of Hamkom, 'I'm no less than anyone'. Hamkom certainly acts that way, perhaps because he is handsome and, at five feet eight inches, rather tall. He wears his curly hair very long, like a rock star, probably a remnant from his guitar-playing days with a local band. I was told that his girl students are forever falling in love with him and that he is very proud of that fact, although, as I was also given to understand, he never takes advantage of it. Perhaps he agrees with what Bah Kynsai used to tell his university friends: 'Do not fish in this pond! The fish will drag you in!'

Hamkom and I nodded when Bah Kynsai mentioned the documentary, and encouraged, he said, 'You see, they have also seen it, so don't give me that crap about not believing me, *ha*, tdong!'

The Khasi 'ha' is not the same as the English exclamation. Sometimes it functions like 'okay', as in: 'We saw these guys, okay, so we went up to them and started talking.'

'But why would they keep the body for so long?' someone asked.

'Because they have to slaughter lots of buffaloes and pigs as part of the ceremony, na? Scores of buffaloes, hundreds of pigs, chicken and fish. And people come at all hours, and they eat non-stop. Can you imagine the amount of money needed for all that? It can take months and years for them to collect enough funds. It all depends on how well-to-do the family is. In the meantime, ha, they preserve the body by rubbing it with special leaves and herbs, and when that is done, they wrap it in layers of cloth and keep it in a *tongkonan*. This is a huge traditional house of bamboo and wood, erected on piles and beautifully designed, like Noah's Ark. I say like Noah's Ark because the roof, na, is so uniquely built, with gables sweeping up dramatically like a pompadour, that it resembles a saddleback or a ship's prow. The tongkonan roof reminds me a little of Donald Trump's hairdo actually. You have seen Trump's hair, na? Like that.'

Raji, who had been listening intently, now said, 'I'm very interested in two things, Bah Kynsai: the keeping of the body for months and years and the slaughter of buffaloes and pigs. I'll tell you the reason later, okay, but right now, I'd like to know why they do it.'

Raji Manai (nobody knows the meaning of his first name, not even Raji himself) is about my height, maybe slightly taller. He has very sharp features and a long, lychee-seed face. Because of his full beard and caterpillar moustache, people often take him for a non-tribal. He is a man of many talents: not only an artist, painter and sculptor, but also a well-known filmmaker, a journalist with his very own cable news network, and a writer with three books to his credit. He is Catholic, but with such a deep love for anything Khasi that he goes to every cultural or religious event organised by the faithful of Niam Khasi. I would grade him as a model Khasi, for though he worships Christ, he has no contempt, only respect for the Khasi religion, and love for Khasi culture. He recognises the fact that, as Khasis, we all share the same ancestors and the same past, regardless of the new faiths we have adopted, and, therefore, always places his community above his religion.

In response to Raji, Bah Kynsai explained: 'Because they want the buffaloes and pigs to join the deceased in the afterlife, na, so his spirit will be able to herd them as on earth, na? The Torajans' belief in the afterlife is so strong, ha, their dead are buried with all the tools they would need to carry on their trade in the next world. If that is not done, their spirits will not be able to live in peace. But as they await their burials, na, the dead are kept in their tongkonans and treated just like people who are sick or merely sleeping. The family members even feed the corpses whenever they themselves eat.'

'*Ish*! Remarkable, remarkable,' Raji said excitedly. 'Khasis who are not Christians also symbolically feed the dead for three days and three nights before they are cremated. Ap can tell you that.'

'Oho, this is not the same, na, Raji?' Bah Kynsai said impatiently. 'These people treat the dead as if they are alive, man! They not only symbolically feed them; they also care for them in every way, washing them, dressing and even taking them out for fresh air now and then.'

'Taking them out?' came a chorus of amused and disbelieving voices.

'*Arre*! Ask them, tdong!' he said, pointing at Hamkom and me.

'True, true,' we replied.

'Bah Kynsai,' Raji interposed, 'I want to know more about the buffaloes.'

'Why are you so obsessed with buffaloes?'

'I have a reason, but after your story … I promise.'

'Well, during the death feast, the *Rambu Soloq*, na, which lasts for several days or even weeks as I have said, na, they first construct a ceremonial site called *rante*, in a large grassy field. There they build shelters for audiences, rice barns and other ceremonial structures, including a new tongkonan for the coffin. But the ceremony truly begins when visitors come to the field to witness the slaughter of buffaloes and pigs. Pigs are given a deep cut just above one leg, and are left hobbling about till they bleed to death. Their stomachs are then cut open, and the entrails and internal organs are removed and placed on bamboo mats. You may crinkle your noses and think it's horrible and gruesome, na, but I'm sure this is what Khasis also do when they slaughter pigs.

'Buffaloes are killed strictly according to custom. Their meat is distributed among visitors, but select portions, and the severed heads, na, are set aside to be placed in front of the tongkonan where the coffin is kept. While the killing is going on, ha, several people, boys included, are busy collecting the blood spurting from the animals in long bamboo tubes. The documentary doesn't show what they do with it, although some are seen smearing their faces with the stuff. When you see it, na, it's all so grisly, yet also fascinating, liah.

'According to the documentary, a Torajan funeral is a very loud affair. There's a lot of music, with flutes and drums, accompanied by dancing, funeral chants, songs, poems, and crying and wailing, and all these, ha, are considered expressions of grief. There are even cockfights and trials of strength between the animals before they are sacrificed. It sounds like one big cultural extravaganza, liah, but it's all true, and all of this is done for everyone, except children, slaves, and the poor. To the Torajans, na, a funeral is a celebration of life. It's not something sad, they don't treat it as a loss—it's simply a journey from this world to the next, and so they treat it as a farewell party. In fact, it is said that a Torajan funeral is much, much grander than a wedding. Among us Khasis, na, we often gauge the wealth of a family based on the weddings it organises ... how many pigs were slaughtered, how many chickens and cows. And if a caterer organises the feast, then people count the plates and boast about the number of guests that were invited. But among the Torajans, na, it is the funeral that determines the status of a family. The splendour of a Torajan funeral is judged by the number of buffaloes sacrificed, and this can be made out from the heads returned to the *puya*, a site for the spirit of the deceased, and the horns placed in front of the death house. The more horns there are, the higher the status of the family.'

Many in the group clucked in wonderment, but Raji raised a finger and said, 'But do they still practise the ceremony?'

'Actually, many things have changed in Torajan society because of Christianity, Islam and the influence of modern lifestyles. Traditionally, na, the Torajans used to organise their activities into life and death rituals. However, the Dutch Christian missionaries and, later, Muslim clerics prohibited members of their flocks from attending or performing life rituals, although death rituals were still allowed. This is the reason why life rituals are practised only by non-Christians and non-Muslims, while death rituals are performed by everybody.'

'Really?' That was Eveningstar Mawñiuh. 'I find it difficult to imagine that Muslims would allow the converts to keep their death rituals, Bah Kynsai. For that matter, I find it difficult to believe that Christians would either. Among the Khasis, ha, Christians are buried, whereas those who are still Khasis are cremated.'

By 'Khasis' here, he meant Khasi-Khasis.

Evening is a very interesting character. A thin fellow of medium height, about five feet six inches tall, fair and not exactly good-looking, he has two bachelor's degrees that I know of, Bachelor of Arts and Bachelor of Divinity, which means that he could have been a qualified preacher in his church. But for reasons not known to any of us, he drives a tourist taxi, that is, a taxi catering to tourists—local, national and foreign—travelling long distances, as opposed to local taxis, which ply within the city or town.

Meghalaya, despite the absence of a functional airport (to be functional soon, they keep saying), good roads (some would say that things are getting better with the Shillong–Guwahati road becoming a four-lane highway, but link roads within the state are still in a terrible condition) and other amenities, like good accommodation and eating places, is a very popular tourist destination, especially for domestic tourists. All this is thanks to places like Sohra and Mawsynram, the wettest places on earth, Mawlynnong, the cleanest village in Asia, the state's magnificent waterfalls, picturesque mountain lakes, delightful river islands, and the wonderful stalactite and stalagmite caves that were formed aeons ago. The panoramic splendour of Meghalaya's landscape, with a sweeping view of the plains of Bangladesh in many places, only adds to the attraction.

Evening, therefore, makes a very comfortable living plying his taxi. In fact, he is so well-off that he picks and chooses his trips and does not work every day. This has given him a lot of free time, which he uses to write articles for the local newspapers, English and Khasi. He is, as we often say, world-famous in Shillong. Evening, or Bah Ning to some, is well known for his pro-Khasi stance as well as his opposition to the matrilineal system, which seems contradictory to many.

'Things are very different with the Torajans, na, Ning,' Bah Kynsai said. 'They always put their community and culture before their religion, unlike many of us. Here, people are drunk either on the Holy Spirit or on real spirits. But the Torajans, na, Christians or Muslims, still perform the death rituals and still bury their dead in the traditional way. By the way, the Torajan burial is also quite fascinating, ha. They do not bury their dead before the eleventh day. And when they do, na, they do it in three separate ways. They may place the coffin in a cave, sometimes large enough to accommodate a whole family, or, if the deceased is a baby or a child, hang it from a cliff or a tall tree with ropes. If the deceased is from a wealthy family, na, they keep the body in a stone grave specially carved out of a rocky cliff. When buried in a cave or a stone grave, ha, wood-carved effigies of the deceased, called *tau-tau*, are usually placed beside the coffin. These are the sentinels of his spirit.

'But listen to this, listen to this, don't interrupt me ... In a further ritual, the *Ma'Nene*, na, usually held in August, the dead—I'm talking now about those already buried, okay—are taken out of their graves and are washed, groomed, put into fresh clothes and taken for a walk in the village, after which they are put back in their resting places ...'

This last piece of information was too much for the group. Irritated, Bah Kynsai bellowed, 'Bew, liah! They think it's a joke, Ap, they think it's a damn joke! Travel, read and watch useful programmes, you buggers, then only will you learn more and not think that everything is a joke.'

'No, no,' Raji said quickly, 'I for one do not think it's a joke, ha, Bah Kynsai, not only because I respect you university people but also because I happen to know of something similar in the Khasi Hills.'

'Something similar in the Khasi Hills!'

'Well, not everything, but two, three things are quite similar ...'

'No, no, that's too much to stomach,' Donald Lachlan Blah said.

Donald is tall, taller even than Bah Kynsai, fair and handsome, like an Anglo-Indian. I didn't know much about him, except that he was Bah Kynsai's friend, although that did not stop Bah Kynsai from calling him 'cosmo', even to his face. When asked why, he said, somewhat cryptically, 'He doesn't think he's Khasi, na?' It was in Lyngngam that the rest of us understood what Bah Kynsai meant.

'Believe me, it's true!' Raji said. 'Have you all heard of Nongshyrkon village in Lyngngam? No? If you haven't even heard of the place, then how can you dismiss something that's been happening there for thousands of years as "too much to stomach"? Remember what Soso Tham said? "Enlightenment we seek around the world; / That of the land's we know but naught." It seems like that to me.'

'Stop preaching and just tell us, na!' Bah Kynsai interrupted.

'Okay, okay. But what I'm trying to say is, if there are strange things in the world, then why shouldn't there be strange things among our people too? That we don't know anything about our own customs is a damn shame! But as I said, two or three things about the Torajans' death rituals are very similar to what the Lyngngams have been performing for thousands of years, okay? Their funeral traditions are different from ours. Among us, for instance, we ...'

'Yeah, yeah, yeah, we know all about what we do with our dead bodies,' Donald said irascibly. 'We keep them for two or three nights and then bury or cremate them.'

'Do you think it's that simple?' Raji replied in an offended tone. 'You may know what Christians do, being a Christian yourself, but do you know what Khasis do before they cremate their dead?'

'What would they do but keep the body for two nights and cremate it? That's all.'

'You see, Bah Kynsai! Soso Tham was absolutely right. People like him know nothing, they don't want to know anything, and they look down on their own kind as people without culture or traditions. I say shame on you, whoever you are! Ap, tell him, tell him about how Khasis cremate their dead, we must teach this fellow a thing or two!'

'What can you people teach me? I have travelled the world, gone everywhere ...'

'You may have travelled the world, but you have not travelled in Ri Khasi!' Raji said hotly. 'Tell him, Ap.'

I did not want to get into an argument with someone I had just met, so I said, 'Why don't you tell us the Lyngngam story first? We can talk about the rest later.'

But Raji would not give up. He looked around for help and spotted Bah Kit sitting outside with some people and called out to him.

Bah Kit is a rather rotund man with beady eyes, completely bald and even shorter than I am. But when he is wearing his hat, which is almost always, he seems quite personable. His full name is Kitshon Lyngdoh: *kit* means 'to carry' and one of the meanings of *shon* is 'burden', so perhaps Kitshon means someone who carries a heavy responsibility. He is a government servant but is well known as an expert commentator on Khasi culture and religion. He is, in fact, one of the people behind the rediscovery of Lum Sohpet Bneng, literally, 'the mountain of heaven's navel', the holiest site in the Khasi religion. He and his Seng Khasi colleagues thus transformed the mountain, which had been forgotten for more than a hundred years, into a modern pilgrimage site. You can see it from the Shillong–Guwahati highway, gently rising away from the road so that its flat-topped summit is completely hidden.

The pilgrimage takes place on the first Sunday of February each year and draws tens of thousands of pilgrims. I too am a frequent participant in the event, not because I am devout but because I enjoy the outing, the trek, and eating *jasong* on top of the mountain. Jasong is lunch packed in a betel nut leaf. Having jasong on the summit of a 1,434-metre-high mountain after a trek of more than six kilometres is deeply satisfying. The simple food I pack is transformed into something incredibly delicious. Besides the religious aspect, in which I don't participate, a fairground atmosphere permeates the whole pilgrimage. Cultural shows, singing and dancing are organised near the sanctum sanctorum, while people mill about buying things from shops that have sprung up overnight or from peddlers, who move around loudly announcing their wares. I have written a short poem about it but, sadly, not anything the faithful would want to hear, for it speaks of how the holy pilgrims, so eager to be the first to reach the sacred site and the first to worship God, bring the highway to a day-long halt.

When Bah Kit came into the room, Raji said, 'Bah Kit, would you please tell us about the cremation rites of the Khasis? This fellow has been saying you people do nothing but keep the body for two nights before you cremate it ...'

'That's the most despicable thing I have ever heard,' Bah Kit said in an offended tone. 'I don't want to hurt anybody's sentiments, okay, but people tend to be dismissive of us Khasis. Our religion, ha, tells us we should always respect others. Why don't you do the same? Take Raji, for example. He's a Catholic, but he knows more about Khasi culture than most Khasis who still practise their own religion. To tell such people anything is pointless, Raji, and anyway, I don't have much time. I'll have to leave very soon.'

Bah Kynsai said, 'Why don't you tell your Lyngngam story instead of squabbling like this, man? Come on, man, we are all waiting. Kit, have you heard of the strange funeral rites of the Lyngngams? No? Not even you? Then don't go, listen. Come on, na, Raji, tell, tell.'

Appeased somewhat by the scolding Bah Kit had just administered to Donald, Raji said, 'Actually, Bah Kit, Bah Kynsai has been telling us of the unique funeral ceremonies of the Torajans, a mountain tribe in Indonesia, okay? Then I told them that our Lyngngam people have a funeral ceremony amazingly like the Torajans'. Not all the rites are comparable, of course, but quite a few are. The most remarkable resemblance is the keeping of the body for months and even years.'

Bah Kynsai cried out, 'Khasis keeping dead bodies for months and years! Unheard of!'

Everyone else agreed with Bah Kynsai. I remained quiet, choosing not to trivialise Raji's revelation: given his work and background, he would know better about such things than most of us.

'Arre, Bah Kynsai,' Raji replied, sounding hurt, 'if you can believe the story of the Torajans, why can't you believe the story of the Lyngngams, our own people?'

'Because the Lyngngams are so close to us, na? How come we have never heard of such a thing, man?'

'You haven't heard of it, with due respect, Bah Kynsai, because you scholars journey the world but are not the least bit interested in your own villages. But you know that I travel to some of the remotest areas of our land, no? Recording cultural events and so on? This is my livelihood, and my interest, okay, that's how I know. And I know for sure that the Lyngngams, not those who are Christians obviously, keep dead bodies for months and even years. That's the reason I was so intrigued by the Torajan story. The Lyngngams cremate their dead, unlike the Torajans, but like them, if the body is still around, they believe that the soul of the dead person is also still around. That's why they too symbolically feed the dead every day.

'Another similarity, okay, is that they hold a feast for several days and sacrifice lots of bulls and pigs and chickens before finally cremating the body. That's why the ceremony is known as Ka Phor Sorat, the feast of the dead.'

'My God, what a remarkable resemblance, man!' Hamkom exclaimed. 'And this, among our own people! You are not pulling our leg, no?'

'No, no, I'm very serious, really!'

The others chimed in with questions. Why did they keep the body for so long? Where did they keep it? How did they preserve it? Did they embalm it? Did it not rot and stink? Why did they kill so many bulls? How many of them? Bulls, not buffaloes, no? For the same reasons as the Torajans'?

Raji admitted he did not know the details but said with a smug grin, 'If you are interested, we can go and see for ourselves.'

'See! Where? Really?'

'A friend told me that such a ceremony will be performed in Nongshyrkon village in February, next month. They will be cremating an old woman whose body has been preserved for nine months. And what's more, this is the last time they will perform such a ceremony, okay, so if we don't see it now, if we don't record it now, it will be lost forever and remain a story that many will not even believe.'

A sudden clamour followed Raji's announcement. 'Let's go, let's go! If there's such a thing among us, ha, then we must definitely see it, *ya*!'

'Ya' is the Khasi version of the Hindi '*yaar*'.

'But how do we get there?' Bah Kynsai asked. 'Lyngngam is so remote, na? Do commercial vehicles go there?'

'That's the problem, Bah Kynsai. I have been trying to find a car for the last week without success. Either they don't want to go because it's so far and the roads are so bad, or they are charging too much: double, triple the normal rate. My friend who told me about the event is not around. He's gone to Chennai, and I am busy with my new film; I have to complete it within the next week or so. I don't know what to do, ya.'

'Why don't we ask Ap to organise the transport? Now that he has resigned from his job, he can't be as busy as we are, na?'

'Don't start, Bah Kynsai,' I replied, laughing. 'I'm even busier now than when I had a job.' And that is true, by the way. Writing in two languages and running a small business can take up a lot of time. But I eventually agreed. 'Okay, okay, I will, but how do I go about it? I know nothing about Lyngngam.'

'If only we could find someone from there or someone who used to work in the coal mines ...' Raji said thoughtfully.

I suddenly remembered someone I knew, a former coal trader. 'Hold on, hold on,' I cried, 'there's actually someone in my locality who used to go to Lyngngam quite often. I can talk to him and find out ... But how many of us are going?'

'All of us, all of us,' Bah Kynsai said.

'What do you mean, all of us?' Raji demanded. 'See, my friend has already contacted the family members of the deceased for me, okay? He said they had no objections. But we must remember we are going to the jungle. There won't be a single shop anywhere, Bah Kynsai, so we have to depend on the family. I don't think too many of us should go.'

'How many of us would there be?' Bah Kynsai asked. 'You, me, Ap, who else? Raise your hands. Okay, Hamkom, Kit, Ning, Donald, seven of us.'

'Eight,' Raji said, 'Bah Su is coming with us.'

I know Bah Su very well. His full name is Sukher Sing Kharakor. Sukher means 'to look after' and Sing, without an 'h', is a common middle name, especially among the Khasi-Khasis. It means 'lion'. Bah Su is long-legged and matchstick thin, but good-looking, despite his age. He walks with a slight stoop, his head bent as if in perpetual thought. He is a well-known journalist and, like Bah Kit, an authority on Khasi culture and religion. He is most famous among the Khasis for revitalising the traditional game of archery by organising an annual tournament in Shillong, which has become so popular that it attracts hundreds of archers, young and old, men and women. He, Bah Kit and Raji are close friends and often travel together: Raji to make films, Bah Su to write for the newspapers, and Bah Kit for his own personal research. Bah Su would be the oldest among us. He is a perfect gentleman during the day. At night, after a few drinks, he tends to withdraw into a world of his own.

Hamkom raised his hand and said, 'I'd like to bring a friend if it's okay with you.'

'Me too,' said Donald.

'You want to bring a friend?' Raji asked aggressively. 'Why do you want to go in the first place? If you think there's nothing worth knowing about us, why do you want to go, huh?'

Bah Kynsai intervened quickly. 'Cool, cool, na, Raji. If he wants to come, let him. He likes adventure, I can tell you that. But no friend, Don. I'm bringing someone, though. Is that all right, Raji?'

'I don't know,' Raji replied evasively, 'we are too many already. I mean, think, ya, we will have to depend on the family, no? Won't it be too much for them?'

'What if we carry our own food, say, a sack of rice, mid-sized, and dried fish?' Bah Kynsai queried. Dried fish is easy to carry and can last for months without going bad.

But Raji thought the family might be offended. As he sat there pondering the matter, I said, 'But Raji, isn't it a feast of the dead, a public event?'

'Oh yes, yes! I completely forgot about that. There will be a lot of feasting, and people will be coming to the village from all over Lyngngam. I suppose ten more will not make a difference; you are right, Ap.'

'Okay then,' Bah Kynsai said, 'ten of us will go. But how will we go and when?'

Raji's friend had said that the ceremony would last for five days. It would begin on the fifth of February and end on the tenth. 'We would have to reach there by the fourth, Bah Kynsai,' he said, 'which means we would have to leave Shillong very early in the morning, say about 3 a.m., then go to Nongstoin, and onward to Nongshyrkon. We should be there by nightfall. And I think we should hire a big car …'

'That means eleven people,' Bah Kynsai said.

'With the driver, yes,' Raji agreed. 'I think it should be okay.'

'Then that's settled. Ap, you'd better start talking to your friend, we have no time to lose.'

Bah Kynsai is an excellent organiser as long as he does not have to do anything himself. But I held my peace and said, 'No problem.'

It was a big problem, however. I went to meet the former coal trader, known in the locality as Bah Ro, probably because his name is Roland. He told me the story of how he had to close down because of the National Green Tribunal—the NGT, he called it—ban on coal mining in the state. He was now selling fish at Ïewmawlong, a crowded part of Ïewduh, or Burra Bazaar, as it is known among non-Khasis. Despite Ïewduh being the biggest market in the state, and despite Ïewmawlong being its most crowded segment, Ro said he was not doing very well. 'Too much competition,' he complained. 'Things are bad, and all because of the NGT ban.'

I felt quite depressed listening to him.

Ro did, however, promise to arrange a vehicle for me. After a few days, he came back, saying, 'I have got a vehicle, but, and it's a big but, the fellow is asking for 35,000 rupees.'

I felt as though I had trodden on the tail of a snake. 'What! I could go to Mumbai by air and back for less, man!'

'I know, I know, but after the coal ban, ha, it's very difficult to find a vehicle going there.'

Was it that, or …? I immediately dismissed my suspicions. Ro seemed genuinely eager to help, but this still sounded like extortion.

'The problem is that even tough vehicles like Tata Sumo and Mahindra Max jeeps, of which there are many, cannot go, no?' he explained. 'Only powerful coal and timber trucks can manage on the Lyngngam road.'

In the Khasi Hills, lorries are called *trok*, from the American 'truck'. As a matter of fact, our English, mine included, is a confusing mix of Indian, Khasi, British and American.

'But how did you go there earlier?' I asked.

'The only small vehicles that can run there are those with four-wheel drives, like Mahindra pickup trucks and Maruti Gypsys. I used to travel in the pickup truck of a friend, but after the coal ban, he's gone to live in Ri Bhoi. I even spoke to my contacts in Lyngngam, but they could not help. The only offer I got was from that fellow who's asking for 35,000. You see, Bah Ap, when people think you are in dire need, ha, they don't want to help; they only want to milk you.'

'Yeah,' I agreed, frustrated. 'But going to Lyngngam is beginning to feel like travelling to another country! Only, it's worse. At least, if you go abroad, you find transport very easily.'

The day for our departure was drawing near. Ro suggested I look around for a friend who could lend us a car with a four-wheel drive: a Gypsy or a Bolero pickup. But who would do that sort of thing for me? And how could I risk taking a friend's car over such frightening terrain?

I had a bright idea then. We would pass Nongstoin, the district capital of West Khasi Hills, about 110 km from Shillong, on our way to Lyngngam. I could phone my lecturer friend, Nick, and ask him to find us a vehicle from Nongstoin to Nongshyrkon in Lyngngam. From Shillong to Nongstoin, I could hire two Sumos for ten people, or we could travel in our own cars. The Nongstoin road, they said, was quite good now.

In fact, if I got a vehicle from Nongstoin to Nongshyrkon, I could even talk Dale into taking us there.

Dale Nongkynrih is one of the tallest Khasis I have ever seen. He stands at six feet one inch in his socks, but because he is so thin—his friends call him *saikor*, literally, 'sewing-machine thread'—he looks even taller. Sometimes he is also derogatorily called *shipiah*, or fifty paise, because his late father was allegedly non-Khasi. Like Raji, he has lots of facial hair, because of which he is often mistaken for a Muslim man. Dale is a local taxi driver, that is, he plies the streets of Shillong. He drives his own taxi but keeps a Tata Winger, which can comfortably seat twelve people, for hiring out to others. (Dale insists that it can seat sixteen people, if not more. As an explanation, he says, 'In Shillong, no, Bah, we squeeze people in like a sack of potatoes. What to do? People also want that, no?') By his own admission, he is doing great business. 'People are always going somewhere in the Khasi Hills,' he told me. 'Catholics to their numerous processions, Presbyterians to their synods or presbyteries or assemblies and whatnot, and Khasis to their dances and annual gatherings, the *lympungs*. As long as people are obsessed with their religion, no, Bah, my Winger will do good business. And of course, there are the picnics and outings during the winter months. Business is good, Bah.'

When people hire his Winger, Dale asks some jobless driver to drive his taxi as a 'tempo', that is, a temporary driver, for as long as is necessary, while he himself drives the Winger and goes wherever his customers want to go. I was sure, therefore, that he would agree to go to Nongstoin, leave the car at Nick's and proceed with us to Nongshyrkon. He would consider it an adventure. Certainly, we would have to pay him a little extra, but it would not be anywhere close to 35,000 rupees.

I phoned Nick, but his phone was switched off. Then, two days later, as I was wondering what to do, I received a call from him. He was at the famous Balpakram Park in the remote jungles of East Garo Hills, where mobile signals can be accessed only from one of the hilltops. He saw my missed calls when he went up a hill to phone his wife and immediately called me back.

Straightaway, he made going to Lyngngam sound quite easy. 'No problem, no problem,' he said. 'I used to go there quite often. I can easily arrange for a pickup truck from Nongstoin. You will have to pay only 4,000 rupees. We'll go together; I have many friends in Nongshyrkon. Don't worry.'

Beautiful, I thought. If we paid 4,000 rupees for the Bolero, we could pay Dale the same amount for a round trip, and a little extra: at the most, we would be paying about 10,000 for the whole package. Beautiful.

But his next words spoiled the fun. 'Only thing is,' he said, 'you will have to wait till I return, on the eighth of February.'

'Oh, no!' I moaned. 'We have to be there by the fourth!'

'In that case, what to do? I'm here, you are there, so sorry, Bahrit.'

Nick used to call me Bahrit, younger brother, a pet name he first used when we were in college together. He asked me if I knew anyone else in Nongstoin who could help, to which I replied 'No' in a very disappointed tone.

As we were speaking, I entered the kitchen where my mother was cooking lentils on the *shawla*, a charcoal-burning stove. We usually use the gas stove, but on winter evenings, we opt for the shawla because it also keeps us warm. The whole room was fragrant with the bay leaves my mother had used to flavour the lentils. When she overheard me saying that I did not know anyone in Nongstoin, she said, 'You don't know?' in her strong Sohra drawl. 'What about Hoi's daughter? Doesn't she live there? Wasn't her husband from there?'

'Oh yes!' I exclaimed. My long-out-of-touch niece, Indalin! How could I have forgotten? 'Thanks, *Mei*,' I said. 'I'll call her family in Sohra for her mobile number.'

Indalin means 'she who would take care of all'. Born and brought up in Sohra, she moved to Nongstoin some years ago to teach at a high school there. She married a local man, who owned a flourishing tea shop, but unfortunately, he died some years later, leaving her a widow with two young sons and a daughter. Indalin, however, is such a forward-looking young woman, bubbling with so much energy, that she refused to be crushed by the tragedy. Living up to her name, she took over the tea shop, supervising things there except during school hours. I had not met or spoken to her for a long time, but I did not doubt at all that she was doing very well.

When I told her about my plans over the phone, she immediately raised my hopes again. 'No problem,' she said. 'I have a friend in Nongshyrkon. He's an educated man with whom I have business dealings. He's working in a government office in Nongstoin besides doing business here and there. I'll talk to him and let you know. He has a Maruti Gypsy.'

When I reminded her of the offer a day or two later, Indalin apologised profusely. Between her work at the school and the tea shop, she had forgotten all about it. 'I'll call him right now. I might forget again.'

After a while, she called back to say that the gentleman would take us to Nongshyrkon in two Gypsys for a minimal fare. 'Just the petrol alone will cost 1,500 rupees,' she said. 'He will take a little extra—not the market rate of 4,000 but, say, 2,500 rupees for one Gypsy, in consideration of our business connections.'

Overjoyed, I asked her to fix for the fourth of February. Indalin suggested that we reach Nongstoin by 8.30 in the morning, to which I readily agreed, relieved that it did not have to be earlier.

Accordingly, I asked our travel group to assemble at Rhino Point, which should be convenient for all of us, by 6 a.m. sharp. How they got there was their business.

On the night of the third, I set the alarm for 4.30 in the morning. But Barrister, our tomcat, came home late, at about 1 a.m., and that, combined with the early alarm, made me restless the whole night through. Barrister is so named because he is entirely black on top, from head to tail, and altogether white below, from chin to scrotum. Since everyone said he looked like a lawyer, I happily named him Barrister. He usually eats his dinner at nine and then goes out, only to return home by eleven or so. But that night, as if to torment me, he came home at 1 a.m. and announced his arrival with loud, sleep-disrupting cries. I felt like wringing his neck and cursed him aloud, 'You son of a bitch, I'll stop feeding you from tomorrow.'

When I got out of bed at 4.30 a.m., the temperature was minus two degrees Celsius. Lawsohtun, on the slopes of Shillong Peak, I must tell you, is always three to four degrees colder than the Shillong valley, which is cold enough. I ran shivering to the bathroom to wash my face and brush my teeth. Thankfully, the water was still slightly warm from being heated in the geyser the previous night. I had a hurried breakfast of boiled rice and tea, followed by a jugful of nutritional shake. I'm a habitual drinker of the stuff because of my stomach problems, which I often had to treat with antibiotics like Norflux TZ and O2. But now, thanks to it, I have been able to bid the drugs goodbye.

That morning, however, I finished the drink with the additional hope that I would be able to *pyllait*, release, before hitting the road. Sadly, it did not work. I have a friend who makes a very big deal about releasing in the morning before going out. Whenever we travelled together and shared a hotel room, I would smile to see him emerge from the bathroom and say with relief, 'Mission accomplished!' Sometimes, though, it was 'Mission partly accomplished!' or a doleful 'Mission aborted!' or 'Mission impossible!'

Breakfast and a quick shave later, I was all set to leave by 5.45 a.m.

I was worried about Dale, though. People say he is lazy, always sleeping in, and always asking tempo drivers to drive his taxi. The fact is that Dale is mad about football and stays up late to watch the English Premier League, the European Cup or whichever game is being shown on TV, so it is often impossible for him to get up early. Consumed by worry, I phoned him at 5 a.m. to make sure he was up and about. To my relief, he was, and as I was considering calling him again at 5.50, he was already at my gate, noisily honking his car.

It was still dark at the time, but off we went. I nursed a growing worry that I might have to release somewhere amidst the bushes along the Shillong–Nongstoin highway. Thinking of that, and of the remoteness of Lyngngam, I had packed several rolls of toilet paper, so I was, at the very least, properly armed. This was also the first thing Raji asked all of us when we met at the Point.

'Have you packed toilet paper?' he asked. 'Last time, I told you to carry plenty of it, no? In Nongshyrkon, we have to do it in the jungle.'

'Open defecation,' Hamkom said.

'No, not just anywhere,' Raji explained. 'You have to go into the jungle. It is especially forbidden to do it near water bodies, that's why you need toilet paper. Using water is out of the question.'

Bah Kynsai produced four rolls. 'Should be enough, na?' he asked.

The others said this was the first item they had put in their bags. And I understood their concern, for otherwise they would have to do it like the locals, using sticks and leaves, or old newspapers when available.

They were all there, Raji, Bah Kynsai, Bah Kit, Eveningstar, Hamkom, Donald, and Bah Kynsai's friend Magdalene Syiem, who turned out to be a former colleague—she and I used to teach in the same college. The only ones missing were Hamkom's friend and Bah Su. All of us were dressed in warm clothes: jeans (brown corduroy trousers in my case), windcheaters and sneakers.

'Where's Bah Su?' Bah Kit asked Raji.

'I don't know. He's usually punctual. Must be on the way.'

'And what about your friend?' Bah Kit asked Hamkom.

'He too must be on the way.'

'What's the name of your friend?' Bah Kynsai asked.

'Halolihim Kyndites.'

'What the hell does that mean? Praise the Lord?' Bah Kynsai asked, genuinely surprised by the name.

'No, Bah Kynsai,' Hamkom replied seriously. 'When I first heard the name, ha, I too was curious. I checked dictionaries, the internet, everything, but there's no such word either in English or Hebrew.'

'No such word in any language, *mɔ, tdong*! Khasis, na, are very fond of such meaningless names.'

As we waited, I took stock of the situation. Of us all, Bah Su was the oldest, at about sixty-five, and Bah Kynsai and Bah Kit were both over fifty-five. Magdalene had just touched thirty, Dale was in his early twenties, and Donald about twenty-eight, according to Bah Kynsai. The rest of us were more or less the same age, between forty and forty-two. We belonged to different faiths and churches: Bah Su, Bah Kit and I to the indigenous Niam Khasi; Raji and Donald to the Catholic church; Bah Kynsai, Hamkom, Magdalene and Eveningstar to the Presbyterian church; and Halolihim to some newly established American church. And oh, yes, Dale belonged to a church that forbade its followers to drink, smoke, or even eat *kwai*, betel nut. Dale, however, did at least two of these forbidden things with apparent relish. In this, he was like most of us, who were wholly unorthodox and liberal in our beliefs, though I could not speak for Donald or Halolihim, of whom I knew nothing at the time. Bah Kynsai was perhaps the most irreligious. He described himself as an outstanding Presbyterian, since, he said, he never attended church but was always standing outside it as a chauffeur for his family. Raji, Bah Su, Bah Kit, Bah Kynsai and I had been brought together by our interest in Khasi culture. The others, I supposed at that time, were prompted by curiosity and a sense of adventure.

That would undoubtedly be true of Magdalene, called Mag or Kong Mag by everybody, kong being, like I said, a respectful address for a woman. Magdalene was pleased to see me and Hamkom, whom she knew very well. We had not met for a long time. Not, in fact, since I quit the college job. We used to get along excellently, though she was in the department of history and I, in English. Actually, Magdalene got along splendidly with everyone. She was always so cheerful and lively, so witty and charming that there was never a dull moment when she was around. Being a divorcee, she lived with her parents and behaved pretty much as she pleased. She was also rather fond of male company, and even used to go hunting in the deep jungles with her male friends, which prompted one of our colleagues at the time to ask her, 'Hunting in the jungle? What kind of animal did the men hunt? The two-legged kind?'

Looking at her now, I found her just as attractive. Dusky and radiant, with her sleek bob cut unspoiled by a single grey hair. Magdalene is a tall woman, taller than my five feet four inches, unlike most Khasi women, whose average height is four feet ten or thereabouts. Embracing her, I said, 'I still remember what you said to me.'

'What, what did I say to you?' she asked, immediately curious.

'I'm not about to tell you,' I replied. But the thought of it brought a smile to my face. One rainy afternoon, I had found her alone in the teachers' room. She looked uncharacteristically despondent and sat with both hands cupping her chin. When I entered, she brightened up, pursed her lips and purred, 'Ap, let's go home, come with me, noo!'

I was too surprised to react immediately, so she said again, 'Come, noo, let's go …'

When she saw me staring at her and smiling foolishly, she added, 'Come, noo, something's better than nothing.'

That was the most deflating comment I have had to endure from any woman.

We had been at Rhino Point for fifteen minutes, and yet there was no sign of either Bah Su or Halolihim.

Rocking to and fro restlessly, Evening said to nobody in particular, 'Indian Standard Time.'

'More like Indian Stretchable Time or Indian Stupid Time, liah!' Bah Kynsai cursed.

'Cool, cool, Bah Kynsai,' Magdalene intervened. 'How can we expect someone with a name like Halolihim to behave like a mere mortal?'

'What is that supposed to mean?' Hamkom asked testily.

'I don't know, maybe he's got a halo around his head or something,' Magdalene responded. 'It's certainly a strange name, isn't it? Even his surname is quite strange, no, Bah Kynsai? I haven't heard of such a Khasi surname before.'

'Must be an anglicised version of Kyndait, na?' Bah Kynsai said.

'Maybe,' Magdalene agreed.

Hamkom, however, did not offer any comment.

'And what about Bah Su?' Evening asked.

'Maybe he's still performing his egg-breaking ceremony or what?' Bah Kynsai replied.

'*Tet*!' Raji protested. 'Do you think every non-Christian is an egg breaker and diviner?'

Bah Kynsai laughed aloud at Raji's offended tone and said, 'He looks like one anyway.'

Most Khasis are terribly untrustworthy when it comes to timekeeping. We were on time right then because we happened to be teachers and professionals. Ordinarily, Khasis are only punctual for school and church— school because of the fear of punishment, and church because they don't want to be subjected to disapproving frowns. In everything else, they simply do not care about being on time. This is most flagrantly reflected in the actions of government employees and our politicians—MLAs, MDCs and ministers—some of whom have been known to delay functions for hours. This unflattering trait has even found expression in our legends, especially in the tale of *Ka Lalyngngi Pep Shad*.

☙

When the world was still young, when animals and all animate things lived in a peaceful community, speaking one language, Lalyngngi was said to have been the queen of flowers, with many attendant flowers to serve her every need. Her beauty and fragrance were unmatched, and her realm was a vast expanse of hills and valleys whose splendour was unrivalled by any other. But one fine day, shamed by her own actions, she fled her kingdom and has since then been found only in the middle of precipices.

The story, however, does not begin with Lalyngngi. In that paradise-like state, there lived three friends who never parted company—Shakyllia the Grass-babbler, Diengkhied the Porcupine and Risang the Squirrel. One day, the three friends, while on a tour of the neighbouring countryside, came upon a circular dancing ground where humans celebrated their annual spring festival. Once or twice, they had been lucky enough to witness the celebrations. They had seen maidens clad in silk and velvet, and adorned with sparkling ornaments, gliding in a slow and solemn dance around the centre of the ground, their gold and silver crowns glinting in the sun with each movement. Young men had pranced in a ring around them, their silver swords flashing, their silver quivers jingling. And around them had stood a multitude of cheering, admiring onlookers. What a charming sight it had been!

The memory put them in a fever of excitement, and they swore then and there to do everything in their power to coax their own kind into organising such a festival. The friends were quite sure they would fare just as well as the humans in their endeavour. In fact, with the variety of skills at their command, the animals might even do a better job.

Back home, they unfolded their plan to other friends and tried to enthuse everyone with a lively display of their brand of music. Shakyllia played a tune on his flute; Porcupine accompanied him on cymbals; Squirrel beat away on his little drums. Soon a crowd collected around them. Seeing how well the three performed and encouraged at finding such accomplished musicians in their midst, everyone present began to think seriously about holding an animal dance festival. The idea was especially popular with the young, who were continually seeking new forms of pleasure and distraction.

A council was summoned to work out the details of the new project, and when everything was finally settled, one among them, one who was young, energetic and wise, was selected to be the chief organiser. The chosen youth was Pyrthat the Thunder, who immediately made a massive drum and went everywhere, beating it and booming out invitations to all fun-loving beasts, plants and flowers to attend and participate in the biggest show on earth. The council had decided to invite plants and flowers too, for their presence would only add to the charm and magnificence of the festival.

When the appointed day arrived, a vast and motley crowd converged upon the dancing ground, which the organisers had made ready after many moons of hard labour. Amidst hooting and laughter, they came from everywhere, crawling, walking, floating, trotting, jumping or swinging from tree to tree, dressed in their very best costumes and habits. When the assembled crowd had taken their seats and the dancers had gathered in the field, the three friends (now accompanied by Hati the Elephant, with his raucous trumpet) took up their instruments and proceeded to kick off the festival. The crowd erupted in applause, chanting praises and urging the dancers to give their finest performance. By prearrangement, plants and flowers, being more fragile, were assigned a place in the centre, while the animals were instructed to dance in a ring around them and not stray into their path. The arrangement was also supposed to reflect the choreography of the human dance festival, where the more delicate women danced in the centre, surrounded by robust and martial men dancing in a protective ring around them.

As the dancing progressed, Shrieh the Monkey and her brood, encouraged by the promptings of the onlookers, let loose with their antics, screeching and making a nuisance of themselves by landing on the backs of the dancers time and again. Of course, they took the burst of laughter that followed to be due approval of their skill, and that only made them even more lively. They did so much leaping that day that monkeys have never been able to be still again.

Exasperated, Kyrtong the Wild Ox blew through his nostrils, pawed the ground and shook his shaggy head vigorously, trying to get rid of the little monkeys that were clinging to his horns. He was so infuriated by their behaviour that he has not yet learned to be agreeable again. Not far from him, some small animals were playing, and ki Sniang the Boars, were wrestling in the dust, oinking and patting each other after every throw.

In all that confusion, Dkhoh the Owl looked ridiculous imitating the human maidens, shuffling over the sand and trying to be dignified while staring into space. Owl stared so hard and for so long, without batting her eyelids, that her eyes became big and round like pebbles, leaving her short-sighted ever since. When he noticed her, Dkhan the Mole laughed so hard and so long that his own eyes narrowed to the mere slits they are today.

There was much fun and merriment during the festival. All sorts of animals and all sorts of flowers, in all sorts of colours, did all sorts of things, so that even the surliest of them were caught up in all the excitement. Members of the council joined in the celebration and impressed everyone with a lively exhibition of sword dancing. Among them were Dngiem the Bear, with his darkly sombre robes, Labasa the Leopard, with his rosetted outfit, and Khla the Tiger, with his elegantly adorned garment. The only animals who felt at a disadvantage were the musicians—between the persistent uproar from the spectators and the din created by the performers, they were having a tough time making themselves heard.

In all that excitement, Kui the Lynx arrived, clothed from head to foot in a brightly spotted costume. On arriving, he swaggered into the dancing ground, produced a dazzlingly radiant silver sword, and began strutting around the circle. Every animal turned to watch. They had never seen such a sword before. It flashed at every twist and turn and seemed to defy the sun itself in its brilliance. The attention he was getting from the crowd turned Lynx's head and made him arrogant. With each passing moment, he began to think that, without him, the whole show would have collapsed. Hearing his vaunts, Thunder was deeply stung and, biding his time, silently vowed to put Lynx in his place before the festival ended.

As soon as Lynx took a break, Thunder approached him and requested: 'My good friend, I have left my sword at home and have nothing with me but my big drum. Would you please lend me your magnificent sword for a moment? I would love to try my hand at sword dancing too.'

Lynx glared at him and said rudely, 'If you want to participate in the sword dance, you should have known better than to come to the field without your sword. Why don't you just go back home and fetch it?'

But some of the animals who were sitting nearby overheard the conversation and condemned Lynx for his selfishness. 'Shame on you, Lynx,' they said in a chorus. 'How can you be so ungracious? If it weren't for Thunder here, there wouldn't be a dance at all.' They threatened Lynx and said that if he did not lend his sword to Thunder, they would take it from him by force. Lynx did not want to part with his precious sword; for one thing, he did not want anyone else to handle it, and for another, he especially did not want Thunder to get hold of it lest he should dance better and win all the praise. In the face of their threat, however, he had no option.

Taking the sword, Thunder went to the centre of the circle and asked all the plants and flowers to vacate the field. He beat on his drum to attract attention and began chanting as swordsmen were known to do. Then, with a sudden motion and the speed of a whirlwind, he pranced round and round the field, furiously brandishing the sword, here, there and everywhere, so that it seemed to the whole throng like one mad, vengeful stick of pure flame, blinding anyone who so much as opened his eyes. Everyone was alarmed. But Thunder was not done yet. He began to beat his drum with such force that the whole area shook as though a mighty tremor had occurred. Frightened out of their wits, all the animals, plants and flowers fled to the nearby jungles to hide in the undergrowth.

Amidst that chaos, Thunder, who was so enamoured of the sword that had given him such power, vaulted into the sky, far beyond the reach of Lynx and the other animals. And to this day, he is often seen wildly striking the heavens with what we have come to know as thunderbolts. Actually, these phenomena are nothing but the gigantic drum of Thunder and the silver sword of Lynx, metamorphosed into elemental forces.

On earth, confusion still prevailed, with each animal blaming the other for what had happened. However, no one was as sad as Lynx, who spent his days moping and seeking out ways to reach Thunder's aerial dwelling so that he might recover his sword. Finally, he hit upon a simple but unique plan. First, he dug a small hole in the ground. Then he went to relieve himself in it every day, hoping that one day the mound would grow as high as the sky. That is why Lynx never strays far from where he is staying, because to this day, he continues to build his mound in this way.

When the story of how Lynx had lost his rare silver sword reached the humans, they felt sorry for him. As a token of respect for this great sword dancer, they decided never to disturb his habitat so that he would be free to continue with his efforts to reach the sky.

Meanwhile, Ka Lalyngngi, being a queen, was busy getting ready. She wanted to look her grandest. She took out all her beautiful dresses and her gold and silver ornaments to choose the best from among them. As is often the case with beautiful women all over the world, she took some time deciding on her outfit and its accessories. When she had finally made up her mind, she went to a spring nearby to wash at the spot where a jet of water spouted from a split bamboo tube. But when she finished washing, Lalyngngi thought that her heels were not smooth enough. Since she was going to dance barefoot like the humans, she wanted to make her heels as beautiful and smooth as possible. Consequently, while all that din and confusion was spreading through the dancing ground, Lalyngngi was busy scrubbing her heels with a bathing stone.

Eventually, she was ready. With all her attendants in tow, she proceeded to the dancing ground, confident that she would be the centre of attraction. Among her followers were the flowers called Tiew Latara, Tiew Larun, Tiew Rtiang and Tiew Laphiah. They arrived in all their colourful glory at the venue, expecting to be the cynosure of all eyes. To their disappointment, they found the place quite deserted. As they stood there, ashamed to have reached after the dance had broken up, they were spotted by the animals who were just then emerging from the undergrowth. Seeing the latecomers standing like lost souls in the middle of the dancing ground, the animals hooted with laughter and jeered and catcalled.

Ka Lalyngngi, proud Queen of Flowers, could not endure the terrible humiliation. Her pain was indescribable. She knew that this shame would haunt her for as long as she lived. Lalyngngi fled from the scene with tears flowing down her cheeks like tiny cascades till she reached the edge of a cliff from which she threw herself headlong into the precipice. Her attendants followed, but luckily for all of them, they fell on a wide ledge sticking out from the precipice and survived the fall without any serious injuries.

The ledge was, in fact, a little hanging valley, watered by a sweet spring emptying into the giddy depths beyond. Lalyngngi took what had happened as divine intervention and decided to settle down in the little valley with all her followers and friends. Since then, when autumn arrives, she can be seen blooming in the middle of the precipice, in all her festive glory, together with Latara, Larun, Rtiang and Laphiah.

When Lalyngngi's story became known, the world began calling her Ka Lalyngngi Pep Shad, or Ka Lalyngngi, who missed her dance. And Khasis have been comparing anyone who is notoriously unpunctual to Ka Lalyngngi Pep Shad ever since. And yet, we never learn.

༄

We had been waiting for twenty minutes by the time Bah Su arrived in a relative's car. The moment he got down, he said, 'I know, I know. Please don't mind. I had left well before time, ha, but then the warrant came and I had to turn back.'

'Ah …' we all murmured.

The warrant is, of course, the call of nature, and everyone understood perfectly well.

Hamkom said, 'I wonder if Halolihim is having the same problem, ya.'

Halolihim made us wait for forty minutes—too long by any standard. Everyone was quite pissed off, and we would have left without him but for Hamkom, who pleaded with us to wait. When he finally came, he wanted to say something in apology, but Bah Kynsai interrupted him and said rather hotly, 'Let's go, let's go. We are late. We have a long way to go.'

When we had all got into the minibus, Halolihim said, 'Let us pray.'

This was too much for Bah Kynsai. He turned in his seat to glare at him and said, 'You made us wait for more than forty minutes and now you have the gall to say, let us pray, liah? Do you think we haven't prayed for ourselves or what? And listen, we belong to different religions here. We pray according to our own beliefs, keep that in mind!'

Many of us shared Bah Kynsai's anger. Nevertheless, we tried to appease him. As for Halolihim, he went on with his prayer, loudly calling on the Lord to forgive our sins and bless us all. Most of us did not pay any attention, but I could see Hamkom and Evening closing their eyes.

In the middle of the prayer, Dale, who had been quiet all along and was now driving the Winger at 80 km/h, suddenly said, 'Shall I close my eyes too?'

Amidst the laughter that followed, Raji and Bah Kit said, at the same moment, 'If you want us to be immortal!'

Taxi drivers in Shillong are well known for their ready wit and brashness.

If I was happy to see Magdalene, I was full of misgivings when I looked at Halolihim. He was tall, thin and loose-jointed, his face scarred by acne. But what made him so unpleasant was the sour look he seemed to direct at everyone. I wondered why Hamkom should want to bring along such a fellow. Just then, Magdalene whispered to me, 'What an eyesore!'

Initially, however, the whispers in the group were not about Halolihim, but Magdalene, because she was the lone woman. Evening, who had always been vocal against what he called the moral laxity of Khasi women, was the first to voice his reservations.

But Bah Kynsai said, 'It's all right, Ning, she is used to travelling with men.'

And Magdalene added rather naively, 'No problem for me, I have even gone hunting with men.'

At 6.45 a.m., when we finally moved out, the road was empty except for the odd car now and then. We were happy to have it to ourselves. But the tragic accident which had caused the death of an official of the North-Eastern Hill University, NEHU, at the very spot where we were and at around the same time, 6.50 a.m., was still fresh in our memory. We told Dale to control his speed.

'What a tragic loss that was, no, Bah Kynsai?' Ham said. 'I knew Je personally. She was an outstanding officer, one of the most efficient in NEHU, they say. Quite young, too. What a loss!'

'It was her own doing,' Bah Kynsai responded unsympathetically. 'You know, Ham, you cannot drive like a cyclone on such narrow, winding roads and expect to always get away with it. These young people driving like maniacs, na, should learn a lesson from this.'

'But was it her fault?' Hamkom asked defensively. 'Even the papers were very vague about it.'

'It must have been her fault,' Bah Kynsai asserted. 'Even inside the campus, she used to drive like a *Fast & Furious* racer, na? People used to call her NEHU Express.'

'It was her fault,' Dale said. 'We are on the road all day, no, Bah. People talk to us, even if they don't talk to the police. All the eyewitnesses said it was her fault. The Sumo was travelling on its side of the road; she was over-speeding on the curve; she hit the side of the Sumo. If you look at the scene of the accident, ha, you would know that the Sumo was clearly on the right side.'

'What was she doing on the road so early? I think she was returning from somewhere, no?' Bah Kit asked.

'She was returning from Mylliem after frost viewing. There were two male passengers with her, a cousin and a friend,' Raji, the journalist, explained.

Mylliem is supposed to be the coldest place in the state. On winter mornings, the paddy fields and valleys are white with frost that does not melt completely until noon. It can be a spectacular sight, especially for city-bound citizens like Je and her friends.

'They survived, no, Raji, those friends of hers?' Hamkom asked excitedly. 'So what did they say? Whose fault was it?'

'They were questioned by the police when they regained consciousness, but they said it happened so fast they simply couldn't tell,' Raji replied.

'You see, you see, it was her fault,' Dale said triumphantly. 'If it had been the Sumo's fault, ha, they would have blamed the driver quickly enough. But they didn't. They said they couldn't tell, which means they were protecting her.'

'Maybe. Who can really say? But what a horrific sight it was! When they pulled her out of the car, okay, she was gasping for breath like a fish out of water.'

'Did you see her?' Bah Kynsai asked.

'I was told.'

'Don't speak like an eyewitness when you are only an ear-witness,' Bah Kynsai snapped.

'Right, right, Bah,' Dale agreed, laughing. 'But you know, Bah? The Sumo driver also suffered terribly. He lost a leg in the accident and cannot drive any more. And he is the family's sole breadwinner.'

'Whatever you say, driving in Shillong is terrible,' Evening observed.

'Not only in Shillong, man, the whole state,' Bah Kynsai said. 'Drivers here are like stampeding animals. Accidents every day.'

'Last year alone,' Bah Su chipped in, 'there were 306 road accidents, which claimed 209 lives according to government statistics, while 586 people sustained serious injuries.'

'Wow, so many?' Hamkom said, amazed.

'What do you think are the reasons?' Donald asked.

Donald was doing his doctoral research in political science from a university in Delhi, Bah Kynsai had told us while we waited for Halolihim. He had also told him about some of us, and as a result, Donald was now 'looking at us in a new light', to use Bah Kynsai's words.

'Underage driving,' Dale said. 'There are so many of them, Bah, fifteen- or sixteen-year-old kids. The moment they know how to hold a steering wheel, ha, they think they can drive, and their parents also pamper them like anything.'

'Unskilled driving,' Bah Su said. 'So many drivers who should only be learners, ha, driving with trainers, ha, are instead driving like professionals and causing so many accidents.'

'And nobody knows or follows any rules,' Raji added. 'If there's a traffic jam, okay, nobody follows the lane; they overtake from right, from left, and make matters worse. They are so bloody unruly, man! If there's a foot of space in front of your car, ha, they try to overtake and squeeze into it, the buggers! And they park everywhere too, even in front of no-parking signs, where they know they will obstruct the traffic.'

'In Meghalaya people simply don't respect the law,' Hamkom lamented. 'They may fear it, but they certainly don't respect it. For instance, if there is a policeman near a no-parking sign, ha, they will never park there, but as soon as he leaves, they literally fight for the spot. They don't give a damn about what the sign says.'

'What I don't understand is why nobody is doing anything about it. Underage driving, unskilled and undisciplined drivers ... Why are the police not doing anything?' Donald wondered aloud.

'The police are too busy controlling the chaotic traffic, no?' Raji said. 'There are more cars in Shillong than the roads can accommodate. A family of three may have four, five cars, no, Bah Kynsai?'

'Or else they take money, ha, Bah Raji,' Dale added. 'The more they penalise, the warmer their pockets. And because everybody gets off with a fine, nobody cares.'

'Let me ask you this question for the sake of argument, okay?' Donald said. 'We have district transport officers in every district of the state, no? So how are they granting licences to unskilled and underage drivers?'

'Many are driving without licences,' Dale said.

'But I have seen the police checking for licences, ya,' Hamkom argued. 'I too have been stopped at least twice.'

'Yeah, yeah, they are beginning to make random checks now,' Evening said, 'and that's a good sign, I think.'

'But that won't help,' Raji said. 'You know why? There are many licensed drivers who cannot really drive!'

'How's that possible?' Magdalene asked, laughing. She had been listening intently to the conversation.

'Arre, Mag, you and Don don't know anything,' Bah Kynsai said. 'You may be a college professor, and Don may have travelled the world, na, but you are too innocent. I have a friend who owns a driving licence, although he cannot drive and does not even own a car ...'

'Really? How come?' Donald asked.

'He bought it! From a DTO, a district transport office.'

'My God, there's corruption everywhere, man!' Donald exclaimed.

'Of course!' Bah Kynsai agreed with feeling. 'We call it *bam pisa*, Don, money-eating ... But tell me, what did you people do to get your driving licence?'

Donald spoke first, explaining that, years ago, he had registered with a driving school for three months, but that he had to get a learner's licence before he could begin learning at all. He applied for a driving licence just before the end of those three months because the school had declared him ready for the test. A motor vehicle inspector from the office of the district transport officer conducted the test, and evaluated him not only on his driving skills but also on his knowledge of road signs and signals. He had to wait quite a while to actually receive his licence.

There were broad smiles on everyone's faces by the time he finished his account.

'Why, why are you smiling?' Donald asked, perplexed. 'Come on, man!'

Bah Kynsai said, 'Don, how many people do you think do that sort of thing in Meghalaya?'

'Everybody, I suppose,' Donald replied.

'Well, I certainly didn't do that,' Magdalene said. 'My father taught me to drive, and he arranged the licence for me.'

'You hear that? Her father arranged the licence for her!' Bah Kynsai cried. 'So why were you playing dumb, earlier, ha, Mag? Crafty, na, you too?'

'No, I'm a very good driver, no, Bah Kynsai? I didn't get a licence for knowing nothing!'

'Anyway,' Bah Kynsai continued, 'hardly anybody here goes through the legal process, Don. First of all, na, very few people go to driving schools, although that is changing now. Many are taught by friends, relatives, or by professional trainers. And I can tell you that they never bother with a learner's licence. They simply talk to an agent who knows the dealing assistants in a DTO. These people, na, arrange everything for them—learner's licence, driving licence, all at the same time. All the applicant has to do is pay the agent and the dealing assistants some money. Of course, he has to pay more than the legal fee, but then he gets his licence much quicker than you did yours, Don, and without any hassles.'

'Did you also do that?'

'No!' Bah Kynsai said emphatically. 'I didn't go to a driving school, but I didn't want to bribe anyone either. I applied through the proper channel. But the point is that most of our people do not do that, na?'

'What about the others?' Donald persisted.

Bah Su said he did not drive. Raji, Hamkom and I said we had used the proper channel, but Dale said with a laugh, 'Why do you ask me? I am a taxi driver, no? We taxi drivers are professionals when it comes to exploiting the system.'

We looked at Bah Kit and Halolihim, but they had their eyes closed, so Raji answered for Bah Kit and said he did not drive.

Bah Kynsai, however, wanted to know how Halolihim had got his licence. He said, 'Ham, Halolihim is your friend, na, ask him, ask him how he got his licence.'

Hamkom turned to Halolihim. 'Hal, *ei* Hal! Wake up!'

'What? What?' Halolihim asked, waking up with a start.

'We want to know how you got your driving licence.'

'Driving licence?' he said. 'I have a friend in the DTO who did everything for me. I'm too busy spreading the Word of God to bother with such trivial things.'

There was a loud burst of laughter and Halolihim, looking quite disgusted with us, went back to sleep.

After the laughter had subsided, Raji said, 'Many people know nothing about traffic rules and signals. They don't yield to uphill traffic, they overtake from the wrong side, they don't dip their lights at night, they don't know anything about road signs. Our channel once asked a driver about the meaning of a zebra crossing, okay, he said he didn't know. When we asked him what it was called, he said, "A cobra or something?" And all this, because people would rather pay bribes than go through the legal process.'

'But why? I don't understand,' Donald lamented. 'People rail against corruption all the time, but they also actually encourage it, no?'

'Why? Because of the bureaucratic formalities and inordinate delays at every stage, na?' Bah Kynsai replied. 'Officials delay because they want money, and the people too would rather bribe someone than run around in circles. Everybody wants everything fast, fast. It's a vicious cycle, Don.'

'I have been listening to you going on about the reasons for bad driving and accidents, ha,' Bah Kit suddenly said. 'But none of you has mentioned drunken driving, and I think I know why,' he added with a smile.

I was under the impression that Bah Kit was asleep, but apparently, he was only relaxing. He was, in fact, absolutely right. According to statistics, drunken driving is the biggest cause of road accidents in the state, and what is worse, there are no checks of any kind. I remember returning from Sohra on Holi last year. It was about 7 p.m. I was following a car that was weaving a line like a seismograph during a tremor. I mean, that guy was causing cars coming from the opposite direction to blare their horns madly and swerve into ditches and footpaths to avoid being hit. When he reached Rhino Point junction, he sent the traffic cones dividing the road flying everywhere, right in front of the traffic policeman. To my amazement, the policeman did nothing, and when we asked him about it, he said, 'What can I do? I'm alone here. Shall I try to catch him or control the traffic? And how do I catch him, on foot?' That is Shillong traffic for you.

Hamkom wagged a finger and said, 'Bah Kynsai, I have always warned you against driving after drinking ...'

Bah Kynsai laughed and said lightly, 'I don't drink much before driving, na, just a peg or two. But Raji also drives after drinking.'

'No, no, nowadays I don't drink and drive, Bah Kynsai, not since that accident,' Raji responded. 'I was hospitalised for almost a month with a broken hand and broken ribs, remember, Bah Su? Nowadays I drink at home before dinner. Before driving, I don't drink at all except a beer or two, no hard stuff.'

That is bad enough, of course, because Indian beer contains between 5 and 8 per cent alcohol. But I didn't say anything. I turned to look at the road and asked Dale where we were.

'We are making good progress, Bah,' Dale said, 'I'm going between sixty and eighty.'

Clearly, our talk had had little effect on Dale. At 60 to 80 km/h, he was going fairly fast on the twists and turns of our highways. But he was an expert driver, and the traffic was light, so I did not worry too much.

When we reached the village of Rangshken, merely 30 km from Shillong, we slowed to a caterpillar crawl, barely making 20 km/h. The road and the entire landscape were blanketed in a thick fog, making it impossible to see further than a few feet, and that too with fog lights and headlights on. I had been warned against this by people living in West Khasi Hills. At night, the frost settles on rivers and streams, on meadows and paddy fields, and when the sun comes out in the morning, it evaporates and rises as a dense cloud to shut out land and sky, making travelling truly perilous.

But Bah Kynsai was untroubled. He shouted to me, 'Ap, who was that minister involved in the fog story?'

'Bah Nit.'

'Yes, Bah Nit. Have you heard the story?'

Raji and Bah Su said they had, but the rest had not.

'It happened quite a few years ago,' Bah Kynsai began. 'Youngsters nowadays do not even know who Bah Nit is, but he was quite a character, ha. People liked him very much; he used to get things done very quickly. He would even beat up IAS officers for not doing their job quickly enough, and doctors for not being in their rural stations. Is he still alive, Ap?'

IAS, of course, means Indian Administrative Service, but among the Khasis it can also mean Iad Step, or morning drink, and can refer to a drunk who has moved up the ladder to drinking early in the morning.

Bah Su answered for me. 'He is, though he's old and doesn't leave his village any more.'

'But what a guy he was, na?' Bah Kynsai enthused. 'One day, while he was the minister of tourism, ha, he was asked to accompany a Union minister to Sohra. Probably the Congress stalwart, Margaret Alva. Somehow, Bah Nit's car, following some distance behind the minister's convoy, got stuck in a dense fog that rose suddenly from the ravines. The entire Sohra road is fringed by deep ravines on one side, you know that, na? So, when the fog came up, the driver, who had never been on such a road before, simply could not drive. It was only when the fog cleared a little, and when Bah Nit scolded him, that he started up again. But even then, he moved like a snail, and as a result, Bah Nit was very late for the function at Sohra Circuit House.

'When he arrived, na, he saw that everyone was waiting for him. He felt so embarrassed that he ran to the minister with both hands folded and apologised profusely. "Oh, madam, madam!" he said pleadingly. "So sorry, so sorry! But fucking, fucking all the way, what to do?"'

Everybody laughed at the story, and Magdalene was so tickled that she rocked to and fro, slapping her thigh. 'He meant to say, "fogging, fogging", didn't he?' she asked, breathless with mirth.

'Yes, yes,' Bah Kynsai said, 'but most Khasis pronounce "g" as "k", na, so he ended up saying, "fucking, fucking all the way".'

After a while, everybody quietened down and concentrated on the road ahead, as if they were in the driver's seat. By this time, about 7.45 a.m., there was a lot of traffic on the highway, mostly Sumo and Mahindra Max jeeps, bazaar buses and small vehicles, all proceeding towards Shillong. There were also lorries carrying coal, building stones, gravel, brown river sand, white hill sand and timber. Most farm produce was packed in pickup trucks or piled high on the roofs of buses. We could barely see anything. Like us, every car coming from the opposite direction had fog lights, headlights and hazard signals on. But every now and then, a Tata Sumo or a lorry would suddenly appear out of the gloom without any lights or signals at all. It was only Dale's alertness that saved us on these occasions. Obviously, we cursed and shouted at them, just to let off steam. We knew they could not hear us.

Another danger was the complete absence of signage. For instance, when we came to a tight bend, we did not know where the road would lead: should we go left or right? Dale kept moaning: 'If only they would draw a white line in the middle of the road and yellow lines on the sides!' In the absence of these, he followed the line of red sand at the edge of the highway.

We were thankful that at least the road was in really good condition, having been laid and tarred only recently as part of the two-lane highway from Shillong in East Khasi Hills to Tura in West Garo Hills. If it had been full of potholes, we would have had it! Imagine cars avoiding potholes, as they usually do, and driving on the wrong side of the road in this fog. Scary!

Dale said, 'An international company made this road, Bah, it's quite smooth. They double coated the tar. Imagine if Khasi contractors had done the job!'

'Khasi contractors?' Evening exclaimed. 'The road would have been full of lumps and hollows. Bumpy like hell! And because many of them would have been involved, ha, some portions would have been completed, while others would not have been built at all. By the time the incomplete portions were built, the completed portions would have become full of potholes. With Khasi contractors, ha, you never get a complete road; you get a road in perpetual disrepair.'

'Not only that,' Raji added, 'the tar would have been washed away by the first summer rains. People in the rural areas, okay, always say that local contractors just paint the road black to mislead people. The motive is always maximum profit for minimum work, never as per the estimates or the plans' specifications.'

'But what about the site engineers, overseers and *maharals*, the section assistants, who are supposed to supervise every project undertaken by the Public Works Department?' Hamkom asked.

'They are all in cahoots, na, they share the spoils,' Bah Kynsai explained. 'And yet we call ourselves *tip briew tip Blei*! More likely, we know demons and thievery. That's all.'

'Ka tip briew tip Blei' is one of the Three Commandments of Niam Khasi, but everybody, including those who no longer practise the religion, uses it to describe a life guided by conscience or the knowledge of man, the knowledge of God. That is, we use it in our everyday conversations, but hardly practise it, which is why Bah Kynsai made that bitter statement. Corruption, or money-eating if you will, is so rampant that it seems we live not in the knowledge of man and God but in the knowledge of Mammon and his demons.

'But why do you say, if the job is given to Khasi contractors, there would be many of them?' Donald asked.

'Two reasons,' Evening replied. 'First, there is not a single Khasi contractor rich enough to undertake the building of an entire highway. Second, politicians try to please everybody so they can extort from everybody. What they normally do is distribute the work piecemeal—so many kilometres, or even metres, to the first contractor, so many to the second, so many to the third, and so on. The excuse is, *ba kin ïa im lang*, so they may all survive. The true meaning is: so they may all steal.'

'That's horrible, man!' Donald said, aghast.

'In your travels, Donald,' Raji said, keen to rub it in, 'have you ever come across anything like this?'

Donald, of course, had nothing to say.

The fog finally cleared as we reached the outskirts of Nongstoin and the headquarters of the Third Meghalaya Police Battalion. It was surprisingly warm and sunny for a winter morning. We all nodded when Magdalene exclaimed, 'Hey! Nongstoin is much warmer than Shillong, ya!'

I could see peach blossoms everywhere. The peach trees in Shillong only begin to blossom in March, but here they were already waving their purple flags in the breeze.

It was almost 10.15 a.m. by the time we reached the heart of Nongstoin. The town itself turned out to be much larger, cleaner, much less dusty and much more organised than I remembered it to be. But then, the last time I was here was some sixteen years ago. There were several government offices and buildings in the outlying areas now. And many more houses too. Like in Shillong, many 'Assam-type' houses had been replaced by concrete structures, some of which were merely square boxes, two or three storeys high. However, there were also good-looking and well-designed buildings everywhere.

The centrally located commercial sectors were clean and not as congested as some of the places in Shillong. The traffic too, to my surprise, was quite orderly, and as we approached Nanbah, the commercial hub, I could see hundreds of taxis parked in an orderly fashion by the side of the broad road.

'Look, Bah,' Dale said, 'can you imagine Shillong taxis as neat as that? Shillong is a chaos of traffic, no, Bah?'

As we cruised through the town, looking for Indalin's shop, some of us wondered aloud at the transformation. Bah Kynsai exclaimed, '*Bong leh*! Ei Ap, where are all the Assam-type houses, man?'

'Bong leh' is almost a swear word, but not quite. Bah Kynsai had often said that one of the reasons why Shillong had become so ugly was because its quaint Assam-type houses had been replaced by squat, unsightly concrete boxes. The Assam-type houses were first constructed in Shillong after *U Jumai Bah*, the great earthquake of 1897. At the time of its establishment as the new district capital in 1864 (the move from Sohra was completed in 1866), most houses in Shillong, apart from government buildings, were of two types: those built of wood and thatch and those of stone and thatch. The migrants from Sohra brought with them their own architectural style, with the walls being built of *maw* Sohra or Sohra stone. This stone is still popular, and is really sandstone hewn into the shape of a *ruti*, rectangular bread, about one foot long and six inches wide.

The people of Sohra never used wood for their walls because of the heavy rainfall. Even after the advent of concrete structures, the stone continues to be used for building houses, fencing walls, making steps, courtyard paving, bridges, decorative pillars, monuments, culverts and drains. Building with maw Sohra does not require the use of either mortar or cement. Since the stones are finely carved, they fit snugly into each other, rendering any cementing mixture redundant. Many structures in the Sohra region, built in this way hundreds of years ago, are still standing without any sign of deterioration. If anything, the Sohra stone has now become even more popular. The arrival of new machines that can cut and polish it into smooth, glossy tiles, used in decorating interior and exterior walls as well as floors, has turned it into a very important export item.

The thatched roofs of Shillong houses, however, were replaced by roofs of corrugated iron sheets, or what we call 'tin roofs', because of the frequent outbreak of fire. (One such fire was the massive conflagration of 1878, which burnt down a significant portion of what was known then as Dukan Pulit, now Police Bazaar.) This style of 'stone-and-tin' or 'wood-and-tin' architecture continued until the great earthquake of 12 June 1897. The quake affected the whole of Ri Khasi and razed all the stone buildings to the ground. The devastation caused the British government to decree that stone houses be replaced by a lighter and safer variety of housing made of wooden frames, roofs of corrugated iron sheets, and walls of bamboo. The bamboo, called *kdait*, was reinforced by mortar—specifically, a mixture of water and lime. These houses quickly came to be known as 'Assam-type' houses, probably because Shillong had become, in 1874, the headquarters of the chief commissioner of Assam, a province carved out of British Bengal.

After 1897, therefore, Shillong was dominated by these humble cottages with their whitewashed walls and tin roofs painted mostly red or green or blue. They were built in the style of traditional English cottages, complete with a rising chimney and wide A-frames gently sloping to a flat roof that often ran along the entire circumference of the house. The flat roof was actually a covering for the veranda, which was made six to seven feet deep to provide effective protection from the wind-driven rain. Apart from the cottages, with their beautiful lawns and gardens full of fruit trees at the back, there were also grand bungalows, larger and more ornate, built almost in the Tudor style with turrets, dormer and bay windows, but using the same materials of tin, wood and mortar. These bungalows were often set in the middle of park-like grounds with tree-lined driveways winding through lawns bordered by flower beds. To look at them was to be filled with dreams and longing: their beauty was such that it smote you.

Thinking of those tranquil days, when there were neither too many people nor vehicles, I was reminded of a haiku by Bashō:

> bird of time—
> in Kyoto, pining
> for Kyoto.

I perfectly understood Bah Kynsai's dismay. The loss was not only of beautiful homes but also of those best suited for life in this part of the world. The Assam-type houses—with their tin roofs, bamboo-mortar walls and wooden floors—were warm and comfortable. They were easy on both humans and animals, unlike concrete houses with concrete floors, which only serve to heighten the winter chill. Bah Kynsai's own house was a modified Assam-type structure; in this respect, at least, he truly practised what he preached.

Donald wondered why people would swap something so suitable for our cold, wet and hilly environment for dreadful concrete boxes.

'Because they want to show off their money, mə, tdong,' Bah Kynsai snapped. He was not cursing Donald, only the general unreasonableness of people, as he saw it.

But Bah Su said, 'It's all very complicated, Bah Kynsai. What you said is partly true. People who have money, ha, obviously want to make big houses and high-rise buildings. But it's also a question of space. With the increase in population, there is a corresponding decrease in living space. Land is very expensive in urban areas like Shillong and Nongstoin. Most people can buy only about 2,000 to 2,500 square feet. But if it's a big family, they would need a house with many rooms. If you build a big single-storey Assam-type house on that kind of plot, ha, there will be hardly any space left for anything else. That's why they prefer concrete houses that can be built upwards—two, three, even four storeys. In this way, they can rent part of the building to tenants and earn some money as well. It is not practical to build a multi-storey Assam-type house because of the wooden pillars. And people also think that concrete houses last forever, ha, without any need for repairs, ha, only painting now and then. All these reasons … very complicated.'

'And now, even if you want to build an Assam-type house, okay, you can't!' Hamkom declared.

'The timber ban by the Supreme Court,' Raji offered as a reason.

'No, no, no,' Hamkom said. 'Forget about the timber ban. Even if there is plenty of wood, okay, you can't build an Assam-type house any more. I wanted to build one, ha, but then, what happened? To the left, a huge building; to the right, a huge building; at the back, another huge building. You see, if I had built a single-storey Assam-type house, ha, I would have ended up living in a sort of hollow, without sun, without scenery. Unless you have a huge plot of land, it's impossible to build such houses again.'

'But even in the rural areas, where they have plenty of space, people have started building multi-storey concrete houses, no?' Evening observed. 'What do you say to that, huh?'

'Fashion, vanity,' Bah Kynsai responded. 'People want to follow the fashion, na?'

'Also,' Bah Su added, 'they might have the same reasons I told you earlier.'

'Or they might want to build something beautiful,' Bah Kit added. 'You people are talking as if all concrete buildings are ugly and all Assam-type houses are beautiful. In Mawlai, where I live, ha, I can tell you there are still many Assam-type houses. Some of them are quite lovely, no doubt, built on extensive grounds and fronted by orange orchards that are wonderful to behold when the fruit ripen in winter. But others, belonging to the poor, or constructed for tenants, are flat-roofed and rectangular. Ugly, I tell you, very ugly. On the other hand, look, look at that concrete building over there, it's beautiful, no? I think it's designed by an architect—wonderful!'

I did not say anything, but I thought, that is what it boils down to: the rich can always build beautiful houses, whatever the materials; the poor must make do with what they can get.

'It may be attractive, but is it safe?' Donald asked Bah Kit. 'I mean, Bah Ap was telling us about the great earthquake that knocked down all the stone buildings in Shillong, no? Aren't people scared?'

'People forget,' Bah Su replied. 'The earthquake happened when? More than one hundred years ago. Since then, we haven't had an earthquake of that magnitude, ha, so people think it will never come again. But if it does, we've had it.'

'I think the situation has changed a bit, Bah Su,' Hamkom reminded him. 'You remember the devastating tremor in Nepal in 2015? After that, we have had a series of earthquakes, at least four, five times a month, across the Northeast. And the last one, Bah Su? That was really scary—6.8, I think. Fortunately, it did not last too long, otherwise terrible consequences would have followed. Whatever you say, people are scared nowadays. And everybody keeps saying the big one will come anytime now.'

'That's very true, Ham,' Bah Kit agreed. 'People are scared now, and those building new houses, ha, are trying to make them as strong as possible. They are, of course, still making concrete houses, but they are also trying to make them lighter by using reinforced tin roofs. They are all nervous, and expecting the big one to come.'

'It will come!' Halolihim said suddenly and with conviction. 'The world has become too sinful. God will send another great earthquake to punish all the sinners.'

'You may be the first one to die,' Magdalene said, laughing.

'Or you,' Halolihim retorted.

'Or you and I together,' Magdalene teased.

'Tet!' Halolihim said in a disgusted tone and turned away from her.

Everyone laughed.

'But coming back to Assam-type houses, ha, Bah Kynsai,' Hamkom said, 'we still have quite a few impressive ones in Shillong, no? What do you say, Ap?'

'Yeah, that's right,' I replied. 'Just around Ward's Lake itself, there are so many magnificent bungalows, like the governor's house, the Raj Bhavan. It's stately in black and white, with sprawling gardens. Then there is the Pine

Wood Hotel—so scenic, the oldest hotel in the city, constructed in 1898, I believe—and many other bungalows which now serve as quarters for ministers and high government officials. And oh yes, there's the famous Tara Ghar, which used to be the chief minister's residence. The English really tried to create a mini-England in that part of Shillong, Ham. All the houses look like Tudor-style manors, and to complete the illusion of an English landscape, they even created an artificial lake.'

'Why is Tara Ghar famous?' Donald asked. 'How is it different from the other Assam-type bungalows?'

'It is famous,' Bah Kynsai said, 'because the government tried to pull it down, na, to construct a new legislative assembly building there, na? But NGOs, prominent personalities and various organisations protested so much, ha, it had to give up the idea.'

'But why were they protesting?' Donald asked again. 'It seems to me there are too many protests in this place.'

'Oho! Tara Ghar is the green heart of this city, na—its lungs!' Bah Kynsai replied. 'They would have to cut down all the trees to build there, that's why. And besides, it is a heritage site, Don, with a lot of history.'

'Seriously,' Evening said, 'our leaders are so myopic, no? I mean, there is so much free space around, and yet they chose a heritage site that is an oasis of green in the heart of the city. When the entire world is talking about climate change, global warming and the need for afforestation, ha, here they are, hell-bent on desertification. Imagine what would happen to our planet if all the world leaders were like them! It would be destroyed in double-quick time. Stupid, really!'

'Leaders or dealers?' Bah Kynsai asked. 'They are good only at making deals, na, auctioning off our land and forests to fatten their own pockets. And they are not only myopic, Ning, but callous and completely without conscience or any moral sense at all, liah!'

'But what happened to the assembly building, Bah Kynsai?' Donald wanted to know. He had been away too long to know all that was happening here. He appeared to have lost some of his arrogance by now.

'The old assembly building was burnt down on 9 January 2001 ...'

'Burnt down, Bah Kynsai?' Hamkom said. 'I thought it was an accident, ya?'

'There are many who believe it was not an accidental fire, Ham. Some people trying to get rid of incriminating files, the rumour goes. But who knows, who knows? Anyhow, it was the most imposing sight in the heart of downtown Shillong. The best Assam-type structure there ever was! Even more beautiful than the Raj Bhavan. It was built about 128 years ago, imagine, 128 years! A real treasure, and they burnt it down, liah! How many years has it been now? Fifteen years! Fifteen years and they haven't been able to construct a new one. What a bunch of clowns!'

'But why, what's stopping them?' Hamkom asked, becoming interested.

'Raji, you tell him, you are the journalist.'

'It's a very funny thing, okay?' Raji began. 'First of all, some years after the incident, they constituted a high-powered committee—HPC, they called it—not to investigate the cause of the fire, ha, but to choose a site for the new assembly building. Yes, a new site, because the Speaker of the Meghalaya legislative assembly at the time, Martin M. Danggo, who was also the HPC chairman, did not think the old site was suitable any more. Why? Because the government had hurriedly sliced away a huge portion from the old site to enlarge and beautify Khyndai Lad …'

'Khyndai Lad?' Donald queried.

'Police Bazaar, man, the commercial hub of the city!' Raji said impatiently. 'An entire hillock, along with the beautiful pine trees planted by the British, was bulldozed to the ground almost overnight. Very suspicious move, many people thought.

'In 2006, the Danggo HPC chose a site in Upper Shillong near the Agriculture Research Station. However, his term as Speaker came to an end, another assembly election was held, a new regional-party government came to power, and Bindo M. Lanong became the new Speaker. His HPC rejected the recommendation of Danggo's HPC and resolved to construct the new assembly at the old site, which it thought was suitable after all, despite the diminished area. That was in 2008, okay? But nothing came of it, nobody really knew why. Then a fresh assembly election was held, the Congress party came to power, and Charles Pyngrope became the new Speaker. His HPC immediately rejected the Lanong HPC's recommendation and resolved to construct the new assembly building at Tara Ghar. Then, because of the public protest, okay, Pyngrope and the government had to give up the idea. Another five years went by, another assembly election was held, and again the Congress came to power, but with a new Speaker: A.C. Mondal. Now the Mondal HPC has finalised a plot of land in New Shillong measuring eighty acres, and this time it seems they mean business. They have already prepared a detailed project report. But still, we'll have to wait and see.'

Raji's report caused some of us to laugh out loud, and Hamkom summed it up by saying, 'What a story, huh?'

'Like Muhammad bin Tughluq's!' Bah Kynsai said. 'Now you know why this state is so backward, na? If the government cannot even build its own house, how can it build a better future for us, huh? You know, Raji, I think we might yet have to wait for another assembly election, man.'

'Why are these people like this?' Donald asked, sounding exasperated.

'Because many of our politicians, especially those from the rural areas, are not very well educated, no?' Evening explained. 'Some, you can even say, are barely educated. And then, many of them are also businessmen, ha, such people are not interested in development or making laws. Profiteering is the name of the game for them.'

'This is why I say that democracy will never work properly in India,' Bah Kynsai said. 'As long as most people are illiterate and unenlightened, na, they will always elect people like these.'

'You know what, Bah Kynsai,' Donald observed, 'the best thing for Indian democracy, okay, would be to make it necessary for all aspiring politicians to have a minimum qualification, a bachelor's degree and above, like they have for the Civil Services exams. That's the only way we can ensure some quality in governance. What do you think?'

Bah Su said, 'Many of our MLAs are graduates, Don, but it doesn't help. A degree doesn't make them well educated, ha, mostly because, as students, they never read anything other than the books in the syllabus ...'

'Most students don't read books, Bah Su, only bazaar notes,' Bah Kynsai said.

'Yeah, yeah, you are right,' Bah Su agreed, laughing. 'So, you see, a degree alone is no good: the problem is much more complex, ha. And we cannot blame only the politicians. In fact, our people are mostly to blame for these corrupt politicians. I have many friends who are MLAs and MDCs, ha, and they tell me that the moment elections are announced, all sorts of people and organisations come to them to demand money and things. A cultural organisation will come for sound systems and whatnot; a sports organisation for uniforms, football boots, cricket bats and gloves; a religious organisation for money to organise this or that function or gathering. Some organisations crop up only during the elections ... Why? So they can demand money from candidates, no?

'All sorts of other people come too—some to request money for tuition fees, textbooks and school uniforms; others for stoves, cooking materials, blankets and corrugated iron sheets. The list is unending. And there are also supporters or purported supporters, who demand feasts and drinks and incidental expenses every day. And these fellows who contest elections have no option but to please them. So what do they do? They spend all their savings and raise more money by accepting contributions from business people, some even borrowing from loan sharks. Therefore, when they win, ha, the first thing they do is cook up schemes to recover their losses and please their contributors and funders. That's how it works. So, who's to blame for the money-eating?'

'That's why I said that people should be educated and enlightened, na?' Bah Kynsai said.

'That's right, Bah Kynsai,' Bah Su agreed. 'In fact, it is because of the voters, ha, that we are not getting quality leaders. People don't look at the larger picture when they elect MLAs or MDCs. They don't care whether the person is going to provide roads and electricity. They don't care about his stand on the influx of migrants, uranium mining or any of the burning issues of the day. They only care about whether he will help them during sickness and bereavement.'

'Very true, very true, Bah Su,' Bah Kynsai said, laughing. 'That's why, in every locality and village, na, every politician has got a person whose only function is to tell them when somebody dies. And you know what? They actually compete with each other to be the first to reach the death house, can you believe it?'

'Yes, yes, correct, correct,' Evening said. 'A politician who is ever ready to visit the homes of bereaved families is what Khasis are looking for.'

Amidst the laughter and head-nodding that followed, Halolihim, who had been quiet thus far, said sourly, 'You people are very funny—from Assam-type houses to politics!'

'Because they are connected, no, Hal?' Hamkom said. 'But if you want us to come back to Assam-type houses, let me tell you of the most beautiful ones around Shillong ... the Tripura Castle, built by the king of Tripura in 1924; the Golf Club Bungalow at Golflinks; the All Saints' Cathedral at IGP Point ...'

'Let me tell you about my favourite one, at Lawsohtun, Ham,' I interrupted. Many of them, apart from Bah Kynsai, whose house is near Lawsohtun, expressed surprise that there could be any beautiful Assam-type houses there, for they thought of it as a mere rural settlement on the fringe of Shillong. 'Have you heard of the sericulture farm?' I asked.

Some of them nodded, but most looked blank.

Bah Kynsai exclaimed, 'Ka Pham Khñiang, mə, tdong!'

Ka Pham Khñiang, literally, 'insect farm', is what the locals call the sericulture farm. Khasis have a knack for that sort of naming. For example, a renowned scholar is respectfully referred to as *u ñiang bam kot*, a book-eating insect.

The farm is a sprawling twenty-one-acre mulberry grove located in a valley enclosed by gently sloping hills on three sides. A reserve forest, thick with Khasi pines and evergreen deciduous trees, fringes its southern slope. The forest, with its many springs and brooks, serves as the water source for many Shillong localities. Just beyond the trees, where the slope levels off to an extensive plateau, there is a small but elegantly designed guesthouse with an immaculate lawn. The lawn is bordered by pink and red roses, white camellias, pink and white azaleas, and two huge pines called *seh Bilat*, or English pines. Adjacent to it are some office buildings; below it are buildings used for rearing and feeding the silkworms, and on the northern slope are more such buildings and employee quarters. On an extensive plateau on the western hill are more employee quarters and the houses of the manager and other officers.

What makes the place so delightful is not only that all the red-top buildings (which date back to 1925, to British rule) are quaint Assam-type houses, often with a double-roof design and black-and-white walls, but also that they are surrounded by a mulberry grove. Two roads lead from the valley into the hills: one goes left towards the guesthouse and the other right, towards the officers' quarters. The only sounds here are people calling out to each other from their hilltop homes, dogs barking, and the melodies of myriad birds and insects that frequent the grove and the forest nearby. This is my sylvan retreat. But not only mine, it seems. There is a poem eulogising the place; I read it in a local newspaper:

> As the moon rises above a precipitous pine forest
> (like our maid's flatbread, imperfectly rounded),
> with motor cars merely as distant glimmers,
> on a road winding through a mulberry grove,
> as birds make their last calls before they sleep
> and countless little creatures come alive,
> the wind speaks to me with diverse tongues at once,
> as if desperate to make itself understood.
> The wind dishevels my hair and licks my face,

pulls at my clothes and frisks my pockets,
and twists about my body like a seductress.
And this too is happiness because
for a brief span of stolen time
(enclosed in the moment,
with firefly blue lights flashing in my face)
I can halt the mad hurtling of days,
and feel the night putting an arm
around my shoulder, protectively.

The poem is aptly titled 'Happiness'.

When I described the farm and recited the poem, many in the group wanted to visit it someday. Even Halolihim said, 'That sounds like a perfect retreat for the one true God.'

Hamkom now spoke of the *dak banglas*, or inspection bungalows, built by the British in strategic villages like Laitlyngkot, which is on the way to Dawki and the Bangladesh border, and Mawkdok, which is on the way to Sohra. He also spoke at length of various buildings, including the famous Circuit House and the Presbyterian Theological College in Sohra, before returning again to Shillong and saying, 'I think the most famous Assam-type houses, at least in Shillong, are Jitbhoomi and Brookside, no, Ap?'

'Why?' Donald asked.

Hamkom reacted rather sharply to his question. 'You really don't know anything about your own state, do you, Don? These houses were associated with Rabindranath Tagore, man! He visited Shillong in … Ap, why don't you tell them, you are more familiar with it, no?'

I was on my phone, trying and failing to reach Indalin. I agreed to tell the story if Raji would keep trying the number.

Tagore visited Shillong three times: in 1919, 1923 and 1927. During his first two visits, he stayed in Jitbhoomi and Brookside, both in Rilbong and both incredibly lovely. I can well imagine the poet sitting on the wide verandas, revelling in their quiet solitude and composing his poems. On his last visit, he stayed in Sidli House at Upland Road, Laitumkhrah. The house belonged to the Raja of Sidli, whose kingdom falls in the present-day Goalpara district of Assam. While in Shillong, the Nobel laureate wrote poems, songs, dramas and novels, and the town featured in all of them. The evocative poem '*Shillonger Chithi*' ('Letter from Shillong'), which he wrote while at Jitbhoomi at the request of two girls from Kolkata, speaks of Shillong with great fondness and admiration. Since I had a prose rendering of the poem, in English, saved on my phone, I read it aloud:

When the heat of the plains could not be assuaged by fans and *sharbat*, I rushed to the cool heights of the hills called Shillong. The mountain ranges with their mantle of clouds seemed to beckon weary travellers to take refuge in the deep shade of woods on their hillsides. The meandering streamlets follow their course with a soft murmur, caressing the heart with their soothing music. Winds blow gently through the branches of pine trees, driving away accumulated poison in the air and rejuvenating the weak and the sick with their life-giving breath.

Nature changes and unfolds a new lively face at every turn of the road cutting its way through rocky hillsides. Compared to Darjeeling, the cold is bearable here, a *kadai* shawl is enough to keep it at bay. Cherrapunjee, with its reputation for rains, though not very far away, the rain clouds do not shower frequently on us here. It is pleasant here to watch the moon play hide-and-seek through branches of trees, but it is more pleasant still when the wind scatters the scent of pine leaves all around. I am quite happy here, roaming leisurely through the woods, picking flowers as I please or watching the dance of nameless birds or listening to the whistles of bulbuls. It is pleasant here during the noonday when the soft and sweet breeze wafts in from the pine groves standing guard on the hills. It is pleasant to watch the mosaic of light and shade fleeting by, or the cultivated terraces on the hill slopes at a distance. It is pleasant to see when the sun is held captive behind clouds or when the sun makes peace with Indra, the rain god, illuminating the sky with its blue and red effulgence.

I concluded my reading by saying, 'The translation is by J.N. Chowdhury, the author of *The Khasi Canvas*.'

Everyone clapped except Dale, who was driving.

He laughed and said, 'Poetry on a mobile, Bah?'

'All my favourite poems are here. Other things too.'

'Why, Dale, is it so strange to have poems on your mobile?' Evening asked. 'You must have music and videos on yours, no? It's the same thing. You have those; we have poems, articles, news clips, anything we find interesting.'

'We all do, man,' Bah Kynsai added. 'It's become part of our culture, na? Haven't you seen people whipping out their mobiles like six guns and quoting stuff from here and there?'

'I have jokes, anything that can make me laugh,' Magdalene told Dale.

'I have the whole Bible on mine,' Halolihim boasted. 'I can read it anywhere, even without network.'

'Yeah, yeah, we all have good stuff and bad stuff on our mobiles,' Hamkom laughed. 'But, man, that was a real gem, ya, Ap! And I think Tagore was the most famous personality ever to visit Shillong, no?'

I wanted to say that was not entirely true. Shillong has had many illustrious visitors, including the viceroy and governor-general of India, Lord Willingdon, and his wife, Countess Willingdon, who came here on 4 October 1933. Another viceroy, Lord Linlithgow, had visited on 28 July 1937. Netaji Subhas Chandra Bose is also supposed to have visited Shillong before Independence. Many years later, during his tenure as the president of the Indian National Congress, he made some complimentary remarks about the Khasi system of traditional democracy, which, he said, he had personally witnessed in action. Swami Vivekananda came to Shillong in 1901 and stayed at a cottage in Laban called Ghouranga Lodge. C.V. Raman, the physicist and Nobel laureate, visited many times, the last time as a guest of the governor at Raj Bhavan. At one point during that visit, he was so lost in gazing at the 'enchanting blue of the Shillong sky' from a quiet spot in the garden that he caused quite a stir among the governor's servants, who were trying to find him for a late luncheon. Nirad C. Chaudhuri, another Nobel laureate, whose wife, Amiya Dhar, was from Shillong, also visited the town at least once and made references to it in his *Autobiography of an Unknown Indian*. In the book, he talks about the 'medley of images formed by the stories of hills, pine trees, gorges, English babies, Gurkhas, pear trees and prayer halls', though disappointingly, nothing about Khasis.

I wanted to say all this, but Bah Kynsai beat me to it. 'Who told you Tagore was famous? He was famous only among Bengalis, na? Most Khasis, apart from those who read books, and they are few, do not know anything about him, you know that? And I can prove it—with a story, a true story.'

This is how the story went. One day, some Bengali tourists from Kolkata came to Rilbong looking for Jitbhoomi and Brookside, where Tagore had stayed when he came to Shillong. The tourists met a Khasi man who was cleaning a wall by the roadside. They asked him, 'Mama, do you know the houses where Rabindranath Tagore used to stay?'

The Khasi looked at them pensively and said, 'Rabindranath Tagore ... I don't think I know ...'

The Bengali tourists were shocked beyond belief. 'What! You don't know where Rabindranath Tagore, our great poet, our *Gurudev*, used to stay?' they cried. 'This is Rilbong, no? The houses are here, think very carefully, Mama.

Rabindranath Tagore is the greatest poet of India, of the whole world even! You must know, you should know!'

Ashamed that he did not know, the Khasi man thought hard. He looked at the sky, thinking intently, all the while repeating, 'Rabindranath, Rabindra, Rabin …' and then he shouted with sudden recognition, 'Oh, you mean Bah Robin! He is working in PWD, come, come, I'll show you his house.'

And with that, he took them to a concrete house up the road and said, 'This is the house of Bah Robin, but I don't think you'll find him at home. Gone to office.'

Bah Kynsai ended the story with a booming laugh, and Hamkom cursed him good-humouredly for telling such a joke. But Bah Kynsai insisted it was a true story. He said, 'There are many Khasis who are named Robin, na, that's why that fellow they were asking about the house of his neighbour, Robin Lyngdoh.'

'But not knowing Rabindranath Tagore is damning evidence of our ignorance, Bah Kynsai,' Donald said seriously.

'Of course it is. Who said it is not?'

Meanwhile, Dale had been driving in circles around Nongstoin, trying to find Indalin's tea shop while I tried to connect with her again and again, without success. Everybody cursed the *phaltu* networks and urged me to keep trying. Finally, I got through to her. 'In, where is your tea shop? We have been going around in circles looking for it.'

'Tea shop?' Indalin laughed. 'I don't have a tea shop any more. I converted it into a general store. It's at Nanbah. Just ask anybody where Kong Lin's general store is, and they will tell you. Or you can ask for the Lyngngam School; my shop is near the school.'

Dale laughed. 'That's why we couldn't find it, Bah. We were asking for Kong In's tea shop, not Kong Lin's general store.'

Hearing the name of Lyngngam School, Bah Kynsai simulated great excitement and said, 'Aha, the smell of Lyngngam already!'

We soon found Indalin's shop with the help of some people whom we stopped and asked. They were very precise in their instructions.

'The way these people gave us directions, no, Ap, reminds me of a story I was once told,' Magdalene said.

The story was about a Khasi woman who was approached by a Hindi-speaking man for directions to an office. The woman wanted to be helpful (this is a common Khasi trait, I'm proud to say), and tried to give clear and exact directions so he would not get lost. However, since she knew only a little Hindi, she decided to improvise and said: '*Mama, yahan aao. Yeh rasta dekha? Aisa karo: shida jao, jao, jao, jao. Phir aisa karo* (indicates a left turn with her hand) *aur shida jao, jao. Phir aisa karo* (indicates a right turn) *aur shida jao, jao, jao, jao, jao, jao, jao, jao … Uder.*'

In English, it goes something like this: 'Uncle, come here. You see this road? You do this: go straight, straight, straight, straight. Then you do this (indicates a left turn with her hand) and go straight, straight. Then you do this (indicates a right turn) and go straight, straight, straight, straight, straight, straight, straight, straight … There.'

The man, it seemed, understood, followed her directions and found his office.

Indalin was standing by the roadside to receive us, looking quite well and prosperous. She embraced me and kissed me on both cheeks and said, 'I never thought I'd see you again. You see,' she added, addressing my friends and laughing, 'he is my uncle, but he remembers me only when he needs me.'

In reply, I quoted from a poem:

> Weak candlelight
> remembered only
> during a blackout.
> We too like you,
> remembered
> like weak candlelight.

After a hearty laugh, she invited us into her shop.

Indalin's shop was in the basement of a two-storey building by the Shillong–Tura highway, right where we had seen a lot of taxis parked. The shop was below the level of the road and not very attractive from the outside. But inside, it exuded an aura of prosperity. Every corner was stocked with foodstuff—sacks of rice, lentils, sugar, salt, flour, potatoes, tins of mustard oil and small household goods of every description. Dominating the far end of the shop was a huge refrigerator in which cold drinks and food items were kept, and near it, cordoned off by a low wooden screen, were books, exercise books and a range of stationery.

'You also sell books or what?' I asked.

She said she had to, since there were not many books or stationery stores in town, and being a teacher herself, she wanted to help students by providing what they needed at reasonable prices. Too often, things were overpriced, she said, but since she bought directly from Shillong at wholesale prices, she could afford to sell them at rates lower than others.

'Waa,' I said to myself, 'a conscientious trader! And my niece at that!'

I asked if business was all right, and she said it was, especially on market days, twice a week. A young man helped her with the shop and looked after it in her absence. In winter, during the two-month school vacation, she spent most of her time in the shop, but during term, she had to divide her time judiciously.

We were all impressed by her energy and drive. She was a small, compact woman, with an affecting friendliness that immediately endeared her to people. She now told us that we should go to her house where Chirag would be waiting, and where we could leave our car until we returned.

We were late by almost three hours, and I worried about keeping Chirag waiting. I'm a stickler for time, a teacher's habit, I suppose. A teacher cannot be late by even a minute; it would be a bad example to set. I dislike being thought of as tardy, and certainly did not want to give Chirag that impression the very first time we met. An explanation about the fog should set his mind at rest, I thought.

I revised my opinion of a cleaner Nongstoin on the way to Indalin's house. Garbage was dumped all over the marketplace. At a point called Khlieh Ïew (upper market), it had taken over an enormous ground, the size of a football field. Nobody did anything, nobody cared, I was told. This is a problem everywhere in the Khasi Hills: in Shillong, in rural areas and urban centres. People just dump their garbage anywhere, as long as it is outside their compound. It has got so bad that all the rivers and streams running through towns and villages are now drains into which tonnes of waste are thrown and effluents from households and septic tanks are discharged. Ironically, Mawlynnong village in East Khasi Hills is considered to be the cleanest village in Asia.

Chirag, we found, had not yet arrived. Indalin's mother, whom everyone lovingly called Hoi, was visiting her at the time, and greeted us warmly. I had not met her for quite some time, so we had a lot of catching up to do, exchanging news about our families and the people we both knew. Indalin showed us around the house, a neat green-and-white Assam-type house, quite roomy and warm.

Meanwhile, her mother said we should have some food while we waited for Chirag.

'How can you feed so many of us?' we protested. 'We can eat in a shop somewhere. It's all right, please don't bother.'

But she simply would not listen to our objections. The food had been prepared, she said, and would go to waste if we did not eat. And anyway, she added, it was a joy to feed a large group like ours. That was a logic I did not understand, but perhaps only someone with a truly big heart could. Then, of course, Hoi owned a jadoh stall in Sohra, so maybe she felt, the more the merrier.

Jadoh is a favourite Khasi delicacy. Literally, it means 'meat-rice', and for lack of a better term, that is what I am going to call it. There are many ways of cooking it across the Khasi Hills. For instance, in Shillong, the rice is cooked with pig's fat and pieces of pig's offal in a mixture of spices, including onions, black pepper, garlic, black sesame seeds and turmeric. In Sohra, jadoh is called *jasnam* because it is cooked with pig's blood, fat and intestines, all mixed with onions ground into a soft paste. Connoisseurs insist that the Sohra variety is tastier. But again, these are only two varieties. There are also chicken jadoh, cooked with chicken blood, pieces of chicken meat and the spices mentioned above, and fish jadoh, cooked with fish heads and these same spices.

Everywhere in the Khasi Hills, jadoh stalls are a common sight. They sell not only jadoh but also plain rice, various types of meat curries, tea and biscuits, and other Khasi foods. I have known many non-Khasi friends who take readily to jadoh, even when they are vegetarians at home. But White people are rarely partial to it. When my friend Nigel was visiting Sohra, I took him to Hoi's jadoh stall. He heard the fellows travelling with us ordering jadoh and *dohkhlieh*, which I explained to him is boiled pig's head, cut into small pieces and mixed with boiled pig's brain, onion, ginger and chillies.

He immediately commented: 'I can't imagine people eating pig's head and pig's brain, can you?'

'Yeah,' I replied absent-mindedly.

'And you, do you eat them?'

'Yeah,' I said again.

Nigel was so disgusted, he cursed: 'You bloody Khasi!'

There was no jadoh this time, though. Hoi dished out an early lunch of steaming hot rice with a curry of fish and beans, served with slices of raw tomatoes. For chutney, we had the famous pickled *ken rakot*, or monster chilli, also known as *bhut jolokia* in Assamese, supposedly the hottest chilli in the world.

Before we could start eating, Halolihim said, 'Let us pray.'

Hamkom said, perhaps fearing that his friend might take too long, 'Hal, let Bah Kynsai say grace.'

Bah Kynsai did not want to do it, but he did not want the food to get cold either, so he said, 'Let us pray.' Closing his eyes, he began, 'Oh Lord, we know you are there, and you know we are here … Have mercy upon us. Amen.'

Before anyone could comment, Bah Kynsai said, 'I learned that from a friend of mine, a Catholic priest.'

'But you are a Presbyterian, no?' Halolihim objected. 'You …'

We never found out what Halolihim wanted to say, for Bah Kynsai interrupted him and said with a deadpan expression, 'Outstanding Presbyterian! However, a prayer to the Lord is a prayer to the Lord.'

It was a beautiful meal that reminded me, after a very long time, of the cooking of my departed uncle, famous for his 'tasty hands'. I thanked Hoi profusely. We all did.

But there was still no sign of Chirag.

As we stood in the spacious courtyard, enjoying the warmth of the morning sun, Donald said, 'You were all talking about the great earthquake of 1897, how big was it really?'

'One of the biggest in the world,' Bah Su answered. He was about to say something more when Bah Kynsai asked, 'Wasn't he supposed to meet us here by 8.30 this morning, Ap?'

'Yeah, and if we had not been held up by Halolihim, the fog and that aimless circling, we would have been here on time. I don't know what's happened to him, but In is taking care of it.'

In fact, while we were eating, Indalin had been calling Chirag, pestering him to come immediately. On the first call, he was in a petrol pump nearby, filling the tank. That was 11.25 a.m. On the second, he was on the way. That was 11.35. On the third, he was coming. That was 11.45. On the fourth, he was nearly here. That was 11.50. I asked Indalin, 'How far is his house from here?'

'Not very far,' she replied. 'Nongstoin is not as large as Shillong.'

Halolihim, who had been restlessly pacing the courtyard, suddenly said, 'What kind of fellow is this? He is late by more than three hours, man!'

Raji remarked, '*Twad shuwa ïa la ka lyngkdong* … feel your own nape first.'

'What is that supposed to mean?' Halolihim asked belligerently.

'It means,' Raji said slowly, 'first think about your own actions.'

That shut him up. But when Chirag kept saying he was coming without actually turning up, even Raji lost patience. 'Ei, Ap, this fellow is taking us for a ride or what?'

We had agreed to meet between 8.30 and 9 a.m., but it was 11.50 and he had still not come! Nongshyrkon was supposed to be quite far, many hours of hard travel over a jungle road that only four-wheel vehicles could traverse. Could we trust this fellow at all?

But Indalin insisted he was okay; he might be tardy, but he was not a swindler. 'He'll take you there all right,' she assured us, 'don't worry.'

Finally, Chirag appeared at noon, after another call from Indalin. He was late by three and a half hours.

He came rattling down the slope from the marketplace in an ancient-looking, blue hardtop Gypsy. The moment he got down, his brown face broke into a guilty grin, and then, quickly addressing Indalin, he said in a loud voice, 'Oooh, Kong Lin, so sorry, so many things to do, is this *Babu* Ap? *Khublei, Babu*, I am so sorry, the car had some problems, no, Babu, I had to take it to a mechanic, but I'm here now, don't worry, you are in my hands, I'll get you to Nongshyrkon before dark. I have brought two Gypsys, one is on top of the hill there, my *kynum* will be driving that one, how many of you are there? Twelve, no problem, six here, six there, who will sit here with me? You better put away your jackets and sweaters at Kong Lin's. Though it's winter, it's very hot in Nongshyrkon … it's like the Garo Hills, Babu.'

Khublei is a popular form of greeting, and kynum means 'brother-in-law'.

Chirag took us all by surprise. He spoke almost without pause. Indalin wanted to reprimand him, but didn't get a chance because he was busy emptying his car of odds and ends, which he dumped roughly at the back— she shrugged and smiled helplessly at us.

Chirag was huge by Khasi standards—taller than Bah Kynsai, who was five feet ten. And also much broader in the shoulders, much thicker in the chest, muscular and taut. His hands were large and rough looking, and all in all, he appeared to be a man of great strength. The bulging stomach should have spoilt the effect, but somehow, it only made him look robust and healthy. He had on a pair of tight-fitting brown corduroy jeans, a sweater and a whitish coat that was not very clean.

We decided that Bah Kynsai, Bah Su and I should be in the same jeep. Donald and Magdalene, who were close friends of Bah Kynsai, wanted to travel with us, and Dale wanted to be where I was. The other group would be led by Raji and Hamkom.

Chirag had finished tidying the car, and he now turned to us. 'Who is going with me? Babu, I think, is going with me, come, come, Babu, we are late.'

I felt like saying that we were late because of him, but what was the point? As he said, we were now in his hands. So, instead, I said, 'We are all babus here, Bah Chirag. This is Babu Kynsai, this is Babu Hamkom, and this one here is Babu Magdalene, a female babu. Babu Kynsai is at the university; Babu Ham and Babu Mag are college teachers.'

Khasis call their teachers 'babu', a term of profound respect. While in the rest of India a babu is a government officer, here such an officer is a *sahep*, sometimes the equivalent of 'sir', at other times more than 'sir', depending on the tone of the speaker. Government employees who are not officers are simply called 'Bah' and 'Kong', or 'Mama' and '*Didi*' if they are non-Khasis. But non-Khasis are also called 'Bah' or 'Kong' often enough. For instance, I have a wonderful Bengali friend whom I call 'Bah Deb'. And he enjoys it because, in this case, it is a term of endearment.

I proceeded to introduce the rest of the group, ending with Bah Kit. 'And this is Bah Kitshon,' I said, 'another kind of babu: he's a government officer.'

Chirag, having shaken the hands of all the others, reached out to Bah Kit and said, '*Kumno*, Sahep?'

Kumno, how are you, is another common Khasi greeting, rivalled only by the term 'khublei', literally 'God bless'. Khublei also serves as hello, welcome, thank you and farewell. There is a poem on the word, written by J.T. Sunderland, a famous American Unitarian minister and reformer:

> KHUBLEI! 'God Bless You' so the
> Simple Khasis say,
> Whenever they meet each other on
> Their hillside paths.
> This is their morning greeting, this
> Their evening word.
> This is their welcome to a friend
> Returned from afar,
> And this is their farewell when from
> Friends they part.
> KHUBLEI! 'God Bless You'
> Is not here a just rebuke to our
> Impiety,

That we, though Christians called,
Habitual meet and part
With speech that hath on it a word
Or thought of God?
Has not the God of all the earth
A lesson deep
Of reverence and humility to teach
To us—to us
Proud Christian ...—by this
Sweet greeting
Of a simple race? KHUBLEI—
'God Bless You'.

When the introductions were done, Chirag escorted Raji's group to the Gypsy driven by his brother-in-law—a much smaller man than him, about five feet eight inches or so, but quite muscular. He had a very confident manner.

After he had deposited them safely in the jeep, Chirag came back down the slope and said, 'Shall we go, Babu? Babu will sit with me in the front, the rest of you, please pile into the two seats at the back.'

Chirag's enthusiastic respect made me warm to him immediately, my earlier unease quite melting away. How easily won over most of us are, I thought ruefully, by a little bit of attention and flattery.

When we were all settled, Chirag started the car with a jolt. But it got stuck in the middle of the slope and he had to reverse again. 'No *spid*, that's why,' he explained, 'but don't worry, I have special gear.'

He used his four-wheel gear and off we went, shooting up the slope as everyone in the courtyard—Indalin, her mother, her two sons and daughter—shouted 'Bye-bye'.

As I was yanked forward and slammed backward by Chirag's sudden burst of speed, I thought what a very funny thing it is that all of us should have forgotten our beautiful traditional greeting of '*leit suk*', go in peace or go happily. Most of us say 'bye', and it is the only English word, I think, that almost all Khasis use without danger of mispronunciation. There are other English words that have become currency, but always adapted to the local tongue, like Chirag's spid for speed, *phun* for phone, *skul* for school and so on. Only 'bye' has truly become a Khasi word in all its Englishness.

The outskirts of Nongstoin, on the way to Lyngngam, were quite lovely, with wide-open spaces, playgrounds and nicely painted houses. Chirag said he owned a plot of land there and planned to build a house on it very soon. He pointed to it as we passed by: a spacious, flat and squarish plot, fringed with a variety of trees, definitely a beautiful spot for a house.

The road, however, began to deteriorate at this point, and by the time we came to what Chirag described as 'the biggest coal depot in Meghalaya', the asphalt had vanished entirely. The jungle road, characterised here by black coal dust, huge potholes and melon-sized stones, had already begun.

Bah Kynsai asked, 'How can the jungle road begin from the very outskirts of a district capital, man?'

Very calmly, Chirag replied, 'Actually, it starts about eight kilometres from here, Babu, there used to be a painted road here, but now you can see only pieces of the blacktopping here and there.'

Khasis refer to a macadamised road as '*surok rong*', literally, 'painted road'.

'But why?' Bah Kynsai insisted. 'Nongstoin is the district capital of West Khasi Hills, na?'

'I think because Maieit, *bam kwai ha iing u Blei*, did not belong to the ruling party, Babu, so he could not do anything.'

Chirag was referring to Hoping Stone Lyngdoh, the MLA who had represented Nongstoin for many years and who was called Maieit, 'loving uncle', by everyone. Hoping had died as recently as 26 September 2015, that is, four months ago. That's why Chirag had appended his words with 'bam kwai ha iing u Blei' ('may he eat betel nut in the house of God'). Khasis do this whenever they refer to a departed person. The practice properly belongs to the Khasi religion, which accords a great symbolic significance to the betel nut (a remarkable story, which I will tell you later). Nevertheless, every Khasi, without exception, uses this invocation as a charm to avert evil or ill luck whenever they mention the dead.

'But that's nonsense, na?' Bah Kynsai said. 'An MLA doesn't have to be in the ruling party to be able to build local roads, man! He's given MLA schemes worth two crore rupees per year, which is meant for small developmental works in his constituency, like building approach roads, link roads and so on, so why didn't he make use of it? And he represented Nongstoin forever, na? In fact, from when we were a part of Assam in 1962 till the day he died, na, Bah Su?'

'Except for five years when he became a Member of Parliament in 1977,' Bah Su clarified. 'He was an MLA eleven times, an MDC seven times and an MP once: he never lost an election, not even once.'

'Never lost, never lost, not even once,' Chirag repeated. 'We love him here, you cannot say anything bad about him, he was a unique person, some say he had miraculous powers. During elections he never gave money to anyone, he never gave food or alcohol like the others, and he never even canvassed, and yet he never lost, people loved him like anything.'

'So why is there a jungle road in the middle of Nongstoin?' Bah Kynsai asked again.

'People say Bah Hoping was not very fond of roads,' Bah Su explained. 'When people came to him demanding good roads, ha, he would say, "Why would you want good roads? Roads will only bring more drunkenness, prostitution, drug addiction, and many more deaths and accidents." I heard he was not in favour of the Shillong–Tura highway either.'

'But how could he have opposed it?' Bah Kynsai asked. 'It's a very important highway, na? Isn't that true, Chirag?'

'I don't know, Babu, people will say anything, but I think it was because he was not in the ruling party in the last few years.'

Bah Su refused to buy that. 'The roads in West Khasi Hills have always been bad, ha, and they were bad even when Bah Hoping was a minister in the state government. In fact, they were bad when he was a deputy chief minister between 2008 and 2009. His contribution to the development of West Khasi Hills leaves a lot to be desired.'

'So, for crying out loud, why was he so loved?' Magdalene asked.

'I'll tell you why, ha,' Bah Su said. 'Bah Hoping ventured into electoral politics in 1957 when he was elected member of the United Khasi Jaiñtia Hills Autonomous District under the state of Assam—that's what it was then. In 1962, he became one of the few Khasi leaders who made it to the then composite Assam Legislative Assembly. He represented Nongstoin. Later, he fought in the Hill State Movement, demanding a separate state for Meghalaya under the leadership of the All Party Hill Leaders' Conference. Following a disagreement with its foremost leaders, he founded his own party in 1968, the Hill State People's Democratic Party, and remained its president till the day he died.

'What endeared people to him, ha, was his integrity. He never once compromised his principles, which were simple and clear. He condemned the formation of the state of Meghalaya, which included the districts of Khasi Hills, Jaiñtia Hills and Garo Hills. He wanted a separate state for the Khasi people without the Garos, with whom we have nothing in common, and till the day he died, he never gave up his demand. He condemned the formation of Meghalaya without a proper boundary demarcation and repeatedly called upon the various governments to solve the boundary disputes with Assam. Initially, he was the only MLA to come out openly against the move of the Union government to mine for uranium at Domïasiat in West Khasi Hills, which he thought would be disastrous for his people. But above all, he was an honest and clean political leader, ha, perhaps the only one in the history of Meghalaya politics.'

'How do you know he was clean when so many of our politicians are greed-infested pigs?' Magdalene asked.

'Well, it's an open secret, Kong Mag. Bah Hoping was an MLA for forty-six years, an MP for five years and an MDC for many years. But he did not even own a house. He lived in his sister's house. He was a bachelor all his life and did not believe in acquiring property or accumulating wealth. There are stories about how he gave away his earnings to the poor and needy in his constituency. Now, how many leaders would you say are like that? As you said, most of them are greedy and self-serving. That's the secret of his undying popularity.'

Bah Kynsai remained unimpressed. 'He may have been honest, but the people around him, na, those who worked with him, were not, and he couldn't do anything about them. Nor could he do anything about the issues that he raised. He couldn't stop his colleagues from including the Garos in the Hill State Movement. Nor could he prevent them from accepting a state without boundaries. But worst of all, to my mind, was the fact that he did nothing to develop either the state or the district. Thinking about him, na, Bah Su, I'm reminded of the story of a very high-ranking bureaucrat who scolded his idle staff by saying, "You people, before you got your own state you shouted, 'No hill state, no rest', but now that you have your own state, only rest, rest, rest, no work!" He went on to say that he preferred a corrupt officer to people like them. According to him, na, a corrupt officer will always do some work, initiate some project or organise some programme so he can also steal a little. But honest officers, because they are afraid to steal, na, see no benefit in working or initiating new projects. They only want to keep files pending. Now, the question is, do we prefer a corrupt but diligent worker or an honest one who does nothing?'

Chirag, for some reason, said enthusiastically, 'That's right, that's right, Babu.'

Donald, who had seemed a bit lost so far, now cleared his throat and said gravely, 'The obvious answer is that we should always look for an honest and hard-working person in public life.'

To which Bah Kynsai replied, 'Needle in a haystack.'

We were passing a coal depot, gigantic and filled to the brim with coal dust and sizeable lumps. There were hundreds of lumbering lorries engaged in loading or unloading, or simply parked about, and hundreds of men with blackened faces and dirty clothes, busy shovelling coal dust. Chirag said proudly, 'All the coal from this side of the state, no, Babu, is coming from our Lyngngam.'

We were all struck by the incongruity of the scene, and it was Bah Kynsai who pointed it out: 'But how can there be so much coal and so many coal trucks, liah? The NGT banned coal mining in the state in 2014, na?'

The National Green Tribunal was set up under the NGT Act passed in 2010. Its objective was to provide for 'the effective and expeditious disposal of cases relating to environmental protection and conservation of forests and other natural resources'. The Tribunal has original jurisdiction on matters affecting the community at large, including damage to public health and 'damage to the environment due to specific activity' such as pollution. Its powers are equivalent to that of a civil court.

The Tribunal had ordered an interim ban on coal mining all over Meghalaya on 17 April 2014, after the Assam-based All Dimasa Students' Union and Dima Hasao District Committee filed a petition before it, complaining about the acidic mine drainage (AMD) from the coal mines of Ri Pnar (Jaiñtia Hills) in Meghalaya that was polluting the River Kupli downstream. After a few months, though, the NGT provided partial relief to coal miners by allowing them to transport the coal already extracted and stored in depots after being duly inventoried by a six-member committee formed by it.

It was a huge surprise, therefore, to see 'the biggest coal depot in Meghalaya' still doing brisk business in February 2016, almost two years after the ban was announced. Chirag said, 'It must be already extracted coal, which can be sold, Babu.'

Bah Kynsai bristled. 'Already extracted? After more than two years of the ban?'

'When there is an understanding, no, Babu, even freshly extracted coal is already extracted coal,' Chirag replied enigmatically.

'Do you think there is an understanding, Bah Chirag?' I asked. 'Do you think the NGT inspectors are taking bribes?'

'I don't know, Babu, perhaps not, but the more coal they take away, the thicker the stock becomes.'

'It's the same thing in Jaiñtia Hills,' Magdalene chipped in. 'We went there about two months ago, and many of the coal depots were still holding plenty of coal, ya, Bah Kynsai. They say it's a miraculous thing: the coal is loaded onto trucks during the day, okay, but the next day the same amount magically reappears in the same depot. It's as if it replenishes itself, you know,' she concluded with a laugh.

Bah Su did not agree. 'No, no, it's very different in Ri Pnar, Kong Mag …'

'Why do you keep calling me Kong Mag, Bah Su? You are much older than me …'

'Okay, Mag it is! As I was saying, ha, we were there just the other day. You must understand one thing about Ri Pnar, okay?' Almost the whole of it is coal producing. In some parts, I agree, it is exactly as you said—people do carry on proxy mining. But the ban is still more than 70 per cent effective, I would say. While there are some depots still holding extensive stock, many others are empty.'

I agreed with Bah Su, for I had been travelling in Ri Pnar very recently. In fact, I had been to places like Khliehriat, Lad Rymbai, Rymbai, Sutnga, Wapung and others, considered to be the very heart of the coal-mining industry. Before the coal ban, in many of these places, especially the Khliehriat–Lad Rymbai area, it was said that the migrant labour force—from all over India, but especially Assam, West Bengal, Bihar, Nepal and Bangladesh—was ten times the size of the local population. And the thriving little town of Lad Rymbai was said to be even livelier than Shillong. Hundreds of shops lined its main and side streets, many of them open twenty-four hours. You could get anything in them, and day or night, the crowds there would easily rival the peak-hour crowd at Police Bazaar.

Like all boomtowns, past and present, Lad Rymbai was characterised by underworld activities dominated by coal barons, armed militant groups and crime rings involved in extortion rackets, kidnappings, robberies, drug smuggling and prostitution. The biggest coal mafia don in the area was a man named Klol. He used to go around with a pistol hanging from his hip, like a gunslinger out of a Western, doing whatever he wanted. He had a terrible weakness for women, and despite having many wives and mistresses, he would ask his bodyguards to kidnap any girl he fancied, and rape her. When he died, not too long ago, the whole town breathed a sigh of relief.

When I recounted some of the stories about him, my friends could not believe that he actually existed. I assured them that he was real and that I myself had had a run-in with him. I was the editor of a Khasi weekly when it happened. Our part-time correspondent from Ri Pnar had sent in a story about the don's nefarious activities. In my absence, the subeditor released the story and had it published under our weekly feature, 'Ri Pnar Diary'. The story was wholly based on hearsay and gossip, with not a shred of hard evidence. I would have killed it had I been there, but it was published because of the sheer carelessness or appalling stupidity, call it what you will, of Nongsiej, the subeditor.

Klol was livid. He took the paper to court, and made every effort to find out who had filed the story. We were not so bothered about the case; it could have gone on for years. But the correspondent was terrified. His voice cracked with fear, and his hands shook so much that, when he ate, most of the rice ended up on the floor. His body trembled like an alcoholic's, and when he stood, he had to hold on to something to keep steady. That was the effect Klol had on him. He called me daily and pleaded with me to resolve the matter amicably and with all haste. He said he would pay any amount that Klol demanded so long as the case was resolved and his identity kept secret.

I took pity on him and sought out ways to contact Klol, although I knew it could be dangerous for me. I did not want to meet his lawyer, for he had been described to me as a *seiñpuh*, a biting snake. In any case, the lawyer was not in favour of an out-of-court settlement, knowing he had us where he wanted us. I spoke to the heads of a few NGOs, but nobody could help. Finally, I went to meet my relations in Jowai to see if they knew anyone who knew Klol. To my great surprise, it turned out that Klol had a liaison with one of my paternal aunts, who was even then raising a six-year-old daughter by him. More surprising still, it seemed that he did not treat her too badly and had built her a big house near her mother's.

On learning of my problem, my *kha*, short for *ñiakha*, paternal aunt, immediately said she would speak to him on my behalf. I asked her if he would be willing to meet me. She said, very confidently, that he had better be: 'Are you not my nephew after all?' It would not be a problem for her to arrange a meeting since he came to her house every Saturday.

I was about twenty-eight at the time, but my aunt was even younger than me, only twenty-seven.

When the date was set, I went (with my brother for moral support) to meet him at our kha's place. When we arrived at nine in the morning, he and his bodyguards were already waiting in the big drawing room. I was asked to enter alone, and when I did, I saw his men standing on all sides, making a kind of ring around Klol, who was sitting on one of the chairs arranged in the centre. He asked me to sit, not on a chair but on a *mula*, a short, round cane stool, deliberately placed so I would look like a supplicant before a master.

I recognised some of his men as members of a local militant outfit who used to deliver press releases to our office. Most of them were wearing jackets and holding AK-47s, or at least that's what I thought they were. Klol himself was dressed in a light blue suit and a grey shirt. He had on a pair of black boots with pointed toes. At his hip was a brown leather gun-belt, and hanging from it, cowboy-style, was a gun—of what make I could not tell. But it looked nasty.

The moment I sat down, Klol, who had been eying me evilly, took out his gun and placed the barrel against my head. He gestured with his other hand to one of his men to close the door. Alarmed at the feel of the gun against my head, I pushed it away with my right hand, saying, 'Hey, hey, cousin, don't do that, there might be an accident!'

'Accident?' he roared, his face contorted with rage.

Klol was a tiny man, in fact, much smaller than me. His face was pinkish— the handiwork of the sun and the wind, no doubt—and, strangely, he had light brown hair, unlike any other Khasi I had seen. When I looked at his beady eyes, pointed nose and fluffy sideburns, I was immediately reminded of a *nai lum*, a hill mouse.

'Accident!' he roared once more. 'This is no accident, you little grasshopper, you worm, you maggot, you termite!' Putting the gun against my head again, he twisted it so hard that it felt like a hole was being bored into my skull. I grimaced with pain but ground my teeth to prevent any sound from escaping. 'I will squash you like this between my fingers!' he threatened, showing me what he meant to do with the fingers of his left hand. 'I will have you cut to pieces and fried, and I will eat you for breakfast, lunch and dinner. You dared write filthy nonsense about me, you little insect! I'll grind you between my teeth; I'll beat you up; I'll drag you through the hills; I'll crush you; I'll pulverise you till nothing but the grass remains!'

I have often relived that scene to examine my state of mind and ascertain precisely what I felt. And I can tell you in all honesty that I did not feel any fear at all. Instead, when I heard his words—and they sounded even better in the Pnar dialect—I thought, how impressive, how imaginative, how delightfully creative they were despite the stark horror of their meaning! I said, 'Cousin, cousin, that's beautiful, that's incredibly poetic!' I took out my pen and little notebook from my shirt pocket and continued, 'You see, cousin, I'm a poet, I write poetry, but I have never heard such words before: wonderfully original, wonderfully imaginative! "I'll pulverise you till nothing but the grass remains!" Absolutely original! Will you repeat them for me, cousin? I'd like to write them down and make use of them in my poetry someday. Please say it again, cousin!'

Klol was so taken aback that he took the gun away from my head, opened his arms wide, looked at his men in bewilderment, and said, 'What kind of fellow is this? I put the gun to his head and threaten to kill him, and all he says is, say it again because your words are beautiful! Is he mad?'

At that point, my kha knocked on the door and said, 'I have brought tea for all of you.'

That served to ease the tension in the room. Everyone relaxed and soon we were sipping the tea and munching on *putharo*, a kind of rice bread, and *pumaloi*, a small rice cake, served with *dohjem*, the curried viscera of a pig. As Klol ate, he kept shaking his head and commenting on the strangeness of my reaction.

One of the men present there was the press secretary of the militant outfit. He said, 'I have come across many such intellectuals, they have no physical strength, but a lot of moral courage.'

I did not know whether I was being brave or foolish or whether the whole thing was simply too unreal for me, but I said nothing.

Klol turned to me and asked, 'What do you want? You have published trash against me, now what do you want?'

I admitted readily enough that we had published trash about him and apologised profusely for it. The paper was ready for an out-of-court settlement, I said. It would give him monetary compensation, plus an unqualified apology that would be published in the next issue.

'This is what I want,' he said peremptorily. 'I want the man who sent you the story, as well as the apology and the money. If you cannot give me these, we will proceed with the case.'

'The fault was not his but the paper's, for publishing what he sent. What do you want with the man?' I asked.

'What do you think? To kiss him, ha, boys? We'll kiss him till there is nothing left of him to be kissed.'

'You see, cousin, that is why we cannot reveal his identity to you. Even the court will never do it.'

Turning to the press secretary, Klol asked, 'Is that true?'

'I think so,' he replied.

'What will the court give me?' Klol asked.

'Your lawyer must have told you: money and an apology, that's all. But if you choose to go to court, the owners will fight you to delay the case. It's a civil case; it may drag on for forty, fifty years.'

Klol told me to leave the room while he consulted with his men. They talked for a long time but finally agreed to my terms for a certain sum of money and an apology. Of course, he said, he would continue to look for our correspondent, but I knew that the money and the apology would appease his offended ego and make his search a half-hearted one.

When I concluded my story, Magdalene said, 'But, Ap, militants are wanted men, no? They are being hunted every day by the police, no? So, how was it that Klol moved around with them?'

'All this happened some years ago, Mag. But that is exactly why the insurgency problem in the state and the Northeast hasn't been solved until now, because businessmen and politicians alike patronise the militants. The police have to fight not only militants, but their patrons as well, and that is difficult because they have political clout. We need the nexus to be broken for the insurgency to end.'

After that, we went back to discussing the coal ban in Ri Pnar. I told the others that the last time I visited Lad Rymbai, some weeks ago, it was almost like a ghost town. Most of the shops, about 90 per cent of them, were closed, and there were hardly any people on the roads. It had a forlorn look, like a millionaire suddenly turned pauper; a depressing sight. There were stories of people selling houses and SUVs for a song, and others withdrawing their children and wards from expensive schools and colleges from around the country. But it was not the barons who were the hardest hit. They had invested in real estate and other businesses all over the state and continued to extract coal by devious means. Those with small holdings and those who depended on the coal mines as labourers and service providers were the ones who found themselves in real trouble.

I thought the ban in Ri Pnar was at least partially effective because the place was not remote or inaccessible. A highway that goes all the way from Guwahati to Silchar, Mizoram and Tripura cuts through it—unlike Lyngngam, which is still an enormous jungle.

Chirag agreed readily. 'You are right, you are right, Babu, it's not working very well here because it is still a jungle, there is no inspection at all. I know because I have a little bit of coal business.'

'Aha, Bah Chirag!' Magdalene said, wagging her finger at him. 'You are not telling us everything, are you?'

'Okay, okay, there's something I don't understand here, huh?' Donald interrupted. 'Lyngngam is in the jungle, granted, but how can they transport the coal so freely, surely there are check gates everywhere?'

'Coal traders pay bribes at check gates, na, Don,' Bah Kynsai replied. 'Check-gate workers are among the most corrupt of government officials, and if there are some who don't take bribes, na, the coal mafias intimidate them into not doing anything. Sometimes they even get them bumped off. Do you remember the case of the police officer who held back thirty-two coal trucks? What was his name? The trucks were illegally transporting coal through the Patharkhmah–Guwahati road, ha, but this officer, na, he held them back. He was quite daring, liah! Come on, na, what was his name? It's at the tip of my nose.'

'Tip of your nose or tip of your tongue?' Donald asked, laughing.

Bah Kynsai was not amused. 'Khasis say "tip of the nose", mə, tdong!' he said.

'Pearly Stone Marbañiang,' Bah Su said, in response to Bah Kynsai's question.

'Yes, yes, Marbañiang. He was a police sub-inspector in charge of Patharkhmah Police Station, ha, very honest, very brave. He refused to let the trucks pass despite a lot of pressure from various quarters, including government officials, contractors and certain NGOs. So, what happened to him? That night while he was on duty, na, he was shot by someone in his own quarters. The initial post-mortem report, ha, from the medical officer of Patharkhmah Community Health Centre, ha, revealed that the bullet had entered from the back of the head, which pointed to foul play. His wife and mother were certain it was murder. Just before the incident, he had a very normal phone conversation with his wife, to whom he had spoken of his determination to uphold the law. But the authorities, na, passed it off as suicide. And his colleagues at the station were in a tearing hurry to clean up the blood, destroying all evidence before the investigation could even start. I ask you, how can any man commit suicide by shooting himself in the back of his head, huh? And how could he have committed suicide when he was in the middle of such a crucial case? The coal business here, na, is as dark and sinister as the colour of the coal itself!'

Chirag agreed about the corruption at the check gates. He said, 'That's why the coal business is much less now, even here, no, Babu, these trucks loading and unloading coal, ha, these belong to the big shots, the big, big *maliks*. Small mine owners cannot afford to pay bribes or take the risk of their trucks being held back, that would simply ruin them, so most of them have stopped.'

'Much less, you say, but there are hundreds of trucks in this depot alone, ya!' Magdalene cried, appalled.

'This is nothing, Kong, believe me, before the ban, there were many more.'

Bah Su said, 'There are two other reasons why the coal miners are getting away with their illegal trade. As Bah Kynsai pointed out, they try to avoid check gates by using side streets and out-of-the-way routes like the Patharkhmah road, which is not part of the Shillong–Guwahati highway.

'The other reason is the NGT itself. It's not that there was no checking by it; inspections were conducted now and then, okay? At one time, the NGT even lambasted the government and threatened to call for paramilitary forces to enforce the ban. But then, the NGT is also at fault, Bah Kynsai. Initially, it allowed the transportation and sale of already extracted coal and set a deadline for it. However, it kept on extending the deadline from this month to that month, which naturally allowed the big coal merchants to keep extracting coal from the mines and pass it off as already extracted coal. And nobody knows why it does that. It's really perplexing.'

Very perplexing indeed, everybody agreed. These things could only happen in India.

Assuming that was the end of the discussion for now, I turned my attention to the landscape outside, holding on for support against the constant lurching and bumping of the car. There was not much to see at this point. We were hemmed in on both sides by the hill through which the road had been cut. I was about to ask Chirag how far we had come when Donald enquired, 'Was the NGT against coal mining per se, or was it only against unscientific mining?'

'Against rat-hole mining,' Bah Kynsai answered. 'That's why there has been a great deal of pressure on the government to formulate a viable mining policy, but so far …'

'What exactly is rat-hole mining, Bah Kynsai?'

'Mining like a rat,' Bah Kynsai replied with a booming laugh.

'Seriously, ya!'

'Bah Kynsai was serious, Don,' I said. 'I'll tell you about it. I used to work in one.'

'Really!' Everyone turned to look at me in surprise.

I told them my story. I was very young at the time, about fourteen years old. As a family, we were quite hard up. Our father had died when I was still in the womb and our mother, a lowly government employee, struggled single-handedly to bring up her three sons and a daughter properly. We boys were forced to look for part-time employment whenever we were out of school during the winter holidays. Those days, in Sohra (we lived in Laitlyngkot then, but spent our winters in Sohra), employment for boys like us mostly meant labouring in the coal mines, collecting river sand, digging white sand on the hills or chipping stones in the quarries. That particular winter, some of us chose to work in a coal mine, where we would be paid much higher wages. The mine was in the middle of a cliff, with a sizeable ledge in front of it. Because we were too young to dig, we were given two choices: haul the coal out of the mine onto the ledge, or haul it from the ledge onto the hilltop from where it would be loaded onto lorries. To take the coal out of the mine, we were offered three rupees per box, whereas carrying it up to the hill would fetch us only two rupees. The box, placed on level ground, was simply a four-sided wooden enclosure without a bottom. It had an area of about six square feet and a height of about two feet.

I chose to go into the mine, though all my friends had wisely decided otherwise. Pulling a small cart, I entered the tunnel, which was about four feet high and led to a spacious circular chamber—about sixty feet or so inside the cave. This is where the coal brought out from the smaller tunnels, which branched off from the chamber in many different directions, was stored. I had to bend a little to pull the cart from the entrance into the chamber. I was also supposed to go into those branching tunnels to bring out the coal that the miners were digging up with their pickaxes. But they were really small, maybe two and a half feet at the most, truly like a rodent's burrow, although a rodent's burrow would have been far safer because it has multiple exits. The miner's burrow is a death trap: only one way in and out.

Leaving the cart in the chamber, I crawled—you have to crawl; there is no other way—into one of the tunnels with a bamboo basket and a piece of tin with which to scoop up the coal. I saw a miner at the end of the tunnel lying on his back and digging away at the tunnel's wall with a pickaxe. Near him was a small kerosene lamp that emitted a feeble light and black smoke that left dark smudges around his nostrils. I tried to crawl nearer to him and the coal accumulating by his side. But the cramped space, the black plumes of smoke and the stench of kerosene were suffocating. I could not breathe. The walls of the tunnel were squeezing me in from all sides. I panicked and crawled backwards like a shrimp as fast as I could, grunting and snorting in terror all the way. When I reached the circular chamber, I felt a waft of fresh air, and a great relief washed over me, as if I had just been released from a strangler's death grip. Controlling my panic, I took the cart, bent double, and pulled it out to the ledge without a single piece of coal in it.

'Now, Don,' I said, 'do you understand what rat-hole mining is? In some areas in Ri Pnar, it's even more frightening because a pit is dug into the ground and tunnels are excavated sideways from the bottom of the pit. It's dangerous not only for miners but also for the environment because of frequent cave-ins that often bring down whole hills. Sometimes, the mines are located very close to villages and the tunnels run under people's homes. You can imagine what would happen in case of an earthquake of some intensity! Even without earthquakes, cases of hearthstones vanishing into the ground have been reported in many places. The worst thing about unscientific mining, however, is the AMD. When the rain comes, coal dust is carried into rivers and streams and water sources, turning them yellowish-brown with acid and carbon. Neither humans nor any other creature can drink the water. There are many such dead streams and rivers in our state because of rat-hole mining.'

My listeners, many of whom had not seen a coal mine up close, shook their heads in amazement.

Meanwhile, Chirag had been manoeuvring the car very slowly, partly because of the bad road and partly because it was uphill. 'We are over the hill,' he told us now. 'From here it's all downhill, so we'll make better spid.'

Chirag kept chattering as he drove and told us all about himself. He was working in a government office as a clerk, but he had a business of his own too, a little bit in coal, a little bit in timber and a little bit in road-making. That sounded like a lot of little bits, but I did not say anything. Magdalene, however, said sarcastically, 'What road-making? There's no road at all, ya!'

To that, Chirag replied matter-of-factly, 'Jungle road.'

Even this trip, he continued, gave him a bit of income on the side, for he took people to Lyngngam quite often, mostly evangelists from the Presbyterian and Catholic churches, but sometimes scientists as well.

It was then that he asked me, 'Why are you going to Nongshyrkon, Babu, so many of you?'

'Why, didn't Indalin tell you?'

'No, Babu, Kong Lin only told me you wanted to be dropped to Nongshyrkon on the fourth and that you wanted to be picked up on the tenth. On the tenth I will not be free, Babu, but don't worry, I'll ask someone to pick you up.'

'We are going to a funeral ceremony called Ka Phor Sorat, Bah Chirag. You must have heard of it. They say it's the very last one.'

'You mean the cremation of our meiduh, Kong We Shyrkon? Yes, yes, she was my meiduh! My youngest aunt! But why are you going there now, the funeral will begin only on the eleventh, that's why I haven't gone yet, I'm waiting for some things I ordered from Shillong, I will be going there only on the seventh.'

'What!' All of us exploded at once and stared at each other in disbelief. 'Are you sure?'

'Of course,' Chirag replied calmly.

'Hey, we have been misled, liah!' Bah Kynsai cursed. 'Stop, stop the car, stop the car, na, Chirag!'

Chirag pulled the Gypsy to a stop. 'Now what?' he asked with a laugh.

'Don't panic!' Bah Kynsai shouted. 'Calm down, calm down, let us discuss this calmly. Where's that Raji *tdir*? He gave us the wrong date, *lyeit*!'

Hearing him curse, we all cried, 'Hey, Bah Kynsai, calmly, calmly ...'

'First of all,' I said, 'we should get in touch with Raji and the rest; we are still in Nongstoin, we can always turn back.'

'How?' Chirag asked. 'There's no network in the jungle, Babu, not even here, take a look at your mobiles ... and they must be at least a kilometre and a half ahead of us, my kynum is a young man, Babu, he drives very fast.'

Chirag was right; there was no signal.

'Bew, liah!' Bah Kynsai said.

'*La bong leh*!' That was the closest Magdalene had got to swearing so far.

Donald went all English on us. 'Gosh! What are we to do now?'

Dale cackled and said, '*La wai leh*! We are goners!'

Only Bah Su did not speak; he simply rubbed the stubble on his lean jaw pensively. As for me, I fiercely uttered the four-letter word three times under my breath.

'Perhaps your brother-in-law has told Raji the same thing, Bah Chirag, perhaps right now they too are turning back,' I said hopefully.

'Not my kynum,' Chirag said firmly. 'He doesn't speak much Khasi, he won't be talking at all unless it is to answer yes or no.'

We Khasis have many different dialects among us. It is not only the different sub-tribes of Khynriam, Pnar, Bhoi, War, Maram, Lyngngam and Nongtrai-Muliang who speak different dialects. Khasi dialects also differ from village to village. What we call the Khasi language, for instance, is in reality the Sohra dialect. It was standardised as the language of reading and writing by Thomas Jones, the first Welsh Presbyterian missionary in this region, who used it when he wrote his *First Khasi Reader*, published in early 1842. Jones is known as the father of the Khasi alphabet, whereas his successor, Reverend John Roberts, is known as the father of Khasi literature because he wrote more books. Which is stupid, if you ask me—every other Khasi book emerged from Jones's little book, so why should he not be the father of Khasi literature as well? Written literature, I mean, for we have always had our stories, songs and poems. But I am getting carried away. What I was really trying to do was to explain why Chirag's brother-in-law did not speak much Khasi.

Anyway, turning back was out of the question. We knew that, but we couldn't come to a decision either. We stood there as if in a daze for quite some time. It was Dale who broke the spell and offered a surprisingly sensible idea: 'Bah,' he said to me, 'would it be so very bad to spend an extra six or seven days in Nongshyrkon? I mean, if there's already a place to stay, we could make arrangements for food with the help of Bah Chirag, no? After all, he's also a local ... What do you say, Bah Chirag?'

'Food and shelter are no problem, lots of people will be coming for the funeral, I think many have already come by now, we will be providing for every one of them, so ten of you will not be a problem.'

Well, come to think of it, Bah Su, Donald (who was on holiday), Dale and I did not really have anything to worry about. We were free agents with lots of time on our hands, and staying in Nongshyrkon for a few days would not be so bad.

Bah Kynsai said, 'I'm worried about my leave.'

'Me too. I haven't even applied,' Magdalene said.

'What leave? Aren't you on a winter break?' I asked.

'We are reopening on the tenth, na?' Bah Kynsai said irritably. 'One or two days of absence is okay, but almost a week is too much ...'

'I'm sure you can work it out with your HOD, Bah Kynsai,' I said. 'And Mag, your principal is very accommodating. I'm sure she'll allow you to backdate your leave application. In any case, we cannot turn back and let the others go ahead.'

'Okay, okay,' Bah Kynsai agreed, 'what to do, liah!'

'Chalo, let's go,' Magdalene said. 'As someone said, "Stop worrying about the potholes in the road and celebrate the journey." We might as well make the most of it.'

'Fitzhugh Mullan,' I said to Magdalene.

'What?'

'Fitzhugh Mullan said those words.'

'Oh, I didn't know that.'

We piled back into the Gypsy and resumed our journey, laughing at ourselves a little.

The road here seemed to have been cut out of a mountain range. On the right was a steep slope, while on the left was a ravine choked with trees and brush. It was not very deep, only a hundred feet or so, unlike the ravines on the road to Sohra, which were thousands of feet deep. Chirag said the road was going to be like this all the way to Wah Rwiang, the River Rwiang. As the jeep rattled down the slope, I noticed the road had become even worse, something I had thought impossible. The coal dirt was replaced by red earth churned into thick layers of dust by an unending stream of empty lorries trundling down, or overloaded ones grunting and bellowing up the slope. Only occasionally did we come across small vehicles, four-wheel drives like ours.

Two things dominated the lorry cargo: coal and timber. Some of the logs were as thick as six feet across. I was about to bring their ample girth to the others' attention when Donald exclaimed, 'What the hell! Both these are banned items, no?' He sounded quite perplexed. 'Is nobody checking? Is everybody blind? Is the law of the land nothing but a piece of paper?'

Logging had been banned in Meghalaya and the entire Northeast by the Supreme Court on 12 December 1996. The court was responding to a 1995 civil writ petition filed by T.N. Godavarman Thirumulpad against the Union of India and Others, concerning the rampant deforestation in Jammu and Kashmir and Tamil Nadu. Taking cognisance of similar destructive activities in the Northeast, the ban was extended to the seven states as well. It was, in fact, only an interim order, directing the concerned state governments to constitute an expert committee within one month to identify all forest lands, irrespective of category or ownership, and to identify all wood-based industries that were operating within their jurisdiction. It further directed the governments to evaluate the sustainability of forests vis-à-vis the timber needs of these industries. Pending the completion of such an evaluation, the felling of trees in the states was temporarily suspended, except for defence purposes and specific requirements by the governments. Twenty-one years had passed since that historic judgement, and the ban was still very much in place.

It had been hailed as a great victory by environmentalists and conservationists all over the country, though it was also fiercely denounced by those whose livelihoods were directly affected by it. In Meghalaya, as the export of timber ground to a halt, and sawmills and woodwork factories were shut down, there was a great hue and cry. Many said the ban had generated untold misery and adversely affected the lives of lakhs of people. I also remember how they blamed the Khasi Students' Union, KSU, for it. Because it had spearheaded the movement against the timber trade in the state, it became a hated name, especially in West Khasi Hills and Ri Pnar, where the logging business was thriving. Was it ignorance or was there a deliberate ploy by timber merchants to rouse people against their perceived enemies?

'Corruption, corruption!' Magdalene exploded.

'True, true, Mag, what else could it be?' Bah Kynsai chimed in. 'But at the same time, na, Don, to be fair to this particular law, na, the timber ban has been quite effective elsewhere in the state, that I can tell you. Only here, it seems to be thriving, liah! But elsewhere, na, when the ban was first imposed, sawmills et cetera were shut down. I remember there were lots of protests, and many even claimed that lakhs had lost their livelihood and were about to starve to death. But funnily, na, twenty-one years after the ban, those people are still alive, they haven't starved to death at all. The rich forest owners, timber traders and sawmill maliks, those who had to shut shop, simply invested elsewhere, and the poor, the labourers, those who depended on the business, found other means of livelihood. They are saying the same thing about the coal ban, the buggers, but most people will survive one way or another—you mark my words!'

But Bah Su argued that the timber ban was cruel. He said, 'It's true that those people have survived, but it's not true that they did not suffer. The ban affected not only forest owners and traders, ha, but more seriously, thousands of woodcutters, labourers and charcoal merchants for whom the forest was the main source of subsistence. It is true that woodcutters and labourers found alternative work, but according to some researchers, they had to work for half the wages they had been getting from the timber industry. That, in turn, affected their ability to support their families, leading to school dropouts and forcing their wives to neglect their children and look for odd jobs here and there.'

'Okay, okay, I admit they suffered,' Bah Kynsai responded, 'but the main thing is that they survived, na? And they weren't in lakhs, Bah Su! To say that lakhs lost their livelihood, ha, would be the same thing as saying that half the Khasi population was dependent on the timber trade. Only a few thousand were directly involved in it. And what did they get? Daily wages! Who got the maximum benefit from the destruction of the forests? A few local traders who also owned sawmills, true, but who got the lion's share? Why do you think the KSU was engaged in a movement against timber trade, huh?

'I'll tell you: because it was mostly the non-tribal contractors who benefited the most. Do you know what those guys did? They leased forests from the local owners and then had all the trees felled: clear-felling, they call it. And do you know that, though the Supreme Court had prohibited indigenous people from cutting down trees, it had exempted contractors and companies that supplied timber and wood to government departments and industries? And who were these contractors and company owners? Non-tribal businessmen! In Meghalaya alone, you have three of them belonging to the Marwari community. Whatever you say, Bah Su, I'm all for the ban.'

'But more than a few thousand were dependent on the forest and the timber trade, no?' Bah Su persisted. 'Think, Bah Kynsai, how many would there be in the charcoal business alone? Thousands. Woodcutters? Thousands. And the poor farmers engaged in *jhum*—cut-and-slash cultivation—how many? Thousands. The figure must be more than a lakh ...'

At that point, I interrupted Bah Su to clarify that the jhum farmers, charcoal dealers and woodcutters who sold firewood were never affected, although the court had also prohibited their activities. The jhum farmers continued to practise their age-old custom as if no law had been passed against it, and the woodcutters and charcoal merchants continued to sell their products everywhere. No governmental authority in the state had ever made any move to stop them, perhaps because they recognised the impossibility of the situation.

Jhum farmers, for instance, need an alternative agricultural practice before they can be stopped from slashing and burning. The people of the state need alternative means of cooking before they can be persuaded to stop buying charcoal for their stoves and firewood for their hearths. It is true that many people in urban areas are using gas and electric stoves; it is also true that many, even in rural areas, have started using kerosene stoves. But they are only a fraction of the population. A vast majority still use charcoal and firewood in their kitchens. Besides, when winter comes, everybody needs their charcoal stoves, which, in addition to warming the house effectively, can also be used for cooking. Very few are satisfied with the limited warmth of electric heaters. As long as the demand is there, there will be no stopping the suppliers. That is why newspapers have daily reports about how lorries and pickup trucks loaded with charcoal are freely roaming the city streets, unloading their cargo at designated locations or directly selling to customers in their localities.

That said, I agreed with Bah Su that the number of people affected by the ban would be more than a few thousand, though not lakhs as he initially said. While farmers, woodcutters and charcoal traders were not really affected, there were others, not directly involved with the industry, who suffered hardships and loss of income. Hundreds of tea shops along the Nongstoin–Shillong road, for instance, were forced to close because the lorries that used to ply the highway at all hours had all but vanished. These stalls were run by women and their hired help, all girls. When they had to close, everyone had to look for alternative employment.

In West Khasi Hills, many women were forced to work as labourers for road builders. Imagine the kind of life they had! They had to follow the road wherever it led, living in tarpaulin tents in proximity to rough, uncouth men who came from every part of the country and who often misbehaved with them. Others flocked to the city to work as housemaids with well-to-do families, and some others were lured outside the state with promises of jobs, only to become victims of the flesh trade. Various city-based NGOs had rescued hundreds of such women in the last few years.

Then there were the small businessmen in the service sector and the luxury market, who had to cease operations because of the economy's sudden downturn.

The government, too, lost crores of rupees in revenue every year. The District Councils used to maintain scores of check gates in Ri Pnar, West Khasi Hills and along the Shillong–Guwahati highway to issue transit passes for timber lorries and to collect royalties from traders. For East and West Khasi Hills, the royalty was mostly collected by a check gate maintained by the Khasi Hills Autonomous District Council at Mawïong, on the northern outskirts of Shillong. The royalty rates were fixed between 500 and 1,200 rupees per lorry, depending on the kind of timber being exported. The lowest rates were for softwood timber and pines, while the highest was for sal and teak. Now, if there were 600 lorries going through the check gate each day, and if the average royalty was taken to be 700 rupees (because most of the timber was softwood), the council's earnings would be about four lakh rupees per day and about fifteen crore rupees per year minus the forty-eight Sundays. But people said that not even half of that money reached the council. Transit passes, where records of all royalty payments were kept, got mysteriously burnt or misplaced. When auditors were sent to audit the check gate, they could not establish anything in the absence of these passes.

'How do you know all this? Are you for or against the ban, liah?' Bah Kynsai asked belligerently.

I told him I was for the ban, but I did want to set the record straight. As for the check-gate keepers, I knew what they used to do from first-hand experience. I explained how the council had decided to lease out the Mawïong check gate to a consortium of private contractors when it found itself incapable of coping with massive losses. That proved to be a win-win situation for both parties. The council increased its earnings from about two crores per year to nearly ten crores, and the contractors also made a handsome profit.

Soon, the contractors began facing the same problems, of course. However, they had one advantage: they could hire and fire staff at will. That was when I came into the picture. A notorious fellow, who had been stealing thousands of rupees each night, had just been thrown out, and the contractors were desperately looking for an honest person to replace him. I had just joined the university as an MA student and was desperately looking for employment because my mother was finding it increasingly difficult to pay for my studies. I planned to support myself by working on a part-time basis. A relative of my brother-in-law, Ma Ni, we called him, introduced me to one of the contractors, Bah Khran. He himself was working with Bah Khran as a manager in one of his vehicle spare-part shops. One day, he took me to his boss for an interview. As it turned out, it was not much of an interview. The man took one look at me and said, 'I like this fellow. He's got an honest, fresh-faced look … When can he start?'

And just like that, I became a check-gate employee, working day shifts from 8 a.m. to 5 p.m. or night shifts from 5 p.m. to 8 a.m. Initially, I did not have to work every day. Since there were two other employees who worked at the check gate, we decided to divide our duties in such a way that each would have at least two days off in a week.

'What happened to the council's staff?' Donald asked.

'They still had a role to play and at least one of them had to be on duty with us. He used to sit in a room adjacent to the one we were in. It was his duty to check and stamp the transit passes and pass them on to us through a window, so we could record the details of vehicles and timber types in a register and collect the royalty. I used to collect two to three lakhs per night, not including the day's collection. At the end of my shift, I handed over the carefully sorted and bound notes to a man sent by the contractors.

I worked at the check gate for three years and gave it up only when I secured a Central government job, although, for some time, I did manage to handle both jobs simultaneously while attending MA classes besides. I was not a very regular student, of course, but the teachers were lenient in those days, and somehow I managed to complete my studies.

During my time at the check gate, I saw many people come and go. Some would last for only a day, but my honesty (the council's employees, because they themselves were crooked, thought it was cunning rather than honesty) was borne out by the fact that, when I wanted to leave, Bah Khran did everything he could to stop me. He even offered me a small investment in his own business and told me that, if I remained honest and hardworking, I would grow to be a very successful entrepreneur in no time at all. But I had a government job already, and I wanted to study further, and so, with many apologies, I declined his generous offer.

Sometime before I left, because of the other employees' constant attempts to steal, I was made a supervisor and asked to check the daily accounts. This required my presence in office every day, but it was not so bad since the work only took a few hours. During that time, the theft trickled down to almost nothing. To almost nothing, because I would ignore people taking a hundred or two now and then for tea money. Was I wrong to permit that sort of thing? Was that not theft too? I feel bad about it sometimes, but at the time, I thought of it as a sort of incentive, a small reward for a good night's work.

Despite the loss of direct control, the council's employees still made a lot of money by charging thirty rupees for every transit pass that they stamped. I did not know if that was legitimate. It seems to me now like extortion, especially because that money did not go to the council's account, but into their pockets. Each employee on duty made between 17,000 and 18,000 rupees per night, depending on the number of lorries that came through. In those days, that was big, big money.

There were four of them under the supervision of a beat officer, who came to the office every day and did night shifts for at least two nights, no doubt for the money. They were a colourful lot. The most sober of them all was a person we called Bah Mer. He was about five feet four and had dark eyes that were always smiling, and a jet black moustache (although he must have touched fifty already). The most remarkable thing about him was his red-and-grey checked flannel shawl, which he was never without, summer or winter. Actually, I do not know if sober is the right word to describe him. He drank every night, sometimes too much, but he was a decent fellow with never a harsh word for anyone, and a loving and responsible father to his six children. Every morning, after his shift, he used to rush home to his wife to hand over the money he had made, for 'safekeeping'. Otherwise, he would say, Kohleng would force him to part with most of it. I will tell you about Kohleng in just a little while.

Bah Mer and I were friends, although he was old enough to be my father, and we used to explore the jungles and streams of the area whenever we could. We loved to laze among the trees, talking about birds and animals and anything else that took our fancy. Occasionally, we even talked about girls, and he would say that so-and-so, living in such-and-such house, would be a good match for me and that he was prepared to act as my go-between. But I was always not ready, or too shy, to apply for a girlfriend.

Oh yes, in those days, when we were smitten with a girl, we had to write a formal letter to apply for her love. The girls thought that much of a person's character could be understood from his letter and, therefore, set much store by how it was written. Often, their acceptance depended on the lover's literary prowess. A poetic letter, with lots of metaphors and similes, which described the girl's beauty and virtuous qualities, used to be greatly prized. I was considered a first-rate love-letter writer. I wrote hundreds of them, to hundreds of different girls, but never for myself, only for friends and acquaintances who would give me 'tea money' for my trouble. And I am proud to say that every one of my letters was a success.

My only regret is not having kept copies of any of them, but I did not see the point then, for they were not even written for myself. In any case, making copies would have been a bit of a problem. I still remember some of the lines I wrote, though. Having 'inspected' a girl from a distance, I would say in the letter, 'When I gazed into your deep, brown eyes, it was like gazing into the very depths of my soul: what you are, I am; what you are, I will be.' Sometimes I would write, 'When your radiant face is like a sunny day with flowers at the park, can you wonder that my soul is desperately clinging to the little black tendrils of delight, the little curls in your hair?' To show how distractedly in love a boy was, I would say, 'How can I eat and sleep when you keep peeping into my dreams again and again like the sun from behind summer clouds? This is how my life is spent: I carry your image everywhere like a hidden birthmark.' Sometimes, I used to begin my letter with an invocation:

> The night is cool
> but windy as my soul,
> as the lone-travelling moon
> races with occasional clouds.
>
> Breathe, oh moon, into my timorous heart,
> the courage of one truly inspired!
>
> Detach from me this crippling shame
> that makes me fear rejection!
>
> Add tongue to feelings,
> skill to tongue!
> I have found an ideal one
> whose very looks
> are the opening of petals,
> the parting of dawn.
>
> The night is cool
> but windy as my soul,
> as the stars glimmer
> like faraway cities.
>
> Hand me, oh stars, a universe of luck
> that I may live my dreams!
>
> And oh, my never-failing muse,
> give me those magic songs again!
> I have need
> to move an alien soul to love,
> to make my own
> that self-denying heart
> and bring to my home the peace of God.

That was how I used to personalise my letters. When Bah Mer saw some of my youthful and effusive poems, he used to flatter me and say, 'Which girl can resist the magic of these lines? You should write for yourself, not for somebody else. Your friends are not worthy of these poems!'

And sadly, he was right, for though my letters never failed to win acceptance, the relationships themselves never lasted long. The romantic ideals in the letters were all my own, and when the girls did not find them in the boys they had accepted, they quickly became disenchanted.

In our deep love for nature, Bah Mer and I were soulmates. Unfortunately, he died of liver failure two years after I joined the check gate. Mawïong held no great attraction for me after that. I still miss him sometimes.

Another person I liked was called Gemstone. When I asked him why he was named thus, he said, 'When I was an infant, I was the most precious thing to my parents. Now when they see me, they spit in my face, they think I have only brought disgrace to the family.' So saying, he rocked backwards and forwards, convulsed with low, rumbling laughter, as if he found his parents' anger very funny.

Gemstone used to take me to all sorts of places when we were on duty together. At about midnight, traffic usually came to a near halt, before starting up again at about 3 a.m. During that hiatus, we would sleep for some time. But when Gemstone was on duty, he would say to me, 'Ap, come, come, let's go. I have asked Mer to look after the office for us, come, we'll go down to the highway for food.'

So off we would go in a timber lorry to one of the tea shops that dotted the Shillong–Guwahati highway in Ri Bhoi district. Everybody called these all-night establishments 'tea shops', but that was a euphemism. They sold rice and tea and all sorts of foodstuff, but their mainstay was alcohol, both the inexpensive *kyiad Khasi*, the local brew, and the Indian-made foreign liquor, *kyiad phareng*. The shops catered primarily to lorry drivers, who plied their vehicles mostly at night to avoid daytime restrictions. (During specific periods of the day, for instance, lorries were not allowed to enter Shillong city, though at night they had a free run.) And these were not merely drivers of timber and coal carriers going from Meghalaya towards Assam, they came all the way from Punjab, Andhra Pradesh, West Bengal and so on, carrying all sorts of cargo for eastern Assam, various parts of Meghalaya and the states of Mizoram and Tripura. That is why, though many such shops closed down after the coal and timber bans, they are still numerous on this particular highway.

At one of these shops, Gemstone would order food for me in the main room while he vanished into the kitchen to seduce the beautiful serving girls. As I ate, he would get busy indulging the one passion that had brought disgrace to his parents, his wife and children, by his own admission. And often, he was successful in his efforts, for I would see a girl going out to a dark corner, to be followed by Gemstone a few minutes later. Whenever that happened, I had to wait in the shop for a long time, entertaining myself by listening to the colourful language and rough banter of the drivers and their handymen. If I was lucky, I would witness a knife fight or two between the drivers, a mixed lot, as I said, of Khasis and non-Khasis from every part of the country.

But one night, when I was just beginning to eat my food, Gemstone came running from the kitchen and said, 'Leave the food, Ap, come, come, we are going!'

Surprised, I asked, 'What happened?'

'There's a beautiful girl in there, and she was willing enough, but when she took me to the bathroom, I counted twenty-one toothbrushes in the rack! It's a big family, man! You cannot fool around with such a family, come, come, let's go elsewhere.

So we left and went to another shop farther down the highway.

Only once did I see Gemstone in action. I was going to a shop in Mawïong that sold *waidong* (betel nut and lime-marked betel leaf) when I saw him sitting with the young woman who owned the little shop. The woman was obviously taken with the handsome, fair-skinned man in front of her. I heard her ask him, 'You are really not married, Bah Gem?'

Gemstone did not say a word; he simply produced a series of quick shakes of the head, much in the manner of a dog, so that his pink lips and ruddy cheeks flapped from side to side in protest, while he looked at her with a pained expression in his eyes, as if hurt that she could doubt his innocence. He went on to have an affair with her that lasted a long time.

'And you approve of people like that, Bah Ap?' Donald asked.

What was there to approve or disapprove? He was what he was. Even his parents could do nothing but spit in his face. I had to work at the check gate, and there were only people like him to work with. But, I must admit, I liked him very much. He was a jolly sort of man who could make you laugh until your sides ached. His life was his own. I valued his friendship because he could turn me away from my own thoughts, too often depressing.

Kohleng was the most terrible of the lot. While all the council's staff were alcoholics, and some of them also philandered, as you now know, Kohleng did everything a person was not supposed to do. Khasis often speak about the three 'Ks'—*kyiad, khalai, kynthei* (alcohol, gambling, women)—the three great vices that afflict Khasi men. Kohleng was guilty of all three, but he was also known as an extortionist, a thief, a gangster and a killer. He had a beautiful wife and two or three children, but hardly ever went home. When he was not on duty, he spent his time in the boozing and gambling dens of Mawïong. His wife often came to the office to beg for money.

Whenever he finished his shift, Kohleng developed a very long tail of dirty and smelly hangers-on who followed him single file wherever he went. His first stop was always the tea shop opposite the check gate, where he would eat breakfast and *khilai*, or treat, his sycophants—still groggy from the previous night's 'quota'—to whatever they wanted to eat. Next, he would disappear into the jungle to relieve himself, with part of his tail in tow, the other part lying about on the road, awaiting his return. I noticed that the council's employees never used any toilet paper. They kept a used exercise book in the office, and whenever they went to the jungle, they simply tore out a page or two from it. But Kohleng never even did that. After his night shift, he had so much money that he used banknotes to wipe his arse. It was an old habit, I was told, which began when the council's staff had complete control of the check gate.

My friends, who like me were hanging on with all their might, trying not to get thrown about in the car, laughed and thought I was kidding them. But I was serious. That was what Kohleng used to do, and he never cared what came out of his pocket: a twenty, a fifty, a hundred—he used them all. Not only that, he used banknotes for his marijuana rolls too.

And then his real routine would begin. Followed by his 'bros', he would vanish into a gambling den—which also sold alcohol—and remain there through the day and night. Now and then, of course, they would emerge to buy food or cigarettes or waidong, and while at it, they would also beat up people who happened to come too close to them.

When Kohleng gambled, he seldom won, because he drank too much. And whenever he lost, he and his bros moved up and down the street to extort money from shops and people, and then went back to drinking and gambling with their ill-gotten gains.

Everyone was afraid of him. But if you did not know who he was, you would think nothing of him. He was even smaller than me and looked quite scrawny and feeble, the result of many years of unhealthy living. So why were people afraid of him? What was the source of his strength? Sure, he had his bros, but they were more or less like him. In a gang fight, they would not stand a chance. As for Kohleng, even I could have easily beaten him up. But then, if I beat him up, I would also have to kill him, and that is something that I, like most people, could not do. It is not easy for ordinary, decent people to kill a man. Not only because they are afraid of the laws of society but also because of their upbringing. Most of us are brought up to respect the sanctity of human life. It has been drummed into us that killing a human being is the most heinous of crimes, punishable with the severest of retributions, not only on earth but also in the afterlife. It would haunt us through life and condemn our soul to damnation after death. The fear of taking a life is as great as the fear of facing death itself.

But Kohleng and his gang thought nothing of killing someone. If you fought with him, you would have to kill him, otherwise he would surely kill you, if not in a day or two, then after a month or a year or many years, but he would do it as surely as night follows day. He had been jailed in the past for killing two or three people, but nothing could be proved, and so he swaggered about intimidating people with a country-made pistol and his reputation as a killer. This reputation was further enhanced by his brother's notoriety as one of the most dreaded gangsters and killers in the Khasi Hills, until he was lynched somewhere in Ri Bhoi, ambushed by friends and relatives of the victims he had slain. The police found his body in a jungle, cut into pieces and stuffed into a gunny bag.

I hated it when I had to share a shift with Kohleng. One night, after he had lost heavily in a game of cards, he came to the office with his drunken hordes, demanding 30,000 rupees from me. Talngung, the beat officer, was with me, but he made himself small as a mouse, and not a squeak of protest did he utter. I was in a quandary. How could I give him that kind of money? I would be accused of theft, and there was no way I could fix the accounts even if I wanted to. I pleaded with him: 'How can I give you that kind of money, Bah Leng, it's not even mine. Please be reasonable. How can I give you somebody else's money?'

He said I had to, otherwise he would cut my throat with a khukri, the ugly-looking dagger used by Gorkha soldiers. He took out the khukri and held it against my throat.

'We don't want any fucking sound,' he said, 'so I'll not shoot your shit head, I'll just cut your fucking throat instead. Will you give me the fucking money or not, you son of a cunt?'

In Khasi, this sounded even more terrible because he was addressing me as 'pha', a term that is used only when speaking angrily to a woman.

The English 'you' cannot even begin to express the offence intended here. Talngung was so alarmed that he actually made some noises of protest. However, someone hit him on the head with some blunt object, and he shut up very quickly.

'How can I?' I pleaded again. 'You know very well it's not my money!'

In response, Kohleng took me by the hair with one hand and pressed the khukri so hard against my throat that a little blood came trickling out. I quickly croaked out my answer: 'Okay, okay, here is the key; you can open the drawers yourself.'

So saying, I threw the key on the table in front of him.

'You piece of shit! *Thloh, liah, stud*! Open the goddamn drawers, now!'

He moved the khukri away from my throat and pointed with it to the drawers while cursing me in Khasi, English, Hindi and Nepali. Now, I was a decent young man, brought up properly by a decent woman who was both mother and father to me, and what's more, I was a respected university student. Nobody had ever spoken to me in that filthy manner. I suddenly lost my temper and became recklessly angry. I'll be damned, I thought, if I allow this son of a bitch to get away with it. Let him do whatever he wants, but I'm not going to open the drawers. Aloud I said, 'The key is on the table, open the drawers yourself.'

When I said that, he jumped on me, beating me with the blunt end of the khukri, overturning my chair and kicking me on the head and in the ribs while I lay on the ground, all the time cursing and threatening to kill me, to chop off my fingers, lop off my ears and ram them down my throat. It was one of his men who pulled him off me, saying, 'Hey, hey bro, we cannot kill the bastard here, we'll have to kill Talngung too ...'

Kohleng, though drink-fuddled, must have realised that killing his own officer was dangerous, for he allowed his men to pull him back. But he pointed a forefinger at me and gave me an ultimatum. 'From tomorrow, from tomorrow, I don't want to see your disgusting face here, you son of a low-born clan! Son of a cunt, shit, son of a penis! If I see you anywhere near Mawïong, I'll have you thrown into the jungle!'

With that warning, he left, followed by his men, one of whom gave me a farewell kick in the ribs. My face was bloody and full of cuts and lumps, and my ribs were bruised, but that was all. Though I had been severely manhandled, the victory was mine, for now. Talngung helped me up and said, 'Well, Ap, I can say one thing about you, you look as soft as dead grass, but you've got balls!'

Before I could go on with the story, Dale interrupted me and asked, 'Bah, I don't understand one thing, ha. You gave him the key, no, Bah, so why didn't he open the drawers?'

I explained to him that if I had opened the drawers and given him the money, it would have been my fault and my responsibility. He could claim I had given him the money willingly. But if he had opened the drawers on his own, that would have been tantamount to theft. And he did not want to do it because his own officer was a witness and because he knew my maliks were powerful people.

'So what happened after that?' they all wanted to know.

The next day, I went to Bah Khran, my employer, and told him what had happened. Bah Khran said I should not worry about it and insisted that I go back to work as usual. 'Nothing's going to happen to you,' he assured me.

It seemed that Bah Khran and the other contractors had sent their people to talk to Kohleng. When next I went to the office, after a few days' rest, Kohleng did not come anywhere near me. Talngung too made sure that we were never on the same shift from then on.

Magdalene found it difficult to believe that someone she had known for so long could have had such an experience. 'Did these things really happen to you, Ap?' she asked incredulously.

Bah Kynsai answered for me. 'You don't know anything about Ap, na, Mag? He's been through a lot in his life. When he was the editor of a daily newspaper, for instance, na, he was threatened by all sorts of people, including militant organisations of every description.'

'But why?'

'Because,' I replied, 'you are not supposed to print anything critical of them.'

Bah Kynsai was not exaggerating too much when he said I had been through a lot. As a boy, I moved from place to place in the Sohra region during the winter vacation every year, looking for work as a labourer. Then, when our family finally moved to Shillong, we lived in a rented tenement. The life of a tenant in Shillong is like that of a cat with kittens. As the cat moves her kittens from place to place, looking for a safe refuge, so must a tenant move from house to house, sometimes by choice, sometimes out of compulsion. And these frequent movements bring him into contact with all manner of people and experiences. But I do not moan about my past poverty: I am much the richer for it as far as my knowledge of life and people goes.

'What about Talngung?' Donald asked. 'You said he was a colourful character, no?'

'And so he was, so he was,' I assured him, 'but to tell his story, I would have to tell you the story of the girl: Chan was her name.'

The girl was sixteen. Tall, compact and with supple curves, she was a dusky beauty, strong and full of the exuberance of healthy, unmolested youth. She worked in her mother's roadside tea shop, and every night, she used to come to our shack of an office to lock away her utensils until the next morning when the shop opened again. The nightly errand was necessitated by the fact that their shop was not an enclosed structure but a roughly put-together shelter of wood and flattened kerosene tin cans without proper doors or windows. In their place, openings had been made in the thin plank walls.

We used to call her the *khatduh* of the office, the youngest child: the one who could do no wrong, the one who could get away with anything. She was well-liked, if not ardently desired, by all of us—an assorted bunch of callow teetotallers and middle-aged veterans of all the vices in these hills, among which, as I have told you, were chiefly gambling, wining and whoring. She was also hotly pursued by lorry drivers who would call out to her: 'Hey, Chan, won't you give me a little *tungtap*?' or 'Come to my car, I'll give you a real joyride'.

Tungtap is a fermented, strong-smelling fish. But somehow, she kept these seekers of young blood at bay with reactions like, 'I'll give you *teiñthap*, you shameless creature!' Teiñthap , as you know, is a species of stinging nettle.

The girl was very attractive with her straight nose, shapely lips and dark eyes that seemed to gleam mischievously all the time. She was also lively, carefree and a great companion, and I would be a hypocrite not to admit that I too was smitten by her. Chan also showed some inclination for me, I thought, for why else did she come to my desk every night, pinching or pulling my nose and saying, 'What a big, long nose you have … a cute nose … a cute duck nose.'

But I was not in that hellhole with all those desperate characters so I could have a girlfriend. Poverty had brought me there, and I was determined to get out of its clutches. I wanted to study hard and make myself fit for an officer's post. I did not want to be sidetracked, though there were times when the temptation became a gnawing hunger, making me gnash my teeth and curse my lot. However, the thought of how I would support her when I did not even have a regular job prevented me from doing anything reckless.

Many among us could not be bothered about such niceties. The middle-aged professionals, for example, tried very hard to have 'a bit of fun' with her. On one occasion, one of them fell drunkenly at her feet and pleaded: 'Take me as your man and I'll tell my wife, right away, I'll tell her to go to blazes.' But none tried as hard or as cunningly as Old Jimmy.

Old Jimmy was none other than Talngung, the beat officer. We called him by that name after the veteran office dog, who was rather fond of young bitches. Potbellied and with pockmarks all over his face, he was not what you would call handsome. In fact, he was called Talngung because his big head resembled an earthen pot. And as if that was not enough to make him an unsavoury candidate for romance, he already had a big family with grandchildren from sons and daughters. Unfortunately, he also had money, for money, as you know now, flowed into the office and into his pockets by the thousands every day.

Seeing all that money always stopped the girl in her tracks. You could see her lovely face screwed up with sudden spasms of desire. She wanted to share it, and the good things it could send her way, the good things that penury and days of drudgery in the shop had so far denied her. Every time she came to the office, she gazed at nothing but the money; she thought of nothing and dreamed of nothing but the joy of having lots of money.

'Ah, what a wonderful thing money is!' she would exclaim to me. 'Think of the things you could do with it. I could buy a new dress for every single day of the year. I could deck myself with gold ornaments, pearl necklaces and diamond rings. I could buy a car and go for beautiful long drives with friends of my choice. I could buy a big house surrounded by a wide-open space. I could live like a *maharani*, the queen of queens … Don't you want that kind of money?'

Sometimes she would simply sigh, 'Oh, what I would not do for money!'

Old Jimmy saw his chance. He eyed her short skirt and long, shapely legs and the firm round breasts taunting him from under her brassiere-less blouse. She would be good to have, he mused, very good indeed. He felt sure she was untouched. Just the thought of it made him crazy.

He gave her small handouts at first, free samples, as you might say. At the end of his shift, before going home, he would shout to her across the road, 'Hey, Chan! Bring me some tea with jadoh and fried pork, would you?' When she came, he would shove a note into her fist, saying, 'Here's a hundred, buy yourself a treat' or 'Go see a movie. There's a Mithun film at Bijou'. These handouts grew larger and larger by the day and, soon, instead of thrusting hundreds at her, Old Jimmy would offer, 'Here's a thousand; buy yourself a nice dress … a mini skirt with a pair of stilettos would be just the thing!' This continued for some time till, one day, he made his move.

'Won't you give me a small hug for all the things I have given you?'

The girl was hooked. She had become addicted to the money he lavished upon her. Nothing else mattered. There was only the fear of losing her daily doses of money. In front of us all, she gave him a hug and became his plaything.

The girl's mother looked the other way, perhaps because she smelled big money. Or maybe she sincerely believed that the excitement of young flesh could persuade Old Jimmy away from his middle-aged wife. Nobody really knew what was going on, what the arrangement was or what promises were made. We only knew that the mother allowed Old Jimmy's midnight trips to her four-room thatched hut, where he visited her daughter as if he were a legitimate and properly married spouse.

News spread, as it always does, and reached Old Jimmy's wife, who fumed, gnashed her teeth and uttered terrible oaths. She was sure that her poor husband was the victim of a deliberate plot hatched by unscrupulous extortionists. She kept telling everybody that it was the girl's debauchery, baiting her husband with fresh meat, which was responsible for the scandal that had brought shame and disgrace to her house. Late one night, she came with an angry mob and went to the girl's ramshackle hut. They dragged out Old Jimmy and heaped curses and unspeakable obscenities on the girl. They spat on her face, slapped her, yanked her by the hair and forced her to kneel at the feet of Old Jimmy's wife. Then they kicked her in the groin to teach her a lesson and whipped her with a broom dipped in ditch water to make her luckless forever.

Dazed and unnerved by his wife's relations, Old Jimmy quickly promised to behave. The next day, he came to the office drunk, to hide his shame and brazen it out, no doubt, and began to blab about money on the ground and other such nonsense to absolve himself. I was too disgusted to listen to the old dog, but this is what I overheard:

'Wouldn't you,' he asked his drink-sodden auditors, 'pick up a hundred-rupee note if you happened upon it on the road? It was like that with me. She was available, and I picked her up. Anyway, I gave her gold,' he concluded with a smirk.

Yes, I could see the gold glittering on her ears and fingers. But I could also hear what they said about her—'SHE IS A WHORE'.

When I concluded the story, Magdalene said, 'My God, ya, are these people for real or what?'

Most of my friends had privileged and protected lives. They knew nothing about the seedy side of life, or the strange characters that crowd such a life. They knew nothing about the kind of existence the poor lead and the evil brutes that are ever ready to pounce upon them. To them, these people were a kind of fantastic story. But I told them that they were all too real, that I had lived with them and that some of them would indeed think nothing of killing a person for a few thousand rupees.

Donald asked me if the check gates were still there.

'Of course not,' I told him. 'That is why I said the government also lost crores of rupees after the ban on timber. Not only the check gates, Don, the tea shops that served them, and the lorries stopping by their side, they too are gone. So are the women who ran the shops. I don't know, for instance, what happened to Chan. I haven't seen her or heard about her at all.'

'I have been planning to ask you, Ap, why do you think it's women who run the tea shops here?' Magdalene enquired.

'It's part of the division of labour between men and women since time immemorial,' I replied. 'While the man was supposed to labour outside the house, in the fields and so on, it was the duty of women to work in and around the house, to clean and cook. Even today, it's mostly considered woman's work to cook and wash utensils. Most men feel it is below their dignity to do this kind of labour. Men take over the cooking only when there's a feast, but even then, the washing of utensils is left to the women.

'But of course, there are also tea shops and jadoh stalls run by men. In fact, one of the most famous jadoh stalls in Ïewduh till some years ago belonged to a man who came to be called Babu Jadoh. He used to teach in a school and went to the shop before and after school hours. His shop was famous not only because the food was delicious but also because of the way he would call out to his serving boys and girls as he charged the customers for their meals. He would shout, "The gentleman with eggs, how much?", "The lady in jeans and high heels, how much?", "The liver lady, how much?", "The kidney gentleman, how much?" Some of his descriptions were really very colourful and added to the cheerful atmosphere in the shop.'

'The liver lady and kidney gentleman?' Magdalene asked.

'Because they ate jadoh with curried liver and kidneys.'

'Oh shit!' She laughed aloud.

Bah Kynsai, however, thought I had given too serious an answer to Magdalene's question about women and tea shops. He said, 'If you ask me, na, women and girls run the tea shops because they are beautiful. They are bait for customers, na?'

'If Evening were here, he would have approved wholeheartedly, Bah Kynsai,' I said. 'In one of his essays, he blames the matrilineal system for the presence of too many women-run tea shops. The matrilineal system, he says, gives everything to women. Because of it, parents do not trust their sons to run the family business dedicatedly, for one day they will leave the house to live with their wives. Therefore, he says, you will always find beautiful girls in the tea shops and "these serve as a snare for the truck drivers" or "as rotten flesh" for every scavenging man. But the ones who actually fall into the trap are not the customers but the girls themselves. It is only Khasi girls, he maintains, that truck drivers and "non-tribals" can play with ... And the result is that the girls have to bear the burden of fatherless children.'

'Nonsense!' Magdalene said hotly.

'The guy is a bloody misogynist!' Donald said.

'Let's not bad-mouth him,' I said. 'I'm just reporting what he wrote because it's public knowledge, but we don't have to attack him when he's not here to defend himself.'

'Okay, okay,' Donald conceded. 'So, what's happening to the ban now? Look at all these trucks!'

'Bah Su can tell you,' I said.

Bah Su told us that, in 2014, eighteen years after the ban, the Meghalaya government suddenly woke up to the problem and framed a scheme for the proper harvesting of timber and the tree plantations in non-government forests. The scheme was prepared together with the North East Space Application Centre at Umïam, mainly to assist the district councils and private landowners in ensuring the effective use of forest produce, especially timber, while also improving per capita income. The two main objectives of the scheme were to see how much timber could be harvested from a forest and how many trees should be planted to replace them. According to it, the beneficiaries who cut down the trees would have to contribute to the plantation programme by way of a 2 per cent green cess, which, it was hoped, would bring about accountability as far as forest management was concerned, and prevent the depletion of forest covers.

Bah Su ended by saying, 'This is what I have been trying to argue all along, Bah Kynsai. Conservation for the sake of conservation will not do, ha. What if the government had enforced the ban? All the jhum farmers, woodcutters and charcoal dealers would have suffered terribly. But with this kind of scheme, ha, we may see a more sensible utilisation of forest produce.'

'But where is all this timber going?' Donald persisted, pointing to the lorries.

'I believe there is a relaxation in the ban,' Bah Su replied. 'As far as I know, about forty-five sawmills have been granted licences, so maybe these are going to them or what?'

Chirag said, 'Only some are going to the local sawmills, Bah, the rest are being taken outside the state, which is illegal, but still, it is much less now after the ban, Bah, earlier there used to be more than a thousand coal and timber trucks per day, now we see only two, three hundred.'

'Imagine the wealth that is being looted from these parts!' Donald exclaimed in frustration.

'People come to Lyngngam only to loot, Bahbah,' Chirag responded.

Chirag called Donald 'Bahbah' because he was much younger. It was like saying 'younger brother'.

Perhaps you are reading this and thinking that we had an enjoyable and comfortable ride—nothing is further from the truth. We were all clinging to whatever we could get a hold of to avoid being bumped about. And when we spoke, we had to raise our voices above the din of the Gypsy.

The road itself had deteriorated further. Bah Kynsai remarked, 'Naturally, na, with so much heavy traffic, how can a dirt track like this endure?'

The jeep had to negotiate huge craters and dried ruts as high as two feet, running like a mud wall, sometimes on both sides of the road, sometimes in the middle. Chirag explained that these were caused by heavy vehicles going over the dirt track after a spell of rain. But hadn't he said there was hardly any traffic during the rainy season, I asked. He replied that it rained now and then during the winter too.

Most worryingly, there were stones of all shapes and sizes on the road, from fist-sized lumps to melon-sized rocks and small boulders the size of chairs and tables. In many places, the road was reduced to half its width by boulders that had fallen from the steep slope on the right. On more than one occasion, one of these could be seen sitting right in the middle of the road, and vehicles had to go around it like water parting before an obstruction.

Chirag had increased the speed a little, just a little, he said, since the winding track was 'all downhill from here to Wah Rwiang'. Just a little or not, we found that we could not carry on an intelligible conversation with each other because of the noise caused by the tyres hitting stones, stones hitting the underbelly of the Gypsy, and all the things that screeched and squealed and clanked inside the Gypsy itself. It was truly terrible, sometimes like a train passing close by, at other times like a giant machine grinding stones and, on occasion, like a jet engine coming to life. Amidst all the creaking, clanking, rattling, screeching and banging noises, there would come, now and then, a weird and shocking sound like a bomb going off. When it first happened, we all cried out in shock: 'What's that?'

But Chirag said it was only the spare tyre. 'I cannot hang it outside because the hook is broken,' he shouted, 'so I keep it inside, in the boot, it's not bound in place, so it sounds like that when it goes up and comes down, don't worry, Babu.'

In the front seat, where I was sitting, all sorts of tools fell from the toolbox in the dashboard. First came a big screwdriver, falling with a thud on my foot and alarming the hell out of me. Chirag said, 'Let it fall, Babu, let it lie on the ground.' Then came a small spanner, then a big one, then a pair of pliers, while other sizes of spanners and screwdrivers peeked out of the toolbox, as if curious to know what was happening outside. When I said I was worried about them stabbing me, Chirag said, 'Pull them all down, Babu.' I did that and left them dancing on the floor.

All this time, we too were jumping up and down in the car, our bottoms merely brushing the seats and our heads hitting the ceiling or the sides of the jeep.

'It's like a mad see-saw,' Donald shouted.

'Like being carried by a flash flood and bobbing up and down in the water,' Bah Su said.

'Like pebbles shaken in a cane basket,' I added. In Sohra, when stones are broken down into pebbles, they are first put in cane baskets to be shaken free of dust before being taken to the stockpile for sale.

'Like being churned in a concrete mixer,' Bah Kynsai shouted.

'Like going on a mountain safari,' Dale cried.

'Only, this is worse,' Magdalene said.

And it was true, for we did not even have seat belts and had to cling to anything we could hold on to, to prevent being thrown to the floor.

We had never experienced such a gut-jerking ride before. I felt as if everything inside me had been shaken loose. My entrails seemed to be flapping about—now left, now right, now up, now down—and I was seriously worried about throwing up all the food I had eaten at Indalin's. But Chirag said, 'You can never get sick on such a trip, Babu, you will be too busy trying to stay in your seat to get sick. Actually,' he added, 'I'm only going at thirty, Babu, but because of the condition of the road, ha, you feel as if I am spiding.'

We were all accustomed to driving and were not a wee bit taken in. I said, 'Let me see the speedometer.' But there was none. The pointer had fallen from its base and was flying madly about inside the glass case. Later, when we arrived in Nongshyrkon, he admitted to having driven much faster than thirty. He said, 'If I had not driven like that, no, Babu, we would have got stuck at many places on the road, and all of you would have had to get out and push, so many times you would have had to push.'

While bouncing in the jeep, I tried my best to observe the countryside. A little further from Nongstoin, there was hardly anything to see. The hills were entirely denuded by years of deforestation, mainly caused by logging, charcoal burning and the need for firewood. Even the ravine that fringed the long mountain range on the left was being stripped of trees. I could see a stream at the bottom of the ravine, almost completely dry, partly because it was winter and partly because of the rampant deforestation. There were trees lying about on its banks, obviously newly felled and left to dry in the sun so they could be used as firewood.

But as we moved deeper and deeper into the interior, the forest became denser. Chirag said, 'All this was bald just a few years ago because of logging, charcoal and jhum. Now, the forest is gaining ground once more, Babu, this is what happens normally if the people let the forest alone for ten or fifteen years, no, Babu, the trees come back.'

Indeed, as we went deeper and deeper into the temperate rain forest, we saw tall, majestic trees, a mixture of soft and hardwood like sal, *puma* (*Cedrela toona*), *dieng kaiñ* (*Rhus succedanea*), iron tree, banyan (*Ficus elastica*), mahogany, *dieng jing* (*Quercus spicata*), bay tree, cinnamon, litchee, jackfruit and the biggest and tallest of them all, *dieng lieng* (*Betula acuminata*, the boat tree, so named because it was used to make boats in olden times). The jungle was so thick in these areas that the sky was almost blotted out by the dense foliage bending down towards the road. For quite some time, we saw nothing but the dark green of the trees coated with the thick brown dust raised by the lorries. Soon, however, we saw more signs of the ravages of jhum cultivation, and more and more bald patches appeared in the otherwise dense and pristine forest. In some places, entire hill slopes were piled with newly felled trees and brush, waiting for the fire.

Chirag pointed to one of the denuded hills and shouted, 'There, you see all those trees and brush being felled on that hill? That's jhum, now they will burn the trees to ashes, the ashes will fertilise the soil, and they will sow the seeds when the rain comes. Previously, when there were few inhabitants and an abundance of land, no, Babu, people cultivated the cleared land for three, four years and then left to cultivate elsewhere. They returned only after ten to fifteen years, and by that time, the jungle would have grown back, Babu, but nowadays, people doing jhum, because of overpopulation and less land, no, Babu, do not wait for more than five or six years before coming back to the same place, hence the jungle cannot recover. When trees are only five to six feet tall, they are slashed and burnt again, and gradually the jungle cannot grow any more, Babu, that's why all the bald hills you have seen.'

Magdalene wanted to know what people were growing on the jhum farms. Chirag told her they grew green vegetables of all sorts, and also yam, taro, eggplant, ginger, turmeric, sweet potato and cassava. He said they also grew grain crops, including rice, but clarified immediately, 'We do not have any paddy fields in our area, Kong, we grow rice on the hill slopes.'

Sometimes, when we came to a higher point on the road, we could see columns of light blue smoke rising from many places deep in the jungle. Donald asked, 'What are those, Bah Chirag?'

'Charcoal burning, that's how people here live, jhum cultivation and charcoal burning.'

'What about logging?' Donald asked.

'That is done mostly by outsiders who lease forests from local landowners.'

The view reminded me of something I had once seen from Kyllang Peak in West Khasi Hills. Kyllang Peak is actually a giant boulder the size of a mountain. It got its name from a spirit who, legend says, used to live on the mountain and whose rage caused a terrible tempest in the rainy months. The malevolent spirit took great pleasure in terrorising humans, spreading measles and misery among them, until he was stopped by his brother, Symper, who fought a terrible battle with him. While Symper threw large boulders at him, Kyllang uprooted trees and dug out all the topsoil from around him to use as weapons against his brother. Symper eventually won the battle and forced Kyllang to flee to his present location on the road from Khatsawphra village to Mawnai.

Standing on the lofty pinnacle of Kyllang, you can see an undulating landscape of low hills, punctuated by pine slopes, dark deciduous forests and the corrugated iron sheets on the rooftops of distant villages. Instead of roads, there are only dusty brown dirt tracks crisscrossing the area like the lines on your palm. And inevitably, you will point to the dark columns of smoke rising from the far forests on every side, and your local guide will say, 'The source of the smog, the solver and multiplier of problems in these parts—charcoal burning!' And if you are a poet, you might ask enigmatically, 'Can the columns of smoke hold up the sky?'

The same predicament seemed to afflict the people of Lyngngam.

After a brief silence, Magdalene shouted, 'This car is worse than a horse cart, man!'

'That's the understatement of the year,' Bah Kynsai replied. 'It's like jumping on a springboard.'

'Don't blame me,' Chirag said. 'Actually, it's better now, Babu, in summer it's simply not negotiable. Do you see all those craters and deep ruts? They are not made by trucks alone, but mostly by water flowing on the road, it's like a river in summer. In summer, no, Babu, pregnant women who want to give birth at the health centre in Nongstoin are advised to get there many months before their due date. Many women who left for Nongstoin near their due dates, ha, used to get stuck in the jungle, and they had to give birth on the road. Very dangerous, imagine giving birth in the middle of the jungle!'

'How did they survive, then?' Magdalene asked.

'They took precautions, Kong, they brought with them a woman, a traditional healer, who could act as a midwife. And also, when such a thing happened, no, Kong, I mean when women gave birth on the road, no, Kong, people from surrounding villages used to come and help as soon as they heard of it.'

Most of the lorries carrying timber and coal belonged to a person called Horkit, who ran a company in Nongstoin called Horkit Company. The lorries carrying timber were marked with the symbol of a buffalo and those carrying coal with an elephant.

'Why are the trucks marked like this, Bah Chirag?' Magdalene asked.

'They are meant to identify the company, Kong,' Chirag replied.

'But why these particular animals?'

'Buffaloes are used to pull out huge logs from the jungle, Kong, I don't know about the elephant.'

To my mind, the answer was not difficult to find. The fellow was boasting of his brute strength as a looter and ravager of the land.

Donald asked Chirag what the company was doing with all that coal and timber. Chirag said some of the timber would go to the company's sawmill, but most of it, and the coal, would go to a depot to be exported. How that could be done in spite of the twin bans was anybody's guess.

But any discussion on the subject was forgotten when Chirag suddenly killed the engine and brought the car to a jerking stop on a heap of dried mud. As we fell forward and cried out in alarm, he said, by way of explanation, 'The brake has stopped working.'

'What! But how?'

Of course, given the road and Chirag's driving, it was only natural that the car should have a breakdown. We had expected something of the sort to happen sooner or later, and now it had, only twenty kilometres outside Nongstoin, in the jungle village of Nong Lyngdoh.

Chirag got down and had a look at the rear wheel. 'Oho! I think the brake oil bucket is broken, Babu, all the oil has spilled out!'

We got down too. The right rear wheel was bathed in brake fluid.

'What to do? What to do?' Chirag kept muttering.

Now, what were we supposed to say? We were not mechanics. This was the middle of the jungle. There was no point expecting any help from this nondescript, dust-coated village of bamboo huts and shacky houses.

'This is terrible!' Donald moaned.

'Does this mean we won't be able to go to Nongshyrkon, after all the trouble we have taken, Bah Chirag?' Magdalene asked.

'For how long will we be stuck here?' Bah Kynsai demanded.

'Will any of the trucks give us a lift?' Bah Su wanted to know.

Chirag only replied to Bah Su's question. 'Haven't you noticed? They are not going to Shyrkon, all of them have gone towards Maweit, the timber and coal will be loaded there.'

We looked around us and realised that the road was indeed empty of traffic. All the lorries had taken the left turn towards Maweit at a little village called Lad Maweit, about a quarter of a kilometre from where we were stuck.

'Can we get a lift back home at least?' Magdalene asked again. She was genuinely worried.

'No need to worry, Kong,' Chirag said, 'we'll travel to Shyrkon without brakes.'

When Dale heard that, he said at the top of his voice, 'Travel without brakes on this kind of road? No, no, no, no, impossible!'

We all protested. Apart from its terrible condition, the road was cut into the side of a long mountain range, hemmed in by a hill slope on one side and with only a forested ravine yawning ominously on the other. Moreover, it zigzagged downwards with chicanes, S curves and hairpin bends everywhere. How could we risk travelling without brakes on such a road? Chirag assured us that he could do it. But none of us agreed. Dale said he would rather trek through the jungle and risk encountering wild animals than travel without brakes. However, being a taxi driver with some knowledge of automobiles, he offered to take a look at the car.

Chirag was pleased with the offer and immediately requested all of us to step away so he and Dale could work without obstruction. We moved away to inspect the place. The village was some distance from where we were stuck. There were about twenty houses, with more huts scattered about the surrounding hills. Only some of the houses had painted concrete walls and roofs of corrugated iron sheets; the rest were mostly shacks of bamboo and wattle with thatched roofs. One or two were built on wooden pillars that were driven into the ground and had walls of thin, rough-hewn planks and roofs of tin sheets made of flattened kerosene cans. Some of the houses had their lights on, although it was about 2.30 in the afternoon. Later I was told that electricity was subsidised for the villagers, which meant that whatever their consumption, the payment was always the same: a small amount fixed by the government. That was why they burned electricity all day.

I was walking up the badly rutted red-dirt track, looking at felled logs lying about, and absent-mindedly watching country chickens scratching for insects by the roadside, when Donald approached me. 'Bah Ap,' he said, 'I'd like to know more about the great earthquake, how big was it really?'

Sources vary in their assessment of the intensity of U Jumai Bah, also known as the Assam earthquake of 1897, which is a misnomer because the epicentre of the quake was the Shillong Plateau within the Indian Plate. While some like Jugal Kalita, a scientist at the College of Engineering and Applied Science, Colorado, placed the intensity at 8.5 on the Richter scale and maintained that it was among the ten biggest earthquakes in recorded history, other sources placed it at 8.3. The most reliable record, from the scientific point of view, was that of the famous British geologist Richard D. Oldham, who wrote about four major Indian earthquakes that took place in 1819, 1869, 1881 and 1897.

According to him, the earthquake took place at about 5.11 p.m. on 12 June 1897. The quake was thought to have happened thirty-two kilometres underground. It left an area of 390,000 square kilometres in ruins and was felt over an area of 650,000 square kilometres, from the western Burmese border to Delhi. Before the shock was felt, there was a rumbling noise underground, which lasted for about three minutes. This was followed by the actual earthquake, which lasted about two and a half minutes. The aftershocks were so severe and prolonged that everything built of stone was levelled to the ground. Some have compared the rumbling noise of the earthquake to 'the approach of an express train' and others to the 'noise of a thousand ship-engines thumping away in the midst of a storm at sea'.

The earthquake was accompanied by an undulation of the ground varying from eight to thirty feet in length and from one to three feet in height. Eyewitness accounts, including that of F. Smith of the Geological Survey of India, who was stationed in Shillong at the time, reported that all the stone buildings collapsed, and about half the houses with wooden frames and reed walls covered with plaster were ruined. However, houses with wooden frames and plank walls that rested on *mawkhrums*, or short foundation stones of about two feet, were untouched. Smith said the earthquake was so violent that the whole of the damage was done in the first ten or fifteen seconds. There were hundreds of aftershocks of varying intensity that lasted for days.

But, considering the violence of the earthquake, the mortality rate was not high, about 1, 542 deaths, with most of them occurring in the Sohra region. In Shella, to the south of Sohra near the Bangladesh border, 600 people died, while all the houses were hurled into the river that ran below. But then, even the biggest earthquake in history, which occurred in 1960 in Valdivia, Chile, and measured 9.5 on the Richter scale, did not kill more than 6,000 people. The deadliest in that sense, although it measured only 8.0, was the one in Shaanxi, China, which devastated an 840-kilometre wide area, and caused the death of 830,000 people on 23 January 1556.

But fatality is not always the criterion by which the awfulness of an earthquake is measured. The great earthquake of 1897 caused terrible suffering to the entire population of the Khasi Hills; not a single person was left untouched. The continuous aftershocks terrorised people for weeks, and the incessant monsoon rains made life even grimmer by denying those who had lost their homes the sanctuary of the outdoors.

When it comes to an eyewitness account of the great earthquake and its effects, nothing is more vivid than the little monograph by the Welsh Presbyterian missionary, Reverend Robert Evans, entitled *The Earthquake in Khasia and Its Effects*. The book was published in India by North-Eastern Hill University as *The Great Earthquake of 1897*. Since I had it saved on my mobile phone, Donald and I read through some relevant sections as we waited for Chirag and Dale to fix the car.

Evans opens the monograph by talking about 'God and Earthquake' in the first chapter, followed by a history of 'Previous Earthquakes' in the second chapter. The detailed account of the great earthquake begins in the third chapter. The following is what Donald and I read together:

When everything was going along in the usual, peaceful way, with no one thinking about anything out of the ordinary, on the 12th of June 1897, between four and five in the afternoon, the inhabitants of Khasia experienced one of the greatest earth tremors known in any country that had not been totally destroyed, along with its people. We know of parts of the world that were completely ruined by earthquakes, places where not a man, not a beast, not a house or a hill were left to show what the land looked like before the earthquake. We give thanks to God for the Khasia earthquake not being of that ilk, but, exceptionally, we can place it amongst the most powerful disturbances mentioned in historical records. A quarter of a minute made the greatest transformation possible to every building in the country.

The very face of the land underwent huge changes. At the end of that short spell, every stone house had become a pile of rubble, while every wooden house was bent and twisted, taking on almost every shape imaginable, until they were totally unsuitable for habitation. Massive landslips took place in every direction. In some places, hundreds of thousands of tons of earth from the hill slopes were carried down—many hundreds of feet and with a deafening thud. Within a few seconds, lofty hillsides, previously made beautiful by grass and trees, were visibly denuded in every part, to the point where the biggest one looked like huge quarries, while those in the distance resembled ploughed land. Great forests were hurled to the valley floors and so were the earth and rocks from under them, until the land was made to appear raw and scarred, whereas, earlier, it looked smooth and verdant. All the roads and paths on the slopes were ripped away, so that getting from one place to another became impossible. For several days, the inhabitants of some villages knew nothing of the plight of those in other villages within a few miles of them because the connecting footpaths had been obliterated. Rice, the natives' means of sustenance, had been blasted away by the earthquake and mixed with soil, leaving next to nothing in the way of food in the villages. And, because communications had been knocked out, food could not be taken in from other places for days, for weeks in some cases. Losing their houses, their refuge from the torrential rain, and their victuals at the same time made the situation far more lamentable. In these two regards, we believe it was worse for the missionaries and other Europeans in Khasia than it was for the indigenous people. Their stone houses had suffered far worse damage—total damage!—while nearly all their comestibles were buried by the disaster. Rain added to the wretched situation, and yet it was nice to have it. Seeing that, generally, the villages were built on hilltops, with the rivers deep in the valleys, going to fetch water was impossible as the paths had been swept away. Rice mixed with earth was gathered and washed in the rain, like washing gold. And although no one could separate it, to an appreciable extent, from the soil and the gravel, still, with things as they were, there was nothing else to do but eat it. Under all those circumstances, it was seen that mercy seems to rejoice in the face of judgement and that men, women and children can live in remarkably unfavourable conditions.

Those were a few of the effects of the earthquake. The cause came like a thunderbolt, creating dread and unforeseen destruction. They had no warning, only in the sense that the earthquake, which was unusually forcible from the start, did not gain full force for six or seven seconds. This was how long they had to flee from their houses. Those who could get away in that short time were spared while the rest were buried in the ruinous mess. Everyone knew from the outset that their end was nigh and fled for their lives to whatever place they considered, in their terror, to be the safest. The houses were shaken until they fell and parts of them broke into pieces as their occupants all ran away. Walls were shifted right off their foundations, floorboards were lifted out of place and the iron bits of the roofs were torn like paper. Not only did walls fall apart but stones were thrown feet away by the sudden force of the earthquake. With every previous earthquake, people felt fairly safe after getting away. But, this time, the danger was everywhere. The face of the earth was like the surface of the sea in a storm, raised up in waves, so that no one could stay on their feet. It would have been bad enough if these waves had come in from one direction, but it was as if they were being pushed and stirred up from all sides. The earth was shaken in this way until gaps of various dimensions were created everywhere, as well as huge chasms many yards wide and many yards deep. Given that the house had collapsed and a column of smoke or dust, as was understood later, was rising into the atmosphere, we believe, at that moment, that the crater of a volcano had opened up beneath the area, so we tried to get further away from the danger. Looking up for a second at the land around us, we could see the earth being shaken for many miles, like a large cloth in a strong wind. The highest hills looked as if they were chasing each other, the one energetically striving to catch up with the other ...

The rain came down really hard and an entire population had no houses to go and shelter in. But they paid very little attention to the rain, which was forgotten because of a far more important matter. Not a second went by without everybody expecting the earth to cave in and bury them alive in its core. Although the earthquake was a very present thing, somehow the significance of the circumstances made the present seem like next to nothing because it brought into view Man's relationship with the past and the future in a frighteningly clear way. In the face of the cataclysm, everyone thought the world was coming to an end and those who knew something about the Second Coming expected to see Him. An unforgettable minute! They all felt their lifetime being squeezed into that very instant. Everyone had to strike out as best they could for themselves, without anyone being in a position to offer help. That was the minute that gave a man some idea of his standpoint before getting to it and a fair degree of certainty as to whether he could stand by it or not. Did I say 'minute'? No! All those things and many more had gone through his mind long before a quarter of a minute had passed. Who can describe the feelings of gratitude of those who were present, those who witnessed the upheaval slowing down, with their children and their own selves in the land of the living? Valuable life had been saved. They had been miraculously delivered from the jaws of death. They felt at the time that being without their houses, their furniture, their sustenance and their clothing was a minor loss when their lives and their relations had been rescued. 'A man will give all for his life'. Everyone was more than happy to forego life's comforts when life itself had been so wonderfully spared ...

God's mercy was truly in evidence in the amazing way the inhabitants were spared. The number of people losing their lives to the earthquake totalled 1542, as far as government officials could tell. Of these, 916 were from the Khasia and Jaiñtia Hills, with 545 from Sylhet district. Almost 600 of the 916 were from Cherraponjee and surrounding villages, and of the 545 lost in Sylhet, the great majority were from Sunamganj region, where many were drowned when the banks collapsed into the surging river. A large number of houses had been built along these banks. They were seen no more ...

In the fourth chapter, Evans talks about the 'natural', as opposed to the 'spiritual', effects of the great earthquake:

After the first big tremor, the one that went on for several minutes, came to an end, a short dream-world pause was experienced for about a minute, during which time we could look around and, up to a point, take in the damage that had been done. We could see we were without a home, without bed and board, without clothing, and that everyone throughout the land was in just about the same situation. We did not know which way to turn. At that point, we thought the worst was over, and we began to plan for the future. But that did not last long, because the earth began to shake and roar again in such a violent way that it would have struck every house down if they had not already been razed to the ground. The earth resembled a child having convulsions. For a minute or so, the assault went on in every direction with unstoppable force, then it calmed down again for about the same length of time. Every commotion caused the earth to rage like a wounded beast in dire agony—or, more as if all the beasts of the earth were groaning together. That was our plight when the evening shadows began to spread across the land. It is not easy to describe the feelings of those who spent that night amid the roaring and the tremors, the rain and the dark. With every disturbance, collapsing sounds were heard all around. The heavy rain made for a very dark night and we did not know what kind of damage was going on around us. We thought it was the earth that was caving in and that some villages were being swallowed up each time—and with the next second, we could be buried in it and lost to sight. A night never to be forgotten! Everyone awaited the morning far more eagerly than night watchmen do. Without a doubt, that was the most drawn-out, anxious and comfortless night we ever spent. And oh! how good it was to see the light of day! We felt it would be better for us to encounter disaster in the daytime than to be hurled head over heels into goodness knows where in the pitch-black night. Our concern was endless, for we got a great number of powerful tremors during the night and hundreds of similar ones during the first week.

In the morning light, the scenes that met our eyes were really weird— destruction of every kind on all sides. The blue-green slopes had been converted into scarred bare rock. The face of the land had changed beyond belief, in as much as some hills had gone down considerably while others had risen. And these transformations kept on happening, although not to the same extent, for months after that. The government sent a surveyor to measure the height of the hills—to compare them with previous measurements and he found there was a big difference in many places. He said that, in one place, a hill had split from the top down and that one side had been lifted many feet above the other. In another place, in the direction of the Garo Hills, he came across one that had risen a few score feet higher than in the previous measurement, and a lake had formed close by, where there had not been one before. When he submitted his findings, the authorities would not believe him and he was sent back to do a second survey. This he did, with the same results. He showed us his observations. He firmly believed that a subterranean explosion of the same kind as a volcano was the cause of the earthquake. But another man, who had been sent to do a particular research into the nature and causes of the earthquake, was of the opinion that the collapse of huge underground caves was the cause.

The emperor of Japan sent a skilful professor to research the nature and effects of the earthquake. We cannot remember asking him in particular for his idea in relation to its cause, but he told us the tremors were in

Category A. In case there was any doubt about their being just as strong as some people had thought, he stated that its surface covered a far wider range than the one that had taken place in Japan. He was the man who told us it was a clear earth movement of ten inches, back and fore, and so it was totally impossible for any kind of stone wall to remain standing. Not only were the walls shattered, but the very stones were hurled several feet from the walls, as if they had been thrown by a man's hand. The official who came here on behalf of the government of India said its effects proved it was one of the biggest earthquakes we have heard about. In his own words: 'That it was one of the greatest earthquakes on record'.

The Khasia Hills are covered with boulders of all sizes. We saw some nearly as big as the largest chapels we have in Wales and some others such as a strong man could pick up. Between these two extremes, there are thousands of different dimensions. But their size made no difference to the earthquake. Nearly all those on the slopes were shaken like corn in a sieve and hurled like sling-stones to the depths below. In many places, the hills had been stripped of them and the valleys filled up with them …

The fifth chapter presents the author's view of the earthquake's spiritual effects, followed by an account of 'Various People's Experience' of it in the sixth chapter. He concludes the monograph with some 'Short Stories' of miraculous escapes and horrible deaths, including 'The Destruction of Shella', to which I referred earlier:

Shella was one of the biggest, hardest and most pagan villages in the land. Its religion was a mixture of the Khasi faith and Hinduism, a kind of impure melange of the one and the other. All the hillsides around Shella were orange groves, which, alongside the limestone quarries, constituted the main living of the native people. They had got a name for themselves for taking each other to court. Owing to there being no clear boundaries between the various orchards, some villains kept on taking advantage of the situation to try and get their hands on their neighbours' land. Let it be said right away that there are good, honest people among them and that justice calls for them to defend their property. But having said that, I have to admit that the inhabitants are getting a reputation for being extremely proud and unprincipled. The village had been built on the slope of a high hill, with a big river flowing below. Near the village, the river flowed slowly except in times of heavy rain because its bed was not much higher than the plains in the direction of Chattuck and Sylhet [both in Bangladesh now]. But at the top end of the village, there was a considerable drop down to the water, which in some places adjacent to the village was very deep.

When the earthquake came, it was very difficult for the locals to escape, on account of the position of the village. Houses were hit, trees were uprooted, the earth caved in down to the depths and the whole lot was swept into the river below. A hideous calamity! Houses, trees, earth, stones, women and children—all jumbled together and lost to sight in the river's watery grave. That was the place where the greatest number of Khasis lost their lives. Hundreds were interred in that dreadful demolition. The strange thing is that no one who was there was saved. Was it that God did not rule 'mercy amid judgement' but gave those who were left behind another chance for eternal life through His Son? Perhaps some will say this was not a judgement upon the village for its sins and that the same would have happened whatever state the native might have been in. That could be the case but God has brought ruin to particular towns before, so that it is safer even in this world not to be 'too ungodly'. Where there was a successful, wealthy village, now there is only bare rock, and the locals who were spared have been scattered. There was such a ruinous mess in the place that no village can ever be built there again. It will stand through the ages as a memorial to that terrifying earthquake and as a warning of what can happen in other places at any moment in the future.

In the course of his narration, Evans tried to put the great earthquake in perspective by recalling other such cataclysmic earth-shakers that had affected India since 1505, including the first recorded earthquakes in the Khasi Hills, which took place in the 'Cherraponjee' area on 4 July and 15 October 1851.

What undercuts the quality of the narrative is the fact that everything is coloured by the author's prejudices and his religious insularity. For instance, Evans speaks of the earthquake as God's weapon to punish the Khasi 'pagans' for their sins and as God's 'purpose' to 'liberate the inhabitants of India from the enslavement of paganism and idol worship to the glorious freedom of God's children, as, through the plagues in Egypt He brought about the complete freedom of Israel from the bondage of the earth stones'.

Evans was especially harsh on Shella when he described it as 'one of the biggest, hardest and most pagan villages in the land'. This is grossly unjust to both the people of Shella and Niam Khasi, the Khasi religion, which calls for the worship of the one true God, U Blei, the Dispenser, the Creator, who is the same for every creature on earth. But such observations are perhaps understandable when read alongside his confession in the 'Foreword' that the tale of the earthquake and its effects were told 'from a missionary's point of view, and how these related to the work of the Mission' in the Khasi Hills.

When we finished reading the monograph, Dale was still lying on his back under the car and tinkering with something near the right rear wheel. I turned back to Donald, telling him about the aftermath of the earthquake as recorded by some Khasi writers. The ugliest thing about it, I said, was the attitude of many Khasi workers and labourers. For instance, they would force a house owner to employ twenty-nine or thirty people to dismantle and rebuild a ruined house when the same could have been easily done by just a few men. And most of them did not even work: they just lazed around and demanded huge wages at the end of the day, while some others came only in the morning to write down their names and return in the evening to collect their money. And that was not all. Everybody claimed to be a *misteri*, a professional carpenter or mason or house builder. In the aftermath of the great earthquake, if a man was able to hold a chisel or operate a saw, he would straightaway claim to be a misteri and demand the wages of a head builder. And such was the desperation of the house owners that they had to submit meekly to the blackmail of these profiteers.

According to one Khasi writer, it was shocking to witness the complete lack of charity and the shameless dishonesty of the Khasi people during that time of great tribulation. He said, 'Though as a community we believe in the Commandments that demand us to live in "the knowledge of man, the knowledge of God", to be guided by conscience and to "earn virtue" in life, yet at that time, we behaved as if we knew only how to cheat and take advantage of the tragedy of others.' In the end, the house owners could only retaliate by calling them *misteri khynñiuh jumai*, 'earth-quaking builders'. And the saying has stuck. To this day, any worker who pretends to be an expert at something he is not and who charges professional rates without being a professional is mocked as a 'misteri khynñiuh jumai'.

'But what about Shella, Bah Ap, is it still there?' Donald asked.

'Of course. It's still a thriving village.'

'So, Evans's predictions did not come true then?'

'How could they? He was not a prophet, was he?'

Dale had crawled out from under the Gypsy by now. He had asked Chirag to pump the brakes while he lay on his back on the dusty road, trying to identify the problem. 'One look and I knew it was the brake pipe,' he said. 'It was completely broken. So I put M-seal on the pipe and then tied it in place with a piece of plastic and cloth. It's quite simple. Fortunately, Bah Chirag keeps many things in his vehicle, otherwise we would be goners.'

Chirag was pleased to be commended by Dale and said, 'When you travel on a jungle road, no, Bahbah, you never know what will happen, so I keep a lot of things in the car.'

Bah Kynsai, who had been dozing beneath a tree all this while, asked Dale, 'If it was that simple, what took you so long?'

'Well, it takes time to actually do the work, no, Bah?' he replied, laughing. 'It's not as simple as it sounds. Doing it and talking about it are very different things. It was very difficult just to get at the pipe without proper tools.' He turned to Chirag and said, 'Bah Chirag, do you have a little more brake fluid? Pour it in the tank and pump the break again; I want to take another look.'

Chirag did indeed have a little brake fluid stored for just such emergencies. He did as he was told, and Dale vanished beneath the car once more.

After a while, Dale shouted, 'It's okay, Bah, it's okay, only a little is leaking.' Crawling out from under the Gypsy, he said again, 'It will do. Once the M-seal hardens, ha, it will stop entirely. But what about the brakes, are they working?'

Chirag tested the brakes while we held our breath. 'Yes, working, Bahbah, thank you,' he said.

Magdalene said, 'Thank God!' for all of us.

Chirag gave Dale a piece of clean cloth on which to wipe his hands, and some of us helped him brush the dust from his clothes. After that, we all piled into the Gypsy, and off Chirag zoomed again.

But Dale was not done talking. He said, 'You know, Bah, if that had failed, ha, I would have broken off the pipe entirely, then sealed it with something so it wouldn't leak ...'

'What would be the point of that?' I asked.

'If I did that, we could have used the front-tyre brakes at least. In any case, I would have been able to get you to Nongshyrkon. You have to thank me for it.'

'Of course,' Magdalene answered for all of us. 'Thank you, Dale, we are very, very grateful to you.'

'But I heard you thanking God, Kong?' Dale said, laughing.

Some kilometres after the village of Nong Lyngdoh, the road became smoother. The Gypsy too became quieter in response. On the road from Nongstoin to Nongshyrkon, there were about six villages, all as small and nondescript as Nong Lyngdoh. The first one outside Nongstoin was Ribiang, followed by Mawlait, Nongtraw, Lad Maweit, Nong Lyngdoh and Rimynñiar. But not one of them had as unusual a name as Maweit: 'shit stone'.

In Ri Bhoi district, in the north Khasi Hills, there is a village called Umeit or 'shit stream'. Once upon a time, there used to be a yearly religious festival involving the sacrifice of goats, chickens and bulls, performed by some villages located near a stream. When the sacrifices were over, people used to go to the stream to wash the animals' entrails, and because all the waste matter and excrement were emptied into it, the stream itself, and a village by its bank downstream, came to be known as Umeit, 'shit stream'.

When Magdalene asked Chirag why Maweit was called by that name, he said he did not know. Bah Kynsai, however, declared that he knew the story. He said, 'Many, many years ago, na, there were only six to seven houses in the village known now as Maweit. At the time, the area around it was almost an impassable jungle. Even today, na, look around you, the jungle is still very thick, so you can imagine the situation then. It used to be the practice of Khasis to crap in the jungle, okay? You know that, na? But in those days, the people of Maweit were afraid to do the job too far away from home because of elephants and tigers and whatnot. So, they chose a spot near the village with a lot of huge boulders lying around, cut down all the trees, and began to do their job there.

'One day, a stranger from another village visited the place. When he saw the spot with a large collection of boulders and interesting rock formations, na, he exclaimed, "Wow, what a beautiful spot! But why are you cutting down all the trees there? Are you trying to turn the place into a picnic spot?" The local guide explained that they did their morning job behind the boulders. "*Ah, ki maweit!*" the stranger exclaimed again. "What a beautiful place in which to do such a dirty job! And what do you call your village?" The guide said the village did not have a name. Since there were only six to seven houses, they had not even chosen a name.

'But when the stranger left the village, na, when he got back home and narrated the story of his journey to his family, na, he referred to the village as Maweit, "shit stone", and since then, everyone has called it that.'

'Is that true, Ap?' Magdalene asked me.

'It's as good a story as any,' I replied.

'Bah Kynsai, you bloody joker!' Magdalene and Donald exploded.

Bah Kynsai burst out laughing, and all of us joined him. Even Bah Su, who had been silent most of the time, grinned from ear to ear.

After Nong Lyngdoh, we reached Rimynñiar, a quaint little village of tin-and-thatch roofs by the banks of Wah Lyngdoh, the River Lyngdoh, whose green pools and meandering flow made the place so picturesque that we all tried to click photographs of it from the lurching car. Then, a little past the village, we came to a simple gate: a bamboo pole laid across the road.

'What is this for?' Bah Kynsai asked.

'From now on, we'll be in Ri Lyngngam, Babu,' Chirag replied. 'There's no PWD road here, no, Babu, this is a private road constructed by us, my family and I, all commercial vehicles plying through here for timber, coal and agricultural produce have to pay a toll, hence the gate.'

Just down the road, we came upon the stunning sight of the River Rwiang, one of the biggest in Lyngngam. At this point, it was a wide expanse of clean white sand, dark boulders and sparkling blue water, more than 310 feet across. Beyond the sand and boulders, on both banks, was the thick jungle with its many shades of green. Where the road vanished into the water, the river was carpeted with small round stones, making it easier for vehicles to cross. It was only about two and a half feet deep in places, but upstream were enormous pools of calm water, crystal clear and blue, with little fish called *shalynnai* milling about. We were told that the pools, as indeed the length and breadth of the river itself, were favourite angling spots, though we could not see anything bigger than the shalynnai near the surface. The big ones were supposed to be down in the depths. Downstream, there was the white of rapids striking boulders, which seemed to fill the river like pomegranate seeds.

Beside the watery road, laid across the river, was a low-hung bridge, long and narrow, made of bamboo poles. Several poles were driven into the river bed to form foundational frames resembling high-backed chairs. Eight poles, tied together lengthwise, were laid on the frames, and several poles were joined to these so they could span the breadth of the river. Bamboo handrails were tied to the protruding posts of the frames for an easy crossing. The entire structure looked like one gigantic chair. The bridge was no work of art—merely a shaky affair that seemed to have been hurriedly put up. The bamboo poles were bound together with cane strips, and in places where the strips had come off, smooth, round river stones kept the poles in position. Nevertheless, it had a kind of antique beauty that appealed to all of us. Later, I learnt why there was no attempt at fine workmanship. The bridge would be carried away by the summer floods when the volume of water increased manifold, and the river itself would become impassable for many wet months. The Lyngngams believe this is the handiwork of Sangkhni, the river god. But that tale is for later.

We asked Chirag to stop the jeep and raced towards the bridge. The loveliness and loneliness of the place made us feel as if we were on another planet, uninhabited and unspoilt. And this was an illusion that persisted despite the road and the bridge. As we posed for photographs, Chirag drove the jeep across and waited for us to finish enjoying the scene. He would have to wait for a long time, I thought. How often do city dwellers find a place like this?

When Chirag had crossed the river and parked the jeep somewhere out of sight, he came back to the riverbank, waving to us and calling out, 'They are all here, they are all here! Come, come, they are all here!'

When we got there, we saw the white Gypsy, with the flaps of its soft grey cover lifted onto the roof, parked beside our blue one. Our friends, we noticed, were in various stages of undress. Both groups shouted in joy, and when we got nearer, we asked them what was happening and why they were undressing. Hamkom told us that Halolihim wanted to have a holy dip in the river, so everyone had decided to have a swim and freshen up.

Bah Kynsai went straight to Raji and shouted, 'Hey, mə, liah! Do you know the funeral will start only seven days from now?'

'We didn't know till we came to the check gate, Bah Kynsai. We spoke to a fellow we met there, and he told us about it. Our driver confirmed the news to us only after that fellow had told us.'

'So what the hell was your friend doing misleading us like that?'

'What to say, Bah Kynsai, I think he also did not know or what?'

Bah Su, Hamkom and I tried to appease Bah Kynsai. Bah Su summed it up by saying, 'It's okay, it's okay, we have settled all that already, Bah Kynsai. We can do nothing now except make the most of the trip.'

Bah Kit came over to where we stood and added, 'It's a huge mix-up, no? But it should be all right, I think. At least we will not be out of food and shelter.'

'Food and shelter are fine,' Bah Kynsai responded, 'but what about this?' He pointed with his thumb towards his mouth. 'I have brought only enough for five, six days, na? What about you people?'

Bah Su said he was in the same spot, but added, 'I think we can make do with the local stuff.'

'That's what I was thinking too,' Raji said. 'There will be plenty of the local stuff, Bah Kynsai, it's part and parcel of the funeral rites, no? And I've heard it's quite tasty, okay, sweet and tasty.'

'Well, all right, then,' Bah Kynsai agreed reluctantly. 'I will miss my stuff, but at least I won't die of thirst.'

Hamkom laughed out loud. 'At least Ap and I have no problem on that score.'

'But what about kwai? I have only this small packet here, na?' Bah Kynsai said again.

Raji replied by asking him, 'You are not going to the mainland, no? There's plenty of kwai here. Everybody eats kwai—look at Chirag's mouth and his brother-in-law's. Their teeth are thick with its stain.'

'I don't mean that, man! I mean, will it be readily available in the jungle?'

'Ooh, I think there will be plenty of kwai, Bah Kynsai, like the local brew, okay, it's also part of the funeral rites.'

'That's okay, then. Without kwai and without *khor*, na, it's impossible to live.'

'Khor' is Khasi slang for alcohol. It means something strong and with a great deal of sting.

What Bah Kynsai said was, unfortunately, only too true of Khasi men, many of whom do not live beyond forty-five because of too much khor. When a man between thirty and forty-five dies, the question most commonly asked is, 'What happened? Stabbed by broken glass or what?'

At that moment, Halolihim, who was dressed in shorts, broke into my thoughts by shouting, 'Come one, come all, let's take a holy dip in this blessed river of God: it's as pure as the River Jordan!'

'Excuse me!' Magdalene shouted back. 'Have you seen the Jordan? I have, and it's quite dirty compared to this!' To us, she added, 'Ignorant bastard. Who's he, Ham?'

Halolihim was already going towards the river and did not respond. Hamkom explained that the man was his wife's relative: 'He works in a government office as a clerk, but mostly travels around with his church people to spread the gospel, as he says. He's not a pastor or anything like that; he's just very enthusiastic about his religion. His church is still very new, ha, that's why.'

'Ah, so that's why he's coming along,' Bah Kynsai said, 'to convert the benighted pagans.'

'Who's a benighted pagan?' Bah Kit asked testily.

'Nobody,' Bah Kynsai said quickly. He had been told umpteen times that Khasi-Khasis could not, by any stretch of the imagination, be called pagans. 'But to Halolihim, na, anyone who is not a Christian is a pagan. He is like the Welsh missionaries.'

To divert their attention, Hamkom urged us to come to the water to freshen up. 'Come in shorts, ha,' he said. 'No underpants!' To the others, he shouted out, 'Hey, come, come, let's have a swim, but wear only shorts, hey Don, only shorts, okay, we have a lady with us.'

We had all brought shorts because we knew it would be warm in the jungle, though just how warm, we hadn't realised until now. The temperature, despite the winter, was about twenty-two degrees Celsius. After the cold of Shillong, the warmth was delightful.

Everyone changed and went towards the river. Even Magdalene could not be kept out of it. After changing into shorts behind some trees, she came splashing in. Only Chirag and his brother-in-law did not join us. They only washed their hands and faces by the riverbank and watched us wallow in the water like excited children. Those of us who could swim—Raji, Bah Kit, Hamkom, Halolihim, Donald, Dale and Magdalene—went towards deeper water and the pools. Bah Kynsai, Bah Su and I splashed about in the shallows, lying on our backs or our bellies, and sometimes dipping our heads in the limpid water.

When we were done, we ate some of the sliced bread and soft drinks we had brought with us, and off we went again, with Chirag's Gypsy leading the way this time.

Soon after crossing the River Rwiang, we came to Phot Jalei junction, a small jungle village somewhere west of the road, and then to Porla. This was a typical Lyngngam village marked by jhum fire. Several bunches of broomsticks hung upside down from a wooden contraption, obviously a drying process.

Everything changed as we arrived in the Lyngngam areas. The boulders were gone from the road, to be replaced by a thick carpet of dust. But this did not make the driving easier, because the craters and the mounds of dried mud were still very much there to torment and bounce us about, though a little less violently. The noise lessened quite a bit, without the stones. The vegetation had also changed, and instead of the thick tropical rain forest, the soaring trees were now mixed with vast expanses of bamboo groves and broomstick plantations. If anything, the jungle seemed to have advanced even closer to the road. In places, it appeared to have swallowed it whole.

There was also infinitely more dust on the road. It seeped into everything. It was difficult to breathe; we had to cover our mouths with our handkerchiefs. We rolled up the windows and asked Chirag to do likewise. But Chirag said, 'No need, Babu, you will not be able to sit in this heat without open windows, and look carefully, when you close the windows, no, Babu, the dust flying in from the floor will not be able to escape, closing the windows will only make it worse.'

We had not thought of that. In our carefully carpeted vehicles, dust never seeped in from the floor. We looked down and, for the first time, noticed that the floor was completely bare, without any kind of covering. And sure enough, dust was floating up in clouds.

'Son of a bitch!' Magdalene cried and hurriedly opened the window at her side.

'Now you know why the cowboys used to wear bandanas,' Bah Kynsai observed.

Many Khasis, especially those of our generation, were fond of reading western novels and watching westerns. Every one of us, therefore, understood what Bah Kynsai was getting at. Actually, the very first novel I ever read, outside my textbooks, was a novel by Louis L'Amour, who became my all-time favourite writer of westerns.

It was now almost unbearably hot. When Shillong was recording a minimum winter temperature of about one degree Celsius, here, in deeper Lyngngam, the midday temperature was in the range of twenty-five to twenty-six degrees Celsius. Wisely, we had taken Chirag's advice and left most of our heavy clothing in Nongstoin.

It was about 5 p.m. when we entered the outskirts of Nongshyrkon. We had passed the odd hut or two when Chirag stopped the car with a jerk. We were all flung forward, clinging to whatever we could to keep from flying out of our seats. Ahead of us was a large flock of what Khasis call *syiar khlaw*, jungle chickens, crossing the road, single file. They were brown with black spots all over.

'*Yiar Khar!*' Chirag announced, naming them.

We all shouted, 'Photos, photos!' but before we could gather ourselves from the jolting we had received, the birds had already vanished into the bushes. Disappointingly, despite driving through dense jungle, these were the only wild creatures we saw on the way. Chirag said it was because we were travelling during the day. That we had seen the jungle fowl at all was because darkness was already rising in waves all around us. And in that gathering gloom, we approached the village of Nongshyrkon.

3

THE
FIRST
NIGHT

THE IDENTITY STORY
AND MORE

'The future of a country is safe
only in the hands of those to
whom her past is dear.'

—William Ralph Inge

Strictly speaking, this was not the first night. We arrived in Nongshyrkon, or Shyrkon, as the locals called it, on the evening of the fourth. That should have been the first night. But there was no time for us to sit around and talk then: we had too many things to do. Besides, we were exhausted. So, the night of the fifth became our first funeral night, when we were able to relax in our spacious hut after dinner, and talk about the Lyngngams and the Khasis in general. That night, we dwelled on the roots of our beloved land, our people's culture, the roots of our times, and most of all, the roots of the past lost to us. We also shared stories, including the tale behind the greatest pastime of the Khasis—the chewing of betel nut.

On the evening of the fourth, before entering Nongshyrkon, we came upon a bamboo gate with a bamboo fence on either side of it, effectively blocking entry to the village. Chirag stopped, opened the gate, crossed over and shut the gate behind us. He would not allow any of us to do it for him because he said we were paying guests. The gate, he explained, was to stop cattle from wandering into the village and into people's fields and gardens. When I observed that they could very well come through the surrounding jungle, he said they had to use the road, like the cars did, because the jungle had also been blocked in places by wattle fences.

When we arrived, Chirag took us directly to his ancestral home. One part of the house was an ancient and rather ill-preserved wood-and-tin affair, though clean and neat inside. The other part, comprising the kitchen and dining room, was a new concrete building with a corrugated iron sheet roof. The two were joined by a short passageway. The house was run by Chirag's kong, or elder sister, a dark, spare-looking woman who did not share the smudgy appearance of the villagers I had seen from the car. Kong Norma turned out to be an educated woman who had lived in several places, including Sohra, before coming back home. Chirag clarified that the house was not hers and that she was only looking after it on behalf of his youngest sister—then living in Maweit, the region's most prominent marketing centre—who would inherit the ancestral property. This is what most Khasi families do now: give away their ancestral homes to the youngest daughter. A big mistake, as we shall see.

Chirag had a brother, a Presbyterian pastor, whose name was Bright Star. The pastor lived with his family in Ri Pnar, but was in Shyrkon at the moment, though we did not meet him immediately, as he was away at one of the jungle farms.

Kong Norma, we were told, had lost her husband some years ago and had no children. She lived here with her cousin, Perly. When I asked what Perly did, there was a momentary—and I thought awkward—pause, and then Chirag said he helped his sister around the house. We came to know later that Perly was a footloose character and would vanish into the jungle, hunting or fishing, for weeks or months, before returning. It seems he was a kind of man Friday (whenever he was around, that is) whom Chirag used in his many businesses concerning coal, timber and road-making. The road from the River Rwiang, which was constructed by Chirag's family, was actually surveyed by Perly.

Perly was quite different from Chirag. With his Tibeto-Burman features, he looked more like a Garo than a Khasi. And unlike Chirag, he was small, merely five feet one or so, but with the wiry frame of the outdoorsman.

Chirag clearly had a healthy respect for the man. He boasted that the road surveyed by Perly was much better and shorter than the PWD road, which nobody used. That was why he had said there was no PWD road: 'because nobody used it.' Perly was also supposed to have travelled extensively in the Lyngngam-Nongtrai-Garo region and was, therefore, well-versed in local lore and knowledge. Communicating with him and Kong Norma was not a problem for us, for they spoke the standard Sohra dialect quite well. Chirag told us that only a few people in the village could speak standard Khasi: 'Only those who have gone to school,' he explained.

Chirag's sister got us *sha saw*, red tea, or tea without milk, and biscuits brought all the way from Nongstoin. To replace these, we gave them the sliced bread we had brought from Shillong. After tea, Chirag instructed his kong to prepare a meal for us. Then, turning to us, he said, 'Now for the most important business of the day, where will you stay?'

We were quite alarmed by the question and looked blankly at each other, fearing the worst. But we need not have worried, for in the very next moment, Chirag said, 'We will have to build a hut for you, Babu, our house will be full of relatives very soon, even now you can see lots of people coming and going, and the death house, as you can see from here—there it is—is already full of people, they are relatives who live in very distant parts of Lyngngam and Nongtrai, no, Babu, hence they try to come early. Come, Babu, we'll choose the site for the hut, I'm thinking that area over there, under the huge jackfruit tree will be nice, no, Babu? Yes, I think we will build there, Babu.'

'Can it be done today? I asked. 'I mean, it's quite late …'

'No problem, no problem, Babu, we have flambeaus, and there are so many men who will do it. Let's see, we'll make it with some poles as pillars, then we'll make a rectangular frame by laying smaller poles on top of them, lengthwise and breadthwise, and then we'll make the walls by tying more poles to the pillars from top to bottom, maybe four poles on each wall. After that, it's simple, we'll simply place branches on the roof and all around and tie them in place with bamboo strings, it will be quite snug and warm, Babu, if it rains, of course, it will be a problem, but I don't think it will, so it's okay. Let's see, there are eleven of you, no? That means we'll have to make the hut very spacious, say sixteen by sixteen feet, that should do, or what do you think, Babu? For your beds we'll simply place a thick layer of rice straw all along the corners, we'll keep the centre clear so we can make a hearth for the fire, it will be cold at night, not very cold for you people, but you'll still need a fire, especially because you have brought only shawls for blankets.'

'That sounds very nice,' I said.

'Even romantic,' Magdalene added.

We thanked him for getting everything organised. We also offered to help, but he said, 'No need, you just stand back and watch how Lyngngam people do things, within hours everything will be done.'

'What will we do for light?' Magdalene asked.

'There will be a fire in the hearth to give you light and keep you warm, do you need any more light, Kong? In that case, we can give you small kerosene lamps, but the smell is not nice and the air will be bad.'

'No need, no need!' she replied quickly.

'Back to the life of our ancestors!' I cried. 'They also did not have any light other than the fire in the hearth. It was everything to them, and the fireside too was all-important, a place to gather around and listen to stories and moral lessons.'

But then, a thought struck me, and I said, 'Won't it be dangerous to build a fire in the hut with so much straw around, Bah Chirag?'

'No danger, no danger, Babu, the straw will be in the corners, kept in place with square logs, and the fire, a small one only, will be in the centre, away from the straw, don't worry, Babu.'

Chirag was as good as his word. Shadowy figures appeared from nowhere, some hammering in the pillars, some making the frame, others bringing in the branches and the rice straw. Very soon, our hut began to take shape. I do not think they took more than two hours to complete the entire structure. And Chirag was right about the temperature. It was getting a bit uncomfortable for us to move about only in shirts. Those of us who had sweaters took them out; others used their shawls. I think it must have come down from twenty-six to about sixteen degrees Celsius.

When the hut was complete, we went in to claim our corners.

'I hope nobody snores,' Magdalene said.

'What about pillows?' Donald asked.

'Use a log,' Bah Su said. 'Our forefathers used to do that.'

'Just pile more rice straw towards the top and put a cloth on it,' Bah Kit advised.

'Reminds me of orangutans, liah!' Bah Kynsai commented. 'Before they sleep, na, they break a lot of branches, pile them together and then lie on them.'

'So, we have been degraded to the level of apes, huh?' Hamkom joked.

'Reminds me of my childhood,' Evening said. 'We used to play in the piles of hay in our courtyard. We used the hay to feed the cattle in winter when the grass was gone.'

But the most positive comment came from Dale, I thought. He sat bouncing on the rice straw and said, 'Hey, Bah, *bes bha*! Enjoy, my friends!'

'Bes bha' is another peculiar Khasi expression. When Khasis want to describe something in superlative terms, they always say 'bes bha', which literally means 'best good' or 'very best good'. The actual meaning is, 'of the very best'.

Only Halolihim did not say anything. He looked down at his spot near Hamkom, dropped his bag to the floor and went out without a word.

Bah Kit suggested that we wash at the village well located in a little valley nearby. We removed our shoes and kept them outside by the hut. Wearing our *chappals* and flip-flops, we trooped down to the well, lighting our way with a flambeau provided by Chirag's family. The well was, in fact, a large pool of spring water enclosed by a brick wall on three sides and covered with a concrete slab on top. The mouth of the pool was open and water flowed from it to form a kind of streamlet meandering its way down the jungle. The water was warm and we revelled in it, sharply reminded of the chilly water in wintry Shillong.

When we got back, Chirag was waiting for us. 'Come, Babu, we will eat,' he said.

We followed Chirag to his house, where Kong Norma was waiting to serve us dinner. She said, 'Just a little rice and something I prepared, please don't mind, we are country people and do not have much.'

With that, she went to the kitchen and brought mounds of rice in large steel plates, followed by a large bowl of mustard boiled with onions and sprinklings of beef jerky ground into tiny pieces. Then she brought a plate of radish cut into small strips and mixed with sesame seeds, onions, lemon juice and chillies. On request, she also brought dried chillies grilled over a fire. Lastly, she brought cups of tea and a bowl of sugar, apologising all the time, as she had done when serving us tea earlier, that it was only sha saw. We responded by assuring her that we liked red tea very much. She explained to us that everything was from her garden, including the sesame seeds, which had been first roasted and then ground into a paste. 'This is white sesame,' she told us. By white, Khasis mean grey, as different from black sesame, which is used only to spice curries and give them a black tint. She also explained that the rice was 'hill rice' from their jhum farm, and that was why the colour was red and not white like *khaw dkhar*, rice from the Indian plains.

Looking at the large teacups and the mountain of food, Hamkom asked, 'Is this high tea or low tea?'

'Lyngngam tea,' Bah Kynsai answered.

Before we could eat, however, Halolihim stood up and said, 'Let us say grace.'

We were all taken by surprise and could not do anything but keep our eyes and mouths shut. Halolihim began to pray. He was an excellent speaker, no doubt about it. But in his enthusiasm to display his skill, he got carried away. Instead of simply giving thanks, he began to sermonise and tell stories about the many miraculous acts of God in America, Korea, Japan, China, Europe and so on.

We were hungry and it was quite late, about 10 p.m., well past our usual dinnertime. But still, Halolihim went on, lost in his own passion. Bah Kynsai lost patience and began eating. Noticing Bah Kynsai eating, Bah Kit, Raji and Magdalene did the same. The others did not realise they had started since their eyes were closed.

When Halolihim finally stopped after twenty minutes, he saw Bah Kynsai eating his food. He shouted at him, 'Waa! You have already eaten!'

'Wuu,' Bah Kynsai replied calmly, 'I started eating when you were in Korea.'

Halolihim spluttered with indignation and anger. Kong Norma pacified him and said, 'Please don't mind, Bah, they must be very hungry, what to do?'

And Bah Kynsai, without any embarrassment at all, said, 'You see, Kong, it's not the length, or the noise, or the skill, or the knowledge of a person that makes a prayer perfect. It is his sincerity and genuineness. I did not notice these qualities in Halolihim, only a wish to show off. I'm an educated man, na, Kong, I cannot stand that. Let me tell you a story to demonstrate what I mean.'

As we ate our food, Bah Kynsai told us the story of a simple farmer who went to a distant market, a day's journey from his village, to sell his agricultural produce. He was so preoccupied with the business of buying and selling that it was evening when he finally set out on his return trip. The night found him still very far from home, so he had to take shelter in a shallow cave formed by an overhanging rock. Because the night was chilly, he built a small fire and prepared to eat his jasong, the rice and meat packed in a large leaf, which he had bought from the market. But when he wanted to say grace, he found that he had forgotten his prayer book at home. What was he to do, poor fellow? He was only a poor, ignorant farmer who could not even recall his prayers. But to eat without saying grace was unthinkable. At last, he turned towards heaven and said:

'Oh Lord, I'm only a foolish man. I cannot remember even one of the prayers in the prayer book. Please allow me to recite all the letters of our alphabet from ABKD to UWY. Please take that as a prayer, for I know no other at this moment.'

The farmer recited all the letters of the Khasi alphabet in a slow, solemn manner, and when he finished, he ate his jasong and went to sleep.

When God heard the farmer's recital, he said to the angels, 'Of all the prayers I have heard today, this one is the most perfect because it comes from the heart.'

Bah Kynsai concluded the story with his trademark booming laugh and said, 'You see, Halolihim, no hard feelings, ha, but you have a lot to learn. A prayer, na, should always touch hearts; it should not generate resentment.'

Everyone, except Halolihim, laughed with Bah Kynsai, and the tension dissipated.

The food was refreshingly tasty. The radish was crisp and crunchy; freshly picked. The boiled mustard flavoured with ground jerky was a new kind of preparation for us, but we took to it immediately, for all of us had simple tastes despite our city living.

Bah Kit said, 'This is the way to eat! Simple and healthy. Imagine, everything boiled, not a drop of oil anywhere, and it's so tasty, no?'

The Lyngngams, we learnt, mostly ate boiled food. This was a necessity because oil was expensive and had to be brought all the way from Nongstoin. Cooking oil was available in Maweit but was much too costly. Even the jerky was ground for the same reason. They could not afford to add whole pieces to the mustard stew, for that would have meant using two or three long strips. Flavouring it this way did not require even a quarter of a strip. When you had to go shopping in faraway places connected by almost non-existent roads, you had to pick and choose from your shopping list very carefully. Only the most essential items could be brought.

The ground jerky reminded me of the War sub-tribe living in the wooded ravines of Sohra. To go to their villages, as I told you earlier, one has to descend thousands of feet using steep perpendicular steps sliding brokenly into the deep jungle. Just to travel up and down those steps is such an ordeal that it makes one's limbs tremble for hours afterwards. What makes matters worse is the fact that the ropeways, which are supposed to make the transport of agricultural and forest produce easier, do not, in places, get beyond the stage of a foundation-stone-laying ceremony. Once every five years, the five-year gods come and make tall promises, but the moment the elections are over, all is conveniently forgotten. They get away with this because they know they can always buy the simple villagers' votes with a few hundred rupees and cheap booze.

My friend Nigel has a rather funny story in his book about an English writer who was trying to go down the vertical steps leading to the ravine hamlet of Nongpriang from Sohra. The steps were made of the famous Sohra sandstone in such a way that they fit snugly into each other even without cement. However, because they had been built ages ago, they were, in many places, in pretty bad shape and could be very dangerous. Mindful of that, the writer cautiously inched forward, clinging to whatever handhold he could find. But just as he was shakily negotiating the steps, he was overtaken by two men with heavily loaded bamboo cones on their backs, running down the sheer slope. He stopped them to ask (not his exact words, mind you), 'How can you run down these steep and broken steps like this when it's so difficult for me just to go from one step to the next? Don't you ever fall?'

'Oh yes, when we are drunk,' one of the men replied.

'You mean you run down these steps, with loads on your backs, after drinking?'

'Yes, often.'

'And do you often fall too?'

'No, only sometimes. Once, my friend here tumbled down this very slope for about fifty feet—he had had too much to drink at the Sohra market—but luckily, nothing happened, except for a few bruises. When he got up, he wrote a poem. He's a poet.'

'He wrote a poem after falling down the slope!?'

'Yes.'

'What about?'

'Falling!'

Because the routes are so difficult and the marketplaces so far away in upland towns, most people from these villages go to the markets only once a week, or at the most, twice. They carry their agricultural produce and commodities in baskets to be sold in the market, and when everything is sold, they buy essentials to last for the week and carry these back home in the same baskets. Meat is considered an essential item, but because they cannot buy enough to last a whole week, it becomes a scarce and highly prized commodity. Many of them, therefore, come up with ingenious ways of meat conservation and consumption, like they were doing in Chirag's house. They binge on meat on market night and the day after, but for the rest of the eight-day week, they make do with the legs of a pig or a bull bought at the market.

Usually, two pairs of legs are bought. Once they have been cleaned, they are hung from a *tyngier*, a bamboo platform suspended above the hearth, to dry. A tyngier is customarily used to keep firewood and other things dry during the rainy months. Like the Lyngngams, the Wars do not fry their food or make curries because of the problem of procuring oil. They simply boil vegetables with onions and salt. But to make the preparation tastier and give it a meaty flavour, they cook it together with one of the legs. After it has cooked for a while, they remove the leg and put it back on the tyngier to dry. The next time they boil vegetables, they use another leg and repeat this process till they come back to the first leg, which is now dry and fit to be cooked again. They do not eat the meat until the day before the next market day.

Sometimes, people simply hide their meat when strangers visit. This we experienced for ourselves when we went to a ravine hamlet called Wah Sohra for something to do with a revision of the electoral rolls. In honour of the 'officers' who had come on such important business, the headman invited us to lunch. But he also told us, 'We don't have any meat; you'll have to make do with boiled vegetables and plain rice.'

We thanked him, for any food is welcome when you are hungry, and had lunch with his family in the kitchen. We noticed that they also ate only rice, vegetables and a lot of chillies. But the headman had a huge pig's blood sausage hidden under his arse, and when he thought we were not looking, pinched a piece from it and quickly put it in his mouth. We ate in silence, suppressing our laughter as best we could, but afterwards, we nearly died laughing. He didn't need to conceal it from us! Who would eat a piece of blood sausage hidden under someone's arse?

The Lyngngam village of Nongshyrkon was not a ravine hamlet, but it was equally remote.

When we finished eating, Chirag took us to the death house to introduce us to the bereaved family. It was a sprawling one-storey structure with bamboo-and-mortar walls and a corrugated iron sheet roof, standing in the middle of a vast compound ringed by massive trees. It was about 11 p.m., but the house was swarming with people, some sitting in the drawing room, others in the adjoining rooms, preparing betel nuts and leaves, and still others in the kitchen, cutting onions and vegetables. The expansive courtyard was likewise full of people moving about, working with wood and bamboo poles, preparing them for use in whatever structure they were making. In one corner of the courtyard, there was a massive bonfire around which people were gathered. In many places, I could see flambeaus tied to trees, for the village had no electricity.

I asked Chirag why there was no electricity when I had seen electric posts in the village. He replied, 'Our village is supposed to be electrified, Babu, but people here say it is more often illuminated by lightning than electricity.'

We were taken to the drawing room, where several men were seated. Some were neighbours, but most were relatives, brothers and nephews of the deceased, and therefore called *burangs*, the uncles of the family. Their role, as you shall see, was all-important.

Chirag introduced us to everyone, and when the purpose of our visit was known, the daughters and granddaughters of the deceased were also called in. The introductions began all over again, the women taking our hands in theirs as a form of greeting. We explained our purpose to them.

I said I had come because I wanted to write a book based on the rituals of Ka Phor Sorat. Raji said he wanted to film and record the event, and then immediately took out his minicam to film the conversation. Bah Su and Bah Kit said they were genuinely interested in the event, as they were in everything related to Khasi culture. Bah Su added that he would write about it in the newspapers. Evening, Magdalene and Donald said they had never imagined that such a unique tradition existed among us, and therefore they wanted to see it for themselves. Only Dale, Bah Kynsai and Halolihim had very different answers.

Dale said rather shyly, 'I'm just a driver.'

Bah Kynsai said, 'I'm neither a filmmaker nor a writer, ha, but I'm here because I want to be a hero in both.' He said this with his booming laugh—everybody in the room laughed with him.

Halolihim said, 'I want to be honest with you, huh? I'm not really interested in these'—he indicated the scene with his hand—'pagan rites. I have come to spread the Word of God and turn people away from such things.'

His statement was greeted with a brief, embarrassing silence until one of the burangs, whose name was Bromson Shyrkon (another English-sounding but meaningless name) said, 'Then you have come to the wrong place, Bah. Everyone here is a Christian except for our sister, who died nine months ago. She was the last *rupyrthei* in the village. We are conducting this ceremony to honour her dying wish: she wanted to be cremated according to the old customs.'

Rupyrthei literally means 'a person of the world'. It was used by the people here to describe followers of the Khasi religion.

There was a moment of silence, then everyone exploded into uproarious laughter while the deeply disappointed Halolihim exclaimed, 'Oh no!' and left the room, punching the air with his right fist and cursing, 'Damn! Damn! Damn!'

When the laughter had subsided, I asked the burangs why the body had been kept for so long. Bah Kynsai chimed in to tell them about the similarity with the customs of the Torajans of Indonesia. Bromson responded, 'Well, we don't know anything about the rajans or the sia, but Kong We, our sister, died in May last year. Our village, and the whole area surrounding it, is bounded by Wah Blei and Wah Rwiang, Babu. These two rivers encircle the area completely. Our village is like an island in summer. From May to October, the rivers are uncrossable. That is one reason why we had to keep the body till winter, when all the relatives living far away could come.

'The other reason is that Ka Phor Sorat is a costly ceremony, Babu. It lasts for six days if we count the bone burial also. We have to feed a lot of people during these six days and before that. Lots of bulls have to be slaughtered as part of the funeral rites. Very expensive. We have to collect a large fund, and that takes a long time because most of us are poor. Some do not have enough to eat, and yet, if they are closely related, they have to donate a bull. It takes a long time for them to collect enough money for a bull ... they have to look for work here and there ... that's why we have to keep the body for such a long time.'

'Moreover,' Perly intervened, 'we have to prepare a special drink made out of rice, and that takes about five to six months to mature and become yellow and sweet.'

'Sounds like mead,' Bah Kynsai observed.

'Mead is made out of honey,' I replied.

'Our kyiad is made from the local rice, Babu,' Perly said. 'No honey is used. Although, when it is fully matured, it becomes yellowish like honey, probably because of the colour of the rice.'

'Is it *yiad um*, Bah Perly?' Raji asked.

Yiad um, or *kyiad um*, is supposed to be the weakest of our drinks. Literally, it means 'water-alcohol', not because it has a watery taste, but because it usually is as colourless and transparent as water.

'No, no, it's different, Bah,' Perly responded. 'It's sweet like *yiad hiar* but stronger.'

Yiad hiar is a kind of rice beer. In the Khasi highland, its colour is usually white.

I thought that was enough talk of alcohol, so I said, 'Does this mean that even if a person dies in winter, the family would have to keep the body for a long time to save enough money and brew the rice beer?'

'That's right,' Bromson replied. 'Sometimes it takes more than a year for us to collect enough money.'

We wanted to ask more questions, but as it was drawing near to midnight, we decided to leave it for the next time. Before we left, the burangs told us that, from the next day, food would be served at the death house. Perly explained the arrangement. 'As soon as you get up in the morning, you come here, Babu. You will be given tea and rice. At about eleven, you can have lunch. In the afternoon, you can have tea and something to eat, and at night, dinner.'

With that, we returned to our hut and immediately went to sleep. I had chosen a corner as far away from Bah Kynsai as possible because I knew he snored; nevertheless, I soon heard him rumbling like a motorbike. I put cotton balls in my ears (something I had to do every night) and went to sleep, too tired to be unduly disturbed by the muffled sound. Luckily, because this was winter, there were no mosquitoes and all of us slept as if cast aside, as the Khasi saying goes.

The next morning, after our breakfast of tea and plain rice, Perly took us on a tour of the village. Chirag had to return to Nongstoin but had left instructions with Perly to take care of us. Perly showed us around the house of the deceased, Ka We Shyrkon, which was now owned by her youngest daughter. After that, we went traipsing through the tropical jungle—which reminded us city folk of the South American forests we had seen in films—to see the Riat Phyllaw (literally, 'courtyard precipice') Falls.

As we walked through the dense undergrowth, someone asked Perly if we should watch out for snakes.

'There are no snakes in winter,' Perly replied. 'In summer there are plenty. But they don't bite. If you leave them alone, they go about their own business.'

After blundering about for some time, we found a track made by people collecting *pashor*, or plantain flower, from wild plantain trees. The pashor is generally boiled, then mixed with white sesame seeds, onions and chillies. We followed the track and came upon plantain trees growing at the edge of a deep gorge. Across the gorge, far away from us, and apparently unreachable from where we were, was the magnificent waterfall whose white waters glowed with astounding brilliance over a dark rocky surface. It followed the contours of a long precipice, fell once over a short drop and then tumbled down the slope into a green pool deep in the ravine.

'Plenty of fish,' Perly said. 'In summer I spend most of my time down there and in Wah Blei.'

Wah Blei, the River Blei, flows on the western flank of the Nongshyrkon region.

'Is there a way to get there from here?' I asked.

'There is, but a treacherous one. Difficult for you, even in winter.'

'Is this part of the River Rwiang, Bah Perly?' Magdalene asked.

Perly nodded.

We took several photographs of the waterfall, some of us with cameras, others with mobile phones. Raji filmed the scenery as part of the visuals for his documentary. After that, we returned to the death house for lunch, and were served plain rice and pork boiled with potatoes. Instead of green salad, we were given tomatoes mixed with onions and chillies. Meat, it seemed, would not be a problem for the next few days, for many pigs and chickens had already been slaughtered.

After lunch, we went to what Perly called Lum Peitkai, the view point. Nongshyrkon was quite far-flung and stretched out. For instance, it could take several hours to go from the River Rwiang in the east to the River Blei in the west. However, most of the houses in the village were concentrated in a mountain valley with a central peak—Lum Peitkai—which overlooked a tableland of sorts and several low hills. On a cloudless day, from Lum Peitkai, one could see as far as Bangladesh in the south, the Garo Hills in the west and Nongstoin in the north. Yet, the view of the village itself was limited, and only the roofs of houses could be seen because the entire valley was thickly wooded, and the houses themselves were constructed among plantain, litchee, jackfruit, bamboo and other trees. This was the most appealing aspect of Nongshyrkon. You entered the village, and you felt like you were entering a park or a jungle made habitable by these dwellings.

Afterwards, when we met Chirag again, he told us about his desire to turn Nongshyrkon into a tourist attraction. 'It is a beautiful place, look at it, Babu, all these houses among the trees!' he said. 'And the waterfalls are so splendid, you have already seen one of them, and Perly told me how impressed you were, and you have also seen the lake and were in love with it. It is much, much bigger than Nan Polok in Shillong, Babu. There are many more beautiful spots around here, we can easily persuade people to come, but we need a good road … If only we could have a good road! Perhaps you people should write something about our village, Babu, make it famous and force the government to do something about our development.'

'That's a tall order, Chirag,' Bah Kynsai said. 'Our government, na, whichever is in power, na, is short-sighted, apathetic, and has no interest at all in formulating policies or initiating development works, unless, of course, the powers that be can pocket a large chunk of the funds for themselves.'

'Is that true?' Chirag asked, his enthusiasm dampened.

'It's common knowledge, Chirag,' Bah Kynsai replied. 'Once, na, we were sitting with a politician at a funeral gathering, talking about this and that, when he suddenly told us about how conscientious he was. He said, "When I implement a scheme, ha, I take only 25 per cent for myself, unlike some people who take as much as 60 per cent. That way, I have always been able to complete all my welfare schemes satisfactorily." The sycophants surrounding him flattered him by praising his thoughtfulness and honesty until an elderly gentleman observed: "You pocket 25 per cent of the funds meant for a scheme? Why twenty-five? Why don't you pocket everything? If you pocket everything, okay, everyone in your constituency will clap their hands and fall in love with you, because then you can buy more blankets and cooking stoves to distribute among them.'"

Nongshyrkon was a village of about sixty-five houses, not counting those in the outlying areas. Chirag's sister, Kong Norma, said there were about 715 people in all, since the average family included seven children, plus parents and grandparents.

The entire local population (apart from Chirag's aunt, the late Kong We Shyrkon, as we have seen) had converted to Christianity. This fact had surprised not only Halolihim but also most of us. We had thought that a village conducting such a unique cultural event would be full of Khasis practising their own religion, but the reality could not have been more different. Every one of the inhabitants, including Kong We's children, was a Presbyterian or a Catholic. But the nice thing about the people here was that divisions along religious lines had not led to them living separately, like in some villages in Ri Pnar. In the Ri Pnar village of Umkiang near the Assam border, for instance, the different religious groups lived on separate hills. They called them Lum Khasi (Hill of Niam Khasi Niam Tre, the indigenous religion), Lum Roman (Hill of the Roman Catholics), Lum Pres (Hill of the Presbyterians) and Lum Trom (Hill of the Trumpet Church or Church of God).

We spent a long time at Lum Peitkai, enjoying the sights and relaxing on one of the platforms built among the treetops. The Lyngngams used these platforms to dry unhusked rice, millet and vegetables like chillies, pumpkin and gourd. We chose an empty platform and dozed off for a while.

When it was about half past three, Perly suddenly said, 'I forgot to take you to the lake, come, come, let's go, we still have a little time.'

It was a half-hour walk, but it was worth it: the lake was a spectacular sight indeed. We spent some time there enjoying the scenery, then returned to the death house, where we dined on boiled rice, chicken boiled with potatoes, and more tomatoes mixed with onions and chillies.

After dinner, we returned to our hut and sat around the fire, talking about the day. The people here, like all Lyngngams (called Megams by the Garos), though a branch of the Khasi tribe, looked like a mix of Garo and Khasi. Many of them had dark brown skin and blunt Tibeto-Burman features, while those with a more Khasi appearance had lighter skin and sharper features in keeping with their Austro-Asiatic origins.

But then, as Bah Kynsai observed, 'What is a Khasi look? Do you remember, Ap, how they treated us in Kathmandu? They spoke to Ap and me in Nepali, man! They thought Ap was either a Bamon or a Chettri, high caste, ha, and about me, they said, "This one *toh* is Gurung". Gurung is one of the hill tribes, liah, hahaha.'

'Right, right,' Evening added enthusiastically, 'Bah Kynsai is right. We Khasis do not have any particular appearance of our own any more. Many of us look like Bengalis, Nepalis, Madrasis or Biharis, some like Europeans or Chinese or Tibeto-Burmans and some like Africans. There are too many types of mothers and fathers among us, no? We have truly become a hotchpotch race. We no longer look like Khasis.'

'What you are saying is only a half-truth,' Bah Kit countered.

'Half-truth!' Evening retorted hotly. 'Can you deny the fact that over many, many generations, our women have been marrying Garos, Assamese, Bengalis, Nepalis, Manipuris, Nagas, Mizos, Keralites, Tamilians, Punjabis, Biharis, whites, blacks and yellows? I think our women have married into every known community on earth except the Eskimos! Only because they don't meet them. If they do, ha, they will no doubt marry them also.'

'That is your first half-truth: you are blaming the women only. What about the men?' Bah Kit countered again.

'Men too, of course, but not as rampantly as women,' Evening admitted.

'Not as rampantly as women, my arse!' Bah Kynsai retorted fiercely. 'What about those clans beginning with "*Khar*", like Bah Su's Kharakor, huh? Soon we will have more "Khars" than pure Khasi surnames, liah!'

When a Khasi man marries a non-Khasi woman, his wife has to take a new surname. But since she cannot take his surname, because of the matrilineal practice, a new name has to be sanctified for her. Customarily, such a name begins with the prefix 'Khar' to indicate that she is not originally Khasi but has become one through marriage.

'Correct, correct, Bah Kynsai,' Raji cried, 'full marks to you!'

Bah Su Kharakor, whose clan had such an ancestress, smiled at them but did not say anything. He only signalled to Raji to pass him the bottle.

Raji, Bah Kynsai and Bah Su had mixed their whisky in a half-litre water bottle and were now drinking from it. The three of them were the real guzzlers among us, but even they, back home at least, never drank during the day. The others, apart from Halolihim, Dale and I, were moderate drinkers, but they had not brought their own drinks. Also, they did not want to have anything strong after dinner.

'You didn't mention the Marwaris,' Hamkom said.

'Marwaris do not marry Khasi women; they make them their mistresses for *benami* transactions,' Evening stated.

In Meghalaya, non-tribal communities cannot buy land in certain areas because of the Land Transfer Act. And they cannot establish a trading company or set up any business without a trading licence from the District Council. This is true to the provisions of the Sixth Schedule of the Constitution of India. To avoid the first problem, as well as to avoid paying taxes and licence fees, non-tribal businessmen had been known to buy land or establish businesses in Khasi names. This was the kind of benami transaction Evening was referring to. But even for this, they had to make some payments to the people whose names they were using. To avoid this, many businessmen married or cohabited with Khasi women so they could use their names as a front. In some instances, they simply kept them as mistresses, as Evening said. But there was no denying the fact that, in most cases, marriages between Khasi women and non-tribal men were the result of mutual attraction and love.

'You see, you are always exaggerating things,' Bah Kit said. 'While I cannot deny what you say, I do condemn your exaggeration and unfairness. Let me ask all of you one thing. If you see a Khasi, man or woman, can you tell whether he or she is a Khasi or not?'

'Everybody can tell a Khasi woman by her *jaiñsem*,' someone murmured.

A jaiñsem is a long cloth draped over the shoulder and worn by Khasi women as an outer garment. Usually, when Khasi women go out of the house, they wear two good-quality jaiñsems of nylon or silk, one draped over the right shoulder, the other across it from the left. When they are in the house, they wear only one, a kind of rough cotton cloth, also called *jaiñkyrshah*.

'Okay, suppose she is wearing a salwar, can you tell?'

After thinking about it for a while, most of us nodded. Bah Kit pressed his point. 'And why can you? Not every one of us, not even most of us, look like the people Ning has just named. The point to remember is that a Khasi is different in appearance depending upon the region or sub-tribe to which he belongs; keep that in mind. A Pnar, a Bhoi, a Maram, a Lyngngam or a Khynriam, all of them look slightly different from each other. I'm not talking about clothes but about faces. And the people with the most distinctive features among us are the Wars. You would know a War when you see one, isn't that so, Bah Su? And yet, even among them, there are differences, okay?

The Wars from the eastern parts, for instance, are generally taller and better looking than those from the western parts, who are mostly short, with a pale complexion and flat features.

'P.R.T. Gurdon has made some interesting comments on the physical appearance of our people in his book. He says the colour of the Khasi skin may be described as brown, varying from dark brown to a light yellowish-brown, depending upon the locality. The complexion of the people who inhabit the uplands, he says, is somewhat lighter, and many of the women who live in the high plateaus possess a pretty, gypsy complexion, as may be seen in southern Europe among the peasants. According to him, and I remember almost every word of this, "The people of Cherrapunji villages are specially fair. The Syntengs [Pnars of Ri Pnar] are darker than the Khasi uplanders. The Wars who live in the low valleys are frequently more swarthy than the Khasi [uplanders]. The Bhois have the flabby-looking yellow skin of the Mikirs [of Assam], and the Lyngngams are darker." The Lyngngams, he says, are probably the darkest complexioned people in the hills, and if one met them in the plains, one would not be able to distinguish them from the other people there, like the Kacharis and Rabhas. The only thing that Gurdon missed is the fact that Khasis who live in the colder regions can be as fair as the fairest Europeans.'

Bah Su agreed with Bah Kit and added, 'The Wars from the east are very fair, Bah Kit. And also, if you are talking about differences in facial features, ha, you must admit that Khasis are different not only according to their sub-tribe and region but also according to the village—people of one village look different from those of another. Take the people of Sohra, for example. They generally have sharp features, are fair-skinned, good-looking, cultured and very well-mannered. But go up only a little towards Laitryngew, the next village, and you find that the people not only look different but also speak a different dialect. And if you go south, below Mawsmai or Mawmluh, you find the Wars with their pale complexion and flat features, speaking a completely different dialect. The appearance and dialect are different, not from region to region, but from village to village. That's why we say the people of such-and-such a village are very good-looking, while the people of such-and-such a village are not. In West Khasi Hills, generally speaking, the Marams are very attractive, but here in Lyngngam, you have seen them, most are dark-skinned and have blunt Tibeto-Burman features.'

Suddenly, Donald erupted, 'I don't know why the heck you people care so much about identity and how we look and speak. I don't care whether I look like a Khasi or not. What is important to me is that I am a human being trying to make the most of my life. That's all.'

'You don't care because you think you look like an Anglo-Indian, na?' Bah Kynsai taunted him.

Donald did look like an Anglo-Indian with his fair and ruddy complexion. Some woman in his family must have married, or at least had an affair with, a Tommy.

'I don't care because I don't care,' he replied.

'You don't care because you are a cosmo,' Bah Kynsai teased.

Evening added with some violence, 'You don't care because you have no loyalty. You identify yourself in the official forms as a Khasi, yet you have not even a little bit of loyalty to the Khasi people. We are beset by so many problems and dangers from everywhere, yet you say you don't care; all you can think of is yourself. You are a disloyal, selfish bastard.'

'How Khasi are you, huh?' Donald retorted. 'Your name is Eveningstar, how Khasi is that name?'

'My name is English, but my soul is Khasi. And I, at least, know the meaning of my name and why my parents named me Eveningstar. Do you know the meaning of yours? Donald Lachlan, do you even know what it means?'

'Even if I do, why should I tell you?'

'You will not tell me because you don't know! We don't need people like you among us. You boast of being a Delhi scholar, but you know nothing, not even of yourself!'

'What don't I know, you self-styled Khasi expert? And why did you call me a bastard? Repeat it and I'll smack you!'

'Bastard, bastard!' Evening shouted.

'Hey, hey, hey!' Bah Kynsai intervened. 'Stop it, you buggers, you are behaving like children, liah!'

'Look, Donald,' I said, 'you are entitled to your opinion, but you cannot deny the fact that every ethnic group on earth cares deeply about its identity. When the Marwaris, Bengalis, Biharis and Nepalis came with the British to these hills, they brought with them their own culture and maintained their own lifestyles. The British themselves created a kind of mini-England in Shillong in what was known as the European Ward. And these were large communities that faced no threat. If even they cared about their identity, why shouldn't it be important for a small community like ours with a population of only about a million? Look at the way the Europeans are treating migrants from the war zones of the Middle East and see how they are closing their borders everywhere ... Or haven't you heard? The only concession I will make is that we should never allow our identity to turn us into fundamentalists and fanatics like the ones causing all the conflicts in the world today.'

'But who are the Khasis anyway? Do you people even know?' Donald asked sarcastically.

'Unfortunately, ha, the origin of the Khasis is a really, really vexed question,' Bah Su responded. 'Nobody knows from where we came. We did have stories once, but they are all forgotten now, except for vague references here and there.'

'Bah Wishing was of the opinion that we came from space,' Magdalene said, laughing. 'Once he came to our college as a chief guest, okay, he rambled on for hours about this and that, throwing the schedule completely out of gear, and then he talked about the Khasis coming from space. And he was very serious about it! He said, initially there were sixteen huts, but because of some internal feud, seven huts came to earth over a bridge—he said a bridge, okay?—located on a mountain in Ri Bhoi called the Navel of Heaven, and decided to settle down here because the hills were so beautiful.'

Bah Wishing was Wishing Stone Kharnoi, one of our prominent political leaders.

'Ooh, he must be talking about the myths of *Ki Hynñiew Trep* and *Ka Jingkieng Ksiar*, ya!' Raji exclaimed.

'But the sacred myth of Ki Hynñiew Trep and the parable of the golden ladder are not about our history, no?' Bah Su said angrily. 'How can Bah Wishing say a thing like that?'

'He says it everywhere he goes, no, Bah Su, strange that you haven't heard it before!'

'Yeah, yeah, people have told me the same thing, Raji,' Magdalene agreed. 'But, Bah Su, are you sure the myth has nothing to do with our history? I mean, I have heard so much about it, no? People are always talking about it, so it should mean something.'

'Of course it means something!' Bah Su said emphatically. 'But it's got nothing to do with our history or geographical roots, only with our spiritual roots!'

'Spiritual roots?'

'Yes! Our religion!'

'How's that, ya? I don't get it.'

'What Bah Su means,' I intervened, 'is that the myth is actually about the Khasi concept of how God created the world and how man came to inhabit earth and be the caretaker of all creation. Unlike the Jewish Genesis, the Khasi myth does not specify how man was created, but simply asserts that his original home was heaven. Initially, sixteen sub-tribes, Khathynriew Treps, lived in heaven with U Blei Nongbuh Nongthaw—God the Dispenser, the Creator—and the spirits who served him. Later, seven of them, Hynñiew Treps, came to live on earth, having made a covenant with God.

'Ki Khathynriew Trep does literally mean "sixteen huts", Mag, and Ki Hynñiew Trep "seven huts", but, as I said, they denote sixteen and seven sub-tribes respectively. The reference to them may well have historical significance and may point to the fact that, in the beginning, we were part of a larger family of sixteen sub-tribes, but that later we split up to go our separate ways. However, we are told nothing more about this, and the rest of the myth mostly emphasises the relationship between man and God.'

'Okay, now that we know we didn't come down from heaven or space over a golden ladder, where does it leave us?' Magdalene asked.

'Most writings about us agree that we are of Indo-Chinese origin— Austro-Asiatic, to be precise,' I replied. 'In the Northeast, we are, to quote C.J. Lyall, "in the midst of a great encircling population all of whom belong to the Tibeto-Burman stock". In other words, we are the only Austro-Asiatic people in the region.'

'Who's C.J. Lyall?' Magdalene demanded.

'Charles James Lyall. He was a British civil servant and a scholar of many Eastern languages, including Khasi.'

Bah Kynsai took up the point. 'That's what many famous linguists, ethnologists and explorers like Dr George Abraham Grierson, Professor E. Kuhn, J.R. Logan, Sir Joseph Hooker, Sir Alexander Mackenzie and others have been doing in trying to identify the Khasis as a race,' he explained. 'You see, Don, the whites were deeply interested in discovering our origins and affinities, but you, na, you are only off-white, and yet you scorn the very idea of Khasi identity.'

'Come on, Bah Kynsai, that's insulting, even for you!' Donald complained.

'Okay, okay, point taken,' Bah Kynsai said apologetically, though he did not apologise.

Bah Kynsai was obviously referring to Donald's Anglo-Khasi ancestry when he called him 'off-white'. If anybody else had said it, there would have been hell to pay. I had heard him on other occasions calling Anglo-Khasis 'Phareng wieh rong', or dipped-in-dye white man. Someday, someone will punch him in the mouth.

Khasis remind me of the men of Gulliver's Laputa, lost in their own little world. They hardly bother about questions of identity and origin. Most believe that the past is better left alone. They are only interested in the history of the diaspora and the holiness of unknown deserts so that, in effect, the people's past has been entirely replaced by an alien one. This may be one reason for the absence, until recently, of any work by a Khasi author investigating the roots of his forefathers. It is no wonder, then, that a poet, risking the ire of his people, penned, in a moment of despair, the following self-deprecatory lines in a poem called 'Laitkynsew':

> I have come here to rinse and replenish my thoughts,
> to forget all the little irritants of my days, only to find
> too much forgetfulness. The bells ring with the glory
> of an alien land, and as we swallow the holiness
> of unknown deserts and follow the history of the Diaspora,
> nobody can tell me the meaning of your name [Laitkynsew].

On my part, I believe that the past should not be treated with such scant respect. Forgetfulness is a kind of blight, and a community without any knowledge of its history, origin and culture is like thistledown, blown hither and thither by a capricious wind. Bhuyan, the Assamese scholar I mentioned earlier, had condemned the Khasis' lack of reverence for their own past in very harsh words indeed:

> Of all the preliterate tribes of Assam, the Khasis are believed to have most rapidly adapted themselves to Western methods of life and manners. This has been made possible chiefly by the establishment of the headquarters of the Province in their midst, which has brought in a large concourse of cosmopolitan population. But the two factors which distinguish all advanced societies, love of literature and love of the past, are not to be generally found among the educated section of the Khasi community. They have been allured by the charms of the culture with which they have come into contact, and never perceive that there is good in their own. They have desisted from building a new structure over the old, nor have they made any organised attempt to lay the foundation of their cultural progress which will serve as a link between the past and the present. Instances of modification and readjustment are rare; annihilation or supplantation is the order in Khasi enlightened society.

The sad truth is that we Khasis suffer from a deep sense of alienation, whether we know it or not. It is not only that we cannot integrate with mainstream Indian culture because of the apparent differences but also that we find it hard to integrate with our own culture. We have truly become what Professor Meenakshi Mukherjee called the exiles of the mind, 'either through loss of the mother tongue or through a system of education that superimposes an alien grid of perception on immediate reality'.

This system of education was none other than the one outlined by Thomas Babington Macaulay for the whole of imperial India in 1835, whose purpose was 'to form a class ... of persons, Indians in blood and colour, but English in taste, in opinions, in morals and in intellect'. Macaulay's scheme worked especially well among the Khasis, more and more of whom deserted their own culture for the charms of Western religion and values. Compounding the problem were changes brought about by the continuing influx of outsiders and the mindless modernisation of lifestyles as a result of rapid developments in communications and information technology. In this situation, as we see ourselves losing our way completely, what should we do?

The answer can partly be found in what Tony Conran said about Wales in the anthology *Welsh Verse*. Methodism, Conran writes, had swept through eighteenth-century Wales like wildfire, destroying in its wake all that was considered pagan and cultural. The Methodists considered 'dancing, harp-playing, public houses, even long hair ... as dangerously profane and irrelevant pleasures. Minstrels and strolling players, last heirs of the tradition, were particularly attacked.' During that period of 'violent cultural changes'—brought about not only by the rapidly increasing evangelisation and Anglicisation but also by the new industries—the Welsh lost much of their heritage as a Celtic nation. But then, Conran reveals, the old Celtic civilisation fought back 'in the work of the antiquaries and scholars, men who first collected and then tried to understand the great legacy of the past'. These scholars turned to the legendary heroes of Celtic mythology to provide moorings for Welsh social and cultural life. There was much speculation about the Druids, attempts to rediscover the Welsh literature of the Middle Ages, and efforts to establish an annual festival of poetry and music, known as the *Eisteddfod*.

I feel that we too should try to rehabilitate the past as high culture, everybody's culture, regardless of our religion, and turn to our legendary heroes and mythology to provide a mooring to prevent our directionless, thistledown-like drift. In every myth is embedded the wisdom of the race and every legend speaks in symbolic overtones. Our quest for the past should be for the sake of this wisdom. In the words of Soso Tham, our national bard:

I do awaken, with words that are clear, for the love of one's own country [seen in] the Virtues and enlightenment of our ancestors. Like a child who absorbs his strength and energy from the mother and who takes care of her in return, we too should first sink our roots into our Past. The Seed that falls on stony grounds—without its roots—wilts as soon as the sun turns hot.

As Tham says, the present should have a symbiotic relationship with the past. First of all, the present should be guided by the lessons of the past and draw its sustenance and strength from there as it journeys into an uncertain future. But for the past to be such a guide, it needs to be treated with filial love and reverence. It is not something dead and 'best forgotten', as many of my compatriots have said. It is forever ancient and new. As Octavio Paz says, '...the search for modernity was a descent to the origins. Modernity led me to the source of my beginning, to my antiquity ... Reflecting on the now does not imply relinquishing the future or forgetting the past: the present is the meeting place for the three directions of time.' Modernity itself is 'today and the most ancient antiquity; it is tomorrow and the beginning of the world; it is a thousand years old and yet newborn. It speaks in Nahuatl, draws Chinese ideograms from the 9th century, and appears on the television screen. This intact present, recently unearthed, shakes off the dust of centuries, smiles and suddenly starts to fly, disappearing through the window.' If we understand all this, we will also understand that to discover the past is to discover our origins, ourselves and the foundations on which we can stand straight and strong.

As things stand now, however, it is only from European writers and others from India (Banrida T. Langstieh, as you will see, is the exception) that we have come to know a little about ourselves. Because of them, we now know that our language is of the Austro-Asiatic family, found mostly in countries located between China and Indonesia and also in countries to the west of this region—in the Nicobar Islands and mainland India. This family includes 168 languages and is subdivided into two branches: Mon Khmer with 147 languages and Munda with twenty-one languages.

While Munda is spoken by the Santhals, Mundas and Korkus living in eastern India, Chota Nagpur and the Satpura ranges of the central provinces, the Mon Khmer languages 'constitute the indigenous language family of mainland South-east Asia. They range north to southern China, south to Malaysia, west to Assam [read Meghalaya] state in India, and east to Vietnam. The most important Mon-Khmer languages, having populations greater than 100,000, are Vietnamese, Khmer [also called Cambodian], Muong, Mon, Khasi, Khmu, and Wa'. This is according to the *Encyclopaedia Britannica*.

This was the closest we came to tracing our roots, for none of the earlier studies by European writers on the Austro-Asiatic languages could say where we had originally come from. Some studies claim that we migrated to the Indo-Chinese peninsula and west into India from southern or south-eastern China between 2000 and 2500 BCE. Invasions by other races split the Austro-Asiatic speakers into several groups. Because of these invasions, not many nation-states developed in the Austro-Asiatic areas. The only exceptions were the regions where Khmer, Mon and Vietnamese were spoken. The rest lived in small tribal groups (this is true even today) and were heavily influenced by the languages that surrounded them. In the case of Khasi, many words were borrowed from the Indo-Aryan languages, mainly from Bengali and Hindi.

Therefore, as far as linguistic affinities are concerned, we are very close to the Cambodians, Vietnamese, Muongs, Mons and the Was. Writers like Logan, Lyall and Gurdon added another community to the list. They maintained that 'the nearest kinsmen of the Khasis are the Palaungs', a tribe inhabiting the Shan State of Burma, the Yunnan Province of China and northern Thailand.

I told the group all this, leaving out only the most exciting bit about Banrida Langstieh's research. I was afraid that the poem I had quoted, and also the views of Bhuyan, Conran and Tham, would get us into a heated religious debate and divert our attention from the question of identity. That did not come to be, however, probably because Halolihim was already asleep in his corner and had not heard what I said. Raji, Bah Kynsai, Bah Su, Evening and Bah Kit, on the other hand, spoke excitedly about applying for travel grants from government agencies so they could journey to these lands to find out for themselves how close we really are with these people.

'What about the migration stories you were referring to earlier, Bah Su?' Raji asked.

'They are not stories. As I said, they are merely fragments. For instance, ha, the old ones used to refer to our migration as "the twelve-year-long journey", but they were not so sure about its direction. One tradition says we came from the east, entering the hills from Assam after crossing the River Kupli, which rises from the Black Mountains in east Ri Pnar and flows north-west towards the Brahmaputra. It is for this reason that Kupli, which marks the boundary between the land of the Hynñiew Treps and

North Cachar, is revered as a goddess and obeisance used to be paid to her through annual rituals and sacrifices till not so long ago. At one point in time, when the kings of Hima Sutnga came under the influence of the Brahmins of Jaiñtiapur, their winter capital in East Bengal, even human sacrifices used to be offered to her.'

'This version of our migration,' I said, 'agrees well with what J.B. Shadwell said about how the Khasis originally came to Assam from Burma via the Patkoi range, having followed the route of one of the Burmese invasions ...'

'Who's Shadwell?' Evening asked.

'John Bird Shadwell,' I explained. 'He became assistant commissioner of the Khasi and Jaiñtia Hills in 1887. He wrote a little book called *Notes on the Khasis*. He claimed that Patkoi Hills was familiar to old Khasis from stories passed on to them. Gurdon corroborated Shadwell's claim with the explanation that all movements into Assam, in the past and up to his time, were from the east. Bah Su's mention of the "twelve-year-long journey" clearly points to the fact that we came to these hills from elsewhere, although we have been here for thousands of years. And this is not just my opinion. Remnants of the iron-smelting work in Nongkrem and Sohra were carbon dated by Pawel Prokop, a professor at the Department of Geoenvironmental Research in the Polish Academy of Sciences at Kraków. He concluded that they dated back to "2040 ± 80 years BP", that is, sometime between 353 BCE and 128 CE.'

'What? Is that for real, liah?' Bah Kynsai exclaimed. 'If the Khasis had the ability to manufacture iron in 353 BCE, more than 2,040 years ago, ha, it would mean that they had settled these hills hundreds of years before that, na?'

'Wow, man, 353 BCE, huh?' Magdalene said.

'That's only about iron smelting!' Evening reminded her. 'My God, man, we must have got here thousands of years ago, ya!'

'That's right, Ning,' I said. 'In fact, a Khasi scholar by the name of Marco Mitri excavated an early settlement on Lum Sohpet Bneng, our sacred mountain. He and his colleagues sent their findings to the US for carbon dating and discovered that the settlement dated back to at least 1200 BCE. That's more than 3,000 years ago. Another carbon dating by him at a place called Umjajew in Upper Shillong revealed that it too had been in existence since 1900 BCE.'

Before my friends could express their amazement again, I shushed them and said, 'Wait, wait, it gets even better. Earlier, I had referred to Banrida Langstieh and her work, remember? Actually, it was a genetic study conducted in 2007 by anthropologists and scientists at the Indian Statistical Institute and the Centre for Cellular and Molecular Biology, Hyderabad. Langstieh was one of them, yes. According to this groundbreaking study, among the first people to have arrived and settled in India were ancestors of the Mundas, who came about 66,000 years ago. Khasis were the first genetic offshoot of the Mundas and appeared on the scene 57,000 years ago. Later, many of these "Austro-Asiatic populations" migrated to South-east Asia through Northeast India, though the Khasis, who represent "a genetic continuity between the populations of South and South-east Asia"—decided to settle in the Northeast itself ...'

'This bloody Ap, you are not pulling our leg, na, tdong?' Bah Kynsai demanded.

'Of course not, Bah Kynsai! Look at this.' I pointed to my mobile. 'Their findings are published in an article entitled "Austro-Asiatic Tribes of Northeast India Provide Hitherto Missing Genetic Link Between South and South-east Asia". You can check it out for yourself when we get back.'

'Bong leh!' Bah Kynsai exploded. 'We are truly, truly an ancient race, man! As ancient as the Greeks, tdir!'

'Perhaps even older, Bah Kynsai!' Raji exclaimed.

In a celebratory mood, Bah Kynsai, Raji, Bah Kit and Evening stood up and began dancing around the fire, chanting *phawars*, our traditional poems, very much like gnomic verses and limericks, which they made up on the spot.

The dancing and chanting went on for some time and soon proved to be infectious. All of us, except Halolihim, Hamkom and Donald, joined in and created such a ruckus that we soon brought Perly and some of his friends to the scene.

When we saw the Lyngngams, we stopped and settled back in our seats. Bah Kynsai explained to Perly why we were celebrating and requested him to bring us some water. While we waited for him to return, Bah Kynsai pointed an accusing finger at me and demanded, 'But why the hell didn't you tell us about this earlier, tdong? Why did you have to lead us on a wild goose chase, talking about all those other theories?'

With a straight face, I replied, 'Because I wanted you to dance, Bah Kynsai.'

I had to duck immediately to avoid a stick that Bah Kynsai threw at me. And of course, after the stick came the curses!

To divert his attention, I quickly turned to Bah Su and said, 'What about the other tradition, Bah Su? You did say there were two ...'

'The other tradition maintains that Khasis came from the north along the Himalayan foothills,' Bah Su said. 'That's why we have our own name for the Himalayas, Ki Mangkashang, sky-mark for a wandering tribe. Sylhet in Bangladesh was supposed to be their destination, but they were driven from there into these mountain fastnesses by a great flood. This tradition also claims that while some of the Khasi sub-tribes entered the hills from the south-east, others came directly from the south.'

'This version of our migration,' I explained, 'is supported by the theory that, once upon a time, the whole region of Sohra was under the sea. The large deposits of limestone in the area point to this possibility. Then there is the village of Laitryngew, located about six kilometres above the Sohra plateau. The meaning of its name is "free onto the shore", or by implication, "shore at last". Why should they give the place that name if not in reference to the sea or, at least, a large body of water?

'Even more remarkably, there is a sacred forest called Law Lieng, or boat forest, in Sohra Rim, a village about two kilometres from Laitryngew. Sohra Rim is about 5,800 feet above sea level, but still a little below Laitryngew. Legend has it that the forest was called by that name because two large boats were found stranded there. Scholars believe the entire area could once have been underwater and must have risen later owing to an earthquake or other natural occurrences, several thousand years ago. Now, could these be some of the boats on which the old Khasis escaped the great flood in Sylhet?'

There was a clucking of tongues and many murmured, 'Amazing, simply amazing!'

Bah Su grumbled, 'The only problem is that, with three versions, including Langstieh's, all of which seem to be equally persuasive, we are left with more questions than answers.'

'No, no, Bah Su!' Bah Kynsai said. 'As far as we are concerned, na, the Langstieh findings are the most genuine. The second story also proves the fact that we migrated to these hills, not from South-east Asia but mainland India ...'

'And what about the first story, which claims that we came here via the Patkoi range?' Magdalene asked.

'That, Mag, could refer to Sajar Ñiangli's migration, which happened much later,' Bah Kit explained. 'I'll tell you his story, don't worry.'

'Great, great,' Bah Kynsai said excitedly. 'You see, Bah Su, I think the question of our origins, na, has finally been answered ... What do you say, Ap?'

I agreed but added, 'Perhaps, as you said, we do need to travel to Southeast Asia, Bah Kynsai. We must discover more.'

Bah Kynsai, Raji, Bah Kit and Evening said together, 'Yeah, yeah, we must do that, we must make it a point to do that!'

Magdalene added, 'As soon as possible, ha, guys?'

Suddenly, Hamkom, who had not been celebrating with us, gave voice to what had been irking him. He said, 'You people have been talking only about the Khasis, what about the Jaiñtias?'

That stopped us short. Then Evening angrily demanded, 'Jaiñtias, what Jaiñtias?'

'The Jaiñtias, the people of Jaiñtia Hills! They are different from the Khasis, no?' Hamkom said sharply.

'What, you ignoramus!' Evening cursed. 'Have you not been listening to what we said? Tell him, Bah Su, tell him there is no such thing as Jaiñtias. We are all Khasis: Khynriam, U Pnar, U Bhoi, U War …'

But before Bah Su could speak, Hamkom jumped up from where he had been sitting and stalked towards Evening. Standing over him, he snarled, 'How dare you call me an ignoramus? I'm a college professor; I have written a book called *A Brief History of the Jaiñtias* …'

Evening sprang up with surprising agility. He said, 'Then you are an academic fraud, a charlatan, a mountebank! There was no such thing as the "Jaiñtias" until the white man gave you the damn word, you idiot! Your book must be full of shit and garbage. And what's more, you are a chauvinistic piece of trash to think you are so special and so different from us all!'

'Who are you calling a fraud and a chauvinistic piece of trash, you ignorant, lowly, miserable taxi driver? How dare you use that kind of language with me? Repeat it and I'll thrash you!'

'First of all, you ignorant bastard, Khasi society is egalitarian: a taxi driver is an equal of the chief minister. Secondly, I'm not only a taxi driver, you academic junk! Do you know how many degrees I have? Three: BA, BD, LLB. And what's more, I'm also a writer; I've got books in Khasi and English. Driving a taxi is a choice for me, not a necessity, you arsehole! And you, just because you are a college lecturer and a Pnar—not a Jaiñtia, you fool!—you think you are superior to everybody else! "I'm not a Khasi! I'm too good to be called a Khasi!" Bloody arrogant piece of shit!'

Hamkom was suffused with rage. I don't think anybody had spoken to him like that before. He clenched his fists and then suddenly kicked out with his right foot, aiming at Evening's groin. Evening, however, almost calmly blocked the kick with his left forearm, karate style, and struck hard with the right. The punch caught Hamkom on the chin and sent him flying to the ground near the fire.

Standing over him, Evening said, 'And that's to tell you that I'm also trained in karate, you arsehole!'

We were all surprised by the power behind the blow. We leapt to our feet and went to help Hamkom. We tried to prop him up against the wall, but he was still too dizzy from the blow. Luckily, his jaw was not broken, although it was badly bruised. We let him lie there in the care of Halolihim, who had been awakened earlier by our dancing, and turned to admonish Evening.

Evening was unrepentant. He said he had not started it; he was only defending himself. We gave him no quarter, though, and told him he should not be bad-mouthing people in the first place.

Hearing the commotion, people came to find out what was wrong. Bah Kynsai told them we were just horsing around, and when things had quietened down again, he gave both Hamkom and Evening a talking-to. He said we should keep in mind that we were guests in a strange village and that we were supposed to be the educated elite. 'Bew, liah, man!' he cursed. 'We are professors, officers and intellectuals, na, liah?'

'Is that the language of the educated elite, Bah Kynsai?' Magdalene laughed.

'That's the language of A-category auditors,' he replied, laughing too. 'But seriously, na, we must not behave in this manner and fight among ourselves, man. What will the Lyngngams say about us? Rotten, second-rate townspeople, they will say! From now on, we should discuss things with a civil tongue, you understand? You two! Come here and make up!'

We watched as the two of them tapped each other on the shoulder as a sign of peace. All of us wanted to move away from the ticklish subject, fearing another outburst, but Hamkom insisted on asking why we would not accept the fact that Jaiñtias were different from Khasis.

Bah Su, who was not only the oldest but also the gentlest, replied in as reasonable a tone as possible, although he too was annoyed by Hamkom's blinkered position. He said, 'Look, Ham, we did not have a written script until 1842, when Thomas Jones designed the Khasi alphabet from the Roman script. All we know about our early history before the white man came is through the stories passed on from generation to generation. These stories have become legendary, and the greatest legend is that which tells us about the Hynñiew Treps, ancestors of the Khasi people. Khasi is a generic term, ha, it relates to the seven sub-tribes: the Khynriams in Ri Khynriam or East

Khasi Hills, the Pnars in Ri Pnar or Jaiñtia Hills, the Wars in the low valleys of East Khasi Hills, West Khasi Hills and Ri Pnar, the Bhois in Ri Bhoi, and the Marams, the Lyngngams and the Dikos (who could instead be Nongtrais and Muliangs), all in West Khasi Hills.

'Now, if you say that a Pnar is not a Khasi but a Jaiñtia, ha, that is a very dangerous thing because then, a War will say I'm not a Khasi, I'm a War; a Bhoi will say, I'm not a Khasi, I'm a Bhoi; a Maram will say I'm not a Khasi, I'm a Maram and so on and so forth. Everyone will claim special status, just as you are doing now, and the entire community will break up.'

'If you are saying we are the same, then why is it that in the list of Meghalaya's Scheduled Tribes, we are listed separately as Khasis, Jaiñtias, Garos and others?'

Evening started to say something, but Bah Kynsai interrupted, 'Not you, Ning. We don't want more trouble.'

But Evening would not be silenced. 'You cannot zip my mouth just like that, I'm sorry, Bah Kynsai, this is something I must respond to. The so-called Scheduled Tribes list was prepared at the behest of arsehole politicians, who knew nothing about their own people or had a secret agenda ...'

'What secret agenda?' Hamkom asked belligerently, the knock on the chin having done nothing to intimidate him.

Magdalene said quickly, 'No more fighting!'

'A secret agenda like yours,' Evening continued. 'To splinter the Khasi people into little fragments. To divide and rule. The bureaucrats are as bad as the British were. Either they are non-Khasis who know nothing or Khasis who have been misled as badly as you have been by the white man. And why? Because, to you, the white man can do no wrong and everything the white man gives you is God's truth.'

'Everyone is ignorant but you!' Hamkom said.

'Everyone knows but people like you! Everyone here, for instance, apart from Donald the Delhi scholar, knows that U Khynriam, U Pnar, U Bhoi, U War, et cetera, are Khasis.'

'If we are all Khasis, then why did we initially have three districts in Meghalaya: Khasi Hills, Jaiñtia Hills and Garo Hills?'

Now even Bah Kynsai was getting fed up. He said, 'You also, na, Ham, you are a historian, but your prejudice has clouded both your judgement and your memory. Initially there was no Meghalaya, no Garo Hills, only Khasi-Jaiñtia Hills in the British province of Assam ...'

'Exactly! Why Khasi-Jaiñtia Hills if the Jaiñtias are not different?'

'Bah Su, Ap, you tell him ...'

'According to C.J. Lyall,' Bah Su began, 'the first contact between the British and the Khasis came about after the acquisition by the East India Company of the district of Sylhet. This was as a consequence of the grant of the *Diwani* of Bengal in 1765. The Khasis, he says, were our neighbours in the north of that district ...'

'He also says,' Hamkom interrupted triumphantly, 'to "the northeast was the kingdom of Jaiñtia". I still remember that, I mentioned it in my book.'

'I know. I have read your book, and it's full of quotations from British writers and non-Khasi historians, but unfortunately, ha, nothing from the Khasi stories or Khasi writers who have knowledge and understanding beyond the reach of British and non-Khasi scholars ...'

Before Bah Su could continue, Hamkom said, 'But Bah Su, earlier Bah Kynsai and Ap said that only non-Khasi writers have written about Khasi identity, so why shouldn't I use them as my source?'

'With our Mon Khmer identity, it's different, Ham. Earlier, Khasi writers did not have the ability or the resources to research the subject, although now we have people like Langstieh and Mitri. But that subject is different, ha. Now we are talking about *our known history*, and therefore, we should listen to our own stories and writers. And in your book, ha, Ham, there is not much information about the establishment of the so-called Jaiñtia kingdom, and nothing at all about Hima Shyllong or Hima Madur Maskut, which occupied a large part of Ri Pnar, Ri Khynriam and Ri Bhoi. I don't know if you are even aware of these states, but if you are not, then I don't think you know much about pre-British Khasi history.'

'There you are!' Evening said triumphantly. 'Go on, Bah Su, go on.'

Bah Su said to Hamkom, 'Tell me, what do you know of the hima that you called the Jaiñtia kingdom in your book? By the way, that is also wrong, Ham. A Khasi hima is never known as a kingdom. It's a state. There's a beautiful story behind this; I'll tell you later.'

'I know that it was one of the oldest kingdoms in the Northeast and that it was quite powerful before the British came.'

'Not kingdom. State,' Bah Su corrected him again. 'And?' he prompted.

'And that it was governed by powerful kings known as the Jaiñtia Rajas, whose capital was Jaiñtiapur, now in Bangladesh.'

'And?'

'What do you mean, "and"?'

'Before that?'

'Nobody knows our history before that!'

'That's where you are wrong ...'

'He means he doesn't know, Bah Su,' Evening said sarcastically.

'It is common knowledge, at least among those Khasis who are the least bit interested in Khasi history and culture, that it was never called the Jaiñtia state or the Jaiñtia kingdom by the Pnars. It was known as Hima Sutnga, ha, ruled by the syiems, the kings, of Sutnga from the dynasty of *ki syiem Sutnga*. And one of its early capitals was the town of Raliang. It was only much later, when Hima Sutnga expanded north towards present-day Assam and south towards Bengal, by capturing the Jaintapur Upazila, that the council of state resolved to create two capitals. One was in Ri Pnar—there was no Jaiñtia Hills at the time, ha—close to the Assam border, for easy control of the northern territories in Assam, and another in the Jaintapur Upazila, for easy control of the southern territories in Bengal. Nartiang was chosen as the northern capital and Jaiñtiapur as the southern capital. Later, Nartiang became known as the summer capital and Jaiñtiapur, in Jaintapur Upazila, as the winter capital because the syiem of Sutnga and his council of ministers spent their winters in Jaiñtiapur, to avoid the cold of the hills, and summer in Nartiang, to avoid the heat of the plains.

'Slowly, however, the syiems began to spend more and more time in Jaiñtiapur and their Bengal territories than in Ri Pnar. The reason was twofold. First, the people of Ri Pnar, who were *u khun u hajar*, the children, the thousands, the citizens of the state, did not pay taxes to the syiems or their council, since they were the real owners of the land. Their treatment of the syiems, because of the egalitarian nature of Khasi society, was also not that of subjects who kowtowed to kings but of citizens with equal standing in the community. All this is corroborated in the works of many Khasi writers. The people of the plains, however, were considered *ki raiot*, the vanquished subjects, and the syiems were empowered by the council of state to tax them. These people treated the syiems with sycophantic reverence and even kneeled before them. In fact, to please them even more, ha, they began calling them the Jaiñtia Rajas—Raja was a Bengali title. And because of that, all the non-Khasi subjects and people in the neighbouring kingdoms also started referring to Hima Sutnga as the Jaiñtia kingdom.

'When the British acquired the district of Sylhet, ha, they had a very uneven relationship with the neighbouring "Jaiñtia kingdom"; sometimes friendly, sometimes hostile. When, eventually, they captured the state after the Burmese War of 1824, they carved it up into three parts. The southern territories were attached to Sylhet and the northern territories to Assam. They allowed the syiem of Sutnga to live in Jaiñtiapur and govern the hilly region of Ri Pnar as a vassal king. But the syiem (Rajendra Sing was his name) refused to be in possession of "any reduced portion" of his state. The administration of the hilly region then passed into the hands of the British, who gave it a new name, Jaiñtia Hills, although it had always been known as Ri Pnar or Hima Sutnga among the Khasis.'

'And the name has not only stuck,' Evening said, 'but has become so much a part of our psyche and has fooled people like this fellow here to such an extent that they now believe themselves to be Jaiñtias—different from the rest of the Khasi sub-tribes. What a bunch of suckers! What is this kind of thing called, Ap? Anglophilia, yes. If the white man says, "eat shit", ha, this fraud would readily do so ... Phooey, historian! Imagine, a historian who doesn't even know his own history! Incredible!'

'Fuck you!' Hamkom said. He was clearly losing all self-control.

'Fuck you, you blinkered idiot!' Evening responded. 'I gave you a punch on the face ... do you want a kick in the mouth now?'

'Hey, hey, hey!' Bah Kynsai came between them, raising both arms and stopping them from coming to blows again.

After they had both settled down, Donald said thoughtfully, 'So, that was the genesis of the word "Jaiñtia"! Frankly speaking, okay, I didn't know anything about it either. Bengali name, huh?'

'The present generation, by and large, knows nothing about it, Don,' Bah Kit said. 'That's why we have the so-called "Khasis and Jaiñtias" in the state's list of Scheduled Tribes. Even the Pnar will accept the name Ri Hynñiew Trep, Hynñiew Trep Land, but not Ri Khasi, Khasi Land. To them, the slogan "Khynriam, U Pnar, U Bhoi, U War, U Maram, U Lyngngam, and so on" means Hynñiew Trep, the seven sub-tribes, not Khasi. That's also why our rebel outfit is called the Hynñiew Trep National Liberation Council, okay? Very cunning, those guys, they knew that only this name would be accepted by all.'

'It has always been like that with us Khasis, na, Don?' Bah Kynsai said. 'We are always too quick to accommodate others and accept what they tell us as the gospel truth. Take many of the places in our state, for instance. Outsiders come, change their names, and we accept these, forgetting the original names. Believe it or not, many people still refer to Sohra as Cherrapunjee, a British-given name. And in Shillong? Khyndai Lad is Police Bazaar; Ïewduh is Burra Bazaar; Lum Laban is Bishnupur; Nongmynsong is Lalchand Basti.'

'Ri Hynñiew Trep or Ri Khasi is Meghalaya,' Bah Su added.

'But isn't Meghalaya a beautiful name, Bah Su?' Hamkom said. 'I find it quite delightful: "The Abode of the Clouds". So poetic!'

'Poetic, my arse!' said Evening. 'Once a fraud, always a fraud!'

'Bah Kynsai, you must do something about this bugger!' Hamkom spluttered with rage. 'He's too much! He's always after me! All I'm saying is that I find the name Meghalaya beautiful, and he starts abusing me!'

'That's exactly why I'm abusing you, you short-sighted idiot of a lecturer!'

'Temper your language, na, liah! If you have a difference of opinion, na, explain yourself without abusing anyone. What the hell is wrong with you, man?' Bah Kynsai admonished him.

'I can stand stupidity from an illiterate person, no, Bah Kynsai, but not from a so-called historian. The name is a damn shame in the first place. It speaks volumes about the folly of our political leaders, the so-called heroes who were responsible for our Hill State Movement. I have no use for any of them. They are not my heroes. They were a bunch of incredibly stupid fools! Firstly, what kind of idiots would fight for a state without borders? Would you buy a plot of land without clear demarcations? Wouldn't you first establish the boundaries and then raise pillars to mark them, if not a fence? But no, those myopic asses had no use for details, they didn't seem to know that the devil is in the fine print. Ask those who live along the Assam border; find out how much they revere those nincompoops! Every day they face one kind of harassment or the other: one day from the Assam police, the next day from the Karbi militants or the Nepali settlers. How do you resolve this muddle now?

'Secondly, how can you fight for a state without a name? What has this stupid name—"Meghalaya, Abode of the Clouds", given by some academic thug from nowhere—got to do with us? Are you a cloud, Hamkom? Does the name connect you with the land, as Nagaland or Mizoram does? Are we a people with no roots in the land? Were they so dim-witted, your heroes, that they couldn't think of a name for their state? Do you see the danger of this silly name? Everyone, migrants and all, is a Meghalayan! We moan about the influx, Bah Kynsai. The silent invasion, we call it. And why not, when our name is so accommodating?

'Thirdly, what have the Khasis or the Hynñiew Treps, if you will, got to do with the Garos? You call them "Garo brethren"! In what way are they your brothers? Do you share the same parentage? Do you have any blood ties with them? Why couldn't they have fought for a state of their own? When most of the struggle took place in the Khasi Hills, why do we have a state for Khasis and Garos? When most of the leaders who went to jail were Khasis, why did we get a Garo as the first chief minister? Doesn't it remind you of the saying, *Ha ka jingïakajia uba bam suk dei u poiei*? In any dispute, he who profits is a stray. The so-called Khasi leaders quarrelled for the post like dogs for a bone, but ultimately, who walked away with it? A "neutral" Garo!

'And what are the problems we have inherited because of this? Job reservation—40 per cent for Khasis and 40 per cent for Garos! Aren't both of them Scheduled Tribes under the Constitution? Aren't both, therefore, equally backward? Haven't they been provided with the same Scheduled Tribe quotas by the Indian government? Then why this reservation within reservation? And why 40 per cent for them when Khasis have double the population? Who is cleverer then, a Khasi or a Garo? And this policy has now been extended to other fields as well, do you know that? Education, for instance … quotas for technical studies. How can your leaders be so blind to all this? And do we ever get on with the Garos? When Khasis pull to the east, they pull to the west. Is there a mismatch worse than that? Where did they keep their brains, those Hill State Movement fools, in their buttocks? *Shish*, leaders, you say! More like dumbasses! You know what? I'm going to organise a group to commemorate the death anniversaries of those idiots. Do you know how we will honour them? We will trample upon their graves like Pathan moneylenders used to do on the graves of those who could not pay their debts—that's what we'll do, sala! And we will heap curses upon them, so they are damned for all eternity, the bastards!

'If you ask me, ha, now is the right time for us to part ways with the Garos. If the politicians won't do anything, we should press for a referendum and see how many Khasis still want to be with them!'

We gaped at Evening, shell-shocked. It was a slap in the face for Hamkom, who had thought so much of a name that now seemed dreadfully inappropriate.

Raji was the first one to react. He said, 'Actually, Ning is right, you know. I have heard others say the same thing, though not with so much intensity or clarity. And about Meghalaya, okay, I'm sorry Ham, but I think Ning is absolutely right. Bah Kynsai is also spot-on when he says we are too accommodating and too ready to accept what others tell us. Take Mawbah, for instance. Now it is Jhalupara; Ïewmawlong is Mawlong Hat; Umshyrpi is Rhino. Do you remember what happened when Khuswant Singh came to Shillong, Bah Kynsai? During an interview with a TV news channel, okay, he asked the interviewer, "What's the name of the huge lake on the outskirts of

Shillong?" The interviewer, a Khasi, replied, "Burrapani, Hindi for Big Water." Khuswant Singh was so shocked that he exclaimed, "Such an ugly name for such a lovely place!" He must have thought the Khasis dim-witted to have given it such a name. But whose fault was it? Solely that of the interviewer! The bugger didn't even know we have a beautiful Khasi name for it!'

'What's the Khasi name for it?' Donald asked. 'I also call it Burrapani.'

'Bong leh!' Raji exploded.

'What do you mean, "Bong leh"?'

'How can you not know the name of Umïam, man? That's what the dam site is called in Khasi. Umïam, it's such a lovely name. How would you translate it, Ap?'

'Weeping Water.'

'See? What a poetic name it is, and that stupid anchor did not even know it. As Bah Kynsai said, okay, we are too quick to accept names given by others and forget our own. It was like that with Jaiñtia also, no? Hima Sutnga became the Jaiñtia kingdom. Ri Pnar became Jaiñtia Hills. And the funny thing is, we think the names given by others are more original than the original!'

'You know what I think?' Bah Kit said. 'Despite the name Jaiñtia, ha, I don't think the various Khasi sub-tribes can be separated from each other. First of all, there has been extensive intermarriage amongst all of us, okay? Khynriams, Bhois, Wars and Marams have been marrying the Pnars for thousands of years. In my opinion, we are too intricately mingled to be different. Secondly, there was a lot of migration in the past from Ri Pnar towards the west of Ri Hynñiew Trep, where the Khynriams, Marams and Bhois live, and vice versa. And these migrations came about mostly because families and clans kept splitting up, necessitating their dispersal. For instance, ha, the Nongkynrihs, the Lyngdoh Nongbris, the Lyngdoh Kynshis, the Passahs and the Shadaps were part of a large clan living somewhere near the River Kupli in Ri Pnar, okay? When the clan split up, the Nongkynrihs and Lyngdoh Nongbris migrated to East Khasi Hills, the Lyngdoh Kynshis to West Khasi Hills and the Shadaps to Ri Bhoi. Only the Passahs stayed behind in Ri Pnar. Although they are now called Khynriams, Marams, Bhois and Pnars, these clans consider themselves to be blood relations even today. Marriage between them is strictly forbidden. And there are many, many cases like that. Too many to name here. So, the question to Ham is, how can we be different?

'And the greatest migration of all, ha, was when U Sajar Ñiangli, or Nangli as he was sometimes known, left Hima Sutnga with all his innumerable followers to establish new himas in West Khasi Hills and Ri Bhoi.'

Bah Kit went on to tell us the story of Sajar Ñiangli.

☙

Sajar Ñiangli was one of the most powerful *mars* of the state of Sutnga. A mar was a strongman, a giant warrior, a warrior leader, oath-sworn to serve the king in peace and war. Some sources identify him as the *lyngskor*, the prime minister, of the king of Sutnga, a long, long time ago, before the king converted to Hinduism. This means that Sajar must have lived earlier than the thirteenth century CE, for by that time, the state of Sutnga was already recorded as the Hindu kingdom of Jaiñtia in the Ahom buranjis, the court chronicles.

It was during his prime ministership that the state of Sutnga achieved the pinnacle of its power and glory. Under his accomplished and daring leadership, many conquests were made to extend the state northwards to Cachar and Nagaon in Assam and southwards to Sylhet. All the other mars, and the people of the entire state, revered him more than they did the king. They loved him and looked to him for guidance and support—not only because he was the most powerful warrior of his time but also because of the nobility of his soul, his sympathetic understanding of their problems and his self-sacrificing love for them. To him, they were no less than members of his own family. His fervent patriotism also meant that he was a great champion of his people's culture and religion, *Ka Niam ka Rukom Tynrai*, as handed down by his forefathers. In fact, it was his attempt to keep them safe that unfortunately brought about the greatest split in the state of Sutnga.

The reigning king at the time had come under the influence of the Bamons, or Brahmins, of the Hindu Tantric branch. The king wanted to convert to Hinduism and issued instructions that all the people of the state should convert along with him. The dark cloud that rose from the king's palace began to spread to the farthest corners of the state. The people of Ri Pnar were caught entirely unawares. A Khasi king was not supposed to take any decision relating to the life and death of the people on his own, nor was he supposed to issue such a momentous instruction without the say-so of the council of state. The dolois, who governed their respective provinces, went to consult with Sajar on the matter, along with all their warrior leaders.

Sajar, the people's champion and the most powerful man in the state, was himself deeply hurt by the king's action. His handsome face contracted in a deep frown as he anxiously pondered the many harrying questions that passed through his mind. How could the king of a hima abandon his people's religion to follow the religion of his conquered subjects? What about all the other customs and traditions? Were they also to be changed according to the canons of the new religion? Would matriliny, for instance, be replaced by patriliny? Would members of the clan take their name from the father? Would inheritance become the son's prerogative? Would everything change with patriarchal Hinduism? Would the Pnars be forced to practise the odious caste system of the Hindus? It was unheard of! Unthinkable!

The dolois and the mars who gathered around him urged him to take immediate action to remove the king, take the throne by force, and thus save the state from the threatening darkness. U Sajar could have easily done that. He was the most powerful warlord in the state and all the provincial chiefs were with him. But one thing stood in his way. He was a mar, a warrior leader, oath-bound to protect the king in peace and war. How could he take the throne he had sworn to protect? How could he raise a hand against the king he had sworn to serve? He was in a terrible quandary: to allow the king a free hand was to let down his people; to remove him from the throne was an act of betrayal. He was in a situation where the cure was worse than the illness.

He told the gathering of dolois, 'I cannot even contemplate an act of violence against my own syiem, despite the grievousness of his action. You know me, and you know my oath.'

One of the dolois reminded Sajar of the oath the king had violated in ignoring the council of state, though the matter concerned the life and death of the people.

Another one said, 'He has also broken his oath to be the king, the mother. He is behaving not like a parent but a tyrant.'

Yet another said, 'He has also broken the oath to be the king, the slave. He is behaving not like a slave of the people but their despotic master.'

Sajar, however, was unable to violate his oath and rise against his own king despite the terrible conflict within his soul: anger against a treacherous king collided with his reluctance to shed his own people's blood. He said, 'A warrior leader's oath is as immovable as a rock, as hard as iron. A word given is a word kept. The old ones used to call it "The Word the Covenant". How can I violate the covenant and still live like an honourable man? The syiem is undeniably behaving treacherously, but how can I shed my own people's blood in removing him from the throne?'

The dolois too were in a fix. They could not move against the king without Sajar for fear of a terrible and prolonged civil war. The king still had his supporters. With Sajar by their side, any serious opposition could quickly be dealt with, but without him, the country would be torn apart.

The dolois then urged Sajar to persuade the king away from his mad scheme. But the king, firmly in the grip of the Bamons and drunk on the new religion, would not budge. Finally, after repeated consultations, and to avoid bloodshed, Sajar and the dolois came to a decision. They permitted the king and his family to convert to Hinduism, but forbade him to force his citizens, ki khun ki hajar, to convert. That, they said, should be left to their free will.

The king was forced to agree to this ultimatum, and for a time, there was peace again in the state.

Then came summer. The king, his council and his entourage, including the Bamon priests, arrived in Nartiang, the summer capital in the western part of Ri Pnar. The Bamons persuaded the king to build a temple dedicated to goddess Kali in Nartiang, as he had done in Jaiñtiapur. Priests were posted at the temple, where they performed many strange rituals and exotic rites almost every day. Many locals became fascinated by the rites, and soon, they too embraced the new religion.

From Nartiang, Hinduism spread to many other villages, strengthening the king's hand with new converts. Seeing his support base growing, the king became more and more arrogant. He began to disregard all the traditional conventions of kingship. He stopped listening to his ministers and was advised only by the Bamons. So strongly was he in their clutches that it seemed as if he could do nothing without their say-so. The master seemed to have become the slave of his own subjects.

The provincial chiefs, the dolois, could not stand by and watch the state slipping into the hands of vassals and foreign puppet masters who were advising the king to do things contrary to the people's age-old customs and traditions and, therefore, contrary to their welfare. The Bamons were only interested in furthering their own ambitions and increasing their own power, but the king seemed to be blind to this.

The dolois once more tried to persuade Sajar to take the throne from the king, but now he was in an even more difficult situation. He had promised the king that he would not rebel against him if he left the people alone and did not force them to convert to the new religion. The king had not done anything to break his promise. The conversion of the citizens was being done through aggressive missionary efforts by the Bamons and their agents. The king was not directly involved. Besides, he was more certain than ever that the state would be torn apart by civil war if he tried to depose the king. The king's followers had increased, and they would fight tooth and nail to defend him. Sajar was not worried about the fighting, but he was concerned about the outcome. If his forces fought the king's in a mutually destructive war, the state would surely fall into the hands of the foreign powers in Assam and Bengal, who were watching the developments with keen and greedy eyes. Once the state was weakened, they would capture it as easily as catching a chicken in its coop.

Sajar could not stand the thought of his beloved people ending up as the vanquished subjects and slaves of foreign kings. He debated with the dolois; he debated with himself; he dithered and could not come to any decision.

Meanwhile, the Bamons who had become the king's eyes and ears whispered lies to him, telling him about an imminent rebellion by Sajar. Under their guidance, the king devised a plan to neutralise Sajar and his followers once and for all. He summoned all the dolois to Jaiñtiapur, apparently to sort out the discontent simmering in the state. But secretly, he also invited all his followers and new converts to come, fully armed, to defend their faith.

Unaware of this plot, the dolois, the mars and the chief supporters of Sajar arrived in Jaiñtiapur. The king had organised a great feast in a large, open ground, ostensibly to welcome them. But he carefully divided the crowd into two groups, those who were with him and those who were against him. His supporters far outnumbered those of the unsuspecting Sajar and the dolois, who had all come only with a few bodyguards. Feeling secure in the midst of so many followers, the king decided to insult the dolois and Sajar's supporters before destroying them. He ordered the two groups to be served different kinds of food. For his followers, there was rice, fish, chicken and vegetables, while for Sajar and his men there was only rice and lentils.

But his actions only served to alert the dolois and their men. They seethed with anger, knowing now that the king was planning the worst for them. They refrained from drinking and made up their minds to kill the king and as many of his followers as possible if it came to a fight. Meanwhile, an old woman employed at the king's palace came to confirm their suspicions. She told Sajar that the king planned to have them all killed that night at the feasting ground. Sajar and the dolois were few, but they were also the best and most ferocious warriors in the state. Some of them suggested that they should not wait for the night. 'Let us strike now and take them by surprise. They outnumber us greatly, but we are men of war, tested in the most brutal and savage of battlefields. Each of us is equal to at least six of them. First of all, let us take the syiem; let us take out the chicken's head and let the rest run amok in confusion.'

Sajar, however, would have none of it. He said, 'We cannot raise our hands against our own syiem. How can we kill a syiem ordained by God to be our leader, a syiem, moreover, whose life we have sworn to protect? How can the protector be the destroyer? And how can we shed the blood of our kinsmen? Look at them. Though many of them are Shilotias and Hindus from these parts, a lot of them are our own too. No, my brothers, the best course is to escape and get away from here before nightfall without arousing suspicion.'

Sajar asked the old woman to bring him a live chicken. When she brought one to him, he cut the hen's throat, drank her blood, then spat it out, making a lot of noise in the process.

His supporters shouted, 'Sajar is vomiting blood, he is very ill! Come, come, let's take him back to his home!'

So saying, they carried him out of there and left the king and the Bamons gaping helplessly.

When the news spread of the king's plan to murder Sajar and the dolois, Sajar's followers flocked to his home, bringing with them their swords and shields, their spears and their bows and arrows. They wanted to storm the palace that very night and kill everyone in it, but once again, Sajar held them back. He said, 'Rather than spilling each other's blood, my people, and allowing foreign powers to subjugate our riven hima like a leashed dog, let us go away and find another place to settle. We are many. We will settle and farm new lands. We will establish new states and give our citizens the love and justice that are sadly absent in this place.'

And so, Sajar and his hordes left Jaiñtiapur before dawn the next morning, marching towards the hills of Ri Pnar, not to capture political power and divide the country, but to leave it for good and find new lands to colonise. On the way to the hills, many people joined him and swelled his ranks. He attracted people to him like bees to a queen, and like a great swarm, they streamed through the land that overflowed with tears of sorrow, for those who could not follow him cried for him, lamenting his unhappy state. When they reached the plain of Thadlaskeiñ, just a few kilometres from the summer capital of Nartiang, Sajar called for a halt. He spoke to his people.

'My people,' he said, 'you the children, the thousands, who have followed me through water, through fire, listen. As a lyngskor and a mar, as a statesman and a warrior leader, I have served my country and my syiem with devotion and fidelity. I don't think it is right for me now to raise my hand against the syiem, ordained by God to serve the people. But the syiem tried to do me harm, tried to harm my chief supporters, the dolois and the mars, the best of their kind. Even now, he might be sending men after us. We are not afraid of these men. We can crush them; we can come down upon them like a hammer on a pebble. But having served my country all my life, I don't feel it is right for me to let its hills and valleys run with the blood of my own kith and kin. To avoid this calamity, I am leaving this land forever. I leave it to you to follow me or tend to your hearths and homes. I release you from all your oaths and obligations. I lay no claim upon your allegiance. I leave it all to you.'

The people said, 'We will live with you and we will die with you; we will follow you through water and through fire; we will go with you wherever you take us, to the ends of the earth, if need be.'

'If that is so,' he replied, 'I thank each one of you, and to every one of you, a thousand bows. We are at a crossroads. Where shall we turn from here? Shall we go west towards the land of our compatriots, the Khynriams, or shall we turn east towards Hadem and Bama, where we will never hear any news of this treacherous syiem any more?'

When the people said it was all up to him, he said, 'Then we will see how the air smells. Wherever there is the smell of *amirphor*, the flower of life, there we shall turn.'

Sajar turned to the west. He said, 'The breeze from the west reeks of rottenness and decay.' Then he turned to the east, and after a while, he said, 'The breeze from the east carries on it a sweet flowery scent ... we will go to the east, but first, we will leave a sign of our passing so that our compatriots will never forget us. Out of the spring that you see before you, we will create a huge lake. Men and women will work together on it, but first, all the warriors will begin digging with the sharp end of their bows. Let a legend grow from this!'

His words turned out to be true. The beautiful Thadlaskeiñ Lake on the way to Shillong from Jowai has become a major attraction for tourists. The legend that Sajar's warriors dug it with their bows survives, and no matter what anyone says, no one will be persuaded otherwise.

From Thadlaskeiñ, Sajar went to Nartiang and then on to Hadem, or Hidimba, the old name of North Cachar in Assam, where he stayed for a while and had another lake excavated in memory of their passing. From Hadem, he went through Patkoi Hills and Manipur to Bama or Burma. Finally, homesickness drove him and his hordes back to the hills of Ri Khasi. However, they did not return to Ri Pnar. They entered the hills from Assam and reached Ri Bhoi in the northern Khasi Hills, where a section of his people stayed back to establish a new state called Hima Jirang. From there, they went to the state of Nongkhlaw in Ri Maram, now part of West Khasi Hills, which was governed by the Syiemlieh clan, a branch of the Syiem Sutnga dynasty. Sajar Ñiangli was warmly welcomed in the state by kinsfolk who had initially migrated from Ri Pnar, and it was there that he spent the rest of his life, helping the king run the affairs of the state with wisdom, fairness and benevolence. His men also won for the state many more territories so that, by the time the British came, it had become one of the most powerful in Ri Khasi, with territorial possessions in Assam to the north and Bengal to the south. But their greatest contribution to Nongkhlaw was perhaps in breeding a race of brave and hardy men, whose descendants were the likes of Tirot Sing Syiem, Mon Bhut, Lorshon Jaraiñ, Kheiñ Kongngor Nongkynrih and many others who fought against British domination and became the first freedom fighters among the Khasi people. Sajar's people also spread across many areas of Ri Bhoi and Ri Maram to found many states, including that of Jyrngam and Rambrai.

When Bah Kit concluded the story of Sajar Ñiangli, Hamkom exclaimed, 'Wow, what a guy, ha, Ap?'

Evening looked like he was about to taunt Hamkom again, so I quickly said, 'Yeah, what a guy indeed! Just compare him with the self-serving pigs that pass for statesmen nowadays. He had a crown offered to him on a platter but refused it because he loved his honour and his people above everything else! He wouldn't break his oath because to do so would harm both country and countrymen. Can you find such a man in these days of greed, rampant corruption and nasty politicking?'

'No way, no way!' Evening said. 'Our politicians are very small people: no stature at all.'

'But what happened to the rest of the people who did not follow Sajar? Did they all become Hindus?' Donald asked.

I said, 'No. Because of the actions of Sajar, the syiem was too scared to force his will upon the people. There were many, of course, who converted, but many more remained true to their ancestral religion.'

'However,' Bah Kit added, 'slowly and slowly, ha, the influence of Hinduism was felt even among them. Instead of only calling upon God, U Blei, the Dispenser, the Creator, sometimes the believers of Niam Khasi Niam Tre would also pray to Hindu deities. And this practice has remained. Another influence of Hinduism among the Pnars, non-Christians, that is, is the avoidance of beef and the naming of their children after Hindu gods and goddesses like Ram, Lakhon, Durga, Lakshmi and so on.'

'You know what?' Magdalene asked. 'Religion can split a nation into two. Living in these times, we should keep that in mind.'

'You are right, Mag, religion is divisive even now,' Bah Kit said. 'But let us come back to the main theme. You see, Ham, many people in Ri Bhoi, Ri Maram and even Ri Khynriam in East Khasi Hills migrated from Ri Pnar. How can you say that we are not the same? Not only that, ha, there are families who now consider themselves Jaiñtias but were originally Khynriams. They migrated east out of necessity or because they were taken there by their fathers. The Lamares are one of them, Ham.'

'What? I have never heard of such a thing! Are you serious? My father is a Lamare, ya! He uses his father's clan name of Lyngdoh, of course, but originally he's a Lamare.'

'I can tell you the story if you want,' Bah Kit promised.

Evening laughed at Hamkom and said, 'Hahaha, a historian who knows nothing about the history of his own father's clan! This is too much.'

But nobody paid him much mind because Bah Kynsai interrupted to say, 'No, no, no! Now, na, Kit, we will talk about us as a people, and the challenges, internal and external, we are facing. Tomorrow we can talk about name stories, nothing but name stories.'

Magdalene, however, did not seem to have heard that. She said, 'I love the story of Sajar Ñiangli, Bah Kit, but I'm also curious about the Umïam Lake. Ap said it means weeping water, no? But why weeping water? Is there a story behind it?'

Still flushed with the excitement of telling the Sajar Ñiangli story, Bah Kit said, 'Yes, there is. It's a story about two river nymphs ...'

☙

A long, long time ago, when the world was still young, when the spirits still rubbed shoulders with humans, two sisters lived on the slopes of the sacred mountain known as Lum Shyllong. People believed them to be the daughters of U Lei Shyllong, the guardian spirit of the mountain. The elder of the two was called Ka Ïam and the younger, Ka Khen. Although they were sisters, they were as different as day and night. Ïam was robust and active and spent most of her time wandering about, exploring the countryside, going on picnics with friends, singing and dancing and banging drums and cymbals.

In short, she was unfit for work and was always leaving her sister and mother to do the cleaning around the house.

Khen, on the other hand, was more of a homebody and was more caring in her attitude to both the house and their mother. Her sister used to tease her for being timid and introverted. One day, after their morning meal, Ïam said to her sister, 'I have never seen a nymph as faint-hearted as you are. You have no sense of adventure at all. Why don't you go out with us today? We are going to explore the northern country up to Kamrup. We have been told there is plenty of fish there, especially *khasaw*, the reddish trout we have been talking about every day. I have not seen many fish here except for the smelts, the little shalynnai and the common carp, who are my friends. Come with us, and we'll bring back enough khasaw to keep us company for a lifetime. But I warn you; we'll be gone for several days.'

Khen was not very keen to go. She said, 'I don't know, Kongkong. You people are going right away, but I still have to help our mother with the cleaning and washing ...'

'It's okay, you can follow us later.'

'That's all right, but what about Mother? We'll be gone for several days ...'

'Why do you worry about Mother? She is more active than you are; she can take care of herself.'

'Still, I don't feel like leaving home for so many days.'

Ïam then tempted her by saying, 'If you beat me to Kamrup, you can keep all the khasaw for yourself, but only if you beat me.'

'How can I beat you if you are leaving earlier?'

'Well, we won't be travelling very fast, we'll dally about. I'm sure you can catch up with us.'

Ïam had no intention of travelling slowly now that a wager was on, but to lure her sister, she said she would not only go slow but would even wait for her somewhere on the way so they could have a proper race.

Finally, after a long argument, Khen was persuaded to follow her sister on the journey. 'You must keep your word to give me all the khasaw if I beat you to the place,' she warned her sister.

Amused, Ïam thought: Hahaha, you beating me, that's a big laugh! But out loud, she said, 'I promise.'

Ïam began her journey immediately. Her friends, the crab, the smelts, the common carp, the tadpole and the little shalynnai gathered around her. Because the route was a difficult one, passing through dense forests and deep gorges, she turned herself into a river to make it easier for her friends. True to form, she and her friends enjoyed themselves thoroughly on the way, exploring the new landscape, singing and dancing and playing music all the time so that the whole countryside along their route echoed with the sounds of their rejoicing.

When they reached a place called Parin Shohksing, Ïam and her friends sat down on a large stone platform to eat. After the meal, they wanted to relax a little and entertained themselves by playing on their drums, big and small, their cymbals and wind instruments, the *tangmuris*. As some of them played, the others sang and danced and had so much fun that they forgot all about Ïam's wager with her sister. But one of her friends spied Khen at a distance, running very fast towards Kamrup. Khen, not knowing her sister's route, had also turned herself into a river and chosen a different, more direct course so that she could make up for lost time. That was how she had got much further along to Kamrup than her sister.

When Ïam came to know of this, she was filled with regret that she had wasted time on frivolities. She had underestimated her sister. Ïam became desperate: how can I allow a feeble thing like her to beat me? It will shame me throughout the world. 'We must go, we must go!' she told her friends. Leaving all the musical instruments behind, she rushed headlong over cliffs and gorges, digging deep pools, excavating caves from the soft earth, and carrying everything before her: stones, boulders and trees. When she reached the territories of Mala Kongngor, the guardian spirit of Raij Nongtung, the Province of Nongtung, she tried to overwhelm farmlands and paddy fields so she could overtake her sister. But Mala Kongngor refused to let her through. He threatened her with dire consequences and blocked her path with huge obstacles.

There was no option but to take a long detour to the left, even though it would make the journey longer and slower. She tried to make up for it by jumping into gullies and ravines to shorten the way, but to no avail. When she got to Kamrup, Khen was already there, collecting all the khasaw.

Ïam was shattered. How could a weakling like her sister defeat her? She was so ashamed that she never returned home but went to hide in a place near the villages of Sohïong and Marpna in Ri Maram, and decided to remain a river forever. Inconsolable, she spent her days weeping, bemoaning her fate. That is why people say that, before the dam was built, when one listened to the rushing of her waters, one could hear a weird weeping sound. This was one reason why the river became known as Umïam Khwan, weeping water, at Khwan. The other meaning of the name is 'the water of Ïam'.

Meanwhile, saddened by what had happened to her sister, Khen also decided to remain a river forever, and from then on, she became known as Umkhen, 'the water of Khen'. Even today, you can find plenty of khasaw in the River Umkhen, but none can be found in Umïam, or so the saying goes.

Magdalene smiled happily. 'I never realised how imaginative our people can be, ya!' she said.

'There are many such stories, Mag,' Bah Kit told her.

'Okay,' Donald said, 'you have been talking about river names and so on, ha, but nobody has told me what the word "Khasi" means.'

That stopped all conversation, as we tried to think what Khasi might actually mean. Donald was one curious son of a gun. Finally, it was Hamkom who broke the silence, and typically, his answer was lifted from some British writer. 'The earliest reference to the name Khasi can be found in James Rennell's map published in 1780,' he said. 'Rennell, now known as the Father of Indian Geography, referred to Khasis as Cussey. Later, Lindsay called them Cusseah, and other colonial writers spelt the word Khasi as Cossyah, Cossia, Khassyah, Kasia and Khyee. Even Thomas Jones referred to us as Cassia. It was only the later Welsh missionaries who first used the name Khasi as we use it. But I haven't heard a single satisfactory explanation about the root or meaning of the word.'

'That's not true,' Evening said. 'You cannot say that Rennell made the earliest reference to the word Khasi. Thousands of years before the white men came, the *dkhars* called us Khasia. Either because the word Khasi sounded to them too much like khasi-sardi or because they could not pronounce it. Many of the white men followed their example.'

A dkhar is a 'non-Khasi'—the term usually refers to people from the plains of India and the rest of South Asia. But Khasis also call the white man a *dkhar lieh* or *kharlieh*, that is, a white non-Khasi. The non-tribal communities of Meghalaya used to consider the word pejorative. But it is not. It can, of course, be used pejoratively, depending on the tone of voice, but mostly it just means non-Khasi. Another reason why it is not always pejorative is the fact that we actually have a clan called 'Dkhar' (Hamkom's clan), which is prosperous and well-respected. How this came about is a story for later, although some mention of it has been made earlier.

'No one should put too much faith in what non-Khasi writers write on the subject, na, Ham?' Bah Kynsai said. 'They are themselves ignorant. What we should do is listen to our own stories, as Bah Su said. In this case, na, one of our stories tells us that we are known as Khasis because our first ancestress was a woman by the name of Si. Kha means "to be born of", and Si was her name. This also explains why our culture is matrilineal.'

'Why didn't you say that earlier, you joker?' Magdalene teased Bah Kynsai.

'Oho! I was trying to recall the story, na?'

'But that is only a story, Bah Kynsai,' Donald insisted. 'What I'm really getting at is why anybody should be proud of his Khasi identity when he is not even sure what the word means.'

'We are sure about the meaning of the word,' Raji interrupted. 'Khasi, born of Si. Bah Kynsai has just told you. We didn't have a written history, okay, our stories have been serving us as history for thousands of years, get that into your thick skull.'

'Besides,' Evening said, 'we have already discussed your views on the subject, no? What more do you want? For me, the name Khasi denotes the seven sub-tribes of Khynriam, U Pnar, U Bhoi, U War, et cetera. I'm quite happy with that. Now, take you, for instance, you don't know the meaning of your own name, Donald Lachlan! But you know that it denotes you and that you are identified by it, aren't you happy with that?'

'Okay, okay, let me put it this way: why are you so worried about Khasi identity? I heard you talking about the problems and dangers that beset our people everywhere; I don't see any of these dangers, what are you talking about?'

'You don't see them because you are blind,' Evening fumed. 'Let me summarise the predicament of the Khasi people today, and when you are truly familiar with it, you too might feel a sense of fear. Even the more populous Assamese are very much under threat from the problem of influx, are you aware of that? About one-third of Assam is, in fact, dominated by migrants from East Pakistan ...'

'East Pakistan or Bangladesh?' Bah Kynsai asked.

'From East Pakistan in the past, and now from Bangladesh, Bah Kynsai. The other parts of Assam are also teeming with people from all over the country, and elsewhere. And, for your information, Donald Lachlan, Khasi Land is faring even worse! We are being assailed from every side. Bangladeshis are infiltrating our urban centres from West Bengal and Assam; they acquire Indian citizenship through a network of corrupt officials. A sizeable portion of Garo Hills is already dominated by them. From there, they come to places like Shillong, the border areas with Assam and the coal belts of Ri Pnar.

'The Assam government is also encroaching on our territories every day. One of the strategies it uses is to push Nepali settlers and ethnic groups like

Karbis and Rabhas into Khasi villages. It backs up this kind of resettlement programme with its own police and paramilitary forces. News of atrocities committed on Khasi villagers, either by the Assam police or the settlers themselves, are published frequently in the local press. Despite that, our leaders offer not even lip service, forget real service, to the villagers. The Khasi public and NGOs raise a hue and cry, only to stop when it falls off the news. That's why Bah Kynsai has often compared us to pine leaves that catch fire quickly but burn out as quickly, no, Bah Kynsai? We have a single infiltration check gate near Byrnihat, and you know what those damn inspectors do? They climb into buses, raise their necks like roosters, and climb down again. At night, they reportedly extort from every "alien-looking" fellow and let him go. It's a bloody joke!

'And that's not all. Added to the influx of foreigners, we have the migration of Indian communities from the mainland to contend with. Ask Raji, ask Bah Kynsai, they'll tell you the same thing. You yourself must have seen the plight of Shillong. It's hardly an exaggeration to say that we are already a minority there, except in some localities. And do you know what is even more worrying? This situation is being replicated in many other urban centres, especially those bordering Assam and Bangladesh. And also, we can never forget the encroachment by Garos on Khasi towns and villages. You are laughing? You think I'm joking? Do you know that some armed Garo outfits have been clamouring for a greater Garo Land that would also comprise about one-third of West Khasi Hills and parts of Ri Bhoi district? Their justification? A Garo population dominates these areas.

'A person has to be deaf and blind and traitorous not to speak about issues that distress our society. Let people say what they will, this is a reality that has to be taken seriously and must be feared, for unless it is feared, no one is going to do anything about it.'

Donald, Hamkom and Magdalene were not convinced. Donald spoke on their behalf when he said, 'I still think you are a fearmonger and too bloody jingoistic by far. This argument that the influx of migrants will swamp us out of existence is just a bogeyman to frighten little children. Since coming to Shillong, you know, Ham, I have heard so many people talk about Soso Tham, our so-called national bard, and how he frightened people by saying that he saw his country on the edge of a terrible precipice. According to him, if we did not wake up, the flash flood of influx would overwhelm us and we would be like the people of Gebion, cutting wood and carrying water for some unknown masters. More than a hundred years have passed since he said that, but has any of it come true? Are we slaves now? Hardly. We have political power. Most of the bureaucrats and police officers are ours. We still have control over our own affairs, no, Ham?'

'Yeah, yeah, very much so!' Hamkom agreed. 'But you know, Don, some NGOs are asking for the Inner Line Permit to be extended here, okay, which means that an Indian citizen would need a permit to enter our state, can you imagine that? Don't you think this is an incredibly retrogressive move? What if other states demand the same, would we be able to go anywhere for studies, treatment, et cetera? These damn NGOs are plain obstructionist, man! When the government wanted to construct a railway head in Byrnihat, ha, they objected because of the fear of influx. When it wanted to expand the airport, they objected on the ground of land-loss for the locals. In fact, they have objected to every big development project the government has wanted to bring in. At this rate, how do you expect the state to progress, man?'

'I heard they are even objecting to the presence of the armed forces here, no, Ham?' Donald asked. 'Don't they know that it's because of the armed forces that the entire country, indeed the world, knows and takes notice of our state as a place of great strategic importance? And if not for the armed forces, ha, Shillong would have lost most of its green cover. Their presence also means much-needed assistance in times of calamity or during a terrorist attack. And that is not such an unlikely possibility, okay? After all, we have many militant outfits in the region, no? The contribution of the forces goes unnoticed, though some people talk about their commendable services, especially in the rural areas ... Everything is ignorance, narrow-mindedness, xenophobia and communal prejudice, Ham, don't you think so?'

Evening was furious. He had tried to interrupt Hamkom and Donald at various points without succeeding. But now he said, 'So, you think Soso Tham was only a fearmongering poet? Let me give you just one example to disprove that. Do you know anything about the timber trade in the state before it was banned? The big gainers were all big-shot non-tribal traders. And what about the Khasis? They were mostly cutting wood for them! Was Soso Tham very wrong then?

'And you think the fear of influx is but a kind of bogeyman? Then you are greater fools than I thought. Go, take another look at Shillong. Go to the border areas with Assam and Bangladesh. Go to the coal belts of Ri Pnar and West Khasi Hills to see what's happening. Go there, and you will see that this is a real and present danger. Haven't you heard about the recent Gauhati High Court ruling? The court has directed the Assam and Central governments to complete the fencing along the state's international border with Bangladesh without further delays and excuses. And why? Because illegal infiltration from that country has to be stopped immediately. While issuing the ruling, Justice B.K. Sharma asked the Centre and the state governments to "seriously attend, not on paper only, but with practical effort", to the grave problem of illegal migration. He also observed that it must be given priority, keeping in mind the duty of the Union of India to protect every state against external aggression and internal disturbance.

'Now, do you still think influx is but a hoax? Even Ap's closest friend, Koiri, who's a first-rate writer, by the way, is dead against influx and all non-tribals, no, Ap? Remember what he said to Nigel Jenkins? "I want there to be violence, blood, deaths and to kick out all non-tribals ..." He said that, no, Ap?'

'I'm sorry to disappoint you, Ning, but he never said any of those things,' I said. 'In fact, he wrote a very long letter of protest to Nigel in which he accused him of putting words in his mouth. I have the letter on my phone. Give me a minute ... Ah, here it is.

'He says, "I never saw you scribbling away on your notepad while I was talking. What you probably did was to recreate our conversation alone at night after a few pints of the potent Indian beer, and in the process, I think you got quite a few things wrong. I still remember what transpired during our taxi conversation on riot-based topics. I remember you asking me if I would like to see an Albania-like situation here. My answer was a resounding 'No!' Later, we spoke about our ancestors, and I remember quoting from the words of Tirot Sing Syiem, our freedom fighter, who said to the British, 'Better to live like a free man than to rule like a vassal king.' I also said that the old ones used to refer to this land as '*Ka ri umsnam u kñi u kpa*', the land soaked with the blood of our uncles and fathers. This is a powerful message, and whenever our very existence was threatened by oppressive outsiders (including the British), the old ones used to remind everyone about it. In fact, the old ones never spoke only of 'peace and development', but laid great stress on 'peace and security', which really means that there can be no peace without security. And if our security is threatened, their message is very clear in the statement, '*Ka ri umsnam u kñi u kpa*'."

'Nigel admitted his mistake and had the words erased from *Through the Green Doors*.'

'That's it, that's it. Ka ri umsnam u kñi u kpa! There must be not only peace and development but also peace and security! And if the migrants threaten our very existence, we must do what we can to ensure our safety, you understand, you idiots? And our demand for the Inner Line Permit is not retrogressive either! Do you know that it is already in place in Arunachal Pradesh, Mizoram and Nagaland? If it is working perfectly well there, why not here? ILP is just another measure to stop the illegal infiltration that the court spoke so strongly about. Also, keep in mind, you two, even the majority Marathis objected to the presence of Hindi-speaking people in Maharashtra, or am I wrong?

'You say that we still have political power? That is a myth! The moneyed class controls political power; you of all people should know that. In our case, that means non-tribal businessmen. And don't pretend to know anything about police officers and bureaucrats! Did you do a count before saying that most of them are Khasis? Do you know that, in both services, we still have a joint cadre with Assam? This fact alone has ensured that most of the top bureaucrats and police officers are not Khasis. Think before you speak, you fools!

'As for the armed forces, Donald …'

At that point, Bah Kynsai intervened and said, 'Ning, Ning, let me speak about the armed forces. But first, let me say that the migration from other Indian states is not as serious as that from the neighbouring countries. Why? Because people from other Indian states have a home they can go back to, na, whenever the situation demands, na? But those from the neighbouring countries are truly down-and-out desperadoes and are, therefore, very dangerous. Don't you agree, Ning?'

Evening did not agree. 'Bah Kynsai, there are so many of them, no? And if we do anything against them, ha, their compatriots in their home states will start fighting for them, and then what will happen to us, huh?'

'That is also there, of course, but I still think they are not as dangerous as the other migrants, Ning,' Bah Kynsai insisted. Then turning to Donald, he said, 'Now, about the armed forces … First of all, na, Don, nobody wants Shillong or our state to be known for its strategic importance. You know why? Because we don't want to be noticed by Ma Shoi, na? You don't know what Ma Shoi means? Chinese Uncle. In case of war, na, Shillong will be the first to be bombed, man! Have you seen what happened to cities in Syria after a bombing campaign? You don't want that sort of thing here, do you? That's the reason why Article 11 of the 1956 New Delhi Draft Rules exists. It's based on international humanitarian law and urges avoidance of the permanent presence of armed forces, military material and mobile military establishments in towns or other places with a large civilian population. The presence of military establishments in the very heart of the city is a direct infringement of this rule, don't you see that, Don?

'Secondly, na, the armed forces have not endeared themselves to the local population. They are seen by many, rightly or wrongly, as the biggest land grabbers around here. Historically speaking, ha, the land occupied by military establishments today was leased out by local landowners to the British Army. When the British left, na, all treaties and agreements between the local authorities and the British government were supposed to be cancelled, and all the land taken and leased by the British was supposed to revert to the original landowners. But what did our armed forces do? Taking advantage of the ignorance and illiteracy of the local landowners, na, they acted as the legal heirs of the British Army, and took possession of all the land that should have gone back to the local landowners. The result? We are now surrounded by so-called defence land.'

'Can't anything be done about this, Bah Kynsai?' Evening asked.

'What can anybody do? Nobody has any papers, na? Only the state government can work something out with the Centre, acquire the land for public use or something, but what can you expect from the buggers that have been governing our state, huh?

'You speak of the services rendered by the armed forces to the local population, Don. I don't know how you came to learn about these services in Delhi, but here, na, we only know of their disservice. Do you remember that time, Bah Su, when the military closed off all the public thoroughfares in Shillong, supposedly because they cut through defence land? A friend and I wrote a long letter to the editor, ha, and among other things, we pointed out that if the military prevents us from going to the market and offices and so on through their so-called land, na, then the military should also stop using roads constructed by our civilian authorities. After that, they opened the damn things really quick, liah!

'Recently, the armed forces rejected the state government's plan to construct flyovers in the city because they would have to go through defence land, does that sound to you like public service, Don? And what is the consequence? Shillong has been staggering every single day under the burden of the massive traffic jams that nobody can do anything about because of the armed forces' arrogance. In Mizoram, na, they have been able to move the military out of the capital, why can't our government do the same here?'

'But has the military actually moved out of Aizawl, Bah Kynsai?' Hamkom asked pointedly.

'The process has already started. But you, na, Don, you speak without knowing anything about the local conditions. You credited the army with maintaining the green cover in Shillong, do you know who planted most of the trees there? All the forest cover that you see on the slopes of Shillong Peak, na, is because of the British government, which had initiated a massive social forestry project to protect the catchment areas, which now supply water to half of Shillong. It's got nothing to do with our military. In fact, the Indian Army is now claiming ownership over these catchment areas as well, and for what? People say the army's top brass are trying to strip the hill slopes bare so they can supply timber for the construction of staff quarters somewhere in the mainland. This may or may not be true, but the very fact that they are claiming the catchment areas as theirs and marking out trees for large-scale felling, ha, has already betrayed their anti-people attitude. Thanks to Laban and its dorbar shnong, the village council, na, till now, they have not been able to implement their plans ...'

'What did the dorbar do, Bah Kynsai?' Evening asked eagerly.

'Through its headman, ha—he died recently, may he eat betel nut in the house of God—the council challenged the army's claims in the High Court and won the case, liah, but the army appealed to the Supreme Court, and now the battle is being fought there, as well as in the court of the NGT. For the sake of the people and their water supply, na, everyone should pray that the army doesn't win. And you, Don, think before you speak, man!'

'Good, good, Bah Kynsai,' Evening said. 'But we must also denounce his accusation of Khasis as xenophobic, narrow-minded and communal, ha! Even your namesake, Donald Trump, is xenophobic. Illegal migrants are a real threat, don't you see? And if they are a threat to the WASPs of America, if they are a threat to the Brits who voted for Brexit, if they are a threat to the Europeans who are closing their borders, if they are a threat to the Australians who set up that infamous camp in Papua New Guinea, should we not see them as a threat too, especially since our community is so small? There's another point I want to raise here: to be communally prejudiced is a very human thing, no, Bah Kynsai? Every community is communal in that sense, except Khasis, the dumbasses! Among us, there are many cosmos like you and Mag and Hamkom, who cannot even see the terrible threat posed by the influx of these migrants. The rest of India is not only communal but downright racist. How can you be blind to that when you live in Delhi? Because you look like an Anglo or what? Many of us who appear Tibeto-Burman or South-east Asian, ha, have suffered racist attacks, verbal attacks at least, from the mainlanders. Do you know that when we go to a hotel, the receptionist asks us for a passport? The plain truth is that most people from the Northeast are not even considered Indians, you know that?'

People from the Northeast are indeed mistaken for Chinese, Japanese, Koreans or South-east Asians. Sometimes this can be quite absurd. Meghalaya's border with Bangladesh, for instance, is guarded by the Border Security Force, but the BSF jawans have little affinity with the villagers they are supposed to guard, since they don't look like them or speak like them or even dress like them. They have much more in common with the Bangladeshis, whom they are trying, half-heartedly, to keep out. This lack of affinity has caused so many misunderstandings between the jawans and the locals that people have started demanding a border force formed exclusively of the local population.

In India, racism is a complex phenomenon. Where does racism end and where does discrimination based on caste or tribe begin? It isn't easy to make out. What is clear is that we, who do not look like the mainlanders, are the 'other'. We are people to be wary of.

I was pulled out of my thoughts by Magdalene, who was shouting something abusive at Evening. I heard only the last part in which she compared him with Donald Trump and declared, 'You should be ashamed of yourself!'

Evening was about to answer back when Bah Su said, 'Just the other day, ha, I was listening to a heated debate. One group wanted to stop the influx; the other group maintained a position exactly like theirs.' He pointed at Hamkom, Magdalene and Donald. 'This group,' he went on, 'said the fear of influx was not only unwholesome xenophobia but also downright unpatriotic because other Indians were being prevented from settling where they liked, as guaranteed by the Constitution. At that moment, it started to rain. You remember the hailstorm that came towards the end of January? It began with one or two big drops. Initially, the raindrops vanished into the parched earth. But soon, the rain came down as if poured from a bamboo tube, and the earth that had sucked in the few drops at first now became completely submerged by the overflowing water.

'When that happened, a friend of mine told the two groups, "Before you continue with your wrangling, have a look at the rain. Can you tell me what happened just now?"

'When no one was able to answer him, he said, "Think back carefully. When the rain came, the first few drops vanished into the earth, didn't they?

But what happened when the rain became a downpour? The ground became sodden and was soon submerged by the water that rushed in like a flash flood. This flash flood, young men, is precisely like the influx about which you have been talking. Migrating people are like rainwater. First, they come in ones and twos, and we treat them with great courtesy and kindness. We give them jobs and land to stay. We say, 'Poor fellows, they have nothing back home, let us accommodate them and treat them nicely.' But when they have become warm in our hearths and homes, they encourage others, their relatives and friends, to come, and soon, before we know what's happening, they are everywhere, like this rainwater."

'You see, Don, when migrants have overwhelmed the local population, what use is political power, what use are your bureaucrats and police officers?'

'But they have not, have they?' Donald countered.

'In some places they have, in some places they have not, but if the problem is left unchecked, they will, eventually. Even the High Court has made that clear. And in a democracy where the majority rules, ha, this is truly dangerous. I think, instead of criticising our people for being worried about the problem of illegal migration, we should think it through sensibly. Is influx only a tool to frighten people? Is it parochialism and communal prejudice? Or is it the Silent Invasion that all of us should fear?'

Hamkom spoke up now. "'Fear," said Francis Johnson, "should not be suffered to tyrannise in the imagination, to raise phantoms of horror, or to beset life with supernumerary distresses."'

"'Early and provident fear is the mother of safety,"' Bah Kynsai said. 'That was Edmund Burke. Here's another one: "Fear is wholesome if it leads to vigilance and circumspection."'

'And that's by?' Raji asked.

'That's by me,' Bah Kynsai said with a laugh.

Most of us laughed with him, and much of the tension visibly evaporated, but then Evening said again, 'Bah Su has hit the nail on the head, ha! Influx *is* a silent invasion; Bah Kynsai also used to say that. And you, Donald Lachlan, who do not even know the meaning of your own name, think deeply before you speak, because you are beginning to sound like the local chatterati.'

'What's wrong with that?' Donald asked belligerently.

'Nothing, nothing at all,' Bah Kynsai said quickly, before another quarrel could break out. 'Just as there's nothing wrong with chattering monkeys, okay, there's nothing wrong with the chatterati either,' he added.

Everyone, even Donald, laughed with him.

The discussion on migration subsided for a while. Donald had borne the brunt of the attack from Evening. However, he was supported by Magdalene and Hamkom, who, in addition to sharing Donald's opinion, maintained that they had plenty of non-tribal friends and that they did not feel threatened at all by them. But that, I thought, is a different matter altogether. I, too, have many non-Khasi friends, some of them among my closest. But you do not feel threatened by individuals. You feel threatened by the abstract idea of a numerous 'other'. The moment this 'other' is broken down to individuals, your reactions become quite different. What you feel is fondness or aversion, depending upon the person's qualities, that's all.

The question of influx, as far as I can see, is a frustrating one. What Evening said is quite true, and the situation is often worsened by the district election officers' overenthusiasm in registering every migrant as a legitimate voter. A case in point was what happened in Sohra in 2015 when the sub-divisional election officer there forcibly registered hundreds of migrants from Bangladesh on the voters' list despite strong opposition from the village authorities. Also, while the governments of India and Meghalaya may be expected to do something about the influx from the neighbouring countries, how are they to tackle the issue of migration from other Indian states? Has not the Constitution of the country guaranteed freedom of movement to all Indians, including us, within the territories of India? The government cannot make a move that contravenes the provisions of the Constitution in any way. But when the people concerned feel threatened by large-scale migration from the more populous ethnic groups, they may resort to direct action. And that is a recipe for disaster.

That's why some people have been saying that if the Government of India is serious about safeguarding the identity of minority tribes, it should adopt a dual citizenship policy. Every citizen of India must also be registered as the citizen of a particular state, and once registered as the citizen of that state, he cannot be a citizen of another. This will prevent migrants (including those of us who have emigrated) from voting in any but their own states. And when they are no longer seen as vote banks, politicians will start taking the problem of influx seriously.

Hamkom started the discussion again by asking why NGOs that were so strongly opposed to the influx had not allowed the Centre to fence the Indo-Bangladesh border. Raji explained that the Co-ordination Committee on International Border, a conglomeration of several NGOs, had not objected to the border fencing per se but only to the government's plan to erect the fence 150 yards inside Indian territory. The committee, Raji said, wanted the government to build the fence along the Zero Line so that local farmers would not lose their agricultural land to Bangladesh. Actually, he added, quoting a statement from the BSF, about 385 kilometres of fencing had been completed in the state, and only about eighty-eight kilometres of disputed land remained to be fenced in.

Hamkom suddenly erupted: 'These bloody NGOs are real pests! As I said before, no, Don, mindless obstructionists, every one of them! They even opposed uranium mining, ya, can you imagine that? Domiasiat and Kylleng-Pyndeng-Sohiong in West Khasi Hills sit atop the largest uranium deposits in India, and these buggers won't allow anyone to mine the ore! Can you imagine that sort of thing happening anywhere else? They would have been arrested and prosecuted, if not shot! These people are nothing but *khynnah tuh*, thieving boys!'

'Mining uranium?' Evening shouted. 'Are you crazy? Do you know what will happen if we allow the mining of uranium? It's not only NGOs that are protesting; a majority of the Khasi people are also against it, don't you know that? And why? Because they know what will happen if uranium is mined, no?'

'What will happen, tell me? Scientists all over India, including those from our university, have written in favour of uranium mining, do you think these scientists are fools?'

'They may not be fools, but they are certainly arse-lickers of the worst kind, and with axes to grind!' Evening retorted.

'This is another example of fearmongering of the worst kind, Ham,' Donald observed. 'Only those who are ignorant and obtuse can raise their voice against uranium mining. They should think of the massive benefits to the country instead of quaking in fear at the supposed evil effects of the mineral.'

'Whom are you calling ignorant and obtuse, you fraud? Delhi scholar, my arse! You are nothing but a fraud!'

'Calm down, calm down,' Bah Kynsai pacified the two, 'let's discuss this in a civilised manner, na, liah!'

'You haven't answered my question: what will happen if the uranium is mined?' Hamkom asked again.

'What will happen?' Evening thundered. 'If the mining of coal and stones and sand can destroy rivers and all aquatic life forms and render the water unfit for consumption, what do you think will happen to the environment when uranium is mined, huh? Have you seen the River Umtyngngar on the way to Sohra? Have you seen what has happened to it because of the stone and sand quarries? It used to be one of the most scenic sites in the whole of the Khasi Hills. The water was crystal clear and fast running. There were flatlands by the banks, lush with carpet grass. Umtyngngar was an ideal picnic spot; everybody used to go there for a day out. Tourists going to Sohra could not pass it without stopping. It was that beautiful! But now? There's hardly any water: sand flows there instead. All the fish and smelts are dead. And in winter, even the huge boulders are clogged with that sickening yellow sand. If this is what sand and stone quarries can do, how dare you talk to us about uranium mining? How dare you imply that nothing will happen to the environment?'

'No, no, no, you don't understand!' Hamkom said. 'The mining of uranium will not be the same as the haphazard mining of coal or sand by some businessmen, don't you get it? It will be done scientifically and with no risk at all to the environment. It's going be managed by the Government of India, no?'

'Who are you trying to fool, Ham?' Bah Kynsai asked. 'Forget about mining, even the exploration for uranium is dangerous, na? Before mining, they need to find out exactly where the uranium is densely located and also determine its quality. But that kind of exploration can be risky, you know that? Taking rock samples can disturb the uranium ore and release its radioactive decay into the biosphere. Once exposed to air and moisture, na, the composition changes and radioactive dust particles can spread through water and air. When drilling occurs, na, Ham, the exploration may disturb underground uranium deposits, which can then leach into underground water reservoirs, potentially contaminating drinking water aquifers … No, no, uranium is too dangerous, man.'

'And I for one,' Evening stated, 'do not believe that the Uranium Corporation of India will care enough about "the ignorant and obtuse tribals" to spend crores of rupees in scientific mining and safety measures. Besides, however scientific the mining may be, ha, there will always be tailings waste dumped in man-made lakes or tailings ponds. These ponds would be full of radioactive components.'

'Like?' Hamkom challenged.

'Uranium waste contains lethal and concentrated dosages of Rodon-222 and Radium-226 in the natural components of soil, water and plants,' Evening continued, evidently recalling some article he'd read on the subject.

'The two are a major cause of cancer in humans, and they can be transmitted through inhalation or through water and edible plants. Not only that, okay, the proposed cosmopolitan mining township of about five square kilometres (equivalent in size to about half of Shillong), along with a mining zone of about a hundred square kilometres, will displace lakhs of people from the area. Where will they go, huh? The Khasi-inhabited districts are small; their total area is only 14,262 square kilometres; what will you do with all those people? If you rehabilitate them elsewhere, what will they do for a living? Jhamela, jhamela! And then, mark my words, the cosmopolitan character of the mining township will also upset the demographic profile of the area. The illiterate and semi-literate landowners and farmers will be forced to move out of their holdings to give way to technologically advanced people from outside the state. The township will become like a cantonment, prohibited to all locals. All this will have a destructive and tragic impact upon our small community, it will be a bitter assault upon us. Are you willing to let that happen, you two?'

Donald responded, 'Think of the positive side, man, why are you people always thinking negatively? Think about how uranium can provide us with clean, safe and cheap energy.'

'Aha, Don, you are speaking like a fool again!' Bah Kynsai said sharply. 'You call everyone who is against uranium mining an ignoramus, na, but you yourself are speaking like one. First of all, it is a myth that nuclear power is safe, ha. Atomic energy is fraught with danger at every step—mining, transportation, storage, utilisation, the management of the end product— danger everywhere. Radiation-related diseases around uranium mines and nuclear facilities are well known. Watch the film *Buddha Weeps in Jadugoda*, and you might also weep a little, liah.

'And, another thing, Don, till today there's no foolproof method of safeguarding nuclear facilities, okay? In fact, India has a very poor track record in this matter ... Wait, wait ...'

Bah Kynsai took out his mobile phone and scrolled down rapidly. Then he said, 'According to this report, ha, about 300 incidents of a serious nature have occurred at Indian nuclear facilities, causing radiation leaks and injuries to workers, though these have remained close-kept official secrets. And around Chernobyl, na, after the nuclear accident, na, it was found that 50,000 to 100,000 liquidators, clean-up workers, working at the atomic plant, died between 1986 (the year of the accident) and 2006 while 540,000 to 900,000 liquidators became "invalids and disabled". Also, 12,000 to 83,000 children were born with congenital deformities during the years mentioned. Nuclear plants are a terrible danger to human lives, and this fact, na, was once again made clear in a study published in the *European Journal of Cancer Care* in July 2007. The study showed a rise of up to 24 per cent in cases of leukaemia among children living around nuclear facilities in Canada, France, Germany, the UK, Japan, Spain and the US. Does all this sound "safe" to you, Don?'

'But are these figures genuine, Bah Kynsai?' Donald asked.

'Uff, this Don! The study was conducted by the International Physicians for the Prevention of Nuclear War and the German Society for Radiation Protection, so why shouldn't they be genuine? And these reports were published in refereed journals, na, tdong! Now, about the other question of cheap energy, ha, that is also a myth, you know that? Nuclear power is actually one of the most expensive sources of energy. The cost of building a power plant based on coal is around 4.5 crore rupees per MW; the cost of building the natural gas-fired, combined-cycle gas turbines is around 3 crore rupees per MW. But the cost involved in producing power from a nuclear plant is around 10 crore rupees per MW. You see that? Do your own calculations now!'

'But would you rather have clean energy or energy from fossil fuel?' Donald persisted.

'I would rather have clean energy from the sun and the wind than from a nuclear power plant. It's too dangerous, man! Think about the horrendous accidents that have happened … Chernobyl, Fukoshima and a hundred others since 1952 …'

'Don't you have any pride at all in your country, Bah Kynsai?' Hamkom interrupted him. 'Don't you want to see India become one of the Super Nuclear Powers? This Domiasiat uranium can help our country humble Pakistan forever.'

'Ha!' Evening cried. 'Now you are warmongering!'

Bah Kynsai added: 'Why should lakhs of our people lose their land, suffer and die from terrible diseases just so our country can become a nuclear power, huh? The greater-common-good argument, na, Ham, does not always work, not when the lives of lakhs are at stake. Besides, don't you think nuclear non-proliferation is a good thing for the world? Or would you rather see an arms race in South Asia?'

'What about development?' Magdalene spoke for the first time. 'Doesn't uranium mining mean development for this incredibly backward part of the state? I heard UCIL has promised to build a hospital and roads to connect the villages with the rest of the state …'

'What development, Mag?' Bah Kynsai asked. 'The road the uranium corporation has promised to build, na, Mag, will be to facilitate the mining and transportation of uranium. I'm not against the road, okay? It should be built, but by our government, not by UCIL. And the hospital that you mentioned, na, UCIL is interested in it only because it will cater to the cantonment-like township of its own workers. First, you bring horrible diseases, and then you say you will build a hospital to treat them? Is that an argument that intelligent people like you should accept? What can a hospital do against cancer anyway? Do you remember what Hoping Stone said on the floor of the Assembly when the government was trying to construct a cancer institute in Shillong? He said, "Can anybody cure cancer? If nobody in the world can cure cancer, then the institute is a waste of time; the money should be invested elsewhere." That is how useful the Uranium Corporation of India will be to the people of Domiasiat, Mag.'

'What I don't understand is why you keep harping on the hazards of uranium mining when qualified scientists have given it a clean chit?' Hamkom whined.

'Yes, answer that, Bah Kynsai!' Magdalene cried triumphantly. 'And don't quote Hoping Stone either! We all know how well-informed he was about cancer.'

'Look, Ham, those scientists you speak of, na, are government agents,' Bah Kynsai replied. 'They draw their salaries and get their grants from the government. What else do you expect? Besides, the local NGOs and the people of Meghalaya are not the only ones protesting against uranium mining, na? People around the world are doing it. In fact, in some of the countries where uranium is found, na, even the governments agree about its ill-effects. There are global protests, not just local obstructionism as you put it.'

Evening added, 'Scientists will always serve the cause of science, ha, keep that in mind, otherwise they would be committing self-immolation. They are not always to be trusted, no, Bah Kynsai? Scientists, you must remember, also made the bomb that was dropped on Hiroshima. Anyway, in the Khasi Hills, ha, though the mining has not really started, the KSU has already reported the death of a large number of fish along the Kynshi and Rilang rivers, owing to exploratory mining activities by a private company working for UCIL. This took place near Porkut in West Khasi Hills. There were reports in all the papers, okay? The mine holes, it seems, were left uncovered, and when it rained, the overflowing water found its way into the two rivers, causing the disaster.'

'The Khasi Students' Union is also one of the NGOs opposing uranium mining, no? What do you expect them to say?' Hamkom said.

'The statement was corroborated by the local press after visiting the area, you fool!' Evening shouted, losing his temper again. 'And this is the main reason why Kong Spelity Lyngdoh Langrin had refused to sell or lease her land to UCIL, though she was offered millions of rupees ... Millions of rupees, imagine! Our crooked politicians would have swooned at the very mention of that kind of money, but Kong Spelity resisted UCIL for many years because she had seen with her own eyes what radioactive pollution caused by test mining could do. For your information, Kong Spelity was a ninety-year-old woman from uranium-rich Domiasiat. And for her, land meant a healthy life and freedom. In a documentary by Tarun Bhartiya ... yeah, yeah, that one, Raji, by the award-winning filmmaker ... In that film, ha, Kong Spelity is seen saying, "Give up my freedom? Can money buy me the freedom which this land gives?" If I must choose one hero from among the Khasi people, no, Bah Kynsai, I would choose her, not our corrupt and greedy politicians. She is my hero.'

Hamkom, however, said, 'I still don't believe the KSU, okay, they are also *khynnah kai*, mischief-making boys, who are always meddling in business that doesn't concern them. What is uranium mining to them? Why should they play politics rather than take up issues relating to students' welfare, huh? And before the High Court banned bandhs, you remember, Mag, they used to call for bandhs, road blockades, night curfews, agitation programmes and whatnot at the drop of a hat. Why should they meddle in politics? Is the KSU a training institute for future politicians or what?'

'No, no, no,' Bah Kynsai interrupted, 'you are wrong, Ham, to blame the KSU for the bandhs and shutdowns and agitations. Everybody was involved: NGOs, militants, and even political parties. But the way I see it, na, it is the media and the public that are to blame. The moment we see a bandh announced in the papers, ha, regardless of the organisation behind it, ha, all of us stop working, liah! Government employees do not attend office, shops do not open, taxis stop plying and everything is closed down. But when you walk on the streets, na, there's no one to stop you. My friends and I used to do that a lot, you know, just to check if volunteers were preventing our movements or not, but we never encountered anyone ...'

'A slight correction, Bah Kynsai,' said Evening. 'When the KSU called bandhs, ha, there used to be several volunteers at every strategic point. Many of their cadres were also arrested, remember?'

'Right, right,' Bah Kynsai agreed, 'but on our side of the town, na, when bandhs were imposed, na, we never encountered any enforcers on the streets, only policemen everywhere. And you know what? When they saw us, they would ask us where the hell we were going. It was as if the police were enforcing the bandh, liah, not the organisation that called it. My point is, if there is not a single volunteer to prevent or restrict our movement in any way, then why the hell should we stop going to work and close our shops? There's absolutely nothing to many of these bandh calls, except for the announcement in the papers. That's all. So why do we close down everything? I'll tell you why. Because we are lousy workers; we love the holidays that the bandhs give us. I'm telling you, even if you and I, in the name of some fake organisation, call for a bandh, na, people will immediately close down everything. The media and the public are to blame, no one else. But as you said, I'm glad the court has prevented the media from publishing announcements about bandh calls. Now we are truly and unhappily bandh-free!'

Bah Kynsai's analysis was received with a chorus of 'Ka dei, ka dei' ('That's right, that's right') and a lot of laughter.

But I fell to thinking about why, indeed, should students and NGOs interfere in governance, and why should young people stick their nose into politics? This question had been debated many times among us. If you think about it, everyone is a part of politics, whether they wish to be or not, unless they live in a vacuum. As Eisenhower once said, politics is a serious, complicated and, in its true sense, noble profession.

The truth, though, is that no government has ever worked conscientiously to provide good governance, and certainly none has truly cared for the well-being of the common person. That is why there have been agitations against governments from time to time, whether organised by student bodies, youth organisations or NGOs. Everywhere, young people who see, to quote H.L. Mencken, 'through shams with sharp and terrible eyes', have become the conscience-keepers of the world. However, I did not say anything, as I wanted to hear Evening's reaction to the tirade.

Evening did not disappoint. After Bah Kynsai had said his piece, he began, 'The question is not why students should meddle in politics, Hamkom, but why the bloody hell should anybody have to interfere? I'll tell you why, because our governments have been unbelievably uncaring and corrupt, that's why. They will not do anything right unless some NGO agitates. Do you know how corrupt our governments have been? I will not give you details, but they are so corrupt, ha, that whenever *India Today* publishes a list of the most corrupt states of India, Meghalaya always comes out near the top. Number two or number three in the list of most corrupt states! And in the list of most developed states? Number two or number three from the bottom! How is that, good enough for you?'

But Hamkom and Donald were not satisfied, and told Evening that if he was going to make such allegations, he should at least provide details.

'You want details? Okay, let me give you details: first, the education scam. In 2009, the education department conducted an exam to select suitable candidates for the posts of primary teachers, do you remember that? When the results were published, hundreds of candidates complained about gross anomalies. The High Court directed the Central Bureau of Investigation to investigate the matter, and what were the findings? The then director of mass and elementary education, who was quizzed by the CBI, confessed to changing marks in the score sheets at the behest of the education minister, can you believe that? The minister, he said, ordered him to apply an erasing fluid to remove the original marks given by examiners—and approved by the selection committee members—and replace them with the marks given by her. From that day, the erasing fluid has been given a new name— Tamperist! The scam itself became Scamperist, after Pamperist, the name of the minister.'

'But that's only an allegation by a corrupt official, no?' Hamkom protested.

'Oh, I forgot! She belongs to your locality! For your information, the director also handed over to the CBI incriminating documents and a file containing the list of names recommended by the minister and her friends and colleagues. Which made it an open-and-shut case for everyone but our rotten government. Instead of taking action against the culprits, it refused to accept the CBI report and decided to institute its own enquiry committee. How can an enquiry committee instituted by the government to investigate one of its own ministers be more authentic than a CBI enquiry, huh? All these years later, the government enquiry has not even started.'

Hamkom persisted with his defence. 'Any accused is innocent until proven guilty!'

Before Evening could respond, Bah Kynsai said, 'Some NGOs are pursuing the matter in court, na, so let's wait and see. If she's innocent, she should prove it in a court of law.'

'The system is rigged, no, Bah Kynsai?' Evening lamented. 'I doubt if the case will ever be resolved ...'

'The system is rigged? You sound like Donald Trump, leh, Ning,' Bah Kynsai laughed. 'But seriously, na, how can it not be rigged when Meghalaya is full of tamperists and scamperists who are led by a chief scamperist?'

Some of us laughed at that, but Evening did not. He only said despondently, 'I really don't know how we can develop such a despicable tolerance for corruption and call ourselves Christians! We should be called money-eaters from now on! Take the Khasi saying about development, for instance: *ka roi ka par*, the progress, the crawl. Do you know who is progressing? The ministers. And the people? They crawl. Ministers are millionaires; their children study abroad, roam about in flashy cars, party and drink, but the ordinary people? They don't have even the bare necessities like drinking water, electricity, roads, medicines and so on. Does that sound like corruption to you, Hamkom?'

'Hey, Ning, before you start crying, okay, listen to this good news,' Raji interrupted. 'You people haven't heard the latest about the education scam. Ning, the Supreme Court has quashed the formation of the high-level scrutiny committee set up by the government, and has referred the case back to the High Court. And the High Court has directed the CBI to conduct a second probe into the scam ...'

'Yahoo!' Evening shouted and punched the air in joy. 'We'll get them, Bah Kynsai, we'll get them yet! Now, let's see, what else do we have? Parliamentary secretaries! Do you remember what happened in 2003? The Ninety-first Amendment Act, which put a cap on the size of a government's council of ministers, was introduced in Parliament. And after that? Our then state government, which had as many as thirty-nine ministers out of sixty MLAs—thirty-nine, just think of it!—had to reduce the number to eleven. Now, imagine that kind of paring down! Who is to stand and who is to fall? Who is to sink and who is to float? Imagine the nights of anguish, the dark machinations, the stealthy calculations, the bitterness and bad blood. Imagine the cuts and the deals, the fawning and the threats, the blackmail and the gifts. Imagine all that racking indecision, the wavering, painful dilemma!

'So what did our scamperists do? To circumvent the Act and continue to keep the party MLAs happy, they appointed them as parliamentary secretaries. Isn't this political subterfuge an insult to the Constitution, especially when these fellows are provided pay and perks that are equal to a minister's? Every month, they receive an assured sum of more than one lakh rupees, plus variable allowances, a government vehicle, government accommodation, an office in the secretariat backed by support staff who are used as personal servants. And all this for what? For no work at all. For your information, parliamentary secretaries receive no files and are not required to assist ministers in any manner.

'And who, Hamkom, is trying to stop this blatant act of corruption and check the massive drain on the exchequer? Not pseudo-intellectuals like you, but a member of an NGO, someone called Madal Sumer. In 2016, he filed a PIL in the High Court, remember, Bah Kynsai? And what is the outcome? The court has declared the appointment of all parliamentary secretaries illegal! Are NGOs merely "mischief-making boys" then, you fraud?

'Do you want more details? What about the eighty "political appointees" that this government has approved, huh? Who are these indispensable people who have to be part of the government? Failed, defeated politicians and obscure sycophants! And what do they do? They head loss-making corporations and unnecessary bodies as chairmen and vice-chairmen, and many of them do not even call for a meeting of their boards. And for this shameless dereliction of duty, these freeloaders are given almost the same perks and facilities as the ministers! Amazing, no, Bah Kynsai?

'And what about the many other cases of corruption? In the Khasi Hills Autonomous District Council, there's a funny story about a check post collecting royalty from lorries along the Assam-Meghalaya border. Though manned by fifteen employees, collectively drawing lakhs of rupees in salaries per month, this check post gives the council an income of Rs 500 per year. Think about that! No one even knows what's going on. Also, in the implementation of the National Rural Employment Generation Schemes, we read of frequent irregularities involving fake beneficiaries, non-payment of wages to "job cardholders" and so on. There are, in fact, all sorts of scams reported in the papers, so many that it seems we have a scam behind every scheme.

'And so, we have pathetic roads, pipes without water, lamp posts without electricity, health centres without doctors and nurses. And of course, to keep people happy and stifle criticism, our politicians have made it a fad to contribute to annual religious assemblies, both in the Khasi-Jaiñtia Hills and Garo Hills. The amounts run into crores. And who are the people trying to stop the politicians from robbing us blind? The NGOs you hate so much, Hamkom!

'Take the uranium mining issue, for instance. Why the hell should any NGO have to protest? Isn't it the government's duty to look after the welfare of the people? If our government had called for a ban on uranium exploration, like some provincial governments in Canada and Australia have done, none of the protests and agitations and bandhs would have been necessary.

'And one more thing, Hamkom. If you say that the KSU has not been taking up issues relating to students' welfare, then you are lying through your teeth. You call yourself an intellectual, but your hatred and prejudice have turned you into a fart bug.'

Hamkom was opening his mouth to make a suitable retort when Raji said: 'So what should we call Meghalaya, Ning? The abode of clouds or the abode of scamperists?'

Magdalene burst out laughing and sang, 'Scamperists, scamperists! The abode of scamperists!'

Bah Kynsai tried to mollify Hamkom. 'You know, Ham, we are lucky we have only the NGOs to contend with, na? In the past, we also had the militants, remember?'

'Now also we have militants!' Hamkom corrected him.

'Yeah, but they are hardly active, na? They are taking a nap. In Garo Hills, of course, it's a different story ...'

'Why do you think the HNLC has become weak, Bah Kynsai?' Hamkom asked.

'Many reasons. But when they first emerged as the Hynñiew Trep National Liberation Council in 1993, na, they were quite a force.'

'What were they before becoming HNLC?' Donald asked.

'They were working with the Garos and were known as Hynñiew Trep Achik Liberation Council, HALC. In 1993, they split up to become the Hynñiew Trep National Liberation Council. Khasis and Garos can never work together, na? I think Ning is right on that score. The HNLC dominated the entire Khasi country—East and West Khasi Hills, Jaiñtia Hills, Ri Bhoi and Ri War. They were formidable in those days. When they called for bandhs, na, there would be a total shutdown, not even cats and dogs on the road. Every year, they used to impose a bandh on Republic Day or Independence Day to stop people from celebrating them, and at night they used to mark their success by firing into the air. There were lots of fireworks in the sky: they must have used signal guns too, I don't really know. We used to go up to our terraces to watch.

'But you know what? When the police went to catch them, ha, backed up by the CRPs, the hated Central Reserve Police Force, ha, they would simply vanish without a trace! People in those days used to call them shadow men. They walked in the shadows. Some even say they were helped by tribal shamans, who performed egg-breaking ceremonies and so on to keep them invisible. But that was bullshit, of course. They could not be seen because the people hid them, na? They had tremendous support in those days; almost everyone was for them. Their greatest support in Shillong came from Mawlai; our Kit is from there, we must be careful what we say,' Bah Kynsai concluded with a laugh.

'But why?' Hamkom asked. 'As far as I know, they were fighting for independence from India, no? Did Khasis really want to be free from India, Bah Kynsai? I know that I don't.'

'It's true that their main agenda is the liberation of Khasi Land, or Ri Hynñiew Trep as they put it, from India. They base their arguments upon the Instrument of Accession. As a historian, you would know—or maybe you don't, liah, you don't seem to know anything—that the Indian Independence Act of 1947, drafted by the British, stated that the suzerainty of the British Crown over the princely states would be terminated on 15 August 1947. This left the princely states completely independent and free to determine their own destinies. But the government of free India, na, did not allow them to do that and instead used the Instrument of Accession to legally annex every one of them. And I say "legally annex" because the document was supposed to be willingly signed by the Government of India on the one hand and the rulers of the princely states, individually, on the other. But that was nothing but a clever ploy, okay? In Ri Khasi, for instance, most of the Khasi states did not sign willingly: they were forced by threats of invasion. That is the basis of the HNLC's fight for independence from India. They maintain even now that India is an occupying foreign force.'

'Do you believe that?'

'You really don't know your history, do you, Ham?'

'No, no, you are getting me wrong. I do know about the Instrument of Accession, but you, do you believe that India is an occupying force?'

'Let me come to that by and by, na. Now, did the Khasis extend such support to the militants because they wanted to be free from India? The answer is no. Nobody believes we can, for practical reasons, exist independently, even if India would let us. We are Indians. It's as simple as that. What the hell do we do, how the hell do we survive outside India? So, back to the question: why did the Khasis support the HNLC to begin with? I'll tell you why: because apart from their stand against India's hegemony, na, they also promised to protect Meghalaya's indigenous population from ...'

'Influx!' Evening put in.

'Hold on, na!' Bah Kynsai snapped. 'I was going to say, from the threat of dkhars migrating in great swarms from outside …'

'Do Khasis really need protection?' Hamkom asked.

'We have been over that already, na, tdong?' Bah Kynsai cursed again. 'It is a fact that most Khasis feel threatened, especially in the border areas. The fear is there, whether we like it or not, and the HNLC took advantage of that. And, if you recall the bloody riots of 1992 between Khasis and non-tribals, you would understand why. Do you remember what happened during those riots, Ham? No? You don't read the Khasi papers, na, that's why. Khasis from Nongmynsong, or what the non-tribals call Lachandbasti, were driven out of their homes. Even house owners were evicted by their non-tribal tenants, and had to flee towards Mawpat and Mawlai. When Khasis became refugees in their own land, na, and when they had to flee from the khukris of migrants, na, no one came to protect them. The police? Most of the police officers, because of the joint cadre with Assam, na, are non-tribals. They, in turn, make sure that non-tribals are recruited as lower-ranking officers and constables. In short, many Meghalaya policemen are non-tribals controlled by mostly non-tribal officers. So why should they protect the Khasis?'

'That is changing now, Bah Kynsai,' Raji interrupted. 'I mean, many more Khasi youth are getting into the police force.'

'To some extent, yeah, but it wasn't like that earlier. The CRPs are worse. They are here to protect the Hindi-speaking population, or that is what most of us believe. For them, maintaining law and order means beating up and arresting anyone who doesn't look like them and who cannot speak much Hindi. So again, I ask you, who was it who came to the rescue of the Khasis during the 1992 riots? None other than the HNLC! I'm not speaking for them, okay, I'm just giving you the low-down on their growing influence.'

'But you said they emerged in 1993, no? So how could they have come to anybody's rescue in 1992?' Donald asked.

'They were there, mə, bew, liah, although they were not yet very active! When Khasis fled from their homes in Nongmynsong, na, and lived in shelters in Mawpat and Mawlai, na, they were the ones who went at night, during curfew hours, to protect those who were still living in their homes.'

Bah Kynsai was swearing freely in Khasi, but nobody minded. It was just how he spoke. People either learnt to put up with his expletives or avoided him. I was reminded of the uneducated villagers of Laitlyngkot and Nongkynrih. As a boy, I had spent some years in these villages, and I used to hear kids using swear words even in front of their parents. Once, as I was sitting with a farmer and his young son near a field of cabbage, enjoying a bit of rest after the hard work of preparing a patch for the winter potatoes, the boy suddenly shouted, '*Labew, liah, Pa! Lah bam lut U Lew ïa u kubi!*' ('Breasts, cunts, Pa! U Lew has eaten all the cabbage!'). U Lew was the name of one of their bulls. The boy was smoking a pipe of tobacco, an astonishing sight for someone from Sohra, where boys were certainly not allowed to smoke! But to hear him speak like that in front of his father made my jaw drop. But the father thought nothing of it and only replied, '*Bom lih, liah, bom!*' ('Beat him up, cunt, beat him up!'). You see, expletives were a part of their speech, and they thought nothing of them.

'The whole bloody thing,' Bah Kynsai said, 'came to an end after the massacre of a non-tribal family near Mawlai. Many people thought it was the work of the HNLC, but the police, na, had no inkling of that and went after all the Khasi boys living nearby. But because of the fighting they had done at Nongmynsong, na, the HNLC militants were hailed as protectors from then on by most Khasis, especially when, after the riots, they eliminated all the non-tribal leaders who were thought to be fomenting trouble in the first place.'

'Are you saying that the 1992 riots were caused by non-tribals, then?' Hamkom asked.

'No, not at all. In these things, na, if you ask the Khasis, they will blame the non-tribals, and if you ask the non-tribals, they will blame the Khasis. But the HNLC militants had their own intelligence, ha, they identified the non-tribal ringleaders and assassinated them. That was why they were hailed as protectors.'

'But that's terrible, Bah Kynsai!' Donald cried. 'How can assassins be hailed as protectors?'

'It has always been like that, all over the world, na, Don? Assassins to others, heroes to their own,' Bah Kynsai said simply. 'That is the nature of conflict everywhere, unfortunately.'

'But what are the real reasons for the conflict here, Bah Kynsai?' Donald asked.

Raji answered for Bah Kynsai. 'The immediate causes were different each time, okay, but the fact is that there was a lot of simmering tension—there still is, sadly—between tribals and non-tribals because of the unabating influx. When Khasi NGOs organised protests against the influx of outsiders, okay, the non-tribal population felt that they were launching a movement against them. And the Khasis were also at fault because they didn't make a distinction between the permanent non-tribal residents and the new migrants, who were coming in droves. Permanent non-tribal residents should be allowed to settle in peace, that's what I think. I hope such a riot does not happen again; I hope we have all learned from 1992, but I'm worried.'

'It's also hard for Khasis to differentiate one non-tribal from another, na?' Bah Kynsai argued. 'To make matters worse, the permanent non-tribals are also known to protect and encourage newcomers in so many ways, man! It's all a bloody mess! But let me come back to the HNLC, okay? Where was I? Oh yes, I wanted to say that there were also other reasons why the HNLC men were hailed as protectors and law enforcers who were much more effective than the sluggish and often communally biased police force. I'll give you two examples. Take Ïewduh. It's the largest wholesale and retail market in the whole of Meghalaya, with the biggest non-tribal traders as well as the smallest, shop-less hawkers, Khasis and non-Khasis, doing business there. All sorts of things are sold there, in fact, everything that a human being could need. But above all, it's a Khasi market: Khasis from everywhere flock to it to buy and sell. Khasi farmers, for instance, have nowhere else to go. It is there that they sell their produce every single day.

'Now, two things used to happen in this market: Khasi farmers, na, were cheated day in and day out by non-tribal traders. These men controlled the prices of all agricultural produce, and they changed them from day to day to suit their needs and their insatiable hunger for profit. To give you just one example, okay, one day they would raise the price of potatoes, say from twenty rupees to thirty-five rupees, and when news of the rising price spread, all the farmers would bring their potatoes to the market. But when the traders saw the market flooded with potatoes, na, they would suddenly reduce the price from thirty-five rupees to ten. Now, what could the poor farmers do? To sell to the traders would mean incurring big losses, but to take the potatoes back home would mean bigger losses. Caught between a rock and a hard place, na, they always ended up selling to those buggers. The police and the government officials never lifted a finger to help them. Year after year, the farmers had to play these cat-and-mouse games with the non-tribal traders until, finally, enter the HNLC! *Tan-ta-naan*, like music in the Hindi movies, na, when a hero comes, na, and the problem was magically solved.

'But there was another criminal thing happening in Ïewduh, okay? The extortion racket. There was a notorious gang with its base in the Sweepers' Colony, na, and it was imposing taxes on all the Ïewduh traders, from the biggest to the smallest. Even small Khasi hawkers selling waidong, betel nut packs, were not spared. The Khasis said to themselves: "Imagine, this is a Khasi market, this is our land, and we have to pay taxes to the Kharmetors!" But what were they to do? Those who didn't pay were beaten up and often stabbed to death. The government did nothing. The police had their fingers in the racket. The NGOs did not have enough influence. So, what happened? Again, enter the HNLC! And everything was resolved within a week. They simply eliminated the ringleaders, and the racket fell to pieces.'

Kharmetors, by the way, are a community of non-tribal sanitation workers.

'Do you recall the shooting of the Kharmetor who commanded the gang, Kit?' Bah Kynsai continued. 'He led a lavish lifestyle, owned several expensive cars, including the most beautifully decorated jeep in Shillong ... and you know what, he was always dressed in a suit and necktie, liah! If you didn't know him, na, you would easily mistake him for a thriving Punjabi businessman. And everywhere he went, he was followed by three, four vehicles packed with bodyguards—the most wicked thugs from the Sweepers' Colony. And yet, the HNLC got him on the very first attempt. They pumped him full of lead!'

'I don't remember any of this, how come?' Hamkom said.

'I was too young, so I wouldn't know,' Donald added.

'Stop speaking, you fraud,' Evening shouted at Hamkom. 'The moment you open your mouth, it stinks of a septic tank!'

'No fighting, no fighting!' Bah Kynsai shouted quickly. 'You, na, Ning, behave like a mad dog sometimes. And you, Ham, if you want to know, just go to the newspaper offices and check their archives. Now, shall I give you another reason for the HNLC's popularity? Okay. Rape. So many we had in the past! Daily we read about them in the papers! Even children of about two, three years of age were raped, ha. And stepchildren were routinely raped by their stepfathers. In some cases, a father would rape his own daughter— perverts like that are also there, na? And nobody was doing anything about it. The police were ineffective or too slow to act. The culprits always got bail, in any case, and would threaten the victims and their families with dire consequences. Everybody got fed up with the police and started complaining directly to the HNLC, and the HNLC always provided them with prompt justice. Within a day or two, na, their cadres would arrest the culprits and give them a good hiding. Not only that, ha, the HNLC clamped locks on rapists' ears and made them stand at busy junctions carrying placards that said "I Am a Rapist". Very prompt and effective justice. That's why those fellows became known as protectors.'

'But why have they become so weak now? That was my question initially, Bah Kynsai,' Hamkom reminded him.

'Wait, na, I'm coming to that. They were the people's protectors, an alternative to the law, providing quick and parallel justice. The people loved and supported them. They gave them places to hide and would say nothing to betray them in any way. Then they became greedy, liah! They set up what they called a "tax-collection network" of their own. At first, they started with non-tribal businessmen, ha, but that was not enough for them. They started collecting from Khasis also. And whenever there was any resistance, na, they exterminated that person. They lost all their so-called principles and forgot their oath to serve and protect the Khasi people. Soon, many more Khasis than non-tribals had been killed by them. Non-tribals, in fact, were protected because they paid their taxes without complaint. The Khasis were killed for resisting, accused of being police informers or suspected enemies. Soon, people began to say the HNLC were behaving like Thlen, the blood-sucking serpent, who would take nothing but Khasi blood. In this way, slowly and slowly, they lost their support ...'

'If I may, Bah Kynsai,' Bah Kit intervened, 'I think that's not all, okay? I believe the main reason why they lost the trust of the people was because they interfered in religious matters. Around the year 2001, ha, there was a quarrel between two religious organisations at Umñiuh Tmar village near the Bangladesh border. It was over a plot of land that both organisations claimed as theirs. A powerful politician and two or three members of an NGO were also involved. These people influenced the HNLC leadership, and soon the HNLC kidnapped the president of the Seng Khasi Ri War Mihngi from his residence in Jaïaw in Shillong on the first of March 2001—I still remember the date. His name was Rijoy Khongsha. But Bah Rijoy was not only a president of the Seng Khasi Ri War Mihngi, ha, he was also considered a prominent leader by the War sub-tribe and followers of the Khasi religion. They should not have kidnapped him in the first place, ha, but instead of realising their mistake and releasing him, they had him killed when he refused to change his stand on the disputed land. Later, of course, they denied any involvement, but nobody was fooled.

'Now, in the HNLC, ha, there were all sorts of Khasis, including followers of our Niam Khasi. These people discussed the matter among themselves and said, "We thought the HNLC was a champion of the Khasi people, but see, it's just another religious organisation. How can we continue to serve an organisation that will have our own religious leaders bumped off like that?" As a result, many of them deserted. Unfortunately for the HNLC, ha, the fallout from the Rijoy Khongsha murder did not end there. Its supporters among the War people, who used to help the militants cross the border into and out of Bangladesh, not only stopped helping them but also started telling the police about the border routes used by the cadres. And that resulted in many of them being arrested and killed by the police within a matter of months.'

'Are you sure about this Rijoy thing, Bah Kit?' Evening demanded. 'Do you have any proof? I, for one, ha, do not believe the HNLC would take sides like that!'

'I don't have any proof, but it's common knowledge. The police also know this. Anyway, this is what every Khasi is saying, except for people like you. And don't tell me they don't take sides! Do you remember what happened in 2008? Actually, Bah Kynsai, the final nail in the HNLC's coffin was the bandh they called on the last day of the Shad Suk Mynsiem Festival. On that day, the fourteenth of April 2008, our people truly realised the anti-Khasi sentiment of the HNLC leadership and turned out in droves to defy their crazy diktat. That year also registered the biggest attendance at the festival, both in terms of dancers and spectators. Now the HNLC is gone! It's in its death throes!'

The Shad Suk Mynsiem Festival is an annual dance festival of the Khasis organised by Seng Khasi Mawkhar, Shillong. The HNLC had called for the bandh ostensibly to protest Sonia Gandhi's visit to the city. But many people did not understand why they did it when it was also the concluding day of the festival.

Unlike Bah Kit, who was thrilled at the HNLC's fading out, Evening was saddened. He said, 'But one thing I will tell you, okay, whether you like it or not, with the decline in the HNLC's power and influence, ha, the Khasi people have also become weak ...'

Hamkom demanded, 'How can you say the weakening of a militant organisation that killed so many innocent people weakens the Khasi people?'

'I'm telling you, the Khasi people are much weaker now!' Evening said doggedly. 'No one is afraid of us now. When the HNLC had their camps at the Assam borders, ha, the Karbi or Mikir or any other militant outfits there never dared raise a finger against us, but now that they are gone, ha, every day, we hear about the atrocities committed by those outfits on our people. Don't you see that? We have no one to protect us now.'

'You know what, Ning might have a point there,' Raji conceded. 'The extortion racket at Ïewduh has raised its ugly head again, Ham. They would never have dared had the HNLC still been powerful.'

'Of course he's right, Bah Raji!' Dale said suddenly, surprising all of us, since he had been listening quietly so far. 'I may not be an intellectual like you all, okay, but ordinary Khasis like me, ha, who are on the road all day, ha, we know very well what's going on. Without the HNLC, I'm telling you, the non-tribals are riding roughshod over us again.'

But Bah Su disagreed with this. He said, 'Let the HNLC become strong again? How can we let the Thlen come back?'

'Yeah, yeah!' Hamkom agreed. 'That's right, Bah Su, the HNLC did not even serve the Khasi people, no? Don't be a fool; don't let the serpent rise again …'

'The fear of influx,' Bah Kit chipped in, 'is a very real thing, whatever anybody might say. What's more, the fear of influx might lead to another riot, God forbid! But to solve this problem, we should put pressure on the government to initiate immediate and effective measures. Turning to militants is the worst possible solution anybody can think of.'

The wrangling could have gone on and on but for a sudden outburst from Halolihim. It seemed like he had not been listening to us and was moping alone in his corner, but now, unable to contain his misery any longer, he said out loud, 'How could all of them have converted to Christianity?'

After a moment of surprised silence, Hamkom responded, 'But isn't that a good thing for you?'

'How can it be a good thing? I came here to preach and evangelise, what am I supposed to do now? Ten days in this place with nothing to do! It's too much!'

'Look at the bright side, Hal,' Bah Kynsai said.

'What is the bright side, where is the bright side?'

'Waa, don't you see? The Lyngngams have only become Presbyterians and Catholics, na? No one belongs to your church. Why don't you try poaching some sheep from them?'

'Don't be so crude, Bah Kynsai,' Halolihim admonished him, but his face suddenly broke into a happy smile. 'That may not be a bad idea at all. My church is the best, after all! I'll see you later,' he said.

Everyone laughed as Halolihim left on his new mission. He was really a very simple person, I thought.

'But how did the Lyngngams become Christians so fast?' Bah Kit wondered. 'I mean, even in places nearer to Shillong, ha, there are still plenty of Khasis, but this place is so remote, and yet everyone has become a Christian!'

'Missionaries have been coming here since the time of the British, Bah Kit,' I said. 'Perly told me that followers of the old faith can now be found only in parts of Nongtrai. Even those who will conduct the ceremony of Ka Phor Sorat are coming from there.'

'The Lyngngams are more enlightened than the Khasis of Shillong,' Evening stated.

'On the contrary,' Raji said, before Bah Kit could open his mouth, 'it's easier to convert the unenlightened than the enlightened. Those enlightened by education are prouder of their own culture.'

Magdalene stopped the discussion from developing further by saying, 'I'm very curious about the Lyngngams, ya, is there anything written on them?'

'Gurdon has written about them in his book,' Hamkom said.

'*The Khasis*? What did he write?'

'How can I remember what he wrote? I read it quite some time ago, no?'

'I have the book on my tablet,' I said. 'I could read out excerpts if you like. Only thing is, he's not very accurate and things have changed quite a lot since he wrote the book.'

'You brought your tablet also? Great, great,' Magdalene said. 'But how do you know his writing is not accurate?'

'Because I have read a book by a Khasi writer from these parts,' I said simply.

In fact, Victor, the Nongtrai elder who was to come with the shamans to perform the Phor Sorat ceremony, was a relative of this Khasi writer. Victor was very well informed about Nongtrai customs.

P.R.T. Gurdon was a British deputy commissioner of Eastern Bengal and Assam and also a superintendent of ethnography in Assam during the 1900s. In his book, he begins the section on the Lyngngams by saying that 'these people differ so very greatly from the Khasis in their manner of life, and in their customs' that they have to be considered in a separate chapter. The Lyngngams, he maintains,

> ... claim [themselves] to be Khasis, they dislike being called Garos; but although it is true they speak what may be called a dialect of Khasi, and observe some of the Khasi customs, the Lyngngams are more Garos than

Khasis ... and possess the Tibeto-Burman type of feature to a marked degree. The Lyngngams are by complexion swarthy, with features of Mongolian type. The men are of middle height and the women remarkably short, both sexes being not nearly so robust as the Khasis, a result due probably to climatic influences, for the Lyngngam live in fever-haunted jungles. The men have very little hair about the face, although a scanty moustache is sometimes seen, the hairs in the centre being carefully plucked out, the result being two tufts on either side. Beards are never seen. The women are ill-favoured and wear very little clothing. The men wear the sleeveless coat of the Khasis and the Mikirs called *phong marong*, which is made of cotton dyed red, blue and white. This custom may have been borrowed from the Khasis. They do not grow their own cotton, but obtain it from the plains. They make their own dyes ... A cotton cloth, barely enough for purposes of decency, is tied between the legs, the ends being allowed to hang down in front and behind. Sometimes an apron is worn in front. At the present day, the men wear knitted woollen caps, generally black or red, of the Nongstoin pattern (a sort of fisherman's cap), but the elderly men and headmen wear turbans. The females wear a cotton cloth about eighteen inches broad round the loins, sometimes striped red and blue, but more often only dark blue. A blue or red cloth is thrown loosely across the shoulders by unmarried girls, but married women only wear the waist-cloth, like the Garos. A cloth is tied round the head by married women, sometimes, Garo fashion. The women wear quantities of blue beads as necklaces, like their Garo sisters ... Brass ear-rings are worn by both sexes; the women, like the Garos, load their ears to such an extent with brass rings as to distend the lobes greatly. Silver armlets are worn by the headmen only, or by those who possess the means to give a great feast to the villagers ... Both sexes wear bracelets. The men also wear necklaces of beads. The rich wear necklaces of cornelian and another which is thought by the Lyngngams to be valuable. A necklace of such stones is called *u pieng blei* (god's necklace). This stone is apparently some rough gem which may be picked up by the Lyngngams in the river beds. A rich man among them, however, is one who possesses a number of metal gongs, which they call *wiang*. For these they pay very high prices, Rs 100 being a moderate sum for one of them. Being curious to see one of these gongs, I asked a *sirdar*, or headman, to show me one. He replied that he would do so, but it would take time, as he always buried the gongs in the jungle for fear of thieves. Next morning, he brought me a gong of bell metal, with carvings of animals engraved thereon. The gong when struck gave out a rich deep note like that of the Burmese or Tibetan gongs. These gongs have a regular currency in this part of the hills, and represent to the Lyngngams 'Bank of England' notes. It would be interesting to try to ascertain what their history is, for no one in the Lyngngam country makes them these days. Is it possible that the Garos brought them with them when they migrated from Tibet?

The Lyngngams do not tattoo. Their weapons are the large-headed Garo spear, the dao and the shield. They do not usually carry bows and arrows, although there are some who possess them. They are by occupation cultivators. They sow two kinds of hill rice, red and white, on the hill-sides. They have no wet paddy cultivation, and they do not cultivate in terraces like the Nagas. They burn the jungle about February, after cutting down some of the trees and clearing away some of the debris, and then sow the paddy broadcast, without cultivating the ground in any way. They also cultivate millet, Job's tears, in the same way. With the paddy, chillies are sown in the first year. The eggplant, taro, ginger, turmeric, and sweet potatoes of several varieties are grown by them in a similar manner. Those that rear the lac insect, plant *landoo* (Hindi *arhal dal*) trees in the forest clearings and rear the insect thereon.

The villages are situated near the patches of cultivation in the forest. The villages are constantly shifting, owing to the necessity of burning fresh tracts of forest every two years. The houses are entirely built of bamboo, and, for such temporary structures, are very well built. In front, the houses are raised some 3 or 4 ft. from the ground on platforms, being generally built on the side of a fairly steep hill, one end of the house resting on the ground, and the other on bamboo posts. The back end of the house is sometimes 8 or 9 ft. from the ground. At the end of the house, farthest away from the village path is a platform used for sitting out in the evening, and for spreading chillies and other articles to dry. Some Lyngngam houses have only one room in which men, women, and children are all huddled together, the hearth being in the centre, and, underneath the platform, the pigs. Well-to-do people, however, possess a retiring room, where husband and wife sleep ... Houses are built with a portion of the thatch hanging over the eaves in front. No explanation could be given me for this ... In some Lyngngam villages there are houses in the centre of the village where the young unmarried men sleep, where male guests are accommodated, and where the village festivities go on ... This is a custom of the Tibeto-Burman tribes in Assam and is not a Khasi custom. There are also high platforms, some 12 ft. or 15 ft. in height, in Lyngngam villages, where the elders sit of an evening in the hot weather and take the air ... There is little or no furniture in a Lyngngam house. The Lyngngam sleeps on a mat on the floor, and in cold weather covers himself with a quilt, made out of the bark of a tree, which is beaten out and then carefully woven, several layers of flattened bark being used before the right thickness is attained. This quilt is called by the Lyngngams 'Ka Syllar'. Food is cooked in earthen pots, but no plates are used, the broad leaves of the *mariang* tree take their place. The leaves are thrown away after use, a fresh supply being required for each meal.

The Lyngngams brew rice beer, they do not distil spirit; the beer is brewed according to the Khasi method. Games they have none and there are no jovial archery meetings like those of the Khasis. The Lyngngam methods of hunting are setting spring guns and digging pitfalls for game. The Lyngngams fish to a small extent with nets, but their idea of fishing, par excellence, is poisoning the streams … The Lyngngams are omnivorous feeders, they may be said to eat everything except dogs, snakes, the *huluk* monkey, and lizards. They like rice, when they can get it; for sometimes the out-turn of their fields does not last them more than a few months. They then have to fall back on Job's tears and millet. They eat arums largely, and for vegetables they cook wild plantains and the young shoots of bamboos and cane plants.

The Lyngngams are divided up into exogamous clans in the same manner as the Khasis. The clans are overgrown families … There do not appear to be any hypergamous groups. As with the Khasis, it is a deadly sin to marry anyone belonging to your own *kur*, or clan. Unlike the Khasis, however, a Lyngngam can marry two sisters at a time. The Lyngngam marriages are arranged by *ksiangs*, or go-betweens, much in the same way as Khasi marriages, but the rituals observed are less elaborate and show a mixture of Khasi and Garo customs. The Lyngngams intermarry with the Garos. It appears that sometimes the parents of girls exact bride-money, and marriages by capture have been heard of. Both these customs are more characteristic of the Bodo tribes of the plains than of the Khasis. There are no special birth customs, as with the Khasis, except that when the umbilical cord falls a fowl is sacrificed, and the child is brought outside the house. Children are named without any special ceremony … The Lyngngams possess no head-hunting customs, as far as it has been possible to ascertain. These people are still wild and uncivilized … Although they do not as a rule, give trouble from an administrative point of view …

At the end of my reading, I told them that Gurdon also wrote of the Lyngngams' death rituals and their religion. However, since we would be witnessing these for ourselves, I suggested that we check what he had to say on the subject later, so we could compare and authenticate.

'That's okay,' Magdalene said, 'but what I want to know is, is it true that married women only wore a waist cloth? Did he mean to say they didn't wear anything on top? Didn't they cover their breasts or what?'

'I knew you would be interested in that,' Bah Kynsai said teasingly.

'Bah Kynsai, are you drunk or what?' Magdalene asked, laughing.

'Drunk on what? I have merely taken a few sips of whisky.'

'Okay, okay, but will somebody answer my question?'

I said, 'According to Lawrence Kharbani's book, *U Sangkhni*—and mind you, Lawrence is a local man—Gurdon must have been speaking of the Hana or Namdaniya Garos who inhabit the low hills to the north of the West Khasi Hills district. The Lyngngam women always dressed like the rest of the Khasi women. Traditionally, Khasi women wore, as a kind of undergarment, a cloth called *jympien*, which was wound around the body and tied at the waist with a strip of fabric. The jympien usually reaches up to the knees or a little below. Above this, they wore *ka sopti-kti*, a kind of blouse, and over this, a pair of jaiñsems. (A jaiñsem, if you recall, is a long cloth draped over the shoulder and worn as an outer garment.) On top of all of that, they also wore a *tapmoh khlieh*, a shawl, either thrown loosely across the shoulders or wrapped around the head and then tied at the neck like Superman.'

'Like Superman?'

'Uh-uh.' I nodded. 'Even now, if you go to the colder places in the Khasi uplands, you'll find both men and women wearing shawls tied at the neck. When the wind blows, their shawls billow around them, and they look like Superman, many Supermen!

'But when the weather was unusually cold, or when they were going out for an important event, the women, it seems, also wore another garment, called *jaiñkup*, over the shawl. It was worn like a cloak with the two ends tied in front and the rest hanging loosely down the back and sides.'

'With the tapmoh covering their heads, na,' Bah Kynsai said, 'and with the jaiñkup hanging loosely down their backs and sides, they must have looked like turtles from behind, liah! Their feminine forms must have been literally kept under wraps. Thank God, now they are wearing much less, and we can see more.'

'Are you talking about miniskirts and sleeveless blouses, Bah Kynsai?' Raji teased.

'I'm talking about how even their traditional wear now consist of skirts, blouses and jaiñsems, much more revealing. After all, what a woman shows is explicit, but what she doesn't show should at least be implicit, na?'

'When it's cold?' Raji asked.

'When it's cold, they can wear sweaters, tapmoh, jaiñkup and even a blanket, who is to object when it's cold?'

'Ap,' Magdalene intervened, 'go on, ya, don't listen to these clowns.'

'The clothes of Khasi women,' I continued, 'as some of you, well, do not know, were made of cotton and silk, either eri or mulberry or *muka* (muga). The cottons were for rough use, and silk for special occasions.

'In the Lyngngam and Nongtrai areas, the women had much the same kind of clothes except for the tapmoh, worn only at night, when it was colder, and the jaiñkup, which was never worn at all, the weather being too hot for it.'

'What are those things I saw around some women's legs today?' Magdalene asked.

'What, haven't you seen those before?' I asked, surprised. 'They were *sopjats*, gaiters. When women go to work in the fields or in the jungle, they wear them to protect their calves from being scratched by thorns, branches, shrubs and so on. The ones you saw were not proper gaiters, of course, merely pieces of cloth coiled around the legs for protection.'

'What about the men, I mean, how were they dressed in the past?'

'Men may well have worn loincloths. This was usually the case with most of the old Khasis living in warm places. But upland Khasis could not have survived in loincloths, especially in winter.'

'Of course not, you joker!' Magdalene said. 'So, what did they wear?'

'*Jaiñboh*, or dhotis, like the people of Sylhet.'

'Aren't dhotis loincloths?'

'Ah, you have been reading the Oxford Dictionary. A dhoti is actually a loose piece of clothing wrapped around the lower half of the body—traditional wear for most men in South Asia.'

'I think it's true that these people are more Garo than Khasi, Ap,' Hamkom said.

'Why? Because some of them look like Garos? According to Lawrence, there was a lot of intermarriage between people from these parts and the Garos. In the process, the culture itself became somewhat amalgamated, but they cannot be described as more Garo than Khasi. They speak a Khasi dialect, and their customs and style of dressing are Khasi too. But here is Perly; we can ask him about some of the other things that Gurdon said … Bah Perly, come, come.'

Raji said, 'Does he have a moustache? Is it like the one described by Gurdon?'

But Perly was clean-shaven. Modernity had caught up with the Lyngngams too. Nobody was wearing loincloths any more; nobody was eating out of leaves, and the gongs, Perly told us, were a thing of the past, although there were still a few around, being used as decorations. When we asked him about 'houses in the centre of the village where the young unmarried men sleep, where male guests are accommodated', Perly said that only Garos, and sometimes those living near the Garo border, had such houses. When we asked him if it was true that the Lyngngams burnt tracts of forest every two years, he said if they had done that, not a single tree would have been left anywhere. He explained, like Chirag had done earlier, that traditionally, land was cleared and left alone for ten to fifteen years to allow the forest to reclaim it, but that these days people were going back to it in just seven or eight years.

About the hunting and fishing methods, he said they did not dig pitfalls any more, nor did they poison the streams for fishes, because both practices had been declared illegal by the government and the king of Nongstoin, who had jurisdiction over these areas. Naturally, he added, you will find violators now and again, but the practice was by and large outmoded.

Perly also decried the allegation that children were named without any special ceremony. When people were practising the old religion, he said, they used to have very elaborate naming rites, similar to the other Khasis. Now, of course, everyone was baptised. He also condemned as nonsense Gurdon's statement that a Lyngngam could marry two sisters at once. If a man's wife died, he could undoubtedly marry her sister, but marrying two sisters at once was unheard of.

After saying this, Perly suddenly held up both his hands and said, 'I came here, Babu, because I have brought something for you. I don't know if I should or not … come, take a look.' He beckoned me over, and Bah Kynsai and Raji too.

We followed him outside and found two large gourds and eleven bamboo containers neatly arranged on a rough bamboo stool by the side of the hut. Raji immediately recognised them for what they were. He cackled loudly and asked, 'Are these what I think they are, Bah Perly?'

Perly smiled and said, 'Yiad Lyngngam.'

It was the Lyngngam rice beer, sure enough, kept in hollowed-out gourds. The bamboo mugs had been made by cutting a four-inch bamboo pole to the size of a mug, with the joint forming a solid base.

Laughing, Raji and Bah Kynsai grabbed a gourd and a mug each and began pouring themselves a drink. Raji sipped his, and went into raptures about it. 'Heavenly, Bah Kynsai, simply heavenly! It's incredibly delicious and sweet!'

Bah Kynsai cried, 'Waa! Wonderful! You are right, leh, Raji, simply wonderful!'

The noise they were making brought the whole group outside. Hamkom took one look at the dancing Raji and asked, 'What's going on?'

Raji pointed to the gourds and the mugs on the stool. 'Our babies! Aren't they beautiful?'

Bah Su, Bah Kit, Magdalene, Donald, Hamkom and Evening each took a sip from their mugs and immediately nodded their approval. I, too, was persuaded to take a sip. I found it to be sweetish but did not like the mild burning sensation it gave me. I have nothing against alcohol; I just don't like the taste of it.

Only Dale did not even taste the stuff, perhaps because I was present. Watching them drinking happily, I said to myself, 'If Halolihim had been here, he would have ranted at them. To him, all drinks are from the devil.'

Bah Kynsai thanked Perly profusely, but Raji had one last question for him. He said, 'Are we getting this ration every night?'

'Every night,' Perly said with a smile, pleased to have made us happy.

Raji started dancing round and round again at Perly's response. Bah Kynsai patted Perly on the back and said, 'Thanks again, Perly.'

He turned to us. 'Come, come,' he said, 'let's enjoy our drinks inside.'

Perly took his leave as we all trooped back inside.

'It's quite strong, leh, Bah Kynsai,' Raji said, 'strong and beautiful. I haven't tasted anything like this, ya, so sweet and delicious. It's rice spirit or what?'

'But Gurdon said Lyngngams don't brew rice spirit, only rice beer, remember?' Bah Kynsai reminded him.

'Either he was mistaken, or things have changed. This does feel like rice spirit, ha. I'm feeling a little knocked already.'

Khasis tend to use the word 'knocked' when they are speaking of being intoxicated—knocked on the head, so to speak, by the drink.

'It's rice beer, man!' Bah Kynsai told him. 'You are gulping yours down like a greedy pig, na, that's why it feels like spirit.'

There is a belief that traditionally Khasis did not drink spirits, only rice beer like yiad um. Gurdon maintained that they began drinking spirits 'only in the last couple of generations'. His book was published in 1906, so that would suggest the 1870s. Nigel claimed in *Through the Green Doors* that Khasis were taught the art of distilling spirits by the first Welsh missionary, Thomas Jones. According to him, Thomas Jones fell foul of his superiors in Wales when he married a Khasi woman after his wife died. Because of that, he had to leave the mission and try his hand at some trade. He did not succeed, as he was hounded out by the villainous Harry Inglis, trader and right-hand man of David Scott, the first British political agent in these hills. Inglis did not want any competition and sent a posse after Jones, who fled to Calcutta, where he died shortly after arrival.

It was supposed to be during the latter part of his life that Thomas Jones taught the Khasis how to distil alcohol.

However, these arguments by Gurdon and Nigel do not stand to reason. Khasis had always had their rice spirit, known as *kyiad paka* or *kyiad pynshoh*, quite different from the weak rice beer, which is of two varieties, kyiad hiar and kyiad um. Kyiad hiar, or yiad hiar, is white whereas kyiad um, or yiad um, is colourless like water. Usually, both these varieties are made out of rice or millet, depending upon the place of origin.

To make yiad hiar, rice is first boiled, then spread on a cane mat or a large circular sieve known as *pdung*, to cool. Meanwhile, the dried leaves of a plant known as *khawiang* are mixed with the boiled rice and squeezed into a kind of gummy ball to form the yeast known as *thit khawiang*. When five of these balls are made, they are shaken together with the boiled rice in a basket. The process is known as *khynrud*. After that, along with some charcoal, the whole mixture is put into another basket known as *sapung*. The charcoal is wrapped in a cloth and kept deep inside the mixture after a prayer has been intoned. Its role is, therefore, both ceremonial and practical, for it is also supposed to stop the brew from becoming weak and deteriorating. The basket is then made airtight by covering it with a cloth, placed in a wooden basin and left to ferment for two nights, after which the alcohol begins to seep into the basin.

To make yiad um, the leftover rice, after the yiad hiar has all oozed out, is put in a tub and mixed with just enough water to make it mushy. This mixture is again left for two nights, after which it begins to froth and turn into a pulpy mass known as *jyndem*. Yiad um beer is nothing but the watery part of the jyndem, and because it is made from the leftover rice of yiad hiar, it is much less potent than yiad hiar itself.

Yiad paka or yiad pynshoh rice spirit is distilled from the jyndem of yiad um beer. In this process, both the yiad um beer and the jyndem are once again mixed with khawiang yeast, poured into a narrow-necked brass pot and cooked over a simmering fire. The brass pot is then covered with an earthen pot, which has two openings, like hollow eye sockets, near its base. It is held in place with a mixture called *jabih*, which also prevents steam from escaping through the joints. The holes of the earthen pot are plugged with the stems of a type of wood called *latymphu*, the pith of which is soft and spongy. The joints between the latymphu stems and the holes are sealed again with jabih to prevent leakage. However, small holes are drilled into the stems themselves, from where the spirit from the brewing pot is channelled into another cloth-covered earthen pot. The spirit is now ready, and it is said to be so potent that a single bottle of it, mixed with two bottles of water, could get a man drunk.

There are two other varieties of spirits even more potent than yiad pynshoh. One of them is *yiad rot*. The preparation is the same, but the fermentation time is much longer. This spirit is so potent that it can even be used to light fires. The other one is the infamous *yiad tangsnem*, which is kept fermenting for a year. This is truly the demon alcohol, for it is fed to *nongshohnohs*, killers hired by the so-called Thlen keepers. A small bamboo cup of it is said to make them not only feel like giants but also make them see others as butterflies and insects to be crushed at will.

Thlen, as I have told you before, is the man-eating serpent of legend that later metamorphosed into a bloodsucking creature dependent on human blood for food. Thlen is believed by many to be both real and mythical and is as old as our creation myths, which originated thousands of years before the British set foot in the Khasi Hills. If the Khasis have had their yiad tangsnem since that time, it stands to reason that they were not taught how to distil spirits by Thomas Jones. What he might have done is teach them a more refined method of distillation, but what I have described just now is a traditional process that distillers still follow.

The most remarkable part of the Khasi alcohol story is the khawiang plant. Khawiang grows to a height of about three feet. Its leaves, with blood-red veins, are shaped like turmeric leaves, only smaller. According to legend, khawiang was specially gifted to man by U Ryngkew U Basa, the guardian spirit of villages and the wilderness. When man pleaded for a drink that was more relaxing and stimulating than water, which would serve him well after a hard day's work in the fields, U Ryngkew gave him a seed and instructed him to plant it in the garden, but to nurture it with the blood of monkeys. Failing this, he said, the blood of a tiger or a wild boar could be used. In this way, the first khawiang was planted and used in the making of rice beer and rice spirit. But because it was nurtured by the blood of three animals, when a man drinks beer or spirits even today, he sometimes becomes a monkey, sometimes a tiger and sometimes a pig. This is also probably the reason why people in the Khatar Shnong villages near Sohra call alcohol *dawai shrieh*, monkey medicine.

When I told them the story of khawiang, my friends guffawed with delight, and Bah Kynsai said Raji was behaving like a monkey right now. Raji responded by saying that Bah Kynsai was acting like a tiger, but nobody dared compare Bah Su to a pig.

As I watched the others giggling over their drinks, I went back to thinking about the Lyngngams.

There was no doubt that Lyngngam had changed a great deal. Even the houses were no longer built entirely of bamboo. Those of the poor were made with walls of bamboo and roofs of thatch; those of the better-to-do with walls and roofs of either corrugated iron sheets or sheets fashioned out of small kerosene tin cans; those of the well-to-do (only a few of these) were made with concrete walls and roofs of corrugated iron sheets. The schools, the village community hall—both constructed with government funds—and the Catholic church were of this last type. But strangely, the Presbyterian church was made entirely of bamboo and thatch. I say 'strangely' because it is a common belief among us that, as individuals, the Presbyterians are the richest and smartest among the Khasis, with many of them in key government positions. Through donations, collections and government grants, they have managed to construct large, palatial churches everywhere. But here, the church building reflected poverty and negligence.

One thing that resembled Gurdon's description had survived, though: the high platform. We saw many of these bamboo structures among the treetops, with pumpkins, chillies, fish and broomsticks laid out to dry on them. The platforms were so sturdy and spacious that several people could comfortably sit or lie down on them. In fact, we spent a lot of time on them during our stay in Nongshyrkon. With plenty of shade and the breeze gently stroking our faces, it was the most relaxing, refreshing experience we'd had. Bah Kynsai wanted us to spend a few nights on them, but when one night, unsteady after a few hours of drinking, he nearly fell off, he quickly gave up on the idea. 'During the day, it's all right,' he muttered disappointedly.

My thoughts went to the kids we had seen earlier that day. They were an unkempt and messy lot, dusty from head to bare feet. Their faces were mapped by dirt and sweat, dried tears and snot. Many had black mucus clogging their nostrils and yellowish rheum collecting at the corners of their eyes. Their clothes were soiled and ragged, and many were only half clad.

Some of the boys were running around without pants and wearing only shabby shirts. They truly seemed to be the children of nature, free and wild. I did not know what they did when they got home, but in Sohra, when we were kids, we were never allowed into the house unless we first washed our faces, hands and feet at the springs or the taps. If our clothes became dirty, we were asked to change immediately, with a little caning so we'd be more careful the next day—a lesson we never learnt.

Among the barefoot kids I saw were two girls and two boys standing together in a straight line, like students waiting to be addressed by their teacher. The eldest was about eight years old. She was dressed in a thin white nylon frock with large red roses printed on it and a pair of yellow jogging pants. On her back was a baby, her sister, I imagined, held in place by a single strip of red cloth. It was a precarious affair, so the girl had to keep her hands on the baby's bottom all the time. Everything about her was dirty. There were black smudges on her cheeks. Her bob cut was bushy and brown with dust. Her once white frock was the colour of brown mud. Only her dark eyes sparkled, staring at us with undisguised curiosity. Next to her was an even younger girl of about six. She was dressed in a pink frock only a little cleaner than her friend's. In her left hand was a piece of blue decorative paper, and with her right she held on tightly to the older girl. With them was a dark-complexioned boy of the same age. He had nothing on but a long, grimy off-white shirt with small grey prints. He was the filthiest of the lot. The area around his gaping mouth was smudged with grime and black snot, while his bare feet were covered with dried mud. But the most pathetic among them was the last one: a boy, only five years old, in dirty red jogging pants, carrying his sister strapped to his back with a dark blue shawl. While the rest were ogling at us, he alone was more concerned with the burden he was carrying. It must have been a terrible weight.

The image of those children remained deeply etched on my mind, and I could not help but wonder what kind of childhood they had. Poverty is a dreadful depriver.

But then, it wasn't just the kids who were dirty-looking. Most people we met were none too clean. This was probably because they spent much of their time in the jungle (reaping its produce or cutting wood) and in their farms, toiling from morning till evening—activities not very conducive to cleanliness. Or it could simply be because the village was watered only by a few springs, all some distance from their dwellings. There was a large lake on the outskirts, but that was too far away for daily use. The surprising thing was that the insides of most houses, like Chirag's, were neat and clean and always had a freshly swept look. So, we thought, the people may not take care of their personal hygiene, but they did take care with their homes and their cooking. This was good to know, considering that we would be spending a few days with them, eating their food.

Some of us kept a lookout for women as we walked through the village lanes—we were curious about whether the Lyngngams were graced with beauty or not.

Hearing us speak of this, Magdalene reacted sharply. 'You guys are sick! I didn't even know you were doing that, and I was with you all the time, you bastards!'

'That's because you are neither a writer nor a journalist, no, Mag?' Raji answered. 'The first thing we do when we visit a new place, okay, is to see what manner of people live in it, so that, afterwards, we can make judgements and say, for instance, that the people of Sohra or Shella or Jowai or Dawki or Mylliem are beautiful, but that the people of many other Khasi villages are not. There's nothing sick about that.'

'Okay, okay, and did you find any great beauty here?'

'I think we were not disappointed, ha, Ap? We did see a few comely ones, no?'

'Then you must have looked very hard indeed. Perhaps you have X-ray eyes like Superman to see through all that grime and dust. Even their faces were grimy, man!'

'You are not a man, na, Mag, that's why you cannot see beyond the dust,' Bah Kynsai said.

'What about their teeth? Did you find those beautiful too?'

'It was only kwai stain, ya. You are also eating kwai, no?' Raji replied.

'Yeah, but my teeth are not red like theirs. I take care to clean them many times a day.'

'You are a spoilt girl, na, you have all the time in the world to clean your teeth. Where do they find the time, always toiling in the jungle and their farms?' Bah Kynsai teased.

'Okay, okay, I get the point, but how can women be beautiful if their teeth are stained red by betel nut juice?'

'We just look beyond all that to the essence of their beauty,' Raji said.

'Red teeth are no obstacle,' Bah Kynsai added. 'They can be made white with vigorous brushing, na?'

'Hey, Ap.' Magdalene gestured to me. When I went to her side, she whispered, 'How are these people kissing, man, with such red teeth and stained lips?'

'Kissing is not a Khasi thing,' I whispered back. 'It came with the TV and affected educated people like you.'

'What about you?'

'I'd rather not say,' I said, for which I was rewarded with a pinch.

But Magdalene was right. We certainly did have to look very hard to see beyond the grime and dust, and we certainly had to ignore the red stain of their teeth. What surprised me most was that even young women here were heavily addicted to betel nut chewing. Elsewhere in the Khasi Hills, unmarried women (unmarried men too, for that matter) do not eat so much betel nut. They take one after every meal, but they also make sure to clean their teeth, if not with a toothbrush, then with a trimmed betel nut peel. From time immemorial, it has been the custom of Khasi men and women, especially those who are still unmarried, to carry betel nut peels with them wherever they go (many still do) so they can brush their teeth at regular intervals. With many married people, however, it is a different matter altogether. Unless they have a keen sense of personal hygiene, they do not clean their teeth at all. They pop one betel nut after another the whole day long until their mouths look like chimneys with burning coals. And what is more, they are very proud of their red teeth and, believe it or not, look down upon people with white teeth. This is because they associate people who do not eat betel nut with halitosis. It is common to hear them say:

'I hate the look of his mouth; it's so pale and sallow.'

'Because he doesn't eat kwai, no?'

'It must stink like a cesspool.'

'It does. I can't stand sitting near him; his breath is like a garbage truck.'

When I meet such people, I remind them that bad breath has nothing to do with not eating betel nut. Unless a person has rotten teeth, it is really a question of hygiene and how often they clean their teeth. But it's like talking to a wall, and all they say is, 'Wuu, for me, kwai is kwai!'

When Khasis begin a speech with the long-drawn sound of 'wuu', it means that they are rejecting what you are saying outright. And so they continue to chew their betel nuts with lime-marked betel leaves and turning their mouths red, like their ancestors did thousands of years ago.

Robert Lindsay has an amusing anecdote about his first contact with the Khasis in his book *Anecdotes of an Indian Life*. Lindsay was quite a manipulator. He was made the government agent and collector of Sylhet after secretly canvassing with members of the Dacca Council, which was then in control of the district. The council eventually gave him the posting, superseding eighteen or so of his senior colleagues in the process. When he arrived in Sylhet, Lindsay was delighted to contemplate 'the wide field of commercial speculation' opening before him through trade relations with the 'Cusseahs'. Describing their contiguous high country, he also enumerated the various resources it was rich in—wood of various kinds (useful in boat- and ship-building), iron of a very superior quality, silks 'of a coarse quality, called *moonga dutties*' (muka or muga silk dhotis), copper in bars, coarse muslins, ivory, honey gums, 'drugs for the European Market, and, in the fruit season, an inexhaustible quantity of the finest oranges'. But the most significant commodity of commerce was '*chunam*, or lime … in no part of Bengal, or even Hindostan … so perfectly pure, or so free of alloy' that the whole of eastern India was 'chiefly supplied' from the Khasi Hills through Sylhet. As the collector, Lindsay saw his opportunity to capture the lime market and monopolise the trade. But to do that, he had to deal with the Khasis directly. In his own words:

My great object was to procure from these people [the Khasis] a lease of the lime-rock, but they previously demanded an interview with me, to consult on the subject. A meeting was accordingly fixed at a place called Pondua [Pandua], situated close under the hills, forming one of the most stupendous amphitheatres in the world. The mountain appears to rise abruptly from the watery plain, and is covered with the most beautiful foliage and fruit trees of every description peculiar to the tropical climate, which seem to grow spontaneously from the crevices of the lime-rock. A more romantic or a more beautiful situation could not be found than the one then before me. The magnificent mountain, full in view, appeared to be divided with large perpendicular stripes of white, which, upon a nearer inspection, proved to be cataracts of no small magnitude; and the river, in which the boat anchored, was so pure that the trout and other fishes were seen playing about in every direction; above all, the air was delightful when contrasted with the close and pestilential atmosphere of the putrid plain below, so that I felt as if transplanted into one of the regions of Paradise. But the appearance of the inhabitants of this Garden of Eden did not enable me to follow out the theory I could have wished to establish; it certainly deserved a different style of inhabitants from those wild-looking demons then dancing on the banks before me.

Lindsay was driven to this conclusion by the Khasis' scarlet lips and the dark-red tint of their teeth, caused by a lifetime of betel nut chewing. He himself confirmed this when he described some of the Khasi women he met as they were bringing 'the produce of the hills' carried 'in baskets supported by a belt across the forehead' and escorted by men 'walking by their side, protecting them with arms'. He said, 'The elderly women in general were ugly in the extreme, and of masculine appearance; their mouths and teeth are as black as ink from inordinate use of the betel leaf mixed with lime. On the other hand, the young girls are both fair and handsome, not being allowed the use of betel nut until after their marriage.' In appearance, he wrote, the Khasis 'resemble very much the Malay'.

Though Lindsay had an awful first impression of the Khasis, he developed a grudging respect for them:

> After a residence of twelve years in their vicinity, and having had much business to transact with them, I can with safety describe the Cusseah, or native tartar of these mountains, a fair man in his dealings, and, provided you treat him honourably, he will act with perfect reciprocity towards you; but beware of shewing him the smallest appearance of indignity, for he is jealous in the extreme, cruel and vindictive in his resentments.

He also admired the Khasis' physique and strength: 'The strength of their arms and limbs, from constant muscular exercise in ascending and descending these mountains, loaded with heavy burthens, far exceeds our idea.' At one point, he wanted to test the weight the Khasi women were carrying. 'I asked one of the girls to allow me to lift her burthen of iron— from its weight I could not accomplish it. This, I need not say, occasioned a laugh in the line of march to my prejudice.'

Lindsay's statement about the vindictiveness of Khasis was backed by personal experience.

> On a certain occasion, when returning to Sylhet, I gave directions to my black officer in charge to permit none of the inhabitants of the plain to soil the beautiful walks or grounds around my dwelling. It unfortunately happened that a hill chief, from a distant mountain, came down a few days afterwards, and, thinking it a favourable situation, he was found by the officer in the very act of offending, and, being laid hold of, he was ordered to throw the noxious deposit into the river. The Cusseah told him that he was a total stranger, and that the offence should not be repeated, but that he neither would nor could act as directed, as it was against the laws of his

religion. Upon this, the officer gave him a few heavy blows with his cane, and compelled him to obey. In a few emphatic words he said, 'This day you have prevailed—it is my turn next'. He immediately clad himself in the garb of despair, (which is a couple of yards of white cotton, with a hole for the head in the middle, the hair thrown loose) and in this manner he sallied out to the Pondua bazar. Towards the evening the shrill war-whoop was heard in every direction, as the Cusseahs retired to the mountains; not a man was seen below for several weeks; at last they descended in considerable force; the offended chieftain singled out the officer who had insulted him,—they fought and both fell.

I had previous warning of what was to pass, and reinforced my small garrison; but the enormities committed by the Cusseahs against the defenceless inhabitants of the plain became very serious. I was compelled, in consequence, to stop all communication and passage of provisions; to retaliate was impossible, for you might as well attack the inhabitants of the moon as those of the mountain above …

I find this narrative diverting as well as illuminating. In these times, when Khasi Land is being encroached upon from every side, and when the inhabitants at the borders (especially the Assam border in the north, north-east and north-west) are being terrorised by the militant outfits of every neighbouring tribe, it is almost unimaginable for the contemporary Khasi—timid, weak and religion-drunk—to visualise that, in the faraway past, our ancestors had extended their territorial possessions far into the plains of Assam and Bengal and subjugated many communities there.

Lindsay's description of the Khasi character is also remarkably insightful. When Bah Kynsai described Hamkom as 'Hum Kisise Kum Naheen', he was unwittingly describing the general attribute of all Khasis. This was substantiated by the late S.J. Duncan, considered to be the finest Khasi short-story writer, who noted in an article that 'We are by nature too individualistic'. He felt this was one of the reasons why Khasis had never been able to establish cooperative societies that lasted for any length of time. I believe this is because of our society's egalitarian nature, which bestows upon every citizen the right to human dignity and gives them the confidence not to bow to anyone, not even to the king or the nobility of the land.

But let me get back to the story of kwai, our betel nut. Lindsay was right when he spoke of our 'inordinate use of the betel leaf mixed with lime', though he forgot to mention that it's always taken with betel nut. A Khasi usually takes as many as twenty to thirty *kyntiens*, or pieces (the literal translation is 'mouthfuls'), of betel nut a day. A kyntien is not the whole nut; as many as eight pieces can be obtained from a large nut. The practice of chewing betel nut is so integrated into the Khasi culture that, even today, distances are measured by the pieces of betel nuts eaten on the way (especially in rural areas). When you ask a Khasi how far Sohra is from Laitryngew, the next village to the north, he might well say, '*Kumba hynriew kyntien kwai*' ('About six pieces of betel nuts'). One kyntien is roughly equivalent to ten minutes, and therefore, one kilometre.

Even old people, toothless or with only a few teeth in their mouth, can be seen munching betel nuts all day long. How do they do it? Traditionally, most Khasi men and women carried net bags made from pineapple fibre, known as *ïarong*. These bags were of several sizes. The bigger ones were used to keep cowries, which were used as coins for trade with Khasis and non-Khasis alike—during Lindsay's time, about 1778, in Sylhet, 5,120 cowries were considered the equivalent of one rupee. The smaller varieties were used to keep betel nuts, betel leaves, tobacco (women usually take tobacco too, with betel nut) and lime, stored in a brass or silver box called *shanam*. Later, the net bags were replaced by haversacks for the men and cloth purses for the women, which were tucked into the jaiñsem. Still later, among the urbanised men, the haversacks were replaced by leather purses, which could be kept in the pockets of their trousers and coats.

Among us, only four people carried such purses: Raji, Bah Kynsai, Bah Su and Bah Kit. Evening, Hamkom, Magdalene, Dale and Halolihim carried their betel nuts in small polythene bags in which their waidongs—the prepared rolls of betel nut, betel leaf and lime—were packed. Donald and I did not carry either. Donald did not eat betel nut at all. Naturally, I like mine and eat quite a bit of it whenever I am at home and can brush my teeth frequently. But outside, I avoid it, not only because of the stain but also because it can be intoxicating. At home, I can always rinse my mouth immediately and sleep it off.

While the tooth-full carry betel nuts, betel leaves, lime and tobacco in purses or pouches, the toothless also carry a *dong khylliat*, a small bamboo tube in which they break up the betel nut with the help of a sharp metal stick attached to a wooden handle. Generally, the metal stick also serves as the lid for the tube. Sometimes old people simply carry a small knife with which they scrape the betel nut into fine shavings before eating.

And yet, betel nuts can take some getting used to. The uninitiated may not like the taste, and it can produce an unpleasant, intoxicating effect, which can make you retch violently. That is why, whenever I take the stuff, I take it without lime, so as to reduce its intoxicating property a little. When we first gave Nigel a chew of betel nut, he described the experience in *Through the Green Doors* as 'going through the Sahara'. This is because the betel nut is hard and dry before it blends in with the paste of lime and betel leaf. When this blending takes place, it becomes quite succulent, although it produces a kind of bitter juice at first that most people spit out to forestall the intoxication. The result is that many public places (roads, walls, toilets, buildings, electric posts, buses, taxis and so on) in Khasi-inhabited towns and villages are defaced by the red stains of betel nut juice. A common sign on buildings, buses and taxis in Shillong is: 'Do not spit or rub lime'. The excess lime is removed from the betel leaf with a finger and rubbed just about anywhere. That is why the sign. But as with all signs in Shillong, this one too is useless.

I remember when Nigel visited our university for the first time, he wanted, as he said, 'to visit the little house'. We pointed him to a urinal nearby. But out he came in a hurry, shouting, 'Who the hell's shitting up the walls? Or is it blood?'

When we went in, we found the walls mapped by beet-red betel nut stains everywhere. 'It's only kwai spittle,' we told him. 'You'll get used to it.'

Khasis have a saying about betel nut: 'I would rather lose a meal than lose my kwai.' People say it is many times more addictive than cigarettes or alcohol. The Welsh missionaries tried to wean Khasis away from its unwholesome influence, but though they were able to convert hundreds of Khasis every day to Christianity, they met with tacit resistance when it came to the betel nut. When they pointed to its unhygienic effect on the teeth, they were told: 'Only the white man and the dogs have white teeth.'

As we sat or lay about inside our hut, warmed by the fire in the open hearth, talking about Lyngngam beauties and their kwai-stained teeth, Magdalene voiced the question that had been raised so many times before: 'Why do Khasis like kwai so much? I mean, I also like it, but if I don't get it, okay, I'm all right. So why is it so difficult to give it up?'

'It's part and parcel of our culture, Mag,' Bah Su replied. 'As Ap said, you can give up your religion, but you cannot give up your kwai. It's too ingrained in our culture.'

'Kwai is God-given, that's why,' Bah Kit added. 'Everything goes back to time immemorial, to our creation myths.'

'What? Does kwai have an origin story too?' Magdalene asked, very interested.

'Of course,' Bah Kit said. 'Some people have written about it, Ap also.'

'Really, tell, tell, no, Ap!' Magdalene begged.

Donald, Dale, Hamkom and Evening had not heard the story either. Making myself more comfortable, I told them the story of *U Kwai, u Tympew, ka Shun bad u Dumasla*, a myth that explains the creation of betel nut, betel leaf, lime and tobacco.

'Actually, this is a tale of friendship, a most ennobling kind of friendship—a story of two men, each of whom would rather have died than hurt the feelings of the other,' I began. The story is set in a long-ago world that was still in a state of innocence; when no discrimination was known between rich and poor. During that time, there lived, in a small and ancient Khasi village called Rangjyrwit, two loving friends, U Nik Mahajon, a rich bachelor, and U Shing Raitoi, a poor man with a poor wife, ironically named Ka Lak, meaning 'great wealth'.

The love between the two friends would be considered extraordinary today. Nik Mahajon was a prosperous merchant who had everything he could possibly need. Shing Raitoi, on the other hand, was a labourer who had to cut wood, break stones and do all sorts of odd jobs just for a handful of rice each day. But his rich friend respected Shing and treated him as an equal. Often, he invited his poor friend to his house, and whenever Shing visited him, Nik never let him go away empty-handed, but always gave him something useful to carry back home. However hard Shing tried to decline these gifts, his rich friend would simply not hear of it.

This state of affairs continued for a long time and quite troubled poor Shing, who realised how one-sided things were. Every time he returned from a visit to his friend, he never failed to talk to his wife about how unequal his relationship with Nik was. 'We are always taking, you see, Lak, we are always taking and not giving him anything in return,' he would moan. 'This is a shameful affair indeed, but how, my beloved wife, how to repay our dear friend for all his kindness?'

Eventually, the couple overcame their bashfulness and decided to invite Nik to their place at least once, despite the bareness of their home.

One day, when Shing was visiting Nik, he said to him: 'My dearest friend, Nik, I have been here so many times, but my home has never even seen your shadow.' Jokingly, he added, 'Is it that you dislike witnessing my poverty?'

'Why do you say that, my dearest Shing,' Nik replied, 'when I have always wanted to visit you in your home to see what kind of things you do in your spare time, and perhaps enjoy an evening meal with you?'

'I'm happy you feel that way, Nik,' Shing replied sincerely. 'You must surely drop in on us one of these days. I hope it doesn't matter to you if we can provide only a simple dish of rice and salt?'

To that meek submission, Nik said, 'Surely not, my friend! When the heart is happy, everything is tasty.'

So overwhelmed was Shing by this assurance that tears welled up in his eyes, and all he could do was embrace Nik yet again. Embarrassed by his own emotions, he left his friend's house abruptly without even finalising the date of Nik's visit to his home. Perhaps, if he had not overlooked that, the ensuing tragedy would not have happened at all.

Sometime after that, Nik called on Shing for the first time in his life. Shing and his wife were pleased with their kind friend's graciousness and received him as only pure and loving hearts like theirs could. After a brief exchange of pleasantries, Lak left the two men to enjoy their time together, and went to the kitchen to busy herself with her own chores.

Having basked for some time in the glory of his friend's first visit, Shing thought it was fit and proper for him to entertain Nik with whatever food they had in the house. Excusing himself for a moment, he went to the kitchen and asked his wife to prepare something for all of them so that they could enjoy dinner together. He was determined that his friend should not leave his house without something to eat, partly because of his love for him and partly because he did not want him to think that he was miserly.

It was with great shock and dismay, therefore, that he learned from his wife that there was not a morsel of food in the house, not even rice enough for one person. Shing had not been working for some days owing to a persistent cold from which he had just recovered. He was planning to go back to work the next day and ask his employer for an advance, but it was already too late: even their stock of rice had run out.

What was he to do? His beloved friend was visiting his house for the first time, and he could not even treat him to a simple dinner! What a shame, he thought, what a horrible shame! 'Go, my dear Lak, go to our neighbours and borrow some rice so we may at least feed our dear friend. Only enough rice to boil for a single meal, just that. That is all we need.'

The faithful Lak went around the village asking for rice, but all the neighbours proved to be as empty of provisions as they were or distrustful of their capacity to return the handout. Consequently, Lak had to return empty-handed and with a heavy heart. To her husband's query, she sadly shook her head and told him how hopeless the errand had turned out to be.

Unable to go back to his friend, whom he had left alone in the other room, Shing suddenly snatched up a carving knife hanging nearby. Declaring to his wife, 'It is better to die than to live with such humiliation,' he stabbed himself in the heart and died there and then.

Lak stood there, a dumb witness to her dearest love's desperate deed. His death was so sudden and shocking that for quite some time, she could only stand there and think of nothing but doors slamming in her face. Then she slowly came back to herself and thought of her life. How full of hardship and privation her whole existence had been. And now that her only faithful companion, her husband, had also deserted her, she did not think it was worth living any more. 'What will I do alone in this wretched world of grief and suffering, shame and disgrace? As I lived with him, so shall I die with him!' So saying, she wrested the knife from her husband's breast and killed herself with it.

While this horrifying scene was being enacted in the kitchen, the sanctum sanctorum of every Khasi home, Nik was getting more and more bored and fidgety alone in the sitting room. He could not understand why his good friend had suddenly disappeared and left him to his own company. It was unlike Shing and, in Khasi society, not at all polite. In fact, it was an outright insult to neglect a guest in this manner. But Nik knew his friend too well to condemn his behaviour without knowing why. Therefore, he got to his feet, determined to see for himself what was happening in the kitchen.

The first thing he saw was the body of his friend, and beside it, the body of his beloved wife. The floor ran red with their blood. Nik was dumbfounded. After such a happy time together, what could have driven his friend to cut short his own life like this! That the two had taken their own lives, he was in no doubt at all. All the evidence pointed to that. But the motive! What could be the motive?

After inspecting the bare and bloodied room, he noticed a rice pot boiling in the fireplace with nothing but water in it. 'Ah, I see now!' he exclaimed. 'Oh my God, Lord and Master, now I see! But why, friend, why? Just because you couldn't feed me! As if I ever expected anything but love from you! What are all my possessions to me now? I have lost the best part of the wealth I had … And who would believe such a story? No, rather than be shamed for this, let me die here with you!' With these words, he also seized the knife, stabbed himself, and fell dead on the spot.

Oblivious of the tragedy that had befallen the house of Shing, the rooster, herald of the sun, sounded his first bugle of the day, announcing the approach of dawn. His crowing caused a roving thief, who was running past the hut, great alarm. He had been trying all night to flee his pursuers from a nearby village. With the coming of dawn so soon, where could he hide? The open hut—which was, just a little while ago, such a happy dwelling for two very poor but deeply loving souls—appeared deserted. It must be an abandoned house, he thought, stealing into it to rest for a while. Because he was so tired and spent, he found his eyes closing against his will.

When he finally awoke, it was morning and most people were up and about. Rubbing his eyes, he looked around at the place into which he had stumbled and which he thought had saved him from sure punishment. But when he saw the dead bodies and the inundation of blood, he jumped up as if bitten by a snake and called out, for the first time in his adult life, the name of his mother. 'Wow, Mei,' he shouted. 'What doom is this for me! From the mouth of the tiger into the jaws of Thlen! If people find me here, they will take me not only for a thief but a murderer, a blood-hunter. What shall I do? Alas, there is no peace for the soul that is black!'

Having quite exhausted himself with cursing his fate, he began to think seriously about his predicament. He knew what awaited him if he was caught—first, the three-patterned shaving of his head, then the parade through the village, with the crowd beating the drums tied to his back, for all to know that he was a killer. And finally, of course, *u tangon u lymban*, the heavy logs with which to break his neck.

'To die after having gone through so much humiliation,' he said aloud, 'and that too for no fault of mine! I would rather die now, a clean, honourable death, along with these unhappy people.' And so, he grasped the very same weapon and ended his thieving career forever.

When the villagers came to know of this terrible tale, they were moved as never before. This could happen to any of them—any one of them might be in a situation where they could not repay a more fortunate neighbour or friend with an act of kindness equal to the one bestowed on them. They called a council of the whole village and prayed to their Creator, U Blei, calling on him to devise new ways of exchanging pleasantries and gifts, and to make something new that was easier to procure than rice so that such a tragic event might never again occur when a rich man visited his poor friend.

God, who was just and kind and saw everything, created from the four bodies lying in the hut a betel nut tree (kwai), a betel-leaf plant (*tympew*), lime (*shun*) and tobacco (*dumasla*) so that both the rich and the poor may use them while socialising with each other. It was from then on that the custom of exchanging kwai, taken together with betel leaf, lime and sometimes tobacco, started among the Khasis. Nik Mahajon, the rich man, metamorphosed into a betel nut, and Shing Raitoi and his wife, Lak, into a betel leaf and lime, which are taken together. The thief turned into tobacco, which Khasi women insert in a corner of their mouths as if to provide it with a hiding place.

Magdalene wiped a tear from her eye and said, 'It's so bloody sad, ya, Ap, like hara-kiri, no?'

'It's sad and bloody, but not tragic,' I replied. 'All the characters, you must remember, metamorphosed into something else: not only into plants and things but also into a beautiful custom.'

'A beautiful custom, he says!' Magdalene laughed through her tears. 'Just look at everybody who eats kwai in this place, man! Has the custom made their teeth beautiful?'

'Not beautiful in that way, certainly, but it's a custom that breaks through all differences in society. It brings together the rich and the poor, the great and the small. When you enter a Khasi home, rich or poor, you will always find a *shangkwai*, a betel nut basket, in the kitchen, occupying pride of place among the most indispensable of utensils and foodstuff. And after you have been in the house for a while, a woman will come into the room with the shangkwai and start peeling a betel nut, splitting it into seven or eight pieces. Then she will rub the betel leaf (already washed and cleaned) dry with her jaiñsem outer garment, divide it into two or three parts, apply a bit of lime to it and offer it to you with a piece of betel nut. This is what Khasis call *shi kyntien kwai*, one chew of betel nut. If you are female, the woman will ask you: "Would you like a piece of tobacco too?"'

'Don't Khasi men chew tobacco, Bah Ap?' Donald asked.

'They smoke, as you know, but they don't chew tobacco at all. The betel nut preparation is given to you when you come into the house and just before you leave it. In fact, you cannot leave the house without a betel nut for the road. And when Khasis meet anywhere, they exchange betel nuts as a sign of trust and friendship. Do you see it now? The whole gamut of human relationships in Khasi society is brought under the purview of betel nut eating and sharing. The rich eat from the poor and the poor eat from the rich. It's a unifying and binding custom. That's why it's beautiful.'

The custom is so integrated into the culture that no important activity in life is complete without it. The betel nut waits for you at the end of every feast. It is our dessert, our chewing gum and, for many, our mouth freshener.

Many Khasis would rather chew a betel nut than brush their teeth after a meal. This is probably because of its detergent-like properties, which give the illusion of a washed and clean feeling.

Because betel nut is supposed to be God-given, it occupies a special place in Khasi culture. When you visit a neighbour, it is the first and the last thing he will offer you. In a courtship, when many are courting the same woman, she will show her preference by giving the man of her choice the first piece of betel nut. At a wedding, when the groom and his male escorts arrive, they are met halfway to the bride's house by her male relatives with pieces of betel nut. And no funeral rite is considered complete unless *ka noh kwai*, the ceremonial offering of betel nut, is made at the pyre by the dead man's relatives, friends, and all those who were close to him. When a person dies, Khasis say, '*U lah leit bam kwai sha ïing U Blei*' ('He's gone to eat betel nut in the house of God'). When I was a kid, I used to ask my elders why they always said this instead of saying, 'He's gone to eat food in the house of God.' Later, I realised that kwai, because of its supposedly divine origin, is a much more potent symbol of divine grace, acceptance and forgiveness.

This saying also points to the Khasi belief that the original home of man is heaven. So, when he dies, if he has earned virtue in life, his soul and his essence will go to heaven to be united forever with all the cognate and agnate members of his clan who died before him.

This is why, when a person refers to a dead man in a conversation, he also says, '*Bam kwai ha ïing U Blei*' ('May he eat betel nut in the house of God'). It's an invocation that wishes the dead well, but also one that asks him not to be disturbed by the taking of his name—he's not being called upon and should not visit the caller, but should remain peacefully in the house of God, eating betel nut.

Magdalene was sceptical. She asked, 'Are we really doing all that with kwai, Ap? I have never heard so much being said about it, ya!'

'Of course,' Bah Kit answered for me. 'Perhaps we are missing something even now. I know, for instance, that some augurs will never begin their business unless the person for whom they are praying and conducting the rituals has brought an unpeeled kwai and betel leaf with him.'

'Betel nut and its associates, betel leaf, lime and tobacco, are even used as medicine, Mag,' I told her. 'When still green, the nut is used for treating stomach ailments and sores. The seasoned nut can be burnt and ground into a powder to serve as medicinal toothpaste. It can also be given to animals for deworming. Betel leaf can be used for treating cuts and minor wounds, to stop the bleeding and also as a healing salve. Lime can be used for all sorts of insect bites and, when mixed with honey, is the best natural medicine for bruises and swellings. It is also excellent for removing a leech that has attached itself to your skin and for treating its bite. Tobacco is also good for this. Sometimes, tobacco juice is used in the treatment of conjunctivitis and other eye problems. And, oh yes, betel nut, betel leaf and lime, when taken together, act as a natural deworming medicine and a great preventer of cavities in teeth. The teeth may look stained and ugly, but they don't stink because they remain healthy and whole. Betel nut paste can also be used to treat minor wounds.'

'Wow, amazing, man!' Magdalene cried, genuinely astonished. 'That's why I have never had problems with my teeth or what? I think I should eat more now, like the Lyngngam women, hahaha.'

But Hamkom said, 'Wait, wait, is Ap pulling our leg or what?'

'No, no, it's absolutely true,' Raji told him. 'There's a book written by a forest ranger named San Blah, published in 1920, which also discusses these things.'

'How come I haven't heard of the book, ya?' Hamkom asked in a lamenting tone.

Before Evening could insult him, I said quickly, 'Because you don't read much Khasi. The book is written in Khasi.'

'Okay, okay, but what about its bad effects? We all know it has many, okay?'

'Haven't you seen those posters with the warning, "Alcohol, Betel Nut, Cigarette and Tobacco Cause Cancer", Ham?' I asked. 'They are put up by the health department everywhere, but of course, no one listens to them. I have heard villagers asking a doctor, "Does it mean that people who don't eat kwai do not get cancer?" When the doctor replies that of course non-kwai-eaters could also be susceptible to cancer, they smile and say, "Then kwai has got nothing to do with cancer." Nobody can wean them off betel nut, and if you try, they will only say, "I would have to stop being a Khasi first."'

'That's true, that's true, I have heard this too,' Magdalene laughed. 'I'm very curious about one thing, though. In the noh kwai ceremony, ha, Ap, why do they throw unpeeled betel nut and unsplit betel leaf, without lime, into the pyre?'

'They don't throw, Mag, they give gently, and utter a short prayer before giving,' I explained. 'The reason is that they are offering them to a dead person. The world of the dead is considered to be the inverse of the living. Therefore, a betel nut for the dead should not be offered in the same way as it is given to the living.'

'Aah, interesting.'

'Yeah, quite,' Donald agreed. 'I think I will also start taking kwai now, Bah Ap,' he added with a laugh.

'So, like the villagers, you are not afraid of cancer?' I teased.

'I thought you don't care for identity,' Evening jeered. 'Kwai is also about asserting your identity, so why should you care for it, huh?'

Ignoring Evening, Donald replied, 'Your story has made it sound too charming not to be taken, Bah Ap.'

At that moment, Halolihim entered the hut, having returned from what Bah Kynsai called his 'sheep-poaching mission'. He asked Donald, 'What has to be taken?'

'Kwai.'

'Oh yes. Look at me, the amount of kwai I have taken tonight is too much. But what to do, if I don't eat their kwai, they won't listen to me talk about God.'

Hamkom smiled. 'How was your night?'

'Hmm, it's a good beginning, I think.'

'Okay, okay, carry on tomorrow night then,' Hamkom said, encouragingly.

'Do they grow kwai here?' Magdalene asked.

I had put the same question to Chirag, and in response, he had pointed to a few areca-nut trees behind his ancestral house and said, 'You see those, Babu? Look closely at the kwai, they are very small, no, Babu? They are not young, they are quite matured, but they don't grow bigger than that. I don't know why they grow only in Ri War when the climate is almost the same, must be something in the soil there, there's a lot of lime in it, no, Babu, here we don't have that, that may be the reason or what? Even oranges, which grow very well there, do not thrive here.'

In response to Magdalene, I simply said, 'No.'

'So how can they have so much kwai when they don't grow it here?'

I had asked Chirag that question, too, and he had given me a long-winded answer. 'You know, Babu, Shyrkon and its surrounding areas, no, Babu, are bounded by two big rivers: Wah Blei to the west and Wah Rwiang to the east. Both rivers have a magnificent waterfall each. The one at Wah Rwiang is called Riat Phyllaw Falls, and the one at Wah Blei is Tongsang Falls. The whole region comprising our village, the farmlands and the vast jungles between these two rivers, no, Babu, easily about twenty square kilometres, ha, is like a huge island. Travel is difficult but negotiable in winter with trucks and four-wheel jeeps, as I have told you, Babu, but it is simply impossible to get in and out of the area in summer when the rivers are in spate. The rivers meet at a place called Shnat Wah Blei, to the south of Shyrkon. So what people do, no, Babu, they stock up on essentials, whatever they have to buy from outside, in spring, for in summer, from about May to October, the road is simply impassable, and even if it isn't, the rivers cannot be crossed. But to stock up on everything you need for an entire season is difficult, no, Babu, it takes a lot of money, so mostly everyone stocks up on rice, salt, dried fish and kerosene. People here have simple needs, Babu. However, they must always have kwai, everyone is addicted to it, and moreover it is part of our culture, no, Babu, so they also stock up on it like an essential item.'

'In winter it's not a problem,' I told Magdalene, 'they buy from Maweit or Nongstoin, but in summer they stock it like they do other essential items— rice, salt, dried fish and kerosene.'

'And the kwai doesn't go bad?'

'They have a way of preserving it.'

'So, in summer, they survive only on rice, salt and dried fish, Bah Ap?' Donald interposed.

'That's what Chirag told me.'

'Amazing!' he said.

'What a terribly hard life, ya!' Magdalene said.

'Could you survive like that, Bah Kynsai?' Hamkom asked.

'Why not?' Bah Kynsai answered. 'Man, na, Ham, can get used to anything, that is his greatest quality. He can get used to the most horrible of conditions. That's how people survive.'

After a brief lull, Bah Kynsai yawned and said, 'Aah Lyngngam! What a pleasantly warm and beautiful place Shyrkon is!'

'In winter,' Bah Kit cautioned.

'But this is the life, no?' Raji enthused, slurring a little. 'Warm in the midst of winter, nothing to worry about, plenty of good food and a sweet, sweet khor. I have never tasted such wonderful brew before.'

'Yeah, me neither,' said Ham. 'And the food is certainly good too. I like boiled stuff. Pork boiled with potatoes is delicious, no?'

'I wonder when they'll give us fish,' Magdalene said.

'You like fish? I doubt they will give us fish. *Ktung*, maybe,' Bah Kit said.

Ktung is dried fish, a very popular food in Khasi villages, partly because it is cheaper than meat and partly because it can be stored for a long time and can be prepared in a variety of simple ways. You can make curries with it, fry it, boil it or simply chargrill it and then mix it with onions and chillies.

'They might, I think, there must be plenty of fish in that lake, no, Bah?' Dale said. He had been listening to us without saying anything for quite some time.

'There are! That's what they told us,' Magdalene answered for me. 'And what a stunningly beautiful lake! Imagine something like that in the middle of this jungle! It's a real discovery, ya!'

'Don't forget the waterfall and the River Rwiang, Mag!' Donald reminded her.

'Who can forget?' Magdalene agreed. 'Shyrkon is full of beauty ... not speaking of humans, obviously!' she added, laughing.

'We should take a swim in it, Bah Kynsai, come on, let's do it!' Raji said, slurring even more now.

'You are asking me, tdong?' Bah Kynsai, who could not swim at all, replied with a curse.

'Wuu, scary!' Magdalene said.

'It's quite deep and dark, not a good place for a swim,' Donald remarked. 'Not for us anyway. But it certainly is a beautiful place, no, Bah Kynsai? We could go there for a picnic, you know.'

'I'm going to swim in it,' Raji declared. 'I don't know about you people, but I'm going to swim! Perly used to swim in it, and if Perly can, so can I, I'll show you!'

'But we went there too late this afternoon, ya,' Magdalene moaned. 'I wish we had gone earlier, no?'

'Why are you worried? We have ten days left, no?' Raji consoled her. 'Ten days, Mag, relax, relax.'

'Tomorrow, we'll go there again, okay?'

We had gone to see the lake earlier, but quite late in the afternoon. Perly, who was supposed to take us there, had remembered only towards 4 p.m. It was quite a walk, as I mentioned earlier, about three kilometres, but we all enjoyed it. We crossed the bamboo gate on the outskirts, travelled a little up the road, and stopped at a place where a path led off towards the jungle on the right. We walked along the brush-choked path for about 200 yards, and then we came upon one of the most astonishing sights I have seen anywhere in the Khasi Hills. There before us, shimmering in the setting sun and completely surrounded by the forest, was a magnificent lake, its dark green waters gently wrinkling in the breeze. The moment we came upon its southern end, a flock of white geese and black cormorants took flight. They had been perched on the branches of some submerged trees in the middle of the lake. We scrambled for our cameras but were too late to capture anything.

'That was an awesome sight!' Magdalene cried.

'*Ki han blei*,' Perly said.

'Ki han blei?' Hamkom asked. 'God-geese? What about the black ones?'

'*Ki han ïong.*'

Actually, they were cormorants, but Perly simply said, 'Black geese.'

'Ah, that's more straightforward. But why are the white ones called god-geese?'

'Nobody knows,' Perly replied.

But Bah Su said, 'Because they are pure white and because they can fly, unlike the ordinary land-bound variety. That makes them unique and wonderful, hence god-geese.'

The lake was about 300 yards wide, but it was quite long, and its dark waters suggested great depth. Perly confirmed this. He said he had measured its depth and found it to be about seventy feet in most places. He also said the lake was much longer than Nan Polok. To be precise, it was 780 metres long, that is, only slightly less than a kilometre. It was called Mlieng Jirang, *mlieng* meaning 'lake' and *jirang* meaning 'streamlet'.

'Streamlet lake!' I exclaimed. 'It's a wonderful name, but why is it called so?'

'*Tip*,' Perly said.

'Tip' is a very curious Khasi word. It means 'know', but when someone says 'tip', like Perly had just now, it's used in the sense of not knowing, like 'I don't know'.

'Are there any fish here?' Bah Kynsai wanted to know.

'The lake is full of fish,' Perly replied.

'Can we fish here now?' Evening asked.

'They don't bite in winter, only in summer.'

'If they don't bite, how do they eat?' I asked.

'I don't know, but they don't bite in winter,' Perly insisted.

'Okay, but if they don't bite and are in hiding, then what were those geese doing here?'

'Wuu, they have their own methods,' he said. 'There are tortoises also here, but they are also more active in summer.'

'How was this lake formed, Bah Perly?' I asked, not expecting an answer.

But Perly surprised me by saying, 'Originally there was no lake in Shyrkon, Babu, only small springs flowing into the jungle as streamlets. But when the great earthquake of 1897 came, no, Babu, this lake also came into being.'

'That's the secret of its name, Bah Perly! Why did you say you didn't know when I asked you earlier?'

'Tip,' he replied.

'Hey, did you hear that, you people?' Donald shouted. 'This lake was formed by the great earthquake of 1897. The earthquake that flattened mountains and turned flatlands into mountains. Incredible!'

'This lake must be bigger than Ward's Lake in Shillong, ya,' Magdalene observed.

'That's what Perly just said,' Bah Kynsai replied.

'He said Nan Polok.'

'It's the same thing, *pha bieit!*'

'Pha bieit' means 'you fool', but Bah Kynsai said it in a playful tone, so Magdalene did not mind at all.

'Is it, Bah Kynsai? I also didn't know that, ya,' Donald said.

Halolihim surprised us by saying, 'What do you know, Don? You know nothing about us.'

'Stop mocking him, Halolihim!' Bah Kynsai said and then turned to Perly. 'Hey, Perly, shall we go, it's getting dark, man!'

Now, sitting around the fire in the hut, Magdalene referred back to our conversation about Nan Polok and asked, 'Is there a story behind Nan Polok, Bah Kynsai?'

'There's a story behind everything in the Khasi Hills, na?'

'Seriously, man!'

'Let the historian tell you. I want to enjoy my booze and listen to you all for a change. Tell her, Ham,' Bah Kynsai ordered.

'She's also a historian, no? And what is there to tell? The lake was made on the orders of the then chief commissioner of Khasi-Jaiñtia Hills, Sir William Ward, that's why it's known as Ward's Lake.'

'No, no, I want to know why Khasis call it Nan Polok,' Magdalene told him.

'That, I also don't know.'

'Phooey, historian!' Evening lashed out at Hamkom. 'Raji, Ap, tell them, tell them.'

Raji responded by saying, 'You think I'm in any condition to tell anybody anything or what?'

'Khasis call it Nan Polok because of the engineer, na?' Bah Kynsai said, deciding to chip in after all. 'His name was Pollock; he supervised the work of constructing the lake.'

'There's more to the story of Nan Polok than that, Bah Kynsai,' Bah Kit corrected him. 'Tell them, Ap, you know the story better than I do.'

'Actually, the history of Nan Polok goes much farther back than either Ward or Pollock,' I began. 'According to a well-known story that was written down for the first time by the Khasi writer W.R. Laitflang, the idea of building a lake was first conceived by a Khasi prisoner from Ri Pnar. He had been brought to Shillong during the chief commissionership of Colonel Henry Hopkinson. Bored with the idle prison life, he begged the authorities to allow him some physical exercise. When asked what kind of exercise, he replied like the farmer he was, that he would like to dig the ground with a hoe. They took him to a field near the present accountant general's office and let him dig. The man began digging a damp piece of ground and carried on as if he were making a paddy field ready. After he had done that for some days, water suddenly gushed out and turned his paddy field into a pool. When the prison authorities came to know about it, they reported the matter to the chief commissioner's office. Colonel Hopkinson himself hit upon the idea of enlarging the prisoner's pool into a lake and work began immediately.

'When the digging was done in earnest by a large labour force, water was found in more than one place, and thus was born a series of artificial lakes known as Hopkinson's Tanks. During the chief commissionership of Sir William Ward, who took a personal interest in the beautification of Shillong, the series of lakes were merged into one big lake. By the way, Ham, Ward was the chief commissioner of Assam and not of Khasi-Jaiñtia Hills. During his time, many other improvements were made. Like the construction of a wooden bridge across the lake—the same one you can see today, yes— and footpaths along its banks. All this work was supervised by an executive engineer named Pollock, who also had trees and flowers planted everywhere. That's why, though the lake became officially known as Ward's Lake, Khasis decided to give credit to the man who actually did the work, and called it Nan Polok. Unfortunately, in the history of Nan Polok, the name of the Khasi man, the Pnar whose boredom in prison had led to the creation of this magnificent beauty spot, was lost through sheer negligence and the disdain of everyone involved.'

When I finished, Evening pointed at Hamkom and yelled, 'And this fellow thought there was nothing much to tell, phooey historian!'

To my mind, Magdalene, the other historian among us, knew even less. But Evening had not been disparaging of her. I think he could not stand Hamkom because he was fanatical about the idea of 'Jaiñtias' as a separate people, although, as we have seen, there is absolutely no ground for it.

I was afraid they would start quarrelling again. Luckily, before Hamkom could react, Bah Kynsai said, '*Kyntur u sniang ïoh nam u ksew.*'

Bah Kynsai was referring to the popular Khasi fable, 'The Dog and the Pig'. According to this fable, a long, long time ago, a dog and a pig went to live as servants to a farmer. They used to do whatever their master asked them to, from the easiest to the most difficult of tasks.

One day, the farmer asked them to till one of his fields on the outskirts of the village. The two left early in the morning, only returning when it was too dark to work. But while Pig worked all day, digging and turning the earth over, preparing it for cultivation, Dog slept the whole day in the shade of some trees nearby. Only when it was time to leave did he get up. He then ran over the tilled section once or twice, and left for home.

After watching Dog do this day after day, Pig decided to complain to their master. 'My Lord,' he said, 'I don't want to work with this Dog any more. He does nothing but sleep the whole day and makes me do all the work.'

The farmer summoned Dog and asked, 'Is it true, what Pig said? Is it true that you don't do any work but sleep all day?'

Dog denied the allegation and said, 'This Pig is a liar, my Lord. I have been working as hard as him, if not harder; I don't know why he would falsely accuse me like this.'

'Tomorrow,' the farmer said to Dog, 'you must work harder, I don't want any more complaints, do you understand?'

Dog readily agreed and said he would work as hard as he had always done. However, when they got to the field the following day, he simply went to sleep, and then, towards the evening, ran over the tilled section, as he used to do.

Pig went to their master and said, 'My Lord, Dog refused to work yet again. If you cannot do anything about him, then I too will be forced to do nothing but lie about like him.'

The farmer decided to take Pig's complaint seriously this time. He said, 'Tomorrow we will go and see the field for ourselves. I want to find out the truth about this once and for all.'

When they got to the field the next day, the farmer examined the tilled sections carefully and found that Dog's footprints were more visible than

Pig's. Angry at Pig's false reports, he said to him, 'You are nothing but a liar and a cheat! You have made allegations against poor Dog without any basis at all. You are nothing but a mischief-monger! What do I see here? Take a look for yourself! Dog's footprints in the fields appear more often than yours. I can see that he has worked harder than you. For spreading canards against your poor companion and for not working hard enough, from now on, you will live in the damp space beneath my hut; only Dog will be allowed a warm place on the porch. That is your punishment!'

The moral of the fable is *kyntur u sniang ïoh nam u ksew*, 'the pig tills, the dog gets all the praise', which always happens when the judge himself is blind.

Bah Kit said thoughtfully, 'This has been the pattern with us Khasis throughout history, no, Bah Kynsai? We always forget our own. The prisoner who created Nan Polok has been forgotten by most of us. But that is not the worst of it. There is hardly any record of our history as a people. Many of us are not even interested in it, nor are we interested in our identity. We don't want to know about our roots or ourselves. We don't have any respect for what is our own. The name of Ri Hynñiew Trep, or Ri Khasi, for instance, has lost out to Meghalaya …'

But Bah Kit could not go on. Evening interrupted him and launched into a long speech, though in such a sad and ponderous tone that he surprised us all, for we had got used to his aggressiveness. It was almost a lament, I thought.

'There are cosmos, Bah Kit, who prefer that alien name to our Ri Hynñiew Trep, and even jeer at people for invoking it,' he mourned. 'Only jingoists and militants, they scorn, can even think about it, not realising that the Hynñiew Treps were our ancestors. How can we laugh at our own parents? What kind of ingrates are we? Ri Pnar has also lost out to Jaiñtia Hills, and some even think, foolishly, illogically, that Pnars are actually Jaiñtias, a name given by Bengalis and beaten into our stupid heads by the white man …

'And what is happening around us? Our border villages are lost, overwhelmed by the neighbouring tribes and migrant communities, and terrorised by their armed insurgents. Think of Langpih, overwhelmed by migrants from Assam. Think of the villages in Block I, Block II, in Ri Bhoi and Ri Pnar, overwhelmed by their next-door neighbours. Think of Ri Bhoi, a quarter of which has been lost to Assam. Think of West Khasi Hills, a quarter of which is lost to our so-called brethren from Garo Hills. Think of villages on the Bangla border, some of them overwhelmed by Shilotias and others terrorised by Bangladeshi goons, who raid their farms and steal their crops day in and day out. Think of Shillong, where migrants can say, "This is Jhalupara, not Meghalaya."

'And what do we do about all this, ha, Bah Kynsai? While the villagers suffer, the cosmos say we are fear-mongering. Blind and deaf, they denounce us as jingoistic, narrow-minded and communal. Our women sell their bodies and souls to migrants. Our men are bought with benami transactions. Our politicians are busy being "tamperists" and "scamperists". All their schemes are directed by their purse strings. Expecting them to make laws and frame policies, to plan and strategise, is like expecting a con artist to do an honest day's work. As our Rome burns, they fiddle and make merry. As our people become refugees in their own land, time and time again, they play musical chairs. Sometimes I really, really feel like wringing their necks, the bastards!'

When Evening finished his dismal speech, Bah Kynsai demanded loudly and none too soberly, 'What the hell was all that about? Are you crying or what, liah?'

His tone made Hamkom and Donald laugh, but Raji said, slurring drunkenly, 'No, no, no, Bah Kynsai, don't say that, don't say that. Don and Ham and Mag and the others may not agree, I don't know, but I agree, I agree ... Totally agree! I'm feeling depressed already; I'm crying already, leh, it's so true, so true.'

'Okay, okay,' Bah Kynsai conceded. 'What now? Shall we call it a night and go to bed on this incredibly depressing note? It's very late, na, almost two o'clock.'

'You go to bed, Bah Kynsai, you all go to bed, only give me that gourd, I'll have another bamboo—I won't say another glass or another cup, ha, this is not a glass or a cup, you understand? This is a bamboo tube, bamboo tube,' he repeated, wagging a finger at us. 'Let me have another bamboo before I sleep.'

Raji took the gourd from Bah Kynsai, who asked all of us, 'What shall we do tomorrow?'

'Tomorrow, Bah Kynsai,' Raji answered for us, 'we will get up, have our breakfast of red tea and plain rice and then vanish into the jungle one by one, as we did yesterday. After that, after that, we will see. Now, all of you can sleep.'

'Come, come,' Bah Kynsai said to us, 'let's put out the fire first, then we'll sleep.'

I had been carefully observing my friends' faces as we listened to Evening's outpouring of grief. Halolihim was lost in a world of his own, probably plotting his next move. Donald and Hamkom appeared soured by all the taunts directly and indirectly aimed at them. But the rest—Bah Kynsai (despite his bravado), Mag (who had not been of the same view as Evening earlier) and Dale ('a mere taxi driver')—seemed genuinely affected. As for me, I was reminded of the following lines from a poem by a friend:

> Let me sit astride a pachyderm and see-saw
> through the reeds in search of the rivet-skinned rhino.
> I would like nothing more than to look it in the eye
> and say, 'Mine too is a vanishing tribe'.

He was talking about the Khasi tribe, of course. I had always thought he was exaggerating, but right now, I was not so sure.

4

THE SECOND NIGHT

NAME STORIES

'A person with a bad name
is already half-hanged.'
—old proverb

On the third day, 6 February, we thought of taking a bath at the village well in the morning. (Khasis always refer to the act of washing one's body as 'bathing' or 'taking a bath' even when there is no bath.) But that turned out to be impossible. The place was teeming with people, mostly women and children. Many of the women were washing clothes by a little stream running from the well. The stream ran over a flat stone surface called *mawsiang*, or spreading stone, which made for a perfect washing spot. The children were mostly fetching water from the well in plastic jerry cans and buckets, used paint containers and bamboo tubes. I had never seen bamboo tubes as big as these—two feet in length and eight inches in diameter—but then, I had never been to Lyngngam before.

Not able to bathe, we made do with cleaning our hands and feet and hair. Then we washed our dusty clothes and returned to the hut. At about noon, we went to the death house and ate a lunch of boiled vegetables and chargrilled dried fish with rice. Perly came to meet us, and when we told him about our problem, he said, 'Go to the lake for a bath, Babu, you can go tomorrow. And no need to rush back for lunch, it's far, no, Babu, I'll pack some for you. You eat there, take it easy, spend the entire day there, no need to rush back.'

'That's an excellent idea, Bah Perly,' I replied. We all thanked him profusely.

After lunch, Perly came to spend the afternoon with us on a high platform among the trees. The platform was the biggest in Nongshyrkon. There were two lines of trees there, with a gap of fifteen feet between them. Their branches met in the middle, forming a natural canopy that was shady and cool. The platform was built to span this gap, resting on the boughs of the trees on either side. As the others slept or chatted, Perly told me the gripping tale behind the founding of Nongshyrkon. Later, sitting around the fire in our hut, after an early dinner of pork boiled with bamboo shoots and green chillies, I narrated the tale to the rest of the group.

Nongshyrkon, Perly had told me, was founded by the Nongsiang clan of Mawliehbah, a village about eleven kilometres from Nongstoin, the capital of the traditional state of Nongstoin in West Khasi Hills, sometime between 1910 and 1920.

☙

The story begins with two Nongsiang brothers, U Puitïong and U Sharïong, famous in those days as accomplished warriors, *ki khlawait*, literally, 'sword-tigers'.

One day, the two brothers, quite by accident, met two men from Lyngngam at the Nongstoin marketplace known as Mawpieñ Mawkhap. The men, U Rin and U Dai from the Shalimar clan, were also brothers. They had never been to Nongstoin before. They roamed about the marketplace and gaped at all the things on sale, until they came upon the two warriors, Puitïong and Sharïong. They were immediately intrigued by the way these warriors were armed. Besides a short sword suspended from their hips, each one carried a bow and a quiver of arrows on his back. They approached the warriors and asked, 'Can we see those things you are carrying on your backs? What do you call them?'

Puitïong explained that they were called bows and arrows. 'Why? Haven't you seen them before?' he asked. 'Don't you have bows and arrows in Lyngngam? You are from Lyngngam, aren't you?'

Rin and Dai replied that they were indeed from Lyngngam and that they had never seen bows and arrows before. Lyngngams, as we have seen, only used spears, swords and shields in battle.

The brothers examined the weapons closely. The bows, made from seasoned bamboo, were quite big, about five feet when unstrung. The arrows, made from a type of reed called *stew*, had iron barbs at the end.

They asked the warriors, 'What do you Maram people do with these?'

Puitïong said, 'We hunt animals and defend ourselves with them.'

'Really!' the Lyngngam brothers exclaimed in disbelief. Then Rin said, 'They don't look like very much, can you really kill animals with these?'

Puitïong told them this was true.

'Show us,' the Lyngngams demanded.

The group moved away from the marketplace to the woods nearby, where they saw two jungle fowl at a distance, a cock and a hen. The Lyngngams challenged the Marams, 'Can you kill those jungle chickens with these?'

The Maram warriors could see that the Lyngngams were simpletons and immediately thought of taking advantage of them. Sharïong told his brother in his own dialect, 'Before we answer them, why don't we make a bet with them, Bah? Let's try to get something out of these fools.'

And so Puitïong said to the Lyngngams, 'What will you give us if we can?'

Rin and Dai did not have anything of value on them. The little money they had was meant for buying essentials to be taken back home. Not wanting to lose their money, they said, 'Land, we'll give you land.'

The brothers thought it was safe to offer land because Lyngngam was quite far from Nongstoin and was difficult to reach. Moreover, it was covered with dense jungle where tigers and elephants roamed. 'Who would want to come to such a land as ours?' they reasoned.

'Are you sure?' Puitïong asked. 'When you make a bet, you should keep your word. The word is everything. We don't know how to read and write, but our word is inviolable.'

When the Lyngngams assured him of their good intentions, Puitïong asked again, 'How much land?'

Secure in the thought that the Marams would never dare come to Lyngngam to make good their claim, Rin and Dai said, 'All the land that we have, between the River Rwiang in the east and the River Blei in the west.'

'How much land is that?' Puitïong asked.

'More than a day's journey across,' Rin replied.

'That's a great deal of land,' Sharïong interposed. 'Are you sure you mean it?'

'We do,' Rin replied confidently.

'All right then,' Puitïong said. 'You keep quiet while we try to creep up on them.'

The Lyngngams, however, told them they should not go too near, for that would be unfair. The Marams assured them that they would go only close enough to be able to shoot with their bows, about fifty yards or so. It was also agreed that the Marams should use only five arrows each. Puitïong was to kill the cock and Sharïong the hen. When the terms were finalised, the Marams took up their positions and prepared to shoot. The Lyngngams went to squat nearby and began mumbling to themselves. They were calling upon the guardian spirit of villages and the wilderness, U Ryngkew U Basa, to stop the arrows of Puitïong and Sharïong from hitting their targets, for otherwise they might lose their land.

Before letting their arrows fly, the Maram warriors also prayed to their *ïawbei*, the first ancestress of their clan, to intervene with God, U Blei, on their behalf so that they might win the bet and enrich themselves with more land than their family had ever dreamt of. It was only after they had said their prayers that they began to shoot. They shot their first arrows in the name of their chickens at home. Both arrows went wide.

Puitïong said, 'The Lyngngams' medicine is very strong, Hep, they must be calling upon some very powerful spirit to assist them.'

'Hep' here means 'younger brother', but it could also mean 'younger sister'.

They took out their second arrows, spoke a few words of prayer, and shot them in the name of their goats. These went wide too. Sharïong said they should renew their prayer to ka ïawbei, which they did. After that, the warriors took out their third arrows, spoke a few imploring words to them and shot them in the name of their cattle. Again, they missed, though not by much. Fortunately for them, the fowls were not disturbed too much since there was only a 'thwack, thwack' on the ground.

'We are getting closer,' Puitïong said. 'See there, the Lyngngams are intensifying their mumblings. Let us shoot the next arrows in the name of our servants!'

They took out their fourth arrows, pleaded with them to be straight and true, and shot them in the name of their female servants. But these were well off the mark.

Puitïong said, 'Let us pray not only to ka ïawbei but also to Ka Mei Hukum, Hep.'

Praying to God in his manifestation as Ka Mei Hukum, or the Mother of Divine Law, they said, 'O Mei Hukum, we did not ask for this land, we only said, if we kill the fowls, what will you give us? It is they who offered, they who named the prize. If they had offered something else, we would have accepted. Now that the prize has been offered, it is not right for them to pray to you and ask you to put obstacles in our way. Help us, O Mei, if we are in the right in this bet, if we are in the right in this wager; help us, if the truth is with us. We are not greedy, O Mei, but if we are warriors, should we not hit our targets, and if we hit the targets, should we not win the prize?'

Puitïong and Sharïong prayed and argued in this manner for a long time. Finally, they took out their last arrows, touched them to their foreheads and prepared to shoot. But first, Puitïong said, 'These arrows we will shoot in the name of *ka niang panpoh*, our mother's "belted sow": she will be our charm, may she bring us victory!'

The sow was referred to as niang panpoh because she had a white stripe like a belt encircling her black body.

With that invocation, they shot their last arrows, and this time they found their mark. Puitïong hit the cock in the neck; Sharïong hit the hen in the chest. With the dead jungle fowl dangling from their hands, the Maram warriors approached the Lyngngams and said, 'We have won the bet fair and square. When shall we come to claim our land?'

Rin and Dai were not pleased with the outcome. In the first place, they had not believed that anything could be killed with a bow and arrow. Secondly, they had not thought that anyone would be serious about claiming the prize, a piece of land in some faraway jungle. What a stupid thing to do, they groaned; in a moment they had thrown away their clan's ancestral wealth and property. However, since they could not wriggle out of it, seeing that they were alone in a strange place, they said, 'We will give; we will give you the land that lies between the River Rwiang and the River Blei, as promised. Come in the twelfth moon, the moon of *Nohprah*, we will meet you there to finalise the deal.'

By that time, the Lyngngams thought, the harvest would be over, and if the Marams should really come, they would know what to do.

In Nohprah, which roughly corresponds to December, Puitïong and Sharïong went to the region of Lyngngam, between the River Rwiang and the River Blei. When they got there, however, Rin and Dai were nowhere to be found. They had finished their harvesting and had gone into hiding deep in the jungle, taking everyone else with them, as well as everything from their homes, including the harvested paddy. Their logic was that, if the Marams could not meet anyone from their extended family, they could not lay claim to the land promised to them. At first, Dai had wanted to wait for them in the village with a group of men and beat them to death when they came. But that idea was given up since Puitïong and Sharïong were accomplished warriors, and there was also the possibility that they might not come alone. Going into hiding was thought to be the safest thing to do. The Lyngngams were confident that when the Marams could not find them, they would return home rather than risk the dangers of the tangled wilderness, looking for them.

When Puitïong and Sharïong did not find Rin and Dai, they were filled with despair. What would they do alone in these jungles? Believing that the Lyngngams would honour their promise, they had not even brought friends or clansmen along. Now, what would happen to them in this strange country? They considered returning home, but then they asked themselves, 'How can we? We will become the butt of everybody's ridicule if we go home empty-handed.' It was this thought that brought anger to their hearts and hardened their determination to search for the Lyngngams till they found them.

Puitïong said, anger and resolve in his voice: 'Those sons of animals! They pretended to be willing to part with their land, but look at them now! They are trying to cheat us out of our prize, Hep. Are we warriors or women, to give up and return home empty-handed? We must search for them through the length and breadth of Lyngngam, and when we find them, we shall claim our land, but if they resist, we must prepare for the worst. However, we must also be cunning, Hep. We are strangers in these jungles; we must pose as their friends, not enemies.'

'How will we live here without food for so long, Bah?' Sharïong asked.

'We will live well enough,' Puitïong said confidently. 'Are we not their friends? We will eat in Lyngngam huts, but failing that, we shall hunt; don't we have our bows and arrows, and don't they have plenty of animals here?'

And so, the two Marams started their search for Rin and Dai, asking anyone they met about them. Some said they had gone west towards Garo Land with their family and belongings. So, Puitïong and Sharïong went that way. When they could not find them there, they returned to the River Rwiang and made fresh inquiries. Some said they had seen them going south towards the plains of Sylhet in Bengal. Puitïong and Sharïong rushed to the south, but when they got there, no one had seen them. In this way, they traipsed through the jungles for months, going west, south and east, looking for the Lyngngams who had cheated them. But give up they would not. They were fearsome warriors; their resolve would not be broken.

One day, as they were resting near a stream, roasting a barking deer they had shot, a woman who was carrying a load of firewood on her back came walking by. They invited her to join them in their meal. 'Khublei, Kong,' they greeted her, 'you look tired and hungry, come and join us, we are about to eat.'

The woman was shy and reluctant at first. However, the meat was tempting. It would be a real treat for her, a wonderful change from the rice and salt she had been eating for many weeks. 'Are you sure you have enough?' she asked.

'Come, come, off with your load,' Puitïong said, helping her place it on the ground. 'The meat is too much for the two of us. Come, come, Kong, let's eat.'

The woman, who now identified herself as a member of the Mawbon clan, living not too far away, thanked them profusely and settled down to eat the meat with wild chillies and onions. She asked them, 'What are you doing in Lyngngam? It's not often that we see Maram people here.'

Puitïong said, 'We are looking for our friends, U Rin and U Dai. We went to their homes, but they seemed deserted.'

'It's a very strange thing,' the woman observed, 'but they decided to leave suddenly, as soon as they had completed the harvesting. Why should they leave their homes, carrying everything with them, and live in a cave? A very strange thing indeed.'

'In a cave?' Sharïong asked eagerly.

'Are you sure you are their friends?'

'Actually,' Puitïong replied, 'we met them for the first time this autumn, when they came to the Mawpieñ Mawkhap market in Nongstoin. We had a long chat, and they promised to give us something if we came to meet them in Lyngngam; that's why we have been looking for them.'

'Ooh, in that case, you should go to the River Blei, cross to the other side, and follow the river down south till you come to a stream known as Sdat Jirang. When you get there, you will see rice husks flowing in the stream. They are pounding their rice in the cave and throwing the husks into the stream. Just follow the trail of rice husks, and you will not fail to find the cave. The entrance is like a crevice, but beyond the entrance, the cave is very big. Every one of them is living there: Rin, Dai, their wives, their sisters, their brothers-in-law and all the children. It shouldn't be difficult to find them; you will hear them pounding rice from quite a distance.'

Puitïong and Sharïong left for the cave early the next day, arriving at about midday. The Lyngngams saw them coming from afar. They were stunned. After quickly talking it over, they decided to receive the Maram duo with an outward show of friendliness and cooperation. 'But,' Rin said, outlining the plan, 'this very day, we must put a stop to this threat once and for all. We will give them food and get them drunk, and once they are drunk, we will cut them up. You women keep the food and drinks ready. As long as these greedy pigs are alive, we will not have any peace at all.'

Having given his instructions, Rin went out to meet the two brothers. He greeted them like long-lost friends. 'Khublei, friends, khublei!' he boomed, opening his arms wide in a warm embrace. 'How did you find us? I'm so sorry I could not send word to you; we had to shift because the jhum farms that side are not fertile any more. We are planning to settle and farm this side of the River Blei from now on. But come in, come in, you must be hungry. We will have lunch together; we will eat and drink to celebrate our meeting once again! Come, come …'

Puitïong was immediately suspicious. He said to Sharïong, 'First they hide from us and now they welcome us as if they love us very much. We must be careful, Hep.'

Sharïong, however, was not so sure. He said, 'I don't know, Bah, his explanation seems plausible enough.'

'Just keep your eyes and ears open,' his brother replied.

Inside the cave, the two men were given wooden stools to sit on. The cave was large and roomy, and shaped almost like an egg, but it was dark, with only a little light entering through a small crack in the roof. A fire burnt in the hearth, right in the middle. At the far end of the central chamber, two openings led to additional chambers, one on the left, the other on the right. The one on the right was obviously used as a storeroom, since the Lyngngams were bringing food and drinks from it. By the opening of the left chamber stood many children—twelve of them, seven boys and five girls—watching the strangers curiously. Near the hearth were three women, preparing the food, while four men, Dai and his brothers-in-law, were by the right chamber, fetching the drinks.

Rin told Puitïong and Sharïong that they would eat as soon as the food was ready. He called out for the drinks to be brought in, excused himself for a bit, and left with one of the women to bring something from outside. At that moment, Sharïong, who was sitting closer to the right chamber than Puitïong, overheard Rin's relatives whispering to each other: 'More, more, bring some more, we need them to be very drunk.' Hearing this, he leant towards his brother and whispered, 'I think you are right, Bah, I think they are trying to get us drunk. After that, I think they plan to cut us up.'

When nobody was looking, Puitïong took out his tobacco container, a bamboo tube about two inches in diameter and four inches in length. He removed the tobacco and put it inside his ïarong bag. He asked Sharïong to do the same, then took out his knife and made a hole in the bottom of the tube. Having done that, he put the tube back in his ïarong and waited.

After a while, Rin re-entered the cave with his wife, carrying some logs. He shouted to his relatives again to bring in the yiad hiar. The men brought the potent Lyngngam brew stored in gourds of various sizes. They put the gourds down on the floor in front of Rin, who said, 'Now friends, shall we have our drinks and celebrate your visit and new-found wealth?'

Puitïong agreed, but said, 'How can we celebrate anything if the others are not drinking? Call them also; we'll all sit in a circle and drink like real friends.'

Rin did not want to involve the others in the drinking, but he could not risk arousing suspicion. So he called Dai and his three brothers-in-law over to join them. When Rin began pouring the yiad hiar into bamboo mugs, Puitïong stopped him and said, 'We don't drink in other people's mugs. It's our custom.' He took out the tobacco container from his ïarong bag, covered the hole with his finger and said, 'We always drink in these.'

Watching his brother and immediately grasping the plan, Sharïong did the same. The Lyngngams, not suspecting a thing, poured the drinks into their tobacco tubes. The Marams sipped their yiad hiar but let most of it out, through the hole, onto the ground, where it was quickly soaked up by the rice husks. In this manner, they kept emptying their tubes, even as the Lyngngams filled them again and again.

At first, the Lyngngams also merely sipped at their drinks, for they wanted only the other party to get drunk, but when they saw the Marams emptying tube after tube, they became quite excited. Dai, the most aggressive of the lot, threw them a challenge, saying, 'You Marams are not the only ones who can drink. We Lyngngams can also drink without getting drunk. What do you say, brothers?'

The others mumbled their agreement. Rin cautioned his brother with a gesture, but Dai ignored him. Seeing Rin hesitating, Puitïong said, 'Why *Koh* Rin, are you afraid of a little drink? Look at us, we have taken so many mugs, and yet we are sober.'

'How do these Marams do it?' Rin said to himself. 'If they can do it, why can't I, a Lyngngam, do the same?' Shortly, seized by the excitement of the moment and the magnetism of the yiad hiar, he began drinking as heavily as the others.

After some time, the Lyngngams, who had been gulping their yiad hiar like water, became so drunk they could no longer stand. When the Marams saw this, they stood up and prepared for the gruesome business that lay ahead. Puitïong said to the Lyngngams, 'We came here in peace to claim the land you had promised us in a bet. But you tried to get us drunk and planned to murder us; now we will cut you up. Your women too were in on it; they will meet with the same fate.'

So saying, he and his brother took out their short swords and began hacking the Lyngngam men to death amidst the cries and loud lamentations of the women and children. The women tried to defend their men by hitting the Marams with burning logs, but what could they do against the strength and skill of two efficient killers with swords? They too died in the bloody melee. The kids tried to escape by running outside, but the Marams, with blood-spattered faces and red-stained swords, were standing at the only exit, and they had nowhere to go. They crouched together in a corner, shrieking in abject terror.

When they had killed all the adults, Puitiong said, 'What shall we do with the children, Hep?'

'What else can we do? We have killed their parents; how can we leave any witnesses here? Besides, how can we take their land if one of them is still alive?'

Puitiong thought for a while and then said, 'You are right … even if they don't go to the syiem to report, they will certainly seek revenge later …'

'It's a bloody business indeed, but we have no option, Bah,' Shariong said. 'We'll make it as quick and painless as possible.'

Shariong went forward, intending to give each one of them a quick end. But the children bawled and cried and ran helter-skelter. The Marams tried to catch them, and in trying to prevent them from escaping, they spun their swords and slashed at the flying bodies, cutting off a hand, a foot, a nose at random. They rushed at the children, hitting one on the head, another in the neck, yet another in the chest. They slashed, they stabbed, they chopped, they killed, they maimed in a frenzy, raising terrible oaths against the pitiable cries of the children trying to escape the butchering. That cave was a scene of absolute horror.

Unknown to them, one of the sisters of Rin and Dai was just outside. A pregnant woman, she had gone out into the jungle to collect firewood. On her way back, she heard the children's harrowing screams. She stopped dead in her tracks and wondered what was happening. At that moment, a bloody boy, with an arm chopped off, came running outside, crying for help. He was followed by a stranger wielding a bloody blade. She realised in the flicker of an instant that the boy was her sister's eldest son, but even as the thought passed through her mind, she saw the stranger raise his gory weapon and bring it down on the head of the running, screaming child, killing him on the spot. She nearly cried out, but managed to stifle the sound. Something was very wrong! Then she suddenly understood. These must be the Marams from whom they were trying to hide. They had found them and were slaughtering her family. Her brothers and her husband must be dead if the children were being massacred. She dropped her load of firewood and fled, and did not stop running for a long, long time.

As night fell, she stumbled across a small treehouse some hunter had built. Walking through the dark jungle at night was simply not an option, so, despite her fear of a possible pursuit, she climbed into the treehouse and fell into an exhausted sleep. When morning arrived, the nightmarish experience of the previous day hit her like a blow. Crying, she hurriedly clambered down from the treehouse, intending to get as far away as possible. She thought about where to go and decided that the safest way lay north-west towards Nongtrai, near the Garo border, where the family had some friends in a place called Nongmihsei. She hurried that way, resting only to beg for food from some remote hut or to bend down for a drink of water at a stream.

Back at the cave, the Nongsiang brothers tried to hide all traces of their butchery. They threw the bodies together in a pile and burnt them for two days till nothing but ashes remained. They covered the bloodstains with sand and earth, freshly dug up, and afterwards went down to the stream to clean and wash. When all traces of their grisly deeds were erased, they returned to their homes in Mawliehbah.

Soon after reaching their village, they called for a clan meeting and organised a big feast at the Nongstoin marketplace of Mawpieñ Mawkhap to celebrate their new-found wealth. They told the clan the entire story, leaving out only the gory details of the killing, and informed everyone that the whole area between the River Rwiang and the River Blei, a vast expanse of about a day's journey, now belonged to them. They offered to share the land with all those female relatives who would like to follow them with their families to settle in the new home. Many of those present willingly and joyously agreed to this, for most of their farmlands around Mawliehbah were scrubby and barren. When everything was arranged, the brothers also authorised the clan members who chose to stay back to make use of the lands vacated by them in any way they thought appropriate.

The travellers were escorted on their southward journey by the entire Nongsiang clan, who accompanied them till the junction of two streams called Nongbah and Nongding. While one group returned to their homes in Mawliehbah, the other crossed the streams, advanced towards Lyngngam and settled in a place called Nongrim Sohpiengrah. This group came to be known as the Konding-Konbah Nongsiangs, or the Nongsiangs who had crossed the Nongding-Nongbah streams.

The clan prospered in their new home. After the death of U Puitïong and U Sharïong, they were led by Thaw Khyllun, a formidable diviner and sacrificer, known and respected throughout the Lyngngam region. It was the practice of the clan to cremate dead relatives at Mawliehbah near Nongstoin.

But when Thaw Khyllun died, it happened to be the month of July, when the rain was a torrential downpour. The clan could not cross the River Rwiang to travel to Mawliehbah. They waited for several weeks, but the rain did not stop and the water did not subside. Consequently, they decided to cremate his body in Lyngngam itself. But the spirit of Thaw Khyllun, the augur, became so angry at this sacrilege that the fire could not be extinguished and the pyre burnt for days. Not only that, it even spread, despite the rain, to the jungle, destroying everything in its wake, including the clan's village. Eventually, a vast expanse of farmland and twelve heavily forested hills were burnt to ashes by the rage of Thaw Khyllun.

The clan left the old village and travelled farther south. After journeying for many hours, they called for a halt to prepare lunch while their scouts went to survey the surrounding areas. Sometime later, the scouts saw a tall tree called *ka kya*, the cotton tree, growing (to this day) on top of a very high hill. They went up the hill to investigate whether the place was fit for habitation. From the summit, they could see that it was a kind of plateau, a beautiful one, and ideal to live in. They went down the hill, looking for water, and discovered three springs to the south, west and north of the plateau. When they reported their findings to the clan elders, a council was quickly convened and soon a new village was born.

The elders found three unique stone formations at different locations on the new village site. They performed religious rites and pleaded with God to transform the stones into the guardian spirits of the village to protect it from the evils of man and beast and the ravages of nature. One of them, in the north-east, called Pyndengbabah, or load-bearing stone, represented the reigning spirit of the village. Another one, in the centre, called Mawkhap, or boundary stone, represented the guardian spirit whose duty was to safeguard the village from attacks by animals and demons. The last one, in the north, called Mawjngoh, or sentinel stone, represented the guardian spirit whose duty was to act as the law enforcer of the village. In Perly's words, the stone acted as 'the syiem's policeman or the Black Cat commando of the deputy commissioner'. He maintained that, even now, 'When thieves and nongshohnoh killers come, the Mawjngoh immediately catches hold of them.' How and in what manner it did that, he did not explain.

After the sanctification ceremony, the elders told the clan not to call themselves the Nongsiangs any more, lest a similar tragedy should befall them too. They directed them to call themselves the Shyrkons, the ones who had gone across, the ones who had crossed the streams of Nongbah and Nongding. The newly established village, they said, should be known as Nongshyrkon, the village of the Shyrkons. Their final advisory to the clan was to always maintain close relationships with their original clan, the Nongsiangs, with whom it was forbidden to have any marital union.

Meanwhile, Rin's pregnant sister had reached Nongmihsei after many days of punishing travel. Her family's friends gave her a place to stay and promised to take care of her in her time of need. After about six months, she gave birth to twin daughters, who were brought up with great care, as if they were 'newly laid eggs', as Perly put it. When they were about the age of ten, the mother told them about all that had happened and warned them to be careful. 'The Nongsiangs might even now be looking for us,' she said. 'Of course, they might not know anything about me, but we should not take even the smallest chance.'

In this way, the girls were brought up on tales of the Nongsiangs' cruelty and grew up in perpetual fear of discovery. To increase their chances of survival, one day, they decided to go their separate ways. It was the elder sister who first raised the issue. She said, 'Hep, if both of us stay here, it will be dangerous. If those Nongsiangs find us, they will cut us up, and our clan will be completely wiped out. I'm the elder, Hep, even if only by minutes, let me stay here since it's riskier. Our mother, too, can stay with me since she is too old to travel long distances. But I want you to be safe. I don't want you to live with this constant fear of discovery. Why don't you go away from here? Some people from the village are going south towards the Bengal border. They are going to settle there permanently to farm and trade with the Shilotias. Why don't you follow them? That will keep you safe. If the Nongsiangs should come here and cut me up, I will be happy in the knowledge that you are still there to continue the Shalimar line.'

The younger sister was reluctant to leave her family, but when her mother also pleaded with her, she finally agreed to go with the other villagers and live near Sylhet. There, she led a happy and prosperous life, and later met and married the deputy king of Nongstoin, the famous Wickliffe Syiem.

Wickliffe Syiem was the only Khasi king to rebel against what he called the forced annexation of Ri Khasi to India through the Instrument of Accession in 1947. Rather than live under foreign yoke once again, so soon after the British had left, he chose to live in Sylhet, which by then had become part of East Pakistan. His symbolic act of rebellion turned him into a heroic figure among the Khasis. The militant HNLC, for instance, claimed to have drawn inspiration from his actions.

When I concluded my story, Magdalene exclaimed, 'It's a sad and horrifying tale, ya, Ap!'

'Like a horror movie!' Bah Kynsai said.

'What amazes me is the Lyngngams making that kind of bet,' Donald remarked. 'I mean, what could they have gained from it? Even if the Nongsiang brothers had failed to hit their targets, they would have got nothing! And in exchange for nothing, they gambled away the entire wealth and property of their clan! There's something wrong with this story, Bah Ap.'

'There's nothing wrong with the story, Don,' I replied. 'It really happened …'

'That's why they say truth is stranger than fiction, na?' Bah Kynsai said.

'Do you know what the rest of the Khasi tribe called the Lyngngams, Don?' I continued. '*Lyngngam bieit*, foolish Lyngngam! It's a horrible label, I certainly do not approve of it, but the story does expose the foolishness of Rin and Dai. The Nongsiang brothers would have been happy with any small thing, but the Lyngngams stupidly offered them all they had. It's really hard to believe, except it happens to be a true story.'

'But the cruelty of the Marams was also terrible, no?' Hamkom said, shaking his head in disbelief.

'Horrifying!' Magdalene said, shuddering. 'And those guys founded this village, huh? Let's go home, chalo, chalo!'

'How can you denounce them out of hand like that?' Raji protested. 'For them, it was kill or be killed, no?'

'No, no, I disagree completely,' Magdalene said. 'The two Marams were greedy and cruel, like Ham said. See, they knew the Lyngngams were planning to get them drunk and have them killed. Who could have stopped them from leaving the place, huh? And again, when the Lyngngams became drunk, the Marams could have easily walked away instead of killing everybody. The fact was that they wanted that land at any cost, and didn't care if it meant killing everybody for it. I cannot sympathise with such greed.'

'The Marams, na, are the most ferocious of all the Khasi sub-tribes, you know that?' Bah Kynsai said with some passion. 'In the past, na, Don, they used to call the Maram-inhabited part of the Khasi Hills, the Wild West. There used to be lots of killings. People were killed over nothing, and the Marams used to brag about how they valued a pipe of tobacco more than human life. That aspect of their nature, na, is clearly reflected in the story.'

Halolihim interrupted us then. 'You people may enjoy talking about killings, but I'm out of here,' he said.

'Don't stay out too late, ha, there might still be a few bloodthirsty Marams out there!' Bah Kynsai shouted after him.

Bah Kit went back to the Lyngngams: 'But finally, ha, it all boils down to the foolishness of the Lyngngams. They not only made that foolish bet, but in the cave also, they foolishly got themselves drunk. Some people should not go near alcohol at all. I have seen it with my own eyes. The moment they get a whiff of alcohol, ha, they become completely crazy. They just cannot control themselves; they have to drink like pigs.'

'So, these Nongshyrkons are not Lyngngams at all, then?' Donald asked.

'They call themselves Lyngngams,' Raji replied, 'and they have adopted the Lyngngam lifestyle.'

'What about Shillong, our capital, Bah Ap, is there a story behind it?' Donald asked.

'There is,' several voices answered him.

'I also know the story, Don. It's nothing like the Shyrkon one,' Magdalene said. 'But what I don't know is why Shillong should be so dead these days, ya! Is there any nightlife at all? By seven or eight, everything is closed, man!'

'Apart from some drinking dens,' Bah Kynsai said.

'Yeah, those,' Magdalene agreed half-heartedly.

'What a coincidence that you should ask that question, Mag!' Raji exclaimed. 'Ap has written an article about it—Shillong's origin, Shillong's nightlife, in fact, the whole history of Shillong, with many little stories and anecdotes thrown in. Ask him.'

Now, many of them wanted the story of Shillong. Even Bah Su, an authority on the subject, was curious about what I had to say, especially about its nightlife, when everybody knew there was hardly any.

The essay Raji was referring to begins with a quote from P.B. Shelley. (Of course I am fond of the Romantics, and I challenge anyone who thinks they have lost their relevance. Romanticism, as Longinus would have you know, has flourished since the time of the Greeks and can still be found in the most contemporary of writers.)

> Swiftly walk over the western wave,
> Spirit of Night!
> Where, all the long and lone daylight,
> Thou wovest dreams of joy and fear
> Which make thee terrible and dear,—
> Swift be thy flight!

For Shelley, the 'Spirit of Night', with its 'dream of joy and fear', is essentially the spirit of life, 'terrible and dear'. But ask a *nong* Shillong, a Shillongite, about the night and he is likely to explain it as a time to rush home, to be indoors, or at least in the streets near home. The spirit of the night, as far as the business districts and commercial hubs are concerned, has come to mean 'the outlaw's day', to use the phrase of English poet and dramatist Phillip Massinger.

Our capital city, with a current population of about 1,43,000 people, was established by the British in 1864, chiefly for two reasons—the hard and relentless rain of Sohra, the first capital of the Khasi-Jaiñtia Hills district, and the Pnar War of Freedom in 1862.

As elsewhere, British advent into these hills began with friendship treaties. These were made on two separate occasions with two different rulers, in 1824 and 1826 respectively. In those days, the Khasi-Jaiñtia Hills district was made up of several democratic states, or himas, ruled by titular kings, the syiems (also called Rajas by neighbouring rulers). Tradition tells us that there used to be thirty states, each under a king, with twenty-nine of them in present-day Khasi Hills and one in Ri Pnar, Jaiñtia Hills.

The first treaty was concluded with Ram Sing, the king of Sutnga, whom they called the Jaiñtia Raja, on 10 March 1824, in anticipation of the Burmese invasion of British Assam. However, after the Treaty of Yandaboo brought an end to the Burmese War, the British picked a quarrel with Ram Sing, attacked his state and captured Jaiñtiapur, his winter capital.

The second treaty was made with Tirot Sing, the king of Nongkhlaw, on 30 November 1826. The British wanted to construct a road through the state of Nongkhlaw—in what is now West Khasi Hills—to link Assam and Surma Valley. However, once permission was granted, the British harassed the local people in so many ways that they were forced to retaliate, resulting in the first Khasi War of Liberation in 1829. The war ended with the capture of Tirot Sing on 13 January 1833 through an act of betrayal. He was offered back his kingship, but refused, declaring: '*Kham bha ba im kum u riew laitluid ban ïa kaba synshar kum a syiem mraw.*' ('Better to live like a free man than to rule like a vassal king.')

The war also resulted in the annexation of all the Khasi states that had supported the cause of Tirot Sing. To facilitate their governance, the British established the Khasi Hills Political Agency on 11 February 1835. Sohra, whose king had assisted the British against Tirot Sing, was chosen as the capital.

Shyllong, which the British later divided into Khyrim and Mylliem, was one of the newly annexed states.

The Agency flourished; peace reigned in the Khasi Hills; Western education was introduced; the Khasi language was cast in the Roman script; and Christianity, proselytised by the Welsh missionaries, spread like wildfire. The peace was shattered only once, in 1862, when Kiang Nangbah led the Pnar War of Freedom, also called the Jaiñtia Rebellion by the British. Kiang Nangbah was a folk hero and one of the greatest freedom fighters of the Khasi people.

'I prefer Hynñiew Trep people, Ap,' Hamkom broke in.

I nodded and continued. Kiang, I revealed, was elected to lead the war against the British by a council of the people following a divine revelation...

'What divine revelation?' Hamkom interrupted me again.

Instead of answering him directly, I said that the Pnars were incensed by the baffling house tax that was imposed on the region in 1860. According to a British official, there was an open rebellion against it, but before it could spread, it was stamped out by 'a large force of troops ... and the villages were awed into apparent submission'. Even before the commotion aroused by the house tax had subsided, the British government introduced another one: income tax. These developments, as well as the arrogance and oppressive conduct of certain British officials, inflamed the whole of Ri Pnar and started another rebellion.

The rebels summoned a council of all twelve dolois, the provincial rulers, at Madiah Kmai Blai on the bank of the River Syntu Ksiar, to discuss the urgent need to fight against the tyranny of the foreigners. At the council, all the bravest men of Ri Pnar agreed that it was time to throw off the foreign yoke. But this time, unlike the leaderless rebellion of 1860, they wanted to make sure they had the right man to lead their resistance. The council decided to leave this to divine revelation, and resolved that whoever managed to obtain a plant called *phlang letang*, found only at the bottom of the deepest pools of the river, would be recognised as the leader of the new uprising.

U Kiang Nangbah, an ordinary farmer and son of Ka Rimai Nangbah (the actual clan was believed to be Susngi) from Tpeppale, Jowai, was the only one who could do it. This was taken as a sign from God himself, and Kiang Nangbah was unanimously elected the leader—

Hamkom broke in again: 'You said oppressive conduct, like what?'

I told him that there were many incidents, but that two were especially offensive. The British had built a police station near a cremation ground, and when people went there for a cremation, the police stopped them, claiming it was unclean and unwholesome. Many clans were thus prevented from cremating their dead. The other incident relates to the traditional Pastieh Dance at Ïalong, also known as *shad wait* or sword dancing. The British confiscated all the swords and burnt them in front of a large crowd that had gathered to watch the festival. This was, in fact, the immediate trigger for the Pnar War of Freedom.

The war lasted about a year and shook the British Empire in the Khasi-Jaiñtia Hills to its very roots. It only ended when Kiang Nangbah was betrayed and captured, and condemned to public execution on 30 December 1862. On the day of his death, he uttered his famous last words: 'If my head turns to the east, you will win your freedom within a hundred years; if it turns to the west, you will remain in bondage.'

As the hangman's noose tightened around his neck, his head slowly turned towards the east, and true to his words, the Hynñiew Trep people won their freedom exactly eighty-five years after his death.

Hamkom intervened yet again and said, 'What act of betrayal?'

Bah Kynsai was pissed off with him by now. 'Will you stop butting in all the time, liah? This is supposed to be a story about Shillong, na, not about Kiang Nangbah!'

Evening said, 'He wants to test Ap's knowledge, he thinks he's the only one who knows about Kiang Nangbah.'

I calmed everyone and told them that it would not take long to explain. The uprising quickly became a fully fledged war and spread to many parts of Ri Pnar. In their desperate attempt to put it down, the British used several forces at once, including the Punjab Infantry, the 33rd Native Infantry, the Assam Light Infantry, the Sylhet Light Infantry, the Sikh Military Police, the Kamrup Regiment and others, including an artillery unit. Yet, Kiang Nangbah and his men were undefeated, with their guerrilla tactics. However, as luck would have it, Kiang was suddenly taken ill and confined to his bed in a place called Umkara. Taking advantage of his illness, the doloi of Nartiang, called U Mon, and his close associate, U Long Sutnga—the bravest among the Pnar warriors—informed the British about Kiang's situation and his whereabouts. The cause of their action was never made clear, though they would go down in history as traitors.

On coming to know that Kiang Nangbah was heavily defended by his men, the British—advised by another traitor, sarcastically called Sinmon Phareng (Sinmon the Englishman)—pretended to launch an attack on the village of Shangpung. When the news reached Kiang, he sent his men to defend Shangpung, and that was the signal for Lieutenant Saddler, guided by Sinmon, to lead a strong contingent to Umkara and arrest him.

Although the Pnar War did not last long, and though all its principal players had been defeated and killed, the British were severely shaken, and that, together with the Sohra rain, which had 'driven many a Company wallah to suicide', made them hasten to look for a new district capital that was 'equidistant north, south, east and west'. They finally found a suitable place in a valley that stretched northwards from the northern slope of Shillong Peak and decided to establish the new capital there in 1864.

Before 1864, there was no settlement in the area that goes today by the name of Shillong. Only the villages of Laitumkhrah, Laban, Mawkhar, Nongkseh and Lawsohtun—which later became some of the major localities of the new city—fringed the chosen valley on the east, south and west. The name of the city itself was derived from U Lei Shulong, 'the self-begotten', patron god of the state of Shyllong, whose divine retreat was U Lum Shyllong, Shyllong Peak, towering about 6,543.45 feet above sea level, to the south of the city. Initially, the British thought of naming Shillong after Ïewduh, the biggest market in the area, which they called Yeodo. But since the city of Tokyo in Japan was also known then as Yedo or Ido, they decided to name the new capital 'Shillong'.

It is easy to imagine what kind of nightlife Shillong would have had in those days. The Khasis, who had just come in touch with outsiders, would have been following a purely traditional way of life. So, after a day in the fields (or the woods, or the marketplace, or the iron forges, or the stone and lime quarries), each Khasi family would have sat around the hearth for some quality time together. These hearths were built in the middle of the thatched cottages—with either stone or plank walls—in a central room serving as both kitchen and living room. The saying, *shong sawdong ka lyngwiar dpei* (sit around the circle of the hearth) is significant for all Khasis, for it refers to our great tradition of storytelling, which goes back to the time of our creation myths and the loss of a manuscript. This manuscript is said to have contained the tribe's philosophical and religious teachings, as well as the script used to record them. Its loss spurred the Khasis into the tradition of storytelling in order to keep the teachings alive.

The function of these creation myths, called *ki khanatang*, or sanctified stories, is to elucidate the Khasi philosophy of life relating to every aspect of culture, and make sure that it reaches and holds captive even the simplest of men. Each myth is invested with symbolic significance, and is rendered in such a way as to beguile listeners into believing they are hearing a story and not listening to a sermon.

Having realised the tremendous potential of the khanatang, the old Khasis invented a story for everything. The phenomenon of lightning and thunder, a gigantic boulder that looks like an overturned conical basket, the name of a waterfall, a hill, a forest, a village … everything. To explain the inexplicable or comprehend the incomprehensible, they found a story. A moral lesson? They invented another story. Young Khasis were instructed thus by their elders; their school was the hearth around which they gathered after a day's labour, to be warmed by both the fire and the tales.

During the dry seasons of autumn and winter, however, the Khasis of early Shillong would have built bonfires in the village greens, where elderly people would have taken on the role of village raconteurs, educating the young about their myths, their past and their culture. Or perhaps, everyone was simply having fun, singing and dancing, swapping anecdotes and discussing matters great and small.

According to Laitflang, the most popular stories in Shillong in those days were of heroic deeds by Khasi warriors in the various wars against the British. The exploits of Mon Bhut, the most ferocious warrior during the war of 1829, and the valiant woman spy, Ka Phan Nonglait, who was responsible for the death of many a British soldier during the same war, were often repeated. The failure of the British to defeat and capture Mon Bhut, and his mysterious disappearance after the war, remained a matter of endless conjecture. Another well-circulated story was that of the notorious bow-toting bandit, U Bansing, a man of extraordinary strength from Mawshut village in West Khasi Hills. Bansing was responsible for many robberies, kidnappings (he used to kidnap women from marketplaces) and murders (including that of the grandfather of the king of Nongkhlaw) before he was captured and hanged publicly. His enormous bow was preserved by the British at the deputy commissioner's office as a testament to his exceptional strength. Unfortunately, nobody knows the whereabouts of it now.

Another night-time tradition that was fashionable among the young Khasis of early Shillong had to do with courtship. Some boys would go to the house of a girl whom one or more of them wished to marry, carrying with them musical instruments like the *duitara*, a traditional stringed instrument, flutes, small drums, cymbals and so on. And they would spend the entire evening singing, chanting phawars, telling stories and sharing jokes around the hearth. This would go on for quite some time until the girl finally chose the most suitable boy from the group.

When the British came, they added their brand of nightlife to the new settlement. In the words of Nari Rustomji, a civil servant during the Raj, 'Assam's capital, Shillong, developed and took shape to become as near a chip off England as could be conceived of any territory outside the British Isles.' Not only did they establish an exclusive European Ward in the heart of the city, build beautiful houses with quaint gardens in the pattern of English country homes, but they also constructed a racecourse, a polo ground and a golf course, the last of which survives to this day. For night-time diversion, they set up social clubs, exclusive preserves of the Europeans, where they enjoyed their evening drinks, played the trios and quartets of the classical period, and danced to Western music.

Of course, the British did not come alone. They brought soldiers, officials, servants and followers drawn from every part of mainland India. And all of them brought their customs and practices, which must have been perplexing to the Khasis, who until then had lived a more or less secluded life. Of the bustling changes that took place during this time, Hughlet Warjri, a noted Khasi biographer, wrote: 'Since that time, slowly and slowly the offices increased in number, new schools emerged, the volume of trade and commerce amplified and the people too ... from all over India came swarming into this refreshing hill station and ... Shillong, that was only a village in 1864—the year when it was made the capital of the district—slowly and steadily became one of the biggest and most populated towns in the northeastern part of India.'

According to A. Hussain, a Shillong resident who had personally witnessed these developments, the most popular form of night entertainment among Shillong's newcomers was drama. The pioneers, he said, were the Bengalis. Nothing could 'deter their enthusiasm even though their spectators saw them in stages [illuminated only] by lanterns, petromax, gaslight, etc'. These were followed by the Marwaris and Nepalis, who used to stage plays during Holi, and the Parsis, who had their own Parsi Drama Company, staging plays in Hindi.

The Khasis too were not far behind and used to perform plays—based on the Western model—mostly depicting myths and legends, but also stories from *The Arabian Nights* and the Indian epics. Famous among them were stories like 'Ali Baba and the Forty Thieves', 'Layla and Majnun' and 'Rama and Sita'. In fact, the Khasis used to organise a dramatic performance at the close of every traditional dance festival. Seng Khasi, for instance, used to enact a moral drama at the Seng Khasi Hall in Mawkhar on the night of the last day of the Shad Suk Mynsiem (literally, 'dance with a happy heart') Festival or the Weiking Dance, performed once a year in the spring month of April. Such performances would last for the better part of the night. Unfortunately, the practice had to be discontinued in the early 1980s because of the drunken rowdiness of the crowd. It does, however, live on in some villages in the not-too-distant fringes of the city.

By and by, drama was replaced by cinema, which first came to the city in the form of Kelvin Cinema, started in 1921 by an Anglo-Indian entrepreneur, known today only as Mr Unger. Kelvin was followed, after a few years, by others like Bijou, Dreamland, Anjalee and Payal. The period between the early 1920s and the mid-1980s could be termed as the great age of cinema in Shillong. The cinema halls used to have at least four shows a day, starting with the first show at 11 a.m. and ending with the last show at 8 p.m., which was also the most popular.

Oldies still recall the mad rush for tickets: the long queues, well before the counters had even opened, and the bedlam that followed when they did. The queues, they say, disintegrated as people pushed, pulled, elbowed, punched and kicked each other to get at the two little counter-slots. Some would crawl between their neighbours' legs and head-butt others out of the way to reach the prized slots. Others, like swarming ants, would climb on top of people, walk on heads and shoulders, and fight their way into the openings. But reaching them was no guarantee that one would get a ticket, as hands already inside the slots would constantly be pulled out by others trying to put theirs in. If the vehicular traffic had been chock-a-bloc as it is today, there would have been absolute chaos everywhere, for the cinema halls were mostly located at the busiest junctions of Khyndai Lad (Police Bazaar), the commercial core of the city.

In all that confusion, it was not unusual, they say, for people to suffer a fracture or lose money, for between the payment and the time the clerks took to cut the tickets, their hands would have been yanked out of the slot. It was also not unusual for fistfights to break out between individuals or groups, and at such times, only the arrival of the police could restore order. Hence the saying, 'The people of Shillong are afraid of the law, they do not respect it.'

But, by and large, Shillong was very peaceful in those days, and this is nowhere better reflected than in the reminiscence of my elderly friend, Bah Kulong:

When I was living in a hostel, I remember some of us, boys between Class VIII and Class X, going for the late shows and returning home at midnight without the least bit of worry. (Normally, we would have been in trouble with the hostel authorities, but the warden was himself a movie buff and never begrudged us a little bit of harmless fun.) Going through the streets at midnight with a procession of other moviegoers, we would loudly discuss the heroics of the Hollywood action heroes or the Chinese martial artists—Bruce Lee and the Shaolin monks—or in hushed tones, crave for the body of Sophia Loren. But if we had been watching a Hindi movie, for Hindi or English did not matter to us, we would wildly imitate the Bollywood numbers we had just learned, and because of that, on more than one occasion, we were mistaken for drunks and taken before the locality headman for disturbing the peace.

Besides the cinema halls, Bah Kulong says, films were also screened every night by individuals with DVD players. Such screenings, usually in courtyards and costing just a fraction more than the price of a ticket at the cinema, were also very popular, as people did not have to venture out of their neighbourhood.

According to Bah Kulong, there was yet another way in which cinema was integrated into the nightlife of Shillong. It was the custom of the city's localities to organise cleaning drives at least twice a year. To celebrate a job well done, the authorities would screen a popular movie at night in some open ground. The atmosphere would be festive, and the locality's inhabitants would turn out in force, young and old. 'For hard-up boys like us,' he adds, 'such an event was a real treat, for it was not only free but also afforded us the rare opportunity of meeting a lot of nice girls in dim surroundings.'

But all that came to an end, for two reasons. The peace of Shillong was shattered by the first ethnic clash in 1979. The influx of outsiders into the city, which started with the British, had intensified as the years went by and became quite alarming during the Indo-Pak War of 1971 when refugee colonies were set up for those who had fled the war in East Pakistan. The East Pakistanis later became permanent citizens of the city. But the matter did not end there. The situation became worse after the war, with more and more migrants coming in from the neighbouring countries and other Indian states. As the demographic profile changed, the Khasis began to fear the prospect of becoming minorities in their own land. The first clash between Khasis and non-Khasis erupted in 1979, followed by another in 1987, culminating in the 1992 riot, the worst that Shillong had ever experienced, when scores of lives, Khasi and non-Khasi, were lost and property worth many crores was destroyed.

The ethnic eruptions effectively put an end to the late cinema shows, and along with them, Shillong's carefree spirit. As soon as it got dark, shops were swiftly closed, and people hurried home, running away from their fears, the darkness and the CRPF jawans, who suddenly became the 'ominous sentinels' of the city's streets. The night, to most people, with their anxieties and suspicions, became 'the outlaw's day, in which he rises early to do wrong', and continued to be like that for many years.

The other reason for the end of the 8 p.m. movie was the advent of television in the 1980s. Initially, the best thing about the TV, people say, was not its entertainment programmes and films, since the only channel available was the hugely uninteresting Doordarshan. From neighbouring Bangladesh, they had access to Western news, entertainment and sports channels. And during the FIFA World Cup events, Shillong's nights came alive with the noise of football-crazy crowds gathered at the houses of the lucky few who owned a television.

The introduction of satellite TV and cable networks, two decades later, brought a sea change in the entertainment scene, and cinema almost received a death blow. It is only recently that it got a new lease of life with the inauguration of a brand-new duplex at the site of the old Dreamland Cinema Hall. Anjalee has followed suit, and we now have two excellent duplexes.

The establishment of these new duplexes, Gold Digital Cinema and Galleria, coincided with some sort of return to normality in the city. The blithe spirit of the late cinema shows is, of course, gone forever, but peace—though fragile, and threatened by both antisocial elements as well as militants—has endured for more than two decades now. Consequently, the city's nightlife has also tentatively picked up again. Some shops are open till 8 p.m. or later, drinking dens and family restaurants are thriving, and four successful 'bars/ clubs' have made an appearance. These places—such as Cloud 9 and Tango in Police Bazaar, Platinum at Polo Grounds and Deja Vu at the Laitumkhrah Point—not only offer good food, drinks and a great ambience but, come Saturday night, dance and Western music are also on the menu. Local bands, some of them known nationally, belt out rock, pop and soul every weekend, and partying crowds sway to their rhythm.

But this kind of nightlife is limited to a few bars attached to hotels, and is confined to the moneyed, the Westernised and, as they say here, 'the hi-fis' and 'hi-byes'. For those without the money or the inclination, for those too fearful of the night so far away from home (and there are still too many who don't trust the peace, who don't believe we have learnt anything from 1992), there is the dark outdoor in the neighbourhood, awaiting them with badminton and a unique urban tradition known as *ïeng kyndong*.

Badminton is a popular form of diversion here. On winter evenings, one can see boys and girls of all ages flocking to the outdoor courts in different localities with their rackets and shuttlecocks, playing for fun, though from time to time, competitive tournaments are also organised. These matches last late into the night, and those waiting for their turn warm themselves by a fire blazing in a corner. One might ask why badminton is played mostly at night. The answer is that although the young do get a two-month winter break, most are busy with domestic chores during the day. Adults, of course, go to work. Chilly winter evenings, therefore, when the wind is gentle and everyone is free, are the best time for the sport.

The tradition of ïeng kyndong, or corner standing, could be said to be an offshoot of the bonfire-making tradition from the old days. Since making bonfires is now nearly impossible in Shillong's narrow and crowded streets, young men are doing the next best thing. They gather in groups in dark corners and build small fires around which they crowd to take stock of the day's events, to converse and to relax under the benign cover of darkness, with the help, in some cases, of a little 'monkey medicine' or a puff of marijuana. This tradition is widely accepted in Shillong, since, generally speaking, the boys cause no trouble, and actually make the roads much safer.

During the rainiest months—April to October—Shillong's nightlife moves indoors, except on those rare nights when it does not rain. People do whatever they can to entertain themselves—read, play games, spend time on their phones or online, and watch TV. Television is, in fact, a treasured friend for most girls and women, many of whom do not play badminton and cannot take part in ïeng kyndong, which is an exclusively male affair. And so, the more educated of them spend night after night with Hollywood movies and the soaps on Star World, while the rest gawk at Bollywood films and the *bahuranis* of Hindi serials.

Two more features of Shillong's nightlife deserve mention. One of these is the wedding feast. Most weddings now take place in winter, probably because the weather is mostly dry during this time. But that does not stop people from joking that it is also because the cold drives lovers to the marriage bed, sometimes prematurely. Typically, two or three weddings take place every single day of the winter months in Shillong. And since all the receptions begin at 5 p.m., the wedding feast, followed by festivities, singing, dancing, and sometimes a performance by a rock band, goes on till the streets are quiet and the stars wane in the sky.

Then there is the Khasi funeral. It may seem bizarre to include funerals in a description of a city's nightlife, but you must understand the nature of this ceremony. The only quiet spot in a Khasi funeral is the room where the body is kept and where the nearest family members keep vigil. Apart from that, all is noise and bustle.

Khasis, as I told you, keep the body of their dead for at least two nights, in some cases longer, before it is buried or consigned to flames. During the two-night wake, relatives from far and near, as well as friends and neighbours, come in hordes to condole and support. They separate into groups engaged in diverse recreations—playing cards, carom, word scrabbles and Ludo, or merely talking, cracking jokes and telling stories—while boys and girls walk around offering tea and biscuits, and of course, the ubiquitous betel nut. Many of them stay late into the night, quite a few for the whole night, establishing a peculiar kind of nightlife. And because people do depart at regular intervals, who is to say that the Khasi funeral is not part of the spirit of the night in Shillong?

After I had summarised the essay for my friends, Magdalene remarked, 'That's your Shillong nightlife, Ap? I had different things in mind, man!'

'Don't worry, more and more bars and nightclubs are coming up, Mag,' Raji consoled her. 'But these are things we do every night, no? However, like you, we do not normally associate them with nightlife.'

'It's certainly not a conventional take,' Donald agreed. 'But packed like a travel bag, ha, Bah Ap? Your article, I mean.'

'The most interesting part, na, is our funeral tradition,' Bah Kynsai said. 'It is quite true, you know, it really is part of the city's nightlife, I mean, people do stay up till two, three in the morning, talking, telling stories ...'

'Like we are doing now,' Bah Kit said.

'Like we are doing now,' Bah Kynsai agreed.

'But the name of Shillong, Bah Ap, you said it came from ...?' Donald asked.

'From U Lei Shulong, the patron god of the ancient state of Shyllong. His divine retreat is Shyllong Peak. The British simply named their new capital after the peak. But they changed the spelling from "Shyllong" to "Shillong". And as always, what the British gave, we swallowed whole.'

'We are great swallowers, na?' Bah Kynsai said. 'At least we are great at that, liah. Okay now, what next? How about the clan-name stories? The Shyrkon story was quite amazing, I thought ...'

'Of course, why not?' Bah Kit chipped in. 'Every clan has its own origin story like that of the Shyrkons', ha. I write my name as Kitshon Lyngdoh, for instance, but actually, Lyngdoh is not a clan name. It's a profession: that of a priest in a particular state or one of its provinces. My clan is Lyngdoh Nongbri. Four other clans are related to us ...'

'Yeah, yeah, you talked about it earlier,' Donald said. 'But what exactly is the story, Bah Kit?'

'According to the story that circulates among us, ha, once upon a time, we were part of a large and powerful clan whose first ancestress, ka ïawbei, was none other than Ka Bor Kupli, the reigning spirit of the River Kupli. Her husband, Ïale, was represented by a beautiful waterfall, now gone, lost forever to the Kupli Hydro Power Project. Even now, when the five clans cross the river, they cannot do so without first making a sacrificial offering to the spirit of this great primal ancestress.'

Briefly, this was the story Bah Kit told us. The clan, being the descendant of a river goddess, was powerful and prosperous. The peculiar thing about it was that there were hardly any deaths among its members. One would have thought this was a happy state of affairs for the clansmen, but it wasn't. They witnessed many deaths among their friends and neighbours, and whenever there was a death, they saw funeral rites performed and great feasts organised. And when a person died old, there was also funeral music and the chanting of gnomic phawars. All this seemed like great fun to many in the clan. They lamented the fact that they never had a chance to organise such rites, feasts and cultural performances in honour of those who had passed on. But most of all, they lamented the fact that there were too many old and sick people among them, who lived in extreme misery and suffering.

One day, the elders of the clan called for a council. When everyone was gathered, the *rangbah kur*, clan leader, rose and addressed the assembly. 'You the clan, you the family, look here, we have convened the council to discuss one crucial matter, and it is this—why does no one from this clan ever die? Some of you may think this is a good thing, something to be happy about, and for which we have to thank our Lord and Master. As elders of the clan, we tell you it is not so. It is a curse rather than a blessing. Haven't you seen with your own eyes how many old, infirm and sick people we have in our midst? Some of our great mothers are so old they cannot even sit without tumbling down unless we keep them in a winnowing basket or rice bin. Think of the pain and wretchedness and desolation of the old ones. How many of you would like to live *shong prah shong shang* like that, to grow so old that you have to be put in a winnowing basket or a rice bin? When you have lost everything that makes life a joyous thing; when you have lost your sense of sight and hearing; when you have lost all your teeth so that you have to drink your food like water; when you cannot walk; when you cannot stand; when you cannot even sit without support; when diseases ravage your body and make you waste away and cause you agonising pain and anguish, I ask you, what use is a long life? It is rather a terrible dungeon, gloomy and nightmarish.

'In such a case, is death to be dreaded? Is death to be avoided at all costs? I tell you, it is rather to be desired, to be sought out like a beloved, whose loving embrace sets us free from the cruel torments of life. It is because of this, my kinsfolk, my flesh and blood, that we have convened this council. In our great pity for the old ones, who suffer horribly and who are but pale shadows of their former selves, we—your augurs, your uncles—have sought the guidance of our first ancestress, Ka Bor Kupli, and of *suidñia*, our first maternal uncle. They, in turn, have pleaded with God, U Blei, the Dispenser, the Creator, to show us the way to ease their agony.

'The signs are neither good nor bad. There is indeed a way to end the suffering of the old ones, but there is also a price to pay. What shall we do, my kinsfolk?'

The gathering asked him what the way was and what the price.

The leader said, 'Our ïawbei and suidñia have indicated that we could pretend a death, conduct our funeral rites and organise our feasts as if someone dear to us has truly died—this should please those among you who look at such things with longing. When this is done, actual death shall follow and come to us, but unfortunately, not only to the old … What say you, you the flesh, you the blood of the clan? This is a serious matter; ponder hard and long before you give us an answer.'

Not one in the gathering was without a few helpless dependants, whose suffering was a constant torment to them. The infirm old were, moreover, a drain on the energy of the youthful and the healthy, who could not properly tend to the daily business of living because they had to continuously monitor the needs of the old and the sick. They thought of the fate that would await them when they grew old and shuddered. Their response was unanimously in favour of the elders' plan.

Not long after, the plan was put into practice. The elders had a green lizard, known as *ñiangbshiah*, killed and proclaimed that one of their old mothers had finally died. The clan was notified, the village was informed and all the paternal relations—sons and daughters of the clan's male members—were apprised of the passing away of one of their great-great-grandmothers. Then the elders constructed an elaborate *krong*, a bier of bamboo, decorated it with colourful silks and velvets and respectfully placed the lizard inside it. After that, they performed all the customary rites and rituals, sacrificed pigs and oxen, and organised a great feast amidst the playing of funeral music and the chanting of gnomic phawars eulogising the sterling qualities of the dead. Three days of funeral rites and feasting followed, and throughout, the clan elders maintained a close watch on the bier, kept in one of the bedrooms of the ancestral house. No one was allowed to come near it. But on the fourth day, just when they were about to carry the bier to the cremation hill, members of a family from the Ryndem clan, whose father was from the bereaved clan, protested that they had not even had a glimpse of the body.

'How can you take our *meikha*, our great-great-grandmother, for cremation without letting us have one last look at her?' they said. 'Custom demands that we say our farewell to the departed soul lest she worry and fret, lest she come to whine and whimper in our rest, in our sleep. We cannot allow you to treat us like this. You cannot deny us a last farewell to our beloved meikha! This is not right! This is not done!'

The Ryndem family also appealed to those gathered, people who had come from all over the village and beyond, to assist them in the funeral. They said, 'You, the people, you, the many, you, the assembly, is it right for them to deny us a last glimpse of our beloved meikha? Is it right for them to deny us our last farewell? Is it the custom? You are the judge, you are the arbiter, give us justice!' they pleaded.

The assemblage ruled that it was not the custom and that it was not just. Confronted by so many, the bereaved clan was forced to open the bier. But when the Ryndems saw what was in it, they shouted in disgust at the obscene trick the clan had played, not only on them but on all those who were present. They called out to the crowd to witness what was going on for themselves. 'Come, see for yourselves, see for whom we are mourning!' they shouted. 'It's not our meikha but an animal!'

The whole gathering cursed the clan and said, 'May you suffer death and grief without end from now on! You have asked for it, may you get it without end! May it come to feast upon you, and may you die like insects and scatter throughout the land like insects!'

The shame of the exposure was something the clan had to bear every day from then on. The ensuing social boycott brought untold hardships and suffering. And then death, which they had sought for so long, came and swept through their ranks, threatening to annihilate the clan. Against the onslaught of these combined forces, they decided to flee, to get away from that place before they were wiped off the face of the earth.

A branch of the clan was entrusted with the safekeeping of its religious practices and therefore came to be known as Lyngdoh Nongbri, the priestly family that kept the clan's religion safe. Another branch set off for *sha ba dap um*, the flooded plains, of Ri Bhoi: they came to be known as Shadap. The last branch migrated to another part of Ri Pnar, *ban sah bad i Pa*, literally, 'to stay with father', and therefore came to be known as Passah, the ones who stayed with the father. The Lyngdoh Nongbris travelled towards the state of Shyllong, stayed in the Nongkrem area in East Khasi Hills, and later served the state as its official priests. Still later, some families decided to move from Nongkrem to establish another village not too far away from there. These came to be known as Nongkynrihs, the shifters, and the village they founded, still thriving today, became known by the name of Nongkynrih. Another branch of the Lyngdoh Nongbris went on to serve as official priests of the state of Nongkhlaw and settled by the River Kynshi in West Khasi Hills. Because of that, it came to be known as Lyngdoh Kynshi.

Bah Kit ended his story by saying, 'But what the name of the original clan was, no one can tell now. That is probably because all the migrating branches of the clan tried to conceal their identity to avoid censure and persecution. What we know for sure is that all five clans came from the east of Ri Pnar and all of them were originally from the same clan. Even today, we consider ourselves *shikur*, or bound by blood in a cognate relationship. Right here, there are three of us, Ap Jutang Shadap, Dale Nongkynrih and myself. Oh yes, I nearly forgot. The green lizard is sacred to all five clans. Our elders forbid us from harming the little creature, our own meikha.'

'Ours too,' Dale said.

'And ours,' I added.

'Interesting, leh, interesting!' Bah Kynsai declared. 'So, by Hamkom's distorted logic, you would also be Jaiñtias, na?' He said this with his booming laugh.

Evening, however, was not amused. He said, '*Tet leh*, Bah Kynsai, you are joking too much! What it means is that we are all the same, no? Imagine, earlier they were Pnars, now they are Khynriams!'

'Okay, okay, who's next?' Bah Kynsai asked quickly to avoid further discussion on the subject.

'Does everyone know the origin story of their clans?' Hamkom asked. 'I certainly don't.'

'I have some idea, but that's all,' Magdalene added.

'We cannot expect anything from Don; he's not even interested in it, na?' Bah Kynsai said. 'Why don't you start, Raji?'

Nobody else seemed to notice that Evening had fallen silent, but before I could remark on it, Raji was already telling us the story of the Manai clan.

According to the story, it all began when the *syiem khynnah* (deputy king) of the state of Khyrim went on a hunting expedition to the Ri War jungles near Nongjri village with many of his warriors. While the syiem khynnah and his men were walking stealthily through the forest, one of his scouts, who was a little ahead of them, heard a baby crying. He went back to the main party to report the matter.

'Pa'iem, Pa'iem!' he said excitedly. 'You won't believe what I just heard!'

'Out with it, man, what did you just hear?' the syiem khynnah said.

'A crying baby!'

'A crying baby in this infernal jungle?'

The syiem khynnah and his warriors laughed at the idea. But the man took them to the spot. When they got there, they saw a leopardess suckling a baby girl beneath a large banyan tree, the stooping branches and massive protruding roots of which had transformed the entire area into a snug and sheltered space. They were transfixed by the sight. No one dared to even breathe, but when the leopardess left, they went to have a closer look at the little creature. They found her lying on the ground, naked and beautiful beyond belief. The syiem khynnah said, 'The child is lucky that these jungles are so warm, otherwise she would have died. Whose daughter could she be? How did she come to be here?'

In response, an old warrior said, 'Pa'iem, this could be an omen. Maybe God brought us to this place so we could find and save this baby! Why don't we take her home to your sister, the *syiemsad*?'

Pa'iem, as you might have gathered, is a respectful address for a king, meaning 'king father', and syiemsad refers to the 'queen mother', who could be the mother of the king or his sister, if his mother is no more.

The syiem khynnah agreed, and they carried off the baby, wrapped in a shawl borrowed from one of the warriors. The queen mother was thrilled to see the baby girl and to hear the fantastic story. Since she was suckling a baby of her own, she decided to keep the child and feed her with her own milk.

Cared for by a queen, the baby girl soon grew into a lovely maiden. Her beauty was such that the prince himself fell in love with her and began courting her. But the queen mother shivered at the idea. The girl was like her own daughter. She and her son had fed from the same breasts; they were like brother and sister; how could they marry? It could never be!

She plotted with her counsellors, who finally found for her a handsome youth from the village of Mairang in the state of Nongkhlaw. Before her marriage, however, the girl was given a new clan name, as was the practice. Because she had been found in the jungles of Ri War near the village of Nongjri, and under the banyan tree called *ka jri*, she was given the clan name of War Nongjri. The queen mother declared that the girl's children would be one of the nobilities of the state of Khyrim, since she had been breast-fed by a queen and had grown up in the queen's palace.

Of this ancestress, three daughters were born, who later became *ki ïawbei khynraw*, the youthful ancestresses of three branches of the family. One of the families migrated to Laitkynsew near Sohra, which was also part of the state of Nongkhlaw. Another went to Nongkrem to become one of the nobilities of the state of Khyrim, as promised by the queen mother. Only the family of the youngest daughter remained in Mairang. This family, as well as the one that went to Laitkynsew, was made one of the nobilities of Nongkhlaw.

The Mairang branch of the family prospered and became so numerous that three branches broke away from it, and went to settle in the villages of Tynghah, Manai and Pynden Nongbri. From that time, they became known as War Tynghah, War Manai and War Nongbri respectively.

Many years later, two sisters from the War Nongjri clan became the ancestresses of yet another clan. The younger one, Ka Konghep, had many sons and daughters, about fifteen in all—

'What, fifteen children! Oh, my God! Did the mother live or die?' Magdalene exclaimed.

Raji explained that, in those days, people used to have as many children as they could. 'Even now,' he said, 'in many villages, people have a minimum of six or seven children. Some even have ten or twelve, okay? Here in Shyrkon too, it's like that; that's what Chirag told us. Khasis used to say that those with many children are *kiba riewspah*, people who are rich.'

'By what logic?' Magdalene asked.

'They claim that a child always brings his own rice. But also, from the perspective of an agrarian economy, it does make sense: the more the children, the more the labour, no, Bah Kynsai?'

'Certainly not!' Bah Kynsai contradicted him. 'Too many hands on the same field are a waste of labour ... Carry on with your story, man!'

The elder sister, Ka Kongthei, did not have any children, Raji said. She was very jealous of Konghep, and whenever there was a family gathering, her barrenness was like a spear-thrust in her breast. At such times, she could not bear the sight of how happy and lively her sister's family was with so many people around, dancing and singing. Her house was exactly the opposite: quiet, cold and lonely.

She also carried the stigma of being a childless woman, and people gossiped maliciously about her barren womb. Not able to stand the torment, one day, in collusion with Konghep (whose heart ached with pity for her sister), she announced to everyone that she had given birth to a baby girl, but that, unfortunately, she had died soon after.

When people came to hear the news, they flocked to her house, as was the custom. Her friends and relatives came from far and near to console and support her in her hour of need. She, on her part, enthusiastically assisted by her sister's family, organised a great funeral feast complete with drum and pipe music in honour of the dead child. When the body was carried to the cremation hill, she even had the drums, big and small, hung on a tree near the clan's large ossuary. But when the cremation was about to take place, it was accidentally discovered that the whole thing was a hoax: there was no child in the bier, only a dead lizard. The sympathisers were incensed by the trick played on them. They spat on the sisters and roundly cursed them and their families before leaving the scene. Not satisfied with that, to remind them of what they had done, everyone, from then on, started calling them Ki War Wahksing, or the Wars who hung the funeral drums on a tree although nobody had died.

Raji concluded the story by saying, 'And so, as you can see, the original clan was War Nongjri, and the other clans—War Tynghah, War Manai, War Nongbri and War Wahksing—emerged from it.'

'But I heard that all these clans have now become Warjri, no Raji?' Bah Kit asked. 'How did that come about?'

'Oh that, wait, wait, I'll tell you.'

Raji revealed that in the years after the great earthquake of 1897, some families from the War Nongbri clan migrated to Sohra, and from Sohra, some of them went on to Shillong. The Shillong lot retained their clan name, War Nongbri, but those who remained in Sohra began calling themselves Nongbri. But that caused a lot of confusion in matters of clan relationships, since there was also the Lyngdoh Nongbri clan, who were often referred to as Nongbri. Therefore, in 1966, a large council of the original War Nongjri clan was convened. Attending the council were representatives of clans like War Nongjri, War Tynghah, War Manai, War Nongbri and War Wahksing. To simplify matters and avoid all confusion, it was unanimously decided that, from then on, all of them would be known by the new clan name of Warjri.

However, Raji said, there were still some people, here and there, who continued to call themselves by their old clan names. Raji himself wrote his name as Raji Manai.

At the end of the narration, Magdalene asked, 'But what is this thing with the lizard, ha, Raji? Khasis seem to have a great penchant for turning the poor thing into a scapegoat, no, Bah Kynsai?'

'Nothing to do with our five clans; it's purely coincidental,' Bah Kit answered for Bah Kynsai.

'With us, it's not the lizard that is sacred, Mag, but the leopard,' Raji explained.

When we had discussed Raji's story for a while longer, Bah Kynsai looked around and asked, 'Anybody else?'

'Why don't you tell your story, Bah Kynsai?' Bah Su said.

'Nothing to tell. My story is the same as Raji's. I'm a War Nongbri actually; I write my name as Kynsai Nongbri to reduce the linguistic burden, na? Why don't you tell yours? The Kharakor clan should have a nice story.'

'It does,' Bah Su replied simply.

'So, tell, na? This Bah Su is also quite funny!' Bah Kynsai said impatiently.

Bah Sukher Sing Kharakor responded with a smile and began to tell us the story of his first ancestress, Ka Akordingla. She was magnificent, he said, the daughter of a British military officer serving in Surma Valley, East Bengal. The officer married a well-educated Sylheti woman and brought up his children in a manner befitting his high official position. Among other things, he equipped them with a proper Western education. The family was quite well-to-do. Unfortunately, their house and almost everything in it was destroyed during the great floods of 1783, forcing the survivors to break up and disperse in different directions.

It was not very clear why the family had to split up and migrate separately like that. Perhaps the parents were no longer alive to keep them together. Whatever the reason, one thing was clear—Akordingla travelled to the Khasi Hills through Jaiñtiapur, carrying with her only a small bundle and a walking stick to ease her travel.

When Akordingla, then merely a teenager, first reached the hills, she went to live as a servant in someone's home. But she never stayed in one place for long, for she wanted to travel up the hills, deeper and deeper into Khasi territory, to get as far away as possible from the terrible memories of the floods and whatever else was haunting her. Perhaps she was fleeing from something sinister, something that had broken up the family in the first place. Nobody knew. At last, she arrived at Lyngkyrdem, where she stayed for some time before leaving to serve in the palace of the king of Khyrim at Khatarblang. By that time, the Khasis, true to their habit of name-shortening, were calling her Akor, which in Khasi also means civility. The name fitted her to perfection, for she was a humble young woman with gracious manners.

At the palace, Akor had to work very hard, getting up at dawn and only resting when it was time to sleep. However, because she was well-nourished and happy in the jovial company of her fellow servants, her natural beauty bloomed, and everywhere she went, people gaped at her, admiring her astonishing loveliness. She was so beautiful that nobody could believe she was a servant. They thought she looked like a princess with her fair European skin, sharp features and commanding stature. She soon had many Khasi men at her feet, wooing her with the earnestness and passion of desperate lovers. Among them was the son of the king himself. However, Akor wanted nothing to do with him, not only because he was the king's son but also because she disliked him, for unlike the others, his intentions were not at all pure. The man she was rather fond of went by the name of Rangkynsai Pyngrope and worked in Lyngkyrdem.

At that point, Donald interrupted Bah Su to ask, 'Why do you call the man "son of the king", Bah Su? Why don't you call him a prince?'

'The son of a king is not a prince, Don, Khasi society is matrilineal, remember? The king's son belongs to his wife's clan, which is not even the ruling syiem clan. Only his sister's son can be a prince.'

'Oh yeah,' Donald said sheepishly.

Bah Su then spoke about how Akor still carried at all times the walking stick she had brought from home. She never let it out of her sight and, even when she was working, it remained by her side. This attracted the curiosity of many, but especially that of the king's son, who wanted to know why she was so attached to it. Whenever he asked her about it, Akor responded with a joke and never gave him a straight answer. But that only fuelled his curiosity, and he decided to keep a very close watch on it.

His chance came one day when Akor was working in the garden. Seeing that she had left the stick standing by the fence, he picked it up and broke it into two pieces. To his astonishment, nuggets of gold and silver fell out of it. He gathered them up and left the broken stick there.

When Akor found her walking stick destroyed, she was heartbroken and cried inconsolably for days. The nuggets of gold and silver, carefully hidden in the hollow of the stick, were all that remained of her family's wealth, and now, even that was gone, for the king's son refused to return them despite her pitiful cries and pleadings. Instead, knowing that she was not merely a poor servant girl, he offered to marry her. However, Akor's dislike for him had only grown; she turned him down and left the palace as soon as she was offered a position elsewhere.

But the king's son would not leave her alone. He began stalking her, forcing her to leave the town and go to a village called Sohrarim, just a few kilometres north of Sohra, in the state of Nongkhlaw. She took an oath never to set foot in the state of Khyrim again.

Rangkynsai Pyngrope, who was deeply in love with Akor, also left Lyngkyrdem and followed her to Sohrarim. Not finding any work there, he moved north to Laitkroh, a village in the state of Sohra, and persuaded Akor to join him. It was in Laitkroh that he married her.

Akor and Rangkynsai were blessed with three daughters. But when the first one was born, a problem immediately arose: what name was she to be given? The mother's family name could not be used since it was not a Khasi name, nor could the father's, since the Khasi matrilineal custom would not allow it. Therefore—

Here Evening suddenly burst out, 'Why not? Why not? I'm using my father's surname! Mawñiuh is not my clan name, but I'm using it, so what?'

'I'll tell you later why you cannot use your father's name, ha, Ning, but for now, let me finish my story,' Bah Su said gently.

Rangkynsai called upon the lyngdoh, the priest in charge of that part of the state, and requested him to sanctify a new clan name for his wife and daughter.

This was eventually done in a big ceremony involving the Pyngrope clan and their friends from the village. The clan name given to Akor and her children was Kharakor: Khar to signify a non-Khasi ancestress and Akor after the name of Akordingla. (The names of Khasi clans with non-Khasi ancestresses usually begin with the prefix 'Khar', though there are exceptions.) The first daughter of Akor was thus named Lyngkjilmon Kharakor. The other two were called Lyngkshilmon Kharakor and Lyngksilmon Kharakor. They were the very first Kharakor children to be born. Meanwhile, because their *thawlang*, their first paternal ancestor, was a Pyngrope, it was also determined during the ceremony that the Kharakors and the Pyngropes should never marry each other.

The family led a prosperous and happy life for some time. Then, when the eldest girl was about fourteen, Rangkynsai felt a kind of homesickness and wanted to go back to Lyngkyrdem. He tried to persuade Akor and the children to go with him, but Akor had sworn an oath never to set foot in Khyrim again, and so, with sadness, she stayed behind when he eventually went back to live with his parents.

When Bah Su finished the story, Magdalene exclaimed, 'What a strange fellow! Imagine, he deserted his beautiful wife and children and went back to his parents. Normally, it's the other way around, no? I don't like the man at all!'

'That's the jilted woman speaking,' Bah Kynsai teased her. 'But to tell you the truth, na, I also find it very strange. I mean, we men used to say, "The mountains will be flattened because of you!" and yet that fellow went back to his parents, and that too when the children were still quite young! His name was Rangkynsai, "the finest man", but he behaved like the most defective ... Unbelievable!'

In his defence, Bah Su said, 'He sent Akor some money every week to help her bring up the kids properly.'

Magdalene began to say something, when Evening interrupted to ask Bah Su, 'What about your promise to answer me?'

Bah Kynsai, however, did not allow the discussion to proceed. 'Ning, we are now talking about name stories, you will have your chance when and if we discuss the matrilineal system. Now, whose?' he asked.

'Who else?' Evening answered with a question. 'I'm using my father's clan name, but ...'

'But you don't know anything about it,' Bah Kit completed the sentence for him.

'Unfortunately, yes,' Evening admitted.

Magdalene said she knew some things about her clan. 'I know, for instance, that we were supposed to have come from a fairy, ha, Bah Kynsai, but I don't know the details.'

'No, no, Mag,' Raji said sharply, 'the origin story of a syiem clan is not the same everywhere, okay? Each state has its own story as to how its ruling syiem clan was founded. For instance, the story of the syiem clan of Hima Shyllong is different from that of Hima Sutnga. Therefore, the syiem of Shyllong is not related to the syiem of Sutnga. Syiem and syiem are not related at all, Mag, unless they are descended from the same ancestress. So, first of all, you have to know to which syiem clan you belong.'

'I give up, I give up!' Magdalene threw up her hands.

'Never mind that, Mag,' Bah Kit said. 'If we have a chance to discuss our traditional democracy, ha, we'll tell you some of these origin tales. One of them might be yours.'

'All right then, that's it, I think, na?' Bah Kynsai announced. 'These three buggers, Ning and Don and Ham, don't know a damn thing, so let's move on.'

Ham interrupted Bah Kynsai to say, 'Bah Kit said he knew something about my father's clan, the Lamares ...'

'I do,' Bah Kit agreed, 'but not everything, only the part dealing with their migration.'

'Let's have it then,' Bah Kynsai demanded.

Bah Kit said he first came to know about the Lamare clan's migration to Ri Pnar when he went to Raliang recently to witness the religious dance festival known as Ka Nguh Blai and Chad Pastieh of Raliang.

Ka Nguh Blai in the Pnar dialect means 'paying obeisance to God'. The ceremony is performed in the sacred forest called Khloo Blai, 'forest of God'. The sanctum sanctorum in the centre of the forest, preserved in its pristine state, is known as 'Poh Puja Kopati'. It is here that the religious rites are conducted between 20 and 22 November every year. And it is after the ceremony that the Chad Pastieh, or sword dance, is held. Incidentally, Raliang Elaka has many sacred forests, including Poh Moorang, Pun Lyngdoh and Khloo Byrsan.

The ceremony, Bah Kit said, was intricately linked with the Lamare clan from Nongkynrih, capital of Raij Nongkynrih, a province of the ancient state of Shyllong. The Lamare clan used to be the custodian of the ceremonial drums of the state, played only during religious ceremonies. But one day, the authorities governing Raij Nongkynrih ordered drummers from the clan to play on an occasion that had no religious significance. The clan elders refused to do so, and this led to a long-simmering dispute between them and the authorities. Rather than live in disharmony, the elders decided that the entire clan should migrate eastward, finally stopping at Raliang Elaka in Ri Pnar. After their drum-playing skills had been tested by the doloi of Raliang, the provincial ruler, they were granted permission to settle in the elaka and were also made the official custodians of the province's ceremonial drums. The place where the Lamare clan first stayed was named Nongkynrih, and it carries that name to this day.

Bah Kit concluded, 'This is all I know about the Lamares, Ham. They were Khynriams but became a very important part of Pnar social and religious life. The story, like the others I told you earlier, clearly indicates that there used to be a great deal of migration, not only from Ri Pnar to other parts of Ri Hynñiew Trep but also the other way around.'

Evening laughed aloud then and said, 'And Hamkom calls himself a Jaiñtia when even his own father was from the Khasi Hills! Hahaha, he's more Jaiñtia than the Jaintapuris of Bangladesh, no, Bah Kynsai?'

This derisive statement could have easily provoked another fight between them but for the fact that Bah Kynsai, ignoring Evening completely, suddenly stood up and said, 'Now we'll take a break. Ham, chal, chal, let's go out for a whistle.'

When Bah Kynsai and Hamkom returned, Evening said, 'We did not hear you whistling ...'

'We whistled on a tree far from here, na, that's why. And that reminds me: nobody does it near the hut, huh? Otherwise, I'll cut it off. Okay, shall we proceed with our name stories, then?'

'What exactly do you have in mind?' Raji asked.

'Well, we have some strange names around, na? For instance, if you read Gurdon, you will be told that the advent of the Welsh missionaries and the partial dissemination of English education produced names such as U Water Kingdom, Ka Red Sea, U Shakewell Bones, Ka Medina, U Mission, Ka India and so on. But English education is not "partial" any more, na, it's universal, so why do we still have these funny names everywhere, huh?'

'Because we are incorrigible anglophiles, that's why, Bah Kynsai,' Bah Kit said. 'The practice most parents follow, ha, especially in the rural areas, ha, is to go through English books and look for nice-sounding words. They use them without even checking their meanings.'

'I have seen people looking for nice-sounding words in dictionaries also,' Hamkom added, 'but mostly, of course, without checking the meaning.'

'That is partially true,' Bah Kynsai said, 'but often parents have specific reasons for naming their children, na? These reasons are the stories behind the names. Now, this is what we'll do, okay, I'll tell you a name story I know of—interesting and funny, of course—and if you also have one, you can do the same after me. But one thing, na, do not use clan names.'

'Why, why?' Magdalene wanted to know.

'Because we do not want to insult anyone, na? You see, I know somebody whose name is Kaligula, okay? Now, that's a funny name to give your son, na? I mean, why should anybody be named after the notorious Caligula? We all know who he was, don't we? Among other things, the Roman emperor was reviled as a mass murderer and a ruthless pervert who converted his palace into a brothel. It's a queer name to give a child, na? However, if I speak of him without the clan name, would you be able to identify him? Impossible. So, no clan names, okay?'

'It's only among us, ya,' Magdalene protested.

'Have you forgotten what these two fellows are going to do?' Bah Kynsai asked, pointing at Raji and me. 'They'll make films and write books and whatnot, remember? No, no, we shouldn't do it!'

'Bah Kynsai,' Donald called out to him, 'earlier you mentioned U Shakewell Bones and Ka Red Sea, et cetera. Are "U" and "Ka" part of the names or what?'

'No, man!' Bah Kynsai answered in mock anger. 'These are gender markers only: "U" to indicate a male and "Ka" to indicate a female … But how do you not know even these simple things?'

'I know they are gender markers, but I'm not sure whether they are part of the names or not, no?'

'Why don't you tell us your story, Bah Kynsai?' Hamkom urged.

'Well, it's like this, okay? Recently, not over a month ago, na, I received an invitation to the wedding of one of my relatives. We used to call her Ka Ness, which is a very feminine-sounding name. I never knew her full name, okay? But when I opened the card, na, I saw this announcement: "Manliness wets Captain". Her name is Manliness, liah! Can you imagine, Manliness for a beautiful woman! And that's not all, ha, according to the card, she would not "wed" the Captain, she would "wet" him. "Manliness wets Captain", and the Captain became *umpi*. Umpi in our War dialect means "brother-in-law", ha, but in the standard Sohra dialect, na, it means "urine". So, "Manliness wets Captain", and the Captain became urine, hahaha.

'When I met the mother at the wedding, na, I asked her why she had named her daughter Manliness. She told me it was her husband's choice. Her husband had been praying for a boy, ha, but when he got a girl instead, na, he wanted her to have all the strength and robust qualities of a boy. Hence the name "Manliness". How do you like that?'

'Oh, like that?' Raji said, laughing. 'We all have stories like that, Bah Kynsai, good, good.'

'Why don't we begin with our own names?' Bah Kit said. 'Mine means someone who would help bear the burden during adversities.'

'I don't think we are interested in nice-sounding Khasi names right now, Kit,' Bah Kynsai replied, 'but okay, we can do that. Don, we can start with you.'

'You cannot laugh at my name; it's a proper English name.'

'No, no, we are not laughing, man, we just want to know the meaning of your name and why your parents chose it.'

'I haven't asked, Bah Kynsai,' Donald replied.

'Donald Lachlan, "warlike world chief",' I said. 'That's what it means. But why did your parents give you that name, Don?'

'That also I don't know.'

'Because they wanted him to be a cosmo, na?' Bah Kynsai laughed.

'True, true, Bah Kynsai, very true!' Evening laughed along.

'What about you, ha, what about you?' Donald demanded angrily. 'Eveningstar! What a name!'

'Oh yeah!' Evening responded scornfully. 'At least I know why my parents gave me the name.'

'Why?' Bah Kynsai asked.

'I was born on a beautiful autumn evening, okay, just when the stars were coming out. I was not born in a hospital, but in my own house in the village. My mother was assisted only by the village midwife and some relatives, but my birth was an easy one, no problem at all. When everything was done, my father, who had been quite tense until then, finally went out to the veranda to relax. He looked up at the cool evening sky and the stars appearing one by one and exclaimed, "What a beautiful evening! Stars peeping out at my son's coming! It's a good omen; I must name him Eveningstar." That's how I was given my name. Laugh if you want to, but I'm very proud of it.'

'Either that or he must have wanted you to be a star,' Bah Kynsai laughed.

Perhaps wanting to take a sly dig at Evening, Hamkom said, 'But Khasis are very fond of stars, there are so many names ending in stars, no, Bah Kynsai?'

'Yeah, yeah, so many of them, na? Starlightersing, Shiningsstar, Plos Star, Wetstarson, Geldingnewstar, Rockystarsing, Morning Lur Star, Upstarwell, Guesstarwel, Roamingfarstar, Balistars, Starlintoi, Starbornes, Twostar … Come on, na, help, help …'

'No, no, Bah Kynsai,' Raji objected, 'by your own say-so, okay, you should also tell us the stories behind the names.'

'Okay, okay … Starlightersing is from a remote village. When his mother got the birth pangs, na, they had to carry her to the nearest health centre where the nurses were. The night was very dark, the torch of bamboo sticks they were carrying burnt out, and they had to stumble onwards, helped only by starlight. That was why, when they got to the health centre, and he was born, na, they named him Starlightersing. They ended the name with *sing*, "lion", so it would sound more Khasi.

'Shiningsstar is simpler. He was born in the middle of the night when the stars were out and shining. Moreover, na, they wanted him to be a shining star in life. Plos Star, meaning "plus star", is the second son of the family. His elder brother is Firstly Star, so he, being the second, had to be Plos Star. Wetstarson is from Sohra. He was born during the famous nine-day-nine-night rain that fell only in Sohra and the adjoining areas. Hence Wetstarson.'

'How do you know all this?' Donald asked, unsure whether Bah Kynsai was serious or jesting.

'Waa, because I know them and their parents, na?' Bah Kynsai replied. 'Where was I? Geldingnewstar … He was named after a horse. When he was only a few months old, na, he was a peppy and bouncy baby. He used to kick away all the blankets covering him. His father thought he was kicking like a horse, so he named him Gelding, without realising that a gelding is a castrated male horse. He added "new star" because Gelding was his first son. Rockystarsing was given that name because his father is an avid *Rocky* fan. You know the *Rocky* movies, na, starring Sylvester Stallone? Right … Morning Lur Star was given that name because he was born in the morning when *lur step*, the "morning star", was still shining in the sky. Needless to say, his father also wanted him to be a star. Upstarwell, like Morning Lur Star, was born when everybody was about to get up in the morning …'

'How can you see the stars in the morning?' Donald objected.

'Arre, Upstarwell is from a rural area, na? People get up quite early there, man, at the crack of dawn, when the stars are still visible. His father wanted him to be always on the up and up in life, that's why the name. Guesstarwel was so named because when his mother conceived him, na, there were lots of guesses as to whether he would be a boy or a girl. The entire family wanted a girl and said the baby would be a girl. Only the father said he was going to be a boy. He had guessed well, hence the name. Roamingfarstar is easy; it means "roaming far star". He was so named because the father, na, who had never gone anywhere outside his village, because of poverty and illness, wanted him to do well in life. He wanted him to be rich and famous and to roam the world like a star. His sister suggested the name. Balistars is a meaningless combination of "stars" and the Khasi-sounding "*bali*"; plenty of names like that in Khasi.

'Now, the rest of the stars are special. I don't know them or their parents, na, so I can only tell you the meaning of their names. Starlintoi means "star of the way" or "star leading the way" because *lintoi* or *lynti*, in Khasi, means "the way". Starbornes was born a star, or so the family must have wished. The name Twostar shows that he is the second son of the family—two sons or two stars, and counting, that sort of thing, na?'

'But why are they special?' Hamkom asked.

'Because, though they are all stars, na, all of them had got arrested by the police. Starlintoi was among a group of six miscreants who allegedly assaulted a woman—it was reported in the papers recently. Starbornes was arrested by the police for violating the NGT's order and driving a truck laden with coal. Twostar was accused of raping a woman and was beaten up in Nongstoin by an irate mob—this was reported in the papers too.'

When Bah Kynsai stopped speaking, Magdalene, who had been laughing loudly, asked, 'But Bah Kynsai, why do you always refer to the father naming the child? What about the mother?'

'You don't know that also? Among the Khasis, na, the name of a child is always given by the father or his family members. It must be different with you, but ask Ap, he'll tell you. Now, who has more star names? Kit?'

Bah Kit responded by saying, 'I know some names … There is one by the name of Bokstarly. The Khasi "*bok*", meaning "luck", combined with "starly". Such names are very common among us; they reflect the parents' wish for their sons to be lucky stars. Another one is Highwaay Star. The fellow is from Ri Bhoi, near Byrnihat. When the due date arrived, ha, his mother was taken to Shillong, as she wanted to give birth in one of the hospitals there. But she went into labour while they were still on the highway and had to be taken to the Nongpoh Public Health Centre instead. Because of that, the father decided to name him Highwaay Star.'

'Let's hope he doesn't become a highwayman,' Bah Kynsai chuckled.

As we joined in the laughter, Bah Kit wrinkled his brow, trying to remember more names. After a while, he said, 'I've got it: Ourstar, Duringlystar, Victorystar, Scamstar, Alivestar, Bumpkinstar, Krismasstar, Duststarwelles, Starry ... Starry also will do, no? Okay, okay ... Nextstarly, Comingstarone, Reverendstar, that's all I can remember.'

'Duststarwelles's name has a rather amusing story, Bah Kynsai. His mother is a teacher in a village primary school, okay? She used to bring the chalks and duster home because they kept disappearing from the classroom. When her son was about eight months old, he became very fond of playing with the duster, and every morning before she went to school, his mother had to bribe him away from it with her *turoi* ...'

'Turoi?' Donald enquired.

'Trumpet,' Bah Kynsai answered. 'Don't ask stupid questions, na, Don. Go on, Kit.'

Bah Kit continued, 'That was why she said they should name him Duster. But the father said, "How can we name him Duster? Instead of that, why don't we call him Duststarwelles? He'll be a star who will do well, perhaps as a teacher, since he is very fond of the duster."'

When Bah Kit ended his story, Bah Kynsai said approvingly, 'Beautiful, leh, beautiful ... Now, who else?'

Evening, however, grumbled, 'You people are laughing at me!'

'No, Ning, we are not, man!' Bah Kynsai pacified him. 'You yourself must admit it's a very curious phenomenon, na, I mean, why should so many people be named "star"? Anybody else?'

'Wait, wait,' Raji said, 'I know quite a few actually ... Pissingstar, Lusfulstar, Myselfstar, Successtar, Bastardingwel, Ohstar, Jonathanstar, Donathanstar (brother of Jonathanstar), Lordstar, Klanstarson, Kaidingstarwel, Homlesstar, Phetstarsing, ...'

'Your stars are not very nice, mə, lih, except for Pissingstar. Anyone with more interesting ones?'

'No, no, some are quite good actually, Bah Kynsai. Take Bastardingwel, for instance. Ba, as you know, is a Khasi prefix, and when we say "*baitynnat*", it means "beautiful". Therefore, when we say "Bastar", it means "like a star".

"*Ding*" is Khasi for "fire". Do you see the point now? By giving him that name, okay, the parents wanted their son to be a burning star.'

'It sounds like "bastard" to me,' Bah Kynsai said.

'It does, and that's the joke, no? Klanstarson is also nice, okay? It means "star of the clan", but as is often the case with us, ha, "clan" is spelt as klan. Kaidingstarwel is also a Khasi misspelling of "guiding star". There are lots of names like this one. And Phetstarsing ... tell me, Bah Kynsai, can you guess why this fellow was named Phetstarsing? Because the father *phet*, or left, soon after the boy was born. To keep the memory of his desertion alive, the mother decided to call her son Phetstarsing.'

'Yeah, these are okay,' Bah Kynsai conceded. 'What about you, Ap?'

'I have hundreds of star names,' I said, 'but I'll try to give you only those with stories behind them ... I know a fellow, for instance, who named his son Testarful. When I asked him about its meaning, he told me he had really wanted to name his son Tester. You see, being an electrician, he wanted to honour the tools of his trade. However, he also wanted good things for his son, so why not change "e" into "a"? That was how Tester became Testar with "ful" at the end to make it more musical. "And a very good name too," he proudly said to me. "Testarful! My son will pass the tests of life and become a star!"

'Another fellow I know wanted to name his son after Sachin Tendulkar, the Master Blaster. But here again, the man was not satisfied with the word "blaster". Why should my son be only a blaster? Why not change "e" into "a" and name him Blastarson? And so he did, and a star blaster was born. And that is not all. According to him, "*bla*" in Khasi means "already", therefore, Blastarson can also mean "a son who is already a star".'

'Who was the little fellow who came to your house for a donation that day, Ap?' Raji asked before I could go on. 'You said he also had a star name, no?'

'Bets Star, son of Fewstar,' I told him. 'His name was the result of his father's fixation with having a male child. Fewstar had ...'

'Why the hell was he named Fewstar?' Bah Kynsai asked, puzzled.

'Because when he was born, in the middle of the night, only a few stars were visible in the sky. But obviously, that was not the only reason. As is the case with most star names, his parents also hoped he would be such a brilliant star when he grew up that only a few could measure up to him—hence Fewstar.

'Anyway, Fewstar had already fathered three daughters, and so, when his wife became pregnant again, the first thing he did in the morning and the last thing he did at night was to touch his wife's belly, then his forehead, with his right hand (a symbol of the father's clan) and intone, "Oh God, let it be a son!" He was so confident that God would answer his prayers that whenever people asked him if he thought the next one would be a boy, he replied, "You bet!" Some of his friends, after hearing this rather smug answer, challenged him: "Why don't we bet on it, Few?" Fewstar willingly took up the challenge and bet his old Maruti 800 against a brand-new car. Every day he went to *ki nongduwai*, the elders who pray, and brought back grains of rice for his wife to eat. And sure enough, when his wife was taken to the hospital, she gave birth to a handsome baby boy. Fewstar was sure it was his belly-touching and all the grains of rice his wife had eaten that had done the trick. Whatever it might be, he had won his bet, so why not name his son Bet Star, or better still, Bets Star?'

Grinning from ear to ear, Raji said, 'Yeah, yeah, I think you told me this story before, it's really funny, no?' He was addressing the rest of the group, though he need not have, for everyone was laughing.

'Do you remember my neighbour's son, Mystarling, Bah Kynsai?' I asked him. 'His name was the result of his mother's excessive love for him. When he was born, she was so completely consumed by her passion for the little guy that she stopped going anywhere so she could always be with him. When he grew older, she became even fonder of him, or so it seemed to the father, who, whenever he came home from office, would see her playing with the child in bed, holding him by the waist and making him jump while chanting over and over again, "My star, my darling". Listening to her constant chanting, he said, "Now I know what to name my boy!" He combined the words and had the child baptised as Mystarling—and delighted he was with the name, for he thought it could also mean my little star. I did not tell him that starlings are, in fact, birds.'

Laughing, Magdalene said, 'You should have, you should have!'

'No, that would have been cruel,' I replied, then continued with another story. 'I know someone who lives somewhere near Sohra, who has eleven children—eight boys and three girls. His first child was a boy whom he named Phasstar ("Phas" being a misspelling of the English word "first"). After getting his first star, he soon got his second, third, fourth and fifth. He called them Twostar, Thristar, Phorstar and Phaitstar. After these, the next three were all daughters whom he called Marbeljone (for Marvel June), Aprilfery (for April Fairy) and Marchwonder, after the months they were born in. The ninth was another son whom he called Naiñstar ("Naiñ" being a misspelling of the English word "nine"). When they had their tenth child, another boy, he said to his wife, "Old woman, I think this will be our last child or what?" His wife said he probably would be. Confident that this would be the last, he named him Lasstar. Unfortunately, Lasstar was not his last star. They had another son. What could he call him? He was in a fix. He pondered over the matter for weeks and months and finally hit upon a great idea: he called him Finishstarwel.'

Magdalene and Dale were slapping their thighs by the time I concluded the story. But Magdalene was also curious about why all these star names belonged to boys and not girls.

'That's because a star is supposed to be male in Khasi,' I told her. 'Of course, we do have girls named after stars too, now and then, but always with modifications like Ladystar and Starlin—"*lin*" being a Khasi word used mostly in girls' names. The only exception is Estar for Easter, many girls, boys too, by that name ...'

'Go on with your story, man!' Bah Kynsai said impatiently.

I said, 'There's a fellow in Polo, a non-Khasi who married a Khasi woman, who wanted to give a Hindi name to his first son. But his wife would have none of it. She wanted only English-sounding names. The man was in a quandary. He could not go against his wife's wishes since he was living in her house and working in her shop. At the same time, he really, really wanted to give his son a Hindi name so he could better identify with him. After many days of worrying about it, one day, he snapped his fingers and exclaimed, "Idea!"

'He went home and said to his wife, "Doreen, Doreen, we will name our son Ekistar, the first *istar*." The not-too-well-educated Doreen heard the word star (pronounced istar by her husband) and readily agreed to his proposal despite the Hindi word at the beginning. When the second, third and fourth sons were born, the fellow adopted the same strategy and called them Rajuistar, Ramuistar and Dilistar. He was very fond of the last son, that's why he named him Dilistar, "star of my heart".

'There's a man in West Khasi Hills who named his first son Morningstar because he was born in the morning. His second son was born in the evening, like our Ning here, so he became Eveningstar. But the third son was born in the afternoon: should he name him Afternoonstar? It didn't sound right at all. Also, friends pointed out to him that stars were never seen in the afternoon. Finally, to make his third son's name rhyme with the others, he named him Porningstar. When he had yet another son, also born in the afternoon, he named him Forningstar.'

'What do those names mean, Bah Ap?' Donald enquired.

'Nothing,' Bah Kynsai answered for me. 'But star is there, na? Go on, Ap.'

'Unless he means Porn Star and Fornicating Star, Bah Kynsai,' Raji laughed.

When everyone had quietened down a little, Donald asked again, 'Bah Ap, are all these star names only common in the villages? What about people in Shillong? Do they not have star names too?'

'They do, Don, they do, but because many of them are well educated, they use names like Bright Star, Shining Star, et cetera. The story of the contractor who built my house is also quite amusing. He lost his first son to a viral disease when he was barely a few months old. He was heartbroken, but then, he recovered his spirit when his second child also turned out to be a boy. In remembrance of the one who had departed, he decided to name his second son Losetarwell. When I asked him about it, he said, "I had lost a star, but now that I have another, all is well."

'When his wife gave birth to another son, it happened at the exact moment that a lorry was unloading bricks at my house. Thinking it to be a good omen, he decided to baptise him as Brickstonestar. Recently, he had another son. He told me he wanted to name him Fullmoon, as he was born during a full moon, but his wife would not hear of it. She said, "If the first two sons are stars, why should this one be only a moon?" The man saw the logic of the argument and therefore named him Fullmoonstar.'

'He still won the argument after all, ha, Ap?' Hamkom laughed.

'That he did. But of all the star names, let me tell you my favourites. In a village in East Khasi Hills, there are four brothers from the Kharkhlam clan who used to be called Jesters, Molesters, Pesters and Monsters. The parents were very proud of these names because they rhymed with each other. As you know, rhyming is a great thing among the Khasis. Even our poets don't write poetry that doesn't rhyme. In fact, even in these days of free verse, they still maintain that if a poem doesn't rhyme, it is no poem at all. Some of them even go to the other extreme of saying that anything that rhymes is a poem. By that logic, Jesters, Molesters, Pesters and Monsters would also be a poem.

'Anyway, despite the parents' pride, when the children were sent to school, the headmistress objected to their names. She called the parents to school and asked them, "Who suggested these names to you?" They said they had got them from an English book. "Did you look for the meaning of the words?" she asked. They replied with a question of their own: "How are we supposed to do that?"

'Realising that the parents had not even heard of a dictionary, she told them that the words had very bad meanings and explained in Khasi as clearly as she could what they meant. However, the father was still adamant, saying, "We like the names, we have been calling our children by these names since they were very young, how can we change them now? They wouldn't sound the same."'

Before I could go on, Magdalene said, 'Wait, wait, wait, Ap, do you mean to say that they sent them to school at the same time?'

'Of course, it's a remote village. It's not safe sending a kid of three or four alone to a school located four or five kilometres away from home. They had to wait till the youngest son was three years old before they could send them all to school. Remember that the parents are farmers who work in the fields from morning till dusk.'

'My God!' she exclaimed. 'These people lead such a tough life, ya!'

'Yeah, real hard, Mag. The journalists here will tell you the same thing ...'

'Though, at this moment, they may not be up to it,' Magdalene said, laughing.

We all looked at Raji and Bah Su, who appeared to be quite drunk.

Raji raised a forefinger, wanting to say something, but I beat him to it. 'Anyway, as I was saying, the father did not want to change the names because he had become too accustomed to them. But the headmistress knew she could not let it be; it would be cruel. She consulted the other teachers and came up with the suggestion that Jesters, Molesters, Pesters and Monsters be changed to Jestars, Molestars, Pestars and Monstars. When she proposed the names to the father, she said, "Now your sons' names will sound the same, rhyme the same, but at the same time, all of them will be stars ... don't you want your sons to be stars?"

'At the mention of the word "stars", the father was overwhelmed with happiness. He could only nod his head repeatedly, giving them a big grin like "a red-mouthed monkey", as one of the teachers put it.'

I was rewarded for my stories with a laugh from Bah Kynsai, who shook my hand and said, 'Beautiful, man, beautiful! And crazy too! I mean, just think about all these terrible stars, man! But what to do? That's how we are, na? Does anyone have any more? No? Okay, I'll tell you a name story of my own, ha?'

Everyone nodded encouragingly and Bah Kynsai said, 'I know a poor couple living near my house, ha, they were originally from Jaiñtia Hills ...'

'Ri Pnar,' Raji objected again.

'Okay, mə, tdong! They have been living in Shillong for many years, ha, and everybody calls them Meikhian, "youngest mother", and Pakhian, "youngest father". They have two children, a daughter and a son, both married and with children of their own. The daughter, naturally, lives with the parents. One day, I went to have a chat with them, ha, and after talking about this and that, na, I asked them for how long they had been married. Pakhian said, "A very long time, let's see, we got married when Meikhian was only sixteen, now she is sixty-four, so, how many years do you think?"

'I calculated the number of years and said, "My God, you two have been married for forty-eight years, you know that? This is amazing! I mean, we have so many broken homes among us, na, but you two have been together for almost half a century! Do you ever have any problems, Pakhian? No? Then what's the secret of your marital bliss? Tell me, na."

'Pakhian replied, "Well, her name is Pani—water, in Hindi—and my name is Bonder Cement."

'I had a laughing fit and then, wiping tears from my eyes, I said to him, "She is Pani, and you are Cement, and the mixture has become an unbreakable bond, fantastic!" We drank a toast to their marriage and I said, "To our concrete spouses, till death do them part!"'

When Bah Kynsai stopped speaking, Hamkom raised a finger to attract his attention and said, 'Bah Kynsai, you remember that lady from Jaïaw, her name is Maya, I think she married a fellow by the name of Darlingson, no?'

'Yeah, yeah …' Bah Kynsai agreed.

'So, what's so unique about Maya marrying a guy named Darlingson?' Donald asked. 'I admit his name is funny, but what else is there?'

Hamkom said, 'Don, you ignoramus, "maya" is a word in the Jaiñtia dialect …'

'Jaiñtia or Pnar?' Raji demanded, slurring his words.

'Okay, okay, in the Pnar dialect, okay, "maya" means "darling", which means that in this case, Darling has married Darlingson, you see that, Don? Now you are laughing, sala!'

'How about this?' Raji said drunkenly. 'A fellow named after Dilip Kumar—you know Dilip Kumar, no, the famous Hindi film star? Don, Ham, Dale … you fellows don't know shit! Anyway, this fellow named after Dilip Kumar was getting married, okay, and to whom? To a woman named Kaflim from the Dkhar clan, in short, Kaflim Dkhar. And what is the other meaning of Kaflim Dkhar? Correct! "Hindi film"! So, during the ceremony, the priest said, you know what he said? He said, "Will you Dilip Kumar take Kaflim

Dkhar, Hindi film, as your lawfully wedded wife?" Dilip Kumar agreed, and they lived happily ever after.'

'He agreed and won the Bharat Ratna,' Bah Kynsai joked.

'There's a very interesting family living in a village near Sohra,' I chipped in. 'When the only daughter of the family became pregnant for the fourth time, her mother prayed desperately for a granddaughter. The last three had been sons, and if her daughter didn't have a female child, the family ran the risk of becoming *kiba duh jait*, a family that has lost the clan name forever. Sadly, her prayers were not answered; her daughter gave birth to another son.

'Feeling sorry for the grandmother, upon whom they depended for everything, the parents decided to name the son Don'tmind, as an apology. When Don'tmind grew up, he married a woman by the name of Pleasemewell. Pleasemewell was given that name because the parents were very pleased with her birth, the first three children having been boys. According to the custom, since Pleasemewell happened to be the only daughter of the family, Don'tmind went to live in her house.

'Pleasemewell's mother is a woman by the name of Highnoon. She was given that name because she was born at noon and because her father remembered his favourite movie, *High Noon*. But in the village, she is known simply as Kong Hi, according to the Khasi custom of name-shortening. Pleasemewell's father is called Bah Morning since he was born early in the morning and was the first son of the family.

'Because of all these names, when people meet one of them on the road, they always say, "Hi, Morning! Oops, sorry, it's Highnoon! Please Dont'mind!"'

After the laughter had subsided, Bah Kit said, 'There's a woman by the name of Ka Jet in Ri Bhoi, okay? On the day she was born, there was a jet flying past her parents' paddy field. Her father, who was working in the field, looked up and said, "How fast and smooth that jet flies! I think it is a good omen; I think my wife will have a smooth delivery."

'Later in the evening, his wife was taken to the Nongpoh health centre, where she had a smooth delivery indeed. In honour of the flying jet, which had been such a good omen for him, the father named his baby girl Ka Jet.

'And Ka Jet really lived up to her name, ha? She grew up very fast. At fourteen, she met a boy of the same age by the name of Pilot, and together they became superfast. They married at the age of fifteen and became grandparents at the age of thirty-one.'

After Bah Kit finished, Bah Su surprised us with a story about another interesting couple. We had thought he was drunk, but apparently, he had only been dozing all this while. He said, 'In Ri Pnar, there's a man by the name of Curiously, okay? He was named Curiously because when his mother was pregnant, everybody was curious whether she would have a boy or a girl.

'When Curiously grew up, he married a woman by the name of Absenteena, who was so named because when she was born, ha, her father was not around: he had gone to work in a distant village. When Absenteena became pregnant for the first time, she kept vanishing into the nearby jungle as soon as she had her lunch. Curiously became very curious about what she was doing in the jungle, ha, so one day, he followed her and found that she was plucking *soh-ot*, a kind of nut. He immediately understood it was a pregnant-woman thing and decided to leave her alone.

'But he grew very keen to find out what soh-ot was called in English, and went around the village asking anyone who might know. Finally, he asked a school teacher, who said that soh-ot was called walnut. This was a mistake, ha, because soh-ot is not walnut but chestnut. Anyway, having got the name, he wrote it down as soon as he reached home lest he forget.

'When his wife gave birth to a baby boy, she asked him, "What shall we name our boy?"

'And he said, "Since you were very fond of soh-ot—hahaha, don't think that I don't know, ha—we will call him by that name."

'His wife was horrified. "How can we name our child soh-ot?"

'Her husband smiled indulgently and said, "We are not going to call him soh-ot, we will use the English name."

'Much appeased, she said, "Ooh! That's okay then. So what's the name?"

'The man fumbled around in his trouser pockets and brought out a piece of paper: Alnot, he said, Alnotstar.'

When Bah Su concluded his story, Bah Kynsai looked around the laughing faces and said, 'Anyone with more stories?'

As everyone racked their brains for more, I decided to speak up again. 'Okay, why don't we listen to this one first? This is also from Ri Pnar. It's about a group of young men courting a woman named Beautiful. Why Beautiful, Mag? Because she really was beautiful. Among her suitors were Blessingson (considered to be a blessing to his family when he was born), Sundayly (you got it, he was born on a Sunday), Welcometoo (a second son, about whom the parents were not overly excited, but who was welcome nonetheless) and

Hasluck (a name badly translated from the Khasi name, Donbok). All four of them were …'

'Donbok doesn't mean Hasluck, Ap,' Bah Kit protested.

'That's why I said badly translated,' I replied. '"Don", literally translated as "has", and "bok" literally translated as "luck". The actual meaning, as you know, is "may you be blessed with fortune". Anyway, as I was saying, all four of them were well endowed with good looks and manly qualities, which made it very difficult for Beautiful to choose. In the end, as advised by her mother, she devised a simple strategy. One day, she said to them: "My dear friends, I have decided not to choose between you since I'm so close to all of you. But if you really want to marry me, tomorrow you will have to find this kwai, which I'm going to hide somewhere in or around the house. The kwai will be marked in a certain way, so you cannot bring me the wrong one. I know this is not according to custom, but the situation demands it, I have no choice in the matter. I will only marry the man who brings it to me."

'The men readily agreed to the adventure and the next evening they arrived at the house to look for the piece of split betel nut. Before they began, each one of them prayed to God for success, each in his own way. Blessingson said, "Oh God, as my name is forever a reminder of your blessing, kindly shower your blessings upon me at this moment, bless me, oh Lord, give me Beautiful, amen." Sundayly said, "Oh God, if you grant me success this day, next Sunday, I will hand over all my week's wages to your Church, amen." Welcometoo said, "Oh God, I welcome this challenge, but please do not give all your blessings to Blessing, nor all the luck to Hasluck. As for Sundayly, today is not his day, so please make it my day, amen." Only Hasluck was not bothered by the challenge. He loved Beautiful, but was also fatalistic by nature, so he said, "Oh God, as I perform this task, may I have all the luck in the world, but if luck doesn't favour me and I don't win Beautiful, what can I do? It's all up to you; I will not blame you."

'When they finished their prayers, they started looking for the betel nut. They turned the house inside out, so to speak, but could not find it anywhere. Finally, they went back to the drawing room to tell Beautiful of their failure. As the others were talking to her, Hasluck noticed that her right hand was closed into a fist. In a flash, he rose to interrupt the others. "You fellows may think of surrendering, but I'd like a final word with Biw … May I have a look at your right hand, Biw?"

'Beautiful, also called Biw by close friends, giggled with delight, opened her right hand and showed them the betel nut. Afterwards, because Hasluck had discovered it, she gave the betel nut to him as custom demanded. And happy she was, for Hasluck was not only handsome but had also proved to be the cleverest of them all.

'Beautiful and Hasluck were married after a few months. Soon (after the mandatory nine months, of course), their first son was born, and in commemoration of the betel nut-finding event, they named him Nutfinder.'

My friends hooted with laughter as I concluded the story.

After a while, Donald asked me, 'Are these names for real, Bah Ap?'

'All real, unfortunately,' I replied.

'All real, Don, all real,' Hamkom corroborated. He turned to Bah Kynsai and asked, 'Bah Kynsai, we have been talking about star names, what about moon names? Do we have as many of those?'

'We have quite a few, but not so many, na, Ap?'

'Not so many,' I agreed, 'and not as entertaining, since Khasis consider the moon to be inferior to the stars. Also, it's male. Apart from the more normal ones, we have moon names like Moonshone, Moonlite, Phullmoon (for "full moon"), Mymoon, Blesshermoon, Julymoon, Marchmoon, Saimoon (in place of Simon), Fishingmoon, Daiamoon (in place of Diamond), Moonsens and so on. The wish, the hope and the logic behind moon names are the same as in the star names.

'In spite of its inferiority to the stars, Khasis have always associated the moon with great masculine beauty, and a handsome man is often described as *u nai khatsaw synñia*, the moon of the fourteenth night. And that's the intriguing thing. If you read *The Arabian Nights*, you will find exactly the same attitude to the moon, and almost the same kind of description of masculine beauty. And this is not something the Khasis got from reading that great book …'

'Yeah, yeah, before the Welsh missionaries arrived, they could neither read nor write, na?' Bah Kynsai said.

'That's right, Bah Kynsai,' I replied, 'but more importantly, "the moon of the fourteenth night" can be found in many of our myths and legends, as old as the tribe itself. And remember what I told you before: according to a new genetic study, the Khasis have been in India for thousands of years, from before the present era. *The Arabian Nights*, on the other hand, was put together during the Golden Age of Islam.

'So how did we have the exact same attitude to the moon as the Arabs of *The Arabian Nights*? Listen to a description in "Night 20" of the book, for instance. After Nur al-Din, the son of a former vizier, and at that time a traveller, had been washed and dressed in the new robes of his patron, he was described in these words: "When he left the baths wearing the robes, he was like the moon when it is full on the fourteenth night."'

'Amazing, amazing!' Hamkom said. 'But tell me, is the moon always full on the fourteenth night?'

'Of course. But I cannot help thinking, you know, that perhaps sometime in our great migration, we passed through the lands of the Arabs. Certainly, there are lots of words of Persian origin in the Khasi language.'

'Back to the moon names, man!' Bah Kynsai demanded.

'The only strange moon name I have come across is that of a girl,' I said. 'Her name is Lady Moon. It is strange because, as I said, the moon is male to us. So why did her father name her Lady Moon? In answer to my question, one day, he took me to his home and simply pointed to a girl cooking in the kitchen. When I looked at her, I immediately understood. She was round like a full moon. And she was not at all beautiful ...'

'How can she be beautiful, liah?' Bah Kynsai interrupted me. 'The moon is more about rotundity and corpulence, na?'

I disagreed with Bah Kynsai. I go for an evening walk every day. The moon is my greatest friend. There is a kind of beauty in a moonlit night that never fails to fill me with a sense of well-being. Everything seems magically transformed. I can never finish my walk and return home without first saying goodbye to the moon and sending it several flying kisses. Just as I can never fall asleep without kissing the picture of my beloved Saia goodnight (I do it every night without fail).

But Magdalene was saying, 'Yeah, yeah, you are right, Bah Kynsai, I for one do not want to be round like the moon, okay, that would be horrible, ya.'

Bah Kynsai, I could see, was pleased with Magdalene's comment. However, he responded by teasing her, 'But you are already like the moon, Mag!'

And then we got the shock of our lives when Donald snapped at Bah Kynsai, 'To you, maybe, not to me!'

'Hey, hey!' Bah Kynsai cried. 'What is this? What have you done to him, Mag?'

Realising that he had given himself away, Donald smiled sheepishly and muttered, 'Nothing, nothing.'

Magdalene had turned red in the face, and Bah Su quickly changed the topic by saying, 'More stories, more stories ...'

Bah Kynsai pointed to me.

Obligingly, I said, 'I know a family from West Khasi Hills who used to live in our locality. They have two daughters. The older of the two is named Babyfive.'

'Babyfive?' Magdalene cried incredulously.

'Yeah, Babyfive. When I first heard the name, I used to wonder why on earth her father had given her such a name. The wife is illiterate and doesn't know the meaning of the name. She's happy enough that it is an English name.

'Then, one day, I met a person who knew the man quite well. When I asked about the girl's curious name, he said, "Ooh, that fellow! This one is not his first wife—she is the fifth! This is his peculiar practice. He named his first child from the first wife Babyone; his first child from the second wife, Babytwo; his first child from the third wife, Babythree; and his first child from the fourth wife, Babyfour. So, his first child from the fifth wife had to be Babyfive, no?"

'I hear he has left his fifth wife also. Doubtless, he will name his next child Babysix.'

Evening reacted to this story with anger. 'Somebody should cut off his thing!' he declared.

Ignoring Evening, Magdalene said, 'I also have a story. Just the other day, okay, my daughter was telling me about how the parents of a student from Jaiñtia Hills ...'

'Ri Pnar, Ri Pnar!' Raji said aggressively.

'Okay, okay ... The parents, as I said, were arguing with the principal about the name of their son. His name is Gayboy, okay, so everybody started teasing and calling him Gay. That was why the principal called the parents for a meeting to discuss the possibility of changing his name. But the parents stood their ground and said the name was a good one; they knew its meaning, and they were not about to change it. Frustrated, the principal asked them, "And what do you think the name means?" In reply, they said, "Everybody knows that gay means happy!" The principal asked them again, "But do you know that gay also means homosexual?" When she said that, the parents were quite shocked. Pressing home her advantage, the principal added, "This is not your generation any more, my dears, you had better change his name." They did change his name then and called him Joyous Forus.'

'Wonderful, Mag, wonderful!' Donald laughed. 'Joyous Forus indeed, for all of us, joyous.'

'Who's wonderful? Mag or the story?' Bah Kynsai teased. 'But what about you, man? I haven't heard any stories from you.'

'Well, I have some internet jokes ...'

'Tet, internet jokes! As if we don't use the internet ourselves. You, na, Don, I haven't seen a man as ignorant as you are on the subject of his own people! Is that why you insist on being a cosmo? To hide your ignorance? But remember this, ha, everywhere you will have to identify yourself as something, and if you identify yourself as a Khasi, it's a bloody shame that you don't know anything about Khasis.'

'Don't be too hard on him, Bah Kynsai, can't you see he enjoys our stories and wants to hear more?' Magdalene defended Donald. 'He's becoming quite interested actually ...'

'He's only interested in you as far as I can see,' Bah Kynsai said with a laugh. Then, turning to Donald, he added, 'You want to hear a story, Don, how about this one? Recently, I went to my home town with my family, okay? As I was parking the car at the bus station near the marketplace, na, two beautiful girls came by and stared at us. Village girls always stare at strangers, na, especially handsome strangers with sunglasses. I smiled at them and tried to be friendly, when all of a sudden, their mother came out of nowhere and shouted, "Lily, Sily! Come here, why are you talking to strangers?" What the hell, I thought, that sounds like Ajit, man! You remember Ajit, the famous villain of Hindi movies, na?'

Only Raji, Bah Kit, Magdalene and I raised our hands.

Gesturing to the others, Bah Kynsai said, 'These guys are hopeless. In many of the movies, na, Ajit used to have a girlfriend by the name of Lily. She was a beautiful woman but rather slow-witted. Whenever she said something stupid, he would say, "Lily, don't be silly!" Anyway, I said to the woman, "No, no, they are not being silly, they are just looking at us, being strangers and all, na, Kong?" But the woman said, "No, no, Bah, both of them are not silly, this one, the older, is Lilyna, the other one is Silyna, in short, Lily, Sily." Amazed that anybody could be named Sily, I said, "Ooh, and why did you name her Sily?" She looked at me as if I was silly to ask, and said with a smile, "The older is Lilyna, so the younger has to be Silyna, no, Bah, so they would match? They do match, no?" I replied with as straight a face as possible that they certainly did.

'Later, when I got to my ancestral home, na, as I was eating my lunch, na, one of my sisters said, "Bah, now that you are here, why don't you go to the funeral of our relative? When I asked her who had died, she said, "Actually two people died in the village yesterday: Mother of Morning and Father of Evening." I told her to be serious and to give me their names. "But I just did that, no?" she said. Mother of Morning and Father of Evening—have you ever come across such a thing?'

Donald was laughing too, but he looked a bit confused. 'Are these really their names, Bah Kynsai?'

We heard Raji snort as he nearly choked on his Lyngngam brew.

Bah Kynsai said, 'Hey, hey, don't laugh and drink at the same time, man.' Then, turning to Donald, he said, 'No, they are not, Don. Khasis, not your kind, of course, have a habit of addressing people as the father or the mother of their first child, na? For instance, because my first child is Brendon, na, many of my relatives call me Father of Bren instead of Kynsai. Okay, now, anybody else?'

Bah Su said he knew the story of a Nepali in Ri Bhoi who became a Khasi merely by changing his religion and his name. Donald became immediately attentive and asked, 'Is that possible?'

'Very much, very much, it's mentioned in a Khasi book also, Don,' Bah Su told him. 'The fellow's original name was Siano Gurung, ha, but it was not very clear why he became a Christian … Was it because of a genuine call, or because he saw it as a way of becoming integrated into Khasi society?'

'But why would he want to become a Khasi?' Donald asked.

'Because of the benefits he would get from being a member of a Scheduled Tribe, no?' Bah Su said. 'Is that the reason why he wanted to change his religion from Hinduism to Christianity? Nobody could really say, ha, except the pastor, who was dead sure that the Nepali had turned over a new leaf. With that in mind, he changed his name to Ripenson, with a Khasi surname.'

Hamkom laughed and said, 'Repent of what?'

Bah Su said, 'Of the sins of being a Nepali?'

We all laughed at that, except for Evening, who became impatient with us. 'No, no, no, you people are missing the point!' he cried. 'What I want to know is, are these things still happening or what?'

Bah Su said, 'There have been quite a few cases in the past of non-tribal families using Khasi surnames and calling themselves Khar this or Khar that. We all know that, I think.'

'But for me,' Donald corrected him.

'But for you,' Bah Su agreed. 'Why do they do that? So they may get the benefits of job reservation policies in the state and the Centre. But now, I'm not very sure. The authorities are quite strict, Ning, and even Khasis with non-Khasi forenames have to produce a certificate from their clan elders before they can be categorised as Scheduled Tribes.'

'Even Khasis with English names?' Bah Kynsai asked.

'No, only those with subcontinental forenames like Amit, Raju, Ahmed and so on.'

'Aah, English names are not non-Khasi, na, who would dare mess with them? Next!'

Hamkom volunteered, 'I don't have a story of my own, okay, but I have some very charming names on my mobile ... let me tell you, hold on ...'

'What names?' Bah Kynsai demanded.

'Actually, these are from a newspaper clipping about the candidates who contested in the last MLA election. One of them says, "Odometer, Daystar, Uproarious, Romeoson, Sunday: all ready for Monday". If you recall, Monday was the day of the election. Listen to this:

> For Sundayevening Dkhar, Monday (February 24) is not an ordinary day as he has to face the toughest battle in his life. But for Vietnamwar Syiem, contests are nothing new.
>
> Sundayevening is contesting as an independent candidate from Sutnga, Jaiñtia Hills, while Vietnamwar from Raliang, is contesting on HSPDP ticket ...
>
> For Uproarious Lyngdoh (Independent) from Nongjngi, and Uproarius Rani (Independent) from Umroi, the election is a very serious matter, and hence they are engaged in a very aggressive campaign. The campaign is such that Uproarious Lyngdoh is too busy to listen to his opponent, Yellingson Kharlum, another Independent from Nongjngi.
>
> Romeosons are waiting for a win in the election ... Romeoson Sano (UDP) from Wahiajer and Romeoson Lyngdoh (Independent) from Mawlai are examples.
>
> Achilles Rumnong (INC), Amlarem, and Hercules Diengdoh (INC) from Nongstoin are not only from the same party but also share another similarity: both their names are from Greek mythology.
>
> But no one it seems is interested in giving ear to Guider Son Marbañiang of HSPDP from Sohïong, or to Serving Lalu (INC) from Barato, although they are ready to really guide and serve the people if elected.
>
> While Daystar Rambrai (HSPDP) from Mairang hopes for a brighter day

on February 24, it may be a sleepless night for Moonlitnight Passah (UDP) from Tuber on the eve of the election.

Amidst the many male candidates, the lone woman candidate from Narpuh, Buttercup Lyngdoh (UDP), promises to make a fragrant difference. But for Uphill Syiem (Independent) from Mawkyrwat, it may be an uphill task to take on the sitting MLA.

While the campaign of Swimmerman Lyngdoh (INC) from Mawthengkut and Odometer Kyndait (INC) from Nangbah gained momentum, it is yet to begin in earnest for Commencer R Pyrtuh (Independent) from Shangpung.

Mawthadraishan will witness a different battle with Almightier Parïong (Independent) taking on Navalmarshal Lyngdoh (Independent) in the presence of Sturdyman Syiem (INC). Langrin will have leaders like Execellentleaderboy Nongrang (HSPDP) and Consultant Lyngdoh (INC) locking horns, while R. P. Thunderstormes Sawkmie (UDP) is longing to storm into power from Nongspung.

While Hopingrock Dkhar (INC) from Mowkaiaw hopes to register a win, Successful Laurelwreath Mushaiñ (INC) from Sutnga is already dreaming of success and laurel wreaths.

'This is exactly as reported in the newspaper, Bah Kynsai.'

'Uproarious like Uproarius, man!' Donald laughed. 'What paper is this, Ham?'

'*Shillong Chronicle*, I think. I'm reading it as it is, okay, the language leaves much to be desired, but I've not changed anything, only some names are not visible.'

Magdalene said, 'But isn't it incredible! How could our leaders have such, such amazing names, man?'

Bah Kynsai drank some of the yiad hiar beer from his bamboo mug, wiped his lips dry with the palm of his left hand, and rubbed the stubble on his chin. When nobody offered any more comments, he said, 'I can only say, do not judge your leaders by their names, na?'

'Arre, Bah Kynsai, these are not leaders, no?' Raji said drunkenly. 'Would-be leaders! You don't know this simple thing also, and you a profeshor? But for our leaders, okay—so-called, so-called, okay, not real, okay—*judge them by their arses*! Our leaders don't have anything; you know that? No heads, no hearts, only arses, hahaha.'

All of us, Bah Kynsai included, laughed with him, genuinely entertained. Bah Kynsai was so impressed by his logic that he said, 'When this Raji is drunk, na, you don't know whether he's talking sense or nonsense! Anyway, shall we move on?'

Bah Kit became rather pensive and said, 'I don't know why people would give such names to their children, you know?'

'For them, anything English-sounding is good, no?' Raji slurred. 'English is always good, gooder, goodest, hahaha.'

Despite Raji's flippant tone, Bah Su agreed with him completely. 'That's very true, Raji,' he said. 'Even people who don't know English, ha, are giving their children English names. But in doing that, what do they end up with? In Ri Bhoi, where I live, there's a man who named his first son U Fas, his second son U Sekon, his third son U Thad and his daughter, also the last, Ka Las. He could not even spell the English words, "first", "second", "third" and "last", ha, he used the Khasi misspellings, ha, but still he wanted to give them English names, can you believe it?'

'But there are even more awful names than those, Bah Su,' Bah Kynsai said. 'In fact, these are quite nice in comparison with names like Pancreasus, Dicklick, Kondombor, Kissmefast, Latrineborn, Kong Pro and Kong Kli.'

Donald exclaimed, 'Are there really names like these, Bah Kynsai! Dicklick is a bit too much to believe.'

'Waa! Of course there are!' Bah Kynsai declared. 'I don't know ...'

'But what's wrong with Kong Pro or Kong Kli?' Magdalene interrupted him. 'They sound respectable enough to me.'

'Hold on, na, I'll come to them later. As I was saying, na, I don't know anything about Dicklick as a person, ha, I found his name in the list of successful candidates published by an open university. But I do know Pancreasus personally. His mother was excessively fond of eating the pancreas of a pig when she conceived him ... You know how women are, na, when pregnant. Anyway, that was why they named him Pancreas. And because they are Catholic, they added "sus" at the end, and he became Pancreasus.

'Kondombor is also personally known to me; he is one of my students, in fact. Initially, na, we told him we wouldn't give him admission ... Why? Because his name is a misspelling of "condom", na? He was so desperate for admission that he submitted an affidavit saying that Kondombor should from now on be known as Kondembor, which is a misspelling of "condemn". We did admit him after that, for everybody said, "If he wants to condemn himself, who are we to interfere?"

'Kissmefast and Latrineborn are primary school students I came across in a rural school in Ri Bhoi while attending a function. Kissmefast could not tell me why he was given that name, but Latrine said her mother had the first birth pangs in a toilet, and because of that, someone from the village suggested the name Latrineborn for her, which he said meant something like "God's wish". That fellow must have been playing a prank on the poor folk, na? I was very angry with the bugger, whoever he might be, and told the teacher that we must change her name there and then. We called the parents, explained the meaning of latrine to them, and got her name changed to Lathrangborn. It means "born with desire", a beautiful name.'

'What about Kissmefast?' Magdalene wanted to know.

'Kissmefast is not as serious a case as Latrineborn, na? I just asked the teacher to do something about his name. Perhaps she has, I don't know.'

'And what about Kong Pro and Kong Kli?' Magdalene reminded Bah Kynsai.

'Yeah, yeah, what about them? They do sound quite normal, you know,' Donald commented.

'The names sounded quite normal to me too until I saw the full versions. Fortunately, they are both dead now ...'

'Were they sisters?' Magdalene asked.

'No, but they were from the same village in West Khasi Hills. I had known them for quite a long time, ha, but like everyone else, I only knew them as Kong Pro and Kong Kli. However, when they died, na, I attended their funerals and was given one of those leaflets containing their names and ages, along with the hymns to be sung. That was when I came to know their real names. Kong Pro was the first to die, and I tell you, my eyes nearly popped out of their sockets when I saw her name proclaimed as Prostitiw, a misspelling of "prostitute". Kong Kli was Klitoris, a misspelling of "clitoris".'

'What? But that's horrible, man! And nobody ever thought of changing their names?' Magdalene asked, shocked.

'They were illiterate people and did not go to school, na? Their parents used to call them Pro and Kli, and when they grew up, they simply became known as Kong Pro and Kong Kli. Nobody ever knew their real names: the Khasi hypocoristic habit saved them from shame.'

'That's true,' Magdalene agreed, 'but still, it's horrible, ya, Bah Kynsai.'

'These must be among the worst, though, ha, Ap?' Hamkom observed.

'Among the worst,' I agreed. 'There are, of course, other names almost as bad. A fellow I know, for instance, named his first daughter Kissdalin ...'

'But Kissdalin is not too bad, Bah Ap,' Donald interrupted me.

'Hold on, Don, hold on. It seems before going into the labour room, his wife kept saying, "Kiss me, darling, I'm afraid, kiss me ..." In memory of that incident, he named his first daughter Kissdalin. Later, when they had more girls, in order to harmonise with Kissdalin, he named them Bissdalin, Tissdalin and Pissdalin. And of course, everybody who knew them called them Ka Kiss, Ka Biss, Ka Tiss and Ka Piss. Now, Don, Biss and Tiss are meaningless, but what about Piss?

'Still, by and large, I find that people usually name their children after someone or something they love. And these might even be possessions or tools of the trade, whatever that trade may be. There's a mechanic in Laban, for instance, who named his sons Piston, Krankshap and Chocosbar.'

Bah Kynsai was very curious about the names. He said, 'Krankshap must be crankshaft, na, but what the hell is chocosbar?'

'Shock absorber,' I replied, 'but he could neither pronounce nor spell it, so he ended up naming his son Chocosbar. Another mechanic in the same area named his sons Steering, Gearing and Ballbearing.

'There is also a driver who named his first two sons First Gear and Second Gear. He wanted to stop because he was the only breadwinner in the family, but both he and his wife wanted a daughter very badly. In our matrilineal society, as I told you before, not having a daughter means not only the end of your clan's line but also that you would be without someone to look after you in your old age. Among us, boys are not considered to be very good carers for the simple reason that their families would not belong to the same clan as their mother's. Therefore, after a lot of thought, he said to his wife, "Old woman, we must fish one more time, okay?"

'But the next time was also a boy. Though he was disappointed, he was determined to give him a good name. He called him Top Gear. However, now they were in a quandary and, for some time, could not decide what to do. It was not until one year after Top Gear was born that the driver said to his wife, "You know, old woman, this time, if we try again, I have a gut feeling it will be a girl!" His gut feeling turned out to be true. The two of them were elated; at last, they could stop having more children. At the hospital, his wife said to him, "Now that we have a girl, we must stop." When her husband agreed, she asked him, "And what will you name her?" The husband looked at her, smiled knowingly and declared, "Now that we are stopping ... what else but Ka Brake?" And so, they finally had three boys and a girl: First Gear, Second Gear, Top Gear and Ka Brake.'

Donald said to me, 'Bah Ap, in the star-name stories I heard people praying for sons, but now they seem to be praying for daughters, I'm quite confused.'

'Don't be, Don. In Khasi society, most families want to have a daughter. But ideally, they would like an equal distribution of boys and girls. When a family has had too many girls, for instance, it's only natural that the parents should pray for a boy, as in the case of a fellow I used to know. His name is Tenshonson …'

'Tenshon?' Magdalene laughed.

'Misspelling of "tension".'

'But why would he be named Tenshonson?'

'When Tenshon's mother was in the labour room of a government hospital in Shillong, his father, Sloli, for "slowly", who was from a remote village, was so tense that he kept pestering the nurses about the condition of his wife. But the nurses would not tell him anything. All they kept saying was, "*Wat tension, Bah, wat tension, phi don bad ngi, wat tension ei ei.*" ("No tension, Bah, no tension, you are with us, no tension at all.") After hearing the same word over and over for half a day, Slo fell in love with it. He thought it would be the perfect name for his child, should he be a son. Many hours later, when a healthy male child was born, he named him Tenshonson, spelling it the only way he knew how.'

'*Tet teri ka,*' Bah Kynsai boomed, and they all laughed.

'*Tet teri ka*' is from the Hindi expression '*dhat tere ki*', meaning something like 'shit, man'.

After they had quietened down, I said, 'Anyway, as I was saying, Tenshon already had eight daughters and didn't want any more children. In fact, he had wanted to stop after the third one, but he wanted to know what his Y-chromosome would be like so badly that he kept trying. He said it was too late for him to stop: he had to keep trying until they had a son.

'Therefore, when his wife became pregnant again, he prayed for a boy as usual. This time his prayers were answered, and in gratitude, he named him Melaai, meaning "you have given". But when his son grew a little older, he felt sorry for the boy. What would he do alone, one boy among eight sisters? Consequently, he and his wife tried again for another son. Once again, he prayed to God, beseeching him day and night to grant him his wish. And this time too, God listened to him and gave him a baby boy. But unlike his brother, who was fair and handsome, the second one was dark and ugly. In frustration, Tenshon named him Melashuai, meaning "you have just given for the sake of giving".'

Magdalene was laughing so hard that she had tears streaming from her eyes. 'We Khasis really have some crazy names, no? I can think of so many I have come across: Hydrophobia, Contempt, Dreadful, Derisiony, Reverend Breakwell, Lord Shakespeare, Suparman, Dentister, Physician ...'

'Hold on there!' Bah Kynsai intervened. 'I have a story related to the name, Mag; it's about three ministers in the Meghalaya government. One day, na, these guys went to meet a Union minister in Delhi for some stupid purpose. When they were allowed into her chamber, na, they introduced themselves one by one. One of them said his name was Noliak and that he used to be a university professor before becoming an MLA. The second one said his name was Marvin and that he used to be an engineer. But the third one simply said, "I am Physician."

'When she heard their introduction, na, the minister turned to a party secretary in charge of Meghalaya, who was also there, and said, "My God, Secretary-ji, did you hear that? One is a professor, another an engineer and the third a physician! Meghalaya politicians are highly qualified, no? Unlike in rest of India, no?"

'Nobody thought of telling her that the third MLA's name was Physician, but his qualification was under-matric.'

Everybody rocked with laughter, but after a while, Magdalene tried to shush everyone. She wanted to give us some more funny names.

At that moment, Halolihim entered and demanded, 'What are you laughing about?'

'Hey, Hal, come, come,' Hamkom responded. 'We have been sharing some very amusing name stories.'

'Have you been laughing at my name too?' he challenged.

'No, no, no,' Hamkom said hurriedly.

'How can we laugh at your name, Halolihim? That would be blasphemous, na?' Bah Kynsai said sarcastically.

Ignoring Halolihim, Bah Su said, 'There are thousands of such names, Mag. Even if we spent our entire stay here naming them, we would not exhaust the list.'

Suddenly, Evening burst out with suppressed anger, 'You people have been laughing at all these names, do you realise that you have been laughing at your own people? What is wrong with using English names? Do you think only Khasis have unusual names?'

Evening had not participated in the discussion at all. From the time we began exchanging stories about star names, he had thought we were indirectly laughing at him because of his name.

His aggressive interrogation took us all by surprise. It was Bah Kynsai who responded. He said, 'The problem with you, Ning, is that you think we are laughing at you. We are not. We are talking about Starlight and Shiningsstar and all the others, not because we think they are funny names, ha, but because we know these people and the stories behind their names. You also told us the story behind your name, na? We are not laughing at the names; we are genuinely interested in the stories behind them, that's all.'

'No, that's not all, Bah Kynsai!' Magdalene contradicted him. 'Starlight and Shiningsstar may be alright, but can you say that names like Kaligula, Sty Son, Apesila, Klitoris, Prostitiw, Pissdalin, et cetera are merely unusual? They are outlandish, bizarre and absurd, man, and they deserve to be laughed at! By laughing at them, we are not laughing at our own people, Evening, we are laughing at some people's foolishness. Don't generalise. And one more thing, we are not against English names per se, okay? My name and Don's and Dale's are English too, but they are names, not some meaningless, completely ridiculous and often shockingly shameful English-sounding words used as names!'

'No, no, no, no, no,' Evening protested. 'I don't agree at all! Do you think only Khasis use outlandish names? What about the English and the Americans? They also have funny names like Fockers, Drinkwater, Bush, Hunt, Couch, Day, Weeks, Forest, Crow, Merchant, Clay, Salt, Rice, Milk, Winter, Summers ... So many of them, thousands upon thousands of them. Why don't you laugh at them too, huh?'

Concerned that the conversation might degenerate into a slanging match, I intervened as gently as possible. 'Look, Ning, we all know about English and American surnames, not first names, mind you, but surnames. However, it's not our business to laugh at other people. You are missing the point entirely. If people don't know English, why should they use English words at all? Why don't they use names from their own language? The English, the Americans and others who use English as a first language are choosing names from their own language. And don't forget that we have funny surnames too, and clans named after animals, just like the English! Shrieh (monkey), Myrsiang (fox), Tham (crab), Ksih (otter), Pathaw (pumpkin), Sohkhia (cucumber), Rymbai (bean), Dohtdong (haunch) and so many others. Yet, we are not talking about them. Why? Because they are in our own tongue!'

'In your own tongue you can name a person anything and, as long as it is not vulgar, nobody will laugh or object. But the moment you choose English words as names without knowing their meaning, you open yourself up to mockery, not only because the names themselves sound ridiculous but also because you are being pretentious. Why are only English-sounding names considered fashionable or trendy? It's an attitude that scorns one's own as inferior, an attitude that should, therefore, be censured by everyone. And yet, we are not even doing that. We are, as Bah Kynsai said, trying to discover the stories behind the names because these stories are genuinely affecting.'

'Whatever you say,' Evening insisted, 'I cannot laugh at my own people ...'

'Not even when they anglicise their surnames and call themselves Conville, Decruze, Dykes, Reenborne, Manners, Soannes and the like?' Magdalene asked.

Evening was adamant. 'No. Let people call themselves whatever they want.'

'Fair enough, it's good of you to not laugh,' I said, 'but you should not stop others if they want to. There should always be scope for debate and the freedom to criticise.'

'Amen to that,' Bah Kynsai said.

'But Bah Kynsai, why do we have so many of these crazy names, ya?' Hamkom asked. 'I mean, Christian babies are baptised by priests who are well educated and well read, no?'

'Maybe they are afraid of upsetting the laity or what?' Bah Kynsai said.

'Maybe ... Is it the same with Niam Khasi, Ap? Do you have as many crazy names as we do?'

Raji answered for me. 'Fewer, fewer, you know why? Because, because in their case, okay, a name given to a child has to be approved by God, by God through signs.'

'Accha, that's interesting! Can you tell us about it, Bah Raji?' Donald asked.

'Me? You must be joking. Can't you see I'm busy with my baby?' Raji replied, pointing to his mug of yiad hiar. Then lowering his voice, he said conspiratorially, 'Wait, wait ... Bah Kynsai, Bah Kyn, can Ap tell the story?'

'You bloody drunk!' Bah Kynsai cursed the cackling Raji.

'You see, Don,' I said quickly, 'the Khasi religion is based on the concept of ïapan, or pleading. The old Khasis never took anything by force, realising that they were not masters of what they beheld. For instance, when they went hunting, they pleaded with God to provide them with an animal from the forest, for it was needed in their kitchen. In the same manner, they pleaded with the animals to forgive them for the needs that had brought them to the jungle. When they sowed seeds, they pleaded with God to give them a good crop, for they needed it to survive. And in this manner, they pleaded for every single thing they needed. They never took anything on their own.

'It's a very different matter nowadays, of course. For instance, when a deer wanders in from the lowlands of Bangla, villages stop every other activity so they can go and kill the animal. What harm is the poor thing doing to us? Why can't it be left alone? Will its flesh feed all of us forever? Are we starving? Do we need its meat at all, or are we just being plain greedy and murderous? All this is because we no longer practise the concept of ïapan. Many of us, including my "brothers of the faith", don't even know about it.

'The concept of pleading also extends to the naming of a child. No name can be given unless God sanctions it. Our naming ceremony is known as *jer khun*, which means, to mark a child. But what is this mark? With what is the child to be marked? Whose is this mark? The answer is, the mark is the name and the name is God-given—it is God's mark upon a human being. This is the reason why, when Khasis "mark" a child, they always choose, along with the name of their choice, two other names, in case God does not sanction the chosen one.

'In the past, the jer khun ceremony was performed by a maternal uncle. The Khasi religion being basically a family or clan religion, uncles also functioned as priests whenever the need arose. Because of this, there used to be many differences in the manner the ceremony was conducted.'

'Are uncles still performing the ceremony, Bah Ap?' Donald asked.

'Tell me, how many uncles would be capable of it now, Don? We have become such a hotchpotch community that to rely on an uncle would be as good as relying on rotten wood. If an uncle is a Khasi-Catholic, for instance, how could he become a Khasi priest as well as being a Catholic? Mostly, Don, people engage a professional priest, who is called *u nongjer*, the marker or the one who marks.

'But let me first tell you about the objects that are most commonly used in this ceremony. There's *pujer*, the marking-bread, which is rice ground into powder; a gourd; rice beer of the purest variety; plantain leaf, if available, and if not, then *lamet*, a kind of leaf; and a marking basket, which is actually *prah*, the winnowing basket. Some priests have been known to use cooked rice and water too, along with the other things. And yes, I nearly forgot, five pieces of dried fish, *khapiah*, are also kept ready, while a basin of water is placed outside the door.

'In addition to these, three *speh khnams*, arrows without metal tips; a miniature bow; a miniature *wait bnoh*, or hooked knife, meant for clearing the jungle and other such work; and a miniature *star*, or cane rope, meant for carrying things, are also used in the case of a boy. For a girl, all these are replaced by a *khoh*, or a bamboo cone, a cane rope and a hoe. And for both boys and girls, in keeping with the changing times, a pen or pencil and an exercise book are also used.'

'What is the significance of all these, Bah Ap?' Donald asked.

'They represent the appurtenances a child would need in his or her adult life, Don, except for the dried fish, which stands for material well-being. Once a date is fixed that is convenient to both the maternal and paternal families, the paternal grandmother sends a quantity of rice to be used as pujer. This is mixed with rice given by the parents of the child, and is soaked in water overnight to endow it with the water of life (what we Khasis call *um-ksiar, um-rupa*, or gold-water, silver-water) and also to soften it enough for grinding. The grinding is done in a wooden mortar at the third cockcrow, which would be around 4.30 in the morning. Why so early? Because the pujer, and there's a lot of it, must be ready by 6 or 7 a.m., the time preferred for the ceremony, although many people have been known to do it as late as 9 a.m.

'On the appointed date, when everything is ready, and when all the paternal and maternal relations and friends and neighbours have gathered round the main room, the priest, sitting just inside the door, begins the ceremony by first performing a ritual known as *ka nguh ka dem*. He arranges all the articles of faith in their proper places, puts his right hand on the marking basket, bows to God, pays homage to him, and pleads with him through befitting prayers to endow him with powers equal to the task at hand. He shakes the basket with its load of ceremonial objects, calls upon the name of God again, stating his purpose for doing so. He shakes the basket for the second time, calls upon the love of God to descend, and pleads with him "to reveal, to disclose the name, the reputation" of the child, and to lay his divine mark upon him.

'Then he takes a pinch of pujer rice from a small container in front of him, lifts his hand towards the child, who is held by his paternal or maternal grandmother, points it back towards the all-important basket and offers his prayer. As he prays, he lets the pujer in his hand drop onto the basket. At this juncture, he reiterates his appeal to God for his love and pleads with him "to reveal, to disclose the name, the reputation and the entitlement" of the child.

'He repeats the ritual for the second time and prays to God and u thawlang and ka ïawbei—the first ancestral father and mother of the clan—calling on them to bless the name chosen by the paternal relations, the name-givers, and gratefully accepted by the maternal relations.

'He repeats it for the third time and prays to God and u thawlang and ka ïawbei again so they would show a sign of approval, so they would let the libation of kyiad um beer and pujer reveal their will, so the name chosen would stick, would stand, would grow, would bring good health, fortune and long life. He prays for the child, so he would grow from strength to strength, blessed with a name given by God, so he would grow in wisdom, in knowledge, in intelligence, so he would grow in fame and fortune, and above all, so he would always be guided by his conscience, his love for man and God, throughout his life.

'When the priest has done this thrice, he slowly pours the libation from the gourd on the pujer he had placed in the basket and then tilts the gourd upwards a little to stop the flow and to see whether a drop of libation is clinging to its mouth or not. If it does, that would be a sign of God's sanction; a sign that the name "has stuck" and can now be marked on the child. But before doing that, the priest repeats the same rituals with the supporting names too.'

'Ah, so that's how God approves a name, ha, Ap? I also didn't know that, ya,' Magdalene said.

'Two of a kind,' I laughed. 'Anyway, after all the names have received God's sanction, the priest wets the pujer in the basket with more of the libation and then mixes the paste with the rest of the pujer in the container. He takes a pinch of the now damp pujer, mutters a few words of prayer for the name to be clear, for the name to be firm, and marks the child with it on his left foot (some priests have been known to mark on the left hand). And with the pujer that remains in his hand, he performs a ritual called *dud skai*. He blows once on the mixture, prays to God to ward off all evil eyes, to ward off all evil spirits, to ward off all curses and ill wishes that may harm the child. Then he blows on the mixture again, and turning it into a ball, throws it out of the door.

'But that is not the end of the ceremony, Don. After marking the child, the priest now marks the mother on her left foot, the father on his right foot, and continues with the ritual of dud skai every time he does the marking. Then he asks the father to eat a bit of the marking bread from the container three times. This is an act of reaffirmation. The father accepts, acknowledges and bears witness to his child being named with God's consent.

'Once the parents have been marked, all the relatives come forward to be marked too—maternal relatives on the left foot, paternal relatives on the right.'

'But why are all the others marked, Bah Ap?' Donald asked.

'It's a sign that everyone is happy and agrees with the proceedings. When all the relatives have been marked, the priest gathers up the plantain leaf on the marking basket, along with everything in it, folds it carefully, and asks the father to go out and get rid of it. The father does that by inserting the plantain leaf in the crook of a tree branch, to prevent it from being messed up by animals, and returns home. Before he can enter, the priest washes his feet with water from the basin, symbolising the water of purity, the water of gold, the water of silver.

'When the now-cleansed father has re-entered the house, a maternal and a paternal uncle jointly take hold of the khapiah fish and break it in two. They do the same with all the five pieces. After that is done—and the articles used in the ceremony, like the bow and arrows, have been carefully placed near the ceiling or hung on a wall—the pujer is eaten together with the khapiah fish. A little of the pujer is first given to the child, then to the parents, grandparents, uncles, and all the other close relatives. After that, it is mixed with the ground rice and sugar is added to make it tastier. Then it is distributed to all the guests, so that *ka bam pujer*, the pujer feast, can begin in earnest. The jer khun feast follows immediately after this and lasts late into the night.'

When I concluded my story, Raji said, slurring again, 'You see, you see, that's why not many Khasis with funny English names, okay? Got it?'

I did not entirely agree. 'It's true that many non-Christian Khasis prefer using Khasi names to English and that, typically, English names are associated with Christians. But that has nothing to do with the Khasi naming ceremony. God is supposed to give consent to a name that will suit the child's *rngiew*, the essence of his personality—a name, that is, which will bring him good health and good fortune. But it's up to the paternal relations to propose the name. And if they propose a funny English name that suits his essence, God will certainly not withhold his consent.'

'You sound so sure about God, tdong! Are you his confidant or something?' Bah Kynsai said sarcastically.

Bah Kit, however, defended me. 'After all, man proposes, God disposes, no, Bah Kynsai?'

Donald raised his hand and said, 'Okay, now we know how Khasis mark a child with a name, and we also know that all Khasis use funny English names. Now what, Bah Kynsai?'

Bah Kynsai looked at his watch. 'It's getting late. Now we sleep.'

'Come on, Bah Kyn!' Raji protested. 'The night ish shtill young!'

'Still young for you. You do what you want, but don't disturb us.'

With that, he went to sleep.

5

THE
THIRD
NIGHT

ROOT STORIES I

'A people without the knowledge of
their past, history, origin and culture
is like a tree without roots.'

—Marcus Garvey

Perly came to wake us up at about 9 a.m. on the morning of 7 February. He wanted us to leave for the lake early so we 'would not be late'. Late for what, we asked. They were going to have a look at the body in the afternoon, he explained. He wanted us to be there unless we had other plans. We had planned to spend the entire day at the lake, but we couldn't miss the body-viewing. Was this not what we had come here for?

We told Perly that we'd love to be there but that we would still like to go to the lake first. No problem, he said, we could go immediately after breakfast. Meanwhile, he said, he would have our lunch packed; the food was already cooked, so it would not take much time at all.

Perly brought us rice wrapped in plantain leaves and pork-and-bamboo-shoot broth in bamboo tubes with lids fitted onto them. Salt, chillies and fish leaves—the chameleon plant we call *jamyrdoh*—were packed separately in large lamet leaves. All of us, except Magdalene, took turns carrying the food, which was stored in two big cloth bags that Khasis call *plaïew*. The sky was hazy, the sun not too strong, but we were sweating heavily by the time we arrived at the lake, making us all the more eager for a bath. But nobody went for a swim except Raji, and even he did not venture too far from the bank. The rest of us wallowed in the shallows, while Magdalene went to a secluded spot to bathe alone.

It was an incredible feeling, having a bath after three days in the humid jungle. We swore, come what may, to visit the lake every day. After the bath, we washed our clothes and left them to dry in the sun and ate our lunch in a clearing carpeted with short yellow grass. The food was simple but heavenly: the exertion, the bath and our hunger combined to make it truly delicious. We were sorry to leave so soon after lunch, but pleasure had to give way to serious business.

Back at the hut, Perly and Chirag were already waiting for us. Chirag had just come from Nongstoin with all the stuff he was supposed to bring. The first thing he said was, 'How are you faring, cooped up in this jungle, are you all right, Babu, is everything all right?'

Bah Kynsai patted Chirag's shoulder and said, 'Never better, never better.'

I asked him about the trip, genuinely curious to know if he had had an incident-free passage.

Smiling expansively, he said, 'No problem, no problem, I had the jeep checked before I came, so no breakdowns this time. Come, come, Babu, are you ready, we have to go.'

We quickly put out our clothes to dry on the tree by the hut and followed him and Perly to the death house.

People were already milling about the sprawling courtyard, getting ready for the procession to the treehouse in the jungle where the body had been kept for the last nine months. There were musicians in the small crowd, adjusting their instruments. Perly told us that some sixteen drummers and four pipers had come with the shamans and elders from Nongtrai, near the Garo Hills border, where a few still practised the indigenous faith. But today, only two drummers and one piper would be playing. Two types of drums had been brought for the Phor Sorat ceremony, of which only the *ksing kynthei* would be used today. A ksing kynthei is a small rectangular drum made from the wood of the rare *lakiang* tree. Its two hollow openings are covered with carefully cured and tanned cowhide, held in place with a network of thongs. A leather string is attached to it from both ends to allow a drummer to carry it suspended from his neck and resting on his belly so it can be played with his left palm and a small stick in his right hand. Although it would not be in play this day, we also saw the small bowl-shaped *ksing padiah*. These drums are placed on the ground and played with two long, thin sticks.

The pipers had brought with them the tangmuri wind instrument, shaped like a trumpet. It has seven openings and is made from the wood of a tree called *lum palam*. By blowing on its mouthpiece, made from a bamboo species called *japung*, and playing on the openings with deft fingers, a musician can produce the most rousing melodies ever heard in traditional Khasi music. But for a tangmuri to produce truly stimulating music, it is said that the japung must be brought from a place far from human habitation; it cannot sound impressive if taken from bamboo cane that grows near where the rooster crows. The Lyngngam tangmuri is called *ka lyhir* and is different from the one used by other Khasi sub-tribes only in that it is made from the horn of a buffalo instead of the lum palam tree.

As we waited, a shaman appeared from the house and walked towards the western part of the courtyard. He was a wizened old man with a quiet dignity about him. Dressed in grey terry wool trousers, a blue tee-shirt and a light grey coat with a pattern of dark grey checks, he wore on his head a rolled-up grey balaclava. All his clothes bore the marks of age and dusty travel, especially his shoes, so completely covered in a thick layer of brown dust that the real colour was no longer visible. A small grey cloth bag hung from his neck. As we watched, the shaman squatted on the ground, bent his head, took out grains of rice from the bag and began intoning a prayer. Perly said, 'Today there will not be many rituals, only *ka duwai khaw*.'

Ka duwai khaw, or prayer with rice grains, is the simplest of rituals in the Khasi religion. When the shaman finished his prayer, he stood up, tossing some rice grains to the left and the right of the entry. That seemed to be a signal to the drummers and the piper, for they struck up a slow, haunting music. The musicians were a nondescript, dusty lot, who looked more like Tibeto-Burmese than Khasis.

As the music began, the shaman led the procession towards the treehouse, now and then tossing a few rice grains to the right and left. This was apparently to clear all obstacles that may hinder our route to the interim resting place of the dead—something, it seemed, that could be brought about by the malice of man or the spell of evil spirits. The shaman was followed by his musicians, the burangs, or uncles, of the bereaved family, and other male and female relatives. As he tossed the rice grains, he also intoned a few words of prayer as a way of letting the soul of the dead, which was still around, know that its relatives were coming to check on the body as a prelude to the final rituals of cremation.

After we had marched for about twenty minutes, the procession came to a halt at a large clearing in the jungle. On the edge of the clearing, there was a very tall tree, easily about sixty feet high. Near the top of the tree, a bamboo platform called *thylliang* had been built, and on top was a little bamboo-and-straw structure, about three feet high, four feet across and seven feet long. The hut-like structure had only one opening, which seemed dark and menacing to us as we looked up at it.

As we approached the treehouse, Bah Kynsai whispered, 'Cover your noses.'

'Tet, don't do that!' Raji whispered back fiercely. 'They may take it as an insult. If it stinks, you'll just have to bear it.'

Fortunately, we were all spared the unpleasantness. There was a kind of eerie silence in the place, but no stench at all, not even a little bit.

When Bah Kynsai asked Chirag about it in a whisper, he said, 'How can there be any smell after nine months? The body is all dried up, no, Babu, maybe bones only without flesh.'

The shaman circled the tree three times, sprinkling rice grains and intoning a prayer. Then he stood in front of the treehouse and addressed the soul of the dead in a very solemn voice: 'Oh you the mother, you the queen, look, we are all here, we have come, we, your kith and kin, your children and grandchildren, your uncles and nephews, we are all here. We have come to give you notice, to give you the good news, do not be disturbed, we have come to tell you, your long wait is about to end. The rites, the rituals are in place, the cleansing of your body is about to begin, so you may be free to leave, so your soul may journey to your eternal abode with our help, with our prayers, with the help of God, U Blei.

'Oh you the mother, you the queen, we have spoken, be prepared, in a few days we will come to lower the body, to have it cleansed with Queen Fire, even as the first body was devoured by her, so your soul may ascend to Krangraij, so it may ascend to your eternal abode, so you may live happily with your ancestors and forebears and share with them the divine kwai, for God has allowed you into your happy home, for God has accepted you as his own.'

With these words, the shaman retreated from the treehouse, walking backwards, as did we all, till we were out of the clearing. Needless to say, I did not understand any of the shaman's words since he was speaking in the Nongtrai dialect. It was only later, when I met Victor, that I learnt the gist of what he had said. Victor, like most people from Nongtrai, was robust-looking and swarthy. Being a schoolteacher, he was much better dressed than his companions, the musicians, who called him Babu Bik.

When we reached the death house, it was about 6 p.m. and quite dark. We were given some water to wash our hands, and after that, we went to the backyard to have dinner, which was much the same as lunch. By 7 p.m., we were back in our hut, sitting around the fire, sipping sweet yiad hiar beer from bamboo mugs. There seemed to be no end to the stuff, and Perly, our supplier, had encouraged us to drink as much as we could. 'There's plenty of it,' he had said. 'We have made a large quantity exclusively for the Phor Sorat.'

With this free flow of alcohol, you might have thought there would be a lot of drunkenness. But as far as I could see, nobody was drinking during the day. They drank before supper and then stopped. Only some, like our friends, continued after supper as well, since they had nothing else to do. They too were only a little high, not drunk. I think this was partly because the drink on offer was not rice spirit, only rice beer, which is not very strong, although Raji did say it was much stronger than the variety brewed in the rest of the Khasi Hills.

The ceremony we had witnessed earlier in the day got us talking about the khanatangs—the sanctified stories upon which rest the foundations of Khasi religious and philosophical thought. The stories, entertaining as they are instructive, provoked intense anger in some but brought understanding to most of us, and I was glad my friends insisted I speak about them.

Bah Kynsai opened the discussion by saying, 'So, that was the beginning of Ka Phor Sorat, ha! Nothing much to it, na?'

'No, nothing much. But that was just for starters, no, Bah Kynsai?' Raji clarified. 'Only ka duwai khaw to inform the soul of the deceased that the cleansing of the body is imminent. I heard that the shamans and the musicians are going to another village tomorrow. They'll be back only on the eleventh now.'

'Not everyone,' I said. 'Victor and some men are staying back to help with the preparations.'

'Coming back on the eleventh—does that mean we'll have to extend our stay by one day?' Magdalene asked.

'No, no,' Raji clarified, 'they'll finish everything by the thirteenth.'

'But that uncle of theirs said it was going to be a six-day ceremony, na?' Bah Kynsai observed.

'The main rituals will last only for three days,' I explained. 'The three days after that are days of mourning and cleaning, followed by a ceremony called *kheiñ sbai*, a strictly family affair, and the internment of the bones after the mourning period is over. Unless we want to see the bone-burial ceremony, we don't have to wait till the very end.'

'We'll cross that bridge when we come to it,' Bah Kynsai said. 'Now ...'

I don't know what Bah Kynsai was about to say, for Halolihim interrupted him mid-sentence. 'What surprises me,' he said sourly, 'is that all those people participating in that ... that *thing* were Christians! How could they? That old fellow was standing there in front of the dead body, worshipping it: it was like demon worship!'

The hut suddenly went very quiet.

Both Bah Kynsai and Raji wanted to say something to normalise the situation, but Bah Kit spoke first: 'I must request you to mind your language. Calling an address to the soul of a dead relation "demon worship" is tantamount to saying that all believers of Niam Khasi are demon worshippers.'

Responding to the hurt in his voice, Hamkom scolded Halolihim. 'Hal, you shouldn't have said that, tet, man, that was too much!'

Raji added, 'He was not worshipping any demon, Halolihim.' Like the Torajans, okay, the Lyngngams also believe that as long as the rite of passage has not been performed, the soul of the deceased is loitering around among the living. The deceased, as such, is still present, the shaman was merely talking to her soul ...'

'If not demon worship, then ancestor worship! The woman died nine months ago, but that old fellow was still talking to her as if she were alive, propitiating her, that's ancestor worship—'

Bah Su interrupted him and said, 'If you say that addressing the soul of a dead relative is ancestor worship, then are you also not guilty of it? Every year, you go to the cemetery, clean it up, put flowers and things on the graves of your relatives, and after that, you pray. Is that not ancestor worship?'

But Halolihim was not even listening. 'Non-Christian Khasis have no real religion, they worship ancestors and all sorts of gods and demons, they are nothing but benighted pagans, they haven't even come to know God, U Blei—'

Bah Kit broke in, appealing to Bah Kynsai. 'Bah Kynsai, if you don't stop this person, I might be forced to do something I'll regret later.'

'Halolihim!' Bah Kynsai shouted. 'If you don't stop this instant, I'll give you a smack on the teeth!'

Raji tried to reason with Halolihim. 'Why do you say non-Christian Khasis do not know God, U Blei? The word Blei is borrowed from the Khasi religion. The name of God in the Old Testament is Jehovah; you of all people should know that!'

At this, Halolihim lost his temper completely. With eyes blazing fanatically and forefinger wagging angrily, he shouted at the top of his voice, 'They do not know God! They worship the cock! Haven't you seen their flags, there is always a huge red cock in the middle of the flag! And their stories about the golden ladder and Sohpet Bneng, the so-called "heaven's navel", are all cock and bull! Their myths are all cock and bull! They are demon worshippers, ancestor worshippers and cock worshippers!' And then, imitating the sound of a chicken and moving his arms up and down as if they were flapping wings, he yelled, 'Kok-kok-ktok! Kok-kok-ktok!'

This was too much for Bah Kit and Bah Su. They jumped to their feet in great agitation. Shaking a finger at Halolihim, Bah Su shouted: 'How could you say something as nasty as that when nobody had said anything against your religion?'

Halolihim, still consumed by righteous anger, yelled back, 'I will say it because it is the truth! You are all bloody heathens, copycat Hindus and RSS agents! And don't shake your finger at me!'

So saying, he walked up to Bah Su and slapped his finger out of the way. Not satisfied with that, he went on to slap his head—the way someone might slap a recalcitrant boy—with all the force he could muster. Bah Su fell backwards into the straw, and seeing that, Bah Kit roared, 'You would even strike an old man, you bastard!' And before any of us could react, he had rushed at Halolihim, ramming his right shoulder into his stomach, American-football style. They went down together, on the fire, sending sparks and burning logs flying in all directions, though luckily, none of the logs landed on the straw.

Bah Kit was on top of Halolihim, who was squirming under him. The fellow was in serious danger. Raji and I rushed forward. He pulled at Bah Kit, and I at Halolihim, dragging them out of the fire as quickly as we could. Bah Kynsai came to help me, and between us, we got Halolihim outside the hut, beating the embers sticking to him with some of the clothes drying outside. His thin cardigan was burnt quite badly at the back, and his trousers had black holes in the bottom. Astonishingly, apart from that and a slightly burnt right hand, he had no other injury. When we finished with him, he was all shaken up and stood there unsteadily, clinging to a tree nearby. We told him to sit down and relax, and he did, all the anger gone out of him. I brought him some water, which he drank greedily, without saying a word.

When I went inside, the others were busy trying to put out little fires that had sprung up here and there from the flying embers. Soon everything was back to normal with no real damage done anywhere. Bah Kit sat in a corner talking with Bah Su. Hamkom took a shawl out to Halolihim outside. And Magdalene, speaking for all of us, exclaimed, 'Shit ya! What a crazy thing!'

Some of us trooped back outside to look at Halolihim. He had not spoken a word. Too shocked, I guessed. He was given his spare trousers and, after changing into them, sat where he was like a hearthstone while Hamkom tried to console him.

We left them there and returned to the hut. Bah Kynsai said, 'We must make peace between you and Halolihim, Kit, and you, Bah Su, must forgive him. We cannot stay in this hut together for days and have that sort of thing happening again. Imagine, the hut could have been burnt down, man, and you two could have been seriously injured, even killed, liah!'

'I'm okay,' Bah Kit said. 'Bah Su is also okay; you just deal with Halolihim if he abuses us again, we'll try to keep quiet.'

At that moment, Chirag, Perly and some others came running to the hut. Chirag said, 'We heard noises and shouting, what happened?'

'Nothing, Chirag, some of us were exercising,' Bah Kynsai replied. 'They got tired of sitting in the hut without doing anything, na.'

Just then, Halolihim entered and said, 'Nothing! How can you say, nothing? That person,' he pointed at Bah Kit, 'was trying to murder me!'

'Why, you lying son of a bitch!' Bah Kynsai shouted at him. 'You were the one who blasphemed against their religion, you were the one who slapped Bah Su when he protested, slapped him as if he was an unruly boy, and now you are accusing Kit of trying to murder you? You are a damn shame to us Christians! I was trying to make peace between them, na, Chirag? Kit and Bah Su have agreed, I was about to talk to this fellow, but after what he just said, na, I think it's useless. We cannot have them staying here together. One of them has to go.'

'What do you mean, one of them?' Raji demanded. 'Halolihim beat up Bah Su; Bah Kit came to his rescue. There are three of them, no? If Bah Kit goes, Bah Su will also have to go.'

'You're right,' Bah Kynsai agreed. 'Chirag, is there a place where Halolihim can stay? I don't think he can stay here with us any longer. This damn Hamkom! Why did you have to bring this Talib along?'

'I think one person can stay with Kong in our house, come, who's going?'

Hamkom took Halolihim to Chirag's, and everyone was visibly relieved.

Bah Kynsai said, 'Where's my mug? Oh shit, lyeit, all the khor is gone! Raji, give me that gourd, man! Now, where were we?'

'We were talking about Ka Phor Sorat, Bah Kynsai ...' Raji began when Hamkom re-entered the hut, and we all turned to him.

'How is he?' Bah Kynsai asked.

'He's gone to wherever he used to go.'

'How can he preach the teachings of the Prince of Peace when he's so violent and intolerant?' Magdalene wondered.

'I, for one,' Donald observed, 'do not understand how people can get so worked up about religion. Personally, I don't care for it. I don't care for identity or culture or religion.'

'I know, I know,' Bah Kynsai interrupted, 'you are a cosmo.'

'I don't care much about religion either,' I said. 'That was why, at first, I was more amused than angry with Halolihim. But this is the great danger

I have always feared, Bah Kynsai. What is happening in this hut, is this not an example of what is happening in Khasi society? Excessively drunk as we are on religion, what if one day we end up clashing with each other? We are such a small community, what will happen if we fight each other because we belong to different religions? We have been discussing the threat of influx, but who will pick up the pieces if we fight among ourselves?'

'You are absolutely right, Ap,' Evening agreed wholeheartedly, 'the poiei, the strays, will pick up the pieces. We have to be careful about this. I'm a practising Christian, okay, I go to church every Sunday and attend all the religious functions that I can, but I get along fine with you people.'

'I have a friend,' I said, 'a leader of an NGO and a devoted Christian, who said much the same thing. We were discussing some of the actions of the HNLC when he observed that the greatest mistake the militant outfit made was to take sides in a quarrel between two religious parties. He was referring to the Rijoy Khongsha case that we discussed earlier. When it should have acted as a peacemaker, he said, it acted as an executioner. That was unforgivable in the eyes of the people. As a public leader, you simply cannot afford to take sides. You have to treat every Khasi the same, regardless of his religion. For me, he said, the fact that I am a Khasi is more important than the fact that I belong to this or that religion. And then he went on to say something profound, I thought. He said, "I can change my religion at any time if I want to, but can I ever change the fact that I am a Khasi?" However, as I see it, there are too few people thinking as he does. Too many are too fanatical.'

But Bah Kynsai thought I was unduly pessimistic. 'If you look at this hut, na, you will see that we Christians outnumber you almost three to one. That's also the case in our society. Yet here, we get along very well with you and Kit and Bah Su, apart from Halolihim. In fact, you are among my best friends, whereas I would never count someone like Halolihim a friend. For me, for Raji, Mag, Donald, and I'm sure for Ham and Ning as well, fighting with you people is out of the question. Halolihim is the only odd one out, na?'

'But you people are well-educated, liberal and tolerant, Bah Kynsai! Others are not like you. Too many are like Halolihim, on both sides of the divide.'

Magdalene agreed with me. 'I think Ap may be right, Bah Kynsai. We Christians are even fighting among ourselves. In villages where a particular church dominates, they persecute all those who do not belong to their church in all kinds of ways. And in some villages where the Khasi-Khasis are few, they are not even allowed to cremate their dead. We read about these things very often in the papers. It's a terrible thing, what's happening, and it's worse in the rural areas.'

Donald was aghast. 'Did that sort of thing really happen? Were people really prevented from cremating their dead?'

'Yeah, yeah, in two such cases at least, the court had to intervene,' Magdalene said.

Raji added, 'Some of us are so fundamentalist now that we behave like some doomsday cult, you know that? All of you must have read about those nine families from Nongthliew village in West Khasi Hills, no? They were so convinced by the doomsday prophecy of a mysterious preacher that they practically stopped living, you remember? It was reported in the press in November 2011. These people, okay, including the families of two government employees and three school teachers, okay, were told by the preacher that it was futile to hold on to wealth, jobs and property, as the world was coming to an end very soon. As a result, they quit their jobs, took their children out of school and, according to the headman, also withdrew all the money from their banks. They even refused to accept the usual ration of kerosene and rice, and threw away their election identity cards. At one point, okay, they left their homes to wait for the Apocalypse in the jungle. It seemed they had been living there for two years before they were discovered and brought back to the village. Even now, they are refusing to lead a normal life.'

'It's true, Bah Kynsai,' Magdalene said again, 'we have become quite intolerant and more and more drunk without drinking. Do you remember that controversy about the Shillong Autumn Festival? Do you remember what happened when the Tourism Development Forum decided to hold its grand finale on a Sunday?'

'Yeah, yeah, we all do, Mag,' Raji replied. 'It caused a terrible uproar!'

'That's right. NGOs like the FKJGP, RBYF, KSU (North), Village Council Umïam and several church forums made a huge noise about how the sanctity of Sunday had been violated. Did any of them even know that, according to the Ten Commandments, the day of the Sabbath is the seventh day of the week, which is Saturday and not Sunday, which is the first day? Did they know that, initially, Sunday was a pagan holiday, declared sacred to the sun god by Emperor Constantine of Rome? It had nothing to do with the Bible, ya! But now, how is it that we cannot even hold a social event on this day? It's incredible how far people can be misled by traditions without knowing anything about them.'

What Magdalene was referring to was Emperor Constantine's edict of March 321 CE:

> Let all judges and all city people and all tradesmen rest upon the venerable day of the sun. But let those dwelling in the country freely and with full liberty attend to the culture of their field; since it frequently happens that no other day is so fit for the sowing of grain or the planting of vines; hence, the favourable time should not be allowed to pass, lest the provisions of heaven be lost.

The edict was first cited by A.C. Lewis in his *Critical History of Sunday Legislation from 321 to 1888* and then by William Blakely in his *American State Papers Bearing on Sunday Legislation,* 1891. However, it must be added that, later, Sunday was declared as the day of worship for the entire Christian world, and in that sense, it is a holy day for all Christians.

I said as much, but Donald countered me by saying, 'That may be true, Bah Ap, but if India is a secular state, with many communities belonging to different faiths, then Meghalaya, as a part of India, should also be secular. And in a secular state, no one has the right to impose their religious views on anyone else.'

Listening to Raji, Magdalene and Donald, Bah Kynsai suddenly became very curious about Halolihim and said, 'Ham, is Halolihim part of the Jehovah's Witnesses or what?'

'No, no, he belongs to some American church. It's still quite new, so everyone chips in to spread the good word.'

'But he certainly behaved like a fundamentalist, na? My God, spitting all those horrible insults!'

Hamkom tried to defend Halolihim. 'I agree he was very wrong in blaspheming against their religion like that, but at the same time, the issues that he raised are also issues that I have always thought about, you know. For instance, please don't mind, okay, Bah Kit, but ...'

'No, no, why should I mind? A rational and reasonable discussion of any religion, yours included, should always be welcome. Even when Halolihim was shouting insults like that, ha, I didn't really intend to get physical with him. It was only when he slapped an elderly person like Bah Su, who can hardly defend himself, that I lost my temper. Bah Su and I go back a very long way, okay? Ask Raji, the three of us used to go everywhere together, no, Raji?'

Raji agreed, and Hamkom, satisfied that he would not be thrown into the fire like Halolihim, said, 'You see, Bah Kit, even I have been wondering about why you object to being called pagans, I mean, a pagan is someone who worships many gods, no? And I have noticed that you Khasis sometimes not only talk about U Blei, that is, God, but also about *ki blei*, or the gods: this is something I don't understand.

'Then, also, you say that your religion is not about ancestor worship, and yet you have gods like u thawlang, ka ïawbei, u suidñia and others to whom you pray. As you and Ap said before, u thawlang is the first paternal ancestor, ka ïawbei is the first maternal ancestress and u suidñia, the first maternal uncle. These are ancestors, no? So why are they revered as gods and goddesses if your religion is not about ancestor worship?

'Hal was also right—though he shouldn't have shouted and disparaged like that—when he pointed out that the flags of organisations belonging to your religion, like Seng Khasi and Seiñ Raij, always carry the symbol of a colourful cock, displayed very prominently. This is the reason many, not just Hal, okay, accuse you of worshipping the cock.

'And finally, the story of the "Golden Ladder at Mount Sohpet Bneng", ha, about how in their Golden Age the Hynñiew Treps used to travel freely between heaven and earth on this ladder, ha, does sound ridiculous. This is perhaps why Hal called the story cock and bull. Now, I'm not accusing your religion of anything, okay, but these things do seem to invite certain allegations, no?'

Bah Kynsai was worried there might be another outburst, so he said, '*Shanti, shanti*, Kit, no tantrums now!'

'Arre, Bah Kynsai, why should I throw tantrums? When did I ever? It was Halolihim who did, no? Not I. And these are quite reasonable questions. It's not only Khasi-Christians who don't understand them, okay, but many among us also. But once you understand them, everything will become clear as day. However, I'd like Ap to do the talking; he has written quite extensively on these subjects.'

'Really?' Hamkom asked in surprise. 'I thought he said he didn't care much for religion!'

'I don't,' I replied. 'But on the other hand, I'm deeply interested in my people's culture, and that includes their religious and philosophical views as well. I rather admire them for it, but as to my personal belief, I'd rather not say.'

Magdalene protested loudly. 'No, no, you have to tell us, Ap. You know all about us. You know that Bah Kynsai is an outstanding Presbyterian; you know that Don doesn't care about religion, though officially he's Catholic; you know that Bah Kit and Bah Su are practising Khasi-Khasis; you know that I am a practising Christian, though not orthodox ... no, no, you must tell us about yourself. Simply saying "I don't care much about religion" will not do. We want to know what exactly you believe in.'

I laughed and said, 'Ham has raised four basic questions about Niam Khasi Niam Tre, the Khasi religion. But I warn you; my answer is not going to be short or simple ...'

'We have all night, na? But make it interesting,' Bah Kynsai commanded.

'I'll try, but also remember that I'm not trying to preach; in fact, I'll tell you later why the Khasi religion doesn't believe in preaching and conversion. For now, let me begin with the khanatangs, the sanctified myths, which Halolihim called "cock and bull". I'd like to do that because most of you don't know anything about them and because, if you don't know about them, you won't even begin to understand what I'm talking about when I try to answer Ham's questions.'

'You did tell us something about them earlier, na?' Bah Kynsai said.

'That was hardly anything, ya, Bah Kynsai,' Magdalene countered. 'Why are they "sanctified", Ap?'

'Khasis have several categories of stories,' I explained. 'These include the *khana pateng* (legends), *purinam* (fairy tales), *puriskam* (fables), *khana pharshi* (parables) and, sometimes, true stories that have worked their way into the hearts of one and all. But the khanatangs are special. They are stories deliberately sanctified because they deal with our creation myths and discuss our religious and philosophical thought. In short, they are the very foundation of our religion. Broadly speaking, there are two sacred myths. One of them is *Ka Khanatang ki Hynñiew Trep* (the sacred myth of ki Hynñiew Trep), comprising the parables of *Ka Jingkieng Ksiar halor U Lum Sohpet Bneng* (the golden ladder on Mount Sohpet Bneng), *Ki Lai Hukum* (the Three Commandments), *Ka Diengïei* (the tree of gloom), *U Khla* (the Tiger) and *I Phreit* (the Wren). The other is *Ka Khanatang U Saw Shyrtong* (the sacred myth of the purple crest), comprising the parables of *U Hati* (the Elephant), *U Kohkarang* (the Hornbill) and *U Saw Shyrtong* (the Purple Crest or the Rooster—a term which I much prefer to the word cock, for obvious reasons). Let me give you the stories as they are, and then we shall see whether they are merely cock and bull or whether they have their own profound symbolism.'

Having given them this brief introduction, I told them the stories, beginning with the sacred myth of Ki Hynñiew Trep, and asked them not to interrupt me until I had finished.

༜

In the beginning, there was nothing but a vast emptiness on earth. God had created only two beings—Ramew, the guardian spirit of the earth, and her husband, Basa, who later came to be identified with the patron god of villages and the wilderness as U Ryngkew U Basa. The two lived happily enough for a time, but by and by, one thing began to plague their minds: they had no children. They wanted children, wanted them desperately, because they realised that life without children would be terribly lonely and monotonous. They prayed to their God, U Blei, to bless them with at least a child or two so that their line could continue.

'O God, our Lord and Master! O God, Dispenser and Giver of Life!' they called upon him. 'We have been living on earth, absolutely alone, for quite some time now. While we love each other and are happy on our own, we wish our love to be fruitful. We wish to have children, the product of our love, children who will lighten our days and ease the monotony of our existence. It doesn't seem right, O God, Dispenser and Giver of Life, that the earth you have created should remain barren and empty like this. O Lord and Master! We have each other now, but what about the future?'

After many such entreaties, God granted them their wish and gave them five children of great powers and accomplishments, five children that people have come to call the elemental forces. Sun was their first daughter, followed by their only son, Moon, and three other daughters, Water, Wind and Fire. Fire was the last born, the womb-cleaning one, and it was her duty to be always at home, to cook their meals and tend to their daily needs as custom demanded.

Ramew was delighted to see her children grow and prosper. She was particularly delighted to see how they worked at reshaping the world into a pleasant land, giving life to tall trees and beautiful flowers everywhere.

And yet, amidst all that plenty and peace, something was wanting. That such loveliness should go untended and uncared for! That such plenty should benefit no one! It was not right, she felt. Ramew turned to God again.

'O God, our Lord and Master! O God, Dispenser and Giver of Life!' she implored him. 'Please forgive me if I seem ungrateful and unhappy with my lot. I am indeed contented and pleased to see my children so powerful and accomplished. They have done wonders here on earth. They have turned it into a pleasant land of peace and plenty. There are trees and beautiful flowers everywhere. There are fruits and plants of every kind and description. But it pains me to see that so much loveliness and plenitude may one day go to waste with no one to benefit from them. O God, our Lord and Master, my children, though bestowed with outstanding gifts, powers and accomplishments, are yet ill-equipped to look after all that they have created. Sun and Moon are too busy roaming the universe, tending to their duties. Water has her limitations and cannot travel the earth freely. Wind is not suited for caretaking on her own, nor is Fire. Both can run wild if not properly tended. You see, my Lord, we need someone who would not only be the heir to all this bounty but also a conscientious caretaker of all creation.'

God, who understood the yearning of Ramew and who had watched her labour hard and long to make the world a fitting place for life, promised to honour her wishes. He created diverse creatures, the first beneficiaries of earth's abundance, and then issued a decree declaring two powerful spirits of the mountains as the guardians of the earth. But instead of seeing to the welfare of the many living things, the sibling spirits began to tussle for power. This resulted in a terrible fratricidal battle, the scars of which can be seen even today.

Responding to Ramew's complaints against the mountain spirits, God then placed the responsibility of ruling earth on animals and made Tiger the presiding administrator. But this also did not work, as Tiger began to rule like a despotic overlord and encouraged the law of 'might is right'.

As anarchy threatened, Ramew once more raised a complaint with God and pleaded with him for wise and conscientious overseers who would be a blessing and not a curse to all the living beings on earth.

God, who is just and benevolent, listened with sympathy to the pleas of Ramew and concluded that none but kinsmen of the sixteen clans living in heaven would be the fitting caretakers of the earth. Accordingly, he summoned the greatest council ever held in heaven, and after days of careful deliberation, he eventually declared that seven of the sixteen clans should descend to inhabit the earth—they would till the land, populate the wilderness, rule and govern and be the caretakers of all creation. And from then on, they would be known as Ki Hynñiew Trep, or the seven huts, the seven families, the seven clans, who would later become the ancestors of the seven sub-tribes of the Khasi people.

God, who had provided for happiness on earth, endowing its soil with riches and the fruits of plenty through the children of Ramew, then made a Covenant with the Hynñiew Treps. As part of the Covenant, he gave them *Lai Hukum*, Three Commandments, including ka tip briew tip Blei (the knowledge of man, the knowledge of God), *ka tip kur tip kha* (the knowledge of one's maternal and paternal relations) and *ka kamai ïa ka hok* (the earning of virtue). As a token of the Covenant, God also planted a divine tree on a sacred mount called Lum Sohpet Bneng, which served as *Ka Jingkieng Ksiar*, the golden ladder, between the kingdom of God and the kingdom of man.

The Covenant declared that so long as the seven clans adhered to the Three Commandments, they could come and go as they pleased between heaven and earth, via the golden ladder at Lum Sohpet Bneng, the mountain of heaven's navel. The mountain would act as an umbilical cord between God and man, for even as a child is bonded with the mother through this thread of flesh and blood, so also is man bonded with God.

Everything was now well with the world. And as long as man remembered God and his divine decree, as long as he behaved in a manner befitting his celestial lineage, he prospered and never suffered any real grief. His life on earth was one long tale of happiness.

But it is not in man to be content with happiness alone. Like everything else in this world, he is essentially two-edged, capable at once of great good and great evil. Soon, he began to tire of following the diktats of God; he wanted to branch out on his own, to determine his life independently, according to his own instincts and inclinations. In this manner, he strayed away from the Three Commandments. Greed, the mother of all evils, sat supreme in his heart, and in his craving for power and pelf, he trampled on the rights of others. He began to cheat, to swindle, to steal and even kill to gain what his avaricious heart desired. Respect for fellow men, through which alone man could approach God, was completely forgotten, as men tried their best to outwit each other for the sake of wealth, their new god.

God, on his part, was vexed by man's rebelliousness. Sorely grieved that man had chosen to ignore and slight the Covenant, he decided to break off all ties and forever closed the golden ladder to heaven through Sohpet Bneng. Away from the remaining nine clans in heaven, and bereft of God's guidance and blessing, the Hynñiew Treps remained helpless orphans on earth, amidst a new kind of darkness that bred all sorts of evil in the minds of men. Their Golden Age had ended.

And that was not all. As evidence of his displeasure, God made an oak tree, located on another sacred mount, grow day by day to a monstrous height and width so that its shadow threw whole portions of the earth into pitch darkness. The perpetual darkness caused by the branches of Diengïei, the name given to this 'tree of gloom', made standing crops wilt and threatened to destroy all plant life while making man himself vulnerable, a prey to all sorts of evils.

Man panicked. But as is characteristic of him, instead of turning inwards to examine his soul, conceding his mistakes and missteps, and approaching God with a repentant heart, he proudly sought his own solution to the ever-worsening crisis that threatened his very existence.

He first convened an extended council to which male representatives from every Hynñiew Trep family were summoned. After hurried consultations, the council resolved to bring down Diengïei, which was still growing alarmingly. In passing the resolution, the council declared:

'We do not know the cause of this terrible darkness, nor why Diengïei has suddenly grown so malevolently huge. But the need of the hour is not to seek the reason. Our very survival is threatened; we must act quickly and decisively. We must bring down this tree of gloom before its foul shadow destroys us. To do this, each family must send at least one man, equipped with a machete and an axe, to carry out the task.'

Work on toppling Diengïei commenced immediately. The men chopped and hacked away from dawn to dusk, lopping off a bit of the trunk each day. But always, when they came back the next day, they found the tree whole again. It was as if it had never been touched.

The men were dumbfounded, and some of them grew apprehensive, for it seemed to them that the tree had mysterious powers. How could they fight something that could heal itself as soon as it was cut?

While they sat brooding, in fear and confusion, a little wren called Phreit came flying to the paddy fields nearby. The bird had never seen men sunk in such gloom before. When she learnt the cause, the wren offered to reveal the secrets of Diengïei:

'It is not what you think, O men! Diengïei may have the power to grow with the swiftness of a bird's flight, but it does not have the power to heal itself. I know its secrets, and I'm ready to help should you wish me to. All I ask is that you allow me to feed freely in your paddy fields so that I too may survive.'

By then, the men were so desperate and so thoroughly demoralised that they were prepared to listen to just about anyone with new ideas. Once the deal was struck, Phreit told them that it was not the tree's magic powers that were responsible for its remarkable recovery, but the licking of its trunk by

Tiger as soon as the men retired to their homes for the night. That was how the gashes filled up as fast as they were made.

Tiger (a symbol of all that was evil and cruel) wanted Diengïei to stand as the expanding eclipse it caused made hunting easier. In fact, he was looking forward to a time when the entire world was blanketed in darkness so that he could start preying on man too. To foil the evil designs of Tiger, Phreit advised the men to fortify the portion of the trunk they had hewn by placing knives and axes against it each night.

Encouraged by Phreit's revelation, the men hustled back to the task, and at the end of their day's work, set their axes against the tree. The next morning, the trunk had not healed at all. Instead, they discovered bloodstains on their axes, and understood that Tiger had cut his tongue to shreds, and terrified, had fled the place for an unknown destination. They were elated. They fell upon the tree with fresh vigour and finally brought it down after many weeks of hard labour. Everyone heaved a sigh of relief.

In concluding my narration, I said, 'The pact made with the little Phreit marked man's first gesture towards repentance and humility. And that was why God granted man success in felling the Diengïei. But this khanatang has to be read together with the sacred myth of the purple crest for the full religious symbolism to be clear.'

Hamkom was instantly dismissive of the myth. 'What religious symbolism? It sounds like a fairy tale, man!'

Surprisingly, Evening sided with him. 'Yeah, yeah, I don't see any religious symbolism at all!'

I told them not to jump to conclusions and continued with the second myth.

After the fall of Diengïei and the return of light, there was much rejoicing among earth's inhabitants: men, animals, birds and all other living creatures. To celebrate the event, man prepared a large dancing ground and sent word to all forms of life on earth about the dance festival he intended to organise. Heavenly beings like Sun and Moon were also included in his invitation.

On the day of the festival, all manner of beings from the four corners of the globe converged upon the dancing ground. They enjoyed the day's festivities as only they can who have lived with much suffering and no pleasure for a long time. Only Sun and Moon arrived at the scene towards the end of the celebration. Sun, on whose good offices depended the smooth running of everything else, could not leave her work untended without first setting things in order. Not to attend the festival altogether, however, would appear arrogant on her part. She thought, therefore, that putting in an appearance would at least be a show of goodwill. That was why she and her brother, Moon, went to the festival and danced on together even when the others had abandoned the arena and were engaged in other forms of pleasure.

But the spectacle of the two dancers created a tremendous uproar. The gathering, especially Owl, Mole, Frog and Monkey, began to ridicule and boo the latecomers:

'Look at those two clowns dancing alone on the empty ground!' Owl hooted.

Mole shouted, 'You insolent hypocrites! If you don't want to dance with us, why did you come at all?'

Frog croaked out, 'You are too early for the next festival!'

But what hurt the heavenly sister and brother the most was Monkey's nasty indictment: 'Hey, you two!' she shouted. 'Are you brother and sister or husband and wife? Look at them dancing so intimately together! Phooey, shameless creatures!'

The two could stand it no longer and left the field, vowing never to show their faces to the world again. Sun, the queen of the heavens, upon whom the universe hinged, felt especially stung by the unwarranted insults heaped upon her and her brother. 'You filthy, vicious creatures!' she raged. 'Is this how you treat your guests? Is this why you called us here, so you could humiliate us? In your beastly rudeness, you went so far as to accuse us of incest, you foul-tongued things! You will never see us in this dirty place again!'

Having hurled these words at the startled gathering, Sun went to hide in Krem Lamet Krem Latang, the cave of the sanctified leaf, situated somewhere beyond the valley of death on the way to the house of God.

From that day on, earth was thrown into perpetual darkness. Man was stupefied. To suffer another period of gloom and despair so soon after his last harrowing experience filled him with dread, and there was much fear, much shedding of tears among the other earthlings too. Everyone was filled with remorse, and they called to Sun and Moon, and prayed to them that they might return to lighten the days of the earth again. But all their cries and pleading were in vain. Sun and Moon would not forgive them so easily and refused to be drawn back into the world.

When the initial shock and confusion had subsided, man, who was more sensible than the rest, convened a council to choose someone from among them, someone with more than ordinary gumption and strength, to bring Sun back to their midst. The first choice was Elephant, the largest and strongest of them all. Elephant personified brute strength and reflected man's pride and his short-sightedness in believing that Sun, who signified heavenly light, could be intimidated by a show of force.

But Elephant quaked at the mere thought of confronting the might of heavenly powers. He said, 'Hear me, O man, my fellow creatures all, before you send me to my doom. I'm big and strong; there's no denying that. But going to the Krem Lamet Krem Latang cave, I will have to go across rivers and seas, bogs and fens, and while crossing them, I fear my hand or my foot may get stuck. Demons may devour me; I may fall into pits and gorges and finally perish without achieving the task you have seen fit to bestow upon me. Forgive me,' he said. 'Let me off this impossible assignment, and I promise to devote myself to serving the interests of the council in every other way.'

After Elephant spoke his mind, there was a sudden hush in the gathering. All of them seemed affected by the simple truth of what he had said; they bowed their heads and were silent.

Then Hornbill, cocksure and proud of his good looks and accomplishments, came forward and said, 'Listen to me, my friends, I will shoulder this responsibility. I will go to the Krem Lamet Krem Latang cave to fetch Sun and Moon. With me to plead for you, they won't be able to resist.'

When they heard this imperious utterance, everyone was relieved and happy that at least one among them dared to undertake the journey to the other world despite its dangers.

True to his words, Hornbill went to Sun's hiding place, where he presented himself as the ambassador of the world, there to discuss her return to earth. At first, Sun treated him with respect and warm hospitality, giving him shelter and food, as she would any honoured guest in her house. But presumptuous and vain as he was, Hornbill mistook her kindness to be a weakness for him, and began to court her, this ruler of the universe at whom no other creature would even have dared to look. Enraged, Sun snatched up a golden stool and threw it with all her might at his beak. 'You shameless creature!' she shouted, and cursed him. 'From now on, you will bear my golden stool wherever you go! You will be plagued with cough and asthma, and you will fly sideways, trying to avoid my golden rays throughout your life!'

Humiliated, Hornbill made his way back to earth. The councillors could hear him coughing and wheezing from far away. They were all curious and plied him with questions the moment he arrived. Embarrassed and feeling small, Hornbill recounted all that had happened to him—and from that day on, he could never look straight at the sun again.

Once more, there was crying and howling all over the land. And once more, the same question was raised: 'Who will bring Sun and Moon back to earth?' After what had happened to Hornbill, no one felt bold enough to offer their services. Seeing that nobody was coming forward, man enquired if anyone was missing from the council. Soon, they discovered that everyone was represented except for Rooster. It appeared that Rooster did not feel qualified to attend since he was a featherless creature hugging the weeds and bushes, too scared of the other animals to venture out. Someone added that he had not even attended the dance festival, at which the whole gathering erupted in an angry uproar. He had defied the entire council of creatures by ignoring an event it had organised. Rooster must be punished, they said, he must be sent to the Krem Lamet Krem Latang cave and be responsible for all the evils and wrongs in the world—in other words, he must bring back Sun and Moon to earth.

Man sent for Rooster, ordering him to attend the council. On his part, Rooster said, 'My Lord and fellow beings underneath the heavens, I'm prepared to go to the Krem Lamet Krem Latang cave and expose myself to all sorts of dangers for your sake. I am also prepared to lose my neck for your faults and failings. But who am I to stand before such royal beings as Sun and Moon? I am only a desperate featherless wretch lying low among small plants and dark holes. Now, if you can give me the forked and resplendent tail of Drongo, if you can cloak me from head to foot in finery and warm feathers bright with all sorts of brilliant colours, I promise to give up my very life, willingly, for the general good. And if you promise to acknowledge my deeds throughout my life, beyond my death, and to let me occupy a place of honour in all your rituals, I'm ready to go at once.'

The council gave him all he had asked for, and at the end, it placed a purple crest on his head to make him look even more like an emissary fit to meet the gods.

On his way to the Krem Lamet Krem Latang cave, Rooster met *Jri*, the rubber tree, whom he asked for shelter. Jri replied, 'Demons live on my branches. They will devour you if you stay the night here.'

Undaunted, Rooster replied, 'If you let me spend the night here, when I return, if I have managed to persuade Sun to relent, I will let you share in the role I will have in the solemn rituals of man.' Seeing that he was determined, Jri allowed him to sleep in a hole in the trunk.

The next night Rooster met *Sning*, the chestnut tree, whom he also asked for a place to sleep, promising to keep a role for him in the religious ceremonies before the altar, if he should return successfully from his mission. Rooster also offered the same thing to Lamet, the leaf, whom he met the following night.

After he had travelled for many days and survived much hardship on the way, Rooster finally reached Sun's retreat, beyond the valley of death. Sun needed only one look to see that Rooster was no randy young fool like Hornbill. She welcomed him gladly and treated him with great benevolence, giving him royal food and a royal bed for him to rest on. But in his humility, he asked only for the leftovers of winnowed rice, which he said he would eat in the courtyard in front of her door, adding that he was only a poor desperate being, not deserving of such good things and royal treatment.

Impressed, Sun said, 'Tell me, why did you come here?'

Rooster answered, 'My queen, O mother, the entire world was thrown into darkness when you left for this holy retreat. Man, animals and all other creatures live in great anxiety and dread. Unless you come back, there will be no peace on earth. Come back, O mother, and I will stand accountable for all the injustices and transgressions of man and his fellow creatures. It was their mistake not to think before they acted, not to limit their scorn to their own kind. But from now on, I will be answerable for all their wrongdoings, and I will see that no other outrage befalls you again. Before you peep into the world, I will shake my shield, and thrice will I sound my bugle as a sign that the world is fit for your divine blessing.

'Come, O mother,' he ended his plea, 'for I have traded my life to be an intercessor with God and his spirits; to be a redeemer of wrongs.'

Touched by the eloquence of one so simple and modest, Sun could not help but give him her assurance that she would return to earth and forgive the misdeeds of the earthlings for his sake. Before she sent him away, Sun bestowed upon him the right to be the Pioneer who would open the way, the Pleader before God, and the negotiator between all things earthly and heavenly.

Thus, Rooster returned to earth in triumph. In a thunderous reception, the victorious fowl was awarded the title of U Saw Shyrtong, The Purple Crest. But glory did not make Rooster forget that it was his humility, his self-abasement before the heavenly being that had carried the day. He remembered his pledge to Sun, and he shook his shield and sounded his bugle, thrice, at regular intervals. And then, like the lifting of a veil, darkness was removed, and light filtered into the world once more, filling it with the joy of living.

Man kept his promise to Rooster as well. To this day, he never begins a ritual or a thanksgiving without the sacrificial blood of Rooster placed before a piece of rubber tree, chestnut tree and lamet leaf, the three to whom Rooster had promised a share in the ceremonies.

When I came to the end of the tale, Hamkom pounced on me. 'They sound like stories for children, Ap, how can you claim these to be the foundations of your religious and philosophical thought?'

As before, Evening agreed wholeheartedly. 'Right, right, they don't amount to much, these stories of yours, Ap. I'm amazed that you should make all those tall claims.'

'That's because you have been listening to the narratives superficially and not thinking of their significance or symbolism,' I replied. 'I insist that like any other religious faith that is known to man, Ka Niam Khasi Niam Tre, the Khasi religion, is also founded upon ki khanatang, the sanctified stories, which constitute the creation myths of the community.'

'What do you mean by "any other religious faith"?' Evening broke in aggressively.

'Well, Hindus, for instance, have their sacred myths as outlined in their great epics, the Ramayana and the Mahabharata, which also contains the Bhagavad Gita. The Greeks have their mythology, which speaks of the genealogy of the gods and their heaven and hell and the underworld ruled by Hades. The Jews have their sacred myths written in their holy book, the Hebrew Bible, or the Tanakh. As you know, this book speaks of the creation of the world, the beginning of life and the history of the Jews. It is upon the Tanakh that Judaism is based, as also Christianity and Islam—'

'How can you compare the Jewish Bible, which is the foundation of the Old Testament, with your khanatangs?' Hamkom asked derisively.

'They are not my khanatangs. They are also yours. Keep in mind that the old Khasis, the Hynñiew Treps, were also your ancestors, unless you deny the fact that you are Khasi ... And why shouldn't I compare? Hindu mythology is sacred to Hindus; Greek mythology is sacred to Greeks; Jewish mythology is sacred to Jews, Christians and Muslims. In the same manner, Khasi mythology is sacred to Khasis. As simple as that.'

'Aw, come on!' Evening exclaimed as if he found the whole thing fantastic.

'What do you mean, "Aw, come on"?' Bah Kit demanded. 'Are you implying like Halolihim that our myths are merely "cock and bull"?'

Before it could get more acrimonious, I quickly said, 'Read Einstein's famous "Letter to God", and you'll know just what he thinks of Jewish mythology ...'

Apparently, no one had read Einstein's letter, but I told them to look it up themselves. 'My only purpose here,' I said, 'is to show you that every religion is based on its own sacred stories. Many of the teachings of Buddhism are based upon the sacred Jataka tales, dealing with the former lives of Buddha. Even the Quran is based upon the sacred revelations to the Prophet Muhammad by Jibril, the angel. All of these are khanatangs, stories sanctified by the very presence of the divine in them, or so each adherent believes. Therefore, remember this, if our khanatangs are cock and bull, then, by the same logic, every other is also cock and bull. But I don't want to quarrel with you or anybody else regarding something I really am not very enthusiastic about. If you don't want me to explain the symbolism of our sacred myths, then I won't. It's up to you.'

'Go on, man,' Bah Kynsai urged. 'What you are saying sounds logical enough.'

'Yeah, yeah, go on,' Magdalene added. 'If the Khasis consider their khanatangs to be sacred to them, who are you, Evening or Ham, to quarrel with that? You two are not even Khasi-Khasis, no?'

'You know, Bah Ap, a person should not ask questions as if he is interested and then quarrel with the answers because they don't suit him,' Donald said, taking me by surprise. 'That's not the attitude of a scholar. Go on, Bah Ap, you people have been speaking of our ancestors' enlightenment so much, I'd like to find out for myself how intellectually advanced they really were.'

Urged on by them, I took up the thread again. 'The great storytelling tradition of the Khasis goes back to the time of their creation myths. One of these myths, *Ka Khanatang jong ki Dak ba la Jah*, the sacred myth of the lost script, tells us about how one of our forefathers lost a manuscript, made of a very delicate material, which contained, among other things, our philosophical and religious teachings, as well as the script used to record these teachings. The man, known as Lyngkor the *Soh Blei*, literally, "fruit of God", had been sent by his people's elders to the summit of a very tall mountain to be in communion with God. On the mountain, he was familiarised with the history of his race and initiated into certain religious rites and moral principles, which were to govern the spiritual, moral and even daily activities of his community. With him was Qurban, a representative of the people from the plains of Surma—'

'Ha, hold on now!' Evening said. 'If the person from Surma was not a Khasi, why were they communing with the same God?'

'Yeah, yeah, explain that,' Hamkom added.

'Khasis believe that God is the same everywhere, for everyone. It's only the manner of worship that is different ... As I was saying, Lyngkor and Qurban received their divine instructions together, and after that, God himself gave them the precious manuscripts to make the propagation of his teachings easier—'

'Manuscripts?' Magdalene cut in. 'Were there two sets of them, Ap?'

'Yeah, each relating to the history, language and culture of a different people but always revolving around the one true God,' I replied. 'On the way home, they encountered a wide, raging river. The man from Surma, used to swimming in turbulent waters, attached his document to a tuft of hair on his head and swam across safely. The Khasi, not wanting to be left behind, took his document between his teeth and, against his better judgement, attempted to cross the river too. But being a hillman and not accustomed to swimming in surging torrents, Lyngkor soon found himself floundering midstream, with his head bobbing in and out of the water. In trying to save himself and gulping air through his mouth, he accidentally swallowed his document, which by then had been reduced to a pulpy mass. And although, after a huge struggle, he managed to save himself, he had to return to his people empty-handed ...'

'But people say that he swallowed the book, na, Ap, that's why, among us, we always talk about the lost book, na?' Bah Kynsai objected.

I said, 'Think about it, Bah Kynsai, can anyone swallow a book, however sodden it might have become? Besides, where would he get a book? The Chinese invented paper in 105 CE, and books became available to the public in Europe only in 1375 after the printing machines had been invented. One more thing you have to keep in mind: do not take the Khasi stories literally. If you do, you'll make the same mistake as Ham and Ning and see them as nothing more than fairy tales. When they say "The Khasi swallowed his script" or "his book", they only mean that knowledge and wisdom had become flesh and blood in him through the teachings and instructive stories orally passed on to him from generation to generation.'

'Ooh, like that, na, liah, go on, go on,' Bah Kynsai conceded.

'On reaching home,' I continued, 'the errant ambassador recounted everything that had happened to a very disappointed people. But he quickly appeased them by assuring them that all that God had revealed to him was still fresh in his mind and could easily be passed on by word of mouth. Consequently, a council of all the members of the Khasi tribe was convened, and each councillor was instructed in God's teachings and his divine laws.

'It was from this time that the Khasi tradition of storytelling is supposed to have started. The stories, as you have noticed, begin with an exposition of the creation of the world and how Man came down from heaven to become its caretaker. From there, they progress to the Khasi world view, our concept of God and religion, good and evil, our matrilineal social structure and clan system, our democratic governance, and so on. These constitute the creation myths, or what we call khanatangs, two of which I have already told you.'

'What about the others?' Donald asked.

'The others are not connected with our religious or philosophical thought; no point talking about them now. According to the sacred myths I've just related, Khasis believe that U Blei Nongbuh Nongthaw, God the Dispenser, the Creator, whose form we cannot even begin to imagine, for that is forbidden, creates everything. He creates man and animals and plants, the earth itself, land and sky and space ... everything. In this, the Khasis are like the Jews, but unlike them, we do not explain how God created man and the world, for that is the work of God, and man should never presume to have any knowledge of it.'

'That's a beautiful concept, Bah Ap,' Donald enthused.

'The stories simply say that God first created Ramew, the guardian spirit of the earth, and her husband, Basa, followed by their children, Sun, Moon, Wind, Water and Fire. Their combined efforts turned the planet into a pleasant and plenteous land, teeming with all sorts of living things. In this, the Khasi view is very close to that of science. The only difference is that Khasis also believe that even these elemental forces were created by God.

'Unlike the other theories of creation, Khasis believe that man was originally an inhabitant of heaven, living with all his kith and kin under the benign guidance of God and his serving spirits, sometimes referred to as the gods. His coming to earth was because of Ramew's pleading. Thus, besides telling us about the creation of the world and the beginning of life on earth, the first story also emphasises one crucial aspect of the Khasis' religious thinking—the concept of ïapan, or pleading.

'This concept points to the belief that man was sent by God to become the caretaker of the earth, and therefore, he cannot act as the master of everything he finds on it. God is the Dispenser and Creator; for that reason, man has to plead with him, to ask him for everything he needs, from the smallest to the biggest. This is crucial. The Jews, for instance, believe that God made man so that he might populate the earth with his countless hordes. "Go forth and multiply," he said. This assertion places man at the pinnacle of all creation. In other words, it argues that man is the master of the earth, while all other creatures are here to serve his needs and his goal, which is to multiply. This kind of anthropocentrism encourages man to indulge in all sorts of earth-wrecking activities in the name of progress and development. He tears down trees in the forest; he quarries the earth; he destroys hills and rivers, land and sea, earth and sky, and thus he places all species of living things, himself included, and the entire planet in terrible danger.

'But the old ones who formulated Khasi thought, in their compassionate wisdom, stressed on the fact that man was sent to earth by God, not to multiply himself, but to be the honourable carer that Ramew pleaded for. Khasis do not believe they are the crown of creation. To them, everything that breathes, and even those without life, like sand and stones, are equal creations of God. That is why the Khasi stories always begin with, "When man and beasts and stones and trees spoke as one". The universe is a cosmic whole that receives its animation and force from the one living truth—God, U Blei. Because of this, the old Khasis held nature in great esteem. They never indulged in acts of wanton destruction. When they went to the forest for tree-cutting or hunting, they bowed low and explained themselves; they prayed and appealed; they asked and pleaded before God.'

I could see everyone was impressed by this, even Hamkom, who said, 'This is what you were referring to in the jer khun story, no? But did they really do that, Ap? I never knew about these things, ya!'

'Not many do, Ham, not even the followers of Niam Khasi, except for people like Bah Kit and Bah Su.'

'So why don't you educate them, Bah Ap?' Donald asked.

'How will they educate anyone?' Raji answered for me. 'They have no churches or temples, no?'

'But you do meet once a week, na, Ap?' Bah Kynsai asked.

'Yes, Bah Kynsai, Seng Khasi has tried to organise instructional gatherings called seng pyni, once a week, but people don't often come. A few do, not many. Ours is not an organised religion, you see, it's a personal religion, a family religion, a clan religion: rules and conditions cannot be imposed on anyone. It's not only a free religion but a carefree one; anyone can do whatever he pleases. He is only supposed to follow *Ka Jutang Blei*, the Divine Covenant and its Three Commandments.'

'You mean the knowledge of man, the knowledge of God, the knowledge of one's maternal and paternal relations and the earning of virtue, Bah Ap?' Donald enquired.

'That's it, Don,' I agreed. 'In practice, of course, nobody follows anything except their selfish interests. And many are not even aware of the concept of pleading. That's why we destroy our hills, rivers and forests with all the living things in them without a care in the world. We have truly become the generation *kaba bam duh*, one that eats till extinction. Only if we remember this teaching and remind ourselves, again and again, that man was sent here by God to be the protector and not the destroyer of the earth, will we be moderate in all things and repay nature for everything that we take.'

'And how will we repay nature for what we take?' Magdalene asked sceptically.

'A tree, for instance, can be repaid with ten trees,' I replied. 'Birds, animals and fish can be saved by the processes of conservation, and nature itself can be made to recover from the onslaught of man in a variety of ways. But, admittedly, and sadly, there are many things that cannot be restored or redeemed … Another aspect of the concept of pleading reminds us of the position of God as *U Nongap Jutang Najrong*, the Keeper of the Covenant from Above, and man as *U Nongbud Jutang*, the Follower of the Covenant. When man follows the Divine Covenant, it means that he fully reposes his trust in God for his well-being on earth. But, for God to help him in any of his difficulties or hardships, man must plead with God; he must let God know so God may release him from all his sufferings. And if man is in need, he must plead with God and let him know so God may come to his aid. Not asking and not pleading means that man does not require the assistance of God, and therefore God may ignore him.'

'That's understandable,' Magdalene commented. 'We pray all the time, especially when we need something.'

'As seen from the first myth, man's descent to earth was not without foundation. Man reached an agreement with God through the Divine Covenant. If the children of Israel have their Ten Commandments, Khasis have their three, which are so far-reaching and profound that they embrace all aspects of life without exception. Now, many of us are aware of these divine laws, but very few of us have really tried to discover the amazing breadth and profundity of their thought. If we go back to the myth, this is what it says:

> God, who had provided for happiness on earth, endowing its soil with riches and the fruits of plenty through the children of Ramew, then made a Covenant with the Hynñiew Treps. As part of the Covenant, he gave them Lai Hukum, Three Commandments, including *ka tip briew tip Blei* (the knowledge of man, the knowledge of God), *ka tip kur tip kha* (the knowledge of one's maternal and paternal relations) and *ka kamai ïa ka hok* (the earning

of virtue). As a token of the Covenant, God also planted a divine tree on a sacred mount called Lum Sohpet Bneng, which served as Ka Jingkieng Ksiar, the golden ladder, between the kingdom of God and the kingdom of Man.

The Covenant declared that so long as the seven clans adhered to the Three Commandments, they could come and go as they pleased between heaven and earth, via the golden ladder at Lum Sohpet Bneng, the mountain of heaven's navel. The mountain would act as an umbilical cord between God and Man, for even as a child is bonded with the mother through this thread of flesh and blood, so also is Man bonded with God.

But though this description establishes the importance of the Three Commandments, it is hardly an explication …'

'Why do we need an explication?' Bah Kynsai asked. 'They are plain enough, na, even we Christians are using them every day.'

'That's what you think. But what are their true implications? Why is ka tip briew, the knowledge of man, placed before ka tip Blei, the knowledge of God? Now, Bah Kynsai, if you think you know everything, tell me, why this is the way it is?'

'Why? It's just an order of words, man! You could very well say ka tip Blei tip briew rather than ka tip briew tip Blei, na?'

'No, you cannot, Bah Kynsai. The Three Commandments are inviolable in their order,' I corrected him. 'And there is a very specific reason why.'

'Really?' Evening said in a disbelieving tone.

'In talking about the knowledge of man, Rabon Sing, one of the earliest commentators on Khasi religion, writes in his book, *Ka Kitab Niam Kheiñ*, that man was sent to this world in consonance with *Ka Hukum ka Kular,* the Commandment, the Pledge. According to this pledge, God wanted man to lead a happy and peaceful life on earth, in harmonious and respectful relations with his fellow men. The knowledge of man points to this stipulation. If man was sent to live on earth together with other men, what must he do to be happy and tranquil? How must he work and earn his livelihood? How will he be strong? How will he prosper? How can he organise his feasts and celebrate his festivals, if he cannot live in harmonious and respectful relations with other men? If he is dominated by the evils of greed and envy, his life will be full of squabbles and disputes, clashes and conflicts. And his way of life will not thrive, it will shrivel and decline, and the society as a whole will weaken and collapse. God is above, but his fellow man is on earth, and therefore the first duty of man is to know, to respect and love his fellow man. Only this can bind men together in a functioning society.

'In such a society, man must know both his rights and duties. That is what the knowledge of man teaches. If he's not aware of his rights, others will take advantage of him, and if he's not aware of his duties, he'll become an obstruction to everyone. To know only one of them is not enough. As an example, if one man plays music at home, that is his right as a citizen. But if he plays the music too loud and disturbs his neighbours, then he has violated the rights of others and disregarded his duties, one of which is to maintain harmony in society.

'But in its deepest connotation, the knowledge of man forms the basis of all human actions. It teaches man to be prudent and urges him to ponder his every move carefully. Will it bring him happiness and joy? Is it good? Will it hinder others in any way and become the cause of ill will and conflict? Is it something that he has to do, no matter what? He thinks these things through—both the task and its outcome—and only then takes a decision on whether to proceed.

'In this manner, a person guided by the knowledge of man is also guided by his conscience, which, by its very essence, weighs all things on the scales of virtue and truth. Therefore, a person blessed with conscience, or the knowledge of man, is also blessed with the knowledge of God, because God stands for virtue and truth. By placing the knowledge of man before the knowledge of God, the Khasi faith indicates two things. One, that man must serve God through service to his fellow man. In other words, service to man is service to God. Two, man must always be guided by his conscience.

'Many religions lay too much emphasis on the knowledge of God. If we take a careful look at what is happening around the world today, we can see how dangerous this kind of teaching can be. The relegation of respect for man to an insignificant corner has been the cause of many conflicts. This little story may serve as an illustration:

Once, in a small village, a religious function was organised in the courtyard of a certain household. As part of the function, many loudspeakers were attached to branches and poles, facing in several directions. So, when the worshippers began to pray and sing, they created a huge racket. As luck would have it, at that time, the children of one of their neighbours were preparing for their annual exams. To make matters worse, his mother, too, was chronically ill. When his children found it impossible to read in that din, and his mother couldn't rest or sleep, the man was left with no option but to approach the worshippers and request them to remove the loudspeakers so the noise was more bearable. But they, in their great love for the Lord, took umbrage and rose as one to bombard him with threats and intimidations, forcing him to flee and report the matter to the police.

When the offending family was later tried in a court of law, the entire village was torn apart, as the population divided itself into bitterly opposing factions. And since then, peace has never come back to that village.

'And so, the knowledge of God without the knowledge of man is indeed a dangerous thing. All the religious conflicts in the world, from the time of the Crusades in the thirteenth century to the present day, have come about because too much importance has been given to the knowledge of God. Such an emphasis without the knowledge of man turns everyone into religious addicts and ruthless fanatics, ready to kill and destroy for the sake of their religion.

'But the ancient Khasis had already seen the harm that fanaticism could breed. Not only that, through the sacred myth of the lost script, to which I referred earlier, they taught us that God, U Blei, is the same for everyone, no matter which ethnic or religious group we belong to. Only the manner of worship is different. The God of the Khasis is thus also the God of Hindus, Muslims, Buddhists, Jews and Christians. And if that is so, where is the feeling of rancour between communities?

'There is another example that further illustrates the principle of the knowledge of man:

Once upon a time, there was a rich man who lived in a beautiful mansion with a lovely garden. The garden was, in fact, the loveliest in the town and the proudest possession of the owner. Even the local priest could never walk past it without admiring its manicured lawn, its many flowering and fruit trees, and the flowers and shrubs beautifully trimmed in the shapes of birds and animals. At such times, he would call out to the rich man, 'Your garden is a thing of beauty. The Lord and you are partners!'

To this, the rich man would always respond with a bow. 'Thank you, sir, you are very kind.'

This exchange went on for days and weeks and months. At least twice a day, on his way to and from the temple, the priest would call out, 'The Lord and you are partners!' Gradually, however, what the priest had meant as a compliment began to annoy the rich man, and so, the next time the priest called out to him, he replied, 'That may be true. But you should have seen this garden when the Lord had it all to himself.'

'You see, the priest—'

Bah Kynsai did not allow me to complete the sentence. Hooting with delight, he said, 'That's true, man, when the Lord had it to himself, na, it must have been a thick and bushy jungle, liah!'

Laughing, I said, 'The priest had actually wanted to compliment the rich man. But the man was irritated because the priest had offered praise to God without giving due credit to his efforts, or to his investment of time, energy and money in transforming the garden into a thing of beauty. The knowledge of man demands that a person should know and perform all his duties as an individual and a social being. But the principle also demands that his fellow men should give him due acknowledgement for his efforts. It is through this kind of spirit that we can best honour God. The inability to acknowledge the work of a fellow man betrays an envious heart, and God does not appreciate such an attitude.

'There is one other implication of the First Commandment. To know man know God also means that man is forbidden to know or follow demons and false gods. This is very important because there are people, even to this day, who are suspected of sheltering demons and evil spirits such as U Thlen, Ka Shwar, Ka Taro, Ka Bih and so on. Is this superstition? Do such creatures exist? Be that as it may, in worshipping such false gods, a demonic spirit is understood to ride in man's heart.'

'My God, Bah Ap, this is unbelievably profound, ya!' Donald exclaimed. 'A very far cry indeed from children's stories. And I had thought—'

'Let him tell the whole thing first, na!' Bah Kynsai interrupted him.

'The Second Commandment, the knowledge of one's maternal and paternal relations, reinforces the knowledge of man. Man must not only love and respect his fellow man but must especially love and respect his maternal and paternal relations. This principle does not advocate insularity, even if it seems to do so at first glance. First of all, it teaches a person how the community organises its clan system and its cognate and agnate relationships. Let me read to you what an early commentator on Khasi religion, Sib Charan Roy, has to say in his book, *Ka Niam ki Khasi*:

> The Khasis determine their clans from the female line (although many of us prefer to say 'from the mother's line'). And these clan relations, however distant they might have become, if they share a common ancestress, called 'ka ïawbei', they would still be taken as their cognate relations or blood ties. Apart from one's own clan, every other person is '*u kha u man*', that is, someone fit for marriage according to the marriage laws.

'As he indicates, Khasis prefer to say they determine their clans from the "mother's line" and not the female's. That is because not all women can be mothers. Some women remain unmarried or, if married, cannot bear children, and therefore, cannot give their surname to anyone. Moreover, when a Khasi marries, he does not take the clan name of a woman but keeps his own, which he has inherited from his mother.'

'It's quite intricate, isn't it, Ap?' Magdalene asked, shaking her head. 'Nothing is as simple as it seems, man.'

Agreeing with her, I said, 'The love of one's cognate relations keeps the clan together, and in the end, also keeps society as a whole together. This, in turn, brings about social unity and the great strength that comes from it. For instance, Khasi clans never abandon any of their members when they fall on hard times. It is because of this commandment, I believe, that it is rare for a Khasi to be begging on the streets like the destitute of other communities.'

'Is that true or what?' Donald asked.

Raji flared up. 'Why? Don't you even know this much, cosmo? How many Khasi beggars have you seen in Shillong?'

'Nobody calls me that but Bah Kynsai! Say that again and I'll—'

'What the hell's wrong with you people?' Bah Kynsai snapped. 'Why are you always quarrelling? Raji, nobody but me calls Don a cosmo, you got it?'

Wanting to come to Donald's rescue and divert attention from the brewing quarrel, Magdalene asked, 'What about the blind beggar in Burra Bazaar?'

'Iewduh, you mean?' Raji asked pointedly. 'He's not a beggar, Mag. He sings and plays his duitara, in case you haven't noticed. That is work, not begging.'

'Raji is right, Mag,' I said, then went on with my explanation. 'To "know your maternal and paternal relations" does not only mean to know who your cognate or agnate relations are but also to have an understanding of the numerous ways by which Khasis determine their clan system, which include *shi kur* or *kheiñ kur*, *kam kur*, *iateh kur* and *ting kur*. When we say shi kur, or cognate kin, we mean that the relationship is an intimate one and that we are of the same blood, the same seed, or ancestor, and the same ancestress. Also, remember, a clan may be in cognate kinship with more than one other clan, as we have seen in the case of the Nongkynrih clan, which is in cognate relationship with clans like Lyngdoh Nongbri, Lyngdoh Kynshi, Shadap and Passah.

'But when we say kam kur, or professed kin, iateh kur, or kin by mutual agreement, and ting kur, or adopted kin, the implication is that we may not be of the same blood and may not share the same seed and the same ancestress. Kam kur and ïateh kur suggest a process whereby two or more clans decide to become cognate relations by mutual agreement, as we have seen in the case of the Kharakors and the Pyngropes.

'In ka ting kur, one clan is adopted by another as a cognate clan. But whatever the manner in which it comes to be, once a clan has become a cognate relation of another, marriage between their members is forbidden, since Khasis are exogamous. There must have been many reasons why the clans settled upon this arrangement, but today, these have become unclear. Perhaps an in-depth study of the histories of our clans may shed some light on the matter.

'The Second Commandment also tells us that a man must always have a deep and genuine respect for his cognate and agnate relationships, so he may not commit any sacrilegious acts. A man who cohabits with a woman of his clan is said to be *uba shong sang*, that is, one who is in an incestuous union, and must therefore be driven out of his home to live like an animal in the jungle. He is also cursed that his children may become lame, blind, mentally damaged, or disabled in one way or another. And yet, this is not only a curse meant to scare people; it is a statement borne out by science. Marriage between members of the same clan is an act of inbreeding that can lead to physical and health defects, including increased genetic disorders.

'The non-observance of the knowledge of maternal and paternal relations can cause numerous problems. This is why, traditionally, Khasis stipulated that a man attracted to a woman should first go through the various processes of courtship, which are solemn, dignified, clean and above board.

'The first thing that happens in traditional courtship rituals is *ka leit kai khynraw*, or the visit of a group of young men to the house of a girl that some of them, or all of them, wish to marry, as I told you earlier. The girl and her family, even as they participate in the proceedings, keep an eye out for the most suitable aspirant, watching the men's behaviour and studying their temperaments carefully. This can go on for quite some time, and when the girl finally picks a man of her choice, she tells her parents about him. If they too like him, the parents ask her to pass the betel nut around, beginning with her chosen one. The others take this as a hint and vanish from the scene the very next night.

'It is only after this thrilling and suspenseful drama has been played out that the parents take over, informing and consulting their relatives and appointing a *ksiang*, a go-between, almost always a maternal uncle, to discuss the matter with the ksiang of the man's clan. Such discussions necessarily involve enquiries about clan ties to ascertain that there is no obstruction of any sort and that the match isn't forbidden on either side. When this is complete, pre-nuptial ceremonies like *ka jingïateh ktien*, engagement, and *ka pynhiar synjat*, exchange of rings, are performed. The wedding itself takes place after the ksiangs on both sides have arranged all that is necessary. Now that this tradition is no longer followed, there has been a proliferation of the practice of cohabitation, which has caused so many complications in Khasi society.'

'That's very true, leh, Ap,' Evening interrupted. 'That's why, ha, my friends and I, ha, are launching a movement for the compulsory registration of marriage. Even live-in partners will have to marry and get themselves registered. That should end a lot of problems, no?'

Magdalene responded to this by saying, 'My wedding was conducted in the church and was duly registered afterwards, Evening, but that did not save me from a divorce ...'

Everybody laughed at that, and Hamkom gave Magdalene the thumbs-up sign. But after a while, Donald asked, 'Did everyone follow that kind of courtship in the past, Bah Ap?'

'Mostly, yes. Except for villages in some remote areas, which followed their own rituals. In some villages on the Assam border, for instance, boys and girls used to meet during the annual dance festivals and pair off to the nearby jungles. Once the deed was done, if they liked each other well enough, they would report the matter to their relatives, who would arrange for their marriage.'

'Really? Was there such a thing among us or what?' Magdalene asked.

'Yeah, yeah,' Raji confirmed. 'I have been to one of these festivals, but the pairing was strictly between locals.'

'Big loss, hahaha,' Bah Kynsai laughed.

'Hold on, hold on!' Magdalene cried. 'This is serious, ya! You said if they don't like each other, they don't report the matter and go their separate ways, no, Ap? But what if the girl becomes pregnant?'

'The child is accepted by the family as—'

'Collateral damage, hahaha,' Bah Kynsai laughed again.

Many of us joined in the laughter, but Magdalene, although laughing too, reprimanded Bah Kynsai. 'Tet, this Bah Kynsai! Be serious, man! Accepted as what, Ap?'

'As legitimate,' I replied. 'And no one is ever forced into a shotgun wedding because of it. There were also some villages in Ri Bhoi that followed a rather rare custom. Men did not visit the girl's house in a group there—they went alone. And to discourage all other suitors, the wooer used to hang his pants on the fence, by the gate.'

'What? What?' everyone cried in amazement.

'If he hung his pants on the fence, then how the hell did he go about? Naked?' Bah Kynsai demanded.

'He must have carried a spare,' I said. 'My sources are not very clear about this little detail.'

'And before pants became the fashion, what did they put on the fence?' Raji asked.

'Loincloths, what else?' Bah Kynsai answered for me and then added, 'Hey, Ap, what about divorce, man, in the past?'

'Divorce was quite difficult, or at least embarrassing, to both parties in the past. Nowadays, couples just move in and out of relationships as they please. But in the past, when couples could not live together any more— because of adultery, barrenness, incompatibility and so on—the matter had to be brought before their clans immediately. If the clans failed to bring about a rapprochement and felt that the two had to separate, the village council would be approached to conduct the divorce ceremony.

'The ceremony always took place at a full sitting of the council comprising all eligible male members of the village. After the preliminary hearing had been conducted—involving speeches by the headman, his officials, the couples and their clan representatives—the ceremony itself would begin, with the wife giving her husband five coins. The husband would add five more coins to his wife's and then return them to her. The wife checked the amount and returned the coins to her husband, who, on being asked by the headman, threw all of them to the ground. This was a sign that their life together as man and wife had ended. After that, the headman announced that such-and-such woman and such-and-such man had officially divorced.

'Later at night, a *sangot*, the village crier, would relay the news from every vantage point of the village. I remember listening to him when one of my relatives divorced his wife. He began by shouting, "Hoooi shnong [village]! Hoooi thaw [community]! This announcement is ordered by the headman and the dorbar, that everyone should know, that everyone should be aware, that from this day forth, U Siew Manik and Ka Sukmon have been officially separated in front of the dorbar. Therefore, from this day forth, may you know, may you be aware that U Siew Manik and Ka Sukmon are free and single again ... Anyone who wishes may now approach them to woo and court for love and marriage without let or hindrance. It is so sanctioned by the dorbar. Hoooi shnong! Hoooi thaw! This is so announced!'"

'Wa! Beautiful, beautiful!' Donald enthused.

Bah Su said to me, 'What were the exact words that he used for divorce?'

'He said U Siew Manik and Ka Sukmon had completed the *pyllait san shyieng* ceremony ...'

'Why, why would he use those words?' Hamkom asked.

'"Pyllait san shyieng" means, literally, "to free with five bones". Originally, the ceremony was conducted with five little bone pieces, hence the expression. Later, the bones were replaced by cowrie shells and then by coins.'

'But why do people also say, "give me back my *pisa saw*" when they want a divorce?' Raji asked.

'That expression was thought up when coins came to replace bones and cowrie shells. In those days, coins were made from bronze, hence "pisa saw", literally, "red coins".'

'Fascinating, fascinating!' Bah Kynsai declared. 'Even I was not aware of all these rituals, man. But what happened to the children?'

'In most cases, they were looked after by the mother and her clan. There were also instances of children being looked after by the father. That normally happened when the children themselves chose to live with their father.'

When all the questions had been asked and answered, I continued with my analysis of the Second Commandment. 'The Khasi instruction on courtship and marriage is clear: every person should be guided by his conscience, and must be absolutely sure about whom he can marry and whom he cannot. He has to learn all he can about the various ways by which the community determines its ties of kinship and organises its clan system. The cognate clan is entirely out of bounds. But when it comes to the agnate clan or paternal relations, he will have to know who the paternal grandmothers and who the paternal aunts are, with whom he cannot marry under any circumstances, and who the agnate cousins are, with whom he can marry under certain circumstances. Agnate cousins, as you know, are the children of sisters and brothers in a family. But—'

'Who the hell would marry their paternal grandmothers and aunts, man?' Bah Kynsai asked sarcastically.

'Have you forgotten what I told you, Bah Kynsai? Klol's wife, my aunt, is one year younger than me, remember? These things happen. Anyway, as I was saying, though agnate cousins are also known as *bakha sang salit*, forbidden only a little, one has to bear in mind that such a union is not encouraged, especially if the uncle is still alive. For example, if a man marries the daughter of his maternal uncle while the uncle is still alive, that would shame (*pynïamrem*) the uncle, weaken the essence of his personality (*pynjem rngiew*) and compromise his role as the minder of his family and his clan. But when the uncle is no more, such a union, though not the most desirable, is not frowned upon.'

'What about marriage between the children of brothers, Ap? They are also agnate cousins, no?' Ham asked.

'Not really. They are known as *para kha*, siblings of the same birth-giver, and hence a no-no. There is also the saying, *Ym bit ban leit ai khaw kylliang*, literally, it is forbidden to exchange rice. This means that if A marries into family B, no one from family B can marry into A's family. Such marriages create confusion in marital relations and are not encouraged. It is because of this that they say a person must always be guided by the knowledge of man when it comes to marriage, so that he will never be led into something taboo and sacrilegious.'

'This is the first time I have heard of terms like "bakha sang salit" and "Ym bit ban leit ai khaw kylliang", Bah Ap,' Donald said. 'It's incredible the things I don't know about my people, ya.'

'Now you admit it!' Raji said.

'It's not too late to learn, na?' Bah Kynsai said, defending Donald.

'Yeah, Don,' I agreed. 'You only need to be interested. You may not care about identity, and you may think that you can get by without any knowledge of your past and culture, but where's the harm in knowing? After all, aren't you a scholar?'

I knew, of course, that once he became interested in his culture, he would also be interested in the question of identity. And I was not disappointed when he replied, 'I have learnt quite a lot already, Bah Ap.'

'There's more, there's more,' I assured him. 'With Mag to help you, you'll be a new man very soon.'

Magdalene pretended to be very angry and said, 'Ap, you bastard!'

I laughed and continued with my analysis. 'When we come to the Third Commandment, the earning of virtue, we will have to go back to what was said earlier about the knowledge of man and God. In the old days, Khasis used to say, *tip hok, tip sot*—know your virtue, know your truth—in other words, earn virtue by leading a good, clean and simple life founded on innocence and truth. And this virtuous life must be good not only for oneself but also for others.

'There is another old Khasi saying, "Do not earn only wealth", for that can only lead to avarice and vice. Thus, to earn virtue also means to avoid doing all things considered criminal or immoral. Not only murder and violence, which are the worst of the worst, but also all acts of transgression that may emanate from a wicked heart or negative qualities like hatred, anger, envy, avarice, lust, selfishness, indolence and so on. By such acts, human relationships may be spoiled, harmonious living may be disrupted, and the very fabric of society may be destroyed.

'This commandment also reveals a profound truth about human nature. We have to ask ourselves why the old Khasis did not say, "live virtuously", but said instead, "earn virtue". The word "earn" indicates that any reward a man may receive is only won after he has worked hard for it, as just recompense. He has to apply himself and toil persistently in order to win a life of virtue. This, in turn, demonstrates the Khasi belief that human nature is not essentially full of virtue. In the heart of man, there are many things good and virtuous, but also many things ugly and bad. And these harmful qualities are always straining to smother and overwhelm whatever is good and virtuous, even as it tries to raise itself aloft.

'This struggle takes place every day in a person's life and reveals itself in everything that he does, but especially in the many temptations to do wrong for the sake of profit and self-promotion. At the same time, virtue, through the operation of conscience, tries to ward off these influences and lead him on to the right path. Thus, the principle of earning virtue implies that there is a hard struggle to be fought daily, and when a person has won such a victory, it may be said that he has truly earned his virtue.'

'Very sophisticated, very sophisticated indeed, Bah Ap,' Donald exclaimed. 'How could those guys, without the benefit of formal education, have thought of something so intricate? Wonderful, wonderful!'

'*Kamai ïa ka hok*, earn virtue,' Magdalene said pensively. 'I have always wondered about that, you know, now it's very clear to me, Ap. Thumbs up, man.'

'Well, make sure you earn it,' Bah Kynsai teased her. 'As far as I can see, you have earned only Donald.'

Magdalene threw a handful of straw at Bah Kynsai and said, 'So what, are you jealous?'

Donald, who was sitting close to Magdalene, put his arm around her shoulder and pulled her towards him. Seeing that, Bah Kynsai teased them again. 'Hey, hey, no fondling in front of us!'

When things had quietened down, I said, 'So, essentially, the Three Commandments go hand-in-hand and complement each other, much in the manner of *ki mawbyrsiew*, the three hearthstones, found in traditional Khasi homes. They stand for the three foundations of social life comprising the family, the clan and the community, which always manifest in the persons of the first ancestress of a clan (ka ïawbei), the first ancestor (u thawlang) and the first maternal uncle (u suidñia). There can be no family or clan without these three initiators, and it is because of this that the Khasis used to construct their hearths by planting three rectangular stones in a kind of triangle, as a symbolic reminder. The Three Commandments are exactly like these hearthstones: if one of them is absent, life loses its foundation, its balance, and collapses like a rice pot that cannot be kept upright on only two hearthstones—'

'Nice comparison, but you need to clarify, na?' Bah Kynsai said.

I nodded. 'The knowledge of man always leads to the knowledge of God, or the path of truth, and keeps a person away from all that is evil and sacrilegious. It is in this way that he earns virtue, and his reward is a happy and peaceful life on earth, and heaven when he dies.

'The saying, *Leit bam kwai ha ïing U Blei*, gone to have betel nut in the house of God, which we discussed earlier, points to the Khasi belief that the original home of man is in heaven. When he dies, if he has earned virtue in life, his soul will go straight to heaven, to live there forever, with all his cognate and agnate relatives who died before him. Also waiting for him in heaven will be those kinsfolk known as Ki Khyndai Trep, literally, "the nine huts" or Ki Khyndai Hajrong, "the nine sub-tribes above".

'The story of the Khyndai Treps, as I said earlier, has at least two meanings. One refers to the people from whom the Khasis descended and from whom they parted thousands of years ago. This is an aspect of Khasi history that needs to be researched urgently, for any discovery made about the Khyndai Treps may also lead to a discovery of our own origins. The other meaning, more spiritual than historical, has to do with the Khasi conviction that heaven is not an empty place or one where only God and the spirits who serve him live. The Khathynriew Treps (the sixteen huts, or the sixteen sub-tribes), who were part of the Hynñiew Treps, forefathers of the Khasi people, were believed to be its original inhabitants. This suggests that man is the son of God, still carrying with him the divine spark, and therefore, when he departs from this world, if he has earned virtue, he will return to the house of God, his original home.

'But what happens to a man who has not earned virtue? Many of us, confused by the teachings of so many religions, have come to believe that such a man will be damned in hell. But the Khasi universe is not three-tiered. There are only heaven and earth.'

'Are you crazy, Ap?' Bah Kynsai said angrily. 'Whoever told you we don't have any concept of hell? What about all those Khasi words signifying hell, huh?'

'Yeah, Bah Kynsai, I have never heard of such a thing, ya!' Hamkom said incredulously. 'By whose authority are you declaring this?'

'By the authority of being Ap Jutang Shadap, who, as these gentlemen here,' I pointed to Raji, Bah Kit and Bah Su, 'will tell you, has written extensively about Khasi religion.'

'No, no, no, no, Ap, this time you are very wrong!' Evening declared. 'We have many words for hell, man—*dujok, nurok ka ksew, myngkoi u Jom* and others too!'

Magdalene added, 'You know, Ap, I wish we did not have hell, ya, but unfortunately, we do, so don't say that we don't.'

A bit fed up with their ignorance, I said, 'Remember that we are talking about my religion. I would never presume to know better than you about the Presbyterian church or the Catholic church, and so, you too should not presume to know better than me about—'

'The Khasi Church,' Magdalene concluded for me.

Bah Kit took that seriously and said, 'We don't have any church, remember?'

'I'm joking, Bah Kit!'

'It's true that you people are obsessed with the idea of hell,' I continued. 'But Khasi-Khasis do not believe in it. It's simply not there in our religion. However, I don't blame you at all, for many of us do not know this either—'

'Explain yourself, na?' Bah Kynsai interrupted. 'You cannot say the idea of hell is simply not there without explaining, na? What about dujok, nurok, et cetera?'

'As Ning said, we do have words like dujok, nurok and myngkoi u Jom, which signify hell to us, and these were already in existence before the Welsh missionaries arrived here. However, these words have nothing to do with Khasi religious thought. Two of them, dujok or *dozakh* and nurok or *narak*, were borrowed from Persian and Hindi, and the last one, myngkoi u Jom, is from Hindu mythology; it points to the abode of Yama or Yamraj, the Hindu god of death. Later, another name for hell was added to the Khasi language—*ki khyndai pateng ñiamra*, the nine storeys of hell. Again, this was borrowed from the Greek description of Hades and the nine storeys of its subterranean world.'

'The son of a gun is right, ya, Ning!' Bah Kynsai exclaimed. 'I remember discussing the etymology of these words with some Khasi scholars, ha, they also said the same thing. Yeah, yeah, now I remember.'

But Evening was not satisfied. 'So what happens to sinners?' he demanded.

'Remember this, Ning: we do not believe in the Christian concept of the original sin. Usually, we do not speak of sinners. However, we believe that a person who has not earned virtue and who has committed *ka sih ka sang*, that which is evil or sacrilegious, will be punished by being denied entry into the house of God when he dies. His *mynsiem*, or soul, and his rngiew, or essence, will be confined to earth to roam the wilderness as a *snaïap*, a ghost or a demon. But this punishment may not be permanent, for even such a one as he may be forgiven if his relatives—haunted by his spirit complaining about its fate—perform certain rites, pleading with God for mercy.'

'But why are Khasis talking about both soul and essence, Bah Ap?' Donald asked. 'Shouldn't the soul be enough?'

'"Ka mynsiem" is the soul, Don, which, as you know, is the spiritual or immaterial part of a human, regarded as immortal. But rngiew is the essence of his personality. Without it, Khasis believe that man will lose his earthly physical appearance, and therefore his identity, when he goes to heaven. Hence, both mynsiem and rngiew must ascend together to the house of God. Rngiew, you may say, is the image of the soul.'

'Whew! All of this is new to me, ya, Ap,' Hamkom admitted in an embarrassed tone. Evening, however, made no comment.

'Of course! You are not from Niam Khasi, are you? Now, if we turn again to the knowledge of man, the knowledge of God and the earning of virtue, we often hear the complaint that Khasis follow these commandments too assiduously and therefore have become timid and cowardly. Others wonder how these principles can be reconciled with the wars and conflicts that the Khasis fought in the past, among themselves and against their neighbours.

'In answer to this, it must be first observed that our forefathers were never tentative or weak, although they were firm believers in their faith. Indeed, they pondered and mulled things over carefully before embarking upon anything serious, and in doing that, they always founded their arguments upon virtue and truth. If, for instance, there were forces that threatened their peaceful existence and terrorised their lives, they raised questions, they conferred, they bowed low before God: was it just that the enemy had come and terrorised their settlements in this manner? What were their own acts of omission and commission? Had they done anything forbidden or dangerous which instigated the enemy in that way? Was it just for them to defend themselves? Should they sue for peace or should they fight against the aggressor? If they understood that justice and truth were with them, they did not waver and faced the enemy resolutely. Everything depends upon the justness of things. It is this that brings about victory and defeat. Thus, even war is but a matter to be thought through with the guiding spirit of the Three Commandments.'

'Bong leh,' Bah Kynsai swore, 'and I thought I knew everything about the commandments, man!'

'Yeah, I also thought the same,' Hamkom agreed. 'My God, man, there's so much more to them than just three dictums, no? How do you get so much out of them, Ap?'

'Because I'm a thinker,' I said with a laugh. 'But seriously, you'd be surprised by the things you can discover through reading and discussions with the right people.'

'But this is not all there is, is it, Ap?' Magdalene asked.

'No, this is just about the parable of the Three Commandments. I dwelt on them in detail because they are the most important in Khasi religious thought. They are so influential that all Khasis use them, regardless of their religion—'

'Yeah, yeah, we also use them all the time,' Raji agreed.

'But,' I continued, 'it is also imperative that we understand the symbolism of the three parables, "The Golden Ladder", "The Tree of Gloom" and "The Purple Crest", because they deal with man's relationship with God. In the first of these myths, greed, the mother of all evils, sat supreme in man's heart, and in his craving for power and pelf, he trampled upon all, regardless of their rights. And so, God broke off his ties with man and forever closed the golden ladder to heaven through Sohpet Bneng, and made Diengïei eclipse parts of the earth in pitch darkness.

'First of all, the myth demonstrates that the relationship between man and God in the *Sotti Juk*, the Golden Age, was very close indeed. This closeness can be seen in the form of the golden ladder and Sohpet Bneng, the mountain of heaven's navel, which were like the umbilical cord linking heaven and earth, God and man, even as a child is linked with the mother—through this thread of flesh and blood, pure as gold and silver. But for the heart of man to be like the golden ladder, it has to be clean and chaste, without any blemish whatsoever. It is only with this kind of heart, full of virtue and truth, that man can be close to God, even as a child is to his mother.

'This closeness between man and God, which had enabled man to move freely between heaven and earth, shrank with the passing of time because of the evil among men, leading, finally, to the severing of the golden ladder and the cessation of all communication between man and God. Reduced to helpless orphans on earth, cut off from the nine sub-tribes in heaven, and bereft of God's guidance and blessing, the Hynñiew Treps lived in a kind of spiritual darkness—symbolised by the abnormal growth of Diengïei, the tree of gloom.

'When man grew tired of this blind groping, he began searching for light and spiritual guidance, using his own knowledge and intelligence. But not once did he look into his heart to try and understand the darkness that enveloped his life, or the many problems that beset him. Not once did he consider his own acts of omission and commission, and not realising his own transgression, not once did he repent, and not once did he bow low before God. Therefore, the gloom of Diengïei was, in reality, the darkness that rose from man's heart to spread through the world, eclipsing it entirely with its impenetrable shade. So, how can man topple the tree of gloom when the darkness has risen from his own heart? The part of man's soul that was good wanted to remove the darkness and the spreading evil, but that part which was wicked resisted all attempts to do so. The Tiger stood for whatever was evil in man, and his attempt to stop the felling of Diengïei was actually the conflict between the forces of good and evil in man's soul.

'Finally, victory came when man became desperate enough to listen to Phreit—a small brown bird, among the smallest of the small. Now at his wit's end, he was prepared to listen even to this insignificant creature. This indicated the first tentative rise of the humble spirit in his heart, and it was because of this that God allowed him to bring down Diengïei, whose fall symbolised the triumph of good over evil. The return of light to the world can be seen as the return of virtue and happiness.

'But darkness and evil had not been wholly eradicated from man's heart. This could be seen in the contemptuous treatment of Sun and Moon. Man had already forgotten that he had won the battle against the tree of gloom through his humility. In his increasing arrogance, he thought he was the equal of the serving spirits of God. This led him to commit contemptuous and sacrilegious acts and transformed him into a cruel tyrant. And it was from his tyrannical heart that evil began to spread once more. The fleeing of

Sun and Moon, who symbolised the light of God, signified that darkness had once again overwhelmed man's heart. It was from there that it spread to the world at large.

'In his arrogance, man tried to make Sun return to earth through a show of strength, symbolised by Elephant. But even when Elephant pointed out his own weakness and shortcomings, man still did not understand. In his impudence, he tried to hoodwink Sun by sending the brash and arrogant Hornbill. It was only after Hornbill had been punished for his presumptuousness and shameless indecency that man began to realise that divine blessing could be won neither by brute force nor by presumptuous cunning. With this realisation, he bowed low and performed the ceremony of *ka nguh dem*, obsecration, to appeal and plead before God with a humble heart. This is what the parable of the purple crest symbolises.

'In this parable, two things are demonstrated. The first is that, though man has fallen into evil and committed foul deeds and acts of sacrilege, he may yet win God's forgiveness if he seeks it sincerely. The second is that, though man's relationship with God is no longer as close as it was during the Golden Age, he can still win God's guidance if he turns to him with a truly humble heart. If man can prove that his love for God is genuine, and if he bows low before him to appeal and plead for all his needs with a self-effacing heart, he may yet win divine grace.

'Humility requires the absence of arrogance and vanity, the absence of pretentiousness or a know-it-all and have-it-all attitude. Love for God denotes not only love for whatever is virtuous and truthful in life but also an absence of qualities that are vicious and destructive. Such a heart is *ka mynsiem ksiar ka mynsiem rupa*, pure as gold or silver. And it is only with this kind of heart that man can approach God to plead for forgiveness.

'The sacred myth of the purple crest clearly indicates that Rooster is only a metaphor for humility, self-effacement, selflessness and self-denial. Khasis have never worshipped the rooster. When people like Halolihim make that allegation, it only exposes their obtuseness and ignorance. To serve as a reminder that the rooster is not an object of worship but only revered as a metaphor for the best qualities in the human heart, Khasis cook his flesh when the sacrifice is complete and make a feast of it. This is why chicken is a must-have on the menu on any festive occasion. This was also what the sixteen Khasi men who founded Seng Khasi had in mind when they adopted the form of a green rooster as the symbol of the Khasi religion.'

'When was it founded?' Mag asked.

'Seng Khasi was founded on 23 November 1899, Mag, to counter the influence of the Welsh missionaries—'

'But, Ap,' Hamkom broke in, 'the roosters that I saw on the flags of Seng Khasi have many different colours, no?'

'Not the flags of Seng Khasi as an organisation, Ham, but the flags of individual believers. And that's because they are as ignorant as you are about the metaphorical significance of Rooster.'

'Do you mean to say that there are people who practise the Khasi religion without knowing anything about it?' Magdalene asked in a somewhat amused tone.

'Unfortunately, yes, but then, how many people really know about their religion? For that matter, how intimately do you know the Bible, Mag?'

Mag laughed and admitted, 'Yeah, yeah, I get your point.'

'But why a green rooster?' Bah Kynsai demanded.

'An all-green rooster does not exist in the real world. It is an attempt to remind all believers that Niam Khasi has nothing to do with real chickens, that Rooster is only a symbol of humility, self-effacement, selflessness and self-denial, which are the attributes of *ka mynsiem ksiar*, the golden heart, the golden ladder that links heaven with earth, man with God.'

'I must say that it does sound quite sophisticated, Ap,' Hamkom admitted at last.

'As sophisticated as anything I have heard,' Donald added, 'and philosophical too. I don't think it's inferior to any other religion that I have read about. Bah Ap is right in comparing it with the others. And there are also many attractive features in it. I like the part about the knowledge of man coming before the knowledge of God, okay, and also the fact that the religion completely lacks any missionary tendencies. The world, as I see it, is too divided by religions trying their best to get people to convert.'

'I like the fact that there's no hell,' Magdalene added. 'A transgressor, as I understand it, will eventually get to heaven once his relatives have completed the necessary rites. But even if he gets stuck on earth as a ghost or a demon, that's not too bad, no?'

Magdalene's comments produced some laughter and prompted Bah Kynsai to say, 'Mag must be thick with sins to fear hell so much, hahaha … But personally, na, Mag, I like its freedom. It doesn't have any dos and don'ts except for the Three Commandments, but even these are mostly an appeal to our conscience. I like the idea of a religion that makes our conscience the guiding principle of life. Other religions, na, they say, don't do this and don't do that, and if you do, they excommunicate you, liah! This can lead to religious tyranny, na?'

Evening, who had been silent for some time, spoke up. 'Ap, you claimed that Niam Khasi doesn't have any missionary zeal, ha, and that it does not believe in preaching, ha, but it seems to me that you have been trying to convert us ...'

'Convert you to what? We don't even have a church or a place of worship, man! Our worship takes place in our homes, in our hearts. It's very personal, like a one-on-one between you and your Maker. As I told you, it's originally a personal religion, a family religion, and at the most, a clan religion. It's very mystical in that sense: an individual trying to reach out to God in his own way and through his own prayers, although there are shamans, faith healers and ki nongduwai, the praying elders, to help you. Nothing is compulsory. And remember, it was you people who requested me to talk about it in the first place. All I want is for my fellow Khasis to learn about their religion so they may understand it, and understanding it, they may learn to respect it. The main cause of tension between Khasi Christians and non-Christians is that too many people are like Halolihim. That kind of scorn needs to be replaced by mutual respect, otherwise, one day our community will splinter.'

'That reminds me, Ap ... you haven't answered my question about why you also pray to your ancestors and the gods, man,' Hamkom said.

'Ah, yes,' I responded. 'Let me tell you about the Khasi concept of God and the spirit world. God, of course, is one—a divine Being whose form and appearance we cannot even begin to imagine. We can see and understand him only in our hearts. God only appears before us in three ways: through his power, through virtue, and through the word that he speaks. Firstly, he appears through his power in the creations that we see around us in nature, the world and the universe; secondly, through virtue, which alone is the guiding principle and sustaining force of all life; thirdly, through the word, that is, the signs and tokens in which he speaks to man from time to time.'

'But why do you also refer to ki blei, the gods?' Hamkom asked.

'Patience, Ham, patience. God is one, but he is also many. That is because he is everywhere and fills heaven and earth with his presence. And that is also why he is sometimes referred to in the plural as "ki blei". He is above gender and number, and because of that, he can be addressed by many names.

'He is U Blei Trai Kynrad, God Lord and Master. He is U Nongbuh Nongthaw, the Dispenser, the Creator, because before he creates, he allocates the portion, or the place, or the role for each creation in the universe. He is U Nongsei Nongpynlong, the Reviver, the Birth-giver, because his life-giving force is continuous. Sometimes he can even be addressed in the feminine as Ka Lei Hukum, the Goddess of Divine Law, or Ka Mei Hukum, the Mother of Divine Law, or simply as Ka Hukum, the Divine Law, because of his quality as the Law, the Decree that governs life. He is U Leilongspah, God the Giver of Wealth, because the observance of his laws, which are based on the guiding and sustaining principle of virtue, brings prosperity in life. He is the feminine Ka Leilongkur, God the Birth-giver of the Clan, because when he sends man to earth, he also gives him full knowledge of the clan and how it is organised. He is U Leimuluk U Leijaka, U Leikhyrdop U Leikharai—names connected with his role as the protector of the village, the land, the gateway and the fortified trenches. In this way, all the names used to address him indicate his various qualities and manifestations, and his different relationships with man. But essentially he is one, and you cannot worship many gods because there is only one.'

'What about the spirit world?' Hamkom asked.

'The spirit world of the Khasis is a three-tier system. At the head of it is U Blei Nongbuh Nongthaw, God the Dispenser, the Creator, presiding in heaven with all the spirits and men and women, who are not merely people departed from this world but also those who belong originally to heaven as Ki Khyndai Hajrong. Below God, there are the spirits, ki blei, the gods, created by God and serving him as his representatives on earth. According to our sacred myths, the first spirits to be created were Ramew, the guardian spirit of the earth, and Basa, the guardian spirit of villages and the wilderness. Then came their children: Sun, Moon, Wind, Water and Fire. They are also addressed as Mei Ngi (Mother Sun), U Ñi Nai (Uncle Moon), Ka Syiem Lyer (Queen Wind), Ka Syiem Um (Queen Water) and Ka Syiem Ding (Queen Fire).

'Besides these, there are spirits like U Lei Shulong (the guardian spirit of the traditional state of Shyllong), U Suidnoh (the god of health), U Mawlong Syiem (the guardian spirit of the traditional state of Sohra), U Lei Synteng (the guardian spirit of Ri Pnar), U Kyllang, U Symper (mountain spirits), and ka ïawbei, u thawlang and u suidñia, the first ancestors of a clan, as you know already, and many others. Being God's representatives, these spirits are often prayed to by people, but only so that they may intervene with God, U Blei, on their behalf.'

'There are people who pray to Hindu gods also, Ap,' Raji reminded me.

'There are. These are the people who have been influenced by Hinduism, introduced, as you know, by the Brahmins of Jaiñtiapur, and they sometimes call upon Hindu deities like Lakshmi, Durga, Vishwakarma and others to plead for them before God. But these have nothing to do with our religion. Niam Khasi is monotheistic. The all-important being is God, U Blei, and the all-important precepts are the Three Commandments that constitute the Covenant reached between him and man. Everything else is peripheral. Ordinary Khasis do not normally pray to the serving spirits, only to God. The spirits are mostly called upon by shamans, faith healers and praying elders during their rituals and sacrifices. But sacrifices to the first ancestors and the other spirits cannot be made without first seeking the consent of God. So, you see, Ham, we do not worship ancestors or gods; we may call upon them to plead with God on our behalf, but we do not actually worship them.'

'Okay, you have God and the serving spirits, that's two tiers, what about the third?' Hamkom asked.

'The last tier is occupied by the lesser spirits called *ki puri*, the fairies. Among these again, there are two categories: the fair-skinned *purilieh* or *puriblei*, godly fairies, and the dark-skinned *puriiong* or *puriksuid*, evil fairies. The evil fairies are also simply called *ki ksuid*, or demons, who are again of diverse types and hierarchies.'

'Do you have names for these demons, Ap?' Magdalene asked. 'I mean, I have heard people talking about them, but always in general terms.'

'The queen of these demons is known as Ka Tyrut. When anyone dies in the wilderness from accidents or acts of violence, his soul is said to become a demon. Ka Tyrut takes charge of this demon, and asks him to stalk the place of his death and moan for more victims so that more souls can come under her control. Such a place is said to be *kaba shong Tyrut*, haunted by Ka Tyrut. That is why certain rites have to be performed by the dead person's relatives to cleanse the place and liberate his soul from the clutches of Ka Tyrut. This practice is followed till today, even by people who no longer belong to the Khasi religion.'

'Is that right?' Donald asked in a tone of wonder.

'Yeah, yeah, very much so,' Raji confirmed. 'Just the other day, okay, some people, not Khasi-Khasis, asked a Khasi shaman to perform such rites near Lyngkyrdem where two of their relatives had died in a car crash.'

'Tyrut,' I continued, 'doesn't have any power over the souls of people who die a natural death, nor does she have any influence over the godly fairies. But she has complete control over all the hill, river and sky demons.

Foremost among these are U Rih in Ri Bhoi, who spreads malaria among human settlements; Ka Ñiangriang, a water demon who fills people's ears with pus, making them deaf; and U Trang U Rwaibah, a sky demon who causes all types of headaches. Others include imps like ki Diaw and ki Boit and demons like Ka Thapbalong, U Kyrtep, U Moïong, U Tynjang and U Jynriew, all of whom can cause different types of illnesses.'

'What about Thlen? Have you forgotten about Thlen?' Bah Kynsai asked.

I raised my right hand, asking him to wait, and said, 'Besides these, there are also spirits that some people are accused of worshipping like household gods. The best known among them are Ka Leikhuri, who protects the house from thieves and robbers; Ka Taro, who punishes people that borrow money from her keepers without returning it, or even those who accept money from them as a gift; Ka Lasam, who causes toothache; and Ka Sabuit, who causes stomach ache in people whom their keepers hate; Ka Shwar, a terrible demon who twists the necks of people that displease her keepers in some way; Ka Bih, a demon who increases her keepers' wealth if they can poison the food that people eat. But the most terrible of them all is U Thlen, who demands that his keepers feed him with human blood. Thlen has an interesting origin story, but we can talk about him later.'

'Do you really believe that these demons exist and that people actually keep them, Bah Ap? In this day and age?' Donald asked.

Before I could reply, Bah Kynsai said, 'Believe it or not, Don, this is true. Most Khasis, na, regardless of what their religion is, na, do believe in demons or household gods. Call it superstition or whatever, but there's nothing you can say or do that will convince them otherwise. It's a very strange phenomenon, Don, and not even Christianity can do anything about it.'

But Bah Su was convinced it was because people had forgotten the core teaching of our ancestors. He said, 'It's all because we have forgotten about the Divine Covenant and the Three Commandments, ha! The First Commandment, for instance, says, "Know man know God", and people who believe in this do not know demons, do not worship them. As simple as that.'

Before anybody else could say anything, I jumped in to ask, 'Don, do you believe in Satan and his demons?'

Donald hesitated for some time and then replied, 'Well, I told you I don't care much about religion, but if you are a Christian, I suppose you have to believe in them ...'

'That's the whole point, isn't it? Every religion has its gods and demons. As far as my personal experience goes, those who believe in God also believe in Satan and demons; those who don't, don't believe in demons either. I have always wondered, which is to be preferred?'

'You got me there!' Donald laughed. 'But you know, Bah Ap, I'd really like to hear the story of Thlen—'

'He said later, na?' Bah Kynsai reminded him.

'Yeah, yeah, that's okay with me, Bah Kynsai. I'll wait. But there's one more thing I'd like to ask you, Bah Ap. In the second myth, you said Rooster stands for humility and all that, okay, but it seems to me he was a bit vain, asking for that ceremonial dress before he would go to Sun. Can you explain that?'

'Yeah, yeah.' Evening was suddenly enthused. 'That's a good question; let's see how Ap answers that. If his answer fails, the whole symbolism of Rooster also fails.'

'The answer is very simple. That part of the parable is really about the power of the right dress for the right occasion. Can you imagine yourself, for instance, going to a job interview in a tee-shirt and shorts? If you do, you will fail even before you have opened your mouth. Therefore, when you think about the parable, keep in mind that Rooster was a "naked and featherless" creature. How could he walk into the presence of Sun and claim he was an emissary of all earthlings? Shouldn't an emissary appearing before a heavenly being dress the part?'

Donald nodded his satisfaction and said, 'Yeah, yeah, I see the point now, Bah Ap.'

'A valid point, a valid point, Don!' Magdalene said. 'I'm okay with it, although I didn't raise the question in the first place. But you know, Ap, I have been thinking about the Khasi religion, ha, it has a beautiful concept, ya. As Bah Kynsai said, it gives you a lot of freedom to worship God in your own way—'

'Right now, na,' Bah Kynsai interrupted her, 'I'm living like a Khasi, Mag. I don't go to church, I pray to God in my own way, and there's no priest to mediate between him and me. I'm truly guided by my conscience.'

'Yeah, that's what I mean, Bah Kynsai. I like that kind of freedom too,' Magdalene told him. 'But what I don't understand is why Ap does not care for it … it's a beautiful religion, man!'

'I don't care much about the idea of religion in general, Mag. My favourite books and writings are those by Charles Darwin, Nietzsche, Bertrand

Russell, Frank Yerby and Samuel Beckett. I consider *The Origin of Species*, *Thus Spoke Zarathustra* and *Waiting for Godot* to be among the greatest books ever written.'

'Is that why you did not become a Christian?' Magdalene asked curiously.

'Why the heck should he become a Christian?' Bah Kit asked. 'He's one of the authorities on Khasi religion, no?'

'No, no, I'm asking because some of the writers he mentioned wrote against Christian beliefs, Bah Kit.'

At that, I said, 'To tell you the truth, I nearly became a Christian when I was young.'

'What?' Bah Kit, Bah Su and Bah Kynsai exclaimed in genuine surprise.

'Ap, a Christian!' Raji added to the chorus. 'That will be the day; that … will … be … the … day!' Raji was beginning to slur, and no wonder, for it was already close to midnight

Magdalene, however, became very interested. She said, 'Why didn't you? Is it because of those writers? Tell us, tell us, no!'

I thought back to the time when I had been asked to speak on this very subject by Seng Khasi members of a particular locality in Shillong. Standing at the podium, I had said to the gathering, 'You have asked me to speak about the causes that make so many of us abandon our own religion and join the innumerable Christian sects, including the BBC. That is what I intend to do. But in the process, I will also explain why I'm not a Christian. It will shed some light on the subject at hand.'

'BBC, Bah Ap?' someone asked.

'Bible Believing Church,' I replied. 'You'll see it on Keatinge Road.'

I continued, 'The great British philosopher Bertrand Russell wrote a superb essay titled "Why I Am Not a Christian". But apart from the title, let me hasten to add, there's nothing in common between what he had to say and the story I'm going to tell you. While his rejection of Christianity was based on certain considerations including his belief in the non-existence of God, mine was because of a deeply personal incident involving my mother's pork.'

'Pork, did you say?' almost everyone said at once.

'Pork, yes!' I replied. 'I will tell you the story by and by. Let me deal now with the topic on which I have been asked to speak …

'According to Russell's 1927 lecture, Christianity in the times of St Augustine and St Thomas Aquinas meant an acceptance of "a whole collection of creeds which were set out with great precision, and every single syllable of those creeds you believed with the whole strength of your convictions". A belief in Christianity therefore, Russell said, also means "a belief in God and immortality"; a belief that "Christ was, if not divine, at least the best and wisest of men"; a belief in hell; and additionally, a belief in eternal punishment for those who do not believe in Christ.

'In the Khasi Hills, Christianity is all of this and more, for it is practised with missionary zeal. "The unploughed fields of the Lord are still vast" and "The seas are still teeming with fishes" are commonly heard statements. These statements, of course, refer to the fact that about 15 per cent of the Khasi population are still Khasi-Khasis, although many of us are already asking ourselves, for how long, when we keep having our *khun langbrot*, our baby sheep, snatched by our Christian, and even Muslim, brethren at the rate of a few heads per year.'

Some of the men and women in the audience tittered at this, but the chairman, Bahdeng Kwar, hushed them sternly, saying, 'This is a serious matter.'

Bahdeng (that is his nickname because he is the middle brother in his family) was a dignified-looking man. His lean brown face seemed to glow against his dark-blue suit, set off by a white shirt and a red tie. Yet, despite his clothes, he looked rather traditional, for he had on his head an embroidered golden silk turban while across his shoulders was a ryndia, a satiny white eri-shawl folded neatly and worn like a sash. In stark contrast to him, I was in my trademark corduroy jeans and blue-and-white checked shirt. My only concession to tradition was a ryndia shawl dangling from my neck.

'Now, why did so many of us desert our own religion?' I resumed. 'The reason lies partly in this often-heard statement: "Because we have been left orphaned, we no longer know much about our own faith; hence we have no option but to convert." Ignorance causes both conversion and scorn. A Khasi who practises his own religion, as you are well aware, is despised as *u bym pat long niam*, a person who has not embraced any religion, as if his religion is not one that counts. He is despised as *u bym pat tip Blei*, a person who has not come to know God, as if his God is not God, or even *u riew pyrthei*, a person of the world, as if everybody else is no longer of this world.

'Even among us here, there are many who do not know anything about our own religion, many who have been misled by borrowed concepts about hell and Hindu gods. As a result, our faith is weak and fragile. If we marry a Christian, we become Christian; if we marry a Hindu, we become Hindu; and if we marry a Muslim, we become Muslim. If we examine the instances of conversion, we will discover that BL, the Bachelor of Love degree, or in Khasi, *Bud Lok*, following the spouse, is one of the primary reasons.'

The house erupted in laughter. After Bahdeng had hushed them again, I continued: 'But a person who has intimate knowledge of his faith, who clearly understands its great source, origin and foundations, as well as its teachings, will never fall easy prey to BL. He is like a full-grown tree whose roots have deeply penetrated the flesh and bones of the earth, and such a person cannot be uprooted or shaken this way and that by the winds of conversion. It is time, therefore, that all of us familiarise ourselves with the chief tenets of our creed so that our conviction becomes strong and secure. It may be a good idea for all Khasis to do so. An understanding of our forefathers' faith, to which we all originally belonged, may encourage us to respect one another and bring about a change of attitude, so that the fact of being Khasi is more important than belonging to this or that religion.'

I could see many heads nodding in agreement. I then changed my tone and said: 'Let me make a small confession to you, let me tell you briefly the story of my love life … I too nearly fell victim to BL!'

There was laughter again, and shouts of 'Tell us, tell us!'

'When I was a young man—not that I'm old now, of course, I'm still a bachelor … I was deeply in love with a beautiful Christian girl. I wrote poems dedicated to her, eulogising her dusky beauty and her charming simplicity. But our different faiths often made us argue with each other till one day she said to me: "How can I love you who have not even come to know God, U Blei?"

'In my youthful anger, I retorted, "Look here! U Blei is ours! Yours is Yahweh or Jehovah! How can you say I haven't come to know God, U Blei?"

'In response to this, she said: "You haven't come to know Jesus Christ!"

'I concurred. "That, of course, is true." And in my fear that I might lose her, I added, "Why don't you give me time to get to know him well … Perhaps, a time will come when I shall …"

'But instead of giving me time, she gave me an ultimatum: "No! If you truly love me, you must follow me!"

'That peremptory demand caused me to think things over very carefully. How could I accept the idea that a particular community is far above all of us, as the chosen people? I loved that girl so very much, and yet I simply could not bring myself to convert because it felt like a betrayal of my ancestors. Isn't this contemptuous attitude towards our own faith, culture, history and myths the reason why many of our sacred places have been occupied and desecrated by the defence forces? I was reminded of the stag in Aesop's fable, who admired his magnificent antlers but derided his legs because they were slender and thin, although he had escaped the hounds with their help. The antlers of other faiths might be magnificent, but it was the skinny legs of Khasi culture that had carried me thus far.

'But more powerful than all these thoughts was the image of my mother's pork, which floated into my mind. So finally, I pleaded with her to give me some time, hoping that when we were truly engrossed in our love, we would forget all these differences.

'However, my beloved was firm in her resolve and gave me another ultimatum: "Either follow me or forget about me!"

'Forget her I could not; follow her I could not. I was left dangling like that for a long, long time. But when the pain was particularly tormenting, I consoled myself with this gnomic phawar:

> *Lama u khun Khasi*
> *Ba kaweh halor u sieij,*
> *Ban duh ïa la riti,*
> *Lah ba duh ïa i baieit.*

> Flag of the Khasi people
> Waving from a pole,
> Rather than lose your culture,
> Better to lose your sweetheart.

'When I think back to that incident, I realise that my sense of belonging to Khasi culture has been exceptionally strong since childhood. And it was all because of my mother's pork.

'My mother is a firm believer in the Khasi religion, but at the same time, she is quite a liberal soul. She would never impose her belief on others. When two sisters who were teaching at a Christian school in Laitlyngkot (although I was born and brought up in Sohra, I spent two years in Laitlyngkot when I was in classes five and six) came to ask me to attend church every Sunday, my mother did not object. She simply asked me, "Do you want to go?" At that tender age (I was about twelve), I was attracted by the sight of other children dressed stylishly and attending church every Sunday. I happily agreed. Soon, I became an ardent churchgoer and was reading both Testaments of the Bible diligently. I came to know many of the stories intimately.

'The enthusiasm rapidly became an obsession, and I started participating actively in evangelistic gatherings held at various places in the Khasi Hills. One day, the two teachers invited me to a gathering at a village called Laitjem, a few kilometres away from Laitlyngkot, on the road towards Dawki and the Indo-Bangladesh border. Because we had to leave very early, my mother worked all night to prepare my jasong lunch. She cut potatoes into small, square pieces and fried them with pieces of pork in a mixture of onion, turmeric and bay leaf. For the chutney, she grilled some fermented tungtap fish and ground them with onions, chillies and ginger. The combination of tungtap, fried potatoes and pork, eaten with boiled rice, was a very popular dish in Sohra.

'Especially exciting was the fact that she had packed several pieces of pork in the jasong, a veritable feast for me, because I was never allowed more than one piece of meat when eating at home. This was part of our policy of frugal living, for we were quite hard-up, my mother being what they now call "a single mom". Sometimes we were even asked to "just smell the meat" because there was not enough to pass around. But this time, because it was an outing with neighbours, she had packed quite a lot of pork. I left home with a feeling of pleasure and anticipation.

'The gathering was a large and exciting one, marked by fervent prayers, rousing hymns and fiery speeches by well-known speakers, who spoke about the intentions of the Lord with remarkable confidence. We listened to them with rapt attention.

'When it was lunchtime, the teachers took us to a small hill so we could eat in privacy. There were six of us in the group, counting the teachers' two nieces and a nephew. I was famished, for it was past my usual lunchtime. And of course, the thought of the fried pork waiting just for me made me feel as if I could eat up a hill or two, as the saying goes. All of us brought out our jasongs and opened them. But before I could eat, one of the teachers began to say grace and launched into a long prayer, asking God to bless the food we were about to eat; to give us all a healthy body; to cleanse our souls and purify our minds; to protect us from the seven deadly sins by reminding us of the Ten Commandments; and to generally make us good Christians.

'When the prayer was done, my right hand immediately went to the nicely browned-and-yellowed pork. I was determined to begin my lunch with a piece of juicy meat and not with a handful of rice as I would do at home. Both the teachers, however, shouted, "Wait!" ("Arre!" I said to myself.

"Why should I wait when the prayer is done? What now?") Then they pulled my jasong towards themselves and looked greedily at my pork. "Your mother must love you very much to prepare this nice jasong for you," they said. I looked at theirs and found that they contained only some boiled vegetables and a small piece of dried fish. Mine was definitely the better fare. Initially, I was rather pleased with myself, but then I became suspicious. Why were they inspecting my jasong like that?

'At that moment, one of the teachers said, "A small boy like you shouldn't be eating so many pieces of pork!" And with that, she took my pork and began distributing it among the group, giving two pieces each to her nieces and nephew and three to herself and her sister. She also took away quite a bit of my fried potato and tungtap. When she had finished the distribution, she pushed my jasong towards me. I found that I was left with only *one* piece of pork!

'All sorts of nasty thoughts passed through my head, and I called them all sorts of names. I felt like crying and telling them to return my pieces of pork, otherwise I would tell my mother when I got home. But what was the use, they were already tearing into the meat.

'I didn't feel like eating any more. They had taken my pork without my consent and did not even give me anything in return. Instead, they had said, "We have only boiled vegetables and dried fish; there's no use giving you any of it." What kind of people were these? They had only just prayed to God to protect and liberate them from the seven deadly sins, and now they were behaving like this! Did the seven deadly sins not include greed … lust, envy and gluttony? Did not one of the commandments tell us, Thou shalt not covet anything that belongs to your neighbour? Did not another say, Thou shalt not steal? So why were these people coveting my pork and stealing all those pieces from my jasong?

'Of course they stole! Isn't taking something that belongs to another without asking and without permission an act of stealing? And I was but a child! These people were frauds! They prayed with the right; they stole with the left! Their prayer was a mere facade, a deception to mislead others into thinking them virtuous. Was it because of this that people said, "*Khristan ka naam*", Christian in name only?

'All these thoughts passed through my mind as I ate my jasong mechanically, without enjoyment. Obviously, when I grew older, I discovered that not all Christians were like those two. I came across many (my relatives included) who were truly simple and virtuous; some have become lifelong friends. But, by then, it was already too late: I had become disillusioned. I could only think: if becoming a Christian is becoming like you, then there is no point in it at all. And from that very moment, because they had stolen my mother's pork, I decided never to leave my own Niam Khasi and convert to any other religion. My mother's teachings are much better, I told myself. My mother used to say, "Wherever you are, remember your fellow man; remember God; behave conscientiously. That is enough." And that is true. The pieces of fried pork had led me to this realisation.'

That was how I concluded my talk that day.

I told Mag and the rest of them the story, and at the end of it, I said, 'That was why I did not become a Christian. I hope none of you is offended; I was only trying to explain to you the reason why I abandoned my attempts to become a Christian, and only since you asked me.'

'Offended? I enjoyed it, mə, tdong!' Bah Kynsai declared. 'Imagine! Even pieces of pork can bring about such a change in a person's life, huh? Remarkable!'

Magdalene added, 'I don't think you were offensive, Ap, on the other hand, you were quite moderate, considering that you were speaking to Seng Khasi members.'

But Evening seemed miffed. He said, 'Your faith must have been quite feeble if you were turned away by pieces of pork!'

'On the contrary,' I replied, 'my faith in my religion became very strong, almost unshakeable, because of my mother's pork. It is only now, because of the influence of all those great writers, that I have become indifferent to the idea of religion as the best guide for life.'

'No, no, no,' Evening insisted, 'this story sounds to me like a criticism of Christianity and Christians—'

'So what if it is?' Donald asked angrily. 'We live in a secular state; anyone is free to discuss the merits and demerits of any religion.'

'Evening *bhi* Halolihim *jaisa*,' Bah Kynsai said in a rather fed-up voice.

'Yes, yes, Evening is like Halolihim, Bah Kynsai,' Magdalene agreed. 'And, Don, I don't think it's a criticism. He's merely telling us why he did not become a Christian. It is *his* story! He has every right to tell it.'

'No, no, no, he must tell us exactly what he feels about Christians! I demand it!' Evening insisted.

'Why the hell should he?' Don asked aggressively. '*You* first tell him what you feel about the Khasi religion, then—'

'It's okay, Don, it's okay. I have nothing to hide. I have already told you, Evening, that I don't give a shit about religion. My relationship with God is my own business. But to answer your question: many of my relatives are Christians, and I get along very well with them. Many of my friends are Christians.' (And my beloved Saia is a Catholic, and she does not give a damn about my religion, or lack of it. But, of course, I did not tell them about her.)

I continued, 'Bah Kynsai, Raji and Mag have been among my best friends for donkey's years. I even count you as a good friend, though you can be a bit too aggressive about your religion, and many other things besides. I have absolutely no prejudice against anyone. Many of my friends are Hindus, Muslims, Buddhists, deists, theists, atheists, agnostics. But if you insist on knowing my attitude towards Christianity, then let me tell you—not because I have to, but because I want to—that despite my distaste for religion in general, the best time of the year for me is Christmas. I love the festive atmosphere and the exchange of gifts, which strengthens family bonds. And I also love the season's songs. As a matter of fact, one of my all-time favourites is a Christmas song.'

One of the greatest poets of the English language, Dylan Thomas, once said this of Christmas: 'The tills in the shops of the town ring out in celebration'. Indeed, Christmas has come to mean precisely that to many people, that is, a time to set the money-making racket in motion. In the city of Shillong, for instance, there are traders selling Christmas stars as if they are bindis for non-Khasi women to wear on their foreheads. There are the woodcutters chopping off pine limbs and turning the town's strategic points into mini-pine groves. There are the confectioners who suddenly decide to make nothing but cakes for the lines of cake-buyers. And, of course, there are the merchants selling dresses and footwear at cut-throat prices to last-minute shoppers, not to mention bootleggers stocking up for the dry days of Christmas. For me, however, Christmas has come to be dominated by one thing alone: a remarkable song and the constant reminder it provides that there is, latent in every human being, a kind of greatness that may surface at moments least expected.

The story goes back to the Christmas of 1818. The day was 24 December. The place was Oberndorf, a snow-sealed little town in the Austrian Alps, about seventeen kilometres north of the city of Salzburg. The town was experiencing the greatest misfortune in its Christmas history. Mice had eaten into the bellows of the church organ, and no repair man could be called in until spring when the snowdrifts melted. There would be no music that

Christmas. People grumbled about it. The organist, Franz Gruber, panicked as he stood at the church door, wondering what to do. Then the minister, Josef Mohr, a quiet and somewhat timid young man, came along. Mohr had gone home to dig up a little piece he had scribbled two years earlier, which he thought the organist could set to music and then teach the children. That way, he surmised, they could still have some music for Christmas.

Rather shyly, Mohr pulled out a crumpled piece of paper and gave it to the organist. Gruber was amazed at the simplicity of the words. He rushed home, strummed the guitar a few times and noted down the tune that came to his mind. That done, he went around town, calling the children together to rehearse.

That Christmas Eve, 1818, as the people groaned their way to church in the dark and cold, disappointed that there would be no music, they were greeted by the haunting notes of a strange hymn. The words and the tune were sheer inspiration. They were delighted. Anybody could hum the tune and sing the words. Soon, they found themselves accompanying the carolling children. The organ was quickly forgotten, but the song lingered in their minds long after Christmas, for it captured beautifully the truth about how God became man to redeem their sins.

It was the repair man, however, who first realised the value of the little poem. With spring, Josef Mohr left Oberndorf for another parish. Franz Gruber was only too happy to part with the silly piece, now that his organ had been repaired. The repair man took it, had it published, and by the following Christmas, all of Austria and Germany were singing the song. Now there is not a church or a chapel in the world where the song is not heard.

In the year of 1992, my friend Nigel and I were standing in the courtyard of the Sohra Inspection Bungalow, on the brink of the gorges, enjoying the moon-presided night air of November and the fantastic view that only the gorges of Sohra could offer. Suddenly, from deep down in the ravines, we picked up the barely audible strains of *Silent Night*. Even in those 'God-forsaken holes', they had heard and made their own that little song that two men in Oberndorf had created 'in a terrible hurry'. But had they heard of Josef Mohr and Franz Gruber? The more the carol grows in fame, the more we tend to forget its creators.

The song made my agnostic friend nostalgic about the church-going days of his childhood, and it moved me too, inspiring me to prayers and a wish to be pure of heart. Since learning of Josef Mohr and his organist, I have never listened to this song without remembering them and their moment of triumph. Remembering is the least we can do for these inspired workers of God.

I shared the story with my friends and was pleased to find that not one of them had heard it before. They were amazed and moved, and some of them asked me for a copy of the essay I had written about it, which I promised to give them once we got back to Shillong.

But Evening gave me a strange look and said, 'I don't understand you, Ap. You rejected Christianity because of some pieces of pork, and yet some of your heroes are, as you put it, "these inspired workers of God". What exactly are you, man? What exactly do you believe in?'

In response, I read a poem to him:

Like Shelley with his 'blithe spirit',
I have often tried to understand
this man who is named Ap Jutang.

How should I describe myself?

A son of a crab, since I fail to suffer
my mother's temper, who, living in my house,
treats me as one of her tenants.

A wicked neighbour, since I object to a toilet
being built against my compound wall, and bark
at window-breaking locality boys.

A felonious councillor, since I attend the village
dorbar without a moustache. A guilty bystander,
since I make myself small as a mouse, even when
riffraff and drunks are drowning out all reason.

A bad relation, since I dislike
clan meetings and spurn playing
mother against aunt,
brother against brother.

An 'evil' administrator, since I forbid
the staff to come at noon
and depart just after noon.

A recalcitrant Indian, since I am buried
too deep in my tribal roots and refuse to be

swept away by the Main Stream. A mutinous
Indian, since I protest army occupation,
uranium mining, influx and *saffronisation*.

A counterfeit scholar, since I write
only poetry, working at a university.

A small-time poet, since I cannot class myself
a small-town writer, since this town judges books
by the weight and writers by their age.

A retrograde, since I want trees on the hills,
birds in the woods, fishes in the streams.
A heathen, since I believe in sacred groves.
An atheist, since I am not a Christian.
A heretic, since I believe in the humanity
of my conscience.

An enemy of the human race, since I believe
in animal rights and birth control. An advancer of the
Malthusian theory, since I wish to include weapons
of mass destruction in the list of natural calamities.

A hopeless believer, since I know not what
is to be done with all that I believe. A hypocrite,
since I pursue private dreams and like a dog,
nod with the head and shake with the tail to everything.

I shall describe myself as that supreme diplomat:
'I am who I am', and that is the ultimate enigma.

'That's who I am, Evening, and that's who everybody is: an enigma.'

'Bong leh, Ap, nice poem, man,' Bah Kynsai said excitedly. 'And it's very true also: each one of us is truly a mystery, na? But when did you write it, man?'

'When I was still at the university—'

'Bah Ap, I wanted to ask you two things,' Donald interrupted me. 'Firstly, is it true that you cannot attend a village council if you don't have a moustache? Secondly, is there really any attempt to saffronise or apply fundamentalist Hindu principles here?'

'Actually, the saying that men without a moustache cannot sit in a village council should not be taken literally. Any person considered to have reached manhood was allowed into the council whether he had a moustache or not. But how would they judge a person's age in those days? They could neither read nor write and, therefore, couldn't keep a record of people's ages. The only way was to look at a person's moustache. What the saying means is that, if you are not a mature adult, you cannot sit in a council and deliberate like a man. As for your second question, I'm not only referring to our state but the whole country.'

Magdalene stood up to stretch. Then she looked at her watch and exclaimed, 'Oh, my God, it's two already!'

Bah Kynsai said, 'Oh yeah … It was that damn fight, na? We lost at least two hours to it. Shall we go to bed? What shall we do tomorrow?'

'Whatever we do, we must go to the lake … Hey, Bah Kynsai, to the lake, okay?' Raji said drunkenly. 'By hook or by crook, to the lake … after drinking the whole night, okay, if we don't take a bath, we'll stink like pigs, leh.'

'We'll do that,' I said, 'but we must hurry back like we did yesterday. Perly said they will be roasting a pig in the afternoon, Lyngngam style—we mustn't miss that.'

But Magdalene's mind was not on the pig. She said, 'That was an excellent analysis of the myths, ya, Ap. I learnt so much today.'

'Me too,' Donald said. 'I must admit that when I first met you guys, you know, I didn't think I could learn much from you. I was not exactly scornful, but I thought, what the hell can one learn from ancestors who could not even read or write? But truly, Bah Ap, as you said earlier, enlightenment did not come to the Khasis with schools and colleges.'

That night, I went to sleep with a smile on my face.

6

THE
FOURTH
NIGHT

LITTLE STORIES I

'Anecdotes and maxims are rich treasures
to the man of the world, for he knows how to
introduce the former at fit places in
conversation and to recollect the latter
on proper occasions.'
—Goethe

On the fourth night, 8 February, as had become our habit, we were gathered around our little fire by 7 p.m. Some of us were nursing mugs of yiad hiar, others just relaxing, thinking, no doubt, about the best dinner we had had in Nongshyrkon.

The day had been bright and sunny. Again, we went to the lake immediately after breakfast, carrying our lunch of beef broth and boiled rice in leaves and bamboo tubes. Halolihim came along, but spoke only to Hamkom.

'He must think we are the spawn of Satan himself, ha, Ap?' Magdalene whispered to me.

When we got back to the village, around 1.30 p.m., we were taken to the backyard of the death house, where they were preparing to roast not one but three large pigs in honour of some burang uncles newly arrived from distant parts. A large pit—about nine feet long, six feet wide and three feet deep—had already been dug. As we watched, it was carefully lined with large plantain leaves so that no soil was exposed, and then it was filled with hot stones. The three pigs were laid on top of the stones. The pigs had already been prepared—the hair burnt off, the skin scraped clean with knives, and the offal removed to be cooked separately. More hot stones were placed on top of the pigs, and after that, the whole pit was covered with neatly cut slabs of turf.

By 5.30 p.m., the pigs were well roasted and removed from the pit. The meat was carved into small pieces and served along with plates of rice and vegetable soup. Our group was given the meat in a large aluminium basin. We had never tasted anything like it before. The meat was tender, juicy, and delicious beyond belief. We ate like shameless gluttons, stuffing ourselves till we could eat no more. Bah Kynsai and Raji hardly touched the rice; they simply ate the meat with shallots and chillies and washed it down with plenty of rice beer.

And now they were talking about it, admiring the feast and confessing that they had never eaten so much before.

Magdalene voiced everyone's thoughts when she said, 'I wonder what they have in store for us next?'

Bah Kynsai said teasingly, 'Dog meat.'

But Raji took that seriously and said, 'No, Bah Kynsai, according to Perly, Lyngngams do not eat dogs. They eat everything except dogs, cats, snakes and monkeys.'

'Then they are like every one of us, Raji,' Bah Kit observed. 'No Khasis, except for some drunks, ever eat these animals.'

'Why?' Magdalene asked curiously.

'Well, most of us fear the poison of the snakes, ha, and we don't eat monkeys because they look too much like humans. But cats and dogs are almost sacred to us.'

'What! Almost sacred?' Magdalene asked in amazement. 'I have never heard of that one before, ya!'

The others hadn't either, and urged Bah Kit to explain. He told them that, when cats and dogs came to live with man, they made a pact with him that required them to guard his house and all his possessions in exchange for his protection.

'The story, the story, man!' Bah Kynsai demanded.

In the beginning, Cat lived not with man but with Tiger, in the forest. She was his servant, following him everywhere and fulfilling his every little wish. Although he was somewhat selfish, never giving her anything, not even scraps from the meat he was eating—always telling her she should hunt for her own food—she was happy enough with him, for, to be fair to him, he did teach her the techniques of hunting.

While serving him, Cat survived by hunting small animals like mice, insects and birds. It was a hard life, especially during the wet and cold weather, and what made it even harder was the fact that Tiger was unpredictable, and would roar at her for the smallest of mistakes. As such, she lived in constant fear and anxiety.

One day, Tiger was suddenly taken ill. He could not eat or drink anything. His wife was terribly worried. She asked him, 'What kind of meat shall I bring for you today? I'm worried that you haven't been eating or drinking anything … Shall I bring you a juicy little rabbit or perhaps a little wild chicken?'

'No, no, no,' Tiger replied weakly. 'I have no appetite for anything. I feel cold and feverish all over …'

'Then what can I do, shall I bring you a little fermented alcohol? There's a place in the woods where some people have left rice spirit to mature.'

'No, no, what I need is a little fire to keep me warm. If I can keep myself warm, I know I'll feel much better.'

'But how will I get you a fire, my dear husband? If I go to people's homes, they'll attack me with their spears and shoot me with their arrows.'

'Why don't you send Cat?' Tiger suggested.

Cat went to a nearby village and entered the first hut she came across. She surreptitiously crept into the hut and stood in a corner by the door, ready to make a run for it should someone attack her. But the family were at their dinner and did not notice her. Watching them carefully, she edged a little closer, lured by the food they were eating. She was so hungry that she forgot all about her errand and could think of nothing but the food in front of her. In her hunger and longing, she meowed, making a soft and pitiful appeal to the group, quite forgetting that she was a wild animal they might harm.

When the family heard her pitiful cries, they were both intrigued and touched. One of the kids said, 'Look, Papa, what a beautiful little animal, can I keep her, please?'

His father said, 'Wait, let's see whether she's dangerous or not.'

He took some of the fish bones from his earthen plate and threw them towards Cat. She pounced upon the food eagerly and ate it hungrily. Seeing how greedily she munched through the fish bones, the family began to feed her more and more scraps of food. They gave her a little fish and later a little rice mixed with fish soup. Cat lapped it all up without leaving even a tiny particle on the ground.

Seeing that, the man said, 'You are a hungry little beast, aren't you?'

Cat surprised them by replying that she was. She told them she was Tiger's servant and that she lived with him in the forest. But she was not happy with him since he never fed her and asked her to hunt for her own food instead. Besides, he snarled and growled at her for no good reason, and that had turned her into a very timid and unhappy creature. At last, she appealed: 'Oh, son of man, will you please allow me to live with you from now on?'

In reply, the man asked her, 'What can you do?'

'If you give me food and shelter from the rain and the cold, I can protect your home, your grains and your vegetables from rodents and insects of all kinds.'

He found her proposition quite attractive, for he had, in fact, been at his wit's end about the rodents ravaging his grains and vegetables. 'All right, I will give you food and shelter you from the cold and the rain; I will protect you from Tiger and all other animals, and what is more, I will not allow other men to harm you. But you too should keep your word. You must protect my crops in the garden, and my grains and vegetables in the storeroom, and you must not allow rats or mice or dangerous insects to come into the house at any time of the day or night. This is our pledge! If you agree to always abide by it, you may live with us from now on.'

And that was how Cat came to live with man and became one of man's best friends, although she also incurred the terrible wrath of Tiger, who swore eternal vengeance against her. It is for this reason, people say, that whenever Tiger finds cats anywhere, he kills and devours them without leaving a single trace of the carcass behind.

However, Cat was well protected by man, not only from Tiger but also from all other animals. Other men, too, respected the pledge with Cat and never killed her for food.

'That was very nice, man, Bah Kit,' Hamkom said. 'It seems that we people have a story for everything, no?'

But Donald wanted Bah Kit to clarify something. He said, 'Don't you think, Bah Kit, the cat behaved treacherously?'

Magdalene pulled Donald's left ear playfully and said, 'Don, you idiot, haven't you been listening? The tiger was a bad master, no? Is escaping from a bad master behaving treacherously?'

'And what about the dog?' Evening asked.

'What, you don't know the story or what?' Bah Kynsai asked sarcastically. 'I can understand Don or Mag or Dale or Ham not knowing it, but you …?'

'What about you, do you know it?'

'Of course I do, but I can't tell it as well as Kit, na?' he responded with a loud laugh.

Evening replied with a sarcastic laugh of his own, and asked, 'Will you, Bah Kit?'

'Let Ap tell you this one, he knows it better than I do.'

'Ap knows everything,' Hamkom said, taking a dig at me.

I hit right back at him. 'I wish you knew at least something, so I don't have to do all the telling.'

'Well said, well said!' Evening clapped, very happy that the man he disliked the most was being put in his place.

But Hamkom chose to be mollifying. 'I was joking, ya, please go ahead.'

I would have refused to tell them anything—I did not like being portrayed as a know-it-all. But that would have defeated my own objective, which was to acquaint them with our culture and past as much as possible, so they may learn to respect them and be more Khasi in thought and feeling. Right now, most of them were too much like 'exiles of the mind'.

Much against my own inclination, therefore, I told them the story of how Dog came to live with man.

In the days when the world was still young, when all animals spoke the same language and lived together in peace, there were fairs and markets where animals bought and sold things, just as man did. The most prominent of these fairs was the one held in the deep forests of Ri Bhoi, adjoining what is now called the state of Assam. It was called 'Ka Ïew Luri Lura', after the anarchy and disorder that prevailed there towards the end.

Every fair day, animals of all sorts from all over the land went to Luri Lura with their distinctive merchandise to trade and barter with one another. Tiger, whom everyone feared and respected, was elected governor, to see that things ran smoothly within the fairground. And so, everything went well for a time. The fair prospered, and more and more animals came to patronise it, each adding to its variety and glamour in his or her own way. For instance, Bear brought her honeycombs, Monkey her fruits and Deer her *sohmylleng* to exchange for herbs and plants and foodstuffs brought by the other beasts.

'Do you know the English name of sohmylleng, Ap?' Bah Kynsai asked.

'In Hindi, they call it *amla*, in English, gooseberry. But there are many fruits found only in these hills that have no English names, Bah Kynsai.'

'Like what?'

Bah Su said, '*Sohphie, sohshang, sohphlang*, so many.'

I added, '*Sohram, sohben, sohum, sohlang, sohramdieng ...*'

'Okay, okay,' Bah Kynsai said quickly, 'I haven't even heard of these fruits, man, forget it. On with the story!'

Only Dog never had anything to sell. He spent most of his time at the fair nosing about for scraps of food the others chanced to drop. Eventually, he became a little ashamed of his habit, and determined to look for something he could call his own, something novel to offer. After days of wandering through the countryside, he came upon a basketful of leaf packets containing bean sauce, a delicacy that humans called *tung rymbai*. Some traders must have hidden it there on the way to their market, perhaps because they found it too heavy to carry.

'Aah, so tung rymbai is a bean sauce, ha, Ap?' Magdalene exclaimed. 'When my friends ask me, okay, I always describe it as a smelly black substance, ya!'

'It's black because it's mixed with black sesame,' I explained and then went on with my story.

Dog began to sniff about the strange substance. The odour was strongly redolent of man's excrement, and as he had once or twice dined on that and liked it, he presumed the other animals would also find the black pulpy mass a rare and delicious treat to supplement their daily diet. Very pleased with his discovery, Dog took it with him to the fair at Luri Lura.

There, he stationed himself in the most prominent part of the fairground and began howling and baying at the top of his voice, extolling the virtues of his stock and inviting all the animals to taste for themselves the only thing of its kind in the entire fair. Curious about the strange and reputedly delicious food Dog had discovered, they all scampered to his side. 'What is it? What are you selling? Let us see,' they asked in one voice.

Feeling important and excited at the attention he was attracting, Dog promptly uncovered his basket and prepared to do business, but no sooner had he done that than a horrible stench issued from the basket, suffocating everyone present. 'It stinks! It stinks!' they all cried. 'What is this you have come to sell in our market?' Maddened by what they took to be Dog's malignant trickery, and assuming that he was trying to con them most shamefully, they chased him out of the fair, trampling on his basket of tung rymbai and reducing it to a filthy, smelly sludge. Dog barked, howled, yelped, protested and argued with them till the whole fair resounded with the din. But their animal passions were truly roused, and there was no reasoning with them.

In all that commotion and chaos, Tiger arrived, muscling his way into the melee to investigate the matter. Dog began to voice his complaints, but before he could say more than a few words, Tiger roared, 'What is this!' He, too, had been smothered by the same fetid smell. 'How dare you defile our marketplace by selling man's dung? If you don't leave this very minute, I will swallow you whole!'

Terrified and humiliated, Dog slunk away from Luri Lura amidst sneers and guffaws, catcalls and boos, which rankled in his mind long after they could be heard no more.

As a last resort, Dog approached man, to appeal for justice and assistance. 'My Lord,' he said, 'you who are wise, who know and understand many things, do you think it is proper for the animals to trample on the rights and property of a weak and helpless creature like myself?'

Man realised that Dog had been greatly wronged, but he was powerless in the matter. 'How can I, a human,' he asked, 'judge the affairs of animals?'

Nevertheless, Dog continued to plead with him. His own kind had turned their backs on him, and worse, they had banished him from their midst. He was all alone in the world, and friendless; everyone would tyrannise him. He begged man to be his master, to allow him to live close to man's house. He would protect the house and be man's watchdog wherever he went. He also promised man that he would do anything for him and asked in return for only food and shelter and a chance to avenge himself upon his tormentors.

As he listened to Dog's desperate pleas, man could not help sympathising with him. Here was a fellow-sufferer, a creature of God like himself. He agreed to Dog's entreaties and said, 'Perhaps you should not have tried to sell them what seemed to them like human dung, but on the other hand, there was no call for them to treat you the way they did and to banish you from their midst. I will give you food, shelter and protection, and whenever I go hunting, I will give you a chance to avenge yourself upon your tormentors. And what's more, I shall proclaim a friendship between us so that no human will ever harm you and eat your flesh. This is our pledge, may it be kept for as long as there is life on earth.'

And that was how Dog became man's most beloved friend, accompanying him everywhere, but especially to the hunting grounds, where he took grim pleasure in noisily forcing animals out of their lairs. And he was very good at that, for the tenacious scent of his tung rymbai clung to their cloven feet after Luri Lura, and was passed on to their descendants.

'So, that's why Khasis don't eat cats and dogs, huh? Wonderful!' Magdalene exclaimed.

'What is even more remarkable, na,' Bah Kynsai said, 'is the explanation about why the dog is so good at stalking and tracking wild animals: the smell of tung rymbai on their feet, unlike humans, *sma tung rymbai hapdeng …*'

'What did you say?' Magdalene demanded.

Bah Kynsai had said, 'unlike humans, smelling tung rymbai in the middle', but realising he might have misspoken, he quickly replied, 'Nothing, Mag, nothing … Okay, so now we know the Lyngngams will never give us dog meat, what next? Shall we tell more stories? The night has just begun, na?'

'What do you have in mind?' Evening asked.

'Little stories. I don't have long or short stories, na? Only little ones. What do you say?'

'If we tell little stories, ha, we must tell something with a moral, not simply jokes and that sort of thing,' Evening said.

'Why are you so interested in morals?'

'Because he's a strait-laced moralist, Bah Kynsai,' Magdalene joked.

'Because,' Evening said firmly, 'I want to learn something more serious than jokes.'

'Ning is right, Mag,' I said. 'We are all here together, how often do we have such an opportunity? This is a golden chance for us to learn something from each other about life, society, human nature and human relationships. I'm sure each of us has a story to tell that is both amusing and meaningful.'

'Yeah, yeah,' Hamkom agreed. 'That sounds good.'

'Okay, that's what we'll do then,' Bah Kynsai said, 'and at the end of each story, na, we must try to find out what lesson the tale has to offer. If there isn't one, the teller must serve us drinks and massage our backs.'

'Not fair, not fair,' Magdalene cried. 'What about those who don't have stories?'

'Okay, okay, we'll keep it simple. Ap, you start and show us what you mean by amusing and meaningful.'

I agreed and began with a story from one of my books, called 'The Ideal Housemaid'.

One day, not too long ago, a Bengali professor issued an advertisement announcing her requirement for a housemaid who would not only look after the house but also help take care of her two-year-old son. Because the wage she offered was a rather generous one, many girls from her locality applied for the job. Seeing so many applicants, she decided to interview them so she could choose the most suitable candidate. But that presented another problem. Most of the girls were Khasi and did not know much English or Hindi. What was she to do? She herself did not know much Khasi. As a last resort, therefore, she sought the help of a Khasi taxi driver who used to drop her at work every day.

Speaking to him in broken Khasi, she said, 'Bah Warjri, you help me choose housemaid, okay, too many of them, *te*.'

'Te' here roughly corresponds to 'you see'.

'Fine, fine, no worry, when is interview?' Bah Warjri readily agreed, also speaking in broken Khasi.

This is one of those strange Khasi traits: whenever a non-Khasi speaks to them in broken Khasi, they respond likewise. Nobody knows why.

'Tomorrow at 9 a.m.'

'Fine, fine, I come, no worry.'

During the interview, the girls, waiting outside on the veranda, were called to the drawing room one by one.

When the first girl came in, the professor and Bah Warjri immediately began plying her with questions: her name, place of stay, age, experience and so on. But the girl was so shy that she stared at the floor, smiled foolishly to herself and refused to say a word. The plumpish professor looked at Bah Warjri, her dark eyes questioning him silently. Bah Warjri, who was sitting on a chair, his folded arms resting on his paunchy stomach, looking very much like a meditating Buddha, shook his head and commented: 'No network.'

The second girl was exactly the opposite. Before the interviewers could ask her questions, she began talking non-stop, boasting of her experience in housekeeping and childminding, and giving them no chance at all to speak. Bah Warjri looked at the professor, shook his head, and said: 'Customer service.'

The third girl was not very nicely behaved. Nor did the interviewers like the way she spoke, especially when she boasted about having worked in many places around India. Bah Warjri gave the professor a sign and said: 'Tourist taxi.'

And so the interview progressed, with Bah Warjri rejecting one girl after another because he did not like the way they spoke or behaved or dressed. This went on for some time, making the professor quite anxious. At last, a girl came in who seemed well suited for the job. She was well behaved, clean and neatly dressed. When they asked her questions, she answered them clearly and politely. She was really perfect in every way. Even Bah Warjri was impressed with her. He looked at the professor, nodded, and said: 'Maruti 800. Best for Shillong conditions.'

Loud laughter greeted the end of my story. Magdalene slapped Donald's back so hard he nearly fell into the fire. After a while, Bah Kynsai said, 'Okay, okay, what about the moral?'

'*Da jied kba ïa ka jinglong briew*,' Bah Su offered. Roughly translated, this means *Human nature must be sifted like rice*, or better still, *Separate the rice from the husk*. Everyone thought this such a suitable moral lesson that Bah Su was patted on the back several times.

By the way, the small Maruti 800 car is considered 'best for Shillong conditions' because the streets here are winding and narrow. Though the company has stopped manufacturing that particular model, it is still the most sought-after vehicle, especially by those who want to use it as a taxi.

Bah Kynsai called for more stories, but since nobody could think of one just yet, I volunteered another.

I had heard this story at a funeral gathering some years ago. The night was cold, and many people were sitting around a fire built in a corner of the courtyard, talking of this and that. Then, suddenly, the conversation turned to the appalling backwardness of our state.

The assistant secretary of the village council, a tall, dark and energetic young man called Hep, said with some passion: 'In my opinion, ha, our state is so awfully backward because we don't have a single *pod* anywhere. Just think about it, what kind of state is this without a functional *erpod*, a *sipod* or even a railway pod? How can it progress without a single pod anywhere?'

As you must have gathered, a pod is a 'port', pronounced as pod by most of us.

The listeners mulled things over for a while and then agreed with Hep.

One of them said: 'Yeah, man, Hep, it's very true, man! Without a sipod or a *relpod*, how can there be any *impod* or *ekspod*? The *transpod* of goods will be completely crippled, no? And without an erpod, how can *turisim* really develop? Impossible!'

But one middle-aged man, small and fair-skinned, whom everybody lovingly called Maduh, or youngest uncle, did not agree with Hep at all. Putting on an air of great surprise, he said, 'Arre, you people, what are you talking about? Who says we don't have any pod in Ri Khasi? Actually, we Khasis have the biggest number of pods in the world, don't you know that? And it is because we have too many that we have become so backward!'

'*Tet phi*, Maduh! What are you talking about?' Hep said, annoyed. And then, pointing a forefinger at the diminutive Maduh, he added rather fiercely, 'Show me, show me, where do we have a pod in Ri Khasi? Even one also we don't have!'

Maduh's long, thin face creased into a broad smile, exposing all his crooked teeth, as he said, 'Arre, you also are very short-sighted, no, Hep? Think very carefully, man, don't we Khasis have many pods? Look here; I'll give you one example, okay? Think of a Khasi labourer—a Khasi labourer always works only four days a week, from Wednesday to Saturday, which is payday. After that, till Tuesday, *u shu bam pod*, he eats hard; *u shu dih pod*, he drinks hard; and *u shu thiah pod*, he sleeps hard. Now, do you dare say we don't have any pod in Ri Khasi, Hep? Actually, we have too many pods here, okay? It's because of them that we have remained backward till today.'

Needless to say, I concluded, Maduh's explanation was met with much guffawing.

Bah Kynsai laughed too. 'Tet teri ka! What a story this Ap comes up with, na?'

'Moral?' Evening asked.

'It's obvious, isn't it?' Bah Su said. '*Don ka sdot haba la than eh ka pod. Atrophy follows overindulgence.*'

Magdalene called out to me and said, 'Hey, Ap, that's exactly what we are doing right now, man … eat pod, drink pod and sleep pod!'

Evening, however, did not like what she said. 'But we are also discussing important matters, no, Mag? And this story by Ap is actually a very serious one. The happy-go-lucky lifestyle of our men, ha, is really very frustrating. When I was constructing my house, okay, I had to fire a lot of Khasi labourers because they simply wouldn't come on Mondays and Tuesdays. I had to hire non-Khasi labourers, what to do?'

'Aha!' Hamkom cried triumphantly. 'I told you, influx is not as simple as driving out all non-tribals!'

But Bah Kynsai, fearing another flare-up between them, quickly came to Evening's defence and said, 'He never said that, Ham. His position is that we should deal with the problem of influx seriously, na? I think he said we should work out a system whereby permanent non-tribals should be given their opportunities while fresh migrants, especially from other countries, should be stopped immediately and deported. That's different from driving out all non-tribals, na?'

'And yet, by his own admission,' Hamkom insisted, 'he is encouraging influx by hiring non-tribal labourers!'

'What I'm telling you about, you trouble-monger,' Evening retorted hotly, 'is the kind of predicament all Khasis find themselves in! I'm being honest, no? I'm against influx, but I was forced to hire non-Khasi men because many Khasis are such lazy workers! Non-Khasi men are not lazy; they work hard, okay, you just have to watch them like a hawk. But Ap's story is very true. It highlights the pathetic absence of a work ethic among us. Not only among labourers, ha, but also among government employees. Many go to work at 11 or 11.30 in the morning and leave by 3.30 in the afternoon. And when somebody dies, they even leave the office at 12.30, so they can go to the funeral and conduct the service. That's the kind of people many of us are, ha, and there's no use defending them. The more we hide the truth, the more the rot will fester.'

Bah Kynsai wanted the heated exchange to stop, so he said, 'Okay, okay, next! Who will tell the next story?'

'Wait, wait, Bah Kynsai,' Donald intervened. 'I think this raises another fundamental question: unemployment. I have always heard Khasis complaining about the massive unemployment problem, but this story and what Evening has been saying seem to suggest exactly the opposite—that Khasis are not worried about it. So what's the real picture, ya?'

'Khasis, na, Don, speak of unemployment mostly in connection with government jobs,' Bah Kynsai explained. 'If they are not working in government offices, they think they are unemployed. But if they were willing to do all sorts of work, na, I don't think there's any unemployment problem at all. In the building sector, for instance, the situation is as described by Ap and Ning. There's plenty of work, but not enough Khasi workers; why else would we have to bring people from outside to build our houses, our roads, our infrastructure projects, or to work in our coal mines? The reason is not simply that many Khasi labourers are not very reliable but also that there are not enough of them. The unemployment problem is mostly with our educated youth, Don, they are unfit for blue-collar jobs, and there are not enough opportunities for the kind of jobs they have been trained to do. That's how it is. Okay, who's next?'

Surprisingly, Dale raised his hand and said, 'I have a small story, Bah, a very short one, it's called "Please Wake Me Up". One day, ha, an officer was planning to go to some faraway village. He had to get up very early in the morning, so he said to his servant, "Arnes, wake me up early tomorrow, okay? Wake me up by four o'clock … I have to leave by five-thirty."

'The servant said, "All right, Bah, I'll do that … Ooh, but how will I know the time? Will you do me a small favour, Bah? When it's four o'clock, no, Bah, you please let me know, and then I will get up and wake you up." That's my story, hahaha,' Dale concluded with a laugh.

'That's a joke, you bloody idiot!' Bah Kynsai said, although he was also laughing.

I said, 'Hold on, Bah Kynsai, it's not as trivial as it may sound to you. I think the message here could be significant too. For instance, if we don't first provide the servant with everything that he needs, how will he serve us at all? *A bad master makes a bad servant.* Don't you think so?'

'When you put it like that, no, Bah Ap, it does sound like a good story,' Donald agreed.

And Dale shook his fist in the air and cried out: 'Yahoo!'

'Okay, okay,' Bah Kynsai said, then added, 'you know, liah, I also want to tell a story, man, but nothing's coming to me right now …'

'It will come,' Raji consoled him, 'you are well known for your stories. Meanwhile, why don't we ask Ap to tell us some more, he's written two or three books of short stories in Khasi, okay, it shouldn't be a problem for him.'

So I told them the story of the fabulous camera.

Maduh Res, a very talented football player, I began, was selected by his office to participate in the All India Office Football Tournament held in Kolkata. Maduh Res was a rather good-looking young man. His full name was Reskiwer Rynjah. Reskiwer, as you might have guessed, is a misspelling of the English word 'rescuer', not unusual for a Khasi name. Reskiwer was called Maduh by his nephews and nieces because he happened to be the youngest uncle in the family. Friends and neighbours simply followed their example and called him Maduh Res.

The trip to Kolkata was Maduh Res's first. In fact, it was his first trip anywhere outside the state, as it was for most of the other players. Knowing this, the team manager spoke to everyone as soon as they boarded the train. He told them of the many dos and don'ts when travelling by train, and especially warned everyone not to buy anything from the hawkers who peddled their wares inside the compartments. When they asked him why, he explained that most of the hawkers were cheats and their products fakes.

Everyone, including Maduh Res, agreed to follow the manager's instructions to the letter. But when the train started moving and the hawkers appeared, Maduh Res was dazzled by all the knick-knacks and baubles they were carrying in their baskets, which they proclaimed were *phorein mal*, or foreign goods. In those days in Shillong, foreign ware was a rarity. The now-demolished Motphran Overbridge, or OB, which, as you know, sold second-hand garments from all over the world, had not been built. The Fruit Market sold only fruits, and not phorein mal like they do today, and the Bhutia Market, which is full of Chinese stuff, had not yet been dreamt of. You can imagine, therefore, what an attraction the hawkers' phorein ware was to Maduh Res, who had never seen such things.

He said to himself, 'Wow, man, there are so many different varieties here, leh! And the price is so low, man, probably because they are from Japan, Korea and China or what? How can they say these products are fake when they glitter like so! Why? Am I a fool or what, not to be able to judge for myself? I know what is counterfeit and what is genuine, no?'

He looked at the glittering phorein products and drooled. 'I will have a look at one of them, leh, no harm, surely, in looking!' He called to one of the hawkers and said, 'Hey, chokra, how much is this lighter?'

'*Sirf do rupaiya.*'

'Gosh man, only two rupees! And that nail clipper?'

'*Sirf panch rupaiya.*'

'La bong leh, ass-wiping thing, man, only five rupees! How cheap, how cheap! Aha, look at this marvellous camera, so beautiful, and so flashy! This camera, how much?'

'*Yeh to mahenga hai … Do hajar, lekin kamti karega.*'

'Oh shit, oh shit, it's only 2000 rupees! Hey Kin,' he called out to his friend sitting nearby. 'This lovely camera is only 2000 rupees, man! In Shillong, it would have been thousands more, if it were available at all! And that too, he said, he would reduce a little bit, leh!'

His friend tried to discourage him. He said, 'Maybe it's fake or what?'

'No man, how can it be a fake when it's so sleek and glossy?' He turned the camera around, examined it from all angles, and said, 'See, see, how beautiful! Foreign is foreign after all, no? Perfect in all respects! How much shall I ask, man?'

Kin knitted his fair brow for some time and said, 'My mother used to tell me, "When you buy anything from a dkhar, you must ask for half the price, always." Why don't you do that? If he gives, fine, if not, forget it.'

A dkhar, like I said, is a non-Khasi.

Maduh Res decided Kin's advice was quite sound. Accordingly, he said to the hawker, 'One thousand!'

The hawker seemed to hesitate for a long time before saying, '*Lijiye, lijiye, bakshish karega.*'

The hawker was essentially saying, 'Take, take, I will give it to you as a gift.'

Maduh Res's handsome face broke into a smile. He giggled with pleasure and exclaimed, 'He has given, man, Kin, he has given! Gosh man, a camera for only one thousand! Hey, chokra, film, film?'

'*Filim andar me. Filim free hai.*'

'The film is already here, man! My God, ya! Camera and film for only one thousand! It's like getting one for nothing, leh, Kin! Why don't you also buy?'

But Kin was not very free with his money, probably because his family had been very poor before he got this job. He said, 'I don't have much money, ya, I have to give all my salary to my mother, no?' He watched Maduh Res counting his money and suddenly shouted to him, 'Hey, hey, don't pay him, don't pay him! First, you test whether it's working or not.'

'Okay, okay, you pose. I'll click one for you … It works; it works!' Maduh Res exulted and took several random photos of people sitting close by. 'It's free film, man, fire at will!'

And so, because the film was free, Maduh Res and his friends took several photos of themselves in various poses inside the train, and when they got to Kolkata, they clicked a photo of whatever struck their fancy until, eventually, the film ran out.

'Come, come, let's buy a new reel,' Maduh Res said to his friends. 'Oh yes, we can also get this film developed at the same time, no?'

They went to a studio and told the owner to develop the used film and replace it with a new reel.

The studio owner examined the camera curiously. He looked at it from the left, he looked at it from the right, then turned it over many times, his eyebrows furrowed. Finally, he opened the camera, removed the film, put in a new one, and told them to come back after an hour or two.

Maduh Res and his friends went to click more photos of Kolkata's famous landmarks, and returned to the studio two hours later.

As soon as he saw them, the studio owner asked, 'Whom did you photograph?'

'Ourselves!' Maduh Res replied. 'On the train, here in Kolkata … Why do you ask?'

'You bought this camera on the train, huh?' the studio owner said, as if he had finally made sense of something perplexing. 'You did not take photos of yourselves,' he explained. 'You took photos of Hema Malini, Dharmendra, Vinod Khanna, Parveen Babi, Zeenat Aman and Shashi Kapoor … all Hindi superstars.'

'Ha!' Maduh Res shouted. 'How can that be? We took photos of ourselves, man! I'm telling you! My God, man, Kin, how can we change into actors and actresses like that?'

'Magic camera,' the studio owner mocked us.

Suddenly a thought struck Kin, and he asked the studio owner, 'What about the new film?'

'Show me, let me check.'

Maduh Res handed over the camera and watched anxiously as the man opened it and examined the film. After a while, he said, 'The film is not going anywhere. When you click, ha, first, it steps forward, and when you click again, it steps backward. That's all. It's dancing.'

Maduh Res smacked his forehead—an action that eloquently expressed the state of his feelings. He was cursing himself, feeling anger, sorrow, regret and shame, all at once.

When I finished the story, Magdalene was cackling with delight and Donald was grinning from ear to ear.

Smiling at them, Bah Kynsai asked, 'Moral?'

Bah Su offered: '*Ignorant disobedience leads to wretchedness.*'

'Or perhaps, *uninformed defiance is sheer pig-headedness,*' Evening added.

Like everyone else, Bah Kynsai agreed with both, and said he had a little story to tell.

One day, he said, an MLA was visiting a village in his constituency. The moment he alighted from his SUV, people swarmed around him like bees around their queen. They demanded that he provide them with drinking water immediately, reminding him that the village had been facing a shortage for many years now.

But the politician, fed up with their pestering, scolded them: 'The whole lot of you are fools! I had promised you a long time ago that I would provide the village with telephone facilities, but now you are demanding water instead! Don't you want your village to advance? Fools, fools, fools! The whole lot of you are fools!'

Bah Kynsai stopped rather abruptly and asked, 'What do you think?'

A smiling Magdalene asked, 'Is that a true story or a tall tale, Bah Kynsai?'

'True, true!'

Raji agreed. 'It may be true, Mag. I can well imagine the scene; politicians are like that, you know.'

'And mind you,' Hamkom remarked, 'he didn't even deliver on his telephone promise, okay?'

But Bah Kynsai said impatiently, 'All of you are missing the point, na? What's the point, Ap?'

'*Give us what we want, not what you want to give,*' I responded.

'Yesss! That's the point, na! The government should give us what we want and not try to deflect our attention to something that we don't need. Okay, next story?'

Raji drawled, 'Ap, from his books.'

'Ap, from his books,' Magdalene mimicked him. 'Are you drunk or what?'

'A little,' he said in the same sing-song tone.

'Go ahead, na, Ap, what are you waiting for?' Bah Kynsai said.

'Okay, let me tell you the story of the recalcitrant quilt. If anyone here has a connection with Shella, I request you to not take umbrage; this is a true story …'

People residing on the Shillong–Sohra road, from Mylliem down to Sohra itself, have a disparaging nickname for the inhabitants of Shella, a village on the Indo–Bangladesh border. This is because of something that happened a long time ago, during the British era, when the Shillong–Sohra road was merely a dirt track used by horse carts and people travelling on foot. In those days, the journey from Shillong to Sohra took several hours. Often, travellers had to make an overnight stop at one of the wayside inns that dotted the route—rarely did anyone risk journeying at night.

One winter evening, a Shella man who had left Shillong rather late, found that he had travelled only as far as Mylliem, reputed to be the coldest place in the Khasi Hills, as night fell. Because of the dark, the loneliness and the terrible cold—especially for him, since he lived in a warm place—he went to look for shelter in one of the wayside inns. Since all the inns were occupied, someone directed him to the hut of an old woman who lived a little away from the main road.

The old woman, who was simply called Men Mahu, welcomed the stranger with the warmth and hospitality for which the people of Mylliem were well known. She said: 'Come, come, Bah, sit near the hearth so you may be warm … Actually, my house is not an inn, Bah, I have never lodged anyone before. You see, Bah, my house is small, I have no spare room, and I don't have anyone to help me. I live with my only son, who is busy working in the fields. But Kong Jngir, my neighbour, said you could not find a place anywhere, so what to do, I have to help you out, no? I hope you don't mind staying in my humble house.'

As soon as he entered, the Shella rushed to the fire to warm his hands, which were so cold and numb that they seemed to be no longer a part of him. Expressing his gratitude, he said, 'Don't you fret, old mother, I'm very thankful to you for giving me board and lodging, otherwise where would I have gone?'

'But as I said earlier,' Men Mahu explained again, 'my house is small, and I have only two bedrooms, one for me and one for my son, which means that you'll have to sleep in this room … I hope you don't mind that. If you sleep near the fire with a nice, thick quilt, you should be quite warm the whole night.'

'It's all right, it's all right, old mother, I don't mind where I sleep. I'm really grateful just to have a roof over my head.'

After he had sat near the fire for some time, and the warmth had returned to his body, the Shella began looking around carefully. The room served, it seemed, as a kitchen and living room and was quite spacious. In the middle was the hearth, and just above it, a bamboo platform where the old woman kept firewood and other odds and ends. In a corner to the west were two doors leading to the two bedrooms. In another corner to the east was a kind of hollow, paved with stones and about eight inches deep, ten feet long and eight feet wide. It seemed to be the washing area. At one end of it, there were earthen pots in which water was stored. The pots were black with age. Indeed, everywhere he looked—he could see, with the help of the firelight and a little lamp on a cornice—the room was black with soot and smoke. The planks on the floor looked as if they had never been washed. He said to himself, 'This old woman really has dirty habits. Look at her clothes, how filthy and ragged! Even an arrow would find it difficult to pierce through all that filth! And what about the food? Ugh, it must be horrible!'

At that very moment, Men Mahu brought in the rice pot, the curry vessel, plates, a wooden ladle and a wooden spatula, saying: 'We'll have our food now, okay, Bah, my son has also come ... The only thing is, I don't have any nice curry to give you, only these mustard leaves boiled with salted and dried fish ... I hope you don't mind. Shall we eat now?'

The Shella looked at the rice pot and the curry vessel, burnt black by the fire, and he looked at the food, and his mood immediately soured. He thought, 'Who would eat this kind of food? Mustard leaves and a potful of water, with only two small pieces of dried fish? And the mustard, did she even wash it? I'm not eating this stuff. The rice, of course, I'll have to force it in, just to avoid this growling hunger, but ...'

In a tone that betrayed his displeasure, he said, 'Give me only rice and salt, it's enough.'

'Why would you eat only rice and salt, Bah? Take the fish broth also, although, I admit, it doesn't seem like much.'

'No, no, no, it's enough,' the Shella said quickly, and then under his breath, he added, 'Even the rice only because I have to.'

'What did you say, Bah?' Men Mahu asked him.

'I said it's enough; I don't eat dried fish.'

The old woman had actually heard that off-colour remark, but she pretended ignorance and only said, 'Oh.'

After the meal was over, Men Mahu took out a bamboo mat for the stranger to sleep on. She also brought some old sacks for him to use as a pillow and a very thick quilt, stuffed with rags and sewn together from old clothes.

The Shella looked intently at the quilt: it seemed old and dirty. What if it was crawling with bugs? Aloud he said, 'It's okay, it's okay, don't give me that quilt. I have a thick shawl, and this fire is quite warm, I'll be all right.'

'How can you be all right with just a shawl in such a frigid place? And when the fire goes out, you'll die of the cold! You'll simply writhe about on the ground. Take it, Bah, take it, don't be so fussy.'

But the Shella stubbornly refused. 'It's okay; it's okay. I'll be warm enough, don't force me ...'

'All right then, if you say so,' Men Mahu replied, now understanding that the sight of the old quilt had made him nauseous. 'I'll just keep it in this corner for now,' she added as she went into her room.

The Shella laid the bamboo mat near the fire, arranged the old sacks carefully and went to sleep, covering himself from head to foot with his shawl. The fire was burning in the hearth, so he was warm and soon fast asleep. But an hour or so later, when the fire went out, he woke up to a raw, freezing cold that he had never before experienced. He shivered all over. His feet were numb and his body felt as if it was covered with ice. He curled into a ball like a pupa in a cocoon, but still he could feel no warmth at all. He clenched his jaws and ground his teeth and shoved his head between his thighs, but the biting cold crept up from the planks, crawled into his feet, bit into his body and penetrated his very bones. Finally, unable to withstand the onslaught of the stinging, hurting wintry chill, he sat up to rub his body and feet. At that moment, he saw the old quilt that Men Mahu had left in a corner and crawled towards it. Dragging it to his makeshift bed, the Shella pulled it over his body and tried to go back to sleep, quite forgetting how old and filthy it had seemed to him earlier. Presently, he could feel the warmth stealing over him again. He made himself more comfortable beneath the quilt, and after a while, fell once more into a deep sleep.

In the morning, Men Mahu and her son saw the Shella fast asleep under the quilt. On the spur of the moment, she decided to teach him a lesson. 'I gave him the broth, no, he was revolted by it!' she said to herself. 'I offered him the quilt, no, he was revolted by that too! But now, who's snoring happily beneath it, huh? I'll teach him some manners, just you wait ...'

She fetched a large stick from the courtyard, dragged the quilt away from the sleeping Shella and began beating it with all the force at her command, cursing and berating it at the top of her voice:

'You shameless creature! You brazen hussy! When people don't want you, why do you force yourself upon them!? Don't you know they find you revolting? Where are your manners? Where is your self-respect? Today I'll beat you till you hop about like a frog! I'll beat you till you remember the lesson for the rest of your life!'

The Shella, who understood that the old woman was really rebuking him in giving the poor quilt a pounding, got up immediately. Gathering his belongings together, he ran away as fast as he could, with Men Mahu's son darting after him, demanding payment.

Soon, the story of this incident spread everywhere, and the man became known from then on as *U Shella tuh nep*, the quilt-thieving Shella.

Hamkom was the first to react. 'This Ap, leh, what strange stories he's getting, no?'

'Strange and diverting!' Donald pronounced, laughing. 'And you said this is a true story, no, Bah Ap?'

'Yeah, yeah, that's what he said,' Magdalene merrily answered for me. 'But what an effective lesson the old woman gave that fellow, ha, Ap?'

'Ingenious, ingenious,' Bah Kynsai declared. 'And what moral shall we draw from this?'

'*Pride leads to disgrace*,' Bah Su responded.

I was not entirely happy with that, so I added, '*The wise know how to counsel*.'

Donald liked that very much. 'Beautiful, Bah Ap, *wa*, *wa*, beautiful!'

'Wa, wa? What do you mean, wa, wa?' Bah Kynsai demanded. 'We are not reciting *shayari*, na?

Ignoring Bah Kynsai, Donald asked, 'But Bah Ap, are the people of Shella as arrogant as that fellow?'

'No, Don. I think the quality of being arrogant, or bad generally, is individual rather than communal. Unfortunately, because of that man's action, his entire community is unfairly called "quilt-thieving" to this day. It has always been like that, Don.'

'Okay!' Bah Kynsai broke in. 'Who's next?'

Raji suddenly remembered a small story.

'One very well-to-do lady,' he began, 'saw a lame beggar walking lamely—'

'Why do you have to say "walking lamely"? It's understood that a lame beggar would walk lamely, na?' Bah Kynsai objected.

'That's what I'm saying, no? You also, no, Bah Kynsai, sometimes you don't understand anything, a lame beggar has to walk lamely, no?'

We all chuckled at that. Magdalene gestured to us to leave Raji alone, for he was clearly a bit drunk.

Continuing his story, Raji said, 'This lady saw a lame beggar walking lamely on the road with the help of a stick, okay? She saw him, and she said, "Ah, poor old man, take this, take this ten-rupee note. Alas, it must be a bitter thing to be lame. But take heart, my poor man, if you had been blind, it would have been even more horrible!"

'And you know what the lame beggar said? He said, "You are very right, *Mai*, yesterday, na, Mai, because I was blind, na, people only cheat me, cheat me and gave me no good money … People very bad, Mai."'

Dale cackled at the story. 'Do you mean to say the beggar was a fraud, that he was neither lame nor blind, Bah Raji?'

'Exactly. But what about the lady? Wasn't she blind also? She said, "poor old man" ignorantly, not knowing anything, okay? So, the moral is, *don't poor this poor that without knowing anything*, and this moral is very significant—'

'It's significant because Raji says it,' Bah Kynsai teased him.

Raji clucked his tongue in annoyance and said, 'Arre, this Bah Kynsai also! You don't know what I'm getting at, no? Earlier, okay, Khasis were very kind, I'm telling you, very kind, very accommodating. If they saw a stranger, okay, they accepted him immediately, they never allowed people to mistreat him, and they used to say, "Don't do that to the poor soul!" Very accommodating, very accepting, and what is the result? Unconto … unconto … uncontollable Influx, with capital I. Now, you see the point, propheshor?'

'We are done quarrelling about influx, mə, lyeit!' Bah Kynsai cursed him. 'Ap, will you tell another story?'

I agreed immediately, wanting to avoid another quarrel between them.

'This story is called "The Command of Mr Hynñiew Skum". And it really happened to me …'

'Really?' Hamkom asked derisively. 'So now we are talking about ourselves too?'

'Don't interrupt, na!' Bah Kynsai said.

'No, Bah Kynsai, if we are talking about ourselves, ha, will it be amusing and meaningful? That's what we said our stories should be, no?'

'Our stories? How many have you told, liah?' Bah Kynsai asked sarcastically. 'Go ahead, Ap, we can do the judging afterwards.'

The incident took place on a Sunday morning, a few years ago, at the bookshop of a friend. I was going to Ïewduh for a haircut—wearing only my house shirt, a pair of tracksuit bottoms and rubber flip-flops—but after the haircut, I thought I might as well proceed to my friend's bookshop to discuss a book that he and I were planning together. As we were talking about possible publication dates and printing presses, a man came into the shop. He was tall and bulging with muscles. His tee-shirt looked as if it would tear any moment because of all those muscles trying to break free. From his conversation with my friend, I realised that he was a Mr Hynñiew Skum, a winner of the Mr Hynñiew Skum Bodybuilding Competition.

Now, Mr Hynñiew Skum had brought a large order for my friend. He wanted to buy hundreds of exercise books, hundreds of textbooks and also many stationery items. It seemed as if he too was a book supplier. And because he was a well-heeled customer with a large order, my friend became wholly preoccupied with him. Seeing that, I amused myself by examining the many titles on display, while keeping an ear tuned to their conversation.

From the way Mr Hynñiew Skum was behaving, puffing his chest and flexing his muscles all the time, I had immediately realised that he was an arrogant man. While talking with my friend, for instance, he did not give him a chance to speak at all. All the time, it was him, yack, yack, yack. Then, suddenly, he asked, 'I want tea, do you want tea?'

He took out a hundred-rupee note from his wallet and said to my friend, who was trying to pull out some money himself, 'No, no, no, I'll take care of it!'

Then he turned to me, assuming I was a non-tribal helper there, and said in a peremptory tone, '*Ei, tum jao to, do cup chai aur samosa le ke ao! Aur haan, gwa pass rupaiya aur sikret ek packet bhi le ke ao!*' ('Hey, you, go and bring two cups of tea and samosas! And yes, also bring me five rupees of betel nut and a packet of cigarettes!')

I was incensed. Not only had this man mistaken me, a lecturer and writer, for somebody's dogsbody, but he had also commanded me to buy tea, samosas, betel nut and cigarettes for him. 'The son of a bitch,' I said to myself, 'to mistake me, *me*, for a daily-wage earner!' But how was I to deal with a thick-bodied man like him? It was pointless to quarrel with him. How could I, frail as I was, win a physical argument with him? 'Stupid son of a bitch!' I cursed him again. 'What to do, what to do?' I racked my brains, and then hit upon an idea.

At that moment, my friend, the bookseller, who had a great deal of respect for me, began to apologise to me. But I made a gesture, signalling that he was not to say anything. I took the money from Mr Hynñiew Skum, with a warning glance at my friend, and left the shop.

When I was some distance away, I directed my feet towards the Palace Diary at Motphran, where they sold excellent tea and *puri*. I ordered one plate of puri, two *rasgolas* and a cup of ginger tea. I was ravenous by that time, and after I had wolfed down my rasgolas and the puri, served with curried potatoes, I called out for one more cup of tea and three samosas with honey sauce. After I had eaten to my heart's content, I bought five rupees worth of betel nut and went home.

'What! You went home? You spent his money and went home!' Magdalene cried out. 'Oh, my God, this Ap is really funny, ya!'

The next Sunday, when I met my friend again, he laughed and asked, 'What happened that day? That fellow was very angry with you. He told me not to employ such thugs, but I told him you were not my employee, just some unknown customer. I didn't tell him anything about you.'

Evening slapped his thigh, laughing. 'Did that really happen to you, Ap? My God, man, what a situation to find yourself in!'

'I still can't believe you did that, Ap!' Magdalene said, still laughing.

'What else could he do against a bodybuilder like that, na?' Bah Kynsai argued. 'You know what?' he added, 'I think the moral here should be, *only ingenuity can prevail over tyranny* or even this, *intelligence is strength*. How's that? I think the story is good, Ham.'

Hamkom, who too was laughing, simply nodded his head, but Donald said, 'Very appropriate, Bah Kynsai, very appropriate. And now, can I tell you a little story? It's not really my own creation. I read it somewhere and found it quite interesting.'

Everybody was pleased that someone other than me was telling a story. We urged him to begin.

'It's really very short,' Donald began. 'According to a news story that appeared on 1 July 1976 in *The Register-Guard*, a newspaper published from Eugene, Oregon, a young Taiwanese sent as many as 700 love letters, in the span of two years, to a woman he loved and wanted to marry.

'His persistence finally paid off, for at the end of the two years, the woman did decide to get married so she could put a stop to all those love letters.

And you know what?' He paused to laugh and then said, 'She married the postman who had faithfully brought her the letters.'

Magdalene laughed delightedly and congratulated him on a very funny story. But Bah Kynsai insisted that Donald should also provide a moral. Without a moral, he said, his story would fail.

As Donald crinkled his brows in concentration, I offered: '*He who serves well shall become a master.*'

'Wonderful, Bah Ap, wonderful!' Donald exulted. 'I accept that gratefully.'

Encouraged by Donald's little story, Bah Kit said, 'If a brief story like that is okay, then I also have one, Bah Kynsai. This is a conversation I overheard between two friends of mine, ha, it was about their son. The mother began it. She said, "You know, Father, you must really get the lock of this cabinet repaired immediately. Why? Because, wherever I keep my money, ha, this thieving son of ours always finds it. Where shall I keep it for now? Can you help me think of a safe hiding place?"

'The father thought for a while and said, "Why don't you keep it in the bookcase where his books are, Mother? I'm sure he'll never go anywhere near it." And from then on, the parents say, their money has always been safe.'

Raji laughed drunkenly. 'But this is very true of our society, okay, very true, Bah Kynsai, even if you don't know it, we don't read books, okay, we simply don't read books. Soso Tham, our national bard, said … What did he say, Ap?'

'He said, "But the Khasi today refuses to read unless compelled to do so at school or the church. And the young people do not read a Khasi book, however good it may be, unless it is a textbook. Is there blindness more opaque than this?" But Bah Kit's story is a bit different; the boy even refused to read textbooks …'

'Exactly,' Raji replied, 'we don't read books, and we don't even read textbooks unless forced to. He said this in, when did he say this, 1932, right, and it's still very true today, Bah Kynsai, even if you don't know it. This is a powerful indictment against our society, okay, as a whole, okay, we especially don't read Khasi books; look at these people, Ham, Don, Mag, Dale, Bah Kynsai—'

'I'm not among them, pha liah!' Bah Kynsai protested, deliberately using the rude feminine marker 'pha'. 'I read a lot of Khasi books too.'

'Okay, okay, point taken, but look at Ham, Don, Mag, Dale, Ning—well, maybe not Ning, I don't know—but these, they don't read, they are too good for Khasi books—'

'I do read books, okay, Bah Raji,' Dale objected. 'I read car instruction manuals!'

'But what's the moral of this?' Bah Kynsai demanded.

'Moral? That's the moral, no?' Raji replied. 'They don't read books; you don't read books; nobody reads at all!'

We all laughed at Raji's drunken clowning, but Bah Su replied, 'There's a moral here, Raji. *He who doesn't read doesn't succeed.*'

'Right, right, Bah Su, you are quite right, that's it!' Raji enthused. 'Any questions, Bah Kynsai?' he challenged.

Bah Kynsai ignored him and said, 'Okay, next?'

'Ap, from his books,' Raji drawled again.

I then told them the story called 'As Per the Rate'.

One day, I began, when the Shillong–Sohra road was still a dirt track—

'What, more Sohra stories?' Hamkom broke in, a touch sarcastically.

'Many more,' I told him. 'Am I not from Sohra, after all?'

One day, when the Shillong–Sohra road was still a dirt track, two men were pulling a horse cart with a heavy load towards Sohra. The cart owner, a man named Kynjreng, was pulling from the front while his helper, Phren, probably a misspelling of 'friend', was pushing from behind. After some time, a friend of Phren's, a man named Mojen, appeared on the scene. The two greeted each other with a lot of warmth, dancing and chanting, giving each other a bear hug and patting each other's backs.

When their greeting ritual was done, Phren turned to Kynjreng, who was waiting impatiently, and said, 'Kyn, why don't you give Jen some work also? See, the poor man is walking without carrying anything, why don't you help him out?'

'What work can I give Jen when two men can easily push the cart?'

'That's what you say. Now that the track is level, we can push easily, fine, but when we come to a steep slope, what will happen then, huh? Come on, Kyn, give him some work also, no? Think of it as a favour to him; how can he walk all the way to Sohra without carrying or doing anything?'

Soon Mojen also began pleading with him. 'Come on, Kyn, do give me a chance, man, if you refuse me now, when I need you, what if you need me sometime, huh?'

With both of them pestering him like that, Kynjreng finally gave in and said, 'Okay, I'll let him work with us, but I'll give him only one *ana*.'

One ana is equivalent to 6.25 paise.

'One ana!' Phren exclaimed in surprise. 'When you are giving me sixty paise, how can you give Jen only one ana?'

'You see, Phren, the two of us can push this cart easily. I need you, that's why I'm giving you sixty paise, but I don't need Jen, I'm doing him a favour, so one ana or nothing … What's it to be?'

'Okay, okay,' Mojen interrupted, 'if he doesn't want to give me more than that, ha, Ren, what can I do? I'll take it just so I can do some work.'

And so, the three of them continued on their journey: Kynjreng and Phren pulling from the front and Mojen pushing from the back. As long as the cart was on level ground, there was no problem at all, but the moment it had to negotiate an incline, the two men in front began puffing and panting and straining with all their might.

On one occasion, when they were going over a particularly sharp slope, the two men in front couldn't move the cart at all. Kynjreng wondered why this should be so when three men were pulling and pushing it. He asked Phren to hold the cart still while he went to check what was happening at the back.

'Phooey, son of an animal!' Kynjreng exploded when he saw what Mojen was doing. 'What kind of pushing is that? How can you push with only one forefinger!'

Mojen did not bat an eyelid. Very casually, he replied, 'Oh, so you need me now? How much are you paying me? Sixty paise for others, only one ana for me, and you still expect me to push hard? As the rate, so the work! One ana, one forefinger!'

'What did you say? Son of an ingrate! I'll give you a hiding; today, I'll give you the hiding of your life!'

But as Kynjreng was running after Mojen, Phren shouted, 'The cart! The cart, it's moving backwards!'

Kynjreng had to leave Mojen alone and hurry back to help Phren control the cart, but he shouted back a warning: 'Don't come near us!'

This only spurred Mojen to walk even closer to the cart and challenge him, 'Why? Is it your road? And how will you move the cart without me? Give me at least twenty-five paise and I'll help you.'

Grudgingly, Kynjreng had to agree to Mojen's rate.

Donald said, sounding quite impressed, 'I have never heard these stories before, Bah Ap, never! You know, initially, when you spoke of little stories, okay, I thought you would be sharing mobile and internet jokes. I have plenty of those. But these, I have never heard, Bah Ap.'

'Moral, moral?' Bah Kynsai demanded.

I said I had composed a little poem to serve as a moral, and quoted it to them:

> *U briew ba khlem kam, u khroh ban ïoh kam,*
> *U tang shu ïoh kam, u sangeh trei kam;*
> *U heh sa ka khñium, ka dawa pisa tam.*

(A man without a job wheedles for one,
But once he gets it, he stops doing it;
He grumbles for one thing only, a little more money.)

Evening said excitedly, 'You are absolutely right, Ap, this is our work culture. This is exactly what we do! To get a job, okay, we would do anything: wheedle as you said, kowtow, beg and bribe ... Yes, *bribe*! We go to politicians, officers and anyone who can help us, but once we get our jobs, ha, especially if we get in through the back door, ha, we stop working. And why? Because we think we are too powerful for anybody to do anything about it. But all the time, we demand more and more money, more and more perks. Take the case of the Mawmluh Cherra Cement Factory, for instance—it has offered the voluntary retirement scheme to as many as 300 employees. Why do you think? Because there are more employees than the factory can support. And why is that? Because the company had to accommodate many people sent by politicians, big officers and anyone with wealth and influence. That's how rotten things are in this state!'

Even though the denunciation came from Evening, there was no quarrel this time. Everyone was aware of the facts.

After a while, however, Donald raised his forefinger and said, 'There's one more aspect to your story, Bah Ap.'

'I know. In fact, that is another good moral for the story: *as the rate, so the work.*'

'Yes, yes, Bah Ap,' Donald responded, 'employers are always taking advantage of workers, always making them work more for less pay.'

'Khasis used to say "*Bam kulai kit hati*", Don,' Bah Kynsai said. 'Eat like a horse, carry like an elephant. That's what all employers would like their workers to do, na?'

The next story was Bah Kynsai's. It was about Header's encounter with a bodybuilder. Header was a prankster who lived in Shillong.

One day, a tall, powerfully built man came to the office where Header was working. He appeared to be a contractor coming to meet the officer-in-charge. The way he carried himself was truly impressive, and because he was wearing a tee-shirt, his biceps could be seen rippling and straining against the short sleeves.

Header, who was working at his table, stopped to look closely at the man as he walked down the passage with a swinging gait. He said to himself, 'This fellow behaves as if he owns the place, sala!' But out loud, he said, '*Uuh, uuh*, what a body!'

When he heard Header's fat-dripping flattery, the man puffed out his chest, looked up imperiously and flexed his arm muscles as he went past. Then he took out his dark glasses from his pocket and put them on his head, perhaps thinking it made him look even more dashing.

Header was annoyed. 'Arre! I was being sarcastic, and this fellow thought I was flattering him! Look at him puffing up like a fish maw! I think I'll pierce this bloated balloon with a pin.' Out loud, he said, 'Uuh, uuh, the body like a bulldozer, but the engine? Like a scooter!'

Everybody in the hall roared with laughter, and horribly embarrassed, the man bent his head in shame and almost ran to the officer's room.

The end of the story was greeted with a loud laugh from Magdalene, who exclaimed, 'What a witty fellow he is, no? "The body like a bulldozer, but the engine like a scooter"! Fantastic! I wish I could use language like that, ya!'

'What a joker, what a joker!' Hamkom agreed, laughing.

'But there are many people like him, Ham,' Bah Kit said. 'I have many stories about such a person, ha. Shall I tell?'

'But first, what moral would you give to the Header story, Bah Kynsai?' Evening said.

'*Muscles without brains cannot pull our life*,' I offered.

'Good, good!' Evening approved. 'Hey, Bah Kynsai, we should always try to make these morals as appropriate as possible, okay?'

'That's what we have been trying to do, na?' Bah Kynsai replied. 'Okay, Kit, why don't you tell us about your man?'

Bah Kit then told us about Stin, a prankster and swindler who died not too long ago.

The strong and robust Stin, with a face as pink as that of a sahep, a European, was a gifted man, according to Bah Kit. He was a skilled mechanic and misteri, that is, a construction worker, mason, carpenter and so on, who could make anything and do anything with his hands. He could speak several languages too, like Nepali, Hindi, Assamese and Bengali. Unfortunately, he was also an incorrigible cheat. Once, he even cheated a Marwari businessman, a thing unheard of. We hear of wily Marwari businessmen cheating their customers, but for one of them to be cheated is indeed a very rare thing.

Stin had been contracted by this fellow to build a garage big enough for three cars. When the day came for him to lay the concrete slab, the businessman and his assistants visited the site to inspect the size of the steel rods being used and the strength of the cement being mixed. The Marwari left, very satisfied. But, not being a trusting man by nature, he asked one of his assistants to stay back and oversee the work.

On his part, Stin did everything as he should, and the overseer left, satisfied. But when the work was done, Stin was unhappy. He had not been able to make much profit from the laying of the concrete slab, as he was forced to use the correct number and the correct size of steel rods. Nor could he make any profit from the cement, which, under the watchful eyes of the overseer, he had to mix according to the specified formula. In frustration, he said to his workers, 'I don't like it one little bit! This Marwari is trying to outwit me. I haven't been able to get anything out of him. You fellows go and bring me some bamboo poles between 12 mm and 16 mm. I'll show him what Stin is made of!'

When the bamboo poles were brought, Stin and his men dug up the cement before it could harden, replaced the steel rods, except for a few, with bamboo poles and covered up the whole structure again with the remixed cement. Stin sold the truckload of steel rods, and when fifteen days had elapsed, and it was time to remove the shuttering planks, he was nowhere to be found.

He had gone to Ri Bhoi to work as a builder under an assumed name. In the Bhoi village, he ate and drank every day at a boozer near the construction site. But he never paid the poor shop owner. He sweet-talked her into believing that he was a big-shot contractor, waiting for the house owner to pay him big money. 'Once they give me the money they owe me, okay, Mei, which is more than ten lakh,' he would say almost daily, 'I will not only pay you what is due but more, with interest. But of course, if you don't trust me, you could keep this watch of mine, very costly, and these expensive clothes as security …'

The elderly woman, whom he had addressed as 'mother', was awed by his talk of lakhs and replied, 'It's all right, Bah Ar, why wouldn't I trust you? If I cannot trust a big-time contractor like you, then whom can I trust? But forgive me for asking, Bah Ar, why aren't they giving you your money?' In the village, he was known as Bah Ar because he said his name was Arthur.

Stin replied, 'They are giving a little bit every week, Mei, but I have to give everything to my workers, poor fellows, they have to eat also, no, Mei? The big chunk they are holding back because we are only digging the foundation now. Once we are ready to erect the pillars and lay the concrete slab for the first storey, they will release the money, Mei.'

Finally, the owners gave Stin money to buy building materials on their behalf. Since they knew nothing about steel rods or steel rings, planks or cement, or indeed, where to purchase these things, they thought he would be the best person to do it, for wasn't he their trusted contractor? Besides, Stin would be leaving behind all his men at the construction site. What the owners did not know was that these men were all new workers he had hired from Ri Bhoi itself. To them too, he was Bah Ar from Mawlai, Shillong.

Stin pocketed the money, about ten lakh, and went home, never to return. In the process, he defrauded the house owners, his own workers, and the poor woman who had given him food and booze on credit.

After about two weeks, the house owners, along with a large group of supporters, arrived at the locality in Shillong where Stin was supposed to be living, with the clear intention of either getting their money back or beating him to death. They asked around for Arthur Pathaw (Arthur Pumpkin), but no one in the locality knew anyone by that name.

Stin was such a compulsive swindler that people said he could neither eat nor sleep if he had not deceived somebody that day. And he was always in need of money because he was a chronic alcoholic. One evening, he wanted drink money so desperately that he caught a hen from his own coop and showed her to his wife. He said, 'Look, old woman, some drunk wants to sell this hen very cheap, local hen, old woman, really cheap, only sixty rupees, why don't you take her? You can easily sell her for 400.'

In the dim light of the small lamp, his wife could not recognise her own hen. Tempted by the low price, she bought her and gave Stin the sixty rupees to be given to the owner. Stin put the hen back in the coop and went to meet his friends at the boozers. In the morning, when his wife looked for the new chicken, she could not find her anywhere. When she asked Stin, he pretended amazement and said, 'But I put her there, old woman, honest I did! Some son of a thief must have stolen her during the night. Wait till I find the fellow! Right now, right now, I'm going to look for him!'

With these words, he left home and spent the whole day in the boozers.

Once, Stin even took his drinking partner, disguised as a faith healer, to treat the ailing father of his Nepali friend. The old man had been suffering for a long time from an illness that made his stomach ache with sharp stabbing pains and rank with swollen gas. No treatment or medicines had been of any help.

'This is definitely Ka Sabuit!' Stin declared. Ka Sabuit, as I told you before, is an evil demon who causes stomach ache in people her keepers hate. 'But no problem,' Stin said, 'you see my friend here? He is a great diviner and healer. He'll cure your father in no time at all.'

Then, turning to his drinking partner, he said, 'These people don't understand Khasi, Momo. What you should do is chant incantations in Khasi, say anything that comes to your mind, even curses and expletives, you are very good at that. Only thing is, you need to mimic the tone our shamans use when performing their rituals, do you understand?'

Momo was so nicknamed because, according to Stin, his face was bloated like the Tibetan dumpling.

Momo did as he was told, and every time he performed his healing ritual, he was paid some money, more than enough for a few drinks. The two of them went to the sick man's house several times, and each time, Momo would apply lime, turmeric and mustard oil on the old man's stomach, all the while cursing the illness and telling it to get the hell out of there or he would literally piss on it. That was the kind of incanting and praying he did. Yet, to everybody's surprise, the old man did get well, and as a reward, Stin's friend gave him 1,000 rupees.

Another day, again to get some drink money, Stin stole a hen from a neighbour's house. After killing and cleaning the chicken, he went to the owner and said, 'Khublei, Mother of Ker, God bless. Will you please help me out and buy this chicken? I'm selling it cheap. You see, we are cooking chicken for dinner, my wife told me to kill one, but by mistake, I killed two. You have to help me out, Mother of Ker, otherwise my wife will kill me. And she would be right too, for what will we do with this extra chicken?'

Mother of Ker was delighted to buy her own chicken at a very low price indeed: only sixty rupees.

On one occasion, Stin borrowed a crowbar from the same neighbour. When he was asked to return it, he waited until the family had sat down to dinner. Going up to the house, he shouted from the veranda, 'Mother of Ker, hey, Mother of Ker! I have brought the crowbar, where shall I keep it?'

'Oh, Bah Stin? We are having dinner; just keep it in the veranda, will you?'

'Okay, here it is,' Stin replied and dropped the crowbar on the veranda's concrete floor so it would produce a loud ringing sound. After that, he said, 'I'm keeping it here, all right? Thank you so much.'

'All right, Bah Stin, thanks.'

Stin, of course, took the crowbar right back and sold it to some misteri for drink money. When his neighbour asked him about it, he simply said, 'But I brought it back, Mother of Ker! You heard me leaving it in the veranda! Perhaps you have misplaced it somewhere, why don't you look carefully?'

One time, Stin posed as a health worker. He went to a village in Ri Bhoi, and with the help of the headman, got people to assemble at the local school, where he administered an anti-measles injection to them. He used an old injection needle that he had brought from somewhere, and for the medicine, he used a mixture of water and blue ink. Stin did not charge anything for the injection because he said it was a government scheme. But he had with him an old camera without film in it, and he asked everyone to pose for photographs. The villagers were very excited about being photographed— no one in the village even had a camera—and so, they requested Stin to take as many photos of them as possible, in singles and in groups.

Stin obliged every one of them. In the end, he announced, 'I have more than 300 photos in this camera: about 220 of them are group photos, the rest are singles. Now, the photo shoot is for free, but to get each photo developed will cost some money, at least two rupees for each one. So, if any one of you would like a photo, you will have to pay me two rupees for one copy. But only if you want a copy, you understand? If not, you don't have to pay me at all.'

Everyone wanted a copy, of course. They gave him the money, and Stin was able to collect a substantial sum from that venture. Naturally, they never saw him again.

Bah Kit ended the story by saying, 'That was Stin, a larger than life character. People in Mawlai still talk about him whenever they gather to talk about the past.'

Magdalene wanted a little clarification. 'But Bah Kit, the cost of one photo is not two rupees, no?'

'Of course not! But Stin knew he could not ask for more. They were poor people; he asked them for what they could give him.'

Evening shook his head in disbelief. 'That fellow was not a trickster, he was a monster! He stole from everyone, young and old, rich and poor, employers and neighbours, friends, and even his own wife. A real monster, if you ask me.'

'Yeah, people laugh at his trickeries now, but think of the people who were cheated by him,' Bah Kit agreed. 'Some people were so mad, ha, they wanted to kill him.'

'But it's weird to have people like him in real life, no? He was real, wasn't he, Bah Kit?' Magdalene asked.

'Yes, yes, that's what I told you! I know his family very well. His wife's dead, but his sons and daughters are still there. Fortunately, they are quite nice people. Nothing like the father.'

'So what moral are we giving to these Stin stories, Bah Kynsai?' Evening asked.

'These are not individual stories, na, Ning, what moral can we derive from them? He was a trickster; that should be moral enough.'

'But then, won't they be a kind of joke?'

'No, Ning, not a joke, a study in human nature.'

'Okay, okay,' Evening conceded, 'so, what's next?'

'Do you remember the stories about that fellow from Sohra, Ap, what's his name?' Bah Kynsai asked me.

'Iso, you mean? He was also a prankster, but not dishonest like Stin. Certainly, now and then, he would play pranks on his fellow workers, but he would never steal or swindle people out of their hard-earned money. The biggest thing he ever stole was dried fish. He was working in a coal mine with his friends then, and had been asked to do the cooking in the little thatched hut outside the mine while they worked deep inside. Their food was very simple, boiled rice and chargrilled dried fish mixed with onions and chillies. But when Iso was cooking, he was tempted to eat all the fish except for one small piece. He knew he would be in real trouble when his friends came up from the mine, and so, he peeled off chips of bark from a dead tree, roasted them in the fire, cut them into tiny pieces and mixed them with onions, chillies and, for added flavour, the small piece of fish he had left for them. He then examined his handiwork. The bark, when roasted and cut into small pieces, did look exactly like salted dried fish, and it did have a fishy smell because of the flavours he had added. Satisfied, he went down to the mine to call his friends.

'He said, "Come on up, you fellows, the food is ready. I'll just go down to the stream for a while. I have already eaten, don't wait for me."

'When the hungry men came up to eat, they realised what Iso had done as soon as they munched on the fish. They looked for him everywhere, wanting to beat him up, but he had already left for home.'

'But that was stupid, no?' Evening cried. 'I mean, how could he risk losing his job because of some dried fish?'

'Iso was like a kid, very impulsive,' I said. 'His favourite ruse, for instance, was tricking boys into scrambling for marbles. He would dig a hole in the ground, put some human excrement in it, cover it with a thin layer of soil, and stick a marble into it, slightly exposed. Then he would call some boys and say, "Look, you fellows, I have kept a lot of marbles in this hole. If you want them, you'll have to run a race. Now, you go to that spot there, about fifty feet from here, okay? Stand there in a line, and when I say run, you run towards the marbles and pick them up, you understand? The first one to arrive will naturally get the most, so try your best." The boys, excited by the prospect of free marbles, would do exactly as instructed and ended up picking up a lot of crap.'

'Didn't he get into trouble with their parents, pulling that kind of prank?' Magdalene asked.

'He did, but that never stopped him. Besides, he was huge and strong as a jungle buffalo; no one could beat him in a fight. Another favourite trick of his was to cover a stone with a paper bag and wait for passers-by, usually boys, to kick the bag.

'He was really like a big baby and played pranks on his mother too. He liked spending time with friends and neighbours, entertaining them all night with his many stories. But that was a torment to his old mother, who had to stay up very late every night, waiting for him to come home. Finally, she got fed up and decided to teach him a lesson. One night, when Iso came home, he found the door locked from inside. He banged on it and pleaded with his mother to let him in, but she only said, "I told you every day not to come home so late because it disturbs my sleep, but you won't listen, so tonight you will sleep on the veranda."

'In response, Iso said, "Okay then, since you won't open, what can I do? I'll sleep here with the dog, goodnight, Mei."

'After that, he was quiet for a long while, pretending to sleep on the sackcloth his mother had left for him. Then, suddenly, he picked up a stick and beat it on a tin sheet and shouted, "*Shu, shu, bam hynroh u bnai! Shu, shu, bam hynroh u bnai!*" ("Shoo, shoo, the moon is being eaten by the toad!") For those of you who don't know, whenever there is a lunar eclipse, as these fellows,' and here I pointed to Bah Su, Bah Kit and Raji, 'will tell you, Khasis believe that everyone should come out of their homes, make a lot of noise and shout, '*Shu, shu, bam hynroh u bnai!*' This, they think, will prevent hynroh from swallowing up the moon. They say that if the moon is entirely swallowed up by hynroh, a terrible year will follow, full of disasters, not only for the family that has not participated, but also for the society as a whole. Old people, in particular, used to believe very strongly in this practice ...'

'That's intriguing, Bah Ap,' Donald interrupted. 'Is there a story behind it?'

'Yeah.'

'Will you please tell us?'

'Please, no, Ap,' Magdalene crooned, 'I too haven't heard it, ya!'

'Nor I,' Hamkom added.

'What about Iso?' I asked.

'No, no, no, after Iso!' Bah Kynsai intervened. 'Go on, go on, man.'

'As I was saying, old people would never stay inside if there was a lunar eclipse. Iso's mother was no different. She opened the door to go out and beat on a tin sheet, but as soon as she did that, Iso went inside and locked her out. The poor woman had to go and sleep with her neighbours.'

'You mean he would do that to his own mother!' Magdalene asked, aghast.

'I told you he was like a big baby. People said he seemed to have difficulty differentiating between right and wrong. Murder and theft of money and valuable items were clearly wrong, but everything else seemed to be fair game ...'

'But there was no problem afterwards, with his mother, I mean?'

'The next day, his mother made him strip to the waist and whipped him with a stinging nettle, first soaked in water to make it sting the more ...'

'But he was already an adult, no? How could she whip him like that?'

'We are talking about the 1910s, Mag, those were innocent days, even grown men could be punished by their mothers ... yeah, incredible but true. Anyway, as you can well imagine, Iso was punished in that manner very often indeed, and every time it happened, people used to flock to the scene. It was quite a spectacle, watching the hulking Iso screaming like a kid, hopping about and grimacing and contorting his chubby face in pain.'

'Hahaha, can you believe that?' Bah Kynsai laughed. 'But it's true, ha, I have heard this from many others.'

'The best known story about Iso,' I continued, 'is about how he defeated a Bengali magician in a *haat*, a marketplace, in Chatok, now in Bangladesh.'

'How could a big baby like that defeat a magician?' Evening asked incredulously.

I narrated the story my mother had told me. Iso had gone to the Chatok market as a coolie, carrying betel nut for some merchant. After he had been paid, he roamed around the bustling market, curiously examining every item like the big child that he was. It was in this way that he came across a large group of people who had gathered around a magician. The magician was, in fact, a snake charmer, yogi and conjurer. And he was brilliant. First, he made a snake dance to his music. Next, he made a rope, which lay coiled in a basket, behave like a snake, rising from the basket, raising its head and peeping at the crowd as if in awe. Then the rope climbed higher and higher into the sky, and from its great heights looked down at the crowd and seemed to laugh at them. Later, the magician, who was dressed only in a loincloth, squeezed through a very small hoop, the size of a boy's head. Later still, he produced small animals from his jute bag and made them vanish into thin air. He performed all sorts of tricks and impressed the spectators so much that they threw coins at him by the handfuls.

When the magician saw that there were many Khasis in the crowd, he shouted a challenge: 'You Khasia! You always boast of having great shamans and diviners among you, do you have anyone as great as me? Do you have anyone who would dare challenge me?' He looked around at their stupefied faces and taunted, 'As I thought, all of you are cowardly savages! Phooey!'

The Khasis were incensed. They had come to enjoy the spectacle of a great magician but had instead been horribly insulted. But what could they do? None of them was a magician. They did have a healer at that time in the market, but he was only a practitioner of traditional medicines and had neither shamanistic nor magical powers. But Iso, always reckless and eager for a challenge of any sort, thundered, 'I challenge you to a competition. I don't think you are that good. If I win, you must give me all the money you have been getting, and you must eat the mud from the riverbank for insulting us.'

The magician was surprised that anyone would challenge him, but he said, 'And if I win, what will you give me?'

'If you win, I'll give you all this money'—Iso showed him the money he had just received as his wage—'plus one large sack of betel nuts.'

'Did he have a sack of betel nuts, Bah Ap?' Donald asked.

No, he was lying, but since most Khasis who went to that market carried such merchandise, the magician did not suspect anything. However, many of the Khasis there knew that Iso had nothing. They all tried to dissuade him from doing something so foolhardy. They said, 'What can you do against a great *jadukar* like this? Can't you see he can even produce animals from his jute bag? And you, you don't even have anything to pay him with, don't be stupid, man!'

But Iso had made up his mind, and there was no reasoning with him. 'No one should speak to us like that,' he said. 'I will not allow it!'

The rules of the competition were quickly drawn up. The magician drew a circle in the sand and said, 'You see this circle? One of us will sit here as the other performs his magic. The one who cannot stay inside the circle, who leaves it for any reason at all, or who gives a sign of surrender, will be the loser. Agreed?'

Iso agreed and promptly said, 'I will begin.'

But the magician said they should toss a coin for the right to begin. The toss was conducted by one of the spectators, who declared the magician as the winner.

Iso's friends and country cousins were now even more worried. Once again, they asked him, 'What magic have you got against him?'

But Iso would not budge and only said enigmatically, 'Mother's magic.'

Iso went into the circle and sat on his haunches. The magician was also on his haunches in front of him, but outside the circle. He began to mumble into his bag and suddenly produced a huge python who immediately crawled towards Iso. In great shock, Iso jumped up and was about to run away when the Khasi healer, who was also watching, shouted, 'The python is not real, Iso! Sit down, sit down! Shut your eyes tight! The python is not real, a mere illusion, sit down and shut your eyes! Whatever he seems to do, shut your eyes tight!'

Iso did as advised. He shut his eyes tight and sat there unmoving. He could feel the python slithering towards him and coiling around his legs and slowly up his body and neck. But the Khasis shouted loud encouragement, telling him to keep his eyes shut tight and not move since it was all an illusion. The magician made the python wrap itself around Iso's body for a long time, but though Iso was on the verge of surrender more than once, he resisted the temptation with a superhuman effort and sat there doggedly, heartened by his compatriots' support.

The magician then made his next move. Mumbling and blowing into his bag, he caused a huge black wolf to jump out of it into the circle in front of Iso. The wolf stared hungrily at Iso with frighteningly inflamed eyes and snarled at him with slavering jaws. Eyes popping, Iso gaped in terror and was about to rush out when the healer shouted to him again:

'Shut your eyes, Iso, don't look at him! He's not real! Even if he jumps at you, don't move!'

When the Bengalis saw the Khasis shouting encouragement to Iso, they also began shouting their support for the magician and urged the big black wolf to pounce on the Khasia and eat him up. The wolf did pounce on Iso, who fell to the ground with a thud. Lying on his back, Iso flailed wildly about and tried to fight off the snarling, biting animal. But once again, the healer shouted, 'Shut your eyes tight and don't move, Iso! If he bites you, let him, he's not real!' Iso made a supreme effort and did as advised. And strangely, when he lay still, the wolf also began to quieten down and withdraw.

The magician shook his head in disbelief and once more mumbled and blew into his bag. He took a long time chanting his mantras, and finally, a huge Bengal tiger emerged from the bag and stood glaring at Iso. Iso stared back, almost against his will. The tiger suddenly gave a terrifying roar and sent him flying to the edge of the circle. Iso struggled up and was about to flee when he suddenly felt something heavy on his back, pinning him to the ground. It was the tiger, holding him down with one paw while emitting deafening roars as if to warn everybody off his victim. Seeing Iso in abject terror, the magician shouted triumphantly, 'Surrender now, Khasia, or the tiger will eat you up!'

Terrified out of his wits, Iso was about to cry out to the magician when the Khasi healer said again, 'No, Iso, no! Shut your eyes tight and don't move! He's not real!'

Iso shut his eyes tight and lay helplessly on the ground. He could feel the tiger growling and putting his huge jaws on the back of his head, trying to chew it off. Terrified, he was about to surrender when the healer said, 'Iso, take a fistful of earth and eat it. Then shut your eyes tight and steel your nerves! The jadukar has brought out his most terrible animal; he cannot do it again!'

His eyes tightly shut, Iso took a fistful of earth, crammed it into his mouth, and swallowed what he could. Then he steeled himself for whatever was to come. But the tiger's grip on his head seemed to slacken and his growls to weaken till, eventually, he withdrew into the magician's bag. Iso lay panting on the ground, relieved. He stared at the magician, waiting for more terror to be unleashed, but the magician announced that he had tried everything and was giving up.

It was now Iso's turn to place the magician inside the circle. 'You, jadukar, sit there and don't move!' he commanded.

When his compatriots asked him what he was going to do, he said, 'Wait and watch ... Khasi magic ... my mother taught me.' With these words, he went to the river for a bucketful of water, which he placed outside the circle, in front of the perplexed magician. Then he fetched a handful of stinging nettles, the most potent of its kind, called teiñthap, and dipped them in the water. When the nettles were nicely soaked, Iso lifted them and, without warning, began flogging the magician's naked back with them. The magician yelped in shock and agony. He jumped up, dancing around the circle, but Iso whipped his skinny legs, his exposed belly and every part of his body not protected by the little loincloth, except the face, for he did not want to harm his eyes. The magician shouted, '*Maago, maago*, I yield, I yield!' He ran out of the circle and jumped into the river. But the water only made the stinging worse. Mad with pain, he ran back to Iso and pleaded with him to remove the Khasi magic immediately.

Iso asked someone to get him two litres of mustard oil, then rubbed the magician vigorously with it. Soon, as if by magic, the pain subsided, and the now-relieved magician quickly begged Iso and the Khasis to forgive him for his insults. Everyone readily forgave him, but Iso also said, 'Don't forget my money.'

That day, the Khasis did not allow Iso to walk home. They carried him in the khoh kit briew, the conical palanquin, and up the mountain paths they went, singing gnomic phawars and shouting slogans in his honour.

Donald was the first to react. 'I'm glad you went ahead and told us the story of Iso, Bah Ap. You know, it all sounds like a different world from ours.'

'It was a different world! Did you think it was not, cosmo?' Raji asked sarcastically.

Bah Kynsai hit Raji lightly on the head with a bamboo stick and said, 'Only I can call him that, you bloody drunk!'

'What was that thing about eating a fistful of earth, Ap?' Hamkom asked quickly to divert their attention.

'The old ones used to say that eating a little pinch of soil in difficult circumstances helps us keep our self-awareness and courage while also toughening our essence, making it impossible for others to take advantage of us.'

'What does "maago" mean, lih, Ap?' Bah Kynsai asked curiously.

'When people from Sylhet are whipped by someone, they often shout "maago, maago" like that. Literally, it's "oh, mother" and is used to express anguish, even surprise. Why do you ask?'

'I thought it means "I surrender". Is that the end of the Iso stories?'

'Yeah, unfortunately. My mother knows many, many more, you know, but I keep forgetting to ask her, much to my regret now.'

'Bah Ap, why don't you tell us the story of the hynroh and the moon?' Donald requested.

'Actually, the story is about a woman by the name of Nam, Don. It is about her ascent to the realm of the stars, which caused a showdown between Sun, who was protecting her, and Ka Hynroh, who was hunting her. Moon came into the picture much later.'

With that introduction, I told them the story of Ka Nam. It all started one hot and sultry day, when a woman who was many months pregnant suddenly developed an intense yearning for lemon or something sour to quench her terrible thirst. As there was no one at home, and as she could find nobody to get some lemons for her, she decided to venture into the nearby forest to look for them herself.

Deep inside the forest, she came upon a large tree laden with the small sour-sweet fruits that Khasis call sohphie. Seeing them, she became mad with desire. But how could she, a woman big with child, get at them? How could she climb a tree so tall and so big? Looking at the fruit with her mouth watering and her eyes tearful, she exclaimed, 'Ah, if only there was someone to shake the tree or pluck the fruits for me! I would give him anything in my power.'

Hearing this, Tiger, who was dozing on the branches, sheltered by the thick leaves of the tree, away from the blazing sun, looked down and roared out, 'If you promise to give me something in return, I will throw down these fruits to you.'

Startled by the deep-throated voice, the woman looked up to see none other than the dreaded Tiger. But, tormented by her craving, she forgot her fear for the moment and asked him what he had in mind. But he refused to say and insisted that she first make the promise. At this, she pleaded with him to take pity on her and to throw down a few sohphie to her so she could return home with her thirst quenched. She added that it was not auspicious for a gestating woman to be denied her desire. Not getting what she wanted, she said, would surely affect the baby in the womb.

But Tiger was unmoved. He reminded her of the cruel trick her kind had played on him, trying to slash his tongue while they were felling Diengïei, the tree of gloom. Tiger told her that he had vowed to avenge himself by killing and devouring any human he met for what they had done to him. So, nothing but a promise to give him whatever he asked for would save her or persuade him to give her the sohphie she so desired.

The woman thought very hard. 'If I shake my head at his demand,' she mused, 'he will surely kill me. On the other hand, if I say yes to whatever he asks, I will not only be saved but also get the fruits. And once out of this forest and his grasp, how is he to find me again?' And so, she said, 'All right, Ñi La, I agree to your condition so long as it does not endanger my life in any way.'

Pleased with her words, Ñi La the Tiger took hold of the tree and shook it with all his might so that the fruits came tumbling down as the hails of Ïaïong—

'Ïaïong, Bah Ap?' Donald intervened.

'Roughly corresponding to April,' I replied. 'It's called Ïaïong, the black month, because of the sudden thunderstorms that come dark as the night, violent as destructive demons. Fortunately, they never last long, never over an hour ...'

'I know about the squalls of April, Bah Ap, it was only Ïaïong that stumped me.'

'Well, at least you know about April,' I teased him.

'On with the story, man!' Magdalene rebuked me in mock anger.

The woman picked up the sohphie one by one, placed them in her jaiñsem outer garment, and ate to her heart's content. Tiger watched her enjoying the fruit with a mischievous twinkle in his eyes and a smirk on his lips. When she had eaten all of it, he shook down some more for her to carry home. But he also reminded her of her promise, and in a voice loud as a thunderclap, he spelt out his evil desire: 'Now that you have taken my fruits, you must keep your pledge. I see that you are two-bodied and about to give birth to your child ... My wish is this: if it is a boy, he may be yours, but if it is a girl, she must be mine.'

Stunned, the woman gaped at him as he glided gracefully away. There was so much beauty in his movements, and yet, such cruelty in his heart. However, she soon took consolation from the thought that she would probably never see him again once she was back in the human world.

One night, sometime after the frightening incident in the forest, the woman began to experience birth pangs. As was the custom, friends and neighbours went to her house carrying flambeaus called 'dongmusas' with them to light their way. Tiger, who had been spying on the house for some time, having discovered it through his own initiative, noticed the neighbours with their dongmusas and instantly guessed the woman was in labour.

He stole to the house and lay in wait beneath it. After what seemed like an eternity, he heard an infant crying and the voices of several people shouting, 'A baby girl! A baby girl!' Tiger, who had been very attentive, was overwhelmed with joy to think that the infant would soon be his. He began to laugh silently, beating his breast with pleasure. Just then, he heard another chorus of voices shouting, 'Oh no! It's a boy, after all!' This news so upset him that he turned tail and returned to his lair with a gloomy face, brooding on his ill luck.

On his way back, Tiger met Fox, whom he despised. He would have walked on without a word but for Fox stopping him with a greeting and commenting on his dark and sombre look. So great was his grief that Tiger found himself relating the whole story to Fox. After listening to everything Tiger had to say, Fox said, 'Why do you worry about such a small thing, my master? I often make forays into the village, picnicking on the villagers' poultry and sometimes their goats. If you allow me, and are so kind as to trust me, I'll find out for you if the baby is a boy or a girl. You see, my master, tomorrow they'll name the baby, for that's what they do the day after a child is born. I'll find out if it's a male or a female name they give to it.'

Tiger's face broke into a smile again. 'Do that,' he said, 'and I will reward you with a big plump goat.'

When morning came, the woman's friends, neighbours and relatives from far and near came flocking to her house for the naming rituals. They took out their wooden mortars to pestle the best variety of rice, after which the flour, along with a gourd of the purest beer, was taken to the priest waiting in the *nengpei*, the front room of the house, for the ceremony. Meanwhile, a big feast was prepared and pigs and chickens were slaughtered, to the delight of one and all—and the even greater delight of the stray dogs that swarmed around the place like honoured guests.

Watching them, Fox, who had been hovering around, thinking of a way to get nearer, saw his chance. He sneaked in among the stray dogs, made friends and mixed freely with them so that it would have been impossible for anyone to distinguish him from the rest of them. That way, Fox was able to take care of both his stomach and his errand, from which he expected an even greater reward.

That night, Fox went to report to Tiger that the baby's name was Ka Nam, a girl's name. On learning how the woman had betrayed him, Tiger became so furious that he let loose a torrent of terrible oaths, roaring and tearing trees around him to shreds and pronouncing the most dreadful threats as he did so. The spectacle frightened even poor Fox, who thought it best to leave and come back for his reward another day. As for Tiger, he growled all night, vowing a terrible vengeance on the woman and her child.

The next day, however, he calmed down and decided it was best to wait and bide his time. If the woman refused to hand over the child to him, he would simply have to resort to other means. So, Tiger resumed his spying on the house, and when Nam grew into a plump and beautiful girl, he began to watch her movements very closely, stalking her and waiting for his chance.

The days flew by, became months and then years. The moon witnessed many changes of seasons in his wanderings, but things did not change with Tiger, who nurtured his vengeance like a treasured possession. Meanwhile, Nam's mother nursed her child with such loving and tender care that she grew into the most attractive girl in the village and made many a mother jealous.

Tiger watched all this from a distance. He observed how Nam's soot-black hair grew so long that it touched her ankles; how her face shone, and her eyes sparkled with such beauty that he was almost afraid to look straight into them; but most of all, he noticed how graceful her movements were, and how her body had begun to fill out. 'Most delightful!' he said to himself. He was sure that, with a little more grooming, she would grow up into a ravishingly beautiful young woman. He resolved all over again to carry her away while she was still young and easy to handle. The proper care to make her even more plump and appealing, he could manage on his own, without any further help from her parents.

Nam's mother had not forgotten Tiger either, and although she was not unduly worried about him, she thought it best to apprise her daughter of his threats. She asked Nam to be careful and especially urged her not to venture too far from home. Naturally, Nam learnt to fear Tiger and never played beyond the boundary of her own courtyard. Gradually, the fear began to prey so greatly on her mind that she never even accompanied her friends to the spring that gushed from a bamboo spout situated only a stone's throw away from the last house of the village.

Seeing how cowardly Nam had become, her friends taunted and ridiculed her, especially when she refused to join them at the spring. Sick of these taunts, one day, Nam decided to put a stop to them once and for all, and so, against her mother's injunction, she took out the bamboo tubes, the cone basket and cane rope, and proceeded with her friends to the spring.

Tiger, who was observing all this from the fringe of the forest, rushed to the spring, pounced upon Nam and carried her away to his cave. It was all done so quickly that the little girls did not even have time to cry out, and when they later reported the matter to the village folk, they said that all they saw was a flash of stripes and yellow, and the next thing they knew was that Nam was no longer with them.

When they heard what had happened, the parents cried their hearts out, stopping only when the elders consoled them, saying it was probably God's will that Nam should seek out her own destiny, for, they said, Nam had been too exceptional a child to live out her life in the village like the other girls. Even her name, meaning 'glory', had been blessed by God himself, and so, they said, it was possible that Nam would not die at the hands of Tiger, but would live on to prove her glory to the world.

Meanwhile, in Tiger's cave, Nam was surprised to find him almost as gentle and affectionate as her parents had been. Tiger gave her whatever she wanted, brought her whatever she asked for, and dressed her up like a princess. It was so unlike what she had heard about him from her mother that she quickly lost her dread of him and lived happily with him as the keeper of his den, till at last, she grew up into a very fetching young woman.

As he watched her grow up, Tiger, too, became even more caring of her. But Nam did not know that Tiger, whom she had come to think of as her adopted father, was observing her the way a farmer would regard his prize pig that was ready for the market, reluctant to part with it, yet thrilled at the very thought of the imminent sale. Thus, when one day, Tiger cajoled her with kind words to clean the den and get ready to prepare for a big feast that he and his friends were planning to hold that evening, she did not, in the least, suspect that she would be the object of that feast. It was little Mouse who whispered the terrifying secret in her ear.

It was quite by accident that Nam met Mouse. Nam was busy cleaning her dwelling and tidying things up according to Tiger's wishes, when she noticed Mouse nibbling away at some of the food she had cooked for the evening feast.

'Get away from there, you naughty little thing!' she shouted at her. 'Don't you see I'm preparing a feast?'

Mouse scurried away, but before she ducked into her hole, she said, 'If you don't allow me to eat a little of the food, I will not tell you what I know about you.'

'What do you know about me?' Nam demanded.

'Something to do with your life,' Mouse replied evasively.

Her curiosity fully aroused now, Nam hastened to give Mouse some food in exchange for her secret. Mouse was not very trusting by nature, so she first ate her fill before parting with the information. 'Your life is in grave danger. Tiger, who you think loves you so much, is right now collecting his friends together to feast on *you*, not on those pots of food you have cooked. His tenderness for you was only an excuse to keep you contented so you would grow faster and become more fetching for his appetite. In other words, he was merely fattening his sacrificial goat.'

Shocked beyond words, Nam stared at Mouse in dumb amazement for a long time. She wished she could laugh in the creature's face and call her a nasty liar. But staring at her in open-mouthed silence, Nam realised the little creature was telling the truth. There was no reason for Mouse to lie. Besides, despite all his apparent kindness to her, she knew, as everyone else did, that her substitute father was a cruel tyrant who was feared and hated by everyone. Dazed and shaken, she asked her little saviour in a small and pitiful voice, 'What am I to do?'

Mouse thought for a moment and then smiled like someone who had made a great discovery. She said, 'I have a solution for you. First, of course, you must leave this cave immediately, and you must disguise yourself in toad skin to avoid detection. Then we shall see about the rest.'

The two left the cave and approached Hynroh, the great toad, who lived in a distant corner of the forest, to beg for a toad skin large enough to fit Nam from head to foot. It was not without fear that they went to her den, for Hynroh was known throughout the forest for her magical and malignant powers. In fact, it was said that her powers were so great that she had once or twice done battle with heavenly beings.

Hynroh was secretly gloating that Nam had been compelled to come to her. She had heard of the girl's great beauty. Once, she had gone to see the girl for herself and had been unreasonably envious of what she saw. She was, therefore, pleased to turn her into an ugly toad—at her own request, as it were—and eclipse her beauty forever. She readily agreed to provide Nam with a toad skin but exacted her word of honour never to remove it for as long as she lived. Hynroh also warned Nam not to venture out of the forest unless she wanted to incur her terrible wrath.

Seeing herself trapped in a toad's life under the control of the evil Hynroh, Nam began to weep bitterly. But her little companion soon calmed her down by saying that she knew of a way out of this unenviable situation.

As she spoke, Mouse took Nam to Kya and Jri, the cotton and rubber trees, and taught her the magic words: *San, san Kong A, pat, pat Kong Ri; San, san Kong Ri pat, pat Kong A* (Grow, grow Kong A, wait, wait Kong Ri; grow, grow Kong Ri, wait, wait Kong A). The chanting of these words would make the two trees grow tall as the heavens and would thus take Nam to the realm of Sun, Moon and the stars, away from the reach of evil creatures like Tiger and Hynroh.

Following Mouse's instructions, Nam climbed onto the branches of the trees and chanted the magic words. And away she went, up and up until she passed through *u mawsiang bneng*, the blue rock of heaven, through a secret passage, and reached the realm of heavenly beings. Mouse, who had been watching the spectacle, wiped away the tears streaming from her eyes—she had grown very fond of Nam—and headed back to her hole in the cave.

Alone in a strange but beautiful country, Nam initially felt a sense of relief and basked in her new-found freedom. But after wandering about aimlessly for some time, she soon began to feel lonely and lost. When night came, her vague sense of loss became a strong surge of anxiety. She hurried towards the first palace she came across, to ask for shelter for the night. There was a faint light emanating from it, and it seemed to her that it was painted with ash. Even its courtyard and surroundings were covered with a fine ash-like substance. It was the palace of Moon, a handsome young god who adored beauty more than anything else in the heavens. When this worshipper of beauty heard someone knocking at his door, he asked his housekeeper to see who it was, but on hearing that it was only a hideous toad, he ordered her off his premises.

Even more worried now, Nam wandered off towards the mansion of Evening Star, but there too, she was refused shelter because she was so ugly. Disconsolate, she moved from palace to palace in search of lodging. In that heavenly realm, however, there seemed to be no place for someone as horrid-looking as a toad. Desperate, Nam thought of removing her toad skin and showing everyone that she was as lovely as any of them. She had no fear of Tiger any more, for she knew that she was beyond his reach, but she dreaded Hynroh, for whom the sky was no limit. Already she had broken her promise to the evil creature by leaving the jungle; she did not care to incense her further by shedding the toad skin. She was thus left with no option but to roam about the heavens for weeks in her ungainly costume, hoping against hope that some kind soul might take pity on her plight.

It was in this way that she finally arrived at Sun's dazzling palace. As usual, Nam asked to be allowed to live in the palace as a lodger, but Sun, like the rest of the inhabitants of that celestial land, could not bear the ghastly sight of a woman who so closely resembled a revolting toad. She was about to send her away when Nam fell at her feet and said, 'My benefactress, queen of the universe! I have been tramping about for God knows how many days now without a roof over my head, eating only fruits and herbs. No one has been kind enough to shelter me even for one night. If even you, a woman, a queen, refuse to help another woman, then what will be my fate?'

Touched by the simple truth of Nam's words, Sun took her into her palace and assigned her a storehouse by the fringe of her compound, where she could live as she pleased. Nam eagerly took possession of the little shed and, expert as she was in housekeeping, quickly turned it into a comfortable dwelling, much to the delight of her benefactress, who then allowed her to work in the house as a servant.

For a time, Nam lived a quiet, uneventful life. As may be supposed, living inside Sun's palace, she felt safe even from the threat of Hynroh. In fact, she was beginning to forget Hynroh altogether: she moved about freely and, when alone in the shed, removed her odious and burdensome toad skin. Very soon, she grew bolder and ventured out daily to a nearby spring to wash without her ugly mask.

Unfortunately, or fortunately, for her, one morning, as she was on her way to the spring, she was secretly observed by Sun's only child, U Lur Mangkara, a dashing young prince, the darling of the blue realm, who had been out riding earlier than usual.

The prince was thunderstruck. He had never seen a creature of such exquisite beauty before. Seeing her as she really was, he ceased to wonder why she was called Nam, glory. To his mind, she was the most glorious woman … But what was he saying? She was no woman; she was a divine fairy, a goddess in her own right. With his heart beating against his breast, the prince hurried home and told his mother what he had discovered, excitedly pleading all the while to let him marry the strange maiden who had been hiding her loveliness under a loathsome camouflage. Sun was equally amazed, but advised her son to be patient, vowing that she would look into the matter herself and find out what awful reason had compelled the fair one to live in the guise of a toad.

The very next day, Sun began watching Nam's movements and soon discovered for herself what her son had told her. She resolved to destroy the toad skin once and for all and make Nam her daughter-in-law. Having been a witness to Nam's modest and sweet nature, and then to her great beauty, she knew she could not have wished for a better woman to marry her son. Consequently, one morning, while Nam was washing at the spring, Sun took away the toad skin, burnt it and replaced it with royal robes and all sorts of precious ornaments.

But Nam was far from pleased. She wept bitterly, complaining to Sun that she was now in grave danger. Nam then recounted the whole story of her life, leading to her flight into this world in deep space. She told Sun of Tiger and his evil scheme to feast on her. And of Hynroh and how she had condemned her to the life of a toad by threatening to devour her if she ever removed her skin. And now, she was terrified of Hynroh, for her dreaded influence was known to extend throughout heaven and earth.

But Sun, ruler of the universe, calmed her fears, saying that she would never allow anyone to harm her future daughter-in-law. At this, Nam quite forgot her worries and was suddenly covered in confusion. Since the time she had set eyes on the prince, she had harboured a secret love for him but had never dared hope, even in her wildest dreams, that he would one day be her beloved husband. Nam lowered her head to hide the happiness that suffused her at that moment. Seeing her agitation, Sun ruffled her long, dark hair and said reassuringly, 'Yes, dear, I intend to compensate for the toad skin with my very own son. And of course, that is also his wish. He loves you with his very soul.'

Shortly after this announcement, Nam found herself the happy bride of a very charming prince at a wedding that was attended by the crowns and coronets of the whole universe. As a special gift to the bride, Sun blessed her with immortality, thus making her an equal partner to her son.

Meanwhile, Hynroh, on learning that Sun had deliberately destroyed the toad skin and transformed Nam into an immortal princess, was so enraged that she flew up into the sky and tried to swallow Sun in one gulp. Sun, an equally powerful being, strove to ward off her onslaught, and a fierce combat ensued, which mankind watched with bated breath.

For a while, the battle remained undecided. Slowly, however, Hynroh began to gain the upper hand. But just when Sun was about to be devoured, the people on earth, who were worried for their life-giver, raised a loud, resounding racket, crying at the top of their lungs, beating on iron utensils, drums and whatever else would make a noise, in order to scare off Hynroh. Although Hynroh was no coward, the deafening din had a draining influence on her magic powers. She was forced to let go of Sun and flee.

Unable to extract her revenge, Hynroh turned to Moon, Sun's brother, and tried to eat him up instead. But this time, too, humans raised a great clamour, forcing her to leave Moon alone and return to her jungle on earth.

I concluded the story by saying, 'To this day, Hynroh has neither forgiven Sun nor forgotten her unsated thirst for vengeance. She is, therefore, seen making periodical attacks on both Sun and her brother, in the hope that one day people will be too preoccupied with their day-to-day lives to notice what she is about.'

'My God, Bah Ap,' Donald exclaimed, 'it's as beautiful and sophisticated a story as any I have heard! To think that such a story was told by ancient Khasis ages ago! Amazing!'

'But earlier, earlier, what did you say earlier?' Raji asked him derisively. Pointing a shaky finger at him, he added, 'We are what? Our ancestors were what? Illiterate savages! You, ha, liah, you are—'

Bah Kynsai broke in. 'Raji, leave him alone, man! He didn't exactly say that, and you know it!' And then to me, he said, 'But to tell you the truth, na, Ap, I too hadn't heard the full version of the story, man. The old Khasis, na, whatever you say, na, did have a lot of imagination, and we can see that in these stories ... But coming back to the unusual characters we have been discussing, ha, there was one very funny fellow who came to our university some years ago, na, Ap? He spoke about the *japih*, remember?'

'Yeah, yeah, the japih man, we called him.'

'Your friend wrote a story about him, na? Why don't you tell us?'

The man was speaking at a seminar, telling us strange things about the japih—they were so strange that my friend Koiri used the incident to write a little story called 'Japih: Scrumptious Meat or Prophetic Frogs?' It's quite funny.

⁂

One day, not so long ago (that is how Koiri's story begins), I took a friend who was visiting from Wales to Sohra, my birthplace, which I love to call 'my Innisfree'. As I always do when I go to Sohra, that day, too, I visited all the spots associated with my childhood, ending with my favourite stream in my favourite sacred grove.

I said to my friend, 'There! There! Do you see those greenish-brown creatures swimming under the water? The ones that look like frogs ... Actually, they are not frogs. Khasis call them japih.'

'Yeah, I see them. What about them?' my friend responded.

'Well,' I said, 'they make excellent food. Clean them, dry them in the sun or over a fire, fry them in oil, and I swear there's no tastier meat on earth. Better than chicken. Surprising, isn't it?'

As I looked at them frolicking in the water, my mind went back to my ancestral home. I could see my uncle draping the dressed japih by the dozens on the clothesline, drying them in the morning sun. I remembered, too, how at first I had refused to eat them because they strongly reminded me of humans hanging naked from a cross, like in the Christian calendars. But my friend was saying, 'Nothing surprising about it. People all over South-east Asia eat frogs.'

'But, Basil, these are not frogs!' I exclaimed. 'We call them japih, whereas frogs are called *jakoid*. And they also look different.'

'You may call them jakoid, and they may look different, but they are still a species of frogs,' Basil stated matter-of-factly.

That stumped me. This ancient white goat had just called me a frog-eater. I fumed. Fortunately, the well-known Sohra courtesy came to my rescue before I could say, or indeed do, anything rash. After all, it whispered, he is a friend from a faraway land, what does he know of our customs? So I nodded instead and said rather glumly, 'I see.'

That was that.

Some days later, I attended a seminar on 'The Role of Waters/Rivers in Khasi Culture and Vision', organised by the Ford Foundation at the city campus of NEHU. One of the speakers was talking about japih. He was saying: 'Japih are greenish-brown frogs—'

'What the …!' I blurted before I could stop myself.

All eyes immediately turned to me in reprimand. I was forced to shut up and make appeasing gestures. What followed, however, was even more shocking than the opening line. To my mind, it was the most outrageous academic presentation I had ever had to sit through. I mean, I knew that japih are greenish-brown in colour, and that they are found in abundance in the Khasi-Jaiñtia Hills. Locals like me love them for the simple reason that their meat is scrumptious. But I had never heard of japih with the combined powers of Michel de Nostredame and the oracle.

If the speaker was to be believed, these creatures not only had oracular powers but had also been acting as his people's weathercocks for ages, besides foretelling some of the social and political events that had shaken India and the world from time to time. Let me try, as best I can, to reproduce for your benefit what the frog man spouted at the seminar:

Once a year, usually in the month of December, it is the habit of Japih to bunch together in the river in which they live. When the gathering takes place deep in the water, this signifies that there will be heavy rainfall. When they gather at the upper level, this signifies average rainfall. When they gather on the surface of the water, this signifies a near-drought condition. In the year 2000, the Japih had gathered on the surface. Because of this, there was little rain in 2001. [Waggling a finger at the audience] Is this true or not, in 2001?

That is not all. Japih, according to this self-appointed specialist, could also predict social and political events. In 1970, at a gathering of these seers, he said, an unknown animal ate up most of them. When this happened, he revealed, a man who had special powers to 'judge' was approached. The 'judge' explained that a great epidemic would occur in the plains. Sure enough, he concluded, in the year 1971, the great epidemic broke out in Bangladesh during the war for that country's independence. Then he continued:

In 1983 at another Japih gathering, there was one leader who led the masses. But his head was cut off. So the judge explained that the leader of the country would be assassinated. True to the judge's words, in the year 1984, Mrs Indira Gandhi, then Prime Minister of India, was assassinated. Last year [2000], the Japih gathered but moved at random. So the man who has the power to judge said there would be war and chaos. Therefore, this year [2001] on 11 September, the great terrorist attack in New York and on the Pentagon took place, and thereafter President George W. Bush declared war against terrorism, where most of the countries of the world took part, causing much death and confusion.

To authenticate the story, the fantastic scholar offered this final revelation: 'This unique gathering of Japih took place at a river in Diwah village, West Khasi Hills, Meghalaya.'

As I listened to him, I was taken back to a story I had learnt in school. It was about a frog who had proclaimed himself the wisest doctor on earth and fooled all the animals of the jungle, until he was put in his place by a cunning fox. In fact, at that moment, as he sat on the podium, the speaker's face was beginning to take on the features of Doctor Frog. I stared at him, amazed at the transformation, but was brought out of my reverie by the sound of a thunderclap.

To my astonishment, everyone was clapping for the joker. What was wrong with these people? How could they listen to such sham and applaud?

Seeing me staring like a zombie, my fellow auditor nudged me. And I, for reasons that I haven't been able to fathom to this day, began clapping too.

❧

Bah Kynsai laughed delightedly, but the rest were more interested in the japih than in the person who had given such a fantastic account of them.

Magdalene said, 'Do you think it could be true, Ap? I know your friend found it fantastic, but—'

Bah Kit interrupted her to say, 'I don't think we should dismiss anything offhand like that, ha, Mag? We need to see for ourselves and study some more.'

'It sounds like a tall tale to me,' Donald declared.

But Bah Kit, Raji, Evening and Bah Su thought the part about the rainfall might very well be true. They were not so sure about the rest.

Finally, Bah Kynsai tried to put an end to the argument by saying, 'The moral of the story is this: *in a seminar, everybody must clap*.'

'Tet teri ka!' They all laughed.

But Magdalene was not easily discouraged. She said again, 'But seriously, what do you think, Ap?'

'I think, like Bah Kit said, we need to see the japih gathering for ourselves and observe what goes on.'

'Okay, enough of that!' Bah Kynsai said. 'Does anyone know of any more colourful characters? If not, we can—'

'I have always been interested in a person named Suhori,' I said. 'He lived near our house in Sohra. When we were young, we thought of Suhori as a madman and used to laugh at him. But now, when overwhelmed by feelings of depression—when recollections of beggars in the streets, as prescribed by Gandhi, fail to lift my spirits—I always think of Suhori, the happy man of Sohra.

'He was always dressed in grimy rags and forever angry with stylishly dressed people, especially girls. Whenever he saw them, he would say, "*Phuit pha ïa leh stail! Pha ïa don pisa tang ma pha*?" ("Phooey, trying to be stylish! Are you the only ones with money?") And shaking his bag of cowries, he would challenge: "Hear that, moneyless brats? I have a bagful of silver here!"

'When the girls giggled at him, he would say, "You think you are the only ones going to school? Can you speak English like me? I can write poetry in English."

'And he would give them a sample of his verse: "I don't know, I don't care, *U Bah Jo u eit ha kper*" ("I don't know I don't care, Mr Jo is crapping in the yard"). If that did not impress them, he would give them his favourite lines:

"My God *long sniang*, I'd like to *kynjih sha bniang*" ("My God, you are a pig, I'd like to leap to heaven").

'Having recited his poetry, he would break into a victory dance and taunt: "You see! You see! You are not as good as me!"

'I sometimes wonder, you know, if life should not be faced with such unbounded optimism, such swashbuckling arrogance!'

'Is he still alive?' Magdalene asked.

'He was quite old when I was quite young ...'

'It's an interesting view of life, no doubt about it,' Donald commented. 'But what did Gandhi say exactly, Bah Ap?'

'He said something about how, when you feel low-spirited and luckless, you should always recall the face of the poorest man or woman you have seen and see how infinitely more fortunate you are. But sometimes even that doesn't help ...'

'But Suhori does?' Bah Kynsai asked sceptically.

'His optimism and defiance, yes. Whenever I remember him, I think, "What the hell! Why not fly in the face of existence?" And it really helps, you know. The only thing is, to be always happy like Suhori, you have to be a complete simpleton or a madman.'

'But he was not always happy, Ap,' Hamkom contradicted me. 'He was angry with those girls.'

'Always happy in the end ... He always won.'

'Talking of madmen,' Magdalene interrupted us, 'have you guys heard of the one who used to live in Laitumkhrah?'

'Which one, which one?' Hamkom, who is also from Laitumkhrah, asked excitedly.

'The one who used to send letters to the sky.'

'Letters to the sky? How?' Hamkom had not heard the story.

'I'm also not very sure, but that's what people used to say.'

I knew the story well enough, so I said, 'He used to go to the local post office to post his letters to the sky, and always he would ask, "A letter to the sky, how much?" To humour him, they would reply, "One rupee ... one rupee for a letter to the sky." He would buy a stamp and tenderly put the letter in a white envelope, then write down his address and put it in a red box, pretty sure it would be delivered to the sky.

'After a few days, he would return and say, "No reply has come to my house, has it come to the post office?" To that, the clerk would say with a smile, "Nothing has come, perhaps in a while." But to her colleagues, she would say, "He sends a letter to the sky and expects a reply, imagine, a letter to the sky, and he expects a reply! Poor, poor fool! Mad! Mad! Mad!"

'They would all laugh at the lunatic or pity him. But away from their post office, they too would go to their places of worship and pray to their gods in the sky.'

'Brilliant, Bah Ap! My God, that's brilliant, ya!' Donald exclaimed. 'Isn't praying to our gods in the sky the same thing as sending letters to the sky?'

'You bloody atheist!' Evening cursed Donald with all the vehemence he could manage.

Bah Kynsai came to Donald's defence. 'It's not about atheism or agnosticism, you idiot! The point is that we pray to God in the belief that he exists and is listening to us. The madman writes letters to the same Supreme Being without any doubt that he will receive a reply. Hence, if we laugh at him and pity him and call him mad, na, then we should also laugh and pity and call ourselves mad. What branch of philosophy is that, Ap?'

'Partly existentialist, partly absurdist.'

'Yeah, yeah, but if you read too much of that, na, you might lose your faith in God completely.'

'Is that good or bad?' Magdalene laughed.

'My philosophy is very simple: to each his own,' Bah Kynsai replied diplomatically.

'That's the most civilised attitude, I think, Bah Kynsai,' Donald observed, 'and certainly, the most tolerant,' he added pointedly.

'Well,' Bah Kynsai said, slapping his thigh, 'we have come to know quite a few characters, but the problem is that most of you did not contribute ...'

'I did,' Bah Kit said.

'So did I ... a little bit,' Dale said, laughing.

'Okay, okay,' Bah Su said, 'but since I don't know of any trickster story, I'll tell you the story of Ka Phan Nonglait, okay?'

'Who's Phan Nonglait?' Magdalene asked.

'Ap referred to her earlier, don't you remember?' Bah Kynsai asked.

Bah Su added, 'The problem with historians like you and Ham, ha, is that you have been reading only Indian and world histories. But no matter, I'll tell you who she was ... The first Khasi War of Freedom in 1829 led by Tirot Sing Syiem, the king of Hima Nongkhlaw, which Ap mentioned earlier, threw up many unexpected heroes, ordinary human beings who performed extraordinary acts of courage and self-sacrifice. But the most remarkable among them, ha, was neither Mon Bhut nor the now-famous warriors, Lorshon Jaraiñ, Kheiñ Kongngor Nongkynrih and Jidor Sing, but a woman, little known before the war. She was a tall, rosy-cheeked young woman with the heart of a sturdy patriot. Her name was Ka Phan Nonglait. This is the story of her amazing feats in the war.

'The account of how the British first set foot upon the land of U Hynñiew Trep and Hima Nongkhlaw is well known. Or, at least, to us it is, ha, Mag. David Scott, the first British conquistador of the Northeast, approached Tirot Sing with folded hands and a humble request for permission to build a road through Nongkhlaw to connect Guwahati in Assam and Sylhet in East Bengal. In exchange, David Scott promised to return to him the territory of Borduar, which the British had seized earlier. Borduar was Nongkhlaw's gateway to Kamrup in Assam. Having received his permission, not only did David Scott not keep his promise but he also encouraged soldiers and all kinds of hangers-on in the British Army to indulge in many acts of provocation ... Why? Because his real design was not to build a road, ha, but to capture the hima. These aggressive acts, which included the molestation and rape of Khasi women, finally led to the outbreak of the war in April 1829.

'As the war raged, and as David Scott made his escape with the help of Tirot Sing's mother, Ka Phan Nonglait burst upon the scene with selfless acts of patriotism, as if to prove that not all Khasi women were son-betrayers.'

'Son-betrayers, Bah Su?' Magdalene asked mockingly.

'Tirot Sing's mother betrayed her own son when she helped David Scott, Mag! You see, Tirot Sing and his council of ministers were planning a rebellion against the British. The people could no longer stand their arrogance and tyrannical acts. Besides, a British *chaprasi*, a peon who ran errands for the officers, had in a drunken state bragged in the marketplace about how the Khasis would soon bear the foreign yoke like beasts of burden. What they had suspected all along seemed imminent: the British were about to capture their hima and enslave the people with oppressive taxes. That was why Tirot Sing and his council of ministers decided to act quickly and take pre-emptive measures right away. A strong contingent of warriors, ki khlawait, the sword-tigers, were supposed to attack the British cantonment that very night. Another contingent was detailed to eliminate David Scott, for they said, "Cut off the head, and the body can only thrash about helplessly." It was a matter of life and death for the nation, and they knew they must act in all haste, in all secrecy, and be ready to take extreme steps.

'Unfortunately, also sworn to secrecy, ha, was the king's mother, Ka Ksan Syiemlieh. "She was still young, still beautiful and still very much capable of loving outside her marriage," to quote a source of mine. Consumed by her passion for her "white god", she crept towards his rest house as soon as it was dark. And she revealed to him not only her son's "murderous plot" but also urged him to flee with all possible haste towards friendly Sohra, and not to Guwahati, which was much farther away. That was how David Scott escaped. He ran away before Tirot Sing's warriors could reach him.'

'As a woman, I find that hard to believe, Bah Su,' Magdalene objected. 'How could a mother betray her own son like that?'

'Hard to believe or not, this is part of history. And it's not only Khasis who have been saying this, Mag. Even Dr John Roberts, who is revered as the father of Khasi literature, attested to the fact that Ka Ksan and David Scott were very friendly and used to meet every time he visited Nongkhlaw. You'll find this in his *Fourth Khasi Reader*. It may be hard for you to believe, ha, but you cannot change history. You should know that.'

'And you should also know that Khasi women are fools for white men!' Evening added. 'But why only for white men? Actually, they are fools for every non-Khasi man, including the scavenging Kharmetors!'

'You are not only a xenophobe, Evening, but also a bloody misogynist! Shame on you for speaking like that about Khasi women!' Magdalene was beside herself with rage.

Bah Kynsai and Bah Su pacified her by reprimanding Evening for speaking out of turn. Bah Su said, 'You should not generalise like that, Ning. The purpose of my telling you the story of Ka Phan Nonglait is to show that not all Khasi women are like Ka Ksan (who will go down in Khasi history as the queen who preferred the enemy's bed to her country) and the women you were talking about.'

'That's right, Ning,' I added, 'nobody can generalise about women, or men, for that matter, be they Khasi or non-Khasi. Human nature is both universal and unique. Every person on earth may share certain qualities, but they also have personalities as singular and distinctive as their fingerprints. Having said that, in fairness to Ning, there does seem to be a preference among many Khasi women for non-Khasi men.'

'A preference, yes, and an unhealthy one, I might add,' Bah Kynsai asserted, 'but not everyone is like that, Ning.' He urged Bah Su to go on, saying, 'Let's not listen to this woman-hater. I think he even hates his own wife, liah, hahaha …'

'As I was saying,' Bah Su continued, 'David Scott took Ka Ksan's advice and fled towards Sohra through Hima Mawphlang, hotly pursued by the determined Nongkhlaw warriors. At Mawphlang, he was assisted in his flight by the lyngdoh, the ruler, who dressed him up as a Khasi labourer so the sympathisers of Tirot Sing would not readily recognise him. This was especially to help David Scott pass through Sohrarim on his way to Sohra, a village that falls under Hima Nongkhlaw—'

'But how did Sohrarim, which is so close to Sohra, come to be a part of Hima Nongkhlaw, Bah Su?' Bah Kit asked.

'By an act of deception,' I said, 'or that's what the story says. It seemed that once upon a time, Syntiew Syiemlieh, the king of Nongkhlaw, requested the king of Sohra (we no longer know who he was) for a small patch of land in his state, near the village of Sohrarim, so he could come now and then to rest. He said, "Give me only as much land as would be covered by a single piece of cowhide; that's all I ask." The king of Sohra agreed, but the king of Nongkhlaw took advantage of his generosity and cut the cowhide into several small pieces and went to place them in such a manner that they eventually covered the whole of Sohrarim. The king of Sohra realised that he had been tricked, but would not go back on his word, for in those days, the spoken word was an unbreakable law. As a result, Sohrarim became a part of Nongkhlaw, but that act of treachery also caused a deep-seated animosity between the two states that ultimately came to be reflected in Sohra's betrayal of Tirot Sing.'

Bah Su picked up the thread of his story again. 'Despite such assistance, ha, there were times when the warriors of Tirot Sing were on the verge of capturing him, especially between the villages of Mawphlang and Mawbeh. But the wily white man tossed thousands of coins at them, and when he saw them stopping to pick them up, he continued to strew his escape route with them. That was how he arrived in Sohra, well ahead of the pursuing warriors. Now, you must keep in mind what Ap has just told you about Sohra's enmity with Nongkhlaw, ha? It was because of this and other territorial quarrels that, even during the Khasi War of Freedom, the syiem of Sohra did not join the freedom fighters but sided with the British. So, when David Scott arrived in Sohra, the syiem, Duwan Sing Syiem—'

'May his soul rot in hell!' Raji cursed.

Magdalene cackled. 'How do you like that, Ap, being from Sohra?'

'Many of us in Sohra don't like him. It is because of him that we are disdained as *Sohra tap thlong*!'

'What does that mean?'

'It means "mortar-covering Sohra". Bah Su will tell you why.'

'Hey, you people, don't interrupt so much, na?' Bah Kynsai said, and urged Bah Su to go on.

'Well, as I was saying,' Bah Su continued, 'Duwan Sing did not like warriors from another state raiding his hima and blustering about as if they owned it. Assuring David Scott of his protection, he covered the white man with a huge wooden mortar, used to pestle rice grains, when he heard the warriors of Tirot Sing entering his palace. Later, when they had left and were busy searching the paths from Sohra to the Sylhet plains, he had David Scott taken elsewhere—'

'To the Rangpungpa Cave,' I pitched in, 'on the precipitous path leading to the ravine hamlet of Nongpriang. They hid him there for months, before taking him back to his people in Sylhet. To this day, the cave is known as the David Scott Cave.'

'You also have a monument dedicated to David Scott, no, Ap?' Bah Kit asked.

'Yeah, we do,' I agreed, 'built by the "Supreme Government". The words of praise on it are a testimony to British falsification of history everywhere.'

'That was the story of David Scott's escape,' Bah Su resumed, 'and because he did escape, ha, he was able to come back later with a large army, the Sylhet Light Infantry, to fight Tirot Sing. Though he died in August 1831, Scott laid a solid foundation for his successor as the architect of British incursion into the hill country. The fight against Tirot Sing was continued by T.C. Robertson, who brought in regiments of Gorkhas, Assamese, Burmese and Manipuri horsemen to strengthen the British position. But finally, it was not British might that defeated Tirot Sing but their betrayal. Through Sing Manik, the syiem of Khyrim, ha, they offered to sign a peace treaty, but when Tirot Sing came to the rendezvous with his men (without arms, as part of the agreement), they ambushed and captured him. This happened in 1833 after a struggle of more than five years.

'Now, before the war, like many other inhabitants, Ka Phan Nonglait had also had loved ones brutishly abused by British soldiers. But, instead of being cowed, ha, she burnt with vengeful anger and patriotic fervour as she bided her time for an opportunity to strike back.

'When Tirot Sing went into the jungles to wage a guerrilla war against the British, Ka Phan Nonglait approached none other than Mon Bhut himself, Tirot Sing's ablest General. Mon Bhut was a giant of a man, ha, and with the strength to match. He was so strong that he used to kill British soldiers by lifting a man in each hand and banging their heads together. Unfortunately, ha, we do not know much more about him. We do not even know what happened to him after the war, although legend has it that he went to live in the thick forests of Lyngngam.

'Anyway, Ka Phan went to Mon Bhut and offered to lay down her life for the sake of the hima and her people. Thus, she became the first and only woman warrior in Khasi history to be actively, and significantly, involved in a war of liberation. As a warrior, ha, her roles were many, and they included dangerous assignments behind enemy lines. Among her many exploits, the most famous, ha, was her involvement in the daring attack on a detachment of British soldiers who were responsible for many instances of murder and mayhem. Working with Mon Bhut and his men, one day, Ka Phan Nonglait, dressed in her loveliest clothes, walked up to the soldiers as they were having lunch by a little stream. She pretended to be a hooch seller with a basket full of the local brew stored in ceramic bottles.

'The soldiers did not suspect anything, ha, for she was a woman alone, with nothing but drinks to peddle. Thinking only of making their lunch more enjoyable, they confiscated the stuff and downed bottle after bottle with wild abandon. Unfortunately for them, ha, the rice spirit was the strongly concocted yiad rod variety. Soon, they were so drunk that they could only stare foolishly as Ka Phan Nonglait gathered up all their guns and threw them into a large crack in the rocks. That was the sign for Mon Bhut and his men, who had been hiding nearby the whole time, to come out and make short work of their enemies. Ka Phan Nonglait did not flinch as she kept watch. Later, she helped the men get rid of the bodies.

'Such was the ugliness of British rule, ha, that it could breed that kind of bitterness even in one of the most beautiful women of her time. But perhaps it was just as well, ha, for without Ka Phan Nonglait's story, Khasi women would certainly have been painted in a bad light because of the betrayal of Tirot Sing's mother.

'Ka Phan Nonglait proved that, even in a matrilineal society like the Khasis, ha, where the woman is supposed to function from the safety of her home, ha, engrossed only in her domestic chores, ha, she could yet take her place among the most audacious of warriors. She also proved that one does not need muscles and strength to be a true patriot. All one needs is pure and absolute love for one's country and all that it represents. It is this unselfish love, ha, that made Ka Phan Nonglait so fearless and so bold. And though the Khasis lost the war, they won many battles through the courage of such warriors as the Brave Maid of Nonglait. May she be worthy of emulation for all time to come!'

Donald wanted to know what became of Ka Phan Nonglait afterwards.

'I'm not very sure,' Bah Su replied, 'but she died on 6 December 1850 in the village of her birth, Nongrmai. Prolonged illness.'

Magdalene was more interested in the British legacy. 'Were David Scott and the English so bad for us, Bah Su?'

Before he could respond, Evening said, 'For us Christians, they were definitely a blessing, giving us the redemption of Christ. And for all Khasis also, they were a blessing, giving us a script and Western education.'

'Are you talking about the English or the Welsh, liah?' Bah Kynsai demanded. 'It was the Welsh who introduced both Christianity and education among us, na, tdong?'

'But without the English, they wouldn't have been able to come here in the first place, no, Bah Kynsai?' Evening said. 'Without their encouragement and support, how could the Welsh even begin their missionary work?'

Bah Kynsai was not impressed. He said the British had introduced us to many things; that was true enough. They introduced the Welsh; they introduced pears, beans, carrots and potatoes, which have become the major cash crops of the Khasis today. But they also brought the people of mainland India and introduced us to our greatest problem today: influx. Then they introduced their iron, which destroyed the Khasi iron industry, but worst of all, they made us dependent on them. We could not have independent trade relations with anyone any more, and we forgot the art of war because the British banned the use of weapons by us. And because we were dependent on them, we became incapable of existing independently after they left. In effect, they turned us into little babies and made us a part of India.

'And gave us a new kind of dependency,' Evening said, forgetting his earlier position.

'Or a new identity,' Donald added, 'as Indians.'

Hamkom looked very dissatisfied. We realised why when he suddenly said, 'You guys did not mention the Jaiñtia War of Freedom!'

'Why,' Bah Kynsai asked, 'did they also have a Phan Nonglait in Jaiñtia Hills?'

'No, but you talked about Tirot Sing without mentioning Kiang Nangbah at all, no?'

'We referred to Tirot Sing, yes, but the story was really about his mother and Ka Phan: two very different women involved in the same war. And Kiang was discussed by Ap earlier, remember?'

To change the topic, I asked, 'Has anybody heard about Smir?'

'What Smir, man?' Bah Kynsai demanded aggressively.

'Well, you know that we had a labour corps serving in France during the First World War, don't you?'

'Of course, that's why we have Motphran, na!' Bah Kynsai replied.

'Ooh, you mean Motphran was built to commemorate the Khasi soldiers who fought during the First World War or what?' Magdalene asked in surprise. 'I never knew, ya. So, Motphran means what?'

'The France Monument,' I replied.

'When and how was it built, Ap?'

Motphran, on the four-way junction adjoining Iewduh in Shillong, was the brainchild of S.J. Laine, deputy commissioner of the British Khasi-Jaiñtia Hills district. In November 1924, Laine called for a meeting of the traditional Khasi rulers—syiems, sordars and lyngdohs—in charge of their respective states and administrative units. The agenda was the funding and construction of a monument dedicated to the memory of the twenty-six Khasi men who worked and died in France during the First World War between 1917 and 1918.

The work, which was to be funded by all the thirty traditional rulers in the Khasi-Jaiñtia Hills, was given to Jumatoola & Sons, a leading construction firm. It took them about three years to complete the monument. The slow progress was attributed to the inconsistent flow of funds. It was not till 1927 that the traditional rulers paid their full contributions, and that too, only after W.A. Cosgrave, the then deputy commissioner, and D. Ropmay, assistant commissioner, issued an order to this effect. The monument was completed that year at the cost of 5,194 rupees.

During British rule, the government used to hold a memorial service once a year, on 11 November, to commemorate the death anniversary of those brave men from the hills. Today we remember the structure, not the men. The wind, rain and sun have even obliterated their names.

Magdalene was flabbergasted. 'You mean to say that we no longer know the names of those people? What about the official records?'

Bah Su said, 'All lost during the separation of Meghalaya from Assam. But some people have reportedly traced their names now, Mag. You can talk to them when we get back.'

'But did you notice something?' Hamkom asked. 'The Khasis did not even want the monument built in the first place, that was why the syiems had to be forced into parting with their money.'

'Maybe because they thought the British should foot the bill or what? After all, those men served the British Empire, no?' Bah Kit said, in defence of the Khasi rulers.

'But still, it was an important piece of history for the Khasi community, no? Whatever you say, I think, as a people, we are quite uncaring about history. See, now we don't even know anything about them. A piece of history lost forever.'

'Not quite, Ham,' Bah Su said. 'I told you some people have already traced their names, no?'

'Khasi, tdir?' Bah Kynsai cursed and, turning to me, said, 'Ap, all this is very revealing, na, and I also didn't know half the history of Motphran until now, na, but what about that fellow, Smir or something?'

'He was a company commander in the Khasi Porter Corps in Burma during the Second World War. I'd like to tell you about him because he was quite a man!'

'In what way?' Bah Kynsai demanded.

The story was first recounted by R. Tokin Roy Rymbai, who was the commandant of the Khasi Porter Corps. It all started when the Japanese invaded British Burma in December 1941 soon after the bombing of Pearl Harbour. The Japanese rolled up in large fleets and immediately seized control of Lower Burma and then moved to where the British had retreated in Upper Burma. The Japanese advance was said to be lightning fast. Within three months, the British had to abandon Burma and flee to India with thousands of soldiers—British, Indian and Chinese—and many more civilians. They set up an evacuation centre at a place called Myitkyina in Upper Burma, from where soldiers and civilian refugees were taken by train towards the Indian border up to the end of the railway line. After that, they had to proceed on foot through dense jungles till they reached Ledo in Upper Assam. From Ledo, they were taken to designated camps by train. To help the evacuees during their gruelling jungle trek, the British government in India set up relief camps every thirteen kilometres along the route, where they were fed, treated for illness or injuries, and given clothes and shelter for the night.

These camps consisted of huts with bamboo walls and roofs of thatch or tarpaulin. The huts were raised a few feet above the muddy ground with bamboo stilts and could be accessed by rough bamboo steps. To organise the camps, build huts and bring in food rations, clothes and medical supplies, and to carry the sick, the old, and the young who could not walk, hundreds of thousands of volunteers were needed. These volunteers came from every part of Burma and India, and were organised into different porter corps. From the Khasi-Jaiñtia Hills, two porter corps were formed comprising 1,000 volunteers each. The Khasi Porter Corps was commanded by Rymbai and the Jaiñtia Porter Corps by Jormanik Syiem, who later became the king of the Khasi state of Mylliem. The Khasi corps was divided into twenty-five companies, each under a company commander. Smir War-Tynghah, from Mylliem-Sadew in East Khasi Hills, was a commander of the Mylliem Company.

The Khasis left Shillong at the beginning of March 1942 and travelled by train to Ledo. It took them up to four days to reach Ledo from Guwahati since the train had to stop at every large station so oncoming trains could pass or others—transporting soldiers or supplies or volunteers like themselves—could go first. From Ledo, they had to travel on foot, carrying food and other supplies through difficult jungle tracks, often thick with ankle-deep mud, or else so rugged and steep that no proper footholds could be found.

As you can imagine, it was a terrible trial just to march with such heavy burdens on their backs on such a route, harried constantly by mosquitoes and jungle flies. But march they did, on and on towards the borders of Burma, making their own shelters wherever they stopped for the night. Day and night, the jungle was like a two-way street. As the porters pushed onwards to Burma, a ceaseless stream of refugees marched towards Ledo in Assam. The Khasis met all sorts of people on the way, healthy, sick and crippled. Army officers in ragged uniforms and civilians in dirty rags walked side by side, and all of them stayed in the same huts for the night before carrying on in the morning. There were makeshift hospitals too along the route, where the sick and injured were given treatment. Despite that, people died like flies from dysentery, cholera, malarial fever and strange diseases of the jungle that affected the brain and killed overnight.

Many of the Khasi porters died. There were quite a few who were perfectly healthy when they went into the jungle for bamboo and rushes, who ate and slept as usual but never woke up in the morning. Rymbai said he would always remember a man who, in his underclothes, suddenly jumped out of bed, crying like a lunatic and running full-tilt towards the jungle. His comrades went running after him, trying to catch hold of him. When they finally caught up with him and shook him out of his trance, he told them: 'My friend, who was sleeping by my side, did not get up. I tried to wake him up, elbowing him in the ribs, but he did not stir. When I touched him, I found his hands and feet were cold as ice. He was dead. That's why I was so shocked!'

The Mylliem Company of the Khasi Corps was put up at a place called Tipang for some time. It was there that the Smir incident happened. One morning, Rymbai, who was in Tipang on inspection, was having lunch with the corps' medical officer, Dr Toberlyne Lyngdoh, and his chief assistant, Prio Davies Laitphlang. Just then, someone came and summoned Rymbai, saying that a British officer wanted to see him. Rymbai said he would finish his meal, then go. But the officer could not wait. He approached the hut where Rymbai was and shouted for him. Rymbai ate calmly, and only when he had finished did he go out.

When the officer saw Rymbai, he demanded harshly if he was the commandant of the corps. At that time, in that valley of death, Rymbai did not care very much whether he lived or died. He only cared about his self-esteem, and he knew that no self-respecting leader would allow anyone to come and shout at him in front of his own men. In as harsh a tone as the officer's, Rymbai replied that he was. Seeing the man not at all intimidated, the British officer lowered his pitch and identified himself as the commandant of the Baluchi Mule Corps. From his insignia, Rymbai could tell that he was a major. The major complained that the Khasis had come to his camp and stolen the bamboo poles his men had brought from far away in the jungle. He said, 'Your men are thieves! My men, who are from an autonomous native state and who are well armed, could easily have shot them down, but I don't want that to happen since we are working for the same cause.'

Rymbai was certain that his men would never steal. They were simply not the stealing kind—and even if they had wanted to, how could they, especially from a corps full of armed and menacing-looking Baluchis?

'My men may not be armed with guns as yours are,' Rymbai replied. 'They may be armed only with knives and cane ropes, but thieves they are not. We, too, are a free people from an autonomous state. We have come here voluntarily, risking disease, injury and death to help the British government, *your government*, and not to steal anything from anybody.'

Angered by Rymbai's unflinching response, the major warned him: 'You take care of your men; if they come again, we'll shoot them down!'

Rymbai replied, 'Shoot if you think you have bullets to waste, but take care, for knives can cut too, especially in the dark!'

Dr Toberlyne and Laitphlang were overjoyed that Rymbai had responded in kind. They, too, were very unhappy at the daily discrimination by the white officers, especially by Captain Hunter, who was in charge of distributing rations and always short-changed them in every possible way. For once at least, they had stood their ground and faced the major down. But they also wondered, like Rymbai, at the strange accusation and urged their commandant to talk to Smir.

Rymbai agreed that there was no harm in asking questions. When Smir returned from the jungle that evening, he summoned him and asked, 'Bah Smir, the commandant of the Baluchi Mule Corps has accused you of going to the Baluchis' camp and stealing bamboo. Is that true?'

Smir replied, 'Yes and no, Sahep. Three of my friends and I did go there, but we did not steal.'

'Why did you go there when it is clearly forbidden to do so?'

'I did not go to the Balut's camp for a visit, Sahep, I went there because I could no longer stand the way they were ill-treating my men.'

'What did they do?'

'Our men are mostly young, as you can see. They are strong and diligent. They go deep into the forest, going up steep precipices and down into the gorges to cut bamboo poles. They bring them up to the track, leave them there and fetch some more from the forest. They do this until late in the evening, Sahep, and then, when it is too dark to go to the forest, they carry all the poles from the track to the camp. That has been their routine every day, and there was no problem till these Baluts came. Lately, we have been missing a lot of bamboo poles. The men told me they saw these Baluts carrying off the poles we had brought from the forest, Sahep, so three of my men and I went to wait for them. And sure enough, we saw three of them stealing our poles and carrying them to their own camp. I yelled and gave chase. Initially, the Baluts ran with the poles, but when they saw me running after them with my hooked machete, they dropped everything and ran like chickens to their coop. I followed them there. I saw many of the poles they had stolen earlier neatly piled in their camp. I took back what I could while the other men carried the poles that the Baluts had dropped on the road. That was what happened, Sahep. We did not steal but tried to prevent theft and to take back what was ours.'

'Weren't you afraid they might shoot you? After all, they had guns …'

Smir looked at Rymbai, surprised, and then he smiled and said, 'We came here for honour, Sahep. I would rather die than let them tyrannise my men and lose my honour.'

When I finished, Hamkom said, 'Either the fellow had exceptional courage or was foolhardy!'

'And that's your reaction to a man who risked his life to stand up for his rights, you goddamn fraud?' Evening spat out.

Alarmed, Bah Kynsai quickly intervened: 'Hey, hey, Ning, zip it! No more quarrelling, you two!' Then, turning to Hamkom, he said, 'But I also think you are missing the point, Ham. As I see it, na, he was a simple man. He saw thieves stealing what they had brought with great effort from the forest. He knew it was wrong, and he knew that to stop them in the future, he had to stop them then. So what should he do? Simple, he ran after them to take back what belonged to him and his men. That's not foolhardiness, Ham, that's courage.'

'He was a great leader, no doubt about it, Bah Kynsai, though only a commander of a small porter company,' Bah Kit asserted. 'He did not ask his men to stop the thieves, ha, on the other hand, he started the chase and put his own life on the line. Though the other side had guns, he had right on his side, and that is a strong ally in the fight against the guilty anywhere.'

'That's it, Bah Kit, that's it,' Evening said eagerly. 'He was a self-sacrificing leader. As Ioannis said, "Greater love hath no man than this, that a man lay down his life for his friends." Though Smir did not die, he was prepared to. I must also say that I was very impressed with Rymbai's conduct as a commandant—'

'Why are you bringing Ioannis into this?' Bah Kynsai asked sarcastically. 'Next, you'll be quoting John the Baptist!'

'They are the same, Bah Kynsai,' Magdalene clarified.

'Oho, you also! I wanted to confuse him, na?'

Smir was a typical Khasi man from Mylliem. He was fair and ruddy-cheeked, and although of average height, he was muscular and had the strength of an ox. He farmed for a living and worked odd jobs to augment his family's income. But adversity brought out the best in him. Alone in a foreign land, inside a dark jungle that even the sun could not penetrate, he and his men did not allow gun-toting bullies to tyrannise them. Smir was lion-hearted—truly a scion of the old Khasis, who were, as a poet put it, 'sturdy, valiant and skilful'.

As for Rymbai, I wholeheartedly agreed with Evening. I added that he was one of the few Khasi writers I truly enjoyed reading.

Bah Kynsai now turned to Hamkom and said, 'These are the kind of people we should talk about, na, Ham, not Tirot Sing and Kiang Nangbah over and over again, as if we have no others. These, na, the lesser-known figures of history, like Ka Phan, U Mon and U Smir, na, with their exemplary courage, na, these are truly worth knowing. But even the wags and pranksters, I would say, are wonderful and edifying in their own way. There are many other characters, you know, who have become part of Shillong's legends ...'

'Like?' Hamkom asked.

Bah Kynsai then told us stories of ordinary people and how they had come to live on in the memory of the community. He spoke of Triet Nongkynrih, the most famous Khasi footballer of yesteryears. Bah Triet of Laban was a rare kind of Khasi. He was six feet two in his socks and fair like an Englishman. But that was not what was so special about him—he was famous both for his skills as a footballer and his exceptional strength. He was so powerful that his shots would cause balls to burst and wooden goal bars to break. In Patiala, Punjab, Triet accidentally killed a goalkeeper when the ball he kicked hit him in the chest. Later, he was allowed to play on the condition that he kicked the ball only with his left foot. However, as has happened to many Khasi sportsmen, he came to a very sad end because of the bottle. In his last days, he became so addicted to alcohol that he ate his dinner of boiled rice mixed with it, as a kind of soup.

Another character, from the same locality, was known simply as Father of Viceroy because his first son was named Viceroy. This man used to walk around barefoot even in the height of winter when everyone else wore thick woollen socks and heavy shoes. Over the years, his soles became so thick and rubbery that he could tread on broken bottles, crushing them into smaller pieces without the smallest cut on his own feet. He would not even be aware of the bottles and would say, 'Arre! How come, frost even in summer?' One day, Bah Kynsai said, and he swore it was not a tall tale, that when Father of Viceroy was returning from a distant forest with a load of firewood, a snake bit him on the heel. But he did not feel a thing. He walked several kilometres, blissfully unaware. It was only when he reached home that his family saw the snake stuck to his heel, dead. But nothing happened to Father of Viceroy.

Bah Kynsai also spoke of the local bully of Laban, a boxer by the name of Denis. At the end of his career, Denis became a ruddy-cheeked alcoholic, and when he was drunk, he would beat up anyone he felt was looking at him queerly. He had a bizarre habit. Every night, on his way home from the boozers, he peed on people's shop fronts. The most peed-upon shop in the locality was that of an old man, also named Denis. One day, old Denis could stand it no longer and protested loudly. Denis looked at him and thought, 'What use is my punching this old fellow in the face?' As he continued with the act, he stared hard at the old man and said, 'Shut up, Denis, son of my penis!'

Old Denis complained to the locality dorbar, but Denis was unfazed. Explaining his problem to the councillors, he said, 'If I don't pee on shop fronts, I cannot sleep … is it because these bastards are overpricing or what? Why don't you buggers look into that first, huh?'

In short, since no one could stop the overpricing, no one could stop his habit either.

There was also a little fellow from Mawkhar, known as Liaw—another of those meaningless Khasi nicknames, perhaps given because he was so small: about four feet eleven only. Liaw was a daily-wage labourer but was well known throughout the locality because of his excessive fondness for praying before mealtimes, especially when there was a big audience. However, Bah Kynsai clarified, he was not a religious person in the conventional sense, and did not even go to church. But at funerals and feasts, he said, you had to listen to his loud prayers before you could eat. Thankfully, though, his prayers were quite unique, and not very long, because they directly addressed the issues at hand, the things he could see or could not see on the plate.

For instance, during a naming ceremony, he and his friends were given a dish of rice and a beautifully prepared beef curry. For dessert, they were given a plate of *gulab jamuns*, which, as you know, are dark-brown sweets, usually the size and shape of golf balls. Looking at the food before him, Liaw began his prayer by saying, 'O Lord, thank you for this plate of rice; thank you for this tasty-looking beef curry; and certainly, thank you for these *liang kulai*, these horse testicles that I so love to eat. Amen.'

At another feast, Liaw was given a plate of rice and pork curry. But by an oversight, he was served only the gravy, potatoes and some bay leaves used to flavour the curry. There was not a single piece of meat on his plate, whereas, on his friends', there were four or five pieces. When Liaw said his prayer, therefore, he began with a loud appeal: 'O Lord! I thank you for this plate of rice and I appeal to you to bless our generous hosts for it, but at the same time, as you turned water into wine, I also fervently pray that you kindly turn these bay leaves on my plate into pork!'

Hearing that, the red-faced hosts quickly produced a plate full of pork for Liaw. And Liaw said, 'Prayers can work miracles.'

Once, a friend of Liaw's, called Knung—because he was so tall and thin— came running to his house in the middle of the night. Knung had recently married the youngest daughter of a wealthy family after long consultations with Liaw and his cronies. The hope was that Knung would be very rich (as per the contemporary Khasi practice, the youngest daughter inherits everything) and the union would bring them great benefits as well. Unfortunately for Knung, his mother-in-law became pregnant again after a gap of many years. The man was in a tizzy. 'What to do, what to do?' he said to himself, and off he went running to Liaw's in the dead of night.

When Liaw opened the door, Knung said without preamble, '*Golmaal, bhai, sab golmaal*! Trouble, big trouble! You have got to help me, man! Please, man, please!'

'What happened? Why are you crying?' Liaw demanded in a stern voice.

'What else can I do? My mother-in-law, man, she's pregnant! Can you believe it? Pregnant at her age! It's shameful, man! But what if she gives birth to a girl? That'll be the youngest daughter, no? Short of murder, what can I do?'

Liaw told him to get a grip on himself. He rubbed the stubble on his chin and asked, 'When is she due?'

'She just learnt about it.'

'Then maybe it's not too late. Don't despair. We'll organise prayer meetings every day, after all, prayers can move mountains, no?'

Liaw and his friends met at Knung's every day after work and prayed for almost nine months that Knung's mother-in-law must on no account be blessed with a daughter. During these prayer meetings, they abstained from drinking, and only indulged afterwards, and that too, only a glass or two to wash off the cement dust from the construction site. And believe it or not, after nine months, Knung's mother-in-law gave birth to a baby boy.

Liaw's fame as a praying man rose phenomenally among his friends. They never tired of telling the story, and also about what happened to him once during a prayer. They were all sitting together in a building site, their lunches, packed in betel nut leaves, spread on the ground before them. As usual, Liaw closed his eyes and began to pray, but perhaps because he was more hungry than usual, he opened his eyes just as he was about to say 'Amen'.

And when he did, he saw a little chicken shit just in front of his jasong. The sight so muddled his thinking that instead of saying 'Amen', he said, '*Ah, i eit!*' ('Ah, shit!')

Only once did Liaw refuse to pray. That was during the funeral of a close relative in Sohra. Liaw had gone there with his usual band of friends, and because they were all construction workers by profession, they were thought to be the fittest people to dig the grave. All morning, till about noon, they worked non-stop at the graveyard, digging and generally preparing everything for the burial. When it was done, they sated their thirst with a few drinks. Then, tired and hungry, for they had not eaten anything for hours, they decided to return to the mourning house and not to wait for food to be brought to the graveyard. On arriving, they immediately headed for the kitchen. The woman helping in the kitchen ladled rice and pork broth onto their plates. But in Sohra, people usually scooper up their rice in thin slices, like pieces of cake. Thus it was that the woman gave them thin slices of rice and a piece of pork each. That done, she said in a friendly tone, 'Okay, Bah Liaw, now you can begin your prayer.'

Tired and hungry, Liaw looked sourly at the small helping of rice and the single piece of pork on his plate. Suddenly he lost his cool and shouted, 'Pray! Pray for this measly rice and this tiny piece of pork! You pray, you miserly woman!'

The woman fled the room in shame, and was replaced by another, who immediately ladled more rice and pork onto their plates. Seeing that, one of Liaw's friends said, 'Hey, Liaw, even refusing to pray can work miracles, huh?'

Liaw had been staring fixedly at the food in front of him, as if trying to make sense of what had just happened. His friend's comment, however, broke the spell. With a low grunt, he said, 'Let us pray.'

It was the shortest and most cryptic of all his prayers. He said, 'O Lord, for this miracle too, we thank you. Amen.'

The last man that Bah Kynsai spoke about was his non-Khasi colleague at the university. He was living in quarters assigned to him by the authorities, a nice stand-alone house. It was big and roomy, and built to suit the requirements of a senior professor. However, owing no doubt to the corruption of both supervising engineers and contractors, the construction was shoddy, and one rainy night, the roof suddenly developed a large leak. Water splashed directly onto the double bed, where the professor, who was reasonably fit, and his wife, who was overweight, were sleeping. They jumped out of bed, threw off the blankets, put a big bucket beneath the leakage, and watched in fascination for a while.

After some time, the professor said, 'I think we can go back to sleep; nothing is wet, and it seems the water is falling safely into the bucket. Only thing is, we'll have to use separate blankets. The bucket has come between us.'

The wife did not like being separated from her husband, but there was nothing to be done; no other solution immediately presented itself. As she put a stone in the bucket to steady it and made the necessary adjustments to the bed, she said, 'Tomorrow, you should complain to the authorities first thing in the morning, okay? Where else can we keep such a big bed?'

She was right—all the other available rooms were taken up by their six children. He promised to attend to it at the earliest.

But, that night, that was how they slept: the wife on the left, the professor on the right and the big bucket in the middle, separating them. The wife tossed and turned the whole night. The professor, on the other hand, undisturbed by his wife's heavy hand on his neck or by her frequent movements, fell asleep almost instantly, and slept peacefully till morning.

Over breakfast, the professor considered the situation carefully. He had never slept as well as he had the previous night. He looked at his middle-aged wife's flabby body with distaste and said to himself: 'No wonder I have had nothing but fitful sleep for the last few years. I don't enjoy sleeping with her any more. The leaky roof has come as a blessing in disguise. Corruption does have its advantages after all.'

His wife broke into his thoughts by asking if he had phoned the people responsible for the maintenance of the quarters. He said he would have to do it from the office since it was too early. When he left for work, his wife reminded him: 'Do it without fail, okay?'

The professor dutifully assured her that he would. However, he said to himself, 'Why don't I wait and see if I can continue to sleep as serenely as I did last night?'

His wife asked him about the call when he returned home, and he pretended surprise. 'Arre, they haven't come? I told them about it! Maybe tomorrow. If they don't come tomorrow, na, I'll give them a piece of my mind, you just wait and see!'

That night, they slept with the big bucket in the middle, and once again, the professor found that he could sleep almost as soon as his head hit the pillow. In the morning, he felt fresh and rested. But his wife, annoyed by the bucket, did not sleep very well. She reminded him to talk to the office people again, and ordered him to order them to come and stop the leak without fail. He promised, but he did not. When he returned home, he pretended surprise again and cursed them a little for being so irresponsible.

That night, there was no rain. His wife wanted to remove the bucket, but the professor said, 'Arre baba, keep it, na, the rain might come in the middle of the night, na, and unnecessarily we will lose sleep again!'

So, that night too, they slept with the bucket occupying pride of place in the middle of the bed, and that night too, the professor slept, as he put it, like 'Sleeping Beauty', dead to the world. He was not entirely happy with the simile, which seemed somehow out of place, but try as he might, he could not come up with anything better.

At the breakfast table the next morning, the professor came to a decision. He would not report the matter to the Estate people. The bucket was affording him such restful sleep; why should he remove it? Was he a fool or what?

His wife nagged him daily about it, and daily he lied to her and cursed the office people for not responding to his alleged complaints. For his wife's sake, he even threatened to take up the matter with the vice chancellor. That was how it went for days and weeks, and soon even his wife got tired of complaining and learnt to sleep better, though the bucket was still in the middle.

The professor was now very happy. The bucket continued to give him a good night's sleep, and his wife had stopped nagging him about it. Only, he dreaded the end of the rainy season and the onset of winter, when he would have to remove the bucket. But then, he consoled himself with his own version of Shelley's immortal line: 'If winter comes, can summer be far behind?'

Bah Kynsai's story reminded me of my granduncle and how he had split up with his wife after living with her for more than fifty years. At the time of their separation, both of them were about seventy-five.

Finding that rather peculiar, my friends asked me to tell them the story.

My uncle's name is Mojen, yes, the very same who had said, 'As the rate, so the work! One ana, one forefinger!' He married a woman from the Ri War village of Nongjri when he was twenty-five years old. He met her on a market day at Ïewbah Sohra while he was buying some yams.

In those days, since the Pynursla road in the east had not yet been built, the main commercial outlet of Nongjri was Sohra in the south-west, and the only route to and fro was a precipitous path through wooded cliffs and deep ravines. It used to take many hours for the people of Nongjri to reach the market in Sohra where they sold their produce of yam, taro root, eggplant, ginger, turmeric, pepper, betel nut, betel leaf, broomstick, cassava and fruits, including lemons and oranges.

Mabah Mojen, as we used to call him, fell in love with his beautiful wife, Ka Kheit Rynjah, at first sight. She was sitting nearby selling oranges while he bargained for his yams. When he saw her, he quickly bought the yams and went to inspect her oranges. Mabah had a ready wit and a smooth tongue, and soon he was in deep conversation with her, talking about everything but the oranges. Kheit's mother, who had gone for tea and the famous jasnam of Sohra, came back to find them laughing together and touching hands. She immediately asked about his antecedents. When she found that he was from a good Sohra family, she encouraged the friendship and left them alone, pretending to be busy with some merchandise nearby.

Mabah courted her for three consecutive market days before telling his parents and uncles, who then took over the negotiations and arranged his marriage. There was only one problem. His wife's family insisted that Mabah should live in Nongjri, the girl being the only daughter in the house. Mabah's uncles tried to persuade him not to go. They said, 'How can you, a Sohra, go to live in Nongjri? What do you know about farming yam and cassava? How will you survive?'

Mabah replied, 'I'm not only a man of many talents, as you all know, but also a quick learner ... why should farming be a problem for me?'

Mabah was indeed very good with his hands. He could build houses, for instance, and work equally well with stone and wood. Incidentally, he was also a talented singer, stage actor and musician, and played the duitara, the flute and the violin equally well. Even after he went to live in Nongjri, the people of the Sohra locality of Khliehshnong used to send for him whenever they planned to stage a *thiatar*. Without Jen, they said, the thiatar would not be 'delicious'. There is a story about an old woman who never missed a performance by Mabah and his friend, Phren, whom you have met before. She would sit in the front row, laughing herself silly, holding her stomach and all the time saying, '*Keiñnoh te Jen, keiñnoh te Jen, ngam long shuh! Ngan sa ïap artat te Jen!*' ('Please Jen, enough, enough Jen, enough, I can stand no more! I will die, Jen, surely I will die!') Mabah Mojen was that good a comedian.

Whenever Mabah came home, he would freshen up and immediately head out to meet Phren. Phren, on his part, would rush out to meet Mabah the moment he heard of his arrival, and so, in that way, they always contrived to meet each other on the road. Between our house and Phren's, there is a long stretch of road, level and straight. When they got to this stretch and saw each other from a distance, it was their habit to break off a branch from some tree, to use as a whisk, and to dance and chant gnomic phawars till they finally met at the halfway point. On meeting, they embraced and danced and sang some more for the benefit of the crowd, which by then would have spilled onto the road to watch them. The Mojen–Phren annual meeting was quite a famous spectacle in Khliehshnong. I had never seen it—for, by the time I was born, Phren was bedridden and Mabah Mojen was too old to come home as he used to do—but my mother and everybody else talked about it often enough. He was quite a character, it would seem.

Because they could not stop him, his uncles escorted him to Nongjri, where he lived very happily with our Aunt Kheit even though they never had any children. The people of Nongjri too adored him, for he was a friendly soul and a great entertainer. No social event in the village could begin without their beloved Bah Jen.

But one fine day, I was about fourteen at the time, our family in Sohra received a message from him through one of the fruit sellers. The message, written on a scrap of paper, explained that he had separated from his wife of fifty years. He did not say why, only that he wanted us to come and take him back to Sohra. He couldn't undertake the hard jungle trek on his own any more. He commanded his nephews, therefore, to come with enough money to hire at least two people to carry him in their conical palanquins.

Eight of us prepared for the journey to faraway Nongjri. There were six men in the group—two of them our kñi, maternal uncles, and four uncles through marriage with our maternal aunts. There were only two boys, my brother and I. Unused as we were to travelling on that kind of rough and precipitous jungle route, we took as long as seventeen hours to reach Nongjri. From Khliehshnong, we walked for about ten kilometres to lower Sohra and the locality of Kut Madan, after leaving home at the third cockcrow, about 4 a.m. From there, we went down a very steep slope over a meandering path until we reached the village of Sohkhmi, located on a low hill near the bottom of the ravine, where we rested, and where the villagers gave us some fruits to refresh ourselves.

The village was surrounded by thick jungle on every side, and the morning was loud with the calls of countless birds, some of which I readily recognised, having heard them in the sacred forests of Sohra. In the village itself were fruit trees like jackfruit, litchee, lemon, orange, papaya, tamarind and, of course, the slim betel nut tree. Overall, the village looked neat and clean and prosperous to me, though many of the houses were mere thatched huts.

From Sohkhmi, we went further down the ravine till we reached Wah Rew, the River Rew, at the bottom. Wah Rew had its sources in the small streams originating from the hills of Sohra and Khatar Shnong, but here it was a sizeable river, easily 180 feet across. Unlike Wah Rwiang of Lyngngam, the riverbed was littered with huge boulders, some of them as big as small hills. We looked to the north, we looked to the south, the sight was the same. The length and breadth of the river, my uncles explained, was choked with stone as a pomegranate is with seeds. 'From where did they come?' we asked. 'Could it be from the time of the great earthquake?' But my uncles said they were there before the earthquake; they had always been there, and nobody knew how. Perhaps some cataclysmic event had taken place thousands or even millions of years ago, causing these rocks to tumble down from the towering cliffs above.

Donald wanted to know how tall the cliffs were. I told him that I didn't have the measure in feet, but from the tableland of Kut Madan up to the bank of the River Rew at the bottom of the jungle ravine, where we were standing, we had travelled about five kilometres. I know that because I remember my uncles saying it had taken us *san kyntien kwai*, five pieces of betel nuts, from Kut Madan to the river.

The banks of the River Rew were quite steep and about a hundred feet deep. My uncles said the water was always full to the brim in summer, completely submerging most of the boulders. But this being winter, it was only a few feet deep and was, therefore, split and splintered into hundreds of channels meandering through the packed boulders. From where we were, there was no path down to the river. We went south towards the village of Suktia, very close to the Bangladesh border, and after ten kilometres or so, we came to a narrow suspension bridge, about two feet wide, spanning the river's breadth. It was called *Ka Jingkieng Doi-doi* by the locals, because when you walked on it, it swung from side to side. It was a scary thing, I can tell you. At the time, it was already modernised with steel cables and iron nettings, but in the old days, the bridge was made entirely of bamboo poles and stoutly woven strings, and anyone crossing it had to pay homage to God first. I was told that it was routinely carried away by the monsoon floods, and had to be rebuilt every year after sacrificial ceremonies had been conducted. These days, hardly anyone travels this route. Nongjri is now accessible by road from Pynursla to the east and Sohbar to the south. The bridge has ceased to exist.

'How can you say the bridge has ceased to exist, Ap?' Magdalene said. 'Those bridges are still very much there, man! My family went to have a look at one of them only last year!'

'Those are not the same, Mag,' I explained. 'They are known as the living-root bridges, made by linking the roots of fig trees together. They are the lifeblood of Ri War, connecting the ravine hamlets with one another. But they are used only where the streams are much smaller, say, about fifty feet or so across.'

That day, we crossed the bridge and found two paths forking from it, one going south towards Suktia and another north-east towards the village of Nongla. We would take the Nongla path, but first, we rested and had lunch. It was terribly hot there, even in winter. But we were inside the jungle, and the trees afforded us plenty of shade. It was 10 a.m. or so when we stopped to eat. We had travelled about twenty-five kilometres in six hours. The War people would have travelled that distance in just three hours, running down the steep steps on nimble feet. For us, running was out of the question. By the time we reached Sohkhmi, our limbs were already trembling with the strain of walking down the steep slope. But from the bank of the River Rew till the bridge, we had some respite: the path was almost completely flat.

Opening our jasongs, we found beef jerky—fried with potatoes—and chillies, raw onions and tungtap fish (roasted and ground) on a bed of boiled rice. The chillies were the tiny variety called *ken khnai,* or rat chillies, which are both hot and aromatic. We ate our lunch beneath the trees. The food felt incredibly delicious, probably because of all that walking we had done. For water, we went down to the river along a very steep path and drank from one of its crystal-clear pools. The water we had brought from home in whisky bottles (no plastic bottles in those days) we were saving for the jungle trek to come.

'From here on,' Madeng, one of our maternal uncles, said, 'it will be all uphill. We'll be exercising different sorts of muscles.'

The prospect of climbing to Nongla, about twenty kilometres up the thickly wooded cliff, was daunting, but I couldn't complain, having pestered them into taking me along. After a short rest, we began the long march up at about 11.20 a.m. Maieit, our other maternal uncle, would not allow us to walk immediately after eating, for doing that, he said, would make our stomachs ache.

The climb was terrible. Our path was made of sheer steps, forcing us to stop and rest every once in a while. I don't think this part of the journey could have been measured in terms of betel nuts eaten, for the progress was very slow. Seven hours later, we reached Nongla, which was perched in the middle of a wooded cliff, on a kind of ledge big enough for twenty houses or so. The people were very friendly. And when they came to know we were related to Mabah Mojen, they treated us with even greater warmth. We were very thirsty and wanted some tea desperately, but there was none to be had in the village—it was too much of a luxury item. They gave us water and taro roots daubed with honey instead. I think the uncles were later given yiad um beer, which made them forget all about the tea.

Donald wanted to know what they did for water on such an impossibly high cliff. I told him that the cliff was thickly forested and had many springs. The jungle was like a huge village in itself, enclosing many villages, criss-crossed by ancient pathways and fed by shadowy springs running through split bamboo poles, like flyovers in cities.

I learnt so much from that walk in the jungle, simple things like the name of *phan dieng* (cassava, or literally, 'tree potato'), with its tall, thin stem and stout, tuberous root. I learnt to differentiate between green and wild pepper. I saw the flaming areca nut for the first time, dangling in bunches from the tousled top of its branchless tree, straight and smooth as a lamp post, and I followed the path of the betel leaf as it crept along the forest floor and up the moss-enfolded trunks for a peep at the sky. I saw giant trees like the shaggy fig or the towering sal and teak, and flitting among them, I saw barking deer and musk deer crossing our path more than once. I saw birds that I had only heard of. I listened to the soft cajoling of *ki slang*, the melodies of *jlaeit*, the distressed call of *jyllob*, the ominous rumble of *pohkrong* and the desolate sadness of *kairiang*: birds that I cannot even name in any language but my own.

Luckily, my uncles were too sensible to get drunk, and at about 7 p.m., we were once again on our way to Nongjri. It was located on a mountain range south and east of Nongla, and we could see its lights from where we were. We could also see the lights of Bangladeshi villages, almost like they lay at our feet. In the morning, it would have been a stunning sight.

Nongjri did not appear to be very far from Nongla, but it took us more than two hours, despite the route now following a slightly downhill slant. We walked on a path cut into the face of the cliff, which would have been terribly frightening but for the fact that we could not see much because of the trees and the darkness.

We had crawled to Nongla in the near-darkness, but now we used the two-foot torches that the villagers had given us. We were given eight but used only four at a time so that they would last us all the way to Nongjri. Perhaps I shouldn't call them torches—they were made of a reed known as *kdait*, bound together and lighted. And that was how we arrived in Nongjri, at about 9 p.m., eight strangers carrying four torches, bathed in sweat and blackened by the sooty flakes from the kdait flames. We caused quite a sensation, arriving so late, but quickly identified ourselves as Mabah Mojen's relatives and were taken to the headman's house, a large hut with a thatched roof like a carapace.

Nongjri was quite unlike Nongla. It was built on the flat summit of a wooded hill. It was much, much larger too. As we stood in the headman's courtyard, quite a crowd came to stare at us. We all wondered why we had been taken to the headman's house, rather than to Mabah Mojen's. But the headman told us that the old man went to bed as soon as the sun went down. 'There's no point going to his house now,' he told us, 'you can eat and stay here with us, but you'll have to sleep in the shed, the hut is too small to accommodate all of you.'

We thanked him and went to a spring nearby to wash. When we returned, food was ready. Neighbours had brought some rice from their homes, and so, the headman's family did not have to cook for us. It was simple fare: boiled rice and a local vegetable boiled with too much water and flavoured with a little dried fish. But we were hungry and ate with relish.

The shed was quite comfortable, with a fair stock of hay, probably for the headman's goats. He was the only one with goats in the village. The others mostly kept chickens and pigs. Goats were rare in Ri War villages as they tend to feed on vegetables and plants. But the headman, whose name was Kren, meaning 'speak', said he kept them tethered and did not let them roam freely.

In the morning, after a breakfast of rice and vegetable, the same as we'd had the previous night, we were taken to Mabah's house.

Madeng recognised the hut and asked, 'But isn't this Aunt Kheit's house, Bah?'

'It is!' Bah Kren confirmed.

'But aren't they separated? Where is Aunt Kheit staying then?' Madeng asked again.

Bah Kren smiled mysteriously and said, 'When you go inside, you will understand everything.'

It was a bamboo-and-thatch hut, with a carapace-like roof, like all the others in the village. It looked rather large, but when we went inside, we found that it had only one big room, say thirty by thirty feet, with two very small lean-tos serving as a washing area and a storeroom.

In the middle of the hut was a large hearth with a tyngier bamboo platform suspended above it. There were not many things on the tyngier, only odds and ends. Clearly, the hearth was not being used, probably hadn't been for quite some time. It had been swept clean, and there was no trace of ash in it.

In its place, two new hearths had been built, one in the eastern corner and the other in the western. A bright fire was burning in both and something was cooking. Near the hearths were pallets with blankets spread over them. In the dim light, we saw an old woman sitting on the pallet in the eastern corner. She was dressed in a bright red frock, and over it a white-and-green checked jaiñsem. Her hair was mostly black despite her age (incredible but true), and signs of youthful beauty could still be seen on her soft, creamy face, which was not as wrinkled as you might have expected. I had seen a few people like that since. Even my paternal grandmother, Beikha Phiw, who is seventy-five, has no grey in her hair, and her face is still quite smooth: simple and healthy living, or perhaps the genes. In the western corner, a very fair old man was bent over the fire. He was dressed in a white cotton shirt and a white dhoti. Old Khasis, in those days, preferred a dhoti to trousers. His hair was completely white, but he too had few wrinkles and seemed quite strong and healthy. Madeng, who was working as a quarryman in the cement factory, had a more furrowed face. When the old man turned to look at us, we could see in him signs of a face that was once very handsome. The face of a Sohra actor. These were my grandaunt Kheit and my granduncle Mojen.

Bah Kren looked at us and guffawed: 'This is their idea of separation: living under the same roof but cooking on different hearths and not talking to each other. They have been living like this for over a year!'

'But why?' all my uncles asked at the same time. They also were laughing.

Before anyone could answer, Mabah came towards us. He had recognised us at once, and crying, embraced each one of us, saying, 'Look, look at how your own flesh and blood has been treated! Now, because I'm old and useless, this is how they are treating me!'

We all looked but could find nothing wrong anywhere, except the two hearths and pallets.

Aunt Kheit said, 'So, so, you have brought your relatives all the way from Sohra, just to malign me? Do not believe a word he is telling you, my sons; no one is ill-treating him.'

Mabah ignored her and pleaded with us, 'You must take me away from here, look,' he pointed to his corner, 'alone, all alone in that corner for a year! Is this any way to live? I'll go back home with you; I cannot live like this any more!'

Maieit, who was a bit of a joker, replied, 'But you are not alone, Mabah! Your wife is in the other corner, just twenty or twenty-five feet away from you!'

'You dare trifle with me, *kharïong*! Jokers like you will always treat even matters of life and death as a joke.' Then, turning to Madeng, he demanded, 'Have you brought money for the carriers?'

Kharïong means 'black non-Khasi'. Mabah was calling Maieit kharïong because he was dark-complexioned. Madeng was as dark as Maieit, and much shorter than his five-nine, but nobody ever called him names—he was a quiet, dignified sort of man who spoke only after carefully weighing his words. His oft-repeated lesson to us was, 'Do not speak without thinking.' And then he would elaborate: 'A word once uttered cannot be taken back. People remember and will use it against you whenever they can.' He himself never once said or did anything that would offend anybody.

Maieit answered for Madeng: 'Hahaha, matter of life and death, he says! Is living under the same roof with your wife a matter of life and death, then?'

Mabah Mojen fumed at that. 'You son of an animal! Have you brought the money or not?'

'We have. But first, you must tell us why you have been behaving like this.'

'Like what?' Mabah demanded.

'Like a spoilt brat, a spoilt old brat, that's what!'

'You son of a black demon! Krokar,' he turned to Madeng, 'tell this mischief-monger not to make fun of my misfortune!'

Before Madeng could say anything, Aunt Kheit intervened: 'You are right, Kros, you have got it perfectly right! All this is because he has been behaving like a kid. He has not spoken to me for one year, imagine! When I speak to him, he does not respond at all. He constructed these hearths because he did not want to eat from the same pot as I. And all because of what? All because, one market day, I forgot to ask my nephew to bring him his favourite jasnam from Sohra. I never forgot, my sons, only once did I forget, and when he could not get his jasnam—that one time only—he began to sulk and has not spoken to me for a whole year! A whole year, imagine! Tell me, isn't he behaving like a spoilt kid?'

I told you about jasnam, remember? It is the Sohra version of jadoh meat-rice, cooked with pig's blood, intestines, fat and onion paste.

When he heard that, Maieit teased Mabah: 'Oho! So you have brought us all the way from Sohra just because of a packet of jasnam? You want to leave your wife of fifty years because of a packet of jasnam? You have not grown old, Mabah, you have grown young; you are a child again!'

Mabah Mojen spluttered with rage and once again cursed Maieit, who was clearly having a good time at his expense.

But now even Madeng asked, 'Is it true, Mabah?'

'It is not *only* a packet of jasnam!' Mabah Mojen shouted at the top of his voice. 'In my old age, it is the only pleasure left in my life! Yet, it's not about that at all; it's about whether she cares for me or not! And when she forgot something so important to me, it means that even she has stopped caring!'

'Of course not, you silly old man!' Aunt Kheit said with feeling. 'How can I not care about you when I have been living with you for fifty years? But I'm also a silly old woman, don't you see? I forget things too, my memory grows short, and I need reminding about many things nowadays. But I'm telling you Kros, and you, Kro, if you carry him away to Sohra, you had better take me too. I'm not living here alone!'

Aunt Kheit was addressing Maieit, whose name was Kroswer, and Madeng, whose name was Krokar, because they were the most influential people in the group. Before answering Aunt Kheit, Madeng asked Mabah, 'So what have you been doing for jasnam all this while?'

'A neighbour has been bringing it to me every week,' he said.

'A neighbour? You silly old man, it is my nephew who has been buying your jasnam, only thing is, knowing your stubbornness, he has been giving it to Khem to pass it on to you. Why else do you think Khem has not been taking your money? And my nephew has been buying the jasnam because I instructed him to bring back a packet without fail, whether I tell him to or not. And we have been doing that because we love you.'

This last revelation was made not only in front of us but also the whole village, for many people had come into the room, and many more were waiting in the courtyard. Mabah Mojen was quite discomfited, and uttered the first words he had spoken to his wife in a year: 'I didn't know that!'

Maieit, making the most of the situation, said, 'Then it's settled. They have not been ill-treating you; you don't have to leave with us. Besides, we cannot carry two old people with us, and we certainly cannot leave Aunt Kheit here alone.'

The crowd of villagers also pressed him to stay. They said, 'You see, Ma Jen, they have not been neglecting you. They are the ones who have been giving you your jasnam. If you had spoken to Mei Kheit or listened to her, you would have known. Not only Mei Kheit, but her entire family loves you. We all love you. How can you leave us?'

Mabah Mojen—who, we suspected, did not really want to leave anyway, and had summoned us from Sohra as a kind of leverage, so he could bring the issue to a head without losing face—finally gave in to the combined pressure of all present. When he agreed to stay, a loud cheer went up through the room and was taken up by those outside. Some of them left immediately to pass on the news to those who could not be there.

Beaming with pleasure, Aunt Kheit asked her nephews to catch two big chickens from the coop and asked her nieces to cook rice for all of us. 'Be quick about it,' she ordered, 'we must hold a feast in honour of our relatives from Sohra.'

Maieit teased her, 'In our honour, Ñia, or your beloved Mojen's?'

Aunt Kheit (or Ñia Kheit, if you wish) simply beamed happily and waved a dismissive hand at him. She looked lovingly at Mabah, who was ordering one of her nephews to build a fire in the big hearth, and sighed contentedly. That was the final sign of reconciliation.

Mabah Mojen and Aunt Kheit lived very happily after that, as they had always done before the jasnam incident. They lived up to the age of ninety-two, and their death was so strange that people talked of nothing else for months afterwards. Even now, it is a topic of conversation both in Nongjri and Sohra. Both of them died peacefully in their sleep, at the same time. They were discovered by one of Aunt Kheit's nieces, who was sleeping in their house for company. The niece was very surprised when the old couple overslept that morning. She knew their habits very well: they slept soon after sunset and got up at the third cockcrow. But that morning, at 6 a.m., they were still asleep. When she went to wake them, they were dead, their hands entwined.

When I finished my story, Magdalene was teary-eyed and Donald had one arm around her. He exclaimed, 'Amazing, Bah Ap, simply amazing!'

Bah Kynsai asked, 'What is amazing? The separation or their death?'

'Everything,' Donald replied. 'I have never heard about so many strange people and incidents in my life, Bah Kynsai. I never dreamt that such people exist in real life. And the travelogue was fascinating too, Bah Ap. Villages in deep jungle ravines, rivers choked with boulders, swinging bridges and villages built into a cliff face ... Amazing! I never knew there are such places in the Khasi Hills.'

Magdalene readily agreed, admitting that she too had never been to such places. 'You know what, I can't imagine myself in that kind of situation, ya. If it had been my husband and I, we would have killed each other, I think. But your uncles are very funny, Ap, both Maieit Kroswer and Mabah Mojen.'

'Say, why don't we organise a trekking expedition to one of these places, Bah Kynsai?' Hamkom asked. 'They sound fascinating, ya.'

'You go ahead and organise one, but if you want me to come along, na, also organise a khoh kit briew palanquin. Look at me, man, do you think I can manage without a carrier?'

Bah Kynsai was certainly in no shape for a gruelling trek like that. He was overweight and tired quickly, even walking around Nongshyrkon. And when we went to the lake, we had to stop and rest now and then to let him catch his breath.

Magdalene, however, thought Bah Kynsai was in much better shape now than before. 'It must be all the walking we are doing, I think,' she said.

Evening interrupted the conversation and said, 'Bah Kynsai, we have been talking only about the lesser-known figures of history, as you said. And they are worthy of note, but what about our achievers? Why don't we talk about them as well?'

Bah Kynsai was not excited by the idea. 'We may know who they are, na, but not much else is known about them—'

'You mean, not known by us here, or by all Khasis?' Magdalene asked.

'I mean by all Khasis: there is only sketchy literature about them, na? I don't think our society has developed the art of biography writing at all, which is a damn pity.'

'We are the Thlen keepers, no, Bah Kynsai? You are forgetting things in your old age!' Raji said. 'Thlen, the serpent—let me refresh your very, very dim memory—does not drink anybody's blood but ours, remember that. That's why we don't write ... what, what, Ap? Biographies, yes: we don't want to promote each other, okay, we only want, we only want to demote each other, hahaha.'

Bah Kynsai hit him with the bamboo stick on the head, but playfully rather than angrily. He realised that Raji was speaking 'incoherent sense', as he put it.

Evening became impatient. 'We may not have well-written biographies, but at least let us pick out our heroes and see what we come up with, no?'

'You do what you like, but don't talk about the living,' Bah Kynsai said.

'Why not?' Hamkom asked.

'We'd be influenced by our prejudices and our relationship with them or someone close to them, na?'

'Very true, Bah Kynsai,' I agreed.

Evening agreed to the condition and said, 'My greatest heroes are the freedom fighters: Tirot Sing, Kiang Nangbah, Mon Bhut—'

'We have already discussed them,' Bah Kynsai interrupted him.

'What about Wickliffe Syiem, the deputy syiem of Hima Nongstoin? He was also a freedom fighter, no? He rebelled against India's horrible Instrument of Accession, ha, and went to live in East Pakistan rather than be a vanquished subject once again.'

'For God's sake, man! Being part of India is not the same thing as being a "vanquished subject"!' Donald protested.

'Wickliffe was a syiem, a ruler, and to him, being annexed to India was like being subjugated. I admire his courage, that's all. It doesn't mean I'm anti-India.'

Hamkom wanted to speak about James Mohon Nichols-Roy, one of the most illustrious of Khasi personalities, but Bah Kynsai protested and said, 'No politicians!'

'But why not?' Hamkom challenged. 'He was the architect of the District Council in the Khasi-Jaiñtia Hills, no?'

Evening added, 'And there are politicians that we must speak about, Bah Kynsai!'

But Bah Kynsai was adamant. 'Not this fellow. You may call him the architect of the District Council, Ham, but he was a divisive politician. When the Federation of Khasi States was set up by all the Khasi syiems and prominent leaders, na, to represent the Khasi cause at the national level, na, Joy refused to join it. As the federation campaigned for the establishment of a distinct administrative system for the Khasi people, based on our traditional democratic form of governance, with the syiems as the titular heads, Joy formed a rival organisation called the Khasi-Jaiñtia Federated States General Conference ... He campaigned for the abolition of the Khasi system and for the formation of the District Council to govern over the Khasi-Jaiñtia Hills district of Assam. The District Council, na, as you know, na, was designed to have absolute power over the syiems and village administrators. And because Joy became a member of the Indian National Congress, his campaign won, and the Federation of Khasi States lost: meaning, we, as a people, lost because of him. I don't think he should be held up as a hero.'

'But Bah Kynsai, do you truly prefer the old syiemship system to the District Council?' Hamkom asked, aghast. 'In the old system, okay, the head of the administration was the king, and he could only be elected from a certain clan, the Syiem clan, whereas in the District Council we have MDCs, members elected directly by the people, and they can be from any clan! Surely the District Council is a much better option!'

'Look, Ham, what do we have now?' Bah Kynsai countered. 'We have headmen in villages. And we still have the old system with syiem raijs, or provincial kings, in the provinces and fully fledged syiems in the himas, our traditional states. On top of that, we have the District Council, and above that the state government. How many authorities do we need to govern a state, man? Don't you see, the establishment of the District Council has not brought about the abolition of syiemship, na? It has only worsened the situation by creating too many authorities, often working at cross purposes. How many times have we read in the papers about the tussle for power between the District Council and the state government, huh?'

'That's true, but—'

'Wait, na, Ham! And what is the District Council supposed to do? It is supposed to protect our culture, our land and our forests and resources! Do you think it has been doing all that? Tell me, how much of our land has been sold to the defence forces, non-tribal businessmen and companies? I'm telling you, na, the District Council is an unnecessary duplication of power and authority. I'll give you one very small example. If you want a house loan from a bank, na, they say you have to go to the District Council and get a No Objection Certificate, an NOC. But when you have done that, na, you are told that, unless your land is registered with the deputy commissioner's office, read state government, your loan application will not be processed. Now, what use is this NOC from the District Council then? It does not even allow us to apply for a house loan, liah! Isn't this a useless duplication of power and unnecessary red tape? Meanwhile, we suffer: we pay fees to the District Council and we pay fees to the state government. It's time they abolished this useless institution. And Joy was its architect! Let's forget about him, man.

'And do you know what the greatest irony is, Ham? Even non-tribals can vote and contest District Council elections, liah! That's how useless it is. Ideally, na, Ham, we should have only one government: the state government!'

'Not any more, Bah Kynsai,' I clarified, 'non-tribals cannot vote any more, not in the Khasi Hills.'

'But what do you think of the District Council, Ap?' Hamkom asked, attempting to enlist my support.

'The District Councils of the states of Assam, Meghalaya, Tripura and Mizoram are constitutional bodies,' I replied. 'They were brought into being by Articles 244 (2) and 275 (1) of the Sixth Schedule of the Indian Constitution. If you want them abolished, then these Articles, as well as the Sixth Schedule itself, will have to be struck off from the Constitution. And that may take some doing. Besides, I believe the intention behind their creation is a noble one. The basic thrust of both the Fifth and Sixth Schedules is really the preservation of the tribal people's "cultural distinctiveness" and the protection of their rights over land and all the resources in it. The idea was to safeguard them from economic exploitation by the more advanced communities. But having said that, Bah Kynsai is also right. Our District Council has not been doing its job at all. The only question is, should we blame the institution or the useless politicians running it?'

'That's the question, Bah Kynsai!' Hamkom said. 'We should think about this more carefully. Ap is absolutely right.' Then, turning to me, he asked, 'But what about Bah Joy, Ap, what do you think of him?'

Before I could reply, Bah Kynsai intervened. 'Joy is no joy, Ham, forget about him!'

'But Bah Kynsai, he was also the founder of the Church of God in Ri Khasi, no?'

'That's a different issue, na? I respect him as a religious leader, but I certainly have no use for his politics. The only politician I would like to name is Mavis Dunn Lyngdoh, who, in January 1937, became the first woman MLA in the history of Assam. She was elected from the Shillong Assembly Constituency. And three years later, na, she became the first woman in India—not only among the Khasis or in Assam, ha, but in India—to hold the post of a cabinet minister in a state government.'

'Who was she, Bah Kynsai?' Magdalene was immediately interested.

'You really should read up on Khasi history, Mag. She was the third daughter of Helibon Lyngdoh of Mawlong near Sohra, and was born in Shillong in 1906. Her father's name? I don't know. She was educated in

Shillong at the Welsh Mission Girls' School and went to Calcutta for higher studies. Later, she studied law at the University Law College, Guwahati, and became the first Khasi woman to hold a law degree. That was the kind of person she was! If you can think of that sort of politician now, na, we can talk about her or him too. But there aren't any, are there?'

Evening agreed. 'We used to have giants in the past, okay, but now we have mostly little men—'

'Little scamperists!' Raji said.

'Little scamperists, yes, little people and scammers ...'

'Old Khasis call it *ka juk shong kulai miaw* or *ka juk kiew dieng sohmynken*,' I commented.

'In English, Bah Ap?' Donald asked.

'The cat-riding age or the chilli plant–climbing age.'

'Why?' Magdalene asked, not grasping the metaphors.

'Why? Because we are so small and petty, na?' Bah Kynsai answered. 'We are so Lilliputian that we cannot ride a horse, we can only ride a cat, and we cannot climb a tree, we can only climb a chilli plant ... Beautiful, Ap, beautiful! Cat-riding or chilli plant–climbing age, wa, very apt!'

'J.N. Chowdhury had said the same thing in his *Khasi Canvas*, you know that?' Evening asked. He consulted his mobile phone, then read out: '"Khasi society has produced many people of undoubted stature who deserve to be known better, especially by a generation that needs inspiration in an age of hopelessness. This has come about because Khasi society has been exposed for a longer period to external influences than any other tribal society in the Northeast. Education, after the first nervous reactions, took hold rapidly, and for a while, this society earned recognition as the most advanced in this region in terms of literacy, including literacy in English. Why this distinction has been lost is for sociologists and educationists to study ..." Whatever you people may say, I fully agree with this,' Evening concluded.

Some of us, including Magdalene, differed quite strongly with Chowdhury's comments. She said, 'I don't agree with that at all, we have many achievers now also, I could name quite a few, but then, we have already decided not to speak about the living, no?'

Bah Kynsai said, 'Yeah, Mag is right, we do have people who have achieved quite a lot, na? Many have gone far afield in their chosen professions. At the same time, it's also true that we lag behind in literacy: we have a high drop-out rate and a huge problem with child labour. And when it comes to politicians, na, Ning and Raji are absolutely right. Most people, because of their lack of education, elect candidates who can wine and dine them, and help them with little things like blankets and cooking stoves. They don't look at the larger picture. They don't look at manifestos and what kind of policies the candidates believe in. They don't even look at qualifications, only at their money. That's why, na, we end up with politicians who give us some *naya paisa* but loot crores.'

'There's only one politician I'd like to speak about,' Evening said, and when Bah Kynsai objected, he protested loudly, saying, 'No, no, Bah Kynsai, please let me finish. I know you said no politician, but this one, to my mind, is exceptional.'

'Who's that?' many voices spoke as one.

'Martin Narayan Majaw.'

'Martin Majaw? Whatever for?' Magdalene asked.

'Three things. Of all the politicians in the state, ha, he was the only one who was really concerned with the issues that troubled the people. When he was revenue minister during the three-party coalition government in 1981—yes, the one led by the foxy B.B. Lyngdoh—he tried his level best to bring about a resolution to the vexed boundary dispute with Assam, and that too, despite the lack of support from his colleagues. Almost every week, he would go to inspect villages affected by the dispute, okay, and try to assuage the sufferings of the people there. Is there anyone like him now? None at all. Secondly, he also tried his level best, on behalf of the civilian population of Shillong, to recover prime land claimed by the armed forces. Ask Bah Kynsai, he'll tell you the same thing. I might add that he was the only minister who tried to do so. Others, then and now, simply couldn't care less. And lastly, he introduced the Land Transfer Act—'

At this, Hamkom jumped up to interrupt him. Waving a finger at Evening, he said, 'How can someone who introduced the Land Transfer Act be your hero? Don't you know that, because of this act, companies cannot set up factories in the state? That Act is the reason our state has remained so backward.'

Evening retorted just as hotly, 'Don't fool yourself into thinking that's why the state is backward, you academic fraud! Despite the Land Transfer Act, companies have been buying land or being granted land everywhere! Just two examples: all those factories in Ri Bhoi and Ri Pnar, so many of them, how are they acquiring land? The businessmen and the damn politicians are using benami transactions and loopholes in the Act, you idiot! And for what? What benefits are they giving to the state and its local population? Nothing. The factories in Ri Bhoi have even been granted tax breaks, but all they do is loot the wealth from here and take it to their own states, so don't talk nonsense, you ignoramus!'

Magdalene joined the debate then. 'Mind your bloody language, Evening! What about the genuine non-tribal citizens who have been here for many generations, huh? Because of the Act, they cannot even buy a plot of land to build their houses on. Is that fair?'

Evening said, 'Let me ask you a question. All of you have houses in Shillong city, no?'

'Count me out,' Bah Su said, 'I live outside Shillong.'

'And me,' Dale said, 'I don't own a house.'

'Okay, but the rest of you do. Now, how many of you could have bought land and houses in Shillong without Bah Martin's Land Transfer Act? I don't know how rich you all are, ha, but I, for one, could never have bought a plot of land in Shillong without it. And why? Because, without it, I would have to compete with rich non-tribal businessmen and officers. And all of them can offer double, triple the amount I can ever come up with. So who would sell me their land? Before the Act came into effect, okay, this was precisely what happened: people sold to the highest bidders! It's human nature, and Khasis, without the Act, ha, would have had to buy only in the rural areas, where the price might be cheaper, *might be*, because there's no guarantee the non-tribals will not go there.

'Even now, people are taking advantage of the loopholes I spoke of, do you know that? Look at what is happening in Upper Mawprem. Many Nepali families who own land and houses have left for Darjeeling and Siliguri and even Nepal. They cannot sell their houses to non-tribals, so what do they do? They use the Gift Deed Act to gift them to the highest bidders. And who are the highest bidders? Not their fellow Nepalis. That's why the population profile in Upper Mawprem is fast changing now. Martin Narayan Majaw, whatever you say, and whatever my non-tribal friends might say, is the only politician I look up to as a hero.'

Bah Kynsai broke into the heated argument. 'This is truly a case of being caught in the shithouse, na? What Ning said is right, but what Mag said is also the humane way to look at it. But what is to be done? If they modify the Land Transfer Act, na, to allow permanent non-tribal citizens to buy land, na, everybody will find a loophole and take advantage of it. Even now, as Ning said, there are so many loopholes. And yet, you cannot have genuine citizens feeling like strangers in the land, can you? They will leave, as they are doing now, only to be replaced by the riff-raff and the undesirables—'

'Why can't they modify it and plug all the loopholes at the same time?' Donald asked.

'How can you ever stop corruption in Meghalaya, or for that matter, in India, Don?' Bah Kynsai asked.

Nobody had an answer to that, and so, shaking our heads and clucking our tongues, we all fell into a long, brooding silence.

After a while, Bah Kynsai said, 'You people are very funny, liah! You wanted to pick out heroes, but you only talked about politicians, tdir! Anyway, it's late—'

Raji suddenly sang out, 'Corruption, corruption, everywhere, nor any drop to drink.'

'What the hell do you mean by that, you stupid sod?'

'Arre, this Bah Kynsai! It means we have nothing to drink but corruption, no?'

Disgusted, Bah Kynsai lay down on the straw. Then, turning on his side, he went to sleep.

Laughing, we all followed his example.

7

THE
FIFTH
NIGHT

ROOT STORIES II

'The frontier regions sank their roots into my
poetry and these roots have never been able to
wrench themselves out. My life is a long
pilgrimage that is always turning on itself,
always returning to the woods in the south,
to the forest lost to me.'

—Pablo Neruda

On 9 February, our sixth night in Nongshyrkon but the fifth of our fireside sessions, we returned to stories about Khasi culture. Not by design; that was just where our conversations led us.

As on the previous day, Perly woke us up in the morning. He did not want to, but since it was about 9 a.m., he thought he had better. Then, as we were washing our faces and brushing our teeth, he asked: 'What plans for today?'

'What would we plan?' Bah Kynsai replied rather roughly. He was always grumpy in the morning.

As cheerily as I could, I said, 'What would we plan, Bah Perly? We'll go to the lake as usual ... We don't have to hurry back today, do we?'

'We are planning to go hill-mouse hunting after lunch; we need all the meat we can get. We'll wait for you if you want to go.'

'Hill-mouse hunting! Nai lum?' Raji asked eagerly. 'That sounds very exciting, leh ... Hey, guys, I think we should all go, ya. This is a new thing for us!'

Bah Kynsai was not very enthusiastic, though. 'We don't want to come rushing back, na, it's too tiring in the heat, man.'

'You don't have to come rushing, Babu,' Perly said. 'See, if you leave for the lake at 10 a.m., have your bath and lunch, you could easily be back by 2 p.m. without rushing.'

Bah Kynsai agreed, though still unenthusiastic about the whole thing.

Before he went, Perly said, 'I'm organising the packed lunch right now. It's quite different today. Chirag bought some oil from Maweit yesterday; we are frying beef jerky and vegetables for you. Should be a nice treat.'

We thanked him profusely and went to have our customary breakfast of red tea and boiled rice. As we were eating, Perly came in with our lunch in leaf packets—no bamboo tubes, since there was no broth or soup. As usual, we went tramping to the lake, had a bath, washed our clothes and ate lunch. The lake was the coolest spot in hot Lyngngam during the day, and we didn't feel like leaving. Even Raji was not so keen, now that he was lying prone on the grass after a heavy lunch. All of us had overeaten, for we had not had fried stuff for some time. However, we had promised Perly, and so, we dragged ourselves up and made the trek back.

Perly and Chirag turned up as we were drying our clothes.

Chirag greeted us: 'Khublei, Babu, are you ready?'

'As ready as we can ever be,' Raji said. 'Shall we go?'

'Where's Halolihim?' Hamkom asked of no one in particular. 'I haven't seen him today.'

We all shrugged, but Perly said, 'I saw him sitting with a girl near the community hall.'

'Sitting with a girl! Maybe he's trying to convert her to his church or what?' Hamkom mused.

Nobody responded. Chirag and Perly called out to the other Lyngngam men and led us north, in the direction of the lake, but after a while, the path turned west towards a large bamboo grove.

Chirag said, 'Nai lum mostly live in bamboo groves, Babu, and that's why, in summer, you find lots of snakes in such places. Like us, they are hunting for mice.'

'Snakes also hunt each other,' Perly said.

Dale found that surprising. 'What? What do you mean?'

'Just like fishes, no, Bahbah, big snakes eat little snakes,' Perly explained.

'Is that true or what? I have never heard of such a thing.'

'Yes, yes, very true. Cobras, especially, eat nothing else but snakes.'

At the mention of cobras, Magdalene yelped, 'Cobras! Do you mean you have cobras here? I'm not going, Bah Kynsai, I'm not going.'

'Me too, me too, I'm not going!' Dale cried.

'Relax, Kong, Bahbah,' Perly calmed them. 'In winter, you won't find any snakes even if you look for them, not here anyway. They all hibernate in winter. It's too cold for them, Kong.'

'But it's hot for us.'

'That's because you are coming from a cold place, Kong,' Chirag explained. 'If you live here for a year, ha, even you will feel cold in winter. Haven't you noticed? Most people wear warm clothes in the evening. The snakes are the same, they feel cold, so they hibernate.'

'Okay then, if you say so,' Magdalene said, still a little suspicious.

'Don't worry, Kong, no snakes in winter,' Perly reassured her.

After walking for about four kilometres, we finally reached the place. It was a massive jungle of bamboo, hundreds of acres. Nothing grew in it but bamboo. Before entering the grove, Chirag divided the men into three groups. Each group was supposed to hunt in a separate area.

Bah Kynsai, who was still panting up the wooded slope, said, 'Count me out. I'll sit here among the trees. I'm too tired after walking so much. From the hut to the lake, from the lake to the hut, from the hut to this place … How many kilometres have we come?'

'About four, Babu,' Chirag said.

'Only? It feels like more, liah,' Bah Kynsai swore. 'It must be more, ten at least.'

'That's because you are tired,' I told him.

Chirag explained to the group what he had in mind. Pointing to a warren of holes in the ground, he said, 'You see these holes? There's a colony of mice living here—'

'Do they live in colonies?' Dale asked.

'Actually, we don't know how they live, Bahbah, but when we start the hunting, you will see quite a few of them emerging from these holes. The holes are all around this particular clump of bamboo, ha, so, this is what we will do, okay, some of us will go inside the grove and burn dry leaves and twigs in front of the holes on that side so the smoke goes in. We will also make a lot of noise, beating the ground and all that. The mice will have no option but to come running towards this clearing, and as they come out, ha, you beat them with these bamboo rackets, specially made for the purpose. Babu, take this one, Babu Kynsai, you can also come if you want, nothing much to do, only beating them on the head.'

Bah Kynsai simply raised a hand in refusal.

Three men readied the fires, while five others, including Victor, the Nongtrai elder, and I, waited near the holes facing the clearing. Soon we could hear the men in the grove blowing smoke into the labyrinth of tunnels, and after ten minutes or so, a small creature with a pointed face and short yellowish-brown hair came running out of a hole that I was guarding. I looked at the little fellow fleeing in terror from the toxic smoke and the deafening noise. He ran towards my feet, probably mistaking my legs for tree trunks. I heard someone shouting, 'There, there, Babu, he's coming towards you, hit him, hit him!' But how could I hit that little thing already half-dead with fright? Hunting is a bloody cruel sport …

Suddenly, I was quite disgusted with the whole thing. I threw away the racket and went to sit with Bah Kynsai, watching the men running up and down, howling like bloodthirsty animals. Bah Kynsai smiled at me and asked, 'Why?'

'I just couldn't do it.'

'You might as well be a vegetarian.'

'I tried many times. But living here, it's difficult, don't you think? We prepare vegetables mostly as supplements to meat. Communities in mainland India, as you know, are experts at preparing nice vegetable curries and chutneys, and when I travel outside, I don't eat meat at all. But here, if you go to a Khasi shop and ask for rice and vegetables, they will stare at you as if you are an oddball. At most, they will give you fried potatoes. How can you enjoy eating only rice and fried potatoes? Sometimes they even bring me raw herbs. Imagine that, Bah Kynsai, rice and raw herbs? Anyway, I'm not really against the humane slaughter of domestic animals. I know that the whole world cannot survive on grains and vegetables alone. And, in many places, people have to eat meat to live. But this,' I pointed to the men beating the poor mice to death, 'what the hell is this about? Why are we raiding their den and exterminating them? What kind of pleasure is that?'

Victor did not seem to enjoy the sport either, and soon came to sit with us. I began a long conversation with him, learning all I could about the Lyngngams and Nongtrais. He told me about his people's culture, especially their funeral practices and the fascinating tale of Sangkhni, which reminded me very much of the Thlen story.

It was growing dark when I heard Chirag say, 'Let's go, let's go, there are no more in here, come, we'll go home and roast them for dinner.'

They came to where we were sitting and rested for a while. Chirag, Perly and some others were carrying the mice tied together in bunches. There must have been hundreds of them.

Our group came too, and flopped down on the ground near us, laughing and panting from the exercise. They were all flushed and excited, apparently enjoying themselves immensely. Hamkom said, 'You should have come, Bah Kynsai, you missed the fun.'

'How many did you kill?' Bah Kynsai asked.

'Quite a few, I think.'

'I didn't kill anything,' Bah Su said, 'but I did take part in flushing them out; I really regret it now.'

'I tried whacking them, you know,' Magdalene said, 'but I just couldn't hit them, they were pretty fast. And just as well, I don't think I would have enjoyed killing them.'

Looking at the bound mice, Bah Kynsai said, 'I'm not eating that.'

'Nor I,' I said.

'Nor I,' Bah Su added.

Donald said he'd try a little bit and see how it tasted. Magdalene was about to say something when Chirag called out to everybody and started to lead us back to the village.

When we were gathered around our hut's little fire after dinner, my friends talked about the hunt and how tasty the meat was.

Raji was especially excited. 'That was wonderful stuff, ha, Ning, I saw you stuffing yourself like—'

'Don't say it, Raji,' Evening said, laughing.

'Okay, okay, but you did enjoy it, no? I rubbed salt on it, anointed it with lemon juice, ate it with onions and chillies, and washed it down with the sweet Lyngngam stuff. Perfect! Better than chicken any day! How about you, Ap? I didn't see you eating?'

'I didn't.'

'Well, if you didn't, you shouldn't have participated in the hunt—'

'He didn't,' Bah Kynsai said.

'He didn't?' Raji asked in surprise. 'Well, I enjoyed it. I recorded it also, some of it anyway.'

Donald was also surprised. 'Oh, I didn't know that, and why not, Bah Ap?'

'As flies to wanton boys are we to th' gods,/They kill us for their sport,' I said.

'Aw, come on!' Raji and Hamkom reacted together, but Donald suddenly became quiet, perhaps thinking about that quotation from *King Lear*.

From food, the conversation suddenly turned to the problem of crapping when Magdalene said, 'Hey, you guys, how are you doing it when you go to the jungle in the morning, ya?'

'What kind of question is that, Mag?' Bah Kynsai laughed. 'How would we do it, there's only one way to do it, na?'

'No, no, what I mean is, it's so difficult for me, you know, and I'm so scared of insects and all, tell me no, what to do?'

Before Bah Kynsai could make another unhelpful wisecrack, I said, 'When we were in Sohra, we used to have the same problem, especially in summer. It was not only insects but leeches—'

'Why? Didn't you have toilets in Sohra?' Hamkom asked in surprise.

'When you were using those service latrines in Shillong—'

'Ah, the service latrines!' Bah Kit interrupted me, remembering those days when the septic tank had not even been heard of in Shillong. 'What a horrible time we used to have, no, Bah Kynsai? The whole compound used to stink, ha, all the time stinking because of the overflowing tins in the latrines. You remember how the Kharmetors used to come in the middle of the night to remove them, Bah Kynsai? In those days, the Kharmetors were kings. You couldn't do anything to upset them; if you did, they would simply stop coming.'

Kharmetors, as I must have told you before, are non-tribal sanitation workers.

'As it is, they were never very regular, na?' Bah Kynsai responded.

'Yeah, yeah,' Bah Kit agreed, 'and worse still, if you displeased them in any way, ha, instead of taking the contents to a truck waiting by the road, ha, they would dump it right there in the compound drain. When that happened, no, Mag, it was simply impossible to step outside the house. We used to plug every hole we could find with rags to stop the stench. Fortunately, my father knew the head scavenger. He used to go to him with a bit of tea money and things got cleaned up pretty fast. But those days were terrible. They can never be the good old days for me! As far as that is concerned, I mean. And yet, when the government wanted to introduce septic tanks and sanitary toilets, do you remember what happened? Everybody in Shillong opposed the move, can you believe it? Many were afraid they might not have enough water, and raised lots of other excuses as well to put off the scheme. People are really funny, no?'

'Change, na, even a good one, is always feared initially,' Bah Kynsai said philosophically.

'Hey, hey, you guys, you are forgetting about my problem, man!' Magdalene reminded us. 'What were you saying about Sohra, Ap?' she asked.

'I said, when they were using their service latrines in Shillong, in Sohra, we were doing it in the sacred groves—'

'Sacred groves! Can you do that sort of thing in the sacred groves?' she asked.

'Well, not exactly sacred groves, but I'll explain that later if you want me to. Right now, let me show you a way out of your predicament. Like you, when we were kids, we used to have problems with insects and leeches in the woods. But not only that … when a large number of people go every morning into the same woods, you'll encounter another problem, Mag: the problem of clean space. To avoid that, most of us kids would go to forests farther away from the suburbs. But there were times when the matter was too pressing, and we had to go to whatever woods we could reach within a few minutes. At such times, to avoid the problem of leeches and clean space, we simply climbed up a tree and did it from the branches. You could do the same thing, Mag.'

'How can I climb up a tree, man?'

'Choose a tree with low branches,' I suggested, 'plenty of trees like that here.'

Magdalene was about to react to that, when Raji demanded, 'Are you saying there are no leeches on trees?'

'In Sohra, there are no leeches on trees, but in the ravines of Ri War, they have a type of big leech that lives on certain species of trees. When you pass beneath those trees, you have to run. The first one to walk past normally escapes them, but the ones that follow, because of the man-smell drifting up to them, could get a sudden shower of leeches. They simply drop from the trees on your head, like raindrops. But the War people know these trees, and when they have to get past them, they run and hold something above their heads as a precaution.'

'But when you did it from the branches, did you ever have any problem?' Magdalene asked me again. 'I want to be sure, ya.'

'Not from insects and leeches. But sometimes, we experienced other kinds of problems. You see, those trees were huge and shaggy, and you couldn't always see what was beneath them. Hence, sometimes, when we dropped our payload, it would fall very near someone sitting in the undergrowth, a few feet from the trunk, and we'd get reactions like, 'Hey, *khun ka tdir*, son of a clitoris! Wait till I get up there!' When that happened, it was a matter of who could get his pants on faster. It was always we boys, of course, since we didn't care much about how we put our pants on. And once we had them on, there was no catching us.'

'Sounds like Ap has some stories for us,' Bah Kynsai remarked.

I grinned at him. 'In those days, we used discarded paper for after-action cleaning. But sometimes, we would forget to bring some along and had to improvise in all sorts of ways. One day, a friend forgot his paper. Before anybody could advise him, he went among the tall grasses and slid his exposed bottom through them. Unfortunately, a sharp stick lying unseen got him in the hole, and he was hospitalised for weeks.

'Another one picked up a large leaf. As a strategy, it should have been fine, but for the fact that instead of picking the leaf from a tree, he took it from the ground. It was a dead leaf, and as he was in the act of cleaning, it crumbled to pieces. One of his fingers was smudged, and in his haste to get rid of the offensive content, he shook it up and down vigorously. Unluckily, the finger hit a stone. He cried out in pain, and without thinking, put the finger in his mouth. From that day, he was nicknamed "Bameit", "crap-eater".

'Ugh, ugh!' Magdalene exclaimed.

But Raji said, 'More, more.'

'Shall I, Mag?'

'If you must,' she replied, in a resigned tone.

I told them the story of why Sohra is so famous for its pork. One day, Everending and I took a friend of ours from Ri Bhoi to have lunch in a well-known jadoh stall in Sohra—

'Everending?' Magdalene asked, amused.

'Don't start, Mag, he's a close friend of mine,' I said.

So, as I said, Kamai Lang, our Ri Bhoi friend (his name means 'earned together', for obviously, it took two to make him), had heard of the famous Sohra pork curry and wanted a taste of it. I asked Everending, who was also from Sohra but lived in Shillong, to contact the owner of the jadoh stall and place an order for two traditional pork curries for three people. Everending asked them to prepare one *syrwa* and one *kylla dish*. A syrwa is a broth-like preparation. In Sohra, it is made in two ways. One way is to boil the pork with potatoes and onions; the other is to simply boil it in hot water without any other ingredients, not even salt. This is generally cooked during feasts and funerals and is called *doh jynlat*.

'Why would they do a thing like that?' Magdalene asked.

'It's delicious, Mag,' Bah Su answered for me. 'You must taste it one day.'

I told Magdalene that that kind of cooking had a long tradition. Before a Khasi wedding could begin, food—usually a large pot of rice and a large pot of meat, customarily pork—had to be sent to the house of the groom. If the groom lived in a distant village, the food would have to be sent a day or two earlier, in which case, the meat was cooked only with water, so as to preserve it. But only hot water could be used; cold water would make it too greasy. Whenever I go to Sohra, I request my relatives to prepare this dish for me.

'Why did it take them so long to reach, Bah? Did they walk all the way?' Dale asked.

In the past, walking was the only means of getting from one place to another, I explained. Then moving on to how the kylla dish is prepared, I said, unlike the broth-like syrwa, kylla is a kind of curry cooked with spices. First, pepper, onions and a little garlic are ground together and fried with turmeric and bay leaves in a little oil. Then pork and potatoes are added, and enough water for the meat to cook. Last of all, sesame seeds are ground into a paste and added to the curry when the meat is almost ready.

These two dishes had been prepared for us when we took Kamai out for lunch. He loved the food, of course, and ate, in his own words, till he was 'stretched tight'. After the meal, as we were relaxing and eating betel nuts, Kamai wanted to know why Sohra pork was so tasty.

Everending explained that it was partly because of the way the pork was cleaned. 'Nobody cleans a pig the way the butchers of Sohra do,' he said proudly. 'First, they pour boiling hot water on the hair and scrape it off with a machete-like knife. After that, they hang the pig on a horizontal bar, burn the entire skin with fire and then scrape it until not even a strand of hair remains. That makes the pork not only very clean but also gives it a nice roasted smell. They don't do that kind of cleaning anywhere else: that's why the Sohra pork is the best.'

'That's true, Kamai,' I said. 'But the main reason is that most of the pigs here are brought from the ravine hamlets of Ri War.'

'Why? What has that got to do with anything?' Kamai asked.

'Not anything—everything, everything to do with it. Firstly, the Ri War pigs have very firm flesh and much less fat than pigs from elsewhere, and that makes their meat much tastier—'

'But why is the flesh firmer, the fat thinner?'

'Because, unlike pigs elsewhere, they are not penned inside a small sty. They are allowed to roam freely throughout the village. Pigs are the natural scavengers of Ri War villages. All edible waste from the houses is thrown to them. That way, the village is kept clean and the pigs are well fed.'

Kamai is very sharp. He asked, 'How can the village be clean if pigs are allowed to roam freely, what about their dung?'

'Good point,' I agreed. 'The dung is collected by the villagers for use in their well-fortified vegetable gardens. But to come back to the point, it's not because they eat edible waste that the Ri War pigs are so tasty.'

'Then?'

'You see, many Ri War villages are built inside the jungle, as an extension of it. In many of these villages, the houses are raised on bamboo or wooden stilts, six, seven feet above the ground. And all these houses have a kind of platform that extends from the back of the house. A part of this platform is screened off by a bamboo partition. And the Wars drop their payloads from behind these partitions, to be gobbled up by the pigs on the ground.'

'But why would they do that? This Ap is pulling my leg, leh. You must think we Bhois are stupid or what?'

I asked him to check with Everending. When he too confirmed my story, I said, 'I think the reason is still very much the same. They don't have toilets and they want to keep their villages clean. The best way, therefore, is to turn pigs into their crap collectors. Symbiotic, you might say. And that, Kamai, is the real reason why the Ri War pork, which is sold in Sohra, is so tasty. Nothing but that.'

When I finished speaking, a customer there suddenly left his food and ran to the back of the eatery to puke. The owner, a woman who knew us well, laughed and said, 'Look at what you jokers have done to my customer! Now he'll never eat our pork again!'

Kamai responded by saying, 'Well, Kong, he shouldn't have listened to other people's conversations. But look at us. We have just had the curry too, but we don't feel anything! Whatever the pigs eat, no, Kong, becomes either energy or dung. It doesn't affect the meat at all.'

'But there might be another reason why people in some Ri War villages do it from platforms like that,' I told Kamai. 'One day, some of us went to a Ri War village for some business and had to stay there for two nights. We were told by the house owner what to do in the morning when we got the warrant. We listened very carefully and nodded. But when morning came, a friend of ours, whom we called Pulit, because he looked like a non-tribal policeman, simply could not do it from the platform. He kept hearing the people inside and felt as if somebody would peep in at any moment. So, against the advice of the house owner, he decided to go to the forest floor. After all, who would see him among the trees and the brush if he did it there?

'But the moment he squatted behind a bush to begin the job, a horde of oinking, squealing animals came rushing from nowhere and pounced upon his deposit. He was scared out of his wits, but since he was in the middle of the act, there was no way he could leave the stage. Some of the squealers were so impatient, they could not even wait for the consignment to drop to the ground. As it dangled like a sausage, they pulled at it and began chomping noisily, the way pigs always do. In the pushing and shoving, one of them mistook Pulit's dangling scrotum for its food and seized it in its teeth. Pulit jumped and cried out in sheer agony. Pulling his pants up in a hurry, he ran away from there as fast as he could, followed by the oinking, squealing horde. All of us rushed out in great alarm, and when we saw what was happening, we chased the pigs away. After patching him up as best we could, we took him to a public health centre in a nearby village. The doctor who treated him said, "He's very lucky, they missed his balls." We all breathed a sigh of relief: the blood, after all, was only from a flesh wound.

'And that, Kamai, may be the real reason why they have been doing it from their platforms,' I concluded.

When I stopped, there was a moment's silence, then Bah Kynsai bawled at me: 'Tet leh, this Ap is making up the damn story or what?'

'Who could make up a thing like that, Bah Kynsai?' I asked innocently.

'Do these things still happen, Ap?' Magdalene asked.

'That was many years ago. Most villages, except for the more remote ones, have toilets now. The pigs in some villages still roam freely and do their cleaning job, but not like before.'

'And is it true that Sohra gets all its pigs from Ri War?'

'Not all the time, no. I was exaggerating a little. Ri War pigs are available only on market days. People keep a lot of pigs in areas around Sohra too … In pigsties, yes.'

Hamkom expressed the fear that many of us felt. 'What about the pigs here in Shyrkon?' he asked. 'I saw some roaming around, are they also feeding on …?'

'Oh shit, oh shit,' Magdalene exclaimed, distraught. 'And we have been eating nothing but pork since we came here!'

'Relax,' I said. 'Many families here have toilets. They dig deep pits in the ground, enclose them with bamboo walls, and do their job there.'

'You mean those roofless enclosures are actually toilets?'

'Yeah, the ones whose openings are covered with sacks. Only some families don't have them. They go to the jungle far from the village, as we have been doing. And there are no pigs there: they only roam around here.'

Magdalene breathed a sigh of relief.

What I did not tell them was that the kids in the village quite likely did it in the open, near the houses, in gardens and so on. They could not be expected to use the pits, or go to the jungle, and well, who was doing the cleaning?

Donald wanted to know more about the sacred forests. 'I never knew talking about crap could be so amusing, but tell me, Bah Ap, you spoke about sacred groves … I don't know much about them. The only sacred grove I know of is the one at Mawphlang. How did they come to be sacred?'

Many villages in Ri Khasi—I said 'Khasi Hills', but Raji insisted I use either Ri Hynñiew Trep or Ri Khasi, which would cover all the districts of East and West Khasi Hills, Ri Bhoi and Jaiñtia Hills—are bordered by what is commonly known here as a sacred grove. In many cases, this is a misnomer, since they are actually enormous forests. Such forests, however, did not become sacred on their own or because of some supernatural visitation. They were sanctified by men through religious rites and solemn prayers, and much pleading with God, U Blei, asking him to bless and consecrate them and charge the guardian spirit of villages and the wilderness, U Ryngkew U Basa, with the task of protecting and preserving them. There might have been a thousand and one reasons why such deliberate sanctification of woodlands was carried out, but I will enumerate only some of the most obvious of these.

At the root of it all is the Khasi pantheistic philosophy and their belief that God exists in all things, animals and people within the universe. In short, to Khasis, God is the universe and manifests most closely through nature. Therefore, to disregard nature is to disregard God, and to deprive forests of trees is to deny God his favourite haunt on earth. Because of this, the old Khasis never indulged in wanton destruction. When they went to the forest to cut wood, for instance, realising that everything must carry God's sanction according to Ka Hukum Blei, the Divine Law, they would do the job only after paying obeisance to God through the ceremony of *Ka Nguh ka Dem*, the bow the homage. As part of the ceremony, the woodcutter would have to intone words of supplication before he could even touch a tree:

> Look here, that I have come to cut you down is not because I detest you or want to destroy you without cause. I have a great need for you. Through Ka Hukum, the Divine Law, God himself has given me his consent that I may cause your fall, so you too may have a role in all my undertakings, so you may live again by becoming a part of my home, a part of my fields and gardens. Therefore, allow me, obey me, bend to my will, so I may fell you with a machete or an axe, for even though you may fall now, yet your fame shall rise and grow before God. Before the spirits, it shall rise, before kings and nobles, before priests and elders, before all the people from generation to generation. So that your seeds, your branches, your trunk may proliferate, may spread, may rise, may grow, hey ho, I have given you my blessing, hey ho, God will give you his blessing, and you too, forgive me. I have spoken.

'Wow, that's sheer poetry, man!' Hamkom exclaimed. 'But did they really do that? Did they really speak to trees like that?'

Bah Su answered for me. 'They used to do that, yes. Even now, in some places, ha, when they have to fetch trees from prohibited forests, they do it.'

It is owing to this unique green consciousness, I continued, that the old Khasis used to maintain forests where the felling of trees was either prohibited or regulated. Foremost among them were the law kyntang, the sacred groves and sacred forests. In this type of woodland, not only is the cutting of trees forbidden, but also, nothing can be taken out of it: not a fruit, not a flower, not even a single leaf. Certainly, crapping in them is strictly forbidden.

'But, Ap, if crapping is strictly forbidden, then what about your story?' Magdalene said. 'I'm a bit confused, man!'

'I'll explain later, Mag, don't worry.'

The most famous law kyntang in Ri Khasi is the Law Lyngdoh sacred grove at Mawphlang, about twenty-four kilometres south-west of Shillong. The grove is so named because it belongs to the Lyngdoh Mawphlang clan (the priestly as well as the ruling clan of the traditional state of Mawphlang), which had sanctified and dedicated it to God and the guardian spirit, U Ryngkew U Basa.

According to legend, the sacred grove had been founded by an enterprising woman by the name of Khmah Nongsai. The legend goes back to the very beginning of Mawphlang's history, to how elders of the Ïangblah clan were one day compelled to perform obsecration ceremonies appealing to God for a sign as to who should be their future ruler.

'Compelled? By whom?' Hamkom asked.

'You see, the clan had originally migrated from Ri Pnar and was in control of the state, but for some unknown reasons, there seemed to be widespread discontent with it at the time—'

'Do you hear that, Hamkom?' Evening cried triumphantly. 'Even the Ïangblah clan, the Blahs who founded Hima Mawphlang, migrated from Ri Pnar! Don't ever say Khasis and Jaiñtias again, you understand!'

'Shut up, Ning!' Bah Kynsai quickly intervened. 'Go on, Ap.'

I told them that the augurs and diviners who conducted the egg-breaking rituals and extispicy, which is the use of animal entrails for divination, declared that a woman named Khmah Nongsai had been revealed to them as the most fitting person to be the ruler of Mawphlang. Nobody knew who she was. Even the diviners had only learnt that she lived in a place called Laitsohma, in the state of Sohra, with her husband, Lyhir Sohtun.

Ka Khmah Nongsai and her two uncles, in fact, had been wandering from place to place for reasons not very clear. One story says she was orphaned after an outbreak of cholera and had to leave home with her uncles to search for new places to farm. Another says she and her uncles had to run away because of a conspiracy to wipe out her family since they were considered a threat to the state's ruling clan. Whatever the reason, Khmah first went towards Ri Bhoi in north Ri Khasi and settled down in a place called Patharkhmah. Later, she left for a village called Nongsai, and that may be why she was known as Ka Khmah Nongsai, after Patharkhmah and Nongsai. Next, Khmah shifted to the village of Mawlieh in contemporary East Khasi Hills, where she met her husband, who took her to Mylliem in the state of Shyllong. However, owing to differences with a powerful clan, they moved away to settle in Laitsohma.

It was to this place that the Ïangblah elders went to meet Khmah Nongsai and offer her the state of Mawphlang. But she did not appear to be interested. She said she would seek divine guidance by planting *diengsohma* (a kind of rhus tree) and *diengsning* (a species of chestnut) saplings, one of each, in Laitsohma and Phiphandi in Mawphlang. She promised the Ïangblah elders that she would settle in the place where both the saplings grew well. When the saplings were inspected a year later, only one was growing in Laitsohma, whereas both were alive and well in Phiphandi. This prompted her to go to Mawphlang to become the first ancestress of Lyngdoh Mawphlang, the priestly ruling clan. Khmah Nongsai also had Phiphandi consecrated as a special place of worship, where the religious ceremonies of the clan could be conducted. As part of the ceremonies, more and more trees were added until the entire area grew to become a large grove that has remained sacred to this day.

This centuries-old woodland is a temperate rainforest with evergreen broadleaved trees. It can be described as a biodiversity wonderland, not only because of the variety of trees in it but also because of the diverse plants, flowers, insects and birds. Enter the grove, and it is like walking into a vast, dimly lit dome with sunlight barely filtering through the canopy of incredibly old trees, many with a thick covering of green moss and lichen, and others with a decoration of wildflowers and orchids of various species. The floor is covered with a carpet of rotting, rufescent leaves, several inches thick, judging from the way one's feet sink into them. The atmosphere is as peaceful and solemn as a house of worship. One can hear only the calming sounds of the forest. The water from its many springs is heavenly.

L.H. Pde, a Khasi writer who has done some research on the sacred grove, tells many stories of how it is protected by the guardian spirit, Basa. He says, for instance:

> Ever since I was a small boy, I have heard tales of the Basa. It comes, they say,
> in two forms, snake and tiger. If a person goes into the grove to do anything
> destructive, such as cutting grass for his pigs, the Basa will appear as a snake
> and position himself in the sty, so that the pig will not dare to venture inside.

When people see such strange happenings, they begin to enquire where the grass came from. Then they say to the snake, 'Go, please. They have done wrong and abuse the grove.' Then, as the people throw the grass back where it was taken from, the snake will disappear.

Elsewhere in the same article, he says:

The locals also consider the Basa, in the form of a tiger, to be a guardian of innocent people. When suddenly, for some reason, people near the grove find themselves overcome with fear, they may cry out, 'O Ñi, O Kong, O Ryngkew, O Basa, please protect us from danger.' Immediately, it is said, the characteristically guttural sounds of the tiger, 'khor, khor, khor', will be heard at their backs and the tiger's spirit felt on all sides. And when they consider that they are out of danger, they send the Basa away.

The kind of total prohibition on the exploitation of forest resources that Pde speaks of is more or less true of all the sacred forests in Ri Khasi, sometimes also known as ki law lyngdoh, where the ruling clans of a state perform their religious rites. There are some, however, like those in the Sohra areas, where the felling of trees for very specific purposes are allowed after the mandatory ritualistic pleading with God. Now, unfortunately, the rituals are not observed except in some places.

'Do you mean to say that the Khasis had entire woodlands consecrated for the love of God?' Evening asked sarcastically.

I answered in the negative. To imagine that, I told him, would be to idealise the community beyond belief. Of course, given their natural respect for trees and forests, the Khasis must have found conservation as a policy easier to implement. But definite and pressing needs for such conservation must also have been felt. That is why, apart from the sacred groves and sacred forests, there are also other types of protected woodlands. Among them are ki law adong (prohibited forests) or law shnong (village forests), controlled by village authorities; ki law raij (community forests), controlled by the state; and ki law kur (clan forests), controlled by elders of the clan. These forests are not subject to total prohibition, although their use is carefully regulated by the authorities concerned.

For instance, when a village allows trees to be cut for firewood from a prohibited forest, only a portion of it is declared open for use. If the east wing is opened, the inhabitants are assigned their shares only in that wing after they have paid the fees to the village council. Other parts of the forests are strictly prohibited. Also protected are saplings and young trees that have not reached a certain prescribed girth. This is how other types of forests are regulated too. Even in the so-called *law pyllait* (unprohibited forests, found mostly around Sohra), which can be freely exploited by citizens for domestic purposes, wanton acts of destruction are not permitted.

There are many complex reasons for the Khasis' veneration of forests. For one, the hills were given to fits of furious rain and wind, which often put houses and the lives of men and domestic animals at risk. The forest surrounding a village formed a natural wind-break that considerably lessened the threat of decimation at the hands of these primal forces.

To the old Khasis, the forest was a temple where priests performed their many elaborate ceremonies connected with faith and culture. It was also an enormous storehouse of everything they needed: water sources, firewood, building materials, fruits, wild vegetables, herbs, medicinal plants, wild honey, flowers and marketable orchids, animals and birds. And all of these form part of the incredible biodiversity of our forests. As an illustration of how rich and diverse our sacred forests are, take the one at Narpuh in Ri Pnar. According to a study by an environmentalist, quoted by H.H. Mohrmen, a local writer, 'More than 400 species of birds, at least 120 species of mammals, which include 37 species of bats, 30 species of carnivores, 7 species of ungulates and 30 species of rodents are endemic to this forest. It is also the source of the three major rivers of Jaiñtia Hills: Ka Kupli, Ka Apha and Ka Lukha.' And this is more or less true of all the sacred and prohibited forests found in Ri Khasi today.

However, the mode of cultivation in those days (unfortunately, still true today) was not very conducive to the conservation of the forest cover. The slash-and-burn method of shifting cultivation, with its large-scale clearing of jungles, had caused the depletion of these sheltering woodlands at a frightening pace. In many places, this had been exacerbated by the production of lime and the manufacture of iron, which necessitated the use of wood in furnaces. One dreads to think what havoc their complete disappearance would have wrought in these hills. Everywhere, dwellings would have been exposed to the ravages of fierce thunderstorms. Erosion on a massive scale would have taken place, and all the covering soil would have been washed away to the plains of East Bengal or Assam. Even more calamitously, springs, creeks and rivers, most of them originating from deep inside the forests, would have dried up within no time, and there would not have been enough water to drink in the dry, windy months between winter and spring. Moreover, no trees would have meant no firewood, and the poor would have been left without a free supply of timber to build their homes and burn their dead. No trees would have meant no birds or animals, no life of any sort—complete desertification.

These must have been some of the most powerful reasons that prompted the ancient Khasis to conserve at least those woods that lay near their villages. And it certainly speaks volumes of their civic wisdom. But perhaps the most unusual motive for conservation is also the least talked about: the call of nature. For, above all else, the forest, to a Khasi, also meant, and still means, in many places, one gigantic loo.

'But not sacred forests, you said, no?' Magdalene interrupted.

'No, Mag, not sacred forests. When we were kids, we used to do it in the prohibited forests. But many people mistakenly refer to them as sacred groves or sacred forests.'

'How come?'

'You see, Mag, having determined the necessity for conservation as a policy, the ancient Khasis sought effective ways to implement it. They settled on sanctification, called on God and his serving spirit, U Ryngkew U Basa, performed rites and pronounced injunctions to prevent anyone from defiling a forest so sanctified. Any surreptitious felling of trees, for instance, would invite upon them not only the wrath of man but also that of God and the preserving spirit. That done, these wise men of the past sat back and dared all possible offenders to call their bluff. But such sanctification, Mag, was done not only in the case of sacred forests, the Khasi temples, where any act of desecration is strictly forbidden, but also in all categories of prohibited forests. Hence, the confusion.

'And if you question the wisdom or effectiveness of sanctification as a strategy, this is what I would ask: is the manner of conservation today more competent? The forest department spends crores every year on the salaries of forest guards alone. Sanctification does not require any guards to protect its trees.

'I strongly feel there's an urgent need to revive the tradition of sanctifying forests to meet the challenges of climate change and global warming, and as a countermeasure to the large-scale commercial logging and charcoal burning in our state, which continue unchecked despite the Supreme Court ban. New forests should be created out of barren hills and unused land. The village forests, controlled by the village authorities, and the community forests, controlled by the traditional state authorities, should all be converted into sacred forests to render them more secure. At the same time, alternative means of livelihood and new modes of cooking and heating homes should be made available.'

'But the question is, will all that ever happen?' Raji asked.

Raji had hit the nerve centre of the problem. Khasis today have lost the green consciousness and preserving instinct of old. What Bhuyan said of the Khasis in 1956 is just as true today: we have no love for the past. The charms of other cultures have enticed us; we never perceive any good in what is our own. We have not built enough on the past; we have not even attempted to link it with the present. 'Instances of modification and readjustment' are rare in our cultural practices—'annihilation or supplantation is the order of the day'.

All of this is borne out by what is happening to the prohibited forests around Ri Khasi. Because of a system corrupted by ignorance and the short-sightedness of village and traditional state functionaries, even prohibited forests like law adong and law raij are being decimated at an alarming rate.

Look at what happened to a sacred forest in the traditional state of Sohra. Permission was given to a local organisation to clear acres of woodland so that a ground for traditional dance festivals could be built there. Then, the ruling council of one of the villages ordered the clearance of acres of the same sacred forest for conversion into a massive garbage dumping ground. These were stupid moves, myopic and heartless beyond belief. There are free spaces everywhere for as many dancing grounds or dumping grounds as we would like to build, because a barren wilderness surrounds the town. What is the need then to destroy forests that have been preserved for many centuries as our proud heritage, forests that are a testimony to the wisdom, the high principles and self-sacrificing patriotism of our ancestors? Their destruction is evidence of what a small-minded, spiteful, ignorant and petty lot we have become.

'That's very sad, man!' Magdalene moaned. 'Why the hell would they do that? If, as you said, the place is full of barren land, they could have constructed a dancing ground or dumping ground anywhere at all, no? Crazy, that's what it is, plain craziness!'

'But this kind of destruction,' I said, 'is everywhere. We really don't build on the past. We destroy our legacy and leave nothing for the generations to come. Look at what's happening to the forests of Lyngngam, West Khasi Hills and Ri Pnar—we are only interested in becoming short-term, single-generation capitalists.'

'During the wars of freedom led by Tirot Sing and Kiang Nangbah, na,' Bah Kynsai chimed in, 'the dense forests of West Khasi and Ri Pnar were a great blessing for the Khasi fighters. For instance, when the British Army took too long to defeat Kiang Nangbah, okay, General Showers was asked by the government why he had not been able to defeat the enemies in all these months. You know what he said? "How can we defeat enemies that we cannot even see?" The forests in those days, na, were not only a means of livelihood but also of defence. But where are those forests now, huh? In our hurry to amass wealth and property, we destroy everything at random, and those in power, na, liah, encourage the destruction as long as it means profit for them too.'

'But, Bah Ap, this sacred grove thing is quite unique, no?' Donald said, wanting to take the conversation back to the sacred forests. 'I don't think there's anything like it in the whole world, ya. I mean, there are sacred forests elsewhere too, but deliberately sanctifying woodlands to preserve them, that has to be a Khasi thing, no? It's a truly wonderful idea. But who was responsible for it in the first place, Bah Ap? The kings?'

'No, Don,' Bah Su answered. 'When we migrated into these hills thousands of years ago, ha, there were no syiems, no kings. We were led by a legendary leader known as Syiem Lakriah, who also featured in our creation myth. He was called a syiem because he was the leader. It was a title of respect, not to be understood in the sense that we understand a syiem now.'

'What do you mean? How do we understand a syiem now? What's the difference?'

'Yeah, yeah, this is something I also don't understand,' Magdalene said. 'I may be from the Syiem clan, ha, but I never knew about this. I thought the syiems were always there, but now you are saying they were not. How can there be himas, or states, as you have been saying, without syiems? There are so many things you have to explain, Bah Su.'

'It's a long story,' Bah Su simply said.

'What do you mean it's a long story?' Magdalene demanded. 'Don't we have the whole night, and several other nights besides, if tonight is not enough?'

'Come, come, Bah Su, tell us, ya,' Donald coaxed him.

But Bah Su pointed at me.

'Yeah, yeah, let Ap do the telling,' Bah Kit said. 'We have listened to him speak of these things before. Go ahead, Ap, we'll help out here and there.'

I told them I would like to begin by quoting from Soso Tham's poetry:

Naduh ki sngi ba rim ba jah,
Hangta ka trai ka jaid ka Spah:

Nangta ki ïeng ka Kñia ka Khriam,
Hangta ki seng ban long ka Niam:
Ka dei ka Ding ba rhem ha Dpei,
Nangta ki ïeng ban saiñ pyrthei.

(Since the days ancient and lost,
There it rested their kinship their Wealth:
Then they raised their Rites their Rituals,
There they founded their Religion:
It was the Fire in the Hearth,
Then they raised their politics.)

Having read these lines from my tablet, which I immediately switched off again to conserve the battery, I said, traditional Khasi democracy has been much spoken of—sometimes extolled in poetry or essays, sometimes vilified in the most insensitive terms. It seems that these adulators and vilifiers, however, have made their cases for, or against, traditional Khasi polity with little knowledge or understanding. Research-based analysis of the subject is what we need at this point when many eyes are trained upon it.

'And your analysis is research based?' Evening asked, as if he could not believe that I was capable of research.

'What do you think?' I asked, just as sarcastically.

'You should know to whom you are talking, ha, Ning,' Bah Kit said. 'Only a handful of people have studied Khasi culture in depth, and Ap is one of them. You are supposed to know him well, no? How come you don't know that?'

Donald sang out, 'Familiarity breeds you know what.'

'I was just asking,' Evening answered Bah Kit.

'The question was alright,' I remarked, 'but the tone was all wrong.'

Evening laughed and said, 'Okay, okay, you got me there. The problem with me is I don't read enough books, only newspaper articles.'

As the lines from Tham's *Ki Sngi ba Rim U Hynñiewtrep* reveal, I continued, one has to draw on the oral tradition to realise that the communal smithy of the Hynñiew Treps was the 'Fire in the Hearth' of the mother's house. It was here that the uncles and fathers, that is, the lawmakers, forged their social and economic systems, their religion and their political system.

It is not by accident that the poet speaks first of the social, economic and religious systems, and then politics. Our folk traditions maintain that the Khasis evolved their political structure, as it survives today, much later, when the need to modify the set-up was felt. But there is no gainsaying the fact that the last item forged in the smithy of 'the Hearth' is also the most important.

'Okay, okay, stop there for a bit, Ap,' Hamkom interrupted. 'Before this political structure was established, what was there?'

'Everything was very rudimentary,' I said. 'The Khasis organised themselves into groups of villages governed either by *ki basan*, the clan elders, or *ki lyngdoh*, the high priests. It was only much later that they founded the himas, our democratic states, republican in nature, monarchical in form. For thousands of years before the birth of Christ, they had survived as provincial entities or raijs—'

'When were the first himas established?' Hamkom asked.

'Who knows, but we definitely know from stories that some himas existed side by side with the Ahom kingdom in the thirteenth century CE. It is said that, among the first democratic states to be established were the states of Sutnga (which was later called the Jaiñtia kingdom by the Bengalis, Ahoms and other non-Khasis), Shyllong, Sohra and Madur Maskut, which disappeared in the fifteenth century.'

'Ah, this is the hima that Bah Su was talking about, no?' Donald said.

'It's a strange thing, you know, but I too haven't heard of it before, ya,' Magdalene confessed.

'What's so strange about it?' Evening said scornfully. 'It's obvious that you two historians know nothing about Khasi history.'

Hamkom bristled at this, but Magdalene readily admitted that she had not tried to discover much about Khasi history. 'It's not taught in schools and colleges, no, that's the problem.'

'We do study many of these things in school, Mag,' Bah Kit told her. 'Not as history but as part of Khasi literature. But if you go to an English-medium school, ha, and don't read Khasi books, ha, you wouldn't know anything about it. Go on, Ap.'

'As I was saying,' I continued, 'the state of Madur Maskut was right there between the states of Shyllong and Sutnga. It had territories both in Ri Pnar and Ri Khynriam (Jaiñtia Hills and East Khasi Hills) as well as in Ri Bhoi (northern Khasi Hills), Assam and East Bengal. I'll tell you more later: there are some fascinating stories about it. Likewise, by the iron-manufacturing age, the state of Sohra was in existence, which we learn from the stories of U Thlen and Ka Likai.'

'You must tell us all these stories later, ha, Bah Ap?' Donald demanded.

'I will, I will,' I promised. 'Over time, about thirty states were established, spread over western, southern and northern Ri Khasi—'

'Ri Hynñiew Trep, man!' Hamkom demanded.

'Okay, okay, Ri Hynñiew Trep, or contemporary East Khasi Hills, West Khasi Hills and Ri Bhoi, and only one large state in eastern Ri Hynñiew Trep, or Ri Pnar. Before that, for thousands of years, Ri Hynñiew Trep had been organised into independent provinces governed by basan clan elders and lyngdoh high priests in Ri Khynriam, Ri Maram, that is, West Khasi Hills, and Ri Bhoi. In Ri War, which is southern Ri Hynñiew Trep, bordering East Bengal, there were provincial chiefs like sirdars. Ri Pnar was governed by dolois.'

Tham had considered this aspect of his people's culture so vital that he introduced it in the very first stanza of his book: 'How in ancient times the Uncles the Fathers/Had fashioned politics, had founded states'. These lines serve to arouse the curiosity of the reader, who inevitably responds with his own question, 'How had our forefathers "fashioned politics" and "founded states"?' But it is not until later (Section VIII) that the poet explains the political set-up of his ancestors. He declares that it began '*Haba ki wad hangno u Syiem*', when they searched for a king who would be accepted as the leader of all, and who would be responsible for all.

This line draws from many legends about the emergence of the ruling 'Syiem' clan. The most famous of these is the legend of Ka Pahsyntiew, considered the progenitress of the first kings of Shyllong. Before this, the areas around what is known now as Shillong Peak were all *ri raij*, community land, and *ri kur*, clan land, organised into seven separate provinces. These were known as 'Saw Kher Lai Lyngdoh' because four of the provinces were under the control of basan clan elders and three under the control of lyngdoh high priests. The basans and lyngdohs governed their provinces independently; there was no central authority. And because each of them was independent, it was inevitable that they quarrelled over trade, land and boundary issues. Often, these disputes, in the absence of a central authority to mediate and reconcile, led to mutually destructive wars. It was to end such divisive disputes and debilitating wars (that could make them easy prey for foreign invaders) that the provinces finally decided to come together in a single state known as Hima Shyllong, though when exactly that happened, nobody can say.

The new state of Shyllong was to be governed by a 'syiem', who would not only conduct the day-to-day administration but would also bind the provinces together under his direction. But who would this syiem, this king, be? Choosing one from among the founding clans of the state, ki bakhraws, the nobles, was impossible as each clan wanted its own member as king. The elders were at their wits' end. What were they to do? How were they to solve the problem? That's when the legend of Ka Pahsyntiew emerged.

'I have heard the story, Ap, but I don't know the details,' Magdalene intervened. She was excited because she belongs to the Syiem clan and might well be one of the descendants of Ka Pahsyntiew. 'Tell, tell the story, no, Ap,' she said.

'At this rate, our discussion will never end,' I protested.

But now, everyone wanted to know. Even Bah Kynsai said, 'The purpose of our discussions is to discover the stories behind them, na?'

'Let me do it, Ap,' Bah Kit volunteered and then told us about Ka Pahsyntiew and how her sons became the first kings of the state of Shyllong.

A long, long time ago, it was said that spirits haunted the forests on the hills around what we now call Lum Shillong, or Shillong Peak. The chief of these spirits dwelt on the highest and most thickly wooded hill. In those times, the people in the surrounding villages did not know much about rites and rituals. It was enough for them to pray to God, U Blei, morning and night. Although they knew about the hill spirits and were afraid to go anywhere near them, they did not think it necessary to make offerings to them. It was not until a village elder, a man of great wisdom and one who understood the mysteries of life, started making sacrifices to the chief of the spirits, that the villagers learnt about paying obeisance to more than the one supreme God that they knew.

The elder had learnt the rites from the people of Sohra, who worshipped God through the mediation of certain spirits. He had seen how the people there prayed to U Mawlong Syiem, the guardian spirit of the villages around Sohra. He had also watched the religious ceremonies performed for U Suidnoh, the god of health, at the sacred forest of Law Suidnoh in Laitryngew. And so, he wanted his village to have its own guardian spirit. He taught the villagers how to pray to the chief spirit of the hills, whom he called Shulong, 'the self-begotten'. From that time onwards, this spirit came to be known as U Lei Shulong, or U Lei Shyllong as he is known today. In due course, U Lei Shyllong became the patron god of all the villages in the seven provinces of Saw Kher Lai Lyngdoh, and everyone paid homage to him.

This pleased U Lei Shyllong. So, when he heard the people of Saw Kher Lai Lyngdoh praying to him for a way out of the impasse they found themselves in, he sent for his daughter and directed her to go and live among his human subjects. The nymph turned herself into a beautiful maiden and went to live in a cave called Krem Marai, near the village of Pomnakrai on the slopes of Lum Shyllong. It was a lonely spot. Only a few boys and girls went there once in a while to graze their cattle and goats. But it did not take the exploring children long to discover her sitting in the sun by the entrance to her cave. The sight of this strange, beautiful woman sitting all alone in the middle of nowhere struck terror into their hearts. They fled the scene to report the matter to their parents and elders.

Word of the mysterious woman at Krem Marai spread like wildfire to the four corners of Ri Hynñiew Trep. Most people, being superstitious, began to avoid the place, believing she was some kind of spirit.

One man among them, however, was not afraid. His name was Sati Mylliemngap, and he was an elder from the village of Bisi, respected for his knowledge and wisdom. The rumour invigorated his adventurous spirit, and he resolved to visit her, no matter what.

Sati set out for the cave on a beautiful spring morning. Along the way, birds sang their love songs; wildflowers, nameless, rainbow-hued, danced in the breeze; the scented air seemed to urge him on, as if to a predestined rendezvous.

He picked his way carefully through the undergrowth near the cave, now and then stopping to look for the maiden. Suddenly, there she was, sunning herself at the entrance—just as the children had described. She had a little orchid in her hand, a *lamat ïong*, the 'black-eyed bloom'.

Sati's jaw dropped as he gazed in wonder at her strange loveliness. Her skin was fair and smooth as spring water; her eyes were blue as the clear sky; long brown hair cascaded down her back. Stranger still, she was not dressed like a Khasi girl at all! Her robe was a creamy yellow, of a cloth quite different from the silk spun by the villagers. She wore no jaiñsem, which was unheard of for a local girl. As Sati stared at her, she caught sight of him and, with a little cry, disappeared inside the cave, which even the bold Sati could not bring himself to enter.

But that was not the end of it. Sati stayed where he was, calling out to her: 'Dear Kong, why do you run from me … don't be afraid … I mean you no harm.'

When she did not appear, he pleaded and coaxed her with gentle words of endearment: 'I'm an old man with neither the strength nor the inclination to harm you. I'm old enough to be your father; come, talk to me. All I want is to help you.'

Nothing worked, however, and exhausted, he sat down for a while to think. It was not long before an idea struck him. He had noticed a bunch of wildflowers called *jalyngkteng* blooming some distance away. Since the maiden seemed to be fond of flowers, he went to pick a handful and fashioned them into a bouquet, which he placed before the cave's entrance. Then he called out to her and said, 'I give up, I'm leaving, Kong, I'll not pester you again. But before I go, here are some flowers as a token of my goodwill. Please accept them. I'll put them here and go.'

Sati left, but having gone some distance, he doubled back and hid quietly by the side of the cave. After a while, the shy maiden peeped out. She looked around to make sure the coast was clear and stooped to pick up the bouquet.

That was just what Sati had been waiting for. He ran up to her and quickly overpowered her, all the while trying to calm her fears and crying, 'I mean you no harm ... don't be afraid ... I just want to know more about you ...'

After a while, the woman calmed down a little.

Sati begged her forgiveness for the trick he had played. Once more, he told her he only wanted to help her. He said the villagers had become very agitated and fearful when they heard about her. It was only to prevent anything untoward from happening that he had come, at the request of the council of elders, to find out more about her, and why and how she had come to dwell in these lonely backwoods.

Reassured by the gentle manner of her captor, and convinced that she was talking to a true representative of the village council, the nymph revealed everything to an astonished and reverential Sati. She told him how her father, happy with the people's unbounded faith in him, had sent her to be the progenitress of the Syiem clan, which would later become the ruling clan of the state of Shyllong. For the time being, however, she urged Sati not to disclose anything to anyone except the council of elders, which must also be sworn to secrecy.

Sati, now excited, made his obeisance to her, and promising to do exactly as she had told him, took her home with him. There, the nymph caused quite a sensation. People, neighbours, friends and relatives flocked to Sati's house to catch a glimpse of the strange woman. Sati introduced her to them as his adopted daughter, Ka Pahsyntiew, the one lured by flowers, because the nymph did not wish to reveal her real name.

Meanwhile, the council of elders met, and on learning everything from Sati, resolved to get her married to the most eligible bachelor in the land: the bravest, strongest, wisest and most handsome youth they could find. After a long, hard quest, they finally chose someone from the Ri Bhoi village of Nongjri, a young man who came to be known as Kongngor Nongjri. They brought him to Bisi for the wedding, which was the biggest and most memorable event of those times.

The moon was new; the moon was full. Time flew by, and life for the couple slipped from one happy year to another. Pahsyntiew gave birth to a charming son, named U Naraiñ, and a beautiful daughter, named Ka Bamon Sari, who grew up to be strong, intelligent and noble-hearted. They were the pride of the land, loved and respected by all. Kongngor, who doted on his divinely exquisite wife and dedicated every day of his life to the welfare of his family, thought their happiness could never end.

Then, one day, Pahsyntiew called her children to her. As they sat before her with their father, she said, 'My dear Kongngor, my beloved children, for so long I have hidden my true self from you, thinking only of your happiness. Now the time has come when I must go back to my own world. I am the daughter of U Lei Shyllong, sent by my father to give the people of Saw Kher Lai Lyngdoh their own rulers. And rulers are what you, my children, shall be. I have done my duty and must return. Your father is a capable man, my dearests. I leave you with him, with my blessing.'

Kongngor and his children were heartbroken. There was much crying and questioning, but since it was decreed that Pahsyntiew should return to her own kind, there was nothing anybody could do about it. With a troubled heart and tearful eyes, Pahsyntiew blessed her children and left the house for her cave in Krem Marai and was never seen again.

Kongngor and his children grieved for a long time. But gradually, with the love and support of the people, they were able to overcome their sorrow. In due course, true to the words of Pahsyntiew, her eldest son, U Naraiñ Syiem, was made the king of the new state of Shyllong, formed out of the provinces of Saw Kher Lai Lyngdoh. The new king ruled his people well. With the help of his *myntris*, or ministers, elected from among the founding clans, his state grew from strength to strength. In no time at all, it became one of the most powerful states in Ri Hynñiew Trep.

The people were greatly pleased with their syiem, and together they built the *iingsad*, the ancestral house, of the Syiem clan, at Bisi. Here they performed all the ceremonies of the state, and here, in accordance with the customs of the land, lived the king's eldest sister, Ka Bamon Sari Syiem, as ka syiemsad, the queen mother, since her sons would later inherit the throne from their uncle.

Having narrated the tale, Bah Kit said, 'Over to you, Ap.'

'But this is not the whole story,' I responded. 'The legend also speaks of how Mylliemngap and the elders of Saw Kher Lai Lyngdoh had brought the divinely beautiful and unusually fair-skinned young maiden from the plains of Sylhet, East Bengal, and had her stay in the cave for a while. Then they floated the story of a fairy living at the Krem Marai cave and made a grand spectacle of her capture. This they had to do because they were finding it impossible to choose a syiem—someone who would have unheard-of powers over their lives—from one of the founding clans without causing a rebellion. So, they, in their wisdom, resorted to this stratagem. And in so doing, they unwittingly propounded one of the earliest theories on the divine origin—but not right, as you shall see—of kings.'

When Bah Kynsai heard this, he muttered: '*Chalu hei sala!* Those bastards were quite cunning, na?' Then he laughed aloud and said, 'So, Mag, you are no royalty, ha, only the descendant of a Shilotia!'

'Shilotia?' Mag asked.

'Someone from Shilot, the Khasi name of Sylhet. You don't know that also or what?'

'So deflating, ya, Bah Kynsai,' Magdalene moaned. 'But what happened to her, Ap? She went back to the cave and then vanished just like that?'

'To bring their deception to its logical conclusion and to convince the people that she had returned to her father, the patron god of Shyllong, they took her back to her own home in Sylhet.'

Evening agreed that they were cunning, but added, 'There's a lesson here, okay? Have you noticed how they simply would not accept a Khasi as their syiem? Envy, jealousy, spite, resentment and mistrust: these are the qualities I see in those ancient Khasis and, unfortunately, among us today. Why do you think the first chief minister of Meghalaya was a Garo, huh? The struggle for the hill state took place mostly in the Khasi Hills, organised by Khasis, so why a Garo chief minister? For the same reason that our syiem had to be a Shilotia, lyeit!'

This might be the unpleasant truth about both the Syiem clans and the rest of us. While some have called it wisdom, others insist it was mean subterfuge. But whatever you call it, it is part of our history. R.T. Rymbai says it was the growing need for an authority that would run the day-to-day administration and regularly preside over the 'dorbar hima' (council of state) that gave rise to 'the institution of families and clans and the origin of titular heads of states called Syiems'. According to him, the syiems 'came not from the Bakhraw clans, the founding clans of the Hima, or from the indigenous clans constituting the citizenry called *u babun u balang* (the many the populace), in whose hands is vested the ultimate authority for the governance of the Hima. As daylight comes after the dark night, we have the legend of Ka Pahsyntiew, a fairy queen emerging out of the cleft of a rock at Pomnakrai to found the dynasty of *Ki Syiem Ka Hima Shyllong*'.

Rymbai also speaks of 'The Legend of Ka Li Dakha', a mermaid who transformed herself into a beautiful maiden and founded the dynasty of ki syiem Sutnga, known later by non-Khasis as the Jaiñtia Rajas.

'Because of Jaiñtiapur and the Jaintapur Upazila, in East Bengal,' Hamkom interrupted, mimicking what I had said earlier. 'I know, I know,' he added, 'you don't have to repeat it.'

But Evening said, 'Every time we talk about the so-called Jaiñtia Rajas, ha, we must remind ourselves over and over that they were known by that title only to the Bengalis and non-Khasis. The old Pnars and everybody else called them *ki syiem Sutnga*, the kings of Sutnga!'

I stepped back in to say that Li Dakha also founded the dynasties of Ki Syiemlieh (called *Safed Rajas* by non-Khasis) and Ki Syiemïong (called *Kala Rajas*) of the states of Nongkhlaw, Maharam, Langrin, Nongspung and others in contemporary West Khasi Hills and Ri Bhoi district.

'You hear that, Hum Kisise Kum Naheen?' Evening demanded. 'The states in West Khasi Hills and Ri Bhoi were also founded by the descendants of ki syiem Sutnga! Now do you dare say that Pnars are different from the rest of the Khasis? Oh yeah, I forgot! To you, Pnars are not Pnars but Jaiñtias. If you have so much faith in the Bengalis, why don't you start speaking in Bangla, huh? Forget your Pnar or Khasi, speak in Bangla, you idiot!'

Hamkom stood up and rushed towards Evening, but Bah Kynsai stopped him. Turning to Evening, he barked, 'Stop it, na, tdir! You go on and on about the same thing, liah! Can't we discuss things without nastiness? Tet tdong! They only want to fight, man, these buggers!'

To divert everyone's attention, Bah Kit said, 'Hey, hey, let me tell you the story.'

In the beginning, Ri Pnar was only organised into a group of provinces, without a king or state. Each province kept to itself under its own administrator, the doloi, who was elected from a particular clan by a dorbar elaka, the provincial council, comprising all eligible male representatives.

The doloi was assisted by elders known as basans, *pators* and sangots, and by lyngdoh priests, who were elected from their respective clans. The dolois ruled their provinces independently and consulted each other only on matters of trade. At that time in Ri Pnar, there were a total of twelve dolois. But soon, for the same reasons that forced the provinces of Saw Kher Lai Lyngdoh to unite under the state of Shyllong, the dolois also decided to come together under one ruler. But finding it impossible to elect this leader from among themselves, their resolution to unite under one state and one ruler had to be put off for some time. It was then that the legend of Ka Li Dakha emerged.

At that time, in a hamlet called Umwi, there lived a very handsome man known as Luh Ryndi, sometimes also called Woh Ryndi. He lived alone, spending most of his time in his field, toiling from morning till night. Like all men in the hamlet, he was very fond of hunting and fishing, and indulged in these pastimes whenever he could.

One autumn morning, when the sky was blue and the sun was brilliant, Luh Ryndi took up his fishing rod and went striding off in the direction of a river called Waikhyrwi. At the river, he took his position by the side of a large pool and settled down for a day-long stint of fishing. Very soon, he could feel something nibbling at the bait and tugging at the line. He took the strain and pulled. Dangling at the end of the hook was a sizeable fish. Catching it with one hand, he unhooked it, placed it inside the basket he had brought with him, and went back to fishing. Strangely, although he tried till the sun sank below the western hills, he did not catch another fish.

When night came, Luh Ryndi returned to his hut with the fish, washed, made up the fire and cooked his meal. Then he took out the fish, put it inside a bamboo basket and left it dangling above the hearth to dry, meaning to boil it in the morning. But when morning came, in his hurry to prepare for the day's work, he forgot all about the fish. Eating a hurried breakfast, he gathered his tools and left for the fields without a backward glance.

When Luh Ryndi came back in the evening, he was in for a big surprise. As soon as he opened the door, the warmth of the room embraced him like a comforting companion. He could see the fire burning in the hearth. The room looked like it had been swept recently, and when he looked at the pots, he realised that food had already been cooked. There was an eerie sensation of an unknown woman's presence in the house. But he brushed that foolish thought aside and guessed that one of his nieces must have come to keep house for him during the day. So he ate his food, which was exceptionally delicious, and went to sleep.

The following day, the same story repeated.

Curious, he went to his sister's place to enquire if she had sent one of her daughters to his house. When she said no, he became quite worried. Who then had been keeping house for him? He could not think of any friend who would do something as inexplicable as visiting his hut to do domestic chores for him while he was away. No, he thought, this will not do. I must find out, by any means. So he hit upon a plan and, comforted by it, retired to bed.

The next morning, Luh Ryndi got ready for work and went to the fields as usual. But once out of sight, he doubled back by another route and went to the back of his hut, where he settled down to wait and watch through a hole in the wall. After a long wait, towards sundown, to his amazement, a stunningly beautiful woman emerged from the fish in the basket. He watched her for some time, gazing with wide-eyed wonder at the unusual fairness of her skin, the brilliance in her eyes and the midnight blackness of her hair, which cascaded down to her heels. He knew, of course, who she was. She could only be one of those fairies called puri, and, from the loveliness of her face, the snowy whiteness of her jaiñsem and her clothes, he guessed that she was a godly fairy, or puriblei, and decided that there was nothing to fear from her. Even as he watched, he saw her sweep the floor, build up the fire in the hearth, clean the pots and prepare to cook the evening meal. But then his patience ran out, and he hastened into the house to confront her.

As soon as the creature saw him and realised she had been outwitted, she dashed towards the fish to take shelter in its scaly skin again. But, rightly surmising what she was about to do, Luh Ryndi jumped forward, snatched the fish from her grasp and threw it in the fire. With her only means of escape destroyed, the strange maiden submitted to his powerful arms and listened to his eager questions: 'Who are you? Where did you come from? What do you want here?'

'I am the daughter of a river nymph,' she said simply. 'I took a fancy to you as you sat fishing by the river alone … I have come to be your wife.'

Hearing this frank admission, Luh Ryndi stared at her, speechless. Presently, his face broke into a smile, and he promised to return her love in full measure by marrying her as soon as he had introduced her to his relations. But first, she had to have a name. After briefly ruminating on the strange manner of his acquaintance with her, he decided to call her Ka Li Dakha, the one who came from a fish.

When all the formalities were completed, Luh Ryndi married Li Dakha in a grand ceremony that the dolois of Ri Pnar organised for him. Over the years, they had three daughters, whom they named Ka Rapungap, Ka Rapubon and Ka Rapunga (also known as Ka Ngap, Ka Bon and Ka Nga), and three sons, whom they named Shyngkhleiñ, Bania and Tetia-ksaw. Eventually, the six children, being the offspring of a nymph, grew into exceptionally beautiful young men and women. The girls were especially adored by everyone, and were courted by the bravest and most handsome young men of the land. Consequently, when the time for their marriage came, the three had a very select band of admirers to choose from and naturally picked the best grooms in the field.

Having seen her children satisfactorily married off, Li Dakha determined to return to her pool. One day, while the family was sitting together, gathered around the hearth, she said, 'My husband, dear children, it is time for me to return home. I can hear my mother and the others calling me back. From now on, you must learn to live without me.'

It fell like a thunderbolt in their midst. Her family gaped at her in disbelief. At length, Luh Ryndi roused himself and said, 'My dearest wife, what foolishness is this? What are you saying? Surely you cannot mean what you said?'

When she affirmed that she did mean it, the daughters joined in the general protest. 'Our beloved mother, how can you leave and render us orphans like this? Surely, you love us more than that! Forget this silly notion, stay on, let us be happy together.'

Although they cried and pleaded with her for days, Li Dakha could not be persuaded, for she argued that it was against the very nature of her being to stay on indefinitely in the land of mortals.

When Li Dakha had gone back to her magic realm, Luh Ryndi tried to lead a normal life once more. But he found it impossible; it was as if the sun had set forever. He began to pine away until, finding the weight of sadness unbearable, and the longing in his heart unquenchable, he visited the pool with his fishing rod once again, in a desperate attempt to win back his beloved. And win back his beloved he did, but in a manner contrary to all his expectations. As he sat by the pool, toying with his rod, suddenly, a big fish took his bait and pulled him headlong into the murky waters.

Luh Ryndi was never seen nor heard from again, but his children and their families prospered and grew in strength. Being the descendants of a supernatural creature, they were looked up to and loved by one and all. And this was a God-sent opportunity for the dolois, who were looking for a syiem to unite their provinces under one state. They sanctified a new Syiem clan for the children of Li Dakha and Luh Ryndi and made Shyngkhleiñ the first syiem of the state of Sutnga. Ka Nga became the first syiemsad, being the youngest daughter.

Raji protested Bah Kit's last statement. 'I know that in Hima Shyllong, okay, when the queen mother is no more, okay, the eldest sister is always made the new queen mother ... So, why are you saying that the youngest daughter was made the first queen mother of Sutnga?'

'No, no, no, Raji, this is different from hima to hima. In Hima Sutnga, ha, it has always been the youngest daughter.'

In later years, Bah Kit said, picking up the story again, the daughters of Li Dakha became the proud mothers of many sons and daughters, who spread out across the land of the Hynñiew Treps. From Ka Ngap descended the clans of Phyrngap, Sutong, Pala, Huwa and Ïongrem, among others. From Ka Bon came the Syiemlieh and Syiemïong clans, whose descendants later became the first kings of the states of Nongkhlaw, Maharam and Langrin, and from Ka Nga came the kings of the state of Sutnga.

At this point, Donald raised his hand and asked, 'But Bah Kit, I don't understand this. You said the first son of Li Dakha became the first king of Sutnga, and yet, now you are saying the kings of Sutnga descended from Ka Nga?'

'The sons of the king cannot be king,' Bah Kit clarified. 'They belong to their mother's clan, remember?'

'Oh, yeah,' Donald said, a little embarrassed.

'But is this story taken to be true, Bah Kit?' Magdalene asked. 'In the story of Ka Pahsyntiew, Ap said it was a subterfuge, what about this one?'

'Your turn, Ap,' Bah Kit said.

Legend says that this, too, was a stratagem, I told her. It was devised by the dolois with Luh Ryndi's support. Luh had actually married a stunningly beautiful Hindu girl from the Jaintapur Upazila, in East Bengal. When he brought her home, because she was so beautiful, like a godly fairy, the dolois, with Luh's approval, spread the story about a river nymph who had emerged from a fish. Later, to bring their deception to a logical conclusion, Li Dakha was supposed to have gone back to her pool in the river, followed by her husband. In reality, both reportedly went back to Jaintapur Upazila, one after the other, to live there for the rest of their lives.

The syiems of Sutnga were given large tracts of land in every province so they could support themselves. Since they could not impose taxes on the citizens, these lands became their main source of livelihood. In those days, the state of Sutnga was confined to the hills of Ri Pnar, but over time, the administrators felt a need to have trading centres in the plains of Assam and Bengal, as well as to have subjects from whom the kings could collect taxes to enhance their income. The Pnars went south to capture the Jaintapur Upazila and the territories of the Bengalis as far as the banks of Surma. Then they travelled south-east, up to the Barak valley and north to Nagaon. Having captured these lands, they established strong forts and trading centres and imposed taxes on the conquered people, part of which went to the coffers of the state and part to the personal income of the kings. It was after these conquests that the king of Sutnga and the dolois decided to establish two capitals to facilitate administration, one in Jaiñtiapur as the winter capital, and the other in Nartiang as the summer capital.

There is a delightful story regarding the Pnar conquest of Jaiñtiapur, known then as Jaintapur or Jointapur. The Jaintapur Upazila used to be governed by Hindu kings, the last of whom was Jayanta Ray. The kingdom was prosperous and the Pnars yearned to conquer it for the sake of its wealth and the trade potential it would open up. However, believing firmly in the Niam Khasi Niam Tre Commandments of ka tip briew tip Blei (the knowledge of man, the knowledge of God) and ka kamai ïa ka hok (the earning of virtue in life), they could not bring themselves to invade it without reason. Instead of an invasion, therefore, they organised a hunting expedition. Hundreds of them, armed with swords and spears, bows and arrows, went towards Jaiñtiapur. After hunting all day, they reached the town in the evening, and being quite thirsty, requested the inhabitants for some water to drink. But the Bengalis, perhaps suspecting their motive, refused to give them any. They said, 'How can we give water to so many of you? If you want some water to drink, you'll have to buy a pond. There's one in the outskirts; buy that pond from us, and you can drink, otherwise, there's no water for you here.'

The Pnar warriors were enraged, but the king and the dolois thought it was for the best. They bought the pond, drank from it, and returned home. After a full moon had passed, the Pnars went back to Jaiñtiapur with thousands of warriors, took possession of the pond they had bought, and chased away all the townspeople trying to take any water from it. News of the Pnars' action spread like wildfire and forced the Raja of Jaintapur to send his army and engage the invading warriors. In the fighting that ensued, the Pnars defeated the Raja's army, and from then on, the Jaintapur Upazila was integrated with the state of Sutnga.

Meanwhile, the children of Ka Bon, who had no part in the governance of Sutnga, left home to wander off towards Kamrup in modern-day Assam. They were led by Shajer and his sister Ka Shaphlong, who crossed the River Kupli and went to a place called Borduar, where they bought a large plot of land from a certain Don Ahom. But before they could take possession of it, the siblings were invited to visit the eight provinces of Phra Lyngdoh in Ri Maram (West Khasi Hills), which was governed at the time by autonomous lyngdoh high priests. These provinces included Mawthangsyiar, Mawsenna, Nongum, Nongkseh, Marong, Marsum, Nongkhlaw and Lawriat.

Having confirmed that Shajer and Shaphlong were indeed from the Syiem Sutnga dynasty, the people of Phra Lyngdoh decided to merge their provinces into one state under their rule. The new state came to be known as Hima Nongkhlaw, which, as you know, later fought the British in the first Khasi War of Independence. And that was how the children of Li Dakha also became the kings of the new state of Nongkhlaw. Shajer became the first king and Shaphlong became the first syiemsad. Because both of them were very fair-complexioned, they were called Syiemlieh, the fair-skinned syiems.

After Shajer had ruled the new state for some time, he realised the importance of establishing a trade outlet in the plains of Kamrup. With some followers, he went to Borduar to take possession of the land purchased from Don Ahom. But Don Ahom refused to hand it over on the pretext that Shajer had not taken possession of it immediately. The syiem returned to Nongkhlaw, gathered his warriors and invaded Borduar. As a result, the whole of Borduar became a part of Nongkhlaw and stayed that way until the British took it away in the 1820s.

Shajer was succeeded by his nephew, U Syntiew, the first son of Shaphlong. Syntiew was a very far-sighted leader. He expanded his state, not only towards the northern plains of Kamrup, but also the southern plains of Bengal. First, he acquired the village of Sohrarim, some kilometres north of Sohra (using the cowhide subterfuge I told you about), and then he bought the village of Mawmluh, to the south, from the Nongkynrih clan. From Mawmluh, he expanded his territories to the plains of Sylhet and established important trade links with the rest of Bengal. Then he turned his attention to the western regions of Ri Hynñiew Trep and annexed many villages in Ri Maram. His successors continued his expansion policy, as a result of which the state of Nongkhlaw encompassed 'fourteen plus eight', or twenty-two provinces, in its heyday. For that reason, it also came to be known as Hima Khatsawphra, literally, 'fourteen eight'. At the time, the state controlled territories from Borduar (Kamrup) in the north to Dewanganj (Sylhet) in the south.

Magdalene wanted to know about the other states in West Khasi Hills that were founded by the children of Li Dakha. But those were minor states, and not much is known about them beyond the fact that they were established much later than Nongkhlaw by the descendants of Shaphlong.

She had one more question about the children of Shaphlong: 'If Ka Shaphlong was fair-skinned and was called Syiemlieh, how come her descendants, who founded the other himas in West Khasi Hills, were known as Syiemïong, the dark-skinned syiems?'

'Why do you think?' I asked. 'It's simple, isn't it? One of her daughters must have married a dark-skinned man.'

Raji wanted to know about the state of Sohra. He said, 'Hima Sohra was one of the most important himas in Ri Hynñiew Trep, okay, but its story is not well known. How was it founded, Ap? You are from there, you should have some idea, no?'

I told him there are two stories relating to the founding of Sohra. But before I could proceed, Hamkom said, 'I have a story about Sohra. It's in English, and it seems to be written by someone who's done a lot of research … Shall I read it to you?'

According to the story, it all began with the migration of two brothers and two sisters from a place in Ri Pnar called Surong-Sumer-Umthli to a place called Swer, halfway between Shillong and Sohra. Their names were U Buhsing, U Sadang, Ka Shan and Ka Jah. Soon, it became apparent to the basan or ruling clan elder of Swer province, which was then under the state of Shyllong, that Buhsing was a real asset to him, for he was both a shaman and an astute statesman. Basan Swer invested Buhsing with the title of lyngdoh hima, the chief priest, so he could officially help with the governance of the province.

Meanwhile, in the seventeenth century CE, during Shong Sing's reign as the king of Shyllong, the basans of Nongkseh and Nongumlong fell foul of Basan Swer. The quarrel ended in a civil war and led to Swer removing itself from Shyllong. With the approval of the people of Khatar Shnong, Basan Swer and Buhsing tried to set up a new capital in various places, finally ending up in Sohrarim. But Sohrarim belonged to the state of Nongkhlaw.

The king of Nongkhlaw, Laitlyngka Syiemlieh, drove them out with a large army of veteran warriors. Basan Swer and Buhsing then went to hide in the Ri War village of Nongsteng and reportedly survived for days on dried peels of citron.

When the war was over, they went to a place called Kyntur Sniang (pig's diggings), north of Sohra. It was there that they sanctified Buhsing's clan of Lyngdoh Sumer as a new Syiem clan, and selected from Khatar Shnong the twelve ruling clans of the new state. It is not very clear what the state was called then, but its first king was Buhsing—not Basan Swer, who was too old—and the first syiemsad was Ka Shan, Buhsing's sister.

It was during the reign of Buhsing Syiem in Kyntur Sniang that there was a fierce land dispute between the people of Mawphu from the Khathynriew Shnong (sixteen villages) province and the people of Laitïam, Ryngud and Sohbar in the south-east.

Buhsing talked to both parties and suggested that their villages be merged with his state to secure lasting peace. The warring parties agreed, and thus, after the war, his state came to comprise the provinces of Khatar Shnong, Khathynriew Shnong and the three villages. As part of the agreement, Buhsing established his new capital at a place called Nonglba, which later became known as Nongsawlia.

Buhsing appointed his nephew, Shan's son, Borsing, as his syiem khynnah, or deputy king. His other nephew, Jah's son, Morsing, was made the provincial king of Khatar Shnong.

When Hamkom finished reading the story, he said, 'That's it, the founding of Hima Sohra.'

Bah Kynsai turned to me and asked, 'What do you think, Ap?'

'I have also read it; it was published in one of the papers. It's not only highly unlikely but also absurd—'

Before I could finish, however, Raji said, 'Why is it unlikely? As far as we know, all these characters—Buhsing, Borsing and Morsing—existed, no?'

Raji did not seem to be affected by the Lyngngam brew tonight. Perhaps he had only been sipping it. In response, I said, 'They did. In fact, there were two Buhsings: Buhsing Tymmen and Buhsing II. This story is silent about Buhsing II, who succeeded Buhsing Tymmen. Anyway, these kings were not the founders of the state of Sohra. They could not have been. During Borsing's time, hundreds of years before the seventeenth century, Sohra was already one of the most powerful states in Ri Hynñiew Trep, so powerful that even the king of Shyllong dared not go to war against it. But according to this story, during the rule of Buhsing and his nephew, Borsing, the state had just been formed and, therefore, could never have challenged the might of Shyllong.

'Also, Sohrarim was given by the king of Sohra to Syntiew, the king of Nongkhlaw. How then could Buhsing and Basan Swer have tried to establish the new state of Sohra in Sohrarim? And how could they be prevented from doing so by Laitlyngka, the king of Nongkhlaw, who ruled much, much after Syntiew? In fact, according to the story, the state of Sohra was established as recently as the seventeenth century CE. This is the most stupid thing I have heard. As I told you earlier, Sohra was among the first Khasi states to be established. The iron-manufacturing business was already thriving in the Sohra region by 353 BCE, and the settlement of Sohra and the ancient village of Rangjyrteh were among the most prosperous trading centres in Ri Hynñiew Trep in those days. In the story of Ka Likai, which you all know—'

'What story? I'm afraid I don't know, Bah Ap,' Donald intervened.

'It's one of the most terrible stories from the Khasi Hills, Don. If Conrad's *Heart of Darkness* is about the darkness in man's heart, the same could be said about the story of Ka Likai—'

'Are you telling us about Hima Sohra or Ka Likai, liah?' Bah Kynsai cursed.

'Likai, Ap, Likai! Please, no!' Magdalene pleaded. 'I have heard so much about her, ya.'

'If you've heard so much about her, why do you need to hear it again?' Bah Kynsai protested.

'Uff, this Bah Kynsai! I know only the skeleton of it, ya, not the whole thing!'

'I think Mag is right, Bah Kynsai,' Raji said. 'Most of us also know only the outline, not the story as the people of Sohra have been telling it.'

'Please, no, Bah Kynsai,' Donald said, 'let him tell us about Likai now; he can come back to the state of Sohra later—'

Magdalene started shouting 'Likai, Likai, Likai' as if at a mock dharna, and finally, Bah Kynsai relented.

And so I began the story. Of all the tragic tales from the Khasi Hills, I told them, Ka Likai is perhaps the saddest of them all, and Mother chose the perfect time to tell us how the waterfall came to be known by the unhappy name, Kshaid Noh Ka Likai (the plunge of Ka Likai Falls). It was one of those dark, pre-monsoon nights in Sohra, during the black month of April. The wind was shrieking with fury as it lashed the houses with pelting rain and hailstorm when Mother suddenly said, 'The howling of the wind reminds me of the cries of Likai.'

Likai was a young widow from the ancient village of Rangjyrteh, about twenty kilometres to the west of Sohra, capital of the state of Sohra. The village was separated from Sohra by sanctified forests and a densely forested gorge several hundred feet deep and about two kilometres wide. At the bottom of the gorge ran a river known as Umïong, 'dark water', since a large portion of its cavernous expanse was covered by the shadows of the thick forest. The river emptied itself into the gorge, hundreds of feet below, forming a powerful, soaring waterfall known then as Kshaid Umïong. Rangjyrteh was located on a hill, some distance away, to the north and west of that waterfall.

Though only the ruins of the village exist now, in that distant past, it was one of the most prosperous manufacturing and trading centres in the area. This was because it was located on a tableland, the meeting point of several villages situated in the tangled and fertile ravines. As a result, the village became the most important wholesale market for agricultural produce in the area, rivalling Sohra itself, to the great envy and unease of the king of Sohra and his council of ministers, who feared the possible emergence of a parallel power hub. Added to this strategic location was the wealth of iron ore in Rangjyrteh, leading to a boom in the iron-smelting industry, which drew business from as far away as Shilot in East Bengal.

It was in the village's heyday that the tragedy of Likai played out—a damning indictment of the spiritual depravity and evil that lurked beneath the exterior of material well-being.

Likai was one of those unfortunate people who was haunted by death throughout her life. Her parents died when she was only a child. They left her nothing except her orphaned state and distant relatives who raised her out of a sense of duty since Khasi society did not allow a clan to turn out members who had been bereaved in this manner. She was raised, therefore, not like a flower, but as a weed that was allowed to grow in the courtyard through sheer negligence. Despite that, she grew strong and, to everyone's surprise, blossomed like an orchid on a tree. Every eligible bachelor in the village began to woo her when she reached the tender age of eighteen. But as soon as she had chosen a man, someone who loved her deeply, she lost him to a disease contracted during one of his business trips to Shilot. Could there be a woman more ill-favoured by fortune?

As the assistant of an iron trader, her husband, U Kynrem, had been working diligently to provide for her every need and to put aside a little so he would be in a position to buy his own iron manufacturing works. His sudden and premature death ensured that Likai was left with nothing but grief, a poor hut standing among *ki dieng sohphie* (trees with small sour-sweet fruits) and a baby girl, who was barely a year old.

What was she to do now? A grown woman with a child, she was no longer the responsibility of her relatives. Likai was supposed to fend for herself, but what could she do, especially burdened with a child that still needed to be carried around?

Her friends consoled and advised her. 'Likai,' they said, 'we know that you have just lost a husband who was more than a husband to you. We know about your orphaned state. You never knew real love until Kynrem gave it to you. You never lived in a real home until he provided it for you. You never experienced peace until he brought it to you. He was the love, the shelter and the hope of your life. And now he is gone, you feel lost like a boat tossed about on the waves without its rower. You feel that your life has come crashing about your feet like a pile of rubble. But take heart, your husband has not died in vain. His spirit lives on in your daughter; let her be your new guiding force. Be strong for her sake, work, scratch the earth, cut the wood, beat the stone. What does it matter? Let her be the new love of your life, the inspiration for your strength.'

With these and many such words, Likai eventually came to terms with her life. She began to take on odd jobs for a living—cleaning utensils in people's homes, sweeping their floors and courtyards, washing their clothes, fetching their water and ploughing their fields; and all the while, she carried the baby strapped to her back with a *jaiñ-it*, a strip of cotton cloth. When the baby became a toddler, she left her to play with her neighbours' children and earnestly began her profession as a piecemeal labourer, finally securing a job as a carrier in one of the ironworks.

In this way, Likai toiled from morning till evening. It was a hard life, but not without its compensations, especially when she came home to the childish prattle of her four-year-old daughter. How lovely her Lasubon, her flower in the crown, was! How like her father—from the curls of her dark hair to the lively twinkle of her dark eyes, and that endearing smile, always lingering in the corners of her little chubby mouth. Oh, she was lovely indeed! 'Come here, Lasu,' Likai would say, 'come, give your Mei a hug. So, you enjoyed playing with Ri and Mai all day, did you? And what about your Mei, did you miss her at all? You did? Oh, my little darling, I missed you too!'

She would wrap the child in her arms and rock her gently, tousling her hair, kissing her head and saying, 'You know, my little flower, when I come home and see you welcoming me so eagerly, I forget all about the aches in my bones, the pain in my muscles, the exhaustion in my body and soul. You are truly the image of your father … Yes, my little princess, your father is in the house of God … What is he doing there? He is persuading God to watch over us; he is telling him to make you grow into the most beautiful woman in the whole hima, to make you forever happy, and to let you marry the kindest and most accomplished man on earth. But run along now, go, wash your little hands and feet by the trough; your Mei will cook some rice and dried fish for dinner.'

After her daughter had gone running off to wash, she would gaze after her and pray to God to keep both of them safe, to guide them through life and to grant them all their dreams and wishes.

That was how Likai spent her days—between back-breaking work and home. This did not leave her free to have many close friends. But between her daughter and her memories, she did not pine for friends and was content to wear out her years in that dull yet tranquil state.

Life, however, had other plans. Now that her daughter had grown a little and Likai had regained some of her charm and youthfulness, young men began to flock to her hut again. Some came with their duitara or flute to try to entertain her with song and music. But things were not the same for Likai. Their presence only reminded her of the nights of courtship with Kynrem, and how of all those wooers she had conferred upon him the traditional 'kwai song' of betel nut and lime-marked betel leaf. Was she the cause of his death, or had he been marked out for an early end so that, by choosing him, she had become the unwitting victim of God's inscrutable ways?

With the support of Deng, her nearest neighbour, who acted as her chaperone, Likai was able to discourage most of her new suitors. She told them frankly that she could never love anyone else again, nor could she think of anything other than bringing up her daughter, whom she loved more than anything else in the world.

Almost all of them left her alone after that. None could love a woman whose heart was fixated on the dead and whose life was lived to honour him.

There was one among them, however, who persisted. His name was U Snar, 'the tough one'—he had been Kynrem's friend and one-time rival.

Unlike the rest, he knew the secret to Likai's heart. He visited her hut every night, not to woo her, he said, but to cheer her up a little and lessen the solitude of the evenings with a masculine presence. Initially, Likai did not welcome his visits, since he had been Kynrem's most serious rival. But Snar was persistent, and Likai began to tolerate his presence in her home because he never spoke of love or marriage and was kind to her daughter, always bringing her something to eat or play with. Moreover, he never really bothered Likai since he spent most of the evening entertaining Lasubon— who seemed to like him too—and would leave as soon as the little girl went to sleep on her pallet of straw.

Friends and neighbours noticed what was going on. They understood Snar's intentions and urged Likai to give thought to the possibility of remarriage.

'Look,' Deng said, 'how can a woman live alone, with only a small child, in these uncertain times when the village is being overrun by strangers— traders, merchants, and dealers in iron, limestone, foodstuffs and farm products? What if some of them, one lonely night, try to force their way into your hut and do both of you harm? You need a man about the house.'

'Don't be foolish,' Likai responded. 'Who would dare do a thing like that when there are so many houses close to mine? Besides, I always bar my door at night.'

'Aha, have you forgotten what happened just a few weeks ago at Bihrit's? Don't you remember how some out-of-town nongshohnohs tried to break into her hut in the middle of the night? And mind you, there were menfolk in the house!' (Just to remind you, nongshohnohs are 'killers' hired by the so-called keepers of Thlen, the legendary demon.)

'I'm not afraid of any nongshohnoh,' Likai insisted. 'Bihrit is in the suburbs; I'm not. All I have to do when threatened is to shout. My compound may be enclosed by the mud wall and the young trees that Kynrem planted, but it is also flanked by neighbours. I have nothing to worry about.'

'Likai,' Nah, her other neighbour, chipped in, 'it's not only a question of safety. A man is visiting your house every night. He is head over heels in love with you. How can you simply ignore that fact and treat him as if he were merely your daughter's pet?'

'But, Nah, you know very well that I cannot bear the thought of another man taking Kynrem's place. Kynrem is special; he is my first and only love. He is my redeemer; he lifted me out of my orphaned state. He is my lodestar, my *maji*, the helmsman of my life. Death has not parted him from my heart. The very idea of another man touching me gives me the shivers.'

'You are being stupid and selfish,' Deng snapped at her. 'And don't talk about him as if he were alive! How can you allow your life to be regulated by a dead man? Have you given any thought to the welfare of your child? You are working very hard for her sake. And yet, where are you leaving her when you go to work? Do you think you are being fair to your daughter, letting her grow up like a plant in the wild? Do you think she will develop into a proper young woman if she is reared like untended goats and cattle? That's what you are doing by leaving her day in and day out with your neighbours. And yes, I, for one, cannot play nursemaid to your daughter forever; I have my work to do, my own kids to look after.'

Nah, too, so readily and so wholeheartedly agreed with Deng that poor Likai became thoroughly dejected. 'Alright,' she replied. 'But supposing we are right in assuming Snar's love for me, and supposing I consent to marry him, how would that solve Lasubon's predicament? I would still have to go to work, and she would still have to sit the day out with her neighbours.'

Sensing victory, the two matchmakers softened their tone and became conspiratorial. 'Listen, Likai, we know for a fact that Snar is desperate for your love,' Deng revealed. 'In fact, he has enlisted our help in persuading you to allow him to propose to you. Look, he loves you, and that is beyond doubt because he was one of your very first suitors along with Kynrem. And most importantly, he loves your daughter ... Isn't that obvious in the way he endears himself to her? Where would you find such a man, a true lover and a devoted father?'

'About Lasubon, don't worry about a thing; we have discussed it with him too. As you know, he is the only son of a rich business family. He is now helping his father run the limestone quarries and ironworks. When you marry him, you won't have to work at all. If you want to, you can take a job in one of the wealthy households, work there for a quarter of the morning or so and return home to Lasubon. For that matter, Lasubon could accompany you to your workplace, so there would be no need for her to be alone any more. What do you say, eh? Aren't things working out rather neatly?'

Thus was Snar able to convince Likai to accept him as her husband, and to persuade the village headman to sanction their cohabitation. This, Snar explained to Likai, was only a temporary arrangement because his parents were not ready to accept the marriage. 'But don't worry about them, dear Likai, they will come around sooner or later. Parents always do.'

To her surprise, Likai did not find her new life so distasteful. She gave up her punishing labour at the ironworks and helped only for a quarter of the morning at the house of a wealthy merchant, mainly washing clothes at the River Daiñthlen nearby. Truth be told, Likai was rather happy at the new arrangement, since it afforded her the hitherto unthinkable luxury of being with her beloved Lasubon, who now followed her wherever she went. Snar too treated her daughter in a gentle and generous manner, although many a night, he was dislodged from Likai's bed by the cries of the little girl for her mother.

Then one day, barely two full moons after their life together had begun, Snar came home in the middle of the day. He said, 'My parents have thrown me out of the family business. It seems they haven't forgiven me. But don't worry, Likai, this is only a temporary setback; I will look for a job elsewhere.'

Days became weeks, but Snar did not find any employment. Likai found that hard to believe, yet maybe, as he had said, his parents had something to do with it; after all, they were influential people. In the meantime, the situation was getting worse. There was no rice even for two meals a day, not to speak of meat, fish and vegetables. Finally, not wanting to see her little girl go hungry, Likai volunteered to go back to her old, harrowing job at the ironworks.

Things were almost back to where they had started. Lasubon stayed at home with Snar, and Likai went to her now even more arduous work. Her employer was expanding his business and dealing directly with traders from Shilot, so porters had to go all the way to Mawmluh, south of Sohra, to deliver the lumps of iron. For Likai, this meant leaving home before daybreak and getting back just before nightfall, since the iron merchant insisted that each porter must make at least three trips a day.

Only this time, instead of cries of joy and welcome, she was greeted with a barrage of complaints from Lasubon. One day, the little girl said: 'Mei, Papa brought home many strangers. They were drinking, and they said bad things about me, and about you. I don't want to stay at home. I want to go with you.'

Likai enfolded her in her arms and said, 'Hush, my little love, don't say things like that. I will speak to your Papa.'

There was no chance to speak to Snar that day, however, for as soon as he heard Likai arriving, he came out, head bent, and not looking at his wife, said, 'I'm going out to meet a potential employer. I'll be home late. Don't wait for me. Leave the door ajar.'

And so, the moon waxed, the moon waned—day after day, Likai came home to more and more allegations and complaints, and night after night, she listened to more and more drunken and abusive clamour. When Likai tried to talk to Snar, coaxing him into seriously looking for a job and putting an end to his excessive drinking, he would push her face back and hiss, 'Oh, you want to quarrel in the middle of the night, do you? You want the neighbours to know what a bad man I am, is it? Job, job, job. Looking after your damn daughter is more than a full-time job. Now leave me in peace and go to sleep. If you can't get up for work tomorrow, how will we eat?'

One day, Likai arrived home to the shrieks of a child in pain, and the sound of dull, recurring thuds. It was a snarling Snar beating Lasubon with a thick stick as if she were a pile of straw, while his bleary-eyed and drooly-mouthed friends cheered him on. The child was howling and cowering in a corner, lifting her small hands in a pitiable attempt to ward off the thumping blows.

At this painful spectacle, Likai flew into a mad rage. She went to the hearth, picked up a burning brand, and attacked Snar and his drunken friends with it. She followed them as they fled outside, shouting terrible oaths after them: 'Why did you do this, you animals? Why did you have to thrash my poor baby as if she were a piece of sackcloth? Look at her swollen little hands and feet! Look at her bruised face and blistered body, you brutes. What did she do to deserve all this, you good-for-nothings?'

'I didn't do anything, Mei,' Lasubon cried. 'I only said I didn't know how to buy kyiad.'

'What? You miserable wretch, how could you ask an innocent little child to go and buy your cursed kyiad? You came to my house with big promises, but you are living like a parasite. Are you not satisfied with turning me into your slave that you now want to turn my poor child into your kyiad-bearer too? I married you in the hope that you would take good care of my daughter, but this is what you do, you shameless polluter! And you, you scum and connivers! Get out of my house and never come back!'

Meanwhile, Snar, who was swaggering about drunkenly, kept waving his forefinger at Likai and muttering, 'So, you want me to take good care of your daughter? Let me take care of her right now.' He lunged at Lasubon, only to be met with a blow to the head from the burning log in Likai's hands. 'Ow!' he yelped, 'what are you beating me for? I only want to take care of your daughter. You just wait. You think I'm bad; I'll prove you wrong. I'll take such good care of your daughter that you will never have reason to complain ever again.' He kept muttering incoherently till he was dragged off to bed by some neighbours, who had come rushing on hearing the commotion.

When things quietened down, Deng and Nah, who had witnessed the whole incident, came to commiserate.

Nah shook her head in amazement. 'I never thought he could be so rotten,' she said in a voice filled with regret.

Deng disagreed. 'I don't think you should take it so seriously. Kyiad can do strange things to men, but that doesn't mean they are not good people at heart. Take Father of Shan, my husband, for instance. When he drinks, he becomes a real tiger. Otherwise, as you know, he's as harmless as a kitten. The thing is how to get them to stay away from the rice spirit and to understand what drives them to it. In my opinion, Likai, you are pampering your girl just a little too much. Perhaps it is that which Snar resents—you know how jealous stepfathers can be. Just think about it: would you have reacted the way you did if it was Kynrem beating Lasubon? But mark my word, when he wakes up tomorrow, he'll be a different person. He did say he'll show you he is not bad, didn't he?'

'Maybe Deng is right,' Likai said to herself. 'Next market day, which is a half working day, I'll have a heart-to-heart with Snar: if he understands, fine, if not, I'll tell him to leave. Nobody can do that to my little darling and get away with it! Do you think Kynrem would do a horrible thing like that? And that too without cause? No, no, this market day, come what may, good or bad, I'll put an end to it all.'

The next morning, before leaving home, Likai, as always, bade her daughter goodbye and said, 'Today, if you don't want to stay home, you can go and play at San Deng's, alright?'

'Alright, Mei,' Lasubon responded happily, 'I'll do that, khublei, Mei. Come back soon.'

That afternoon, when Likai returned home, she found the house unusually quiet. Lasubon did not come running to meet her. As Likai washed her hands and feet in the water trough, she called out: 'Lasu! Lasubon! Where are you, khun, daughter of mine?'

Nobody answered. She went to her nearest neighbour, Deng. 'Have you seen Lasubon?' Likai asked anxiously.

'I saw her with the kids earlier. But I haven't seen her since. She must be playing around here somewhere. Maybe at Nah's,' Deng replied casually.

There was smoke rising from the hut, so Snar must at least be close by, Likai reasoned. The door was not barred, either. 'Yes,' Likai mused, 'they must be somewhere nearby. Let me go inside anyway. Arre! Surprise of surprises! Snar has cleaned the house and cooked the food! The blow I gave him on the head has done wonders, it seems. He must have felt bad about the quarrel yesterday and is trying to make up for it. Hmm, what an aroma!' She lifted the lid off the vessel. 'Aha! Chicken curry, or is it a young pig? Delicious fragrance! From where did Snar get this wonderful meat?' She picked up a piece and put it in her mouth. 'Very tasty. Somebody in the village must have called in the faith healers and sacrificed a piglet or something. Yeah, that must have been it; they must have distributed the meat, for, after all, it has to be finished within a single day. Ah, I'm dying of hunger. Lasubon must have eaten already; yes, some rice has been scooped from the pot. Let me also eat now and look for her afterwards. There's still some light, let her play a little while longer.'

Her appetite whetted by the unusual fare, Likai fell upon her food with gusto. When she had had enough, she went out to wash her hands, then stood back to rub her belly and burped a little with delight. 'What a hearty meal,' she said to herself, 'all I need now is a nice little pack of kwai to round it off.'

Inside, as she used to do after a meal, she reached for the shangkwai, the round bamboo basket, where they kept the betel nuts, betel leaves, lime and tobacco needed to prepare a chew of kwai. She pulled the basket towards her and placed it on her lap, only to spring up, recoiling in terror. For a while, she stared stupidly at the objects that spilled from the overturned shangkwai, until a loud and piercing cry of '*Wow rap!*' broke out from the very depths of her being. It was a heart-rending cry for help, a cry from the pits of despair, so loaded with anguish and torment, so shrill with horror that it flew over the hut to smite the darkening roofs around and cause an enormous shudder of foreboding to rise from the entire village.

Likai's world came crashing down. Heaven and earth darkened in an instant, and she was aware of nothing but the little hands, the sweet little hands of her sweet little child. Yes, they were Lasubon's. She would know them anywhere, dead or living, whole or in pieces. There they lay with the betel nuts on the floor before her, still longing for her loving touch. In a wink, she understood the foul crime that the unseen power, that unpitying and unjust arbiter of her fate, had seen fit to make her commit. Was this the ultimate reward for a life burdened by grief, suffering and bereavement? Yes, she understood now: that vicious savage of a stepfather had cut the child to pieces, prepared a curry from her flesh and trapped her into eating her own daughter, her own soul, her own life.

'*Wow rap!*' she shrieked again and threw herself on the floor, howling like a dog in pain. She tore her hair loose, rent her clothes off and tore at her belly, retching and writhing on the ground like a butcher's sow in the last painful throes of life.

People came rushing to her hut, agog with excitement and apprehension: 'Why? What's wrong? Bring a flambeau! What happened?'

When they saw Likai, squirming naked on the floor and weeping huge violent sobs that racked her whole body, they admonished her, 'Why are you doing this to yourself? Are you mad? What is it that has happened that you should behave in such a manner?'

Likai only wailed more shrilly: '*Wow, Mei!* My mother!' she called out. 'What life is this you have given me? What wrong have I done? What misdeeds, what transgressions, what sacrilege have I committed that I should be marked out for this abominable crime?'

'But what happened? Tell us what happened!'

'*Wow, Mei!* The fiend! The monster! He has killed my daughter; he has cooked her flesh; he has made me eat it … *Wow, Mei!* What shall I do?'

The confession caused an uproar in the crowd. While the women, who were now weeping themselves, tried to calm and console Likai, the headman called out angrily, 'Hey, ho! You, the menfolk, you, the real sons of your mothers! Let us go and hunt down this demon, this offspring of Thlen! This very night we shall purge the village of this evil!'

At these words, Likai suddenly snatched the long, hooked knife that was hanging from the wall, the very knife that was perhaps used to chop up Lasubon, and vowed, 'Hunt him down, that's what I'll do.'

With the wood-cutting knife in hand, she ran outside, crying, 'Where is he? Where is that child-killer? Where is that cannibal? I'll avenge you yet, my child!'

The men and women followed her through the dark lanes, calling to her, trying to hold her back. But nobody could go near her because she would swing the knife at anyone who came too close. After looking everywhere in the village, Likai, followed by the crowd, went towards the River Daiñthlen, where someone said he had spotted Snar earlier in the evening. Not finding him there, she crossed the river and followed the path down towards the River Umïong. Finally, she reached the outer edge of the Umïong forest and stood there, on a hill looking out over the Umïong waterfall, staring intently into its impenetrable darkness.

Then, exhausted by her mad rush, Likai, still holding the knife, fell to the ground, beating it with her hands and shrieking like one who has truly lost her senses: 'Oh, my child! My black-eyed bloom! My soul! My most beloved on earth! Flesh of my flesh! Blood of my blood! Bone of my bone! I cannot even find the brute who has done this to you, who has done this to us! Your flesh is churning in my stomach, and I cannot even find the demon. What use, my flower in the crown of queens, what use is my living without you, in shame and torment? How stupid of me! You wished me khublei this morning—you said, "Thank you, Mei, farewell and God bless you"—and I did not know it was your last greeting … I am an ill-omened companion of death! At the mere touch of my flesh, my parents died, my husband died, and now you, the very purpose of my life. What is the point, then, of living in this accursed place that dispenses only sorrow and tears, and where fortune scatters only the seeds of misery and death? Yes, death is the only true and constant comrade of my wretched life. Death, yes, only in death will I ever find my peace.'

And with that, she sprang up and dashed towards the waterfall, all the while crying forlornly, 'Why? What dreadful wrong have I done him? Heart of stone, heart of iron! What dreadful wrong have I done to God? If God is everywhere, where was he in our moment of need? Where were the guardian spirits of my ancestors? My mother, my father, ka ïawbei, u thawlang, u suidñia, where were they all? Heartless is man, heartless is God! Why? … Why? … Why? This godless world … Why? … Why? … Why? …' Those were the last words the villagers heard before Likai plunged headlong into the waterfall that would bear the terrible burden of her name for all time to come.

Meanwhile, Snar, who was all this while skulking among the trees by the edge of the Umïong forest, took a last look at the unfolding scene. He gnashed his teeth and, with a grim smile, turned away into the dark fastness of the forest, never to be heard of again.

I had to stop here, for Magdalene was crying noisily. We all tried to comfort her. Donald took her in his arms and let her sob into his chest, whispering all the time, 'It's okay, it's okay, it's only a story—'

Raji, his own eyes moist like most of ours, interrupted him. 'It's not only a story, man, haven't you been listening? It's a true story; Likai did suffer that horrible fate and did jump into the waterfall, that's why it's known as Kshaid Noh Ka Likai, no?'

'My God, what a cruel fate!' Magdalene exclaimed tearfully.

'My God, your God, but not her God, na? That's why,' Bah Kynsai said bitterly.

Even Dale was deeply affected. He said, 'What a fiendish beast, no, Bah?'

I wanted to ask, who—Snar, or the arbiter of her fate? But I thought better of it. Whenever I reflect on the story, I cannot help thinking, like Bah Kynsai that, for people like Likai, God certainly did not exist.

As Donald consoled Magdalene, some of us went outside to stretch and whistle among the trees. When we returned, Magdalene had composed herself and apologised for her behaviour. Bah Kynsai said to her, 'Crying is cathartic, Mag, you should never apologise for it. Anyway, most of us were also dewy-eyed, na? So, Ap, is it over?'

'The worst is over,' I said, 'there's only a little left.'

Ka Likai's story spread far and wide and moved to tears all those who heard it. But for the king of Sohra and his ministers, it was an opportunity they had long been waiting for. The king convened the council of state to discuss the ghastly incident at Rangjyrteh and to decide the fate of the village that had allowed such boundless evil to take place. Every adult male citizen of the state attended the council. During the day-long deliberation, many viewpoints were articulated. Eventually, however, it was resolved by a majority sanction that the village of Rangjyrteh be derecognised with immediate effect. The inhabitants of the village were advised to disperse to surrounding settlements, and the chief priest of Sohra was instructed to perform sacrificial rites at the Rangjyrteh market so that the evil would not repeat itself.

After the unhappy story of Ka Likai, I went back to the founding of the state of Sohra and said, 'You see, Ham, this was in the age of Kamarupa, as the elders used to say. Kamarupa in Assam, yes. Even in the legendary story of Thlen, the man-eating serpent, which was much more ancient than Ka Likai, the state of Sohra was clearly mentioned. That would make it one of the most ancient states in Ri Khasi, and yet that stupid story you read put it down to the seventeenth century CE! Incredible!'

'Are you saying that Khasi writers are not dependable?' Hamkom demanded.

'No, of course not. We have already spoken about pioneering Khasi writers like Rabon Sing Kharsuka, Radhon Sing Berry Kharwanlang, Jeebon Roy Mairom, Kissor Sing and Soso Tham. There are others like Token R. Rymbai, Primrose Gatphoh, Father H. Elias, Father J. Bacchiarello, Mondon Bareh, Kynpham Sing Kharsawian, H. Onderson Mawrie, Hipshon Roy Kharshïing and others, who are genuine authorities on Khasi history and culture. But many others write without proper knowledge or research. The point is, when you read a book or an article about us, in Khasi or English, you have to compare the story with versions of the same story recounted in other books and articles. More importantly, see whether the story is in accordance with our cultural practices or not. Of course, this means you have to be well versed in your people's culture as well—'

'From the perspective of culture, is there a problem with the story Ham read to us?' Raji asked.

'Two things,' I said. 'In the story, Buhsing supposedly belonged to the Sumer clan. When they made him the lyngdoh of Swer, he became Buhsing Lyngdoh Sumer. Later, it was said that his clan was sanctified as a Syiem clan. This is not according to Khasi culture. Khasis, as you have seen, would never sanctify an existing Khasi clan as a Syiem clan. Another thing to keep in mind is that all Khasi himas were founded by clans which ruled the provinces and wanted to merge these into a new state. The founding clans then searched for a king. In this story, however, Buhsing was first made a king, and after that, clans were selected to be in his council of ministers. This is an upside-down view of Khasi culture.'

'Yes, yes, Ap is absolutely right. The story is stupid,' Bah Su declared. 'Rymbai and Soso Tham said this too. Himas were established by the founding clans of provinces, and only afterwards did they look for a syiem.'

'I know the writer, I have read the story and have always condemned it,' Bah Kit said. 'You see, this is what happens when books are written by people who have converted to other religions. They know nothing of our religion and culture, and they write all sorts of nonsense.'

I did not agree with that, for writing well or with proper research has nothing to do with religion. However, before I could say anything, Bah Kynsai said, 'So what is Sohra's history then? If Hamkom has been telling us an incorrect version, then tell us the correct one, na? Why are you going on and on about how it is incorrect?'

I laughed. 'I would have, but then I was asked all those questions, remember? The correct version is much simpler and more in keeping with our customs and the practical demands of the times ...'

Having given them that opening, I told them the story I have already told you, right in the beginning, about the founding of the state of Sohra by the twelve clans from Khatar Shnong and Khathynriew Shnong. I told them how, when they were sitting in an open council, trying to decide who their king would be, a mysterious woman suddenly appeared before them to declare that her sons would be the future rulers of the state. The woman had identified herself as Sohra, taking her name from the characteristic feature of the land, as a place where nothing grew. And that was how the new state came to be known as Hima Sohra. Buhsing I, Buhsing II, Borsing and Morsing were very much a part of Sohra's history, but they came much later and were descendants of the mysterious woman, Ka Sohra. I told them that this was the version Rymbai favoured when he wrote about the divine origin of the Sohra kings.

Of course, some states were founded without a divine king. In such cases, the founding clans would go down to the plains of East Bengal or Assam to kidnap the first couple they came across, so they could become the forebears of their ruling Syiem clan. This is precisely what happened in the state of Mawïang in West Khasi Hills, whose first king was the son of a Muslim woman.

It is partly because of these origin myths and legends that our ancestors, the Hynñiew Treps, attributed certain qualities to their kings. For instance, they called them *ki syiem ki blei*, the kings, the gods; *u syiem u kmie*, the king, the mother; and *u syiem u mraw*, the king, the slave. As a god (or, at least, a person with a supposedly divine origin), the king must be just and deliver equitable justice to all citizens, regardless of their wealth and position in society. As a mother, the king must look after all his citizens with love and tender care. And as a slave, the king must work selflessly and untiringly for the welfare of one and all.

This is the kind of political wisdom that made a poet like Tham sing in praise of the old Khasis: 'So they learnt to forge their Politics; / So they learnt to found a State'. They discovered their first lesson in politics when they tried to find a 'king'. Having found him, they began organising their provinces and villages into a 'state', which they vowed to protect at all costs. In this way, 'because their blood surges, / Alive the Name the Glory stays'. In other words, because of their patriotism, their states flourished and grew in name and glory.

Donald raised a finger to ask, 'Sorry to interrupt, Bah Ap, but what are these himas, or "states", that form the basis of Khasi politics? I'm quite curious about why a syiem can be called a king but a hima cannot be called a kingdom.'

I told him that once, during his visit to these hills as viceroy and governor-general of India, Freeman Thomas, Earl of Willingdon, had observed: 'It is a proof of the stamina and virility and competence of your people that when greater Empires in the East and in the West have throughout the ages come and gone, you still maintain in your pleasant hills the freedom of your small republics, based on your ancient ways and the tenets of your race.'

The viceroy referred to the Khasi states as 'republics', not kingdoms, implying thereby a comparison with the Greek city-states. Rymbai and Hipshon Roy, both writing on this subject, explain why. The political organisation of the Khasis, they say, 'is basically democratic, where separate states, independent of one another, coexist. Fundamentally, they are all republican in nature, but monarchical in form'. This is because the king, as head of state, is not endowed with any power to act on his own authority but must rely on the consensual decision of the people expressed through the dorbar hima. The people of a state, upon whom real power is vested, are not raiots, or subjects, of the king, but citizens known as *u khun u hajar*, the children, the thousands.

As I have told you, there used to be thirty states, each under a titular head called syiem. Of these, twenty-nine were in contemporary East and West Khasi Hills, Ri Bhoi and Ri War, and one in Ri Pnar. In the Khasi polity, power is distributed in a three-tier system. At the village level, there is the *tymmen shnong* or *rangbah shnong*, the village headman, who, with the help of the council of elders, administers all its affairs. Matters of policy affecting the village as a whole are referred to the dorbar shnong, the village council. All adult males, except for drunks and known criminals, have the right to attend the council. The headman, the first among equals, is elected by the collective will of the people during an annual session of the council, and his appointment is confirmed by the king.

A group of villages constitutes a raij, or province, with a titular head called syiem raij or syiem shnat, the provincial king. Like a tymmen shnong, he has no authority to act on his own, and only administers the province with the help of a council of elders called basans. He settles disputes between villages or between individuals belonging to different villages within the province. But matters of policy affecting the province as a whole are referred to the dorbar raij, the provincial council. All adult males, except for drunks and known criminals, have the right to attend the council. Like the king, he customarily belongs to the Syiem clan of that particular state and is elected by its members through consensus.

Several provinces make up a hima, or state. The number varies according to the size of the state. The king is elected by members of the Syiem clan through consensus, and is usually accepted by the myntris if he is not otherwise ineligible because of a physical handicap or moral turpitude. If, however, members of the Syiem clan cannot agree on a candidate, the matter is referred to the myntris, and should they also not reach an agreement, then the council of state is approached for the final decision.

According to Rymbai and Hipshon Roy, writing in *Where Lies the Soul of Our Race?*, the republican nature of the Khasi political system derives its strength from the Khasi social structure. In the social order, the Syiem clan (this also applies to the founding clans of a state) is no higher than any other clan; Khasi society is strictly egalitarian. The difference is functional and only relates to the part they play in governance and administration. The king of a state is assisted in day-to-day administration by a council of ministers whose members are elected from the founding clans. In matters of ordinary administration, he carries out the people's consensus as conveyed to him through members of his council in session, and in matters of high importance affecting the state, as conveyed by the councillors in an open session of the council of state.

Tham describes the republican nature of the Khasi states thus:

> *U Syiem kam pher la dei 'u Maw';*
> *Ka Hima kit u Rit u Khraw;*
> *Bishar-khadar ryngkat bad ki;*
> *Ha u ki ai ka Nar-bili:*
> *Te kum u Tiew Myngngor Lyngsyun,*
> *Kumta ka ïaid Dorbar pyllun.*

> (It matters not the King may be 'a Stone';
> The State is borne by Small and Great;
> Justice with them collectively;
> To him the Fetters:
> And so, rounded as Marigold,
> It runs the Council of the State.)

The poet's understanding of the traditional political set-up is absolute. Since governance and statecraft are dealt with by the 'Great' ('u Khraw', the nobles) and the 'Small' ('u Rit', the citizens), it does not really matter what kind of 'King' heads the state, as long as he is acceptable to one and all. It is the 'Dorbar', with its open-air, circular seating arrangement, the marigold in full bloom, that is all-important.

Tham was not the only one who was full of admiration for his people's brand of democracy. In one of his speeches as president of the Indian National Congress in 1938, Netaji Subhash Chandra Bose said, 'those who wanted to see true democracy in action must go to Khasi-Jaiñtia Hills and learn from the people out there its soul and spirit'. Even David Scott, the greatest enemy of the Khasis in British India, only had good things to say about the Khasi 'democratic dorbar'. As Nongkhlaw's council of state was discussing his request for permission to construct a road from Guwahati to Sylhet through Nongkhlaw's territories, he had these observations recorded:

> The attendants came up the Hills, armed with swords, bows and quivers. The *Rajah* proceeded to explain the subject of the meeting and required the different orators to express their sentiments on the proposition of the British Government. The leading orator, on the part of the opposition, immediately commenced a long harangue in condemnation of the measure, expressed in a continuous flow of language accompanied with such animation of manner and appropriate gesticulation. This was replied to by an orator of the *Rajah's* party and in this way, the ball was kept rolling until evening. I was struck with astonishment at the order and decorum, which characterised these debates. No shouts of exultation, or indecent attempts to put down the orator of the opposite party [were made]. On the contrary, every speaker was fairly heard out. I have often witnessed the debates in St. Stephen's Chapel, but that of the Cossya parliament appeared to be conducted with more dignity of manner.

This system, founded in 'the days ancient and lost', is still practised today. For instance, the king's economic role and functions remain much the same. He can collect tolls from markets and produce on the way to markets. He can impose fines and try criminal and civil cases for specific fees and see to the day-to-day administration, but he cannot impose taxes of any sort, since the land and its resources belong to an individual, a clan, a village or a province, and not to him.

The exception now, apart from qualitative degeneration, is that the District Council has assumed to itself a constitutionally sanctioned supervisory role over and above the council of state. No king can be appointed without its approval. This state of affairs has given rise to at least two conflicting demands—one, calling for the abolishment of the District Council and the restoration of these institutions to their former relevance and glory, though subservient to the state government, and the other calling for their replacement with the panchayati raj system.

Donald, being a political scientist, was the first to comment when I concluded my account. 'It's a good set-up but for a few things. The king, for instance, is elected only from a particular clan—'

'You know the reason why,' Bah Kit countered.

'You see, Bah Kit, the problem is, they were thinking in terms of establishing a ruling clan for all time to come. If they had thought of electing an individual syiem instead, as in a modern democracy, they wouldn't have had to go to Bengal or Assam for a king—do you see that? Candidates could have been fielded from all the Khasi clans for a certain term of office, rather than a lifetime.'

'There is a term of office for the headman,' Bah Kit responded. 'In some villages, it's one year, in others, it's two or even four years. But defining a term of office for the syiem in those days, in those circumstances, when everyone was preoccupied with their livelihoods, when life was precarious at best, and wars were a constant threat, was simply not an option, Don. That was why they had to invent the Syiem clan—they needed a man who would be completely devoted to the day-to-day administration of the hima.'

Raji added, 'In the British system today, the monarch is from a certain family, no? And he or she assumes office for a lifetime. So how is it good for the British but bad for Khasi democracy? We should be full of praise for our system, man! What the British learnt in the modern period, okay, we had always been doing it, no, Bah Kit?'

'But don't you see the difference? The king or queen in Britain is only a titular head with no executive power, but among the Khasis, he is also an executive.'

'You are quite wrong, Don,' Bah Kit insisted. 'The syiem is only an executive when it comes to running the administration, no? And in that too, he is dependent upon his myntris from the founding clans of the hima. He cannot make or change policy. That was why, when the British asked Tirot Sing for permission to construct a road from Guwahati to Sylhet through Nongkhlaw, ha, Tirot Sing, ha, could not decide alone, he had to call for the dorbar hima.'

'Quite right, Bah Kit, quite right,' Raji added, 'our syiem is not an executive like the American president, okay? In essence, he's only a titular head. The bakhraws in his council of ministers, ha, Don, sometimes can be more powerful than him because they represent the founding clans of the state.'

'I don't approve of that either,' Donald said. 'Why should only a few clans be part of the king's council of ministers?'

'Because they were the founding clans of the hima, no?' Bah Kit replied.

'But when the state grows in size, there would be many more than the founding clans living in it, no? Why shouldn't they be given a chance in its governance through free and fair elections?'

Bah Kit tried to defend that too. 'They may not be given a chance to become ministers, ha, but remember, as citizens, they are powerful, and their voice and influence can be expressed through the various dorbars: the village dorbar, the provincial dorbar and the dorbar hima. For instance, ha, if the citizens in Nongkhlaw's dorbar hima had denied the British permission to construct the road, ha, there was nothing the syiem could have done about it.'

'No, no, no, Bah Kit, whatever you say, it is not a complete democracy, and it needs to change and modify—'

'Yeah, yeah, you are quite right, Don,' Magdalene supported him. 'It must change. For instance, why should only men be kings and ministers? And why should only men be allowed in the councils? Why only "adult males", huh? Why not adult females too?'

This is yet another growing demand, for the participation of women in all the policy-making councils.

Addressing Magdalene, Bah Su said, 'Traditionally, ha, Mag, the exclusion of women from the dorbars was the result of the peculiar structure of the Khasi matrilineal system. The woman is the manager of all household affairs and the custodian of wealth and property, though not the proprietress, okay? She is the receiver and the custodian and, therefore, must not stray into the field of politics. She is not to take part in the affairs of the state; her domain is the home—'

'Why not? Why not?' both Donald and Magdalene cried out.

'This division of functions was based on the ground realities of the past,' Bah Su explained. 'The constant threat of war, ha, was the most prominent factor. For instance, could a woman go to war? If not, then how could she participate in the dorbar discussing war and strategies of war? For her own safety, she was put in charge of the household.'

'That might have been true then, Bah Su, but times have changed, no? Women should be allowed to participate in politics without any discrimination,' Magdalene argued.

I was about to say that customs must evolve with the changing times, for this is the only way to ensure that our culture stays vibrant, but Evening spoke first. 'If you women are so hell-bent on change, ha, then we men must also demand the same. We must demand, for instance, that the culture be changed, so that clan names and surnames are passed on through the father and not through the mother. We should also demand that an equal share of property and family wealth be given to male children. If you agree to all of that, then, no problem, we'll let you sit in our dorbars and be our kings and ministers.'

'No, no, no,' Magdalene declared. 'No chance of that.'

'Then no chance of women in dorbars either!'

There was much laughter following that impasse until Donald said again, 'One more thing about the Khasi democratic set-up that I need to say, okay? Sometimes, I think, it does bear a likeness to the system of the Taliban, as someone said.'

'Why the hell would you say a thing like that, ha, Iyeit!' Evening said sharply. Bah Kit and Bah Su, too, were quite upset.

But Donald ploughed on. 'Because I have read of so many cases where families have been ostracised by village councils, no? And for what? For merely making use of the Right to Information Act to find out things about welfare schemes, government grants, public distribution of rice, sugar, kerosene, and so on. Why should families be ostracised, ha, Ham, for trying to expose the corruption of the headman and his executive council? Isn't that dictatorship?'

'That's a different matter altogether, you idiot!' Evening exploded. 'If a few people in control of village administration for a year or two are corrupt and behave like despots, how is the system to be blamed as a dictatorship? Because modern democracy is full of corrupt politicians, should we condemn it as a system run by thugs and the Taliban? Democracy, whether Khasi or modern, is not perfect, no? But it's still the best. You, of all people, should know that!'

'In this case, ha, Don, you are very wrong,' Bah Kit said. 'I think your prejudice has misled you completely. Corrupt headmen cannot serve forever. They have a limited tenure; for how long can they be dictatorial? Even syiems can be removed from office. No one is above the voice of the people.'

'I think they do have a point there, Don,' Bah Kynsai broke in. 'Let's forget it, okay? Why don't we tell some more stories, ha, just to calm our frayed nerves?'

Donald promptly said, 'Bah Ap, you promised to tell us about the state of Madur Maskut; you said there are fascinating stories about it.'

'So I did, Don. The story of Madur Maskut is basically the story of two of its most powerful rulers and their conflicts with the kings of Sutnga. U Kyllong Raja's story, in fact, is so strange it sounds like a fairy tale. However, everybody who spoke and wrote about it swore it was true.'

'You mean U Syiem Sait Snier?' Bah Kit asked.

'Yes, the king who washed his intestines, none other!' I replied. 'But let me begin at the beginning.'

Once upon a time, the state of Madur Maskut was said to be the most powerful state in Ri Khasi—

'Ri Hynñiew Trep,' Hamkom reminded me.

'The same thing, man! Chalo, Ap,' Bah Kynsai responded.

Madur Maskut lay between the powerful states of Shyllong to the west and Sutnga to the east. It extended from Nagaon, Assam, in the north, to the plains of Sylhet in the south. But the most unusual thing about it was that its territories encompassed areas belonging to the Khynriams in the west, the Pnars in the east, the Bhois in the north and the Wars in the south. Thus, it truly represented a unified Ri Khasi, where the four sub-tribes lived as equal citizens under a single ruler. The capital of the state was a place called Thangkhri in the Sung valley, but its most prominent trading centre was Ïaw Dai Ja or Ïew Die Ja, about sixteen kilometres from Jowai, the district capital of contemporary Jaiñtia Hills.

Not much is known about the history of this state, only that its rulers were the descendants of a nymph, born of a mythical sow. The nymph was discovered by a village elder who brought her up as his own daughter and later arranged her marriage with the most eligible young man he could find. The villagers saw the presence of the nymph and her children in their midst as an act of providence, and soon, other villages in the area were inspired to join together and form a new state to be governed by the nymph's 'God-sent' children as the first kings. They called them ki syiem Malngiang since they were born of a sniang, a sow. But beyond that, the history of Hima Malngiang, the state of Madur Maskut, is hidden in the gloom of unrecorded time. It was only towards the end of its existence, during the reign of the last two kings, U Kyllong Raja and U Mailong Raja (known by those titles because of their subjects in Assam and Bengal), that it became famous.

Madur Maskut was said to be so powerful that neighbouring kingdoms in Assam and East Bengal were in dread of it. No one knew when its rulers would come swooping down from the hills to raid and plunder, to maim and kill and carry off everything they could, including men and women whom they kept or sold as slaves. Even the kings of Shyllong and Sutnga had to keep their borders well guarded.

But it was with Sutnga that the conflicts and battles were most frequent, owing to its proximity to the Madur Maskut capital of Thangkhri. The cause was mostly Madur Maskut's incursions into Sutnga villages to loot and plunder. And they were at their worst during the reign of Kyllong Raja, U Syiem Sait Snier, the most powerful of Madur Maskut kings, because they were carried out by his warriors in roving bands as well by him on his own.

Kyllong was a huge man—tall as a bamboo pole, they said, and wide as a banyan tree. His body was packed with muscles made iron-hard in battle. Being the descendant of a nymph, he was also a handsome man with radiant good looks and an unusually fair complexion. Women were very fond of him, as he was of them. Indeed, he was too fond of women, and that was the cause of his eventual downfall.

Although Kyllong was a king, he did not spend much time in his palace. Blessed with the strength of a hundred warriors and the skill to match, he thought it was a waste of time to spend his days managing administrative matters, sometimes as petty as the quarrels between neighbours. He mostly left governance to his young nephew, Mailong, and his able ministers and elders. He only came home to take stock of things and then quickly left on more raids. On these incursions, he went alone, for he required no help, except for porters to carry his loot. He usually took his sword and shield and a long spear, while his porters only carried bows and arrows and never entered the fray, except to shoot from a distance. When he returned, Kyllong invariably brought back gold, silver and women, some of whom he kept as mistresses, despite having a lawfully wedded wife.

He was a terror to his neighbours, especially the state of Sutnga, which was closer to home for him. The Pnars tried many times to trap and kill him, but without success. It was true that, once or twice, he was in a tight spot, or badly cut up, but always Kyllong would escape, and return to loot and plunder.

One night, the Pnars succeeded in capturing him. While he was resting in a wooded spot after plundering a Sutnga village, thousands of them came, surrounded the place, and tried to kill him. Though hundreds died in the fight, the Pnars managed to overpower him, and hacked him to death. That night, they left for their homes singing and chanting. In the morning, however, Kyllong was seen burning more than a dozen Sutnga villages as revenge for what the Pnars had done. From then on, the Pnars fled whenever they saw him, convinced he was a monster, not a man.

This was when Markusaiñ, the king of Sutnga, summoned the state council to discuss Kyllong Raja's incursions. After lengthy deliberations, everybody agreed that the only way to fight him was to find out how he had been able to return to life after being hacked to pieces. But how were they to pry out his most precious secret from him? It was one of the elders who finally came up with a suggestion. 'We know that this man, this monster, has one weakness,' he said. 'He is a notorious womaniser. Whenever he raids our villages, he carries off the most beautiful women he can find and keeps them as mistresses. When he tires of them, he sells them off. We also know he has several non-Khasi concubines in Shilot and Damera in Nagaon. This, it seems, is his greatest weakness. So why don't we find the most beautiful woman in our hima and convince her to become his lover?'

Markusaiñ was sceptical. 'How are we to convince the woman?' he asked. 'How are we to persuade her to sacrifice her chastity and perhaps her life for something that does not directly affect her?'

Undeterred, the elder said, 'We could talk to her about patriotism and the need to protect our people from the onslaughts of this terrible fiend. We should certainly offer her wealth, or whatever she wants, and if all else fails, we could resort to blackmail, perhaps even hinting that her family will be in danger if she doesn't do it.'

The rest of the council agreed with the elder, which forced Markusaiñ to relent. 'Alright, we'll do that,' he said, 'but there will be no blackmail. If we find such a woman, we'll convince her that her sacrifice is for the country, and that she will be rewarded for her deed with our gratitude and all the wealth that she wants. But if she is not willing, no one should force her. I suggest that headmen start looking for such a woman in their villages immediately.'

The search for the most beautiful woman in the country, who would also be willing to sacrifice everything for the sake of her people, began in earnest and lasted for a long time, but find her they did, in a village called Shangpung. Her name was Ka Phuh Langbang, 'the blooming one'. She was indeed in the full bloom of youth, and her beauty was beyond description. Think of a sunny spring morning, think of the black-eyed-bloom orchid, think of clear skies, crystal waters and a fragrant breeze, it was said, and you might have an idea of her immaculate beauty and her fresh, natural grace.

The king of Sutnga directed the women of his household to dress her as a princess and to give her the best of everything. The women made her wear a blouse of satiny white silk, a jympien undergarment of the same material, topped with glossy silk jaiñsem of the deepest red, and a checked shawl of black and gold. On top of all that, they gave her gold necklaces, lockets and bracelets. When they were done, even the king fell in love with her and had second thoughts about sending her to Kyllong Raja.

After Phuh had been adequately trained to behave like a princess, she was escorted to Ïew Die Ja on a market day when Kyllong was around. She was accompanied by two servants, a woman and a man. Phuh caused quite a stir with her beauty and the splendour of her dress and ornaments. She was introduced to people as a distant cousin of the king of Sutnga, fleeing from his unwelcome attentions. Everywhere she went, eyes followed her in admiration, lust and envy. The women admired and envied her; the men lusted after her. Kyllong's spies saw her and fetched the king to the market as soon as they could.

When Kyllong Raja saw her, he was immediately struck by her loveliness. There she was, towering over most people in the market. The black curls of her long hair seemed to dance as she moved her head, talking to sellers, laughing and flashing her even white teeth. Her eyes were dark as the night, her lashes long and curly, her nose straight and sharp, her lips neither too thin nor too full, and her face, the colour of peach blossoms, seemed to glow like the sunrise, set off as it was by her gold ornaments and the combination of white blouse and maroon jaiñsem. 'Whose daughter or granddaughter could she be?' Kyllong wondered as he watched her. He was not exactly awestruck by her beauty, being the kind of man he was, but he yearned to have her in his arms, and his yearning was an ache.

Kyllong asked his servant to bring her to his retreat in a village not far from the capital. It was there that he kept most of his concubines. He would have gone to speak to her himself, right there in the marketplace, but appearances had to be kept up, for he was the king after all, and the people should not see him openly courting beautiful women in public places. What they heard and what they knew were two separate things. At no time should he disrespect his *mahadei* (a title given to a king's wife) or his people by flaunting his romantic liaisons openly.

When Phuh was brought to him, and when she looked him full in the face like the princess she was supposed to be, his heart went wild with excitement. She was not only extraordinarily beautiful; she was also fresh and unsullied. That he could tell immediately. His servant introduced him to her as the king of Madur Maskut. He watched her reaction closely; she was not awed. She smiled warmly and even looked a little amused. 'It is true then, what they are saying,' Kyllong told himself. 'She is used to royalty. She must really be the distant cousin of the syiem of Sutnga, as my spies have told me.'

Phuh greeted the king by taking his right hand in both her hands and said, 'Khublei, Pa'iem, I'm much honoured to have an audience with you. I hope you don't mind my coming to your hima like this; I had to. I'm running away from my distant cousin, the syiem of Sutnga—'

'Your name is?' Kyllong interrupted her.

'My name is Ka Phuh, from the family of Ka Libon Phawa and U Krot Syiem, may he eat betel nut in the house of God; I'm his youngest daughter.'

'And yet you had to run away, why is that?'

'The syiem of Sutnga has been paying me unwanted attention, Pa'iem. My mother gave me what she could and asked me to run away to your hima. She said it was not right for the syiem, married as he was, to court his own cousin.'

'And aren't you afraid someone might do the same here too, beautiful as you are?'

'I seek your protection, Pa'iem. If you should give it, who would dare do that against my will?'

'What if it is I?'

'Pa'iem?' Phuh said, pretending to be confused, but when Kyllong repeated his question, she said, 'Pa'iem, everyone has heard of your great fame. I'm one of your admirers—'

'And I'm not your distant cousin, nor as ugly as him,' Kyllong said. 'Now tell me more about your family's enmity with the syiem of Sutnga. I heard the king's men killed your father?'

'Yes, Pa'iem. My father was a very popular warrior in Sutnga. The king feared he could be a rival to the throne. And now that he's no more, he's trying to persecute us further.'

'Alright, Kong Phuh,' Kyllong said, 'you may live in one of my houses in the village. My servant will take you there. You are free to move about and travel where you please. I'm only too happy to grant refuge to the daughter of U Krot Syiem.'

After she had left, Kyllong asked his men to investigate her story. Everybody knew about Krot Syiem and how he had been killed at the behest of the king of Sutnga, but Kyllong wanted to make sure that Phuh was really his daughter.

The report came one week after Phuh's interview with Kyllong. It confirmed her story to the letter.

Kyllong, of course, did not wait for the report. Having had Phuh's acceptance at the first meeting, he spent almost every night with her, to the envy of all his other concubines. Kyllong had known many women, Khasis and non-Khasis. And all his women were beautiful, but no one was quite like Phuh. Not only was she the most beautiful of them all, and the youngest, but she was also the most loving and the least demanding. She seemed to understand his every mood. Phuh was sweet. She was caring; she was playful;

she was sympathetic; she was sensual: and all of it accorded with his humour of the moment.

Soon, he began to neglect his other concubines and spent all his free time with her. Even when he travelled up and down the state, he took her along. He never left her alone except when he went off on one of his incursions. He even found himself confiding in her and discussing political problems with her. And always she would surprise him with clever and sensible suggestions.

What endeared Phuh most to him was the fact that she never seemed to want anything for herself. It was as if she had made his pleasure and needs her only purpose in life. Eventually, he, who had never loved any woman before, and to whom a woman was a mere plaything, grew to love her genuinely, deeply.

Indeed, he doted on her and offered her anything she might care for. But she wanted nothing beyond his love and attention. Her only fear in life was losing him. She seemed haunted by that fear, and as time passed, she began to speak about it more and more often.

One night, almost two years after she had met him, while they were lying in bed, she suddenly crooned, 'Oh, my dearest love, my precious Pa'iem, what would I do if something were to happen to you? How am I to live when I love you so much?'

'Why, what would happen to me?' he asked, surprised.

'Anything could happen to you, my love. You are forever going on these raids, and all alone too, accompanied only by porters! Do you think I do not worry? When you leave me and go to fight in distant lands, I cannot eat, I cannot sleep. Have you thought what will happen to me if, God forbid, someone should slash you with a sword or shoot you with an arrow? The mahadei, your wife, will give me to her dogs. Or the other women will, who blame me when you neglect them. I'm the unhappiest woman on earth, worrying about these things all the time.'

Kyllong took her in his arms and said, 'Come here, you foolish girl. Nobody will kill me, not in peace, not in war, so stop your foolishness and let us enjoy ourselves.'

But Phuh pulled away from him. She said, 'It's so easy for you to joke about it, my love, but think about me. It would be alright if I didn't love you so much, I could joke about it too, but unfortunately, my heart is inextricably entwined with yours. When you live so dangerously, I shiver all the time.'

'I'm not joking, my dearest,' Kyllong assured her. 'I said nobody will kill me because nobody can.'

'What are you saying, Pa'iem? Anybody can be killed, so why not you?'

'Why, haven't you heard the story of how the warriors of Sutnga captured me one night and cut my body into little pieces? In fact, they threw pieces of my flesh into a gully, thinking they were done with me, but in the morning I was there, in front of their houses, burning their homes. Nobody can kill me, my love. Stop worrying and let's be happy together.'

'My dearest love, of course I have heard the story, who hasn't? But do you seriously think I would believe a thing like that? I have been with you for almost two years, and I know that, despite your great strength, you are only flesh and blood like anybody else. So please don't tease me with these tales of immortality, my love.'

'But it is the truth, my dearest Phuh, I swear to you on the great love I bear for you, nobody can kill me, stop worrying.'

But Phuh worried and fretted. She sat up in bed, holding her head in her hands, and began to cry. Through her tears, she said, 'How can you ask me to believe in such a thing? If I take a knife and cut your skin, will you not bleed? And if you bleed, how can you not die? I worry, my love, not only about you, but about myself too. You know very well what my position would be without you! Maybe you don't know this, but I worry so much about us that, when I get up in the morning, the first thing I do is pray to God and the last thing I do, before I sleep, is pray to him again, asking him to always, always keep you safe.'

Moved by the great love she had for him, Kyllong took her in his arms once again and said, 'If I tell you a secret, will you keep it to yourself, come what may?'

'Why, what are you saying, my love, haven't your secrets been my secrets all this time?'

'Now, be serious,' Kyllong said. 'What I am about to tell you is a secret like no other. It concerns my very own life! You have to swear to me that, even under pain of torture, you would never reveal it to anyone.'

Phuh took Kyllong's face in her hands and looked straight into his eyes. 'You can trust me with your life,' she said. 'I swear it! What am I without you? What life do I have without your life?'

It was on that fateful night that Kyllong told Ka Phuh Langbang a secret he had not even shared with his mother. He said, 'When I was an infant, a nymph, my ancestress, appeared to my mother in her dream and said she would bless her son with great powers. "Your son will be big and strong," she said, "but even more, he will be immortal, until and unless the secret of his life force is revealed to his enemies. For that reason, this secret cannot be revealed even to you. When he grows up, he will know what to do." So saying, the nymph vanished. My mother told no one about the dream, not even my father. She told me about it when I was about ten years old and warned me not to reveal it to anyone else …'

Here Kyllong paused for a long time, remembering his mother's words. Phuh did not say anything at all, afraid to even utter a word. Finally, Kyllong gave a deep sigh and ploughed on: 'It was when I was fifteen that I realised where my life force lies. From that time, I have been taking care of them very carefully, washing them every morning before I do anything else. But even that needs a lot of secrecy. I had to look for a really secure place. With that in mind, one morning, I went for a long walk in the woods until I came to a stream with a clear pool in it. It was there that I first started cleaning them. I still do that, which is why I always leave you at the third cockcrow—'

'What are you talking about, Pa'iem, my love?'

Kyllong opened his shirt, exposing his stomach, and said, 'Do you see this line running from the base of my chest to my hip? You have always taken it for a battle scar, but it is not. I use it to open my stomach and wash my intestines. It is there that my power lies. Unless my enemies can cut them into pieces and destroy them completely, I will always come back to life, even if killed.'

'My God, Pa'iem, washing your intestines! But that's a dangerous thing! Supposing, God forbid, your enemies happen upon you as you are cleaning them and strike you with a sword or a knife or a spear, right at that moment when you are completely helpless, won't you fall and die on the spot? I do fear for you, my love, what if such a thing should happen?'

'You need not fear, my little Phuh, nobody knows where I do it, and besides, a thing like that cannot kill me; the intestines have to be destroyed completely.'

'It still sounds very risky to me. Are you certain no one knows about the place where you clean them? Where do you do it, exactly? You mean the source of the stream flowing through the village? But that's a very lonely spot, my love, supposing people follow you and find you there, washing your intestines, all alone and helpless … It's terrible, even thinking about it.'

'That's the place, my darling, but don't worry, it's still dark at the third cockcrow, nobody will come. And they would have no reason to: the woods are sacred, access to them is strictly forbidden. Anyway, there are only two people who know about my secret: you and I. What is there to worry about? Come here now; we have done enough talking for one night.'

At last, Ka Phuh had discovered what she had come for. She waited till Kyllong had gone on one of his incursions before sending her servant with explicit instructions to one of the Sutnga spies living in Jowai. The servant was instructed to return as soon as possible so he would not be missed. Having done her job, she waited for Kyllong's return with bated breath and, at times, copious tears. She had done her duty, but a part of her wanted them not to succeed. Kyllong had loved her above all else in the world; she doubted she would ever find another like him. But the deed was done. She had been true to her country, though being true to it had also killed a part of her, the most important part, as it turned out.

Having got what they wanted, at long last, 600 of the hardiest warriors of Sutnga kept a daily watch at the pool where Kyllong washed his intestines. Finally, the day came when Kyllong returned from his incursions and visited the place. He took off his clothes and revealed a body corded with muscles. Despite themselves, the men of Sutnga were filled with wonder that such a man walked the face of the earth. There he was, tall as a pine tree and shaggy as a bear! And they shivered to a man, for Kyllong exuded raw power, and they avoided looking into his eyes, for his gaze, it was said, could transfix people like a cat can do to a mouse. They took large sips from their gourds of rice spirit to steel their nerves and whispered to each other that everyone should rush him at the same time when the moment came.

Kyllong looked all around once before entering the pool. But his survey was quite cursory, for he suspected nothing. The place had always been safe for him, and he had no reason to think it should not be so that morning. Sitting on a half-submerged stone by the side of the pool, he opened his stomach and began washing his intestines. As he was bent over his task, the warriors of Sutnga crept forward, and when they reached the clearing near the pool, they rushed towards him, yelling at the top of their lungs to drown out the fear that was threatening to overwhelm them. Kyllong heard them, but he was quite helpless: his stomach was open and his intestines exposed. He could not even stand up to defend himself. He could only utter one last cry: 'That I love a woman, forgive me, Mother!' The Sutngas attacked him with swords and spears, beginning with the neck and the head. When they had knocked him senseless, they severed his head, took out the entrails, cut them into pieces, put them in a sack and left the place for their own territory.

Later, they fed the pieces of entrails to the dogs. And that was how Kyllong Raja the Mighty, the King Who Washed His Intestines, met his end.

When news of his murder became known, there was universal mourning in the state of Madur Maskut. But even as the pieces of flesh from Kyllong's body were collected, Mailong wisely took measures to secure all the borders of the state and prevent potential enemies, especially the Sutngas, from taking advantage of the situation. Then, the remains of Kyllong Raja were cremated with all the rites befitting a great king. And when the mourning period of three days was over, Mailong Raja, his youthful nephew, was formally crowned the new king of Madur Maskut.

Meanwhile, since nobody knew Kyllong's secret, there were no suspicions of foul play. Phuh, being now unwelcome in Madur Maskut, had the perfect excuse to leave. She returned home to a heroine's welcome and was given all that had been promised to her: wealth, property, and men and women to serve her every need. But there was no rejoicing for her; her heart had turned to stone. She is said to have led a very secluded life, living alone in her new home with her servants, meeting no one and going out nowhere. She died a year after that—from self-imposed starvation.

Magdalene was crying again when I concluded the story. 'It's so bloody sad, ya!' she offered as an excuse.

'Yeah, no, Kong?' Dale, also teary-eyed, agreed.

But Hamkom, being from Ri Pnar, laughed loudly and said, 'Ka Phuh was like Mata Hari, no?'

Donald, one arm around Magdalene, said, 'Do you believe Kyllong had that kind of magical power and that he could really wash his intestines, Bah Ap?'

'Kyllong Raja was a historical figure. That he existed and was a hulk of a man is true. That he had great strength and great skills as a warrior are also true. All the stories point to that. It is also true that the Sutngas had mortally wounded him several times, and that he somehow survived to exact terrible vengeance afterwards. The bit about his life force and his intestines are probably part of the legend that grew around him.'

'And Ka Phuh?' Magdalene wanted to know.

'That's also true. He did fall because of her treachery.'

'But how was the hima itself destroyed?' Bah Kynsai asked. 'You did say it disintegrated in the fifteenth century, na?'

'The destruction of the state of Madur Maskut took place afterwards, Bah Kynsai, during Mailong Raja's reign,' Bah Kit said.

I agreed. 'But it was not immediately after the death of Kyllong Raja. The state was still strong then. After Kyllong's death, the Sutngas did launch attacks against it but were driven away each time with heavy casualties. If anything, the state became even more powerful under Mailong's able leadership.'

'If it was so formidable, na, why didn't they avenge the murder?' Bah Kynsai demanded.

'They wanted to, but they knew they could not afford an all-out war with Sutnga for fear that the state of Shyllong might take advantage of it to invade from the west. Mailong did send punitive forays into Sutnga, burning villages, destroying crops and killing all the men they could find. But he was not a warrior like Kyllong. He was a cunning statesman who paid more attention to defence than offence. However, even as he grew older and more influential, he never once forgot how cruelly the Sutngas had dealt with his uncle, chopping up his flesh as if he were an animal, not a king.'

Besides the desire for revenge, Mailong was driven by an ambition to be the greatest and most powerful king of Ri Khasi. To realise his dream, he had to destroy Sutnga first and then deal with Shyllong. Since an all-out war was not an option, he plotted and schemed with the elders who assisted him as ministers, and looked for a way to overwhelm Sutnga by subterfuge.

About ten years after the death of Kyllong, Mailong finally hit upon a good plan, or so he thought. He sent a message to the king of Sutnga, saying he was tired of the quarrel between them, which did not even have anything to do with him. 'Let us bury all our past differences and disputes,' he pleaded, 'why should we fight over a piece of land here, a piece of land there, when the plains of Ri Dkhar are open to us for invasion and conquest? If we are united at home, if we can live in peace among ourselves, the plains will soon become our rice plate to feed our citizens and enrich our himas. I, therefore, offer you a treaty of peace and friendship in the hope that we can avoid bloodshed among brothers and expand our himas to where the foreigners are. As a sign of my seriousness, I would like to invite you, your family, your dolois and provincial rulers, your basans and elders, your mars and warrior leaders, and anyone else you deem important, to a feast I will organise in Iew Die Ja in your honour and in honour of the peace and friendship that will follow our treaty. I also invite you and all your men to stay with us for a few weeks after the feast so you may have a first-hand experience of our hospitality. For our entertainment, I propose to organise a hunting trip in the jungles of Madur Maskut where you will find plenty of elephants and tigers. For the sake of lasting peace between us, I hope you will accept this offer. Please let me know your thoughts on the matter.'

Markusañ, the king of Sutnga, and his chief doloi, Salong Ked, were excited when they received this unexpected offer from Mailong. They immediately sent off a message of acceptance and summoned all the provincial rulers for a meeting in Raliang, where the king was then living. They all came to the meeting, except the doloi of Jowai, who was ill. In his place, he sent two warrior leaders and brilliant statesmen by the name of Ïang Lato and Bula Toi.

Both warriors were huge men by Khasi standards. Ïang was easily over six feet while Bula, at five feet eleven inches, was only slightly shorter. The two of them were often mistaken for brothers.

As soon as they arrived in Raliang, Ïang and Bula demanded that the meeting be held in utter secrecy to avoid word being carried back to Mailong Raja.

When the meeting had been called to order, they declared that they did not trust the intentions of the king of Madur Maskut. If he was inviting their king to come with all the provincial rulers, elders and warrior leaders, there must be some hidden motive behind it. 'We doubt very much that he has forgotten the killing of his uncle, Kyllong Raja,' they said. 'Therefore, we move that the syiem, the dolois, the elders and the mars should not respond at all to the invitation.'

Salong, the chief doloi, who was like the state's prime minister, retorted angrily, 'Who are you to contradict the decision Pa'iem and I have taken? We have already sent word to Syiem Mailong, accepting his invitation and promising to come in three weeks … Do you think it is right to violate the word of a syiem like that? As far as I'm concerned, the killing of Kyllong is in the past. If Syiem Mailong is ready to forgive and forget for the sake of peace and unity, who are you to stand in the way? If we can have peace with Hima Malngiang, our hima will prosper, for we will then be able to expand our territories towards the northern and southern plains.'

The rulers of the provinces bordering Madur Maskut realised that both arguments had merits. They said, 'What the chief doloi has stated is true. If there is peace, our hima will prosper in many ways. However, we live close to his state and so we also know Mailong very well. He is wily and untrustworthy. We believe that Ïang Lato and Bula Toi may be right, and we ask the council to consider their suggestion with an open mind. Just because the syiem and the chief doloi have given their word, it doesn't mean that the council should accept it. This is a matter of state; it is for the council to decide what is to be done.'

However, the council too felt that it would be most improper to go back on the king's word. It was suggested that the king, the provincial rulers and the warrior leaders refrain from going to the feast. Instead, the king should be replaced by a double. Other men could be asked to masquerade as the provincial rulers and warrior leaders. The rulers of the border provinces, who were known to Mailong and others in Madur Maskut, were asked to find excuses for not attending.

Accordingly, a man who resembled the king was found and brought to Raliang, while the king himself went to hide in a cave near Jowai so that the ruse would work smoothly. To this day, the cave is known as Krem Syiem, king's cave.

When the day came, about 300 people, including the fake king and several fake provincial rulers, left Raliang for the feast in Ïew Die Ja, somewhere on the Shillong–Jowai road between the villages that we now know as Mokyndur and Modymmai. They arrived at the walled town towards nightfall to find that the king of Madur Maskut had kept his word as far as the feast was concerned. Vast quantities of food and drink awaited them. There were huge pots of boiled rice, jadoh meat-rice, and a variety of meat, including beef, pork, chicken, wild fowl, goat's meat, venison and fish of many kinds, curried, boiled with vegetables and fried. Also on the menu was a dish of dried fish curried with black sesame, a favourite of the Pnars. There were also all sorts of chutneys, from pickled chillies and pickled fruits to tungtap fish, roasted and ground, and tung rymbai bean sauce.

Mailong himself greeted the fake king and his entourage. Because they had never met before, because the feasting ground was lit only by flambeaus, and because the man resembled the real king so closely, nobody realised he was a double.

The Sutngas were immediately plied with the strongest rice spirit, specially prepared for the purpose. The men of Madur Maskut, on the other hand, most of whom were warriors with weapons hidden nearby, were given drinks diluted with water. Most of the Sutngas set upon the food and drink with gusto. They were convinced by now of Mailong's good faith, for they had seen no armed men on the feasting ground, only celebrating men, women and children. Soon they became hopelessly drunk, except for some like Ïang and Bula, who had accompanied the false king so they could spy on the town and its famous fort. These few managed to stay sober by furtively pouring the rice spirit, given to them again and again, on the ground.

When the warriors of Madur Maskut saw that the Sutngas were completely drunk, they picked a quarrel with them, fetched their weapons, and then started the massacre. When Ïang and Bula and their few followers saw the warriors of Mailong hacking the feasting Sutngas right and left as if they were slaying goats, they hastily fled the scene, taking advantage of the darkness and confusion to escape towards Jowai. In the terrible commotion and chaos, nobody noticed them leaving. Ïang and Bula were followed only by the awful cries of their compatriots. Those who witnessed the massacre said they had never seen anything as horrible: severed heads flew onto wooden plates of rice, and blood spurted like fountains into rice and meat and drink. It was truly a feast of the dead.

When the last man had been despatched, Mailong gathered his warriors together and asked them to prepare for an invasion of Sutnga, to destroy it and wipe it off the face of the earth. 'Eat and rest,' he told them, 'tomorrow, at the crack of dawn, we march! Their king and dolois and dreaded mars are dead, they have no one to defend them now.'

Of course, a rude shock awaited Mailong and the men of Madur Maskut. When the bodies were examined in the morning, Mailong's spies told him that the dead were not who they were supposed to be. There was no king, no provincial chief or warrior leader among the dead, only common men masquerading as chiefs. They shivered now to think of the consequences. Abandoning their planned invasion of Sutnga, the king and all the state elders dispersed to their forts and walled towns and villages to prepare for any possible retaliation.

But the Sutngas were too shocked, and too worried about a follow-up action from Madur Maskut, to think about retaliation. When word of the massacre reached them through Ïang and Bula and the six others who had made good their escape to Jowai, the entire state was thrown into such gloom and loud lamentations that no one could think of anything but the poor souls who had died while drinking and feasting. The savagery of it shocked everyone. Amidst the universal lament, the king, Markusaiñ, vowed vengeance. But for now, it was the ruler of Jowai and his two warrior leaders who took the initiative of spreading the word among the provincial rulers, directing them to secure their borders and prepare for the worst.

When the state council of Sutnga met soon after, many provincial rulers wanted the king to prepare for immediate war. But Ïang and Bula, who had seen with their own eyes the strength of the Madur Maskut forts, advised caution. They said, 'We cannot win against them with might alone. Their forts are too strong and too well manned. Their men are too well trained and armed. If we attack the heart of their hima, their forces from the north or the south could attack us at will. We need to defeat them with cunning.'

The king asked what they had in mind. Bula replied, 'If we can take two men with us, men of rare talents, we will try to infiltrate Madur Maskut— first Ïew Die Ja and then the palace of the Malngiang syiems in Thangkhri. Once in, we will keep in touch with you and plan for the overthrow of the fort from within. But the men who come with us must be prepared to sacrifice their lives, for if discovered, our heads will roll.'

In response to Bula, Salong, the chief doloi from Raliang, stood up and said, 'We are not afraid to seek vengeance, but it won't be easy to find men whose talents are so rare that they will attract the attention of the syiem of Hima Malngiang … men who are intelligent, cunning, and above all, ready to lay down their lives. However, I agree with these brave warriors: we must begin our search immediately.'

Two brothers by the name of Tonkha and Buitkha Laloo volunteered their services. They were not only expert masons and carpenters who could build anything with wood and stone, but also smiths who could work equally well with iron, gold and silver. That was not all. Like all Khasis of their time, they were accomplished warriors, with muscles as hard as stone—the result of daily physical labour and the many battles they had fought. Unlike Ïang and Bula, Tonkha and Buitkha were handsome and had nothing of their cunning appearance, and for that reason, they were more charming and infinitely more dangerous.

The brothers were briefed about their mission and warned about what they should expect if discovered. But neither was in the least bit worried, for in their hearts, vengeance was like a raging thirst. And so, when all was ready, they left for Ïew Die Ja with Ïang Lato and Bula Toi, as their assistants.

Here I had to pause, for Donald wanted to know why it was so easy for the spies of Sutnga to enter Madur Maskut without any suspicion being raised.

I replied that, in that part of the state, the citizens were mostly Pnars, and so it was easy for them to pose as Madur Maskut citizens from some remote village. Their choice of place was perfect too. Ïew Die Ja being the most important trading centre for Madur Maskut, it was where anyone wanting work would go. In any case, they could not have gone directly to the capital in Thangkhri, for it was not so easy to get in, especially for strangers.

The brothers set up shop in Ïew Die Ja, selling iron tools, gold and silver ornaments, pieces of furniture, as well as wooden implements like ladles and spatulas. They were an immediate hit. The people of the town had never seen anyone who could do so many things equally well. The brothers were hard-working, and orders were delivered on time. Their rates were cheap, but the quality of their products was so good that soon they became the talk of the town. By and by, their reputation as quality workers and conscientious businessmen attracted the attention of the king himself.

One day, when they were in Ïew Die Ja, Mailong and some of his ministers visited the brothers' shop. Tonkha and Buitkha went out to greet them, and bowed low, saying, 'Khublei, Pa'iem, may God bless you and may he bless your noble ministers! We are humbled and honoured that you have come to our shop, please take whatever you want as a gift from us.'

Khasis do not bow to the king or anybody else. But the brothers were deliberately trying to impress him with their humility. The king was indeed pleased with their flattery. He returned their greetings magnanimously and began to examine their various creations, impressed with the extraordinary workmanship on display. As he scrutinised each one carefully, he thought, 'These fellows are not only experts in their trade but also humble and respectful. I like them; I think they would be good for us.' There and then, he made them an offer: 'How would you like to become the official smiths at the king's palace?'

The brothers were thrilled. In a grateful tone, they said, 'This is an honour beyond anything we could have dreamt of, Pa'iem. An offer from you is a command for us. However, kindly allow us some time to sell off the shop. If you permit us, we will come as soon as we have settled our business here, Pa'iem.'

The brothers sold their business in Ïew Die Ja and moved to Thangkhri. They trekked down a steep and densely wooded path, thousands of feet into the Sung valley. When they got to the bottom, this being autumn, they were greeted by golden rice fields everywhere. As far as the eyes could see, rice stalks, heavy with ripening grains, waved at them in the breeze. Among the low hills, here and there, they could see huts and green vegetable fields. They stopped in their tracks.

'What an incredibly beautiful place this is!' Bula exclaimed in sheer amazement. 'And incredibly fertile too! No wonder the hima of Madur Maskut is so rich and powerful.'

Ïang agreed. 'This land is worth fighting for. Imagine, all this will be ours if we succeed in our mission!'

They stood at the foothills, scanning the valley. 'It's an extraordinarily deep and wide valley,' Tonkha observed. Shading his eyes with his right hand and looking towards the northern plain, he said, 'I think I can just see Thangkhri from here, do you see that hill, the one that seems to be dotted with trees? That's Thangkhri, I think, and those must be the houses. How far do you think it is? Six pieces of betel nut?'

His brother Buitkha said it could be, and then said something that quite startled the two warrior leaders, Ïang and Bula. 'But you know what I'm wondering about? Why is all this left unguarded?'

After thinking about it for a while, Ïang said, 'I think I know why. This path leads directly from Ïaw Dai Ja, which is a walled town, that's why. You cannot access it from anywhere else.'

Bula said, 'No, Ïang, it can be done. Warriors can bypass the fort at Ïaw Dai Ja, climb down the wooded slopes—'

'But the slopes are sheer, and it has to be done at night, Bu,' Ïang said. 'Do you think it can be done in the dark, without flambeaus?'

'By trained woodsmen, yes,' Bula insisted, 'and we have plenty of those from the War regions.'

'But they cannot win a war by themselves, can they?'

'What about the western and northern sides of the valley?' Buitkha asked.

'The western side is a no-go zone,' Bula replied. 'It's Shyllong territory. On the northern flank bordering our Nartiang province, there are three forts. However, if they leave the forests unguarded at night like this and watch only the approach lanes, our warriors could easily creep in and slip into Thangkhri, if we manage to open the gates from inside. That's something we'll have to find out. Come, come, let's see what the place is like.'

They walked along a well-trodden path towards the capital town. Near the capital, they had a good view of the fort, and were struck with wonder. It was quite large, a little bigger than Ïew Die Ja, with about 400 houses within its high walls. But it was the breathtaking beauty of the setting, much more magnificent than Ïew Die Ja, that impressed them. The houses, though roofed with thatch as elsewhere, were made of timber and planks, and painted white or red or black with natural dyes, a thing unheard of among the Khasis in those days. Nor were the roofs made in the shape of a carapace as in other Khasi villages. These houses had a double roof, perhaps influenced by the style of architecture prevalent in the Malngiang territories in the plains.

The fort was built on a sprawling plateau about 500 cubits high and covered an area so large that it would take nearly half a day to traverse it. There were trees everywhere on the hill slopes, and they could see at least two little streams flowing down into the rice fields. But near the plateau itself, all the trees had been cut down and replaced with sharp wooden stakes. Only two pathways led into the fort, one from the east, another from the north. When the four of them took the eastern pathway, paved with granite blocks, they found that the fort was surrounded by deep trenches with sharp wooden stakes at the bottom. The only way in was via a land bridge connecting the pathway with the entrance. The fort itself was constructed with strong oak poles, about one cubit in diameter and thirty cubits in height, and solid stone blocks. The portions near the gates were made of stone; the rest of it was made of oak poles driven deep into the ground. The tops of the poles had sharp edges, and as the group studied the stockade, they saw sentries pacing near them.

'You see, Tonkha, these people cannot be defeated with military might alone,' Bula remarked.

Just then, the sentries called out a challenge and they had to identify themselves quickly. When they told the sentries their names and purpose, the gate—also made of oak poles held together by stout logs hammered into them with wooden pegs—was dragged open by three armed men and pushed back in place as soon as they entered. Once inside, they saw how the sentries were able to walk near the top of the stone-and-wood wall. Built alongside it was a wooden platform about twenty-five cubits high. This not only strengthened the wall but also served as a walkway around the rampart, standing on which the defenders could shoot arrows or sling stone missiles at possible attackers. The spies looked at each other and shook their heads in wonder. By comparison, their forts were primitive works indeed! They did have strong forts of wood and stone, but nothing as elaborate or as sturdy as this. 'This would be impregnable!' they whispered to each other.

In Thangkhri, the Sutnga warriors quickly made themselves popular. All of them were hard-working, sincere, outgoing and friendly, and were always ready to help anyone with anything. They soon became the most trusted handymen in all the town. The king's family liked them, for they were always making things for them with gold and silver. They were also very friendly with the guards manning the palace and the fort gates, and often gifted them gold and silver ornaments to take to their wives or female relatives. Soon, they were able to move in and out of the fort without restrictions, except at night, when the gates were closed. Nevertheless, they made sure never to venture out together so as to not arouse suspicion. If one of them was outside the fort, the others were always inside, busy with their work.

It was in this way that they were able to send word to the ruler of Nartiang, the Sutnga province closest to the Madur Maskut capital, about the fort of Thangkhri. They met spies posing as fruit sellers and merchants, and told them all about the fort: the number of warriors present at any given time, the number of guards at the palace and manning the gates. They also reported details about the guards' roster, where they slept, where they kept their weapons, and how many actually stayed up throughout the night. More importantly, the four warriors told the spies that the woods outside the fort were unguarded and that Sutnga warriors could easily slip into them at night, provided they avoided the farmers' huts that dotted the length and breadth of the Sung. The ruler of Nartiang passed on all their messages to the king at Raliang.

Tonkha, Buitkha, Ïang and Bula spent several months in Thangkhri. Finally, when they had won the complete trust of the king and his guards, and when they had learnt everything there was to learn about the place, they sent word through the spies about their readiness to act.

Meanwhile, the Sutngas had infiltrated the forts of Lyrnai, Maskut and Ïew Die Ja. When every one of their people was ready, they sent word to Thangkhri, enquiring about the best time to launch an attack on it. Thangkhri must be the first to go, they said, since it was not only the capital but also the strongest of the Madur Maskut forts.

The spies in Thangkhri waited for Mailong to go on one of his tours with his chosen warriors before sending a message to the king of Sutnga. They told him that Mailong had left for the fort of Madur to the east and would be staying there for fifteen days or so. The king then set a date for the attack. He said the best of his warriors would be hiding in the woods near the fort by midnight. The duty of the four warriors was to find a way to get at least a few of the Sutnga men inside so that the gates could be opened and maximum confusion created in the town. The same was being done at the forts in Lyrnai, Maskut and Ïew Die Ja.

Tonkha, Buitkha, Ïang and Bula devised a plan that would get the Sutnga warriors inside. They sent word to the king that at least fifty warriors should carry a large piece of meat with them. As for themselves, they already knew what to do.

On the day of the attack, Tonkha announced that he had come down with dysentery and showed the palace guards spots of blood staining his thighs. Lifting his dhoti, he groaned, 'Look at this … and there's such a terrible pain in my stomach!'

The guards took pity on Tonkha and reported the matter to the minister in charge of the fort, who straightaway ordered that Tonkha not be allowed to relieve himself in the communal pit inside the town. That day, Tonkha went outside the fort several times, ostensibly to go to the woods nearby for his business. Towards evening, he complained that his illness was getting worse and that he was too weak to go out alone. The guards, who were his friends, allowed his brother, Buitkha, to accompany him. Soon Tonkha and Buitkha were going out so frequently that the guards complained: 'We are tired of opening and closing the gate for you. We'll just leave it open and rest in the hut. Let us know when you are finally done. But also, watch out for any suspicious movement anywhere. We don't think it's likely, but you never know.'

The guards opened the gate and retired to the guards' hut nearby to rest with their sleeping colleagues. The brothers had their chance. They went out several times, and each time they returned, they smuggled in some warriors, who were immediately led to a safe hiding place by Ïang and Bula, who were waiting nearby. Ïang and Bula appeased the dogs that were loitering about by asking the warriors to feed them the meat they were carrying. The dogs did make some noise, fighting over the meat, but who was interested in the quarrels of dogs?

Once fifty warriors were inside the fort, they attacked the guards' hut, first killing the four guards who were warming themselves by the fire and then cutting the throats of all the others who were sleeping. A signal was sent to the other warriors, who poured in through the unguarded gate and spread out soundlessly to every part of the town like black shadows of death. The guards manning the other gate of the fort, equally unsuspecting, were quickly overpowered, and then the palace guards, who were fooled by the familiar sight of Tonkha and Buitkha, were also quickly dealt with. After the gate and palace guards had fallen, the attack began in earnest. The Sutnga warriors let out terrible war cries as they began entering houses and attacked the sleeping men. Their shrieks alerted the king's family, who, realising what was happening, gathered up their gold and silver and fled the place through a secret passageway. But the capital's inhabitants were not so lucky. The Sutnga warriors plundered their belongings, killed any man they could find and spared none but women and little children.

But the reputation of Thangkhri as the sturdiest fort of its time was not for nothing. The gate and palace guards had fallen because of treachery. Initially, the citizens were taken by surprise and many were butchered in their sleep. But soon, they rallied. These were hardy men, scarred and battle-hardened, who had fought everywhere: in the hills, in the woods, and the faraway northern and southern plains of Ri Dkhar. They grabbed whatever weapons they could find and organised themselves into small bands to engage the Sutngas in every lane and every corner of the town. Soon, there were pitched battles everywhere. The defenders were fighting not only for their lives but also for their families—their women and children. They hit back with all the force of desperation and, in many places, got the upper hand and either slaughtered the Sutngas or made them flee for their lives.

Heartened by these victories, they shouted encouragement to other defenders saying, 'Hey ho, brothers of the flesh! Hey ho, brothers of the blood! Don't give up! We have slain all the Sutnga dogs here; we are coming to help you! Fight, brothers of the country, fight, brothers of the clan, fight as you have never fought before, we will make mincemeat of these animals yet!'

And they would have done that too, but for more Sutnga warriors pouring in from the Nartiang borders after their compatriots had laid siege to the Madur Maskut forts in that part of the state. When the defenders saw themselves hopelessly outnumbered, they were forced to surrender, although here and there were fighters who fought to the death, each taking four or five enemies with him. At last, Thangkhri fell, its streets awash with the blood of defenders and invaders alike. The town had exacted a terrible toll on the Sutngas too, who lost hundreds of warriors and warrior leaders, the finest they had. Also dead were the four spies, whom the defenders specially sought out.

When the fighting was finally over, the Sutngas herded all the survivors outside and burnt the fort to the ground. The fire from burning Thangkhri was seen from the highland forts of Lyrnai, Maskut and Ïew Die Ja. When the sentries in these forts raised the alarm, people went up the ramparts to look and wonder at what could have happened to their capital. In the panic and confusion, nobody noticed the Sutnga spies opening the gates and letting in warriors who had been hiding in the woods nearby. A hard-fought battle ensued in these forts too, until the Madur Maskut men were finally overwhelmed and had to surrender.

The Sutngas burnt these forts as well to the ground. Mailong saw the fires from Madur. He rushed in that direction, but was ambushed on the way by

2,000 or more Sutnga warriors. He had only a few hundred men with him, and though they fought hard to save their king, they were wiped out almost to the last man. At the end of the battle, the Sutngas found themselves with only 800 survivors. Angered by the death of so many of their friends, they dragged Mailong into their midst and beheaded him there and then. His head was stuck on a pole and taken in procession to Markusaiñ, the king of Sutnga.

Soon afterwards, the fort of Madur surrendered and was burnt to the ground like the others. And that was the end of Hima Madur Maskut, the greatest of the Khasi states, for many, many years. Its territories in the plains declared their independence, while the Sutngas tried to seize its provinces in the hills. They were, however, thwarted in their attempt by the king of Shyllong, who came with thousands of his fiercest warriors to demand his share of the state of Madur Maskut.

Markusaiñ, his provincial rulers and surviving warrior leaders did not like this one little bit. The Khynriam king had not done anything to deserve a share in the division of Madur Maskut. He had not fought any battles; he had not lost a single man. How could he come and demand a share of the vanquished state? But there he was, waiting with his warriors, ready to take his share by force should the Sutngas be unwilling to negotiate. The Sutngas knew this. They had just fought the bloodiest war in the history of their state. About three-quarters of their warriors and warrior leaders were dead. Those who had survived were too weak and exhausted to do any fighting. The sight of thousands of warriors hovering over them like ravenous vultures, willing them to make a false move, was truly intimidating. After a lengthy discussion among themselves, they sent word to the king of Shyllong, agreeing to a peaceful negotiation.

The outcome was that the Khynriam-inhabited areas of Madur Maskut went to Shyllong, while those inhabited by Pnars went to Sutnga. Thus, the western part of the Sung valley, where the capital of Madur Maskut once stood, went to Shyllong, while the eastern part went to Sutnga. The Ri Bhoi and Ri War areas were likewise divided equally between the two states, keeping natural boundaries in mind. And these divisions, done in the fifteenth century, were later recognised by the British when they established a new district, within Assam, which they in their ignorance called the Khasi-Jaiñtia Hills.

No one interrupted me while I was telling the story. They seemed riveted, and perhaps they found it hard to believe that such ghastly things could happen among our own people.

Now, Bah Kynsai said: 'Perhaps it was a good thing, after all, that the British came among us and stopped that kind of bloody infighting, na?'

Evening, forgetting that he had hailed the British as do-gooders earlier, hotly opposed him. 'How is it a good thing, Bah Kynsai, when they imposed the Bengali name of Jaiñtia on us and brought about the most damaging division between us?'

Bah Su and Bah Kit agreed with Evening. Bah Su added, 'But imagine what would have happened if the two himas had clashed at that time! It would have been quite a different history for our people, no? I think we are very lucky that both the syiems showed such maturity and decided to negotiate in peace—'

'I don't think it was maturity, Bah Su, the Sutngas had no choice, remember?' Donald corrected him.

'But the Malngiang kings of Madur Maskut were not very attractive, no, Bah Kynsai?' Hamkom commented. 'I mean, one was a tyrant, the other was treacherous, no?'

'What do you expect, man, after all, they came from a pig, na?'

'Careful, Bah Kynsai,' I warned him, 'there are still some Malngiang kings around.'

'Where?' Donald asked

'I told you that Mailong's family escaped, didn't I? Among them was the family of Mailong's sister, the queen mother. They fled west and later became the rulers of the state of Mawsynram.'

'Mawsynram is in?'

'Western East Khasi Hills, mə, lih,' Bah Kynsai said.

Magdalene did not think the Malngiang kings were detestable. 'I don't agree with you at all, Ham, Bah Kynsai … I think Kyllong Raja was a wonderful lover. He may have been a frightening warrior, but he was true and gentle to Phuh.'

'I agree with you, Mag, you are quite right,' Evening said. 'He found someone he could really love, and he was completely faithful to her. And I don't condemn his so-called tyrannical deeds either, ha, he was a man with supernatural powers, it would have been the most natural thing for him to harass his enemies in that way. The Sutngas, on the other hand, were quite treacherous and repulsive.'

Donald said, 'I still want to know about the states of Shyllong and Sutnga, Bah Ap. You said they were wary of each other, but did they ever fight?'

'Never a full-scale war, for that would have been mutually destructive,' I replied. 'They engaged in skirmishes often enough. There is an account of the army of Sutnga invading Shyllong under the command of U Ksan Nangbah.

But neither the date of the invasion nor the reasons for it are known today. Why did the king of Sutnga send his army on such a bloody and risky errand? We only know that Ksan took his massive army west towards the Shyllong territories, intending to march up to the capital town of Nongkseh in the western suburbs of contemporary Upper Shillong. On the way, he seized towns and villages and forts, killing and plundering as he went. It was only at the fort of Nongjrong that he was checked. Nongjrong, as you know, is a village some kilometres from the present Shillong–Jowai road.

'The people of Nongjrong held off the army of Ksan, numbering in thousands, for months. The Sutngas tried every trick to overcome them, but without success. The village was on top of a hill and was well defended. The people of Nongjrong tied huge boulders with stout creepers and dangled them from the hilltop on all sides. When the Sutngas rushed to attack their fort, they cut the creepers and the boulders rolled down the slopes with terrifying speed, killing and maiming hundreds of warriors at a time. Each boulder was like a scythe cutting through rice stalks. Added to this onslaught were arrows that rained down on the Sutngas like a death-dealing swarm. Finally, when they had suffered too many casualties without injuring a single Nongjrong man, Ksan decided to change tactics. His men surrounded the village, intending to starve it out. Unfortunately for him, Nongjrong had fertile fields around it, and the crops had just been harvested when his army got there. When there was no sign of the village surrendering, even after several months, he left it to itself and proceeded west towards Nongkseh.

'Village after village fell to the might of his army. But when he reached a place called Law Jynriew, at the time a dense jungle, as its name implies, he was met by the army of Shyllong, led by a commander-in-chief called U Bor. A fierce battle took place right there, on what is now the Shillong–Jowai road, and eventually reached the village of Laitkor. The battle lasted for the better part of the day without any clear sign of victory on either side. But towards evening, Ksan and his warriors inflicted very heavy casualties on Bor's army, which became so demoralised that it was about to disperse and take flight. Just at that moment, reinforcements arrived from the Ri War areas under the command of an able warrior, whom we only know as U Nongrum, his clan name. The War warriors, still fresh and hungry for combat, rushed forward in a solid shield wall, their spears raised for throwing or jabbing. Foot by foot, they pushed back the Sutngas, who tried in vain to attack them with their swords. Many Sutngas perished as they were speared in the ribs or the neck or the stomach, making the ground slippery with blood and spilt entrails.

Meanwhile, the War archers, famous for their nimbleness, climbed trees and hillsides and let fly at the enemy with their arrows. The fierceness of their attack forced the Sutngas to flee, pursued hotly by the Shyllong fighters, who hacked them down like goats and cattle. In the end, only a small number of the invading army escaped with their lives.

'But the Shyllong army had also suffered terrible losses. Even their commander-in-chief had been slain in the battle. Nevertheless, it was a decisive victory, and the king of Shyllong and his ministers planted monoliths on the spot in memory of the fallen heroes. One of them— dedicated to the memory of the commander-in-chief, and known as Maw Ïap U Bor, the death stone of Bor—still exists. If you sit by the stone in the evening, you have a fantastic view of Shillong, with the lights coming on one by one to illuminate the city and make it sparkle like millions of fireflies on the wing.'

Hamkom was unhappy that the Pnars had lost to the Khynriams and the Wars. 'I'm sure there were other clashes where the Pnars won against Shyllong, no?'

Evening laughed sarcastically, but I said, 'There might have been, but nothing important, or stories would have been told about those too. The only other time the two states came close to a full-scale war was when the famous king of Sutnga, Borkusaiñ, came on a sightseeing tour of western Ri Khasi, or Ri Hynñiew Trep, for Ham's sake, with his sister, Ka Rimai—'

'Why, Bah Ap, was not the one you spoke of just now a full-scale war?' Donald asked.

'Not really,' I said. 'Many provinces in Ri Khynriam, Ri War, Ri Bhoi and the Mikir Hills were under the state of Shyllong, and they did not participate in the war at all because it came to an end before they could turn up. If they had all come and invaded Ri Pnar, it would have been a terrible, terrible thing indeed. And in an all-out war, there would have been alliances too, with other states. Just think about that: a people torn apart!'

'So what happened when Borkusaiñ and his sister came to see the rest of the Khasi states?' Magdalene asked.

'What could happen? They came, they saw, they left,' Bah Kynsai joked.

'Uff, this Bah Kynsai!' Magdalene exclaimed in an exasperated tone. 'Ap said a full-scale war nearly broke out when they came to these parts, no?'

'Did he? Then let's hear about it, na, what are we waiting for?'

Once again, I found myself telling a story—this time about Borsing, king of Sohra, and Borkusaiñ, king of Sutnga. Borkusaiñ and Rimai travelled to western Ri Khasi because they wanted to see for themselves how prosperous and developed the famed states of Shyllong, Sohra and Nongkhlaw were. As the state of Shyllong was the closest to his summer capital in Nartiang, he thought he would begin his tour by inspecting its capital town, which had just been shifted from Nongkseh in the west to Nongkrem in the east.

Borkusaiñ and his sister arrived in Nongkrem on a market day. Curious to know how Khynriam markets were run, they went to have a look. Standing at the edge of the market, they examined the neat rows of stalls, where clothes, groceries, meat and cooked food like jadoh were sold. They saw that the stalls had wooden frames and thatched roofs, but that their sides were left open. Then they turned their attention to the wide-open area surrounding the stalls, where people sold vegetables, fruits, yam, cassava, taro root and other odds and ends.

Borkusaiñ observed to his sister, 'It's not very different from our markets, is it?'

Rimai agreed, 'Yes, it's very similar.'

'Shall we, Hep?' Borkusaiñ asked his sister. 'I'm quite hungry, I'd like to have some jadoh. I hear it's terrific …'

'Are you sure they don't cook it with beef?'

By that time, the royal family of Sutnga had converted to Hinduism and did not eat beef.

Borkusaiñ reassured her, 'I'm sure. They cook it with pig's fat and its viscera.'

'Eating jadoh at a market stall! It's not very kingly, is it?'

'Well, Hep, we are not here to be kingly. We are here as pilgrims and travellers, remember?'

As they stood there, two tall and imposing figures, people openly stared at them, for they were clearly strangers in the land. Borkusaiñ, a handsome man with sharp features, was dressed very much like any other Khasi man of means, in a white dhoti and a white turban to match. However, on his feet were sandals of a kind the locals had never seen before, because they were made in Jaiñtiapur by Bengalis. Another thing that marked him as a stranger was his Pnar-styled jacket, which was visible under the neatly folded white ryndia silk shawl he wore around his neck.

His sister had the same sharp features as his. She was dressed in a green velvet blouse with a yellow-and-black checked shawl wrapped loosely over her shoulder. But she wore her yellow silk jaiñsem like a Pnar woman, almost like a sarong, not draped over the shoulder like the Khynriam women did.

People could see that the couple were quite well-to-do, too, despite the absence of any gold or silver ornaments.

Borkusaiñ and his sister were just moving into the thatched stalls when they were suddenly seized and dragged away. They had been recognised as King Borkusaiñ and his sister, Rimai. The men took them to a large pigsty with a sturdy door and made them sit on the floor, which was covered with cowhide. A deliberate insult, since it was known that the royal family of Sutnga, being Hindus, considered the cow a holy animal. After that, they were locked up and guarded by a strong band of warriors, who had strict instructions not to allow anyone to approach the place.

It was not very clear why Haiñ Sing, the king of Shyllong, had them suddenly arrested like that. But that he kept them in that carefully guarded pigsty, whose floor was covered with cowhide, is still a widely told tale. In fact, he kept them there for as long as a year, feeding them nothing but rice and salt.

'What about ransom,' Donald asked. 'Did he demand any ransom?'

'He was not an extortionist or a mere warlord to demand ransom, Don. He was the king of a powerful state, why would he demean himself by demanding ransom like a common criminal? No, no, he must have hated them—'

'But why?' Magdalene asked.

I told her that he may have been angry because they had turned away from their own religion to embrace the faith of a vanquished subject. He might also have remembered the treatment meted out by Borkusaiñ's ancestors to Sajar Ñiangli, who had to leave his country to roam like a refugee till he finally settled down in the state of Nongkhlaw. Maybe that was why he made them sit on a cowhide.

Meanwhile, in Sutnga, people mourned the mysterious disappearance of their king and his sister, the queen mother, and raised a hue and cry about the inaction of their provincial rulers, the dolois. Following the outcry, the dolois called for a sitting of the state council, which finally decided to send their lyngskor, the prime minister, towards western Ri Khasi to find out what had happened to the king on his pilgrimage. Potiphas or Pati Kharsapuid, the lyngskor, was one of the most influential leaders in the state of Sutnga. Some said he was even more powerful than the king himself. His power came from the people's love for him, for he was a brave, wise and honourable man.

Potiphas started his journey west as soon as he could. On the way, he kept asking people about the king and his sister without mentioning their true identities. But no one seemed to have any idea. Finally, he reached Nongkrem on a market day and began to ask around discreetly about Borkusaiñ and his sister. He offered anyone who could help him a large sum of money. But most people refused to even speak to him. Frustrated by their hostile attitude, he finally decided to approach a group of drunks, sitting in a dim corner outside the marketplace, although he knew it could be risky.

On seeing him, one of the drunks said, 'Out of here, you bloody … Hey, you are not from here! Hey brothers, he's not from here! Out, out you son of a cunt, out, before I kick you in the balls!'

One of his friends held up his hands and cried, 'Wait, wait!' Then, whispering, he said, 'He's a Synteng, a rich Synteng, let's get some money out of him.' Turning to Potiphas, he demanded, 'What do you want?'

After Potiphas had explained that he was looking for his missing friends, the drunk asked again, 'What's in it for us if we tell you about your … your friends?'

Potiphas produced a handful of cowrie shells and some silver coins. 'These,' he said.

'Okay, come here, squat right here!'

And then he whispered the story of the two Pnars who were being kept in a pigsty. On Potiphas's request, he described them, but also warned that nobody could even go near the place. 'And, you didn't hear it from us, you understand?' he warned.

From the drunk's description, Potiphas immediately knew that the two Pnars in the pigsty were none other than his king and queen mother. His heart burnt with a terrible rage. How could Haiñ Sing treat a fellow king like an animal? But what was he to do? He was alone in a strange place and he knew no one would raise a finger to help him. Potiphas considered returning home to gather an army and terrorise Shyllong till Borkusaiñ and his sister were released. But that was wishful thinking. He still remembered the story of Ksan Nangbah and what had happened to him during the war against Shyllong. Of the thousands of warriors, only a few hundred had returned home. An invasion was out of the question.

In this troubled state of mind, he wandered towards a jadoh stall. Being hungry, he went in and ordered some jadoh with a curry of pig's liver. As he ate his food from a leaf packet, Potiphas listened to the conversation around him. The locals were bragging about the achievements of their king, U Haiñ Sing. They said he was the greatest. But a man from Mawkdok village, in the state of Sohra, disagreed. Of all the kings then ruling in Ri Khasi, he said, there was none as brave or as skilled in both the art of governance and the art of war as the king of Sohra, U Borsing. Not even the king of Shyllong could mess around with him, the man said. Potiphas ate his jadoh in silence. He finished and left without a word but did not go very far. He pretended to be looking at the wares in the market, all the while keeping an eye out for the man from Mawkdok.

When he saw him leaving the stall, Potiphas followed him and politely greeted him: 'Khublei, friend! I couldn't help hearing what you said about Pa'iem Borsing. I'd like very much to go to Sohra to meet him—'

'Who are you, friend, that you would like to meet our Pa'iem? What makes you think he would want to meet you?'

Since the man was from Sohra, Potiphas decided that honesty would be the best policy. He identified himself and requested him once again to take him to King Borsing. He also promised to pay the man handsomely for his assistance.

When Potiphas met Borsing, he told him everything he knew and finally said, 'I'm sure our syiem and his sister are the ones being held in the pigsty of Haiñ Sing. I desperately need your help, Pa'iem. Without your help, they'll continue to languish there for the rest of their lives.'

Borsing replied, 'I do feel pity for your syiem, but what can I do? If a hima as powerful as yours doesn't want to test its strength against them, what do you think I can do?'

'I know of your reputation, Pa'iem, as a very resourceful man. Perhaps you could think of something. If you are willing to help us, we will gladly part with half our territories in the plains of Surma. What do you say, Pa'iem?'

'Your promise is certainly tempting,' Borsing replied. 'Who wouldn't take such an offer seriously? But the job at hand is a very tricky one. Why don't you get your offer confirmed by your king?'

'But how do I do that, Pa'iem, when they will not allow anyone near the pigsty?'

'Do what I tell you. Dress as a Hindu fakir, use a red dhoti. Smear your head and face with ash, put prayer beads around your neck and carry a sitar in your hand. Can you play the sitar? Good, play it in the marketplace and sing a song, any song, in Bengali. This will be such a novelty that you will be asked to sing in front of Haiñ Sing, and doubtless in front of Borkusaiñ too, to provide him with some rare entertainment, for what harm can a Hindu fakir with only a sitar in his hand do? When they have brought you in front of Borkusaiñ, sing a song identifying yourself and tell him about your offer to me. If he agrees to it, let him give you a strand of hair from his head as a sign of his agreement. Go, and you will find things turning out exactly as I have said.'

And so they did. Potiphas was not only able to sing in front of Borkusaiñ and his sister, but also to get a strand of hair as a sign of his willingness to let the king of Sohra have half his territories in the plains of Bengal. Potiphas then returned to Sohra to finalise the agreement with Borsing.

Borsing sent Potiphas back to Nongkrem with detailed instructions. 'Go to the marketplace as before and sing your song there. Towards evening, go and sing before the prisoners. The guards will not object to you now since you were already asked by Haiñ Sing himself to sing before them. Reveal the plan in your song, tell them about how you intend to get the guards drunk, break the lock on the door and take them away to the southern fringe of the town. From there, two of Sohra's strongest porters will carry them to where my warriors and I will be waiting across the River Umïam.'

Even today, this river marks the boundary between the state of Sohra and the state of Shyllong. Emerging from Shillong Peak, the river flows south into the village of Kyrdemkhla in Sohra territory, turns north towards Mylliem in Shyllong, and then south again to Mawbeh in Sohra till it reaches the plains of Bengal.

'Wait, wait, wait, Ap,' Hamkom interrupted. 'You said the fakir would sing to them and then you said he would have to break the lock. Is he singing to them from outside?'

When Potiphas sang, he did so in front of the prisoners. But after that, the guards escorted him out and locked the door. That was when he gave them the alcohol, laced with some tranquilising agent, ostensibly as a reward for having been so kind to him. While the guards lay in a drunken stupor, Potiphas broke the lock and took the prisoners away to the town's southern fringe, from where they were carried towards Borsing and safety.

'Did they have locks in those days, Ap?' Magdalene asked.

I reminded her that Khasis had been manufacturing iron and ironwork since 353 BCE, perhaps even earlier. Then I said that the guards woke up as soon as the drug had worn off, only to find that the prisoners had escaped. They ran to the palace to report the matter to their king, who sent town criers everywhere to rouse all his fighting men with their drums.

By then, however, Potiphas and the carriers were well on their way. When the Nongkrems finally caught sight of them, they were already across the River Umïam with Borsing and his army. The Nongkrems were enraged when they realised that it was Borsing who had planned it all. Why should he interfere in their hima's business? They tried to cross the river, determined to teach him a lesson, but Borsing's men let fly a few arrows and shot at them with the cannons they had brought along. They hastily retreated, swearing great oaths of revenge.

Borkusañ and his sister spent some time in Sohra to recuperate. When it was time for them to leave, he requested Borsing to go with him, so he could show him the areas in Sylhet that would be given to him. Borsing took with him only Phiah Lyngskor, the prime minister, and a few servants to help them on the long journey back to Jaiñtiapur.

When they reached the Sutnga town of Angajur, now in Bangladesh, Borkusañ said, 'All this, Pa'iem Borsing, is part of the Sylhet plains that I'd like to hand over to you. But all in good time. We'll rest here till my ministers arrive, and then we'll go on to Jaiñtiapur.'

Borsing was delighted with Borkusañ's promise. But when Borkusañ kept putting off finalising the agreement even after they had been in Jaiñtiapur for a few weeks, he became impatient and a little suspicious. Deciding to take up the matter once and for all with the Sutnga king, he went to meet him, and said, 'Pa'iem Borkusañ, it's time that I go home, why don't we settle our business now?'

Borkusañ said, 'Why the hurry, Pa'iem Borsing? Stay awhile, enjoy my hospitality, we'll do our business soon enough.'

The fact was that, now that he was safely home, Borkusañ did not feel the need to part with even an inch of his land. He regretted having made the promise to Borsing. He thought, 'Why should I honour a pledge made when I was in such desperation? I'm back home and safe now. No one can touch me here; I can do as I like.'

The very next day, Borkusañ visited Borsing in his quarters and said, 'Pa'iem Borsing, I'd like to show you that part of our hospitality which you haven't experienced yet. We'll go on a boat ride on the River Jaiñtiapur. When we return, we'll finalise our arrangement. Is that alright?'

Borsing was reassured by his words and replied, 'Whatever you say, Pa'iem Borkusañ, I await your pleasure.'

Borkusañ arranged for two boats, one for him and the other for Borsing. The rowers of Borsing's boat headed downstream and started to paddle very fast towards the distant town of Sylhet. He protested, asked them to stop, but they went on rowing as if they had not heard him at all. Borsing realised that he was being kidnapped. The river was big and the current was strong: it was impossible for him to swim across. There was nothing he could do.

In Sylhet, he was taken to the fort of a powerful zamindar by the name of Sujlar, and kept under house arrest. He was free to move about inside the stone fort but not allowed outside it.

Meanwhile, Phiah Lyngskor was alarmed when his king did not return home in the evening. He went to meet Borkusaiñ to enquire about Borsing, but Borkusaiñ refused to meet him. Desperate now, he went to Potiphas, who instantly understood what had happened. Livid with rage, he confronted Borkusaiñ and demanded that Borsing be released at once. Borkusaiñ, however, refused to do so. He tried to persuade Potiphas to forget about the matter, but Potiphas raged and ranted and said he would take up the matter with the other ministers and the state council if need be. Giving the king an ultimatum, he left the palace in a huff.

Potiphas now realised that even the lives of Phiah Lyngskor and his servants were in danger. He advised Phiah to leave immediately, with the assurance that he would do everything possible, not only to have Borsing released, but also to see that the land agreement, one he himself had been instrumental in making, was honoured fully.

Phiah and the servants left Jaiñtiapur for Nonglba, the capital of Sohra, in the dead of night. When news spread about Borkusaiñ's appalling treachery, the whole state rose as one and prepared for an invasion of Jaiñtiapur. But the ministers from the twelve founding clans advised patience. Pleading with the warrior leaders, they said, 'If we rush into a war right now, when our syiem is still a prisoner, we will only endanger his life. Potiphas is an honourable man. He has promised to get our syiem released; let us wait to hear from him.'

The warrior leaders were not convinced. 'How do you know our syiem is still alive?'

The ministers told them that the shamans had already performed *ka khan ka shat*, the divination ceremony. They had done it with cowrie shells and rice grains, with ka shanam, the silver lime container, and with eggs. To reassure them further, they said, 'We, the myntris, have seen them perform the extispicious rites. Many roosters were sacrificed, and their entrails were examined for the signs. And all the signs pointed to the fact that our syiem lives, although we know not where.'

Somewhat placated, the warrior leaders agreed to wait. They also urged the myntris not to rely on Potiphas alone, but to send spies to Sylhet and Jaiñtiapur to look for the king.

In the meantime, true to his word, Potiphas pestered Borkusaiñ every day. Borkusaiñ tried to appease his prime minister in various ways, and when all else failed, he finally offered him huge bribes of money and land. Shocked by his king's meanness, Potiphas lost his temper and railed at him: 'You dishonourable wretch! How can I even call you my syiem when your word is dung and your heart is a dung pit? The king of Shyllong kept you in a pigsty for a year, and yet you don't even feel a tiny bit of gratitude for the man who made your liberation possible! Instead of rewarding him, you put him in prison, you shameless creature! Or have you had him killed already, you miserable wretch? And when I plead with you to release him, what do you do? You demean me with offers of wealth! Do you think it is treason for me to speak like this to you? I risked my life trying to rescue you. I sacrificed my honour for you. But now, despicable thing that you are, you are no longer my syiem! Tomorrow I'm going to Nartiang, and when I get there, I'm going to convene the state council. We'll make sure you no longer rule us!'

Having given his king a blistering tongue-lashing, Potiphas stormed out of the palace. Borkusaiñ had never been spoken to like that in all his life. His subjects in the plains kowtowed to him, and that had made him feel like a god, no less! He visibly blanched at being thus berated and seethed with rage. But there was nothing he could do, for Potiphas was truly all-powerful. He also knew that if the prime minister were to reach Nartiang, the provincial rulers would listen to him and do what he wished. In desperation, he called for the Bamons, his Brahmin priests and secret advisers.

The Bamons straightaway said, 'Your Majesty, if you are to save yourself, Potiphas must not be allowed to leave Jaiñtiapur. Why don't we secretly summon his wife here? She is an ambitious woman—'

'What do you have in mind?' the king snapped. 'If Potiphas will not listen to me, what makes you think he will listen to his wife? He's not that kind of man.'

'Your Majesty, what we have in mind is something different. How do we keep Potiphas from travelling to Nartiang? You are quite right, Your Majesty, we cannot, unless we keep him here by force. But how do we keep a powerful myntri like him by force unless …'

'I get your meaning. Do you think his wife would be willing to kill her own husband?'

'Not kill him, Your Majesty, merely assist. She's an ambitious woman, Your Majesty, and very beautiful, as you know. We can offer her three things: absolution from us, wealth and power from you.'

'Power?'

'Forgive us for suggesting this, Your Majesty, but if she were to become your … how do we say it, Your Majesty?'

'My concubine, you mean? Yes, I see your point. And why not? I have always nursed a secret longing for her; as you say, she's beautiful. But if we should fail, have you thought of the consequences?'

'Forgive us, Your Majesty, but we don't think we will fail. We know that she's not very happy where she is. Potiphas is too honest and clean, whereas she wants riches, influence and the freedom to live life as she pleases. Besides, what else do we have, Your Majesty? Potiphas will leave tomorrow. He must die tonight, or you will lose everything, Your Majesty.'

As the Bamons predicted, Potiphas's wife readily accepted Borkusain's offer. She drugged her husband's food and also that of the three guards securing the back of the house. When Potiphas and the guards had fallen fast asleep, she signalled to the king's men, who were waiting among the trees nearby, to climb stealthily onto the roof from the back. They could not enter the house itself because of the other guards on the veranda and those indoors, who refused to eat or drink while on duty.

When the king's men were on the rooftop, they made a hole in the thatched roof and lowered a long spear to Potiphas's wife, who pointed it right at the sleeping man's heart. When that was done, they pushed the spear home, and Potiphas never even knew what killed him.

News that Potiphas had been executed for treason began to spread across the state. The people of Sutnga were surprised that he could be accused of treason. However, they did not know the facts of the case and had to take the king's word for it.

Borsing's men in Sohra also heard about it. The news hit them like a thunderbolt, bringing gloom and hopelessness. Nevertheless, they did not give up the search, for their shamans still insisted that Borsing was alive.

It was now three years since Borsing had vanished without a trace from Jaiñtiapur. The Sohras searched for him everywhere in the eastern plains of Bengal, pinning their hopes on their shamans' divination. But when he was discovered at last, it was quite by accident.

At that time, there lived in the village of Mawlong a prosperous merchant named Kon Sing, who used to go to Sylhet quite often. One morning, he decided to see the famous fort of Sujlar. He stared with great interest at the stone structure. It was about twenty-five cubits high and seemed to be quite sturdy. At the very top, there appeared to be a kind of platform, on which a sentry strolled. But the sentries were very casual and mostly sat in an enclosure on the platform that was meant for their use. As the merchant walked around the fort, he came across a deep canal, about four feet wide. It was meant to divert water from the river into the fort. He went to the point where the canal entered the fort and, out of curiosity, bent down to look inside. To his surprise, he saw a very handsome man, fair and tall and well built, washing his face in the water. The man looked to him like Borsing Syiem. But because his beard was untrimmed and his hair was long, Kon Sing was not very sure and said nothing. When he got home, however, he reported the matter to the ministers of Sohra.

The ministers were very excited. They had no doubt it was their king, for who else in Sylhet could resemble Borsing? They requested Kon Sing to take their men to the place. But the merchant warned them that too many warriors would attract unwelcome attention. Finally, it was decided that only Kon Sing, Phiah Lyngskor and four of the state's greatest warrior leaders should go to Sylhet, while more of them would wait in the town's north-western fringe.

Kon took Phiah for a morning walk at precisely the same time as he had gone previously. They casually followed the course of the canal like morning strollers, and when they got to the point where it vanished into the fort's compound, they squatted down to wait. Soon, they saw the same man, carrying a small brass pot, coming towards the canal to wash his face. Phiah knew at once that it was none other than Borsing himself. But he could not speak to his king for fear the sentries might hear him. Instead, he tied a large leaf to a thread he had brought along and let it float into the compound.

Borsing saw the leaf tied to a thread. He bent down to wash his face and took the opportunity to look towards the canal's entrance. When he saw it was Phiah, he cried silently, shedding copious tears, which he quickly disguised by splashing water on his face. He gave Phiah a sign that there was a sentry nearby. But through hand gestures, Phiah managed to communicate that they would come back that night to rescue him. When Borsing indicated that he would be ready, Kon and Phiah left to make the necessary preparations.

At about midnight, the Sohras crept into the opening where the canal entered the fort, carrying a small canoe to which they had tied strong cords made from creepers woven together. They floated the canoe inside, and Borsing, who was waiting in the shadows, got into it and lay flat at the bottom. The warriors pulled him out of there and fled the scene as fast as they could. They walked all night, and by morning, they were safely in the wooded countryside, where thirty more warriors met them. They walked the whole of that day, stopping only to eat their jasong. At nightfall, they made dry camp among the trees, posted a watch and slept for a few hours. Just before midnight, they got up and walked again through the night. By the time people were up and about in the morning, they were already entering territories controlled by Sohra.

'Was there no pursuit?' Evening asked.

There must have been, I replied, but it would have been chaotic because they would not have known where to look in the first place.

A month after Borsing's arrival at Nonglba, the biggest state council of Sohra was summoned. It was attended by all the provincial kings, their ministers, and by all the eligible male citizens of the state. There was only one agenda at the council: the incarceration of their king and the betrayal of Borkusaiñ.

First of all, the council listened to first-hand accounts by Phiah Lyngskor and Borsing about what had happened. The harrowing experiences of the king at the hands of Borkusaiñ and his zamindar, Sujlar, were highlighted. Borkusaiñ's treachery and his ingratitude were roundly condemned. Everyone present there felt the insult to their king as their own, and most of them called for war with Sutnga. They argued that, even if they could not invade the entire state, they could easily take the Sutngas' territories in Sylhet by force. There was nothing Borkusaiñ could do about it. His warriors from the mountainous provinces were too far away to offer any protection, but Sohra being so close to Sylhet, all they had to do was swoop down there, overcome what opposition there was, and take what was promised them.

At first, the council seemed to be unanimous in this decision, and everyone chanted and raised war cries that echoed through the hills and the deep ravines nearby. But suddenly, amidst that warlike passion and rage, a section of the councillors disagreed with the decision. The dissenters were led by Morsing, the son of Ka Jah, and his two brothers (also provincial kings like Morsing), U Rai and U Jiei. They were supported by the five founding clans of Tham, Umdor, Dohling and Sohkhia. A majority of the councillors were astounded by the turn of events. They could not understand how, after learning of the awful and demeaning treatment of Borsing by the Syiem Synteng (as they called Borkusaiñ), anyone could stand by without wishing to avenge it. There was amazement, then anger, then a heated quarrel, followed by the drawing of swords and the unslinging of bows and arrows. The supporters of Borsing wanted to wipe out Morsing and his men there and then. They said these bastards were as treacherous as the Syiem Synteng. 'Hey ho!' they shouted. 'You, the true sons of your mothers! You, the chosen men! You, the magnificent warriors, the true pride of Sohra! Come, let us take out this pus-filled wound, let us finish the job right here, right now!'

However, Borsing was an honourable man. He cried out to his people to stand down. Appealing to them, he said, 'My beloved people, brothers of the flesh, brothers of the blood! Please think awhile before you draw your swords or let loose your arrows. These are your fellow citizens! Morsing and the syiem raijs are my own flesh and blood. How can you wage war against your own brothers? How can I have my own flesh and blood slain? Rather than fight among ourselves, you who love me and are ready to fight for me, let us remove ourselves from these traitors! Let us leave this place and set up another state elsewhere! What say you, my compatriots, brothers of the flesh, brothers of the blood?'

Dale suddenly made one of his rare interventions. 'Who are these people again, Bah? I mean, Morsing and Ka Jah?'

Briefly, I told him about King Buhsing, his brother Sadang and his two sisters, Ka Shan—also the queen mother—and Ka Jah. But I made it very clear again that Buhsing was not the founder of the state of Sohra, but a distant descendant of the mysterious woman, Ka Sohra, whose sons became the first kings of the state founded by the twelve clans from Khatar Shnong and Khathynriew Shnong. Borsing was Shan's eldest son, and being the queen mother's son, was made the king of Sohra after Buhsing. Morsing was Jah's eldest son. He was made a provincial king in charge of the province of Khatar Shnong by Buhsing.

After that explanation, I picked up Borsing's tale again. His supporters finally acquiesced, and followed him and the seven founding clans of Diengdoh, Khongwir, Shrieh, Myrboh, Majaw, Nongtraw and Mawdkhap, as they moved south, away from Nonglba. A few kilometres from their former capital, they came across a likely spot, well-watered and fringed by fields and woodlands. There they decided to settle down and establish a new state. Borsing and the seven founding clans swore an oath to always stand by each other in prosperity and adversity, war and peace, life and death. As a token of their commitment, they planted a massive monolith called *Mawsmai*, the oath-swearing stone. From that time, the settlement also came to be known as Mawsmai, and the new state as Hima Mawsmai.

When Borsing moved out of Nonglba, Morsing wanted to put some distance between himself and his cousin. He and his supporters moved the family seat from Nonglba to Sohra Twa in Upper Sohra, where it has remained. It must be kept in mind that Morsing was not the first to inhabit Upper Sohra. The market at Madan Umleng and the settlement of Sohra were established hundreds of years before his time. And so was the state of Sohra—by the time of Borsing Syiem, it was already one of the most powerful states in Ri Khasi. It weakened quite a bit after the departure of Borsing and the civil war that followed, but it recovered later, when Mawsmai reunited with Sohra under Duwan Sing Syiem.

'What civil war, Ap?' Magdalene demanded. 'Earlier, you said they did not fight, no?'

Only much later did Borsing discover the reason why Morsing, his brothers, and the five founding clans had refused to go to war against Borkusaiñ. The treacherous Syiem Synteng had bribed them. This discovery so enraged Borsing that he declared war against his cousin. In one of the battles that followed, Morsing and his warriors attacked Mawsmai and killed one of its warrior leaders, U Thaw Mihngi Mawdkhap, father of U Myntri Khongwir, the Mawsmai minister from the Khongwir clan. After his death, they were able to enter the fort, but unfortunately for them, during the fighting that ensued, Morsing had his right leg slashed by Borsing and fell to the ground, a helpless prisoner. When his warriors saw that Morsing had fallen, they lost heart and fled home to Upper Sohra.

U Myntri Khongwir wanted to kill Morsing as revenge for his father's death. But Borsing forbade him from doing so. He said, 'Morsing, whatever he may be, is still my own flesh and blood.'

Hearing that, the entire Khongwir clan went berserk and shouted, 'Let us break all our bows and arrows; let us break our oath! What is the use of fighting for this kind of syiem?'

When Borsing's brother, Buhsing II, realised that the enraged Khongwirs would not be appeased unless Morsing was given to them, he winked at them as a sign that he was with them. Encouraged, the Khongwirs took hold of Morsing and dragged him away to a secluded spot, where they killed him and cut his flesh into long, thin strips like jerky and left them hanging from a tree to dry in the sun.

Magdalene shivered and said, 'Ugh, that was gross, man! How can our own people be capable of all that, ya?'

'Because,' Bah Kynsai replied, 'they were not angels, na?'

But the state of Mawsmai did not last long. After Borsing died, the throne went to his brother Buhsing II. But since he did not have a nephew of his own, he went to Morsing's nephew, Duwan Sing, in Sohra, placed his hand on his head, and said, 'My kingship shall fall on you.' And that was how Mawsmai came to be reunited with Sohra, until the British turned it into an independent province under their direct control. Mawsmai is now governed by a provincial ruler known as the sordar or sirdar.

'What about the status of the Khasi states today, Ap?' Magdalene asked.

'We told you about them, no?' Bah Kit said. 'They signed the Instrument of Accession and merged with India—'

'Were forced to sign,' Evening interrupted.

'Were forced to sign,' Bah Kit agreed. 'But they were not abolished. They were simply put under the control of the District Council. We have already discussed all that, no?'

'You mean, all thirty states still exist?'

'There are twenty-five himas right now, Mag, but besides them, there are independent provinces, elakas, governed by lyngdohs and sirdars. Most of these were created by the British.'

Donald observed, 'I find the stories of the Khasi states very impressive, but they are also full of intrigue, treachery, internal strife and war—'

'Like everywhere else, Don,' Bah Kynsai reminded him.

'Yeah, maybe, but I think it must have been terrible to live during those times, no?'

'Being governed by kings and tyrants was always terrible in any part of the world, Don,' Bah Kynsai reminded him again. 'Imagine a world where the king can do no wrong! At least among us, the kings were only titular heads, na? We should be thankful for that.'

Bah Su, however, clarified that the Khasi states did not always fight among themselves. 'There was free movement of people from one hima to another,' he said, 'not only for trade but also to settle down in a place of one's choice. For instance, a Pnar could decide to live in a Khynriam hima and a Khynriam could freely settle in a Pnar hima, as you have seen. Besides, whenever there was conflict with a non-Khasi hima, the Khasis always came together. The best example of this was when Ram Sing Syiem of Sutnga was captured by an Ahom king in the seventeenth century CE—'

'Yeah, yeah, I remember that, Bah Su,' Hamkom said.

According to Bah Su, there were conflicting accounts about how and why Ram Sing was captured. But the most likely story, mentioned in the Kachari buranji, and also corroborated by Pnar oral traditions, was that he and the Kachari king, Tamradhvaj, were trying to mount a combined attack on Ahom territories. The Ahom king, Rudra Singha, sent two powerful expeditionary forces, one under the command of Bar Phukan, which took a direct route from Gobha to Ri Pnar, and the other under the command of Bar Barua, which proceeded through the valley of the River Kupli and the Kachari territories. It was Bar Barua who first reached the outskirts of Nartiang, the summer capital of Sutnga. There, he set up camp and decorated it as if for a festive occasion. He then sent word to Ram Sing that he had brought a beautiful Ahom princess for him to marry. Ram Sing, who was said to have an irredeemable weakness for attractive women, fell for the ploy. He and Tamradhvaj responded to Bar Barua's invitation and were summarily captured and taken to the Ahom king under heavy protection. But the armies of both Bar Barua and Bar Phukan were ordered to proceed to Jaiñtiapur and to remain there until further orders.

The story of this treachery provoked outrage not only in Sutnga but across the length and breadth of Ri Hynñiew Trep, as Bah Su put it. Scores of Khasi states, including Hima Shyllong, and hundreds of Khasi provinces joined forces to dislodge the invaders from their land. Their initial plan was to assail the forces escorting Ram Sing to the Ahom king. But they found the army to be too large and turned their attention to Bar Phukan and his soldiers as they were passing through the hills. Although they could not stop Bar Phukan from reaching Jaiñtiapur, they managed to destroy eight of the forts he constructed along the way and massacred all the defenders. A detachment taking away the graven image of Jaiñteswari and other treasures from Jaiñtiapur was also attacked, and the idol and the treasures were recovered. Hundreds of Ahom soldiers died in the fighting. Those who survived fled north towards Nartiang and tried to regroup there. But when the Khasis came, they fled and were pursued clear out of the land. Many more died while fleeing, and only a handful reached Surapani in Ahom territory.

The Ahom king sent massive reinforcements to fight the combined force of the Khasis, but they could not even engage them in battle. The Khasis adopted guerrilla tactics, hitting them with arrows and spears from hillsides and forests, and immediately withdrawing, only to return later to harass them again. Meanwhile, both Bar Barua and Bar Phukan, not wishing to be in a hostile country while the rainy season approached, withdrew from Jaiñtiapur and tried to return to Assam. Before leaving, they put to death more than a thousand inhabitants, many of them Bengali subjects. Angered by this act of cruelty, the Khasis pursued and harassed the two retreating armies all the way to the Ahom territories, killing hundreds. When they reached their own kingdom, the armies were such a depleted force that the Ahom king became mad with rage and tried to put his commanders to death. They were saved only by the intervention of the nobles.

Although the Khasis were able to drive the Ahoms out of Ri Pnar, they could not rescue Ram Sing himself. In the Ahom court, the Kachari king, Tamradhvaj, submitted meekly to Rudra Singha, but Ram Sing refused to bow down, saying that Khasis do not bow to anyone, and as a king, he would certainly not bow to another king. Rudra Singha then told Ram Sing that he could return home if his nobles appeared before the Ahom court and submitted to him. But while these talks were going on, Ram Sing contracted smallpox and soon died of the disease.

The point of the story, Bah Su said, was to show that the Khasi states did not just fight among themselves. 'When external forces threatened them, ha, they always came together to defend their country,' he concluded.

Donald wanted to know if the Khasis often lost to the kings from the plains.

'Not often,' Bah Su responded. 'And even when they lost, ha, it was only some of their territories in the plains. No one could venture into the mountain fastness of the Khasis. The Ahoms tried but did not last long. Only the British succeeded, but they had plenty of help from the locals.'

'Bah Ap and you have spoken of the Khasi territories in the plains, Bah Su, what exactly are they?' Donald asked.

Before Bah Su could respond, Hamkom said, 'I can tell you that the state of Sutnga was divided into three sectors, as Ap said: the Assam plains in the north, the hills of Ri Pnar and Surma Valley in the south. In Assam, it controlled areas like Raha, Cuppermukh, Jagi Road, Neli, Shara and Gobha. The western part of Gobha was controlled by the state of Shyllong, which also controlled Sonapur and Beltola. The other states with territories in Assam were Nongkhlaw, which controlled places like Borduar, and Nongstoin, which controlled some *dwars*, or trading centres, in Goalpara district—'

Evening suddenly put his hands together and clapped. When Bah Kynsai asked him why, he said, 'Didn't you notice? He said "the state of Sutnga", not the Jaiñtia kingdom.'

Before anybody could say anything, Bah Su intervened and said he agreed with Hamkom, though he also gently corrected him. 'Actually, ha, Ham, there were more Khasi himas with territories in Assam. Among them were the hima of Nongpoh and those in West Khasi Hills (Nonglang, Nongmynsaw and Rambrai), which controlled areas like Panbaree and Boko. In the plains of East Bengal, ha, Hima Sutnga ruled the Jaintapur Upazila from the Cachar Hills, along the north bank of the River Surma, to the boundaries of Sylhet town. Sohra ruled areas like Chhatok, part of Pandua and Bholaganj, while Nongkhlaw controlled large tracts around Dewanganj in Sylhet district.'

At this, Evening said jubilantly, 'Do you hear that? Why shouldn't we be proud of the Khasi himas? Whatever their shortcomings, ha, they were also glorious. Just think about it, they had territories in the northern plains of Assam and the southern plains of Bengal, man! What a feat that was! Especially when you look at how, these days, everybody—north, south, east, west—is pinching at Khasi Land, I think that was a great, great feat indeed!'

While the rest of us nodded in agreement, Raji, who was by then quite drunk, said something rather profound: 'On the glories of the past, let us sleep!'

8
THE SIXTH NIGHT

LITTLE STORIES II

'Ieit la ka jong, burom ia kiwei.'
('Love one's own, respect the others.')

—Khasi saying

On the sixth night, 10 February, it was Magdalene who opened the discussion. 'That was a fantastic day we had today, ha, Bah Kynsai?'

We had spent the entire day lazing around the lake. It was perfect from the start: no Perly to rouse us before we had had our fair share of sleep. We woke up at about ten, had our breakfast of tea and boiled rice at 10.40, and then proceeded to the lake after Perly had brought us our packed lunch of boiled rice and pork boiled with mustard leaves. For greens, he gave us *bat moina* (gotu kola), a locally grown herb, and sliced cucumber.

At the lake, we bathed, washed our clothes, ate lunch, and then lazed about, enjoying the scene and the cool breeze wrinkling the lake's surface and ruffling our hair. It was a truly tranquil day in the warm sun, and we quite forgot that, back home, it was blustery winter. Even Halolihim's presence could not spoil the mood. To be fair, he was quite unobtrusive, keeping to himself and speaking only to Hamkom. We did try in the beginning to make him feel at ease, but he scorned our efforts, so we left him alone. When we returned at dusk, we went to the death house for dinner—boiled rice and boiled pork again—and then retired to the hut.

Magdalene sighed contentedly, reliving the day.

Bah Kynsai agreed. 'It sure was good. I hate the hurrying back and forth. When you are sweating so much on the way, na, even taking a bath is useless. But today was perfect; everybody was happy, except Halolihim.'

'Well, he didn't disturb anyone,' Hamkom argued.

'No, he didn't,' Bah Kynsai agreed. 'But he behaved like someone with measles, na?'

Raji, a mug of yiad hiar beer in his hand, muttered, 'Like someone visited by the gods.'

'What is that supposed to mean?' Hamkom asked belligerently.

'Hey, Bah Kit, he doesn't even know what that means, leh!' Raji said sarcastically.

'I also don't know, ya, Raji. Tell no, what does it mean?' Magdalene asked.

'When people come down with measles, okay, Khasis say they are being visited by the gods and, therefore, must not be bothered or offended in any way. Normally, patients become quite capricious, ha, and they can ask for all sorts of things. Some children have been known to ask for real aeroplanes and ships, while others insist on being carried on their mother's back the whole day. That sort of thing, no? And if you don't do what they say or give what they ask, the disease becomes worse. It's the gods, they say, who are upset. That's why patients are never disturbed in any way.'

'In what way does it get worse? I really don't know, ya, my daughter hasn't had the measles, no?'

'Well, if the patients don't get what they want, okay, they cry and sulk and fuss, and that can make the fever much worse, even fatal.'

'But if they are asking for aeroplanes, how can parents satisfy them?'

'I have known parents who bought toy aeroplanes and tried their best to fool their children. You just need to sweet-talk them. Ap has a story about this.'

'Really, tell, no, Ap. Tonight we'll have another night of little stories, ha, Bah Kynsai?'

Bah Kynsai agreed, and Evening added, 'But like the last time, they must have morals, okay?'

'Come on, Ap, you start. We'll all chip in later,' Bah Kynsai prompted.

I told them the story called 'The Boy with the Measles and a Can of Worms'. But first, I explained that Khasis always refer to the illness as *mih blei*, literally, 'to grow god', or *wan ki blei*, 'the gods are visiting'. Although there is a proper word for it—*mih ñiangpyrsit*, afflicted with measles—they never address the illness directly when someone is suffering from it, for fear of offending the visiting gods. And this is something most Khasis believe, regardless of their religion.

Bah Kynsai said impatiently, 'Just tell us the story, na!'

'I, for one, needed that explanation, ha, Bah Kynsai,' Magdalene said. 'By the way, Ap, your story should be called "The Boy Who Grows God and a Can of Worms", no, Don?'

'Good one, Mag, good one,' Donald laughed.

'Good one because Mag said it, na?' Bah Kynsai teased him. 'To you, everything that Mag says or does is a good one, liah. Chalo, Ap, chalo!'

One day, I began, a boy of about eight, living in our neighbourhood, started running a high fever. The worried parents took him to a doctor, who explained the cause of the illness and gave the boy some medicines.

He also told the parents not to worry too much since it was only a case of measles. Pointing to the red rashes on the boy's face, he said, 'Do you see that? Measles.'

As soon as they heard that, the parents were even more worried: the gods were visiting their child; they had to be very, very careful. They began treating him with kid gloves as if he were something brittle, an egg perhaps, that might break if mishandled. They spoke to him in cajoling tones and made sure not to raise their voice when speaking to him, lest the gods were offended and the illness worsened. They also warned his brothers and sisters not to shout at him or make him angry in any way.

'Look here, my children,' the father said, 'U Deng has been visited by the gods, so don't upset him in any way, understand? If the gods are upset, we'll truly have a hard time caring for him. It might be dangerous for you too: if offended, the gods might come to you next.'

Deng, on his part, began behaving like a spoiled brat, or rather, a capricious despot. Sometimes he asked his parents to carry him on their backs and go for long walks outside, even in the middle of the night, and at other times he made them crawl on all fours like goats or cattle, while he sat on top of them, whipping them with a rope. Sometimes he asked them to buy an aeroplane, and when they bought him a toy aeroplane from Police Bazaar, he refused to accept it and said, 'Give me the big one that flies in the sky.' When the parents explained that the police would not allow them to buy a big aeroplane, he said, 'Give me a ship, then!' When they said that a ship could only float in the sea, he said, 'Give me chow!' When they brought him a plate of chow from the best Chinese restaurant in Shillong, he said, 'No, I don't want it, give me momos!'

Thus Deng tormented his parents every day. Sometimes his mother got so angry she wanted to spank him. But what to do? She grit her teeth and bore it, lest the gods get offended.

One day, when Deng got tired of asking them for chow and momos to eat, he asked them for worms instead. Thinking this was some kind of food, the mother asked him gently, 'What kind of food is that, Deng, darling? Is it some kind of sweet, son? I haven't heard of any sweet called worms—'

His pinched face contorted with rage, Deng shouted angrily, 'I don't want sweets! I want worms! Dig them up from the garden!'

The mother was now beside herself with rage. Red like a hornet from suppressed fury, she went to the father and told him, 'No, no, this cannot have anything to do with the gods, *Kpa*! It must be him trying to torture us.

I'm not going to tolerate this kind of behaviour any longer. He's asking us for impossible things—aeroplane, ship, machine gun, tank and, now, worms! No, no, I won't—'

The kpa, the father, his face showing great concern, pacified his beautiful wife. 'Calm down, *Kmie*, keep cool now. Don't do or say anything rash, okay? If the gods are offended and the poor child comes down with a terrible fever, what will you do? Cool, cool, Kmie.'

Leaving the kmie, the mother, he went to his son, who was lying in bed, and crooned to him, 'So, you want some worms, darling? Okay, okay, don't worry, Papa will dig up some for you, okay, just you wait, okay?'

After some time, the father came back with a can full of worms. 'Look, son, I have brought you the worms. Do you see these? A can full of them.'

Deng looked at the worms and said, 'Fry.'

'Fry!' the mother shouted at the father. 'How can we fry worms? Where do we fry them? I'm not giving you a frying pan, Kpa, don't even think about it! If we fry the worms, we'll have to throw away the frying pan also ... I'm not giving it ... I'll not allow it!'

The father placated her once more. 'Cool down, na, Kmie, you also are too touchy, te! You know very well you cannot upset someone like Deng! Look at the poor kid, thin and pale, and plastered with those ugly rashes! And yet, what do we say to him? He's *bhabriew*, handsome! Why? Because we cannot upset him, Kmie, you know that? He's been visited by the gods, no?'

'No, but it's really too much, no, Kpa?'

'Cool, cool,' the father said again and patted her on the shoulder. He thought for a while and then asked, 'Do you remember that old frying pan we never use any more, Kmie? Take that one out.'

'Okay, I'll take it out, but I'm not going to fry them. You do it!'

The father took the frying pan, poured some oil into it and fried the worms with onions till they were nicely brown. Then he took them to his sick son and said, 'Deng, son, look at these worms, Papa has fried them for you.'

Deng glanced at them once and said in a monotone, 'Eat them.'

At this, Evening burst out laughing. Magdalene slapped her hands together and said, 'Oh my God, what a son!' Everyone was in splits. Bah Kynsai asked, 'From where did you get such a story, lih?'

Hamkom wanted to know if the father really ate the worms.

Well, the father was quite shocked, but controlled himself and said, 'How can I eat them, you are the one who wants them, no, son?'

'No, you eat them!' Deng insisted in the same monotone. 'I don't want them; I want to see you eat them.'

The father tried to talk Deng out of it, but the boy would not listen. Caught in a terrible dilemma, he stood there for a long time, staring stupidly at the worms, grimacing and wincing, and then, in a piercing voice, cried out to his wife, 'Kmieee!'

Hamkom asked again, if the father ate the worms.

'What do you think?' I asked. 'The gods wanted him to, didn't they?'

Laughing, Bah Kynsai said, 'Moral?'

Bah Su immediately said, '*The child cannot be the father of the man.*'

Bah Kit added, '*All beliefs should have their limits.*'

'You are thinking of Halolihim or what?' Bah Kynsai said, teasingly.

'I'm thinking of all of us, Bah Kynsai, no one should get carried away by their religious beliefs.'

Raji stroked his black beard and said, 'No more religion-talk, please! What we need are more stories.'

'Why don't you tell one?' Bah Kynsai asked.

'Because, Bah Kynsai, right now, I have no story, only this mug of yiad hiar!'

'Tet sala!' Bah Kynsai swore. 'Ap, one more, come on!'

I told them the story called 'Fifty for One Forefinger'.

In the early 1950s in Sohra, there weren't many non-tribals, except for the Bengali families that had come with the British. Therefore, many people, unless they had been to Shillong, did not know what non-tribal Indian women looked like. They had only seen Bengalis, whose saris covered them from head to foot. So, when a Nepali family with two young daughters settled down in the locality of Khliehshnong, they became an immediate sensation.

One day, a man named Jreng, who was returning from one of the stone quarries, met one of them as she was fetching water from a spring in the northern outskirts of the locality. When he saw the young woman, Jreng was quite amazed. 'Arre! Who's this?' he exclaimed. Then to himself, he said, 'I have never seen such a woman before! Look at her! Rosy and tall and well-formed ... such a beauty! My God, but look at the way she's dressed! A short blouse and a skirt! And the stomach and navel exposed like that! Unbelievable!'

He watched as she put the pot on her head and walked home ahead of him. Overtaking her, he looked at the woman with undisguised curiosity as she twisted her hips sensually, causing her navel to move up and down her flat, firm stomach, as if it was taking a little walk of its own. He ogled at the dancing navel, fascinated. 'Waa,' he cried, 'what kind of dress is this? I have never seen Khasi women dressed this way; I have never seen them showing their navels like this!'

Jreng was suddenly overwhelmed by an urge to touch the voluptuously twisting navel. It was a strange fascination for him, and almost against his will, he found himself going near her and giving the frisky little thing a hard poke.

Shocked by his sudden action, the woman cried out in fright, and throwing her pot to the ground, she went screaming all the way home. Her family came out and asked what had happened. When she told them everything and showed them the tall, powerfully built man who had poked her in the navel, the father wisely decided to report the matter to the headman.

He, in turn, convened an urgent meeting of the village council and summoned Jreng to appear before it. As he stood in front of all the attending male members, Jreng was asked by the headman, 'You, Jreng, tell us, is the complaint of this Didi true? Is it true that you poked her in the navel with your forefinger?'

Jreng, who was a simple-minded fellow, told the council the truth. In that drawl for which the people of Sohra are well known, he said, 'Poke her in the navel, te, I did, of course.'

'Why did you do that?'

'How should I know?' he countered, as if he too was perplexed by his action. 'But when she showed her navel like that,' he continued, 'when she twisted it up and down like that, wouldn't any of you also feel tempted? Wouldn't any of you also want to poke at it and see what happens?'

Hearing his answer, the entire council roared with laughter, which lasted quite a while. The headman, whose face was streaming with tears, stood up to his full height of five feet three, raised both his hands, and tried to silence everyone. When order was finally restored, he said, in as stern a voice as he could manage, 'Because of your inappropriate action against a woman, you will have to pay a fine of fifty rupees!'

Jreng was so shocked by that judgement that he blurted out, '*Labew! Sanphew shi tidew!*'

This could be translated—without the beautiful alliterative rhyme that makes it sounds so good in Khasi—as 'Bloody breast! Fifty for one forefinger!'

There was deafening laughter again. When it had subsided a little, the headman said (this time in a tone still shaking with laughter), 'And for using foul language in front of the dorbar, you will be fined another fifty!'

Of course, after he apologised, Jreng was excused the fifty for cursing, but he had to agree to pay the fifty for navel-poking in easy monthly instalments.

Shaking with laughter, Bah Kynsai said, 'This Ap, tdong! What kind of stories are these, man?'

I thought that Bah Kynsai quite liked Jreng because he was the cursing type. But I simply said, 'True stories, Bah Kynsai. No one could have invented them but life itself.'

Hamkom, who was still laughing, said, 'People were very naive in those days, no, Ap?'

'But I admire the conduct of the dorbar!' Evening declared. 'You see, Donald, you cannot compare our dorbars with those of the Taliban. When the people who run it are honest, ha, there's nothing despotic about it. Look at what happened in this story: the complainants were not even Khasis, and yet they had their justice, and the Khasi man who committed an unbecoming act was punished with a fine.'

'But why was he allowed to pay in EMIs?' Donald objected.

'Not EMIs, Don, just easy monthly instalments, whatever he could manage in a month. Fifty rupees was a lot of money in those days, and Jreng was only a poor labourer.'

'So, what's the moral?' Bah Kynsai asked.

Bah Kit said, '*Do not poke your finger into the wrong hole.*'

'Or,' Bah Su added, '*it's not the seriousness that defines the nature of a crime.*'

'That's a good one, Bah Su,' Bah Kynsai said approvingly, 'that's what the dorbar was also implying, na? Okay, guys, now it's my turn, okay? I'll tell you a little story.'

Bah Kynsai told us about a government employee who went to see a doctor, complaining about extreme fatigue. The man said, 'I don't know why, doctor, but I feel extremely weak, and my whole body seems to be aching.'

The doctor listened to his complaints attentively and then examined him carefully. He placed his stethoscope on the patient's chest and back, asking him to breathe in and out. After that, he inspected the eyes, asked him to open his mouth and show his tongue. At last, he made the man lie on a cot and squeezed his stomach a few times.

When he finished this meticulous examination, the doctor asked his patient, 'Since when have you been feeling weak and tired like this?'

'It's been almost a month, Doctor.'

'Hmm ... but I cannot find anything wrong with you; I don't know what medicine to give you.'

'Nothing wrong, Doctor?'

'Uh-uh, nothing at all. It may be a case of overwork ... Are you keeping late hours in the office?'

'Actually, I took leave from office for two months; there are urgent things I need to do at home—'

'Ooh!' the doctor exclaimed. 'Now I know why. What you need is complete rest. No exertion of any kind at all. This is what you must do. From tomorrow, you must go back to the office immediately; if you don't, your health will break down completely.'

Everybody guffawed with delight. Laughing still, Hamkom asked, 'What the hell are you trying to say, Bah Kynsai? Are you saying that people don't do any work in office?'

'Isn't it true?' Bah Kynsai asked. 'When you visit government offices, na, what do you see? Most people are busy playing computer games or knitting sweaters and whatnot for their children, or simply sitting around and chatting.'

'True, true,' Evening concurred. 'I have personally seen people coming to work at noon, and the moment they sit in their chairs, ha, they take out their knitting ... very true, very true, Bah Kynsai.'

Raji added, 'I think of all the people working in government offices, okay, only a quarter of the total strength is needed. The rest are there because of political appointments. They are not needed, and so, they don't work at all.'

'So what should be the moral, Bah Kynsai?' Evening asked.

'*Should one's place of work be a place of rest?*'

'Perfect,' Bah Kit said. 'I also have a very similar story, Bah Kynsai.'

The story was in the form of a conversation between two government servants. One of them, U Nang, was telling his friend about a meeting of the Association of Government Employees. He said, 'Yesterday I went to listen to the speech of our president ... You weren't there, were you, Tang?'

Tang said he could not make it as he had to leave the office early to buy some medicines for his wife. He asked, 'So, what did he say?'

'He told us that we should always do our duties sincerely, "a hundred out of a hundred". And then he explained what he meant, that we should work 12 per cent on Mondays; 23 per cent on Tuesdays; 40 per cent on Wednesdays; 20 per cent on Thursdays; and 5 per cent on Fridays.'

Tang laughed. 'He's very witty, ya!'

'He is, he is, but I think he was being sarcastic, you know,' Nang responded.

'Why do you say that?'

'Because a little later he asked us, "Do you know why the government has made the road from IGP to Kachari into a one-way street? Let me tell you … because the government employees going to the office should never ever run into those already leaving the office."'

Magdalene laughed aloud and said, 'He was making that up, surely!'

'Perhaps,' Bah Kit said, 'but the message is true all the same.'

'Which is?'

'*A government job is not a job.*'

'If it isn't a job, then what is it, Bah Kit?' Dale asked.

'You remember that song by Dire Straits?' Bah Kynsai asked. '*Money for Nothing*. To many employees, that's what a government job is, Dale.'

He looked around. 'Okay, anybody else?'

'I have one,' Evening said, 'but it's got a strong moral content—'

'That's okay, as long as it doesn't point a finger at us,' Bah Kynsai laughed.

The story was about a woman with two sons. Her husband had left her for someone else when the boys were still quite young.

Financially, the woman, a government servant, was not badly off. But she could no longer afford a housekeeper and had to leave her sons unsupervised while she went to work.

Therefore, when they returned home from school, it was the boys' custom to prepare their own food, make their own tea, and do the housework— sweeping the floor, cleaning the utensils and, more importantly, fetching water from the roadside taps.

All in all, the boys were remarkably well behaved. The older one was in Class VII, the second in Class VI. The only complaint about them from their neighbours was that they quarrelled almost daily. But since the mother had never personally witnessed them fighting, she chose to ignore the complaints, preferring to give her sons the benefit of the doubt.

However, one day, she returned home from the office earlier than usual because of a sudden headache. When she entered the house, her sons were in the middle of a heated quarrel, trading insults and calling each other horrible names. They were, in fact, about to come to blows when the mother entered. She demanded to know why they were fighting.

The younger son immediately replied, 'How can I not fight? Bahbah has stolen my cigarette!'

When she heard the cause of the quarrel, the mother shouted at her elder son: 'Bahbah, why did you steal your brother's cigarette? Take this money; go and buy your own! Never ever steal your brother's cigarette again, do you hear?'

When they heard the end of Evening's story, almost everybody cried, 'What! How can that be? How could they smoke at that age? How could the mother actually approve of it? Unbelievable!'

'I swear it really happened,' Evening said. 'They are my neighbours.'

'It's possible,' I said, 'if they come from one of those villages where kids, especially those who don't go to school, are allowed to smoke at quite a young age.'

'You are right, Ap, you are right,' Evening said eagerly, 'they are from a place near Nongkynrih.'

'That explains it,' I said again. 'In those places, believe it or not, you will find very young cowherds not only smoking cigarettes but even pipes. *Shilims*, they call them, and carry them around everywhere in their cloth bags.'

'Really? That's very strange, man,' Hamkom said.

'Yeah, so many things we don't know about ourselves, no?' Magdalene added.

'So, moral?' Bah Kynsai demanded.

'*Do not treat a boy as a man*,' Bah Su offered.

Magdalene was impressed. 'Wonderful,' she declared.

Raji turned to me and said, 'Ap, why don't you tell that story about Sohra's etiquette? It's also got a strong moral, no?'

'Oh, so now you are presiding?' Bah Kynsai asked, annoyed.

'No, no, I'm just … Arre, Bah Kynsai, why are you taking your role so seriously?'

'Any role given to a man should be taken seriously, and those around him should respect his role, otherwise, how are we going to run things?' Bah Kynsai said earnestly and then added, 'Okay, Ap, why don't you tell us that story?'

Everyone, including Bah Kynsai, roared with laughter at that.

I began by explaining that, in the past, Sohra was well known, not only for its good manners, but also for its cleanliness and the neatness with which people maintained their homes. But as more and more people migrated to

Sohra from the neighbouring villages, things changed. Old Moren, or Men Moren, as he was known, was among those who lamented the decline in Sohra's moral standards. He hated to see people, especially the young, forgetting their manners. Eventually, he decided to do something about it.

Men Moren had his first chance one evening when some boys, local and non-local, visited his house in Lum Maha locality, Khliehshnong, to spend time with his beautiful granddaughters. Because it was a cold winter evening, the boys were invited to sit in the spacious kitchen, where a fire was blazing in the hearth and a charcoal stove was also kept burning. Happy at the prospect of sitting near the fire, the boys quickly fetched some cane stools from the drawing room, where they were kept in a very neat row.

Men Moren observed them closely, and whenever he thought they were out of line, he very subtly put them in their place. For instance, when one of them sat too near the stove and denied his friends to his left and right their due share of the warmth, Men Moren said to him: '*Peit ïoh ih!*' ('See that you are not cooked!') When another one spoke too loudly, he asked the group, 'Is anyone hard of hearing here?' And when another bragged about things obviously not true, he said, 'Hmm, what smell is that? Do you fellows smell anything? Very unpleasant too!'

After some time, when the boys realised they were being watched so closely, they got up slowly and said, 'Bih Thei, Bih Rit, we'll have to go … it's getting dark and getting on to supper time too. Parad, we are going … Sleep well, everyone.'

The girls did not want the boys to leave so soon. They objected and said, 'Wuu, why are you leaving so soon? It's still quite early, no? Come, come, sit for a little while longer!'

But Men Moren didn't like the boys very much. He had noticed that, despite his gentle reminder, they were all crowded close to the stove, pushing and shoving against each other. Etiquette dictated that they should enlarge the ring so that everyone would get a fair share of the heat from the fire. But these boys, he thought, were behaving like selfish animals. So he said, 'The boys are right, girls, it is getting late.'

The boys, realising that Men Moren wanted them to leave, excused themselves, wishing everyone goodnight. As they were leaving, Men Moren shook his head sadly but kept his peace. However, when the boys were some distance away from the house, he shouted to their dark silhouettes: 'Hey, boys, come back, come back, you have forgotten something!'

The boys thought they had left something important behind and ran quickly back. When they arrived, they asked Men Moren, 'Did we leave something behind, Parad? We really don't remember ...'

Men Moren pointed to the cane stools around the stove. 'Those! You forgot those!'

A short burst of laughter from my friends followed Men Moren's announcement, but Magdalene raised a hand and asked, 'But why did he wait till they had gone so far from the house, Ap?'

'Would I have told you this story if he hadn't done that? Would there be a story? Would it be so memorable or so effective?'

'I see what you mean. What a way to teach, huh?'

'Yeah, Mag, I can tell you that those boys never forgot the lesson. Men Moren never tired of telling us that when we visit people's houses, we should always return everything to its rightful place. That's the unwritten rule of etiquette. If you don't do it, he would say, you'll expose not only yourselves but also your families as people without manners.'

'Moral!' Bah Kynsai demanded.

'That's the moral, Bah Kynsai!' Bah Kit replied.

I added, '*Civility, like character, reveals itself in all the little things we do.*'

'Good one, good one,' Hamkom approved. 'We must have revealed ourselves quite a bit by now, ha, Bah Kynsai?'

'Especially Bah Kynsai with his expletives,' Raji teased.

'Yeah, yeah, Bah Kynsai and his liahs and lyeits,' Magdalene agreed.

Bah Kynsai laughed and said, 'Next!'

When he was met with silence, Raji said in a sing-song voice, 'Ap, from his books.'

'Ap, from his books,' Bah Kynsai mocked him. 'Are you drunk again? Go ahead, Ap.'

I talked about something that had happened one day in our MA (English) class while I was a student at the university. A bunch of boys and girls were coming in from their lunch break when they saw a typewritten poem left on one of the benches. They picked it up to check the name of the poet, but there was no name.

One of the girls said, 'This must belong to that know-all over there! She's always claiming to be a poet, you know.'

One of her friends agreed, 'Yeah, it could be, she's always acting smart, ya, that one! When teachers ask questions, okay, she always has to be the first to answer. She is a first-first kind of girl!'

But a boy sitting with them said, 'I'm not so sure, you know, it could even be that *dohlab* sitting at the back … Yeah, that one, he's always trying to impress people by quoting poetry, no?'

Dohlab means spleen, but here it was used in the sense of arsehole.

'Oh yeah, yeah,' the first girl agreed, 'he's also ego number one!'

Another boy said, 'The writer of this thing must be looking for free comments, ya, why else would he, or she, leave it around? Come, come, let's see if it's any good.'

Calling to the others to join them, they read the poem through carefully. When almost half the class had examined it, they began discussing its literary merit. But because they all thought the poem was written by one of their classmates, not one among them had anything good to say about it. One of the girls wrote 'Room for improvement' on the margin. Another wrote, 'This a poem?' Yet another wrote, 'A cheap, sneaky way of getting free reviews'. In this way, all the others, too, came up with all sorts of nasty condemnations and began defacing the poem with them. One of them even wrote, 'Touting this thing as a poem! You are lucky I cannot shove it down your throat and cause you indigestion for a month.'

When they were done with it, they left it on the teacher's desk. When the teacher came in after some time, he read the poem and all the comments on it. Then, smiling, he asked, 'Who made all these nasty comments here?'

Everyone was silent, so he read out their comments and asked again, 'Do you know who wrote this poem?'

Many voices said, 'No, sir.'

'Pablo Neruda, the great Chilean poet, wrote this poem. He won the Nobel Prize for Literature in 1971.'

The class erupted into gales of laughter, and all the resentful critics turned red in the face.

My friends too guffawed with delight and said, 'What a lesson! What a lesson!'

'But it's very natural, isn't it?' Hamkom stated. 'I mean, when something is done by someone we know, we tend to think about the person rather than the work, no?'

'It's a common tendency, yes,' Donald agreed, 'but it doesn't always work like that. I have a classmate who's an excellent writer, and my judgement is not at all influenced by my knowing him. But when we don't like the person, as in Bah Ap's story, our judgement can be clouded by prejudice and jealousy.'

'No, no, no, Don, in fact, when we like a person, we become even more prejudiced, isn't that so, guys?' Hamkom insisted.

'I agree,' Bah Kit said. 'We tend to shower him with unjustified praise.'

'But when the person is neither liked nor disliked?' Raji enquired.

'Then, too, we tend to be prejudiced,' Bah Kynsai said. 'Because the person is one of us, na, we are reluctant to believe that he can rise above us—that's human nature.'

'So what's the moral of this?' Bah Kit asked.

'Isn't it obvious?' Bah Kynsai countered. '*Do not rush into judgement lest your ignorance is exposed.*'

'Or *lest you do others an injustice,*' Bah Su chimed in.

'Right, right,' Bah Kynsai agreed.

'Hey, Bah Kynsai, shall I tell a dirty story?' Magdalene suddenly asked. 'I have hundreds of them, ya.'

Evening protested. 'No dirty stories, Bah Kynsai! We agreed to tell only stories with morals, remember?'

'Right, right, if we have clean stories that are amusing, why should we resort to dirty stories?' Bah Kit said.

Bah Kynsai shrugged helplessly. 'I'm overruled, Mag, sorry. Personally, I do enjoy dirty stories.'

'You people are prudish!' Magdalene said disapprovingly.

'Okay, okay, let me tell you a very, very short story,' Raji said, not wanting a quarrel to break out. 'I was an eyewitness to this one, okay? It happened in a Chinese restaurant. While I was enjoying my fried pork chow, a cabinet minister from the state government and his friends suddenly came barging in. At the same moment, a man at one of the tables stood up. When the minister saw that, okay, he puffed up his chest and went to him and said magnanimously: "Sit down, sit down! I appreciate it, but you don't have to stand up!" The man was utterly stupefied: "Why? Can't I even take the water jug from that table?" Many of us who heard the exchange, ha, chuckled softly, and the red-faced minister quickly went towards another part of the restaurant.'

'Was that you standing or what, Raji?' Magdalene laughed.

'Why does it have to be me?'

'But this little story of yours, what moral can it have?' Evening asked tartly.

Raji creased his brows, trying to think of an appropriate moral, so I helped him out: '*A man who is full of himself does not understand the world.*'

'There you are,' Raji said triumphantly, 'and a beautiful one too!'

'Okay, who's next?' Bah Kynsai asked.

'Bah Kit, since he's so full of "clean" stories,' Magdalene said, still miffed.

Bah Kit, however, said he could not think of anything right then and pointed at me.

I told them a story about Bah K.

During elections, it is the custom for politicians to find out if there are any funerals in their constituencies so they can attend them and meet a large number of people without having to go to their homes. At such gatherings, they make a great show of their generosity by donating money and goods to the bereaved family, though their actual motive is to buttonhole the others who have come to console, talking about politics and what they would do if elected.

One day, Mr N, an MLA candidate from the Congress party, hearing that somebody had died in a locality on the outskirts of Shillong, decided to get to the death house as soon as he could. He arrived very early, at about 9 a.m., because he said he would have to go to some villages for election-related meetings. At that time, there were quite a few men from the locality sitting in the drawing room, dressed for the office, for they planned to proceed to work directly from there. There was only one man in the room who was dressed in house clothes—a tee-shirt, sweatpants and rubber flip-flops. That man was Mr K, a college teacher and a well-known columnist, respected for his extensive knowledge, and much sought after for advice. He was dressed informally because he happened to live nearby and did not plan to go to work that day.

Mr N—a tall, handsome but arrogant-looking man—was contesting for the first time and therefore did not know many people in the locality. When he came in, he went directly to where the body was kept. After whispering his condolences to the family and surreptitiously handing over some money to the next of kin, he came to the drawing room to sit with the locals. He gave them a big smile, introduced himself and shook their hands, saying to each, 'How are you? I'm Mr N from the Congress, you are …?'

He did that with every one of them, but when he came to Mr K, he grimaced in distaste. He thought, 'Why should I shake this dirty fellow's hand? He doesn't seem to have much, look at him, a tee-shirt, sweatpants and rubber flip-flops! What can this fellow do for me?' He ignored Mr K completely and went to sit in the easy chair someone had vacated for him. Soon, he began to discuss politics in a loud voice, quite forgetting that he was in a death house. Mostly, he bragged about how the national leaders—Sonia-ji, Rahul-ji and the party leadership—loved him so much that they had given him the ticket despite stiff opposition from the local factions.

Mr K had heard it all before. He felt like saying, 'How can you claim to be so close to Rahul and Sonia when even senior Congress ministers have described both of them as "Sonia, yet so far?"' But he decided to not engage. He left soon afterwards, not only because he was fed up with Mr N's boasting but also because the insult had soured his mood.

At home, Mr K busied himself with tidying up his little garden, weeding it, and pruning the plants and flowers. Some time later, he was startled by someone calling loudly from the gate. He looked up and found that it was Mr N. He was saying, 'Hey, Bah, is this the house of Mr K?'

Mr K politely replied that it was.

'Is he at home?' Mr N asked.

'You want to meet him, Bah?' Mr K countered.

'I do want to meet him very badly, yes,' Mr N said. 'I was thinking of requesting him to help me with this voters' appeal.'

'Ooh!' Mr K exclaimed as if greatly disappointed. 'Just now, just now, he left home! You missed him by a thread, Bah! You'll have to come back some other day, please don't mind.'

'That sounded like Ap to me,' Bah Kynsai laughed.

'It was a trick well played and well deserved too,' Magdalene declared.

'But why should such a man run for election?' Hamkom wondered. 'His PR is lousy, ya!'

'How did he fare, Bah Ap?' Donald asked.

'He got the lowest number of votes and lost his security deposit,' I said.

'As he should, as he should,' Bah Kynsai said. 'So what about the moral?'

'Two,' Bah Su said, 'I would give two: *do not look at anyone with prejudice*, and, *he who would be great should first be humble*.'

'Nice ones, Bah Su, nice ones,' Donald commended him.

'Okay, next,' Bah Kynsai shouted.

Dale raised a hand and said, 'I'll tell the next one, Bah, just a very short one.'

His story was about a boy who was asked to kiss his mother's visiting friend. And this, according to Dale, was something that really happened—to his neighbours actually. The visiting friend was just leaving, and the mother wanted her little son to kiss her goodbye. Calling out to him, she said, 'Bahlit, come here, son, come and kiss your auntie goodbye.'

But little Bahlit refused to come. When the mother tried again in a sterner voice, the boy replied, 'No, I'm not kissing her!'

'But why not? Come here, don't be so naughty—'

'No, no, I'm not kissing her,' little Bahlit insisted, his voice getting more desperate.

'But why not, you little devil?'

'She might slap me like she slapped Papa yesterday.'

We all laughed at the story, but Bah Kynsai pretended to be angry and said, 'Dale, you are telling us a bloody joke, you dummy!'

'But a good one, Bah Kynsai,' Magdalene defended Dale. 'Imagine the shock of the mother!'

I added, 'It's not a pointless story either, Bah Kynsai. Look at it this way: *a child sees what adults have not even dreamt of.*'

Dale shook his right fist and said, 'Yeah! Good, Bah, good.'

'Who's next?' Bah Kynsai asked.

'Ap, from his books,' Raji drawled.

I told them about an incident concerning two colleagues, one from Sohra, the other from Pariong, West Khasi Hills, who were carrying out an official inspection in the house of a wealthy woman in Mawsynram. The woman had applied for a grant from their office.

'But why should a rich woman apply for a government grant?' Magdalene protested.

'That's the question, isn't it? Why, indeed?' I replied.

'The rich want everything, na, Mag?' Bah Kynsai stated. 'They know all about the loopholes in government schemes, and more importantly, na, they know how to make themselves seem poorer than the poor before the government. I know a woman who's a high-ranking officer, ha, whose husband is a stinking rich businessman, ha, but when he went for treatment to a super-speciality hospital in Mumbai, na, his wife claimed reimbursement from the government. Because he did not work as a government employee, na, she declared him as her dependant. Dependant, my arse!'

'They also bribe people, Bah Kynsai,' Raji chimed in. 'They'd do anything to hoodwink the government.'

'There's your answer, Mag,' I said.

Magdalene did not say anything more, only shook her head in disbelief. So, I continued.

The two friends arrived in the morning and worked without rest till noon. Then, they sat with the woman in the drawing room to ask her some final questions.

By this time, they were famished, for they had eaten nothing since morning. They consoled themselves with the thought that the family, being well-to-do, would surely give them some food very soon. In their experience, whenever they went on inspection duty to remote places, the families— because of the problem of procuring food, and out of gratitude—always gave them lunch. Even the poorest among them would share whatever food they had.

After the interview was over, the woman asked, 'You two must be very hungry by now, no?'

Their hearts immediately warmed to her. The Sohra answered for them both: 'Actually, yes, Mei, we were so busy since morning that we weren't able to eat anything at all.'

When you are hungry, they thought, you should not try to be polite; always admit the fact.

'Hmm,' the woman responded, 'so, will you take tea or kwai?'

The question was so shocking that it soured the Sohra's mood completely. 'Waa! What kind of question is that?' he thought. 'This woman is truly, truly stingy. In Sohra, we would never ask such a question; it's downright insolent. We came here for her grant and have been toiling hard, and yet, she has not offered us a single piece of betel nut until now. And when she should be showing us a bit of hospitality, she's asking us this shameless question instead! To accept anything from such a woman would be to demean ourselves.' Aloud, he replied: 'No, it's okay, it's okay. We'll go and have our food in the shops …'

But the Parïong was fuming at the woman's shameless lack of gratitude. Unlike the Sohra, who was taught to behave politely even under testing circumstances, he thought it was time to teach her a lesson. Interrupting his friend, he said, 'Eat in the shops? They are about three kilometres away, man! By the time we get there, on foot, in this heat, we will collapse.' Then, turning to the woman, he said, 'We will take both, and also give us lunch, otherwise …'

He left the sentence hanging in the air, but the woman understood, and so, scowling all the while, she grudgingly brought them lunch, tea and betel nuts. When she gave them only a piece of pork each, the Parïong immediately said, 'Give us some more meat, otherwise …'

Magdalene chuckled and shook her head. 'I haven't come across any Khasis as miserly as this woman,' she said. 'Ap must be kidding us or what?'

'All my stories are true stories, Mag,' I told her.

'Aw, come on!' she said.

Evening intervened. 'Have you ever been that side, Mag? Many people there are like the woman in the story: miserly, self-seeking, and very cunning. I know. I have had the same kind of experience myself.'

Then, Raji, mimicking Bah Kynsai, said, 'Moral?'

'This Raji, liah, is drunk again, I think!' Bah Kynsai swore.

Bah Su was very fond of supplying morals. Once again, he offered: '*To be polite with the impolite is self-defeating*.'

Evening added, '*Only daring can give you victory*.'

Donald, however, was not entirely satisfied with the story. He said, 'Bah Ap, the Parïong spoke about walking to the shops, didn't they have a vehicle? How did they get there in the first place?'

'Long-distance bus service. But there was no means of transport around the place.'

'Okay,' Bah Kynsai declared, 'now I'll tell you a story called "What Did You See at Nan Polok?" You remember Nan Polok, na, Don? Ward's Lake, yes?'

One day, a school in Shillong took a bus full of kids to see the beautiful Nan Polok Lake. This was part of the school's plan to show its students the interesting places in town and to acquaint them with their history.

The following day, their class teacher asked the students, 'So, what did you see at Nan Polok yesterday? Was it beautiful?'

'Yes, miss, it was very beautiful,' they all said.

'And what was it that you found most beautiful?'

Some said they loved the trees and the many varieties of flowers growing in the manicured lawns and well-kept flower beds. Others said they liked the colourful wooden bridge across the lake, and all of them said they loved the fish, silver and red, and how they caught the *chana*, fried chickpeas, that visitors threw down to them.

But one group of boys said nothing at all. So, the teacher turned to them and asked, 'What about you? Why did you not say anything?'

The biggest of them stood up and said, 'We saw kissing.'

'What! Who was kissing?' the teacher yelped in surprise.

'Some boys and some girls in a corner.'

Everyone laughed at Bah Kynsai's story, but Evening scoffed. 'What do you expect from Bah Kynsai?'

'Why, Evening, it's not a dirty story, man!' Magdalene protested.

'No, no, I'm not saying it's a dirty story, but only Bah Kynsai could turn a children's story into something like this, no?'

'It's actually a serious story, Ning,' I said.

Bah Su nodded. '*A public place should not be a place of infamy,*' he said.

'These things are still taboo to us, but in the West, ha, people are doing it everywhere!' Donald observed.

'What do you mean by "doing it", man?' Bah Kynsai demanded.

'Aw, come on, Bah Kynsai,' Donald laughed, 'you know I mean making out and nothing more!'

'But here, ha, once it gets dark, ha, people go to public places and do more than make out,' Evening lamented, 'and no one is doing anything about it.'

'What can anybody do about it, anyway?' Hamkom countered.

'There should be a law against it,' Bah Kit replied.

'And who will enforce the law?' Bah Kynsai asked. 'There are so many laws in Meghalaya already, na? There's a law against smoking in public places, a law against drunken driving, a law against using mobile phones while driving, a law against polythene bags, a law against littering and pollution, a law against noise pollution and late-night partying … But nobody gives a damn.'

'Hey, Bah Kynsai, we are the outlaws, leh, the outlaws! And we don't like in-laws, hahaha,' Raji cackled. He was drunk again.

'So, what can we do about debauchery in public places?' Bah Kit wanted to know.

'What can we do about anything?' Bah Kynsai asked. 'We can talk and talk and write, but finally, we're like prophets in the wilderness. This is India, na?'

'Worse, Bah Kynsai, this is Meghalaya,' Raji added. Apparently, he was not so drunk.

'Hamkom, Donald, Magdalene and Raji'—Bah Kynsai pointed at them— 'they haven't told us any stories at all, don't you have anything, you buggers?'

'Why, Bah Kynsai, I did tell one tonight!' Raji protested.

'Bah Kynsai,' I said, 'have I told you the story about Phron?'

Phron lived in Khliehshnong, Sohra. Everybody called him *Khaweit*, a shit-himself coward. Phron acquired this unenviable reputation because of his irrational and intense fear of the dark. If he walked alone in the dark, Phron felt as if a demon, a Thlen, a tiger, a thief, a robber or a killer would suddenly come out of it and pounce upon him. He tried his best never to be alone outside after dark.

But Phron also needed to leave the house and make his nocturnal rounds, or he would not get a wink of sleep. And so, every night after dinner, he would visit one of his neighbours, invariably escorted by his wife and one of his children, who would return home after seeing him safely to his destination.

While at the neighbours', Phron would hang around until people began to yawn. But because he had a ready wit and was well-stocked with amusing tales, most people loved his company and enjoyed chit-chatting with him. They were also mindful of his nyctophobia and, therefore, when it was time for him to return, they made sure to drop him back to his doorstep.

But one night, the neighbours he was visiting decided to play a prank on him, just to see what would happen. When it was time for Phron to leave, they said, 'Phron, tonight, whether you like it or not, you'll have to go home alone.'

'Go home alone!' Phron yelped. 'But you know I cannot walk alone in the dark! The lanes are pitch dark, horribly frightening, and I don't even have a torch or a flambeau!'

'In that case, you'll have to sleep here; we simply cannot drop you home.'

'But why?' Phron protested.

His friends pretended to be angry and said roughly, 'Can't you see how busy we are? Are you blind or what? And you know very well tomorrow is market day! If we don't get these lime packets ready, what shall we sell?'

'How can I sleep here in this wintry cold without proper blankets and quilts?' Phron protested again. 'And what will my wife say, huh? Can you answer to my wife for me? Tomorrow she won't even let me in, and worse, she'll never escort me out again.'

'That's up to you, we cannot drop you home tonight!' they said and refused to discuss the matter any further.

With no way out, Phron went outside and stood shivering in the dark, for his friends had refused to loan him a flambeau. He turned his attention towards home, but his feet refused to take even a single step. He stood there for a long time, asking himself feverishly, 'What to do, what to do?'

Suddenly, an idea struck him. He took out two cigarettes and lit them both. He held one in his right hand, the other in his left. Then, spreading his arms wide, he took his first steps home.

He took a drag of the cigarette in his right hand and said to himself, 'So, where are you going tomorrow, Deng?' Pulling on the other cigarette, he replied in a different voice, 'Tomorrow, Phron? I don't have anywhere to go. Shall we go bird-catching or what?'

Another drag of the first cigarette and he said, 'Not a bad idea, Deng, not a bad idea at all.'

Thus he walked on—arms spread wide, two cigarettes glowing in the dark and two voices speaking to each other—until he was within sight of his own house. But as luck would have it, Phron was spotted by a neighbour, who was standing by the fence of his house. Curious about this strange behaviour, he peremptorily demanded: 'Why are you spreading your arms like that and talking to yourself like a lunatic?'

The neighbour's stern voice, coming out of the dark like that, gave Phron a terrible fright. He cried out in alarm, jumped as if he had stepped on red-hot coals, and, losing his balance, fell flat on his face. Lying on the hard-packed soil, barely able to breathe, he tried to steady his heart, which was hammering wildly in his chest. It was only when the neighbour spoke again that he recognised the voice and was slowly able to bring his fear under control. He regained his wits, and getting up, cursed the fellow: 'What the hell, man! *Tdong, mrad*! Arsehole, animal! Can't you see I'm practising for a drama? When a man is focused on something, never do that! Damn you, lyeit, now I have forgotten all the lines! And where are my cigarettes?'

Shaking with laughter, Bah Kynsai said, 'Tet teri ka, your people are quite something, man!'

'I like this fellow, very ingenious,' Hamkom declared.

'I like him too,' Donald said. 'And what I like best about him is that, though he had a phobia—nyctophobia, no, Bah Ap?—he devised a strategy and overcame it. True courage, they say, is not the absence of fear, but the ability to overcome fear. Who was it who said, "There's nothing to fear but fear itself"? Was it Roosevelt? I think Phron proved that.'

'What I learnt from this,' Bah Su said, 'is that *fear is a means of defence.*'

'Or it can be linked to the question of influx,' Evening added. '*The man who fears makes himself secure*. We should really learn to fear influx and devise a strategy to make ourselves secure.'

'You and your influx!' Hamkom and Donald said together, sounding disgusted.

'The morals are good, though,' Bah Kynsai observed. 'Next!'

Magdalene said she would tell the next story, a classroom story she had been told by one of her colleagues. It was about a boy with a repulsive habit. He sat in class all day, with his forefinger in his nostrils: poking, digging, scraping and scratching. No one knew why he did that, perhaps he was naturally mucus-rich or had a perpetually itchy nose or was worm-infested, which people say can make your nose very itchy. No one really knew, but everyone was thoroughly sick of it.

One day, while one of his teachers was giving a lecture on a poem by John Keats, the boy, as always, was busy with his nostrils. The teacher, who had seen him do it far too often, thought it was time to put a stop to it once and for all. Intending to shame the boy in front of everyone, he suddenly stopped his lecture, turned to him, and asked, 'Did you get it?'

Without any hesitation, the boy replied, 'Yes, sir.'

Incensed at his impudence, the teacher addressed the entire class and said, 'Look at him! He has been picking his nose since I entered the room, and when I ask him if he has got what he was poking for, his answer is a brazen "Yes, sir". Have you come across such a shameless creature before?'

Now honestly embarrassed, the boy said, 'I thought you were asking about the poem, sir.'

Laughing at her own story, Magdalene asked, 'What do you think? What do you think?'

The story was rather abrupt, and the punchline a little tame, but Donald patted her on the back and laughed with genuine pleasure. Hamkom, too, smiled and asked, 'And was the teacher able to stop his habit?'

'Whenever he saw the teacher and remembered the incident, the boy did try to remove his finger from his nostrils. But mostly, he forgot.'

Bah Su offered the moral of the story: '*When hardened to a bad habit, we harden.*'

'I hope, Bah Su, you are not talking about me or Bah Kynsai because we are always drinking, especially Bah Kynsai?' Raji said drunkenly.

'I'm not soaking up drinks like you, Raji! I don't become shit-faced and piss drunk like you!' Bah Kynsai retorted hotly.

'That's too much, Bah Kynsai, too much! I have never pissed in my pants, okay, however drunk I may be, okay, not in my pants! But you, Bah Kynsai, you are drinking too much! Even now, you are *jawsheh*, drooling drunk ...'

Bah Kynsai threw a piece of wood at him and said, 'Why, you *lwa pei*!'

A lwa is an earthen pot used to store alcohol. A lwa pei is a pot with a hole. Khasis often describe an alcoholic as a lwa pei.

Raji would have said something nastier because he was really rat-arsed, so to speak, but Bah Su interrupted them and said, 'Actually, I had myself in mind.'

'Oh, yeah, yeah,' Raji agreed. 'You too, Bah Su, you are as fond of your drink as drooling-drunk Bah Kynsai.'

Bah Kynsai rushed towards Raji, but we held him back and asked him not to pay any mind to someone not in his senses. However, he was really, really angry. As he struggled to break free from our grasp (Hamkom, Donald and I were holding him), he said, 'Let go of me, na, liah! He should know his place before insulting me, na, stud! I'm a professor at a university, who the hell is he?'

'Why, I'm a journalist and a filmmaker, and I stand on my own two feet, I—'

'Shut up, Raji!' we all said.

After a while, we managed to calm Bah Kynsai down and consoled him by saying that Raji was a bit of a joker when he was drunk and that he was sure to apologise once sober.

To tell you the truth, Bah Kynsai and Bah Su were also very fond of their drink. Even now, Bah Kynsai was at a stage we call *shongshit*, that is, fervent with drinks. But to be fair to him, he never got beyond this point. Bah Su had downed quite a few mugs too, but he always managed to seem so calm and quiet that no one really knew whether he was drunk or not.

To change the tone of things, Hamkom said, 'I also have a classroom story, personally experienced.'

One day, while Hamkom was invigilating at his college, a huge Naga fellow with shaggy hair like Samson suddenly stood up and rapped very hard on the desk.

Thinking he wanted an extra script, Hamkom quickly went towards him. However, the fellow said he did not want an extra script. He produced a little piece of paper the size of a postage stamp. When he unfolded it, it turned out to be a long, thin strip folded many times over. Hamkom saw that it was full of notes written in very small writing. As he looked at it in amazement, the fellow said in a peremptory tone, 'I'll copy from here, okay?'

Hamkom was so surprised by the question that he found himself asking the student, 'But the writing is so small, can you read it? You'd need a microscope.'

'I can see well enough. I'll copy, okay?'

Hamkom took a moment to think this through carefully, and said to himself, 'Just yesterday, a friend of mine was beaten up by one of the cheating students for taking away his script. Now, if I scold and threaten this fellow, without a doubt, it will not go well. Besides, he will be expelled and not allowed to write the remaining papers. So far, he hasn't done anything wrong ...'

Instead of scolding him, Hamkom asked, 'If you copy from that paper, is it okay for me to write on your script that you have copied from it? If it is okay for me to do that, then it is okay for you to copy.'

The fellow scratched his head, sat down and exclaimed in frustration: 'Ashh!'

But he did not copy.

Bah Kynsai praised Hamkom for handling a potentially dangerous situation so well. Magdalene said she had come upon a few students trying to copy from books and pieces of paper, but always on the sly. She asked Bah Kynsai, 'There is a word for such a piece of paper, no?'

'A crib sheet.'

'Yes, yes, a crib sheet. Many students in our college use crib sheets during exams.'

'Is cheating that rampant in Shillong colleges or what?' Donald enquired. 'I saw a recent TV news report about cheating in a Bihar college, okay? On the screen was a three-storied building where an exam was in progress. And you know what? Hanging from every window of the building, ha, were scores of male relatives of the examinees, handing them crib sheets or whispering answers to them from books and mobile phones. And they continued to do that in spite of the TV crews filming them from outside. Is it like that here too?'

'Oh no, no, no, Don!' Magdalene said quickly. 'Here, okay, only in some colleges will you find students attempting to cheat, and we always catch them and either give them new scripts to write on or expel them if they are repeat offenders. Nobody from outside is even allowed into the college compound during examinations.'

'Meghalaya is definitely not Bihar in that sense, Don,' Hamkom said. 'In fact, Shillong is the best educational centre in the Northeast. Students come from all over the region to study here. These are all exceptions rather than the rule, no, Bah Kynsai?'

'Bihar has a terrible reputation, ha?' Bah Kynsai said. 'But what happened during that particular incident, na, was a national shame. I think they finally cancelled the exam and rescheduled it.'

Taunting Bah Kynsai, Raji drawled, 'Moraaal.'

We thought Bah Kynsai might explode again, but he only laughed and cursed: 'Stud, liah, how can I be angry with this bugger? When he's drunk, na, he's so damn funny!'

Bah Kit offered the moral: *Diplomacy averts disharmony.*

'Nice, nice, Bah Kit, thanks, ya,' Hamkom said.

'Bah Kynsai,' Magdalene said, her hand raised for attention, 'if you don't mind, I have a little story. It's very, very short, but—'

'Just tell it, na!' Bah Kynsai told her.

Magdalene told us of a young man who wanted to study theology and train for the priesthood. Since his family was really hard-up and could not support his studies, he went to his maternal uncle to plead for help. The uncle was willing to support him, but said, 'It's going to be very difficult for you to prepare yourself for the priesthood if you continue to hang around with that girl of yours ...'

The nephew assured him, 'It's all right, Mabah, I'm exercising a lot of control.'

A little annoyed by his cocksure attitude, the uncle replied, 'What you say may be true, but when there is too much *control*, the *black market* is also there, no?'

A short burst of laughter followed the little story, and Bah Kynsai himself tried to come up with the moral. When he failed, he said, 'No, no, no, that won't do. Give us another.'

I volunteered: '*Only those who have trodden the path can truly point the direction.*'

'That's a good one, Ap,' Bah Kynsai said. 'Hey, you guys, why don't we try telling love stories? Is there anyone with a love story?'

Everyone shook their heads.

I had two that might pass as love stories, so I proceeded to tell them the first one, 'The Bride'.

The boisterous wedding procession wound along the wide footpath of Ïingkhrong, down the ancient steps, spilled out onto the Shillong–Sohra road and flowed along the sacred forest of Khliehshnong. It was heading towards the Presbyterian church at Ïewhat. Viewers, young and old, men and women, stood along the fringe of the sacred forest, forming a line about half a kilometre long. Many had just emerged from the forest, where they had been preoccupied with their own affairs. Some women came with water pots, carried in bamboo cones on their backs, while others carried wet clothes in large aluminium basins, which they had been washing at the *shyngiars*, the springs gushing from bamboo pipes. At the very last moment, a group of men and young boys came from their hiding places among the trees, where they were trapping winter birds with birdlime.

'This is definitely a white man's wedding,' Parum said.

Parum worked as an office clerk in Shillong. He and his friend and co-worker, Pareh, had just alighted from a bus. They were dressed in terry-wool trousers and tweed coats and looked every inch the brown Khasi gentlemen they were.

'Look at the dress of the bride!' Parum continued. 'She's in white from head to foot: white satin frock, white satin gloves, white tiara, white lace for the veil and even white beribboned shoes. I wonder how the groom is dressed.'

'He must be waiting near the church,' Pareh answered, 'and he must be wearing black ... Most Christian weddings are black and white.'

'What's the symbolism of these wedding dresses, do you think? Why is the bride always dressed in white?'

'Virginity, chastity, purity of heart, all sorts of feminine virtues—'

'Then why would the man dress in black?'

Pareh laughed aloud, struck by the incongruity.

A shifty looking woman overheard them and laughed along too, showing teeth stained dark red-and-orange from years of betel nut chewing. She said, 'You men are always making fun of serious issues.' Then, turning back to her friend, she added, 'You heard what these two just said, didn't you, Ieit? Anyway, as I was saying, everyone knows about it. Eva was actually going around with Gavin, had been for quite some time, and no one had raised any objections. In fact, Eva's parents, Kong Mad and Bah Bro, had seemed happy enough to have someone like Gavin as their son-in-law, you know, someone who's young, good-looking, well-mannered and quite well educated ...'

When Parum heard the woman's story, he whispered to his friend: 'Listen to these women, sounds intriguing.'

'So why is Eva not marrying him today?' Ieit asked. 'Why is she tying the knot with that *metïaw*? I mean, look at her, so fair, so tall, so stunningly beautiful, why would she marry a middle-aged outsider?'

Ieit was a simple-looking woman in house clothes, with teeth as stained as her friend's. She had a basinful of clothes on the *kynroh rel* by her side. A kynroh rel, in case you do not know, is a low parapet of stones—2.5 feet wide, 2.5 feet high and 5 feet long—constructed by the side of a road for safety. The people of Sohra call it kynroh rel, a train wall, because a series of them running parallel to a road do look like the bogies of a train.

Her friend, Lor, scoffed: 'You mean you don't know? Living in the same locality, and you don't know!'

Lor's full name was Lorna, but because she was so gossipy, everybody called her Lor for Lorni, the Khasi word for gossipy.

'I'm not a *ksew-bna-lat* as some people seem to be, you know,' Ieit replied testily.

'Alright, alright,' Lor cut her short. 'I'm not a feast-knowing-stray-dog either, but I happen to be close to a friend of the family, that's how I know more than most about the matter. That metïaw you referred to is none other than Bah Bhoi, the new works manager at the cement factory. Do you see the picture now? Bah Bhoi is from Ri Bhoi, that's why he's called Bah Bhoi, although I'm not sure from which village exactly. Anyway, as I was saying, Eva was very much in love with Gavin. They were always together. Eva's parents, as I told you, had even encouraged them, for Gavin is considered a very eligible bachelor with good prospects, having passed his BSc. But everything changed when Bah Bhoi came on the scene. My friend, Rit, was in the house when Bah Bhoi came calling.

'It was late afternoon when he visited Kong Mad's. He had timed his visit very well. Everyone was in the house. The father had just returned from the market where he has a vegetable shop. Nowadays, he comes home early, letting one of his sons look after the shop after 5 p.m. You know that he's a devout church elder, no? He spends his evenings in church or at other people's homes on church affairs. Kong Mad was there too, busy cooking the evening meal with her friend, Rit, who was peeling potatoes. The eldest son, Phroming, had just come in from work. He's a labourer at the cement factory, I think, but drawing good wages, the factory being government-owned. Most importantly, Eva's uncle, Bah She, was also there. I mean Bah Shedrak, ei, you don't know him or what? He's a responsible uncle, you know, visits his sister's house every evening. It was a good thing too that he was there, for Khasi uncles have a very important role to play in such matters.'

'They used to, but not any more,' Ieit said. 'As I see it, their roles have been taken over by fathers and priests.'

'I shall ask you to explain that someday, but for now, shall I continue with the story?'

'Hold on, Ap, hold on!' Bah Kynsai suddenly shouted. 'Is this just a story or a true story?'

'True story.'

'Okay, so Lor told Ieit the story, but how did you come to know?'

'The story has become quite a legend in Sohra. I'm narrating it in my own inimitable style, that's all,' I said, laughing.

'Inimitable style indeed! Go ahead, mə, liah!' Bah Kynsai swore.

Lor said that when Bah Bhoi came to the house, they were all in the kitchen, including Eva, who was helping her mother clean the fish for frying. While the women were busy working, the men sat by the charcoal stove, drinking tea. Just then, they heard a gentle knock on the door. Kong Mad, looking at the others with questioning eyes, said, 'Who could it be? Eva, *khun*, go, see who's come.'

Khun means child, but it is also used as a term of endearment.

Eva washed her hands and went to the *nengpei*, the front room adjacent to the kitchen, to open the door. Her eyes dilated with surprise at the sight of a smiling Bah Bhoi. He was a 'big' officer at the cement factory ... everyone called him sahep ... what was he doing in her house? She had been seeing him around. She had also noticed the way he looked at her but had not given it much thought, partly because he was so much older than her and partly because she was used to the admiring and covetous stares of men.

But now he was saying: 'Kumno? How are you? I'm sorry to bother you like this ... Are your parents at home?'

Eva recovered herself and said politely, 'Yes, they are, Bah, please come in.' She seated him in a comfortably cushioned bamboo chair and went to fetch her parents. 'Bah Bhoi,' she whispered in a tone of amazement. 'He wants to meet the two of you.'

Kong Mad and Bah Bro exchanged glances as if asking each other, 'Why?', and then hastened to the front room. Kong Mad was a beautiful woman still. Clearly, Eva had inherited her good looks from her. And from her father, she had her height.

'*Waa, i Sahep! Kumno kumne!*' Kong Mad exclaimed. 'How is this? What a surprise!'

'Yes, indeed, what a surprise!' Bah Bro echoed his wife.

Greeted with such apparent disbelief, as if his visit was something of an incongruity, Bah Bhoi became quite embarrassed. He was a tall, big-boned individual with a friendly face. He had a snub nose but was not bad-looking at all. Perhaps his affluence and authority as an officer also helped to make him appear more attractive than he really was. He said, 'Please don't mind me, Kong Madeline, Bah Broming. I came just like that. Perhaps I should have used a friend, but I hardly know anyone here. Well, I do know a lot of people, many of them work at the factory, but I don't think I have a friend who's that close to me, if you know what I mean.'

'Aah!' Kong Mad and Bah Bro exclaimed, nodding their heads, but with eyes clearly not in agreement. They said, 'Sooo …?'

'Sooo … I'm here on very personal business, something very close to my heart, uff, it's quite difficult, how to put it? It's quite awkward.'

At that moment, having cut the vegetables, Rit came into the room. Rit was a small, pasty-faced woman, although surprisingly full of restless energy. She exclaimed, '*Waa, Sahep! Shano kumne*, where to now?'

'Oh, it's Kong Rit! You are here too? I have come for a very personal matter, but I quite don't know how to explain myself.'

'Wait, Sahep, wait. I think I know what you are about. Your clerk, Bah Jrin, hinted to us.'

'You mean Jrin talked about me to you and your husband? But I didn't discuss anything with him!'

'He knows, Sahep, he knows,' Rit reiterated. 'Believe me, he knows.'

'But I only asked him a few questions,' Bah Bhoi responded.

'Aah, there you are!' Rit said knowingly. 'But never mind all that. If you give the word, I can do the chirping for you. Shall I, Sahep?' When Bah Bhoi nodded dumbly, Rit said, 'Come, Kong Mad, Bah Bro, come.'

Rit took the bewildered parents back to the kitchen and left Bah Bhoi wringing his hands in the front room.

'Oh my God! Oh my God!' Rit exclaimed in a fierce whisper. 'It's true! It's true! Father of Heh is right. He told me it was only a matter of time before Bah Bhoi called on you!'

'Call on us for what?' Kong Mad asked impatiently.

'Eva, please go and keep Bah Bhoi company for a while,' Rit commanded. When Eva had left, she said slowly, excitedly, emphasising each word, 'Bah Bhoi has been smitten by your Eva for quite some time now. He wants to marry her, and he has come here to ask for your permission. Think about that, a manager! The boss of the Mawmluh-Cherra Cement Factory!'

The works manager is not exactly the boss of the factory. There are people above him, but only one or two.

In response to Rit's announcement, they all exclaimed, 'What?'

Kong Mad's tone was one of excited amazement. The rest were mostly incredulous.

'Do you mean it, Rit? Is this for real?' Kong Mad asked, taking her friend's hands in her own, in a gesture of pleading.

'Of course, of course, it's for real! You'll know it soon enough. But are you willing?'

'Are you crazy? What a question to ask! How often do you get a manager asking for your daughter's hand in marriage? Of course I'm willing, the moment he asks, I'll say yes!'

'Hold on, hold on for a second!' Bah Bro, her husband, intervened. 'Have you thought about the fact that he's almost twice her age? Why woman, he's only a little younger than the two of us!'

Shedrak, the uncle, as handsome as his sister, said, 'And what about Evelina? Do you think she would be willing just because you are? In our custom—'

'Damn your custom!' Kong Mad snapped at her younger brother. 'Are the two of you mad? So what if he's older than her? For God's sake, he is *the manager* of the cement factory! He's drawing a salary of thousands and thousands, not to speak of cars and servants and whatnot! And Eva is but an unemployed girl! Being only matric-pass, what do you think her chances are of getting a job in these hard times?'

'I think we should consider her feelings too; we cannot be mercenary about this,' Bah Bro insisted.

'I agree,' Shedrak asserted. 'And if she's already in love with someone else, it could be dangerous to force her—'

'With whom is she in love, Bah She?' Rit asked, as if this was news to her.

'Don't you think I know, Rit? The whole locality knows she has been dating that nice young man, Gavin. If she's in love with him, how will you persuade her to marry your Sahep? And as I recall, Thei, you yourself encouraged her to be friendly with Gavin!'

'Look, Gavin may be a nice young man, but he is unemployed right now,' Kong Mad objected. 'God knows when he'll get a job, and when he does, if he does, he can still never be a big officer like Bah Bhoi. I know I encouraged the match, but things have changed now. If Eva marries Bah Bhoi, she doesn't even have to look for a job. She's got it made for life!'

'That's okay, but how will you part them, woman?' Bah Bro demanded. 'If Eva is so in love with Gavin, as you well know she is, how will you make her forget him?'

Suddenly, Phroming, the son, spoke for the first time. Almost as if to himself, he said, 'My God, the manager of the factory to be *my* brother-in-law! Me, a mere labourer, to have the boss as *my* brother-in-law!'

Phroming was not a pleasant-looking person. He was tall and broad-shouldered like his father, but he had inherited the hard ambition of his mother. Turning to her, he said, 'Think about your other sons, Mei, four of them unemployed! We could ask him to give all of them a job at the factory.

If Eva marries Bah Bhoi, Mei, she's not the only one who's got it made; the whole family has got it made!'

'Yes, yes, son, you are absolutely right! I had not thought so far ahead, but yes, yes, you are absolutely right! No, no, by hook or by crook, Eva has got to marry Bah Bhoi!'

'But how?' Bah Bro asked. 'If Eva does not agree, I will not agree either. And I don't see how she will agree if Gavin is still with her.'

'Leave Gavin to us, Papa. We'll take care of him.'

'What do you mean you'll take care of him?' Bah Bro and Shedrak asked, quite alarmed by the menace in Phroming's words.

'Relax, Papa, relax, Marit, I don't mean to do him any harm; there are five of us, and with a few friends to help, we'll just persuade him to ditch Eva.'

The father looked thoughtfully at his shaggy-haired son and asked, 'Why would he ditch Eva when he dotes on her?'

'He will, Papa, he will—'

'I forbid you to do anything unlawful—'

'Don't worry, Papa, nothing unlawful, just a little persuasion. You don't have to know anything, and we'll certainly not do anything that will spoil your standing as a church elder. Just leave it to us.'

'And if you succeed in persuading Gavin to dump Eva, what will happen to her?' his father asked.

'Oh, she'll cry and moan for a few weeks, maybe longer, but I know women … when the man they love turns out to be a betrayer, not worthy of their love, they tend to get over him quicker than you think.'

'And since when have you become an expert on women's behaviour?' Shedrak asked caustically.

But Phroming only said, 'You old people are out of your depth here. Just leave it to us.'

Kong Mad and Rit were delighted with Phroming's plan. Kong Mad because of the advantages and the status the marriage would bring, and Rit because she, as the woman who made it possible, could extract something from Bah Bhoi, maybe even a job for her son, as a quid pro quo.

Only the men were more than a little worried. First of all, they were concerned about Eva's feelings, and secondly, they were even more worried about the scandal Phroming's actions might bring upon the family. Nobody gave much thought to Gavin.

Phroming did not lose much time putting his plan to action. One night, he and three of his brothers, along with a few friends, went to wait for Gavin in a lonely spot as he was returning home from a meeting with Eva. One of Phroming's brothers, Draining, the second one, was as big as him, but even uglier because of his unhygienic habits. The other two, Taining and Blinding, the fourth and the fifth, were of average height and rather good-looking, but for the hardness around their mouths. The third one, Priming, who was more like his father, had refused to participate. Phroming's friends were a shabby lot, and all marked with the purple blotches of heavy drinkers.

When Gavin reached the spot, the brothers emerged from behind the trees and blocked his path. Without so much as an explanation, they asked him to write Eva a letter, telling her that he had decided to stop seeing her since he had met someone else. The night was dark, the spot was secluded, and Gavin was all alone. But he was not afraid. And why should he be? Were these not the brothers of his beloved, whom he had known forever? His initial reaction, therefore, was amazement rather than fear. He said, 'Are you mad? Why should I do a thing like that? I love Eva and Eva loves me; we plan to marry as soon as I get a job—'

Even as Gavin was speaking, Draining and one of his friends suddenly caught hold of his left hand and held it up in front of Phroming, who took one of the fingers and bent it back till it broke. Gavin screamed in sheer agony—quickly muffled by several hands held tightly over his mouth—doubled up in pain and fell fainting to the ground. The brothers left him lying there for a while, but when they were sure nobody was coming, they slapped his face a few times to wake him up.

When Gavin woke up, he immediately grabbed hold of his broken finger as if that would lessen the pain. It did not help, but after a while, he somehow controlled himself enough to look up at the men through his tears and ask through clenched teeth, 'Are you people crazy? I have known you since I was a child, why would you do a thing like that?'

'This is just a taste of what will happen to you if you don't write that letter,' Phroming answered. 'We don't want you anywhere near Eva from now on. Write the letter and stay away from her, otherwise—'

'Otherwise,' Draining intervened, 'something may happen to your little sister, say, while she is fetching water from the shyngiar or washing clothes at the stream—'

At this, Gavin shouted at them, 'You bastards are monsters! I'm glad you have shown me what you really are before I became your brother-in-law. I'll write your damn letter, but not because I'm afraid. If anything happens to my sister, you will answer to my relatives; I'll make sure of that. But I'll write it because I don't want to be related to thugs like you! I love Eva above all things, but I don't want to live with the likes of you for the rest of my life.'

Phroming and his brothers took Gavin to the megaliths nearby, so he could sit on a table stone lying at the feet of the standing stones. They gave him an exercise book and a pen, and ordered him to write his letter.

Gavin wrote just two brief sentences, ending his relationship with Eva. He could not manage any more while his left hand was throbbing with such terrible pain. But he refused to tell her that he had met someone else. He merely said that family circumstances had made it impossible for him to carry on with their relationship, although he would continue to love her for the rest of his life.

The brothers objected to that last sentence, but there was nothing they could do. Gavin refused to tell an untruth. 'I love her and will continue to love her for as long as I live. But I don't want to be anywhere near fiends like you!'

When it was done, they let Gavin go with more warnings about what would happen to his sister should he squeal on them.

Looking at the letter, Phroming embraced everyone and said, 'Well, that was rather easy. Let's go and celebrate in the boozer, shall we?'

Gavin's letter was given to Rit, who gave it to Eva in the presence of Kong Mad. As predicted by Phroming, Eva cried and moaned for weeks, refusing to eat anything. The family had to take her to a hospital in Shillong, where she was put on a saline drip. Even after she recovered, Eva continued to be grief-stricken for more than two years, which was why the marriage with Bah Bhoi could not take place earlier. Phroming had miscalculated the strength of her love for Gavin. His words declaring eternal love for her touched her to her very soul. But eventually, she got used to the fact that Gavin would never come back to her despite his self-proclaimed love. Her mother, too, constantly questioned whether Gavin's passion for her was real. She would say, 'If he really loves you like he said, why would he put his family above your love? I think it was only a ploy not to make you think the worst of him. And look at the terseness of the letter! Do you think he really cares for you?'

But Eva was not convinced. She knew Gavin as she knew her own heart. She knew that he loved her, as he had said. Something terrible must have happened with his family to make him stay away from her. And so, in her heart of hearts, she still pined for him. Eventually, though, she agreed to marry Bah Bhoi, partly to put an end to her mother's pestering and partly because of the hopelessness of her situation.

After Lor had told Ieit all this, Ieit asked her how she knew about what Phroming had done to Gavin. Lor said, 'Phroming confided in Rit and Rit confided in me, but no one else knows. You are only the fourth person to know. Sometimes I thought of telling Eva about it, but what good would that have done? And so, there she is, dressed in white and about to marry the boss of the cement factory!'

'I don't believe you haven't told anyone else, Lor,' Ieit said bluntly.

'Let's not talk about it now,' Lor replied quickly and tried to draw Ieit's attention back to the wedding procession.

Parum, who had overheard everything, said, 'What a story, ha, Pareh? Do you think she will be happy with him?'

'She'll get used to it, I'm sure, especially because Gavin, who seems like an honourable fellow, would never come to disturb her life again. But if he does, married or not married, there will be disastrous consequences.'

'Even if Gavin leaves her alone, do you think Eva will be all right in this marriage?'

Before Pareh could speak, there was a sudden commotion in the wedding procession. 'What happened, what happened?' someone shouted.

Soon the answer was relayed back to them: 'The bride has run away!'

'What?' they all cried, surprised, shocked, and then pleased that something fantastically dramatic was taking place. 'Where, where has she run away to?' they all asked.

'Into the sacred forest,' the answer came.

'Oh my God, Ieit, I think she's still in love with Gavin after all!' Lor exclaimed. 'I think she's going to run away; I hope she doesn't do anything stupid ...'

Parum was really concerned. 'Come, come, Pareh, they must not allow her to go too deep into the jungle, she might try to harm herself.'

'Yeah, yeah,' Pareh agreed, running after Parum, 'she might even try to commit suicide, man!'

When they got to the place where the bride had rushed into the forest, they were stopped from proceeding further by her relatives, who said, 'Ten men have gone after her, please don't go into the jungle and complicate things further. Let's wait here; they should be able to catch up with her soon enough.'

Parum and Pareh waited with the crowd. They saw the mother, surrounded by her relatives and friends, including Rit, sitting on the ground and crying bitterly. The father, Bah Bro, and the uncle, Shedrak, were standing beside her. Bah Bro was berating her: 'I told you, woman, not to do it! Look at what your greed has done to us. Oh, the shame of it! If they catch up with her, what are you planning to do? Tie her with a rope and drag her to the wedding like a sacrificial lamb? And what if they don't find her soon enough? Have you thought of what she might do to herself? Oh, my poor baby! I should never have listened to this greedy woman!'

Shedrak added bitterly, 'She may not have time to hang herself, what with the men pursuing her and all, but there are plenty of gorges and deep gullies in the jungle from where she could throw herself to her death, have you thought about that? God, oh God, what a mess!'

Kong Mad's cries became louder. She took off one of her shoes and hit her head with it again and again, as a gesture of regret and repentance, or perhaps as a sign of her ill fortune. Rit, the matchmaker, herself pale and frightened, tried to comfort her by stroking her back.

Shedrak left the group, and going to the edge of the forest, shouted, 'What news? What's happening now?'

Meanwhile, inside the sacred forest, the bride lifted her trailing skirt above her knees and ran down the steep path as fast as she could. The men gave chase, shouting and telling her to stop and not to do anything foolish. Phroming, who led the chase, called out to her, 'Eva, please don't do anything stupid. Come back to us; we'll talk things out nicely. If you don't want to marry Bah Bhoi, we won't force you, only please come back. If anything happens to you, what will happen to all of us? Think of our family's reputation! The world will talk about this for as long as we live. Please come back and stop this nonsense. We'll do whatever you want!'

But the bride only ran faster. Once or twice, she picked up stones or sticks and threw them at her pursuers, saying, 'Go away! When I told you to go away, why are you still running after me? How can I do anything when you are running after me?'

When she let fly with her missiles, the men stopped for a moment to avoid them, then continued the chase. 'We don't want you to do anything foolish, that's why we are running after you. Stop it, come back here, we'll do whatever you want!'

'Go away, you stupid men!' the bride responded, sounding frantic. 'You don't understand anything, go away right now!'

The men, however, did not go away. They kept running after her in a determined bid to stop her from killing herself. When the bride had run some distance into the forest, and saw that she could not outrun her pursuers, in her desperation, she squatted right there on the steep path, lifted her skirt, pulled down her panties and let rip a sound like a tyre exploding.

When the men saw what she was doing, they immediately understood and let out a collective sigh: 'Aah, that is why!'

Phroming was the first to recover. He shouted to the men: 'Go back, go back, let's go back outside!'

When the people milling outside the sacred forest saw the men coming back without the bride, they immediately feared the worst. 'Where's Eva?' they cried. 'Why have you come back without her? What happened to her?'

The women heard these questions and started crying and howling at the top of their voice. Then the men coming up the jungle path shouted back their answer: '*Ka leit eit*!' they said. 'She's taking a crap!'

The answer was relayed to everyone, and they, like the men in the sacred forest, heaved a collective sigh. 'Aah, that is why!'

Soon, in true Khasi fashion, some of the men composed a gnomic phawar and began chanting and dancing:

> *Ooooo!*
> *Ba ka tieng i'u Bhoi Sahep,*
> *Ngi nang mut mo ka la phet,*
> *Thab kti, kynhoi kynheit,*
> *Ka khlem phet ka shu leit eit,*
> *Hoooi Kiw! Hoooi Kiw!*

> (Ooooo!
> Scared of Bhoi Sahep,
> We all thought she had fled,
> But now let's sing and clap,
> She only ran to take a crap!
> Hoooi Kiw! Hoooi Kiw!)

And all through the evening, after the wedding ceremony, the drunks kept dancing and chanting the refrain:

> *Ka shu leit eit,*
> *Ka shu leit eit.*

> (Only to crap,
> Only to crap.)

By the time I finished, everyone was in paroxysms of laughter.

Finally, Bah Kynsai managed to say, 'This Ap, sala! I thought he was telling us a tragic love story, na? Who would have guessed the bride was not trying to kill herself? Who would have guessed she was only going to take a crap? Shit, man! You took us all by surprise, tdong!'

That summed up everybody's reaction. After a while, Bah Kynsai added, 'Ap, you promised us two love stories; what's the other one called?'

'"The Courtship". One of the men involved told my brothers and me the story when we were young. This too features the cement factory. Life in Sohra, at one time, did revolve around the factory, Bah Kynsai. But the narrative itself is about one of my uncles—no, no, not the funny one, the serious one, Krokar.'

'Okay, *suru, suru*, begin, begin.'

It all began immediately after the establishment of the Mawmluh-Cherra Cement Factory in 1965. Many young men from Sohra found employment there as skilled as well as unskilled workers. But those managing the office and running the administration were mostly experienced people from Shillong.

My uncle, Madeng Krokar, and two of his friends from Khliehshnong, Kelan and Reng, were working as unskilled labourers. Humble though their jobs were, to the mostly poor local people, they instantly became highly eligible bachelors, for the company was government-run, and those working there were ensured a good and steady income.

Madeng used to get up at the second cockcrow every day, and by the third cockcrow, he was ready and waiting for his friends, who would give him a shout from the footpath nearby. That was their daily routine, leaving home by the third cockcrow or thereabouts, walking the distance of more than six kilometres to the factory, starting work at 6 a.m. and returning at dusk. Until they met Bulbul.

Bah Reng, the man who told us the story many years after the incident, said they first met Bulbul in a tea shop, quite by accident. It seemed that every day at noon, they had a one-hour lunch break. The three of them always ate their packed lunch on a hill near the limestone quarry where they worked. When they had eaten, it was their custom to wash the food down with boiled water carried in glass bottles. But one day, Bah Kelan forgot to bring his water bottle and had to ask his friends for some. However, since they had been sipping from the bottles all morning, there was not enough water for them all. For a change, therefore, Bah Kelan insisted that they go to one of the tea shops near the main office for tea.

When they entered the shop, the first person they saw was a beautiful young woman sitting at the counter, taking down orders from customers and collecting payments. She reminded them of an apple they had seen their boss eating. Her cheeks were that kind of pink, probably because of the fire in the kitchen behind her. But she was not plump as an apple. She had sharp, well-cut features, or as the Khasis say, '*mih khmut mih khmat*'.

'Exact meaning, Bah Ap?' Donald asked.

'Translated literally, it sounds terrible, Don, it could mean someone with "protruding nose and eyes"—'

'Like Bah Kynsai,' Raji suddenly said.

We all looked closely at Bah Kynsai and noticed, as if for the first time, that he did have a jutting nose and big, bulging eyes. Bah Kynsai knew exactly what Raji was getting at. Before any of us could make any comments, he said, 'With all that hair on your face, has anybody told you, Raji, that you look like Jihadi John?'

'Tet leh, Bah Kynsai, that's too much, too much!'

Laughing his big, booming laugh, Bah Kynsai replied, 'When you insult people, it's not too much, but when others do it to you, it's too much, huh? Stud, liah!'

'You cannot even take a little joke?' Raji whined.

'I'm laughing now, na? Go on, Ap, go on.'

Addressing Donald, I said, 'But that's not how the phrase should be understood, Don. "Well cut" is its true meaning—'

'Get on with the story, man!' Bah Kynsai said impatiently.

Bulbul was pink as an apple, I said, with a chiselled figure and with black hair that flowed in curly cascades. What held the three men spellbound were her eyes, radiant and black, with a kind of lingering gaze and a teasing smile that set their hearts on fire. They were immediately love-struck. But none of them made any attempt to speak to her that day, although, from then onwards, they suddenly developed the habit of drinking tea after lunch.

My uncle and his friends soon became very familiar with Bulbul. With familiarity came courage. They began to have frequent conversations with her and sometimes even teased her about this and that. When her mother saw what was happening, she said, 'Why don't you boys come to visit us at home after work? At home, we can talk about so many things we cannot freely discuss here.'

It was an open invitation. The next day, when they went to work, they took with them their best clothes, so they could change out of their work clothes after washing in a stream nearby.

When they went to Bulbul's for the first time to formally court her, they were treated like honoured guests, entertained in the drawing room, and given comfortable armchairs. They might only be unskilled workers, but they were workers in a government factory and, therefore, quite a catch for someone who was only the daughter of a tea-shop owner. For weeks they went to the house, and were always treated with great respect and friendliness, and always given comfortable armchairs in which to sit. But Bulbul simply could not choose between them. Bah Kelan was tall and handsome, but she thought he was too bold and perhaps just a little bit roguish. Bah Reng was fair and attractive in a rugged kind of way, but he was too fond of his own tall tales. He told endless jokes and made them laugh, but would he be serious enough as a husband? She showed a marked preference for Madeng, my uncle, who, though not as striking as the others, was good-looking in a quiet and dignified sort of way. But still, she held back—perhaps she was holding out for a bigger catch than them. She was, after all, one of the most beautiful girls in Mawmluh, and people were forever admiring her good looks and flattering her endlessly.

A bigger catch did come in the form of a slightly built clerk with a roundish face, smooth as butter, and almost of that colour. He had just joined the factory's office staff. When the clerk from Shillong saw Bulbul, he too fell head over heels in love with her, and from the very next day, he too started going to her house to court her. Being an educated man and an office clerk drawing a much bigger salary, the fellow was always neat and well dressed. Compared with the other three, to the parents at least, he was like a full moon to a distant star. Bulbul, however, did not fall for him, probably because he was not very good-looking, though the parents showed their immediate preference.

The next evening, when the wooers went to visit Bulbul, they found only two armchairs in the drawing room. The clerk was asked to sit in one of them, while Bulbul sat in the other. My uncle and friends were given mulas, those low cane stools I told you about. Their faces immediately reddened. This was a sign for them to make themselves scarce. But how could they? They were in the throes of an awful infatuation that would not let them eat or sleep in peace. So obsessed were they that they thought of the insult as a trial to be borne stoically, or even with bravado, for the sake of love. In short, they were in the grip of La Belle Dame sans Merci, and could neither be shamed nor intimidated.

Things continued in this manner for some time, and they too soldiered on, thinking that this was not Bulbul's doing—for she kept flirting outrageously with them—but that of her family. And what could the family do if Bulbul herself should prefer one of them to the clerk? Nothing. In our custom, a person's choice is all, nothing else matters.

But still, Bulbul would not make a choice. When the family asked her what she was waiting for when she had such a respectable and well-matched suitor like the clerk eating out of her hand, she simply said, 'I like their company.' It was actually another way of saying that she liked flirting with all of them, and choosing one of them would spoil the fun.

Soon, however, the family was thrilled that she had delayed, for there was a new arrival from Shillong, an accounts officer, much, much superior to all the others: 'The sun to the moon', as the parents put it. Not very tall, he nonetheless looked quite powerful with his sturdy arms and legs, and though not handsome, he had a pleasant face and friendly manners. This man, too, was stricken by Bulbul's beauty, and after only a few days in the village, started going to her house to court her.

Initially, both the officer and the clerk were asked to sit in comfortable armchairs, but that seating arrangement did not seem appropriate to the parents, who thought that the officer should be shown preference. They were in a tizzy, until the mother suggested: 'Why don't we adopt the same stratagem as earlier?'

'You mean, make the Sahep sit in an armchair and the rest on mulas?' the father asked. 'But it didn't work, did it? Look at those stubborn labourers still polluting our house with their presence. If they had taken the hint and scrammed, Bulbul would now be happily married to the clerk!'

'You stupid man!' the mother shouted, her fat face red with suffused rage. 'Marry the clerk when a big officer is courting her! I think it was a blessing in disguise that they did not leave. But now, it's time to make them disappear.'

'How? What do you have in mind?' the father asked again, his long, thin face creasing.

'Just leave it to me.'

Almost a week after the accounts officer's visit, a new seating plan was devised in Bulbul's drawing room. The officer and Bulbul were given the only comfortable armchairs in the room; the clerk was demoted to the low cane stool; and my uncle and friends were further demoted to the very low wooden stools, just about seven inches from the floor.

When they heard this, my friends hooted with laughter. 'What a thing, what a thing to do, man!' they cried.

'Unheard of, no, Don?' Magdalene said, giving Donald a hard push on the shoulder.

Bah Kynsai said, 'If somebody had done a thing like that to me, na, I would have cursed them and said to hell with them, right there and then!'

'All of us would have done that, I think,' Donald responded.

But Bah Su said, 'You are saying that because you are not in love. I have seen worse things being tolerated in the name of love.'

'So what happened, Ap? Let him tell the story, ya, liah!' Raji slurred.

'You are cursing, Raji,' Magdalene observed.

'Am I?' he asked in surprise.

'Yeah, you said "liah"!'

'Oh, sorry, sorry, I thought I said leh, sorry, Mag. Ap, chalo, man, full steam ahead!'

When that happened, I continued, the clerk's face immediately lost colour. He was already embarrassed by the fact that his own officer was courting the same girl, but now, being so openly told that he was not welcome cut him to the quick. However, he, too, was in the grip of La Belle and simply could not bring himself to get up from the mula and leave. He sat there, smiling inanely and looking at Bulbul for a sign of favour. She too smiled back at him and seemed to tell him with her eyes not to lose hope just yet. When he saw that expression, he took heart and forgot all about the insult.

But when Bah Kelan saw how they had been further lowered, almost to the ground, he signalled to the others to follow him outside for a serious powwow. To Bulbul and her mother, they said, 'Excuse us for a moment,' and left for the courtyard.

Standing there in the dark, they debated in whispers about what they should do in the face of this new challenge. Bah Reng was for dogged resistance. But Bah Kelan said, 'Look, even the clerk, who's so much above us, has been demoted to a mula! Personally, I don't care about clerks or officers, okay? I have known women choosing for love rather than wealth and status, but what I don't like is the family's behaviour. What if a bigger officer comes, what happens then, huh? I'll tell you what will happen: the bigger officer will get the chair; the accounts officer will get the mula; the clerk will get the low wooden stool; and we, what will happen to us? We'll be squatting on the floor, man! Would you like that to happen? I vote that we leave this place immediately and look elsewhere for a wife!'

Madeng said he loved Bulbul with all his heart; however, if she did not return his love, it was pointless to keep coming to the place and be lowered from chair to cane stool and from cane stool to an even lower wooden stool. 'Ke may be right, Reng,' he concluded, addressing Bah Reng, who still wanted to brazen it out. 'If we don't leave immediately, we'll soon find ourselves on the wooden floor.'

With the vote standing two to one, Bah Reng had no option but to give in. That very night, they all left, never to return.

The family heaved a sigh of relief.

After that day, the three friends lost their habit of having tea after lunch. They drank water and never went near the tea shop again. Therefore, they had no way of knowing what was going on in Bulbul's drawing room. Did Bulbul make her choice? Did the clerk give up? Or did she somehow choose the clerk over the officer? The clerk was, after all, a dignified-looking sort. They talked about it every day but were too shy to go down to the shop to find out.

Only three months later did they hear the news. A friend of theirs, who knew about their courtship, came up to where they were having lunch one day. He smiled at them and said, 'Look at you three, on a self-imposed exile! Haven't you heard the news?'

'What news, Sten?' Bah Kelan asked.

Stender, who had been given that name because his elder brother was called Tender, said, 'After you three left, when the clerk kept coming to the house, Bulbul's mother—'

'Why would he do that if—?'

'That's just it. Bulbul liked flirting with them both, and refused to choose between them. Finally, it was the parents who brought the matter to an end. To discourage the clerk, they demoted him to the wooden stool. That proved to be too much for him, so he left, leaving the field clear for the accounts officer. His name is George something; I don't know the surname. Instead of proposing marriage, George tried to seduce Bulbul into a premarital relationship. However, Bulbul's mother, Kong Merin, was like a hawk; she saw everything and thwarted him at every attempt—'

'But why did this George fellow try to do that?' Bah Kelan asked with surprising fierceness. 'Why didn't he marry her?'

'Here's the best part,' Stender said smugly. 'He's a married man!'

'What?' they all exclaimed. 'So, we lost out to a married man, then? Of all the damn luck!'

Stender nodded, looking amused. 'But Kong Merin found out from a friend about George and threw him out. She even threatened to set the local boys on him if he ever came near the house again.'

'What about the clerk?' Bah Reng asked.

'He's already courting another one now; her name is Linda. Nice girl.'

They were all silent for a while, thinking about how Bulbul was now without a suitor. Should they go back? But the image of the cane stools and the even lower wooden stools loomed large in their minds.

After a while, Bah Kelan said, 'You know what, it serves them right for being such fools for officers, fools for money and status! Who the hell are they, treating us like lowly dogs to be summoned and shooed away like that?'

'Kong Merin,' Stender said slowly, 'has been asking after you three. She said you behaved like perfect gentlemen, true sons of Sohra!'

'No, no, no, no, no!' Bah Kelan shouted and raised both hands as if trying to physically stop his friends from going to Bulbul's house. 'Don't even think about it, you two! Think instead of the cane and wooden stools! Have we ever been treated like that by anyone? Anywhere we go, we are treated with respect. We are men with our own standing in society. What she did to us was mean, mean as hell. The arrogant hag! When we were infatuated, we didn't think much about it, but now, the memory of it makes me feel like reaching out and throttling the life out of her. You two, please promise me, never, never go anywhere near that house again! Swear it to me right now! If you do, I'll never speak to you again!'

Madeng and Bah Reng said the insult still rankled with them too, although they did not hold any grudge against either mother or daughter and certainly did not wish them harm. But they were reluctant to swear the oath, for a part of them was still pining for Bulbul. Without the clerk and the officer around, it would almost be a walkover for them. And they were sure they would now be treated differently; they were sure the cane and wooden stools would be a thing of the past. Hadn't the family learned a hard lesson already? But Bah Kelan berated them for being such weak and shameless creatures until they were finally persuaded to swear never to go anywhere near Bulbul again. As a final warning, they were told to always bear in mind what a wise man said, 'Once bitten, twice shy', or something to that effect.

When Stender saw the three of them taking the oath together, he said, 'In case Kong Merin asks me about you, what shall I say?'

Very quickly, Bah Kelan replied, 'Never again!'

A week after that, Bah Kelan was suddenly taken ill. When Madeng and Bah Reng went to see him in the evening, he was in bed, moaning like a dying man. He said in a feeble voice, 'The doctor told me it's dysentery, and probably stones in the kidneys too. I'm applying for medical leave, Deng, will you please take the application to the office for me?'

Madeng agreed. The leave was for two weeks.

And so, Madeng and Bah Reng went to work without Bah Kelan. In the evening, when they tried to see him, his mother did not let them into the house, saying the doctor had forbidden her son from seeing anyone. He needed complete rest, it seemed. After that evening, they tried to see him once more, but when they were not allowed in, they decided to leave him alone so he could recover faster.

But even after two weeks, Bah Kelan did not report for work. Worried about him, they went to his house again, only to discover that his mother would not allow them in even now. They shrugged and carried on by themselves.

Soon, two weeks became one month, but still, there was no word of Bah Kelan. Eventually, it was Stender who told them the news. One day, coming up the hill during lunch break, he said, 'What are you two doing here? Aren't you going to the wedding of your best friend?'

'What are you talking about? Who's getting married?' Bah Reng demanded.

'Why? You don't know? No wonder it's such a hush-hush affair. Only the closest of relatives, no one else invited. But I thought at least you, being his best friends, would have been called!'

'Just tell us what you are talking about, man!' Bah Reng urged.

And Stender said, as if announcing the greatest news of the year, 'I'm talking about Kelan marrying Bulbul. Today!'

'What?' Madeng and Bah Reng cried out in shocked surprise. 'Are you serious?'

When Stender nodded and said it was taking place right then, Bah Reng cursed at the top of his voice. 'The son of a bitch! The son of a bloody, bloody bitch! I'll kill the cheating son of a low clan with these bare hands! Just you wait! Let the son of a thief come back to the quarry, I'll kill him with these bare hands, I'll kill him!'

'Oh, one more thing,' Stender said. 'He won't be coming back here. He's been transferred to the clay works, and you won't be meeting him in Khliehshnong either. From today, he'll be staying in Mawmluh with his wife.'

Infuriated by the news, Bah Reng let loose a string of the choicest expletives, ending with a frustrated cry: 'The piece of dog shit!'

Even Madeng, who had kept quiet so far, and who never cursed, exploded: 'The son of an animal!'

Madeng never spoke of it to us. But whenever he warned us against bad friends and treacherous people, he always compared them with Bah Kelan. His favourite refrain was, 'Never keep a friend like Kelan; he will make a spiced curry out of you.'

Bah Reng, who was telling us the story, ended by saying, 'Now you know why your Madeng has remained a bachelor for life.'

'What about you? Were you not as disappointed?' I asked.

'I don't take things so seriously, my boy. If a woman rejects me, I simply move on and try another one. *Never let anyone make your life miserable.*'

Bah Reng proceeded to compare courting a woman to eating jadoh meat-rice in a shop. 'If the jadoh is not to your taste,' he said, 'you move on to another shop, and another, till you find the right one. The taste of jadoh depends on the hands of the cook. That's all.'

Hamkom was the first to react. 'My, my, my, what a story, ha, Bah Kynsai? From being demoted to a low wooden stool to being stabbed in the back by a friend. It's both hilarious and sad, ya!'

'It's full of hateful people,' Magdalene declared.

Playfully pinching her cheeks, Donald said, 'No, no, my dear, Mag, there are good characters too: Madeng Krokar and Bah Reng are nice people, honest and simple.'

'Too honest and simple in a world full of small-town vanity, arrogance and treachery,' Magdalene countered.

'It's a story without poetic justice,' Bah Su chimed in. 'The treacherous rogue won the damsel!'

'As if there is any poetic justice in life! There's no such thing, Bah Su,' Magdalene argued.

Evening said, 'A treacherous damsel too, Bah Su! I think they deserve each other, no?'

'But I like this fellow, Bah Reng, ha. His attitude to life is very positive,' Bah Kynsai observed.

'What about morals?' Evening asked. 'Are we looking for any morals here? We did not provide one for the other story either, Bah Kynsai.'

'Why should we need morals here?' Donald responded. 'These are short stories, not little stories, Evening. You can read so many things into them. We don't need to talk about morals here.'

'Don is right, Ning,' Bah Kynsai said. 'And now, if we don't have any more love stories, na, we can move back to little stories. Who's next?'

'Why don't we take a little break, Bah Kynsai?' Bah Kit proposed.

Bah Kynsai looked at his watch and said, 'What time is it? It's only 10.20 … yeah, yeah, why not? Come, come, let's have a little bathroom break!'

We all trooped out into the darkness, returning to relax by the fire. It was not cold, but the little fire, with its frolicking flames of orange illuminating the hut, and its dark, tremulous shadows providing a magic lantern show, added greatly to our comfort. Everyone was inside, except for Magdalene and Donald. Bah Kynsai asked Raji to fill his and Bah Su's mugs; Evening fiddled with the fire; Dale and I lay back on the straw, stretching our backs; Bah Kit sat stroking his hairless head and holding his cap in one hand. All of us were waiting for the missing pair so we could resume our storytelling, when suddenly we heard thunderous remonstrations.

'You spawn of Satan! You shameless creatures! How dare you do this sort of thing here, for the whole world to see! You godless things! I will report you to your churches and get you excommunicated at once! Jezebels! Prostitutes! Pimps! Procurers! Gropers! Exhibitionists! Shameless, godless fiends! How dare you shame us all in front of the entire village! You …'

By then, all of us had rushed out. We found Halolihim shouting at Magdalene and Donald, but before we could say anything to stop him, Donald stepped forward and gave him a hard punch on the mouth that immediately stopped the flow of all that filth. Halolihim fell to the ground with a loud thud. Donald bent down to drag him up and punch him some more, but we all dashed forward and pulled him back.

Donald was shaking with anger and indignation. He said, 'Nobody calls us names like that! I'm going to kill this bastard tonight!'

We held him fast and pinned his hands to his sides. Unfortunately, we forgot about his feet, and Donald kicked the still groggy Halolihim a few times in the ribs before we could pull him away. By then, Chirag, Perly and a bunch of locals had also reached the spot. I shouted to Chirag to lend Halolihim a hand. Chirag and Perly took him by the arms and helped him up, but as they were doing that, a thoroughly maddened Magdalene, whom everyone had forgotten about, rushed at him, grabbed his hair and raked his face with her fingers. Bah Kit let go of Donald and went to pull Magdalene away with the help of the other Lyngngam men.

Donald and Magdalene were now shouting abuses at Halolihim, who was still too weak and too shocked to speak. Bah Kynsai and I eventually got them to calm down. Hamkom was with Halolihim, trying to stop the bleeding from his mouth. With the help of a flambeau, Perly picked some herbs growing nearby. He chewed on them for some time, then pressed the mixture firmly against Halolihim's lips and told him not to move at all. Meanwhile, some other Lyngngam men chewed more of the herb and wrapped it in a piece of cloth to make some sort of poultice. They made Halolihim lie flat on his back and pressed the poultice against his lips.

Perly said, 'This plant is very powerful. It will soon stop the bleeding, and not only that, Babu, it will prevent any swelling also.'

'That's good, that's good,' Hamkom said, sounding relieved.

'Will he be able to speak?' Bah Kynsai asked Perly.

Perly said confidently, 'Yes, yes, but he should not open his mouth too wide, otherwise his lips will bleed again. Also, depends on how serious it is, no, Babu?'

I asked Perly to show me the herb. Just like I thought: *sohlakthem*! We have it in Sohra too. Plenty of it. In spring, the hills are glorious with its violet blooms. We use its evergreen leaves for all sorts of wounds—it can stop the bleeding almost immediately. We also use it to treat diarrhoea. Halolihim was quite lucky.

As we waited for him to recover, we stood around in small groups, feeling thoroughly ashamed that we had caused such a ruckus, not once but twice in the village. 'What the hell will these people think of us, huh?' Bah Kynsai demanded. 'For God's sake, man, we are supposed to be scholars and teachers and whatnot, na! What's wrong with us?'

'What's wrong with us!' Magdalene, who was standing with Donald—clinging to him, in fact—at some distance from us, shouted. 'Ask that arsehole over there! Calling us all those horrible names, lyeit!'

She was crying again, and Donald put his arms around her. Magdalene comes from a wealthy family. All her life, she has been pampered and treated like a sweetheart who can do no wrong. Tonight was a dreadful shock for her.

After comforting Magdalene as best he could, Donald added to what she had said. 'And you know what, Bah Kynsai, if he hadn't shouted so loud and awakened the entire village, we would not have felt so bad. Somehow, we could have sorted it out among ourselves. But look at all these people crowding around us, how did they come to be here? Because of him! You should have seen him! His ugly face with all those scars, livid with rage, his eyes flaring with all that mad frenzy, it was simply horrible! I think there's something wrong with him, Bah Kynsai.'

'But what happened?' many of us asked at the same time.

'You ask the bugger,' Magdalene said. 'I'd also like to know what wrong we did.'

We waited for almost an hour for Halolihim to recover. When they took away the poultice, we could see that the bleeding had stopped, and as Perly had predicted, there was not much of a swelling. Halolihim was lucky the punch had not landed plumb on his mouth, but to the right side of it, which left his lips largely undamaged.

When Bah Kynsai saw that he could speak, even if only in a kind of mumble, he demanded, 'What the hell happened, Halolihim? Why were you thundering like the devil and abusing these two like that?'

Halolihim pointed to Magdalene and Donald with a finger shaking with anger and said as malevolently as he could manage, 'They were having sex right there by the lane!'

As he said that, the crowd of villagers gasped in shock. Making love by the lane! That was unheard of! Sacrilege!

When they heard the accusation, both Magdalene and Donald rushed towards Halolihim, and we had to grab hold of them again. Trembling with anger, they shouted abuses at him. Donald ended with a threat: 'You lying piece of shit! Wait till I get my hands on you again!'

Pointing an accusing finger at Halolihim, Magdalene said, 'You saw us standing by that tree, how can you say we were having sex?'

But Halolihim insisted that they were making love. 'They did it standing!'

That brought some more angry reactions from Magdalene and Donald, who stopped only when Bah Kynsai said, 'Okay, okay, now you two, why don't you tell us what happened?'

It was Magdalene who spoke. She said, 'We were both standing by that tree.' She pointed to a tree by the lane leading to Chirag's sister's house. 'We were standing very close no doubt; Don had his hands on my shoulders ... We were discussing how best to approach my father ... Don and I are planning to get married ...'

'Aah!' Most of us heaved a sigh of relief.

'And this bugger,' Donald said, 'came out of nowhere and poured all that filth on our heads!'

'What have you got to say to that?' Bah Kynsai asked Halolihim.

'It looked like they were having sex to me!' Halolihim said sullenly.

'The problem with you is that you are too bloody suspicious and narrow-minded!' Bah Kynsai rebuked him.

Chirag interrupted him and said, 'It was dark, that's why, Babu.' Turning to the crowd, he said, 'Go home, go home, it was nothing but a misunderstanding, these two were standing very close discussing their marriage, we should congratulate them for that, but this Bah here thought they were doing something wrong because of the dark, go home, go home, it's nothing at all.'

'Yeah, yeah, it was nothing, please go home,' Bah Kynsai added. Then, turning to us, he said, 'Earlier, na, it was Halolihim and "the ungodly pagans", and now it's him and "the ungodly Christians". This fellow is too much, man.'

When the crowd had gone, I turned to Halolihim and said, 'You shouldn't have jumped to conclusions like that, Halolihim, and you shouldn't have used that kind of language.'

'I thought Bah was coming here to preach,' Chirag added, 'but that kind of language, even our labourers do not use—'

'Chirag, Chirag,' Raji interrupted him, 'that's called righteous anger, no?'

'But a righteous man should not speak like that, no, Bah? And why is he coming here when he is staying with our kong?'

Hamkom answered for Halolihim. 'He was coming to meet me.'

'You are the culprit, Ham,' Bah Kynsai said. 'You shouldn't have brought him here in the first place—'

'No, no, no, Bah Kynsai,' Raji protested, 'without Halolihim, okay, there would have been no fun. What are we doing here? Sitting and talking and telling stories, but with Halolihim around, ha, lots of excitement, we are also fighting, *dichum, dichum!*'

Bah Kynsai gave him a playful kick in the arse, and Raji cried, 'Ouch, ouch!', as if in great pain.

'Well, Bah Chirag,' I said, 'sorry about that.'

'It's all right, Babu, it was nothing, as Bah Raji said, let the people have some fun also.'

With that, he and his friends went back to the death house, and we trooped back into the hut. Hamkom accompanied Halolihim to where he was staying, though he returned almost immediately.

When we were back inside, Bah Kynsai said, 'So, you two are planning to get married, sala! Why didn't you tell us also, huh?'

'We were planning to,' Magdalene replied. 'In fact, we were planning to tell you tonight.'

All of us went up to congratulate them. But Bah Kynsai was also curious about Donald. He said, 'How can you marry, Don, you are not even employed yet?'

'I have two job offers, Bah Kynsai, sorry I haven't told you before. I meant to, but forgot—one from a college in Shillong, another from a college in Delhi. I guess I'll have to take the one in Shillong now.'

'What about your research?'

'That can go on, no problem.'

'Good, good.' Then, slapping his hands together, Bah Kynsai added, 'Okay, shall we go back to our stories?'

'On with the show!' Raji said, mimicking Bah Kynsai again.

Bah Kynsai ignored him and asked me, 'Ap, do you remember the story you told me about the student who explained why his English was no good? Why don't you tell us that one?'

The story was about one of my classmates at the university, when we were studying for an MA. He was so bad at English that, one day, he was summoned by one of our teachers, who asked him in Khasi, 'Kingson, why is your English so bad? You are at the university, studying English literature, but you write like a student of Class IV! Aren't you ashamed of yourself? Haven't I told you to read as many books as you can and to look up the meanings of words you don't know? And haven't I told you to try writing? Write anything, anything at all—an essay, a short story, a love letter, anything. Why? Don't you have a girlfriend? Write a love letter to her every day. You see, it doesn't matter what kind of writing you do, but you should write. Only writing will improve your language skills … Haven't I told you all this? But it seems you haven't learned anything; your English is as horrible as ever!'

'I didn't get a good foundation, no, sir?' Kingson replied. 'I went to school in Government Boy's High School, which was no good; then for college, I went to St Ant's, which was also no good in those days … You see, sir, that's why.'

'Listen to me,' our teacher told him. 'Do you know which school I went to when I was a kid? You people are from the city; you have excellent schools here. I was from a village. When I was in Class IV, I went to a school that also served as an animal shelter at night—for cattle and goats. Before we could begin our classes, we had to sweep the rooms and get rid of the dung.

Besides, there were not enough benches for us, so what did we do? Many of us had to kneel on the floor to write—heads down, bottoms up, like Muslims at prayer. Do you get the picture?'

Kingson laughed. 'You are very funny, sir.'

'Funny!' our teacher thundered. 'This is no joking matter! It is the truth! And do you know where I went to school?'

'No, sir.'

'Do you know where I went to college?'

'No, sir.'

'Because I won a merit scholarship, I came to Shillong ... I went to Government Boy's High School and after that to St Ant's: the very same institutions you went to, and which are no good according to you!'

'Oh!' Kingson exclaimed. He could only gape at his teacher as if he was seeing him for the first time.

'Oh, oh?' our teacher responded. 'Now, do you understand the significance of my story? Do you remember the story about the bad workman who quarrelled with his tools? This is a lesson for you: never blame schools or colleges for your shortcomings, do you hear? Now go and do as I tell you: read and write. Overwhelm your girlfriend with love letters! But if you lose her, don't blame me, blame your English.'

When I finished, Bah Kynsai said, 'Good counsel, good counsel. That's what I used to tell my students too.'

'What? About losing their girlfriends?' Raji teased him.

Bah Kynsai threw some straw at him.

Ignoring them, Hamkom said, 'But, Ap, schools that also served as animal shelters! And without benches! Are these things for real or what?'

Before I could reply, Raji said, 'Hamkom, Hamkom, poor Hamkom, you don't know anything about our villages, do you, poor Hamkom? In some remote places, okay, such schools are many, many, I tell you, with my own eyes I have seen. Some years ago, I even heard of schools without schools; you know that?'

'Meaning?' Hamkom asked.

'Hamkom, Hamkom, poor Hamkom, schools on paper only, man!'

'Really? In Meghalaya? I don't believe it. I have heard about these things in other Indian villages, but Meghalaya? No, I don't believe it.'

'Well, what can I say?' Raji replied. 'You are a man with a lot of faith, blind faith, hahaha.'

'So what's the moral of this?' Evening asked.

'What moral?' Bah Kit countered. 'The teacher already talked about a bad workman, no? What more do you need?'

'Or we can say,' Bah Su said, '*persistence is the difference between excellence and mediocrity.*'

'What about talent, Bah Su?' Donald asked.

'Talent is important, of course, but persistence is equally important.'

'But what I don't understand is, why should we be obsessed with the English language?' Evening said. 'Whether we are good or bad at it, what does it matter? English is neither our mother tongue nor father tongue, no?'

'In this case,' I replied, 'it's because the student was studying English literature. But you are right, Ning, most Khasis are obsessed with English. I have another small story to demonstrate the point.'

A man was drinking tea in the dining room with his young son. He called out to his wife in the kitchen. 'Old woman, hey, old woman! The tea is not sweet, could you please bring me more sugar?'

His wife shouted back from the kitchen in Khalish. 'Sorry, Kpa, *ka shini lah* out of stock!' ('Sorry, Father, the sugar is out of stock!')

The son did not understand what his mother was saying. He asked his father, 'What does "out of stock" mean, Papa?'

The father explained its meaning. 'You see, son, when something is used up, and there is none of it at home, we say it's "out of stock". Now, please go and buy some sugar from Bah Ro's shop, will you? Can you go there alone?'

The son said he could, and ran off to the shop.

Some days after that conversation, the boy's maternal uncle visited the house. After greeting everyone, he came to the boy, tousled his hair playfully and asked, 'Bahbah, where's your father? I don't see him anywhere?'

'Papa, Marit? He's out of stock.'

'Hahaha!' Evening laughed. 'This is something I have always wanted to discuss, okay? Why can't we speak pure Khasi? Why do we have to mix it with English? Always. Even here, most of us are speaking Khalish, isn't it strange?'

Bah Kynsai said, 'There are things that cannot be expressed in Khasi, Ning. We don't have words for many things—computer, telephone, mobile, TV ... So many things, mə, lih. Khasi is very poor, na?'

'But that's not the only reason, no, Bah Kynsai?' Evening argued. 'Even with things we can easily express in Khasi, we use English. For instance, we have many expressions for "out of stock", but the woman in Ap's story didn't use any of those. This is what we do.'

'Maybe because of the English-medium schools or what?' Bah Su suggested. 'Many Khasis send their children to such schools nowadays.'

'But other communities do that too, ha, and yet their children are equally proficient in their mother tongues, Bah Su,' Evening insisted. 'Who has analysed this, ya? Anybody?'

Raji pointed at me and said, 'Ap used to teach in the English department, but he writes in Khasi, he's the best person—among us, among us only, ha, Ap, don't inflate your nostrils just yet—the best person to speak about it.'

Ignoring Raji, I said, 'I have, in fact, written something about it. As far as I can see, there are, broadly speaking, five categories of Khasis—'

'You see, you see?' Raji said with mock excitement. 'Now he'll give you categories and whatnot.'

'Shut up, man!' I laughed. 'As I was saying, there are uneducated Khasis who speak nothing but their dialects and only a little bit of the Sohra dialect that we call Khasi. There are uneducated Khasis who speak their dialects, Khasi and Shillong Hindi. There are educated Khasis who speak their dialects, Khasi and English. Among these, quite a few speak Hindi as well. There are educated Khasis who speak their dialects, Khasi (both falteringly) and English. And there are educated Khasis who speak only English and almost no Khasi or anything else. Do you agree with me? Obviously these are only broad categories—'

'I think that's a very good division, yeah,' Bah Kynsai agreed.

Even Hamkom said, 'Hmm, I think so too, yes. But how many would you say speak this so-called Khalish?'

'A vast majority, including many of us here,' I replied. 'There's no gainsaying the fact that English has become something of a requisite in the modern world. Research shows that about one billion people worldwide are learning English, either as a mother tongue or a second language. It has emerged as the language of business, politics, international relations, culture, entertainment, science, technology and, most importantly, the internet—where about 80 per cent of the content is in English. Whatever the historical reasons for it, today English is the only language that can be described without exaggeration as a global language.'

'Hmm … agreed,' Hamkom said.

'In India, despite vigorous attempts to propagate and promote Hindi as the national language, English remains one of the most crucial links between regions and communities. In the Northeast, the language has become indispensable, I would say. Without it, there would be no interaction among the diverse tribes.

'To a Khasi, English is a saving grace, for what would he do without it? His knowledge of Hindi is almost non-existent. Apart from the "bazaar Hindi" spoken in Shillong and elsewhere, he can, as a rule, neither read nor write the language. And this "bazaar Hindi" is incomprehensible to people elsewhere in the country, for who would understand a man if he says, "*Aw mama, khaw la ka khaw, surom burom bhi nei*?" A Khasi has a strange—'

'Hold on, hold on,' Bah Kynsai and Hamkom shouted at the same time. Bah Kynsai barked at Hamkom: 'Will you stop interrupting?' Then turning back to me, he said, 'I wish to dispute you on this, Ap: there are many Khasis who can speak pure and beautiful Hindi, na? We even have Khasis who have done their PhDs in Hindi—'

'Out of the total Khasi population, what number would you say these people constitute?' I asked.

Raji raised his finger and said, '0.1 per cent, hahaha.'

'Raji may be right, Bah Kynsai. These people are exceptions, and we are not talking about exceptions, are we? As I was saying, Khasis have a strange reluctance to learn Hindi or any other foreign language in school, with the exception of English. And this is a historical fact. Around 1832, Krishna Chandra Pal and Alexander B. Lish of the American Baptist Mission of Serampore had used Bengali orthography to cast the Khasi language in written form. Before that, Pal's mentor, William Carey, using the same orthography, had translated the Bible into Khasi with the help of some Khasi scholars. Both endeavours failed because people simply refused to learn the complex Bengali script. However, when Thomas Jones introduced the Roman script in 1842, they adapted to it readily and became, for the first time, literate.

'Even more than his newly scripted mother tongue, it was English that caught the Khasi's imagination, and he became an enthusiastic learner of the language almost from the very beginning. The reason is not hard to see. The comparative simplicity of the Roman script, used for both Khasi and English, did the trick.'

Raji clapped his hands and shouted, 'Shabash! Bravo! Very good knowledge of history. Go on, go on …'

Ignoring him, I said, 'As for Hindi, the Khasi remains stubbornly unwilling to learn it even now. There are scholars who have excelled in the language, but by and large, the extent of Hindi-learning for a Khasi student is confined to painstakingly copying exam questions.'

Magdalene laughed and spoke for the first time since the incident. 'Yeah, yeah, in our time, that's what we used to do.'

'So,' I continued, 'English has become the Khasi's medium for interaction with the outside world. Without it, he cannot even connect with the Garos, who share a state with him. It is his instrument of education, without which he has no hope of acquiring a well-paying job; it is his gateway to learning, without which his intellectual world would shrink to nothing; it is the measure of his creative talents, without which even his writings would languish in his own little world, unknown and unsung. In short, it is his voice, without which he cannot make himself heard.'

Raji stroked his full beard and said, 'Hmm … yes, yes, certainly very true of me.'

'But English also poses a serious threat to a Khasi, his language and his cultural life. The first casualty is naturally the mother tongue. A UNESCO survey once predicted the impending death of the Khasi language because of this obsession with English. That might have been an alarmist forecast not based on ground realities. Nevertheless, a Khasi's attitude to his language can be deeply disturbing. For instance, a Khasi will refuse to speak to another Khasi in Khasi just because he teaches English literature. Educated Khasis generally refuse to read anything Khasi, for they look down on Khasi newspapers as yellow journalism and on Khasi books as biblia abiblia, books that are not books. And students who study in English-medium schools generally refuse to speak Khasi even at home because they cannot or because "it is not cool". To such a Khasi—'

Raji clapped his hands again and shouted, 'Shabash! Bravo! You have hit the head on the nail! That's the problem; that's the problem.'

Everyone burst out laughing, and Bah Kynsai cursed him for good measure, telling him to shut up.

But Raji said, 'Arre! You should thank me for giving you a running commentary, no?'

'Good, good,' I said, to keep him quiet. 'To such a Khasi, the mother tongue has suddenly become, as Czeslaw Milosz says in one of his poems, "a tongue of the debased,/of the unreasonable, hating themselves". In such a situation, should we not say that the English language represents a clear and present danger to the very survival of the mother tongue? And no one in his right mind can make light of this danger, for the mother tongue, heard and spoken from birth, represents the sound of a people's ways and manners, that is, the sound of life itself—'

'Who's this Surf Wash, he's very good, very good, leh!' Raji enthused.

'Czeslaw Milosz, a Polish poet and Nobel laureate. I have already spoken to you of Meenakshi Mukherjee and the "exiles of the mind", the outsiders "in their own community either through loss of the mother tongue or through a system of education that superimposes an alien grid of perception on immediate reality". There are many such exiles among us. A Khasi today does not know much about his own language, culture, myths, history, philosophy, even geography. He has truly become what Thomas Babington Macaulay wanted him to become, an Indian "in blood and colour, but English in taste, in opinions, in morals and in intellect". But the still greater tragedy—'

'Hey, Ap, these two, you see these two lovebirds?' Raji intervened. 'They are exiles, and oh yeah, Hamkom too, they are all exiles ... Hi, exiles!'

A burst of laughter followed, and Bah Kynsai, though also laughing, shushed him: 'This Raji, sala! Go on, Ap, don't listen to him.'

'As I was saying, the still greater tragedy for a Khasi is that, despite being an incurable Anglophile, and despite a lifetime of focus, he has not acquired mastery over the English language. At the same time, he has largely forgotten his own mother tongue. A Khasi reminds me of a parrot that has just been taught how to speak—only, the parrot knows his own language quite well. What we hear in the streets is neither English nor Khasi, but something that is increasingly called Khalish:

> You going *ne em*?
> (You going or not?)
> You know *ei*, *ngam ju lah* decide *khlem da* think *te ei*.
> (You know what, I can never decide without thinking, ya.)
> Then decide *wut wut seh ei*, what's taking you so long *ei*?
> (Then why don't you decide quickly, what's taking you so long, ya?)
> *Hooid ei*, it's a very bad habit ... tomorrow *thik thik mo ei*?
> (You're right, ya, it's a very bad habit ... tomorrow for sure, okay?)

'Or this:

> You know *ei*, my mom made tungtap yesterday, so *sat*!
> (You know what, my mom made dry-fish chutney yesterday, so hot, ya!)

'You see—'

'That sounds like my friends and me, man!' Magdalene said, laughing aloud.

Raji said, 'Aah, she admits it, you see, Ap? Proud to be an exile!'

'Hey, you, shut up!' Magdalene said playfully.

'When we listen to such conversations,' I resumed, 'we cannot help but think that a Khasi is not a complete human being speaking a complete language. His patchwork, macaronic prose has given rise to many amusing stories, but the dilemma he faces is hardly funny. That English is of paramount importance to his survival and growth in modern life is unquestionable. But that it can also alienate him from his own environment and turn him against the mores and language of his own people is also undeniable. The most important thing to redress this situation is an attitudinal change towards the mother tongue—'

'Change!' Raji said sharply. 'How? Show me how we can change when we have exiles like these, right here in front of us?'

'A Khasi must realise that the mother tongue is, besides being the sound of his life, the root of his very existence,' I said. 'His first duty is to the nourishment of this root. It is from here that he must build his life upwards. It is from here that they will grow, the trunk and branches of all other languages that he may acquire in the succeeding stages of his life. The worst thing he can do is to groom the trunk and branches without watering the root. Rake up the soil, keep the root well watered and well nourished, and the tree of life will grow tall and sturdy. Only then can he think of grooming the trunk and trimming the branches—'

Hand on chin, Raji asked, 'Can we do all that with exiles like these around?'

'That's why he said we need a change of attitude, no?' Evening said.

'Aah! That we need, *that* we need,' Raji agreed.

'To speak plainly,' I went on, 'what the Khasi needs is to be equally good at both his mother tongue and English. Let him be large-hearted enough to accommodate both languages, and as many other languages as he can learn. There can also be no harm in remembering the saying, *Ieit la ka jong, burom ïa kiwei* (Love one's own, respect the others).'

'That's it, that's it!' Raji enthused. 'Like you and me, ha, Ap? I'm good at both Khasi and English. Like Ap, I also write in both. Am I not good at both, Ap? Say it, say it!'

'I'm much better at Khasi, but you are, you are, Raji,' I humoured him, and we all had a good laugh.

'I don't know why Raji is so talkative tonight,' Evening wondered aloud. 'Normally, he becomes rather quiet after he has had one too many.'

'He's mixing his drinks tonight: foreign and local,' Bah Kynsai said.

'Spot-on, Bah Kyn, spot-on, for once, only for once, you are spot-on!' Raji said, emphasising his point with a raised forefinger. 'But it's making me wittier too, no?'

'It's making you lousier,' Bah Kynsai said.

'Jealous, now, are we?' he taunted. Then he turned to Magdalene and said, 'Mag, Bah Kyn is jealous, look at him, jealousy written all over his face, hahaha.'

Before Bah Kynsai could react, Hamkom said, 'You know, Bah Kynsai, I'm struck by what Ap said about how, despite being incurable Anglophiles, we, all of us included, have not acquired real mastery of the English language. There are quite a few funny stories about our usage of English, you know. I have heard stories of MA students writing "sky crappers" instead of "skyscrapers" and that sort of thing—'

'Yeah, yeah,' Magdalene responded excitedly, 'I have come across many howlers by students; I wish I had collected them, ya, just to show you how funny their English is.'

'I know of some at least, Mag,' Bah Kit said. 'Not so long ago, ha, there was a procession of students in West Khasi Hills. They were protesting the opening of wine shops adjacent to a school. And this is what they wrote on the placards they were carrying …'

Bah Kit located a file on his mobile phone and read, 'Love wine store, it will kill you, go kick it out. Profit to the state government, greatest lost to the public, stop it at once. Alcohol destroy the society. Hell a Wines Store in our area … What I don't understand is why the teachers didn't correct them first.'

'Yeah, yeah, they should have, but they never do,' Hamkom agreed. 'I remember seeing a bus full of students from a rural school recently, okay? They were going on an annual excursion to Guwahati. Do you know what was written on the banner? "Execution Trip to Guwahati". Can you believe it?'

'Maybe the teachers also don't know or what?' Bah Kynsai surmised. 'Some of the teachers in rural schools, na, are really, really bad. Political appointees, mostly.'

'Those in the city are the same, Bah Kynsai,' I said. 'A friend of mine told me a story of some schoolteachers playing carom in the teachers' common room … One of them asked his partner: "Can you pocket this dice here?" And his partner replied, "There I used to can."'

'Tet mə, liah!' Bah Kynsai laughed.

'I'm not joking, Bah Kynsai. Even one of your university colleagues, your friend, in fact, the tall, fat one who used to be a politician—'

'I know who you mean, Renhi, na?' Bah Kynsai asked.

'Yeah, that one. While campaigning for one of the MLA elections, he asked some boys in his village to prepare the community hall for a public meeting. When he went to check later, he saw them trying to put up the banner. But it was too low. Calling out to them, he said, "Take it upper, upper!" The boys said they could not reach any higher. Renhi got angry and said: "You fools, go and bring a bridge! How can you reach upper without a bridge?"'

That set the group laughing, but Hamkom wondered: 'Why should he speak English to a bunch of village boys, though?'

'That does, Ham, that he does, every time,' Bah Kynsai confirmed. 'That's the problem with us, na, even those who don't really know English insist on speaking in English. Renhi was trying to impress the boys, I think.'

'With bad English?'

'How the hell would they know whether it was good or bad, man?'

'There's a teacher at your university, Bah Kynsai,' I said, 'who published a short story in a local paper recently. Her protagonist is the leader of a Village Defence Party, who, according to her, "used to go every night with the youths of his village on a crime petrol".'

'I read it, I read it too,' Bah Kynsai laughed. 'Sometimes, na, I wonder how people like these got a job at the university, I mean, I'm not perfect myself, but I'm not as bad as these buggers, na?'

'No, you are not, Bah Kynsai,' I replied with a smile. 'Back when I was teaching in college, one of my colleagues wanted to apply for casual leave. She wanted help translating the name of her illness. She said, "*Nga sngew kumno re kumno.*" To that, I replied, "But feeling *kumno re kumno* is not an illness, Kong. It means that you are merely feeling uneasy. How will the principal give you leave for feeling uneasy?" Finding me of no help at all, she went off in a huff. Shortly afterwards, the principal, a non-Khasi, called me to his office. I was a little anxious, wondering what it could be about. When I entered his room, the principal waved a piece of paper at me and said, "Professor Ap, could you please take a look at this casual leave application? It's written by one of your colleagues. I cannot make any sense of it." Relieved, I took the application and read aloud: "Sir, I shall be obliged if you would grant me one day CL since I cannot attend duty since I am feeling how-re-how." You see, she translated the peculiar Khasi expression "*kumno re kumno*" literally, and the result was utter confusion.'

Magdalene chuckled. 'That was Overjoy, wasn't it?' she asked. 'I heard of this incident. She's an odd one, that woman. And what a funny name, huh? One day, she went to meet a minister from her constituency, okay? She wanted something or the other from him, but the minister was not really listening to what she was saying, he kept on talking about the things he had done. "I have put a lot of inputs into these projects," he boasted. And Overjoy, who was thoroughly fed up by then, said, "I know, I know what you ministers have been doing. You put in lots of inputs here and there, but there are no outputs anywhere, instead of outputs, you have only *put-put*!"'

Put-put in Khasi means 'arse'.

Magdalene laughed herself silly at her own story. She was quite resilient, I thought, unlike Donald, who seemed subdued and downcast. He had never punched a man in the face before, and it still disturbed him.

Just then, Bah Kynsai said, 'Hey, Don, perk up, man! No need to think about it. If he had said those things to me, na, I would have done worse.'

'Don, Don, listen to this story,' Raji said. We thought he had gone to sleep, for he had been quiet and lying on his back for some time. But now he sat up and said, 'These guys have been talking about literal translations, okay, but you listen to this.'

English-medium schools in Shillong do not allow students to speak in their mother tongue, Raji said. If teachers catch anyone speaking in his own language, they immediately shout: 'English, English.'

One day, a teacher caught a Khasi boy speaking in Khasi. Irritated, she admonished him, 'You there! Speak in English only!'

'Yes, ma'am,' the boy replied obediently.

The teacher then asked him his name: 'What's your name?'

The boy thought for a while and said, 'Gang Rape.'

The teacher scolded him. 'Are you joking with me, boy?'

Scared, the boy quickly replied, 'No, ma'am, my name is Batborlang, but you asked me to speak in English only, so I translated that as "gang rape": Batbor means "rape" and Lang means "gang".'

When the entire class burst out laughing, the teacher cried out in alarm, 'No, no, no, that's not the translation of your name. Don't translate it literally; your name means "together we will hold power", you understand?'

Raji ended his story rather abruptly and said, 'Laugh, Don, laugh, hahaha.' He did, as did we.

'You don't sound so drunk any more, Iyeit,' Bah Kynsai said, 'were you really drunk before or what?'

'It's very sad, Bah Kyn,' Raji answered, 'I'm becoming sober little by little.'

Bah Su said, 'But that was only a boy, no, Raji? He can be excused for saying something like that. Kit and I have seen something written by a professor and a so-called expert on Khasi culture … Show me, show me that piece we got from the Directorate of Arts and Culture magazine … Here it is … Listen: "Once there was an old woman and an orphan in the Jaiñtia Hills district, her parents died when she was at a tender age. She lived with her maternal uncle along with his wife and helped them attending the cattle when they were busy in agriculture. She lived a village life full of simplicity. Her house was just at the outskirt of River Syntu Ksiar. She had three cows to her possession inherited from her grandmother and these cows made her earn her livelihood till she grew into a young beautiful lady. As she loved those cows and treated them as human beings, the girl used to call them by their respective name. The first male cow she named 'U Sah', to the second cow who was also a male she named it 'U Neh' and to a female cow she named it 'Ka Rom.'" And so it goes. What do you think? Male cow and female cow? Can you believe it?'

'That's not the only funny part, Bah Su,' Evening laughed. 'The whole thing is written like an essay by a Class IV student.'

'I have heard about this too, ha, though I had not read it,' Bah Kynsai said. 'Reminds me of an essay I had to correct once. In certain government offices, na, peons have to undergo a departmental exam to be promoted to the rank of lower division assistant, LDA. After one such exam, ha, I was asked to correct the papers. One of the questions required them to write an essay on the cow, and do you know what one of the peons wrote? He began his piece by saying, "The cow is the wife of the bull."'

Everyone burst out laughing.

'We may laugh at it, na,' Bah Kynsai said, 'but I seriously think that that peon was better than this professor, tdir, at least he knew a cow is female and a bull is male, na?'

'What's the name of this female-cow professor, Bah Su?' Hamkom asked.

'No names, we agreed on that,' Bah Kynsai quickly intervened. 'We are talking about issues, na? We are not gossiping. We can use names also, no doubt, but only when the issues are not slanderous.'

'But if you want to know the name,' Bah Kit responded, 'you can check out the magazine for yourself. It's foolishly called *Khasi, Jaiñtia and Garo Folklores*. Read it; you'll know everything.'

Bah Su added, 'And you know what, Ham, the Directorate of Arts and Culture and the state government, ha, have been routinely giving literary awards to such people, including this professor.'

'Did he really win an award or what?' Hamkom asked incredulously.

'Of course! And very recently too!' Bah Su confirmed. Then he added, 'It's not a he.'

'As I said earlier, na, here they award people, not their work,' Bah Kynsai said.

'What about you, Ap, have you been awarded by them too?' Hamkom asked.

'So far, I haven't written an essay like a Class IV student, you see. Once I do, I'm sure I'll be rewarded too.'

'Well said, Ap, well said,' Magdalene laughed. 'Uff, these government people are too much, ya!'

'But are all the state literary awardees as bad as that?' Hamkom wanted to know.

'No, no,' I replied quickly. 'There are some who do deserve their awards, but there are many more, too many, who would put the entire community to shame if their works were translated into other languages.'

Bah Kynsai now moved the discussion back to students and their translations. 'Students can be quite funny sometimes, na? One of my friends told me about a boy who was asked to translate an English sentence into Khasi, okay? The sentence was, "If an opportunity comes your way, grab it!" The boy translated it as, "*Haba don ka bu khem beit!*" And when you retranslate it into English, na, it becomes, "If there's a breast, squeeze it!"'

'That's a dirty story, Bah Kynsai, and we promised not to tell dirty stories, remember?' Evening protested.

Magdalene laughed and said, 'It's not a dirty story; it's a translation by a boy.'

'Exactly, Mag, exactly: a translation by a boy,' Bah Kynsai said approvingly.

'Translation can be a dicey thing, no?' Raji said. 'Hey, Bah Kynsai, Ap has done a lot of translation, leh, he must know a lot of stories, ask him to tell us some, no?'

'Why don't you ask yourself?'

'I'm scared to ask without your permission, no, Bah Kynsai?' Raji laughed.

Bah Kynsai chuckled and shook his head as if to say, 'What an impossible character!'

I told them the story of a Khasi teacher who bragged to his students about Khasi being a far richer language than English. One day he—may he eat betel nut in the house of God—told his students, 'You fellows are always looking down on your mother tongue; do you know that Khasi is actually a very rich language? Do you know that many Khasi words cannot even be translated into English? But all English words, I'm telling you, can easily be translated into Khasi, you know that?'

His students were taken by surprise. They said, 'How can that be, Babu? Other teachers have told us that English is the richest language in the world since it borrows from every other language. And they also told us that everything can be translated or transcreated into English, so how can Khasi be richer than English, Babu?'

'You fellows would even disbelieve your own babu?' he lamented. 'Okay now, if you don't agree with me, try translating these two expressions— *khmat lbong* and *jrong kti*. See if you can!'

The students thought for a long time and at last translated the words as 'eye thigh', 'eye of the thigh' and 'long hand as translations'. When the teacher heard that, he exclaimed: 'Is there such a thing as "eye thigh"? And if you say *jrong kti* is "long hand", the meaning is completely different, don't you see that, you fools? They are untranslatable! The first one means the best meat from a cow's thigh, and the second means someone who has the tendency either to molest a woman or to steal. You cannot translate them, you have to explain them. Do you see that, you fools?'

The students knew that their teacher's claim was rather far-fetched, but they had no answer to the problem he posed. There was one among them who was considered a bit of a wag. He challenged his teacher, saying, 'But, Babu, there are English words also that cannot be translated into Khasi, no? For instance, how do you translate "honeymoon"?'

'*Dur khun ka bieit*, damn you, son of a fool! You cannot even translate that little word?' the babu retorted. 'It means the moon is eating honey!'

'What does that mean, Babu?' the wag asked.

'You will know when you grow up.'

Laughing, Raji pointed at Magdalene and Donald, and said, 'Ap, Ap, look at these two, soon the moon will be eating honey, hahaha.'

Magdalene and Donald threw straw at him, but everyone was laughing good-humouredly again.

Then Bah Su said, 'You know, Ap, we can give a moral to this one: *a clever man makes himself safe.*'

'Good one, Bah Su,' Bah Kynsai said, then turning to me, he added, 'Go on, Ap, you said you had some more, na?'

'One or two more. This one is also about a literal translation, Bah Kynsai.'

A headman was rushing home from Shillong so he could be in time for a meeting with the local MLA and some non-Khasi government officials visiting his village. But he arrived very late at the venue. Feeling hugely embarrassed, he apologised profusely: 'I'm sorry, sir, I'm sorry, everyone … A truck translated on the road … massive traffic jam!'

You see, the man was translating the Khasi word *kylla*, which can mean either 'translate' or 'overturn', quite literally, without placing it in the proper context, and hence the hilarity he provoked after his hurried explanation.

'That's a good one, Bah Ap!' Donald said, smiling. 'A truck translated on the road indeed!'

I was glad to see Donald recovering. Although he had started off rather full of himself, as a scholar at a Delhi university and all that, he was now becoming a truly interested listener. It was as if he was trying to learn everything all at once, to fill the tabula rasa of his mind—as far as Khasi culture was concerned, I mean—with all that he could learn from us. For what was happening to him, I was very thankful.

'There's another aspect of English that we need to discuss when Khasis use it,' I said, 'and that is mispronunciation—'

'Yeah, man!' Bah Kynsai agreed. 'Even at the university, na, there are teachers—not Khasis, of course—who pronounce "government" like "garment", and "blurred" as "blue red". One fellow even said, "Unlike in the West, in India, we have collision garments."'

I laughed and clarified, 'But that is not the sort of mispronunciation I had in mind. I was speaking about the coining of words.'

Like the Native Americans, I said, we too are very good at coining new words based on the basic features of things. For instance, not too long ago, a dramatic society was trying to translate Agatha Christie's *The Mousetrap* into Khasi, but could not find a suitable translation for the title, something equally potent and effective. As they were grappling with the problem, a few of its members came upon a metal mousetrap in a small hut in a Ri Bhoi village. Excitedly, they pointed to it and asked the owner what it was called. Quick came the answer: '*Ka miw nar.*' The iron cat. And that was how *The Mousetrap* became *Ka Miw Nar* in Khasi.

'Yeah, yeah, that's very Native American too—"iron horse" and all that, no, Bah Ap?' Donald agreed.

'There are many more such examples, Don. For instance, a pressure cooker was described by an illiterate housemaid as "*U khiew siaw*", the whistling pot. I used that in one of my stories.'

When the first Khasi to come in contact with a kettle was asked to bring the utensil to his English master, he did not know what to do. When the Englishman persisted, he brought to him all sorts of things, but not the kettle. In exasperation, the Englishman fetched the utensil himself and snapped: 'This is the kettle, you blithering idiot!' Then, poking the thing in the Khasi's face, he said again, 'K.e.t.t.l.e, kettle, got it?'

And the Khasi responded, 'Oh, *ketli*! I got it.'

'Not ketli, stupid man, kettle!'

The Khasi snapped back, 'No, no, no. You spelt it as k.e.t.t.l.e, so ketli, not kettle!'

And that was how the kettle came to be known as ketli among the Khasis.

'Is that really its etymology or are you just pulling our leg?' Hamkom asked.

'Hey, Ap,' Raji said conspiratorially, 'he's always complaining that we are pulling his leg, leh, as if it's gorgeous, like a model's, hahaha.'

'Tet leh!' Hamkom protested, though he too was laughing.

I told Hamkom that the story was true. 'By mispronunciation, I'm actually talking about this kind of linguistic corruption. Khasi was initially a poor language, but over the years, it has enriched itself by borrowing from Hindi, Urdu, Persian, Bangla, Assamese and English. And all these borrowings have been in the form of linguistic corruption. Take the words *pap* (sin) and *juban* (commitment), for instance, these are from the Hindi words *paap* and *zubaan*. There are so many others; in fact, hundreds of them. And from English, we have even more: *bos* from bus; *trok* from truck; *rel* from rail; *eroplien* from aeroplane; *skul* from school; *pomkranet* from pomegranate; *apil* from apple; *presbin* from French beans ... And all of these have become a part of Khasi vocabulary because people mispronounced the original words.'

'You see, Ning,' Bah Kynsai observed, 'you were talking about corruption earlier, na, but not all corruption is bad, you see? Think of the Khasi language—without corruption, na, how would it enrich itself, huh?'

'Tet, this Bah Kynsai is always joking, leh!'

Bah Kynsai laughed and said to me, 'Hey, Ap, you people in Sohra are always talking about *Phareng miet ïew*, what does it mean, man?'

'The saying is actually, *Wat kren Phareng miet ïew*, meaning, do not speak market-night English. In the past, in Sohra, a market night was full of out-of-town drinkers from the ravine hamlets of Ri War and the surrounding upland villages. When they were drunk, whether educated or not, they would all start speaking in English. And they would say something like, "My darling sweetheart, *dohnud tah kyiad*" ("My darling sweetheart, liver to be taken with alcohol"), or "*Sming smong in the eit tyrkhong*". Sming smong to them meant the sound of the English language. And they clubbed it with eit tyrkhong, or dried crap, for no other reason than that the words rhymed. If they were angry with a friend who had a habit of disappearing every now and then, they would say, "Only basket, basket, I'll forest your eyes, potato finish!" This is a literal translation of "*Tang ka shang, ka shang, ngan khlaw ïa ki khmat phan dep artat!*" which means, "Only roaming, roaming, I'll gouge out your eyes, you'll be damned for good!" But mostly, market-night English is full of English swear words. The mildest among them are "bloody hell!" and "bloody swine!" The favourite expression of most drunks was, "Damn you, bloody swine!" and the retort from the other drunk would be, "Damn you, swine *naraiñ pukyllaiñ*!" Pukyllaiñ is a kind of twisty bread, but naraiñ is a meaningless word.'

'But that kind of language doesn't make any sense, na?'

'Exactly, Bah Kynsai. That's why when people speak nonsense, or use too many expletives, or speak Khasi mixed with too many English words, the people of Sohra say, "Out, out of my sight, don't come speaking market-night English to me!" I think it's an excellent way of discouraging Khalish among us.'

'Also of discouraging Bah Kynsai's English,' Raji added.

'My English is not full of nonsense, you bloody drunk!'

'Yeah, but it's full of expletives, and just now also you expleted, hahaha!'

Bah Kynsai picked up a burning log and threatened to hit Raji with it, but he was clearly amused.

'My God, Bah Ap!' Donald exclaimed. 'The things that go on in Khasi villages are amazing, no? I have never heard of these things at all!'

'Not many have,' Bah Kit said. 'Even we do not know enough.'

Hamkom defended Khasi English by saying, 'But it's not only us who use the English language badly, okay? Others, all over India also do the same. While in Guwahati once, ha, I saw a sign in a shop saying, "Framing done here. God photo available". And one day, while travelling with a Mizo on a train, ha, I overheard this conversation, okay? The Mizo was talking to someone from Punjab, who was sharing some food and drinks with him. He was so impressed with the person and his kindness that he invited him to Mizoram and said, "Come to Mizoram, I'll kill you pig!" Do you see what I mean?'

Everyone laughed, but Bah Kynsai said, 'We should not point fingers at others, na? We should only talk about ourselves. We will praise ourselves when we can, but we should also criticise and laugh at ourselves when necessary.'

Most of us agreed, but Hamkom was a little put off by the reprimand. Perhaps because of that, or because he wanted the conversation to move on to other things, he started objecting to what I had said earlier about 'bazaar Hindi'. 'You know, Bah Kynsai,' he observed, 'I don't agree with Ap at all about us speaking "bazaar Hindi". Do you? I mean, speaking for myself, ha, my Hindi is understood well enough, even outside the state, okay?'

'Of course we agree with him!' Evening said, before Bah Kynsai could answer. 'My Hindi is also quite alright, but we are the exceptions, no? Most people speak the kind of Hindi that nobody but a person from here, who also knows some Khasi, would understand. Let me tell you about a conversation I overheard in a bus station, then you can decide for yourself.

'A Nepali coolie was asking a Khasi woman, "*Ye baksa aapka,* Kong?"

'And the Khasi woman replied, "*Ha, aapka.*"

'Her companion told her, "What are you saying? He's asking you, is it yours, and you just told him, yes, it's yours."

'When she heard that, the woman corrected herself quickly and said, "*Hei* sorry, sorry, *apnga, apnga!*" She simply combined the Hindi aap, you, with the Khasi nga, me, to form a new Hindi word. Would anybody who is not from here understand that?'

'Another example,' I announced, and then told them a story my friend Pyllait had told me. A Khasi man wanted to buy a duck from a non-Khasi vendor. Approaching him, the man said, '*Hey, Mama, kitna ithu pani ka phum phum?*' ('Hey, Mama, how much is that thing that splashes in the water?')

The vendor did not understand the man at all since he was mixing broken Hindi and Khasi in his speech. He asked him, 'Kya?' ('What?')

The Khasi customer replied, '*Ithu mə, ksheng ksheng ka chalta.*' ('That one, man, that walks like a drunk.')

The vendor still did not understand, so he asked again, 'Kya?'

In frustration, the Khasi shouted, '*Ithu mə, kwak kwak ka bolla!*' ('That one, man, which says quack, quack!')

The vendor finally understood. 'Oh, ithu! Five hundred rupees, no discount!'

'And that, Ham, is the bazaar Hindi spoken by most Khasis,' I concluded. 'It took even a resident non-tribal some time to understand it.'

'I have another,' Bah Kynsai said. 'Robin, a friend of mine, na, told me about a conversation between a Khasi fishmonger and a non-tribal customer, okay? When the woman told him the price of a particular variety of fish, ha, the customer asked for a discount. But he was so shameless, na, he asked for half the price the woman had quoted. The woman replied, "*Aap thik thik baat he, nei thik thik baat to ham haath,*" which means, "You speak properly, ha, you no speak properly, I'll hand.'"

Hamkom laughed. 'If you don't speak properly, I'll give you a slap! That's something everybody would understand.'

'But it's not *pukka* Hindi, is it?' Evening asked.

'And here's yet another example, Ham,' I said. 'Ravi, another friend of mine, told me the story of his mother-in-law watching a Bihari who was sewing her quilt. The man was so quick that his needle, it seemed to her, was faster than lightning. And she did not like it even one little bit. She thought it was hastily done work and was sure the quilt was not properly sewn. Stopping the Bihari, she told him, '*Bhaya! Jao-jao-jao mat karo. Jayega-jayega-jayega karo!*' ('Brother! Don't do go-go-go. Do going-going-going!')

At this, Raji said, 'So, Bah Kynsai, we also should do *Jayega-jayega-jayega*. If we do *jao-jao-jao*, okay, we won't have any more stories left for the next night.'

Bah Kynsai looked at his watch and said, 'This bugger really must be sober! He's right, it's quite late. Must be that damn incident with Halolihim! So ...'

'So,' I agreed, 'tomorrow to fresh woods and pastures new!'

'Why do you say that?' Bah Kynsai asked.

'It's a quotation from a poem,' I explained. 'They are bringing down the body tomorrow, so let's see what happens.'

'On that very auspicious note,' Bah Kynsai said sarcastically, 'let us go to bed.'

9

THE SEVENTH NIGHT

ROOT STORIES III

'Example isn't another way to teach,
it is the only way to teach.'

—Albert Einstein

'I never thought I'd see anything like that!' Raji declared as he entered the hut and packed away his mini video camera.

'Exactly like the dead of the Torajans!' Bah Kynsai stated. 'Like Skeletor! I thought it was grinning at you, Mag.'

'Wuu, crap! I hope I don't have nightmares tonight!' Magdalene said, as though shaking off an unpleasant sensation.

'How will you have nightmares with Don by your side?' Bah Kynsai joked.

We had seen the body of Ka We Shyrkon earlier that day, brought down from the tree house where it had spent over nine months. That morning, 11 February, Perly came by at 8 a.m., and we had to get up in a rush, have a quick breakfast, and hurry to the death house for the beginning of the ceremony.

Inside the house, we found most of the burang uncles and other relatives already assembled. They were waiting for the shaman to finish his breakfast. It seemed that only one of the shamans and some of the musicians had returned. The rest would come the next day.

Perly and Victor told me that today there would only be the duwai khaw, the prayer with rice grains. That began as soon as the shaman was ready. They made a place for him in the middle of the drawing room. As he sat on a cane stool facing the door, a brass basin filled with water, a winnowing basket containing rice grains, and a rooster were brought to him. Surrounded by burang uncles and male and female relatives of the deceased, the shaman began the ceremony. He took a fistful of rice grains, cupped his hands and touched them to his bowed forehead. Then he put back the rice grains, took a handful of water and did the same with it. Having thus made his obeisance to God, he began his prayer by formally invoking God and the guardian spirits of the Shyrkon clan, ka ïawbei and u thawlang. He informed them of the family's intention to bring down the body of Ka We Shyrkon from its temporary lodging, and into the house, where it would be prepared for the final rites so that the soul of the deceased could finally undertake its journey to the other world. He introduced to the spirits the *yiar kong*, the rooster, who would show the path, who would lead the way as the soul proceeded on its journey to the abode of the spirits at Krangraij, its final resting place. Having introduced him, the shaman threw some rice grains and water on the rooster as a sign that he had been cleansed and was ready to perform his solemn purpose.

After that, the shaman pleaded with God and the guardian spirits, asking them to bless the cremation rites, which would begin with the homecoming of the body. He informed them that everything in the house had been kept ready to receive the body, and so saying, he got up to throw a few rice grains and sprinkle water in all the rooms—especially in the bedroom where the body would be kept. He then gave thanks to God and the guardian spirits and led the way to the tree house.

The procession was very quiet, without music and the usual chatter that accompanies a Khasi cortege. We (minus Halolihim, who did not come) were the only outsiders, for the ceremony was supposed to be conducted exclusively by the relatives of the deceased. That we were allowed to accompany them at all was because we were considered special observers.

When we got to the tree house, some men were already waiting with a tall bamboo ladder they had made on the spot. Before the men went up the ladder to bring down the body, the shaman again invoked God for his blessings. He also addressed the soul of the deceased and asked it not to worry, for we had only come to take the body home to prepare for the cremation rites. He held the way-pointing rooster aloft so the soul could see that a guide was already at hand. After invoking God's blessings once more, he told the men to bring down the body.

Six men clambered up the ladder. While three of them went into the tree house to bring out the body, the others waited on the ladder to help bring it down. The body, wrapped in an elaborately woven bamboo mat called *tliang*, was brought down slowly and with extreme care. Chirag and Perly were among the body fetchers. When later I asked them how they had managed with only six men, Chirag said the corpse was very light: 'As light as popcorn, nothing but skin and bone.'

Once the body was on the ground and placed in a bamboo bier, the shaman went forward to sprinkle a few rice grains and water and mumble a few words over it. Then he asked the men to carry it home. The bier was covered with a white cotton cloth, unlike the one that would be used for the cremation.

Back home, the body was unwrapped from the bamboo mat and laid on the bed. It was then bathed and dressed in the deceased woman's best clothes:

a white blouse, maroon dhara silk jaiñsems and a grey-and-black checked shawl. On a low table by the bedside, the family placed food on a plate and a burning candle. Finally, the way-pointing rooster was tied to the left foot of the deceased.

It was while they were doing all this that we saw the condition of the corpse. It was truly only skin and bone, all shrunken and dried up. Like Skeletor, as Bah Kynsai had said.

When the ceremony was over, we went to the usual place for lunch, where we were served rice and pork boiled with mustard leaves. As usual, we ate the food with lots of green chillies and raw vegetables, mostly jamyrdoh, mint and radish. Surprisingly, our appetite was not spoilt at all by the sight of the grinning corpse. After lunch, we went to the lake to bathe and sleep the afternoon away.

Hamkom said he had never seen a corpse being bathed before. 'I had always thought they would wash it the way a living person would take his bath, you know, taking it to the bathroom and pouring a lot of water on it.'

'The bathing is always symbolic,' Raji explained, 'that was why they only rubbed it lightly with a damp cloth. So is the feeding. Only the dressing is real. They even put gold rings on her fingers, did you see?'

'What will happen to those rings, you think?' Magdalene asked.

Bah Kit said they would be cremated along with the body.

'Such a waste!' Magdalene lamented.

Bah Kit explained that it was not. 'Actually, the melted gold will be collected later by *ki nongkylla-thang* ...'

'Nongkylla-thang?' Don asked.

'Body-turners or cremators. It's the family's way of giving them something for their services. Direct payment for cremation is forbidden in our custom.'

'Aah, I see. It's a beautiful custom after all, no, Don?'

'It certainly is, Mag,' Donald agreed. 'But what happens when the family is poor and doesn't have gold?'

'Simple,' I said. 'No gold is given or expected. But then, before the body is taken to the cremation hill, there is a ceremony called *pynkham pynsoh*, where family members, friends and well-wishers give some money to a priest or an elder who sits beside the body. The elder places each contribution to the left of the body if given by maternal relatives, and to the right, if given by paternal relatives, friends and well-wishers. Later, the money is wrapped in a muslin cloth and kept inside the bier with the body. Although offered as a parting gift to the departed, it is not burnt at the pyre, but is kept aside for the body-turners. The family is not supposed to know this, since no payment is supposed to be made. The family shows its appreciation when the cremators come home to report on all that happened at the cremation hill. At that time, they are always offered food as a sign of gratitude.'

'And do you always have willing cremators even when the family is poor?' Donald asked again.

'Yes, yes,' Bah Kit assured him. 'That way, in matters of life and death, ha, the Khasi community is completely lacking in mercenary tendencies. In such matters, everyone is always willing to help.'

As we were talking, there was a deafening sound, as of a gun going off. We all rushed outside and saw a large group of people gathered at the main entrance to the courtyard of the death house. They were standing around a kind of mini cannon, and as we drew closer, it gave off another booming sound. Bluish tendrils of smoke curled upwards from it. The little cannon, about three feet long and four inches in diameter, is called a *narlong*. It functions much like a cannon, but no ball is used, only gunpowder stuffed into it with an iron rod.

Chirag told us that some burang uncles from the far west had arrived. They were firing the narlong to announce their arrival. 'There will be more of them arriving tonight and all through the day tomorrow, Babu, the other burangs who live nearby and who are already here have gone to welcome them home, I cannot go because I'm operating this gun, we'll be firing four times since four burangs have arrived so far.'

After some time, we saw a group of people coming towards the death house, leading at least eight bulls. The burang uncles, each with a mug of yiad hiar beer in one hand, were escorted by resident clan members and musicians playing their drums and tangmuri wind instruments. When they reached the house, they were welcomed so noisily that it seemed as though they had come for a grand feast, not a funeral. The bulls were taken away to a temporary enclosure, to be housed with the others that had been brought earlier by other relatives.

When we were back in the hut, Donald exclaimed, 'My God, man, what a grand affair it seems to be! Already I'm counting twenty-five bulls in the pen. What are they going to do with them?'

'They'll sacrifice them on the cremation day,' Raji replied.

'Whew, twenty-five bulls to be sacrificed at one fell swoop!'

'There will be more, Don,' Raji explained. 'And don't forget that several pigs have already been slaughtered, and many more will be. Why? Haven't you noticed? Almost the entire village has been eating at the death house for the last few days. That's why it's called Ka Phor Sorat, the feast of the dead, no?'

'Is it because the dead person was a woman that they are doing all this?'

'No, no, it's not that at all, man,' Raji replied.

'Actually, Ka Phor Sorat is observed only when an old person, woman or man, dies,' I clarified. 'But it's also a fact that the most important funeral ceremony among the Khasis is performed when a paternal grandmother dies. Kong We would have been a paternal grandmother to many, many Lyngngams, and that, perhaps, is the reason why there is such a large gathering here. And many more people are expected. The better-off relatives will bring along at least one bull with them. Perly said they are expecting not less than eighty bulls to be brought in by tomorrow.'

Donald, now ever curious, asked, 'But why would a paternal grandmother be given the most important funeral rites, Bah Ap? Shouldn't mothers and maternal grandmothers be given more importance since we follow the matriarchal system?'

'The matrilineal system, Don, not matriarchal,' I corrected him. 'The mother may be loved by her children and grandchildren, but she is revered almost like a goddess by her paternal grandchildren—'

'Really?' Evening sounded incredulous.

Raji said impatiently, 'What a question to ask, Ning, you have lived here all your life and you don't even know that?'

'How would he know when he doesn't have a paternal grandmother?' Bah Kynsai said derisively.

'How can that be, Bah Kynsai?' Donald asked curiously.

'How? Don't you know he uses his father's clan name?'

'He did tell us that, but—'

'Oho, this Don! Because of that, na, his paternal relations have become his clan, and his clan has become God knows what!'

Evening began to protest loudly, but I interrupted him and said, 'Nobody can exchange clans like that, and I shall tell you why if you want me to.'

Donald said he would very much like to know about this strange matrilineal system where the paternal grandmother is revered like a goddess.

Evening, however, wanted no part of it. 'Why do you want to know about a system that pampers the woman and denies the man everything?'

'Speaking as a research scholar,' Donald answered, 'I have to know the system intimately before I can even begin to talk about it. As it is, I know barely anything. All I know is that I belong to my mother's clan.'

'It's a system that should be thrown to *ka nurok ka ksew*, the place of the dog!'

'Look who's talking!' Donald responded sarcastically. 'Hey, Ham, when we were talking about the influx, do you remember how fanatical about Khasi identity he was? But now he doesn't even want us to talk about a system so crucial to that identity!'

Evening, Hamkom, Bah Su and Bah Kit were all about to say something when I intervened. 'Look,' I said, 'if I speak about it, I don't want any interruptions. I could tell you how it used to be and how it is practised today. The rest is up to you. I'm not going to take sides, not because I'm afraid to, it's just that I have my reasons. If you agree to that, I'll do it, otherwise, not.'

When most of them said okay, I told them what I knew about the Khasi matrilineal system and why the girl child is so beloved.

I have already told you how the old Khasis considered their social structure to be so important that they included it among the Three Commandments, the Divine Laws, which are the guiding principles of Khasi religious and philosophical thought. The reference to our social structure comes in the form of the Second Commandment, *ka tip kur tip kha*, the knowledge of one's maternal and paternal relations. If the First Commandment directs man to love and respect his fellow man, the Second asks him specifically to love and respect his maternal and paternal relations. This principle, as you know, does not advocate insularity; it instructs a person in how the community organises its clans and its cognate and agnate relationships. A Khasi always says he determines his clan not from the female line but from the mother's, because of all the reasons I have already told you.

To understand our clan relationships more clearly, we must keep in mind that a Khasi clan grows out of one family, tracing its lineage to a common ancestress. This ancestress is called *ka ïawbei tynrai*, or simply *ka mei ka ïaw*, the queen, the mother of origins, very different from the queen mother who is the mother or sister of a king. The use of the word 'ïaw' or 'kyïaw' implies that the Khasis organised their social system around the mother, whose status was like that of a queen in a beehive. Ka ïawbei tynrai is, therefore, the ancestral mother of a particular kur, or clan. Below the clan comes a division called *ka kpoh*, literally, 'the belly', meaning a branch, which may comprise many families. The mother of this tributary-clan is called *ka ïawbei tymmen*, literally, 'the old queen mother'. Below the tributary-clan is *ka ïing*, or the family, whose mother is called *ka ïawbei khynraw*, literally, 'the young queen mother'.

To explain this, I said, I would like to cite the story of the Diengdoh clan of Sohra, as it was told to me by some of its elders from Ri Pnar.

'That's my mother's clan,' Evening said.

'Is it?' Bah Kynsai asked. 'And do you know anything about the story Ap is about to tell?'

'No, I—'

'Then shut up, mə, tdong!' Bah Kynsai said in mock anger.

Before Evening could retaliate, Donald asked, 'Bah Ap, you said the Diengdoh clan of Sohra, but mentioned elders from Ri Pnar, how is that? The two places are very far apart, no?'

The Diengdohs had their roots in Ri Pnar. According to the story, the first ancestress, or ïawbei tynrai, of the Diengdoh clan came in the form of a river nymph emerging from the River Kupli to the east of Ri Pnar (or, I added with a smile, Jaiñtia Hills, as it was called by the British and everyone else now). The nymph married a local man, and one of her favourite resting places in the house was an earthen pot called *lalu*, into which she would often crawl to spend the night. Because of that peculiar trait, she and her children became known as 'Lalus', the origin family of the Lalu clan, which prospered during the heyday of the state of Madur Maskut.

With the disintegration of Madur Maskut, the Lalu clan migrated back across the River Kupli into areas now claimed by Assam. There they prospered for many generations until the outbreak of a plague that wiped out the entire clan, except for one woman by the name of Ïaw Ïaw, who, although she had lost her family, became fantastically rich, having inherited all of the clan's wealth. Because of her new-found wealth, suitors flocked to her house and drove her to distraction with their persistent wooing. Ïaw Ïaw then fled to Jowai (now the capital of Jaiñtia Hills district) and sought refuge in the house of the lyngdoh. Instead of providing her sanctuary, the high priest of Jowai, not knowing anything about her, treacherously tried to sell her off as a slave, encouraged by his wife's repeated prompting. He was unsuccessful in his attempt, however, since nobody was willing to offer more than *shibdi ki sbai*, or twenty cowries, the currency of the time. Later, when he came to know of her great wealth, he immediately arranged for her to marry his own son. By that time, Ka Ïaw Ïaw had become known as 'Ka Ïaw Shibdi', or the woman who was offered the buying price of twenty cowries only.

Ka Ïaw Ïaw and the lyngdoh's son came to love each other deeply and lived happily together for some time. But some fortune hunters from across the Kupli turned up in Jowai and tried to carry her off as a rich trophy bride.

That forced the lyngdoh to arrange for the couple's speedy escape to the state of Shyllong, where they settled in a place called Sohphoh Kynrum near Nongkrem, which was then the capital of Shyllong. Here the family soon flourished, for Ka Ïaw Shibdi proved to be an astute businesswoman. She founded a market in the area and invested heavily in the iron-manufacturing industry as well as in farming and animal husbandry. In fact, she owned the biggest piggery in the area, and became famous for feeding her numerous pigs in a large trough carved out of the *diengdoh* tree. And that is how the Lalu family came to be known as the Diengdohs, the people who fed their pigs in a diengdoh trough.

But from here too, the family had to flee south towards a place called Umthli because of a covert attack by the king of Sutnga, U Long Raja. The new place proved to be unsuitable for the family, and as a result, it decided to split up and migrate to five different regions. One branch made its peace with the king of Sutnga and returned to Jowai, where it retained its original clan name of Lalu, whose spelling its members later changed to Laloo. Two branches went towards present-day West Khasi Hills. One of them settled in the state of Nongkhlaw and retained the name Diengdoh, while the other settled in the state of Mawïang and became known as Parïong. Another branch, led by Ka Ïaw herself, went east towards Dawki, bordering East Bengal, and became known as Lamin. The last one went further south towards Sohra and, like the branch in Nongkhlaw, retained the name Diengdoh. This branch increased and multiplied in the area and prospered so much that they eventually became *ki bakhraw batri*, or one of the ruling clans of the state of Sohra. Though the Diengdohs later splintered into three groups, called Diengdoh Bah, Diengdoh Shngaiñlang and Diengdoh Kylla, to the rest of the world, they were still known as Diengdohs.

Magdalene laughed out loud. 'Ning, you and Ham were fighting about the name Jaiñtia, remember? But now it turns out that your maternal ancestors were originally Pnars, while Ham's paternal ones were originally Khynriams, what an irony!'

Evening laughed ruefully and shook his head as if in disbelief. But he did not challenge the story because he knew nothing of it.

I told them that every Khasi clan has a similarly interesting story to tell. And each one of these stories establishes the family as the nucleus of the clan, with the first mother called 'ka ïawbei tynrai'; the first father called 'u thawlang'; and the first maternal uncle, that is, the first son of ka ïawbei tynrai, called 'u suidñia'. The spirits of these forebears are greatly revered in

Khasi society, and are also prayed to and given ritual offerings to ensure the family's welfare. But these offerings are only made after permission has been sought from God, U Blei, for the three are not gods but only intercessors between God and the living. There is no such thing as ancestor worship among the Khasis, who are monotheistic.

A Khasi family, therefore, is not merely a unit of husband and wife, but uncle as well. These three have very clear-cut roles to play. The mother, ka kmie, is, of course, central to the family, being the source of the family name as far as the children are concerned. She is *ka nonglum ka nonglang*, the safekeeper, the caretaker, the one who collects and keeps what is brought to the house and the one who runs the daily affairs of the household. But she is not the head of the family: Khasi matriliny should not be confused with matriarchy. Though the family is of matrilineal descent, it is not even matrifocal. The authority and responsibility for running the family are not hers alone. They are shared by the father, who is the head of the family, the 'master in war and peace'. The father, who retains his surname, different from that of his wife's and children's, is *uba lah uba ïai*, the one who is capable, the one who provides. And his responsibility is not only basic—to provide the family with food, clothing and shelter—but also progressive, that is, to work towards the family's economic welfare and see that it prospers in every respect. His burden is weighty, and as far as matters of the house are concerned, his authority is final, for he is also *u nongri u nongda*, the keeper, the guardian.

This is traditionally the division of labour between the mother and the father, but in many Khasi homes, it is very common for both the parents to work together for the family's well-being. It is only in matters directly related to the mother's clan that the father has no say at all. For instance, he can have no role in the running of his wife's ancestral property. Nor can he attend her clan's periodic gatherings or participate in any of its religious ceremonies. Nor would he want to, for he has his own clan's affairs to look after as an uncle.

Contrary to common understanding, the Khasi family is not matrilocal, or at least not entirely so. When a man marries, he does go to the house of his mother-in-law to live. However, unless his wife is the only daughter, or the last daughter in the family, he moves out after some time to set up his own family. This is true of many Khasi sub-tribes, except for the Pnars, where the man continues to live in his mother's house and only makes nightly visits to his wife's until such time as a child is born or, in many cases, until the children are grown up.

It is only when a man marries a khatduh that he lives with her in her mother's house, where both her parents and some of her unmarried brothers may be living together. The khatduh is not necessarily the youngest daughter—

'What, what?' Magdalene interrupted hotly. 'Everybody knows that the khatduh is the youngest daughter of the family—'

'Listen, na, Mag,' Bah Kynsai said gently. 'Ap knows much better than you. He and Kit and Bah Su still practise the culture as it is, all of them are Khasi-Khasis, remember?'

I told Magdalene that what she was saying was a widely held misunderstanding. But before proceeding to explain why, I asked, 'Why do you protest, Mag? Are you the youngest daughter in the family? Do you have unmarried sisters?'

'No, I'm the only daughter,' she responded.

'Then you have nothing to worry about!' Everyone laughed, and Bah Kynsai teased Donald about managing to catch himself a rich heiress.

I said the khatduh is definitely not the youngest daughter to be born, but the last daughter in the house. Among the Khasis, there is no custom whereby the elder daughters have to marry first. In many cases, it is actually the youngest daughter who does so. In this situation, she has to move out with her husband to set up her own family. In this way, the daughter who marries last, or the one who does not marry, becomes the khatduh, the one who waits upon her parents, who looks after them and the ancestral house. The concept of ka khatduh is, therefore, the result of the process of elimination through marriage, and not the question of being born last.

Even if a man marries the khatduh, his position is not a subservient or subordinate one. While he is expected to respect his in-laws as he would his parents, they and their children respect him too, not only as a provider for, and a guardian of, the young family but also as a nongkha—literally, 'the one who gives birth', the one responsible for the propagation of the clan. It is not only the father who is given this respect as the propagator of the female clan but also his entire family, especially his mother. His mother is called ka meikha, literally, 'the mother who gives birth', and is revered almost like a goddess by his children. The other members of his family: his father (parad, or 'old father'), his sisters (ki ñiakha, 'the aunts who give birth') and his brothers (pasan, or 'elder fathers', in the case of elder brothers, and pakhynnah, or 'younger fathers', in the case of younger brothers) are all given the same reverential treatment. All of these members constitute the paternal relations, who must not only be accorded the highest respect but must also never be offended, for that is taboo.

Donald nodded briskly to show that he now understood why the paternal grandmother is so much revered. And then he surprised me by asking about an article that had appeared in the May 1997 edition of *Femina* magazine. He said, 'But, Bah Ap, if this is the case, then why would that *Femina* fellow say that Khasi men are "good for nothing"?'

'Yeah, yeah,' several voices cried. 'Who was that fellow?'

'That was Vivek Ghosal,' I replied. 'He also said, "While women earn for the family, men just eat and drink. They are parasites." How did you know about that, Don?'

'My father showed me the article.'

'That damn so-and-so, liah, tdong!' Bah Kynsai swore. 'I wrote a strong letter against the article, you know, but I never saw it published ... the bastards!'

'That was why the KSU got so angry, no?' Bah Kit chimed in. 'Its members burnt copies of *Femina* in the Khasi-Jaiñtia Hills, remember, Bah Kynsai? They made a huge bonfire in Police Bazaar—'

'Of course I do! I was there too, taking photographs—'

'I believe most of us were there, you know,' Bah Kit said. 'Though these fellows may have been too young, I think.'

Raji, Evening, Hamkom and I said we were in our late teens at the time and were very much there, for the incident had caused quite a stir among young Khasis.

'Served them right, if you ask me!' Bah Kynsai declared.

'What about freedom of expression and the freedom of the press?' Donald asked.

'Freedom of expression! What the hell are you talking about?' Bah Kynsai snapped. 'If tomorrow I say to the press that you are a good-for-nothing, that you don't do any work and that you only eat and drink on your wife's wages, what would you do, liah?'

'I would certainly not resort to violence.'

'You would not because you would be alone!'

'No, Bah Kynsai, it's not that, I mean, we have the law to take care of these things, we could always go to court—'

'Go to court? Who would go to court against a powerful media organisation? The case would go on and on until there's not one of us left to fight it. And who would fund a court case like that, huh?'

'The government could have taken the initiative—'

'Don, Don,' Bah Kynsai said, sounding tired, 'we have been talking about the kind of government we have in Meghalaya, don't you understand anything? Governments here are only interested in three things: maintaining law and order at all costs, keeping themselves in power at all costs and looting money from every scheme they implement. Even when an entire society is unjustly maligned, na, our so-called leaders are not moved from their callous indifference! So what do we have left? The KSU, NGOs … If not for them, na, *Femina* would have got away with it!'

Raji added, 'No, Don, this is not about the freedom of the press. Bah Su and I are also journalists, okay, but we would never write anything without verification, and we would certainly never malign an entire community without basis, no, Bah Su? That's not only yellow journalism, ha, it's downright malice!'

'You see, Don,' I chimed in, 'the KSU did not take the extreme step of burning those copies of *Femina* immediately—'

'How do you know?' Donald asked.

'I was a student at the time, remember? A Khasi student! Many of us sent letters to the magazine, but somehow all these letters simply vanished into thin air. We also know that the KSU sent a letter to the management of the magazine, demanding an immediate apology. But their letter was ignored. It was only then that they resorted to burning copies and banning the magazine's circulation in the state. When its management realised that its commercial interests would be affected, only then did it finally issue an apology. And that brought an end to the confrontation. If they had behaved more ethically in the first place, there would not have been such an ugly incident.'

'But was Ghosal justified in saying that about Khasi men, Bah Ap?'

'What a question to ask, Don! Now, look at us here. Who are you? You are a research scholar from a university in Delhi and you are about to join a college as an assistant professor. Bah Kynsai? He's a university professor. Bah Kit and Halolihim are government employees; Raji and Bah Su are journalists and writers. Ning and Dale are entrepreneurs, among other things, and Ning's wife is a housewife—'

'So are ours,' both Raji and Bah Su said.

'Yeah, so they are. Can you say therefore that any one of us is a good-for-nothing, a drunk, a parasite? Can you say that our friends here are the kind who would let their women work while they do nothing but eat and drink? In a group of ten men, there would have been at least a couple of good-for-nothings if Ghosal was right. What would he know of anything if he came here like "the snapping of fingers"?

'When I was young, my family was quite badly off. My mother tried to bring us up on her own—all four of us, three brothers and a sister—and all she had was a low-paying, fourth-grade government job. That was not because my father was a parasite, but because he was dead. She struggled very hard to raise us, providing us with a proper education and so on. But it was never enough, so all of us, except my sister, had to work odd jobs as piecemeal labourers during the holidays to supplement the family's income. That's not the way that parasites treat a sister, is it?

'When we grew older, we were, if anything, even harder up. By then, we had migrated to Shillong, and were living a squalid life in a wretched tenement, paying more for the rent than we should have. I can tell you, life was harsh and ignoble for this rustic, who struggled to be a day-time student, a night-time labourer. Those were the most miserable years of my life, and everything seemed to ridicule me, from rich girls giggling on the road to loud boys on bicycles and young louts playing badminton. Like those rich boys, I too wanted to ride bicycles and play badminton, but where was the money? Where was the time?

'Instead, I would sometimes climb up the branches of a pear tree and indulge in a kind of vicarious enjoyment while watching those rich kids play. But then, I got lucky. In the nick of time, I learnt the enchantment of books, the relief of stories and the pleasures to be conjured up behind closed eyes—'

'What is the point, man?' Bah Kynsai demanded impatiently.

'The point is that my brothers and I toiled very hard on behalf of the family. Thanks to us, our sister had a regular education and is now doing very well. These are not the actions of parasites, are they? If some journalists weren't lazy, insensitive, presumptuous hacks, they would know that Khasi men are no different from hard-working, conscientious bread earners found elsewhere in India. Both men and women share the burden of earning for the family, though in many cases, the man may be the sole breadwinner. Indeed, you would be hard pressed to find a husband who stays home without working, unless he is chronically sick or disabled in some way.

'All Ghosal had to do was to take an approximate census of men working in government and private offices, men working as farmers in the fields, as labourers, miners, woodcutters, stonebreakers, builders, businessmen, traders and so on. But no, he preferred to touch only the surface and fly away to write a hurried piece, passing judgement based on market gossip. It is only fitting, I think, that he is compared to a dragonfly, a *ñiang-kynthah-um*, the water-toucher, or a *ñiang-shih-um*, the water-fucker.'

'That's it, Ap, you've hit it on the head, he did behave like a bloody water-fucker,' Bah Kynsai swore.

'People like him,' Bah Kit said, 'come here, talk to one or two people and go back to write all sorts of nonsense about us, it's really too much, Bah Kynsai.'

'I know, I know, Kit, I feel like cursing that bugger all over again.'

'We too, we too, Bah Kynsai,' Raji put in. 'Come on, shall we go outside and curse him at the top of our voices?'

'And what will the Lyngngams say about us, liah?' Bah Kynsai replied. 'Let's forget about him, man. Ap, go on.'

'I have spoken of the role of the Khasi man as a father,' I continued, 'a far cry from the parasite that Ghosal wrote about, now let me speak of his role as an uncle.'

The role of the uncle in the family is a unique one. While the father is 'the capable provider' and 'guardian', the maternal uncle, especially the eldest one, is *uba kit ha ka ïap ka im*, that is, one who bears the burden of the clan in matters of life and death. But first, it must be kept in mind that *u kñi rangbah*, the eldest maternal uncle, is not the same as u suidñia. Suidñia, literally, 'spirit aunt', is the first maternal uncle and the eldest son of ka ïawbei tynrai, as I have said. He is a *suid*, or spirit, because he is no longer in the world of the living but exists, with his mother, the first ancestress, as the guardian spirit and an intercessor between God and his clan. His role is to plead for the clan and its members' well-being whenever they reach out to him through prayers and ritual offerings.

'But why is he called "spirit aunt", Bah Ap?' Donald asked.

'Good point,' I observed. 'He is "spirit aunt" because he belongs to the spirit world, where things are the wrong side up from the world of the living. But another reason is the Khasi custom of interchanging genders, in which feminine markers are sometimes used to address a man and masculine markers to address a woman. Like, *u syiem u kmie*, the king the mother; *u ñi u kong*, the uncle the sister, though it means the uncle the brother-in-law; and *u kong rangbah*, the eldest brother-in-law, but called u kong rangbah, the eldest sister, when addressed by his sisters-in-law. I suppose you know that "suidñia" is often misspelt as "suidnia", but that is a practice from the past when the letter "ñ" was written as "n". Even now, in the computer age, many people use "n" because they cannot find "ñ" on the keyboard.'

'Some people also spell it as "suitnia", Ap,' Raji stated.

'That is pure nonsense, or sheer ignorance of Khasi spellings,' I told him. 'Suit does not mean spirit. It means the pouring of libation in honour of a god or a dead relative.'

Anyway, I continued, u kñi rangbah is a maternal uncle—and very much alive. It is he, with the support of his younger brothers, who runs those affairs of the family that are connected with matters of the clan. He is the chief priest of the family and conducts all religious ceremonies relating to birth, the naming of children, marriage and death. He is also the elder who performs sacred rites and pleads with God or the guardian spirits of his clan whenever there is sickness or misfortune in the family. In this way, he is both diviner and healer. And that is not all. When it comes to the management of the family's ancestral wealth and property, he and his brothers have the final say. For instance, though the khatduh or the last daughter in the family is given custody of most of the ancestral property, she cannot actually take any important decisions concerning it. She may work the land allotted to her and enjoy the income that accrues from it, but she cannot lease or sell it without the say-so of the uncles.

'In some cases, it's not only the khatduh who gets the ancestral property, na, Ap?' Bah Kynsai asked.

In many Khasi sub-tribes, I agreed, ancestral wealth is shared, if there is enough to share, with the other daughters. But the largest portion still goes to the khatduh. Some Khasi sub-tribes like the Wars are also known to share their ancestral wealth equally among the children, including sons.

Coming back to the khatduh, I clarified that far from being the lucky heiress, she actually has the most onerous responsibility of all the daughters. She must, for instance, accept into her home and care for any family member who suffers a misfortune. Her house is also the *iingseng iingniam*, or the religious house, where everyone assembles whenever the eldest uncle conducts rites relating to the well-being of the clan.

'Wuu, crap, taking care of all my relatives? Doesn't sound like fun at all, man!' Magdalene lamented.

We all laughed at that but offered no comment.

Despite the emphasis on the equally important roles of mother, father and uncle, there is no denying the fact that in any Khasi family, when it comes to children, the daughter is the most beloved and cherished. When the first child of a family is a daughter, there is an immediate easing of stress, for the family does not have to keep hoping for a girl child to be born. Usually, though, the attitude is, the more the number of daughters, the merrier. It is a common saying among the Khasis that those with many daughters are *kiba khraw jait*, people who have a large clan, and therefore, are also *kiba riewspah*, prosperous. On the other hand, when the first child is male, it is normal for the family to hope for a girl the next time the mother becomes *armet*, or two-bodied, as they say. The angst-ridden words most commonly heard in such circumstances are, '*Ban da ïoh noh da i kynthei te hooid sieh!*' ('If only we could get a girl this time around!')

The anxiety is not only because the line is passed on from the mother to the daughter but also because daughters, especially ka khatduh, are supposed to look after their parents and the family's ancestral wealth and property. Besides, families without a daughter are usually scorned as *kiba duh jait*, the ones whose lineage has come to an end. All this contributes to making the girl child a beloved prize, the queen of children, in Khasi society. This is also reflected in the names frequently given to daughters: Ibanylla ('the pure, the perfect'), Ibaphylla ('the wondrous'), Phibakordor ('you, the precious one'), Phiba Angnud ('you, the desired one'), Phibasiewdor ('you, our recompense'), Naphisabet ('from you, it will be sown'), Meba-Ai ('God-given'), Mebari ('protected by God'), Barilin ('you, who will care for all'), Damonlang ('loved by all'), Pynhunlang ('you, who satisfies all'), Pynkmenlang ('you, who gladdens all'), Medariker ('God, protect and care'), Wanrilin ('come to care for all'), Larisa ('exulted') and Imynsiem ('my soul').

In English, too, it is customary to come across female names like Miracle, Adorable, Memorable, Darlinica, Desiree, Grace, Godgift, Joyful, Rejoiceful, Plentiful, Marvellous, Wonderful, Delightful, Brilliancy, Lovely, Sweetie and so on. These names reflect the sense of wonder and joy that God has graced the family with a girl child. Can there be anything like this anywhere in the world?

'Why not?' Evening asked. 'There are matrilineal communities in other parts of the world, also, no, Ap? The Tonga of Zimbabwe and the Ashanti of Ghana, for instance, and in India itself, we have the Nairs of Kerala and the Garos of our state—'

'These people may follow the matrilineal system, but do they have the same kind of reverence that Khasis have for the girl child?' Bah Kit countered. 'Do they have the same kind of reverence for the father and the paternal grandmother as ki nongkha, the birth givers? Most importantly, do they follow our unique hearthstone system of mother, father and uncle? I doubt it, Ning.'

Evening did not know anything about the peoples he had just named, so he kept his peace. To be fair, the rest of us didn't either.

The modern Khasi family has undergone a great transformation, I told them. Modern life has badly corrupted our traditional system and grievously eroded our traditional values. The most significant changes can be seen in the roles of the khatduh and the maternal uncle. The influence of Western education and values, and the new religions, have left a large section of the Khasi society in ignorance or with only a modicum of knowledge about its own culture. The result is confusion, leading to a perversion of almost all traditional practices. The khatduh, for instance, is now misunderstood as the family's youngest daughter, and not the one who stays in the house by marrying last or not marrying at all. And that is not all. She is also misunderstood as the heiress and proprietor of ancestral wealth and property. This has brought about unwholesome changes in the family hierarchy and the way children are treated by their parents, for they look at the youngest daughter as the owner of everything from the moment her status as the youngest daughter is established.

Magdalene raised her hands and shook them in the air to celebrate this with cries of 'Yeah, yeah!'

Because parents expect the youngest daughter to look after them in their old age, they also tend to give her special treatment and allow her priority in everything. In this way, she becomes spoilt and, in many cases, loses all respect for her elder siblings, who become alienated and are made to feel insecure in their own home. This feeling is even more palpable among boys, who are often referred to as *ki ban leit sha ïing ka briew*, those who will go to a woman's house, and therefore, do not belong.

It was now Evening's turn to be jubilant. He said, 'You see, you see, what did I tell you? The system is stacked against men!'

'Hold on, na, hold on!' Bah Kynsai silenced him.

But this particular corruption of the system, I continued, has come about because the maternal uncle has lost his traditional importance and status. With the conversion of a majority of Khasis to Christianity, the maternal uncle's religious role also came to an end. The priests now conduct baptism and christening, marriages and funeral rites. And this development has affected even those families practising the Khasi religion. In many cases, because the uncles have adopted the new religion, these families have no option but to turn to *ki nongduwai*, the elders who pray, or *ki nongshat nongkheiñ*, the augurs and diviners, to perform the religious ceremonies for them. These people, together with the Christian priests, have become, in a manner of speaking, the new uncles in Khasi society.

With the loss of this most critical function, for which he was revered and feared, the position of the maternal uncle as the administrator of the family's ancestral wealth also weakened dramatically. The youngest daughter, in many families, knowing that she is no longer dependent upon her uncles for religious purposes, does pretty much as she pleases with the ancestral property. And thus, the Khasi man at present finds himself in a much reduced role. While he remains the father, who is a capable provider (*uba lah uba ïai*), a guardian (*u nongri u nongda*) and a birth-giver and nurturer (*u nongkha nongpynlong*), he is no more the uncle who bears all burdens in matters of life and death (*uba kit ha ka ïap ka im*). He is now an uncle with not too much of a role in his own clan. Of course, there are exceptions, but by and large, this is what is happening in Khasi society today.

Bah Kit and Bah Su did not agree with my analysis at all. They were still very important uncles in their own clans, and there were many others like them, they argued.

'That's because everyone in your family is a follower of Niam Khasi,' I said. 'Take the case of one of my friends, a follower of Niam Khasi like you. When his niece, a Catholic, was getting engaged, his sister invited him and all his brothers to her house to meet the groom-to-be and to arrange things, he thought, as in the old ways. When the boy and his uncles arrived, my friend and his brothers wanted to begin the proceedings immediately. But their sister said, "No, we must wait for Father to come." The Reverend Father, from South India, came late, and the moment he entered, he said in broken Khasi, "The people, where? The girl and the boy, where? Bring them to me." When the two young people were brought to him, he took them to another room and spent about twenty minutes with them there. Finally, when they emerged, the Father declared, "Me done everything, no need for anything else now, only to eat some food and celebrate!" My friend and some of his brothers refused to stay back. He said he had never been made to feel so useless before. A Khasi uncle, he said, is now like a monolith, he is there, but nobody gives a damn about him any more. And this is how it is in 95 per cent of Khasi homes. Even you Bah Kit, you Bah Su, you said you still play an important role as uncles in your own families, tell me, are you also diviners and augurs?'

'You know very well we are not!' Bah Kit replied testily.

'Then how can you say you still play an important role as uncles in your family? You are no longer the family priests. When an uncle loses that role, he loses everything, unless he can support his sisters' families financially. And how many uncles can do that when they have to provide for their own families too?'

'Ap is absolutely right,' Bah Kynsai said. 'In our Christian families, na, uncles don't have any religious function any more; that has been taken over by the priests. Sometimes we do feel like useless monoliths.'

Evening laughed aloud at that and said, 'You see, you see, this system is *faltu*! You know why I hate it so much? It's a woman-pampering system! The Khasi woman gets everything: family name, children, wealth and property … everything. And she can do as she pleases. If she wears miniskirts that reveal her bottom, it's okay. If she wears pants like a boy, it's okay. If she wears jeans that are so tight that they trace every part of her legs, her pelvis and her arse as if she is not wearing anything, it's okay. If she cuts her hair like a boy, it's okay. If she gives it the colours of the rainbow, it's okay. If she wears ornaments in her nostrils, it's okay. If she wears a salwar kameez that reveals her navel, it's okay. I think even if she wears only bras and panties also, it would be okay; nobody would say anything because she's a woman—'

'That's too bloody much, you bloody misogynist!' Magdalene shouted at him. 'You know, Evening, you are nothing but a disgusting pig!'

Bah Kynsai tried to calm them down. 'Cool it, na, cool it! Let's discuss the issue calmly; we don't want another scandal, do we? And you too, Ning, temper your language, man!'

'No, no, Bah Kynsai, what I'm saying is true! We are pampering the women too much. I have a friend who used to be very religious, okay, very regular churchgoer, but now he doesn't go any more. You know why? This is what he said, "How can I go? In front of me was a girl wearing jeans that exposed the crack between her buttocks all the way to the hole. To my left was a girl wearing a skirt so short that even her panties could be seen; to my right was another whose blouse was so tight that her breasts looked like footballs, and so low that all her cleavage was visible. So, what could I do? How could I concentrate on what the pastor was saying?" That's why nowadays he doesn't go to church any more. You see, Bah Kynsai, Khasis will let the woman do whatever she wants—'

'So what the hell do you want Khasi women to wear, you bloody Talib? Hijabs and burkas?' Magdalene demanded.

Donald also protested. 'You cannot interfere with the way people dress, man! That's moral policing and a violation of their fundamental rights! If you do that, then what is the difference between you and the various fundamentalist groups in this country that are trying to regulate even the food we eat?'

'And so damn unfair too, Evening!' Hamkom chipped in. 'It's not only girls who are allowed the freedom to dress how they please, you chauvinist pig! Have you seen the way Khasi men deck themselves up? Have you seen their hairdos? Whatever they see being done on TV, they also do. Why speak of only girls, you loud-mouthed bigot!'

But Evening was not even listening. He said, 'Khasi women should wear only Khasi clothes—'

'Then what about Khasi men, huh?' Magdalene demanded hotly. 'They also should not wear trousers and coats! They should only wear loincloths and ryndia shawls!'

'Khasi men used to wear dhotis, shirts, traditional jackets and ryndia silk shawls, not loincloths, you fool!'

'So wear them, you pig, why are you wearing trousers?'

Before Evening could reply, Raji said, 'I think Ning is not against modern clothes as such, I think he only wants the girls to dress respectably—'

'No, no,' Evening interrupted, 'Khasi women should wear only Khasi clothes. But that's not the whole point. Khasi women not only dress as they please, but also behave as they please. If they marry, it's okay. If they merely cohabit, it's okay. If they bring a man home at fifteen, it's okay. If they keep him, it's okay, and if they don't, it's okay. If they marry one man, it's okay. If they marry one man after another and produce twelve children from twelve different fathers, it's okay. If they bring home a Khasi, it's okay. If they bring home a non-tribal scavenger, it's okay too. And Khasi women can marry anyone they please: white, black, brown, yellow and any other colours in between—'

'Aren't Khasi men also free to marry whom they please?' Magdalene challenged.

Hamkom added, 'Why all the rules only for women? Why interfere with people's fundamental rights?'

Ignoring him completely, Evening continued: 'And because nobody is doing anything about their loose behaviour, non-tribal businessmen are taking advantage of them, turning them into second wives and concubines, over and above their legal wives from their own communities. To them, Khasi women are nothing but trading licences and benami transactions.'

I think I have already told you about this. In Meghalaya, as per the Sixth Schedule, non-tribal communities cannot establish a trading company or set up any business without a trading licence from the District Council. To avoid the taxes and the hassles involved in this, many businessmen are simply marrying or cohabiting with Khasi women, or sometimes, even merely keeping them as mistresses. But, of course, in many cases, marriages between Khasi women and non-tribal men are the result of love and mutual attraction.

Magdalene said as much: 'Have you done a survey of how many non-Khasi men have married Khasi women? Do you know how many of them married Khasi women for love? Do you know that the most prosperous businessmen, the most brilliant teachers, scholars, officers and scientists in the Khasi community are children of such interracial marriages? Does that sound like mere benami transactions and trading licences to you?'

'And do you know how many bastards Khasi women have produced because of their loose behaviour?' Evening countered, just as angrily. 'According to the 1981 census, there were 27,072 of them in the Khasi-Jaiñtia Hills, but by 2001 the number went up to 324,864, and out of these, 108,288 were from non-tribal fathers. If we do a survey now, I'm sure the number of bastards would go up to ten lakh, and of these, I'm sure those from non-tribal fathers alone would be six lakh at least!'

'Really! Is that true?' Bah Kynsai was quite taken aback by the statistics.

'Unfortunately, it's true, Bah Kynsai,' Raji said. 'The surveys were carried out by SRT. But stop calling them bastards, Ning! You know damn well Khasis don't have any issues with children born out of wedlock.'

SRT is Syngkhong Rympei Thymmai, an organisation of modern Khasis. It is actively campaigning for the replacement of the matrilineal with the patrilineal system.

'But why is Evening saying that the number of children from non-tribal fathers would cross six lakh?' Hamkom challenged.

'Why?' Evening asked scornfully. 'Because of influx, you idiot!'

'Mind your language, na, lyeit!' Bah Kynsai snapped.

Evening carried on as if he hadn't heard the reprimand, 'And such bastards are mostly born in areas like Shillong, Ri Bhoi, where the national highway is, and in the coal belts of Jaiñtia Hills and West Khasi Hills—'

'No, no, no, how can you say that these children are the result of the loose behaviour of Khasi women?' Magdalene interrupted angrily. 'Have you thought that it's nothing but the exploitation of their simplicity, innocence and gullibility by both Khasi and non-Khasi men? You are a bloody male chauvinist, Evening! Have you analysed why Khasi women prefer non-tribals to Khasi men, if at all they do? I'll tell you why, because most Khasi men are drunks and have no sense of responsibility whatsoever! Do you know that about 90 per cent of Khasi men who die young, before forty-five years of age, die because of too much liquor? What do they call such deaths, Ap?'

'Stabbed by a broken glass!'

Evening snapped back, 'And do you know why they drink? I'll tell you why, because of the matrilineal system! They—'

Bah Kit and Bah Su were furious when they heard that. 'How can you blame our age-old customs for everything?' Bah Kit retorted. 'When women dress indecently—by your standards—you blame the matrilineal custom! When men drink too much, you blame the matrilineal custom! Now I know your secret agenda, Evening, all you want to do is wreck our culture completely!'

Bah Su added, 'You cannot say that, Ning, how can you? Who has done a proper study of the causes of alcoholism? Nobody! I know you want to turn our society into a patriarchal system, ha, but don't speak out of hatred and prejudice; speak with reason.'

Evening did not deny that his agenda was the restructuring of Khasi society. He said, 'Of course I want to replace the matrilineal with the patrilineal system! That's why I have taken my father's surname! I hate this matrilineal thing! It's undermining our menfolk completely! Why shouldn't our men become drunks, tell me? They are getting nothing. As Ap said, even in their own homes, they are made to feel like strangers, people who don't belong, "who will go to a woman's house". And—'

'But that's exactly what your system will do to us women, you bloody misogynist!' Magdalene shouted.

'And that's not the system, Ning,' I said. 'That's the corruption in the system. In the past, because the uncles had the ultimate control over both religious and temporal affairs as far as clan matters were concerned, they also had a tremendous sense of belonging to the family, and, certainly, a tremendous sense of responsibility towards their maternal relations. Whenever they visited their ancestral home, they were treated with the love and respect due to the most important persons in the clan. Now, of course, because of our ignorance and mistaken beliefs, everything has changed, everything has been corrupted.'

'Exactly!' Evening declared. 'Everything has been corrupted. The man does not get anything from his own family. Nor does he have any say in any of the family affairs, religious or otherwise, as we have seen. Family businesses are never given to sons, or only rarely. And why? Because their own families do not trust them! I have personally heard people say that if they let a son run the family's business, ha, he might take it all away to his wife. This is the truth, nobody can deny it. So how will the society prosper? Haven't you noticed? Because Khasis do not trust even their own sons, their businesses do not survive for more than one generation!

'And then, when Khasi men marry, what do they get out of wedlock, huh? Nothing! Their children are not their own! They cannot even identify with them. For instance, if your son gets an award, ha, Bah Kynsai, and if his name is mentioned in the papers, ha, who would know he's your son, huh? He doesn't carry your name! Nobody would ever connect him with you. Now that you are alive, perhaps some people will refer to your house as Bah Kynsai's! But the moment you die, okay, they will say, oh, this is Kong Nancy's house! And that, after you have spent your entire life building it. Phooey, what a system! When a Khasi man dies, ha, no trace is left of him anywhere, have you thought of that? Not in his children, because they don't bear his name, and not in his house because his wife's clan will immediately claim ownership. The only thing that will remain is the nameplate on a tombstone. But in the case of Bah Kit or Bah Su, ha, they will not even get a tombstone because they will be cremated, and everything they stand for will turn to smoke!

'I ask you, is that any incentive for a man to live a responsible life? If his wife knows how to respect him, and if his children love him, he may work hard for their sake. But if they treat him like an outsider in his own house, ha, which Khasi women and their families normally do, ha, then he will either leave or drink and say, why the hell should I slave for somebody else's children? They are not of my clan, so why should I waste my life slaving for them? Thomas Laird and Paul Andrews were right when they wrote "Where Women Rule and Men Are Used as Breeding Bulls". We are not only breeding bulls; we are also our wives' beasts of burden! If we want our society to progress, we must change this system! If we want to stop the exploitation of our women, we must change this system! If we want men to stop drinking themselves to death, we must change this system!'

Bah Kit and Bah Su were seething with rage. But it was Magdalene who spoke first. 'You know what, Bah Kit, recently a friend of mine read something to me from a book by Apol Mawñiuh, okay? The book is filled with the most extraordinary hate speech I have ever come across, ranting against women and the matrilineal system, as if they are the cause of every evil in Khasi society. Evening is speaking exactly like that fellow!'

'Why shouldn't I speak like Apol? His book inspires me—'

'Inspires you with a load of dog shit!' Bah Kit snapped back angrily. 'How can you be influenced by stray visitors who come here and say crazy things like "Where Women Rule and Men Are Used as Breeding Bulls", huh? Where did they say that, Bah Kynsai? Yeah, yeah, in an Australian magazine. Are Khasi men nothing but "breeding bulls", Evening? How can you be influenced by madmen such as these? Are you a breeding bull? Are you a mere beast of burden toiling for your wife? You make it sound as if your wife is a slave master, whereas, in all probability, she must be making herself small as a mouse before you! How else could she live with a tyrant like you? And just because your children do not carry your name, are they not your flesh and blood? Do they not carry your genes?

'Tell me, when you work as hard as you are doing, is it because your wife has forced you? Look into your soul, man! Can any woman force a man like you to do anything against your will? When a man struggles and gives his best to succeed in life, it is because of his own drives, his own dreams and ambitions, not because he's slaving for his wife or anybody else. That's the most ridiculous thing I have ever heard! A man works hard as much for himself as for his family, for his wife and children. They are the flesh of his flesh, the blood of his blood. What does the name matter?

'And no Khasi man is a mere breeding bull. You know why? I'll tell you. While it is true that most of the ancestral wealth and property are given to women to look after—not to own, mind you—it is not because Khasis hate their sons. Khasi laws were made by men, and when they made these laws, they wanted to protect the interests of the weaker sex. I think that is the most generous thing Khasi men could have done for their society, the most humane thing I can think of. Our ancestors deserve praise for it, not anger or resentment! And they did not deprive us of anything either. A Khasi man was the master in war and peace. He was the provider and the master in his family, and the controller of ancestral wealth and property in his clan. He—'

'That was in the past; now, he is nothing!' Evening retorted. 'Bah Kynsai, do you remember the story of that guy in Laitumkhrah? Because his only sister had abandoned their mother and followed her non-tribal husband to Mumbai, ha, he and his family had to stay in the ancestral house to look after her, remember? He took care of her for many years, but when she died, his sister came, and like a whirlwind, she sold off the house within a week of the funeral. And what happened to the poor guy? He had to look for a rented house in a hurry—that's your damn matrilineal system!'

'But was that the fault of the custom, Evening?' Bah Kit asked. 'The mother could have made a will in the son's name, and he would have—'

'Of course it was! Even though her son had taken care of her, the mother did not give him the house because she was following the custom!'

'No, no, no, in such cases, the custom is very flexible, you dumb fool!' Bah Kit said indignantly. 'Mothers are free to give their houses to whomever they please. If that particular mother did not leave the house to her son, it could have been because of very personal reasons. Maybe she didn't like her son's wife and children? Maybe they only took care of her out of a sense of duty, resentfully, without any love? You never know!

'But let me get back to the point: why did you say a man is now nothing? Are you nothing, then? In the past, the Khasi man was not tasked with looking after his family's ancestral wealth and property because of the constant wars and also because he was considered a *khatar bor*, a person with twelve powers, the stronger member of the family. He could make his own way in life and create his own wealth. And all of us here are very proud that we have bought properties on our own, created our own wealth. And thanks to the education and skills our families made it possible for us to get, we have made our lives prosperous. Our families are thriving because of our hard work. We are not living with our wives' families. We have our own homes. This is a matter of great pride for us. Khasi men, far from being their wives' servants and mere breeding bulls, are self-made men. Shame on you for not being proud of that! Shame on you for being led by the nose by the likes of Laird and Andrews and Ghosal!

'And when we make our own wealth and build houses, these are not in our wives' names—unless yours is? They are ours, registered in our names. We can give our self-earned wealth to anyone we wish. Our custom may say that ancestral wealth should go to women for safekeeping, but it does not tell us what to do with our own wealth. We can give it to our wives and children, daughters or sons, but we can even give it to our nieces and nephews, or charity if we so wish! You cannot even think for yourself; you have to be told what you are by strays and fly-by-night operators! Breeding bulls indeed! What does a breeding bull do? He breeds with one cow after another. How many of us Khasi men behave in such a manner? Think before you speak, man!'

Raji added, 'You know, Ning, if we think there's a problem with the system, okay, we should not think in terms of rejecting it, because that's impossible. We should rather think in terms of reforming and modifying it.'

'No, no, no,' Bah Su interrupted, 'we must not do that! We don't need to change or modify the system. It's true that it has been corrupted, but what we need to do is bring it back to its original state.'

'How do we do that?' Bah Kynsai asked. 'Ap has spoken of all those corruptions in the system, na, how do we remove them?'

'Bah Kynsai, Bah Kynsai,' Raji intervened, 'we agreed that the uncle, both in Christian and Khasi families, has lost his religious role, no? But can't he still be made the director of ancestral property?'

To that, I replied, 'Look, Raji, when the uncle lost his religious role, nobody gave a damn about him any more. Besides, because of our ignorance, we have corrupted the system almost beyond recognition. We don't even know who the khatduh is any more. And what is worse, she is no longer the custodian but the owner of all ancestral property; she does whatever she likes with it. What can the uncle do?'

'But what if the uncle's power as the controller of ancestral property is restored by a will?' Raji insisted.

'That can only be an individual arrangement, unless, of course, there's a mass movement for creating awareness, making parents understand the role of both uncles and daughters as custodians—'

'Yes, yes, that way, we can bring back the power of the man, not only as a father, the capable provider, but also as an uncle who carries the burden of the clan in matters of life and death,' Raji said excitedly. 'If you want our men to be more responsible, okay, that's the solution, I think. And as Ning said, we must also have a compulsory registration of marriage to avoid the exploitation of women—'

'That alone will not help, Raji,' Bah Kit said. 'As it is now, ha, all marriages, whether conducted by the churches or Seng Khasi, are legally registered. The real problem is that men are avoiding marriage by simply cohabiting with their partners. What do we do about that?'

'But what if cohabitation is treated as marriage and those who cohabit are forced to register by law?' Raji asked.

'How can you have something that is not a marriage registered as marriage?' Bah Kynsai asked scornfully. 'Speak sense, man!'

'You cannot, you cannot, Raji!' Magdalene asserted. 'If you try to register cohabitation as marriage, okay, then the guy will simply move out and say, "I have nothing to do with this woman, she's not my wife!" If he admits to anything at all, he will claim she is his girlfriend. How can you force a friendship to be registered, huh?'

'You are right, Mag,' Bah Kynsai agreed, 'nothing will help but a mass awareness campaign. In the past, na, cohabitation was neither recognised nor sanctioned by our society. Do you remember our courtship tradition? Marriage had to have the sanction of parents and that of the respective clans. Even divorce was not a personal affair: it was both legal and social. So what we must do today, na, is to get society involved again. And society must derecognise cohabitation once again! We must not only frown upon it but also stop it wherever it happens. We have our village dorbars, na? They can once more be empowered by a popular mandate to stop cohabitation. That's the only solution I can see.'

'No!' I said emphatically. 'Cohabitation is not the problem, Bah Kynsai, the lack of protection for women is. But there may be a legal solution very soon. The Supreme Court is hearing a case of a Karnataka woman whose live-in partner has left her, and it seems that "strict proof of marriage" may not be needed for "maintenance proceedings under Section 125 CrPC". All that is required is proof that the couple had lived together and that children had been born out of the relationship. If that happens—'

'If that happens,' Magdalene said excitedly, 'all our problems are solved! Our women can sue their live-in partners right and left. Good, ya, Ap, good!'

'No, no, no!' Evening shouted. 'How can all our problems be solved? Cohabitation is not our only problem, is it? No, no, no, we must change this damn system to patriliny! Change or bust, I say!'

'But how can we change it, you cranky arse?' Magdalene demanded. 'That's not possible. You have seen it for yourself, no?'

'It can be done,' Evening claimed. 'Look at me, I'm taking my father's surname, and I'm doing all right—'

'You are doing all right?' Bah Kit asked scornfully. 'You are Eveningstar Mawñiuh when you should have been Eveningstar Diengdoh! What does that mean? You don't consider your clan as your own any longer, which means that now you and your children, who take the surname of Mawñiuh, like you, can marry into the Diengdoh clan, which remains your clan despite your denial. So what happens now, huh? In a not too distant future, your children may end up marrying Diengdohs, their very own paternal relations, which is incestuous and taboo in our society. Soon our exogamous society will be full of incestuous rogues, you myopic fellow! And you dare say you are doing all right?'

'Not only that, ha, Bah Kit,' Raji added. 'Ning has done something very funny, okay? His sons are using his adopted surname of Mawñiuh, and his daughters are using his wife's surname, Decruze—actually Dohkhrut, okay, but anglicised as Decruze. Do you see the implications?'

'Of course we do!' Magdalene declared. 'It means his sons and daughters are no longer related. Now they can even marry each other because they belong to different clans, hahaha, what a bugger this Evening is!'

'And he's not the only one doing it; you know that?' Raji continued. 'There are many, many others doing the same thing now. Can you imagine the confusion this sort of thing will create? Truly, truly dangerous.'

'There's also another side to asking the children to adopt a father's surname,' I said. 'Take Dale, for instance. He made his two children use his clan name. But that does not make them Nongkynrihs because the Nongkynrihs are saying, "His children are not Nongkynrihs, they are only using the name. We cannot and will not accept them as our clan members!" At the same time, their maternal relations, the Mawrohs, have rejected his children because they feel insulted. So, where do his children end up? They are neither Nongkynrihs nor Mawrohs. *Shong ruh jhieh, ïeng ruh kynduh.* Sit they get wet, stand they hit the ceiling, as the saying goes.'

'What a terrible dilemma to put your children in, no?' Magdalene said. 'Why the hell did you do that, Dale?'

'I have changed, Kong, I have changed their names back to Mawroh!'

'There you are, Ning, you also should do the same, man!' Bah Kynsai told Evening. 'But do you know what could really help us now? As far as I'm concerned, na, this is what we should do: reinvest the uncle with traditional secular power, make the khatduh the custodian of ancestral wealth and not the heiress, and by a popular mandate through the dorbars, either forbid cohabitation or legalise it. That should do it, na?'

'That's about it, Bah Kynsai,' Bah Kit agreed.

Evening said, 'I don't agree with it at all. I want patriliny. And I also want any woman who marries a non-Khasi not only to be ostracised but also to lose her clan name and her status as a Scheduled Tribe!'

'My God, listen to this guy!' Magdalene exclaimed, frustrated.

'And what if a Khasi man marries a non-Khasi woman?' Bah Kynsai asked.

'That's simple,' Evening said, 'we continue to do what we have been doing: sanctify a new surname.'

'And according to you, the children of a non-Khasi mother are more Khasi than the children of a Khasi mother, liah?' Bah Kynsai demanded. 'And that too, when we are following the matrilineal system?'

'In the past, Khasi women did not marry outside the tribe,' Evening argued.

'What do you know of our history or culture, ha, when you have already thrown them away?' Bah Kit challenged. 'Do you know that old Khasis used to have a practice called *tan kongngor*?'

Evening said nothing.

'But that is only done in the case of the Syiem clans, na?' Bah Kynsai asked.

'No, Bah Kynsai. It was also a practice of forcing a non-Khasi woman to marry a Khasi man or a non-Khasi man to marry a Khasi woman. When a Khasi woman could not find a Khasi husband, ha, and when the clan was worried that the woman might not have children to continue the line, ha, they would go down to the plains to catch hold of a likely man and bring him back to marry her. But most people don't know about it because no new surname ever came into being from such an alliance. Why? Because the mother was Khasi, no? So don't ever say that Khasi women did not marry outside the tribe in the past, Evening! You know nothing about our past. And I, for one, like Bah Kynsai, will never accept that the children of a non-Khasi mother are more Khasi than those of a Khasi mother, just because a new surname has been sanctified for her!'

'This Ning is crazy, na?' Bah Kynsai added in a disgusted tone.

'Why?' Evening asked belligerently.

'Why? Have you thought about what your proposal would do to our small tribe, liah? If we ostracise Khasi women who marry non-Khasi men, do you think that will stop anyone from marrying outside her community? It won't. When people fall in love, they will marry if they want to. Your own daughter might end up marrying a non-Khasi man, then what will you do, huh? Ostracise her? We'll just grow smaller and smaller by the day, man! Right now, we are like a mouse in the jungle of India, but soon we'll be like a flea, and people will have to use a microscope to see us. Think before you speak, na, tdir!'

'But some village dorbars have already implemented this thing, Bah Kynsai, you know that, no?' Raji asked.

'That's because they are run by myopic, ignorant, narrow-minded and bigoted men like this fellow here, na?'

'And who know nothing about our past!' Bah Kit added.

'Or our present, Bah Kit,' Raji put in. 'For instance, okay, what happens to women who are victimised by non-Khasi men and are left with bastards, huh? If they lose their status as a Khasi woman and a Scheduled Tribe, what will happen to them? How will they live? Non-Khasis who marry Khasi women are not as bad as those who merely cohabit with them, or those who merely keep them as mistresses, as you yourself said, Ning. Don't you see that? What will you do about them, huh?

'And one more thing, okay, you must also define who a Khasi is. All of us, apart from Ham, know that Khasi means Khynriam, U Pnar, U Bhoi, U War, U Maram, U Lyngngam, U Diko, isn't that so? Okay. But according to the state's official list of tribes, Pnars (because we are so unbelievably ignorant about ourselves) have been listed as Jaiñtias or non-Khasis. So, what does that mean? It means that if a Pnar, who is one of us, marries a woman from any of the other sub-tribes, that woman will also lose her status as a Khasi. Do you see how dangerous and divisive this kind of talk is?'

'This is too bloody much, ya!' Magdalene cried in impotent rage. 'Supposing I, a full-blooded Khasi, marry a non-Khasi man, okay, should that be any reason to ostracise me and say that I'm no longer of the Syiem clan? Bullshit! I would challenge that kind of bigotry in a court of law, and I would ask all Khasi women to rise and fight against this Talibanisation! It is Talibanisation, nothing less!'

'Yeah, yeah, Mag, quite right, quite right!' Donald supported her.

'Say what you will,' Evening persisted, 'but if we don't tame the Khasi woman and turn to patriliny, our society will one day implode!'

'Tame the Khasi woman, he says!' Magdalene shouted. 'Is she a wild animal that she has to be tamed?'

'Many of my friends would say she is worse!' Evening replied.

At that unwarranted statement, all the men in the room spat at Evening and said he had gone too far. Some, like Hamkom and Donald, were for making him physically eat his words. But Bah Kynsai and I calmed them down.

Finally, Bah Kynsai said, 'At this rate, we'll never get anywhere, man. But the good thing, na, is that most of us agree that we have to stick with the matrilineal system, although we need to revitalise it.'

'There's only one thing that men who want to adopt patriliny, or patriarchy, can do,' I said.

Evening looked at me with renewed hope.

'They should marry non-Khasi women, but when they sanctify a new surname, the surname should not only be for the non-Khasi woman but the Khasi man as well. For example, if you are a Nongkynrih and you marry a non-Khasi woman, the new surname should be ...'

'Kharnong,' Bah Kynsai said, laughing.

'No, no, no!' I also laughed. 'It should simply be Nong, and it should belong to both the Khasi man and the non-Khasi woman, so that they can write their names as Mr and Mrs Nong. Their children can also be Nongs, and there will be no risk of incestuous relationships with anyone since the mother is a non-Khasi. Additionally, to prevent such relationships, the Nongs should have an alliance with the Nongkynrihs. And the new clan so created can adopt patriliny as a way of life.'

'Hahaha, this goddamn Ap, sala!' Bah Kynsai burst into booming laughter.

Evening said, 'Hey, I don't think that's a joke, ha! I think it will really work, ya! It will; it will! And if nobody will sanctify it, we can simply opt for an affidavit in a court of law. Perfect, Ap!'

'The only problem is, we'll eventually end up with two kinds of Khasis,' I said, 'matrilineal and patrilineal Khasis—'

'But that's happening now also, no?' Evening replied, his enthusiasm not a bit dampened. 'I think we'll do that, leh, Ap, I'll suggest it to my friends.'

'But it's too late for you. You have already married a Khasi woman,' I told him. 'On the other hand, I, being single—'

Everybody laughed at that, and with the laughter came relief that everything had ended amicably despite the acrimonious exchanges. Taking advantage of the new-found bonhomie, Bah Kynsai said, 'I think now we should discuss something less controversial, na, unless we want Ning and Mag to start clawing at each other again.'

'We didn't exactly do that, Bah Kynsai!' Magdalene protested.

'Okay, but you did turn him into a pig, na?' Bah Kynsai teased her.

Before Magdalene could respond, Hamkom said, 'Just one more question, Bah Kynsai. As a matrilineal society, okay, we say that our name is derived from the mother, and of course, we have also seen the mother's important social and economic roles, that's true enough. And yet, it seems to me, ha, that her position in Khasi society is a bit diminished by her lack of a political role. What do you say, Bah Su?'

'Diminished nothing!' Bah Su reacted hotly. 'Do you remember what Soso Tham said in his poem? The old Khasis forged their social, economic, political and religious systems in the hearth of the mother's house. Nowhere else. That was their smithy. Everything emanated from the mother, remember that. And according to our belief also, the first creation of God was Mother Earth, and from her, we got everything: Sun, Moon, Wind, Water and Fire, who were her children. Everything material—food, shelter, everything—is from this mother.'

'Also, Bah Su,' Bah Kit added, 'even our divine laws, which constitute the basis of our religious, social and political thought, were given by Ka Mei Hukum, the Mother of Divine Law—'

'That's what I wanted you to say, Bah Kit!' Raji exclaimed. He had not been drinking very much tonight and was still quite sober. 'Earlier you said that Khasi laws were made by men, no? That's true enough, but if we go further into the sacred myths, okay, we will find that the laws were handed down by God in his manifestation as Ka Mei Hukum! And that,' he pointed at Evening, Hamkom, Magdalene and Donald, 'is how revered the mother is in Khasi society, do you understand, you fellows?'

'Correct, Raji, absolutely correct,' Bah Kit said, giving him the thumbs-up sign. 'And there's one more thing, neither material nor spiritual, but recreational, that was handed down by Ka Mei Hukum. And that is ... anyone?'

Bah Su, Raji and I knew the answer but did not want to spoil Bah Kit's fun.

Finally, when the others had given up, Bah Kit announced, 'None other than our national game!'

'Our national game? How is that?' Hamkom protested. 'Our national game is football, no?'

'Is that right, Bah Kit?' Donald asked. 'Is football our national game?'

'It could be,' Magdalene said. 'It's the most popular game among the Khasis, no?'

'*La bong leh*, what the hell, man!' Raji cried, surprised and a little bit angered. 'You mean you don't know what our national game is?'

'Why? Is it not football?' Dale asked.

'Football may be the most popular game now, na, but it was introduced by the British; it cannot be our national game,' Bah Kynsai said.

'No, Bah Kynsai, before that, we had our own brand of football!' Bah Kit clarified. 'It was played especially in Ri Pnar during the Beh Deiñ Khlam Festival. It was called "Dat La Wakor". But because the ball was made of wood, the game never became popular, until the British gave us a less painful ball to kick with.'

'So what's our national game, then?' Magdalene asked impatiently.

'My God, Ap,' Raji cried again, 'these people don't even know what our national game is, man! Why don't you tell them that story you wrote about it? It's called "The Story of Khasi Archery", no?'

'Archery!' they all cried.

'Why? Are you surprised?' Raji asked. 'It was the most popular game in the past, and it still is in the rural areas. Even in Shillong, we have an annual tournament organised by Bah Su, yes, our Bah Su here, and some of his friends. And of course, there is *thoh tiim*, the archery-based gambling that's popular everywhere in the state, you know that, no?'

'Who doesn't know that?' Magdalene replied.

'That's right, everybody knows, and many, many people play it. But do you know that the numbers are purchased based on dreams? I'm telling you, Ap has written a beautiful story about it!'

'I don't know about beautiful,' I said, 'but it's a long one. You'll have to bear with me.'

And the reply, as usual, was, 'We have the whole night.'

When we were children, I began, archery was simply one of the games we played, throwing arrows made of bamboo at a soft target in the open spaces surrounding our homes. Then we progressed to playing with real arrows, throwing or shooting with bows that we made out of bamboo shafts and jute fibres plucked out of used gunny bags. Later, we were allowed to go to the archery matches where contending teams, localities and villages played for pigs, chickens or cash wagers. These matches were held once a week, generally on Sundays, on the outskirts of Sohra or the adjoining villages.

We used to enjoy them immensely, not only for the excitement of the game or the gnomic phawars chanted by competing groups but also for the tea shops and the variety of food hawked around the shooting ranges. Apart from seasonal fruits like oranges, lychees, starfruits, pineapples, chestnuts and the brilliantly white *soh phlang* (flemingia vestita), the most popular food item was the black caterpillar called *ñiang phlang*, or grass insect. These were cleaned in a stream to rid them of their bristles and then curried with spices. The ñiang phlangs were especially popular with drinkers, for they were said to combine very well with the local brew. Of course, drinking was prohibited on the grounds, so those who did not dare drink on the sly would buy the curried insects for later.

As children, we were also introduced to the other aspect of the archery game: gambling. Not that we actually witnessed how archery gambling, or *ïasiat tiim*, as it is known, was done. We were only 'runners', running to the bookies' counters at the Sohra bus station to buy numbers for our families and neighbours.

So, yes, we grew up with the game. But not until I learnt English and read books written by the British did I know that archery is considered the Khasi national game. Still later, I came to know from elders that it also occupies a central place in our culture, for it is supposed to be God-given. There is a story behind this, not very well known even among the Khasis, particularly among those who do not read Khasi books.

ༀ

The Tale

One of the basic tenets of the Khasi religion, as you have seen, is the concept of ïapan, or pleading. The old Khasis believed that everything must emanate from God, the Dispenser, the Creator, and carry his sanction. This is Ka Hukum Blei, the Divine Law. It is for this reason that the invention of the bow and arrow, needed for their very survival, is attributed to divine providence. And this goes back to the beginning of time.

You already know how the seven sub-tribes, the Hynñiew Treps, ancestors of the Khasi people, came to live on earth, and how God had made a Covenant with them. The Covenant declared that so long as the seven clans adhered to the Three Commandments, they could come and go as they pleased between heaven and earth, using the golden ladder. God, through one of his attributes as the motherly Mei Hukum, also decreed that the same Spoken Word would prevail among all creatures on earth so that man and beasts and stones and trees could speak as one during that Golden Age.

But this happy coexistence between man and the other creatures did not last long. When U Syiem Lakriah, the leader of the Hynñiew Treps, grew old and infirm, his powers began to wane and his hold over *ki laiphew jingthaw*, the diverse creatures, began to fail. U Thlen, the serpent, who represented the spirit world in his council of ministers, was the first to rebel against him. Thlen had always been greatly envious of Lakriah and the Hynñiew Treps. He believed he was superior to them in every way and much more deserving than them to rule. One day, during an open session of *Ka Dorbar ki Laiphew Jingthaw*, the council of diverse creatures, he openly contested the sanctity of the Covenant. To everyone's shock and horror, he proclaimed:

'From this day forth, I will cease to live by the Covenant made between Ka Mei Hukum and the Hynñiew Treps. I find that living in the knowledge of man and God, in the knowledge of one's maternal and paternal relations, or earning virtue, does not suit my purposes. From now on, my sustenance is humankind; my earning is pelf.'

'Hold on, Bah Ap!' Donald interrupted me. 'This is the third or fourth time I have heard about Thlen, when are you going to tell us about him?'

'I will, I will,' I told him, 'but not right now. I'm on a different topic, remember?'

Seeing that Lakriah could not control Thlen, the animals also rebelled against him and clamoured for their own interests. The Divine Covenant was now completely forsaken. Before things could get out of hand, Ka Mei Hukum intervened and called for a council of diverse creatures to decide the fair share of God's blessings for each being. In the council, she directed man, the spirits and the animals to appear before her after 'nine days and nine nights'. The animals, however, impatient to know of their portion, went to her after only seven days and seven nights had elapsed. Seeing that they had violated her directive, she gave them an inferior share, comprising great strength but little ingenuity. She reserved for mankind, which had acted according to her wishes, the superior portion, comprising great ingenuity, though only a little strength. Ka Mei Hukum also took away the Spoken Word from animals and ended their verbal interaction with mankind forever. And Thlen, who did not turn up at the council, was condemned to live in the wilderness as a demon, who, later, true to his vow, fed on human flesh.

During that parting of ways, the animals sought to destroy the Hynñiew Treps with their brute strength. But the Hynñiew Treps, who still retained their link with Ka Mei Hukum through the Covenant, pleaded with her to come to their aid. Ka Mei Hukum appeared before them and taught them how to make *ka tiar ka sumar*, the weapon the protection, to defend themselves from animals. These were the names then given to the bow and arrow, which later came to be known as *tieh kpong* and *nam pliang* respectively. The bow was made from a five-jointed seasoned *shken*, a type of small bamboo known for its tensile strength, and cut between the middle of *Kyllalyngkot*, January, and the end of *Rymphang*, February, while the moon was on the wane. The arrow, on the other hand, was made from a type of reed called *stew*, and because it was meant for warfare and hunting, it carried a triangular, barbed metal cap much like a spearhead, and was fletched with eagle feathers in a five-sided pattern.

Thus, with the help of the bow and arrow, the Hynñiew Treps gained the upper hand over all animals. As a show of respect for these God-given gifts, the bow and arrow were declared the lifelong companions of every male child, to be used not only for warfare and hunting but symbolically in all ceremonies that denoted significant events in his life. For instance, during the naming ceremony of a male child, a miniature bow *(tieh jer* or *tieh lymboit)* and three miniature arrows, without metal caps *(nam jer* or *nam lymboit)*, are used to serve as a reminder both of man's lordship over animals and the qualities of manhood that he must cultivate in life. The three arrows represent the weapons used in defending himself, his family and clan, and the territorial rights of his village, province and state. And so too, when he dies, three funeral arrows, *nam tympem*, are shot from a funeral bow, *tieh tympem*, to the south, north and west. The arrows are meant to protect his soul from demons and evil spirits as it journeys to the house of God—as a reward for a life well lived—to be forever with all his maternal and paternal relations departed before him.

'Will they shoot funeral arrows here too, you think?' Hamkom asked.

Raji did not think so. 'The Lyngngams don't use bows and arrows, remember?'

'Oh yeah, I forgot.'

Donald asked me why the funeral arrows are not shot to the east.

'The east is considered the source of life, Don,' I replied, 'being the direction of sunrise, the birthplace of Mei Ngi, Mother Sun. The soul must not travel back to the source of life, but onwards towards the house of God through the western route. Arrows are also shot to the south and the north to prevent demons coming from those directions.'

'So, no demons in the east, then?'

'No demons in the east,' I agreed.

Bah Kynsai added, 'Even in real life, na, Don, demons always come from the west. People all over the world were enslaved by whom? Demons from the west, na, liah?'

To commemorate their victory over the animals, I continued, the Hynñiew Treps organised a mammoth dance festival, which later became an annual celebration. It was because of this that Khasi archery as a sport came into being.

In that early age in the history of the Hynñiew Treps, somewhere between Sohra and Mawmluh in southern Ri Khasi, lived a couple whose names were U Mangring and Ka Shinam. Shinam was a fairy sent by Ka Mei Hukum to live with humans. The legend says that she was oviparous, born from an egg, and was discovered by U Sormoh and U Sorphin, legendary heroes, who became her brothers. Later, she married Mangring, one of the most accomplished young men in the area. The couple lived happily together and had five daughters and two sons, who shared the exceptional qualities of their parents—devotion to virtue and their people's culture.

Like everyone else, Shinam and Mangring used to participate actively in the annual dance festival. But when their sons grew a little older, they experienced a little problem. The boys wanted to go too and could not be persuaded to stay at home with their grandparents. But taking them along was not an option since the dancing arena was very far. The parents felt sorry for the children. They pondered long and hard and tried to create new forms of diversion for them. Failing to do so, they finally turned to Ka Mei Hukum, who appeared before them in the form of a mother carrying a child on her back.

Approaching the couple, Ka Hukum said, 'You have pleaded with me for days; your devotion to the cause of virtue is worthy of praise and reward. I appreciate your deep love for your children. I appreciate your desire to make them grow strong and healthy, for in the strength of children rests the strength of the race, the resurgence of the land. You have worked hard, devising exercises and games for them; I appreciate you for your efforts, for what else would make them fit, in body and soul, and keep mischievous idleness away but simple pastimes such as these? So, I will give you what you want. Now that they grow tired of the old games, I will teach you a new one, and you will teach your children, and you will give them a game that will ignite their passion and keep it burning for the rest of their lives. And so it will continue until the end of time, for your children shall spread it far and wide. It will be called *ïasiat khnam rongbiria*, and it will be played with a bow and arrows.'

Bowing before God, Shinam and Mangring replied, 'Ko Mei Hukum, we genuflect before you with gratitude and humility. We are immensely pleased to hear about the new game that will hold the entire tribe captive for as long as they adhere to the ways of the old ones, which are based on the principles of virtue outlined in the Covenant. But forgive us that, in our ignorance, we seek further illumination. How can boys, O Mei Hukum, play with devices meant for hunting and warfare? They are dangerous weapons that have caused the death of many a warrior. We are afraid, in our little understanding, we are anxious, for we know of no method of getting a barbed arrow out of a wound without causing more laceration and fatal injuries to internal organs. Forgive us that, in our inadequacy, we are asking questions of you.'

To this, Ka Mei Hukum replied, 'Indeed the bow and arrows are not things to play with. In their present shape, they are certainly too dangerous for sport. You are fully justified in your fears. We will change their shape, and I will teach you how to make *ka tieh lymboit, u nam lymboit*—a simple bow made from a bamboo shaft and cane string, and harmless arrows without fletches or barbed metal tips. With these, your sons can play; with these, they can shoot at a target fashioned out of wood and placed not less than sixty paces away. The target will be called *ka liang dieng*. Teach them this game; they will stop wanting to follow you to the dance. Teach it to them and think of the possibilities. Come, we will make the new bows and arrows, and when we are done, teach them, support and inspire them, I will come again if you should need me.'

Shinam and Mangring bowed low to Ka Mei Hukum and said, '*Khublei shihajar nguh*, we thank you with a thousand bows.' Then they looked at the new bows and arrows and thought of the possibilities. 'If all boys become fine marksmen at a tender age, do you realise what this would mean for the tribe?' Mangring asked.

They taught their sons the new game of ïasiat khnam rongbiria, recreational arrow-shooting. Sometimes, for the sake of variety, they taught them to use their arrows as javelins to be thrown at the target. They called this *ïasum khnam*, arrow-throwing.

The boys were happier than they had ever been before. They played with their bows and arrows from morning till evening in a field by their hut, stopping only for food and when they were needed at home. They forgot all about the dance festival. And so, when the day for the festival arrived, when all those who could walk the distance were flocking towards the lympung, a circular dancing ground covered with pure white sand, Batiton and Shynna were preoccupied as usual with their new game.

But they were not the only ones who forgot about the festival. As the dance-goers passed by the hut, many of the young men stopped to watch the boys shoot their arrows at the liang dieng, a kind of wooden plate. The game that Shinam and Mangring had invented, with the inspiration of Ka Mei Hukum, was such a novelty that it soon drew a large crowd of onlookers. So mesmerised were they by the new game that they gathered around the boys and cheered them on, forgetting all about their original destination.

Among the spectators was a shifty youngster by the name of Kajang. After watching the boys at their game for a few days, he called out, 'Hey, Batiton, hey, Shynna, can I play with you? Can I, can I?'

'No, you can't!' the boys said haughtily. 'These are made by Mei and Papa for us!'

Seething with rage and envy, Kajang left in a huff. But the next day, he was back again to watch. Climbing onto the earthen wall demarcating the boys' courtyard from the field, he began a running commentary. First, he praised Batiton and then Shynna. After the first round, he said, 'Batiton wins; he has shot the most arrows into the liang dieng.' After the second, he said, 'Batiton loses; Shynna has completely outplayed him.' He continued in this manner until a violent quarrel ensued between the two brothers. Batiton being the elder, tried to browbeat Shynna into accepting that he had shot the maximum number of arrows into the target. Shynna refused to admit defeat and maintained that he was the better shooter. In this way, the game that was God-given, to delight and benefit body and mind, became not only a fierce contest but a source of bad blood between the brothers.

The parents were dumbfounded. 'What is the cause of this?' they wondered. 'How can a game inspired by God for the pleasure of man degenerate into this vicious conflict? How can something meant for good turn into this vile acrimony? Surely, we will let Ka Mei Hukum down if we allow this to continue!'

They questioned the brothers closely and discovered that the cause of it all was that the arrows of both boys were identical in appearance. Earlier, when their only objective was to hit the target, and their only pleasure was the thrill of the bull's eye, they had experienced no problem at all. But since Kajang had sown the seeds of discord and conflict, that simple pleasure was no longer adequate—they also had to know who was better than whom. But in the absence of differentiating marks on the arrows, the result was only confusion and disagreement. Shinam and Mangring thought of a simple solution. They marked the arrows with lime paste: Batiton's at the top, Shynna's at the base. Thus, the two arrows became known as *thoh-khlieh*, top-marked, and *thoh-trai*, base-marked.

The game of arrow-shooting became once again a happy event played in the spirit of healthy competition. The brothers ceased to quarrel now that they could tell whose arrows had hit the liang dieng. They realised they were well matched and that victory would come to one or the other by a very slender margin. Sometimes it was Batiton who had the edge, at other times Shynna, but there was no animosity between them any more.

The only sufferer was Mangring, a hard-working man with a big family. Amidst his back-breaking labours, he was often pestered by his sons for help. This was because the lime paste fell off every time it dried and would have to be pasted again. Seeing how harried her husband was, Shinam prayed to Ka Mei Hukum to intervene.

Ka Mei Hukum appeared before the couple for the second time and said, 'I know of your difficulty and will come to you whenever you plead before me according to the pledge that mankind made with me. Now that you seek my help, I will teach you how to mark the arrows with colours that will last. Take this beeswax and these herbs that are plentiful around here and mix two sets of colours, one black, one red. The arrows marked with black will henceforth be called *namïong*, black arrows, and those marked with red will be called *namsaw*, red arrows. Let your sons choose a colour each time they take to the field. Let this become a tradition.'

Following Ka Mei Hukum's advice, Shinam and Mangring took the newly marked arrows to their sons. Shinam said, 'Sons, here are two sets of arrows, one marked with red wax and the other with black. From now on, before you take to the field, you must first choose your colours. And by the colour of your choice will you be identified. Let this be a tradition. Ka Mei Hukum wishes it to be so.'

From that day on, Batiton and Shynna always followed this practice before they played. But Batiton, being the elder, would demand the first choice, and his choice would always be red because he said *saw*, red, rhymed with *ksaw*, good luck.

One day, Kajang came to see how the two brothers were getting on. An unpleasant surprise awaited him. The new game was thriving, and improvements had been made. He seethed with rage to see the brothers playing cheerily, free from the ill will and discord he had sown. Seating himself on the earthen wall, he bided his time and pretended to enjoy the game. Just when the two archers were busy looking for their discharged arrows among the weeds, he got down hastily, broke the liang dieng, and fled from the scene.

Once more, there was disquiet in Shinam and Mangring's family. The boys could not play without a target. What were they to do? Mangring raged and threatened to punish the perpetrator. But who had done it? Nobody seemed to know. Even the onlookers who were present said they did not see anything. 'Envy! That's what it is!' Mangring thundered. 'And I'm not referring to the offender alone. Wait! Let me find out who it is! Just you wait!'

Shinam calmed him down and asked him to make another liang dieng. In his anger, Mangring said, 'What's the point? Whoever it was will only break it again! And again, nobody will see anything.'

Once again, Shinam thought the only thing to do was to call on Ka Mei Hukum. The Divine Mother, who saw and understood everything, came to the couple with two ready-made targets. They were fashioned from a fat-stemmed grass with a three-sided pattern, like a file, known as *langtylli*. The grass was wrapped in a cylindrical shape around a small pole and belted together in six places with bamboo thongs. Handing the targets to Shinam, Ka Mei Hukum said, 'These shall replace ka liang dieng as the new targets. I have fashioned them from the fat-stemmed langtylli that are plentiful in and around marshy grounds. You may call them *ki skum hynriew panpoh*, the six-belted targets. Let your sons shoot into their separate skums from now on. The counting can be done jointly to decide the winner.'

Kajang was not about to give up, though. Seeing how things had changed for the better every time he sought to make them worse, he tried to sabotage the game one more time. Climbing onto his usual place on the wall, he noticed that Batiton was always shooting red arrows. 'Aha,' he exclaimed, 'now I understand why Batiton is always winning!'

'How can you say that?' Shynna retorted. 'We always win by turns.'

'You are wrong,' Kajang replied. 'You have not been keeping count carefully, and how can you, when you are so caught up in the shooting? But I have, and I know that Batiton wins much more often. And I understand why.'

'Why?' Shynna asked.

'Why? Because he is always shooting with red arrows,' replied Kajang. 'Don't you know that saw also means ksaw? Colours always signify something deeper than themselves. In this case, the colour red signifies victory. But it's up to you to solve the problem; after all, you are brothers. And, oh yes, the old people always say that colours can also relate to your rngiew, your essence, so be careful.'

Having injected that poison, Kajang left with a smirk on his face, for he had already seen the beginning of a quarrel between the brothers. The quarrel soon degenerated into a fierce struggle, which resulted in one of the skums being torn apart. Fortunately, the parents came on the scene and stopped the fight before it could get any worse. Deeply disturbed by this fresh outbreak of hostilities, they called upon Ka Mei Hukum again, and she appeared before them for the fourth and last time. Ka Mei Hukum instructed Mangring to cut the skum that was still intact into two pieces, thereby turning the six-belted skum into a three-belted one. She taught him how to make skums and how he should make them always in an open-ended pattern of three or five or seven belts. She instructed him on the materials to be used and how he should cut the fat-stemmed langtylli in the middle so as not to damage the plant permanently. This, she said, was in keeping with the provisions of the Covenant, for what is taken from nature should be done in the spirit of tip briew tip Blei, that is, in the spirit of a conscientious being.

Ka Mei Hukum also taught Mangring how to make a new type of arrow from the reed that was used to make the arrow of war. She showed him how to cap it with a round, pointed metal cap without barbs, and to fletch it in a four-sided pattern instead of a five-sided one. For fletching the arrow, she advised him to use the feathers of birds like eagles, hawks, hornbills, cranes and even ducks, but warned him not to harm them by plucking too many feathers from any one bird. All these modifications, while hugely improving the speed and accuracy of the arrow, rendered it much less dangerous and, therefore, very suitable for the game. And this is the arrow that is used in all Khasi archery competitions even today.

'You mean, Bah Ap, they never killed the birds, but simply took their feathers?' Donald interrupted me. 'But how did they catch them without killing them?'

'They trapped them,' Bah Kit answered.

'But many did not listen to Ka Mei Hukum,' Raji added. 'They simply killed them: easier, no? We are human, after all.'

Ka Mei Hukum then gave them some words of advice, I said, returning to the story. She said, 'Seek your own means; I empower you to do so. Seek your means, choose your colours, but before that, always address yourselves to me. Say what is in your mind, speak your needs, inform me, plead, appeal before me. Everything will be done according to my law through the word of man. And since this is a game for pleasure, founded in the spirit of fair play and healthy competition, forbidden is anger, forbidden is rage, forbidden is coercion, forbidden is force. Play, compete, amuse yourselves. I will bear witness to all, in the middle of all, I will intercede and judge for all. I, the Divine Law, have gifted you this sport, I will watch over it, my presence will be felt, for what is God-given must remain.'

Before leaving them, Ka Mei Hukum told the couple that this would be the last time she appeared to them in person. But she would always watch over them as they developed the sport; she would speak to them through signs and indications; her word would be for those whose pleas were founded on merit and the principles of virtue. 'In this manner,' she concluded, 'the game will continue until the end of time.'

And so it did, for when Batiton and Shynna outgrew their childish possessiveness, they coached many in the art of archery as a sport. In this way, the Sohra–Mawmluh areas to the south of East Khasi Hills became the first to adopt the new game, and it was from there that it spread to other parts of Ri Khasi and the adjoining regions. The propagation of the game started with the travels of Batiton and Shynna as young men. With the blessings of their parents and Syiem Synriang, the king of Sohra, the two champion archers gathered together their best marksmen and followers, and prepared for a journey that would see not only the propagation of the game but also the conquest of many territories. Batiton, with his followers, including Barikor and Karikor, two nobles from the court of Syiem Synriang, went towards the east. His brother, Shynna, together with Khyndai Kamar and Biskorom, also two of Syiem Synriang's nobles, took his followers towards the west.

Shynna's journey was especially fraught with dangers and difficulties because Kajang, envious of the brothers to the end, always went ahead of him to poison the minds of kings and rulers so that his march to propagate the sport was misconstrued as the march of an invading army. Consequently, he had to fight many unwanted wars and became an unwilling conqueror of many territories, especially in the plains of Bengal. Towards the end, Shynna installed Khyndai Kamar and Biskorom as the new rulers of the conquered lands and returned home to a hero's welcome, where he was reunited with his brother, who likewise had had a successful expedition. As a reward for their triumphs, the state council of Sohra bestowed upon them the title of 'bakhraw' in the court of Syiem Synriang, where they served as state ministers in his administrative council.

As for Kajang, he was slain in one of the wars, and his body was cremated with hundreds of others without ceremonies or prayers.

When I concluded the first part of my story, Hamkom said, 'Remarkable story, ha, Bah Kynsai? I think the Khasis have a story for everything, no?'

'Of course they do, that's what they have been telling us, na,' Bah Kynsai replied. 'Why do you always forget?'

'Not forgetting, Bah Kynsai, just—'

'At least he hasn't forgotten to say Khasis,' Evening taunted him.

'Enough of that damn quarrel, man! Whatever anybody says, na, we are "All for one, one for all".'

'Who said that, Bah Kynsai?' Evening enquired.

'The three mosquitoes,' he replied with a straight face.

෴

The Game

> *Pyllun kawei ki shad ïasiat,*
> *Ki kad ha shkor, ha sop ki wiat;*
> *Ba kiew u Khnam ba lieh ba ïong,*
> *Halor Sohpdung ne ha ka Thong;*
> *Ki seng phawar, ki sin sngewbha,*
> *Ban ïeng dawbah ka Rongbiria.*

> (Together as one they dance in a ring,
> They pull till the ears, on the tip then they draw;
> That the arrow white and black,
> Mount on the Tuber or the Target;
> They invent their phawar, for fun they slander,
> So may it flourish a Celebration such as this.)

There cannot be a more picturesque description of Khasi archery than this. Almost in the same breath, Soso Tham describes the scene of festivity at the archery ground and the concentration of the archers; the flight of white and black arrows to the targets; the slogans and gnomic phawars of the supporters; and the good-natured war of words. Is it any wonder, then, that the game of archery is called *ka rongbiria*, the colourful celebration?

The poet speaks about archery with such enthusiasm, not only because he was known to be fond of it, but also because it represents the greatest pastime of the Khasis. Other Khasi writers like Donbok T. Laloo, J.S. Shangpliang and W.R. Laitflang have also declared it to be one of the greatest and oldest cultural events of the Khasis that still survives. The British writer P.R.T. Gurdon was fascinated by Khasi archery and has given an elaborate description of it in his book, *The Khasis*, where he proclaims it to be 'their principal game', which 'may be said to be the national game'.

According to the traditional model, the archers of one village always challenge those of another through their leader, *u nongkhang khnam*, the arrow-blocker, or *u nongkhan khnam*, the arrow-diviner. The village so challenged then sends its nongkhang khnam to negotiate the terms of the meeting with his counterpart. Thus, between these mediators (I use this word for convenience, though it does not even begin to describe the role and significance of the nongkhang khnams), the conditions of the contest are laid down much before it commences. Among the most important of these conditions are the day and place of the contest, the number of participating archers, the number of arrows to be shot by an archer in a single round, the number of rounds to be played and the distinguishing colour of each side's arrows. Usually, the choice is between red and black, though other colours are also known to have been used. Another crucial requirement is an agreement on the nature of the bet: what prize they would be playing for, and if it is for money, then how much?

Initially, when two villages met on the archery ground, there was nothing more than the reputation of the village and the archers at stake. Later, however, the question of a wager was introduced to make the contest more exciting and intense. The first known wager was in the form of a kwai song, which the losing side had to serve the winner. This may seem like a strange wager, but as you know, a piece of betel nut and lime-marked betel leaf, kwai song, is a very important cultural symbol.

As time went by, kwai song gave way to more significant forms of betting as competing villages began to play for domestic animals like pigs, chickens, cattle and goats, and for agricultural produce like rice, millet and so forth, until finally, money came into the picture. But even now, there are archery contests where the wager is not monetary, though side-bets are prevalent.

When all the conditions have been agreed upon, the two sides gather in an open field in front of their separate skums, the targets, made of the same material and in the same manner as specified by Ka Mei Hukum. The target, fastened to a small three-foot pole, is about one foot long by four inches in diameter. Sometimes, although this is getting rarer and rarer, the target is made from the root of a plant called sohpdung, and hence a reference by the poet to a 'Tuber'.

Before the shooting can begin, the nongkhang khnams sit in front of their respective targets with some rice grains, a small bamboo mug filled with water, and the bows and arrows to be used in the competition. Spraying a little water and some rice grains on the target and on the bows and arrows (this they keep doing at regular intervals), they invoke Ka Mei Hukum, utter incantations and plead for her aid. While thus imploring, they recite the shortcomings of the opposite side, vividly laying out the reasons why it should not be granted victory. This business usually lasts for more than an hour, during which there is silence all around, for the nongkhang khnams are looked upon with awe. They are men with shamanistic powers, diviners who possess the power to prevent the arrows of the opposite party from hitting their mark, or even to claw out the arrows that have already hit it.

The tradition of this 'verbal contest' involving the nongkhang khnams is derived directly from Ka Mei Hukum's words of advice to Shinam and Mangring, which their sons, Batiton and Shynna, had taught to every potential archer during their travels. Its existence not only proves that Ka Mei Hukum's divine words have been carefully nurtured and followed to the present day but also exhibits the Khasis' firm belief that he who is on the side of virtue will triumph. It is for this reason that it is accorded the utmost respect, for the outcome of the competition is believed to depend mostly on the outcome of the verbal contest.

'That sounds impossible, man!' Hamkom said.

'You just wait and see,' Raji responded. 'On with the story, Ap!' he commanded, and then rather sheepishly, added in a kind of sing-song, 'Sorry, Bah Kynsai.'

In uttering his incantations, the nongkhang khnam always refers to the pledge of Ka Mei Hukum to bear witness to all, to be in the middle of all, to intercede and judge for all. He also refers to her pledge that 'her word would be for those whose pleas are founded on merit and the principles of virtue'. He promises that his side will uphold the honour and dignity of ka rongbiria, that anger, rage, coercion and force are forbidden, for this is a game for pleasure founded in the spirit of fair play and healthy competition. As winners, he says, we will sing, shout, cheer and also jeer, but as losers, we will take it all in a sporting spirit. He finally restates the shortcomings of the opponents and pleads for victory for his side.

When the nongkhang khnams finish their pleadings, the gathering erupts in a loud cheer, and the match commences. The archers take up their positions about forty to fifty yards away from their targets and arrange themselves in a straight line facing them. Then each side begins shooting at its own target amidst the chanting of phawars, dancing, the mutterings of the nongkhang khnams and the general din of the milling crowd all around. These days, the use of a single target has become more common.

Khasi archery is high-speed by nature. A description in Dhruba Hazarika's *Bowstring Winter* shows just how fast it can be:

John Dkhar heard a hum, as of bees droning, the arrows smacking into the skum in such quick succession than he had believed it possible. One after the other, the feathered sticks were transferred from the ground to the bowstrings and just as quickly were homing in on the skum. There was something casual about the effort, a fluidity born of experience and practice. But despite the apparent ease with which the hands and fingers functioned, there remained a rigid concentration of spines, of bodies caught in the tension of the 180 seconds during which the shooting had to be completed.

Usually, the time allowed for each round is two minutes, except in *ïasiat tiim*, professional-gambling archery, where archers can take up to four minutes. But Khasi archery is not only remarkable for its speed. Hazarika speaks of 'a fluidity [of skill] born from experience and practice', and Gurdon speaks of the strength of a Khasi bow, which 'carries a considerable distance', and the prowess of a Khasi archer, who can shoot 'an arrow over 180 yards'. Robert Lindsay has also borne witness to this ability.

In his *Anecdotes of an Indian Life*, he recounts an incident from the 1770s, when he was invited to a hunting party by the king of Sutnga, whom he referred to as the Raja of Jaïntiapur. Lindsay was taken to an enclosure not less than thirty acres and surrounded by a stockade where he was made to sit on an open balcony, with the king to his right and the king's prime minister to his left.

In Lindsay's words, 'A huge number of wild animals had been driven into this enclosure previously, it being the highest ground in the plain.' Among these animals were more than 'a couple of hundred of the largest species of buffalo, hundreds of the large elk deer, a great variety of smaller deer and innumerable wild hogs'. The animals were galloping around the enclosure in great agitation when Lindsay was asked to begin the hunt by taking the first shot. Although, by his own admission, a bad marksman and a reluctant 'shekar' who did not wish to betray his want of skill 'in so public manner', Lindsay aimed, and to his astonishment, dropped a large buffalo dead on the spot. It was now the turn of the prime minister, for the king, he said, would not be persuaded to participate, probably because of the apprehension that he might fail before his own people. Lindsay describes the incident in these words:

On my left hand sat his *lushkar* [lyngskor] or prime minister; his quiver, I observed, only contained two arrows. 'How comes it, my friend,' said I, 'that you come to the field with so few arrows in your quiver?' With a sarcastic smile, he replied, 'If a man cannot do his business with two arrows, he is unfit for his trade.' At that moment he let fly a shaft, and a deer dropped dead—he immediately had recourse to his pipe, and smoked profusely.

In traditional Khasi archery, the counting is done after each round by representatives of both sides. At the close of day, the side with the maximum hits wins the contest, and the successful party returns home in a boisterous procession.

As you can see, Khasi archery is not just a competition between two groups or two villages. It is an important community event, a unique cultural festival around which many other traditions have grown—the shamanistic war of words, the spontaneous gnomic phawars, and all the other ceremonies and festivities.

The story by Shangpliang about an archery competition between Sohra and the adjoining village of Mawsmai gives us a glimpse into how important it was considered to be. Sohra was losing the match, and Mawsmai was already rejoicing, when, amidst all the chanting and jeering, someone from among the glum Sohra crowd suddenly declared, 'O you people of Mawsmai! Do not rejoice yet; we still have one more!' The last archer was none other than the famed marksman and king of Sohra, U Ram Sing Syiem, who had removed his kingly turban and was proceeding to the shooting circle to rescue Sohra from the losing contest. To cut a long story short, Ram Sing won the day for Sohra, and the thunderous victory aria of the day was: 'Only one was the champion! Only one was the champion!' The moral of the story? Even a king becomes a common man when caught in the thrill of the bull's eye.

Donald was amazed. 'It was that important, ha, Bah Ap? Even the syiem would come down to the field to participate? Unbelievable!'

'It's true, Don, it's true,' Bah Su assured him. 'When you are in the field, ha, you forget everything, all your hardships and struggles, everything except the thrill of the game. You even forget who or what you are: it's a different world out there!'

'I like the stories about Ram Sing and the lyngskor of Sutnga, you know,' Raji said. 'What incredible marksmen they were! No wonder the people of the plains used to dread Khasi warriors in the past.'

'And you are not fascinated by the story about the stockaded animals?' Bah Kynsai asked.

'Yeah, yeah, I am. Sounds so strange to us, no?'

'Like a story from the pages of the Mughal Empire!' Hamkom added.

'The story of the nongkhan khnams is also fascinating,' Donald said. 'Are they still around?'

'Of course,' Bah Su replied. 'How can you have an archery competition without them?'

'And is it true that only he who is on the side of virtue will triumph, Bah Su?'

'That's right. But you have to prove it to Ka Mei Hukum. You have to persuade her as to why your side deserves to win and why the other side deserves to lose. You have to prove to her that their shortcomings are more serious than your own team's—'

'What shortcomings?'

'They could be small things, you know. The way the opposing team speaks and behaves in the field, its archers' temperaments, the quality of its poets and nongkhan khnam ... So many things actually.'

'It's an interesting belief, you know, that only he who is on the side of virtue will triumph,' Magdalene observed. 'But is it relevant now?'

'We discussed this already, no, Mag?' Bah Su replied. 'In the past, Khasis would not even go to war unless virtue was on their side. But now, nobody believes in the Three Commandments. They invoke them all the time, without either conviction or understanding.'

'But is it true that the outcome of the actual competition is dependent mostly on the outcome of the verbal contest?' Hamkom asked for the second time. 'Ap did not address this question at all—'

Speaking for me, Raji said, 'He'll come to that, he'll come to that, patience, Ham.'

❦

The Poetry

Ki seng phawar, ki sin sngewbha,
Ban ïeng dawbah ka Rongbiria.

(They invent their phawar, for fun, they slander,
So may it flourish a Festivity such as this.)

The line 'They invent their phawar, for fun, they slander' should not be taken to mean that the traditional form of Khasi poetry known as ka phawar was invented in the archery field. Ka phawar is an occasion-inspired poem and was created to celebrate occasions much before archery existed.

Among the many types of phawar that the Khasis have, some relate to *Ka Phawar Shad* (dance phawar), *Ka Phawar Leit Thep Mawbah* (bone-burial phawar), *Ka Phawar Ïam Meikha* (phawar mourning the death of the paternal grandmother), *Ka Phawar Ksan Thma* (victorious-war phawar), *Ka Phawar Dngiem* (bear phawar), *Ka Phawar Siat Thong* (competitive-archery phawar), *Ka Phawar Ring Maw* (stone-fetching phawar) and *Ka Phawar Khleh* (mixed phawar).

Because most phawars, including the competitive-archery phawar, share the same metrical structure, I proposed a brief discussion on the subject. Everyone agreed, for many of them did not even know what a phawar is.

The phawar is a six-line traditional Khasi verse form. It can be described as a limerick because, although it is not a five-liner, it is often humorous. It can also be described as a verse epigram that expresses a clever thought, usually funny and satirical, and as a gnomic verse because it comprises pithy and sententious sayings, embodying some moral principle or precept, some of which can be quite witty. Sometimes ka phawar has also been referred to as 'a combination of couplets' because of the short lines rhyming in a certain manner.

Ka phawar is, of course, not a set of couplets. Despite the short and concise lines, it is neither composed in the English iambic pentameter nor in the rhyme scheme of aabb, which is generally associated with rhyming couplets.

In essence, ka phawar combines the characteristics of the first three kinds of verse mentioned, with the gnomic verse bearing the closest resemblance to it. However, ka phawar is also different from all of them in the fact that it is primarily a kind of performance poetry. The following may serve as an example:

> *Oooo!*
> *U jhur mo shi pirit,*
> *I pylleng mo shi ana,*
> *I dur te la ibit,*
> *I rynñieng i dang duna,*
> *Hoooi kiw! … Hoooi kiw!*

> (Oooo!
> A saucerful of vegetables,
> One anna of scrambled egg,
> The appearance is graceful,
> The height not quite correct.
> Hoooi kiw! … Hoooi kiw!)

The origin of the competitive-archery phawar goes back to the legend of Ka Shinam and U Mangring. The ancient Khasis had a unique way of calling out to each other when they were working in the woods or the fields. When the first person called out '*Hoi*', the second would respond from afar with '*Kiw*'. And thus, slowly, the phawar chanting of 'hooooi kiw' evolved: the two words were combined and a tune was adapted from the crowing of the rooster.

Shinam and Mangring were also familiar with this kind of chanting. So, when they noticed the 'Ohs' and 'Ahs' of their daughters, as they reacted to the game Batiton and Shynna played, they encouraged them to use the proper phawar chanting of 'hooooi kiw' as a substitute to celebrate with their brothers. But it was during Batiton and Shynna's wanderings that this phawar was fully developed. Both of them were followed by twelve humourists called *rang biria*, whose function was to animate the game of archery with their chanting. They composed witty phawars on the archery grounds to amuse their auditors and to reinforce the spirit of the archery game as ka rongbiria, a colourful celebration without end, without closure, as Ka Mei Hukum had ordained.

As it stands now, the competitive-archery phawar is in the form of quick repartees between rival groups. Usually, one group tries to defeat the other with fervent appeals to Ka Mei Hukum and, with sharply satirical and cleverly coined words, mocks the prowess of the rival group's archers and ridicules their impudence in presuming to challenge the champions. The other group listens and responds in kind. The use of abusive language is strictly forbidden, for Ka Mei Hukum had gifted the game for amusement and recreation, to be played in the spirit of fairness and camaraderie. As may be gathered, the actual phawar is not made up by archers but by composers, including shamans, priests, professional poets and anyone, including women, with talent. These composers are always surrounded by a crowd of dancing supporters whose role is to drive home the message of the phawar with the chanting of 'hooooi kiw'. But the dancing is not to be performed near a target or a rival group, for that might lead to unpleasant incidents.

On the archery ground, the poets begin their phawars only after the nongkhang khnams have finished their opening ritual and the game has been set in motion. The leading poet always begins with invocations to Ka Mei Hukum, soliciting her blessing and then commencing with a phawar such as this:

Oooo!
Ynda khroh i'i Ïawbei,
Ï'u thylliej ynda pynsum,
Ïa ïoh te i'u namshei,
Ba i ieit i Mei Hukum,
Hoooi kiw! ... Hoooi kiw!

(Oooo!
We will coax the Ancestral Mother,
The tongue we will wash,
We get the arrow that strikes,
For the Divine Mother loves us.
Hoooi kiw! ... Hoooi kiw!)

Because the game is God-given, because the divine spirit of Ka Mei Hukum is ever-present, because victory goes only to the deserving, therefore, the poet says, we will first plead with ïawbei, the ancestral mother. Ïawbei is here equated with Ka Shinam, the ancestral mother of the game, as well as with Ka Hukum or Ka Mei Hukum, the Mother of Divine Law. And because such pleading cannot be done with profane words, therefore the tongue must be washed—the pleaders must be pure and truthful. It is only thus that they may be loved by the Divine Mother and granted the arrows that strike the target true and fast.

'Wa, wa! Beautiful, really beautiful, man!' Hamkom said, responding to my analysis.

'The "tongue we will wash"—uff, beautiful!' Raji added. 'You hear that, Bah Kynsai?'

Bah Kynsai laughed and simply said, 'Take it easy on the booze.'

This opening gambit, I continued, is immediately followed by a quip from the other group, which, after its own invocations to God, would let fly as under:

Ooooo!
Thylliej ynda pynsum,
Kba u khaw jong ki kynthei,
Ba ieit i Mei Hukum,
Ba kynmaw tang ïa ngi hei,
Hoooi kiw! ... Hoooi kiw!

(Ooooo!
The tongue we will wash,
Rice is for the women,

That the Divine Mother loves us,
She remembers none but us.
Hoooi kiw! ... Hoooi kiw!)

The second group has cleverly used the second line of the rival party's verse to develop its argument, which is equally steeped in metaphor. We, too, the poet says, understand the need to plead with the Divine Mother. We, too, will be pure and truthful before her, but remember this, 'Rice is for the women', that is, only unskilled archers depend upon fortune. And because we have skill added to our purity and truthfulness, the Divine Mother will remember none but us.

This exchange continues and builds up in intensity, but as the game progresses, the phawars become more and more non-spiritual:

Ooooo!
Narsuh ïa doh masi,
U biseiñ ïa ka syrdeng,
Haba kynduh bad ngi
Ngin pynkheiñ sa ïa ka reng,
Hoooi kiw! ... Hoooi kiw!

(Ooooo!
Roasting spit to a beef slice,
A snake to a bamboo fence,
When colliding with us,
Even the horn will be broken.
Hoooi kiw! ... Hoooi kiw!)

The imagery used here is designed to mock the rivals and put them out of composure. The poet refers to them as 'a beef slice' to be roasted on a spit or a 'snake' to be kept out with a bamboo fence. And because of this unique strength of attack and defence, his party will not only defeat them on the field but will humiliate them in the wider world by turning them into bulls with broken horns.

To this, the rival party hits back:

Ooooo!
Siej lung u thew sha bneng,
U siej ïaw pat sha khyndew,
Kat bym pat wan kynrem

Phi ïa jlew kum ki phyrbew,
Hoooi kiw! … Hoooi kiw!

(Ooooo!
Bamboo shoot points to the sky,
Old bamboo trunk bows to the earth,
As the champions haven't arrived,
You howl like jackals.
Hoooi kiw! … Hoooi kiw!)

Far from losing their composure, they respond with disdain. They liken their opponents to a 'bamboo shoot', and very subtly denounce their childish and ignorant vanity. Since the champions have not yet taken to the field, they are full of vainglorious taunts and are howling emptily like jackals, but soon they will learn just how hard it is to meet in a real fight. Having bragged about their strength, the opponents will have to bow their heads in shame like an 'old bamboo trunk', burdened by the hard realities of life.

In this manner, the competitive-archery phawar proceeds, going back and forth until the end of the match when only the winning party is left with its victorious chants.

It is a general belief that the outcome of any archery competition involving equally skilled archers from rival groups, villages, provinces and so on, depends upon the skill of the poets—who complement the verbal contest of the nongkhang khnams—to kill the counter-arguments of their rivals. A story recounted by Madeng illustrates how strong this belief is among the practitioners.

'You see, Ham, you see, now he comes to it!' Raji enthused. 'Now he will answer your question.'

Donald asked, 'Madeng, your uncle?'

'Madeng Krokar, yes.'

'Was he also an archer?'

'Almost every adult male was an archer in those days.'

'But your uncle seems to be everywhere, Ap, he seems to be doing everything,' Hamkom said.

'In fact,' I said in response to the jibe, 'you could say that Khasi men in those days were complete human beings: they could do almost everything. They had all the skills needed for a self-sufficient rural life. One man could be a skilled mason, a joiner, a carpenter, a roofer, a thatcher, a glazier—in short, a builder who could build houses, walls, roads, bridges, fishponds and so on. Additionally, he could be a skilled blacksmith, a farmer, an expert angler, a weaver, or a craftsman capable of making all sorts of things with cane and bamboo. He could also be a woodsman who knows all about trees, wild vegetables and herbs, and all sorts of birds and animals. My uncle was like that. Nowadays, even in rural areas, it's very difficult to find people like him.'

'Are you kidding or what?' Hamkom asked, not knowing whether to take me seriously.

'I never joke about these things. Ask Bah Kit and Bah Su, or even Raji. They all know such people. I might add that many of them were also healers, not shamans, but people who could treat minor ailments like diarrhoea, cold, cough and so on with herbs and their own concoctions. They could set bones and treat sprains, minor cuts and wounds, including snake bites and scorpion stings. That's why, whenever I read about the pioneers of the American Wild West, I was always reminded of Madeng and his ilk.'

'So what did your uncle do?'

'He could have done anything, but as I told you, he worked in the cement factory. However, when the house needed repairing, or the large vegetable garden needed tilling, I tell you, we never had to call anyone else. He did everything on his own.'

'I'm glad I asked that question, Bah Ap,' Donald said. 'This is amazing!'

'Before the British came, everyone was self-reliant. The British made us lose many skills, the greatest of them being—'

'—the art of manufacturing iron,' Bah Su completed the sentence for me. 'Before they came, we used to export the best kind of iron to Bengal. Now nobody knows anything about it.'

When everyone was silent again, I told them what Madeng had told us about an archery competition in Umstew, a place between Sohra and the village of Laitryngew, where the party of archers from Sohra were experiencing a strange difficulty. Many of their arrows, which had struck the target, fell off the moment their rivals' arrows, in turn, hit the target. The murmur that spread through the field put it down to the work of the nongkhang khnam and the phawar leader of the Laitryngews, men with a formidable reputation in these matters. As the Laitryngews won one round after another, their phawar too became more and more vigorous and passionate, quite overpowering the Sohras, who seemed to be losing steam with every defeat. This continued until the Laitryngew poet made a false move. To capture the phenomenon of the Sohra arrows falling off the target, in his excitement, he composed the following phawar:

Ooooo!
Ngan am na ka nyllong,
Bang ym bang ruh ngan da mad,
Ba la tam la ka nong,
Nang ym nang ruh ngan da shad,
Hoooi kiw! … Hoooi kiw!

(Ooooo!
I'll bite from the anus,
Delicious or not I will taste,
Because the wage is in excess,
Whether I can or cannot, I will dance.
Hoooi kiw! … Hoooi kiw!)

Uncharacteristically, the Sohras let this one pass, and thinking that they had admitted defeat, the Laitryngew poet continued:

Ooooo!
Ngan shanem na nyllong,
Ngan da khlaw ïa ki kynthei,
Haba la ïashem ngong,
Men da khie kyang wow ko mei,
Hoooi kiw! … Hoooi kiw!

(Ooooo!
I'll assault from the anus,
I'll haul out the women,
When we meet face to face,
You will scream for your mother.
Hoooi kiw! … Hoooi kiw!)

'Wuu, that's incredibly dirty, man!' Magdalene protested. 'How could he say something like that while pleading to Ka Mei Hukum?'

I held up a hand, signalling for a little patience. There was nothing dirty or abusive or immoral in those two verses, I said. Admittedly, he used violent, even brutal, sexual imagery in both. But in the first one, when he said he would 'bite from the anus', he merely meant the base of the target, where the arrow could bite directly into the pole. This was a tough feat and could be achieved only by accomplished archers such as those from Laitryngew. But when an arrow did hit that point, the entire target was shaken, causing arrows to drop from it. If that happened, the poet would rejoice by dancing regardless of whether he was a good dancer or not.

Superficially, the second one seems even more vicious than the first in its imagery, as though the poet was hell-bent upon committing acts of savagery against women. Yet, here again, he was merely restating his intention of aiming the arrows at the base of the target and pulling out 'the women', or the arrows, clinging weakly to it, by vigorously shaking it. What the poet really wanted to imply was that the Sohra archers lacked both skill and strength. Therefore, when they met with real champions, they would, like women, cry out for help to their mothers, or symbolically to Ka Mei Hukum.

Despite the verses being only superficially offensive, the Sohra nongkhang khnam and phawar leader saw in them an opening for a counterattack and shot back immediately:

> *Ooooo!*
> *Men shanem na nyllong,*
> *Men da khlaw ïa ki kynthei,*
> *Ha sngap ko Mei Hukum,*
> *U kren sang ïa phi Ka Blei,*
> *Hoooi kiw! … Hoooi kiw!*

> (Ooooo!
> He'll assault from the anus,
> He'll haul out the women,
> Listen oh Divine Mother,
> He even abuses you, our God.
> Hoooi kiw! … Hoooi kiw!)

Ka Mei Hukum, as you know, is the feminine attribute of the one supreme God, Dispenser and Creator. For this reason, women and especially mothers are treated with the utmost consideration and respect in traditional Khasi society, and any offence against them is frowned upon by the entire community. The Sohras appealed to Ka Mei Hukum on these grounds. 'It is true,' they said, 'that symbolically the Laitryngew verse is neither offensive nor immoral. We are aware of that, but when one refers to women and God, one should not only be pure in intention but also in words.'

After many such phawars and arguments by the Sohra poets and nongkhang khnam, the Laitryngew arrows began, in turn, to fall off the target with every hit by the Sohra archers. At the end of the competition, the Sohras emerged as champions. Every one of them was convinced that it was *ka ktien hok*, the virtuous word, which had carried the day for them. And so, their slogan for the day was *Ka ktien hok kaba jop* (The virtuous word that wins).

At the end of my account, Raji said to Hamkom, 'You see, Ham, you see, the outcome of an archery competition can really depend on the outcome of the verbal contest … It's clear now, no?'

'Quite clear, quite clear,' Hamkom agreed. 'But it's still very strange that a game can be won or lost with words, no? What do you think, Don?'

'Very strange indeed,' Donald said with a thoughtful expression on his face.

Bah Su said, 'Not only games, ha, but many things in life can be won with words. It all depends upon the justness of your cause.'

'Unless, of course, you are dealing with corrupt officials, unscrupulous lawyers and tyrannical rulers,' Bah Kynsai added with a laugh.

෴

The Gambling

Khasi archery as a form of gambling can also be traced back to the legend of Ka Shinam and U Mangring. After Kajang had failed in his repeated attempts to wreck the God-given game of archery, he resorted to polluting it by tempting Batiton and Shynna to play the game in a new format, which he said was 'delicious without eating, sweet by merely holding'. When the brothers, who always listened to their parents, refused, Kajang taught this new format to some of their followers. It was from these men that archery gambling started.

But this is not the same as the friendly wagers between villages and groups that we see in rongbiria. It is something else—a game of chance and numbers, which developed separately from rongbiria, but almost side-by-side with it. It is known today as *siat tiim*, literally, 'shooting by teams'. Unlike the sport of rongbiria (or *siat thong*, shooting for a bet, as it is also known), which is popular in many parts of Ri Khasi, siat tiim is held only in places like Shillong, Jowai and the village of Mawngap, a few kilometres from Shillong. Tiim shooting in Jowai takes care of the betting in Ri Pnar in east Ri Khasi, and that in Mawngap is confined to the village and its adjoining areas. The one organised in Shillong is the biggest.

By the evidence of Morningstar Jyrwa, general secretary of the Khasi Hills Archery Sports Institute (KHASI), whom I met in his office, tiim betting, also simply known as *teer* in Hindi, has now been centralised in all the remaining districts of the state. The results are based on the shooting that takes place at Polo Ground in Shillong at 4.15 p.m. every day, except Sunday. And that's not all. The KHASI president, P. Laloo, who was also present, revealed that all the major cities of India are connected to the Shillong tiim archery through what he called 'hidden counters'. He added, rather smugly, 'That is how big we really are!'

Hamkom interrupted me to say, 'Wait, wait, wait, I want to be very clear about this: do you mean to say that you actually went to interview the archery gambling officials?'

'Yes, I did,' I confirmed, although I did not understand the urgency in his tone. 'I went there with Everending.'

'You mean Everending of the Sohra pork story?' Magdalene asked.

'How many of them do you think there would be, Mag?'

According to Laloo, or Bah Tutu, I said, modern tiim archery began in the 1950s simply as a competition among a gathering of eight clubs under the supervision of the Archery Board of Control (ABC), and the only betting that took place was among the spectators—

'Shouldn't it have been the Board of Control for Archery, Bah Ap?' Donald asked.

'Should have, but that's how good we are, na?' Bah Kynsai answered for me. 'Go on, Ap.'

ABC's betting went on to become what was called *tiim pynlang*, or betting by collection. The shooting, according to Bah Tutu, used to take place at Kper Koidi, the garden of convicts, where the Polo Supermarket now stands. In this version of tiim betting, a customer may buy a number for say, twenty-five paise, but if he fails to 'get' the winning number, only fifteen paise is returned to him. In this way, ten paise is collected from all those who do not win, to pay the winners.

Bah Tutu spoke of how the Assam government, then ruling the Khasi-Jaiñtia Hills district, completely dismantled the shooting range at Kper Koidi and arrested the archers, bookmakers and players en masse. 'But that did not put them down for long,' he said triumphantly. 'They shifted the shooting range to a small field by the River Umkhrah, opposite the Polo Ground, and conducted their business as usual. Many of the oldies still recall how quaint and lovely the site used to be, located as it was in a bend of the picturesque and crystal-clear river. But look at it now!'

'You mean this was the very same spot?' I asked.

'Exactly,' he replied. 'In the late 1970s, four more clubs joined the archery fraternity, and ABC reorganised itself as KHASI.'

'Was it also then that tiim betting was restructured into the fully fledged form of gambling it is now?'

The KHASI officials around us in their small office bristled at the description of the game as gambling. Everending, who was helping me with photographs, looked up with a nervous expression, but he need not have worried. Contrary to the commonplace image propagated by the self-righteous, of foul-mouthed and ruffianly *nongkhalai tiim*, tiim gamblers, and despite their loud protests, those elderly officials were the most gentlemanly Khasis I had ever met. I felt quite at home with them.

Perhaps they were right in thinking of themselves as the keepers of their people's culture. Although the betting part of the game has completely overshadowed all the other elements, and although the game has been thoroughly commercialised, is it fair to discount the sporting part of it altogether? Besides, were they not the most natural propagators of rongbiria, since they were also among the most enthusiastic participants in the game? To them, tiim was a game of amusement; betting was only coincidental. Be that as it may, even after Meghalaya gained statehood in 1972, tiim archery was deemed illegal by the government, and those involved in it had to play a hide-and-seek game with the law enforcers for many years.

'I have many personal recollections of those days,' one of the officials said. 'My father was a tiim steward, and I used to be scared witless whenever I saw a policeman.'

In the Sohra locality of Lum Maha, where I grew up, almost every parent used to be a tiim player, that is, a buyer of tiim numbers. There was nothing wicked about them. They were all God-fearing people who would make us pray before we ate and pray before we slept. They played the numbers for the thrill of it and also because 'the game' provided good money for the little investment of twenty-five paise or one rupee. The tiim counters used to be at the bus station near the marketplace, where they still are. And because Lum Maha was about half a kilometre from there, many of the women would turn us boys into their runners. Invariably, we used to run about three or four times for the same person because, after she had bought a set of numbers, she wanted to buy the same ones as her neighbour, or because someone had told her of a 'making' number or a new dream. And we were happy to oblige for several reasons: the chance to get out of the house, to run away from household chores and the chance to gape at vehicles at the station. But most exciting of all was the chance of a reward, for when the women *pom tiim*, or won their bet, they used to give the runner a little tea-money, as they called it.

Once, my eldest brother and his friend Tnin, so nicknamed because he was very thin, ran into the middle of a police raid. They were put in a police truck with the bookies and driven away towards the district jail in Shillong. On the road, however, the cops realised that they had crying children on board. When they reached Laitryngew, about six kilometres from Sohra, they promptly transferred the two boys to a Sohra-bound bazaar bus, with instructions to the driver to get them home. Were they scared? They did raise quite a tearful ruckus inside the truck but returned home to become heroes for days and the most sought-after runners for years.

Back in the KHASI office, the general secretary, Morningstar, or Bah Ning as he was called, told me, 'Two factors eventually saved it from sustained persecution. The persistence of gamers proved too much for the government, especially when, as always, many of its inspectors were more interested in making a quick buck than in arresting bookies. Secondly, it realised belatedly that a lot of money could be collected from the game in the form of taxes. And that was what finally prompted the government to declare tiim archery legal by an act called the Meghalaya Amusement and Betting Tax (Amendment) Act 1982, which became effective from October of the same year. You see,' Bah Ning added with evident pleasure, 'even the act calls it "amusement and betting", not gambling!'

Someone else added, 'For this, we have to thank Dr F.A. Khonglam, the then revenue minister, who got the Act passed despite strong protests from some holier-than-thou elements in the Cabinet.'

'How much money do you think the government collects from the game per year?'

'Not very sure of the exact amount, but quite a lot,' Bah Tutu said. 'We are paying 15,000 rupees annually as shooting-licence renewal fee. The bookies have to pay a licence fee of 850 rupees quarterly, or 3,400 rupees annually, plus 200 rupees for every tiim book they buy from the government. That's quite a lot of money, given the hundreds of tiim counters in Shillong alone. But you would have to ask the taxation department of the government for an exact figure.'

His estimate agreed with the amount of 6,042,735 rupees that the government had (according to M.M. Khymdeit, who has done some research on the subject) collected for 2003–04. Strangely, Tynshaiñ Dohling, the tax superintendent who spoke to someone I had sent, said that the average annual income was thirty lakh rupees. Of course, Dohling did not even bother to check the records; his figure was produced from the air, like a conjuror's trick, and I suspect, about as reliable.

Today, tiim gambling is run by KHASI, which was formed by the thirteen original clubs of Jaïaw, Kynthuplang, Laban, Laitkor, Laitumkhrah, Malki, Mawlai, Pynthor, Rangbiria, Sengbiria Iabeitlang, Senglang and Wahingdoh. It functions through tiim counters, found everywhere in the state, especially in the commercial areas of Shillong and other urban centres.

'What does KHASI get from running the game?'

'Nothing,' was Bah Tutu's humble response. 'As we have told you, we are paying a large licence fee to the government, as well as a hefty rent of 6,000 rupees per month for the ground. We are also paying 3,400 rupees to a club per shooting; besides, we are defraying the expenses of all the tiim officials. And all we get is an average of fifteen rupees per day from each tiim counter in Shillong. We get nothing from counters outside Shillong.'

'How many counters does Shillong have?'

'Roughly 800,' said an official.

'That sounds like a lot of money. Let's see, 800 multiplied by 15 would be 12,000 rupees per day. Multiply that by 26 days, since you don't shoot on Sundays, that would be 312,000 rupees per month.'

'I don't think there are 800 counters in Shillong. More like 600,' another official quickly interrupted. The others promptly agreed with him. But the bookies themselves told me later that 800 was a more accurate figure.

'How much do you spend in defraying the expenses of the officials?'

'Leading officials like us,' Bah Ning said, 'are paid 300 rupees per day plus incidental expenses. Others get a lump sum amount of 2,000 rupees per month.'

'What about the stewards?'

'The stewards are not our people. They represent the three unions of bookies. They are paid 100 rupees per day plus money to repair arrows and so on.'

I made a mental calculation, deducting the association's expenses from its earnings, and came up with an income of over one lakh rupees per month. Big money certainly. No wonder all sorts of people are interested in this business.

The tiim counters are run by bookmakers, who either work for an employer or are investors themselves. The bookmaker is called *u nongthoh tiim*, literally, 'one who writes tiim'. He has two sets of books, one containing tables of numbers from one to hundred, the other made up of blank sheets with detachable betting slips. The book of tables has several columns, rows and boxes, which are referred to as ki ïing, or houses. In a small book, each number is allotted ten boxes; in the bigger one, twenty-five. When a customer comes to *thoh nombar*, or write a number, a red cross or a circle is marked in one of the boxes. This means that that particular box is full. The number, together with the rate of purchase and date, is written down on a betting slip, which is then detached and given to the customer, who invariably, and I speak from personal experience, pockets the slip with a warm, hopeful feeling in anticipation of the result in the evening. The bookmaker keeps a carbon-copy record of the purchase.

The lowest purchasable rate of a number used to be twenty-five paise, for which a customer got twenty rupees. Now it is fixed at one rupee, for which he gets eighty rupees. This amount increases as the rate of purchase increases. As the bookies put it, 'Double the stake, double the prize money.' Customers are free to purchase a number at a rate of their choice. One may buy for one rupee, another for five, and yet another for ten and so on. This means that when the entire row of ten or twenty-five boxes, depending on the size of the book, is sold against a number, the total money from it is never the same. There is, of course, a limit that bookies enforce, depending on their ability to pay. For instance, one bookie may sell a number for lakhs of rupees (Believe me, I too was shocked by this revelation), while another may limit his sale to fifty rupees only. The lucky bookmaker on a particular day is the one who has sold all the numbers except the winning number of the day. The unlucky one is he or she who has sold the winning number without selling many other numbers.

'He or she, Ap?' Magdalene asked with sudden interest.

'There are several women bookies in the Khasi, Jaiñtia and Ri Bhoi districts,' I told her. 'In fact, many customers are known to favour women bookies. To them, women are *kham jem rngiew* and, by buying from them, they believe they are more likely to win than by buying from men.'

'Damn, ya! This is the first time I have heard about women bookies.'

'Plenty, plenty of them, Mag,' Raji assured her.

Bah Kynsai staggered everyone by saying, 'I like buying from women too, ha, but not because they are jem rngiew … Some of them are really beautiful. I admire beauty, na?' he concluded with a laugh.

'Don't tell us you play the numbers too, Bah Kynsai!'

'Why not? It's rather fun; you should also try it,' he said simply.

The others laughed and shook their heads, surprised to discover that Bah Kynsai was a tiim player.

But Hamkom was otherwise occupied. He asked, 'What exactly is rngiew, man? Till now, I'm not very clear about it.'

'The essence of one's personality, partly like Jung's anima,' I said. 'So, *jem rngiew* would mean someone with a weak essence.'

'Explain that anima thing, na!' Bah Kynsai demanded. 'Can't you see you are leaving poor Ham speechless?'

'You or Ham?' Raji asked.

'You and Ham,' Bah Kynsai retorted.

'Scholars explain Jung's concept as the "soul image", the spirit of a man's élan vital: his life force or vital energy. According to Jung, in the sense of "soul", the anima is the "living thing in man, that which lives of itself and causes life". The Khasi mynsiem, or soul, and rngiew, or essence, taken together, are almost exactly like Jung's anima.'

'So, that's rngiew, huh?' Ham said. 'But I'm telling you, some Khasi words are really difficult, no?'

'For people like you, yes,' Bah Kynsai said, and added, 'Chalo, chalo, Ap.'

I went back to describing the way it all worked. The sale of numbers is for two rounds—the first or morning round, *kylla step*, and the second or evening round, *kylla miet*. For the morning round, the sale is open throughout the day and closes at 4 p.m. in summer and 3.20 p.m. in winter. The evening round opens for only half an hour, from 4.30 p.m. to 5 p.m. in summer and from 4 p.m. to 4.30 p.m. in winter. This is because the shooting times are different for summer and winter. In summer, shooting for the morning round takes place at 4.15 p.m. and for the evening round at 5.15 p.m. But in winter, because it gets dark much earlier, the shooting begins at 3.30 p.m. for the morning round and 4.50 p.m. for the evening. The rates of payment in the evening round are also lesser, and a player gets only sixty rupees, instead of eighty, from one rupee.

The numbers are sold in four ways: as a single number, ending, booking and forecast. A player may buy a single number as shown earlier, or he may use the ending method by which he purchases all the numbers, from one to hundred, which end in a particular digit. For instance, if he asks for 'ending four', it would mean 4, 14, 24, 34, 44, 54, 64, 74, 84 and 94. For this, he will spend a minimum amount of ten rupees, and if he wins, he gets ninety-five rupees. In the booking method, a player books a particular number for days, weeks or even months, in rates that increase every day, until it is finally shot as the winning number. The forecast method is quite different and requires the player to buy the same number for both morning and evening rounds. The player only gets paid if the number he has bought is shot as the winner for both rounds. In playing the forecast, a punter will get 5,000 rupees from one rupee, 10,000 rupees from two rupees, 25,000 rupees from five rupees and 45,000 rupees from ten rupees. But hitting the forecast is a rare phenomenon indeed, and is usually an occasion of great jubilation for the punter. At the same time, it is an occasion of grief for the bookie because the payment he has to make far exceeds his earnings.

After 4 p.m., all attention shifts to a small field opposite Polo Ground. It is a field by the Polo–Nongmynsong road at a place called Saw Phurlong, or fourth furlong. Although the field is by the roadside, it is not easy for a first-time visitor to find because it is completely hidden from the road by shops and squat, ugly buildings. When I visited, a long, narrow path about two feet wide led up to the field, and I felt immediately disappointed about having to slink through such cheerless access to witness such a well-beloved sport. And then I was at the entrance, looking down at an incredible scene, and I thought, is this a marketplace or a fairground?

Towards the west of this circular ground, half the size of a football pitch, were several tin shacks selling tea and food. At the northern end, near the bank of the River Umkhrah, was a newish little cottage made of concrete and corrugated iron sheet that I later learnt was the office of the archery association. In the far south-eastern corner was a long shack with a black tin roof, partitioned into three rooms, which served as tea shops and tiim counters. One of the rooms seemed to be a favourite meeting place of the tiim officials and was mysteriously referred to by someone as 'the house of inspiration'. At the north-eastern end, by the bank of the river, was an open shed where the target-striking arrows were counted. In front of it was the *skum tiim*, or tiim target, much larger than the rongbiria target, though it was made of the same materials. But what made it look like a marketplace were the little open huts with no walls and corrugated iron sheets for roofs. There were about ten of them, arranged in a semicircle, all facing the target. Just behind them were more open huts, which served as tiim counters. These were swarming with last-minute purchasers.

When I entered, I saw several bunches of arrows, with a bow for each bunch, neatly laid on the floor of the huts. There was no one near them. It was only 3.50 p.m. People were still milling about, having tea and conversing animatedly. At 4.10 p.m., when the whistle blew, the archers emerged from the crowd to take up their positions in the shooting huts.

On this day, only two out of the thirteen clubs would be shooting. One club fielded fifteen shooters, and these were joined by thirty stewards who represented the three unions of bookmakers, taking the total number to sixty. One shooter was given thirty arrows, which meant that a total of 1,800 arrows would be launched at the target, which was set sixty feet from the shooting huts. On Saturdays, I was told, they had a slightly different set-up: all thirteen clubs, with three shooters from each club, were involved, along with the thirty stewards. The target was of an average diameter of forty-two inches, varying between forty and forty-five inches, and stood on a thirty-four-inch-long pole.

The archers were a mixed bunch. There were elderly men puffing on tobacco pipes from which thin blue smoke wafted up in spirals; there were middle-aged men chewing betel nut; young men in their teens, and even boys. The youngest archer was an eleven-year-old by the name of Edward Kharumnuid. He was shooting for Jaïaw Club, but lived in Khap Tynring, a village in Ri Bhoi district, far from Shillong.

Hamkom raised his hand and asked me excitedly, 'Are you serious? Are you serious? A boy of eleven!'

'You sound exactly like Robert Vadra, liah, Ham!' Bah Kynsai teased him.

Almost everybody went into fits of laughter, except Dale, who did not understand, and Magdalene, who asked, 'Why, why? What did Vadra do?'

'When Vadra was questioned by Times Now about his land deal, na, Mag, he reacted exactly like that.'

'Aah, I did not see that, ya,' she said, joining in the laughter.

'Who's Vadra, Bah?' Dale asked me.

'Rahul Gandhi's brother-in-law, man,' Bah Kynsai answered. 'Chalo, chalo, Ap.'

I told them that, at a shouted instruction from the whistle-blowing steward, all the archers nocked their arrows and took aim. Inspecting them carefully, the steward waited for a while before barking out: 'Four minutes for thirty arrows. Begin!'

Suddenly, the air was abuzz with whooshing sounds and the thwack-thwacks of arrows as they hit the target. Like swarming dragonflies in Sohra, I thought.

The steward was shouting again, 'Two minutes ... One minute ... Half a minute ... Stop!'

'Like lappraw!' I exclaimed. Lappraw is one of those showers that comes and ends abruptly. You have to be absolutely absorbed to enjoy this game. It is over before you know it. Like haiku. I remembered a Welsh friend telling me about David Cobb, one of the best haiku poets in the UK. Having won a haiku-writing competition, Cobb was interviewed by the BBC. Towards the end, the interviewer asked him to read the winning haiku. Cobb read. And the interviewer said, 'Is that all?' You might well ask the same question about siat tiim archery.

Immediately after the shooting, the area around the target was cordoned off by a three-foot-high tarpaulin curtain tied to a thick string. It was a well-planned precaution, for the crowd of spectators suddenly surged forward, eager to know the winning number. The head steward, an erect old man, supervised the process of counting. He had all the arrows that did not hit the target collected and put away. Then all the target-striking arrows were pulled out by chosen officials and carefully kept in the counting shed. The counting itself was conducted by six reckoners, the head steward, a scorekeeper and fifteen witnesses standing behind the squatting reckoners. The reckoners were casual employees of KHASI, selected from among the stewards of bookie unions. They were paid a hundred rupees per day. (That is not a bad deal at all in these parts, since these people have to be in the field only for about two hours in the evening. They, like almost all the other KHASI employees, work elsewhere during the day. Many are government employees.) The first reckoner initiated the counting, which was cross-checked by the other five. They passed on the counted arrows to the scorekeeper, who kept them in a counting frame in bunches of ten. All this was done in front of the gawking, impatient crowd.

On that day, the reckoners tallied up 695 arrows hitting the target. Of these, 690 were given to the scorekeeper to be kept in the counting frame. The remaining five were taken by the head steward, who rose from the ground, took a few steps towards the anxious spectators, and with great dignity javelined the five arrows one by one into the ground in front of them while announcing, 'Ninety! One, two, three, four, five. The target-number for today is *ninety-five*.'

The announcement broke the crowd into a pocket-groping frenzy as everyone rummaged for their 'slips' to check the numbers they had purchased. And suddenly you heard suppressed curses like '*Stud! Shu lait thaw!*' ('Stud! Just about missed it!') or a doleful exclamation of '*Shish, tang shi dak!*' ('Shish, only by a number!'). The man who had spoken was inconsolable. 'See, see,' he said, thrusting the slip in his friend's face. Another cursed, '*Ka nusip ksew!*' ('The luck of a dog!'). But you could also hear shouts of triumph like '*Pom sanphew! Pom sanphew, liah!*' ('Got fifty! Got fifty, liah!') or '*Yahoo! Leit noh sha ïew, tdir!*' ('Yahoo! I'm off to the market, tdir!'). Not just in Khasi, for there were among the crowd Biharis, Nepalis, Bengalis and others, cursing or rejoicing in their own languages.

'Strange,' Everending observed, 'people curse in joy and curse in sorrow.'

A KHASI official replied, 'Some of them come from the lower strata, and that's how they speak. It's part of their vocabulary, quite normal for them. They may not even be aware they are using expletives. But not everyone speaks like that; many are very courteous. But you must have noticed that yourselves.'

'Like Bah Kynsai, ha, Ap?' Raji teased. 'I think he is also from the lower strata or what?'

I picked up my narration before Bah Kynsai could explode.

I was curious about why so many arrows had been shot. To find out, I sought out Bah Ning and asked, 'If you count only the last two digits for your result, why do you shoot so many arrows, Bah Ning?'

'So that the game is more beautiful.'

'Is that all? I mean, the numbers on sale are only from one to hundred, so why don't you shoot only a hundred or a hundred and ten arrows?'

'Oh, that is to avoid making.'

'Making?'

'You see, elsewhere the booking counters close by 4 p.m., but here on the ground, bookies sell numbers till the very last minute, even after the shooting is done. As the arrows are being shot, the crowd tries to count the number hitting the skum. If only a few arrows are used, it would be quite easy for them to know the winning number and take advantage of the bookies.'

'You know, Bah Ning, since I was a child, I have heard complaints about this "making" business ... that the number was predetermined in such cases. How is it done?'

'Do you think that kind of "making" is possible? You have seen for yourself, is it possible? Everything is done in the open, in front of everybody, is it possible to predetermine the number?'

'But what of the people who used to be involved so heavily in this "making" thing in the past? We have heard so much about them, and so much has been reported about their activities too. Some of these people are still alive. You know what I'm talking about.'

'Oh, in the past, there were those people, yes. They were gangsters. But as I told you, "making" is not possible. Their "making" was different. They used to come to the ground in hordes, all of them armed, and by force, they used to have a number in which they had invested heavily declared as the winning number. Nowadays, we don't have such things.'

'What about militants? Just a few years ago, we read about the involvement of the HNLC in the tiim business. I remember that after its organising secretary confessed to the police, members of your association were also arrested. Is there a nexus?'

One of them said, 'Nothing like that. No nexus. Those people also adopted gangster tactics.'

Bah Ning added, 'They would buy a certain number very heavily from all parts of the state and then come here to get it declared as the winning number. As you can see, they did that by force, no nexus with us.'

How heavily these people invested in a number can be understood more clearly if you remember that some bookies are big-time gamblers and would sell a single number for lakhs.

'What about now?' I asked.

'Nothing.'

'You are not even paying protection money now?'

'No. Since the arrest you spoke of, okay, we have had no interference from anyone. It's very clean now; it has truly become the common man's game.'

During the break between the first and the second round, we noticed the youngest archer, Edward, wrestling on the grass with another youngster: 'That's Jib Kharumnuid, Edward's uncle. He is thirteen years old,' Bah Ning explained.

'Great,' I said, 'a thirteen-year-old uncle with an eleven-year-old nephew! But how come, Bah Ning, such young boys are used in such a game?'

'I told you, siat tiim is not gambling. It's a sport. A young fellow like Edward knows nothing about the betting side of it. Look at him playing; he's still an innocent kid. The club selected him because of his skill. That's a great privilege. Imagine being a professional shooter in an archery club at such a young age! In archery, we don't judge people by their age, Bah Ap, only by their skill. Also, he gets 110 rupees whenever he shoots. People often talk about child labour, but this is not labour, it's a sport, and talent should always be recognised in sport.'

He had a point, I thought. If only such kids were picked up by the government and trained in the art of modern archery, we might even win gold at the Olympics. But our politicians never plan, never formulate, never conceptualise; they only feel their pockets—or as they say here, they only eat our money—all the time.

'What now, Bah Ning?'

'Now for the second round.'

The second round began at 5.15 p.m. The process was the same, but the target was smaller, with a thirty-two-inch diameter, standing on a thirty-inch-long pole. And the number of arrows shot also was only 1,200. I asked Bah Ning about the use of targets with different sizes.

'This,' he said, 'is to prevent people from calculating the average number of arrows hitting the target.'

When targets of different sizes are used, apparently it becomes much harder to make such a calculation.

The archers were lining up once more to shoot for the evening round when someone proposed that we retire to the small office to talk about dreams.

'Now, it gets even more interesting,' Raji promised the others.

❧

Dream Numbers

Like most cultures, the Khasis have also held dreams to be of considerable importance. Like the Babylonians in *The Epic of Gilgamesh*, we see dreams as mantic. Like the Jews in the Old Testament, we believe that many incidents in dreams are a form of divine revelation. And like the ancient Egyptians, we consider dreaming a supernatural communication or a means of divine intervention, the message of which can be decoded only by those with certain powers. Among us, it is ki nongkhan, ki nongkñia and ki nongduwai (faith healers, diviners, augurs and elders who pray) who play the role of professional dream interpreters. Their interest here is related to disease diagnosis. That is why their interpretation follows a pattern that resembles the dream classification of the early Islamic scholars who recognised three kinds of dreams: false dreams, pathogenetic or disease-producing dreams, and true dreams.

'Hey, I never knew about all this, ya!' Hamkom said, genuinely surprised. 'What are these true and false dreams, man?'

'I'll explain everything, Ham, just hold on.'

To a Khasi, a false dream is motivated by wish-fulfilment and instigated by events of the preceding day, which Freud called the 'day residue'. Dreams caused by a traumatic experience or those resulting from some morbid fear are also considered false. These are, therefore, discounted for diagnosis. Pathogenetic dreams are those predominated by certain symbols, animal or human, and by certain types of activities. These symbols and activities (I will explain them more clearly later) relate to certain types of illnesses needing cures both at the level of medicinal administration and faith healing. These dreams may or may not have mantic qualities. True dreams, however, are mantic by nature and are considered both a form of divine revelation and a means of divine intervention. These dreams are believed by faith healers to be necessary, not only for man's physical health, but also for his spiritual well-being.

'And your faith healers can interpret these dreams accurately?' Hamkom asked incredulously.

'As accurately as Joseph interpreted the dreams of the Pharaoh,' Raji responded.

'Based on your dreams,' I added, 'they can predict things that will happen to you in the future. For instance, if you are a politician and if you have had a certain dream, they can tell you whether you will win or lose an election. That's the reason why so many politicians, regardless of their religion, flock to diviners during elections. They can also see whether you have enemies, and through the process of pleading, neutralise all ill wishes and plots directed against you—'

'Are you serious about politicians going to them, Ap?' Hamkom asked again.

'They not only go to them; they even promise huge sums of money if the diviners can bring them victory. In this, faith healers and diviners act like nongkhan khnams do in the archery field—'

Bah Su objected to what I was saying. 'Our nongkhans do not demand money, Ap!'

'I did not say they do. Genuine faith healers never fix a price for their work of divination or obsecration. When you ask them, "How much shall I give?", their reply would invariably be "As you wish". So, if you give them nothing (and many people cannot give them a single paisa because they are poor), it's fine; if you give them fifty rupees, it's fine; but if you are a rich man, like our politicians, for instance, and decide to offer them 50,000, that's fine too. It's all up to you and how much you can or want to give.'

Apart from this, we also have a unique dream tradition directly connected with tiim archery, which is generally referred to as *pynkup tiim* or *pynkup nombar*, clothed with tiim or clothed with a number. Sometimes it is also known as *kheiñ tiim*, to calculate for tiim. This means that all types of dreams are taken into consideration and broken down or related to numbers, which are then purchased at the tiim counters.

Previously, I referred to how tiim numbers are sold in four ways: single number, ending, booking and forecast. All these methods are related to dreams. Even the booking method, involving the booking of a favourite number for days, weeks and months, is not entirely dream-free since a number may become someone's favourite as the result of a dream.

Does this mean that everyone who plays the numbers must dream?

I put the question to the roomful of KHASI officials, and one of them said, 'Maybe not everyone, but most people.'

There are, it seems, gamers, especially the big-time ones, who do not rely solely on dreams; they also have their own secret system of numerical analysis and calculation. But for most players, dreams are the only way of predicting numbers that could emerge winners, which is why this tradition has become such a vital part of tiim archery.

'How did it come about?' I asked the officials.

'We don't know. The old ones must have begun from somewhere, but none of us knows about it now.'

That was Bah Ning. Very disappointing. I did learn the history of it later, of course, but not from the KHASI officials. Their biggest handicap was the absence of any written record on the game, surprising when you consider that it has for years been their chief source of livelihood and the reason for their organisation's existence. I see this deplorable attitude among Khasis in general: we simply do not think much of books. This would be especially true of a government official like Dohling. Though his department gets lakhs of rupees from the game annually, he sat in his chair, showing no interest in providing it with either a permanent ground or authentic literature. When others wanted to do the job for him, he only asked, 'Why does he need to write about such things?' Like the men of Laputa, he too was badly in need of a 'flapper', just to remind him where he was.

'At least tell me how it works. If a man dreams of something, how is that dream converted into a number?'

'Ah, that we can tell you,' Bah Tutu said, 'we do that every day.'

'So, say you dream of colours?'

'Black is nine; white is eight; blue or any darkish colour is seven; red is four; green is seven; gold is four.'

'Yellow?'

'We still don't know what number to give it.'

'Some people give it three,' one of the elderly men chimed in.

'If you dream of God, Bah Tutu?'

'God is nine; heaven is nine; death is nine; evil spirits, nine; famous people, nine; aeroplane, nine.'

'If you dream of a man?'

'Man is six; woman is five; child is three; baby is two; bride is eight; groom is nine. But if the man is a dkhar, the number is seven; if he's a sahep, the number is eight.'

Dkhar, you'll remember, is a non-Khasi. That is why we have words like kharlieh and kharïong, white non-Khasi and black non-Khasi. But dkhar is also used to expressly denote a non-Khasi from the Indian subcontinent. Hence, a dkhar is seven, and a sahep, a white man, is eight.

'A policeman?'

'Four,' Bah Ning said.

'No, no, he's no longer four. Now he's seven,' Bah Tutu corrected.

'How can he change from one number to another?' I asked.

'Earlier, when the Assam government was in charge, the police used to wear red berets, hence four; now, under the Meghalaya government, they are wearing green berets, therefore seven,' Bah Tutu explained.

'Ah, I see, a change in government can also bring about a change in numbers. What about water?'

'Seven. Fish is eight; fishing rod is seven; ship is seven; a woman taking a bath or swimming is seventy-five or fifty-seven, but a naked woman is fifty.'

'What about a naked man?'

'Whoever dreams of a naked man?' Bah Tutu asked, and we all burst into laughter.

'Trees?'

'Tree is one; fruit is zero.'

'Vehicles?'

'Two-wheelers are two; small vehicles are four; big vehicles are eight; wheels are zero.'

'Animals?'

'Dog is seven; cat is five; horse, three; cow, four; goat, four; pig, four; chicken, two; tiger, eight; elephant, nine; snake, seven; insects, seven; birds, nine.'

'Do you have a number for everything, Bah Tutu?'

'For most things. House is eight; hands and feet are five; bad dream is fifty-six or sixty-five; nightmare involving demons is nine.'

'What about a computer?'

'We don't have a number for it yet. It's still too new, but some people are giving it four because it's shaped like a TV. TVs and squarish machines are four.'

'On what basis do you assign numbers to dream objects, Bah Tutu?'

'This is a long-established tradition; we can explain some, not others. You take number nine, for instance, it's used to represent God, heaven, death, evil spirits, famous people, aeroplanes, elephants, birds and the colour black. What do all of them have in common? Greatness, pre-eminence, immensity, distinction … Aeroplanes, for instance, represent human achievement; birds have their enviable power of flight and black is the strongest colour. That's why they have been given the greatest number.

'Then, number six … In Khasi, man is *briew*; six is *hynriew*. Phonetically, the two words rhyme, hence six for man. But a dkhar is seven because he's non-Khasi, different from a Khasi. A sahep is eight because he's white. White in Khasi culture symbolises something *bha*, something good. Bha rhymes with *phra*, eight, that's why white is eight. But a woman is five because she's regarded as weaker, not inferior, just physically more delicate than man. We have a saying in Khasi: *U rang khatar bor, khatar buit; ka kynthei shibor shibuit*, so, you can see why she's five, a number smaller than six.'

'Interesting,' I interrupted. '"Man of twelve powers and twelve skills; woman of one power and one skill", and this, even though we are a matrilineal society. But maybe we are matrilineal precisely because of this, Bah Tutu, because we want to provide for those whom we perceive as the weaker sex. Interesting.'

'That's for you people to look into. The colour red is four because the Khasi word for both red and four is saw, so, anything red, including blood, is calculated as four. Because of this, though death is represented by nine, when a man dies in an accident or is murdered, involving a lot of bleeding, the numbers calculated are sixty-four and forty-six.'

'Why sixty-four and forty-six?'

'A tiim number is always bought in pairs. Man is six; accidental death is four, so sixty-four. But blood, four, may very well come first, followed by man, six. The numbers must be reversed, you see? The player always has to buy in pairs.

'Hands and feet are also easily explained. They are five because of the five fingers and toes. A house is something needed, you know, *roti, kapda aur makaan*—food, clothing and shelter—and therefore something bha, good, which rhymes with phra, eight. A tree is one because it's upright like 1; fruit is zero because it's round. Anything round is zero. That's why a naked woman is fifty; five for woman, zero for the roundness of her frame; also for her nakedness, of course.

'Horse is *kulai* in Khasi, so it's *lai*, or three; dog is *ksew*, so it's *hynñiew*, or seven; tiger is *khla*, so it's *phra*, or eight; cat is five because it's associated with feminine qualities; hen is two because it's two-legged. Otherwise, most animals are calculated as four, because they are *mrad saw kjat*, or four-footed animals ... Ah, do you hear that? They have just finished shooting for the evening round.'

The noise of the crowd drove us outside. I drifted through the mass of people and spoke to an old man, who identified himself simply as Bah Tai. He turned out to be very knowledgeable; I asked him about bad dreams.

'When it comes to bad dreams, ha, Bah, what you call pathogenetic dreams, we Khasis have a very peculiar attitude. A bad dream is calculated as fifty-six/sixty-five, and that which involves demons or dead people, as nine. But there is more to it. When we dream of a snake or a leech, or when we dream of a cat, we interpret that in two ways—the presence of enemies and ill-wishers trying to do us harm, or that we are suffering from an illness known as "*pang thlen*". Thlen, as you know—or maybe you don't—is a man-eating serpent of legend that used to stalk the wilderness of Sohra, and later metamorphosed into a dependent creature that some people kept, in return for riches, in the form of a leech. That's what they say, anyway. They also say Thlen can assume many forms, and when disappointed with its keepers, it climbs onto the roof and reveals itself in the shape of many animals, but especially a cat. But then, how can we be sure? We don't know what Thlen looks like, do we? Anyway, that's why these animals are associated with pang thlen,' Bah Tai explained.

'I'm dying to hear the story of Thlen, ya, Bah Ap!' Donald broke in.

'You will, you will,' I promised.

Magdalene was shaking her head and saying, 'My, my, what a fascinating business this is, no, Raji? I mean, the way they analyse the dreams and break them down to numbers! But the most amusing one was the naked man, ya. Did you finally find out the number for him, Ap?' she asked with a laugh.

'Unfortunately, no, I didn't.'

'Maybe they should try hundred or what?' Bah Kynsai suggested.

'Why? Why?' Magdalene was immediately interested.

'Well, a tree and two fruits, na?'

'Tet sala, this Bah Kynsai!' We all exploded into laughter and curses.

After a while, Bah Kynsai turned to me and said, 'Come on, man! What else did the old man tell you?'

'When we dream of a pig,' Bah Tai said, 'we believe that there are definitely enemies out there who are trying to turn us into victims of their evil plans. When we dream of a bird in a cage, we know that we are grappling with a very serious illness indeed. But the worst kind of bad dream that we can have … Do you know what it is? A broken tooth. A broken tooth presages death, either in our own family or among relations, and always necessitates a visit to the faith healers. But for those who are tiim players, ha, Bah, such a visit may not be necessary, for they may simply say, *pynkup noh ha ka tiim,* convert it into a tiim. The belief is that if a nightmare is converted into a tiim number, and if that number turns up as the winning number, then the nightmare will never come to pass in real life. Having come true on the archery field, it loses its evil influence. The dreamer is, therefore, happy for two reasons: money and respite from death. So, who says, Bah, that tiim is bad?'

Not I, of course. It is not a widely known fact, not even my closest friends know about it, but once upon a time, I too was a counter owner. My elder brother, a government employee, had just married, and because his wife was unemployed, he wanted to improve his income by opening a counter. A distant relative who was in the business persuaded him to join. Taking a bank loan, he started operations and reported excellent initial earnings. He persuaded me, in turn, to join. I was a student at the time, but already working at the toll gate, as I told you. Not able to sit at the counter myself, I hired a man to do it for me. I was not doing too badly, but then, one day, I won an essay-writing competition and my photos were all over the local papers. I was pleased with all that attention until I visited the counter. The fellow had plastered the entire place with the newspaper photos and was telling all his customers that I was his boss. I decided to shut shop from the very next day. My brother employed that enterprising man.

'You are leading us on, mə, tdong,' Bah Kynsai exclaimed. 'I can't imagine you running a tiim counter!'

I assured them it was the truth, and returned to Bah Tai's stories. Another remarkable thing about the dream of a broken tooth, he told me, is that it is believed to be directly related to the winning number of the previous day. For instance, if one tooth breaks, then one number will fall from the winning number of the previous day. That means, if it was forty-four, then the next day's number could be forty-three. As Bah Tai put it, 'More teeth breaking, more numbers falling.' A dream about climbing up or down the steps also works in the same way.

Clearly, Khasi dream interpretation, as far as tiim archery is concerned, is heavily influenced by our cultural beliefs and the phonetic sounds of the words. But it is also more than that. I know for sure that people do win when they buy a number revealed by their dreams. When they dream about fishing, for instance, they will buy eighty-seven and seventy-eight, for water and fishing rod are seven and fish is eight. But they will also buy fifty-eight/eighty-five or fifty-seven/seventy-five because the hand that holds the rod is five. And quite often, as if there is a mysterious relation between dreams and tiim, one of these numbers turns out to be the winning number. If it does not, the dream is said to be *ka bym kup*, that is, not accurate.

Now, the question is, how do people know that one of these numbers will be the target-number? An old man I met recently had an answer to that question. He used to be an avid tiim player and knew most of the pioneers of tiim archery. But he had converted to Presbyterianism and stopped playing altogether. That is why he asked me not to reveal his identity.

According to him, the unique tradition of dream numbers started when one of the early associates of tiim archery, Bah Lon, had a dream about the winning number of the previous day. The number was sixty-four. Convinced that sixty-four would turn up as the winning number again, Bah Lon invested heavily in it that afternoon. The dream came true, and he won quite a large sum of money. Later, he kept waiting for numbers to appear in his dreams, but when that proved to be infrequent, he started analysing whatever dreams he had and converted their objects and symbols into numbers. And that practice soon became popular and was adopted by others in the fraternity.

Those early pioneers were unknowingly following the idea of condensation that Freud spoke about, where one dream object is believed to stand for several associations and ideas. But in their case, these associations and ideas were converted into numbers. They observed an object over a long period before finally giving it a dream number and establishing it as a representation of that object. It is precisely because of this that no number has been assigned to the computer yet. The process of observation is ongoing.

In their 'do-it-yourself dream interpretation', which Ann Faraday had popularised in the West, the Khasi pioneers followed, again unknowingly, the Jungian doctrine of the importance of context in dream analysis. For instance, a vehicle is two if it's a two-wheeler, four if a small four-wheeler, and eight if a big one. But if, in the dream, attention is focused on the wheels and not on the body, then the number would be none of the above but a zero. In the same manner, if the colour of a vehicle is seen more prominently than any other aspect of it, then the number will relate to the colour. On the other hand, if a vehicle appears in the dream with its registration number clearly marked, then the tiim numbers will be based on it. For example, if the number is ML 05E 1364, the tiim numbers would be thirteen/thirty-one and sixty-four/forty-six. The number '05' is not counted, being a common denominator.

Certainly, there are people, not only big-time gamblers but also frequent players, who buy a number daily, with or without dreams. A close relative of mine, whom everyone calls Bahdeng, is one such man. Being a shopkeeper, he asks everyone who comes into the shop for a dream. If no one has had a dream, he simply looks for whatever number may be printed on their clothes. It is customary for him to say, 'What is that on the lapel of your jacket? Let's see, let's see … Aha! A number ten!' And with that number he makes a round of the nearest tiim counters. Believe it or not, he often wins too.

When I reached the end of my account, Donald said, 'Mag's right, it's truly fascinating, Bah Ap. And very well researched too! I mean, you bring in almost everybody who counts on the subject, from Freud to Jung to Faraday, not to speak of *Gilgamesh*, the Old Testament, and the Islamic scholars. But what I like most about it is that it's not merely academic—'

'It's a story, man,' Raji declared, 'full of mythic tales, little stories and dialogues and whatnot.'

'That's right, that's right,' Donald agreed. 'Do people still buy dream-based numbers, though?'

'Very much,' I told him. 'People who play the tiim numbers never get tired of asking you, "Did you have a dream last night?" Bahdeng, for instance, asks me the same thing every day.'

ॐ

The Last Words

As it exists today, many enthusiasts of the traditional game of *ïasiat khnam rongbiria*, the recreational arrow-shooting, consider tiim archery a fake form of archery. When asked why, they always say, 'What kind of shooting is this? It lasts only for three to four minutes. The distance is only sixty feet, and the skum is huge. Apart from that, there's no nongkhang khnams, no phawars, and even the arrows are numbered instead of carrying the traditional distinguishing marks.' It is nothing, they claim, but a game of chance and numbers, depending very much on luck, like any other form of gambling.

Socially, tiim archery is both popular and frowned upon. Its popularity can be determined by the large number of tiim counters doing business in the state, by the enormous amount of revenue collected from it annually, and by the participation of a large number of women (both as counter-runners and customers) as well as a cross-section of the society. I have personally seen people from various communities, including Khasis, Bengalis, Biharis, Nepalis, Marwaris and others in the archery field, but I also have an anecdote to serve as further proof.

Some young men were loitering around Ïewduh, the largest marketplace in Shillong, when they heard a commotion at one of the tiim counters. The counter was operated by a Nepali, who was, at that moment, quarrelling with a Chinese customer.

The Chinese man was asking for a number, or numbers, in broken Hindi. He said: '*Shi nga eh shi nga pa.*'

'*Kya bola?*' ('What did you say?')

'*Ham bola,*' the man repeated, '*shi nga eh shi nga pa.*'

'*Kya shi nga eh shi nga pa? Jao yahan seh, sala!*' ('What *shi nga eh shi nga pa*? Get lost, you stupid bugger!')

The old man got angry at that and shouted at the top of his voice, '*Shi nga eh shi nga pa ham bola!*'

The bookie appealed to the young men watching the drama: '*Bah, aye to aye ... Kya mangta hei yeh?*' ('Bah, please come here ... What does this fellow want?')

The young men spoke to the Chinese man, but when they too could not understand what he was saying, they asked him to write down what he wanted. And this was what he wrote:

'Single eight, single *pas.*'

Paanch, which he wrote as '*pas*', is Hindi for five.

The incident clearly shows that all kinds of people not only participate in tiim archery but do so very passionately indeed.

'I can well imagine the situation,' Hamkom said. 'When the Chinese speak Hindi, okay, it's really horrible, much, much worse than Khasi Hindi.'

Everyone agreed, and Bah Kit said, 'Khasi Hindi can at least be understood, ha, but if that Chinese guy had not written down the words, no, Ham, nobody would have figured him out.'

The Khasis who play tiim numbers, I said, come from every stratum of the community. Among those belonging to the Khasi faith, the attitude towards it is generally one of tolerance, though not everyone is a participant, for participation, like in any other game, depends very much on personal inclination. Among the Christians, Catholics are more likely to participate, both as players and counter-runners, since it is considered a means of livelihood like any other. In fact, on my visits to the tiim archery ground, I came across many acquaintances belonging to the church who officiated in the proceedings. But other Christian denominations, especially Presbyterians, strictly forbid any kind of contact with it, for they view it as gambling, an evil. To them, 'tiim' (although taken from the English word 'team') is the same as the Khasi word '*tim*', 'to curse', and so they look at those who indulge in the game as accursed souls. One of their pastors often tells the following story as a 'joke' and a deterrent:

Many years ago, in Shillong, there was a man by the name of Pankwah, literally, 'ask-for-it'. He was such an inveterate tiim gambler that the first thing he would do in the morning was to ask his wife and children about what they had dreamt the night before. One morning, as usual, as soon as he had finished his morning ablutions, he asked his family about their dreams.

'Tymmen, old woman, what did you dream last night? You, Bahbah? Rit? And you, Thei?'

Bahbah and Rit were his two sons, Thei his daughter.

When none of them had dreams to offer, he pleaded with his wife, 'Tymmen, why don't you go back to sleep? Sleep with the baby and dream, Tymmen, dream well so I can buy a number. Go, Tymmen, go.'

'Are you mad?' his wife replied angrily. 'Who will look after the children? Who will do all the work? Even a hen cannot incubate the whole day long, go and sleep yourself, you shameless idler.'

Taking that as sincere permission, Pankwah climbed back into bed immediately after breakfast. He said: 'Mind you now, do not disturb me, no noise, and don't rouse me; let me wake up on my own.'

Pankwah slept for a long time and dreamt that his wife was run over by a truck. When he woke up, he said excitedly: 'Aha, what a beautiful dream! Now, a truck is eight, a woman is five, so eighty-five and fifty-eight should be sure shots. Also, because my wife died, I had better buy fifty-nine and ninety-five as well.' Then, addressing his wife, he said, 'Tymmen, I'm going for the numbers, I'll be back in a moment, okay?'

But Pankwah did not come back in a moment. He was so happy with his dream, and was so sure about the numbers, that he wandered from counter to counter trying to buy as many as he could afford. While he was loafing about in that manner, someone came running to him:

'Bah Pan, Bah Pan, your wife has been run over by a truck!'

And all this, the sermoniser used to say, was because of the accursed tiim archery.

When I finished, Raji said, 'Hey, Ap, you said Presbyterians are against tiim archery, but what about Bah Kynsai? He plays the numbers too, no?'

'So do you,' Bah Kynsai responded.

'I'm a Catholic, Bah Kynsai!'

'I was speaking about the policy of the church,' I responded. 'But as I said, it all depends upon personal inclination.'

In fact, the Presbyterians are not against tiim archery alone. From the time of the Welsh missionaries, they have strictly forbidden any kind of participation even in the traditional and God-given game of rongbiria. In his book on Soso Tham, Hughlet Warjri speaks of Tham's great love for the game despite being a Presbyterian:

U Soso Tham loved going on fishing and hunting trips and used to watch the game of archery, involving a wager between the people of Shangpung and Raliang at the foot of Lamare Hill [in Ri Pnar] with great delight ... So, one day elders of the [Presbyterian] church went to persuade him away from it [archery]. There were three of them. In response to their admonitions, Tham replied:

Tang lai: phin lah ïa nga?
So bad So long phra,
Sa bad ka Tham lei lei
La long ha nga khyndei.

(Only three: you would overcome me?
Four and Four are eight,
Add to that the crab
All with me are nine.)

Tham reportedly ran into many such difficulties with the church leaders because of his love for indigenous customs.

'Hey, Bah Ap, does "Soso" mean "four and four" or what?' Donald enquired.

'In the Pnar dialect, yes. But Tham was named Soso because his father was in love with the English word "so-so". He heard it from the Welsh missionaries.'

'Tet leh, this Ap!' Bah Kynsai laughed. 'But tell me, is that one of the reasons why he had to leave the Presbyterian church?'

'Definitely,' I replied. 'Warjri thought he did so of his own free will, although others said he was hounded out. But even if he did leave on his own, the reasons are not hard to understand.'

'If you ask me, I don't see why we cannot practise another religion without hating our own culture. It's very sad, ya,' Magdalene said.

'Very sad, but that's how things are, mostly,' Bah Kynsai responded. 'Do you see him?' He pointed at Evening. 'Why do you think he hasn't been saying anything? Because he too doesn't like archery, na? He's a strange creature: sometimes he's pro-Khasi to the point of being fanatical and, yet, he actually hates many aspects of Khasi culture.'

'I think he's a bloody fake!' Magdalene said.

Evening became quite angry at that and retorted, 'I'm not a fake, you—'

'Don't say it!' Bah Kynsai warned.

'Fine, I'm not saying it! But I don't hate Khasi culture, only this stupid matrilineal system!'

'You are deluding yourself, mə, liah!' Bah Kynsai countered. 'But let's forget it ... So, what's the status of archery as a sport now, Ap?'

The God-given game of recreational arrow-shooting, rongbiria, is still very much the national game of the Khasis. This huge community event, a unique cultural and colourful festival, is still played everywhere, together with all its attendant traditions. There are still archery meetings between villages and groups every week in the countryside, accompanied by the traditional shamanistic war of words; the singing, dancing and chanting of men, women and children, all rallying behind their champions; the spontaneous composition of gnomic phawars; and the hurling of derogatory names by supporting groups. In Shillong, there are several big archery tournaments held every year, involving teams and individuals vying for prizes and monetary rewards. Bah Su can tell you more about those. It is a measure of the Khasis' great love for this ancient tradition that the sport thrives to this day despite Kajang's subterfuge, the suppression of the Welsh missionaries and their followers, the stigma of gambling, and the onslaught of modern forms of entertainment. As Ka Mei Hukum said, 'What is God-given must remain.'

'What is God-given must remain! That's a good way of calling it a night, I think, Bah Kynsai?' Bah Kit suggested.

Bah Kynsai looked at his watch and said with surprise, 'Arre, it's very late … That quarrel with Ning must have taken up more time than we thought. The good thing is, we didn't end up fighting, na? But truly, Ning, I wonder what your relationship with your wife is like. If you hate women so much, how can you bring yourself to sleep with a woman?'

Bah Kynsai laughed at his own joke, and even Evening, recognising it as one, let it pass.

Raji, however, could not help saying, 'That's different, no, Ning?'

Ignoring the banter, Bah Su said, '"What is God-given must remain" is undoubtedly a good ending. And I'm not referring to archery only. You see, even our matrilineal culture was God-given, ha, that's why it's also mentioned in the Three Divine Commandments as ka tip kur tip kha, the knowledge of one's maternal and paternal relations. And so, it too must remain.'

Evening responded with fury: 'Don't give me that—'

'Don't say it!' Bah Kynsai warned again.

'Okay, okay,' Evening said. 'But, in my opinion, ha, the greatest mistake the Welsh missionaries did was in not changing the matrilineal system. If they had, I guarantee you that every one of us would have become a Christian by now. What man would not want to convert and get his children to adopt his surname, huh? And when all men become Christians, what could the women do but follow?'

'You are taking too much for granted, you fool!' Magdalene retorted. 'Supposing they didn't want to follow, what then?'

'I think the missionaries also thought about it, ha,' Bah Su said, 'but realised the dilemma that Mag is pointing to … So, I say again, what was God-given must remain.'

'Given by what God?'

'Why, Evening, God is the same for everyone, isn't he?' Magdalene asked.

Before Evening could answer, Bah Kynsai said quickly, 'Of course he is! God, Godot, he's all the same, na?'

'Come on, Bah Kynsai!' several voices were heard protesting.

'Alright, alright!' Bah Kynsai said. 'Now, Evening, God is the same for everyone, do you hear? Unless you want to say, there is no God but God, and his name is—'

'Tut!' Evening said angrily.

'Okay then, that settles it! Let's go to sleep!'

'If we can,' Raji pointed out. 'Listen to all that noise!'

Raji was referring to the sound of the gun being fired every few minutes, followed by the raucous music of drums and the pipe instruments.

'It will stop, they also have to sleep, na?' Bah Kynsai replied. But as soon as the words left his mouth, the gun went 'Boom!' and Bah Kynsai said, 'Bew!'

After a while, he said again, 'Let us try anyway, cursing these fellows is useless.'

10

THE
EIGHTH
NIGHT

LITTLE STORIES III

'Ka jingieit kam ithuh jingïapher.'
('Love knows no otherness.')

—from the Khasi book
Ki Kyrwoh: Ki Khana Phawer

The noise of celebratory gunfire had kept us up until late the previous night. We finally caught a little sleep towards 5 a.m. but were woken up at 8 a.m. by another round of firing as more and more burang uncles arrived. The noise only stopped at 10 a.m. It was 12 February; we were drawing closer to the final ceremony.

Since we could not sleep any more, we got up, performed our morning ablutions, and went for breakfast. After that, we went to see the bulls in the pen. The number had gone up to sixty-five. We asked Chirag if they had all been brought by the uncles. He explained that each uncle had brought at least two bulls, one from him and one from his wife's family. The rest were brought by his dead aunt's grandchildren, nieces, nephews and paternal grandchildren, that is, the children of the deceased's sons and nephews, many of whom had arrived during the night. Chirag also told us that, by noon, they would begin the ceremony called *on-kti shaw-kti* or *ka tawla tawjien*. This is a formal fund collection to meet the estimated expenses, as calculated by the uncles.

The ceremony began with one of the shamans performing a simple prayer with rice grains, followed by the fund collection. Five burang uncles, sitting on a low bench with a desk in front of them, oversaw the operation. Each had a register in which every voluntary contribution received was noted down along with the contributor's name. This process is called on-kti, or lending a helping hand. Anybody can lend a helping hand: relatives, friends, well-wishers. And the contribution is reciprocated whenever there is a death in the family of any of the contributors. Such reciprocation is known as shaw-kti, or the return of the helping hand. The collection took all day and continued late into the night, for people from far and near came at their own convenience.

We also took up a collection among ourselves. Each of us gave Bah Kynsai 1,000 rupees, except for Halolihim, who refused to contribute, quoting religious reasons, and Dale, whom we did not ask since he was our driver. The amount came to 9,000 rupees, but Bah Kynsai said the family would not consider nine an auspicious number, as it is connected with death. So each of us added some more to take the total up to 10,000, and gave the money to Chirag, who gave it to his uncles. As they dutifully put down our names in the register, one of them said, 'If anything happens in your family, let us know, we will reciprocate your helping hand.'

Having done our duty, we ate our lunch of boiled rice and chicken broth with jamyrdoh herb and radish mixed with onions, chillies and lemon juice. After that, we went to the lake for a bath and a well-deserved siesta. Halolihim, however, left as soon as he had bathed, citing urgent business back in the village.

When we returned, the collection was still in progress, and it continued well after dinner, which was the same as lunch, without the radish, but with ground dried fish for chutney. All the money was handed to a shaman, who performed a thanksgiving ritual using rice grains from a winnowing basket and yiad hiar beer from a gourd. After the ritual, we returned to our hut.

Once we'd settled in, Raji said, 'That was a rather strange affair, ha, Bah Kit?' He was referring to the fund collection.

'Why?' Donald asked. 'Is there no fund collection among other Khasi sub-tribes?'

Instead of answering him, Raji asked, 'Do you remember what you said when we were discussing Khasi funeral rites? I do. You said, "Yeah, yeah, yeah, we know all about what we do with our dead bodies, we keep them for two or three nights and then bury or cremate them as the case may be." But lately, you seem to be asking a lot of questions, how come, huh?'

'Look, I admit I was a bit full of myself, okay, I didn't realise there was so much to know about our people at first, and at that time I didn't know any of you guys, except Bah Kynsai, who—you must admit it, Bah Kynsai—never spoke much about any of this. But since coming here and listening to all of you, okay, I can see how very wrong I was. And I don't mind admitting it at all.'

'Good for you, Don.' Magdalene patted his back, evidently pleased by his attitude.

Moved by Donald's openness, Bah Kit said, 'Among the rest of us Khasis, no, Don, whenever death occurs, the closest relatives assemble immediately and contribute large sums of money to the bereaved family so that the shopping of essential items can begin—'

'By essential items, na, Don, he means rice, meat, onions, oil, tea leaves, biscuits, cakes and so on,' Bah Kynsai interrupted. 'All essential for a feast, not a funeral.'

We all laughed, and Bah Kit said, 'They do this for everyone except for rich people who can fend for themselves. Then, when distant relatives, friends and neighbours come, the first thing they do is meet the family members sitting by the body, not only to console but also to surreptitiously hand over some money to the main person there—'

'The main person?' Donald asked.

'You know, if it's the mother who dies, then the main person sitting there would be the daughter living with her, and if it's the husband, then the main person would be his wife … Yes, it's always a woman watching over the body. As I was saying, when they come, they surreptitiously hand over some money—'

'Surreptitious in what way, and why? Believe it or not, I haven't really experienced these things.'

'Why, haven't you been to funerals before or what?' Raji asked, a hint of sarcasm back in his voice.

'I have, once in a while, whenever I was home, but I mainly sat with friends outside and did nothing but talk.'

'And drink tea,' Bah Kynsai added. 'But that's because you were only a student, na, Don? Only working people are supposed to contribute.'

'Well,' Bah Kit continued, 'surreptitious because the giver keeps the money hidden in his fist and passes it on to the main person under her shawl. The taker also receives the money surreptitiously and puts it in her bag, hidden by her shawl, without looking at it. All this is done with as little movement of the hand as possible. You see, the main person and the other two or three female relatives keeping her company are supposed to be in deep mourning, receiving whispered consolations—not something as businesslike as money. In this way, nobody ever knows who is giving how much. Anyway, this money is rarely used during the funeral itself. The expenses, as I said, are met from the family's own money and contributions from close relatives, except when the family is really poor. Usually, it's only after the funeral that the collection from consolers and well-wishers is brought out and counted. The amount is compared with expenses spent, and if the receipt is less, the relatives try to make up for the deficit. And if it's more, it's either used to repay relatives who have given money or kept aside for use during *ka khawai dap snem*, the first death-anniversary feast. Here, as you can see, an estimate is made in advance and the fund collection is done one day before the actual cremation ceremony.'

'You know, Don,' Bah Kynsai said, 'I have a friend who's got a shop at Ïewduh, okay? He's a hardcore businessman, miserly through and through, cunning, and I would even say, unscrupulous—'

'And yet he's your friend?' Raji asked, laughing.

'And yet he's my friend,' Bah Kynsai affirmed. 'He's quite entertaining, very witty, na, I like his company, and because I know him so well, I can always avoid being conned by him. We call him Bukhir the Miser. Bukhir has one very curious trait. He loves funerals, and whenever he goes to one, he always makes it a point to give the bereaved family some money—'

'But you just said he's a miser?' Hamkom protested.

'Hold on, hold on, na! Because of that, people think he's very generous and treat him with a lot of respect. And of course, Bukhir also enjoys that very much. He also had me fooled me, ha, and initially I thought he was, after all, not as miserly as I had believed him to be. I was reminded of a story about a great writer—I can't recall his name right now, tet teri ka! Anyway, one day, when some nuns came to him for a donation, na, he immediately blew out two of the four candles he had been using while writing. When they saw that, the nuns looked at each other and thought: from such a man, what kind of donation will we get? To their surprise, na, when they had explained everything to him, the writer gave them a very generous contribution. With many apologies, the nuns told him what was on their minds. The writer laughed and said, "To write a book, I need four candles, but why should I need four to talk to my guests? I practise parsimony precisely so I can save up to help noble causes like yours."

'So, initially, I also thought Bukhir was like that, you know, generous with noble causes … until, one day, we visited a death house together. That whole evening, he was very restless, okay? And why? Because he couldn't get any small change for his ten-rupee note. After a while, he went out to ask at all the shops in the locality until he finally got four two-rupee notes and two one-rupee notes. He slyly turned the whole lot into a fat roll and went to give it to the woman sitting by the body. The poor woman who took the money under her shawl thought the respected and generous Bukhir had given her a huge amount. But I had seen everything, na? He had given her only ten rupees, the bugger! From that time, he has been buying me a peg or two whenever we meet, hahaha.'

'Why, Bah Kynsai, are you blackmailing him or what?' Magdalene asked, laughing.

'No, no, no, it's his way of bribing me into silence, na? But he need not have bothered, for what could I do? I couldn't very well go to a bereaved woman and say he had given her only small change, could I? He's quite chalu and unscrupulous, that fellow. He even takes advantage of his relatives, can you imagine? When they come to buy anything from his shop, na, thinking he will give them the best prices, being a relative and all, na, he actually overcharges them. When I asked him why, he said, "Business is business." He's quite a thug.'

'So, what moral shall we give your story, Bah Kynsai?' Evening asked. 'This one definitely sounds like a moral story.'

'*To an impostor, even misfortune is an opportunity for deception,*' Bah Su offered. 'Will that do?'

Nobody could come up with anything better. But Magdalene thought that perhaps the moral should be, 'A man is known by the company he keeps.' She was obviously teasing Bah Kynsai, who laughed it off.

Donald also laughed and then said, 'Bah Kynsai, did you see how the shaman prayed this afternoon? It was as if he was in a trance—'

'That's how he has been praying all along, haven't you noticed?' Bah Kynsai asked impatiently.

'Yeah, yeah, I have. And this afternoon, I became so curious that I asked Perly about it. He said the shaman acted like that because he actually saw the deceased's ancestors—ka ïawbei, u thawlang, u suidñia. He was talking to them as in real life. Do you know what amazes me, Bah Kynsai?'

'What?'

'The fact that when Khasis speak of these things, and also of their myths, they seem to believe them implicitly. The golden ladder on Mount Sohpet Bneng and all that, for instance, Bah Ap clearly said that they are only parables, but most people speak of them as if real. That's why Bah Wishing suggested that we came from space. And Thlen, the serpent? Many of us really believe in his existence—there are even hired killers collecting blood for him. Everyone seems to live in a world of magic realism … I don't really know how to put this, but a world, you know, where reality seems to mix freely with the surreality of dream and fantasy. Even you people, educated as you are, seem to believe in this kind of world—'

'But we don't believe that the myths are real, no, Don?' Bah Kit cut in. 'As you said, we have made it clear that they are only symbols and metaphors.'

'That's true, but in the archery game, for instance, you all seem to believe that there are people who can stop arrows from hitting their target or even make them fall from it by using words and chanting some mantra!'

'But we explained that, no?'

'Yeah, but are there really people like that?'

As Bah Kit hesitated, Bah Su jumped in and said with absolute confidence, 'Of course there are! I organise archery tournaments every year, and I witness this sort of thing regularly. But it's not a mantra, Don. The same word is not repeated again and again to aid concentration as among the Hindus. In the archery game, ha, the nongkhan khnams pray to God as Ka Mei Hukum, they plead with her and argue their case and show why their archers deserve to win and why their rivals, because of their shortcomings, deserve to lose. And if the rivals are really guilty of these shortcomings, ha, and cannot prove otherwise before God, ha, then they lose the game despite their superior skill.'

'And the power of the word, ka ktien, can be felt in all aspects of life, not only in archery, Don,' Raji added. 'Khasis call their shamans by different names: in the archery game, he's a nongkhan khnam, but otherwise, when he's involved in the business of healing, he's *u nongduwai*, the elder who prays—'

'Or the praying elder,' Bah Kynsai added. 'Like the praying mantis, na?'

'Tet!' Raji said, annoyed. 'He's *u nongkñia*, the sacrificer, the augur, who performs extispicy. He's *u nongkhan*, the diviner, who uses rice grains or cowrie shells or shanam, the silver lime container, for his work, and *u nongshat nongkheiñ*, the egg-breaker, who divines by breaking eggs on a wooden board. Many say that going to these faith healers is nothing but superstition, okay, but people do go to them when they fall ill or have something important to do, like taking exams, constructing a house, moving into a new house, travelling, contesting elections and so on. I also go to them sometimes—'

'Really?' Donald, Magdalene and Hamkom asked at the same time.

'Yeah, I do, and I find them very helpful, so there! Whenever I had to go to a doctor, okay, my mother used to tell me to first go to these elders so they could plead with God on my behalf and neutralise all ill wishes and pave the way for a successful treatment. One of the most amazing of these people, ha, is a woman from Mawlai. She's not really a faith healer, she's a diviner and uses playing cards—'

'To tell fortunes? That's not very unique!' Hamkom interrupted.

'Shut up, man!' Raji said in mock anger. 'I'm not talking about fortune-telling. This woman has a very remarkable ability, okay? If you are ill, for instance, she can tell you who the best doctor would be. It all depends upon your luck, she says, and with whom your luck lies. And when she tells you about a doctor, okay, she explains everything about him: his name, his place of work, his specialisation, his residential address, complete with locality names and street names and whatnot.'

'How does she know all that?' Magdalene demanded.

'That's the thing, no? How does she know all that? And mind you, the doctors she recommends are not only local but those who work in Vellore, Mumbai, Delhi, Kolkata. She's amazing, I tell you!'

'Perhaps she has a secret address book or what?' Hamkom suggested.

'And memorises thousands of names and resumes? Don't be stupid, man!'

'Is there really such a woman, Raji?' Bah Kynsai asked, suddenly interested.

'Yes, she lives in Mawlai Kynton Masar—'

'And she's not a fake either,' I said. 'I also went to her with my brother once. At that time, I was still teaching at the university. She first started with my brother and asked him to cut the cards. When he'd done that, she laid them one by one on a small table in front of her, studied them carefully, and after a while, told him he had a serious health problem. She advised him to first go to a particular faith healer, to strengthen his essence, and then to a Bengali doctor in a certain Shillong locality for treatment. She gave him the names and complete addresses of the two people without consulting anything but the cards in front of her. When my brother went to meet them, he found them exactly where she had told him they would be. But when it was my turn to cut the cards, she took one look at them and told me, "You have no problem at all. No major illness, and economically, you are very well-placed. You don't need anything. You have a teaching job at the university, don't you?" And believe me, she had never seen me before!'

'You two are not fooling around, na?' Bah Kynsai demanded. When we assured him we were not, he said, 'You must take me to her too, huh? She sounds fantastic, man!'

'Me too,' Hamkom said, 'I'd like to see this for myself.'

'And me,' Magdalene added.

Even Donald said he would like to see the woman. But he was not done with his questions about shamans yet. 'Bah Su, Bah Raji, if you say that these faith healers have the power to neutralise your enemies' ill wishes, doesn't that mean they can also do you harm?'

'Shamans cannot harm anybody without cause, Don,' Bah Su replied. 'They have to have a cause. Besides, shamans must swear an oath before God to fight against evil, disease and misfortune by pleading before him on behalf of anyone coming to them for help. Causing anyone ill luck is taboo for them, you understand? But sometimes, being human, they might have a personal quarrel and may use their power against their enemies, but that too, only if their cause is just—'

'Like in the story of Liar Sordar Mawdem, no, Bah Su?' Raji asked.

'Yes, yes, exactly.'

Liar was the ruler of the Ri Bhoi province of Mawdem in the state of Nongkhlaw, which is why he was known as Liar Sordar Mawdem. He was a famous faith healer, respected by friends and dreaded by foes. There are many stories about him and his extraordinary powers. Once, for instance, when Kine Sing, the king of Nongkhlaw, sent two of his ministers and their followers to request Liar to attend an important state council, Liar decided to play a trick on them. He welcomed them to his home very warmly, though they had to camp outside and prepare their own food since there were so many of them. Liar provided them with rice and four very fat hens. The men boiled the rice and curried the chickens. But when it was time to eat, something strange happened—as the men ladled the meat onto their plates, they could see it was chicken, but when they put it in their mouths, it turned into boiled plantain flower, very soft and mushy. Shocked and scared witless, they jumped to their feet and spat it out as fast as they could. When Liar, who was watching them closely, saw that, he pretended to be enraged and roared, 'How can you insult me in my own home like this?' Even more scared of Liar than they were of the meat, the men forced themselves to eat it and said it was the best chicken they had ever tasted.

At another time, a jadukar came to Mawdem and bragged openly to the local inhabitants about the things he could do. He went on to run down Khasi faith healers, calling them charlatans and daring them to prove him wrong. Overawed by his self-glorification and his magic tricks, many ignorant villagers flocked to him with their problems and gave him money and valuable items as payment.

When Liar heard about this, he immediately went to confront the jadukar and challenged him to a contest. He gave him a rifle and said, 'If you are as good as you say, let us shoot each other with this gun. I'll give you the advantage of shooting first, what do you say?'

But the jadukar trembled at the thought. If the rifle worked and he killed the sordar of the place, he might be lynched by the crowd. On the other hand, if Liar managed to *ban* the gun, that is, put a spell on it so it would not work, he would surely be killed when it was Liar's turn to fire at him. He refused to accept the challenge. But Liar would not let him off so easily. He said, 'If you are too scared to accept the challenge, then let us shoot at our shirts. You can begin.'

The jadukar took the gun and shot at Liar's shirt, which had been hung on a bamboo fence for the challenge. To his amazement, the gun made a loud explosion, but no bullet came out of it. When it was Liar's turn, the jadukar took off his shirt, hung it on the same fence, and then, as Liar picked up the gun, the jadukar muttered his mantra to cast a spell on it. But his spell did not work and his shirt was soon full of holes. When Liar left the place, he told the jadukar: 'For cheating the poor of their hard-earned money, you will live only for a week.' And that was precisely what happened. One week from that day, he died unexpectedly while washing himself on the banks of a river.

But then, Liar Sordar Mawdem converted to Christianity and gave up his practice as a faith healer. This angered some of the other faith healers in the region, who made several attempts to punish him. But Liar was too powerful for them, and no one could do him any harm. One day, however, one of them nearly succeeded. Liar was going to a neighbouring village with his grandson for a religious meeting. When they reached a river called Khri, they stopped by its banks to have their lunch of boiled rice, chicken and fried vegetables packed in large lamet leaves. But when the grandson opened the packets, he found nothing there but a bunch of cat's hair. When Liar saw that, he smiled and said, 'The fellow is trying to send this hair into our stomachs, my son, but because my essence is so strong, the food turned into hair even before we could eat it. I could easily return the favour, but why indulge in this pettiness when I am about God's work?'

'So,' I concluded, 'that was how an offended shaman could use his power against his enemies.'

'But Bah Su said they can do that sort of thing only if their cause is just, no?' Donald said. 'How is the cause of that shaman just, in this case?'

'From his point of view,' Bah Su explained, 'Liar Sordar had betrayed him and the rest of the shamans by turning his back on his own kind. It was an act of betrayal and desertion as far as he was concerned.'

'Ah, I see,' Donald said. 'But apart from that kind of thing, what else can they do?'

'They can do quite a lot of things, you know,' I said. 'I was very young when this happened to us …'

I told them the story of our fishing trip to Ri Bhoi near Umïam Lake. My neighbours and I, four men and six boys of varying ages, left home soon after lunch, at about 9.15 a.m.

'Lunch at about 9.15 a.m.?' Donald asked in surprise.

'Khasis eat lunch at 9 or 10 a.m., Don,' I replied. 'I know you eat lunch after noon, but most Khasis don't. We normally have a very light breakfast of tea and a little rice or tea and biscuits or whatever, and then eat lunch by 9 or 10 a.m.'

Returning to my story, I said we took no food with us since we planned to be back early, by 3 p.m. or so. But before we could start fishing, a sudden downpour drove us to a rocky crevice nearby. The rain lasted for hours and stopped only in the evening. When we left our shelter at about 5 p.m., all of us were cold, miserable and hungry. We struck out across the hills and headed for the distant highway, hoping to have some tea in one of the shops there. But in the hills, we came across a field full of pumpkins and cucumbers. Ordinarily, we would not even think of touching anything growing in other people's fields. But that evening, we were so cold and hungry that the men leading us thought it would be okay if we took three or four cucumbers to share among the ten of us, just to keep the biting hunger at bay.

The men peeled the cucumbers, cut them into small round slices, and distributed them among us. We ate and headed back towards the highway. But we were only some distance away when the owner came and saw what we had done. He shouted horrible curses at us and finally said, 'From tonight, all of you thieves and free-eaters, all of you, one by one, will carry my cucumbers wherever you go!'

One of the men thought we should go back and talk to him, but the others said we should not make the situation worse by going back. 'What if he thinks we are going to beat him up and goes bawling for other locals?' they asked. 'No, no, it's best that we hurry up and get away from here.'

That was what we did. We had tea at one of the highway tea shops and, after that, caught a bus for Shillong and home. None of us gave any serious thought to the curse of the Bhoi farmer. In the morning, word spread throughout the building we lived in that one of the men had grown a large boil on his left buttock. The next day, another man had a similar boil high on his left thigh. And soon, all of us, one after another, were nursing a large boil in the most inconvenient of places. Some of us went to doctors, others to *ki nongpyrsad*, literally, 'the blowers', who treat such ailments by chanting passionate incantations while blowing on a fingerful of lime or a little mustard oil, and on the boil itself. When these actions have been performed several times, the lime or mustard oil is applied around the affected spot, and the rest given to the victim so he can use it at home.

However, nothing helped. My mother took me to two doctors and some nongpyrsads. Instead of getting better, the boils began to multiply and grow thick and fast. It was not until Meirad (old mother) Masile, our family friend from Sohra, intervened that I was cured. Before treating me, Meirad Masile said a prayer with a few rice grains, which she moved around on a winnowing basket. The moment she finished, she said, 'Ap has offended someone very powerful; he has been cursed by him. I can cure him only by asking God and the offended man's forgiveness. We cannot confront the man since we are in the wrong.'

So saying, Meirad Masile took a fingerful of lime from the container in the betel nut basket, muttered long incantations, and blew on the lime and the boils by turn. Finally, when she was satisfied, she applied a little lime around the spot where the first boil was. Having done that, she very confidently said, 'By tomorrow, they will all begin to burst.'

'What about the other boils? Didn't she apply anything on them?' Raji asked in surprise.

We had asked Meirad Masile the same thing, but she said they were not important.

True to her words, the boils began bursting one by one, and within a week, they were all gone, except for the scars, which also disappeared after a month. Needless to say, all the others also went to her and were soon cured.

When I concluded my account, many of my friends said it was indeed an incredible story.

'If true!' Evening added.

'*A false man sees falsehood everywhere*—old Khasi saying,' I responded, then turned to the others. 'And you know what? Meirad Masile was not even a professional nongpyrsad, I mean, she did not make a living from the practice. In fact, she did not take money from any of us. She was a betel-leaf seller at Ïewbah Sohra. And believe it or not, she was a devout Christian too!'

'And yet she could tell what was wrong with you by just praying with a few rice grains, Bah Ap?' Donald asked in amazement.

'That's right. She had a remarkable gift indeed.'

'And she was a Christian?' Evening wanted to make sure.

'She was,' I confirmed. 'May her soul rest in peace, and may she eat betel nut in the house of God! She was very good with burns too. I was treated by her more than once.'

'Unbelievable!' many of them said again.

'You had better believe it,' Raji said. 'Most Khasis don't go to doctors when they have boils and carbuncles, okay? They go to such faith healers. I also went to one of them, not a doctor. Bah Kynsai also. In fact, I was the one who took him to the faith healer in Smit, remember, Bah Kynsai?'

Bah Kynsai nodded and said, 'When my son had one, na, I took him to the same guy, and in just three visits, it was gone and has never come back. You too, Mag, Don, if you happen to get a boil somewhere on your buttock, na, just tell me, I'll take you to him.'

'Tet, this Bah Kynsai!' Magdalene and Donald said, pretending annoyance.

'What to do, boils are very fond of such places, na?' Bah Kynsai laughed.

I interrupted to say, 'I have one more story about offended shamans, experienced personally, with my uncle Madeng Krokar.'

One day, Madeng and I went on a bird-catching trip to a place called Jingdih Um, deep in the jungle ravines of Sohra near the famous Likai Waterfall. As usual, we left at the third cockcrow, and by sunup, we had already laid our birdlime traps by the banks of a rivulet emerging from a spring. I am not going to speak about the birds that we caught. I hate thinking about that now. However, Jingdih Um, which literally means 'the source of drinking water', was an interesting place. Right from the source of the spring, which was on a slope four feet above the ground, was a channel of split bamboo that followed the meandering course of the rivulet. The bamboo channel, Madeng told me, was used to supply water to a village located thousands of feet below the spring, right at the bottom of the ravine. There was a big river flowing by the village, but Khasis generally do not drink river water.

At about 8 a.m., Madeng told me to fetch some water from the spring so we could cook rice at the campsite we had set up. While fetching the water, I knocked down a length of bamboo by mistake. I took the water to Madeng and went back to replace the bamboo on its pole. It turned out to be not so simple because some of the bamboo strings holding it to the pole had rotted and were no longer useable. The result was that I took quite some time fixing it, and that must have badly disrupted the water supply to the village.

When I had done the job as best I could, I went back to the camp and sat by the fire, watching the rice boiling. At that very moment, an irate villager came storming up to our camp, brandishing a large knife and swearing horrible oaths at us in his War dialect, which we could not understand. When Madeng finally got him to speak in the Sohra dialect, he told us that we had disrupted the water supply to the village, and for that thoughtless and uncaring act, we deserved to be cursed in the harshest of terms. So saying, he blasted us again in his own dialect, refusing to accept Madeng's apologies. We did not understand much except for the last part, which was said in the Sohra dialect, 'This water will refuse to serve you!'

After he was gone, Madeng scolded me for not telling him about what had happened, but then he shrugged as if to say, 'Anyway, what's done is done.' He asked me to build up the fire and mind the rice while he went to check on the birdlime traps. After some time, he came back with a few lovely birds that were squealing pitifully. He took a stout stick and knocked them on the head one by one, explaining, 'We should always kill them quickly, never prolong their agony.'

He then removed the lid from the rice pot to see what was happening. The rice was boiling quite nicely, but the water seemed to be at the same level as before. Not a bit of it seemed to have dried up. And it had been more than an hour since we boiled the rice. Madeng was very surprised. He said, 'It should have cooked by now, the water should have dried up … Arre!'

He bent down to check the fire, but there was nothing wrong with it. It was blazing brightly. He shrugged again and returned to cleaning the birds. After half an hour, he took another look at the rice. It was still boiling quite briskly, but the water had not receded even a little bit. He told me to build up the fire some more. Soon, it was blazing so high that it completely engulfed the pot, lid and all.

Madeng said, 'Let's leave it like that for some time and see what happens.'

While he went back to cleaning the birds, I went up the slope of the forest to pluck some sohum fruits that I had seen earlier. When I returned after half an hour or so, Madeng said, 'Let's have a look at the rice again.'

He took out some of the burning sticks to reduce the blaze and removed the lid from the pot. It was now more than two hours since we had put the rice to boil in the small pot that was only big enough for two people. But would you believe it? The rice was bubbling happily as before, but without any sign that it was getting cooked. The water level too was the same, not a whit less. Madeng suddenly lost his temper. Using some rags, he took the pot and overturned it in the fire. 'Let's see how you boil now, you lousy thing!' And he stormed out of there into the trees for a whistle.

I stared at the pot, not knowing what to do. After some time, I began eating the sohum I had plucked. Then, feeling restless, I also went into the trees for a whistle. I returned to see that Madeng was not back. He must really be angry, I thought. Mechanically, I began to build up the fire, which had almost gone out, and stretched my hands towards it, though it was not cold at all. Just then, I heard heavy footsteps lumbering up the slope towards me, and the same man who had cursed us appeared through the trees. He was puffing and panting as he came, his face red as a wasp. Sweat ran down his face and neck, wetting his shirt and making it stick to his flesh. I was frightened and shouted out to Madeng, who came running at full speed. He saw the man and immediately realised that something was very wrong. Thinking he had come to do us harm, Madeng picked up a stout stick and waited in a posture of readiness. I did the same. However, when the man finally reached our camp, he fell at Madeng's feet and pleaded, *'Law noh, law noh ïa ka ban!'* ('Remove, remove your spell!')

At first, Madeng did not understand what he was saying. The man said again, 'I was angry that you stopped the water; I didn't mean to curse you that way, now please remove it; my body is burning with the fire you sent!'

At that, Madeng looked at the overturned pot and suddenly understood what was happening. By overturning the pot in the fire, he had unknowingly returned the man's curse to him and was causing him to burn with a terrible heat. In response, he said, 'All right, I'll remove it … But you too must remove yours. Now go, let me do my work!'

When the man left, almost crawling down the slope, Madeng removed the pot from the fire. Most of the rice had fallen out. He emptied it in a corner and prepared to cook a fresh pot of rice. Because we were quite late for lunch, he cooked it with a little salt and pieces of dried beef and pork we had brought from home.

It was the best jadoh I had ever eaten.

'Wow, what a story, man!' Magdalene exclaimed. 'The rice that would not be cooked!'

'And that man, Bah Ap, he did all that with mere words?' Donald asked.

'Yeah, as far as I could tell,' I replied.

'But how could he? It seems so strange—'

'Of course he could!' Bah Kit declared. 'But don't ever say "mere words", Don. The word is everything to Khasis. Even our religion is called Niam, meaning *nia im*, the living word. True, things have changed a lot now, but in the past, ha, when we had no written documents, the word was everything. Pledges were made with words, or when they were really important, oaths were taken by licking salt from the tip of a sword. Such oaths could not be broken even under pain of death. Trade, buying and selling, business deals, contracts, all were done with words, you understand? Education was through the spoken word. We had nothing but the word; the whole society was run based on the spoken word. And a man whose word could not be trusted was as good as ostracised. No one would take him seriously; no one would have any dealings with him. That's the power of the word, Don. And the communion between man and God and man and the spirits could certainly be done only through the word—'

'But how could they give people boils and cat's hair and stop them from cooking rice by merely incanting curses?' Donald asked.

'I don't know,' I said frankly. 'I can only tell you what I have personally experienced. The boils, of course, could have been a coincidence. However, what happened in the forest of Jingdih Um is something that I cannot even try to explain rationally.'

'Are there such people still?'

'The gifted woman in Mawlai is still there,' Raji answered. 'And there are plenty of others too.'

'Even the Jingdih Um man should still be alive, no, Ap?' Bah Kit asked.

'Yeah, he should be, old maybe, but still around, I think. I'm not so sure about the Bhoi who cursed us with boils, though. He was old even then.'

'The Khasi Hills sound dangerous, ha, Mag?' Donald said.

'No, nothing like that, Don,' Bah Su told him. 'The business of these people is basically to ward off evil and cure illnesses, or at least help in the process by strengthening your essence. Unless you have personally wronged them, they cannot do anything to you. They cannot harm people without cause, ha, nor would they do it, because it's taboo. They would be ostracised even by their own kind. Also, they believe that their gifts are God-given, and whatever they do must be done by pleading with God, and God is always on the side of the just. That's why the old woman who cured Ap, ha, was able to do so only by pleading for forgiveness since he had committed a wrong.'

Bah Kit raised his hand for attention and said, 'Victor, who came with the shamans, told Ap and me that there are people in Nongtrai who can turn themselves into tigers—'

'Not only in Nongtrai; in Ri Bhoi also,' Raji added.

'Tell, tell, no!' Magdalene pleaded.

'That story is connected with the Thlen and Sangkhni stories,' I replied, 'so—'

'Right, right,' Bah Kynsai said. 'Now we will tell little stories only, ha? Let them tell you about tiger-men, Thlen and Sangkhni later. Okay, let me begin.'

One day, Bah Kynsai said, a woman by the name of Prohibit, but called Ka Bit by everybody, went to the village council to complain about her husband. Addressing the headman and his executive members, she said:

'Look here, Bah, these are my children, yes, all of them are mine, from this little toddler to this thirteen-year-old boy, all mine. So many children, and he still had the nerve to leave! And he doesn't even give me any food money. You'll have to help me, Bah, please, you and the dorbar, please lend this unfortunate woman a helping hand. Really, Bah, you'll have to do something, please make that rogue give me some money, otherwise, poor as I am, how am I going to raise so many of them alone?'

The headman asked her, 'When did your husband leave you, Kong? Your husband is Rit, no? The one they call Rit Shrieh, who drives a taxi, no?'

'Yeah, yeah, that's him, Rit the Monkey,' one of the councillors put in.

'Right, right, Bah, it's him!' the woman confirmed. 'He's really one very callous bastard, Bah! Sorry about my language, Bah, but he really gets my blood boiling … Look at these, Bah, so many of them and—'

'No, no, but when did he leave you?' the headman asked her again.

'Oh, about his leaving, Bah? Wuu, he left a long time ago! Twelve years now, Bah!'

'Twelve years!' they all cried. 'How is that?' Everyone present was dumbfounded. 'Tet teri ka, how is that?'

The headman hushed everyone and asked the woman again, 'But how come you have so many children? You said these are also Rit Shrieh's, no?'

'Of course they are his! I have told you that already!'

'No, but if these are his, and if he left twelve years ago, then how did you get them?'

'Oooh!' the woman responded with a long-drawn exclamation. She stepped a little closer to the headman, and obviously embarrassed, said in a small voice, 'You see, Bah, it's like this, Rit used to come, you know, whenever it was flat,' she pointed to her stomach and added, 'Sorry again about my language, Bah. But what to do, I don't know how to express myself … You see, whenever it was flat, he used to come and beg for forgiveness …'

Bah Kynsai had to stop here, for many of us were roaring with laughter and crying out, 'Tet teri ka, this Bah Kynsai!'

After a while, Hamkom added, 'So, Prohibit did not prohibit Rit Shrieh, ha, Bah Kynsai?'

'How could she?' Bah Kynsai asked. 'She's called Ka Bit, na, and in Khasi the word means "available", hahaha.'

'Hey you, mind your language!' Magdalene playfully scolded Bah Kynsai and then asked, 'but did the dorbar manage to make that fellow pay?'

'Initially, Rit refused, okay? You see, they call him Rit the Monkey not only because he's red-faced like a monkey's arse but also because he cannot stay put in one place and is always changing his taxis and his wives. So, which wife should he pay, na? What if the others also complained to the dorbar about him? He was thinking about all that when he refused to comply. But the dorbar threatened to ostracise him, and he was forced to pay his wife 800 rupees every week as alimony. You see, Don, you accused our dorbars of Talibanisation, Mag also referred to it, but sometimes such a dictatorial action is also needed, na? Rit had to pay because of it.'

'But how would the woman manage with 800 rupees a week, Bah Kynsai?' Donald asked.

'She was also doing some menial labour, but I would say it's a case of the bare minimum, na? Many survive on less. It's terrible, but that's a fact.'

'Why couldn't the dorbar make him pay more?' Magdalene wondered.

'He's only a taxi driver, na, he earns only about 2,400 a week.'

'What about the other wives? Did they also complain?' Bah Kit asked.

'Luckily for him, na, they were what the taxi drivers called "tempos", temporary wives without children … they could not complain.'

'But Bah Kynsai, did this Rit not try to deny that the children were his own?' Hamkom asked.

'How could he? They all looked like him, na?'

Laughing, Magdalene said, 'You know, Bah Kynsai, I had wanted to ask you why the woman would agree to have so many children when she knew her husband was like that.'

'I have already explained that, na, he came to ask for forgiveness—'

'No, no, I don't mean that. I mean, why didn't she insist on protection?'

'Aah!' I intervened. 'I'll tell you why. Poor and uneducated people are very reluctant to use protection. Firstly, they are too shy to go to the pharmacies. Secondly, they don't have the money—'

'But it's quite cheap, man!' Hamkom said. 'It's only some 150 rupees for ten.'

'Cheap?' Bah Kynsai responded sharply. 'That's fifteen rupees for one, na? A lot of money when you earn only 2,000 or so per week. And also consider this, ha, ten condoms would not even last them for one week.'

'Tet leh, Bah Kynsai!' they all cried out, scandalised by his statement but also amused.

'Arre, you are laughing?' Bah Kynsai protested. 'They have lots of stamina, na, don't you know that? Two, three times also they can manage per night!'

More laughter followed. Magdalene picked a stick and threw it at Bah Kynsai, saying, 'You shameless creature!'

Bah Kit said, 'But I heard the government is providing free protection to poor folk, no?'

'But even that doesn't work, Bah Kit, that's what I have been trying to tell you,' I said. 'How do I know? I'll tell you a little story. Recently, in a West Khasi Hills village called Mawkohngei, a woman was given several packets of "protection" by the secretary of the village council. The secretary felt pity for her because she was giving birth to a child every year. As a kind of suo moto action, he donated to her some packets given to him by the block development officer and told her to ask her husband to use them. But when her husband was shown the stuff that night, he said, "*Araa*, is the government so rich or what to supply shirts for that thing also? It should give us real shirts instead, no?" He opened one of the packets and took out a piece. He looked at it very carefully, turning it over and over in his hands. Finally, he threw it and the rest of the packets in the fire and said, "I'm not a kid to play with balloons."'

'Tet leh, this Ap is also like Bah Kynsai!' Magdalene admonished, laughing along with the others.

'When I have to be, Mag,' I replied. 'The story must dictate its own language.' Then turning to the others, I said: 'You see, it would never work with many of them because of this kind of ignorant pride.'

'Well,' Bah Su said, 'protection or no protection, the moral should be, *to forgive is divine, but to keep on forgiving is a kind of prompting*. How's that?'

'Nice, Bah Su, nice!' Hamkom said.

Bah Kynsai said, 'Or, it could be, *to forgive is divine, but to keep on forgiving is bovine*, hahaha.'

Evening did not like Bah Kynsai's story very much. He thought it was too hard on the Khasi man in general. To counteract the story, he told us another one about a husband and wife having a heated altercation. The quarrel was so loud and furious—accompanied by objects being thrown around—that onlookers began to gather on the road near their house. Some of them wanted to go in and intervene before the couple could cause each other serious injury, but others stopped them, saying they should not interfere in a quarrel between husband and wife.

At that moment, the door of the house opened, and a small boy, sobbing and snuffling loudly, came running out. One of the elderly women on the road caught hold of him and said, 'Son, what is all that terrible noise? Is it your parents fighting?'

Through his tears, the boy replied, 'Yes. They are always fighting like this.'

'Who is your father, son?' the woman asked him.

'That's what they are quarrelling about, Mei.'

Evening concluded his story by saying, 'You see, it's not only the man who errs and has relationships with more than one woman. Women do the same and try to pass off bastards as their husband's children.'

'That may be true,' Bah Su said, 'but in this case, it seems more like a matter of suspicion than fact, Ning. The moral, therefore, should be, *do not build your home on suspicions*. If you are not sure about the person you are marrying, it's better not to marry at all.'

'Quite true, Bah Su,' Raji said, 'but what Ning says is true too, and all of us know it, apart from these two lovebirds and Ham, maybe. In fact, I have a story to prove the point.'

The story that Raji told us was about a woman who left her husband and promptly married another man. But the husband still missed his wife very much and would not look for another wife. Whenever the other man was at work, he used to go and visit his wife on the pretext of missing his children.

One day, he stayed longer than he should have, and was discovered by the man when he returned home in the evening. Seeing the first husband sitting by the hearth and his wife cooking rice gave him such a shock that he stood transfixed where he was, by the door. All he could do was stare at them speechlessly, wondering what was going on. When the first husband saw him staring like that, he demanded, 'What are you staring at? *U phas te u phas!*'

Everyone laughed, except Donald, who asked, 'Meaning, Bah Raji?'

'First is first!' Raji said.

Being the first, he believed he had every right to be there. Later, the second husband demanded that his wife choose between them. And he warned her that if she chose him, then she should never allow the first husband into the house again. From that time on, whenever the first husband came visiting because he missed his children, the woman quickly closed the door, but made her children stand by the window so he could look at them from outside. She did that until he gradually got tired of the window-gazing and vanished forever.

Another round of laughter followed Raji's story. Then I said, 'I have something similar.'

A man by the name of Returning, who had been married for many years, heard a rumour that his wife was seeing somebody else while he was at work. One day, he confronted her with this, but his wife denied everything. 'How could you even think I am capable of such a thing? Look, how many children do we have? Four? How can I have an affair with another man?'

Returning was not convinced. His source was very reliable. He gave her an ultimatum and said, 'Look, Wishful, if you tell me the truth, I'll forgive you, as long as you promise not to do it again. If you don't tell me the truth, I will leave right now and never come back!'

But Wishful still denied everything and protested her innocence. In anger, Returning gathered all his belongings and left for his mother's house that very night.

His mother tried her best to persuade him to go back to his wife. She said, 'Look, son, you have four children, you should not behave like this on the basis of mere suspicion. If you leave her, who will look after them? How will they grow up without a father, especially when their mother does not even have a job? Tomorrow you must go back home and make peace with your wife, do you hear? Think of your children, son, forget everything else.'

Returning thought his mother might be right, after all, and agreed to go back home. He said he would go that evening since he could not take leave from office because of some urgent work.

In the evening, Returning collected his suitcases from his mother's house and left for his own home. When he got there, the door was closed. He knocked and waited. When his wife opened the door, he said aloud, 'Surpriiise!' and then in a kind of sing-song, he continued, 'Wish, darling, did you miss me?'

But Wishful just stood there, staring at him with her mouth open. She was indeed surprised.

Returning pushed his way into the house and said, 'Come, come, my love, don't stand there as if you've never seen me before! Let's forget everything and make up. I'll never be such a bad husband again, come, darling, come!'

But when he went in, it was his turn to be struck dumb. A man was sitting by the hearth, playing with one of his children. Returning stared at the man and turned to Wishful for an explanation. And Wishful finally found her voice. 'I thought you had left for good!'

'Tet teri ka!' Bah Kynsai laughed aloud. 'And all in one day! But what happened after that?'

'What would happen? He was a self-respecting man. He did leave for good, but the new man did not stay for long. After that, the woman had to do menial work in people's houses to survive.'

Evening cursed the woman. 'Serves her right, the damn—'

'Don't say it, Evening, don't say it!' Magdalene warned him.

'I was only going to say she was a damn fool, why, is that also offensive?'

'Oh, sorry, I thought you were going to abuse women again. Yeah, yeah, you are right, she was a damn fool.'

Raji responded by shaking his head and saying, 'What a story, what a story! But I have heard of quite a few cases like this, you know, Ap. Did he support the children, though?'

'At first, he paid for their education only. He didn't have to, you understand, he was the aggrieved party here, but he was also a good man, and he loved his children above all. That was why, after a few months, he started taking care of their every need. The children too loved him very much, and when they were older, they came to live with him, for he never married again.'

There are indeed many stories of unfaithful women like Wishful. I know the story of a very rich man, for instance, who was dying of lung cancer when he was only forty-five or so. His name was Wanphai. He went to Vellore in Tamil Nadu for treatment, and after that to Guwahati, which is much nearer, for regular check-ups.

But Wanphai did not live long. He died only a few months after his treatment, and his passing was greeted with a sigh of relief. Everybody— relatives, friends, neighbours—thanked God for his mercy, for Wanphai had suffered extreme physical and mental agony during those last months.

A few hours after his death, because of some special instructions left with the lawyer, his wife and relatives were asked to gather in the drawing room for a will-reading. The dead man was survived by his wife and a young daughter, and everyone expected that all his wealth would go to them. And when the lawyer read the will, the dead man did mention his wife first of all. He said, 'To you, my dearest Hellweena, I have a gift; I was inspired in my gift for you by none other than the great Shakespeare. Shakespeare had left for his wife only his second-best bed. I, too, leave for you this putrefying body of mine. Part of my wealth shall go to the state cancer institute, and the rest shall be placed under the care of my sister, who will pass it on to my daughter when she comes of age. My sister will be given a generous monthly allowance for her trouble.'

When Hellweena first entered the room, she had trouble hiding her happiness. She was enjoying the thought of all the wealth that would come to her and was making all sorts of delightful plans. But when she heard what was written in the will, she broke into loud lamentations, beating her chest and tearing her hair and asking the lawyer, 'But why, why would he do a thing like this, tell me, Bah, why would he do a thing like this to me?'

Unable to hide her hatred any longer, Wanphai's sister shouted at her: 'Why don't you ask your lover with whom you have been having an affair since my brother was diagnosed with cancer, huh? With my brother gone, you thought you could live openly with him, huh? And enjoy my brother's wealth as you please, huh? And what did you say? Why did he do this to me? Phooey, you shameless slut!'

At this tirade, Hellweena suddenly stopped crying, got up and left the room. As a parting shot, she said, 'The vindictive son of a bitch!'

Bah Su raised his finger and said, 'I have a nice moral for this one, Ap: *as you give to the living so shall you receive from the dead*.'

'Beautiful paradox, Bah Su, beautiful!' Donald declared. 'But tell me, Bah Ap, did Shakespeare really leave his wife only his second-best bed?'

'That's what they say.'

'I enjoyed the story too, you know,' Magdalene said, 'but you guys behave as if only women cheat, ya.'

'No, that's not true at all, Mag,' Bah Kynsai contradicted her. 'You heard the story of Rit Shrieh, na? And all of us have had to listen to Evening telling us about all those kids Khasi women have to bring up on their own, so what more do you want? If a story is nice, na, Mag, we tell it, we don't care whether it's pro-this or pro-that.'

'Okay, okay, Mag, this one is definitely pro-woman,' I said and told them the story called 'Who Wanted a Divorce?'

Some years ago, a couple from Khliehshnong, Sohra, went before the headman and his executive committee to discuss their divorce. The headman asked the husband, 'What happened, Ex?'

Exstarson replied, 'Let her tell you about it, Bah. I'd like you to talk to her and find out for yourself.'

The headman turned to Peril, the wife, and said, 'What happened, Kong Pe? Both of you are still quite young and quite handsome too, well matched for each other, I must say, so what's happening? *Balei phi kwah pyllait san shyieng?*' ('Why do you want a divorce?')

Peril looked very surprised that such a question should be asked in a council and said, '*Shyieng! Oh, hooid nga bang bam doh shyieng.*' ('Bones! Oh yes, I love eating meat with bones.')

The headman ignored that, though the other men present started tittering. He asked her again, 'I said, why do you want a divorce? *U Ex u shait shoh ïa phi?*' ('Does Ex ever mistreat you?')

'*U Ex? Um ju ong phi-phi ïa nga, u ong beit pha-pha.*' ('Ex? He never addresses me lovingly as phi, he always calls me pha.')

Pha, as I have told you, is used when one addresses a woman rather roughly.

'I'm asking you,' the headman repeated, 'if your husband has ever mistreated you. *Lada u leh, phi shait leh kumno?*' ('If he has, how have you been coping with it?')

'*Kumno? Ïaei kumno?*' ('How? How about what?')

Irritated, but realising that she was hard of hearing, the headman shouted, 'Do you or don't you want to divorce your husband?'

Because the headman had shouted his question at the top of his voice, Peril heard him loud and clear and replied quite reasonably: 'It's not me who wants to divorce him. I love him. He's the one who wants to divorce me. He says he cannot have a meaningful conversation with me.'

'You see, Bah, you see?' Exstarson cried triumphantly. 'How can I live with her? You have to give me a divorce!'

Some of the executive members were heard sympathising with Exstarson: 'Yeah, yeah, how can the poor man live with such a person?'

But the headman looked sternly at Exstarson and said, 'Shame on you, Ex! Your wife is a beautiful woman, but she also has a problem. How can you abandon her in her misfortune? How many children do you have? Three? Now, how do you expect the poor woman to take care of your children on her own, in her condition? Your wife is hearing-impaired; instead of coming to me for a divorce, you should take her immediately to a doctor. Get her treated and report to me regularly! I shall monitor this case personally. The dorbar can never allow such an inhumane act. Get her treated, get her a hearing aid. You cannot divorce her just because she is hard of hearing. You should care for her! Now go, and don't waste any more of our time!'

Reacting to the story, Magdalene clapped her hands: 'Bravo, bravo! I wish we had more headmen like him, ya!'

'I wish our dorbars had that kind of power now, ha, Bah Kynsai?' Evening declared.

'Why not?' Bah Kynsai asked. 'It all depends upon the will of the people, na?'

'No, but people don't go to the dorbar for a divorce any more, no? They go to court, and that too, if their marriage was registered. If it's cohabitation only, then gone case: they can get help from no one, neither court nor dorbar.'

'They still go to dorbars in some areas, na, Ap?' Bah Kynsai asked. 'Anyway, come, come, let's move on.'

Dale surprised us again by saying, 'Since you people are talking about marriage, and men and women living together, no, Bah, I also have a small story.'

His story was about a young man who went to meet his girlfriend's father to ask for her hand in marriage. Well, not exactly marriage, but we'll come to that later. When his prospective father-in-law walked into the drawing room, the young man, without even introducing himself, said, 'I know that what I'm going to say to you is only a formality, and you may not like it, but, Bah, will you allow your daughter to live with me?'

The girl's father was livid. 'Live with you! Are you crazy? Who the hell are you? And who the hell said my permission is only a formality?'

Without batting an eyelid, the young man said, 'The gynaecologist!'

'Hahaha, you see, Bah, she was already pregnant!' Dale ended his story with a loud laugh. 'And that really happened, ha, Bah, to one of my friends.'

Magdalene asked, 'So, what did the father do?'

'What could he do? He had to give his permission, of course. Later, he went to beg his church leaders to conduct—'

'A shotgun wedding!' Bah Kynsai laughed.

'I was going to say postnatal wedding.'

'Do they do that sort of thing here, Bah Kynsai?' Donald asked.

'Some churches do, some don't. They call it *iathoh tymmen*, literally, "old people's wedding".'

'What about Niam Khasi?'

'We do perform such weddings,' Bah Kit answered. 'It's better than cohabitation, no? The problem is, when young people make mistakes like that, there are normally only two options, either cohabitation or desertion—the man running away.'

'Don't forget infanticide, Kit,' Bah Kynsai reminded him. 'At fifteen or sixteen, they want to have boyfriends, na, but when they have babies, they throw them into drains and leave them in toilets and dumping grounds, the little so-and-sos!'

'And who's to blame, Bah Kynsai, the girls?' Magdalene asked aggressively.

'Remember that song, Mag? "Oh girls, they wanna have fun." But seriously, na, everybody's to blame, boys, girls, parents, everybody.'

'I told you,' Evening cried, 'Khasi society is in deep shit, and all because—'

To stop Evening from returning to his favourite punching bag, Raji said quickly, 'On the same topic of wife, husband and dorbar, ha, Bah Kynsai, I also have a story, but it's quite different from your Rit Shrieh story.'

Raji told us about a woman with six young children, three boys and three girls, the youngest of whom was only a few months old. The woman had been married for about twelve years. Her husband was a good man, a misteri who worked with a building contractor, but for the last three years, he had been drinking heavily and not giving her money for housekeeping. She had to make do with what she earned from her work as a washerwoman. Fed up with the situation, she went to meet the headman of the locality and said, 'Bah, I'd like to complain about Nah, my husband.'

'Why? What did he do?' the headman enquired.

'Lately, he has fallen into the habit of drinking heavily, he comes home drunk every night, and at the end of the week, he never gives me any rice money.'

'So, what do you want me to do? I cannot stop him from drinking.'

'I know that, Bah, but you have the power to make him give me rice money, no? Failing that, I would like a divorce immediately.'

'Okay, but I'll need to convene a meeting of the dorbar. I'll arrange it for this coming Saturday, if that's all right with you. I'm sending a separate summons to your husband. Both of you have to appear before the dorbar, especially if there's going to be a divorce.'

The woman thanked the headman and went home.

The headman announced an emergency meeting of the council and sent summons to both husband and wife.

On the appointed day, the council gathered at the local football ground at 8 a.m. The meeting was scheduled early because many people, who were not employed by the government, had to go to work.

However, neither the woman nor her husband showed up. The councillors waited till 8.30 before they decided to disperse. Everyone was angry with the couple. The headman wanted to impose a hefty fine on them, but after careful deliberation, they decided to let the couple off 'just this once', for the sake of the woman who was so hard up and had so many mouths to feed on her own.

A week after that, the headman, while walking in the locality's commercial quarter, spotted the woman walking hand in hand with her husband, laughing gaily and looking like someone in love for the first time. They were headed in his direction, so he immediately crossed to the other side of the road, not wanting to embarrass them. The woman, however, saw the headman and crossed over to him. Then, coming very close, she whispered in his ear, 'He has given rice money.'

Magdalene laughed softly and said, 'All's well that ends well.'

'Yeah, because of the dorbar, Mag,' Raji replied. 'The husband was afraid of being punished.'

'Also, in this case,' Bah Kit added, 'the dorbar acted humanely. What the woman and her husband did, not appearing before the dorbar, was a serious offence, okay? But considering their poverty, the councillors did not impose a fine on them. Certainly not a Taliban-like act, ha, Raji?'

'But according to this story, Bah Raji,' Donald observed, 'it seems that there truly are Khasi men who behave like Ghosal's parasites: drinking away all their wages and living on their women's earnings.'

'There are many, many drunks, Don, no one denies that, but no one can live on their women's earnings, you know why? They would be promptly kicked out by the women's families, plus the dorbar is also there, no? Whatever you say, Ghosal has no right to accuse every Khasi man of being a parasite, no way, Don.'

'We have already discussed that, na?' Bah Kynsai said. 'Instead of quarrelling about the same thing again and again, let me tell you a story about a politician who was the chief guest at a football match.'

Bah Kynsai told us about a minister who was invited to give away the prizes at the final of a football tournament in a village in East Khasi Hills. The game was an exciting one, with both teams equally matched. Team A scored in the fortieth minute through a corner kick headed home by its centre back, and team B responded with an equaliser through a spectacular back kick by its centre forward. But after that, neither could score another goal, although there were plenty of very thrilling near misses on both sides. That forced the match into extra time in which there were some dramatic near misses again, but no goals. Eventually, the match had to be decided by a penalty shoot-out that was won, four to three, by team A.

There were many prizes to be given: 20,000 rupees and a silver cup for the winner, 10,000 and a copper cup for the loser, medals for all the players and cash prizes for the best player, the best scorer, the best goalie and the most disciplined player of the tournament. But before giving away the prizes, the minister was requested to speak a few inspiring words to the players and spectators.

The minister stood before the mike, puffed up his chest and said, 'I feel very privileged that you have called me to be your chief guest at this football tournament. However, I also feel disheartened a little bit. You see, football is the most popular sport in our state. There are hundreds of clubs, and everybody plays football, from kids on the streets to men and women in the fields. The game is so popular that we have all sorts of tournaments going on all the time, even in the cold of winter. We have inter-pig football tournaments, inter-bull, inter-goat, inter-rice and even inter-chicken or inter-duck football tournaments. But I am a little disheartened this time, you know why? I am disheartened because, despite the immense popularity of the game in our state, only two teams have reached the final this time. Therefore, I urge both players and team organisers and managers, et cetera, that next time they should make sure to see that more than two teams reach the final. Then it will be a truly exciting final! This time, as I said, I am a bit disheartened.'

'Tet leh, Bah Kynsai,' Hamkom protested, 'this is another tall tale, ya!'

'It's not a tall tale, mə, tdir!' Bah Kynsai cursed. 'Ask Ap, we were there together.'

'Yeah, yeah,' I confirmed, 'that was what he said. You know what our politicians are like, don't you?'

'Yeah, but how could he be that stupid?'

'There's another story about him, even more outrageous. But if I tell you, you will only say it's a tall tale.'

'Tell, tell, no, Ap,' Magdalene chimed in.

'Bah Kynsai's story is about NS, no?' Raji asked. 'I've heard it too. He's quite a crazy fellow that one, Ham, you have to believe it. Of course, there are plenty more like him.'

'Chalo, chalo, Ap,' Bah Kynsai ordered.

NS had been invited by one of the premier city hospitals to inaugurate a brand-new operation theatre. At the time, he was the minister of health and family welfare. The hospital's administrators thought that being invited to cut the ribbon would make him more amenable to their requests for financial help.

When the appointed day arrived, everything was ready by 10.30 a.m., thirty minutes before the scheduled time. By then, most of the invitees were assembled. Everyone was eager to see the operation theatre, which was being touted as the city's first state-of-the-art centre, with sophisticated equipment specially imported from Europe. All, that is, except the chief guest. But since it was only 10.30, nobody gave it much thought. However, when he did not make an appearance even by 11.15, everyone began to fidget. The organisers assured the guests that the minister would be coming very soon. 'He may be a little late, being a very busy man and all, but he'll be here soon enough,' they said.

But NS was not a little late. He was very late. By noon, everyone began to grumble, and many openly and loudly insulted him. 'Why, is it only his time that is precious? What about ours?' The organisers tried to reassure the guests again by saying that he was probably on the way. 'Please be patient and wait for just a little longer,' they said. 'We know that he's more than an hour late, but he'll definitely come, someone has already phoned him. He'll be here very soon.'

When some of the guests complained about the man's shamelessness, the organisers said, 'What to do, we also need him, no? He's in charge of the health ministry, after all. As they say, "No one is more desperate than those in dire need." Kindly wait for a little while longer, okay?'

When NS finally arrived at 12.30 p.m., and had been properly garlanded and bouqueted, everyone breathed a sigh of relief. The chairperson led him and the other guests of honour to their seats on the dais, and said, 'We will begin, okay, sir? We are a bit late—'

Ignoring her gentle reminder about his tardiness, NS replied peremptorily, 'Begin, begin. I also am in a hurry.'

The chairperson explained the programme to him. 'This is what we will do, sir. First, there will be a welcome song by members of the nursing staff, then our madam director will give a welcome speech, to be followed by a keynote address by the chief surgeon, who will tell us all about the operation theatre. Finally, we will call you to deliver your speech as the chief guest. Will that do, sir?'

'I know that's the usual programme, but today, don't mind, I really am in a hurry, I have another meeting outside town. Very urgent meeting! You do like this, after the welcome song, let me speak. After I have spoken, I'll cut the ribbon and then leave. You can continue with the programme as you wish.'

The chairperson did not like the arrangement one bit. They had been waiting for him for so long; the bugger could at least stay through the programme and give them some inspiration, she thought. But no, he would like to speak first and leave! What a pest! But what could she do? Necessity never makes a good bargain, as they say.

And so it was that after the welcome song, NS promptly took the mike.

'Whatever you say,' he began, 'I am full of praise for this hospital. Not only is it the best hospital in town, which is also very ready to help the poor and the needy, but, as you yourselves, respected guests, have seen, it is also very advanced in its thinking. You see, whenever I came to visit patients in a hospital, I used to feel pity for them. I used to think, what would these poor souls do alone in the hospital after their relatives have gone home? They have nothing to do but sleep in their beds. Many of them have even got bedsores from too much sleeping. Therefore, I tell you, I'm full of praise for this hospital, which is really, really advanced in its thinking. You see, so that the patients will not feel bored, this hospital has constructed for them no less than a theatre! I firmly believe that, with the presence of this theatre, the patients will be able to entertain themselves with all sorts of dramas.'

The other guests—among whom were nurses, doctors, scholars, well-known personalities and journalists—started giggling softly. When the giggles threatened to explode into roaring laughter, some of them covered their mouths with their handkerchiefs and shawls. Others laughed softly into their coats or sweaters, and still others bent their heads and buried their faces in their hands, shaking with laughter and streaming tears. But NS never noticed any of that. He went on and on, extolling the hospital theatre that would entertain the patients.

Hamkom exclaimed, 'That's too much, Ap, that's too damn much, man!'

'I knew you wouldn't believe me,' I said. 'But it happens to be the truth.'

'It's true, it's true, Ham,' Raji corroborated. 'Why, haven't you heard about NS and the crazy stories about him?'

'I can well believe it, Ham,' Magdalene said. 'You know why? Last year, my colleagues and I were asked to attend a workshop organised by the District Institute of Education and Training, okay? You were also supposed to be there, I think, but you didn't come. Everybody knows that this institute is known simply as DIET, no? Okay, so, when the minister of education came to inaugurate the workshop—'

'It was MD, I think?' Raji asked.

When Magdalene nodded, he said, 'Yeah, I remember it well. It was so stupid that we decided not to telecast her speech.'

'You should have, man, that would have taught her a lesson. Anyway, as I was saying, when she came to inaugurate the workshop, she ... do you know what she spoke about from the beginning to the end? She spoke about nutritional diets. She thought DIET was all about proper diets for the sick, hahaha.'

After everyone had stopped laughing, Raji said, 'You see, Ham, that's the kind of people we have as leaders. And why? Because most of our rural folk, ha, are either illiterate or semi-literate. They don't know whom to choose. Most of them are happy with those who wine and dine them during elections and those who help them with small things during feasts and bereavements.'

'I absolutely agree, Raji,' Evening said. 'One hundred per cent. But what moral shall we give to all these stupid-politician stories?'

'*Choose a leader who is a leader*,' Bah Su said.

'Or,' Bah Kynsai added, '*what can we expect from a leader who doesn't know his arse from his elbow?*'

'I like that, Bah Kynsai,' Evening laughed. 'Fits some of them to perfection, the buggers!'

'That may be true,' Donald responded, 'but you seem to really dislike politicians, no, Bah Kynsai?'

'Who doesn't dislike them, lih? They call themselves servants of the people, na, but they only serve their own pockets.'

'That reminds me of a little story about a politician from Ri War, Bah Kynsai. Shall I tell?' Evening asked.

One of Evening's friends had drawn his attention to this man. 'Look at that big fat man, Ning,' his friend said. 'Do you see him, the one speaking on his mobile, yes, the one who's followed around by two bodyguards?'

When Evening nodded, his friend told him: 'That fellow used to be matchstick-thin and dog-poor, okay? He had no job prospects at all. So, what did he do? He started following the local MLA around. Having a glib and oily tongue, and a ready-to-lick-arse attitude, he soon endeared himself to the MLA, who gave him most of the lucrative building contracts from the MLA Local Area Development Scheme. After he had made some money, ha, he bit the hand that fed him and contested the next MLA election against his own patron. And everywhere he went to canvass, he said, you know what he said? He swore that he would get rid of poverty, roots and all. He has already won two terms now. Look at him, a crorepati, and bursting at the seams. He really has kept his pledge!'

Evening concluded his story by saying, 'Bah Kynsai is absolutely right. That's the kind of politicians we have! They speak with the tone of a murmuring brook, but their hearts are laced with venom, like the arrows of war. They have nothing inside them but a cold, hard indifference that has driven students to the streets and boys to the therapy of the gun! They have nothing but the kind of rottenness that would sell even our holy mountains for a car and a few concubines—'

'Since when did you start caring for our holy mountains?' Raji interrupted tartly.

'I'm quoting from a poem by someone,' Evening replied rather lamely.

'Ah, that explains it! I was wondering how a man like you could—'

'No, quarrelling, no quarrelling!' Bah Kynsai said quickly. 'Moral?' he demanded.

Bah Su responded immediately. '*When a crook keeps his promise, it is still a broken promise.*'

'True, true,' Bah Kynsai said excitedly. 'Once, na, I went with an MLA, a friend of mine, to a Ri Bhoi village that falls in his constituency … We went there to canvass for my friend's party candidate, who was contesting for Parliament, but when we got there, na, we were immediately mobbed by the entire population. I was scared shitless, I tell you. But you know what? My friend coolly asked them what the problem was. Speaking for them all, the headman said, "Three years ago, you said if we elected you MLA, you would make sure our village got electricity. But till now, there's no sign of a single electric post anywhere. What have you got to say about that?"

'When I heard that, na, I thought we were goners. But my friend was quite unmoved. His dark, fat face showing great surprise, he said, "Waa, how is that? I myself had promised you that your village would get electricity immediately, do you remember? How come you haven't got it till now? You should have come to report the matter to me immediately! Without a doubt, someone who hates me, or hates your village, has sabotaged the project. I will look into it the moment I get back. I will look into it! But for now, please elect our party candidate as your member of Parliament, okay? I will solve all your problems, don't worry, I'm here, no?"

'And the poor villagers were fooled once again by his promises. But from that time, na, I never went anywhere with the bugger again.'

'Most of them are incorrigible hypocrites, Bah Kynsai,' Bah Kit said in a tone of disgust. 'In fact, I have a story called "Hypocrisy", which also deals with politicians.'

In the story, some friends were discussing the topic of hypocrisy. One of them, Muthok, declared, 'What I hate most in a friend is hypocrisy.'

Everyone agreed, but after a while, many of them felt a bit uneasy about the statement, for who is completely free of this common failing? At one time or another, all of them had behaved like hypocrites. Therefore, they tried to qualify Muthok's declaration. One of them said, 'Hypocrisy is indeed repugnant, Bah Mut, but we don't really think it's evil, or what do you think, Bah Shem?'

Shemphang agreed with Muthok all the way, but he also understood why the others were asking that question. So, he decided to answer with an example. He said, 'The government has always spoken of the blessings of ecotourism, hasn't it, my friends? It spends lakhs of rupees every year advertising the need for ecotourism and organising seminars and conferences to highlight its virtues. Yet, about ten years ago, it also allowed eleven factories in Byrnihat to use charcoal as their power source. According to reports, these factories have consumed more than 5.61 lakh metric tons of charcoal so far. Now, can you imagine the number of trees that were felled for this? Lakhs and lakhs, certainly. But not only that, okay, the same reports say the government contracted an out-of-state company to distribute the charcoal without calling for a tender. And it did all that *after* the Supreme Court ban on timber-felling across the country.'

They all cried out angrily, 'What a rotten government we have here, no? Instead of implementing the court ruling, it helps factories to violate it, tet teri ka, what kind of government is this? Why is it always like this in our state, Bah Shem?'

'This is hypocrisy, don't you see? The keeper of the law is also its violator. Now, would you still say that hypocrisy is repugnant but not evil? You ask why it is always like this in our state; the reason is that we have chosen leaders who are not only stupid but also hypocritical and greedy. Have you heard what one minister said about the environment during the last World Environment Day? When journalists asked him what he understood by the word "environment", he said, "Environment is planting trees, and now that I have planted one tree, you can say that I love environment." Then he went to his office and signed documents permitting fourteen cement factories to be opened in one district alone. And on the wall behind his desk are these words from the Bible, "let not thy left hand know what thy right hand doeth". You see, a man who is a hypocrite does not even hesitate to misuse words from holy texts … Now, would you still say that hypocrisy is merely repugnant and not evil?'

When his friends nodded, Shemphang said, 'Actually, this also depends upon the position that one occupies. *In a man with power, hypocrisy is equivalent to evil.*'

Magdalene laughed and said, 'Thank God we don't have any power!'

'Yahoo, our hypocrisy is harmless!' Raji said.

Bah Su, however, took them seriously. 'You are missing the point completely, you two. That was a very good moral, in fact. It's the common practice of our government, ha, to make laws and then to violate them at will. I have a little story to prove the point.'

In his story, two men were sitting together in a bus. One of them was a chain-smoker, while the other did not smoke at all. The smoker, whose name was Pullingstone, kept lighting one cigarette after another, filling the entire bus with smoke. The non-smoker, simply known as Dei, had to keep his nose covered with his handkerchief all the time. When he could stand it no more, he said, 'Please stop smoking, Bah. Don't you see that sign? It says, "No smoking inside the bus!" Why don't you follow the rule and think about people who don't smoke?'

Pullingstone pretended not to hear and went on puffing furiously. Earlier, he took at least a short break between cigarettes, but now, because Dei had complained, he smoked without pause. As soon as one cigarette was burnt to the stub, he immediately lit up another. Dei was getting more enraged by the minute. His handkerchief did not help at all. He was literally choking on Pullingstone's cigarette smoke, but because he was the decent type, he merely said again in a polite tone, 'Do you know that a large portion of this smoke is getting into my lungs, Bah? Please stop, will you?'

Pullingstone, mistaking Dei's politeness for weakness, said, 'Really? In that case, since one cigarette costs me five rupees, you'll have to pay me two rupees fifty paise for every cigarette I smoke.'

Dei was now absolutely incensed. He shouted, 'Why should I pay you, you shameless creature? You have not an iota of civic sense! You are puffing non-stop like a factory chimney and spoiling my lungs in the process, and you have the nerve to ask me to pay for your cigarettes! Don't you have any manners at all? What do you teach your children if this is how you behave in a public place?'

Soon, there was a terrible row between the two. They would have come to blows too, but for the fact that the other passengers came to separate them after asking the driver to stop the bus.

Pullingstone was asked by the driver to sit somewhere else, and calm was soon restored. But before the driver returned to his seat, Dei asked, 'Bah, why do you have that "No Smoking" sign if you allow your passengers to smoke?'

Because the driver was himself a smoker, he replied morosely, '*Shu buh.*' ('Just keeping.')

Bah Su ended the story by saying, 'You see that? *A law only for show is nothing but a cause of discord.*'

'Many laws are only on paper, Bah Su,' Evening said, 'but you are right, Khasis have no civic sense at all. When it comes to hypocrisy, we are worse than our politicians. And yet, we call ourselves a community that follows the laws of man and God! I think we rather follow the laws of thieves and cut-throats.'

Bah Kynsai took a sip from his bamboo mug and said, 'What to do? We are what we are, but we don't know what we are ... Anybody else?'

I said I had a short one and told them a story called 'Model Code of Conduct'. This was partially a found story, in the sense that I had overheard it on the street in Police Bazaar. It was a conversation between a beggar and a politician, who had just emerged from the old Legislative Assembly building, the one that was later burnt to the ground.

As the MLA was walking out of the entrance facing Khyndai Lad, the nine junctions of the bazaar, a beggar, who was sitting by it, pulled at his coat and said in a broken and mournful voice, '*Babu, paisa de na.*' ('Babu, please give me some money.')

'Tet, you bloody fool!' the politician said harshly. 'Don't you know that the Model Code of Conduct has come into effect?'

'*Eh, kya bola, Babu?*' ('Eh, what did you say, Babu?')

'The Model Code of Conduct, you idiot! MCC, you understand? It's imposed by the Election Commission of India. Do you know that, according to this law, anyone contesting the MLA election cannot give any money to anybody after the announcement of the polling date? This is mentioned in Article—eh, what article is it?—anyway, an article in the Constitution of India, you know that? The election is drawing very near, you understand? And I am a candidate, if I give you money, ha, I will be immediately disqualified. Go, don't ask anything from us when MCC has been invoked! Go, beg elsewhere!'

Hamkom laughed. 'This one is a tall tale for sure, don't deny it, Ap!'

'Most stories about our politicians sound like tall tales, Ham, but actually, they are not. You should know that by now.'

'You cannot expect anything from a politician,' Raji sang out, 'unless he thinks it will benefit him too. A beggar cannot scratch his back, no?'

'Hey, Raji, that could very well be our moral, man!' Evening enthused.

'Or we could say,' Bah Su said, '*he who doesn't want to give has many excuses to give*. And this does not apply only to politicians.'

'You mean it could also apply to Halolihim refusing to donate, Bah Su?' Magdalene asked.

'To anybody with excuses like that.'

Evening raised a finger and said, 'I also overheard an interesting conversation, ha, between a politician and a locality headman at a funeral gathering.'

A local MLA was lambasting a colleague who had left the party with some of his followers. He called him all sorts of names and finally condemned him as a traitor.

The headman, who was listening patiently, finally asked him, 'Why do you call Bah Dry a traitor, Bah Las?'

Lasting, the MLA, put on an air of great astonishment and replied, 'Why, Bah Ton? Because Dryland left our party and took some of our MLAs with him, of course!'

The headman thought he had him trapped, and asked again, 'But recently some MLAs also defected to your party, no? So how would you describe them?'

Gesturing expansively with his hands, Lasting replied, 'They have turned over a new leaf, Bah Ton! They have finally seen the light! Our party is the best, after all.'

As he said that, his fat, round face broke into a broad smile, and everybody, including the headman, laughed at his unassailable wit.

'This reminds me of my friend, Winwell,' Bah Kynsai said. 'I think you know him, Ap, he completed his Master's in English from our university. He's quite a joker, that guy! Now he's a lawyer, but earlier, na, he used to be an active politician. Do you know how he entered politics? One day, he applied for the post of junior spokesman at the local branch of a national party, okay? After an in-person interview, he was asked to submit his résumé. A week after that, na, he received a letter from the party's general secretary. And the letter said something like this: "Dear Mr Winwell, we find the write-up about yourself to be full of exaggerations, roundabout explanations, confounding half-truths and downright lies … So, when can you join us?"

'That's the nature of politics in Meghalaya, na?' he concluded with a laugh.

'That's the nature of politics everywhere, Bah Kynsai,' Donald responded. 'But certainly, it's better or worse in a particular place, depending on the nature of the electorate.'

'That's very perceptive, Don,' I said, 'you—'

'He doesn't need your praise, man, but we need your stories,' Bah Kynsai intervened. 'Come on, tell, tell!'

I told them the story of Joyly Lyngdoh, a parliamentary candidate for the Shillong Lok Sabha constituency. Badly mauled at the hustings, having got only a small fraction of the votes, he was inconsolable for days. Watching him cry day after day, his wife was becoming quite depressed herself. Finally, when she could take it no more, she decided to give him a little pep talk.

'Actually, you know, Kpa,' she said, 'you should rejoice. Just imagine, 1,017 people gave you their votes! Isn't that something? With so many people loving and trusting you with their hearts and souls, how can you not be happy?'

'Come on, Kmie, why do you jest about a serious thing like this? Do you know how many voters there are in the constituency? About eighteen lakh! Aren't my bitter tears moving you to pity at all? Why are you mocking me instead?'

'Waa! Why should I mock you, Kpa? Of course I feel pity for you! That's why I'm giving you this advice. Personally, okay, I never knew we had as many as 1,017 people who love us. Look at the bright side, Kpa, always. Do you remember those two friends of yours? What are their names? Bah Parodyli and Bah Lorens, no, Kpa? You remember what they said when they met you after a long time? I still remember it perfectly. Parodyli said, "Waa, U Joy! What's happening to you? Your hair is all white, man?" But the very next day, when you met Bah Lorens, what did he say? "Arre, Joy, how are you, ya? You look good, you know that? And your hair is still almost black, ya! Look at me, completely bald!" Now, Kpa, what kind of man would you like to be, like Parodily or Bah Lorens? It's the attitude that counts, don't you see, Kpa?'

Joyly thought his wife's words made sense. He cheered up a little, and then, more than a little. Soon, he was infused with a kind of zest again, and in his excitement, he cried out, 'It's true, Kmie, it's true, it's the attitude that counts! Next time, okay, Kmie, next time we will see … Next time we will show them, Kmie, the two of us will show them! Just you wait!'

Donald chuckled and said, 'This one is a very different story, Bah Ap, not politician-bashing. It shows us quite a different side to them: the never-say-die attitude.'

Bah Kynsai protested. 'Don, Don, you are getting us all wrong. You see, when we say that politicians are corrupt, self-serving and greedy, we may be politician-bashing, but the stories we have told you, na, these are true stories, man!'

'Why, Don, don't you know what they say of people in the Northeast?' Raji asked.

When he shook his head, Raji said, 'In the Northeast, no, Don, they say, "The 1st Divs become doctors, lawyers and engineers; the 2nd Divs become bureaucrats and control the 1st Divs; the 3rd Divs enter politics, become ministers and control the other two. The dropouts join the militants and control all the above!" Hahaha.'

Many of us laughed and said, 'That's true, that's true, man!'

But Donald disagreed. 'That sounds like exaggeration, ya!'

Raji took a sip from his mug and replied, 'You think so? Then go ahead and think so. But remember, there is no exaggeration without foundation.'

'Wa, wa, what a profound statement, Raji!' Evening laughed.

Raji smiled self-contentedly, took another sip and said, 'Now what, Bah Kynsai?'

'What do you mean, now what? More stories, of course! The night is still young, na? Are there any more stories about politicians? If not, we can tell any other stories; it doesn't matter—'

'As long as they are entertaining and have a moral,' Evening reminded us.

Dale raised his hand and said, 'Bah Kynsai, earlier Bah Kit was telling a story about hypocrisy, no? I'll tell one about the same thing, okay?'

A bus conductor had told Dale this story. A male passenger was sleeping on the bus. The man had, in fact, shut his eyes as soon as he saw women board the overcrowded bus, and did not open them again for hours. When the bus neared its destination, the conductor noticed the sleeping man and went to wake him up.

The conductor said, 'Hey, Bah, wake up, wake up, we are nearly there.'

'It's okay, it's okay,' the man replied, 'I was not sleeping.'

'You were not sleeping? But your eyes were shut, no?'

'Oh, I was just shutting them because I couldn't bear the sight of women standing while many of us men are sitting.'

Dale concluded the story with a laugh. 'If that is not hypocrisy, then what is?' he asked.

'Your story doesn't sound like much,' Evening said dismissively. 'What moral can we have from this?'

Bah Su said, 'Actually, this is a good one, ha, Ning. It's not only about hypocrisy but also about how we tend to ignore problems, be it at home, in the workplace or society at large. Many of us behave like tortoises, withdrawing our heads into our half-dome shells at the first sign of trouble. The moral of the story can be: *ignoring our problems will not make them vanish on their own.*'

'But shutting his eyes did work for the guy, didn't it, Bah Su?' Magdalene asked.

'The women were still standing, weren't they?' Bah Su countered. 'Their problem was completely ignored, wasn't it?'

Evening, who could now see sense in Bah Su's explanation, said, 'Like the problem we are ignoring in our matrilineal society, ha—'

'Not that again,' Bah Kynsai broke in.

'No, Bah Kynsai, this is not the same thing,' Evening said emphatically. 'The fact is that this system is imploding, and we must never, never ignore it. If you listen to the story of Men Kiri, you will see what I mean.'

Men Kiri, 'old' Kiri, was deserted by her grandchildren and had to live all alone in Shillong. But it was not always like that. She had a daughter who lived in their village with her husband and many children: four sons and five daughters.

When Men Kiri moved to Shillong to take up a job there, her daughter, Twinty, sent her second daughter, Lilymerry, to live with her grandmother. The two were very happy together, and loved each other very much. When Twinty died of tuberculosis and left her children to the care of her husband, nothing changed for them. But then, Lilymerry got married, and her husband, a non-Khasi, refused to live in the same house as his grandmother-in-law. Lilymerry was forced to follow him, for, being unemployed, she depended on him for everything. The other granddaughters, because their mother was no more, did not feel obliged to go and live with their grandmother either. Their father did try to persuade them, but no one wanted to go. Some had husbands and children of their own; the others did not want to leave their village.

Meanwhile, Men Kiri retired from her job and continued to live alone, although many more of her grandchildren, male and female, had by then moved to Shillong to work in government offices.

One day, Men Kiri fell very ill. All alone and confined to bed, she could not eat or drink anything, not even a glass of water. She would have died, had it not been for a neighbour, who discovered her condition and took her to a hospital, where she was put on a drip and given all sorts of injections.

The neighbour informed Men Kiri's grandchildren, who came flocking to the hospital. Their reassuring presence and the care she received at the hospital soon helped her regain some of her health and strength. When she was almost fully recovered, Men Kiri was discharged from the hospital and taken home by her grandchildren.

At home, her eldest grandson, Buheh, called for a meeting to discuss the situation. In the presence of his brothers and sisters, and their children, he opened the discussion by saying, 'What happened to our Meiieit must never happen again. She could have died if Kong Mai had not found her.'

The others readily agreed, and the thin, wrinkled face of Men Kiri broke into a beatific smile, for, at last, her grandchildren were about to make a decision never to leave her alone again. Then Buheh added, 'From now on, we must provide her with a mobile so she can call us should she fall ill again.'

His words were like a thunderclap and instantly erased the smile from Men Kiri's face. Her eyes hardened as she looked at them. 'These ungrateful wretches, these *khun jynreiñ*, children of a louse, who come from the flesh to feed on the flesh, how can they be my very own grandchildren?' she asked herself. When she spoke aloud, it was in the harshest of tones. But she did not say much, only this: 'A mobile? Why not a gun so the business would be quicker?'

Evening's last statement was as shocking to us as it must have been for Men Kiri's grandchildren. There was something both chilling and ridiculous in it, and we did not know whether to laugh or to shake our heads in disbelief.

Finally, Bah Kynsai said, 'Deadly sarcasm, Ning, deadly!'

As soon as the spell was broken, Magdalene asked, 'Then what happened?'

'Why do you keep asking what happened and spoil the punchline?' Raji asked her, annoyed.

But everybody else wanted to know too, so Evening said, 'Men Kiri is now dead. She died alone.'

Magdalene felt so bad about it that she cried out, 'Crap, man! What a shit thing to do to their own grandmother!'

'And there are many more cases like this, okay?' Evening claimed. 'More and more elderly people are ending up in old-age homes, and more and more children are ending up in orphanages. Something must be done about this. Even our clan system, which used to make sure that each took care of its own, seems to be failing.'

The story had us all depressed. It is true, more and more old-age homes and orphanages are beginning to emerge in Khasi society. But Bah Kit insisted that it was not because of the matrilineal clan system. 'It's rather the confusion that prevails among us and all that systemic corruption we talked about,' he said. 'All we have to do is make some corrections—'

'Yeah, yeah,' Raji supported him, 'replacing the system with patriliny would only cause chaos greater than that caused by the partition of India.'

'Why?' Evening demanded.

'Because of the hopeless confusion it would bring, man! I'm talking about the confusion in the process by which we determine our cognate and agnate kin. And then, what if half the population agrees to the change and the other half opposes it? Think about that chaos too!'

'Let's forget it,' Bah Kynsai said. 'Evening's system will never work. He himself has been rejected by Mawñiuh, his father's clan, and Diengdoh, his mother's clan, so what is he then? Even he doesn't know. But we have already discussed all that, na? Let's talk about something else. Let me give you a little comic relief, okay? After Evening's depressing story, na, I think we all deserve it.'

Bah Kynsai told us the story of a woman who was working in a private company, or rather, not working at all. She came to office very late, and immediately set about disturbing the other staff by telling them gossipy stories about her friends and neighbours. And that's what she did until the canteen people came with their tea and snacks. After tea, it was her habit to take out her knitting materials.

The manager was thoroughly sick of her. He reprimanded her every day, but the moment he turned his back, she went back to her gossiping or knitting. And there was nothing he could do, apart from shouting at her. The woman was related to one of the directors on the company's board and her contract with the company did not allow him, for the time being at least, to sack her. Therefore, after consulting with some other officers, he came up with a plan. One day, he called her to his room and said, 'Kong, after long deliberations with the other officers, the management has chosen you for a special incentive; it has decided to promote you and raise your pay—'

Overjoyed, she asked excitedly, 'With effect from when, sir?'

'Hmm,' the manager drawled, 'we decided to promote you and raise your pay the moment you start working, but, and this is a big but, we will put you on probation for the entire term of your contract.'

The story did succeed in making us laugh, but Donald, wanting to tease Bah Kynsai, said, 'And of course, this is also a true story!'

'Of course! That's why, na, in many of these stories, we haven't mentioned the characters' names or their descriptions. We don't want to expose them, understand? Some of them may even be your friends or relatives, who knows? After all, Khasi society is very small, na?'

'Does that mean that the stories with names and descriptions are not true?' Donald asked smugly, thinking he had Bah Kynsai cornered.

'Haven't we told you they are true, liah?' Bah Kynsai exploded. 'When we give you names and descriptions, na, it means that the stories are not potentially defamatory. That's why we spoke of all those political and historical characters, na? But in this story, for instance, do you think I should reveal her identity?'

'You cannot trap this old fox, Don,' Raji said matter-of-factly.

'I think whether this story is true or not is beside the point,' Evening said impatiently. 'The fact is that most office workers, especially those in government offices, behave exactly like that woman.'

'That's it, Ning,' Bah Kynsai agreed. 'Next.'

Dale raised his hand and said, 'I will tell, Bah Kynsai.'

A beautifully dressed woman entered an overcrowded bus. Dale's friend, the bus conductor from his earlier story, was immediately smitten by the woman, who was fair and tall and, in his words, "*kaba ibang bha*", very tasty-looking. Wanting to be chivalrous, he looked around the bus, trying to find an empty seat for her. But there was none. As a last resort, he requested a woman sitting nearby to make room for the tasty-looking newcomer. He said, 'Kong, could you please make room for this Kong also?'

But the woman taunted him: 'Just because she's stylish, you want me to make room for her? What about all those other women standing? And if I make room for her in my seat, will you charge me only half the fare?'

Behind this woman sat an elderly man, who did not look very well at all. When he overheard the conversation, he felt pity for the tasty-looking woman and gave up his seat for her.

The woman sat down very quickly, as if afraid somebody might take it from her, and then, making a dig at the other woman, said, 'And you, Bah, how much should I give you?'

The man, who was standing by the seat he had just vacated, was taken by surprise. He did not like the question at all, or the tone she used. However, he only said, 'Why should you pay me anything?'

After some time, though, he suddenly turned to her and said, 'Excuse me! What did you say, Kong?'

The woman looked up at him and said gruffly, 'I didn't say anything.'

'Oh,' the man replied, 'I thought you said *khublei shibun*, thank you very much, are you sure you did not say that?'

Reacting to the little story, Magdalene said, 'Wow! That's what you call a subtle put-down, man!'

'Because the man was from Sohra, no, Kong, that's why,' Dale explained. 'People from there can be very subtle in their censure.'

'Is that true, Ap?' Magdalene cross-checked with me.

'Many of them are,' I agreed. 'If you visit somebody's house in the evening, for instance, and if the host thinks you have overstayed your welcome, he might say, "Uff, I really enjoyed that! When you are having fun, you know, time just flies." If you are a sensitive person, you will catch on very quickly, but if you are not, and you decide to stay on, the host might pretend to yawn and then immediately say, "Oh, I'm so sorry, I don't know how that one got out at all."

'But if you still don't get the point, then the host might well do what my uncle Madeng used to do when his friend Bah Kelan visited him on the weekends and lingered late into the night. Madeng, as I told you, was used to getting up at the second cockcrow even when he was not going to work. So, he couldn't afford to let anyone disturb his bedtime. Whenever Bah Kelan came calling, therefore, he tried his best to get rid of him as soon as possible. But because anything subtle would be lost on his rascally friend, Madeng adopted a more direct method. As Bah Kelan was enjoying himself, gossiping with the rest of our family, he would vanish into the kitchen, soak some logs in water and then burn them in the fire. Soon the whole house would be full of smoke, and everyone would be heard coughing and opening doors and windows. When that happened, Bah Kelan would say, "There goes Deng!" and saying that, he would leave immediately, for it was impossible to carry on a meaningful conversation with all that smoke going for their eyes and lungs.'

'Hahaha,' Magdalene guffawed in delight. 'Smoking out your own guest! There's your Sohra subtlety!'

'Your Madeng seemed to be quite a character, ha, Ap?' Bah Kynsai laughed. 'But you did say the two were close friends, na?'

'Yeah, thick as thieves, so to speak, until that matter with Bulbul. One day, having heard the smoke story from my mother, I asked him about it. In response, he said, "Some people have to be literally smoked out." When I reminded him that Bah Kelan was supposed to be his friend, he replied, "A true friend shouldn't mind a little smoke."'

'Yeah, that's true, Ap,' Evening said. 'But what could be the moral of Dale's story, huh?'

'*Gratitude is all that counts,*' Bah Su promptly replied.

'Good, good,' Bah Kynsai said and added, 'Hey guys, from Sohra's subtlety to Laitmu's vanity, okay?'

'Hey, hey, careful, Bah Kynsai, you are talking about our locality, man!' Magdalene warned.

Bah Kynsai playfully gave her the thumbs down and went ahead with the story, which he called 'With a Song'.

One evening, he told us, some of his acquaintances were discussing the relative merits of the various localities of Shillong. After moving from locality to locality for a while, one of them suddenly declared, 'But as dirty a locality as Laitmu I have never found anywhere, man!'

'Dirty? Is it really that dirty, Jied?' Mang asked in surprise.

'No, no, I don't mean that it's full of filth or anything like that, Mang,' Jied clarified. 'I mean its people, man. Because most of the English-medium schools are located there, okay, they act as if they are the most modern, the most knowledgeable, and the only ones who can speak English or sing English songs. They are so arrogant that they won't even speak their own language: only English for them!'

'Ah, now I understand,' Mang said. 'You mean their vanity, right? Yeah, you are quite right, Jied. But they are not really all that good, you know. For instance, you said they act as if they are the only ones who know English, but if you look at the university, most of the Khasi teachers in the various departments are not from there. And in the English department itself, there's not even one. Even in the colleges, only a few are from Laitmu. Furthermore, when you look at Khasi writers writing in English—I'm referring only to those who have made their mark on the national scene, mind you—most of them are from elsewhere. They are just dreadfully conceited, that's all.'

All of them nodded in agreement. Encouraged, Mang went on, 'And do you know what they are saying about them now? Because they feel so "standard", they are not even allowing the chana wallah to use his little bell.'

'The chana wallah is not allowed to use his bell!' they all exclaimed in surprise. 'Why, why?'

'Because they say it's adding to the noise pollution.'

'Tet leh!' they all cried in an incredulous tone. 'So what are the chana wallahs doing, then?'

'It seems that the dorbar has issued an order asking all peddlers to sing a song instead of using their bells.'

'But what song can a chana wallah sing, man?' they asked.

'Their place is the rock-and-roll capital of India, isn't it? So, what else but pop?'

'A pop song for a chana wallah! How? Do tell, man!'

'He's supposed to sing, "*Chana-na-na-na! Hey! Chana-na-na-na!*"'

Magdalene, Donald and Hamkom protested loudly. 'Tet leh, Bah Kynsai! You cannot tell that sort of joke about our locality, man! And don't say it's true, because it's not!'

Bah Kynsai laughed his big, booming laugh.

Raji, however, said, 'The story about the chana wallah may not be true, but it's a fact that everyone in Shillong thinks the people of Laitmu are vain and pretentious.'

'But why? We are not like that! Are they really saying that sort of thing about us, Ap?' Magdalene asked.

'Unfortunately, they are.'

'But why?'

'Mostly, I think it's plain envy,' I replied. 'It cannot be denied that Laitumkhrah is the most developed of all the localities in Shillong—'

'No, no,' Evening interrupted, 'what Mang said in the story is very true. Most of the officers and professors and writers are not from Laitmu.'

'That may be so,' I argued, 'but that doesn't make the place any less developed or any less enlightened—'

'Or any less liberal-minded,' Donald chipped in. 'You are right, Bah Ap, it's plain envy.'

'But you cannot deny that most people from there speak more English than Khasi, Ap, and that's what has been putting people off, no?' Evening persisted.

'That's true, unfortunately. But to be fair to them, most educated Khasis in Shillong, regardless of where they live, pretend to know more English than Khasi—'

'Ap, Ap, I can see two morals in this story,' Bah Su said excitedly. '*Vanity provokes censure* and *envy sees no good even in the best*. Okay?'

'I was just thinking of the same thing myself, Bah Su,' I replied. 'Takes care of both arguments.'

All of a sudden, Dale said, 'I don't know what you big people are arguing about, for me, ha, it was a beautiful story. I shall remember "chana-na-na-na" forever.'

Bah Kit, who was enjoying it all, said, 'Do you see what kind of quarrel your story has provoked, Bah Kynsai?'

'It's not a quarrel; it's a healthy debate, Kit,' Bah Kynsai replied. Then, turning to me, he added, 'Hey, Ap, why don't you tell them a story that will stop all this yapping?'

So I started on a story about a coolie's medical operation.

Once, not so long ago, a Nepali coolie, whom everyone called Daju, met with a serious car accident at a place called Stand Jeep, one of the busiest commercial hubs in Shillong. His friend, Samlem, a Khasi coolie, hired a taxi and rushed him to Civil Hospital. He then informed Daju's relatives, using the numbers saved on his friend's mobile phone.

When the relatives arrived at the hospital, they were informed that Daju had to be operated upon immediately. For that, blood was needed urgently. The relatives straightaway had themselves tested, but none except one shared Daju's rare AB+ blood type. However, he was not eligible since he had a large tattoo on his right arm. It was then that Samlem offered to donate his blood, which turned out to also be AB+.

Daju was operated upon with all the haste that his severe injuries demanded. The operation was successful, and Daju, after about two weeks in the Intensive Care Unit, was declared out of danger and brought to the General Ward, where they kept him on a drip for some more days. When they finally told him that he could eat some solid food, Daju demanded a bowl of beef soup.

His relatives begged him not to ask for beef soup. They said, '*Bhaiya*, how can we give you beef soup? You are a Hindu; we are all Hindus!'

But Daju refused to eat anything else. Not wanting to displease the sick man, the relatives finally brought him a bowl of beef soup from one of the shops nearby. Daju was given the soup with a little soft-boiled rice, which he ate with great relish. He thanked his relatives and lay back to let the food, the first he had had in a long time, work its wonders. Soon, he did feel a lot better and stronger. In fact, he felt so good that he started to hum a Nepali tune. But then, all of a sudden, he switched to chanting Khasi phawars and ended each gnomic verse with the long-drawn concluding chorus of 'hoooi kiw', repeated twice.

When I came to this part of the story, my friends roared with laughter and, wagging their fingers at me, said, 'Impossible, impossible!'

I asked them not to jump to conclusions. When Daju started chanting Khasi phawars like a pro, his relatives got scared because, before the accident, he spoke but a few words of Khasi. They called his doctor and told him everything. The doctor examined Daju carefully but found nothing wrong with him. He talked to him, asking him many questions in Hindi. The patient answered him quite normally but his Hindi was mixed with a lot of Khasi.

The relatives asked, 'Is he all right, Doctor? What's wrong with him? He's not losing his mind, is he?'

The doctor turned away from the patient and said, 'There's nothing wrong with him. And no, he's not losing his mind. He's quite normal … but it seems he has become a Khasi!'

My friends laughed and threw straw at me. 'Damn you, Ap, you told us not to jump to conclusions, but the conclusion is the same, man! That's the tallest tale we have heard so far!'

Donald, however, responded passionately, 'What are you talking about? This is the best story, the most significant story I have heard so far! The—'

'What! Are you crazy?' Evening snapped. 'How can a Nepali daju suddenly become a Khasi just because he has been given some Khasi blood?'

'Again, you are falling into the trap of taking the narrative literally!' Donald countered. 'Think of the story as a Khasi myth or even an Aesop's fable. Aesop's fables are not true, are they? I mean, animals do not have conversations with each other and behave like humans, no? And yet the morals about human nature and human life are profoundly true. Think about the message of this story, and you will agree with me that it's the best story we have heard so far!'

'And what is its message?' Evening asked sceptically.

'Why, can't you see? *Love knows no otherness!* That is its moral—'

'Yeah, yeah, I see it now, great, Don, great! He is my Don, after all,' Magdalene said proudly.

Hamkom said, 'True, true …'

'What is true? That Don is Magdalene's?' Bah Kynsai laughed.

'Tet leh, Bah Kynsai!' Hamkom protested. 'But it's true, Don, it's true. The story does carry a message of selfless love and pure friendship!'

'And can't you see what such a message could mean for a cosmopolitan place like Shillong?' Don asked. 'Shillong has been described as a mini

India, hasn't it? What do we have there? Khasis, Garos, Bengalis, Assamese, Nepalis, Biharis, Marwaris, South Indians, Punjabis, UP wallahs, and tribal communities from every Northeastern state, isn't that so, Mag? For the peaceful coexistence of these communities, okay, this is the kind of message that should be propagated: love to defeat hatred; service to fellow man to abolish all differences and break down all barriers—'

'Yeah, absolutely right, Don, this is the kind of writing I have always admired, you know,' Magdalene agreed. 'In fact, some time ago, I came across a beautiful poem that carries a similar message, okay? It's a short poem but beautiful. Wait, wait, I have it on my mobile …'

Magdalene switched on her phone and began to read the poem aloud:

> Beloved Sundori,
>> Yesterday one of my people
> Killed one of your people
>> And one of your people
> Killed one of my people.
>> Today they have both sworn
> To kill on sight.
>> But this is neither you nor I,
> Shall we meet by the River Umkhrah
>> And empty this madness
> Into its angry summer floods?
>> I send this message
> Through a fearful night breeze,
>> Please leave your window open.

Magdalene said, 'I read this in a national magazine. It's titled "Sundori". According to the reviewer, the poem was written during the 1992 riots in Shillong. Look at the horror of the first few lines, Don. Everyone was mad with hatred! Everyone had become a bloodthirsty monster, and then suddenly, towards the end, you have a message of love sent "through a fearful night breeze" to a beloved from another community. And the message says, let us "empty this madness" into the "angry summer floods" of the River Umkhrah; let us defeat all this bloodthirstiness and barbarism with our love. With love, let us cross barriers, let us make bridges and unite so the world will learn again to be sane and human. Lovely, lovely poem, no, Don?'

'Ultimately, no, Mag, amidst the madness and gore, the poem is as refreshing as the night breeze it speaks about. Beautiful, beautiful,' Donald enthused.

'It's a lovely poem indeed, especially when analysed like that,' Bah Su agreed. 'But who's the poet, Mag?'

'That's the thing, no … I was so taken by the poem that I forgot all about the poet!'

'I also have a poem which I found in one of the local papers,' Hamkom said, surprising us. We didn't know he read poetry. 'The same kind of message, ha, beautifully written, but I too photographed only the poem; I don't know who wrote it. It's called "Canine Lesson". Shall I read?'

Hamkom, like Magdalene, read the poem on his mobile phone:

Every day on the way
to a mulberry grove for his evening walk,
two dogs always come rushing out of a house,
yapping at him and snapping at his heels.
Angered by this senseless aggression,
he throws stones at them, hits them with sticks,
and shrieks at the top of his voice,
speaking a language
that puts his salt-and-pepper head to shame.
Still, the dogs keep at it,
if anything, a little more enraged every day.
One day, on a sudden inspiration,
he changed his strategy.
When they came barking at him,
he stopped, clucked his tongue, clicked his fingers,
and crooned to them.
To his surprise, they too stopped, confused,
then whined and wagged their tails.
Astounded, he patted their heads:
'It's true,' he exclaimed,
'make friends, not enemies!'

Hamkom was not as good a reader as Magdalene, who understood the rhythm of her poem and read with feeling. But he was quite oblivious to all that and said, '"Make friends, not enemies!" Isn't that magnificent? Isn't that what we need in a place like Shillong? Everybody speaks about communal tension and worries about the return of the 1992 riots, ha, but if all of us follow this policy of making friends and not enemies, wouldn't that solve a lot of problems?'

Evening objected to this interpretation. He said, 'Do you think what worked with dogs would work with humans?'

Donald said, 'If it works with animals, why shouldn't it work with humans? As someone said, human nature is like a looking glass: smile at it, and it will smile back at you; frown at it, and it will frown back at you. I tell you, if you offer people an olive branch, okay, they are likely to accept it with warmth and friendship. *Love knows no otherness!* This should be our message for our people. If we want to see the end of the communal riots, this is it!'

'Love cannot be one-sided,' Evening persisted. 'What happens if they don't return our love, huh? Do you remember the Rit Shrieh story? His wife kept forgiving him because she loved him, but what did he do? He simply took advantage of it and visited her only when her stomach was flat. In our enthusiasm to offer an olive branch to others, we should be careful not to end up like Rit Shrieh's wife. What do you say, Bah Kynsai?'

Before Bah Kynsai could respond, Bah Su said, 'The way I see it, the message of love and fellowship is a good one, ha. And it has the potential to bring lasting peace to our anxious city, with its fragile peace and the ever-widening divide between tribals and non-tribals. But Ning, too, is justified in asking for caution and reciprocity. For instance, love and goodwill can be offered to the citizens already here, but how can we welcome all migrants with open arms? Not even Europe and the USA are doing that, ha. Our community is too small; we are too few. When migrants, especially from foreign countries, flock to these hills, it is the duty of the government, and all of us, to stop them. But when it comes to our permanent non-tribal residents, ha, by all means, love should know no otherness.'

Evening was not satisfied. He said, 'Even the so-called permanent residents should be meticulously vetted, Bah Su, otherwise—'

'Okay, okay, that should be enough,' Bah Kynsai cut in. 'We have already discussed the issue twice, na? It's time to move on—'

But Dale said, 'Wait, Bah Kynsai. Before we move on, I want to know why Daju was hit by the car. Was he drunk or something?'

'You bloody chauvinist!' Bah Kynsai said good-humouredly. 'Just because you are a driver, you think the fault is always that of the pedestrian, sala? If you ask me, na, it must be the driver who was drunk!'

'No, no, no, that's unfair, Bah Kynsai,' Dale protested. 'I never drink at all, and I certainly would never drink and drive—'

'I always do. I take my quota in a restaurant at Jhalupara at about 7 p.m. and drive home from there. And nobody ever stops me.'

'That's because you were not drunk when driving, Bah Kynsai,' Raji said. 'Nowadays, they have started checking—'

'Nonsense!' Bah Kynsai pooh-poohed the idea. 'How many drunken drivers have the police ever arrested? If there's such a thing as a check on drunken driving, na, almost half the male population would have been arrested.'

'Half the male population?' Donald asked.

'Of course! In a society where 50 or 60 per cent of the male population drink themselves to death by the age of forty-four or forty-five, don't you think—'

'I get it, I get it,' Donald said quickly. 'But why do you think there's so much drunkenness in Khasi society?'

'That's what I've always wanted to talk about—'

'You have already talked about it, Ning,' Bah Kit interrupted, 'and you blamed the matrilineal system for it, remember?'

'Well, if you don't think the matrilineal system is the cause, then what is?' Evening challenged.

'Nobody has done any research on the subject, Ning,' Bah Su said. 'We can only speculate.'

'No, no,' Evening insisted, 'when a man—'

I did not want the discussion to veer towards the matrilineal system again, so I said, 'Wait, Ning, wait, I have a story called "Reasons for Drinking".'

'Good, good,' Bah Kynsai enthused. 'Now we are getting somewhere, na? Chalo, chalo, Ap.'

It is an undisputed fact that alcohol is a terrible curse to Khasi society. Its abuse is so rampant that any Khasi man dying between the age of thirty and forty-five can safely be said to have died of eating too well (*bam bha palat*), a Khasi euphemism for drinking too much.

Every time there is a drink-related death, the most common and perplexing question that we hear is: 'Why did he abuse himself like that?' or 'Why did he drink himself to death?'

But does one really need a reason to drink? Evening may very well have singled out one of the fundamental reasons why Khasi men drink so much. However, the little anecdote related to me by my friend, Kamai, had an entirely different take on the issue.

One Saturday afternoon, Kamai bumped into a group of young men— the oldest about twenty-five and the youngest about fifteen—who were hopelessly drunk. They were stumbling up the village road as if blown by the wind, now swaying left, now swaying right. All of them were raucous and abusive, chattering loudly about what they had been doing in so foul a language that Kamai wanted to cover his ears in shame. But being a responsible citizen, he decided to speak to them.

In a friendly but firm tone, he said, 'Hey, hey, stop using that kind of language! You are in the middle of the village street, not in the jungle! And tell me, why are you so drunk this early in the day?'

The boys stopped and stared at him aggressively. When they recognised him, their leader said, 'What to do, Bah Mai, we just lost a football match and had to give the winners a pig … We were in such low spirits, ha, so, we thought we should take some spirits to cheer ourselves up.'

Next Saturday afternoon, Kamai met the same group of young men in the same drunken and rowdy condition. He said to them, 'What did I tell you about using foul language? And what is it this time? Did you fellows lose again?'

'No, no, Bah Mai, not this time, not this time!' the leader declared triumphantly. 'This time, no, Bah Mai, we beat them good and got 5,000 rupees! See, our prize money!'

'So, why are you drunk then?'

'Arre, Bah Mai! When you win, you have to celebrate, no?'

'You fellows are very strange: lose, you drink; win, you drink. You are exactly like Drainij Lyngdoh—'

'Drain, the village drunk? Come on, that's too much, too much, Bah Mai! Why compare us with him? We only—'

'I'll tell you why. When his uncle asked him why he was drinking so much, do you know what he said? He blamed his wife. "How can I not drink when, the moment I come home, my wife starts barking at me, *hew, hew, hew*?" But when his wife left him, Drain did not stop drinking, if anything, he drank even more. When his uncle asked him about it, he blamed his wife again. "How can I not drink when my wife has left me?" You fellows beware, see that you don't end up like Drain, or even like Drippingjoy Dkhar, the gambler! Do you know what Drip said when asked why he was drinking so much? He said, "I drink because I lose; I lose because I drink. The more I lose, I drink; the more I drink, I lose."'

'Tet teri ka, Bah Mai, you are so funny, so funny!' They all laughed drunkenly.

'Funny? You fellows take care unless you want alcohol to have the last laugh.'

My friends were laughing too. And I said, 'Those are some of the reasons why people drink.'

'But they don't seem like reasons at all, Ap!' Bah Kit said. 'People drink when they win, drink when they lose, drink when their wives are with them, drink when their wives leave them … Those are not real reasons for drinking. What do you say, Bah Su?'

'Quite right, quite right,' Bah Su agreed. 'And those reasons, ha, if they are reasons at all, have nothing to do with the matrilineal system. Those boys would have been too young to think—'

'But Bah Su,' Evening interrupted, 'you are taking it for granted that Ap was telling us a true story—'

'It is true!' I asserted.

'There you are,' Bah Su responded. 'So, as I was saying, ha, those boys would have been too young to think about marital relationships and the matrilineal system. And, as you have heard, they drank to console themselves in the first instance and to celebrate in the second. The other fellow, Drain, obviously did not drink because his wife nagged him. He must have been rebuked because he was always drunk, ha, but when he did not mend his ways, his wife had no choice but to leave him. So, what are the real reasons for drinking?'

'Why don't we ask Bah Raji and Bah Kynsai?' Dale suggested with a laugh.

'Why only us?' Raji asked belligerently. 'Why not Bah Su also? He's drinking as much as us, no?'

'Yeah, yeah, let's ask the three of them,' Hamkom said. 'So why do you drink?'

'No, no, you first,' Raji told Hamkom. 'Why do you drink?'

'At home, I don't drink much. I have a peg or two before dinner, that's it. It's a kind of relaxation for me.'

'The same thing for me!' Raji declared. 'I don't drink much at home. I drink only before dinner, also for relaxation.'

Everyone laughed at the idea of Raji not drinking much at home, but Bah Kynsai said, 'That's true, that's true … We drink a little more than a peg or two, of course, but only to make the food tastier, na? We don't drink till drunk. Till a little drunk, maybe, but not till very drunk,' he concluded with a loud laugh.

'And all for relaxation and as an appetiser?' Magdalene asked.

'Absolutely.'

'Well, it certainly looks like nobody drinks because of the matrilineal system, no?' Donald observed. 'Evening will have to give us an example if he insists that people drink because of it.'

Not wanting another quarrel, Bah Kynsai said, 'So what's the moral of Ap's story? What about this? *A drinker justifies his drinking with reasons but gives only excuses*. Should do, na? And that's exactly like the song Ap used to tell us about a Sohra man … what was that song, Ap?'

'You mean Phamos's song? Yeah, he—'

'Hahaha, what a name!' Magdalene laughed.

'That was how his parents spelt "famous", I explained.

'And what about the other names you gave us earlier? Exstarson, Hellweena, Drainij, Drippingjoy, are they real?'

'Yeah, yeah, all real. Their stories are public knowledge, you know, so no harm done. As for Phamos, he was a habitual drinker, but people loved him because of his jovial ways. The only unhappy person was his wife, who used to yell at him whenever he came home more drunk than usual. But Phamos never lost his temper. He simply sang a song to justify his drinking and mollify his wife. And the song was always the same: *Dih te nga u ba dih, tangba nga dih teng teng, ta ruh ym ka yiad Khasi, hynrei ka yiad Phareng.* (Drink, it's true I used to drink, but only now and then, and that too, not the Khasi brew, but the whisky of the Pharengs.)'

Bah Kynsai laughed. 'According to him, na, because he drank the whisky of the Englishmen, and not the local brew, it was okay to drink.'

'Speaking of justifications,' I said, 'Kamai told me once about the drunks of Nongpoh. Defending their drunkenness, they used to say, "Drinking? Who says we are drinking? We are actually engaged in Education, and we are studying three very serious subject-combinations: Comic, Logic and Plastic. In the morning, we relive the Comic scenes of the night; during the day, we apply Logic to find ways of earning money for a drink; and in the evening, we go to buy Plastic in which the local brew is kept."'

'That's a really good one!' Bah Kynsai said, roaring with laughter, as were the others.

Only Donald was a bit confused. 'What exactly do you mean by plastic, Bah Ap?'

'Polythene bags.'

'But why polythene bags?'

'The sale of the local brew is illegal, Don. Makers and sellers in most places operate without a licence. That's why they keep it in the most innocuous containers they can think of. At Ïew Polo in Shillong, for instance, they sell in plastic bottles kept in cloth bags carried by men and women who move up and down the street, on the lookout for thirsty people. It's uncannily like soliciting. At a place in Jaiñtia Hills—'

'Ri Pnar,' Raji reminded me.

'At a place in Ri Pnar,' I said with deliberate emphasis, 'where the largest concentration of coal mines is, girls are forced to peddle on lonely roadsides because the sale of alcohol is banned in the village. Which, of course, is a really stupid idea because it places the girls at the mercy of their drunken customers.

'However, speaking of ways to avoid getting caught, the most ingenious one is definitely practised in the uranium-rich Domiasiat areas of West Khasi Hills. According to my friend Tarun, women keep their rice spirits in tyre tubes. The tubes are bound with strings, which allow the women to carry them like bags dangling from their shoulders. When the tubes are properly in place, the women cover themselves with thick shawls and sit somewhere, pretending to sell betel nuts and cigarettes, or simply walk about. When a drinker comes, he puts his head under a woman's shawl and is allowed to drink directly from the tube by removing the valve cap. For twenty rupees, the man gets one long pull—'

'Tet leh, this Ap!' Bah Kynsai laughed. 'What if he pays twenty rupees and takes more than one pull?'

'Impossible. The women hold their customers by the neck, so they know precisely how many pulls they take. Tarun said it was a sight to behold! A man putting his head under a woman's shawl, the woman cuddling him, holding him between head and throat—it was exactly as if she was suckling him. And that's why, when the men want to go for a drink, they always say, "*Hai dih buiñ noh, hai!*" which means, "Let's go suck a breast, come on!"'

I wanted to continue, but Magdalene cackled loudly and said, 'This is too much, man, too much!'

Raji said, 'But it's true, Mag, it's true. I have also done it. It is as Ap has described, exactly. I wish I had told you the story rather than him, but it never crossed my mind.'

'But why are they banning the local brew and giving licences for Indian-made foreign liquor?' Donald asked. 'These liquor stores are everywhere, ya!'

'Now they have started putting restrictions on the sale of IMFL too,' Raji replied. 'But you are right, Don, banning the local brew is a foolish thing to do. Instead of banning it, okay, they should regulate its manufacture and sale. That way, ha, they would earn revenue from taxes as well as stop the terrible adulteration.'

'Adulteration?' Donald asked.

'Yeah, yeah, the local stuff is not sold in sealed bottles, okay? It comes to distributors in all kinds of containers—tyre tubes, jerry cans, pots, plastic bags, all sorts of things. This gives the distributors a chance to adulterate the content freely. Normally what they do, ha, they double the quantity by adding water to the liquor. Then, to give it sting and zing, they add DDT, carbon from newspapers, poison from lizards, acid from used batteries, camphor, methylated spirits and other stuff that we know nothing about.'

'What! How can they do all that crap? Don't people know about it?'

'They do it, Don,' Bah Kynsai assured him. 'It's an open secret. Everybody knows it, but when you are an addict, na, what can you do?'

'They could buy foreign liquor.'

'The local brew is a poor man's drink, man. It's cheap!' Bah Kynsai said. 'IMFL is too expensive … Poor people have no option but to buy the local stuff, although they know it's contaminated.'

'But don't they die?'

'Not right away,' Raji said. 'First of all, okay, those who drink from places like Polo soon have purple maps on their faces. And then, after a few years, they die of cirrhosis, jaundice, kidney failure, cancer, TB and whatnot.'

'It's terrible, ya!' Hamkom exclaimed. 'Like a slow poison, no? I think Raji is right, you know, I think it's high time they legalised the local brew and regulated its production and sale.'

'The best thing to do, na, is to regulate its production and then put it in sealed bottles like the IMFL,' Bah Kynsai asserted. 'That's the only solution.'

'They will have to do it eventually,' Bah Su said. 'We will not allow our yiad um beer and yiad rot spirit to be banned. We need them for most of our religious rituals. Sometimes, I feel that the attempt to ban the local stuff and not the foreign liquor, ha, is just a gimmick to destroy our religion.'

'Maybe we shouldn't go so far, Bah Su,' Raji objected gently.

'I know, but sometimes, I do get this feeling.'

'It's definitely a foolish move!' Raji said again. 'And it's not bad stuff at all, if not contaminated. Look at this Lyngngam brew! How beautiful it is!'

Evening disagreed. 'You are saying it's a foolish move, but didn't we agree that alcohol is a curse for the Khasi people?'

'True, true, but by banning the local stuff only and not the foreign liquor, they are causing more harm than good, no?' Raji argued. 'That's what we are saying.'

'By "they" you mean the government, don't you?' Donald enquired.

'Actually, it's not only the government, Don, it's the NGOs too,' Raji clarified.

'Ah, of course! Meghalaya cannot function without NGOs,' Donald said sarcastically.

'In fact, they are the most active prohibitionists in the state,' Raji explained. 'They hold meetings everywhere.'

'They held two meetings in our locality,' I said. 'They held two meetings and never came back.'

'Why, what happened?'

The first meeting was organised by an NGO called Alcohol Prohibition Society, together with a women's welfare organisation. The meeting was held at night in the locality's biggest junction. Members of the two organisations sitting on the hurriedly made wooden platform came up to the lectern one by one to hit out against the evils of alcohol. Finally, it was the turn of the NGO's president, who spoke eloquently and with such thought-provoking metaphors and examples that he held the whole gathering spellbound.

One of the things he said was that, though man claims he is a rational being, a 'thinking reed', capable of both thought and emotion, unlike animals, he still behaves in a manner that is often irrational and unreasonable. Often, the president said, we find that man eats and drinks stuff that is poison to his system, while animals will never do that, although they are not supposed to be sentient or sensible. Animals like cats and dogs, for instance, do not eat what is pungent, sour, spicy or oily. And when it comes to anything intoxicating, he asserted, they never, never touch the stuff!

He asked the crowd, which was hanging on to his every word: 'Supposing I keep a bucket of water and a bucket of alcohol right here, and then I bring an animal to them, say an ass ... Now, you tell me, what will the ass drink?'

With one voice, the crowd replied, 'The water.'

'Tell me, why would he drink the water and not the alcohol?' he asked again.

The crowd was silent, thinking about the right answer. Unfortunately, among the audience were also many alcoholics standing in a separate group in the junction's darkest parts. They were enraged by what the NGO's president and the other speakers had said about drinkers in general, but they had not dared say or do anything to disrupt the meeting for fear of reprisal. Now they saw an excellent opening. They pushed one of their friends to the front and said to him, 'Say it, say it!'

The drunk straightened himself and shouted out his reply, 'Why? Because he is an ass, that's why! Don't you even know that, liah?'

There was an explosion of laughter from the crowd that drowned out everything the prohibitionists tried to say afterwards. Most of the listeners were actually for the cause of prohibition, but that moment of explosive laughter undid all the excellent work of the president and the previous speakers. The prohibitionists left in a huff, never to come back.

The second meeting—

'Wait, Ap, wait,' Bah Su stopped me. 'I think I have a nice moral for this story. But first of all, are those who do not drink asses? Are those who drink all evil men? Food and drink are good or bad depending upon moderation. *Make no rules about another's habits.*'

Evening was very pleased with the moral. 'Beautiful, Bah Su, beautiful! I'm a sipper, I drink in moderation; you cannot call me an evil man.'

'You sound like the Buddha, leh, Bah Su, with all that moderation stuff,' Bah Kynsai grumbled. 'Luckily, you don't practise what you preach. Go on, Ap.'

Bah Su's face broke into a wry smile, but he did not say anything.

The second meeting, I went on, was held in the community hall. It was a much smaller affair, organised by a smaller prohibitionist group. Here too, quite a few speakers expounded on the evils of alcoholism. One of them was a masterly orator. He told us the story of a boy who asked someone about the power of alcohol.

According to the story, one day, while buying a few things from a local shop, a boy dropped his polythene bag to the ground, spilling everything. With the help of the shopkeeper, the boy tried to pick up the items one by one. However, among the things he had dropped were a packet of sugar and a bottle of mustard oil, half of which had flowed into the sugar when the cap flew open. Being only a boy, he did not think much of the loss. He poked at the oil and the sugar with his finger and soon became more interested in the fact that the sugar did not melt. He asked the shopkeeper, 'Bah, how come the sugar doesn't melt? It's mixed with the oil, no?'

'Oil cannot melt sugar. Only water can,' the shopkeeper replied.

The boy was filled with wonder and asked him again, 'Bah, what about other liquids like, like alcohol?'

'Alcohol?' the shopkeeper asked, taken by surprise. Then after a while, he said, 'Alcohol can certainly melt sugar, son. In fact, alcohol can melt all sorts of things—gold, silver, cars, houses, family, happiness, love … everything.'

'How's that?' the boy said in even greater wonder.

'Do you see that man there, the one dressed in rags and sunning himself by the roadside? That man used to be very rich. He had houses, cars, gold, land and a loving family. But then he fell under the influence of alcohol: from morning till night, he did nothing but drink. Do you see what has happened to him now? He has lost everything, including his family. Now he sits in the sun and begs people for money so he can buy a few drinks.'

When the speaker finished, all the men in the hall applauded. But the drunks present there resented the picture he had painted of the fate of drinkers. One of them, an elderly man who was known to everyone as Bah No, because his name was Knowell, stood up and said, 'You fellows, you claim to be prohibitionists, you claim to abolish alcohol, but what have you done? Nothing but talk, talk, talk, nothing but meeting, meeting!' Slapping his chest with the palm of his right hand, he continued, 'We are the real destroyers of alcohol—me and my friends here. The moment they make it, we drink it! They make more; we drink more! We destroy it the moment they make it! What about you? Talk, talk, talk!'

There was loud laughter from the crowd, and complete confusion for a while. Finally, Bah No and his friends were thrown out and order was restored. However, by then, the mood of the speakers had soured. They blamed the gathering for laughing with the drunks, and they blamed the local authorities for allowing them inside in the first place. And they never came back.

Raji, who was just a little drunk by then, said, 'There's some logic there, I think.'

'Where? In Bah No's speech?' Hamkom asked. 'A warped kind of logic, if you ask me.'

'But logic, nevertheless,' Raji insisted.

'So, what's happening in your locality now?' Evening asked.

'Plenty of drunks in that place,' Bah Kynsai answered.

'Some of them are drunk right from the morning,' I agreed, 'and you can see them lying about on the grass like caterpillars. It's not the council's fault. The sale of alcohol has been banned in the locality, but that doesn't help. They still get it from commercial areas nearby, places like Bishnupur, for instance.'

'But some drunks are quite funny, no?' Magdalene observed.

'Most drunks are funny, Mag,' Bah Kynsai said. 'Haven't you seen what happens to Raji when he is drunk? Even you and I might become funny when we are drunk—'

'Not all, Bah Kynsai, not all,' Raji objected, 'some can be very quarrelsome, okay, you also know that!'

'True, true,' Bah Kynsai agreed, 'that's why I said, most drunks, na, not all—'

'Bah Kynsai,' Dale interrupted him, 'I have some little stories about how funny drunks can be.'

One of Dale's stories was about a drunk who had been hit by his taxi. Some people going for a picnic to Umïam Lake had asked Dale to drop them at the picnic spot and return to pick them up in the afternoon. As they cruised down the highway off Mawlai, an early drunk suddenly came swaying onto the road out of nowhere. Dale slammed the brake, but it was too late. The man was hit plump on the rump, and flew into a ditch by the roadside.

Dale was scared out of his wits. He was not at fault, but he knew that in Mawlai, if a pedestrian was hit, the crowd simply beat up the driver without asking questions. To them, the driver was always in the wrong.

It was with great trepidation, therefore, that he stepped out of his car to check on the drunk, who was trying to climb out of the ditch. Dale peered at him and asked anxiously, 'How are you, Bah, are you all right?'

The drunk looked up at him balefully and said, 'All right, all right? Go, look at your own car, see if it's dented or not!'

When Dale heard this, he was flooded with relief. He jumped into his taxi and drove away at full speed. After they had travelled some distance, they all let out a sigh of relief and began laughing at the drunk's strange reaction.

We also laughed and Bah Su dutifully provided the moral. He said, '*When under the influence, even the frailest can feel like a tank.*'

In the other story, Dale was standing by his taxi on a busy street in Shillong, waiting for a passenger who had gone to buy something, when a drunk came lurching up the footpath towards him. When he reached Dale, he said, 'Hey, bro, can you tell me where the other side of the road is?'

Suppressing a smile, Dale pointed to the other side. 'There it is.'

But the drunk suddenly lost his temper and let out some of the worst expletives Dale had ever heard. Angry now, Dale demanded to know what the matter was.

'How can I not bawl at a damn liar like you?' the drunk replied. 'A few minutes ago, I asked a fellow, and he pointed this side, but now you are pointing that side, sala! You think I'm a stupid pig?'

Hamkom shook a finger at Dale and laughing, said, 'No, that couldn't have happened!'

Dale protested loudly, also laughing, 'I swear it did, Bah Ham, it really happened, I swear it!'

'I'm sick of you fellows saying we are telling you tall tales!' Bah Kynsai said. 'This shows what, you know? That you don't know anything about life. Life is strange, man, it's full of strange characters, but just because a story sounds strange, na, it doesn't mean it isn't true. When we tell you a tall tale, don't we say so?'

'Actually, most of our tales, barring one or two, have been true stories, Bah Kynsai,' I reminded him. 'I too have a few stories about drunks, which I'm sure everyone will find hard to believe. But as you said, what can be stranger than life?'

'Hold on, Ap,' Evening said. 'I have a moral for Dale's story: *helping an ingrate is asking for trouble*. How's that, Bah Su?'

'Good, good!' Bah Su nodded his approval.

'Okay, now your stories, Ap,' Bah Kynsai ordered.

The first story was about a person in Sohra whose name was Khlaiñbor, or 'great strength'. This fellow was of a very peculiar character. The moment he drank, he developed a strange desire to kill himself. His wife and children lived in constant dread, for whenever he returned home from the boozers, he would start looking for knives and machetes to cut himself. The instant they saw him coming up the path to the house, they would say to each other, 'Hide, hide all the knives and sharp objects … He has come, he has come.'

One day, Khlaiñbor came home even more sozzled than usual. As always, the first thing he did was look for knives and machetes. 'Where's the knife? Where's the machete?' he demanded. 'I will make myself gone, deceased, this very day! Goddamn, wife! Spawn of a low-born clan! Not even a little love does she feel for me! Only cursing, cursing every day! Where are you hiding the knives, you ugly hag?'

His wife, Bluebell, was really scared, for he seemed to be quite mad. His bloodshot eyes stared at her as if he would eat her up, while the purple maps on his face seemed to blink off and on as if they too were reprimanding her. Khlaiñbor bunched his small right hand into a fist and shook it at her, demanding again, 'Where are the knives, you spawn of a demon?'

In her fright, the wife blurted out the first thought that came to her mind. She said, 'Kong Rosydaisy has taken all the knives, they are holding a feast tomorrow—'

'You would give everything from the house to your neighbour, spawn of a cunt! Spawn of an arse! Where's the hammer? Where's the crowbar? I'll stab myself to death right here, right now!'

Saying this, he began looking for the hammer and the crowbar, cursing and swearing terrible oaths and kicking everything that lay in his path. But finding nothing with which he could wound himself, even after searching for a long while, he left the house and lurched down the path towards the garden.

Bluebell was very concerned. She asked one of her nephews to go and check what he was doing. 'Go, go, Ever, go, see what your pakha is doing! Don't let him do anything to harm himself, you hear?'

When Ever entered the garden, he saw his pakha, in only his underwear, trying to sling a *gamosa* over the low branch of an oak tree. He shouted: 'What are you doing, Pakha? Why are you slinging that little cloth over a branch like that?'

Khlaiñbor turned to glare at him and cried petulantly, 'Ehhhh, I'm trying to hang myself, she comes to spoil it all instead!'

Magdalene laughed heartily, but Donald asked, 'Ever is a boy, no, Bah Ap?'

'Ever is our friend, Everending. His pakha addressed him as "she" because he was angry.'

'What a terrible guy,' Hamkom remarked, 'I mean, terrorising his wife and family like that every day!'

'Most drunken husbands are like that, Ham,' Bah Kynsai said. 'This fellow at least did not beat her up, na? I know others who abuse their wives both verbally and physically.'

'Is this why many Khasi women prefer non-Khasi men or what?' Magdalene asked.

'I think it's natural, you know,' Bah Kit said. 'If a Khasi drunkard and a non-tribal man were to come to ask for my sister's hand in marriage, ha, I would also choose the non-tribal! Who would want to entrust the fate of his own sister to a drunk?'

'If a suitor is already a drunk, yes, I would never encourage my sister to marry him,' Evening chimed in. 'But you are forgetting that most Khasi men take to drinking after marriage. Have you considered why? Isn't the woman to blame in such cases?'

'We have already discussed that, Evening, and we have also acknowledged the fact that many Khasi men take to drinking while quite young and unmarried,' Bah Kit responded. 'Have you forgotten Ap's story about the drunken footballers?'

'What happened to the Sohra guy eventually, Ap?' Magdalene asked. 'Did he manage to kill himself?'

'No, I don't think he really wanted to kill himself, you know. How can you try to kill yourself with a thin gamosa slung over a low branch? I suspect that, even if he had been given a knife, he would only have pretended to stab himself. He must have had some psychological issues. Maybe all he wanted was to see if his family would really be alarmed by his threats of suicide. That could be his way of finding out whether they loved him or not. I don't know. But no, he never killed himself with a knife. He didn't have to. Alcohol did the job for him.

'Strangely, during the day, he was a perfect gentleman and had a very cordial relationship with his wife. He was also very witty. One morning, for instance, when his wife saw him sunning himself on the veranda, she teased him: "Arre, arre, look at you! The way you sit with folded arms … like a babu, an officer!" Laughing, he replied, "Why don't you finish the sentence, Mother? Why don't you say babuaid, a drunk, as you really wanted to?"'

'You mean, he shared that kind of bonhomie with his wife in the morning?' Magdalene asked.

'Yeah, it was only when drunk that he became a loathsome brute.'

'What about our drunks here?' Magdalene teased.

Raji took no offence at all. 'You have seen me, no? Always at my best when a little drunk.'

'A little witty, a little roguish,' Bah Kit elaborated.

'Bah Kynsai?' Magdalene asked again.

'I don't know, I have never been really drunk in my life, na?' he replied innocently, and then laughed at his own joke.

Bah Su said, 'I become reticent when very drunk. I don't even want to speak; I just want to sleep.'

'I think, one day,' I said seriously, 'I'll drink myself blind just to see what I do.'

'Hahaha, that will be the day!' Magdalene laughed. 'But come to think of it, okay, you are right, Ap. It would be good to see what kind of demons we have hidden inside us, no?'

'That's what I mean, Mag,' I agreed. Moving on to another story, I said, 'When I was young, there was a fellow in our locality who used to become extremely quarrelsome when he was drunk. His name was Kmonding, because his parents could not spell "commanding" correctly. He was quite small, and because of his excessive drinking, very thin too, his limbs like chicken legs. The only thing big about him was his stomach. Probably bloated with gas and alcohol. He reminded me a little of Garfield. Like Ever's pakha, when sober, he was quite all right. But when drunk, he would pick a quarrel even with his friends at the boozer.

'One market day, as he emerged from a roadside boozer, Kmonding started quarrelling with his companion. Angered by his foul language, the other man gave him a hard punch on the left temple. Kmonding fell into a ditch. He tried to get up and retaliate, but only managed to rise a few inches before plopping back in. As he was struggling to get out of the ditch, another friend came on the scene and said, "Arre, Ding, what happened to you?" And Kmonding replied, "*Khyllie lih khyllie; ngan buh ….*"

'Meaning, Bah Ap?' Donald demanded.

'It means "Lift me, man, lift me; I'll thrash …."'

Donald laughed. 'He couldn't even get up on his own, and he was threatening to beat people up!'

Evening added, 'Ap, I have a good moral for this one: *think very carefully, is it the companion who hit you or the alcohol?* What do you think?'

'Ask them,' Donald replied, pointing at Bah Kynsai, Raji and Bah Su.

We all laughed at Donald's little joke, and cursing him good-humouredly, Bah Kynsai said, 'This Don, liah, is also getting over-smart, na?'

Next, I told them about Cunning Star from Ri Bhoi. He was a chronic drinker and always came home drunk at night. The family lived in extreme poverty and subsisted on boiled rice and salt since Cunning, a daily-wage earner, never gave his wife much money at the end of the week. But every night at dinnertime, he would say loudly to his children, 'You Dro, what will you have, chicken? And you Sweety, Rit, Hephep, what will you have, chicken or pig's head? What the heck, old woman! Let them have both; let them have both! Plenty to go around anyway.'

Cunning did this every night so the other tenants, living in the same wood-and-tin single-storey tenement, would hear and think his family was very well off. But his wife, Bhentinora, was sick of him and complained about his behaviour to her parents and uncles. By the way, Bhentinora was so named because, when they took her mother to the hospital in a taxi, her father had to sit in the boot, or *bhen*, since there was no room inside. To commemorate the incident, when she was born, he decided to call her Bhentinora. Anyway, one night, Bhentinora's relatives came to her home and waited for Cunning. When he entered the main room, Cunning was confronted by his wife's parents, uncles and brothers, who berated him with the harshest words they could think of without actually using expletives, for they were from a respectable family. Finally, they said, 'We are warning you, Cunning, if you don't stop drinking from tomorrow, you will have to take all your belongings with you and leave the house, never to come back. If you do, our family will have you thrashed like the dog that you are.'

Cunning gave serious thought to the matter. In the evening, after work, he hesitated for as long as five minutes before entering the *pata*, the local boozer. The result was that he came home drunk as usual. His wife's relatives, who were waiting in the house, took one look at him and said, 'Take all your belongings and go!'

Cunning went out to the veranda, took a cane rope, strapped his wife to his back, and carried her off to his parents' home.

'Why the hell did he do that?' Magdalene exclaimed.

Bhentinora's family was too surprised to react. But then they went to complain to the headman, who summoned Cunning to appear before the village council.

At the council the next morning, the headman asked Cunning why he had kidnapped his wife and kept her the whole night in his mother's house against her will.

In response, Cunning said, 'Arre, Bah, we in Ri Bhoi call a wife *ka marïung*, no? Part of our goods and chattels, no? You see, my in-laws asked me to leave the house at once with all my belongings. Since my wife is my marïung, one of my most valuable belongings, I took her with me.'

The whole council erupted in laughter. When it subsided somewhat, the headman forced a tone of dignity into his voice and demanded, 'Do you love your wife and children, or do you love alcohol?'

Cunning thought for a while and replied, 'I love them both.'

Another round of laughter followed the answer. Ultimately, the council had to take the matter seriously and ruled that as long as Cunning continued drinking, he should go nowhere near his wife or children. If he did, he would have to face severe consequences.

Donald reacted to the story with some surprise. 'This is indeed a bizarre thing, Bah Ap. We live in a matrilineal society, and yet the woman is called ka marïung!'

'The expression is used only in certain places in Ri Bhoi, Don, not everywhere,' Bah Kit explained. 'But look at how the story played out. The woman was not left to fend for herself. She was supported by both her family and the village dorbar. All this is possible because of our unique social and political systems. That's why, whatever anyone says, ha, our systems are still functioning—not as well as in the past, true enough, but they are still quite effective.'

'Back, back to the drunks, Ap,' Bah Kynsai commanded. 'These buggers might quarrel again, na?'

So I told them about two drunks, one from Jaïaw and another from Malki (both Shillong localities), to illustrate how sharp-witted some of them could be.

The first incident, about 'Bah Tiplut', 'all-knowing', a celebrated drunk from Jaïaw, took place in 1992. I was very young then and living in a place called Mission Compound, adjacent to Jaïaw. An indefinite curfew had just been imposed on the entire city owing to the communal riots. That was a tough time for all of us. There was a shortage of everything. We had to eat sparingly, and many of us subsisted on rice and salt.

But if it was hard on us, it was harder still on the drunks. Delirium tremens sets in if they do not get their quota. But what were they to do? The streets were being patrolled by the much-feared jawans from the Central Reserve Police Force, infamous for their severity, especially with those who did not speak Hindi. The drunks were truly caught between the devils and the drink.

Ultimately, however, the clamouring demands of alcohol proved to be far greater than their fear of the CRPs, and so, when darkness set in, they played a cat-and-mouse game with them. A group of CRPs used to patrol about a kilometre of the twisting, turning street. Taking advantage of this peculiar topography, the drunks waited in the dark by-lanes till the security men had turned a corner, and then sprinted across the street to vanish into the local boozers. They did the same thing when they returned home.

Unfortunately, Bah Tip was caught mid-street by the CRPs. When they saw him violating the curfew, they came rushing at him, brandishing their terrible *lathis*, readying their guns. The frail Bah Tip was shaking with terror. He knew he would be hit on the head and kicked in the ribs, and dumped in a jail if he was lucky. If not, he could be beaten to death on the spot. 'What to do, what to do?' he asked himself desperately. An idea suddenly came to him. He dropped his pants and went to squat by the roadside ditch. When the CRPs came up to him, they were a bit confused since he was not running away. They asked him in Hindi, 'What are you doing here, you motherfucker? Don't you know there's a curfew, you sister-fucker?'

Bah Tip pointed to his bottom and said, '*Paiñkhana phi mama!*' ('Toilet, respected uncles!') And then in broken Hindi, he explained, 'People inside toilet, no mama, that's why; cannot stop this!'

On hearing Bah Tip's explanation, my friends cackled like hens in a coop, and it was a while before I could explain that the CRPs understood his predicament very well. After all, patrolling the streets day and night, they too had found themselves in similar difficulties. So they let Bah Tip be, but warned him to go home as soon as he had finished the job.

Magdalene threw a stick at me and said, laughing, 'Did he really take a crap, or just pretend?'

'My dear Mag,' I said, 'when CRPs came rushing at you like that, there is no question of pretending. Of course he did it for real! He was literally crapping with fright. It was because they saw the real thing that they let him go.'

'So, did he go home after that?' Raji asked.

'Of course not! You should know better than to ask that sort of question—'

Bah Su chimed in, '*In a tight spot, only a quick wit can save the day.*'

Evening gave him the thumbs up, as did I.

I had more stories about Bah Tip, who really was a funny, funny character. One night, he met a priest from a nearby church. Seeing that he was unable to walk properly, the priest helped Bah Tip reach home. But before entering the house, the two of them spent a long time sitting on a stone parapet by the gate, talking about religion and God. The priest was very eloquent. He spoke to Bah Tip about sin, immoral living, the need to repent for redemption and so on. The priest's concern for the welfare of his soul so touched Bah Tip that he cried and promised to repent. Through his tears, he said, 'From this night, from this moment, I'll never touch the accursed stuff again! I'll come to your church and be your follower from tomorrow!'

The priest patted his back gently and said, 'Go home now, but if you want, I'll come back early tomorrow morning, and then we'll go to church to pray and arrange things properly.'

Bah Tip readily agreed, and shedding copious tears, thanked the priest and went inside.

As promised, the next morning, the priest went to Bah Tip's house. Bah Tip was still sleeping, but his mother was up, and she was pleased beyond measure to know from the priest that her son was ready to turn over a new leaf, as the priest put it. She rushed to her son's bedroom and woke him up. She said, 'Tip, Tip, up, up quickly, Reverend S has come!'

Shaken out of his sleep much before his usual wake-up time, Bah Tip felt quite faint. He sat in bed for some time, rubbing his bloodshot eyes and trying to recover from his grogginess. Reaching below the bed, where he had kept a bottle of the local stuff, Bah Tip took a long pull. He always did that to reduce the shaking of his hands. He called it 'rinsing last night's leftovers'. After that, he got up slowly, washed his face, brushed his teeth, combed his hair and, finally, after a long delay, went to the living room where the priest sat fidgeting. On entering the room, Bah Tip cried out, as if in great surprise, 'Arre, it's Reverend S! How now, Reverend? Where to?'

'Good morning, Bah Tip! I came because of our conversation last night. Remember, you said you would come to church with me this morning and start living a new life—'

'Shish, you also, no, Reverend!' Bah Tip exclaimed, laughing softly as if he found the whole thing very funny. 'How can you take a night talk so seriously? I'm like figure 8, no? You cannot suddenly turn me into figure 1!'

Evening exclaimed, half in anger, half in amusement, 'Tet teri ka, the bloody joker!'

'What do you expect from a chronic alcoholic like that?' Bah Kit asked. 'How can he give up drinking overnight? Impossible. Even those who go for treatment, ha, do not always succeed.'

I agreed with Bah Kit and continued. When Bah Tip's wife died—

'Wait, wait, wait, Ap!' Bah Kynsai interrupted. 'If he was married, why was he living with his mother?'

That happened after his wife's death, I told him. When his wife died, Bah Tip was despondent and angry with God and life for giving him such a bad deal. He cursed all the doctors and nurses at Civil Hospital for being such incompetent and uncaring bastards. On his way out of the hospital's compound, though tiny and usually gentle, he kicked a doctor in the arse for blocking his path, and when he fell to the floor, tried to kick him some more. When a non-Khasi police officer, who had come to intervene, asked him why he had done that, Bah Tip replied, 'He threw rocks at me!'

'Rocks!' Magdalene cried in amusement. 'And what happened to him?'

'Considering that he had just lost his wife,' I told her, 'he got away with only a stern warning.'

Having lost his wife's steadying influence, Bah Tip started drinking even more heavily than before, leaving home immediately after breakfast and returning only towards midnight. His mother was so tired of staying up late every night and waiting for him to come home that, one night, she decided to teach him a lesson he would not forget. She waited for her son's return by the door, with a broomstick in her hand. When Bah Tip arrived, he took one look at his mother and immediately knew what she was planning to do. Going to her side as quickly as he could, he said, 'Waa i Mei! Why are you sweeping the floor so late at night? Give me, give me the broom; I'll do it for you, you shouldn't work so hard, go to bed, let me handle everything.'

'And he got away with it?' Raji asked, laughing.

'He got away with it.'

There were many stories about Bah Tip. The most memorable one, to my mind, was about the time when he and his friend Bah Shngaiñ, 'the comforter', took some of us boys for an overnight angling trip to a river that flowed into the Umïam Lake. They used to call that sort of thing *khwai sah miet*, staying-the-night fishing. But Bah Tip said it was not going to be a simple fishing trip; it was going to be a picnic: 'Something that you boys will remember for the rest of your life!'

The first thing we did was to go to Ïewduh to buy rice, beef, pork, potatoes, onions, mustard oil, salt and turmeric. While in the market, Bah Tip found a bull's head on the market floor. He picked it up and told us to carry it. He said we would have a terrific time feasting on it the next day. After we had done our shopping, we left for the river in Bah Shngaiñ's jeep, driven by one of his friends. If we had gone straightaway, we would have reached the river by three o'clock and everything would have been all right. But the three men stopped at a roadside watering hole to buy what they called 'supplies'. The problem was, they did not simply buy. They filled up as well. They made us wait for a long time in the jeep and came out only towards 6 p.m.—when it was already dark.

We reached the riverbank by about 7 p.m. It was a dark, cloudy night, and we could see only with the help of a small torch that Bah Shngaiñ had. We set up camp quickly, first building a fire so we could have some light. When the fire was burning, the tipsy men started preparing our dinner while sipping from their glasses all the time. As they cooked the food, they boasted to us about making the best dinner we would ever have. They curried the pieces of beef, pork and potatoes together and also prepared fried rice with turmeric, ginger and lots of chillies.

By the time the food was cooked, the men were completely rat-arsed. Bah Tip fell into the river while fetching some water. After he was rescued, he bragged about it and said, 'I swam in the ocean!'

It was a wild night. The men cooked and drank and danced at the same time. They even gave us a few sips of whisky. Bah Shngaiñ lost one of his rubber flip-flops and went about with only one of them the whole night.

When the food was finally ready, it was as good as they had promised. We ate as we had never eaten before, for the men told us to help ourselves to as much meat as we wanted. 'Don't worry about tomorrow,' they said, 'we still have the bull's head.'

Finally, the merriment came to an end, and we all went to sleep on the grass near the fire, covering ourselves with thick blankets.

When we got up in the morning, the first thing we did was to go to the river to wash. The water was the colour of yellow clay, and thick with mud and debris from the recent rains. We could not even bring ourselves to wash our faces in it.

'Did we cook with this water last night?' Bah Tip asked, knowing fully well that that was precisely what they had done.

'Yeah,' Bah Shngaiñ confirmed. 'There's a spring nearby, but it was impossible to look for it in the dark. Come, come, we had better find it now.'

'But what about the food we cooked last night?' one of the boys asked.

'What has been eaten has been eaten, forget about it,' Bah Tip told him. 'But if you don't want to eat the rice for breakfast, then you'll have to wait for more to be boiled. That will be at about eleven.'

Bah Shngaiñ found the spring and made tea for breakfast. But should we have the rice or not? Our stomachs were growling; we felt faint with hunger. Seeing our reluctance to eat, one of the men said, 'What harm can it do to you when it is properly cooked?'

In the end, hunger won out, and we decided to have some rice too. Bah Shngaiñ ladled generous helpings of it onto our plates. But on the third serving, he brought up not only rice but also his missing flip-flop. He said, 'Ooh, here is my flip-flop! I was looking for it the whole night last night!'

He had cooked our rice with his rubber flip-flop. All of us boys ran to the trees to throw up. And that was the last time I ever went night fishing.

Magdalene shuddered and said, 'Yuck! Cooking rice with a chappal and using that kind of water! Wuu, horrible!'

Evening solemnly said, '*When drunks organise an event, it can only become a drunken affair.*'

'Good one, Ning,' Bah Su said approvingly.

The other story I remember was about the time when Bah Tip was rebuked by an executive member of the locality council. It was about 7 p.m.

when he was discovered lying in a ditch by the official, whose name was Frolein—a meaningless name that sounds as if it was derived from Fräulein. Frolein, a tall, handsome man, was a known womaniser. However, his wealth and influence succeeded in rendering many people blind, and that was how he was able to get himself elected onto the council's executive committee.

When Frolein found Bah Tip lying in a ditch as early as seven in the evening, he launched into a furious tirade against him. 'You lazy good-for-nothing! You do nothing all day but drink! Aren't you ashamed of yourself, you son of an animal? Look, it's only seven o'clock, and you are already falling into ditches and lying in drains! You shameless creature! It's time we banish you from the locality!'

Bah Tip was not at all impressed by this outpouring of anger. He opened one eye to look at the official and said, 'Shameless creature? Who's a shameless creature? Me? I at least am falling into large ditches, but you? You are falling into those little gashes all the time! This big,' he measured the size with his fingers, 'only this big, and you keep falling into them all the time! And you call me shameless?'

Frolein left the place in a hurry, followed by the derisive laughter of the crowd.

Hamkom said, laughing, 'Your characters are really something, man! From the fringes of society, no doubt, some of them even lowlifes, perhaps, but colourful, strange and engaging! I wish I had met some of them myself, you know, Ap.'

'You are meeting them now, man, be thankful!' Raji responded.

'But how did you meet so many people like these, Ap?' Hamkom asked.

'Thanks to my childhood in Sohra, my poverty and my days as a tenant in Shillong, moving from one slum to another.'

'It's hard to imagine you had that kind of background, Bah Ap,' Donald remarked.

Some of our gang, especially Hamkom, Donald and Magdalene, were born into wealthy families and had led sheltered lives. To them, all of this must have sounded like a different world. That was why they kept asking us if we were telling tall tales. As for me, I'm thankful to have lived the kind of life I have. I cannot imagine anyone being a writer without an intimate acquaintance with life and the people that inhabit its many different layers. Poverty of experience would have killed my creativity.

But I was not done with Bah Tip yet. He remained a memorable character to the very end, I told them. When he died, his drinking buddies refused to let anybody help with the gravedigging. They insisted on doing it themselves in honour of his memory. Consequently, on the day of the burial, they drank and ate and dug till 2 p.m. When they sent a message to the house that everything was ready, the body of Bah Tip was carried to the graveyard by another bunch of his drinking buddies. But when they reached the cemetery and tried to lower the coffin into the grave, it simply would not go in. Bah Tip's drunken friends tried it from one end of the grave and then from the other, but it was no use; it just could not be squeezed in. After that, everybody stood back to have a better look. The grave was dug in the shape of an 'S'.

'Tet sala!' Bah Kynsai boomed.

The others laughed aloud. But Magdalene wanted to know what happened next.

'Why do you want to know the obvious?' I asked her.

'Tell, tell, no?'

'What is there to tell? The locality boys took over and straightened out the grave, but it was not till 7 p.m. that Bah Tip could be lowered into his little hole.'

'*A crooked grave for a crooked life!*' Evening announced. 'How's that for a moral, Bah Su?'

'A drunk he may have been, but crooked he was not,' I defended Bah Tip.

Hamkom was a bit confused. 'But, Ap, you said he refused to become a Christian, so how was he buried and not cremated?'

'Perhaps I didn't make myself clear, Ham. Bah Tip was already a Christian. Reverend S wanted to reform him and take him into his own church.'

'Oh, okay,' Hamkom said.

Hearing the disappointment in his voice, Raji said, 'Why, do you think only non-Christians are alcoholics, Ham? Look at the hard drinkers in this room, how many? Three: Bah Su, Bah Kynsai and I. And how many are Christians? Two. And what about the sippers? Everyone is a sipper here except for Dale, Halolihim and Ap, maybe—'

'I also sip, sometimes,' I told him.

'Okay, so how many sippers are Christians? You, Ning, Don, Mag. Four to two.'

'See, Ham,' Bah Kynsai added, 'we are in the majority everywhere, na, that's why, among the drinkers also we are in the majority, hahaha … Anyway, let's forget about all that, na? Ap, what about the other drunk?'

'The story of the other drunk is not a very long one,' I said. 'It's about another drunk–priest encounter and took place at a funeral gathering in Malki not so long ago.'

According to a friend of mine, on entering the compound of a death house in the locality, a priest noticed a group of drunks sitting in the courtyard, talking loudly and laughing even louder. Obviously, they were having a good time. The priest thought it might be a good idea to sit with them and talk some sense into them. He went towards them and said, 'Hello, young men, may I join you?'

Immediately the conversation died down, and the drunks became respectful and made room for him. Soon the priest began speaking to them about sinful living and the terrible punishment that awaits such people in hell. 'Imagine the heat of a thousand suns!' he visualised the torment of hell for them. 'Imagine that agonising pain for eternity! Would you not fear that kind of eternal damnation? Think very carefully, young men, before you choose what kind of life you want to lead.'

Every one of the drunks bent his head in shame, feeling crushed by the priest's frightening sermon. But one of them, called Boit, because he was pint-sized, was not very bothered. Changing the topic, he asked, 'Reverend, I heard you went to Chennai recently, no?'

'Yes, I did, Boit, how did you know? I got back only yesterday.'

'How was Chennai, Reverend?'

'Terrible, simply terrible this time of the year! Impossibly hot, I tell you, forty degrees Celsius and above! Imagine, here at twenty-four or twenty-five degrees, we grumble about the heat. But in Chennai, forty and above! Terrible, terrible!'

'So what did you do? How did you bear that kind of heat, Reverend?'

'Initially, I thought I would go mad. The fan in my room did not work. It was stiflingly hot. I had to remove all my clothes and went about with only a little loincloth. I bathed several times a day. I wet a towel and covered myself with it; I did all sorts of things just to get a little relief from the heat. Outside, it was even worse. I had to discard my suits and went about in only a tee-shirt and shorts and chappals. And of course, I had to carry an umbrella everywhere. But even with all that, you cannot stay outdoors for any length of time. It was the worst time of my life. But thankfully, after a few days, I got used to it and was able to cope with it much better.'

'So, after a few days, you got used to it, Reverend?' Boit asked with a knowing smile on his thin, dark lips.

'Yeah, I ... Wait a minute, what are you driving at, you little imp?'

'I'm not driving at anything, Reverend,' Boit said innocently. 'But it's nice to know that a man can get used to all that heat, no, Reverend?'

All my friends laughed at Boit's punchline, except for Evening, who said angrily, 'Bloody drunks! How do we get rid of these drunks?'

'They may be bloody drunks, but that was witty, man!' Magdalene countered.

'Ning,' I called out, 'your statement reminds me of a woman in Upper Shillong.'

With Bah Kynsai's permission, I told them the story of a woman called Kong Lieh (because she was very fair) and the unique way in which she dealt with her son's drinking problem.

The woman was a prosperous fish supplier. Since she was so rich, she gave her only son, the handsome Jonathan, whom she doted on, everything that he asked for. This gradually spoiled him to such an extent that he refused to study or do any sort of work at all. He was encouraged in this by his friends, who kept telling him, 'Why study or work when your mother is so rich? Enjoy life, spend her money, otherwise all her wealth will end up with your sisters, or worse, with your brothers-in-law!'

Jonathan did exactly that, spending his days enjoying life, going out with women and drinking with his friends. Soon, he became a chronic alcoholic. The women were quickly forgotten, and the only mistress he knew was alcohol. Kong Lieh tried to control his excessive drinking, and whenever Jonathan asked her for money, she used to say, 'Son, I cannot stop you from drinking. It's too late for that. It was my fault, spoiling you with money in the first place. But at least try to control your drinking. Take a peg, or two, or even three or four at night before dinner. But stop this kind of binge-drinking! Every night, people find you lying in ditches and roadsides … We are a God-fearing, religious family, Son, stop putting us to shame like this. Come and work with me in the shop, learn the business, be your own man, stand on your own feet. If you want to drink, drink at night, in your own home, I won't object to that.'

But Jonathan always responded with expletives and all sorts of unfounded accusations. 'You are giving me, your only son, only this, liah! Three hundred rupees, tdir! Only for half a bottle, lyeit! What are you trying to do with all the money? Save up for my brothers-in-law? My friends are right. You don't love me; you only love your daughters!'

Saying this, he would go berserk, throwing things around, breaking them, thrashing his sisters and threatening to hack his brothers-in-law to death with the machete he always carried, and with which he slashed at tables, chairs, window shades and curtains.

And that was not all. When Kong Lieh tried to ration his drinks, Jonathan beat her up and threatened to cut her throat, for he was convinced that she loved her 'stray dogs', the sons-in-law, more than she loved him.

Kong Lieh was fed up. One day, she said, 'Jo, since you think I hate you for trying to control your drinking, I will stop doing that. From now on, I will give you whatever you want. I will even buy for you the most expensive drinks available, however much you want. My only condition is that you drink at home, in that shed. I will keep you supplied with food and drinks from morning till night, but don't go out to drink in the boozers and don't ever beat up your sisters and throw tantrums around the house again. Do you agree?'

Jonathan thought for a while and then said, 'There's no fun drinking alone—'

'Bring your friends, it doesn't matter, but don't go out. We'll keep all of you happy, but don't make any trouble around the house.'

Jonathan agreed. Every day, Kong Lieh bought at least fifteen bottles of the best whisky available for him and his friends. Jonathan was very happy. He thought his mother had finally seen the light. 'Blood is blood. How can she love the stray dogs more than me?' he bragged to his friends.

What he did not realise was that his mother was feeding him slow poison in exchange for a little peace of mind. And it was not so slow either, for, within a year, Jonathan developed all sorts of problems and finally died of multiple-organ failure.

I concluded the story by saying, 'Perhaps, Ning, this is what you have in mind?'

'Damn it, Ap, that was a horrible story, man!' Magdalene swore. 'A mother doing that to her own son!'

'I don't see what choice the mother had,' Evening said, defending Kong Lieh.

'What choice! Why man, she should have helped him instead of poisoning him like that, no?' Magdalene cried with indignation.

'But how?'

'Yeah, there's the rub, isn't it?' Bah Kit asked. 'How do you help drunks? And there are so many of them, no?'

'You know, Mag,' Raji said, 'Khasi men have tattoos like tigers and so on drawn on their arms when they're young, okay? They feel like heroes, you know, sitting on their bikes with only their black tee-shirts on and showing off their tigers. But by the time they are twenty-odd years old, okay, because of alcohol abuse, okay, their muscles become flabby, and their tigers become little kittens.'

'They should have had the tigers drawn on their cheeks, na?' Bah Kynsai laughed.

'Why, why?' Magdalene asked.

'Because the more you drink, the more your cheeks puff up, that's why! No chance of tigers becoming kittens.'

Hamkom asked, 'What percentage of Khasi men would you say are drunks?'

'Maybe 30 per cent or a little more. We can only guess.'

'That's a huge percentage, ya, Bah Kynsai,' Donald observed, 'but I seem to remember that Mag mentioned 90 per cent—'

'What?' we all cried. 'That's crazy, man!'

'No, no, I didn't say that, dear Don,' Mag clarified. 'I said about 90 per cent of Khasi men who die below the age of forty-five die because of heavy drinking. That's different.'

'Ah, I see, sorry, Mag,' Donald said apologetically. 'So why doesn't the state government try prohibition?'

'Yeah, there have been many attempts to … it's no use,' Evening said.

'But those were not real attempts at prohibition, Evening! They were trying to abolish the local stuff, but what I mean is a total clampdown by the government on the manufacture and sale of all types of liquor.'

'That would never work, Don,' Bah Kynsai asserted. 'In the US, na, the period from 1920 to 1933 was known as Prohibition, you also know that, na? The production and sale of liquor were completely forbidden during that time. But it didn't work, did it? Closer home, in the state of Mizoram, na, the prohibition policy was followed for seventeen years. But now the Mizoram Liquor Total Prohibition Act of 1995 has been lifted, and the sale of liquor has been allowed with effect from January 2016.'

'But why didn't it work?' Donald persisted.

'Why?' Raji asked. 'Because most people are like us, no? As long as people want to drink, okay, there will always be sellers and black marketeers, and they will simply charge three, four times the usual price. Consumers pay through their nose and the government gets nothing.'

'Not only that, Don,' Bah Kynsai added. 'Total prohibition, as was the case in Mizoram, na, can lead to worse problems, like drug abuse … And then, think of the adverse economic effects, man! The first to be hit would be the tourism industry.'

'So, what is the solution then?'

'Control,' Raji responded. 'For instance, in Mizoram, okay, the Prohibition Act has not been completely lifted. It has only been replaced with the Mizoram Liquor Prohibition and Control Act, 2014, which strictly prohibits drunken driving and drunkenness in public places—'

'Here, our government has moved in the right direction,' Evening interrupted. 'And it deserves praise, despite my earlier condemnation, okay? Its recent order to disallow the sale of liquor within 200 metres of educational institutions, hospitals, places of worship and within a hundred metres of the national highway has really been very effective, no, Bah Kynsai? I think many liquor shops have closed down already.'

'Closed down and caused me untold misery, liah! Imagine, they have even closed down my usual watering hole, man!'

'Well, if that's the case,' Donald said, responding to Evening, 'it shouldn't be difficult to shut down the liquor shops altogether, no? All you have to do is open a little school or a little place of worship near them, and voila, the boozers are out of business.'

'No, no, it may not work like that at all, Don,' Raji said. 'Many of the liquor shops that have been closed down in Shillong, okay, are fighting in court now. They are claiming that their shops were established well before the schools or hospitals near them. If they win, okay, it will not be the liquor shops that go out of business but the schools or hospitals established after them.'

Bah Su said, 'The government has amended the Act recently, Raji, I don't know how you missed it. It has allowed liquor stores near the highway, ha, although they should not be visible from it.'

'Has it, Bah Su? Ah, it must be because I was so busy preparing for this trip, ya! I did not even go to the office before heading out here, you know.'

'Well, it seems all the liquor stores, ha, are taking advantage of this new rule,' Bah Su disclosed. 'They are simply putting up screens in front of their entrances and changing their signboards. You know what they write now? "Shop Open" or "Open Shop" in large letters, instead of "Wine Shop".'

'Tet teri ka!' We all laughed. And Evening added, 'The bloody sons of so-and-so!'

After a while, I said, 'There are certain measures adopted by the village councils that are quite good actually. In Sohra, for instance, drunkenness used to be a real problem. During market nights, especially, certain localities like Khliehshnong were crawling with drunks speaking their market-night English. Noisy disputes and drunken brawls were rampant. The streets were not safe for kids and women after dark. To stop all that, Khliehshnong imposed a ban on the manufacture and sale of alcohol, local or foreign, inside the locality. Long-established boozers were given licences to manufacture and sell, but here's the catch, they were asked to set up shop about eight kilometres away from the locality, in the wilderness—'

'Really?' Magdalene laughed.

'Yeah, yeah, and this has dramatically reduced the number of drinkers because only the "hard-cores" will trudge those many kilometres to the boozers. And because of economic compulsions and the absence of public transport, most of them do really have to trudge. By the time they get back, they are already sober again. This also serves to reduce cases of drunkenness inside the town, which has been forbidden in any case. Those who have had too much to drink are forced to sleep it off elsewhere, which means there is no disturbance within the locality. The scheme is quite effective.'

'Aah, the poor drunks of Sohra!' Magdalene chuckled.

'To drink and become sober on the way home is no fun, mə, tdong!' Bah Kynsai said.

'That's the whole point of the scheme, no, Bah Kynsai?' Donald responded. 'Bah Ap is right, you know, if drunkenness in public places is forbidden, and if the authorities are really strict about drunken driving, the situation would be much better.'

'Hey, Bah, hey, Bah Kynsai,' Dale suddenly called out. 'Sorry to interrupt and sorry to say this, okay, but I find it amusing, you know, listening to you all.'

'Why?' Bah Kynsai demanded.

'I mean, forgive me for saying this, but it strikes me as very funny to listen to drunks discussing the evils of drinking for so long ... Please don't mind.'

Bah Kynsai let loose at him. 'We are not drunks, mə, tdong! We drink, but we are not drunks. Look at them,' he pointed to us, 'are they drunk? I'm also not drunk! I'm merely shongshit, a little heated up. Even Bah Su and Raji, for tonight at least, are merely a little more than tipsy. Can't you see that, liah? Remember this, Dale, we are not against drinking; we are against drunkenness, although I'm not sure what Raji feels about it.'

'But how many people can drink without getting drunk, Bah Kynsai?' Dale insisted.

'That's the real problem with us Khasis, no, Bah Kynsai?' Hamkom added.

'When I went to Wales in 1995, na, some of my friends' houses had minibars,' Bah Kynsai informed us. 'The moment we entered, ha, we were offered our choice of drinks. We drank, had dinner, and that was it. Nobody got drunk. If that had been in the Khasi Hills, na, nobody would have stirred from the bar until they had slurped up everything. It's indeed a problem with us, Ham. But still, you cannot go for total prohibition, that will only drive them to the black market and ganja and drugs and whatnot. Also, among the educated drinkers, you know, things are not so bad. I mean, look at us. This is free booze, but nobody has got really drunk, apart from Raji, these last few nights. And Raji was drunk because he chose to be, but tonight, because he doesn't choose to be, he's not drunk. Like me, he's only a little heated up. So, like I said, na, we must fight against drunkenness, not drinks—'

'Yeah, yeah, Bah Kynsai!' Raji readily agreed. 'The fight must never be against drinks but drunkenness! And not through total prohibition, okay, but through effective controls. What do you think, Ap?'

'I suppose so. And Mag is right too. We should help drunks and not try to kill them off. There should be fewer NGOs clamouring for prohibition and more support groups for addicts. The problem should be approached with sympathy, not anger.'

'And it is a big, big problem, okay?' Bah Kynsai stressed. 'I think we should sleep on it, na, rather than try to solve it in one night? What do you say?'

Before anyone could answer, Chirag and Perly came into the hut and said, 'Khublei, Babu, you are still up?'

'Come, come, Chirag, come, Perly, sit, sit,' Bah Kynsai welcomed them.

But they said they were busy and had only come to tell us that the ceremonies would begin very early in the morning. 'So, if you want to record it all, you have to come by 5 a.m.,' Chirag concluded.

'Oh no, 5 a.m.!' Magdalene cried out in surprise. 'And now it's already what? Close to 2 a.m., man!'

Before anyone else could say anything more, I intervened. 'Thank you, Bah Chirag, we'll certainly be there.' When they were gone, I added, 'Those who can't wake up in time can come later. It's not a problem.'

'Chalo, chalo,' Bah Kynsai said. 'Let's try to get some sleep now.'

11

THE
NINTH
NIGHT

ROOT STORIES IV

never knew bulbuls
feeding at dawn, noisy as
Khasi funerals.

—From *Time's Barter: Haiku and Senryu*

'It was quite an exciting day today, ha, Ap?' Raji said, clearly still fired up. 'I got it all on film, man! Very unique, very unique, I haven't seen anything like it in my whole life.'

It was about 7.30 in the evening when we returned to the hut after dinner. Undeniably, 13 February was a day to remember. Someone had come to wake us up at 4.30 a.m. Raji, Bah Kynsai, Bah Su, Bah Kit, Donald and I were the only ones who had decided to go. We had a quick breakfast of tea and boiled rice and proceeded to the death house, where people were already gathering in the courtyard. At that hour, it was lit only by the dim light of a single flambeau suspended from a wooden pillar on the veranda. The burang uncles and all the relatives were there, though Chirag and Perly were nowhere to be seen. The two shamans and other elders from Nongtrai were also in attendance. Everyone appeared to be waiting for something to happen.

Suddenly, the music of drums and lyhir pipes and the noise of people shouting and chanting filled the air. Victor, who had been acting as our interpreter, whispered, 'They are bringing the monolith. We'll start the ceremonies by planting it in the courtyard, over there, near the east entrance, where the shamans are.'

Soon, we could see musicians playing and dancing, spurring on a group of men who were carrying the monolith and other stones. The monolith was a single upright stone about 2.5 feet tall and about sixteen inches thick. The men were also carrying a squarish flat stone, with an area of about 2 sq. feet and a thickness of about eighteen inches, as well as four vertical ones, about a foot tall. The granite monolith—its base wider than the top, which narrowed to a rounded point—and the flat stone were each strapped to two bamboo poles with bamboo strings and were carried by a group of four men. Other men carried the four small vertical stones on their shoulders.

When all the stones had been deposited near the designated site, the men started digging a pit where the monolith would be planted. By the time they were done, the sky had begun to lighten in the east. Suddenly, the senior shaman raised his right hand and the music and the noise stopped. He took a handful of rice grains from a winnowing basket, cupped his hands and touched them to his forehead. He replaced the rice in the basket, took an egg and did the same. Victor explained that no religious ceremony could begin without paying homage to God, the Dispenser, the Creator. After that, the shaman started his prayer by calling upon God, and upon ka ïawbei, u thawlang and u suidña, the guardian spirits of the Shyrkon clan.

Victor gave me the gist of his prayer. The shaman began with an invocation, saying, '*Ko Blei Trai Kynrad*, oh God, Lord and Master, look, I have come here, look, we are all gathered in this spot so we may begin the ceremonies; so we may begin the rites; so the body of Ka We Shyrkon departed some nine moons ago may be devoured, may be cleansed by Ka Syiem Ding, our Queen Fire. We will begin the ceremonies so her soul may be free at last to make its final journey to the abode of the spirits at Krangraij. We will begin the rites so Ka We may live and be happy with all her ancestors, ka ïawbei, u thawlang, u suidña. We will begin them so she may be happy with all her mothers and grandmothers, with all her fathers and grandfathers, with all her relations, maternal and paternal. Look here, oh God, Lord and Master, we will begin, we will plant a monolith in honour of Ka We's memory. We will plant it as a token that we have begun the ceremonies, as a token that we have done all that should be done, so the passage of her soul, from this world to the next, would be smooth, would be free, without obstacles, without hindrances. Bless me, oh God, bless all of us present here, bless this hallowed ground that has been dug, bless it, oh God, so Mother Earth may take this stone into her own bosom; so we may begin; so we may finish the rite of passage for the soul of the departed; so she may live again in the abode of the spirits. Look, I sprinkle these golden grains, these silver grains upon the hallowed ground, accept them, receive them, oh Mother Earth, a token of our prayer to God, a token of our worship, a token of our love. Accept them and let them pave the way for the coming of the male stone, the monolith, who will stand upright in your bosom, now and forever.'

The shaman sprinkled a few rice grains in the pit, took an egg, touched it to his forehead and said, 'Oh God, Lord and Master, you, the Dispenser, the Creator, I have taken this golden egg, this silver egg, attached to our sai hukum, the dispensing thread, the divine decree that defines our lives, that determines our portions, that specifies how long we should live and when we should leave. This golden egg, oh God, Lord and Master, I will break upon this hallowed ground, show me through signs, show me through ciphers, so I may know that you are pleased, so I may know that you bless us, so I may know that everything is all right, that no hurdle stands in our way, so we may go ahead and begin for the sake of the deceased, who has waited these long moons so she may journey to the blessed habitat of those departed. Hear me, oh God, bless me, show me, I have asked, I have pleaded, and now I will break this golden egg so I may read, so I may see.'

So saying, the shaman threw the egg with great force into the centre of the shallow pit. But instead of breaking, it bounced and flew onto the gravelly ground of the courtyard. A gasp of shocked surprise rose from the onlookers. 'How can an egg—so fragile, so brittle—not break when thrown with such force?' they asked each other. 'Something is terribly wrong …'

The shaman raised a hand for silence. Squatting in front of the winnowing basket, he consulted his colleague, then took some cowrie shells from his pocket and put them in the basket along with the rice. Muttering a few indistinct incantations, he moved the shells and rice grains around and studied them carefully. Then, after consulting his colleague again, he stood up, took another egg, touched it to his forehead, and resumed his prayer. 'Oh God, Lord and Master, you, the Allocator of our portions, you, the Giver of our rights, you tell me you are not pleased; you tell me the spirits are not pleased; you tell me Mother Earth is not pleased; people in this village are not pleased. They grumble, you say, they complain, you say, that these ceremonies should be performed. It is true, there have been disruptions; it is true, there have been commotions. The peace of the village has been shattered by the noise of mourners and consolers, with the music of drums and lyhirs; life has been thrown out of gear; people cannot perform their daily routines in peace. Their comings and goings have been interrupted; they cannot sleep properly; they cannot go to their fields and plough the ground; they cannot harvest their crops; they cannot wash their clothes, for the funeral of Ka We Shyrkon demands their attention, demands their help. It is but natural for some people to be displeased, to grumble, to complain. We ask their forgiveness, we ask their indulgence, today we will begin the main ceremonies, today we will conclude them, their inconvenience will be short, their trouble will be short—this we promise. Ko Blei Nongbuh Nongthaw, you, the Dispenser, the Creator, give us our right, give us our due since we have expressed regret; since we have said sorry, bless us, give us a sign.'

So saying, the shaman blew on the egg, touched it to his forehead and threw it into the pit again. But for the second time, the egg bounced and didn't break, and for the second time, the crowd gasped. 'This is horrible,' some said. 'A bad omen,' others said, and still others believed it was an act of witchcraft. 'Some sorcerer has definitely cast a spell,' they proclaimed.

The shaman called for silence as his colleague and he spoke to each other again. Both squatted by the winnowing basket and proceeded to divine why the egg had not broken. After some time, they stood up and the head shaman invoked God again. 'Oh God, Lord and Master; and you, ka mei ka ïaw, the first ancestress; you, u thawlang, the first ancestor; you, u suidñia, the first maternal uncle; look here, the people who are laying these hurdles, who are casting these spells, are hard to please and will not accept our apologies and regrets. They want to stop us, they want to impede us, they want to cross swords with us … We have no right to perform these ceremonies, they say, when the woman died so many moons ago. But the woman, Ka We Shyrkon, oh God, wanted us to give her body to Queen Fire, and had asked her children to conduct the funeral rites according to the old ways. Who are they, these saboteurs, to stand in the way and speak of right and wrong? According to the wish of the departed woman, we will conduct these rites today, so her soul may proceed to Krangraij and meet her happy ancestors. We have implored them, we have pleaded with them, but since they would not be moved, oh God, Lord and Master, we ask your permission, we ask your indulgence, for as virtue is with us, as right is with us, we will give them warning and we will give them notice that we will not be stopped. Threats we will send, curses we will send, so they retreat, so they depart, oh God, Lord and Master, since virtue is with us, we will have to do this.'

Having pleaded with God, he squatted by the basket, took out some objects from his cloth bag, including little pieces of elephant tusk, tiger bone and dried herbs, and placed them with the rice grains and cowrie shells. While he muttered incantations and stirred the objects around in the basket, his colleague was doing his own pleading and divining, blowing into a mug of yiad hiar beer and a cup of water now and then. They did this for quite some time. Meanwhile, the crowd waited, looking on with bated breath. Raji, of course, was recording it all.

When the shamans were done, they got up and went to stand by the pit. The head shaman muttered a short incantation and sprinkled the pit with rice grains, consecrated water and yiad hiar beer. Then he stood back and bowed low, making his obeisance to God. 'Oh God, Lord and Master,' he intoned, 'since virtue is with us, since right is with us, we have given the warning, we have given notice, we have even sent the threat. We have told them of what we can do, of what we must do, should they still stand in the way, should they still try to stop us. And now, I bow low before you, bless us, since virtue is with us, help us, since right is with us, give us a sign, give us a cipher, so we may proceed, for the soul of the departed must be sent on its way.'

So saying, he took one of the eggs that had not broken earlier, blew on it, touched it to his forehead, muttered a few words and threw it into the pit. The egg broke into pieces and sprayed those nearby with fragments of shell and a pulpy mess of white and yellow. The shaman bent to look into the shallow pit and examined the largest piece, which lay with its inner surface facing up. He referred to it as *ka lieng*, the boat. Then he looked at the pieces that had fallen around the boat. Almost all of them lay with their inner surface facing down. He nodded to his colleague and pronounced, 'The way is clear.'

After that first egg, the shaman broke two more eggs in the pit, just to make sure, and then bowing low, said, '*Khublei shihajar nguh*, thank you a thousand bows, oh God, Lord and Master! We thank you, oh ïawbei, we thank you, oh thawlang, oh suidñia! The way, you say, is clear, the path, you say, is free, now that you have given the command, oh Dispenser, oh Creator, we will plant *u mawbynna*, the male stone, we will plant *ki mawshan*, the vertical stones, let them lend their support, let the female stone rest upon them. We will do all this in honour of Ka We Shyrkon, the mother, the grandmother of the Shyrkon clan and ka meikha, the paternal grandmother, of the hundreds and thousands who were born of the Shyrkon men. We will do all this as a sign that we have begun the cremation rites, that we have done what is necessary according to our faith and our religious practices ... Khublei, khublei, khublei.'

The shaman concluded his prayer by thanking God three times and three times bowing low before him. After that, the other shaman said, 'Now, men, plant the monolith!'

At this, the music began again. The lyhir pipes wailed their shrill, mournful notes; the ksing kynthei drums belted out regular, solemn beats; the small bowl-shaped ksing padiah pitched in with their thin, distinctive choir. It was a strange mix of mournfulness and raucousness, which made us feel simultaneously troubled and excited. I tapped my feet and nodded my head, while also feeling strangely haunted.

The planting of the monolith—the menhir, or the upright male stone— was not a difficult matter since it wasn't very large. It was planted in such a way that it faced west, looking directly at the east-facing house. The small vertical stones were planted in front of it, two on each side, and lastly, the flat female stone, the dolmen, was laid on them. The whole construction, when finished, looked like a little chair with a straight back.

After the monolith (called *mawnop*), which would serve as a bone receptacle, had been raised, they washed it with water and poured a libation of yiad hiar beer on it in honour of the deceased. After that, using lime, they drew two vertical parallel lines on it, with a dot at the bottom between them, and placed five pieces of betel nut and five betel leaves on the flat female stone as an offering to the soul of the dead. Lastly, they broke an egg and poured it on top of the leaves.

We noticed that this kwai offering was not prepared as usual. As we have seen earlier, kwai consists of a properly cleaned and peeled betel nut (split five ways or more from the whole nut) and a piece of betel leaf (split two or three ways from the whole leaf) marked with a little lime paste. But because the world of the dead is the inverse of the living, the betel nut placed on the mawnop was unpeeled and split into two pieces only while the betel leaf was unsplit and unmarked by lime at all.

The monolith-planting came to an end at about 9 a.m. By then, the rest of our gang had also had breakfast and came to join us. Magdalene asked us what they had missed. Donald excitedly told her about the eggs and was trying to explain why they would not break when Chirag arrived and said, 'Now we'll have the first bull sacrifice, Babu, come, let us watch.'

The crowd's focus shifted to a large bull tethered separately from the others. This bull, belonging to the family of the deceased and called the *pahja* bull, was supposed to be *u si lam lynti*, the guiding bull, the trailblazer, who would lead the way and escort the soul of the departed to Krangraij, the abode of the spirits. Perly, as one of the nephews of the deceased, was asked to bring the bull into the courtyard. When the bull had been brought before the shamans, the musicians were asked to stop playing so as not to spook him. The shamans fed the bull some boiled rice as well as *jyndem*, the fermented rice used to brew yiad hiar. When he started eating, the shamans asked the crowd to stand back and make room so they could begin the ritual.

The head shaman now spoke to the bull. He said (as summarised by Victor later), 'Oh God, Lord and Master, you, the Dispenser, you, the Creator, look here, oh God, we have brought before you the pahja bull. To us, the living, this bull is but a beast of burden to help us in the fields, he is but an animal to give us meat for the kitchen, but the world of the dead, oh God, as you yourself had revealed to our ancestors, is the reverse of our own, inverted and upside down. This beast of burden, this beast that gives us meat, this beast without awareness, without the thoughts and feelings of a sentient being, becomes the most understanding, the most knowing in the world of the dead. He knows the way to Krangraij as unerringly as we know our way to our hearths and homes. He knows every twist and turn in the trail. He knows the safest paths, and he knows the most dangerous, where demons wait to obstruct, to hinder. He has this knowledge, oh God, as you yourself had revealed a long time ago, as you yourself had advised the ancient ones of our race. We propose, oh God, that this day too, as he has done in the past, he should lead the soul of Ka We Shyrkon, lead it, escort it and take it to Krangraij, the abode of the spirits.

'Let him accompany the yiar kong, oh God, the *yiar krad lynti*, the guiding rooster who will point the way, the rooster who pledged his life to be an intercessor between heaven and earth, between you and us. Let them keep each other company, let them help each other, let them take the soul of Ka We Shyrkon to its destined abode, where Ka We, together with all her kinfolk, gone before her, may be happy, may be joyful.'

He paused to sprinkle the bull with some water. 'This golden water, this silver water,' he continued, 'I sprinkle upon the pahja bull. I wash him with it; I clean him with it; so he will be spotless; so he will be pure; so he will be suitable to be an attendant; so he will be fit to journey into your world. I ask you, oh God, Lord and Master, I ask you for your blessing, for your permission, allow us to send this great and knowing pathfinder to the world of the departed. Let his spirit join the soul of Ka We Shyrkon, so both can wait for the yiar kong, who will join them this very day, so they can all undertake together the long and arduous journey. His sacrifice, oh God, will not be a wanton waste, for his flesh will feed the multitude, and his spirit will live like others to graze in the valley near the abode of the spirits. I ask, oh God, with humility, with self-abasement, bless us, I bow to your will.'

When the shaman finished his pleading, he sprinkled some more water on the bull and asked the family to send a nephew of the deceased to carry out the sacrifice. Perly stepped forward. He carried a sharp axe and stood ready by the bull. When the shaman raised his hand, Perly raised his axe, and when the shaman dropped his hand, Perly slew the tethered bull with a single blow to the back of the neck. Blood spurted like a red fountain, and the huge beast, his neck dangling loosely, sank slowly to the ground, almost in slow motion. Perly had specks of blood on his face and tee-shirt, but the jet of gore had missed him, for he had jumped aside after striking the bull. Apparently, he was very experienced at this sort of thing.

Some of our friends gasped and moaned when they saw the bull falling to the ground in a bloody heap. But Bah Su said it was a humane way of killing. The bull, he maintained, could not have felt anything.

When the pahja bull fell, the shaman directed one of the avuncular relatives to collect the blood and wash the mawnop monolith with it. It was Bromson, the head burang, who came forward. Collecting the blood in his cupped hands, directly from the gushing wound, he ran to the monolith and splashed it with the blood in a symbolic gesture of washing. This act also accomplished the symbolic linking of the spirit of the bull with the soul of Ka We Shyrkon. As Bromson ran, drops of blood fell to the ground, forming a trail of red spots which soon attracted a few ants.

Now, the shaman called for silence. He bowed low and prayed to God: 'Oh God, Lord and Master, the deed has been done, the pahja bull is gone, his spirit waits upon the soul of Ka We Shyrkon, we thank you for your blessing, a thousand bows for your consent. But now, oh Lord and Master, we must plead again. The journey of the soul is a long and arduous one, full of hurdles, full of hardships, full of dangers, full of demons and malignant spirits who will try to stop it and try to deflect it from its destined abode. The soul of Ka We Shyrkon will need more attendant spirits to accompany it, to keep it safe and be its foot soldiers in the other world. We fear the pahja bull and the yiar kong alone may not succeed, may not achieve their purpose, may not accomplish their mission with so many hurdles and dangers on the way. We plead for more attendant spirits, oh Lord and Master, we plead for more of them, as strong and knowing as the pahja bull, to help him, to ease his burden and be a comfort to him. We promise you, oh Lord and Master, their sacrifice will not be a wanton waste, for their flesh will be distributed among the multitude, and their souls will live like others to graze in the valley near the abode of the spirits. I ask, oh God, with humility, with self-abasement, bless us, I bow to your will.'

The shaman then performed a short divination ceremony and prayed with the rice grains and cowrie shells that had been kept in the winnowing basket. When he was done, he stood up and told the burang uncles, 'We can have fifty bulls.'

When someone explained what the shaman was saying, Magdalene yelped, 'Fifty bulls! What does he mean by fifty bulls?'

Chirag, who was nearby, said, 'Shush!' and then, speaking in whispers, clarified: 'All in all, we have eighty bulls in the enclosure, Kong, brought by the burangs and our paternal relations, the children of the burangs and those of Aunt We's sons. Out of these, fifty will be sacrificed to accompany the pahja bull.'

Magdalene grabbed her head. 'Oh my God! Fifty! I'm not going to watch this, you guys do what you like, but I'm not going to watch!'

Chirag smiled and was about to say something when Bromson called out to him: 'Hey, Chirag, you and Perly go and select the bulls of the most elderly burangs and paternal relations ... Lead them out here; keep the others inside.'

After Chirag had left, we all turned to Magdalene. But before any of us could say anything, Evening cried, 'Bah Kynsai, look, look!'

When we followed the direction of his finger, we saw Halolihim among the crowd of onlookers. He was standing with a girl. She was unlike any of the Lyngngam girls we had seen, and very clean. Her skin was rosy; her hair was black and glossy, worn in a bob; her lips were pink and full; and her eyes were sparkling black and lovely. Her nose, though, was rather small and rounded.

'What the hell is he doing with that girl?' Bah Kynsai blurted out. 'And where did he find her? She's beautiful, man! The bloody scoundrel! They are behaving like lovebirds, liah! He's married, na, Ham?'

The girl was holding on to Halolihim's arm as they watched the musicians performing in a corner. I had not realised it, but there were quite a few of them—about thirty. Many of them were sitting on the ground with the lyhir pipe players and the ksing padiah drummers. At least eight others were playing the rectangular ksing kynthei drums and dancing in front of them. It was an absorbing sight.

'He is, Bah Kynsai,' Hamkom responded thoughtfully. Then, after watching them for some time, he added, 'But I don't think you should jump to conclusions like that, no? She must be from one of those families he's trying to convert ... Maybe he has already converted them or what? Does look like it.'

Bah Kynsai snorted but said nothing more. Magdalene and Donald said nothing either, and Bah Kit and Bah Su had no interest in Halolihim. Raji was busy filming. Only Evening and Dale kept staring at him and his female friend. After a while, I also lost interest and strolled over to where Victor stood.

While Chirag and Perly were busy selecting the bulls to be sacrificed, Victor took me to where the pahja bull was being skinned. He said, 'The meat from this bull will go only to the family and closest relatives, the shamans and the body-turners in charge of the cremation. Everyone else will be fed with meat from the other bulls, Babu. The family of the deceased will get the front right leg and meat from the right ribcage. The jaws and horns will be hung on that bamboo pole. You see that one, Babu, behind the monolith? There.'

The pole I saw was adorned with a white cloth and little figures of a fish and a winnowing basket made from matted bamboo. I pointed to them and asked, 'What about those things? What do they stand for?'

'The cloth signifies purity, Babu. The fish represents food for the deceased, and the basket for the accoutrements that she would need in the afterlife.'

'What about the jaws and horns?'

'They represent the spirit of the pahja bull, who is now guarding the soul of the deceased.'

The men had already removed the skin from the bull and were hacking at the body, cutting flesh and bone into large pieces. They reminded me of an army of ants dismembering their prey. Disturbed, I turned my attention back to the musicians. Pointing to the ones sitting on the ground, doing nothing, I asked, 'Why are there so many of them when there are not enough instruments to go around?'

'You see, Babu, from now on, the music must not stop; it must go on till the body has been cremated, so the musicians have to take turns playing.'

'I see. But why must the music be played non-stop?'

'This is a phor, a feast, Babu Ap, or *phur* in your dialect—'

'Yeah, but Ka Phor Sorat is a feast of the dead, Bah Bik!'

'A feast of the dead, yes, Babu, but a feast nonetheless, a celebration! And why? Because the body of Ka We Shyrkon, dead so long ago, is finally to be cremated. Her soul, loitering in these jungles for so long, will finally be able to undertake its long-awaited journey to the valley of the dead, where Ka We will be happily reunited with her parents, grandparents, and her maternal and paternal relations. Even for the living, it is a kind of freedom. At last they have been able to collect enough funds to perform the funeral rites; at last they can liberate the soul of their relative from the ties of the flesh, and that is a kind of liberation for them too, Babu. That is why, although in one way it is a sad event, it is also a celebration. And what is a celebration without music? It would be an insult to the dead.'

Suddenly, there was a loud cheer. We looked up and saw Chirag, Perly and their male relatives leading the first ten bulls to the sprawling courtyard. The crowd seemed to be hungry for blood, frenzied by the gory spectacle to come. The only thing keeping the excitement in check was the fact that it was happening as part of a funeral ceremony. Victor took my arm and said, 'Come, come, let us watch.'

When we got closer, we heard Bromson asking Chirag, 'Have you chosen carefully? What have you done with the rest?'

'We have tied a *rijanop* vine around their necks so they are not slaughtered by mistake.'

'Good, good, let's start, it's getting late. Who will do the slaying?'

Chirag pointed to Perly and four other men.

'Good, good, let's take them to the shamans.'

When we got to where the shamans were waiting, I asked Victor their names. He said, 'The head shaman is Bigod Borchugrei, the other one is Alfred Francis Nachugrei.'

Bigod? Perhaps they were thinking of 'By God' when naming him? I asked Victor why they had English names.

He said, 'Many of us have Christian names though we may not be Christians. It's a fashion.'

The shamans went to each tethered bull, muttering a few words of prayer and sprinkling a little water on their heads to symbolically cleanse them. After that, the slaughtering began. One by one, they were slain with the stroke of an axe to the back of the neck. The blood spurted and flew in the wind like long strips of red bunting, and as the bulls sank to the ground, it gushed into the sand with a gurgling sound like water spilling from some narrow-necked vessel. While it gurgled and gushed, the owners of the slaughtered bulls, burang uncles and male paternal relations collected it in their cupped hands and washed the mawnop with it.

The scene was quite chaotic. As they ran to the monolith, sometimes they bumped into each other and sometimes they slipped on the blood and gore that was now flooding the entire area. If they lost the blood, they returned to their bulls for another handful and ran back. The slayers, taking turns, were soon covered with blood, and sweat flowed down their faces so fast, it was as if someone was pouring water over their heads. Other men pulled the slaughtered bulls away, shouting directions at each other. Still others shouted to them to do the butchering as quickly as possible so the meat could be cooked for lunch. And in that confusion, the crowd gasped in horror or prattled loudly (commenting on the butchered bulls and the skills of the slayers) or laughed (whenever a burang uncle fell) or simply gawked at the gory spectacle and all the bloodletting with an avidity that made me sick.

But finally, it was over. It had taken them less than two hours to slaughter the fifty animals. The crowd dispersed in different directions, some going away to mind their own business, others to watch the dancing musicians and a few to watch the butchering. Victor and I went towards the butchers to see the horns and jaws being stripped of flesh. The moment one was properly cleaned, one of the men went to hang it on the bamboo pole. By the time all the fifty jaws and hundred horns were hung, the pole was bent nearly double with the weight.

I checked my watch; it was 11.40 a.m. I asked Victor what would happen next. 'Now they are busy with all this butchering, Babu. They'll start the next phase after lunch,' he replied.

We could see that some of the meat was being cooked in large cauldrons in the expansive garden. As we watched, more fires were made as more meat was brought for cooking. Rice was also being cooked in large pots in a different part of the garden. It seemed as if all the relatives and the entire village, numbering in their hundreds, would be taking part in the feast.

Victor said, 'It's slightly different in Nongtrai. We don't feed the crowd until the *shad stieh* has been performed, no food at all, people have to bring their own food.'

Shad stieh means shield dancing, except that in a Nongtrai funeral, it's more than a dance. As the clan elder of the deceased stands in the doorway with a shield blocking everyone from entering the death house, the clan elder of the deceased's spouse, symbolising the outsider, fights him for the right of entry. The outsider hits the shield of the house owner with his own, and the owner pushes him back. And they continue to spar like that till the outsider overpowers the owner who guards the door. Sometimes such a clashing of shields can go on for hours if the dancers, or fighters, are evenly matched.

When the clan elder of the deceased's spouse has been able to overwhelm the house guard, he enters and dances with his shield around the deathbed three times. This is followed by a sharing of betel nut and rice beer and a discussion on *beilet*, the money that must be contributed by the outsider's clan for the funeral. It is only after all that has been done that the crowd can enter and take part in the feast.

'But here we have been eating in the death house since we came, nine days ago,' I said.

'It's different for you and us, Babu, but you are right, even the locals have been eating here for days.'

We saw some people covering the blood of the slaughtered bulls with fresh soil brought in gunny bags.

Victor said, 'When the blood is dry, they will scrape it out and burn it.'

We wandered around the courtyard, listening to the music and watching the dancing drummers. Some of them seemed to be quite drunk, and were dancing as if in a trance. Bunching together, they glided around the courtyard in a circular motion, beating the ksing kynthei drums with sticks and palms, lifting their hands in graceful, wafting movements from time to time before letting them fall to the drums again. Circling the rough dancing area, they made little circles of their own.

'It seems to me,' I said, 'as if the dancers are imitating the motions of the earth, revolving around the sun and rotating around its own axis.'

'You are right, Babu Ap …'

'And then, if you watch carefully how they bow to the ground and look up at the sky, it seems as if they are imitating the floating movement of a gentle breeze.'

'This dance is about life and death, God and his creation, Babu, that's why this particular pattern is always followed. While the earth's revolution and rotation give us warmth and light, water and ice, the earth's atmosphere enables us to live.'

'That was a beautiful interpretation, Bah Bik. And the music and the dancing are truly mesmerising, you know … But tell me, how long can they continue with this when some of them seem so drunk?'

'They will continue for as long as it is necessary, and they will continue drinking too. But nothing will go wrong; these are professionals, Babu Ap.'

Suddenly, soaring above the music and the noise of the crowd, we heard the shrill, piercing cry of a woman, followed by the most heartrending chanting I had ever heard. Before I could ask, Victor said, 'Ah, the mourning! It will continue until the body has been cremated. In Nongtrai, it begins the moment the person dies …'

Unlike the westernised parts of Ri Khasi, where it is merely a spontaneous act of crying and sobbing, the mourning here was no less than a song of lament. I don't know how inconsolable the woman really was, but it felt as if her sorrow was stabbing her heart with the spear of despair over and over.

'We call it Ka Lu Ïap Bru, the funeral phawar,' Victor explained. 'There are two mourners, both daughters of Kong We, but they take turns, so you will hear only one voice at any one time. I know some of the words.'

This is one of the funeral chants we heard in Nongshyrkon, but the agony in the singer's voice is impossible for me to render on mere paper:

> *Ani, ni, ni, ni!*
> *Ko Mei khlem ma phi bad no sha ngan shong ngan sah?*
> *Phi la ieh lyndet mo ïa nga Mei!*
>
> *Ani, ni, ni, ni!*
> *Phi la pynlehraiñ sha mo ïa nga?*
>
> *Ah Mei, phim ieit phim peit sha mo ïa nga?*
> *Ïa nga phi la ieh thylli ieh lyndet mo Mei?*
> *Ban bam ngam kwah, kren briew ngam kwah*
>
> *Ani, ni, ni, ni!*
> *Ko Mei balei phim sngew phim sngap sha*
> *Ïa ka jingkyrsiew jingkhot jong nga?*
> *Leit lyngkha wan lyngkha ruh badno shuh?*
>
> *Ani, ni, ni, ni!*
> *Ko Mei mano ban pyllait ïa nga na u riewsniew,*
> *Ha bym don sha ma phi ko Mei baieit?*
>
> *Ani, ni, ni, ni!*
> *Wow, Mei, wat leit marwei wat wan marwei ho!*
> *Sa leit ryngkat bad ki hynmen para ho!*
>
> (Ani, ni, ni, ni!
> Oh Mother, without you, with whom shall I live, with whom shall I stay?
> You have forsaken me, you have left me behind, ha, Mother?
>
> Ani, ni, ni, ni!
> You have really caused me shame, huh?
>
> Ani, ni, ni, ni!
> Oh Mother, you don't love, you don't care for me any more, do you?
> You have left me empty, you have left me behind, ha, Mother?
> To eat, I don't want; to speak, I don't want.
>
> Ani, ni, ni, ni!
> Oh Mother, why can't you hear, why can't you listen
> To my call, to my rousing?
> With whom shall I go to the fields, with whom shall I return?

Ani, ni, ni, ni!
Oh Mother, now that you are no more, who will protect me
From evil men, who, my beloved Mother?

Ani, ni, ni, ni!
Oh Mother, do not go alone; do not come alone, all right?
Go with your brothers; go with your sisters, all right?)

Victor said the mourners would go on like that till the very end, recounting their association with the deceased, lamenting their loss and voicing their loneliness in words steeped in sorrow. He told me that the custom was very much alive in 'these western parts'. Girls are taught by their mothers from a very young age to perform such funeral chants.

I wanted to ask him if that was also true of those who had converted to Christianity when I heard the booming voice of Bah Kynsai saying, 'Bew, liah! Did you hear that, Ap? So touching, man!' Then, typically, in the next breath, 'Come, come, let's have lunch, they are serving lunch right now.'

When I turned to look, I saw that all of my friends were together again. Excusing myself, I followed them to the dining area. When we got there, we found all the benches occupied. But there were scores of people sitting or squatting in groups on the brown winter grass. Each group was sitting in a kind of circle around the rice and meat placed in the middle. We decided to do the same and went to squat in a part of the garden far from the crowd.

One of the servers saw us and came over. She wanted us to go to one of the benches, where she would ask people to make space for us. Bah Kynsai looked at the crowds around the benches, people eating, spilling food, shouting for more rice or meat, for salt and chillies, and quickly said, 'No, no, no, please don't bother, Kong, we'd like to sit here, away from the crowd. Besides, sitting here on the grass, na, is like a picnic.'

The woman went away, promising to bring us our food very soon. After she had left, Raji laughed and said, 'Why did you have to say "like a picnic"? Have you forgotten where we are?'

'Listen to the noise, man!' Bah Kynsai replied. 'The music, the dancing, the people shouting, talking and laughing gaily ... It is a bloody picnic!'

'It may be a picnic for you,' Magdalene said, 'but I'm not eating any meat! I don't want to eat anything—'

One arm around her, Donald explained: 'She's very upset by all that killing.' Then, turning to her, he added, 'You have to eat something, honey, some rice and vegetables at least—'

'Yeah, Don's right, Mag,' Bah Kynsai said. 'If you don't eat anything, na, you'll go hungry the whole day.'

'But that's it; I'm not hungry, no?'

'Hungry or not, you'll have to force something in, Mag,' I responded. 'I'm also sickened by the sight of all that blood, I don't really feel like eating anything. But if we don't eat, we might even collapse in this heat. Think about that, what if we fall ill in this place without doctors and medicines, huh?'

The others too pressed her to eat at least a little rice. Magdalene agreed listlessly: 'I suppose you are right.'

Presently, the food arrived. Two men brought the still steaming boiled rice in a large basin, placed it before us and went away. Two women brought us plates and vegetables—radish, sliced into big pieces, jamyrdoh, raw onions, salt and plenty of green chillies. Then they ladled the rice onto our plates. While they were doing that, the two men returned with another, smaller basin full of beef soup, boiled with potatoes but no meat.

Looking at the food, Donald said, 'See, Mag? You can eat this; there's no meat at all.'

The serving women thought he was worried about having to eat without meat. They quickly assured him: 'Meat will come, meat will come, Bah, they have gone to bring it.'

Donald was trying to explain what he meant when the two men came back with a large basin full of boiled beef cut into huge pieces. As we stared at the basinful of meat, shocked by the sight, Bah Kynsai exclaimed, 'Bew, liah!' But then, realising he should not have said that in front of women and strangers, he quickly apologised: 'I'm sorry, Kong, I shouldn't have said that. But I'm so shocked, na, Kong, we have never been served like this anywhere before. Look at this mountain of meat! My God, you Lyngngam people can really make a man happy!'

The two women laughed happily. They asked us to enjoy the food and to give them a shout should we need anything else.

'Bong leh, Bah Kynsai, look at the size of the meat!' Raji exclaimed.

'The size of papayas!' Bah Kit said.

'Eat, my friends, eat!' Bah Kynsai urged us with great enthusiasm. 'With this much meat, na, we don't need any rice at all.'

He picked up a piece of the meat, bit into it, and then suddenly let out a string of curses, ending with a loud 'Stud, liah! These bloody buggers!'

'What happened, what happened!' we all asked.

'Tdong, man, didn't you see? My teeth bounced off the damn thing, man! It's like chomping on rubber, sala!'

'Huh?' Raji asked.

He, Bah Kit, Hamkom, Evening and Dale took a piece each, bit into the meat and immediately cried 'Bong leh!' in great disappointment.

Bah Kynsai cursed again, and said, 'But look at those Lyngngams over there! Look at the way they are tearing at it!'

'They must have extremely sharp teeth, ya, these fellows!' Hamkom said in a tone of wonderment.

'Tiger teeth!' Bah Kit proclaimed.

'Lyeit! They are treating us like Tantalus, liah!' Bah Kynsai cursed yet again. 'You know the story of Tantalus, na?'

I told the story briefly, at which Dale exclaimed, 'Yes, yes, Bah, it's exactly like that! They are putting all this meat in front of us, knowing full well it cannot be eaten! Hahaha, what a thing to do!'

'Actually, they don't know that, Dale,' I defended our hosts. 'They think we have shark teeth like them.'

Some of our friends tore at the tough, leathery meat, cursing it all the while. As for me, I never touched it at all. I have never approved of animal sacrifice of any kind, and the sight of fifty bulls being slaughtered at once had really grossed me out. I hoped the incident would turn me into a vegetarian. But I knew it would not, not only because it is difficult to be a vegetarian in the Khasi Hills but also because I would probably forget all about it and start eating meat again by dinner time. Even at that moment, I would not have turned down a little dried fish.

Magdalene, Donald and Bah Su did not touch any of it either. (Bah Su's abstention, I suspected, had nothing to do with squeamishness, only the weakness of his teeth.) While Donald and Bah Su ate the rice with the beef soup and potatoes, Magdalene and I ate it with only salt and some raw vegetables. But the rest of them did not give up. They selected a piece of meat, gnawed on it for some time, then threw it away. As Bah Kynsai put it, 'Just to get the juice.'

After lunch, we went to where the betel nuts and lime-marked betel leaves were kept in a large basket.

As we stood there, Hamkom said, 'That was a memorable lunch, ha, Bah Kynsai?'

'Never tasted anything like it before,' Bah Kynsai said, laughing loudly.

We went to the courtyard to see what was happening, and met Chirag there. He explained that the cremation ceremony would begin as soon as the shamans, the elders and the musicians had had their lunch. 'The musicians will take some time, Babu, they have to take turns eating. The music must not stop, no?'

We dozed for a while under the shade of a massive tree and woke to a flurry of activity on the spacious veranda of the death house. It was about 2.15 p.m. They were bringing out the body in a krong bier. It was not an elaborately constructed thing like those back home, which are wrought in bamboo in the shape of a rectangular trunk with a lid swelling out convexly like a carapace so that it becomes easy for coffins to be put in. Traditionally, only very rich Khasi-Khasis used coffins. Everyone else simply wrapped the body in a bamboo mat and then put it inside a krong bier. But these days, everybody uses coffins although, unlike the Christians, Khasis place the coffins inside the krong bier. The krong bier elsewhere in Ri Khasi is not only elaborately constructed but also beautifully decorated with colourful silk jaiñsem and traditional ryndia silk shawls. Cane loops are attached on both ends so that pall-bearers can insert long bamboo poles into them. But the krong bier here was a very simple affair without even a lid on top. The body, wrapped in a bamboo mat called tliang, was kept in it and simply covered with a maroon silk jaiñsem.

The nearest relatives were all assembled on the veranda on either side of the krong bier—maternal relations to the left, paternal to the right. The chief shaman, standing at the head of the krong bier with the other shaman and some elders, began to pray under his breath, sprinkling rice grains, water and yiad hiar beer on the body. Then he stood back and called for eulogies. There were two speakers, one, a burang uncle from Kong We's clan, and the other an elder representing her paternal relations. The two spoke eloquently, recounting Kong We's life story, their association with her, and the great emptiness her demise had left in them. They highlighted exemplary events in her life and ended with prayers of their own that her soul may travel smoothly and be accepted gladly into the abode of the spirits.

The music toned down for the speeches, a subdued sound in the background. The chanting of the funeral phawar too had quietened to a low moaning emanating from one of the two women who squatted near the krong bier. The women had their heads and faces covered. I could see the red mouth of the chanter, stuffed with masticated betel nut, opening and closing as she chanted her lament quietly.

When the eulogies had been said, the head shaman came forward again to begin his prayer in earnest. He started by invoking the aid of God, U Blei

Trai Kynrad, and pleaded with him on behalf of the deceased. He said, Kong We, as a human being, may have had faults and failings like the rest of us. Through omission and commission, she may have blundered in her life; she may have displeased and offended neighbours and friends, and so, he pleaded for God's forgiveness on her behalf. Her faults, if any, he said, could not have been very serious, for she was loved by all. Finally, he implored God for his blessing so Kong We's soul would be allowed free entry through the golden gates of Krangraij into the blessed abode of the spirits, where the hardships and sufferings of the world would all be forgotten.

After the prayers, his colleague gave the head shaman the red rooster, the yiar kong, that had been tied for the last few days to the dead body. Accepting the yiar kong, the head shaman bowed low, touched him to his forehead, and then twisted his neck. He let a few drops of blood drip on the body and began praying again, pleading with God to bless the yiar kong—who had just sacrificed his life in the service of man, as he had pledged a long time ago—so he could be a true guide for the soul. He also prayed for the well-being of Kong We's family, her clan, her paternal relations, her friends and neighbours, and all those with goodwill who had come to see her off on her final journey. He ended his prayer by sprinkling some more rice grains, water and rice beer on the body.

When all that was done, he signalled to the pall-bearers to approach. Two men came forward and tied a cane strap to both ends of the krong bier's two bamboo poles. Meanwhile, the assisting shaman picked up a bag (roughly fashioned out of a white cotton sheet) from the wooden floor and dangled it from his left shoulder. Taking some rice grains from it with his right hand and holding the yiar kong rooster in his left, he went to stand behind the krong bier, his weather-beaten face composed and still. When the head shaman raised his hand, the pall-bearers put the cane straps on their heads, gripped the bamboo poles in their hands and stood up; when he lowered it, the horn-blower responded. Three times the horn sounded, after which the assisting shaman threw some rice grains and the rooster forward, signalling the beginning of the funeral procession. As the cortege moved out of the courtyard, the assisting shaman moved to the front, sprinkled some more rice grains, picked up the rooster and threw him ahead again. And he did this throughout the procession, not only to mark the route but also, symbolically, to clear the way for the soul's journey.

The sounding of the horn was also a signal for the music and the mourning to intensify. And so, we followed the krong bier through the village. It was a noisy, confused kind of procession, not at all the solemn and dignified affair that you would expect in a cortege. The mourners walked directly behind the krong bier, crying 'Ani, ni, ni, ni' in a high-pitched wail and chanting their funeral lament in a mournful voice. The musicians came after them, dancing and beating their drums and playing their lyhir pipes. All of us moved in a ragged line, with children raising a dust cloud, running around us and fighting each other for the coins being thrown by someone from the family. Men shouted loud instructions to each other and the crowd gossiped loudly, joked and laughed.

But the procession did not head directly to the cremation hill. It wended its way to Chirag's ancestral house and stopped at the courtyard. The krong bier was placed on sticks laid on the ground. Chirag's sister came out of the house and presented the assisting shaman with an egg and a bottle of yiad hiar beer. The rice beer was poured on the body, while the egg was given to an elder who circled the krong bier once before returning it to the shaman to be broken at the pyre later.

Victor told me the ceremony was called *kaikong*, literally, 'visiting houses'. Before the body could be taken to the cremation hill, he explained, it had to be carried to the houses of the maternal and paternal relations of the deceased as a kind of leave-taking. The body of Ka We Shyrkon was taken to almost every home in the village, for everyone was either her maternal or paternal relation. Incongruously, the visit reminded me of a politician on a door-to-door election campaign.

Eventually, at about 4.15 p.m., the procession reached the cremation hill. The krong bier, now thoroughly soaked in yiad hiar beer, was placed on a stack of sizeable logs, and the crowd gathered around it, watching the musicians and mourners. Meanwhile, some of the men proceeded to make the *thyrnang*, or pyre. Four thick posts about two feet high, called *dpha*, were planted on the ground in the shape of a rectangle. The top ends of the posts had been cut out in a 'Y' shape, and within their hollows, two smaller logs, called *snoij*, were laid lengthways and tied to the posts with bamboo strings. Two others, called *bajilan*, were laid sideways on top of the snoij and tied securely to them. The process of laying and tying poles lengthways and then sideways was repeated until the pyre was about three feet high. Four bamboo poles were then planted at the four corners of the pyre. They were tied together at the top with liana and decorated with large leaves. Finally, firewood was piled on the pyre, which was now ready to receive the body.

First, however, the krong bier was taken around the pyre three times. Then, the body, wrapped in its bamboo mat, was lifted from it and placed on the firewood. A white rooster called *yiar tha thyrnang*, or pyre-marking rooster, was handed to the head shaman, who cut his throat and let his blood drip on the body together with some more yiad hiar beer. Victor told me that the pyre was never lit until it had been marked with the blood of the pyre-marking rooster. This was because, according to the sacred myth of the purple crest, Man had made a promise to Rooster never to begin any important religious rite without the offer of his sacrificial blood. The promise was an acknowledgement of Rooster's success in bringing back Sun to earth—symbolically, his success in winning God's forgiveness for Man through his humility.

Once the pyre was marked with the rooster's blood, the head shaman signalled to the male relatives of the deceased to set it alight. When the fire was ablaze, and orange flames soared from it, he took the guiding rooster, the yiar kong, and threw him three times across the pyre from right to left, left to right and right to left again, after which he tossed him into the flames together with the pyre-marking rooster. This signified that the yiar kong was ready to lead the soul of the deceased, through fire as it were, to its final resting place. The shaman then took the eggs collected during the kaikong ceremony and broke them on top of the pyre one by one. All that done, the musicians and the mourners circled the pyre three times as a sign that all the funeral obsequies were complete. The female mourners now returned home, while the male relatives stayed behind to make sure that all would go well.

Meanwhile, the musicians continued to play and dance until, at last, the fire burnt out. The body-turners poked around in the coals to see if any lumps of flesh were left unburnt. Satisfied that all was well, they spread the coals thin and sprayed them with water to extinguish them. Then bone fragments were collected in a large gourd and kept in a bamboo enclosure covered with maroon silk jaiñsems. They would be taken home and placed beneath the female stone of the mawnop after three nights had passed. Near the pyre, a miniature straw hut was built with bamboo poles planted upside down, the thicker base facing up. Offerings of food and drinks were placed inside together with all the accoutrements the deceased would need in the afterlife. The hut was intended as a temporary spirit lodge, where the soul of Ka We Shyrkon would spend the night before going to its eternal abode at Krangraij when the guiding rooster sounded his bugle three times in the morning.

As we waited by the pyre, the stars came out one by one. Darkness crept along the ground, climbed up the trees and rose to the sky in thick waves. Flambeaus came to life, casting weird shadows on the people still milling about in the dark. Finally, the funeral rites for the passage of Ka We Shyrkon's soul were complete.

The Lyngngams believe that the soul of the deceased has to overcome two obstacles before entering the blessed abode of the dead. First, it would have to scale a sheer precipice by the name of Phok Sohlait, and then, before reaching the top, it would have to climb a tree known as Diengpun Diengsohlait, or the ladder tree of Sohlait, which is guarded by a malevolent spirit. If these rites of passage are not performed, it is believed that the spirit guarding the Diengpun would prevent the soul from getting through to the top. That is why Ka Phor Sorat, the feast of the dead, used to be of such paramount importance to the people of Lyngngam.

Once the soul has succeeded in scaling Phok Sohlait, it is a downhill journey until the River Umbylleiñ. Before crossing this river, the soul has to cleanse itself by bathing in its waters. And when that is done, it emerges as a new being, cleansed of disease and suffering, of failings and transgressions. Above all, it is cleansed of memories, for no spirit can be truly happy unless the memories of the living world have been completely washed away. That is why the river is called Umbylleiñ, the river of forgetfulness.

Once the soul crosses this river, it can enter the eternal abode of the spirits, but the spirits of the animals accompanying it will have to stop at the valley of Diengphieng, the tree of awe, where they will spend their lives in eternal bliss. The soul-ushering bulls are believed to be initially tethered to this tree before they are released by the spirits guarding the valley. The Lyngngams insist that the tree truly exists in a place just outside Balpakram National Park. They say it bears the marks of the countless bamboo strings used to tether bulls to it.

That, then, was the exciting day Raji was referring to when we got back to our hut that night.

Hamkom asked, 'And you really got it all on camera? Don't forget to give me a copy of the CD, okay?'

'I'll give everyone a copy, don't worry, but at the right price,' Raji said, laughing.

'No problem,' Hamkom agreed.

'You bloody mercenary!' Bah Kynsai teased him.

'Only make sure you don't put too much of the bull slaying in it, okay?' Magdalene requested him.

'I can't, even if you want me to. It's too gory.'

'But why slaughter so many of them? Do the Torajans do this too, Bah Kynsai?' Donald asked.

'The Torajans' belief in the afterlife, na, is so strong that their dead are buried together with all the tools they would need to carry on their usual trade in the other world. The Lyngngams, I gather from the things they put in the little spirit lodge, have a similar belief. But about the bulls, I'm not sure ...'

'Their reasons for the bull sacrifice are very different, Don,' I explained. 'The Torajans believe that the slaughtered buffaloes and pigs will join the deceased in death, so he can continue herding them in the spirit world as on earth. But for the Lyngngams, the pahja bull is the guide for the soul of the deceased. The other bulls are slaughtered to accompany him, since the journey is long and dangerous. The smearing of the mawnop with their blood is to symbolically link their spirits with the departed soul. It is also to let the deceased know that the relatives have contributed to the funeral rites. But the slaughter also has a very practical reason—to feed the massive crowd of mourners who will be in attendance for the next few days.'

'For how long will they be here, do you think?' Donald asked.

'For as long as the food lasts,' Bah Kynsai said with a straight face.

We all laughed, and Donald said, 'Tet leh, Bah Kynsai, be serious, ya!'

'After three nights have passed, Don,' I replied. 'After the end of the mourning period.'

'We call it "*lait ïa*", the free day, when we are all free from mourning,' Raji explained.

'Bah Raji, I realise that all this is quite unique, but exactly how different is it from the traditional funeral of the Khasis elsewhere?' Donald wanted to know.

Raji gestured to Bah Kit, who said, 'Well, everything is different. Our funeral rites now are comparatively simple. We don't have sacrifices and music any more—'

'But the noise and the confusion are still the same, okay, even without the music,' Raji remarked. 'And that is true of both non-Christian and Christian funerals—'

'Not so much Christian funerals,' Evening protested.

'You think so?' Raji challenged. 'The only quiet spot in a Khasi funeral is the room where the body is kept and where the closest family members keep vigil. Apart from that, all is noise and bustle, and you well know it, Ning. But as an additional reminder to you, let me read you a poem written by a friend of mine.'

Raji looked through his mobile phone for a few moments, and said, 'Here it is: "Requiem (Remembering Meri)". Mag, you read, okay, you are a much better reader than me.'

'There are two parts, shall I read both or just the part relating to the funeral?' Magdalene asked.

'If you read both, I think it will be clearer, no?'

Magdalene agreed and read the poem in a well-modulated voice:

I

The moans that floated
into the still autumn nights
were borne by the cold winds
onto the season of carols.

I heard them nightly,
beating against the window panes
like disembodied tenebrios
pleading to be let in.

I heard them as I went to sleep,
and heard them as the rooster
sounded his first call to the sun.

I heard them as the cockcrowing clocks
summoned schoolboys to their texts,
and heard them as the muezzin
loosed his azaan into the murky air.

What was wrong with Meri?

Her very name calls upon God to protect,
but there she was,
moaning as naturally as a sleeper, snoring.

No doctor came …

And finally, only two titanic tarantulas,
one black, the other with a crimson chest,
crept with slow hairy steps, like skulkers
of the night, and hauled her off
to their invisible lair.

II

Love broke into loud lamentations.
The mother cried for divine explanations.
Mourners swarmed her deathbed.
A tent was erected, the courtyard illuminated.
A tearful vigil was kept up
for two consecutive nights.
Packs of cards were bought,
raconteurs joked, sympathisers guffawed.
Her body was washed and scented.
Utensils were rented.
She was dressed in her favourite clothes
adorned with her favourite trinkets.
A funeral feast was hosted.
Church elders were invited.
The cortege assembled.
Prayers were offered.
Kwai in dishes was ordered.
Sermons were shouted.
Gossips were floated.
Psalms were read.
Tea and biscuits were distributed.
Then, her sudden demise was sadly lamented:

such a young girl,
such a sweet girl,
such promise ....

But the eschatologists offered some comfort.
They were happy she had gone so peacefully.

When Magdalene finished reading, Bah Kynsai said, 'That second part,
na, Mag, describes our funeral practices exactly as they are!'

'Yeah, no, Bah Kynsai?' Hamkom agreed. 'That's what we do exactly, ya.'

'Don't try to say Christian funerals are quieter, Ning,' Raji added.

'Who's your friend, Raj?' Magdalene asked.

'Not Raj, Mag, please, I hate being called that. But about my friend, okay, he could be me also, who knows?'

'Oh, like that, is it? I didn't know you write poetry as well, ya.'

'Actually, you don't know anything about me, whereas I know many things about you—'

'Such as?' Donald asked testily.

Raji took a sip from his mug of rice beer. 'Don't give me that evil eye, you bloody fool!' he said, laughing. 'I know things about people because I'm a journalist. But I don't know anything bad about your Mag. Just a little bit maybe, but nothing to worry about.'

Magdalene threw a fistful of straw at him, and laughing, said, 'Can't you see, Don, he's drunk again, he's toying with us?'

'No, I'm not drunk! This is only my first sip, Mag, don't insult me like that. But it's true, Don, I'm only joking.'

'Hey, you three, we are getting distracted, mə, tdong! Don's question about the funeral of the Khasi-Khasis has not been answered, na?'

'Traditional, Bah Kynsai, not as it is now,' Donald corrected him.

'Let Ap explain,' Bah Kit said. 'He gave a talk on it recently.'

'Actually, I dreamt about my own death, you know, a few months ago,' I told them. 'And what they did to my body was exactly what my ancestors would have done to a dead relative. When I thought about it, I was reminded of the words of Jorge Luis Borges: "The dead one, alien everywhere, / is but the ruin and absence of the world. / We rob him of everything".'

'Profound, profound, but who's he, man?' Hamkom asked.

'A famous Argentine author,' I replied and then narrated my dream.

When I died, I saw people swarming about my bed, looking down at me, like a crowd at an accident site. Among them were my mother, my sister, my wife and daughters (in my dream, I was married and had two daughters) and all my closest relatives. They were too unpleasantly curious for my taste. My two brothers pushed them back, however, and told them to sit down and be quiet. Then my eldest brother—whom we call Bah, and who does not look anything like me, being taller and browner—bent down to my ear and called my name. He said, 'Ap Jutang Shadap, can you hear me?'

I thought that was very strange, you know. Why should my brother call me Ap Jutang Shadap when he used to call me Ap? But now he was calling to me again, 'Hey, Ap Jutang Shadap, wake up, everyone is here.' He waited for some time, and when I did not respond, he called for the third time: 'Hey, Ap Jutang Shadap, if you can hear me, show me a sign!'

He waited for a while, and when there was no sign from me, he turned to the assembled family and shook his head, indicating that I was dead. That gesture was like a gun going off at a racecourse, and my whole family erupted in a terrible cacophony of crying and bawling. My mother and my wife threw themselves on my body and cried inconsolably. 'Why are you leaving us like this, all alone in the world? Why are you going away so soon? You have spent but half your season here, why do you have to go? What will we do, how will we carry on without you?' They went on and on with such questions and accusations as if I were to blame for it all.

One of my daughters climbed onto the bed, took my face in a warm embrace, and sobbed desolately into it. My other daughter cried less forcefully, though she did keep a hand on my body all the time. I looked very closely at my teenage daughters. They were quite beautiful. The one who was sobbing into my face was dusky and had sharp features like her mother, while the other had inherited my fair complexion and features. But both were beautiful, and I was delighted to have sired children such as them. The other relatives crowding around the bed, including my plumpy sister, were also crying. My sister kneeled near my feet and covered her sobbing face with her jaiñsem. There were others too, who had come in, obviously attracted by the noise. They stood around the room, speaking in whispers and putting on sad expressions.

As all this was happening in my bedroom, outside, my brothers, cousins and nephews were discussing what to do next. Bah, my eldest brother, asked, 'What shall we do, shall we wrap his body in a bamboo mat, or put it in a *shyngoid* as the rich people do?'

A shyngoid is a kind of lidless coffin hollowed out of a tree trunk. I was pleasantly surprised that, in my dream, I was considered a rich person.

One of my cousins, a tall, big-boned man whom we call Bah Son (I suddenly realised with regret that I did not even know his full name) said, 'If we do that, we'll have to sacrifice a *niang shyngoid* ...'

'That's okay; a shyngoid pig is not a problem, he's put money aside for his own funeral. We always thought he was crazy, but now we know why ... he must have sensed it all along, you know.'

'Well, if the money is there, we can even buy new clothes for him. In the past, they used to dress the dead in new clothes: white shirt, white dhoti and white turban. And the turban is coiled from the left, not from the right as we do with the living—'

'I don't think we can do that,' my other brother, Bahnah, argued. He is very different from me in appearance; in fact, he looks nothing like me. 'First of all, he wouldn't have liked being put in those clothes, and secondly, we may not have the time. How many nights are we planning to keep him, two?'

'No!' Bah Son said emphatically. 'Either we keep him for one night or three, never an even number. Only non-Khasi-Khasis keep the body for two nights. I'm Christian; you are Khasi-Khasi—how come you don't even know that?'

'Mei would want to keep him for three nights, I'm sure,' Bah mused. 'But let's forget about new clothes, okay? We'll dress him in his favourite clothes instead: blue corduroy trousers, the blue-and-white checked cotton shirt and his navy-blue coat. Come, come, let's make up the bed and get everything done before more people arrive.'

At that moment, the scene vanished. It was as if I had gone to sleep. When I next opened my eyes, they had already made up the bed and changed the position of my body. I was now lying with my head pointed westwards and my feet eastwards, something we are not supposed to do when alive. The body was washed, dressed and scented, and screened from view with a white muslin cloth adorned with white ryndia shawls, dhara and muka silk jaiñsems. I understood that all this was done because the ugliness of death must be kept hidden at all cost. My brothers, cousins and nephews had done an excellent job. I looked as if I was peacefully asleep, and that was what everybody who came to look at my body said. I was very happy my brothers did not make me lie directly on the bulrush mat, called *japung*, but had thoughtfully covered it with a white cotton sheet. It would have been quite uncomfortable, I thought, to lie directly on the prickly-looking japung. I was also pleased they did not put around my head a wreath of corn (made out of nine fried grains of Indian corn) as they used to do in the past. I could not imagine myself smelling like popcorn.

A lamp burnt within the enclosure, for the soul, still very much about, must not linger in the dark. An egg, called *leng kpoh*, was kept on my umbilicus, not only a reminder that my sai hukum, my thread of life, had been severed by a divine decree, but also to bond the funeral obsequies with my soul. A shaman must have done all this, I thought.

And I was right, for outside, at that very moment, the shaman was preparing to sacrifice the yiar krad lynti, the rooster who would scratch the way for my soul. They had not done it yet because Bahnah, my middle brother, was protesting, saying, 'I don't think we should sacrifice any animal, Ap was always fiercely against such things.'

But the shaman disagreed. 'If we don't do it, then how do we perform the funeral rites?' I did not like the shaman very much. He was a shifty-looking fellow with a moustache like a little black thread. 'The yiar krad lynti must especially be sacrificed,' he asserted, 'otherwise how will his soul find its way to the house of God? It will be lost; it will get stuck here on earth as a ghost or a demon. We have to do it.'

'I think we better call Mei, let her decide,' Bahnah said.

'No, we shouldn't call her. Let's go to her,' Bah replied.

My mother, a very short but good-looking woman, was sitting with my wife and daughters in my bedroom. Her head was covered with a dark green shawl. I could see that her eyes were swollen from crying. The shaman explained the situation to her and concluded by saying, 'The cock is not the only animal we'll have to sacrifice, Mei. We'll have to kill a *masi pynsum*, a spirit-cleansing bull, then two other cocks plus a goat just before we carry the body to the cremation ground. Luckily, we don't have to sacrifice the *blang mawlynti*, since the cremation ground is not that far. Otherwise, if it is far, no, Mei, we would also have to plant the midway mawlynti monolith and sacrifice a goat before that. So, what do you say, Mei, you don't want your son's soul to be stranded here on earth as a demon, do you?'

I called out to my mother; I shouted at my brothers; I gestured wildly in front of all of them, trying to get their attention and saying all the while, 'No! Say no! Don't do it! I don't want it; I'll hate you for the rest of my life!' But to no avail. Nobody could see or hear me. And my mother, being a practical woman, after thinking for a while, asked, 'We would have to kill some animals, wouldn't we, to feed all these relatives and friends?'

'That's right, Khaduh, especially those who have come from far away,' Bah Son said quickly. 'After all, they have come here to help us and be with us in this hour of need, no? Since we need meat to feed all of them, we might as well observe the obsequies and sacrifice the animals. That's what I have been telling them, Khaduh. And the meat will not be wasted, we all know that!'

Bah Son addressed my mother as Khaduh because she is his youngest paternal aunt.

Now, Bahnah became quite insolent. 'You are not even Khasi, and you are speaking of sacrifices?'

'I may not be, but Khaduh is, and my father is. When he passes away, God forbid, I will have to perform these ceremonies. If not, his spirit may come to haunt us.'

The shaman added, 'Also, think, Mei, what if your family gets blacklisted for being non-compliant and rebellious? No shaman or praying elder will ever come here again.'

Between them, the shaman and Bah Son, they finally persuaded my mother, and I cursed them, feeling quite disconsolate.

Before sacrificing the rooster, the shaman bowed his head and touched it to his forehead, paying his obeisance to God. Then he said, 'Oh listen, oh Lord, since I do not know the cause or the judgement, since I do not know the cause of ruin, the cause of defeat, Tyrut, the demon, might have caused it, heaven or earth might have caused it. Now, I stand here and leave everything to the yiar krad lynti. He will scratch the way, he will find the way, that the soul of this man, U Ap Jutang Shadap, might get to where the ancestral mother is, to where the uncles, the fathers are, according to the rites, the rituals of his very own religion. Oh Lord, I have spoken, let it be so, I thank you a thousand bows.'

Having said his prayer, he twisted the rooster's neck and asked them to get him cleaned and cut into small pieces. Then, that very evening, he slaughtered the masi pynsum, the bull that would cleanse my soul with his blood. My brothers bought him from a cattle-rearing Bihari family living nearby. The Biharis used to be very friendly with me, and so, for my sake, they did not overcharge my family, although it was an urgent affair.

Somehow, I did not see the sacrifice itself. I only saw that the left leg of the rooster and the jaw of the sacrificed bull were carefully saved, to be kept later, along with my bones, in a little cist called *mawshyieng*, literally, 'bone stone', which would be built the next day in the garden. It seemed that I was no longer living with my mother but had moved out with my family to one of the houses I owned.

When next I opened my eyes, I was lying in my bedroom, in a beautifully made shyngoid coffin, quite smooth and sparkling with polish. So, I thought, the bastards had sacrificed the shyngoid pig too! A small basket containing pieces of the sacrificed animals was hung over my head, and on a small table by the bed was a dish of my favourite food. This offering, I knew, would be made each morning and evening as long as my body was in the house. A brass jar full of water and a brass plate containing five pieces of unpeeled betel nut and five unsplit betel leaves were also kept near the food plate, although I was never a great betel nut chewer. By the side of the bed, divided by the thin screen, were the living—among them, my mother, my wife and our two daughters—who mourned my passing. People kept coming in and going out of the room. They came in, talked to my mother and wife, and gently pushed their closed fists under their shawls. Obviously, they were giving them some money, as I used to do when going to a death house.

I was not feeling very pleased. Even though the customary practices had been observed diligently, the animal sacrifices had soured my mood. Yet, I was also very touched that my family seemed genuinely sorry that I had ceased to be.

Then, it was the third night, and I could hear the sound of a gun going off three times. In a corner of the courtyard were some musicians playing on their small rectangular ksing kynthei drums and the seven-mouthed *sharati*, a kind of long, slender flute carved from seasoned shken, the small-stemmed bamboo. At that moment, the drums were rather subdued, although the sharati was emitting some of the most plaintive notes I had ever heard. From the conversation, I realised that they had been playing every night for the last three nights.

As always, the scene outside the death house disgusted me: some teenaged girls, relatives and friends were moving about with kettles of tea and trays piled with cakes and biscuits, offering them to the loud-talking, loud-laughing and shamelessly irreverent crowd—'Tea? Red tea or milk tea?' Behind them were very young girls and boys with plastic packets of betel nuts and betel leaves, shouting, 'Kwai, Bah? Kwai, Kong? Betel nuts, anyone?' They reminded me of tea sellers in a railway station and betel nut hawkers in a cinema hall. But the real feast was set up behind the house, in the garden. An open-sided tent had been erected there and huge fires were burning inside it, with pots of rice, beef, pork, chicken and vegetables being cooked. Away from the fires, seated on long benches, people were shouting for more rice or meat and loudly commenting on the quality and taste of the food. Some even said: 'The food at a funeral is always tastier than at a wedding.'

There was plenty of food, it seemed, for apart from the animals that had been sacrificed, my paternal relatives had gifted me with a large pig, while others had brought several chickens with them. Only the poorest of my clan members had brought no food, just the rice beer called *ka yiad rong*, which would be sprinkled on my body before setting it alight.

The scene shifted; it was my cremation day. A man I knew, someone from Seng Khasi, was speaking into the mike in a solemn tone. 'Brothers and sisters of the clan; brothers and sisters of the paternal clan, friends, and any of you who would like to have a last look at the deceased, and who would like to contribute to *ka pynkham ka pynsoh*, are kindly requested to come and do so now before we begin the service. For those of you who would like to contribute, one of our elders is at hand to guide you.'

Ka pynkham ka pynsoh, as Bah Kit explained, is the ceremony of giving farewell money to the dead.

Following the announcement, many people, I was surprised to see, lined up to enter my bedroom. I never imagined so many would be eager to see my dead body or to give my spirit some parting money. I went inside the room to see what was going on. The praying elder sitting beside my body was someone I knew. He guided the body-viewers carefully and directed them to leave from another door so as to not bump into those coming in. It was all done in a very sombre, orderly manner.

When that was done, they put the shyngoid coffin inside the krong bier. The bloodthirsty shaman sacrificed the *yiar syngkhong*, the bier-raising rooster, after paying homage to God. Holding the poor creature in both hands and touching him to his forehead, he said, 'Oh listen, oh Lord, now that the body has been raised to the krong, the bier, now that the bamboo strings for the tying, the binding have been put in place, I stand before you with this yiar syngkhong, so he may untie, so he may unfasten the soul from the tying and the binding, so he may protect it from the shame, the defeat, the dangers along the way. Oh Lord, bless this creature that U Ap Jutang Shadap may reach in peace, may arrive in peace, where his uncles, his fathers are, where u suidñia and ka ïawbei are. I have pleaded according to the rites, the rituals, oh Lord, let it be so, I thank you with a thousand bows.'

The shaman touched the rooster to his forehead again and twisted his neck. He then let him bleed on the ground and smeared some of the blood on little sticks about three inches each. These were bound together and put inside a small basket to be thrown away near the cremation hill. The shaman smeared some blood around the krong bier, after which it was firmly closed and tied with bamboo strings and taken to the courtyard, where the main part of the funeral service would be conducted. The krong bier had been beautifully decorated with a maroon dhara silk jaiñsem and white ryndia silk shawls. The shawls were tied crossways over the jaiñsem, making the bier look truly magnificent. Even the non-Khasi-Khasis present were heard commenting on its beauty.

In the courtyard, the krong bier was placed on two benches right outside the front door. My relatives sat on benches on either side of it—maternal to the left, paternal to the right. At its head stood the leaders of Seng Khasi who would conduct the service, various speakers who would say the eulogies and read condolence messages from different organisations, and the elder who would lead the prayer. Everyone stood in readiness, but first, they had to wait for the animal-killing shaman to sacrifice a black ram called *lang sait ksuid*, the demon-cleansing goat. Holding a machete, the shaman led the goat to a corner of the courtyard and, after paying obeisance to God, killed him with a single blow to the back of the neck. I could not hear what he was saying as I was standing near my mother, waiting impatiently, like them, for the obsequies to begin.

When the purificatory ceremony was done, the chairman took over and started the service. My mood improved now, for the obsequies were being conducted strictly in accordance with tradition. The elder conducting the ceremony was a man I had always admired for his dignified eloquence. The other leaders of my faith and the rest of the speakers were also well known for their oratorical skills. There were quite a few speakers. One of them spoke on behalf of my religious organisation. I had never been a very religious man and had disagreed with many of my organisation's views and practices. Despite that, he said the organisation had lost one of its strongest pillars, and consequently, at that moment, he and his colleagues were feeling like helpless little orphans. Another spoke on behalf of the Khasi writers who had turned up in considerable numbers, and declared that I had been a giant among them. However, I had heard him making spiteful remarks behind my back, denouncing my writings and stating that they must never be awarded by the government since 'they are not polite and contain many curse words'. But now, in my death, he asserted, 'not only the community of writers but also Khasi society as a whole has lost one of its leading lights'. I was reminded of the words of Horace, who famously said, '*exstinctus amabitur idem*'.

'Meaning?' Bah Kynsai demanded.

'The same man, maligned living, when dead, will be loved.'

The speaker who followed the writer was a professor who spoke on behalf of my former colleagues. She said I was one of the best and most dedicated teachers she had known, although I had left the profession early. The next speaker was no less than the headman, who spoke with 'a glib and oily art' on behalf of the village, and described me as the best friend, guide and adviser the village dorbar had ever known. There were a few more speakers, Khasis and non-Khasis, from organisations I had helped in one way or another. The head of my clan lamented my loss with a tearful farewell, and lastly, Bah, my eldest brother, thanked everyone for coming to the family's support 'at this darkest hour', when every consolation and commiseration was a comfort and a reassurance. He concluded his speech by requesting all the funeral attendants—those who would be going to the cremation hill as well as the others—not to leave without partaking of the food and refreshment that the family had specially prepared for the occasion. When I heard that, I gave him the 'up yours!' sign, for I had never approved of that part of the funeral speech. It made the funeral sound too much like a feast. But otherwise, I thought he did an outstanding job. On the whole, the service was a resounding success.

As they were speaking, the music became quite muted, and now and then sobs escaped my mother, wife, daughters and sister, the women closest to me. At that point, the funeral was truly solemn and dignified.

The elder who had been called to conduct the prayer was so eloquent and fluid that somebody later said, 'Did you hear that guy who prayed? My God, like being played from a tape recorder, man!' The prayer included the invocations we had heard from the head shaman here in Nongshyrkon. However, my priest also asked me, or rather my spirit, not to forget my family, relatives and friends, and to plead with God for their health and welfare. You see, unlike Kong We Shyrkon, I would not be going to the eternal abode of the spirits at Krangraij, nor would I be bathing in Umbylleiñ. I would be going to eat betel nut in the house of God and meet my ancestors, long dead and happy.

As part of the prayer service, the elder emptied the plate of food by my bedside outside the boundary wall. (I could see some of my nieces carrying fresh food in baskets meant to feed my spirit at the cremation site.) Then he came back and sprinkled the last few rice grains and water on the krong bier while at the same time making his invocations to God and the guardian spirits of my clan in clear and ringing tones. He ended his prayer by bowing low and paying obeisance to God. After that, the chairman took over the service again, and called to my male relatives and friends to carry 'the krong forward'.

The procession then lined up, led by one of my nephews, who carried a *dieng tyllaw*, a smouldering brand, to be used for lighting the fire at the cremation site. With him was a relative carrying a coil of thread meant to symbolically bridge a stream on the way to the cremation hill. In the past, I thought in my dream, they must have used branches or grass or woven thread, but now everything is ready-made. These two were followed by the pall-bearers, who were followed by the musicians, with their subdued drum and doleful sharati flute music, and the family mourners. This part of the procession was solemn, but the crowd that brought up the rear was as rowdy and disrespectful as any I had seen at Khasi funerals. Their loud chatter and wild laughter were made even worse by the constant ringing of mobile phones, the regular 'boom boom' of gun salutes, and the throwing of copper coins that attracted all the street urchins from the neighbourhood. The behaviour of the crowd irked me at first, but then I remembered Wislawa Szymborska's funeral-procession poem, 'Funeral (II)', and was immediately struck by the irony of it. I quoted a few lines to myself:

> 'so suddenly, who could have seen it coming'
> 'stress and smoking, I kept telling him'
> 'not bad, thanks, and you'
> 'these flowers need to be unwrapped'
> 'his brother's heart gave out, too, it runs in the family'
> 'I'd never know you in that beard'

People everywhere are the same, I thought with a smile.

At the cremation hill, I saw that the *jingthang*, my pyre, was tastefully decorated. The rectangular enclosure of huge plantain trunks was covered with pure white cotton sheets, adorned with dark red velvet and festooned with golden tassels. The corners were topped with *siarkait*, the figures of plantain flowers carved from seasoned teak. The *shanduwa*, or the high canopy, of deep red satin cloth was raised above the pyre on four long bamboo poles. The sight of it made me cry out in happiness: 'Yay! This is a rare honour, given only to the very few!' But then, realising that my delight was somewhat inappropriate, I turned away to watch the ceremonies more closely.

They, too, were carefully conducted. First of all, a fire was kindled in a corner using the burning brand brought from home. Then the body-turners broke open the krong bier after stripping it of its expensive decorations, which they wrapped in a cloth. They carefully stashed away the money given as a parting gift to my spirit, lifted my body and placed it on the sticks, already piled high on the fine-looking pyre. My head was towards the west, for that was the direction my soul was supposed to take on its journey to the house of God. More sticks were piled on top of my body. When everything was nicely arranged, the head body-turner signalled to the bloodthirsty shaman, who came forward, paid his obeisance to God, and twisted the neck of another rooster, the *yiar padat*, to be thrown across the pyre three times.

When the shaman had sacrificed the rooster, he smeared his blood all around the pyre three times. Then he and the head body-turner called my relatives to start the fire. Bah, being the eldest brother, was the first to insert a burning brand into the hearth beneath the pyre. He was followed by Bahnah, and all my nephews and male relatives.

I shuddered with fear. 'Next time, if I ever have another chance, I'll choose burial.' Even that thought gave me no comfort, however. 'But wouldn't I suffocate under all that dirt?' It is not a very pleasant thing, watching yourself being despatched like that, I can tell you.

The function of the yiar padat rooster was much like that of the pyre-marking rooster of the Lyngngams, the yiar tha thyrnang. But he was also like their guiding rooster, the yiar kong, because when the fire was blazing nicely, the shaman threw the rooster three times across the pyre—a symbolic gesture to show that the way for the soul had been cleared through the fire. After that, the pieces of meat from the path-finding rooster and the spirit-cleansing bull, which were hanging above my head in the house, were consigned to the flames.

Some of the body-turners broke the krong bier into pieces and threw it away. The bloodthirsty shaman, meanwhile, complained to the body-turners about my relatives, who had not allowed him to sacrifice another goat called *lang duhalia*, the musicians' goat. It turned out that my brothers had disallowed it since the musicians did not want it. The body-turners consoled him and asked him to carry on with the ceremony.

The shaman started with the leng kpoh, the egg which was placed on my umbilicus, breaking it at the head of the pyre after paying obeisance to God and invoking his blessings. Then he took the tieh tympem, the funeral bow, and three nam tympem, the funeral arrows without metal tips, turned his back on the pyre and shot them one by one, first to the north, then to the south and lastly to the west. The arrows would keep the soul safe from any demons and malignant spirits who tried to obstruct its journey to the house of God. Having done that, the shaman took the bundle of clothes used to decorate the krong bier, passed it through the fire three times, and returned it to my relatives.

Next, he asked my relatives to perform the noh kwai ceremony, which, as you know, was meant to give me my farewell kwai, comprising a piece of unpeeled betel nut, split into half, and an unsplit betel leaf. My mother began the ceremony, followed by my brothers, my sister, my wife and daughters, my maternal and paternal relatives, and all my friends and well-wishers, quite a few in number. I rejoiced to see my friends, Khasi-Khasis and non-Khasi-Khasis alike, honouring me like that, and watched them passing the kwai three times through the fire while intoning the words, '*Khublei, khie leit bam kwai ha ïing u Blei.*' ('God bless, go, have your betel nut in the house of God.')

That marked the end of the obsequies, and many took their leave of my family. I was reasonably pleased with the proceedings, though I did see a few in the crowd impertinently blocking their noses and saying they would not eat grilled jerky again for months. After a while, only my closest relatives and friends remained. But when it got dark, towards 6 p.m., even my family members went away. Only my two brothers, my cousin Bah Son, some nephews and some of my closest friends stayed behind to keep the body-turners company.

By about 7.30 p.m., my body was completely burnt and the fire was reduced to cinders. The head body-turner invited my relatives to come and see for themselves if the body had been completely consumed or not. He turned the coals three times, and each time he did so, he asked my relatives to carefully check lest there was a piece of flesh anywhere that was not incinerated. When my relatives were satisfied, the body-turners killed the fire by sprinkling water three times, starting at the foot of the pyre. Then they carefully sifted through the coals, collecting bone fragments and also looking for what they called 'the yellow', a euphemism for the melted gold from the ring they had placed on my ring finger. When the bones were washed and collected in a piece of white muslin cloth, and the gold had been found, they dismantled the pyre and cleaned the hearth.

At the head of the hearth, the body-turners constructed a *raksha*—a little enclosure in the form of a square bracket, using three pieces of bamboo—and prepared for the ceremony called *ka jer ka thoh*, meant to mark my name as finally dead and gone from this world. The head body-turner placed a little ash and coal inside the raksha as a sign that the body had been thoroughly cleansed by fire. Then he took the plate of food brought from home, which contained three loaves of rice bread, or *pu japha*, some powdered rice, or *pu jer* (for the name-marking), some boiled rice and meat, and placed a little bit of each inside as a sign that I, the deceased, had now been fed. He made invocations to God and informed him that my body had been cleansed by Queen Fire and that I was gone for good from this earth. Hence, my name should from now on be marked as dead and that, whenever anyone called out the name, he should follow it up by saying '*Bam kwai ha ïing u Blei*' ('Eating betel nut in the house of God'). He sprinkled some water from a brass jar on the raksha as a sign that I had been washed. He poured a little mustard oil from a bottle and placed a comb inside as a sign that I had been oiled and combed and duly spruced up for the house of God. Lastly, he emptied the rest of the food from the plate by the side of the raksha and placed some betel nuts and betel leaves near it as the last supper and the last kwai for me.

He then sprinkled some more water from the brass jar on the raksha and prayed to God that my journey be easy and free of obstacles and that I be quickly united with the first ancestors of my clan in heaven. He also prayed that I should not pine for this world, that I would have no regrets or complaints, that I would not return to my family to whine or protest about anything since the funeral rites had been conducted according to the customs of the tribe. He sprinkled more water on the raksha and prayed that the body-turners and all those who were involved in the cremation be washed and cleansed and blessed with good health and prosperity.

After the closing prayer was said, my bones were handed over to my eldest brother, who led the procession towards the mawshyieng in my garden, with a person who strewed the route with rice grains to help my spirit find the way to its own bones. My brother was sternly warned not to take even a single backward glance towards the cremation site, for that was highly inauspicious. That warning suddenly reminded me of Lot's wife and I urged him to take heed lest he too be turned into a pillar of salt. But, of course, he could not hear me.

When we had to cross the stream again, the person with the rice grains made a rough bridge with branches and tall grass. After that, we proceeded straight to the little mawshyieng cist on which the head body-turner sprinkled rice beer and made more invocations to God. He took the bones from my brother, placed them inside a small black earthen pot, and covered it with the same white muslin cloth. Then he put my bones inside the cist together with three pieces of boiled egg yolk, three loaves of rice bread, the left foot of the yiar krad lynti and the jaw of the spirit-cleansing bull. That done, he closed the opening of the cist with a specially carved stone and put some food, water and betel nuts with betel leaves on top of it as offerings, should my spirit come to visit.

The ceremony completed, the body-turners washed their faces and their hands and feet very carefully at the tap near the garden and entered my drawing room to give their account of my cremation. My family members were sitting on one side of the room, waiting for them. They were shown to their seats on the other side. The head body-turner reported every detail of what had transpired at the cremation site, and concluded by telling my family how beautifully my body had burnt and how quickly it had turned to ashes. Everything, he said, had gone off smoothly: nothing untoward, no cause at all for worry.

The next morning, when the crow was still red, as the saying goes, that is, when the light was still faint, my brothers, Bah Son and some nephews were at the cremation site. They were looking for any sign that I might have come during the night to eat the food they had left there—or for whatever reason a dead man might have to visit the scene of his cremation. I shouted to them, 'Hey, fellows, do you really expect me to come and lap up that food from the ground? Like a dog?'

I was only teasing them. I knew they had come to check for my footprints— the belief is that one can foretell future events from them. However, there were none, which made them very happy, for it indicated that I was content and had not returned, or if I had, had not left them any sign of complaint or dissatisfaction. I felt pity for them. The poor guys had not had any proper sleep for the last few nights, and when they could finally relax because the job was done, they had to get up at this unearthly hour to check whether my phantom had visited. But what to do? That is the custom.

After three days had passed, that is, after the mourning period was over, my family gathered in my drawing room. They were engaged in the ceremony of *kheiñ sbai*, literally, 'counting the cowries', but meaning calculating the expenses. The ceremony is a private affair, and so, only the closest maternal and paternal relations were invited to it. My mother, wife, sister, brothers, aunts—maternal and paternal—first cousins and some grown-up nephews were all there.

In the absence of uncles, for we had none, Bah had to lead the proceedings. After offering a brief prayer, he began by saying that they should first calculate the expenses. They did that by asking the people in charge of buying things, hiring utensils, getting the marquee done, et cetera, to present their total expenses. After that, everyone was asked how much they had contributed towards these and other miscellaneous expenses. Each one submitted their carefully recorded accounts. Bah Son, however, refused to oblige, saying that what he had given was a gift to me and that he did not want to be reimbursed. On the other hand, if the money was short, he was willing to contribute some more. But Bah would have none of it, and so, even Bah Son had to submit his accounts. At the other extreme, Bahnah, my own brother, who I somehow knew had not contributed anything, presented a long list of expenses adding up to a large amount. I shook my head in disbelief and said, 'Once a trickster, always a trickster. Even in matters of death and misfortune, he has to have his ill-gotten gains.'

Bah Son looked at Bahnah, and like me, shook his head in disbelief. It seemed he also knew. But he could not say a word in protest since this was a solemn ceremony where people were not supposed to quarrel.

After the expenses had been calculated, the financial contributions received from relatives and friends were taken out. Mostly, they had been given to the female relatives who were sitting in the room where my body was kept. Some of Bah and Bah Son's friends had given money directly to them. They now took it out and put it on the table.

Only Bahnah was quiet. Bah Son asked him pointedly, 'Did no one give you anything, Nah?'

Bahnah simply shook his head, although many of his friends had been spotted giving him money. I wondered how such a person could have been born of the same parents as us. Bah and my sister are generous souls. And while I may not be as large-hearted as them, I'm open-handed enough when I have to be, and I would certainly never cheat.

Bah invited Bah Son to count the money with him. The contributions received far exceeded the expenses incurred, and everyone heaved a huge sigh of relief. The various people who had contributed to the expenses, including the deceitful Bahnah, were promptly reimbursed. But Bah and Bah Son refused to accept any reimbursement. They said their share of the money should be used for my first death-anniversary feast.

I was infuriated by the despicable falsehood of Bahnah, but Bah and Bah Son showed me that for every bad person in the world, there were two good ones. Or so I hoped.

My dream now skipped ahead. I was in my own house. None of my relatives was there, only some of my wife's. I saw with deep anguish that my little library, painstakingly built over the years, was already overrun by worms, which were swarming in and out of my beloved books. They were everywhere, on the table, the shelves, the floor, feasting on every scrap of paper. Only some of the books I had written, those included in school and college syllabi, were carefully preserved in glass cases, obviously because they were still bringing in some money.

As I left the room in forlorn sadness, it occurred to me that my house, built by the sweat of my brow, for which I had sacrificed my youth (even resisting the temptation of love and the pleasure of girlfriends) and my health (at times simultaneously working three full-time jobs) was now referred to as my wife's house. It seemed that, along with my body, my name had also turned to smoke. My erasure was complete and total.

It was then that a terrible melancholy gripped me. *I cannot be another 'mute inglorious' dead*—uba rim uba jah, *the ancient the vanished.* I fervently prayed to God to grant me a few more days of life so I could plant, with all the mandatory rites, a small monolith to myself, right there on the green spot in front of the house, where I could inscribe these words of remembrance:

> This house is bequeathed to us
> By our beloved father, U Ap Jutang Shadap,
> Son of our beloved meikha, Kong Rit Shadap.
> Let no one disdain what has been given,
> Let no one destroy what has been built.

And as a postscript, in smaller letters:

> This stone has been ritually sanctified,
> You may tamper at your own peril.

When I was done, Bah Kynsai burst out laughing. 'Excellent story, Ap. No one even interrupted you. But you were asked to talk to us about the funeral rites of the Khasis, na, not the story of your dream, man!'

'No, no, no, Bah Kynsai!' Bah Kit interrupted him. 'You see, it may only be a dream, but the details of the funeral rites, ha, are exactly like that of the old Khasis. In fact, as I said earlier, we still observe most of them, except for the sacrifices, the music—'

'But what about the gun salutes, the throwing of coins and the collection of bones?' Raji asked. 'They don't do these things any more, I think?'

'Most of us don't collect bones any more, that's true, but some still do, Raji,' Bah Kit clarified. 'Even here, they are still doing it. As for gun salutes and coins, they were the practices of the rich anyway.'

'The description of the pyre in Ap's story is quite interesting,' Hamkom remarked. 'I have never been to a Khasi funeral, you know … Is it really like what Ap described?'

'The jingthang is exactly like that, in every detail,' Bah Su answered. 'But the shanduwa canopy is erected only for the elderly and the famous. In the past, there used to be three types of pyres: the simple *dieng tylli* pyre made of poles (like the one we have seen here) and used by the poor; the *bait wait* pyre made of planks roughly shaped by a machete, used by people with moderate means; and the *lyntang* pyre made of well-planed and polished planks, used by the rich. This last is decorated exactly as Ap described it. And yes, pyres can also be made with plantain trunks, Ap is right.'

'But how exactly are they made?' Hamkom asked.

'Perhaps I didn't explain that clearly enough, Ham,' I said. 'The plantain trunks, logs or planks are used to make a spacious rectangular enclosure, open at the bottom and the top. The enclosure is firmly fixed to the ground with fist-sized wooden spikes in such a way that it fences in the wooden latticed platform of a makeshift hearth. This hearth is the foundation for the pyre. It's called *ka kpep*. The fire begins from the hearth and is directed up into the body by the rectangular enclosure.'

'What about the mawshyieng? Is it like the monolith they made here for Kong We's bones?' Evening asked.

'Why, Ning, you haven't seen a mawshyieng before or what?' Raji asked in surprise.

'Just tell me, ya!' Evening replied.

'A mawshyieng is a cist, not a monolith, Ning,' I said. 'It's built like a small square box with an opening in front of it. The opening is closed with a specially carved stone.'

'Well, Bah Ap,' Donald observed, 'I think your story is a very clever technique—what you told us could have been quite boring otherwise.'

'It's not a technique at all, Don. I really had the dream: perhaps because I'm always thinking about death and the desire for remembrance, like the elegiac poets. For instance, I'm obsessed, possibly unhealthily, with the question of how to develop a language of remembrance for myself.'

'That's exactly what I was talking about earlier, no!' Evening cried. 'When a Khasi man dies, his erasure is complete and total. Even his name vanishes without a trace. And all that he owns is gobbled up by his wife's clan. That Argentine author is quite correct, Ap, we rob the dead man of everything!'

'Unless he has made an indelible mark in the world,' Hamkom said. 'But then, how many of those can there be?'

'I think the dream, na,' Bah Kynsai broke in, perhaps to deflect attention away from the topic of Khasi men, 'contains a deadly satire about the way we conduct our funeral services. Like that part about the speakers, na? There are many stories about such eulogies—'

'Such as?' Hamkom asked.

Bah Kynsai told us three. One was about the death of an officer whom everyone called a 'big shot'. There are two things a big shot with plenty of money would most likely do in the Khasi Hills: drink and womanise. That was what this chap—a big man with bloodshot eyes—did. He was horrible to his wife and kids. When he came home at night, he *byrthen kum u laren*, that is, roared like laren the monster, in the words of his own family. Everyone at home, including his mother-in-law, lived in constant dread of him. Any false move would get them the boot. Luckily for them, his debauched living ensured that he did not live very long. He died at the age of forty-six.

During the funeral service, which took place in the courtyard in front of the house, there were many speakers: a fellow officer spoke on behalf of his office; one of his rich friends spoke on behalf of his drinking buddies; his first cousin spoke on behalf of his clan; a locality functionary spoke on behalf of the locality dorbar; a church elder spoke on behalf of his fellow believers. They all paid glowing tributes to the dead man. The officer said his colleague had been the most brilliant, the most dedicated and the friendliest officer he had ever known. His drinking buddy cried during his speech and had to be led away, which was more expressive than anything he could have said on behalf of the dead man's goodness. His clan elder spoke about how he was a good father, providing for 'this large family of sons and daughters'. The children, he said, should forever remain grateful to him for the kind of life and upbringing he had given them. The locality functionary recounted his generosity and how he had always donated liberally to the many functions the dorbar organised. And lastly, the church elder, probably thinking of the reputation of the family as a God-fearing and religious one, spoke glowingly about the man and lamented that the Lord had taken such a good soul so early.

That proved to be the last straw for the wife. She called out to her son and said, loud enough for everyone to hear, 'Bahbah, go, go, look in the coffin … See if the man in it is really your father or not?'

The whole gathering burst into peals of laughter despite themselves, and the service was brought to a very quick end.

Hamkom laughed and protested at the same time. 'Tet leh, Bah Kynsai! Did it really happen or what?'

'Arre, this Ham!' Bah Kynsai replied indignantly. 'Can anyone make up a thing like that? I'm not a creative writer, na?'

Raji and Magdalene declared that they believed Bah Kynsai. They had been to quite a few funerals and could well imagine the scene.

The second story was about another drunk, a small, thin man with bulbous red cheeks and black eyes that were turning yellow, perhaps because of jaundice. He too had married into a God-fearing and religious family. Apart from the alcoholism, however, he was not a bad sort of man. And when he drank with his many buddies, he never used any of the money from his salary, only his 'side income', which he was regularly getting from people who respected his position as an excise inspector. His salary went towards the upkeep of his family, whom he loved dearly, though it was forever a bone of contention between him and his wife, who used to say, 'If you really love your family, you should stop drinking this instant!'

Undeniably, he loved his two sons and daughter very much. But how could he listen to his wife or anyone else when he was in the grasp of such a powerful and jealous mistress? The upshot of it was that he drank himself to death.

During the funeral service, because the family was rich and respectable, the speakers said many good things about the dead man. As the family sat by the coffin in the courtyard, surrounded by relatives, friends and neighbours, the speakers paid their tributes, carefully avoiding his problem with alcohol and dwelling on his generosity, his gentle manners and his qualities as a good provider.

But just when they were heaping praises upon the dead man, a thin little fellow, probably one of his drinking buddies, timidly came forward, and then, bending almost double out of respect, ran towards the coffin, heavy with its many floral wreaths. When he reached it, he took out a half bottle of whisky and laid it reverently among the wreaths.

Many in the crowd shamelessly erupted in loud laughter, others giggled and immediately covered their mouths with their hands. But the relatives were furious. Some male members dragged the man out of there. Thrusting the bottle back into his pocket, they chased him and his five or six friends away from the place. Some were for beating him up, but others pacified them by saying that a funeral was no place for such a thing.

The drunks, fearing for their safety, left, but not for home. They went to the cemetery and hid in a corner. When the body was buried, and everyone had gone away, they emerged from their hiding place, addressed a few words to the dead man and inserted the bottle deep into the grave's soft earth.

Bah Kynsai concluded his story to much laughter.

The last story was about a man who was so thoroughly nasty that he was a nuisance for everybody, not only when alive but also when he died. The fellow was a drunk, a drug addict, a wife-beater, a troublemaker, a terror at home, a bully and a menace in the locality, who picked fights for no reason at all. He was also suspected of involvement in some of the locality's unsolved robbery cases. As a result, when he died, the church elder organising the funeral service did not find any speakers to deliver eulogies; no one knew what to say.

Eventually, the elder decided he would say a few words before the religious part of the service got underway. 'Friends, we are gathered here today to mourn the passing of Bah Ramen, the father of this house. As human beings, we have many faults and failings, but at the same time, we are not without our merits and admirable qualities. In my experience, Bah Ramen used to be, eh, eh, he used to, eh, eh … Well, the best thing I remember about him is that he used to have beautiful handwriting …'

The laughter that followed this desperate statement made the elder's ears quite red. He called for silence and immediately asked for the prayers to begin.

We too laughed at the story, and Raji exclaimed, 'Tet teri ka! That one even I haven't heard, leh, Bah Kynsai!'

'But I have,' Bah Kit said. 'A friend of mine told me this story actually. It happened in Laban, no, Bah Kynsai?'

'Yeah, yeah,' Bah Kynsai agreed. 'You see, this is the nature of our funeral speech, na, we would never say anything bad about the dead.'

'Not only ours, Bah Kynsai,' I told him. 'The Romans used to say, "*de mortuis nil nisi bonum*", say nothing but good about the dead. It's a common thing. But you know, Bah Kynsai, on one occasion, I was in the same situation as the elder in your story.'

'What happened?'

'You see, a fellow known as Bah Robin had just died in our locality, and since he lived alone, his distant relatives, to save some money, decided to keep the body only for one night before cremating him the very next day. During the funeral service, they ran short of speakers. The chairman requested me to help out by saying a few words about the dead man. So, I composed an impromptu speech:

Friends, neighbours, kith and kin, Bah Robin was a good office-goer and very much a gentleman. Soft-spoken and mild-mannered, he never had a harsh word for anyone. But very sad to say, he listened to the tavern's song and began walking like a seismograph. His eyes took on the rustiness of betel nut stain, the watery glaze of a nitwit. His head became the tangled nest of a crow, his cheeks a pair of buttocks, and his nose a glowing tomato that constantly dripped so that the teeth of an elephant seemed to grow from his nostrils. His lips were moist and swollen like rotten brinjals, his teeth like a dog's feasting on excrement, his breath like menstrual blood and his body odour like the scent of a cobra.

In this way, he led a most despicable and miserable life, speaking the language of A-category auditors and deserting his wife and only daughter. For the last fifteen years, he had so devotedly given himself up to drink that his medical report said there was no more blood in his alcohol. What good can be said about him now?

'As I was thus preoccupied—'

'Did you really say all that, Ap?' Magdalene interrupted me excitedly. 'And what happened after that?'

'Of course not! I only imagined the speech. How could I say all that about the dead? The relatives would have beaten me up.'

'So?'

'So, when the chairman repeated his request, I recoiled in horror and left in a hurry.'

'Hahaha! But that's the most graphic description of a Khasi alcoholic I have ever heard, ha, Mag?' Bah Kynsai said.

'Yeah, no?' Magdalene agreed. 'You do have a vivid imagination, Ap.'

'Unfortunately, I meet this type of man every day in my locality, Mag,' I told her. 'But speaking of eulogies, the most bizarre one I heard was when my brother-in-law's relative died. He was about to retire from work, which means that he must have been touching fifty-eight. There were lots of people at the funeral since he was an enormously popular man from a very big clan. There were many speakers too, and the service went on and on. Fortunately, in the middle of all those tiresome speeches, we were provided with the most unexpected entertainment.

'A former colleague of the dead man was asked to read a condolence message from his office. He was a big, tall man with a swarthy complexion. Although he was working in a government office, everything about him told us—I was standing with some of my friends—that he was from a rural background. His accent, when he read the message, written in Khasi, proved the point quite clearly. One of us complained, "It's astonishing, you know, that after a lifetime of schooling, these country bumpkins cannot even speak Khasi properly!" Before anyone could react, the man was saying, "That was a message from our office, but before I step down, I'd like to say something from my side ... A final farewell." So saying, he produced a piece of paper from his shirt pocket and proceeded to read:

> So swit to mit,
> So sat to pat,
> So hat to se,
> gudbai swit hat.

'The whole gathering was utterly overwhelmed. Exploding into roaring laughter, we quite forgot that we were in the middle of a funeral service—'

'But what did he mean?' Magdalene asked. 'Was that English?'

'That was the worst kind of Khasi English I have ever heard, Mag. But it's not about his English accent. This is what it means:

> So sweet to meet,
> So sad to part,
> So hard to say,
> Goodbye sweetheart.

'I tell you, when he finished—'

But Magdalene was laughing and saying, 'Oh my God, oh my God! What the hell was he to the dead man, lover or what?'

'That was what people at the funeral were asking as well. But I think it was plain stupidity, nothing more. But the funniest part about it was that, despite all the laughter, when the man came down from the veranda, he actually asked his friends, "How did I do?" It was incredible.'

Donald now raised a hand and said, 'Bah Kynsai, if we don't have any more stories about eulogies, I'd like to ask a few questions about Ka Phor Sorat—'

'How will we have any more stories when you people do not contribute at all?' Bah Kynsai interrupted him sarcastically.

'I don't have any story, ya, I have been living outside, I hardly know anything—'

'At least now he's asking questions,' Raji said pointedly.

'What do you want to know?'

'First of all, ha, Bah Kynsai, what do you make of those eggs not breaking?'

'I have seen it many times,' Bah Su replied. 'The faithful of Niam Khasi used to have these lympungs, or assemblies, in different places, ha, Don. Each lympung begins with the planting of a monolith. But monoliths cannot be planted without prayers and obsecrations by shamans, who first have to plead for permission from God. And in the many places I visited, ha, shamans had been having such problems. When there are ill-wishers around, cursing the activity, ha, eggs do not break. In such situations, the shamans have to plead their cases before God very hard indeed.'

'And you think there are ill-wishers in this village?'

'There are bound to be, no, Don? Kong We was the last person in the village who belonged to Niam Khasi. And to be fair to the villagers, the whole thing is also quite disruptive.'

Raji, Bah Kit and I also said we had seen it happen before. Bah Kynsai added, 'This afternoon, na, I forgot to tell you, I told Perly that the eggs did not break because the ground was soft. Perly, though a Christian, got mad at me. He dug a hole in the garden, ha, then brought six eggs to me and asked me to throw them on the soft ground. All the six eggs broke, liah! Dale was also there; he saw everything, na, Dale? We are witnessing something strange here, something beyond rational understanding, I'm telling you!'

'Yeah, it was quite strange,' Donald agreed. 'I also recall the head shaman saying something about how the body of Ka We Shyrkon ought to be cleansed by Queen Fire, even as the first body was devoured by her ... What did he mean by that?'

'How do you know that? Can you understand Lyngngam now?' Bah Kynsai asked, surprised.

'I overheard Victor summarising the speech for Bah Ap,' Donald explained.

'I did ask Victor about it,' I said. 'You see, like us, the Lyngngams also have a story to explain why they cremate their dead, rather than burying them.'

'You mean we also have a story?' Magdalene asked. 'I've never heard of it, ya, tell, tell, no, Ap!'

'In fact, we have two,' I told her.

One story, prevalent among the highland Khasis, is that it all started with the legendary Syiem Lakriah, the leader of our ancestors, the Hynñiew Treps, when they came to live on earth. Lakriah went to God to complain about the infertility of the soil. God directed Lakriah to plead with Ramew, the guardian spirit of the earth, the first being he had created. Ramew felt great pity for the Hynñiew Treps, for they had come to their new home as a result of her pleading with God. However, she told Lakriah the truth: 'I can rectify the matter only if Man himself removes the cause of the soil's infertility.' When Lakriah asked her what the cause was, she replied, 'Your people's practice of burying dead bodies beneath the ground.'

The putrefying bodies, Ramew explained, had contaminated the earth and adversely affected its fruitfulness. She advised Lakriah to direct his people to cremate the bodies instead, so that Queen Fire would devour them without leaving behind a single morsel of rotting flesh to harm the earth.

Lakriah readily accepted Ramew's advice, and soon the soil became fertile and fruitful again, regenerating plants and trees everywhere. The crops of the Hynñiew Treps, too, for so long stunted and small, thrived once more.

According to this story, the first person to be cremated was a woman by the name of Ka Lisan, mother of the legendary hero, U Synriang, who is reputed to be the originator of Niam Khasi. Synriang is also supposed to have been the first to initiate the practice of bone burial when he collected the bones of his mother and kept them in the mawshyieng bone repository.

'And what is the other version?' Bah Kynsai asked.

The second story speaks of the death of Ramew and her children's attempts to dispose of her putrefying body. But the question was, who among them was the fittest to do so? After days of bickering among themselves, they finally decided to give Moon the task, since he was the only son.

Moon laid Ramew's body reverently on a beautifully constructed platform. He prayed to God, the Dispenser, the Creator, pleading with him to bless his mother and accept her soul into his house, for he was about to get rid of her body, now empty and lifeless without her soul. Then he directed his brightest rays on it and waited. To his astonishment, though he worked the whole night, nothing happened.

Next, it was Sun's turn, since she was the eldest daughter. Unlike Moon, she decided to start early in the morning, working slowly, as was her habit, and turning on the heat gradually as she progressed through the sky. Like Moon, she too was astonished to find that even after training her strongest rays on the body, she could not get rid of it. It only bloated up and became even more decomposed and foul-smelling than before. Towards evening, she gave up and asked Wind to take over.

Wind began her work the very next day. She blew a strong gust from the east and kept at it for hours. When nothing happened, she changed course, blowing fiercely from all directions. All she could do, however, was move her mother's body around and spread the foul smell everywhere until all of earth was filled with it. Men and animals choked on the stink and cried out in protest.

In desperation, the siblings asked Water to intervene, but she too only managed to break up the body and pollute the streams, streamlets and springs, so that earthlings were deprived even of water to drink. Having no other option, Ramew's children pushed the youngest daughter, Fire, into doing the job even before Water had given up.

At first, because the body was still soaked in water, Fire had a tough time of it. But slowly, as the water dried up, the body shrivelled and then burst into glorious flames that devoured everything, not leaving a single morsel of rotten flesh on earth. The air and the water became pure again. All the earthlings rejoiced in Fire's resounding success, and so grateful was Man to her that, from then on, he entrusted to her the task of disposing of the bodies of all dead humans. It was also from that time that he reverently started calling her Ka Syiem Ding, Queen Fire.

The Lyngngams and the Nongtrais have a different version of this story. When Ka Ramew, whom they call Meiïawlong, died, the children dressed her in her best clothes and laid her to rest on her bed, treating her as if she were merely ill. During the day, when they went to work in the fields, they took turns watching over their dead mother. This went on for a very long time. The rotting flesh fouled the air and rendered their life miserable. But she was their mother, and they refused to get rid of the body, preferring to suffer stoically. Fire did suggest that they reconsider their course of action, but was reprimanded for it, and so she kept her peace and went about her business.

However, one day, when it was her turn to watch over her mother's body, Fire decided to get rid of the rotting flesh and make their home liveable and wholesome again. She went to the bedroom, looked at the body, and said, 'Mother, I know you are not in there any more. What we have here is only your decaying flesh. Your spirit is haplessly loitering about, unable to go to its eternal abode because your body is still rotting here. Let me devour it, let me release you from its bondage so you may peacefully proceed to the land of the spirits at Krangraij.'

So saying, Fire devoured her mother's body and then set about cleaning the entire house.

When her siblings returned, they were immediately struck by how clean and fresh everything was. Fearing the worst, they rushed to the bedroom, only to find an empty bed. Fire had indeed devoured their mother! They raged and ranted and tried to throw her out of the house since she had committed a sacrilege. But Sun, who dearly loved her youngest sister, defended her fiercely, which led to a terrible war of words between the siblings. Not wanting anybody to get hurt, Sun took Fire with her and fled to the holy cave of Krem Lamet Krem Latang until she was persuaded to return to earth by the humble pleading of Rooster. In fact, the last part of the Lyngngam story is exactly like that of the sacred myth of the purple crest.

Bah Kynsai said, 'Now you are confusing us, leh! Which one is the correct version, man?'

'Not difficult to tell, obviously the first one, no?' Raji replied.

'Why?'

'Because Ramew, a spirit, cannot experience death like a mortal, can't you see? It doesn't stand to reason, Bah Kynsai.'

'Raji is right,' both Bah Su and Bah Kit agreed. 'Ramew is the guardian spirit of the earth. How can she die?'

'Ap?' Bah Kynsai asked.

'Yeah, the first story is the more likely one. Only thing is, Synriang cannot be said to be the originator of the Khasi religion—'

'Why?'

'Because, according to the sacred myth of Ki Hynñiew Trep, the Khasi religion was God-given and was founded upon the Three Commandments, which were part of the Covenant between Man and God.'

'That was quite a tale I got for my question, Bah Ap, thanks so much,' Donald remarked. 'But I've been wondering … After witnessing Ka Phor Sorat and listening to your funeral story earlier, okay, I'm still baffled about one thing: are Khasi funerals really funerals or feasts?'

'You need not be. Death for a Khasi is not a tragedy—'

'I don't buy that argument, Ap,' Magdalene objected. 'How can death not be a tragedy? What about the living?'

'You are right, Mag. Death is always a matter of great sorrow for the living, and if the dead person happens to be the sole earner in the family, that's a real tragedy. But not for the deceased. We believe that the soul goes to eat betel nut in the house of God unless the person has committed a serious crime. This is another way of saying that, through death, man attains eternal life. The living draw consolation from this belief. However, Khasis also believe that, as long as the funeral rites have not been performed, the soul will not be able to begin its journey to its heavenly abode. That is why, in the past, a Khasi funeral was both an occasion for sorrow and a celebration, for it was intended to liberate the soul from the confining ties of the world. And then, of course, as you have seen, there is a practical reason for all the feasting at a Khasi funeral.'

'Why do you say in the past? What about now? We are still feasting, no?' Evening protested.

'Here, yes. This is the last ceremony of its kind—'

'No, no, elsewhere too.'

'You are right, Ning, but only partly. Since we don't have sacrifices and music any more, a funeral is no longer a celebration in that sense. Nowadays we treat it as a sad event, but without succeeding, because we still offer people, not merely close relatives, tea and betel nut and food. And so, more people become involved in shopping, cooking, eating, feeding the crowd and cleaning utensils than in the real business of mourning and consolation. And this feeding is not done, as in the past, because they had to feed relatives and friends coming from far away to stay till the mourning period was over. Now we give food to everyone because we feel grateful that they have come—'

'Though why people come to funerals, na, nobody knows, liah!' Bah Kynsai swore. 'They come, sit around and do nothing, only joking and laughing, eating free kwai, drinking free tea and cake ... What is all that about, man? Meaningless, meaningless.'

'Like us,' Evening laughed.

'Like us,' Bah Kynsai agreed, smiling.

'No, no, no, I must protest!' Raji shouted. 'You know very well why we have come here!'

'Right, right, Bah Raji,' Donald agreed, 'we have come here with a purpose, remember, Bah Kynsai?' Then turning to me, he said, 'But, Bah Ap, is there a story about the beginning of these funeral feasts?'

'Yes, it all began with the story of U Synriang and his mother, Ka Lisan—'

'But you said that story was untrue, no?' Hamkom pounced on me, triumph in his voice.

I disappointed him immediately. 'I said the claim that Synriang had originated the Khasi religion is false. However, stories abound about how he was the initiator of the funeral feast, which is a different thing altogether—'

'Tell, tell, no,' Magdalene said impatiently.

I said the story began when the world was still young, when people were not so numerous and when the villages were not so densely inhabited—that was when Synriang and his mother, Ka Lisan, lived. Lisan lost her husband when she was very young, and lived alone with her son in a small hut. She struggled very hard to bring him up properly and eke out a meagre living from her fields. But her hard work, supported now and then by her aunt's children, was richly rewarded when her son grew up into a strong and handsome young man, packed with muscles from all the physical labour he did. With him as the defender of the home, the clan and the community as a whole, she earned the respect of the whole village.

But one day, at the very height of her happiness, Lisan—frail at the best of times because of all the years of hard struggle—suddenly fell seriously ill. Her son went to all sorts of faith healers and medical practitioners, but no one could do anything for her. She wasted away day by day and was soon reduced to a skeleton, with sunken cheeks and hollow eyes. Finally, Synriang was left all alone, a heartbroken wreck at a very young age. For a time, after his mother's cremation, performed in a corner of his garden, he lived like an outcast, wearing only rags and bathing himself with ash from head to foot. He did not go to the fields; he did not clean his hut; he did not cook, only eating whatever his relatives and others brought him. Such was the burden of his grief.

His uncles went to talk to him. At first, Synriang refused to listen to them, but his eldest uncle was a wise man. He drew Synriang's attention to his mother's life and to how she had struggled single-handedly to bring him up to be the young man that he was. 'What is your hardship compared to hers?' he asked. 'What is your sorrow compared to her loss through death? What is your sorrow compared to her anxiety about life, alone with her little child? Do you want all her struggle to go in vain? Get up, wash, clean, cook, eat, and go to work like a normal human being. Otherwise, your mother's sacrifice would all have been a waste. Get up and make your mother proud!'

His uncle's words seeped into his grief-stricken heart and made him realise what an unworthy son he had been. 'I must put down this burden of sorrow,' he told himself. 'I must let go of my mother's memory, though it hurts. I must look forward; I must move forward; I must not stand still, for to do so is to stagnate and rot.'

From that day, he returned to normal life. He washed and cleaned, he cooked and ate, and went to the fields to till and plant from dawn to dusk.

One day, while he was preparing a portion of the fields for his millet crop, Synriang saw a sow coming towards him. He watched curiously as the sow began digging the soil with her nose as if she wanted to help him. He was intrigued by her actions and allowed her to do as she pleased.

This went on for several days, and the two of them became quite close. When the tilling was done, Synriang planted the millet seeds and moved on to another part of the field to prepare for other crops and vegetables. But the sow did not understand what was happening and continued to dig up the fields that had been sown. Synriang tried to stop her, but she kept doing the same thing. In his anger, he took up his bow and shot her in the leg. The sow squealed in pain and ran away, frightened and dragging the arrow with her.

Synriang immediately felt bad about what he had done. He went after the sow to try and remove the arrow and dress the wound. But she thought he wanted to finish her off and fled as fast as she could, going into rougher and rougher country, till she reached a wooded hill where she seemed to vanish into thin air. Synriang looked for her tracks everywhere but could find none, for the ground was hard and stony. There weren't even any traces of blood. He climbed up the hill and searched through the woods, checking every hiding place, but she was nowhere to be found. Eventually, he climbed down and circled the base of the hill very carefully. It was then that he saw a small cave hidden by some natural projections and rocky outcrops. He went into it and was pleased to find the sow's tracks clearly etched in the sand. He followed them and quite unexpectedly emerged into a world he had never seen before.

From his vantage point at the cave's entrance, he could see that it was a vast and expansive valley, green with thriving crops and trees growing in neat rows, almost as if someone had planted them. Between the trees and the crops were colourful houses with lawns and lovely flower beds. Everything seemed to sparkle. Amazed, he said aloud, 'This surely must be heaven!'

To his even greater amazement, a voice like his mother's replied from behind him, 'This is not heaven, my darling son, but very close to it. It's the abode of the spirits. I have been sent here to live for a while.'

Synriang turned to find his mother smiling at him. She did not look like the sick woman he had last seen, but the healthy, youthful and beautiful woman he had loved so much. He took her in his arms and kissed her forehead, and cried for sheer joy. His mother, too, was thrilled that the spirits had allowed him to visit her in this forbidden place. She returned his embrace and kisses but let go rather abruptly, crying out in pain.

Synriang looked down and saw an arrow sticking out from her left foot. Now he understood that the sow was actually his mother's spirit, taking that shape so she could come to help him in his work.

'Look what you have done!' she exclaimed, fondly ruffling his hair. 'Instead of being grateful for my help, you shot me with an arrow! Wicked, wicked boy!'

While he removed the arrow as gently as he could, she pointed to a strange shrub growing nearby and said, 'Give me the leaves of that plant there, will you?'

She chewed the leaves to a paste and applied it to the wound. 'Within minutes, it will heal, my darling, don't worry about it,' she assured her distressed son.

Synriang went to live with his mother in one of the lovely houses made of beautifully polished wood and painted with colours extracted from plants growing nearby. It was a wonderful world, neither too hot nor too cold, and never subjected to the vagaries of wind and rain as on earth. However, when he met the other inhabitants, he discovered that everything in this world was the opposite of what it was in the land of the living. The language was different: what was black on earth was white here. The food was different: what was good on earth was inedible here. The clothes, too, were worn differently. Jackets, for instance, were worn inside out, and sandals were always on the wrong foot—left on the right and right on the left.

In dealing with the other inhabitants, Synriang found himself continuously making mistakes and thus causing them much vexation. They soon complained about him to his mother and asked her to send him back to his own world.

Succumbing to their combined pressure, one day, Lisan said to Synriang, 'My dear son, you have been allowed here with us because the spirits felt pity for me. However, only those who come through death can stay here forever. Though you have enhanced my happiness a thousand times, I will have to send you away now. Go, my son, go back to your home and be a good man. Marry, raise your own family, work hard. Earn your virtue and adhere to the truth in whatever you do, respect your fellow man and worship God always, and when your time comes, you too will travel through this happy place and be united with us in the house of God. Go now. My blessings will always be with you.'

Synriang responded by saying, 'But back home, I will miss you terribly, Mei. Tell me, what can I do to please you? What can I do to console myself, feel as if you are still with me on earth?'

Lisan brought out several drums, including the large, round *nakra*, and the small, rectangular ksing kynthei and ksing shynrang made out of the

Lakiang tree and cowhide. She also took out a tangmuri pipe and said, 'I will teach you how to play all these instruments, and I will teach you how to dance, and you will learn the *Symphiah* dance, wave a whisk with your left hand, flick a sword with your right, cut a caper with your feet. When you have mastered both music and dancing, you will go back and teach members of our clan, and when they also have learnt these skills, you will organise a funeral feast for me. Collect my bones, which you have left scattered at the cremation site. Put them in a small cist built of stones, then later, collect the bones of all our departed clan members and put them together in a large ossuary. While doing all this, pay obeisance to God, offer sacrifices to the guardian spirits, play music, dance and make merry, for by performing these rites, you will be helping our souls in their journey to the house of God.'

When Synriang had mastered the arts of music and dancing, he was escorted out of the enchanted valley through the same cave. But when he reached outside and turned to look back, the cave had magically vanished, as if it had never been there at all. Synriang understood that he was not supposed to look for it ever again. He went home to a startled community that had given him up for dead, for he had been absent for so many moons. Synriang simply told them that he had been travelling and learning new skills, which he was now prepared to teach them all.

After a few months, having taught his kinsmen the new skills, Synriang collected and washed his mother's bones and those of all the departed clan members carefully and kept them in small mawshyieng cists. To commemorate the occasion, he organised a funeral feast, which from then on came to be known as *Ka Phur Ka Siang*. Later, he organised another phur to mark the transfer of the bones from their little cists to the large stone ossuary called *mawbah*, or the great stone. Synriang built the mawbah in the shape of a square box with an opening in front of it, very much like a mawshyieng but many times bigger. To commemorate these two events, he planted the first Khasi monoliths (three upright male stones and a flat female stone at their feet, supported by small vertical stones) near the mawshyieng and the mawbah. And that was how Ka Phur, the funeral feast, started among the Khasis.

'Whew,' Donald exclaimed, 'our people seem to have a story for everything, man!'

'And what did you say earlier, liah?' Raji, who was now a little 'heated up' with rice beer, cursed him light-heartedly.

Donald laughed. 'That seems like a long time ago, Bah Raji.'

'In the jungle, no, Don, one week can seem like a year,' Hamkom observed.

'You should say just the opposite, mə, tdong,' Bah Kynsai said. 'Since coming here, na, I have enjoyed myself so much that I'm not even aware of time passing. Time is not important here. This is a beautiful life, man; you don't have to hurry anywhere; you don't have to worry about schedules, lessons, research, publications; you just live from moment to moment, from one day to another. I have even forgotten about my wife, liah!'

That sent everyone into shrieks of delight, and Raji exclaimed, 'True, true, ya, Bah Kynsai! I also don't remember my wife at all now. Forget my wife, I don't even remember my life in Shillong any more!'

Laughing and nodding our heads, many of us said, 'Yeah, yeah, this is beautiful ...'

After a few moments of silently luxuriating in this happy feeling, Evening suddenly said, 'Say, Bah Su, do we ever perform phawars at our funerals?'

It was Hamkom who answered. 'Nope, we don't! I have never come across the kind of funeral lament they chanted here, completely unique.'

'So, you are suddenly the expert now?' Raji asked.

'I'm merely saying I haven't come across that sort of thing before,' Hamkom replied irritably.

Bah Su said, 'In many places in the Khasi uplands, ha, the chanting of funeral phawars is no longer practised, that's why Ham has never seen it before. But in certain areas of Ri War, Ri Pnar and Ri Bhoi, they still do it.'

'Is it the same kind of thing as the lament here or different?' Hamkom asked.

'It's different,' Bah Su replied.

'But how is it different, Bah Su?' Bah Kynsai asked.

'I'll give you an example,' I offered. 'In the places Bah Su just mentioned, the chanting of phawars is performed especially after the death of the paternal grandmother. The gnomic chant itself is called Ka Phawar Ïam Meikha.'

This phawar is a unique one, enacted by two people, one representing the son, standing on the veranda, the other representing the paternal grandson, standing outside in the courtyard, each holding a whisk of yak's hair used for dancing. The chanting, performed amidst drum and tangmuri pipe music, is in the form of a verbal exchange, recounting the life story and extolling the virtues of the paternal grandmother.

In the enactment of this phawar, the son, or someone representing him, begins the chanting by saying something like this:

Ooooo!
I shoiñ ïa lyngwarku,
Ka phireit ïa u khun kbeit,
Rynñieng ne ka ja pu,
Meikha te iba peit,
Hoooi kiw! … Hoooi kiw!

(Ooooo!
A finch to a cuckoo,
A wren to a hawk,
Manhood or rice ball,
Meikha gives them all,
Hoooi kiw! … Hoooi kiw!)

This is followed by the response of the grandson, or someone representing him:

Ooooo!
Dohkha kum ïa ka kyrbei,
Ka lapadong ïa u dkhiew,
Ko Meikha ko Ïawbei,
Da kyrkhu ba ngan long briew,
Hoooi kiw! … Hoooi kiw!)

(Ooooo! A fish to a pangolin,
A lapadong leaf to an ant,
O Paternal Grandmother, O First Ancestress,
Bless me that I may flourish,
Hoooi kiw! … Hoooi kiw!)

This verbal exchange goes on till the life story of the paternal grandmother has been recounted fully and her virtues extolled fittingly. The choral invocation of 'Ooooo' and the choral rounding-off of 'Hoooi Kiw!' are also done by a group of supporting voices, men and women, standing with the musicians in a corner. It is only after the phawar has been performed that the cortege can proceed towards the cremation hill. Even during the procession, the phawar continues, accompanied by the music and the male dancers in their traditional attire.

'As you can see, it's very different,' I concluded. 'The chanting is not a lament but a glorification of the paternal grandmother.'

'Can you tell me more about the traditional dancing attire, Bah Ap?' Donald asked.

'A Khasi male dancer is usually dressed in a luxurious dhoti of deep purple eri silk, with silver edging,' I said. 'Over it, he wears a white shirt and a sleeveless velvet jacket adorned with ornate designs and the golden tassels of muka silk. And over this is draped an X-shaped chain of silver inlaid with rubies. He usually wears a necklace of gold and red coral stones, and on his head is a magnificent purple-and-gold mulberry-silk turban topped with feathers from the tail of a rooster, or sometimes from that of an eagle. He also carries a miniature silver quiver, full of silver arrows, on his back. In his right hand, he holds a polished sword, and in his left, a whisk of yak's hair.'

'Wow, that sounds incredibly expensive, ya!' Donald cried.

'It is. Unless you are rich, okay, you cannot be a Khasi dancer!' Hamkom said.

'That's not true, Ham,' I corrected him. 'I have been describing how most of them dress, but there are dancers who simply wear cotton dhotis, shirts and turbans, all white, without any ornaments. Some dancers from rural areas even use handkerchiefs instead of whisks. Too costly for them—'

'And nobody looks down on them?' Donald asked.

'Khasi society is not like that, Don,' Raji explained. 'Everybody is free to dance and have fun. You will only be laughed at if you dance without knowing how to.'

'Hey, Ap, are you saying that other Khasi sub-tribes do not have funeral chants of the kind the Lyngngams practise?' Evening asked.

'They do, but it's practised only in a few places now. In the past, of course, it was prevalent everywhere, and in fact, we even used hired mourners—'

'Hired mourners!'

'Oh yeah, I remember hearing them last in Sohra when I was a boy of eleven or so. And they were terrific, I tell you. Horace was right when he said, "Hired mourners outstrip in word and action those whose sorrow is real."'

'You mean there were hired mourners in ancient Rome?' Evening sounded surprised.

'In Rome, in Greece, and in many parts of India too. Do you remember that Hindi film, *Rudaali*? There also they have hired mourners—'

'But why would Khasis use hired mourners?' Evening asked.

'Khasis believe that a dead person should always be mourned before he is cremated, if not, his spirit may come to pester his relatives since it will not be able to make its journey to the house of God—'

'You people keep talking about the dead complaining and pestering the living. How do they do that, ya?' Magdalene asked.

'Through nightmares mostly, nightmares about the dead person,' I replied. 'But sometimes unearthly moans can also be heard at night near the houses of those who had in some way displeased their dead relatives. For this reason, a person must always be mourned. My first experience with a hired mourner was when a one-year-old child near my house in Sohra died. Since the mother was very ill, her relatives hired a woman to mourn for him. When she came, she started howling and crying in such mournful and heartrending tones that she even drew many of us kids away from our play. And the words she used were so poignant and touching that many of the people present there cried. But then, amidst all that woeful wailing and chanting, she suddenly stopped and said, "*Ai, ai lem uto u kwai!*" ("Give, give me that betel nut also!") After that, she immediately went back to her crying and howling, but she had spoilt the effect completely, and people were laughing instead of crying.'

Magdalene was amused. 'This Ap, you know, he always manages to mix the most serious with the most comical, ya!'

Smiling, I said, 'They used to say that the best mourner in Sohra was a woman by the name of Sumari. But Sumari was also a famous stage actress, playing comic roles. When she was asked to mourn for someone, she could never resist the temptation to use funny comparisons in her laments. One day, mourning for a four-year-old child, she chanted:

> *Ani balei mo ieit*
> *Phi shu wan mo tang shipor?*
> *Ani balei mo ieit*
> *Phi shu leit noh khlem dei por?*
> *Phngong jak phi mih,*
> *Phngong jak phi rieh,*
> *Kumba phon ïa i khlieh shrieh!*

> (Oh why, my love,
> Why did you come for a little while only?
> Oh why, my love,

Why did you leave me so abruptly?
Up you came
And down you went
Like a monkey's head boiling in a pot!)

'When they heard her say that, even people who had been crying started laughing, for it sounded hilarious, especially with all that rhyming. I wish I could reproduce the exact thing for you in English, Don, but I can't, unfortunately.'

Donald, Magdalene, Hamkom and Dale could not understand the simile. Donald asked, 'But why "monkey's head", Bah Ap?'

'When a monkey's head is cooked in a pot, the boiling water causes the head to bob up and down rhythmically,' I explained. 'Like the dead child, coming up into the world and sinking into oblivion after no time at all. It was apt enough but also inappropriate given the context.'

They all laughed now, and Magdalene said, 'Sounds like fun.'

'If you are not the bereaved.'

'Hey, Ap, do you remember that funny Lam Sniang ceremony we witnessed together?' Raji suddenly said.

The Lam Sniang, or 'escorting the pig' ceremony, is performed only upon the death of the paternal grandmother. Raji and I had witnessed one recently in Shillong. The pig was escorted from the house of the paternal grandchildren, where he had been kept for one night, to the death house, which was not very far from there.

On the morning of the cremation day, the paternal grandchildren gathered with relatives and friends in the courtyard and directed the minders to bring the pig there for washing. The washing was merely symbolic: a mugful of water poured on the pig's back, followed by vigorous rubbing. But the pig squealed and protested loudly. The uncle of the family, a fellow called Bran, who was washing the pig, spoke to him in cajoling tones. Rubbing the pig's back up and down, he said, 'Oh uncle, oh brother, look, we are washing you, we are cleansing you, not because we are your enemies. We are doing this by the will of God, the Dispenser, the Creator, who had given us leave, so we can take you to the house of our paternal grandmother, who is gone from this world to eat betel nut in the house of God. This is our way of showing our love, our reverence for her. Your purpose is to participate in the obsequies, the spiritual ceremonies, so her soul may journey peacefully to its heavenly abode. Do not squeal, do not protest. Cooperate with us, do not resist, for yours is the honour, yours is the fame, yours the enviable duty of helping the soul on its journey.'

The pig quietened down, probably because he was reassured by the soft, droning voice and also perhaps because he liked the rubbing and scratching he was getting. When the washing was done, he was driven to the death house, flanked by his two minders and followed by the rice-bearers (male relatives carrying a large pot of boiled rice meant for the death house) and the rest of the family.

Raji and I were very surprised to see the pig walking peacefully in the direction he was guided, as if he had grasped the uncle's words perfectly and had accepted his fate. His legs, I could see, were swollen, and his haunches were all bloodied from the ill-treatment he had received at the hands of his previous owners. The poor thing walked with great difficulty, but went meekly enough. Everybody admired his intelligence and said he must have had a divine prompting to make him walk so quietly to his own death.

Somebody in the crowd said, 'If a shaman had been called to perform acts of obeisance and obsecration, I guarantee you that this pig would, of his own volition, without minders, go to the death house.' He sounded bitter. 'They made a mistake. They should have called for a shaman; the ceremonies would have been more dignified with him conducting them.'

His name was Shan, I think.

Just then, we came to the first fork in the road, and the pig tried to take a turn in the wrong direction.

Shan immediately cried, 'See, see, I told you! We should have called for a shaman!'

Constantine, his cousin, replied, 'It's okay, it's okay, he just made a mistake.'

However, each time we arrived at a junction, the pig tried to take the wrong turn. Now, even some of the others were worried. One of Shan's brothers, Shin, said, 'I think we spoke too soon about the pig's cooperation, you know, Bah. I think he knows what's in store for him; he's avoiding it, see, see.'

The minders used a combination of force and gentle coaxing to persuade the pig on his way. Finally, after a few such diversions, we reached the stone steps leading to the death house. The pig looked up at all the steps and stopped dead in his tracks. He simply did not want to go on.

'He can smell death in the air, I think,' Shin remarked.

But Constantine said it was probably because of his injured legs. 'The pain must be excruciating. Look at them, all purple and swollen!'

'No, no, it's not that!' Shan said again. 'We should have called for a shaman.'

When the pig refused to move any farther, the minders dragged him up by the ears, which caused him to squeal at the top of his lungs. Meanwhile, the family and close relatives of the deceased waited to welcome him by the gate of the death house. The eldest uncle of the family, called Scot, was asked to make a welcome speech. But he was not a good speaker and only managed to stutter a few words of welcome, which he concluded by saying, 'Come in, pig, please come in.' But when the pig did not enter, he lost his cool and shouted, 'Why don't you come in, you son of a pig?'

The crowd laughed, but the relatives were embarrassed. A nephew scolded him for using such language and whispered some words in his ears so he could properly coax the pig.

Shan was furious. 'This is a bloody farce! There should have been a shaman to send off the pig and another to receive and welcome him. What a farce!'

'Why didn't you do that, then?' I asked.

'Because we allowed our women to crow like roosters, that's why! They said the ceremony should be performed by the uncles, who are supposed to be the official priests of the families. That's fine, but these guys don't know anything. Look at him'—he pointed at Scot—'he cannot even say a few words of welcome.'

The pig had to be forced into the compound. Eventually, he was led to the room where the body lay. The stuttering Scot sprayed him with water and, after being coached by his nephew, said, 'I wash you with this golden water, this silver water, so you may be cleansed and be ready to be with my sister's spirit, which will shortly travel to the house of God.'

After that, on the nephew's prompting, he prayed to God and addressed the spirit of the deceased, telling her of the arrival of the sacrificial pig from her eldest son's family. He sprinkled some rice grains and prayed again that everything might go smoothly, and then told the deceased not to worry or pine for anything or complain about anyone since they had tried to do everything according to the rituals of her religion.

Having said his prayer, he asked the minders to lead the pig away for slaughter. But the pig did not want to leave. He smelt the feet of all those present, probably mistaking their smelly socks for food, and then began to lap up the rice grains from the floor. The minders tried to move him out again, but somebody in the crowd shouted, 'Leave him be, he's having his breakfast, can't you see?'

When he was done, they tried coaxing the pig to leave. He started to, but all of a sudden, fled back in, went to the body, sniffed at it for a while and then lay down on the floor and went to sleep.

The sisters of the deceased tried to sweet-talk the pig. When that failed, they prayed to God, pleading with him to instruct the animal to go peacefully to his slaughter. Bran, the uncle of the paternal grandchildren, also started praying, but what he was saying nobody could tell, for he was muttering his prayer under his breath.

Bran's nieces thought it was a sign of displeasure from the dead. They were so worried they became jittery. One of them, Missiful, thought it was because the deceased was pining for her eldest brother, who was in Delhi. She phoned him from her mobile, told him about what was happening and said, 'Bu, please talk to the pig, tell him not to pine for you … Here, talk to him, I'm keeping my phone against his ear …'

The brother, Bu, spoke to the pig, and because the loudspeaker was on, everybody could hear what he was saying. 'Look here, oh uncle, oh brother, we have brought you to the house of our meikha, not because we hate you or desire your death, but because it is the custom, permitted by God, that you do not die in vain but go with honour, a sharer in our rites and rituals. Look here, uncle, look here, brother, that I cannot be with you at this most important moment in your life is not because I disdain your sacrifice and selflessness but because I can't. My duties had brought me here, and there's no way for me to travel back and be with you in time for the funeral. Do not pine for me, brother, I honour your sacrifice, do not sulk that I'm not there. I ask for the same indulgence from meikha, who lies there before you, I ask her to forgive me and not pine for me since my absence is not deliberate. Dear uncle, dear brother, go in peace now. I plead with you; please go in peace.'

But the pig only grunted and shook his head in annoyance at the noise in his ear.

Meanwhile, the spectacle of someone from Delhi speaking on the mobile phone to a pig set off such a tumult of laughter and unseemly banter that the death house began to resemble a marketplace.

Someone standing near me wondered aloud: 'Does he understand he's going to die? Is that why he's not budging? Or is he simply too tired and scared by all this noise?'

At that moment, Scot's children brought another pig into the bedroom. Seeing the other pig sleeping, he also promptly lay down on the floor. But he lay in such a strange position, with front feet folded, that Scot teased his children, who were Catholics, and said, 'Look! Your pig is also a Catholic, you see, he is genuflecting!'

This brought on another round of uproarious laughter. By now, it was as if a comedy was being staged there.

Eventually, though, the pigs were forced out of there and slaughtered. Their meat was cut into two halves. The upper portion was cut into pieces and boiled with potatoes, while the lower was kept back for distribution among the deceased's blood relatives and the paternal grandchildren. This would be done at night, after the body was cremated.

When the meat was cooked, the deceased was offered the first ladleful together with the boiled rice—top of the pot—brought by the paternal grandchildren.

And that marked the end of the chaotic and entertaining Lam Sniang ceremony that Raji and I witnessed, although entertainment it certainly was not supposed to be.

Many of my friends were amused, but Bah Kit and Bah Su were annoyed. Bah Kit said, 'The ceremony was a farce! All that noise and laughter has no place in such a solemn event!'

'That's what Shan also said,' Raji explained. 'He was furious and called it a bloody circus.'

'And all because the womenfolk wanted to revive the ancient status of the uncle as a family priest,' I added. 'Unfortunately, they only managed to turn those particular uncles into clowns.'

'I told you, I told you, because of the matrilineal system, hens are crowing like roosters and the men—'

'Enough, enough!' Bah Kynsai interposed. 'We have been there already, na?'

Taking advantage of the sudden lull, Hamkom changed the topic. 'You know, Bah Kynsai, I have been thinking about this Phor Sorat affair, okay, and I can't help wondering why these people did not develop a method of embalming the dead when they have been practising the custom for donkey's years. I mean, keeping the body for so long without preserving it … Initially, it must have stunk to high heavens, no?'

'They developed something much better than embalming, na, Ham?'

'What's that?'

'They simplified matters and simply put the body on top of a tree in the jungle, na? How offensive can it be, on top of a tall tree in the jungle, huh?' Bah Kynsai laughed loudly.

'Tet leh, this Bah Kynsai!'

I said, 'In Sohra, they used to practise embalming.'

'What? They keep the body for this long in Sohra too?' Hamkom asked in disbelief.

'Not now, in the past—'

'I know,' Bah Kit intervened. 'Ap is talking about the cremation of the syiems of Hima Sohra. Only the body of a dead syiem was kept for a long time, sometimes years.'

'Why?'

'One of the reasons,' I said, 'was because the body of a syiem must be cremated by his successor—'

'But how long would that take? Not years!' Hamkom asked.

Bah Kynsai added, 'Yeah, why should it take time at all? You yourself said the king of a state is elected by the Syiem clan, na, and these guys normally elect the eldest nephew of the dead king, so—'

'Yes, yes,' Hamkom pressed home his point. 'And you also said whoever is elected by the Syiem clan is accepted by the nobles and ministers, unless he is physically handicapped or morally depraved, so why the delay?'

'All of this is true, Ham. It is also true that the man so chosen can govern the state with all the usual powers allowed to a king. But in Sohra, the custom is a little different. The syiem-elect is not considered a true or fully fledged king unless he has been formally enthroned by the ministers from the twelve founding clans of the state according to established religious customs. And he cannot be enthroned unless he has cremated the body of his predecessor—'

'So what's the problem?' Bah Kynsai asked. 'Cremating the body of his predecessor couldn't have been that difficult, na?'

'That's what you think,' I replied. 'The cremation of a Sohra king is the most elaborate of all the Khasi funeral rites, since it is also connected with the enthronement rites of his successor. And both these rites can cost a lot of money. The cremation of the last king, for example, more than a hundred years ago, cost about 50,000 rupees. Imagine what that kind of money would be today! Not less than fifty lakh. In fact, when Ram Sing Syiem died in 1875, his successor, Hajon Manik Syiem, could simply not collect enough funds for his cremation. As a result, Ram Sing's body had to be kept in the house for thirty-three years till Roba Sing Syiem ascended the throne and cremated him in 1908. And for that reason, Hajon was never considered a proper king by the people of Sohra. He was called *U Syiem Thok*, the charlatan king.'

'My God, man, thirty-three years! Are you serious?' Hamkom exclaimed.

Evening said, 'Of course he is serious, this part I also know, it's recorded in the history books.'

'But how did they preserve the body, Ap?' Magdalene asked, bringing us back to the original point.

'The body is embalmed in a shed at the queen mother's palace, where it is first wrapped in a cloth and put in a shyngoid, a coffin hollowed out of a tree trunk. In this case, however, the shyngoid is made like a trough with a hole at the bottom, which can be plugged and unplugged as the need arises. When that is done, the shyngoid is filled with rice spirit until it covers the body completely—'

'But I heard they used honey, no, Ap?' Raji asked.

'Initially, the body was kept in a shyngoid full of orange-flavoured honey, but when the British came, they spread the rumour that the Sohras were selling honey that had been used in the embalming of a king. That affected the honey trade so severely that, from then on, they started using only rice spirit.

'The body is kept in the rice spirit for three days, after which the plug is removed and the putrid content allowed to drain deep into the earth through a bamboo tube. The body is then washed with lukewarm water and dried for a day or so. When it is quite dry, it is put back in the shyngoid coffin, where it is completely immersed in fresh lime juice. After a few days, the content is again emptied through the bamboo tube. This process of immersing the body alternately in rice spirit and lime juice continues until all the fluid has been drained out of it. Once the process is complete, the body is dressed in royal garb and placed in a coffin covered with a close-fitting lid and, additionally, made airtight. The coffin is placed inside the palace—with no offending smell at all—till the cremation can take place.'

'Wow!' Magdalene exclaimed. 'Whatever you say, no, Bah Kynsai, I'm very proud of my people. Imagine having that kind of know-how, ya!'

'I didn't say anything, Mag, why did you say, "whatever you say"?' he protested.

Magdalene laughed. 'No, no, I'm just saying—'

'Yeah, yeah, it's truly wonderful,' Hamkom interrupted her, 'but what I want to know is, why would it cost so much to cremate a Sohra king?'

'In the first place, the process of curing the body could take several weeks and months, involving a considerable amount of money. Then, there is the kpep to be considered. This box-like cremation structure, made of specially hewn, close-fitting stone blocks, could take twenty masons about four to five months to complete. They had to mine the stone, prepare the blocks, build the four walls of the structure and fill the space inside with stones and sand till the top became completely flat. Then the stone walls had to be decorated with carvings. Can you imagine the kind of expenditure that went into all that?'

'What is the size of the kpep, Bah Ap?' Donald asked.

'It could be thirty feet long, more than twenty feet wide and about eight feet high.'

'That's huge, man!' Hamkom agreed.

'Next, there is the *lyngkhason*, both coffin and pyre, made of beautifully polished and carved wood. The lyngkhason is made in the form of a large coffin about four feet wide, seven feet long and four feet high. Three handsomely polished square logs are vertically attached to each side of it. The top of the logs is carved like an eight-cornered vase crowned by a figure in the shape of a plantain flower, the siarkait. The siarkait is covered with gold leaves.'

'Oh, shit! Did you hear that, Don?' Magdalene cried in genuine surprise. 'Gold leaves and all too!'

'All around the rim of the lyngkhason coffin is a kind of ornately carved cornice, while on the flat top are nailed more figures carved in the shape of a vase, a comb, a cleaning brush, a bed, a canopy, a tobacco pipe and so on. Each of these figures, about three feet high, is topped with a siarkait flower covered with gold leaves. The six square logs are painted with different brilliant colours, while the body of the lyngkhason itself is covered with a wine-coloured flannel.'

'Whew! That's why they say the people of Sohra are the most cultured of Khasis, no!' Raji exclaimed. As an artist, he was clearly impressed by what he was hearing.

'But that's not the end of it. A *tabut*, or a three-storey lid, has to be made for the lyngkhason coffin. And this is yet another intricate affair—'

'A three-storey lid, Ap!' Magdalene yelped.

'Yeah. It's made from bamboo and cane and is at least the height of three bamboo poles, or approximately sixty feet—'

'Wow!' they all exclaimed in unison.

'The first storey is the shortest and is made in such a way that it fits the coffin-cum-pyre lyngkhason snugly. This part is made in the shape of flowers or human figures and is fixed to the coffin with stout, woven bamboo strips inserted into specially drilled holes in the coffin's cornice. The next storey is much taller, made in the shape of human figures or some beautiful objects. These figures are usually decorated with bits of coloured cloth, replaced in later years by coloured paper. The last storey contains the shanduwa high canopy of dark red satin cloth, raised on four long bamboo poles. The borders of the shanduwa are decorated with tassels and little pearl-like decorations dangling from strings and painted in, most often, red, yellow, white and green. These same decorations are also hung all around the tabut lid. The lyngkhason coffin and its tabut are said to be so heavy that they had to be carried on a specially designed wooden platform by about 300 men. Now, my friends, can you imagine how much all of that would cost?'

'But how did they take such a thing up the cremation kpep, which you said is about eight feet high?' Evening asked.

'By a bamboo ramp, dismantled afterwards ... But to return to the point, these are only the things that have to be made, Bah Kynsai. What about the numerous rites and sacrifices? For instance, more than twenty *lang basas*, or market-stall goats, have to be slaughtered. These are white goats whose horns are covered with leaves of gold or silver, Don. They are so named because they are meant to be sacrificed in the king and the ministers' market stalls at Ïewbah Sohra. And then there are roosters, bulls and pigs brought from all over the state, which must be ritually slaughtered according to long-established and very expensive customs. Added to all this, there are ceremonial dances that must be organised at Rikhana near Ïewbah, every day, three weeks before the cremation day. At night, funeral music has to be played in the queen mother's palace without pause. And think of the mourners, consolers, duhalia musicians, professional phawar chanters and funeral attendants coming from all over the state. All of them have to be fed for weeks! Do you see now?

'To compound the expenses, all these obsequies have to be combined with the new king's enthronement rites! That's why, after Roba Sing in 1926, no other Sohra king has been able to cremate his predecessor. And that's also why the Sohras have been calling all of them *ki syiem thok*.'

'The charlatan kings! What a pity, ya,' Hamkom said, almost sadly. 'The cremation of the Sohra kings sounds a hundred times more fascinating than our Phor Sorat, no?'

'Yeah, it must have been a sight to behold!' I agreed. 'Just imagine the multitudes walking in a cortege with all that music, phawar chanting, gun salutes and crackers going off! It must have been several kilometres long at least!'

Raji, however, defended the Phor Sorat ceremony and said, 'This is also quite unique, okay? As far as I'm concerned, ha, this day has been the most memorable of my life.'

'Yeah, yeah, this too is unique, Raji, no doubt about it,' Hamkom conceded. 'But tell me, in this Phor Sorat, okay, I noticed the mourners circled the pyre three times, why is that, ya? In fact, almost everything they did, ha, they did it three times ... What's so special about the number three?'

Raji looked at Bah Su.

'The circling of the pyre,' Bah Su responded, 'was a sign that the obsequies were over. And number three has a special meaning for Khasis, ha, Ham, because of the sacred myths. For instance, ha, the Commandments that govern our lives are three. And then, when Rooster made his pledge to Sun, okay, he said, "Before you peep into the world, I will shake my shield and thrice will I sound my bugle, as signs that the world is fit enough for your divine blessing." That's why three is a special number.'

'And this is the last Phor Sorat to be performed, huh? What a shame, man!' Raji lamented.

'But why has it got to be the last?' Hamkom asked.

'Isn't it obvious to you, tdong?' Bah Kynsai cursed him. 'Ka We Shyrkon was the last Lyngngam to practise the indigenous religion, na?'

'No, but in Nongtrai, there are still some who belong to the Khasi religion, no, Bah Kynsai?' Hamkom argued.

Raji said, 'It's the last in Lyngngam, but it may not be the last in Nongtrai, no one can really say. In the early twentieth century, the British banned the keeping of corpses for a prolonged period, and that was later reinforced by Sib Sing Syiem, the king of Hima Nongstoin. These bans, together with the huge expenditure involved and, of course, the advent of Christianity have all combined to make the observance of Ka Phor Sorat less and less frequent.'

'But something has been troubling me about the story of the first funeral feast, Bah Ap,' Donald said. 'It was for a bone burial, no, not a funeral?'

'You are quite right. Initially, Ka Phur was conducted only during bone burials, but later it was also performed whenever they cremated elderly or prominent people.'

'But even Synriang's bone burial seems to be quite different from this. Here, they will place the bones inside the monolith. But Synriang, you said, planted the first Khasi monoliths after the bone receptacle had been built to commemorate the event.'

'Right again. In the Khasi uplands, bones were never buried inside monoliths. It was only after mawshyieng cists and mawbah ossuaries had been built, and the bone burial ceremonies had been performed, that monoliths or megaliths were planted some distance away from them, as commemoration. And there's one more difference: here they planted just one small monolith, but in the uplands, the standing male stones are always in groups of three or five or seven and so on ...'

'Why don't you tell us about these monoliths, Ap?' Bah Kynsai asked. 'You see them everywhere, na, but nobody seems to know what the hell they stand for.'

Bah Kit replied, 'You are right, Bah Kynsai, even the faithful of Niam Khasi, ha, do not know about them any more.'

'But they are all connected with death and funerals, no, Bah Kit?' Hamkom asked.

'I think you had better tell them, Ap,' Bah Kit said.

The Khasi word for monolith is *mawbynna*, which implies a stone that marks or records or announces something important so that it remains *bynna*, forever etched in human memory. Even the word *kynmaw* means 'to mark in stone'. And since the Khasis did not have a script of their own and were not literate till 1842, every significant event was marked with stones. That's why the profusion of monoliths and megaliths dotting the landscape of Ri Khasi—

'Comprising East Khasi Hills, West Khasi Hills, Ri Bhoi and Jaiñtia Hills districts of Meghalaya,' Raji said.

'We have clarified that many times, pha!' Bah Kynsai scolded him.

Raji was offended. 'Don't call me "pha", Bah Kynsai, otherwise—'

'Otherwise, what?' Bah Kynsai challenged him.

'Otherwise, I'll pull off—'

'Don't say it, Raji!' I interrupted sternly. He was about to say 'I'll pull off your wig'—Bah Kynsai's most closely kept secret. Even to his closest friends, he never admitted to wearing one.

Quickly returning to my story, I said that Gurdon had borne witness to this profusion of monoliths when he wrote, in 1906, that the first objects which struck the eye of the visitor to the Khasi Hills were the 'monoliths, table stones and cromlechs' that could be seen 'almost everywhere'. This was despite the fact that many of them had been toppled by the great earthquake of 1897 and by the rampant vandalism of ignorant and uncaring people, which had forced the chief commissioner of Assam, Sir Charles James Lyall, to instruct the deputy commissioner of Khasi and Jaiñtia Hills to 'place the stones under the protection of the village authorities' and to punish those responsible for destroying them.

Perhaps it was thanks to measures like Lyall's that we still come across numerous monoliths and megaliths of varying sizes in every part of Ri Khasi. They stand erect, alone or in odd-numbered groups, and always with flat and round table stones in front of them. We see them by the roadside and on country tracks, atop lonely hills and in secluded valleys, in marketplaces and the most central spots of villages. The menhirs or standing stones are called *ki mawshynrang*, male stones, and the flat table stones lying at their feet, very much in the form of dolmens, are called *ki mawkynthei*, female stones.

'Wait, wait, Ap, wait!' Raji said, his palm raised. Looking around at the others, he asked, 'Did you boneheads know all this?'

We all looked at each other and chuckled, realising that Raji was drunk again.

Raji glared at the others and shouted, 'I'm asking you!' When they smiled and shook their heads, he waved at me and said, 'Go ahead, Ap, they don't know anything.'

Most of these stones are rough-hewn from either granite or sandstone in such a way that they taper gradually towards the top, although there are some, such as those found in Sohra, which are more or less rectangular, with only the top neatly rounded off. In some cases, the middle male stone is ornamented and carved with figures. Such is the Mawsmai monolith, south of Sohra, which is decorated with a crown, and the Mawsngi, or sun stone, at Longwa in West Khasi Hills, which is decorated with an image of the sun.

But perhaps the most unusual menhir in Ri Khasi is the one in the ruined village of Rangjyrteh to the west of Sohra—

'Wait, wait, Ap!' Raji broke in again. 'I'd better clarify matters for these boneheads. Children, Rangjyrteh is the village where Ka Likai used to live, okay? You remember the story, no? Good, good, go on, Ap.'

Everybody laughed. Raji was funny when he was drunk.

This menhir, I continued, is in the shape of a perfect rectangle, and its top is completely square. Rangjyrteh itself is a famous megalithic site and has a large collection of monoliths, cromlechs, cremation kpeps and stone troughs for iron smelting. This is the only place around the Sohra districts that has been well protected by the Soil Conservation Department of the Meghalaya government—

'And do you know why, little children?' Raji asked. 'Because, because Rangjyrteh is very important, historically very important … But why is it important?' When they shook their heads to tease him, he declared: 'Bloody boneheads! Tell them, Ap.'

Because, I said, it used to be the greatest iron manufacturing and trading centre of southern Ri Khasi thousands of years ago—

'Thousands of years ago, he says. Be specific, man!' Raji commanded.

'How can he be specific about the past like that, *pha buaid nguid*?'

Buaid nguid means 'greedy drunk'. Raji did not like that at all. Wagging his forefinger at Bah Kynsai, he retorted, 'Don't start, don't start, Bah Kynsai, otherwise—'

I intervened again. 'Do you remember what I told you about Prokop and Mitri's radiocarbon dating? Prokop dated the iron smelting and megalithic memorial monuments in the Khasi Hills to a period between 353 BCE and 128 CE, while Mitri dated the settlement at Umjajew, near Shillong, to 1900 BCE, about 4,000 years ago. God only knows exactly how old Rangjyrteh and the first Khasi monoliths are.'

'Well, Ap, one thing I can say about you, okay, you know your stuff, man, you know your stuff, unlike Bah Kynsai here,' Raji said.

Bah Kynsai did not take the bait and only asked me to go on.

The size of these stones varies from place to place, I said. In height, they range from three or four feet to thirteen or fourteen feet, although many could be taller than twenty-five feet. The typical thickness of an ordinary male stone is between eighteen inches and two feet. The size of the female stones, raised about two feet above the ground, also varies with the size of the male stones, that is, the bigger the male, the bigger the female.

The Khasi monoliths have been a matter of great curiosity even for us. For instance, why are female stones made to lie flat at the feet of male stones when ours is a matrilineal society? This could be a reminder that the Khasi matrilineal system is not a true matriarchy, and the man is not only the head of the family but also the one who takes upon himself the burden of protecting his family, clan, village and state. All this we could say, but the fact remains that Khasi monoliths were also meant to be useful, and were designed in such a way that they could serve as resting places for wayfarers.

That is why they were planted beside trails and pathways leading to villages and markets, or places of work in the fields, hills, rivers and jungles. (Khasis always say 'plant' a monolith, and never 'erect', since it is to them a living memory, something alive, like a plant that grows with time.) Quite often, one sees men and women breaking their journey on them, laying their burden of firewood or market produce aside to sit for a while on the flat stones, enjoying a chew of betel nut or a smoke.

'You see, Ning, he can even explain the matrilineal system through monoliths,' Raji teased Evening. 'And what is he saying? The woman is lying flat and the man is erect. Why don't you like such a system, huh? Do you want to lie flat instead and have the woman erect over you? Do you want that, Ning? Say it, man!'

'Uff, this Raji is too much, ya!' Magdalene complained.

And Evening cursed: '*Riewkai tdong!*'

Riewkai means 'joker' and tdong, as you know, means 'arse', but Raji only cackled, delighted to have got under Evening's skin.

I decided to ignore them.

That they serve as resting spots is not why there are so many monoliths and megaliths everywhere, even now. There are different types of monoliths, and each type was planted for a specific purpose, one of which was to raise a memorial for those who had passed on. The old Khasis had great respect for the dead—which is not to be misunderstood as ancestor worship. As Gurdon says, the erection of gravestones, to mark the spot where the remains of the dead are buried, is an almost universal practice. But, though raised as memorials, Khasi monoliths and megaliths are not gravestones, for they do not mark the place where the remains of the dead lie buried. The old Khasis, as you know, cremated their dead, as do Khasi-Khasis like Bah Kit and Bah Su—

'What about you?' Raji demanded.

'I'd like to be buried, so my children can come and bring me some flowers once a year,' I replied.

'From where will you get children, ha, so far you haven't even got a woman, na?' Bah Kynsai said, laughing.

'He's only forty, Bah Kynsai, and forty for a man is still very much okay, no?' Raji defended me. 'Hey, Ap, Bah Kynsai doesn't even know that, leh. From now on, we'll call him the ingenuous professor, okay? Hi, Professor Ingenuous!'

I was afraid Bah Kynsai might be angry, but he only laughed and cursed light-heartedly. 'Enough, *pha lyeit*! On with it, Ap.'

'Wait, wait, wait! Something you should know, Bah Kynsai ... I remembered just now,' Raji said again. 'Ap has a secret ... You know what it is? He has a girlfriend, yes, a girlfriend! And this bugger hasn't even told us about her! You know how I know? I know because I know, and you don't know what I know ... I saw them at Ri Kynjai resort, yes, at Umïam! Sitting by the lake and holding hands, sala, and you would not even tell us about her! But beautiful, man, stunningly beautiful! Brown hair, curly like Maggi noodles, brown eyes, straight nose ... Like a white girl, I'm telling you, like a pukka white girl! Sala! Ask him to tell us, Bah Kynsai, ask him!'

'Oh Saia, my beloved Saia!' I took her name silently, overwhelmed by a sudden longing for her. We love each other, it is true, but she is so young. And I? I am running to seed ...

Magdalene asked, 'Is that true, Ap? Do you really have a girlfriend?'

Overcoming my sadness with a supreme effort, I said, 'Look at him'—pointing to Raji, who was quite drunk—'can you take him seriously in this condition?'

'Okay, okay, enough of that!' Bah Kynsai said impatiently. 'On with it, man!'

Bah Kynsai had been quite irritated when I did not take a fancy to his relative, introduced to me as a potential spouse. I could see he was still a little sore about it.

I promptly returned to my narration. Many Khasi memorial stones could be called cenotaphs—monuments to someone cremated or buried elsewhere. Several are also in the nature of cromlechs, serving as a charnel house where the bones of dead relatives are kept. This class of memorial stones is again of many kinds and are generally called *mawniam*, religious stones, because their planting is done only after the performance of certain funeral rites. Among them are the permanent cremation kpeps and the mawshyieng ossuary where the bones of a person are kept—

'Description, for the children!' Raji drawled, gesturing to Hamkom, Magdalene and Donald.

'I have already told them what they look like, remember?' I replied.

'Oh yeah, yeah, sorry, *dost*.'

Taking up the story again, I spoke briefly about the large mawbah ossuary where the bones of all the deceased clan members from a particular kpoh—belly or branch, comprising many families—are finally interred. The process of taking the bones from mawshyieng cists to the mawbah ossuary is known as *Ka Thep Mawbah*, or the ceremony of burying the bones in the large ossuary. The mawbah, as we see now, is built with several upright stones planted close together in the shape of a large, circular fence. A part of the fence is left open to form an entrance covered with a specially carved stone, and its top is covered with a large flat stone, like a cromlech.

'How large is this mawbah, Bah Ap?' Donald asked.

'Its actual size depends on the size of the clan using it, Don,' Bah Kit answered.

'But earlier, Ap said it was built like a mawshyieng cist, no?' Hamkom objected. 'This one, however, is different, ya!'

'Synriang, mə, tdong, Synriang built it like a mawshyieng cist,' Raji said. 'Later, except for the rich, most mawbahs were built like this. Understood?'

The Thep Mawbah ceremony could be organised only after due consultations among brothers and sisters, uncles and nephews in the house of the last daughter in the family, which was the religious house of the clan. In this gathering, they raised their prayers to God as the Mother of Divine Law, and pleaded for his permission through divination rites performed by the eldest uncle. If God so decreed through signs and tokens, they would begin the fund collection for building the mawbah and the gathering of the bones, which must be done with feasting and due pomp and ceremonies.

But all of this is in the past. Things have changed now. In Pomsohmen, where the cremation kpeps of the kings of Sohra are located, there are hundreds of these monuments on both sides of the Pomsohmen stream. The place could easily have been turned into a treasured heritage site, but through the callous negligence of our traditional rulers and locality authorities, these incomparable legacies have instead been destroyed and treated with such ignorant discourtesy that it makes one weep. The entire area has been given over to settlement, and the result has been rampant vandalism. There's a particularly heartbreaking sight here. The area's biggest mawbah, believed to be the common ossuary of the Sohra royal family, has been converted into a part of their stone fence by one of the settlers. If you enter the settler's compound, you can see that the family is using the mawbah to store odds and ends.

Raji bowed and shook his head, looking genuinely sad. 'I shed bitter tears, bitter tears, I have seen that place also, liah, I tell you, it's tragic.'

The others looked at Raji, who was now snuffling. It was hard to tell whether he was crying or merely fooling around.

There are many more kinds of mawniam religious stones, I told them. But the most common are the market stones or *mawïew* monoliths, like those found in the marketplace of Ïewduh in Shillong.

Mawïew monoliths were planted to commemorate the founding of a market and had nothing to do with funeral rites or ossuaries. They are, in fact, a separate category of mawniam, and religious ceremonies are performed in some of them even now; most Khasi markets are also known as *ïewniam*, or religious market, since their establishment was dedicated to the guardian spirit of villages and the wilderness, U Ryngkew U Basa, through religious rites. The most famous of these ceremonies today is the one at Ïewduh, the megaliths of which are intricately connected with the history of the state of Shyllong.

There are almost as many mawïew monoliths as there are marketplaces in Ri Khasi. Such mawïews are ordinarily in the form of three menhirs planted alongside a large table stone. The biggest existing mawïew is in Laitlyngkot, which is 28.5 feet high. But perhaps the most famous is the one in Nartiang, which is associated with the story of U Mar Phalyngki, the Pnar strongman and warrior leader of the state of Sutnga. According to the story, the market in Nartiang was established by accident. Mar Phalyngki married a woman from a clan appointed as the custodian of the sacred stone at Ïew Mawlong in Raliang village. One day, when the skies were pouring as if from huge bamboo tubes, Mar Phalyngki asked his wife for a *trab*, a flat circular rain shield made of bamboo and large leaves, so that he could return home to Nartiang. It was the Pnar custom for a man to sleep in his wife's house and to return home during the day. But his wife was very busy at the time, and without even looking at him, she said rather morosely, 'I have no trab to give you, if you want a trab, go, take the flat mawïew from the market, use it as a trab.'

Mar Phalyngki took her seriously, for, after all, was she not the custodian of the sacred market stone? He went to Ïew Mawlong and lifted the massive table stone to use as a rain shield.

'He was that strong or what?' Mag asked incredulously.

'That strong, that strong, Mag!' Raji said drunkenly.

When Mar Phalyngki reached Nartiang, he went to place the table stone at the centre of the village and then went on home as if nothing had happened. But when people saw that the sacred market stone had been brought to Nartiang, they shifted the marketplace from Ïew Mawlong in Raliang to the new location. To commemorate the event, Mar Phalyngki, with the help of his followers and another strongman by the name of Luh Laskor, planted one of the tallest menhirs to be found in Ri Khasi—it was twenty-seven feet high. Mar Phalyngki also planted hundreds of other menhirs, big and small, and little table stones called *mawlyngknot*, or stool stones, which were used as seats when the religious rites to consecrate the new market were performed. Later, these rites became an annual commemorative affair known as Ka Pomblang Ïew Nartiang, or the Nartiang market goat-beheading ceremony, an intricate and expensive affair involving animal sacrifice (scores of goats, hundreds of chickens and doves) and the performance of the *chad pastieh* sword dance, culminating in a large community feast.

In this category of monoliths are also those known as *ki mawklim*, or stones of adultery. In the past, Khasis believed that when a man and a woman married, they did so for life. Even after the death of one of the partners, the marriage was considered to be still binding. Therefore, if, for instance, a man died and his wife married again, especially before the mourning period of one year had elapsed, she was considered to have committed an act of adultery. As punishment, she had to return the deceased husband's bones to his clan and pay a specified amount of money to defray the expenses of conducting the ceremony of cleansing the sang, or sacrilege. As evidence that the impure deed had been purified through mandatory rites, three small male stones were planted.

'Was such punishment only for a woman, Ap?' Magdalene asked.

'No, no, no, Mag!' Raji answered for me. 'He said "for instance", no? And take this as a lesson, you boneheads, in the past, okay, neither marriage nor divorce nor adultery were easy things to do. We have discussed this already, no? I hope you haven't forgotten what we taught you, little children? Go on, Ap.'

Mawnam, or stone of fame, stone of honour, commemorates an important event. As a rule, these monoliths are bigger and taller than the religious mawniam stones connected with funeral rites and ossuary sanctification. The menhir at Nartiang could also be called a mawnam since it was specifically planted to commemorate Mar Phalyngki's shifting of the market from Raliang to Nartiang. Among the other mawnam monoliths, which could be as tall as fifteen to twenty-five feet, are *ki mawlum*, the hill stones.

The most famous mawlum monoliths are Ki Mawphonsyiem at Mawphonsyiem Peak in Sohra, easily the highest point in the entire region, with a breathtaking view of the town and the far plains of Bangladesh. There used to be four large menhirs together with a few smaller ones, fronted, as usual, by large table stones. All but one were knocked down by the great earthquake of 1897.

The literal meaning of Mawphonsyiem is 'the king's treachery stone'. According to the story, when the central stone was planted to commemorate an important event in the state of Sohra, it simply would not stand and stay in place, although several attempts were made. The king consulted some of his hierophants, who told him that the stone was craving blood. Following their advice, the king deliberately dropped a silver lime container, his shanam, into the pit and asked one of his slaves to fetch it. When the slave was inside, the twenty-two-foot stone, easily weighing tonnes, was dropped on him, to the horror of all the onlookers. True to the words of the hierophants, the stone stood firm, paving the way for the rest of the menhirs to be planted. The irony is that people have forgotten the event for which they were planted and only remember the monoliths as the king's treachery stones.

Sometimes the mawlum monoliths are also called *ki mawkait,* or banana stones, especially if they were planted by members of a wealthy family to honour their dead parents. This is because the gnomic phawars they chanted while planting the stones kept referring to the parents as capable feeders— *Phi kiba lah ka kait-im ka kait-ih* (You who could provide the green banana, the ripe banana). Among the Khasis, infants are customarily fed with certain species of bananas, including kait mon, kait syiem and kait shyieng, which have no, or very little, acidic content. Hence, metaphorically, a capable parent is someone who can provide the bananas.

'Wa, wa, shabash, Ap, I didn't know that, man!' Raji said happily.

The other memorial monuments found in Ri Khasi are *ki palong,* literally, 'beds' or 'couches', and *ki kor,* 'stone benches'. The most famous palongs are Ka Palong ka Ber and Ka Palong u Ronsing in Khliehshnong, Sohra, built to commemorate the passing of Ka Ber, believed to be one of the queen mothers of the state of Sohra, and of Ronsing, one of the early kings. Constructed in the form of large circular platforms by laying carefully hewn stone blocks on top of each other, up to a height of three feet or so, these palongs were meant to be used as relaxing spots for travellers and sightseers and had nothing to do with funeral rites.

Ki kor, the stone benches, built with carefully hewn stone blocks fitted tightly together, are in the form of two square brackets facing each other, with a large gap between them. The most famous kor is Ka Kor Nongpriang on the trail from Sohra to the ravine hamlet of Nongpriang, which offers a spectacular view of the sylvan slopes, the tumbling white waterfalls and the deep valleys below, cut by a crystalline stream flowing all the way to Bangladesh.

There are also stone bridges and monuments sculpted in the form of animals and certain implements to memorialise specific events or simply to remind people of things that are integral to their culture. In the planting or construction of these monuments, religious ceremonies may or may not be performed, depending on the inclination of the people concerned.

From the plethora of menhirs and dolmens in these hills, some of which are huge, the question that arises naturally is how the old Khasis had raised these mammoth structures. A million visitors a year to Stonehenge are reportedly awestruck by the primitive technology and muscle-power which must have been used in transporting the enormous monoliths and raising them on Salisbury Plain. Should we not wonder then at the primitive technology and muscle-power of our own ancestors, who planted these menhirs, some of which are not only much bigger than those at Stonehenge but also located in more treacherous terrain?

'Correct, Ap! Absolutely correct!' Raji exclaimed. 'Now, children, listen very carefully.'

With menhirs, table stones and dolmens of small sizes, I said, there was not much difficulty, even though they might have had to be brought from faraway places where the stones were found and carved. In such cases, the old Khasis simply tied the stones to bamboo or wooden poles, much as the Lyngngams had done with their mawnop monolith, and then carried them to their designated locations. However, when the stone was a large one, the *ring maw*, or stone-fetching, became a community event. The men used to make a bamboo or wooden platform, with or without wheels, known as '*ka po*', for transporting it. If the po had no wheels, they put round logs underneath it to help it move. Once the stone was firmly fastened to the po, a man holding a leafy branch, whose duty it was to chant an inspirational phawar, was made to sit on it. Beating the stone with the branch, he would say, '*Kawei ka bor ba lang*' ('In one collected strength'), and the pullers and pushers would respond with the refrain of '*hui hah*'. The whole verse goes like this:

> *Kawei ka bor ba lang, hui hah,*
> *Kawei ka buit ba lang, hui hah,*
> *Pynbeit ïa u thiri, hui hah,*
> *Pynbeit ïa u jyrmi, hui hah.*

(In one collected strength, hui hah,
In one collected talent, hui hah,
Straighten the bamboo twine, hui hah,
Straighten the liana line, hui hah.)

And that was how they would proceed till they reached their destination.

'Beautiful, beautiful!' Raji cried excitedly. 'I haven't heard this phawar either. Bong leh, you should have warned me, man, I could have filmed your recital, no?'

'We'll do it, Raji, we'll do it,' I consoled him, 'when your hands are more stable.'

'Tet sala!' he cursed.

Now, more than ever, the monoliths are under threat, not only from vandalism and urbanisation but also because of the collective indifference of the community. It all began with the coming of the British. When the Khasis were living among themselves, cut off from the outside world, except for their immediate neighbours in Assam and East Bengal, and when everyone was practising the same culture and religion, there was much respect for, and even awe of, the menhirs and dolmens. It was said that illness and misfortunes would visit anyone who trifled with them. But when the British came, they brought with them their followers from mainland India, who practised their own religions and cultures and knew nothing about these strange stone structures. Consequently, they and the British, having no regard for the stones, were among the first to wreck and uproot them from their moorings. The need to construct more and more houses and develop more and more roadways forced the destruction of any monoliths that stood in the way. It was only in 1894, as I have told you, that the British government woke up to the need to preserve the stones, not only as monuments of 'great interest from an anthropological point of view' but also 'as memorials of the dead'.

But then, the great earthquake of 1897 came, and many of the menhirs that were still standing came toppling down or split or couldn't stand straight any more. Following closely upon this cataclysmic event was another development that changed the nature of Khasi society forever. And that was the large-scale conversion of Khasis to Christianity. Reverend Sister Philomena Kharakor of the Catholic church took cognisance of this when she wrote, in one of her essays, 'The conversion of Khasis to Christianity since the 19th century more and more blunted their love for their culture.'

'But why, man?' Raji demanded aggressively. 'Why should this be a cause to "blunt" our love for our own culture, our own history, huh? Quite a few of us have become Hindus or Muslims, but is that any reason to deny our own heritage, liah? Sorry, ha, Mag, but this thing is getting under my skin, ya! Whatever our religion now, okay, did we not come from the same ancestors? Did we not come from the same maternal ancestress, ka ïawbei, and the same paternal ancestor, u thawlang? Tet lyeit! Can we ever change that fact?'

'Is he still drunk, or has he suddenly become sober, this fellow?' Bah Kynsai wondered aloud.

'There *is* method in his drunkenness,' I said. 'And he's absolutely right, you know. Just think of the stories that the monoliths and memorial stones can tell us! Think of the history they may reveal if we can delve deep into the events behind their planting. Whatever our religion, we cannot change our past or our history. Without these, we are like thistledown, scattering every which way, at the mercy of the wind. It is because we cannot erase our past and implant a brand new one on top of it that Tham said, "The Seed that falls on stony grounds—without its roots—wilts as soon as the sun turns hot." He reminds us that the present and the past have a symbiotic relationship, supporting one another like mother and child.'

'Quite right, Ap, quite right!' Bah Kynsai enthused. 'And if we want our cultural heritage to survive, na, we should also learn from Christian nations like Great Britain. Why? Don't you know that the British government has spent millions to reconstruct, preserve and maintain the famous Stonehenge monoliths? And those monoliths were not even erected by the English, man! Why then can't we feel a little pride for our own, equally unique and equally ancient monuments, and try to do our bit for their safekeeping and maintenance, huh? Even our drunken friend here cried at their sad fate, na?'

'Right, right, Bah Kynsai,' Bah Su said. 'And we should try to get UNESCO to declare some of them as World Heritage Sites, ha, it's high time.'

'Bah Kynsai spoke of learning from Great Britain, I agree,' I said, 'but I also think we should pay heed to Reverend Sister Philomena. To her, these ancient stone monuments are "our priceless heritage … we must preserve and maintain them as handed down to us by our ancestors". This thought, coming from a Catholic nun, should be taken to heart by all of us. After all, only philistines do not respect the legacy of the past and its irreplaceable treasures.'

'What a coincidence, man!' Raji cried. 'I was also about to say that, you know? We are all like the philistines, man! Khasis are the philistines, liah! Hoooi kiw!'

We all chuckled at Raji's comment. Then Bah Kynsai suggested we take a break. We all trooped out, stretching and bending and exercising our limbs and necks. The night sky was an enormous blue tent with so many holes in it that the sky above could be seen twinkling with yellowy lights. I breathed in the aromatic jungle air until the scent of wood smoke from the death house drifted by to spoil it. We could see a crowd still milling around in the courtyard and the garden.

Bah Kynsai said, 'The Lyngngams are still eating, leh!'

'Second round; must be the second round!' Raji declared.

Dale, who was looking at the night sky too, suddenly said, 'Bah, how come those stars are red? And they are quite near, you see them?'

'Those are satellites, man,' Bah Kynsai explained. 'I hope the time doesn't come when there are more satellites than stars in the sky.'

'That can never be, Bah Kynsai,' Donald responded, 'but I understand the sentiment.'

Magdalene, who was not wearing anything warm, shivered in the cool night air and said, 'Let's go back inside, ya, it's cold outside. Not cold, actually, but uncomfortable, come, come, Don.'

We all followed them back inside and settled down on the straw again. The night air seemed to have sobered Raji a little. He reached for the gourd again, then thought better of it. Bah Kynsai took a sip from his mug. Bah Su did the same. Bah Kit took off his cap and rubbed his bald head with the palm of his right hand. I noticed that he did this often. Donald and Magdalene were sitting very close to each other. Evening and Dale, who were sitting side by side, now leant their slender frames against the wattle wall. Hamkom did the same on the opposite side. I looked around and wondered how there could be so many tall people in this room when the average height of Khasi men is about five-four. It must be one of those strange coincidences.

Bah Kynsai put down the mug and said, 'Now what?'

'We can talk some more about Ka Phor Sorat, Bah Kynsai,' Hamkom offered.

'What about?' Bah Kit asked. 'I think we covered everything, no?'

'Except for one thing,' Magdalene said. 'You guys said it was the most remarkable funeral ceremony you had ever witnessed, and I agree, but not because of the dead body on the tree house or the bulls or the chanting or the music.'

'Then?' Raji asked, staring blankly at her.

'Why, haven't you noticed or what? For me, it was unique because not a single mobile phone rang through the entire event.'

Everyone laughed at that.

'Mobile phones can be so irritating sometimes, no?' Hamkom said.

'Sometimes? All the time, man,' Bah Kynsai replied. 'Indispensable, but—'

'We have become a slave to them,' Evening concluded.

'Khasis used to call people talking to themselves lunatics or sorcerers, ha,' Bah Su said, 'and parents used to forbid children from doing so. But now, because of the mobile, ha, everyone is talking to himself. Are we then a generation of lunatics and sorcerers, or have the old maxims lost their relevance completely?'

'Hey, Ap,' Bah Kit suddenly said. 'Do you remember what happened during Madeng's funeral? That was a crazy thing, huh?'

Bah Kit told us about what had happened during the funeral of our clan elder, Madeng Nongkynrih. Just when the priest was rendering his homily, the mobile of a woman sitting close to the microphone rang at full volume. The woman made a frantic search for it in her bag, one of those single-slit cotton satchels rural people carry to the market. But because the bag was cluttered with odds and ends and also because the woman herself was becoming nervous, she had a great deal of trouble locating her mobile. While she was rummaging inside the bag, the mobile kept bawling, drawing many giggles as well as angry mutterings. Eventually, she found her mobile and everyone heaved a sigh of relief: at last, the priest, whose ears were turning increasingly red, would get some respite. But no! The woman took the mobile in her hand, lifted it to her left ear, ducked her head beneath her shawl and began a parallel homily of her own.

As the priest was saying, 'It is only God who knows about everything in this world,' the woman said into the phone, 'No, no, I also know it very well! I know that.' As the priest was saying, 'I ask you then, isn't life just a dream?', the woman said, 'No, it's not like that; it cannot be like that at all, in fact ...' And as the priest was saying, 'Now, can anybody say where the soul of man will go?', the woman responded, 'Waa, where else will it go? It's there on the tyngier, yes, the bamboo platform above the hearth!'

And that was how it went for some time. A few people ran out, holding their stomachs, while others got very angry and hissed at her to shut up. At last, an elderly woman broke off a stout branch from a tree and stabbed her arse with it, hissing, 'Will you stop it or not, you brazen beast!'

When the stick hit her, the woman lifted her shawl and said, 'Oh, you could also hear me or what?'

Because she had gone under her shawl, she had thought it was all right to speak on her mobile, no one would see or hear her!

When Bah Kit concluded his story, Magdalene chuckled and said, 'Oh my God! Oh my God! How can there be people like that, ya?'

'It's true, Mag, it's true,' Bah Kit said. 'Ask Ap, he was also there.'

Dale raised a hand and asked me excitedly, 'Do you recall the incident at Bor's house, Bah? Tell them, tell them.'

It was very much the same thing, I suppose, but on that occasion, the person involved was no country bumpkin but an elegantly dressed woman. She was carrying a very trendy and expensive-looking brown leather handbag, one of those many-chambered things that seemed to have been made from crocodile skin. She was beautiful too. Perhaps she was one of Bor's close relatives. She was sitting with the family, right there by the coffin, just behind the priest.

Here too, the priest, quite young to be one, was in the thick of the action, rendering his homily with upraised arms and jumping up and down in the heights of his passion, when the beautiful woman's phone sang out raucously.

I could see that she was a sensitive woman. She must have forgotten to silence her mobile. Her face flushed like a cherry blossom in early winter (oh yes, cherries do bloom in winter here) and she delved into her bag with panicky hands, opening one zip after another, but not finding the thing anywhere. People ogled at her, some giggled, and many burst into loud laughter, but the poor woman simply couldn't find her mobile in all those compartments and pouches.

And so, as the priest shouted out his sermon even more aggressively, no doubt to drown out the competition, her mobile kept asking: 'Who let the dogs out?'

'Who let the dogs out? You mean that song by Baha Men!' Magdalene asked, incredulous and laughing. 'Why would a woman like that keep such a ringtone?'

'It sounds like an insult to me!' Evening said sourly.

'Yes,' I replied, 'the poor woman was so ashamed that she left the place soon after.'

'No, but what a ringtone, Ap!' Magdalene said again.

'I have a friend who teaches in a college, who has a very low-key ringtone on his phone, in keeping with his position. One day, however, while he was bathing, he absently sang Bappi Lahiri's Hindi-film song, "*jile le jile le aayo aayo jile le*". His sons heard their father's funny, off-key song and recorded it on his mobile phone. Then, unknown to him, they set it as his ringtone. In the class that day, he forgot to put it on silent mode. And as luck would have it, just when he was explaining some intricate point about physics, his phone rang and gave him the shock of his life, for he seemed to be hearing himself singing, "*jile le jile le aayo aayo jile le*". The class exploded into ear-splitting laughter, and from then on, he became known as Professor Jile Le. He's your colleague, Mag.'

'I was about to say that too,' Magdalene laughed. 'Everybody in the college knows the story. Yeah, you are right; we call him Jile Le now.'

'Something like that could have happened to the woman too.'

'Interesting, interesting,' Bah Kynsai said, stifling a yawn. 'God, I'm so tired tonight. We got up too early, na? Shall we call it a night?'

'Before we sleep, ha, Bah Kynsai, let me just say how grateful I am—' Magdalene said.

'For?'

'You guys are full of stories, ya.'

'How can we not be full of stories?' Raji demanded. 'I'm a writer, no? A well-known Khasi writer. And so are Ap, Bah Suh and Bah Kit. Even Bah Kynsai and Ning write a little. But oh, wait, you guys don't read Khasi books, you are too good for them! Learn from this, you boneheads, Khasi books are not as bad as you imagine.'

'We have two problems, Raji,' Evening remarked. 'First, we have educated people who don't read Khasi books, and second, we have educated people who don't read any book—'

'Sorry to interrupt, Bah Ning,' Dale said, 'but I have a friend who loves books so much, ha, he finds it hard to sleep without reading. For that reason, ha, he always keeps a book by his bedside, and whenever he has trouble sleeping, he takes the book, reads a few words, and immediately falls asleep …'

'Tet sala! This Dale is also funny, na?' Bah Kynsai said, laughing.

But Evening was not amused. 'You see, that only reinforces the point. Now, you tell me, how do we develop the language in such a scenario? How do we get it recognised by the Government of India, huh? Isn't it funny that many less developed languages are in the Eighth Schedule of the Constitution but Khasi is not?'

Nobody had an answer to that.

After a while, Donald remarked, 'You know, Bah Raji, I think I'll start reading Khasi books too. It sounds as if I could learn quite a lot from them.'

Raji cried excitedly, 'With that kind of attitude, okay, we should not give up hope—'

'He's only one man, Raji, and he has to learn the language first,' Evening said, to dampen his enthusiasm.

'Make that two,' Magdalene said.

'There we are, Ning!' Bah Kynsai declared. 'As Lao Tzu said, ha, "The journey of a thousand miles begins with one step." A nice thought to sleep on, na?'

With that, he emptied the last dregs from his bamboo mug and went to sleep. We looked at him, then at our watches, and followed his example.

THE TENTH NIGHT

SERPENT TALES
(THE METAPHOR GONE WRONG)

'It is with antiquity as with ancestry, nations are
proud of the one and individuals of the other;
but if they are nothing in themselves, that
which is their pride ought to be their humiliation.'

—Caleb C. Colton

The last night of our stay in Nongshyrkon, 14 February, began on a sad note. It was Magdalene who started it. 'I don't know about you guys, but I feel quite sad we are leaving tomorrow, ya! I'm going to miss this place so much.'

'It's not only the place, Mag,' I said. I, too, had been feeling low. 'It's also the time we have had together, and the fact that we are heading back to the struggle and strife of our lives—the real jungle.'

'Yeah, man, the real jungle! I also feel terrible, ya,' Hamkom admitted. 'Back to the grind.'

'What to do? Everything has an end, na?' Bah Kynsai said philosophically.

'By tomorrow evening, they will have dismantled this hut and there will be no trace of us left whatsoever,' Raji said woefully.

'Yeah, it's like a kind of death, no?' Bah Kit observed.

'Reminds me of a poem called "Life" by Kojo Gyinaye Kyei, a poet from Ghana,' I said. 'It's quite beautiful. Life, he says, is "the only wayside inn" on a "rough and tumble safari", and every one "of our party / stops here overnight". After that, "he is only a memory".'

'That's very sad, ya,' Magdalene interrupted in a weepy voice.

'True, but the last three lines also offer some consolation—'

'How, Bah Ap?' Donald asked.

'Let me answer you with another poem. It's called "A Farewell Letter of Cherries":

> Dear friend, this is a letter
> of cherries, this is a poem
> born of cherries and my affection,
> when the town is pink
> with their blush.
>
> This is a poem
> born when summer greets winter
> under a compassionate sky,
> like two old-timers,

like you and me
before we go our separate ways.

This is a poem
born of sadness,
for the cherries will yield
to a blasé green
and the cold will finally conquer.

This is a poem
born of consolation,
for the business of man
is not to possess,
and the only part you can keep
of things that come and go
is that which you have photographed
with your mind.

Dear brother, we live in our memory,
in the memory of the world:
stoking that memory with fondness
is all that we can do.
We can do no more,
we can do no less.

'You see, memory, though often a source of sadness and a "longing like despair", is also a form of consolation.'

'Ah, yes.' Donald nodded. 'Earlier, too, you spoke about developing a language of remembrance for yourself, no, Bah Ap?'

Before I could respond, Raji said, 'We could stay back till the end of the mourning period, you know.'

'Till the sixteenth?' Bah Kynsai asked.

'No, nobody would take us back on the sixteenth. They'll be busy with the bone-burial ceremony.'

'If we stay back, we'll have to wait till the seventeenth,' Bah Kit said.

'But what do we do till then?' Hamkom asked.

'We don't have to do anything!' Raji replied. 'We enjoyed ourselves today, no?'

Raji was right. This morning, we had slept till about 10 a.m. and lazed about till lunchtime, watching the family cleaning the house, washing their clothes and tidying things up. In the past, in the Khasi uplands, relatives were not allowed to close the house or clean it or wash themselves or their clothes before the mourning period had passed. But things have changed. Even in the uplands, relatives carry out the cleaning on the day after the cremation or burial. However, they do still keep the house open and will not go anywhere before the mourning period has ended.

As we stood in the courtyard, talking to Victor and some elders from Nongtrai, we saw men scraping out the blood from yesterday's bull sacrifice. They collected the blood-spattered dust in bamboo baskets and dumped it in a large hole dug in a corner of the garden. When everything had been scraped clean, they covered the hole with fresh earth. They did not burn it after all, though Victor had said they would. But of course, this was Lyngngam, not Nongtrai.

Lunch was quite good thanks to Chirag's intervention. We were given pork boiled with potatoes and served with some bitter herbs and radish, sliced and mixed with chillies and lime juice. After lunch, we went off to the lake for a bath and a siesta, and returned only towards dinner time.

Perly had told me that today and tomorrow would be spent mostly on cleaning up. But on the sixteenth, after three nights had passed since the cremation (the cremation night is also counted), they would have the bone-burial as well as the meat-distribution ceremonies.

He also said the fetching of bones from the cremation site and their burial under the mawnop monolith, whose flat female stone would serve as a receptacle, would be done early in the morning. The procession, accompanied by music and dancing, would be taken out after a rooster had been sacrificed, and homage to God had been paid through invocations and prayers. When the bones were brought to the mawnop, they would be transferred to an earthen pot, covered with a white cotton cloth, and buried under the female stone. The meat distribution would begin after that.

A large portion of the meat from the sacrificed bulls had been left uncooked, he explained. This would be smoked and dried and distributed among the uncles and other relations. The immediate family of the deceased would keep the thirty bulls that were not sacrificed as special assistance for all the expenses they had incurred.

All in all, it was an enjoyable, relaxing day for us.

Hamkom developed cold feet when Raji suggested that we stay on till the seventeenth. 'Much as I enjoy being here and dread going back to the drudgery of work, ha, I don't think I can afford to remain here for another three days, ya, Raji. Bah Kynsai and Mag also would have problems—'

'Don't speak for me, Ham, I don't mind—'

Before Bah Kynsai could finish his sentence, we heard the dreadful shriek of a woman, followed by a man's plea of 'Forgive, forgive' and the angry shouts of numerous people. Some of them were saying, 'Beat him up, beat him up, son of an animal, mutilate the bastard' and other terrible oaths in Lyngngam, which we could not understand.

All of us rushed out to see what was happening. To our shock and horror, we saw Halolihim being punched and kicked and dragged by some men towards the courtyard of the death house, while a group of women were trying to beat his head with their flip-flops. We ran towards them. Bah Kynsai and I jumped into the melee, shouting, 'Stop it, stop it! What are you trying to do, kill him?'

Some people tried to punch and kick us too, as we pulled at the men and women, shouting and trying to stop them from beating Halolihim. Fortunately, at that moment, Chirag, Perly and their relatives came out and stopped the crowd's frenzied attack.

Chirag asked the crowd what was going on, while we examined Halolihim to see what damage the Lyngngams had done him. His hair was dishevelled and sticking up like a pig's bristles. His face was bruised, but he was bleeding only slightly from a cut above his left eye. He moaned about the pain in his ribs and shins, although nothing was broken. All in all, he was very fortunate. The Lyngngams were either bad boxers, or else too many of them had been trying to get at him at the same time and ended up obstructing each other.

We took him to a tree nearby and made him sit, leaning against its trunk. Hamkom and the others came to look at him. When Bah Kynsai saw Hamkom, he lost his temper. 'Where the hell were you, liah?' he shouted. 'He is your relative, na, lyeit! You bloody coward!'

God knows I did not like Halolihim, but he was with us, and when I saw him being beaten up like that, my only thought was to save him. It was a kind of reflex response. It must have been the same with Bah Kynsai. I did not blame some of the others for not interfering: Halolihim had had a run-in with Bah Kit, Bah Su, Donald and Magdalene. But Bah Kynsai was right, Hamkom *was* a bloody coward. Halolihim was his relative, and he was the one who had brought him here, and yet, he did not even try to help him. However, this was not the time for recriminations, for the crowd was coming towards us.

Bah Kynsai and I picked up a stout stick each and stood in front of Halolihim. But Chirag said, 'Don't worry, Babu, we'll not allow them to touch him again, we just want to find out what happened, this Kong here has accused him of raping her daughter—'

'What!' Halolihim shouted in shock. He tried to stand up but was held back by Hamkom. 'What are you talking about?'

The accuser, whose name was Antina Shyrkon (a misspelling of the English word 'antenna'), shouted at Halolihim in Lyngngam. She bent down towards him, eyes blazing, red lips flapping and spitting, red teeth grinding and grimy forefinger shaking at him violently. She was a terrifying sight to behold.

Chirag translated for us. 'According to her, you were found lying on top of her daughter on the grass behind her garden, and she challenges you to deny it if you dare.'

'Wait, wait, calm her down, Bah Chirag,' I said, raising my hands. 'We'll talk to him and find out what happened.'

As Chirag tried to calm Antina and her relatives down, Bah Kynsai and I turned to Halolihim.

'We are in a very dangerous situation here, Halolihim, do you understand?' Bah Kynsai said. When Halolihim nodded, he continued, 'If it's really true that you raped her, nobody can help you, so tell us exactly what happened.'

Chirag and Perly came to listen while some of the others held back the yelling woman and her threatening husband, Late Riangtim.

Halolihim shook his head emphatically. 'I did not! What a terrible thing to say!'

'So what happened, mə, tdir?' Bah Kynsai cursed.

'Rosina and I love each other—'

'What? How can you love her when you are married and have children of your own?' Hamkom asked, scandalised.

'When has that ever stopped anyone, you blockhead?' Bah Kynsai demanded. 'Who is Rosina? Is it the same girl we saw you with?'

When Halolihim nodded again, Bah Kynsai turned to me. 'It's the girl we saw holding his arm yesterday. She's quite beautiful, na, I don't know if I can blame this bugger—'

Some of the men laughed, much to the displeasure of the relatives. I said quickly, 'Okay, so you love each other, but what did you do to her? Did they find you lying with her on the grass?'

'Yes, but I did not rape her—'

'Are you saying that you had consensual sex with her?' Bah Kynsai demanded.

'No, I did not!' Halolihim said adamantly.

'So what the hell were you doing with her on the grass?' I snapped.

'Do I have to tell you that?' Halolihim shouted back at me.

'Would you rather Rosina's mother asked you these questions?' I retorted. 'Or perhaps you would prefer her father, look!'

Late had got hold of an ugly-looking curved machete from somewhere and was looking threateningly at Halolihim.

Halolihim swallowed hard. 'I … we were not doing anything.'

'Arre, this bugger!' Bah Kynsai exclaimed in frustration. 'You admitted you were lying with her on the grass, na? So what were you doing? Just lying there looking at the night sky?'

Chirag interrupted to say, 'Kong Antina said he was lying on top of her!'

'I did not rape her!' Halolihim shouted. 'We just—'

'We just what?' Bah Kynsai asked.

'Please don't … Do I have to tell you?'

'Yes, every single, lurid detail,' I said unsympathetically.

'It's true, I was on top of her,' he said, crying and bowing his head in shame. 'But I was merely kissing her—'

Chirag interrupted again. 'Kong Antina said he did more than that.'

'I was, eh, I was not kissing her lips … Please, we did not even …'

'Are you sure?' I asked more gently.

When Halolihim nodded, Bah Kynsai insisted, 'You mean you did everything else but that?'

'Yes,' Halolihim replied in a broken voice.

Chirag spoke up. 'Kong Antina does not believe he did nothing, she said she saw it with her own eyes.'

'She could have been mistaken in the dark,' I said. 'I think this fellow is telling the truth, Bah Chirag, why don't we call the girl here and question her too?'

Chirag spoke to Antina and Late and then shook his head. 'They refuse to let you speak to her, and say that, even if it was consensual, he will still have to face the consequences—'

'Which are?' Bah Kynsai asked.

'They'll speak to their daughter, and if it is rape, they said they'll have to, at the very least, cut off, you know what, and if it is consensual, they'll file an FIR because she is only seventeen, unless of course, he marries her—'

'Marry her? How can he marry her when he's already married?' Hamkom shouted.

'Shut up, you fool!' Bah Kynsai growled. 'Okay, tell them to talk to their daughter, we'll wait here.'

When they had gone, Raji came over to us. 'We are in a pretty pickle, actually!' he said in a whisper. 'If Rosina says rape, okay, they'll cut it off, and there's nothing we can do about it. And if she says consensual, they won't let him leave unless he marries her.'

'You know what, I believe the bugger is telling the truth, man,' Bah Kynsai confided. 'I don't think they did it. They could have got to it, but they were discovered, na!'

'But if the girl wants to marry him, she could say anything,' I said.

'That's what I don't understand,' Raji said. 'How can she fall for someone as ugly as he is?'

'He's ugly to you, but to her?' Bah Kynsai said pointedly. 'And he's tall, na, liah, women like tall men. And besides, think of the good things that a well-placed government employee like him could give her … In this poverty-ridden jungle, na, she'll simply waste away like the rest of them.'

'And yet, we love it here,' Raji observed.

'We are escaping from city life and our daily toils for a while, na? For her, it's the other way around.'

At that moment, Antina, Late and their relatives returned to the scene, led by Perly. They seemed to be less angry and threatening than before. 'Could be good news,' Hamkom said hopefully.

When they arrived, Chirag went to talk to them, and then came back to report to us. 'According to the girl, it was consensual; they want him to marry her or face an FIR.'

Bah Kynsai went near Halolihim and asked, 'Do you hear that? What do you want to do?'

'Believe me, please, we did not do anything,' he insisted.

'But the girl is saying you did and the parents are saying they saw you do it, no, Bah?' Chirag accused him.

'But I did not do it, Bah Chirag, please believe me,' Halolihim said in a small voice.

'Nobody will believe you,' Chirag replied harshly.

'So, will you marry her or what?' Bah Kynsai enquired.

Halolihim looked at Hamkom and said, 'How can I marry her? My family, my church—'

'Your family, your church, hahaha!' Bah Kynsai laughed angrily. 'Now you think about those things, sala! But just now you said you loved her, na, liah?'

'I don't think I can marry her …'

'You don't think you can marry her!' Bah Kynsai mimicked him. 'Then what you felt was not love, you dog shit! It was lust! And the moment you were found out, all the heat went out of you!'

Bah Kynsai turned to Chirag and asked, 'What to do, Chirag? Can you help?'

'What can I do, Babu, look at the crowd …'

The crowd was indeed getting restless, and Antina and Late were beginning to shout and gesticulate wildly again. When our friends saw that, they came and stood in front of Halolihim in a show of support. Seeing them, Halolihim said again, 'We did not do it!'

Nobody responded to that. They did not think he was innocent. However, they did not want to see him harmed either.

'Actually, it's not a bad idea, Ham,' Bah Kynsai said. 'How many men have such a young and beautiful girl as Rosina forced on them? I'm sure his wife is as ugly as he is, na?' he concluded with a loud laugh.

'Tet leh, Bah Kynsai! How can you joke about a thing like this?'

'He deserves it.'

'How can he marry another woman when he's already married?' Hamkom asked.

'The Lyngngams are saying he should marry Rosina now and divorce his wife later,' Bah Kynsai replied.

'How can that be?'

I paced up and down, trying to think of a way out. Like Bah Kynsai, I thought the fellow was telling the truth—they had not got to it. Of course, he was guilty as hell! He must have dazzled the poor girl by bragging about his position as a government employee and the salary he drew per month. To her, who probably had never even seen a 1,000-rupee note in her entire life, it must have seemed like fabulous wealth. Perhaps the son of a bitch had claimed he was an officer! And she must have taken his vows of love seriously too, and thought that, by marrying him, she would escape the deprivation of the jungle for a world of beautiful houses, satellite TVs and cars. That must have prompted her to say they had made love when they had not actually got that far. Perhaps she even thought she was doing her lover a favour.

I discussed this with my friends, who all seemed to feel the same way. We felt no sympathy for Halolihim, but how could we let a married man marry again? If only we could verify the fact that they had not gone so far, we could save this fellow ... That's it! A medical examination!

I approached Bah Kynsai and Chirag. 'The way I see it, only a medical examination can prove who's telling the truth. Is there a doctor in Maweit?'

'A doctor? Why, we have a doctor in Shyrkon, Babu! She came to the funeral, I thought of introducing you to her but forgot, she is our relative—'

'Where is she?' Bah Kynsai demanded. 'Why didn't she come forward, she should have come, na, being a doctor?'

'She is staying at her relative's house on the outskirts, near the lake, Babu, she did not want to be disturbed by the noise, I'll take the jeep and fetch her immediately.'

Chirag explained the matter to Rosina's family and left with a couple of other men.

Halolihim looked up at me and said, 'Thank you, Bah Ap.'

'Are you sure?' I asked.

'I'm sure,' he said confidently.

We did not have to wait very long before Chirag returned with the doctor. He took her to Antina's house to see the girl. We waited with bated breath, but Halolihim seemed quite relieved. Although, even if he was telling the truth, there was still the matter of the seduction and molestation. After all, Rosina was a minor.

Soon, too soon, Chirag, Perly and the others returned from Antina's, but without Antina and her husband. When he got near enough for his voice to carry, he said, 'It's all right, Babu, the girl refused to be examined and told the truth, she said they had not really done anything.'

When Halolihim heard that, he put a hand to his chest and breathed a huge sigh of relief. Then he started praying loudly, ending each sentence with 'Hallelujah!'

The spectacle so sickened Chirag that he spat and said, 'Phooey, son of a bitch!'

I had never heard him curse before. He had always been polite with us, calling us 'Babu' all the time, but there is a limit to anybody's patience.

We also turned away from Halolihim in disgust and headed back to the hut, except for Hamkom. Chirag called out to me: 'Hey, Babu, Babu Ap, don't leave this person here, it's not safe, the parents are still angry, he violated her person, no? Take him with you. Some are even saying they will cut off one of his ears, but Rosina's uncle did not agree, otherwise he would have lost one ear by now.'

We walked back to Chirag. The hut was not very safe either, we said. If Antina and her friends decided to come and get him, there was nothing we could do. Perhaps he could be given a place to stay in the death house? Chirag agreed and asked Perly to take Halolihim to the house. I also suggested a visit to Antina's, so we could apologise to her family. Chirag agreed to that too.

Antina and Late were quite sullen at first, but Chirag told them that none of us was Halolihim's friend, and when we apologised to them with all sincerity and concern, they became more responsive. Bah Kynsai felt so bad for the girl, who was a school dropout, that he said, 'Look, Kong, if you agree, I can speak to my sister. She's a doctor. Right now, she needs an office attendant to help the other girl who works with her. If you say Rosina has studied up to Class IX, then she can easily take care of the work. She can also stay with my sister. What do you say? And if she wants to, na, she can attend evening school. The clinic closes at 5 p.m.'

When Chirag translated the proposal, her parents were receptive to the idea but also rightly suspicious. After all, they did not know any of us, and Halolihim, whom they had allowed into their home with his talk of God and heaven, had let them down horribly. It was only when Chirag volunteered to take the girl to Bah Kynsai's sister and make sure that everything was okay that they agreed with genuine pleasure and gratitude.

They spoke to Chirag for a while, all the time smiling happily. Towards the end, Chirag said, 'Ooh, they are full of praise for Babu Kynsai! They say he is a true Christian—'

'Although his language is a bit unconventional, to put it diplomatically,' Raji broke in.

'So what if Babu's language is a little rough, his heart is great, no, Bah?' Chirag said.

Hearing that, Bah Kynsai boomed out his trademark laugh and patted Chirag gently on the shoulder. We were all happy. Because of Bah Kynsai, something good was coming out of this whole mess.

When we got back to the hut, it was about 8 p.m. Raji said, 'It's only a quarter to eight. It felt like a long time, no?'

'We ate early this evening, na, that's why,' Bah Kynsai replied.

'But what a scary thing, ya!' Magdalene exclaimed. 'Did you see the father with that huge, curved knife? I thought our man was a goner for sure!'

Hamkom shook his head from side to side and said in a tone laden with sorrow, 'How could he swing from one extreme to the other like that? He always seemed to be interested in nothing but religion, no?'

'Nothing surprising in it,' Bah Kynsai stated. 'If Adam could fall at the hands of Eve, na, why not Halolihim at the hands of Rosina?'

'No, no, no, that's not fair at all, Bah Kynsai! How can you blame Rosina for what Halolihim did?' Magdalene said fiercely.

'I'm not blaming her, ya. I'm not saying she seduced him. I'm merely suggesting that her youthful beauty was too much of a temptation for him, na? There's no doubt that he was the seducer, Mag.'

'Oh, okay.'

'But you know what amazes me, Bah Kynsai? How is it that we never noticed these romances until they came out in the open?' Raji asked.

'Don't compare us with Halolihim!' Donald warned.

'I'm not, I'm just saying that we never noticed anything,' Raji said quickly.

'That's because you were mostly drunk at night,' Bah Kynsai replied. 'We have been noticing the little things between these two for a long time, na, Ap? And we never missed noticing the fact that when one went outside, na, the other always followed after a while, hahaha, we saw everything, okay, Mag? And about Halolihim and the girl, na, we were told about them quite some time ago, remember? Only thing is, we never dreamt he would do a thing like that, being holier-than-thou and married to boot.'

Donald quickly changed the topic. 'You know, Bah Kynsai, what you are going to do for that girl is a great thing, ya. Now they will not think so badly of us any more.'

'Yeah, yeah,' Bah Kit agreed. 'But that fellow was incredibly stupid, you know—'

'When you are thinking with that particular body part, na, Kit, you are always stupid,' Bah Kynsai said.

We all laughed, but after a while, Bah Kit said again, 'I'm saying he was incredibly stupid because this is a very dangerous place, no? In the past, the upland Khasis used to call these people *ki Diko bam doh briew*. Halolihim could have died a horrible death tonight!'

'*Ki Diko bam doh briew*, Bah Kit?' Donald asked.

'Human-eating Dikos.'

'Let's forget about how horribly Halolihim might have died tonight,' Bah Kynsai said. 'Let's talk about … What shall we talk about? Why don't we share stories about the most horrible deaths we have witnessed or known?'

'No, no, Bah Kynsai!' Magdalene protested. 'Why should we talk about such horrible things?'

But Raji seconded the motion. 'Why not? We are at a funeral, no? I can go first, but tell me, when are we leaving?'

'When?' Bah Kynsai asked. 'As soon as possible, if we don't want some angry Lyngngam to cut off that bugger's thing.'

'That means tomorrow at 5 p.m., then?'

'Why can't we leave earlier?' Hamkom asked, clearly worried.

'Because the man who is to drive us back to Nongstoin will not be free till 5 p.m.,' I explained.

'You mean Chirag is not going with us? If Chirag is not going, then what if they stop the car in the middle of the jungle and attack us?'

'Chirag cannot go because the mourning period is not over—'

'Who would attack us, you goddamn coward?' Bah Kynsai said. 'I have promised to help the girl, na? If we continue to stay here, of course, some angry relative might want to cut off Halolihim's ear, or worse, but who would organise such a deliberate attack when I'm going to help their daughter? Think straight, man! Go ahead, Raji, tell us the story. This fellow is getting under my skin.'

Raji told us about Shrimp Lyngdoh and how he was murdered by his relatives in a village called Thangbnai, literally, 'moon burning' or 'monthly burning'. Apparently, he was involved in a land dispute with his clan members, who claimed the community land he was farming as their own. They asked Shrimp to vacate it, but he refused, saying that he had been permitted by the proper authorities to cultivate the land.

His relatives approached the village council, then the lyngdoh raij, the provincial ruler, and finally, the king of Khyrim to complain about Shrimp. But they all confirmed that the plot was indeed community land, and that Shrimp had been given due permission to cultivate there. Not satisfied with the ruling of these local bodies, the relatives took the matter to the District Council Court. After hearing the case for months, the court passed its verdict on 9 October 2012 in favour of Shrimp.

Despite all the rulings, the land-greedy relatives continued to stubbornly claim that the land was theirs and continued to ask Shrimp to vacate it. When he refused, they decided to have him killed. It was the manner of his killing, Raji said, that made the crime so chilling.

It happened one Monday morning while Shrimp and his wife were walking down the street in the village, heading for the weekly market in the neighbouring village of Mawlyngngot. One of Shrimp's relatives suddenly appeared out of nowhere and hit him on the head with a thick stick. When

Shrimp fell unconscious, he was dragged to the house of Spoke Lyngdoh, who was the main man behind the attack.

All this happened in front of Shrimp's wife, who cried out for help. Hundreds of villagers, including the headman, rushed to the scene, but by that time, Shrimp's relatives, numbering six in all, had already dragged the unconscious man inside Spoke's house.

The crowd outside raised a hue and cry, pounded on the door and demanded that Shrimp be let out. But the six men inside bludgeoned him to death instead, right there. The killers opened the door only after the police arrived, hours after the incident.

A senior police official, speaking to the press, admitted that the case was one of the strangest and most gruesome he had come across. 'How is it that such a heinous crime was committed in broad daylight before so many people?' he asked. 'Why did the villagers not break down the door and attempt to save the man?'

'This seemed to me like an open-and-shut case,' Raji concluded, 'but the last I heard, the accused had been released on bail.'

'If you ask me, the whole bloody village is guilty of the murder!' Bah Kynsai said with feeling. 'Who are the others?'

'Bastards and killers! May they rot in hell!'

'Wuu!' Magdalene shuddered. 'I don't like such stories, ya, they give me the shivers.'

As if he had not heard her, Bah Kit said, 'The most horrible death I have ever come across was in Mawlai …'

Bita was a young and beautiful woman with a two-year-old daughter, who lived with her hard-drinking husband, a daily-wage labourer by the name of Stick Lyngdoh. Stick was known throughout the locality of Mawlai as a quarrelsome bully and a wife-beater. Despite that, Bita was loyal to him and always defended him when people said terrible things about him. That, unfortunately, never stopped Stick from suspecting her of flirting with other men, and he would beat her up every night when he was drunk.

One day, Bita's little girl developed a high fever. Scared by the rapidly rising temperature, Bita rushed her to a doctor. That was at about 5 p.m. Meanwhile, Stick returned home to a locked house. He opened it with a spare key and asked the neighbours where his wife was. They told him that his daughter was ill and his wife had taken her to a doctor. Bah Kit and his friends were loitering on the road nearby and heard everything.

Stick was a little drunk and was heard complaining that he had to make his own tea. Next, he began cooking rice for dinner, whining that his wife had forced him to do a woman's job. When it was 6 p.m., Stick came out to ask the neighbours at what time Bita had left. The neighbours told him that she had left at about 5 p.m. 'The damn slut, 5 p.m., and she still hasn't returned!' he complained loudly and went back inside.

When it was about 7 p.m., Stick was heard cursing his wife, calling her all sorts of nasty names and throwing things around. Just at that moment, Bita came in, carrying the baby on her back. When Stick saw her, he got up from where he was sitting near the hearth and threw a glassful of rice spirit on her face. Then, without even questioning her, he proceeded to give her a few resounding slaps that sent her and her daughter sprawling on the floor. After that, despite the fearful wailing of the little girl, he shouted and screamed horrible obscenities at Bita, accusing her of going to meet imaginary lovers.

Through her tears, Bita tried to explain that there were too many people at the clinic. 'Even now,' she said, 'there is still a long line. You can go and see for yourself if you don't believe me.'

He began beating her again.

When Bita was heard howling at the top of her lungs, Bah Kit and his friends wanted to intervene, but one of them said, 'Come on, guys, how can we interfere in a quarrel between husband and wife? Come, come, let's get away from here.'

Persuaded by him, they all left the place to loiter somewhere else. It was only later that they heard what had happened. Stick was not satisfied with the beating he had given Bita. He poured a jerry can of kerosene on her and the baby on her back, set them on fire, left the house and locked the door from outside. His wife cried for help and tried to get out. People came rushing but could not get in. By the time they managed to break the door down, both mother and child were dead.

'Even now, when I think about it, ha, I can feel tears in my eyes,' Bah Kit concluded, wiping his eyes. 'Imagine, if we had intervened, the tragedy would never have happened, no?'

'This is the problem with us Khasis, na, Kit?' Bah Kynsai said. 'People keep saying, why should we interfere in husband-and-wife affairs, but when the quarrel becomes violent, is it not our duty to stop it? And this is another thing we do, ha, when we see a person lying on the road, we always dismiss him as a drunk. That's also terrible, man. One day, at Motphran near Iewduh, ha, I saw a man lying face down on the road. Many people were standing nearby, shopkeepers and loafers. I asked them, "What happened to him?" They told me he must be a drunk. When I asked again how they knew, they replied, "If he's not a drunk, then why is he lying on the road?"

'I was so angry, I gave them a piece of my mind ... And you know what that means, na, the language I tend to use? Finally, I told them, "Have you ever thought that he might be ill? How long has he been lying here?"

'They said he had been there for quite some time. I turned him over and saw there was foam on his lips. I knew then that he must have had an epileptic fit. With the help of some of the men, I put him inside my Maruti van and took him to Civil Hospital. But it was too late. He died soon after because he had been left for too long in the winter cold. Sometimes, na, Khasis can be quite inhuman, liah!'

We all agreed with Bah Kynsai. Dismissing people lying on the road as drunks does seem like a convenient excuse for not doing anything. People just do not want to go out of their way to help others any more.

'But that bloody bastard was worse than Likai's husband, ya!' Magdalene suddenly exploded. She was still thinking of the wife-killer, it seemed.

Dale raised his hand and indelicately said, 'Speaking of people dying in a fire, ha, Kong Mag, we have two stories from our locality.'

He told us about Paulus, a daily-wage labourer and a drunk who lived with his bedridden father. He had no immediate family save his father, and was a good son but for his night-time drinking. In the morning, when he was sober, Paulus would leave home only after he had taken care of his father's needs. During the day, his niece, the daughter of a distant relative, used to come and help out for a fee, leaving only after her uncle returned.

When he came home from work, Paulus usually cooked the evening meal on an electric stove and served his father dinner before settling down to drink, sometimes with friends, at other times alone. But one Saturday evening, being payday, and probably because of his friends' promptings, he was already drunk when he returned home.

When he entered the house, his niece teased him about his drunkenness and left after she had received her weekly wage. Alone and drunk, Paulus scratched his head, trying to remember what he had to do. Then he said, 'Cooking, yes, I have to cook.'

He turned on the electric stove to fry some fish. But because he was so drunk, he poured too much mustard oil on the flat frying pan, which spilled onto the stove, causing a fire to break out. Paulus tried frantically to put it out, but he was too far gone to think straight and act quickly. First, he tried blowing out the fire with his mouth, then he tried beating it down with a rag, but nothing worked and the fire got worse. He then staggered from one end of the kitchen to the other, trying to douse it with cupfuls of water. Finally, when the flames rose to the ceiling and engulfed the entire kitchen, he staggered outside and sat in the courtyard holding his head.

When the neighbours saw the house on fire, they rushed to help. By then, it was too late. The fire had grown too fierce, and the house, a single-storey wood-and-tin structure, was completely burnt to the ground. When his niece and her mother arrived on the scene, they asked Paulus about his father. Paulus, who had not once stirred in all that commotion, looked up at them with dazed and bloodshot eyes and said in surprise, 'Father? I forgot!'

They found the bedridden man burnt to cinders.

Another story was about a couple who locked their two children, a boy of five and a girl of four, inside their rented house while they went to wash their clothes in a nearby stream. The house was situated on a hill slope, and since there was no one to look after the children, the parents decided that it would be best to lock them in.

Neither Dale nor I knew the name of the mother, but the father was called Bu. The parents did not plan to be away for long, since there were not too many clothes to wash. So, they left the fire burning in the hearth and water heating in a pot so they could wash the children when they returned.

It was an incredibly stupid thing to do. The children must have tried playing with the fire and set the whole house ablaze. When the neighbours saw the house on fire, they tried to put it out. They could hear the children screaming inside, but the door was locked from outside. By the time they broke down the door, the little bodies were burnt beyond recognition.

'I was among the rescuers,' Dale said, 'and sometimes, even now, I have nightmares about those screaming kids. We tried so hard to save them, no, Bah? It was horrible!'

Bah Kynsai then brought up the issue of infanticide and told us stories about newborn children who had been discovered in drains and behind school toilets.

'It is this boyfriend-girlfriend culture young people see on TV these days, Bah Kynsai,' Raji chipped in. 'This is one big cause of infanticides. Only recently, okay, an eighteen-year-old girl was arrested from Lad-Mukhla in Ri Pnar in connection with a case of attempted infanticide.'

'What happened?' Bah Kynsai asked.

One morning, Raji told us, a man by the name of L. Rymbai was going to the open-pit toilet in his unfenced garden when he heard the sound of a baby crying inside the pit. The shock was so great that he lost the urge to crap. He shouted to his wife and others in the family, who came rushing to the toilet, thinking that something untoward had happened to him. When they got there and heard the baby crying, they also received a jolt. They realised the baby must be pulled out immediately. Rymbai himself volunteered for the task. Wearing a mask, gumboots, rubber gloves and a plastic raincoat, he was lowered with a rope into the pit, where he discovered a baby boy inside a black polythene bag.

Having rescued the baby, Rymbai's family cleaned him up, cut his umbilical cord, wrapped him in a soft, warm shawl, and took him to the community health centre nearby. Later, the baby was taken to the Dr Norman Tunnel Hospital in Jowai, where he was kept in an intensive care unit. Luckily, he survived and was promptly adopted by Rymbai's family, who thought the little fellow was nothing less than God's gift to them. And that was also why they named him God Gift.

'And the mother?' Bah Kynsai asked.

'She was a Class X student in a local school,' Raji replied. 'She was staying in a hostel. Her friends informed on her. Initially, she denied committing the heinous crime, okay, but on medical examination, it was found that she had given birth just a few hours earlier. The case is in progress.'

'Hey, Ap, what about you?' Bah Kynsai enquired. 'Don't you have a horrible-death story?'

'No, no, no, no!' Magdalene protested. 'No more for now, please, Ap, don't say anything, man!'

'Okay, okay,' Bah Kynsai conceded. 'How about some strange deaths instead?'

'That's better,' Magdalene agreed.

'The strangest death that I know of, na, was of an elderly woman, a neighbour of mine. It was a Sunday, ha, and many of us were sitting in her courtyard, talking about this and that. Suddenly the old woman got up and said, "I'll bring the betel nut basket, please wait, okay?" But then, her foot hit a small stone sticking out from the ground, and she fell and died on the spot, liah! And you know what? The ground was completely flat, man!'

'That's certainly very strange, no?' Hamkom said. 'Maybe she had a heart attack or what?'

'No, no, she was a very healthy woman. The doctor who came to examine her, na, said she could not find any cause of death. She had to make up something—'

'Aw, come on!' Hamkom objected.

'Really, man! You are always disbelieving my stories, tdong!'

Dale raised his hand, which he always did when he wanted to say something. 'The strangest death I know of, ha, Bah Kynsai, was during a road accident—'

'What's so strange about death in a road accident?'

'Just listen, no, Bah, please!'

The accident happened one evening on the Sohra–Shillong road during the dead of winter. A young man was travelling from Sohra on a motorbike. When he reached a place called Lad Mawphlang, the cold really gave him a nasty clobbering. He was especially feeling it in the chest since the zip of his leather jacket was not working any more. To protect his chest, he stopped the bike, removed the jacket and put it on again back-to-front.

A little way up the road, however, perhaps because of the cold and his numb fingers, he drove the bike into a shallow gully. The local people who witnessed the accident rushed to the young man's rescue. When they got there, they found him lying flat on the ground, unconscious but still very much alive. They turned him over and saw that the head was facing the wrong way. It was rather dark in the gully, and they all thought the young man had twisted his neck.

'Why don't we set it straight?' one of them asked.

Another man said, 'No, I don't think we should tamper with the body in any way. We should wait for the ambulance to come. Nah has already phoned 108. It's on the way from Sohra.'

Most of the men were worried that it might be too late by the time the ambulance came. They said, 'The ambulance will take at least twenty-five minutes to reach here. By that time, the poor man might be dead. Why don't we straighten his head and ease his pain, at least?'

And so, in their eagerness to help, the villagers took the young man's neck and twisted it hard towards the zippered side of the jacket. The young man grunted once and breathed out a sigh.

The villagers thought he was sighing with relief. 'There, he's much better now!' they said.

When the ambulance arrived, the attendants found the young man dead. The cause of death was a twisted neck.

'Tet teri ka, this Dale is joking, sala!' Bah Kynsai laughed.

The others thought it was a joke too. I said, 'He's not joking, Bah Kynsai. The story was actually recounted to me by Everending. Ever was also in the rescue ambulance. The detail about the dead man's jacket was gleaned later from his friends.'

'Oh, so it was you, Bah, who told me the story! I was wondering who it was,' Dale exclaimed.

Hamkom had a story too, about B. Sushang of Shangpung village, Jaiñtia Hills. Sushang and another woman named Whinnied Kharlukhi were invited by Badamon Ryntathiang to stay with her in Rynjah for some time, so they could put into practice their staunch belief that they could fast like their saviour for forty days and forty nights.

'What kind of fool game is that, man?' Bah Kynsai asked.

Hamkom said they belonged to a particular religious sect—very radical. According to police sources, Sushang, who was forty years old, volunteered to go first. She started her fast reportedly in April 2015, not even taking a drop of water, and subsisting only on prayers. However, after only a week of fasting, Sushang died. Her two friends did not report the matter to anyone, for they were sure she would come back to life after forty days and forty nights. They held a vigil for her soul every day, burning candles and praying that she would come back to life after the allotted period. But the stench from the putrefying body drove them out of the house and forced them to take up residence elsewhere, though they returned daily to offer prayers for Sushang's restoration.

Well before the end of the forty days and forty nights, the odour had permeated to the houses nearby. The neighbours reported the matter to the headman, who, in turn, reported it to the police. It was the police who discovered Sushang's body, and after seizing the diaries that the two surviving women had been keeping, promptly arrested them.

When Hamkom came to the end of the story, Raji deflated him by saying, 'That was reported in the newspapers, Ham, we all know about it.'

To defuse the awkwardness, I said, 'One of the strangest deaths I know of is that of Pran Shangpliang. He was from Borsora in West Khasi Hills, and his business was the manufacture and sale of the local rice spirit, which had been banned by both the local village council and the excise department.

'Of course, by now, you all know that such a ban does not really mean anything in these hills. Pran continued to peddle his illicit alcohol, pouring it into tyre tubes and taking the tubes to the various vendors every morning in a large cloth bag. One morning, as he and five of his men—all of them carrying bagfuls of spirit—were passing over a bridge spanning a chasm about hundred feet wide and fifty feet deep, he suddenly saw a police lorry coming towards the bridge. Just the day before, Pran had heard of the police raiding boozers in a neighbouring village. He thought the police were now coming for him. He panicked and jumped into the chasm before his men could stop him. Pran died, bathed in all that spilled spirit. As it turned out, the lorry had nothing to do with the police. It was carrying some Home Guard personnel on their way to cut wood from a forest nearby.'

'That's a really strange one, leh, Ap,' Bah Kynsai laughed. 'I mean, why was he so scared of the police? Selling illicit liquor is not even a serious crime, na? He could have got off with a fine, man, why the hell did he jump to his death?'

'This happened in April 2010, no, Ap?' Raji asked. 'I also remember this.'

Evening was sure the death had to do with the way rural folk bring up their kids. He said, 'How can illiterate Khasis not fear the police, Bah Kynsai? Parents always try to scare their children with them, no? I remember when we did something our parents did not want us to do, ha, they would say, "Don't do that lest the police come and catch you!" They would even say, "Don't play too far from the house lest the police come and catch you!" I mean, that sort of thing can affect a person for life, no? Especially if he is uneducated, no?'

Bah Kit then told us of a woman in West Khasi Hills who met her death in an incident that could only be described as bizarre. Ialdoris Nongspung, of Seiñduli village near Nongstoin, was having a difficult pregnancy. She was admitted to the Nongstoin Civil Hospital on 5 May 2011, but because her condition was critical, an ambulance was sent to bring her to Shillong Civil Hospital immediately. It was about 2 a.m. Only twelve kilometres from Nongstoin, the ambulance ran out of petrol. And there was not a single car on the road so early in the morning. Eventually, a car did come by at 7 a.m. and loaned the ambulance some petrol, but the woman could wait no longer. She died soon after the ambulance started moving again.

'Oh God, oh God!' Magdalene cried. 'What a horrible thing to happen! How can they run an emergency ambulance without petrol, man?'

'Three reasons,' Bah Kynsai said. 'Carelessness, indifference, corruption.'

'The family should have sued the hospital authorities. Did they, Bah Kit?' Evening asked.

'They were poor, ignorant people, ha, how can they even start thinking about such things? They only said, "What to do? It was meant to happen. It's God's will." That's the kind of thing we Khasis always say.'

'Any more stories? Anyone?' Bah Kynsai asked.

I told them the story of a fifty-year-old woman who killed her sixty-five-year-old husband, July Lyngdoh, who happened to be the headman of Um Rakhia village in Ri Pnar. The relatives and the entire village were enraged and wanted to lynch the woman on the spot. Fortunately for her, the police arrived and took her into custody. As she was being taken away, people shouted curses and spat at her, calling her a husband-killer, a cold-blooded murderer and other abusive names.

But if you listen to what she told the police when she confessed to her crime, you'll find it quite intriguing. She said, as if in a daze, 'We were sitting by the hearth, the fire burning high to keep the chill at bay. We had just returned from the fields ... Having cooked the rice, we boiled beef stew and filled our cups, as we used to do, with yiad lieh. We sat sipping our spirit with a little salt, we talked, told stories, and then we quarrelled. Something insignificant, I don't remember what about, but we quarrelled, and in my anger, I hit him on the head with a bronze blower, but not too hard, not too hard, how could I ever hit him too hard? Just a little bit, just *phlok*, like this ... The damn fool! Just phlok on the head, and he died! Didn't he know I cannot carry on without him?'

'Whew, that's very touching, ya, Ap!' Magdalene exclaimed.

'Yeah,' Donald agreed. 'It's tragic, indeed!'

'Isn't it?' I concurred. 'I took her words from a poem actually, a poem based on her actual confession. How can you condemn the poor woman, now that you know her story? The real tragedy is hers.'

'It really is,' Bah Kynsai agreed. 'Are there any more?'

'There are plenty, Bah Kynsai,' Bah Kit said, 'but should we spend the entire night talking about such stories?'

Magdalene promptly seconded that opinion. 'Let's move on to something else, Bah Kynsai. If they happen to crop up in the course of the discussion, so be it, but for now, let's move on, okay?'

When Bah Kynsai agreed, Donald said, 'Okay, since we are moving on to something else, ha, I would like to ask Bah Kit why the people here were called "human-eating Dikos".'

'Let Ap tell you,' Bah Kit responded. 'He spoke at length with Victor on the subject.'

I said the old Khasis never referred to the Lyngngams as human-eating Dikos. So, the question is, who were these Dikos, originally named among the seven sub-tribes of the Khasi people? Very hard to say. But it's true that they referred to many people living in these parts as human-eaters. According to Victor, there are two reasons for this.

First of all, in the past, people from here believed that when a dead body was cremated, it should be totally consumed by the fire. However, there were times when pieces of flesh would simply not burn or would take an inordinately long time to do so. This was taken as a sign that the soul of the deceased was restless and pining for something. In such a case, the body-turners, after paying obeisance to God, used to address the spirit directly, naming all the possible things that it might be pining for. If, even after all the possible causes had been specified, the pieces of flesh were still not carbonised, it was incumbent upon the body-turners to eat them with their rice spirit. That was one of the reasons.

The other was the existence, in the past, of a ferocious clan called Matsadu-Matsadei. The Matsadu-Matsadeis were like other people in every respect except one: they had small tails growing from their bottoms, though these were covered by their clothes and could not be seen. All the men from the clan were supposed to be able to turn themselves into tigers as soon as it became dark. Victor's friend maintained that they could do so even during the day if the sky was overcast. And when such a transformation took place, they acquired the strength, skills and feeding habits of tigers, and would pounce upon beasts and men alike to eat them raw. The Matsadu-Matsadeis do not exist any more. They were wiped out in a protracted conflict with other, more numerous and more powerful clans.

But Ondromuni Kharngapkynta, who was writing about the history of his clan, had a different story to tell—

'Tell us more about the tiger-men first, no, Ap,' Magdalene urged.

I asked Magdalene to hang on. Ondromuni's story traces the origin of the Kharngapkynta clan to a Brahmin priest from Jaiñtiapur, brought by the Sutnga kings to look after the Durga temple in Nartiang, their summer capital. The priest had four daughters called Ka Tuli, Ka Tula, Ka Haji and Ka Haja. All of them married local men and went to live in different places in Ri Pnar. Ka Haja, for instance, settled down with her husband near Jowai. She had three children: a daughter, whose name is unknown, a son called U Barman, and another daughter called Ka Pankon.

Haja's grandchildren from the eldest daughter lived in Nartiang and later spread out towards the villages of Nongbah, Tuber and others. Barman and Pankon, however, were kidnapped by warriors from Shyllong, who brought them to their king in Nongkrem, who later sold them as slaves to a family from the Lyngngam–Nongtrai areas—it is not very clear whether the family was Lyngngam, Nongtrai or Diko. That family also bought another female slave and made all three of them work in their jhum fields. It was back-breaking work, toiling from morning till dusk, but on the whole, they were treated and fed very well. In fact, the combination of good food and hard labour soon made them strong, healthy and physically very well developed indeed.

One day, many moons later, Barman and Pankon were asked to go to the fields without their companion, who was needed at home. After working until dusk, as usual, they returned home to find a large number of people feasting and merrymaking with the family. Their companion, however, was nowhere to be seen. Thinking that they would look for her later, Barman and Pankon went to have their dinner, which was being served in the courtyard. But feeling shy with so many strangers around, they decided to eat at the back of the kitchen. It was there that they saw some discarded body parts that were being eaten by stray dogs. In a flash, they understood what was happening: their companion had been butchered! Those people were feasting on her flesh! They, too, would have become the unwitting victims of cannibalism had they not seen these remains.

As the masters and their guests were drinking and feasting, oblivious to all else, Barman and Pankon decided to run away as fast as they could. They went east towards Nongstoin and Ri Maram in West Khasi Hills and travelled through the dense jungle for many days, surviving only on roots, herbs and fruits.

Meanwhile, the next morning, their masters discovered the duo's absence. They immediately organised a huge manhunt, using woodsmen and hunting dogs, who straightaway found their tracks. But after their initial success, the pursuers lost the trail completely when they came to a stream. Barman and Pankon, knowing what their masters would do, had walked for a long time in the water, emerging from it only when they could step on stones that would leave no trace at all. And they resorted to this strategy as far as they could. Even at night, they did not sleep on the ground, but climbed a tree, made a crude platform of leaves and branches and slept there.

It was by these tactics—and with a lot of help from the summer rain, which wiped out some of their tracks—that they were able to delay their trackers and make it as far east as the River Rilang. But the river proved to be their greatest obstacle: it was running in spades, and there was no way across. They were stuck by the river for two days, going up and down the bank, trying to find a ford or a shallower spot where the water was less turbulent. But it was hopeless. The river was a roaring, angry, frightening thing.

Meanwhile, the pursuers arrived. Barman and his sister could hear the dogs barking, the sound coming nearer all the time. They were trapped and had nowhere to go. In their desperation, the siblings kneeled by the riverbank and prayed to God and the guardian spirit of villages and the wilderness, U Ryngkew U Basa, to come to their aid, for they were about to plunge into the roiling waters and place themselves at God's mercy rather than face certain death at the hands of the cannibals behind them.

By the time they finished praying, the pursuers were only about a hundred yards away; the barking, snarling dogs were even closer. When the men saw the two of them genuflecting by the riverbank, they shouted in triumph. But Barman strapped Pankon to his back with a cloth and jumped into the river, leaving the murderous Dikos, or whoever they were, staring in disbelief.

While Barman was floundering about in the churning river, a huge tiger suddenly jumped into the water beside him, also trying to swim across. Perhaps the tiger too had been frightened by the men and the baying dogs, but Barman did not doubt that he was U Ryngkew, coming to his aid. He grabbed the tiger's tail and clung on for dear life, and in this way, he and his sister were hauled safely across.

On reaching the other bank, the tiger quickly vanished into the thick jungle, leaving the two humans to lie exhausted in the mud. Across the river, the cannibals were shouting and cursing and throwing spears at them, but in vain, for the river was a vast expanse that no spear thrown by human hands could ever span.

From there, Barman and Pankon kept travelling east until they reached a village called Sakwang in the state of Nongkhlaw. On learning their story, the people there gave them shelter and treated them as their own. Later, Barman became a trader and was called Bartep by the locals. When he was well established in his business, he married Pankon off to a fellow trader by the name of Shan Maram Marbañiang. The couple had two daughters. The older girl continued to live in Sakwang, and from her came the clan known today as Kharsyntiew. The younger left Sakwang with her husband to live in Sohrarim village near Sohra, which belonged to the state of Nongkhlaw. She had four daughters: Ka Sa, Ka Phan, Ka Wan and Ka Ngap. Ka Sa married a man called Wian, Ka Phan married Buh, and Ka Wan married Lang. Their children became known as Kharsawian, Kharphanbuh and Kharwanlang. Ka Ngap married a non-Khasi man from Pandua called Kynta; her children became known as Kharngapkynta.

This means that the five clans had relatives in Ri Pnar, Ri Maram and Ri Khynriam. All of them used to come and store the bones of their departed relatives in the great mawbah ossuary in Sohrarim, until the great earthquake destroyed it. After that, the clans decided to construct their own ossuaries in the areas where they were living.

Evening immediately cried out, 'You hear that, Hamkom? More and more evidence that we came from the east and Ri Pnar. Don't ever say Jaiñtias are different without knowing anything, you fraud!'

'Forget it, man!' Bah Kynsai said. 'This story is about why the Dikos, or whoever they were, were known as human-eaters, na? Let's stick to the point.'

'Do you think the people from Lyngngam–Nongtrai really were cannibals in the past, Bah Ap?' Donald asked.

'Ondromuni's story suggests that there were people in these parts who were cannibals. And Victor did tell us that the Matsadu-Matsadei was a cannibal clan. Perhaps Barman and Pankon were their slaves. Who can say for sure?'

'What about the tiger-men, Ap?' Magdalene asked. 'Raji also said there used to be tiger-men in Ri Bhoi, but how can men turn into tigers like that? Even in X-Men, this does not happen, no? I mean, in X-Men, once changed, the characters cannot become normal again!'

'According to the Khasi belief,' I replied, 'when a person sleeps, his rngiew, the essence of his personality, leaves the body to roam freely in his form. But Khasis also believe that some people are given the power to change their essence into all sorts of animals: tigers, bears, otters, even snakes. The change is not a physical one, it is his essence that is changed. Among the Lyngngams and Nongtrais, there are certain people who, they say, can change their essence into a tiger or a Shwar or a Sangkhni. I had referred to Shwar, the demon, earlier, I'll tell you about Sangkhni later.'

'Are these people the same as the Matsadu-Matsadei clan, Ap?'

'No, Mag, these are different. The Lyngngams and Nongtrais believe that a person's power to change his essence into a tiger is God-given, meant for his own good and that of his family and friends. This is because, like a tiger, he can protect not only himself but also others from all sorts of enemies and dangers. At the same time, the man could misuse his powers, and if that happens, he becomes a ruthless destroyer of men and animals: a curse to mankind.

'A person who can turn his essence into a tiger is said to be often restless in his sleep. As the tiger stalks the jungle and people's farms to hunt and kill, the man twists and turns all night, asleep, yet awake. Sometimes, his stomach becomes bloated with gas from eating rotten flesh that has been lying on the ground for days—'

'Did they ever kill humans, Bah Ap?' Donald asked.

'Bad tiger-men can be ruthless destroyers of men and animals, but normally, they kill only their enemies or humans mistaken for animals. That's why tiger-men, Victor said, often appear in the dreams of their relatives to warn them not to wear red clothes so they may not be mistaken for a deer. It is also said that a tiger-man has alliances with other tiger-men and that, when he dies, the others try to get rid of the body by eating it. When a tiger-man dies, therefore, the relatives have to guard his body very carefully indeed.'

'And you believe this, Bah Ap?' Donald asked again.

'Victor swore by it. He said even now there are many people with such a gift—'

'And not only here, okay, in Ri Bhoi as well,' Raji intervened. 'I personally know one of them; I'll take you to him if you want. I can promise you a fascinating conversation, Don.'

'What about people whose rngiew can turn into a Shwar?' Magdalene asked.

'Do you remember what I told you about Shwar? Khasis believe she's a terrible demon who twists and deforms the necks of those who displease her keepers in some way. The Lyngngams and Nongtrais also have their Shwar legends, though their idea of her seems to be quite different. They say she's a man-eating demon who looks like a human but is many times larger. She has red eyes, shaggy hair, fanged teeth, a large nose curved like a parrot's and huge talons instead of fingernails. Her favourite method of eating people, especially children, is to wrap them in plantain leaves and have them like a human roll.'

I then recounted the story of the Shwar-men as Victor had told it to me. Unlike a tiger-man, whose power is God-given, a man can turn his essence into a Shwar or a Sangkhni only if he is possessed by them. According to Victor, the first Nongtrai man to turn into a Shwar was Agreng or Akreng.

It happened one day as Akreng was taking Kong, the eldest of his five sons, to his jungle farm. Father and son were very happy together, singing and whistling and shooting birds with slings as they went along. They tilled the fields all day long and spent the night at the *lengphan*, a bamboo hut that stands on bamboo stilts. But as soon as he was asleep, Akreng's essence turned into a Shwar. His eyes grew red, his fingers and toes became talons, and his body swelled out with muscles like small hills. He looked at his son like a tiger would look at a deer and pounced upon him, tearing him to pieces with his talons and fanged teeth and devouring all the flesh, leaving only the bones and hair.

When morning came, Akreng woke up as a normal human being. When he realised what he had done, he was devastated and cried his heart out. But, after a while, fear hit him like a mighty blow. He shuddered and trembled all over when he thought about what his wife's relatives would do to him if they found out what he had done to his own son. How could he return home without the boy? But how could he not return? Their relatives would start looking for them and discover the truth. Finally, he hit upon a plan, and after cleaning the hut carefully, he went home as if nothing had happened.

When he reached home, his wife, Ka Lot, asked, 'Where's Kong?'

'He's at the lengphan. The boy's obsessed with bird-catching and hare-hunting; he doesn't want to come home just yet.'

A day after that, Akreng took his second son, Pyrdi, to the jungle farm. 'I think I'll take Pyrdi with me today so Kong will have a companion,' he explained.

The mother, who did not suspect anything, let Pyrdi go with her blessings. Again, father and son were very happy together on the way, singing and whistling and shooting birds with slings. When they reached the farm, Pyrdi asked for his brother, Kong. Akreng told him he must have gone hare-hunting somewhere and asked him to concentrate on the work at hand. They worked through the day and went back to the lengphan only in the evening. Pyrdi was very surprised not to find Kong at the hut, even though it was getting dark. He asked his father about his brother again, but just then, Akreng turned into a Shwar, tore him to pieces and devoured him. When morning came, and he woke up as a human once again, he cried his heart out like before, lamenting the loss of his second son.

The next day, he again returned home as if nothing had happened and said to his wife, 'Wuu, you should have seen those two! They are so delighted with the jungle life; they don't want to come home at all.'

Akreng did the same thing with his other sons. He knew that taking them would be the end of them, but the spirit of the Shwar had taken over his entire being, and there was nothing he could do but respond to its terrible urges.

When Akreng had eaten his last son, he stopped going home altogether. Ka Lot waited for a week or so, and when neither her sons nor their father made an appearance, she became sick with worry and went to the farm herself to see what was going on. But when she got there, Ka Lot found no one at all in the fields or the hut. She went around shouting for them without getting any answer. Finally, she climbed a hill nearby so she could see better. That hill, however, was a place of horror—in a hollow at the top, she found a pile of bloodstained bones. Her head spinning with terror, she fell in a swoon.

When she came to, Ka Lot took a handful of earth and ate it so it would toughen her essence and prevent her from being overwhelmed by the sudden rush of panic and paralysing fear. Thinking that some monster had massacred her entire family and devoured them, she fled home, crying and sobbing all the way. Back in the village, she recounted all that she had seen to her relatives and friends. 'My poor sons, my poor husband, tell me, who has done this horrible thing to you?' she sobbed.

But one of her neighbours said, 'How can your husband be dead? I saw him in the jungle this morning, near my farm!'

'What!' they all cried. 'What was he doing in the jungle? Why didn't he come home to report the terrible thing that has happened to his sons?'

'I don't know,' the man said, 'I saw him from a distance; he seemed to be stalking something—'

'Could it be that he was pursuing whoever has done this to his family?' Lot's father wondered.

'Perhaps he's mad with grief and is aimlessly roaming the jungle,' another man suggested.

'He was stalking something,' the first man insisted.

'God forbid, has he been possessed by a monster? Is it he who has devoured his own children?' the village headman wondered. 'Is that why he's not returning home?'

The thought was so horrible that Ka Lot fell in a swoon again. While Lot's family was carrying her into the house, the headman organised a posse of twelve spearmen, the best in the village, and went to the jungle to investigate.

When they reached the farm, they first inspected the hut, but finding nothing, went to the hollow in the hill. Poking around the bones, they discovered the heads of the children, but not that of the father. They understood then that it was Akreng who had killed and devoured his own sons. The next day, they began scouring the jungle, looking for him. Finally, not finding him anywhere, the headman and the spearmen decided to return home, believing that he had left the vicinity for good. On the way home, they had to cross Akreng's jungle farm, and because it was late, they decided to spend the night in his lengphan hut. But when they went inside, they got an awful shock, as though they had stepped on the tail of a snake: Akreng was sleeping on one of the makeshift beds! When he saw them, his essence turned into a Shwar, and he looked at them like a cat looking at a bunch of mice. He sprang down from the bed and attacked them, trying to kill them with one swipe of his outstretched talons.

The men fled outside so they would have more room to manoeuvre. Akreng thought they were fleeing for their lives. Roaring with triumph, he went after them, a truly terrible spectacle—bared fangs, sickle-shaped talons and bloodshot eyes. But when the men reached level ground, they formed a semicircle and faced him, attacking him with their long spears. When Akreng pounced on one of them, the man thwarted him with his spear while the others stabbed his exposed flanks. They were thus able to inflict massive injuries on him. Strangely, however, the wounds healed almost as soon as the spears were drawn out. The men were at their wits' end. All they could do was keep blocking and stabbing him with their spears.

The battle continued in that manner the whole night long. The men became weak with exhaustion, and many of them were scratched and lacerated, bleeding profusely and hopelessly waiting for the inevitable to happen. But one of them, whose name was Jop, was so enraged at the prospect of being devoured by the demon that he went after him with renewed energy, blindly stabbing wherever he could. Akreng responded by swiping at him with sharp talons and opening his mouth wide to maul him with his fangs. Quite by chance, Jop's leaping spear pierced Akreng's tongue, and Akreng suddenly fell dead. The men stood stock still, staring, not daring to believe. But it was true, Akreng was dead. They concluded that the Shwar's life force was in his tongue, and when Jop accidentally stabbed it, his heart simply stopped beating.

Before they could recover from the shock, another strange spectacle held them spellbound. The enormous demonic body became smaller and smaller before their eyes until it was reduced to nothing. Fear gripped the wounded men, and some of them began fleeing from the scene. But, just in time, Jop and the headman realised what was happening. They called out to the rest, explaining that what they had been fighting against was not Akreng, but his essence turned into a Shwar. His real body, they said, must be lying inside the hut.

It was true. The men found Akreng's body inside the hut with its tongue completely shredded. They dragged it out, cut it up and scattered the pieces on the hill where his children's bones lay. That is why the hill is called Lumshyieng, or bone hill, to this day.

The death of Akreng did not mean the end of the Shwar-men. Members of his Naphak clan inherited the curse and continued to terrorise the Nongtrai areas for hundreds of years. And though the Naphak clan has now been wiped out, the Lyngngams and Nongtrais believe that there are men, somehow related to the Naphak clan, whose essence can still turn into a Shwar.

When I came to the end of the story, Evening remarked, 'This could be one more reason why people from here were called cannibals, no?'

'Could be, could be,' Bah Kynsai agreed. 'But what about these Sangkhni-men, Ap, do they also kill people?'

'They do, but unlike the Shwar-men, they don't seem to be evil. Like the tiger-men, they are restless in their sleep, especially in the rainy season when they are busy destroying bamboo bridges—'

'Destroying bamboo bridges?' the others asked, laughing.

'Yeah, like the one across the River Rwiang—'

'But why would they do that?' Magdalene asked.

'A Sangkhni is a serpent, like our Thlen—'

'Ah, Thlen at last! Don't forget, Bah Ap, you promised to tell me about him,' Donald said.

'Why do you want to know about Thlen, lih?' Bah Kynsai demanded.

'Because I have heard of so many Thlen-related killings in the last few years, no, Bah Kynsai? I want to understand—'

'Hey, hey, you people are forgetting the Sangkhni story,' Magdalene said. 'Let's come back to it, Ap.'

'As I was saying, a Sangkhni is a kind of serpent, and his natural dwelling is a deep river pool. He's especially active during the summer, making rivers swell with floodwaters and destroying the bamboo bridges across them because they obstruct his free movement—'

'And Sangkhni-men do the same thing?' Magdalene asked.

'Exactly. But that's not all. They also kill people by drowning them in the rivers they are trying to cross. However, they don't kill at random, only those who have committed sacrilegious offences—'

'Like?' Hamkom asked.

'The greatest sacrilege among us, Ham, is incest. In the past, the upland Khasis not only ostracised such people but also put a curse on them, so they would be devoured by a tiger or struck by lightning. The Lyngngams and Nongtrais, on the other hand, simply called on Sangkhni and the Sangkhni-men to punish them—'

'But a Sangkhni can kill them only when they cross rivers, no, Ap?' Magdalene asked.

'According to Victor, in the past, there was only one Sangkhni, and he was known to destroy villages where such offenders lived. He did that by tunnelling through the earth and making houses and farmlands collapse and sink into a crater, which he then flooded with water from rivers and lakes. The belief that Sangkhni and Sangkhni-men are the destroyers of sacrilegious offenders comes from the story of Adynga and his two nieces, Gerjei and Ajei.'

A long, long time ago, there used to live in Nongtrai a giant by the name of Adynga. He was famed throughout the region for the many heroic deeds he performed in the service of the people. But this is not the story of his rise or greatness, rather of his fall.

One day, while he was preparing his wild-fowl snares in the jungle near the banks of the River Rdiak, Adynga suddenly heard the *mieng*, a bamboo musical instrument much like a Jew's harp, being played by two people. He was so captivated by the enthralling music that he just had to find out who the players could be. Adynga went up to the hump of a hill for a better look, but because of the dense jungle, he could see nothing. He fetched a boulder as tall as a two-storey house and about a hundred feet across, and placed it on the summit of the hill. When he could still see nothing, he uprooted a huge banyan tree and placed it on top of the boulder.

Climbing to the top of the banyan tree, he shaded his eyes and looked in the direction from which the music was coming. Now he could see two women sitting on a hill on the opposite bank of the river, playing their miengs. He could see the village of Nonglangsaw on a plateau below the hill, some distance from the river. Ah, the women must be from there, he thought idly. I wonder what they look like. Must be beautiful to make such delightful music!

Having seen them and satisfied his curiosity, he tried to go back to his own work. But the enchanting mieng music kept intruding into his thoughts, making it impossible for him to concentrate on his task. He abandoned his snares and responded to the call of the music even as a bird might respond to the call of a *simpah*, a caged singing bird used to attract others of his kind to a trap. And the comparison is not far-fetched either, for unknown to him, he too was heading towards a sort of trap, not unlike the ones he was preparing for the jungle fowls.

When Adynga reached the hill across the river, he saw that the two mieng players were young and beautiful beyond description. As he watched them, their silky black hair was blown back by the breeze, revealing smooth dusky faces and large, dark eyes that shone with pure delight as they swayed gently to their own music. Adynga was smitten by their loveliness. He picked up a huge boulder and went to sit near them. The two young women were so shocked by the sight of him that they stopped their music, and for a long time, could only stare dumbly. They were, in fact, awestruck by his great strength, his huge, muscular physique and his majestic appearance. They had never seen a man like him before. Could this be, they thought, the great Adynga we have heard so much about?

Adynga introduced himself. In response, the two girls told him they were sisters, Gerjei and Ajei. When the introduction was done, Adynga requested them to continue playing their miengs, for he had left his own task to come and listen to their mesmerising music. 'Play on, please play on, your music is like a soothing massage for my soul,' he pleaded.

Gerjei and Ajei were pleased beyond measure by the praise from this great man. They played their miengs, both trying to outdo each other and both looking at Adynga with adoration in their eyes. They, too, had fallen in love with him on the spot.

Adynga went to the hill every day, drawn not only by their music but also by their love. He made a giant swing for them so they could enjoy their outing all the better and watched them as they played on it, happy like little children. And so the days came and the days went, until one day, Adynga openly declared his love for them. The two women also confessed their love for him and said they were prepared not only to accept him but also to share his love between them. It was only later, after proper introductions had been made, that they found out how closely related they were. Not only did they belong to the same clan, but further inquiries revealed that Adynga was essentially their uncle, albeit a distant one. However, by then, it was too late. Their love was truly blind, even to clan ties and incest. Adynga married Gerjei and Ajei, and though they were ostracised and banished from their villages, they lived happily together in the jungle. Music, as with Manik Raitong, had trapped them into an improper relationship—

'My God, you are right, man!' Raji exclaimed. 'The story does remind me of him ... What do you think, Bah Kit?'

'But in this case, they were happy, no?' Bah Kit objected. 'In the case of Manik Raitong and Ka Lieng Makaw, it was tragic. They both died, remember?'

'What are you people talking about?' Donald asked. 'Who's Manik Raitong?'

'What!' Bah Kynsai, Bah Kit, Raji and Evening exclaimed in unison. 'You haven't heard the story of Manik Raitong?'

'Don't be too hard on him, ya,' Magdalene defended Donald. 'For that matter, I also don't really know the story, ya, I mean, I know the skeleton of it, so to speak, but not much more.'

'Same here,' Hamkom admitted. 'I'm not very proud of it, but I must confess, I also don't know much about it.'

'How can you not know, man? Manik was a beggar who won the love of a queen, na?'

Bah Kit, Bah Su, Raji and I hooted with laughter at Bah Kynsai's statement. Raji, who was swigging from his 'mug of happiness', actually choked on the beer.

After Raji had recovered and was settling down to tearful giggles, Bah Kynsai demanded, 'What are you buggers laughing about?'

'Because he was not a beggar, Bah Kynsai!' Bah Kit said. 'You have got it all wrong.'

'Oh shit! That means I also don't know it, tdong!' Bah Kynsai said in disbelief. 'You had better tell us the story, Ap.'

I protested, 'How can I tell you about Manik Raitong when I haven't even finished the Adynga story?'

'Then you shouldn't have mentioned Manik Raitong at all and made a fool of me, na, tdir!'

'Tell the story, Ap. You can always come back to Adynga later,' Magdalene advised.

Bowing to their combined pressure, I told them the tragic tale of Manik Raitong and Lieng Makaw.

U Manik Raitong, or Manik the Wretched, is the archetypal lover of Khasi society and is at the heart of the tradition of love and music. He lived sometime in the remote past, in the capital of one of the biggest Khasi states in those days, located in the contemporary Ri Bhoi district. The names of both the capital and the state are unknown, perhaps deliberately kept a secret to protect the identity of the king. Manik was an orphan, a young man all alone in the world, having lost not only his family but also every other member of his clan. Yet, he was neither poor nor wretched in the material sense, for he had inherited all the property of his clan—a spacious hut on the outskirts of the town and large tracts of cultivable land bordering a nearby village.

Manik spent almost all his time in his extensive and partly wooded fields. He would leave at the third cockcrow and return at nightfall to a lonely hut, never enlivened by the company of friends, for he had none.

In the fields, where he grew a little rice and millet, a little of this and a little of that, his routine was never rigorous. He would work on a furrow or two till his midday meal and then retire to the hills and woods to listen to the songs of birds and the melodies of insects. He did not need to work hard, having only himself to support. His sole ambition was to learn how to recreate the countless sounds of Nature, which had strangely brought such restful consolation to his bruised soul.

It was while wandering about in this manner that Manik met a stunningly beautiful girl. Straying absentmindedly towards a shyngiar spring on the fringes of a neighbouring village, he quite literally bumped into her as she emerged from another lane.

Surprised, they stared at each other and then blurted out at the same time, '*Oh, mab!* Forgive me!' A nervous laugh followed and the girl turned to proceed down the lane. But Manik, like a man afraid that his dream might come to an abrupt end, blurted out: 'Wait …'

She waited, looking him full in the eye, as if daring him to speak his mind. Manik gazed at her, enthralled. He had never seen such a beautiful woman before. Not that she was dressed differently from the girls he had seen in the fields. Like them, she wore a jaiñsem over her sarong, and like them, she had, slung across her shoulder, a ïarong, one of those small net purses woven from the thread of pineapple leaves. Nonetheless, he could see that she was no ordinary woman. She had about her an elegance, a confident grace that no clothes, however commonplace, could obscure.

Manik was even more fascinated by the peach blossom on her face. Her thick black hair was pulled back firmly and tied in a bun at the back of her head, only intensifying the effect of her cerise complexion, her luminous dark eyes and her smiling thorn-berry red lips, so that she seemed aglow like an early sunrise.

'Forgive my rudeness,' he finally said when he saw her blushing uncomfortably under his intense gaze. 'I'm sorry to embarrass you like this ... you are so ... I ... I have never seen you before.'

Seeing him ill at ease, the girl giggled happily and said, 'But we have been watching you every day. You never seem interested in anything except the singing of birds and the loud chirping of the cicadas. Are you a poet?'

'No, I'm only trying—'

'Someone's coming,' the girl interrupted, 'I have to go.' And with that, she turned towards the shyngiar.

Manik shouted after her, 'Will I see you again?'

'If you want to see me, come to my house tomorrow,' the girl called back. 'Ask for the house of the lyngskor.'

'What?' Manik said to himself. 'The lyngskor? Is she the daughter of the prime minister? No wonder she looks high-born. Anyway, lyngskor or no lyngskor, I will go. After all, she has invited me, and come to think of it, I'm not so badly off myself.'

The next day Manik tried to appear as respectable as he possibly could in his clean work clothes since he did not want to dress formally and draw undue attention to himself. Arriving at the house of the prime minister late in the afternoon, he was received by the mother herself, who said, 'Oh, so you are the man my daughter has fallen for? No wonder ... Look at you, like the moon of the fourteenth night.' She called out to her daughter: 'Bring us the shangkwai.' Then, turning back to Manik, she resumed, 'Now tell me about yourself.'

Manik introduced himself.

'What! You are the sole surviving son of Ka Phrin and U Sherin! Please wait here,' she said and left the surprised Manik to wait alone.

In the kitchen, she reprimanded her daughter and told her not to bring the betel nut basket to the main room. 'And all of you,' she said, addressing her family, 'stay out of sight. What I have to tell the young man is not for your ears. You are lucky your father is not here.'

Back in the main room, she addressed Manik in peremptory tones: 'I'm extremely displeased that you, a miserable orphan, could be so presumptuous as to court the daughter of a lyngskor. What have you got to offer her except misfortune, and perhaps, God forbid, untimely death? Don't you know what people say about you? You carry with you the touch of death. You have caused the death of your parents, your family and your entire clan; now you want to bring ill luck into my house too? When Ka Phrin, your mother, died, she left her only daughter in your care. What happened to her? You are a death dealer. Your name shall never be spoken in this house. Your presence here shall never be permitted. Now go, cast your ominous shadow elsewhere.'

Poor Manik, his love had ended as soon as it began. He did not even know the girl's name, but what was the use of knowing it? He had not realised until then that there was so much hatred for him in this world. It had always seemed to him that God and the dead had been cruel to him by deserting him, leaving him stranded in this unfriendly world, but now that same world was turning everything upside down by blaming him.

'Ah, my dearest sister, you were the last to go,' he said aloud to his departed sibling. 'How I tried to save you! Surely everyone knows how much it meant to me that our clan would live on and prosper through you! When you fell ill, I collected every plant and herb known to man for your cure. I brought all the shamans, healers, diviners from every nook and cranny of the hima, so they could plead for your life with their ritual egg-breaking and their sacrificial roosters. I desperately wanted you to live so that you might, in turn, be my companion and caretaker. But the world is blaming me even for your death.

'I'm like an animal in his lair, sad and lonely, yet the moment I try to step out, people chase me away, they hound me out as a dirty and dangerous creature. Alone then, alone I shall live from now on, alone as long as I breathe, and since I am treated as an outcast, as an outcast shall I live. I will dress in sackcloth and dust myself from head to foot with ash from the hearth of my burnt-out life. Let me give the world a reason to denounce me as a pariah. Let it shun and leave me alone. But away from meddling eyes, in the friendship of the night, let me be pure and spotless. Let me be true to myself. Let me be true to my quest. Let me speak with the musical sounds, the healing tones of nature.'

In truth, many a young woman would have been only too happy to be courted by Manik. He was young, handsome and a man of property. Since everybody has to die one day, surely the thought of future death would not have been as important to a young woman in love as her present well-being? But who was to tell Manik that the feeling of one indignant mother did not represent a collective truth?

From then on, Manik began to appear in sackcloth and ashes. That was how he walked through the lanes of the town, whistling to himself or playing the seven-mouthed sharati, the long, slender flute he had invented, carved from seasoned shken, the small-stem bamboo. That was how he went to his fields or roamed the woods to find new tunes for the instrument, which had become his only companion. But unknown to the world, he waited for the night, to wash, dress in his best clothes and play his sharati, sharing with the crickets the sad story of his life.

And that was how the world came to call him Manik Raitong, Manik the Wretched, Manik the Forsaken.

Manik lived the life of a recluse, oblivious to what was going on in the world. It was as if the town's life passed him by completely, and except for the occasional jeering of children, who branded him 'a madman playing mad music', he was completely ignored. There were tremendous changes in the world around him, but he remained blissfully unaffected by them.

Meanwhile, a young king, a strong ruler and a mighty warrior, had taken over the governance of the state. Under his leadership, the state, and consequently its capital, were growing in fame and prosperity. The king had won many battles and annexed many territories. The state had expanded on all sides, but especially northwards, where its territories extended far into the plains of Kamarupa, from the Koch kingdom (Goalpara) in the west to the Kachari kingdom (Cachar Hills) in the east. To govern these territories, the king appointed many provincial rulers, the syiem raijs, who reported directly to him at the capital in Ri Bhoi.

The king was a hero, loved and respected in the whole state, and feared throughout the length and breadth of Ri Khasi, also known in those days as *Ka ri u laiphew syiem bad u khatar doloi*, that is, the land of the thirty kings and a dozen dolois. He was also still a bachelor at twenty-eight, a bachelor every young woman dreamt of and whose marriage was the subject of endless speculation.

The king was in no hurry to marry, had no desire to settle down and grow old just yet. He was a man of action, who thrilled at being in the thick of battle and whose ambition was to go down in legend as the greatest conqueror and nation-builder among his people.

His mother, however, had different plans for him. She realised that he was living a dangerous life and wanted to curb his restless spirit by diverting some of his energy towards the responsibilities of raising a family. Besides, as she told the king, she would like to see him happily married before she grew too old to perform her part in the nuptial rites.

Following the queen mother's wishes, several matchmakers were engaged to look for the most eligible bride in the state. But, as it turned out, their services were not required, for the king had taken a fancy to Ka Lieng Makaw, the unmarried daughter of the prime minister, who had been introduced to him by her father.

Lieng Makaw became officially betrothed to the king after the engagement ceremony, called pynhiar synjat, was performed. The wedding was fixed for six full moons from then, to allow everyone time to gear up for the grand event. Invitations were relayed to every part of the land through special messengers. Weeks before the occasion, representatives from villages and provinces arrived with gifts of goats, cattle, pigs, poultry, rare birds and wild animals, as also basketfuls of rice, millet, maize, fruits and foodstuff of every description. They poured into the capital from every direction and occupied every bit of space in the suburbs, singing and dancing to the accompaniment of the raucous pipe music of ka tangmuri and the booming sound of ki ksing, the big and small drums.

On the wedding day, everyone was curious about the mahadei-to-be. Had their syiem chosen the right woman? What did she look like, to win the approval of such a king and his mother, the queen? Was she fair? Was she tall? Did she have the grace, the refinement, the sterling qualities required of a true mahadei of the people?

The wedding was held in an open field so the citizens could have a glimpse of the bride. The ceremonial rites were conducted by the lyngdoh hima, the chief priest, in the presence of ministers, provincial kings, nobles, representatives of the council of state and countless other dignitaries from neighbouring states.

And yes, Lieng Makaw was all that the people expected, and more. She was dressed in a brilliant yellow velvet blouse over which were draped, across the shoulders, a pair of chaste white mulberry-silk jaiñsem, the dharas, with gold designs near the hem, just above the flowing tassels. Over these, she wore a milky satin cape. On her feet were slippers made from specially treated deerskin. On her arms were bracelets, bangles and armlets of solid gold inlaid with rubies. Her necklace was a *konopad* made of flattened gold and adorned with topazes and rubies; her earrings were dangling gold leaves; her crown was a tiara of gold and diamonds, holding down her copious hair, which flowed down her back like a cascade of black silk.

There she was, sitting beside the majestic king in the specially decorated, gem-studded love-seat. To say that she was beautiful would have been an understatement. She was the snow on a summit of Ki Mangkashang, the Himalayas, kissed by the golden sunlight of the afternoon. The revellers heaved a collective sigh of happiness, and many of them started dancing and singing paeans to the queen consort.

Lieng Makaw moved into the palace of the king, an exception the matrilineal Khasis allow their rulers. Since, customarily, a married Khasi woman would never go to settle in her in-laws' house, it is hard to describe Lieng Makaw's feelings at that moment. She was living in a strange place (not exactly with the in-laws, but in a palace in the same compound), bound to a man she hardly knew, a man, moreover, with whom she had not fallen in love at first sight. But that man was also a king, regal, celebrated and revered. It would be false to say she was unhappy; nevertheless, it would be untrue to say she was thrilled.

Adjusting to the new life, with its protocols and decorum, its duties and responsibilities, was rather awkward for her, used as she was to the freedom of the hills. Her new family assured her that she would grow accustomed to her altered circumstances with the guidance and inspiration of the king. And so, perhaps, she would have, and perhaps she would have grown to love him dearly too, but for the fact that he never seemed to have much time for her.

Barely a week after the wedding, the king announced: 'My dear mahadei, there are rumblings of discontent in my provinces in the plains. I have to head there immediately. I cannot risk a full-scale rebellion at this point … No, I cannot take you along, too dangerous. Besides, I don't know when I'll be back. I'll leave tomorrow with the lyngskor and some of my most trusted ministers and swordsmen. I have appointed a deputy king to administer this part of the hima in my absence. Please look after the affairs of the palace. I don't want any indiscipline among the servants. Keep everyone on a tight leash. My mother and sister will help you carry out your duties in a manner befitting a mahadei.'

That night, Lieng Makaw could not sleep for a long time. 'Why is he leaving me alone so soon after the wedding?' she asked herself. 'Why can't he take me along? Could it be that dangerous? How can I live here without him? I'm still almost a stranger here …'

As she was moping in this fashion, Lieng Makaw heard a strange sound carried on the wings of the night breeze. What mournful music, she thought. I have never heard anything like it before … it cannot be the raucous tangmuri, nor is it the moan of the three-stringed duitara … What can it be?

The music seemed to creep in from cracks in the wall to tug at her heartstrings. She sat up and wakened the king. 'Pa'iem! Pa'iem! Listen … can you hear that?'

The king woke up and listened. Just at that moment, however, there was a sudden lull in the light wind and the music stopped. 'It must be the wind,' the king said. 'Go back to sleep.'

By and by, Lieng Makaw dozed off. Just before she fell asleep, she thought she could hear snatches of the music again, but try as she might, her eyes would not stay open, and she fell asleep almost against her will.

The king departed at the third cockcrow, accompanied by his most intimate advisers and a large number of fighting men. Lieng Makaw felt forlorn. Despite the king's explanation, she felt vaguely, inexplicably, let down and unwanted. She was so depressed by this desertion, as she saw it, that she moved about as if in a trance. Her loneliness owed itself, in no small measure, to the indifference shown by the king's family living in the ancestral mansion at the centre of the palatial compound.

One day, towards nightfall, after a perfunctory dinner, she found her loneliness so overpowering, the sense of neglect so unbearable that she ran out of the suffocating confines of the palace to go for a stroll in the fields nearby.

Outside, fanned by the cool, fragrant breath of autumn, she felt immediately better. 'Let me see,' she said to herself, 'the palace is on the outskirts in the east. Where shall I go from here? To the north where I can get a glimpse of the woods from those clusters of monoliths, or the south where I can climb the low hills for a view of the town?' Her lady-in-waiting, who had followed her, suggested it might be too late to go anywhere. Indeed, a light moon was up in the eastern sky and a few stars were making their appearance, but Lieng Makaw walked towards the knolls and dismissed the woman, instructing her to appear only when called for.

When she got to the nearest hill, the night was already bathed in the flaxen light of the moon, and the surroundings were clear as day. The town was quiet and glimmering with flambeaus and hearth fires. She turned her gaze north-east to the clusters of monoliths—the male stones standing erect like alert sentries, the female stones at their feet, a calming place of rest. She felt strangely drawn to them, and in spite of the advancing night, made her way towards them.

Lieng Makaw sat on a flat slab and leaned back against a standing male stone, sighing as she brooded over her life and a husband who seemed to have lost all interest in her within a week of their marriage. And I'm bound to him for life, she thought bitterly. How will our years together be? Will I always be left to myself like this till the fire in my blood slowly dies for the lack of caring hands?

As she sat there brooding, the air abruptly came alive to the strains of the extraordinary music that she had heard the previous night. It rose as if from the depths of the earth and was picked up and carried forward by the light wind to be distributed among the lonely creatures of the night. Lieng Makaw tried to gauge the direction it was coming from. Perhaps it was from that hut she could see standing alone between the monoliths and the woods. She ran towards it eagerly. Yes, the delightfully sweet, incredibly sad music was emerging from it. In her excitement, Lieng Makaw shouted, 'Hey, Bah! Hey, Kong! Who's in the house? May I come in?'

In response, the music stopped and there was only silence, even after Lieng Makaw had repeated her call several times. Uncertain and a little nervous, she retraced her steps and ran back towards the palace.

At the palace, she called her attendant and casually enquired about the solitary hut she had seen near the woods.

'That, Mahadei, is the hut of Manik Raitong. Yes, Mahadei, he is the one who goes about in sackcloth and ashes. He even smears his face with soot; nobody knows exactly why, but everyone thinks it is because he has suffered so much in his young life ... Yes, he lives completely alone. All his relations have died. He is the most miserable creature on earth.'

'Hmm,' Lieng Makaw said to herself, 'so that is the hut of Manik the Wretched. But if he is what they all say he is, how can he be the creator of such haunting music? And why does his music affect me so profoundly? It is as though it knows me intimately, as though it is my long-lost friend and that, deep inside me, I also know it, and that is why I react to it with such spontaneous joy.' She rubbed her chin. 'Could he be the one ... No, how could it be? He was so good-looking ... and yet, could it be possible? It was so long ago ...'

There was no sleep for Lieng Makaw that night. She was grappling with a different kind of restlessness, no longer the misery that had been gnawing at her, but an excitement induced by the music and provocative thoughts about Manik Raitong. She tossed and turned in bed, and then, at about midnight, suddenly sat bolt upright. Yes, she could hear faint snatches of the melody beckoning her like the barely audible voice of a friend calling from far away.

The palace was asleep. She tidied herself, crept out into the moonlight and ran to the hut, and then stopped at a distance to listen.

The music was full and round as if it gushed from some hidden spring and emerged surging into the air, riding the waves like a silver thread. It soared above the trees, now high, now low, like a gliding eagle ... It was the wind whispering dolefully among the trees, the rain pattering softly among the dead leaves of the forest, a brook gurgling eerily among the bushes ... It was the rolling wail of a cicada, the distressed call of jyllob in the deep woods ... It was the cry of a soul in despair, translated into this sweet, unceasing lament.

The music seemed to be all of these to Lieng Makaw. She was moved as never before by this melodious outpouring of grief. It reeled her into the mysterious world of the musician, as if at the end of a hooked line. She ran lightly onto the porch. She peeped into the hut. 'What! This is no Manik Raitong in sackcloth and ashes!' she exclaimed.

Indeed, the man who sat on a wooden stool facing the hearth was in the finery of a king. The enthralling music that had possessed her was flowing from the man's breath through the seven openings of a thin bamboo tube— the seven mouths of the soul, the seven outlets of sorrow, the seven wonders of music created by the very breath of life. It was by flickering his fingers over the openings that he was creating the most hauntingly poignant tunes that Lieng Makaw had ever heard. Every time the man exhaled into the tube, a string tautened in her heart and tugged at her painfully.

She knocked loudly on the door. 'This is your mahadei, Ka Lieng Makaw, please open the door,' she demanded.

The door did not open, but this time, the music did not stop either. Lieng Makaw peeped through the chink in the plank wall again, and without taking her eyes off him, beat the timber frame with the palm of her hands, pleading, 'Please open the door, I only want to listen to your music. Please let me in, I only want to watch you playing your instrument.'

The man turned his face towards her. It *was* the handsome youth from the shyngiar! The youth who had asked for her hand in marriage many years ago! He was older, more mature, otherwise he was the same: serene and attractive as ever. Yes, her very first love! With her heart hammering in her chest, she banged on the wall more fiercely and shouted, 'Manik, it is I, the woman at the shyngiar! My name is Lieng Makaw, don't you remember me? You even came to my house to meet me!'

Manik was startled, she could see that, but then he simply turned away and began playing another eerie tune. As she listened, spellbound, she seemed to understand everything. She was the last straw in his cheerless life, the last straw that broke his back. It was she who had turned him into the despised creature that he was now. She understood this as plainly as though he had recounted his story in clear and lucid words. She became even more desperate. Manik's sharati drew out her very soul, which swirled about the porch like a mad spirit trying to find a way in. That was when she spotted a large machete leaning against the wall. She grabbed the broad, heavy knife and began battering the door with it till it finally broke.

She entered. Manik had stopped playing. He was staring at her in amazement.

Lieng Makaw looked up at him with adoration in her eyes—how she had secretly admired this fair, finely etched face, manly and majestic, framed by a light-yellow turban of muka silk. How fascinated she had been with these striking dark eyes, shining with such a sad, gentle light. She said, 'Don't you remember me? We met at the shyngiar years ago; you said you were in love with me; you—'

'I used to love a woman, not a mahadei,' Manik interrupted sadly. 'If you had shown your rebellious spirit then, we would have been happy. But now you have only condemned me to death.'

It was a portentous statement from a man who had gained much wisdom from much suffering. But Lieng Makaw did not stop to think. 'What wrong have I done?' she replied. 'I have only come to listen to your mournful and mesmerising music, which has not allowed me to sleep or to rest even for a moment since I first heard it. And no wonder. Now I understand. Your sorrow is my sorrow. But I have done nothing wrong by coming here. We have done nothing wrong, and besides, it is midnight. Nobody knows, and nobody needs to know.'

Lieng Makaw started visiting Manik every night to hear him play; to listen to his magical sharati flute; to wonder how on earth he could conjure up such enchanting notes. Nobody knew that Manik Raitong, Manik the Wretched, Manik the Forsaken, had won the heart of a queen.

Time flew, the seasons passed over the land, and passed again. But the king did not return. It was only at the end of the third winter that he sent word of his homecoming. The entire state got ready to give its great and noble king a reception befitting a conquering hero. There was great rejoicing in the land when he reappeared. Every village received him with festivities and much show of affection. In the capital, however, the tone of welcome was muted. And in the palace, there was only a dreadful hush.

When the king arrived at the palace, he first asked for his mahadei: 'Where is Ka Mahadei? Why isn't she here to receive me?'

A frightened household gave him the answer: 'She is suckling the baby, Pa'iem.'

'Baby! What baby?' the startled king thundered.

The servants replied, 'Ka Mahadei's, Pa'iem.'

'What? Ka Mahadei has a baby? How is that? Why was no message sent to me?' he bellowed.

At that moment, the queen mother appeared. 'Welcome home, son,' she said quietly. 'Come, we will talk in private.'

When they were alone in the main chamber, the queen mother asked, 'How long have you been absent?'

'Three winters, of course,' the king said impatiently.

'Then the baby is definitely not yours,' the queen mother said. 'We have always known that, of course, that's why we have put her under house arrest. I just wanted to make sure. The child is male. He is about six full moons old. The question is, what is to be done now?'

The king clenched his fists and hissed with suppressed rage. 'I'm going to destroy the man who has brought this shame upon me, upon my house, upon the entire hima. And I'm going to destroy them both.'

'That's how I feel too,' the queen mother said. 'But first, you should find out from her who the man is. Not that she will tell you, knowing what you will do. But you could try.'

Lieng Makaw was summoned before the king. As the queen mother had predicted, there was no disclosure forthcoming. Here was no repentant woman. She came before the king with her head held high—proud, stubborn, unashamed and even happy. Seeing that, the king thought, is she naively expecting me to merely throw her out, release her from her nuptial vows, so she can live happily ever after with her paramour? Or does she believe her father, the lyngskor, will protect her? A hard, cruel smile played on his lips as he dismissed her.

But what was to be done? He could not possibly torture her into a confession, for she was, after all, his lawfully wedded wife and the daughter of the hima's prime minister to boot. Later, he could devise an appropriate punishment, but for now, what was to be done?

It was the chief priest who suggested that a test be carried out to uncover the identity of the wrongdoer. 'On my instruction,' he said, 'the shamans have performed an egg-divination ceremony, Pa'iem. God, U Nongap Jutang,

Keeper of the Covenant, the Pledge between Man and Him, has indicated through signs a way by which we can expose the offender and right all wrongs.'

To implement the test, a council of state, comprising all villages within striking distance of the capital, was convened. All marriageable men were ordered to attend without fail and to bring with them a banana apiece.

On the appointed day, the men were made to form a circle around a large field. At the head of the circle sat the king, the chief priest and other ministers (the prime minister, Lieng Makaw's father, was not present since he had fallen ill due to the shock and the shame). To their right and left, extending for thousands of paces, sat the councillors from the villages. The middle of the circle was left bare, except for a cane mat where Lieng Makaw's baby lay. The purpose of the council was explained at length by the chief priest, following an instruction from the king. Each man was required to hold up the banana he had brought and offer it to the baby. The man whose banana the baby accepted would be declared his father and would be punished as deemed fit by the whole council.

Many objected, pointing to the possibility that the baby might accept more than one banana or accept it from the wrong man. But the chief priest argued that the test was according to the signs and tokens indicated by God, and assured everyone that justice would be carried out only after a further careful investigation. The man whose banana was accepted by the baby, he said, would be subjected to additional examination and questioning, so that the absolute truth was first established.

After these assurances, the council unanimously agreed to put the test into operation. The men, starting from the right, approached the baby with great trepidation.

The first one, a scrawny middle-aged man, hand extended in a gesture of offering, crouched and slowly crept towards the baby. His posture was that of a man trying to appease an angry and dangerous animal. With sweat dripping from his forehead, he reached the baby and presented the banana, cooing softly and grinning foolishly. The whole council held its breath. The baby looked at the man and then at the banana but continued to suck his fingers. The man stood up, gave a loud sigh of relief, raised his hands and shook them in the air in jubilation.

And so, one by one, to the last man, each was subjected to the test— the younger men sweating under the strain, while the elderly were more perfunctory. One of them, a joker in the pack, even tried to thrust the banana into the baby's hands so he could be suspected of having made love to the mahadei. The baby, however, showed no interest in the banana. Frustrated, the king nodded an instruction to the chief priest, who stood up and asked, 'Is there anyone from anywhere who hasn't attended? Respected headmen, please answer for your groups.'

Each headman stood up and testified that every marriageable man from his village was in attendance. But one headman from a locality of the capital said, 'Everyone has attended, Pa'iem, except Manik Raitong. He lives like an outcast and goes about in sackcloth and ashes. His face is always covered with soot and grime. He is truly a wretched creature. Should such a man be called to the dorbar?'

At first, the council was divided in its opinion, but the chief priest intervened. 'I have just consulted with the other priests, Pa'iem, and they are unanimous that every man, regardless of his circumstances, must be called before the dorbar. I, therefore, move that Manik Raitong be brought here.'

Manik was brought to the council and handed a banana. Timid and shy, he cut such a pathetic figure in his ragged and ash-covered sackcloth that everyone present clucked in sympathy and annoyance that such a one should be subjected to this test. How could the mahadei consort with such a poor thing? 'Shish!' they uttered in derision, 'he looks like one of those beggars from the plains.'

Manik walked towards the baby with his banana. He was no longer timid and shy. Erect as a menhir, he advanced. When he reached the baby, he kneeled and offered him the banana. As soon as he saw Manik, the baby giggled and gurgled, clapped his little hands, kicked his little feet and reached out towards him. Manik took him in his powerful hands, raised him aloft and announced imperiously, 'This is my son!'

A deafening roar went up from the council. The men jumped to their feet in amazement. They craned their necks for a better look at Manik and exclaimed in sheer disbelief, 'How could such a stinking wretch have cuckolded our syiem?'

The king called for order. How could this filthy half-human have undone him? He instructed the chief priest to question Manik closely. He sent one of the ministers to have Manik's claim confirmed by Lieng Makaw. When everything was done, and the truth was established beyond the shadow of a doubt, the council sentenced Manik to immediate death by u tangon u lymban, that is, by crushing his neck between two heavy logs.

Manik, unperturbed, requested the council that he be granted a dying wish. He began: 'You the syiem, the mother; you the ministers, the advisers; you the priests, the nobles; and you the councillors, true sons of your mothers, in whom true power is vested; please hear me out. You consider me a criminal to be condemned to death by u tangon u lymban. But in my heart of hearts, for reasons that you will come to know in due course, I know that I am not a criminal. It is life's design that I should suffer and, through suffering, create and conquer, and then suffer again for my very achievements. I'm not a lawbreaker the way a thief or a murderer is. My heart is pure, pure as a mountain stream. If someone is attracted to that purity and tries to drink from it, that does not render the stream impure. I'm not trying to justify my actions, nor plead for clemency. Death is the natural end of all sorrows. All I ask is that I am not slain like a common criminal. Please allow me to choose the manner of my death.'

The council was surprised by Manik's fluent self-expression. Even their renowned ruler had never managed to speak with such solemn eloquence. Amidst the hushed silence, the king enquired, 'How would you like to meet your death?'

Without hesitation, Manik said, 'I would like to die by the cleansing power of fire. What I have done is unclean to you. What life has done is unclean to me. Let fire destroy every trace of my life, let my soul rise like the blue smoke and become one with the blue sky. And let me build my own pyre, so I may go in peace, having died by my own hand.'

Moved to pity despite his unpardonable crime, the council granted his unusual request. Even the hard-hearted among them said, 'Since he's going to die anyway, it does not matter to us how he meets his end.' A day was appointed and some men were assigned to assist Manik in making the pyre. Guards were also posted to monitor his every movement.

Manik went about building the pyre as though he was preparing for the happiest, most important occasion of his life. He selected a site on a small hill on the western edge of the town and had a large rectangular strip cleared. Then he proceeded to make the pyre very much in the manner I described last night, and beautified it with dark red velvet, golden tassels, siarkait flowers and the shanduwa high canopy.

When all that was done, Manik stood back to survey the place of his last repose. Satisfied with his handiwork, he went home to prepare for his final journey.

On the day fixed for Manik's self-immolation, people streamed into the capital from every corner. They started arriving at the first cockcrow and continued to flow in till the sun stood at the zenith. It was shortly after they had all settled down and chosen their vantage points near the funeral pyre that they heard the sound of music floating towards them. They had never heard anything like it before. Onwards, the eerie music came, its notes like creeping tendrils stealing invisibly through the afternoon sky. It grew strong, fuller, more dismal. It was now wheeling like a hawk, up and down, high and low, swirling about them, conveying anguish, a vast grief and deep lamentation.

Many of those present asked, 'What is that? Is it the wind whispering sadly among the trees? Is it the rain pattering softly among the dead leaves? Is it a brook gurgling eerily among the bushes? Is it the rolling wail of a cicada? Is it the forlorn sadness, the distressed call of a bird in the deep woods?'

They soon saw it was Manik Raitong, playing his sharati, the very same instrument the townsfolk had dismissed as the plaything of a madman. But now it haunted them with the repertoire of mournful, gently stabbing, yet deeply wounding melodies Manik had fashioned from his singular sorrow. And how magnificent he looked! He was washed and clean and handsome beyond belief. Tall and sinewy, he strode forward gaily, his head slightly tilted to the left, his lips kissing the mouth of the sharati and both his hands fondly fingering the rest of its slim body.

He was dressed like a royal dancer in a dhoti of deep purple eri silk with silver edging, over which he wore a white shirt and a sleeveless jacket adorned with ornate designs and the golden tassels of muka silk. Over this was draped an X-shaped chain of silver inlaid with rubies. Around his neck was a necklace of gold and red coral stones, and on his head was a magnificent purple-and-gold mulberry-silk turban topped with eagle feathers.

The gathering was wonderstruck.

'Is this Manik the Wretched or Manik the Prince? Look at him clothed in the ceremonial robes of a king!' cried one of them.

'Yes,' cried another, 'in the finery of a spring dancer!'

Yet another asked, 'How is it that we never knew we have this prince of princes in our midst? Not only is he a well-endowed youth but an accomplished musician as well! Why did we treat such a gem like a pariah?'

It seemed as if Manik had come to life in all his splendour just before the hour of his death. Many thought it was neither just nor honourable to destroy such a God-gifted talent. They went to the king to plead on Manik's behalf, to beg him to spare his life and change his death sentence to life in exile. But the king sat there, flanked by his ministers, near the pyre, hard-faced and unmoved as a rock, silently watching Manik's curious behaviour.

Having reached the top of the hill, Manik turned his back to the pyre and walked backwards towards it—he was withdrawing from life, having a last look at it, while his sharati sent its last greetings to his mahadei. He was playing his heart out, piping the most poignant and affecting dirges. The sweet-bitter tunes, tinged with black despair, drew tears of pain from the regretful eyes of the onlookers.

When he arrived at the pyre, Manik set the dry logs on fire, then turned to circle the blazing flames three times. As he began his slow circular motion, the music abruptly changed. His sharati was no longer mournful but festive and triumphant, shaping a new image of Manik, the consummate artist. Having won the love of a queen through an art that was also winning the hearts of all those who had initially come to enjoy the spectacle of his fiery end, Manik was now happy to sacrifice his life.

After he had circled the crackling pyre three times, Manik passed the sharati through the fire three times and then threw it across the pyre another three times. Next, he went to a corner and planted it upside down—a powerful and profound gesture, a denouncement of society and how it had treated him and his art. Then, without further ado, he jumped into the roaring inferno.

All this time, Lieng Makaw had been confined to her room in the palace. Her guards had strict instructions not to let her out of their sight. But the spectacular metamorphosis of Manik, dressed in royal robes and playing what seemed to them a transformed and mesmerising sharati, had caused such a frenzied tumult that all the guards deserted their posts for a glimpse of what they thought was the spectacle of a lifetime.

Lieng Makaw heard the familiar lingering notes of sweet sadness and her heart broke into a dust-devil dance. She moved about the room like a restless spirit, and without knowing why, she found herself putting on her best clothes. When the music stopped as Manik passed out of earshot, she also stopped, wondering fearfully what had happened to him. She was suddenly assailed by an empty feeling, as though everything inside her had been scraped out, leaving her with nothing but a hollow shell. She wailed in despair, 'What use is this cage without its *maina*? Oh, my beloved Manik! I'm coming, I'm coming! Forgive me, my son, my little darling; my mother will look after you, forgive me, my love … Oh, my beloved Manik! I'm coming, I'm coming!'

So saying, Lieng Makaw rushed out, flying like the wind, towards the cremation hill. When she arrived there, almost unnoticed by anyone, Lieng Makaw was in time to see Manik throwing himself into the fire.

'Maniiik!' She let out a shrill, agonised cry, and before anyone could stop her, jumped into the burning pyre to be with the only love of her life.

A deep gloom fell upon the gathering. They had never witnessed such an event, nor known such extraordinary souls before. They dispersed slowly, with a bitter taste in their mouths and an unclean feeling in their hearts.

'Bong leh!' Raji exploded at the end of the story. 'I have never heard the story in such graphic detail before, have you Bah Su?' When Bah Su shook his head, he added, 'I'm sorry I laughed at you, Bah Kynsai. The way Ap told it, okay, proves that I hardly know the story myself, leh.'

'Wrinkle not thy face with too much laughter, lest thou become ridiculous.' Bah Kynsai laughed aloud. 'Thanks for making this fellow eat his own laughter, man,' he said to me.

'But you are wrinkling your own face right now, no, Bah Kynsai?' Raji said.

'This is different, na? He who laughs last, laughs last.'

'Bah Kynsai and his quotations!' Evening laughed.

'Speaking of quotations,' Donald commented, 'how about this one: "To believe heaven fits into hell, that's love, and those who have tasted it, know it"? Isn't this very fitting for the Manik Raitong story?'

'Who said that?' Bah Kynsai asked.

'The dramatist, Lope de Vega, I believe,' Donald replied.

'Yeah, it's quite fitting, no?' Magdalene agreed. 'But I must tell you, Ap, the story made me cry again, man. I also love your description of Manik's music, wonderful!' she added, flashing both thumbs.

'It's a truly, truly moving story, no doubt about it,' Donald reiterated. 'I can easily understand why you said it's the most famous love story among the Khasis, Bah Kit.'

'Yeah, that it is,' Bah Kit agreed. 'Traditionally, ha, Manik Raitong and Lieng Makaw were condemned as adulterers, but the way Ap has told it, no, Don, has transformed them into tragic and heroic figures.'

'Hindus would love this story, liah,' Bah Kynsai said. 'You know why? Because they would take it as an example that sati was practised in these hills, na?'

'No, no, no!' Evening objected firmly. 'This has got nothing to do with sati. It's a matter of love, pure and simple.'

'Okay, Ap, back to Adynga,' Bah Kynsai said. 'I can see why you made the comparison with Manik, but back to Adynga and his love for the two sisters now.'

Adynga and his wives, I told them, were happy, though ostracised and banished, but their happiness did not last long. To begin with, Adynga found that he had suddenly and mysteriously lost his power to move boulders and uproot trees. His infraction had diminished him to the status of an ordinary man with ordinary strength, without, however, an ordinary man's self-esteem. Soon afterwards, Gerjei and Ajei's mother died from the shame and sorrow. His wives asked Adynga to purchase a bull for sacrifice during the funeral rites. However, nobody would sell him one since he was considered uba shong sang, someone guilty of a sacrilegious act.

Adynga had no choice but to travel very far from home to a place where no one had heard of him and his misdeed. He went towards the plains of Assam and stopped at the dwelling of a Nongtrai man by the name of Ara, the founder of Aradonga village. Ara sold him a prime bull. However, on the way to Nonglangsaw, the bull became intractable and ran away into the jungle. Adynga had a tough time finding him and leading him towards the village, and when he finally managed to do so, it was too late. On the way from Langdongdai village to Nongkonghur, he met several people returning from the cremation hill: the body of his sister-cum-mother-in-law had already been cremated. In anger, he beheaded the bull on the spot. Gradually, the bull turned to stone, and came to be known as *mawmasi*, the stone bull.

Frustrated and thwarted at every turn, Adynga directed his steps homeward, a defeated man. But, as he was crossing the River Rdiak, Sangkhni came to drag him away. His body was found by the people of Nonglangsaw three days afterwards, with the ears, eyes, nose and nails missing.

Gerjei and Ajei tried to cope with the tragedy of their husband's death as best they could. One day, as they were sitting on the giant swing Adynga had made for them, the liana rope that bound it was struck by lightning coming out of a clear blue sky, and their bodies were thrown several kilometres into the wilderness.

'And this too, Bah Ap, is a true story?' Donald asked playfully.

'As far as Adynga being the first man in these parts to marry his own nieces, and as far as the manner of their death is concerned, yes. Victor swears by it. Even Perly and Chirag, and in fact everybody here swears by it. But you must have noticed one thing about the Khasis; even when they are telling a true story, they bring in supernatural elements. But then, why fault them? Even Shakespeare was guilty of it.'

Donald was not convinced. 'But this does make some of them hard to believe, doesn't it, Bah Ap? Except, of course, as allegories and parables. And what about Sangkhni? Is that a true story too?'

'Why don't we listen to the story first and then decide whether it's true or not?' Bah Kynsai said. 'The same thing is being debated about Thlen also, na? Chalo, Ap.'

Sangkhni is a river god and the eldest brother of Ñiangriang, a river nymph, who, among other Khasis, is considered a water demon. Many creatures of the river, such as smelts and fishes, are his servants, while others like pangolins, scorpions and snakes are his slaves. Before the covenant between him and man was broken, Sangkhni had a human form and was one of man's most trusted friends, helping him in every way he could. He even upheld the sanctity of human relationships by destroying those who committed sacrilegious crimes like Adynga's. At the time, Sangkhni could not kill a human being without the permission of Ka Lei Sam, the equivalent of Ka Lei Hukum, God as the Goddess of Divine Law. If he did, he would be struck by lightning. But after man violated the covenant, everything changed, and Sangkhni became one of man's worst enemies. Even his appearance altered as he transformed into a creature with the head of a cat and the body of a snake. The head is said to have been about two feet in diameter, the body the size of an elephant whose length was about the width of the River Rdiak, or about eighty yards.

'What is this covenant you are talking about, Ap?' Hamkom asked.

'It's a long story; I'll come to it later,' I said.

'Ap, Victor also spoke of many Sangkhnis, no?' Bah Kit asked.

'That's right. Initially, Victor said, there was only one. But after the violation of the covenant, when Sangkhni became man's enemy, he multiplied like the summer floods, spreading all over the region so he could inflict maximum damage.'

'But when Sangkhni became the enemy of man, what happened to the Sangkhni-men, Ap?' Evening wanted to know. 'Did they continue to kill only those who had committed incest?'

'That's what Victor said.'

'What's the meaning of Sangkhni, anyway? You haven't told us that, na?' Bah Kynsai complained.

'Actually, the name was derived from Adynga and his crime, Bah Kynsai,' Bah Kit explained. 'Adynga was a *khni*, an uncle, ha, who committed a *sang*, or incest, ha, and since the river god killed him because of it, the river god himself became known as Sangkhni. Go on, Ap.'

The covenant between man and Sangkhni, I said, came about because of Stepïong, literally, 'dark morning', a farmer from the village of Nongmyllng. Stepïong had a vegetable field near the River Rdiak, where Sangkhni lived with his sister, Ñiangriang. One day, as the nymph was taking a stroll in the wooded hills and valleys nearby, she came across Stepïong's field and saw mustard leaves and aubergines growing in profusion. The sight made her mouth water. She plucked as many of them as she could and ate them as she ambled along.

When Stepïong visited his field the next day, he discovered the theft. Enraged, he began to keep watch every day, determined to find and punish the thief once and for all. But when, after one week, he finally saw the thief, he did not know what to do. 'Shall I seize and punish her or shall I speak sweet words to her?' he wondered, as he watched Ñiangriang walk among his plants, plucking and eating them with apparent relish. He had never seen such a stunningly beautiful woman before. Stepïong fell in love with her on the spot.

'But still,' he thought, 'she has stolen, *is stealing*, my vegetables; I must do something about it.'

He crept up silently, and as she was bending down to pluck some mustard leaves, bound her flowing hair to the aubergine plants, and said with all the anger he could simulate, 'Aha! Now I've got you, you thieving woman!'

Shocked and trembling with fear, Ñiangriang spun around to see who was calling her a thief. But now it was Stepïong's turn to be shocked. Up close, she was even more dazzlingly beautiful! He gaped at her with his mouth open. When Ñiangriang saw that she had made a conquest, she promptly lost her fear and began in turn to study him. She found herself looking at a tall, well-built man, his handsome face burnt brown by the sun, his features strong and rugged. She liked what she saw very much and said in as pleasing a voice as possible, 'Please forgive me, Bah, I didn't know it was your field. I thought they were wild plants.'

Stepïong was so surprised by that answer that he lost his bashfulness and cried, 'What kind of woman are you if you cannot even tell the difference between vegetables and wild plants?'

'I come from another world; I don't understand your ways. But if you will untie my hair and let me go, I will take you to my brother and he will compensate you for everything.'

'Another world? Who are you? And who is your brother?' Stepïong asked in a puzzled tone.

'Come, I shall tell you on the way.'

As Stepïong followed Ñiangriang down towards the river, he could not help letting his eyes rove hungrily over her body. This was unusual behaviour for him. 'It's an extraordinary dress, indeed,' he said to himself. 'Look at that, only a tight golden blouse and a golden miniskirt, covered by a single jaiñsem as short as the skirt! Unheard of! But who am I to complain? Look at her fair and shapely legs! Could she ever be mine? I'll certainly speak to her brother about it.'

Stepïong kept staring at her legs, which were exposed when her long, glossy hair that partially concealed them parted with every step she took. He blushed with shame but simply could not take his eyes away. It was while he was staring at her like that that he suddenly noticed her feet. They were quite unlike any feet he had seen: their heels were to the front.

'Very strange! What kind of feet are these?' he wondered. But when he took his eyes away from them and back to her legs and sensual body, he thought again, 'Who cares about her feet when she is so divinely lovely?'

And so, the two of them carried on till they reached an enormous pool, dark and deep, in the River Rdiak, known even now as the Stepïong Pool. When they were standing by the edge of the pool, Ñiangriang said, 'Here we are. We have reached my dwelling.'

Stepïong looked around in bewilderment. He could not see any house anywhere. He asked, 'Who are you? You haven't even told me who you are. And your brother, who's he?'

'My name is Ñiangriang; my brother is Sangkhni.'

'What? Sangkhni!'

'Yes, and this is our home, come.'

So saying, Ñiangriang took Stepïong's hand and jumped into the pool. One moment they were in the water and the next they were in front of a beautiful palace made of stone and decorated with gold and all sorts of gemstones. Stepïong stared open-eyed at the wondrous structure, which glittered with a strange light. Then he turned his attention to the surroundings. He saw that the palace was built in the middle of a vast field. Trees and flowers grew all around it, neatly arranged, as if by a master creator. The ground was covered with grass that was more like a green mat. Further afield, he could see birds flitting from tree to tree and deer grazing peacefully. He turned to Ñiangriang and asked in wonder, 'What is this place?'

'This is our home,' she said simply. 'Come. Let's go inside. I'd like you to meet my brother right away.'

But Sangkhni was taking a nap and could not be disturbed. Ñiangriang took Stepïong outside for a walk among the trees, some of which were blooming with flowers while others were heavy with fruits he had never seen before.

As they were strolling along, Stepïong suddenly said, 'But wait, I haven't even introduced myself, how silly of me. I'm—'

'I know, you are Stepïong from Nongmyllng; I have been watching you for a long time. In fact, I was the one tampering with your fish traps and releasing all the fish.'

'Aha, so you were the one! What shall I do with you now?' And to himself, he added, 'No wonder I wasn't able to catch the culprit! How could I, when her feet are back to front like this? I followed the tracks in the wrong direction.' And then, suddenly, a thought occurred to him. 'But why have you been doing that to a poor man like me? I was only trying to earn a living, you know.'

Ñiangriang smiled mysteriously and responded with a question of her own. 'Why should any girl do a silly thing like that?'

'You tell me.'

'Because I wanted to meet you, of course. But when I failed, I started going to your field to feast on your vegetables—'

'Aha, so that entire thing about mistaking them for wild plants was just—'

'A ploy. I hope you are not angry?'

'How could I be? I also followed you not because I wanted compensation from your brother; I wanted to see where you live; I wanted to know you better.'

'So, you too are—'

'Yes, I'm madly in love with you!'

Stepïong moved closer to Ñiangriang, but just then, a servant came to announce that Sangkhni was ready to see them.

Stepïong was asked to wait in a massive hall while Ñiangriang went to speak to Sangkhni alone. After some time, Sangkhni himself appeared before him. Stepïong shivered when he saw him. He was huge, like a giant, and had the imperious appearance of the god that he was. However, Sangkhni's cordial greeting soon dispelled some of Stepïong's fear.

'Khublei, Bah,' Sangkhni greeted him. 'I welcome you to my home. My sister has told me everything. I must apologise to you on her behalf. I'll compensate you for whatever you have lost through her childish actions.'

Stepïong was relieved that Ñiangriang had not told him about their conversation. He said, 'I'm not really angry with her, Pa'iem, you don't have to pay me anything—'

'So why are you here then?' Sangkhni asked him pointedly, but when he saw Stepïong's confusion, he smiled knowingly and added, 'It's all right, I understand. But now that you are here, I'd like to make a pledge with the people of Nongtrai through you … Are you willing to do that?'

'What kind of pledge, Pa'iem?'

'A pledge that will be mutually beneficial.'

Stepïong agreed. 'I'm sure the people will accept and honour the pledge, Pa'iem, as long as it's truly beneficial.'

Sangkhni outlined what he had in mind: 'I will come to your aid whenever you need me. I will help people in every way I can. I will save them from drowning. I will help them when they cross rivers and streams. I will keep human society free from serious crimes like incest and murder, and most important of all, I will ask my most valued assistants, Ki Kharynñiaw, to weed the fields of the Nongtrais so their crops may thrive and flourish. In return, the people of Nongtrai must pledge that they will never destroy my homes or wantonly kill my slaves and servants. Ki Kharynñiaw are especially sacred to me; they must never be harmed in any way. If anyone should harm them, I will visit upon them the worst punishment imaginable. If you agree, we will execute the pledge tomorrow before Ka Lei Sam. I will send a messenger to her immediately. We will seek her permission and plead for her divine presence as a witness to the pledge between us: man and the river spirits. Everything will be done according to the necessary rites and rituals. For tonight, you will stay here and dine with us.'

Ki Kharynñiaw are an extinct species of fish that used to be found in plenty in the River Rdiak. They are so named because their tails resemble the beautifully forked tail of a songbird called *rynñiaw*.

Although he agreed to the pledge, Stepïong did not want to spend the night in the palace. He was in awe of Sangkhni, and the prospect of spending the night under his roof was not a very pleasant one. He said, 'There's nothing more pleasurable than the anticipation of spending the night here with you and your sister, Pa'iem, but I'll have to be back home before sunset. I haven't told my parents anything; they'll be worried about me.'

But Sangkhni said, 'If you don't stay the night, then how will we discuss the matter relating to my sister and you? I'm sure your parents will think you have spent the night at the lengphan, your field hut.'

A blush of embarrassment crept up Stepïong's face. He said, 'Well, I—'

'We will wait for my sister before we talk about it. She's preparing some special dishes for you.'

As they waited for Ñiangriang to finish cooking, they talked of this and that, but especially of matters relating to angling and the various techniques used by man to kill fish, which Sangkhni said were destructive to his homes and must end immediately. Stepïong agreed with him completely, for he too had been very vocal against some of these techniques, especially the poisoning of rivers and streams.

As they chatted, Stepïong lost his awe of Sangkhni a little, and Sangkhni too warmed to him, finding him a sensible young man. Finally, Ñiangriang and the servants appeared with the food, and they all sat cross-legged on a golden mat to enjoy it.

Commending Ñiangriang, Stepïong said, 'This is excellent, the best dinner I have ever had. You are a wonderful cook, Riang.'

Ñiangriang smiled with pleasure. 'Well, if a girl cannot cook, she'd be laughed at by everyone, wouldn't she?'

Sangkhni observed them closely and was pleased to see Stepïong looking at his sister with such adoration. Clearing his throat, he said, 'Ahem, so, Bah Step, my sister has told me everything ... Is it true that you love each other?'

Stepïong readily declared his love for Ñiangriang: 'I love her with all my heart.'

When Ñiangriang made the same declaration, Sangkhni said, 'Then it is settled, I will entrust her welfare to your capable hands. Tomorrow, immediately after the pledge-making ceremony, we will organise your wedding as a symbol that the bond between us has been sealed forever by the fact that now we have become kinsfolk.'

Stepïong was shocked by the suddenness of the proposal. He said, 'Pardon me, Pa'iem, this is a matter of great consequence not only for me but also for my family. I will have to consult my parents—'

'Why? Don't you love her enough?' Sangkhni demanded.

'Of course I love her, Pa'iem, heart and soul, but in our custom, no son or daughter can marry without the prior consent of their parents and their uncles, the khnis and burangs. I will have to consult my parents to seek their blessings, and my uncles will have to meet you and Riang to arrange for my wedding—'

'But this is a matter between the two of you, what have your relatives got to do with it?' Sangkhni asked in a displeased tone. To his mind, the wedding would be an excellent symbolic conclusion to the pledge between the river spirits and man, but this fellow seemed bent on thwarting his wishes. He simply could not understand it.

Stepïong, on his part, could not imagine marrying anyone, not even his beloved Ñiangriang, without the knowledge of his parents. Such was his upbringing that even the mere suggestion of such a thing was deeply shocking. Sticking to his position, he said, 'Pa'iem, we Nongtrais follow the custom of always respecting our maternal and paternal relations. A wedding is such an important occasion that every one of our relations must be involved. But above all, we believe our parents are God's representatives on earth; to turn away from them is to turn away from God himself. Please, Pa'iem, allow me to go back home and inform my family of this matter. I love your sister very much. I promise to come back with my family to marry her.'

After much persuasion, Sangkhni reluctantly agreed to postpone the wedding. Ñiangriang was terribly upset and fled from the room without a word to Stepïong. However, he just would not change his mind. The idea was too foreign to him.

The next morning, the pledge was executed between Sangkhni, on behalf of the river spirits, and Stepïong, on man's behalf, in the presence of Ka Lei Sam. The agreement outlined the previous evening was repeated aloud to the gathering, and as a token that it had been made willingly by both parties, two monoliths were planted, one on each side of the River Rdiak. At the end of the ceremony, a big feast was held, and cultural events, including Ka Shad Ai Ïaw Rei, the peace-making dance, were organised. During the dance, people in the crowd embraced each other, saying repeatedly, '*ai ïaw rei, ai ïaw rei*', till all anger and ill will were purged.

After the function was over, Stepïong went back to Sangkhni's home to say goodbye to Ñiangriang, who had left the scene of festivity a little earlier. She made him promise to come back to her as soon as possible, and before letting him go, packed for him the food he had loved so much, so he could share it with his family.

On reaching his village, Stepïong first went to the headman to tell him of the pledge made between him and Sangkhni. The headman and his council of elders readily agreed to it and promptly had it announced throughout the length and breadth of Ri Nongtrai and the adjoining regions. The announcement especially forbade the killing of any Kharynñiaw fish from the River Rdiak.

After having discharged his civic duty, Stepïong went home and excitedly told his family all that had happened to him. He also gave them the packed food, which he said was the most delicious in all the world. His mother opened the leaf packet, but instead of the delicacies that Stepïong had bragged about, she found only pebbles and sand and pieces of bark in it. She looked strangely at him and said, 'Step, what is wrong with you, are you mad? Why do you call this rubbish the best food you have ever had?'

'Why do you condemn the food my beloved specially prepared for me with such harsh words, Mei?' Stepïong asked in a hurt tone.

'Well, what do you want me to say to all this, then? See for yourself.'

When Stepïong saw the pebbles and sand and pieces of bark in the packet, he was dumbfounded. Shaking his head in disbelief, he said, 'But it really was the best feast I ever had, Mei, I swear it was!'

His mother did not say anything more. She only told him to go to bed, for he looked quite exhausted.

In the middle of the night, Stepïong developed a very high fever, throwing the whole family into a state of panic. They fed him the juice of several herbs, put wet rags on his forehead and did everything to control his fever and save him. But nothing helped. Stepïong tossed and turned, moaning in agony, and only asked for Ñiangriang all the time. Shamans were called to break eggs and perform divination ceremonies all night, but his fever did not subside.

In fact, it became worse the next morning. The family tried everything that was suggested to them, but his condition did not improve. The young man hovered between life and death for several weeks. At last, they sent for a renowned shaman from a distant village. After sacrificing a rooster and inspecting his entrails, the shaman told the family that Stepïong had trespassed into the world of the spirits. Since this had taken place at the River Rdiak, the only cure for him, he said, was to drink the water from the very pool where he had committed the transgression. The water, he said, must be collected by someone at the crack of dawn before that person had washed his face or spoken to anyone.

Stepïong's elder brother was sent to collect the water, and true to the shaman's words, as soon as Stepïong had taken a few sips of the water, his fever began to gradually subside. So remarkable was his improvement that, within a week, he was back on his feet, though still very weak.

Fearing that Stepïong might go back to the River Rdiak, his family called for a clan meeting and unanimously resolved never to let him go anywhere near the river again. They took away his farm by the river and gave him another

plot far away. When Stepïong protested and said that he had to go back to
Ñiangriang, whom he loved with all his heart and whom he had promised to
marry, they responded, 'How can you, a mere mortal, marry a river nymph?
How can we let you go and live with them to eat pebbles and sand and pieces
of bark? Have you forgotten your illness and why it happened? Do you want
to go back to your death? We will never let you go. Your uncles have already
picked a beautiful woman for you to marry within a week. For your own sake,
all our male relatives will be staying here to stop you from going to the river.'

And so, Stepïong's dream of marrying Ñiangriang, the divinely lovely
river nymph, came to nothing, all because—

'All because he did not value his love more than his life, the son of a bitch!'
Magdalene broke in angrily.

All of us laughed at her outburst, except Donald, who agreed with her.

Raji teased them: 'If you two are so angry with Stepïong, can you imagine
how Sangkhni must have felt?'

'Burning with rage, of course!' Magdalene replied.

Sangkhni did burn with rage when Stepïong did not return as promised.
After months of waiting, he raged and ranted alone in his palace: 'The son
of a cheat! The son of a rogue! The despicable double-dealer! She dares toy
with me, me, a river god? She is not a man; she should wear a jaiñsem like
a woman! The son of a low-born clan! Wait, wait till I get my hands on him
and his kind!'

His sister, however, reminded him of the pledge. 'I am the one who's
suffering the most because of that shameless betrayer! But his promise to
marry me is not part of the pledge, Bah. If you move against him or any of
his kinsfolk, Ka Lei Sam will strike you down with lightning. Think carefully,
Bah, before you act. Do not let anger cloud your mind.'

Sangkhni was quiet for a while and then said, 'You are right, of course,
Hep, but I will prepare for the time when this traitor and his descendants
do violate the pledge … Right now, we are confined to Rdiak, but shortly I
will send my children and grandchildren and all my relatives out to every
nook and cranny of Nongtrai. I'll be prepared to pounce upon all humans
the moment the pledge is violated … May it please God that they do it soon!
My punishment will be terrible! I will change my shape at will to confuse
these humans. I will turn into a cat, a snake, a buffalo, even a log spanning
across the rivers. And when they least expect it, I will strike. I will tunnel into
the earth; I will cause floods and turn villages into lakes. Once the pledge is
violated, I will not spare anyone!'

The violation of the pledge, however, did not happen during Stepïong's lifetime, because he kept reminding people about it. As a matter of fact, it did not happen for hundreds of years after his death. Sangkhni had to wait a very long time indeed for his revenge.

But eventually, it did come to pass. Many, many years after the death of Stepïong, one of his descendants went to farm on the left bank of the Rdiak. After slashing and burning the jungle, Jang and his wife, Jynnam, planted rice, millet, Job's tears and vegetables like pumpkin, cucumber, aubergines, mustard leaves, chillies, radish and sesame. Their crops thrived and flourished, as Sangkhni had promised, for his Kharynñiaw fish went there at least once a week to weed the fields and keep them free of any unwanted plants.

One day, Jang and Jynnam, who was pregnant at the time, went to the farm much earlier than they usually did, as they planned to return home immediately after they had eaten their lunch. When they arrived, an amazing sight awaited them. They saw hundreds of Kharynñiaw fish busy weeding their fields. Jynnam, who was some months into her pregnancy, suddenly developed a craving for their meat. She said to Jang, 'Kpa, I want to eat some of these fish, why don't you catch them? Please, kpa, please, will you do it for me? I'd like to cook them with chillies in a bamboo tube ... They'll taste wonderful!'

But Jang remembered the pledge and said, 'How can we catch and cook them when the pledge has forbidden us to do so?'

'Think of what will happen to the baby in the womb if you don't give me what I want!' Jynnam said petulantly. 'Do you want the baby to be deformed because my craving is not satisfied?'

Jang was in a dilemma. He did not want the baby to be deformed in any way, but he also dreaded the thought of what would happen if the pledge with Sangkhni, witnessed by Ka Lei Sam herself, was broken. He said, 'Wait, let me ask for special permission from the river god,' and so saying, he prayed aloud to Sangkhni to allow him and his wife to kill a few of the Kharynñiaw fish since a pregnant woman's craving had to be satisfied.

Sher, a little fish, smaller than a smelt, who was acting as the Kharynñiaws' attendant at Sangkhni's behest, immediately went to report the matter to Sangkhni. Rumbling with rage, he told Sher to direct the farmers not to touch a single one of them, for they were sacred to him.

Jang was now at his wits' end. While Sangkhni had forbidden him to kill his servants, his wife was forcing him to do so. While he was standing there, not knowing what to do, Jynnam, annoyed by her husband's indecision, took matters into her own hands and began knocking down the Kharynñiaw fish with the top edge of her curved machete. Putting them in the conical basket she was carrying on her back, she called out to Jang, ordering him to help her. When Jang saw what was happening, instead of stopping her, he joined her in the killing. 'If one fish has been killed, many more might as well be killed,' he thought. And so, together, they began killing in earnest. His wife was especially bloodthirsty. She told him: 'Let's kill them all. We'll organise a big feast in the village; we'll be famous, nobody has ever tasted Kharynñiaw before.'

When he saw what was happening, Sher, crying and heartbroken, fled for his life. The old ones used to say that the spots on his back were the tears of anguish that drenched him when Jang and Jynnam slaughtered the Kharynñiaw fish.

On reaching his master's house, crying and sobbing, Sher recounted the whole tragic tale to him. He described the greed and cruelty of the woman, who had started the massacre, and the hypocrisy of the man who had assisted her in the wanton killing.

Sangkhni's rage was a terrible thing to see. He gave out a mighty roar that caused hills and mountains to tremble and rivers and lakes to surge with giant waves. He had hoped that, one day, humans would violate the pledge by killing one of his sacred Kharynñiaw fish so that he could exact revenge on them for Stepïong's betrayal, but even in his wildest dreams he had never imagined they would dare wipe them all out in one fell swoop. He summoned all his relatives, servants and slaves for an assembly in the great hall of the palace and told them to stop their loud lament. Their brothers and sisters, Ki Kharynñiaw, he said, would not be avenged by useless weeping and howling. What they needed to do was to compose themselves and work out a practical course of punitive action.

Addressing them, he said, 'This is what I will do. I will slay Jynnam and her unborn child, and I will crush Jang to a pulpy mash! But I need to know who else feasted on my beloved assistants. Sher will go to find out. If the entire village of Nongmyllng is guilty of breaking the pledge, I will wipe it out once and for all! I will tunnel the earth below it; I will create a crater beneath the houses; I will pull them and all the people in them into it; I will flood it with water from the Rdiak; I will turn the entire village into a lake! I will give them a real reason for calling it Nongmyllng, the "lake village". And if there is anyone else, outside the village, who is guilty, that person and his entire household will be destroyed. Your duty, my children and relatives, is to pull everyone down into the flooded crater, so no one escapes our punishment. And you, little fishes, the weakest and smallest of my servants, you will nibble on their eyes, ears and noses, you will pull out their nails, and thus you will show the people of Nongtrai how I have punished these betrayers. Now, Sher, go to Nongmyllng and find out the truth.'

Sher arrived at Nongmyllng towards evening. He went to watch the village from a vantage point near a spring to which all the villagers came to fetch drinking water. He saw many people coming and going, and all of them had the smell of Kharynñiaw fish on them. Even their pots, when dipped in the water, were greasy with Kharynñiaw fat. Only one old woman by the name of Ganda was free from the Kharynñiaw smell. Knowing that the woman was innocent, Sher came out of hiding and spoke to her.

The woman told him, 'No, my son, I did not eat any of the Kharynñiaw fish. I'm only a slave at the house of Jang and Jynnam; I was not given any of the meat. But even if I had, I would not have taken it. I hold the pledge between Sangkhni and the Nongtrais as sacred as the covenant between man and God himself—'

'Tell me, old mother,' Sher interrupted her, 'how come you to be a slave? I thought you people believe in the divine law of the Three Commandments that enjoin you to earn virtue in life and to always live in the knowledge of man and God and the knowledge of maternal and paternal relations. So how can such people have slaves? That is against the implied teaching of the Commandments, is it not?'

'It is, my son, but our people also believe in the sanctity of the word. When my grandmother died, my parents did not have enough rice to swap for a bull for the sacrificial rites. They borrowed from Jynnam's grandmother, but when they could not repay the loan, I was given to the family as a slave.'

Sher felt pity for the old woman, who told him that Jynnam and Jang were terrible masters, overworking her, beating her often, and feeding her only leftovers and rotten food. He asked her if he could trust her, and when the old woman gave him her word of honour, he told her that Sangkhni was going to destroy the entire village of Nongmyllng since everyone in it had feasted on creatures sacred to him. He instructed her to leave the village immediately after the first cockcrow but warned her not to reveal the secret to anyone, lest Sangkhni's wrath should fall on her too. Before he left, Sher asked her if anyone else from outside the village had participated in the feast.

The old woman thanked him for taking pity on her. To his question, she said, 'Only one woman from a village near the River Randi. She also took away a packet of Kharynñiaw for her family. Her name is Synnup.'

After Sher left, the old woman walked homewards, filled with anxiety and dread. That night, she did not sleep a wink, fearing that she might oversleep and die with the others. She did not pity the villagers, who had all been unkind to her. Besides, they had violated the pledge, and to her mind, the wrath of the river god was just punishment. However, she could not leave Jynnam's two-year-old son to his doom. 'The poor little soul,' she said to herself, 'knows nothing about his parents' transgression. I will take him with me and save him at least.'

By the first cockcrow, Ganda, the old woman, was already out of the house with the baby. By the second, she was on top of the highest hill that overlooked the tableland where the village was. And as she stood there watching the sleeping houses and the place which had been her unhappy home for so many years, trying to make up her mind in which direction to go, she heard a tremendous explosion the like of which she had never experienced in her life. It shook the very ground beneath her feet, and she was thrown violently into the bushes by the force of it. Miraculously, she found the wailing baby still firmly clutched in her arms. When she was able to stand again, Ganda looked down at the village and found that the tableland, with all the houses in it, had vanished into a gigantic crater, flooding before her very eyes with swirling red water.

Shocked, the old woman exclaimed, 'Oh my God, oh my God! Water on top of a hill! From where did it come?'

As she stood there, watching the scene in horror, a torrential downpour began. Covering the baby with her shawl, she ran towards the surrounding jungle to seek shelter among the trees, like an animal. But she could not stay there forever. There was nothing there to live on, and after what she had seen of his terrible power, the fear of Sangkhni struck panic into her soul despite Sher's assurance that she would not be harmed. 'Where can I go?' she asked herself. Eventually, she came to a decision. 'Anywhere, but far away from Rdiak. Let God, the Dispenser, the Creator, guide my feet to a human settlement.'

Trusting in God's mercy, the old woman walked away from that place of horror, enduring the driving rain and trying to avoid wild animals by keeping to higher ground and hill slopes. She walked like that for many days, resting among the trees, eating only herbs, which she also fed the baby after chewing them to a soft, wet mass. When the baby cried and demanded milk, she gave him her withered breasts to suck on. A hard time she had of it: the rain, the cold, the hunger, the fear of animals and the leeches that clung to her by the dozens made her wild wandering one of unrelieved misery. But finally, by the grace of God, as she firmly believed, she reached a village nesting on a tree-covered plateau overlooking the River Randi, where she was given food and shelter and was cared for till she finally made a full recovery.

Unfortunately for her, this village happened to be the one where Synnup lived. It was not long before Sangkhni reached the area and identified Synnup's house. He dug a crater beneath it, and one night, while everyone was sleeping, pulled the house and everything in it into the crater, which he flooded with water from the River Randi. The booming explosion caused by the destruction brought the entire village to the spot. There they saw a large crater filled to the brim with swirling red water that was swallowing up everything—house, sheds, people and animals—till no sign of them was left anywhere. What they had found so hard to believe in Ganda's story about Nongmyllng was happening right before their eyes.

The inhabitants panicked, and although none of them had eaten the Kharynñiaw fish and violated the pledge, they were sure that Sangkhni would come back and drag their village into the quagmire of mud and churning water as he had done with Synnup's house. The very next day, except for half a dozen families, everyone shifted out. Those who remained believed Ganda's assurances that Sangkhni would not harm them since they had not harmed the creatures sacred to him. Ganda stayed behind with these families and raised the baby till he grew up into a strong and hard-working young man. And because Ganda had stayed on, the place came to be known as Nong-Ganda, the Village of Ganda. But not long after she and the older generation died, the younger folk left to live in a more prosperous village nearby. Nong-Ganda has been a deserted village ever since.

At this point, Magdalene cut in to say, 'This story is absurd, Ap. I mean, why should that Jynnam woman want to kill the Kharynñiaw fish? Just imagine, wouldn't the sight of fish weeding their farm be a wonderful and miraculous thing? Wouldn't it fill anyone with awe and reverence? But that woman only wanted to kill and eat them, isn't that incredible? And why should she want to destroy creatures that were keeping her farm weed-free and helping her crops grow and flourish?'

'She was a pregnant woman, remember? Pregnant women do have unreasonable cravings, no?' Raji said.

Magdalene was about to respond when Evening said, 'You cannot blame it on her pregnancy alone, Raji. She wanted to kill every one of them, okay, not just a few, to eat and satisfy her craving, but every one of them, so she could hold a feast and enhance her reputation in the village. That's greed, man, greed, plain and simple!'

'You people forget that this is a fairy tale; you cannot look for credibility or logic in such a story, no?' Hamkom asserted.

'That's the point I made earlier, Ham, when I asked whether the Sangkhni story is true or not—'

'No, no, no, Don, it cannot be a true story,' Hamkom said emphatically. 'How can it be?'

'I think it's much more than a fairy tale, Ham,' Bah Kit protested. 'People here actually believe in the existence of Sangkhni. When their makeshift bamboo bridges are carried away by the summer floods, ha, they say it's the work of Sangkhni, since he has the power to increase or decrease the volume of water at will. And when people drown, they say it's because they have been dragged into the water by Sangkhni, who has become man's enemy since the violation of the pledge. It's like our Thlen story, no? Many people say it's only a fairy tale, but many more believe in his actual existence.'

'Hey, hey, what about my questions?' Magdalene cried.

'I'll answer your questions, Mag,' Bah Kynsai offered. 'As I see it, na, the story is definitely more than a fairy tale, but not because people believe in it. It's like a parable with a profound moral lesson, na? Mag asked us why Jynnam did not find the sight of fish weeding her fields miraculous. That's simple. It reflects man's loss of faith in God and the supernatural. Then she asked why Jynnam would kill creatures who were helping her crops grow and flourish. That one, na, has a profound thought behind it. It reflects the very nature of man. What kind of creature is man? He's the most ungrateful being on earth; he will even bite the hand that feeds him. Now, think of mother earth and what we are doing to it … Isn't that the same? And why are we doing it? Need is one of the reasons, that's true, but is it need alone? No, my friends, as Ning said, it's greed with a capital G. We are never content with satisfying our needs alone, we always have to get more, more than we need, because we want to show off our possessions to the world. Vanity, that's what it is! But there's one more reason why Jynnam killed the fish— bloodthirstiness. Man is a natural-born killer … Hey, Ap, what is that poem we read the other day?'

'Killer Instincts.'

'Yeah, yeah, this guy in the poem, na, he is asked by his relatives not to kill anything because his wife is pregnant. Khasis believe that if you kill anything when your wife is pregnant, ha, the child will become deformed in some way. Now, this fellow sees geckos scouring the walls, rats scouring the kitchen, and spiders and mosquitoes everywhere pestering his sleep, okay? So what does he say? "For nine long months, it was maddening not to be a killer!" You see, man is an instinctive killer! And because of all the repulsive qualities in his heart—monstrous ungratefulness, greed, vanity, bloodthirstiness—man is also suicidal. He destroys the very place where he lives. And when he has finished with it, na, he will finish himself off, mark my words. That's why this story is more than a fairy tale.'

'But Bah Kynsai, human nature is also more than this, no?' Hamkom countered.

'That's true, but mankind is primarily dominated by these impulses, na, or at least, that's what this story is trying to say.'

'Victor also believes that Sangkhni is part-real and part-parable,' I said.

'Why?' Hamkom asked.

'According to him, the creature has been spotted many times over the centuries. Sangkhni bodies have also been found after they were struck by lightning. The other reason is that the Nongtrais—before the pledge was violated—used to call on him for help whenever they found themselves in any difficulty. For instance, when they got stuck on one side of an overflowing river, they used to call on him, and soon a *diengpun,* a bridging log, would appear out of nowhere and enable them to cross the river—'

'And what do their bodies look like, Bah Ap?' Donald asked.

'From Victor's description, it sounds to me like an anaconda, or some sort of a giant snake. But we must keep in mind that Sangkhni can assume many forms—'

'What about him as a parable?' Donald asked again.

'According to Victor, the Sangkhni lore is partly a parable because of what the river god himself said soon after the destruction of Nongmyllng and Synnup's house.

'Soliloquising, Sangkhni said, "I had thought the destruction of Nongmyllng and the slaying of Synnup and her family would satisfy my vengeful anger, but no, I find myself more and more hating all humans ... Every one of them seems to be reeking of the smell of Kharynñiaw. I thirst for their treacherous blood. No one can stop me now; they were the ones who violated the pledge. I have been destroying all their bamboo bridges; killing anyone who crosses rivers; killing as a snake, a buffalo, a cat and a diengpun. But killing one or two here and there is no longer enough—'"

'How can he kill in the form of a cat or a bridging log?' Hamkom interrupted.

'As a cat, he can enter people's homes easily and kill them by assuming other forms. As a bridging log, he can lure people to walk on him and throw them into the raging floods. But Sangkhni was not content with that any more. He said, "From now on, I will also assume the form of a human, for it is as a human that I can do the maximum damage to humans, that I can do the maximum damage to their dwellings, their fields and farms, their streams and rivers, their woods and forests, their hills and valleys. I will be a timber trader and destroy their forests and denude their mountains. I will be a surveyor and look for the most precious minerals, and as a mine owner, I will dig up hills and valleys and destroy them along with their rivers and streams, their fields and farms. But most of all, because, of all humans, I hate the Nongtrais the most, I will be a local guide, I will bring my relatives from faraway places, I will tell them to assume a human form. I will show them where to settle, farm, trade, mine, and how to exploit the locals by marrying their daughters, the keepers of their wealth, so all of it can be siphoned off to me and my kinsfolk. I will do all that and slowly we will overwhelm the Nongtrais, destroy their culture, their livelihood, and wipe them off the face of the earth."'

'Bong leh, Ap, this is a deadly story, man!' Bah Kynsai exclaimed. 'See, it's saying that all the evil in this world, na, happens because of man's own fault. Sangkhni was man's friend, but he became an enemy; he was a helper but became man's destroyer; he was a protector but became an exploiter, all because of man's own fault. Now, think about these evils—the destruction of forests, animals, water bodies and aquatic life, the death of rivers and streams, the loss of drinking water, the destruction of cultivable land, air pollution, and the slow killing of the atmosphere—all these evils, na, are not because of outside agents but man's own doing. That's why Sangkhni says he will assume a human form. The greatest enemy of man is man, and the greatest destroyer of the planet is also man!'

'It does sound a lot like the message of the Thlen story, no?' Raji remarked.

'There are similarities,' I agreed. 'For instance, the emphasis on the evil in man's heart is the same. But one of the most important morals in the Sangkhni story is the warning against the influx of outsiders, their exploitation of local resources and their complete domination of the area. The symbolism of Thlen carries a very different warning—'

'Come on, Bah Ap, this will not do at all,' Donald complained, 'you cannot talk about the symbolism of Thlen without first giving us the story!'

'Okay, okay, with Bah Kynsai's permission …'

'Are you trying to be like drunken Raji or what?' Bah Kynsai asked.

Before I could reply, Raji said, 'I'm not drunk yet, Bah Kynsai, but I will be, I'll make sure of it, after all, this is our last night here, no?'

'And after that, you'll be as shameless as—'

'After that, you'll be snoring like an auto-rickshaw, Bah Kynsai. I'm taking it easy now, but later, I'll go to one of the bonfires and show the Lyngngams who's the best drinker—'

'Whatever you do, don't cause another scandal, ha, liah?' Bah Kynsai warned.

'Are they drinking or what, the Lyngngams?' Evening asked.

'Of course, what else will they do through the night? They drink and tell stories like us—'

'Only one or two, Raji, not all, and outside the death house,' Bah Su said emphatically.

'Of course outside, no one would dare drink inside, no? But how do you know only one or two are drinking?'

'I went out earlier, remember? I spoke to them—'

'Well, okay, I'll go and make it three or four then!'

'You do whatever you like, just remember what I told you, otherwise I'll personally shave off your beard,' Bah Kynsai threatened.

'Not my beard, please, Bah Kynsai, anything but my beard!' Raji said, raising his hands in fake horror.

'You would look more handsome, Raji. Seriously, right now, na, you look like an ISIS fighter,' Bah Kynsai teased him.

Raji did not respond. He was listening intently to the sounds outside. 'But how come we are not hearing any Hindi film songs?'

'Why should we?' Bah Kynsai asked.

'Someone told me that in Lyngngam, okay, people sing hymns when going to the cemetery, but Hindi film songs when returning,' Raji said seriously.

'Tet leh, Raji!' Evening protested.

The rest, however, laughed and said, 'It must be a joke, ya.'

Bah Kynsai agreed. 'It is a joke. I've heard it before. Well, Ap, when are you going to tell us the damn Thlen story?'

The legend of Thlen, swallower of humans, lives on to this day, and people speak of this man-eating, bloodsucking serpent as they would of the plague, cancer, tuberculosis, or any other killer disease. That is what this monster represents now: the cause of a deadly illness where a person loses his natural colour and grows thin and weak except for his bloated face and belly. They say the keepers of this creature and the killers in their employment, whose business it is to hunt men for their blood, are still very active in some parts of the Khasi Hills.

At first, Thlen did not need a keeper or a hunter to feed him with the blood of humans. But the story of how he metamorphosed from a man-eater into a blood-drinker and a dependent creature lies somewhere in the dim past, when man was still rubbing shoulders with the spirits.

According to the legend, Thlen was an evil creature with supernatural powers, who lived in the wilderness of Sohra. In those days, it was said, he could change his shape and size at will. His favourite form, however, was that of a gigantic python lying with his enormous mouth open in a cave at Pomdoloi Falls, in the western fringe of Sohra, his tail tapering off towards Iingkhrong, some kilometres away in Sohra proper. But how did Thlen come to live in that tunnel? Where did he come from?

Thlen's origin is traced to dubious though superhuman parentage. He was the son of Ka Kma Kharai, depraved daughter of U Mawlong Syiem, the chief god of the area around Mawsmai, to the south of Sohra.

Ka Kma Kharai herself was a spirit presiding over caves and trenches, but her name was associated with such licentious and immoral living that she was shunned by all the gods, except the most inferior and malicious in their world. Having led a debauched life and degenerated into an evil spirit, Ka Kma Kharai was cursed with a bastard, a deformed demon whose birth so roused the wrath of her father that she had to flee and look for a new place to settle. At last, she came towards the northern territory of Sohra and decided to make its beautiful gorges her permanent home. But, a harlot by nature, she soon found her child a burden and tucked him away in a cave near the Pomdoloi Falls.

Ka Kma Kharai chose the cave for a reason. Being a malignant spirit, an enemy of mankind, she was determined that her son should grow up on nothing but human flesh. The cave was ideal as it lay on the route to Rangjyrteh, which, as you know, was a large town to the west of Sohra and had the biggest and most popular marketplace in the Khasi Hills in those days.

It was Thlen's practice to lie in wait for passers-by, and whenever they came through in groups of three, five or seven, he would suck in the straggler and swallow him whole. And that was how he earned his name: by the manner of his feeding. He could polish off a full-grown man in a matter of minutes, leaving not a trace behind.

The first man to vanish was a trader from Sylhet—a Shilotia, as the Khasis described him. The market-goers and traders in the area, from Rangjyrteh to Sylhet, organised a big search party around the Pomdoloi Falls. They searched for weeks, but instead of finding the man, or at least recovering his body for the funeral rites, more and more men were reported missing from the search party itself. This so alarmed the searchers that they gave up and went to the augurs to seek from God the reason for this strange and evil phenomenon.

God, who saw everything and who understood that Thlen intended to wipe out the human race from these beautiful hills, revealed to the augurs the cause of the mysterious disappearances and directed them, through signs and symbols, to seek the help of U Syiem Syrmoh in the avatar of Suidnoh. Suidnoh had many other manifestations too. Throughout the length and breadth of Ri Khasi, he was prayed to as U Syiem Kyrsan, the chief of all the guardian spirits and the restorer of health and virtue. His favourite haunt was believed to be the sanctified grove of Laitryngew, to the north of Sohra, known as Ka Law Suidnoh, whose fame as a holy place was such that even the Shilotias used to come and perform their religious rites there.

The augurs invoked Suidnoh with many offerings and sacrifices, painting a vivid picture of Thlen's cruelty and ardently pleading with him to end the malevolent creature's savage onslaught on humankind. As the restorer of health and virtue in the world, Suidnoh could not ignore their plea or tolerate Thlen's monstrous deeds. He readily agreed to help and showed them signs, urging them not to lose hope.

Having committed to the task, Suidnoh, appearing in human form, made his first stop at the house of the chief priest of Law Suidnoh. He commanded the priest to build a smithy some distance from Thlen's cave and there to make a huge iron ball and a pair of giant tongs. When the implements had been readied, Suidnoh waited for the next market day at Ïewbah Sohra before approaching Thlen and greeting him like a long-lost friend. There was nothing unusual about this, for the two knew each other well, both being from the spirit world.

'How are you, *Um*?' Suidnoh called out to Thlen, referring to him as brother-in-law, not because they were related, but merely as a show of respect. 'It's been a long time since we met, ha, Um?'

'I know, Um, I know,' Thlen replied from his hole. 'It's been ages, in fact, since I last set eyes on you.'

'I'm on my way to the market of the gods at Ïewbah Sohra. Would you care for something to eat, Um?' Suidnoh offered.

'I wouldn't mind, Um, I wouldn't mind at all,' Thlen said. 'Only, make sure you bring me a piece of that famous Sohra pork, I have grown a little sick of human flesh lately.'

Suidnoh took his leave of Thlen and went back to the smithy, happy to have set his plan in motion. He ordered the priest to heat the iron ball to the highest degree possible.

Towards evening, when the iron ball had turned white-hot, Suidnoh went back to Thlen's cave, carrying the ball of iron between the giant tongs, and said, 'Ahoy, Um! I have brought you the pork. Open up, Um, open your mouth; it's a rather large piece.'

Thlen, who had grown enormously fat from eating so much human flesh, had become rather sluggish and did not stir from his cave, neither did he have reason to suspect that anything was amiss. Thanking Suidnoh for keeping his promise, he opened his mouth to swallow the pork in one gulp. But Suidnoh was not satisfied. He said, 'Open up some more, Um, open up some more … It's larger than you think.'

Thlen opened his jaws wide, till they entirely shut out his eyes. That was the moment Suidnoh was waiting for. With a mighty thrust, he shoved the burning-hot iron ball down Thlen's throat and promptly left the spot. The ball burnt up Thlen's insides, and he began to writhe and squirm and thrash about with such violence that his movements caused the earth to quake all across Sohra and the surrounding country.

So powerful were his death throes that they made deep cracks in the land and created one of the most famous gorges in Sohra. This later came to be called Ka Riat Mawïew. The hour of his death was quite traumatic for the people in the area: the earth shook, hills came tumbling down, houses and all, and the air was filled with so much debris that the sun was completely blotted out. Fortunately for them, the quake did not last long—the iron burnt quickly through Thlen's vital parts and he died soon after.

After Thlen's death, Suidnoh directed the chief priest of Law Suidnoh to call all the people from around Sohra, and those from Sylhet who were looking for their missing relatives in the area, to gather by the river near Thlen's cave the very next day. Suidnoh said the monster's flesh must be cooked and consumed by all those who had been tyrannised by him directly or indirectly, and all of it had to be eaten within a single day, at the exact spot where he had been killed. Not even a tiny bit of the flesh, he said, should be taken anywhere else or left for another day. He offered no explanation—only a warning that his instructions should be obeyed strictly if they really wanted to be rid of the evil creature forever.

The people obeyed his call. They converged upon the sinister cave, hauled Thlen's body from his lair and cut it into pieces, cooking the portions that could be eaten in large cauldrons and burning to ashes all the rest: skin, bones and every other part that was not edible. They celebrated the end of his tyranny on a grand scale, with rice beer and rice spirit flowing freely to kill whatever reluctance they may have felt about making a hearty meal of the creature's flesh. Appetite thus roused, one and all, young and old, ate to their hearts' content, leaving not a morsel anywhere.

After the feast, the gathering broke up and all went their separate ways, except for the local elders, who stayed behind to complete the ritual part and pay obeisance to God, the Dispenser, the Creator. They carved out on the rocks the figure of Thlen, the serpent, and all the cooking articles used in the feast, to enable future generations to learn the story of the demonic creature. Before leaving the place, they renamed Pomdoloi Falls as Kshaid Daiñthlen or Daiñthlen Falls, meaning the place where Thlen was killed and carved up.

Unknown to the revellers, an old woman had kept back a bite of the serpent flesh for one of her sons who could not attend the feast. At home, she put the meat in a basket where she kept dried fish, intending to give it to him as soon as he returned home. However, as if confounded by some mysterious power, the woman kept forgetting about it, until one day, when she was alone, the piece of flesh called out to her: 'Old woman, keep me and I will make you rich. I have the power to give you all the gold and silver in the world. Keep me, and I will make you prosper in everything that you do.'

The old woman turned towards the basket and saw a small snake looking at her and talking to her as if it were a human being. She suddenly remembered the piece of flesh and understood what was happening. Thlen had been resurrected. That was why Suidnoh had been so particular that the last of the creature's flesh be consumed.

But now Thlen was in her house. The old woman was gripped by a feeling of great dread and would have rushed out of the house had Thlen not spoken again.

'I have promised you riches, old woman, but think carefully about what will happen to you if you inform on me. You are as much an enemy of mankind as I am, for you have given me back my life.'

That stopped the woman. She knew only too well what would happen to her if the people discovered her error. She would be stoned to death. On the other hand, if she kept Thlen a secret, there were all those riches ... The thought tilted her mind in favour of preserving the demon.

Thlen, on his part, made her wealthy and prosperous, as promised. Then, one day, when he thought he had finally won her over, he called out again: 'Old woman, look, I have made you prosperous and given you whatever you wanted. Now return my favour. Bring me a *lang-thoh-khlieh* so I can eat too.'

The old woman brought him a goat with markings on its head. But instead of being pleased, Thlen thundered, 'I asked you to bring me a goat with a spotted head, what animal is this you have brought? Bring me someone like you.'

When the old woman understood that by lang-thoh-khlieh he was euphemistically referring to humans to eat, and not to a real 'goat with a spotted head', she trembled from head to foot and replied, 'Forgive me, my Lord, but from where will I get humans for you to eat? They surely won't come by themselves?'

'That is your business,' Thlen replied sternly. 'But if you don't do as I say, I shall begin feasting on your family.'

A couple of days later, the old woman found that her daughter's youngest son had died for no apparent reason. Now thoroughly frightened, the woman began to look around for desperate men who would kill for money and bring back the blood of the victim so she could feed it to her serpent. The task was not easy since Thlen refused to accept anything but Khasi blood, saying, 'They tried to destroy me ... It is no longer a simple matter of feeding on humans ... My thirst is for Khasi blood alone.'

This is how the practice of hiring paid killers, or nongshohnohs, for Thlen came to be. The old woman used kyiad tangsnem, the special brew of rice spirit, to spur on the killers and to render them ruthless and utterly devoid of conscience, so that a human would seem to them no more than a flitting butterfly. In this way, the old woman and her children propagated the practice of keeping Thlen for riches until it grew into a prevalent evil practice in some parts of Ri Khasi, notably Ri Sohra.

It is said that Thlen punishes the keepers who cannot keep him fed by killing one or two of their children and also by shaming them before the world by climbing onto rooftops and assuming the form of a cat, a smelt or any other animal. The keepers, on their part, try to keep him happy by offering sacrifices in the way of blood, or when blood is hard to come by, in the form of hair and a piece of cloth cut from unsuspecting victims. Thlen then converts this hair or piece of cloth into the likeness of a particular victim, which is made to dance on a silver plate to the eerie throbbing of a small drum at midnight. At the end of this evil ritual, the serpent feasts on the image, starting from the feet upwards. And he continues to do this for weeks. When nothing is left, the real victim, who would have been suffering all the agonies simulated on his image, dies.

But Thlen is supposed to be powerless against those from the Syiem clans because the forebears of these clans were not Khasis, and also because Suidnoh, his destroyer, was himself a syiem, a king, a ruler among gods, servant of the one God.

At the end of the story, Donald exclaimed, with some satisfaction, 'So, that is the legend of Thlen, huh? Hmm, fascinating. But then, Bah Ap, it also sounds like a fairy tale, no? Like the Sangkhni story, no? So how is it considered a "living legend", something that really exists?'

'Superstition!' Hamkom stated.

'Whose superstition?' Bah Kit asked testily.

Surprisingly, it was Evening who replied. 'When we spoke of the spirit world of the Khasis, do you remember, there were all those fairies and demons like Tyrut, Rih, Ñiangriang, Shwar, Bih, Thlen, et cetera? We Christians do not believe in them—'

Bah Kit was enraged by this insinuation. 'Are you insinuating that we—'

Donald raised a hand and said, 'Wait, wait, Bah Kit, let me handle this. We were talking about the spirit world of the Khasis, Evening, not about who believes in what. Do you remember what Bah Ap asked me then? He asked me whether I believe in Satan and his demons. I can tell you that made me examine myself very long and very hard indeed. Finally, I realised the truth of what he was trying to say—if I believe in the existence of God, then, whether I like it or not, I have to believe in the existence of Satan and his demons too. All religions have their gods and demons, as he said, and only those who don't believe in God don't believe in demons either. So, who are we to accuse others of being superstitious?'

Bah Kynsai was also quite miffed with Evening. 'And do you remember what I said, tdir? I said most Khasis, *regardless of what their religion is*, still believe in these demons or household gods. Call it superstition or whatever, but there's nothing you can say or do that will convince them otherwise.'

Bah Kit was still simmering, but Bah Su patted his knee to quieten him and said, 'And I also explained that it was all because we have forgotten about the First Commandment, which says, tip briew tip Blei. People who believe in this, who live in the knowledge of man and God, who are guided by conscience, do not know demons, do not worship them. As simple as that.'

'You know what I think?' Magdalene asked. 'Now that Halolihim is no longer with us, okay, Evening has taken his place as the new fundamentalist—'

'And what did you say when we were talking about influx, lyeit?' Raji asked hotly. 'Didn't you say that influx is the number one enemy of the Khasis? How the hell do you fight against influx when you are turning Khasi against Khasi? Bloody hypocrite! And do you think I give a shit about you because you are a karate kid? Up yours!'

Evening blushed a deep red and was about to react angrily when Bah Kynsai said, 'Shut up everyone. Let's cool down. Just keep quiet for a while.' He raised his hands to silence everyone, then said, 'Now, you see what Thlen is already doing to us? What did Thlen say in the story? "My thirst is for Khasi blood alone", na? There, that's a message of vital importance. It is also a great parable, leh, Ap!'

'Don called the Thlen story a fairy tale,' I said, 'and Bah Kynsai called it a parable. I believe that both of you are right. And yet, strangely, most of us, irrespective of religious affiliations, do not read it as either. We believe in the reality of the creature, although, apart from the legendary serpent that was slain by Suidnoh, nobody has really seen what he looks like. Even now, we beat up people, we lynch and murder them, we burn their houses and destroy their properties on the mere suspicion of being *ki nongri Thlen*, keepers of Thlen, or nongshohnoh, killers hired by such keepers.

'On 26 January 1993, I still remember that date, a man by the name of Bris Kharpuri was stoned to death in Khliehshnong, Sohra. His crime? A girl who was suffering from epileptic fits and mental illness suddenly called out his name and cursed him while she was having one of her fits. His viscera were pulled out and roasted and eaten by drunks.'

I took out my diary to check the draft article I had written on the subject.

'Three years earlier, in the same locality in Sohra, someone called Kan Swer was stoned to death by three people but tacitly supported by others, all because a girl who was suffering from some illness had called out his name during a nightmare.

'On 15 March 2006, five friends, including three young women and two young men, were branded as nongshohnohs by villagers of Laitkyrhong, East Khasi Hills, and were beaten up severely. They were saved only by the timely arrival of the police. Their crime? They went for a picnic in a lonely spot near the village—'

'Hey, Bah Ap, sorry to interrupt, but what exactly is the meaning of nongshohnoh?' Donald asked.

'He explained that, na?' Bah Kynsai said impatiently.

'I know he did, but I want to know exactly what the word means.'

'Let me see,' I said. 'Nongshoh means "beater", noh means "instantly", so, perhaps nongshohnoh means "instant beater" or "instant killer".'

Raji burst out laughing. 'While the world has instant coffee, instant soup, instant noodles, et cetera, we Khasis have instant killers! Wa, wonderful!'

All of us laughed, but Bah Kynsai said, 'Let him get on with it, na!'

I consulted my diary again.

'On 17 June 2007, an angry mob torched five houses and two vehicles belonging to D. Nongkynrih of Mawbseiñ village, Ri Bhoi district. His crime? He was extremely rich, and extremely rich people, especially in the rural areas, are often suspected of being Thlen-keepers—'

'Is that a fact or what?' Hamkom and Donald cried out in surprise.

'Yesss!' Raji replied. 'Unless you have a source of income that is known to everybody, okay, people are likely to accuse you of being a Thlen-keeper, as in the case of D. Nongkynrih. There's even a popular song in Khasi that says, "La duk ngi sha kren beiñ, la riewspah ki ong uba ri Thlen". If poor, they scorn us, if rich, they call us Thlen-keepers.'

'I never knew about that, ya!' Hamkom exclaimed.

'That's because you are a town-bound historian,' Evening said.

'Hey, Ning, stop that kind of talk, man!' Bah Kynsai said.

'Are you referring to me too, Evening?' Magdalene asked, irritated.

'Why? You also don't know or what?'

Before Magdalene could reply, I said, 'On the night of 7 October 2011, a large crowd at Maraikaphon, Sohra, lynched Timingstar Khongsit, all because the women in the village insisted that he was a hired killer sent by some Thlen-keepers. The reason? Being a stranger in a strange place. As it turned out, poor Khongsit was a mentally challenged man from Laitlyngkot who was on his way to meet a Catholic priest in Sohra.

'On the same day, two other men, Warless Nongrum and Batskhem Rynjah, both from Nongkynrih village, East Khasi Hills, were lynched by a mob at Mawkisyiem, Sohra, because they were suspected of being nongshohnohs—'

'Instant killers,' Raji added.

'Instant killers,' I agreed. 'According to a headman from Nongkynrih, Warless and Batskhem were actually men of "spotless character".

'On 28 April 2012, Johnson Marak, a resident of Joiram, West Khasi Hills, was asked to leave the village because five women dreamt about him giving "something" to some people who had died recently. But he was among the lucky ones and got away with his life.'

'That is because he was not a Khasi, Ap!' Evening said. 'If he had been a Khasi and not a Garo, okay, they would have killed him. That place is so full of Garos, ha, they were afraid of a backlash, I think.'

'Are you saying that those people were also like Thlen, Ning? Nothing but Khasi blood?' Bah Kynsai laughed.

'Ning is right, Bah Kynsai,' I said, 'that is exactly why he was not bludgeoned to death.

'On 23 February 2013, J. Khongwet and her family were attacked by a crazed mob at Wahlyngkhat village, East Khasi Hills. Their crime? Khongwet was suspected of being a Thlen-keeper ... Of course, there was no proof, Don, how can there be? I told you, nobody has ever seen what Thlen even looks like.

'On 27 May 2014, two people, Nes Salahe and his younger sister, Desment Salahe, were killed by a mob at Umkyrpong village, East Jaiñtia Hills. Their crime? A woman who was attacked by a disease similar to epilepsy had accused them of being Taro-keepers—'

'What is that, Bah Ap?' Donald asked.

'Taros are demons supposedly kept only by people from Ri Pnar, Don, and they are supposed to have the power to twist their victims' necks, permanently deforming them ... Later, Ribhamiki Salahe, the victims' sister, who was saved by the arrival of the police, said they were sitting on the veranda, enjoying the morning sun, when a group of people armed with guns and machetes attacked them. First, they dragged her elder sister, Desment, out of the house and stabbed her to death. Nes tried to run for his life, but they shot him with a gun, and when he fell, they hacked him to death. Ribhamiki, who was also injured in the incident, revealed that Desment was not even living with them. She was only visiting with her daughter and one-year-old grandson.

'These are just some of the incidents I have jotted down, but of course—'

'Ap,' Bah Su said, 'if you are done, I have a story to tell, okay?'

I nodded and he began.

Muiang Khang was the founder of Jalyiah village in the Ri Pnar province of Tuber. His name means 'forbidder of evil'. Muiang's parents were killed by four hired killers while they were tending their cattle and goats in the hills. The murderers then came to the hut where the young Muiang was waiting alone for his parents' return. But he was a very clever lad. When he saw them approaching the house with their bloodied machetes, he took a pot of boiling water up to the *tympan*, a platform above the hearth very near to the roof, and quietly hid there.

The murderers came in and looked for him in the hut's three rooms. But finding him nowhere, they gave up the search, thinking he had fled for his life when he saw them coming. Seeing pots of steaming rice and meat in the kitchen, they crowded around the hearth and began to eat the food that Muiang had prepared for the family. Even as they were eating, Muiang emptied the pot of boiling water on them, wounding them critically. When he saw them writhing in agony on the floor, he came down from the tympan and killed them with their own machetes. Then he hacked their bodies to pieces, called out to his cows and oxen by name, and ordered them to eat the flesh, not leaving a morsel behind.

After this incident, Muiang devoted his life to fighting crime and evil wherever they occurred, and thus singlehandedly made the province of Tuber a much safer place to live in. Towards the end of his life, he simply vanished without a trace. The hill where his hut used to stand is considered sacred by believers of Niam Khasi Niam Tre, who still perform certain rites there as a token of respect to him.

Bah Su concluded his story by saying, 'That's it, that's the legend of Muiang Khang!'

'It's a great story, Bah Su, but what is your point?' Bah Kynsai asked.

'My point is that the people of Ri Hynñiew Trep have believed in the existence of nongshohnoh from time immemorial.'

'We know that, Bah Su,' I said, 'but the incidents I've recounted happened in recent years.'

'And what happened to the perpetrators of all those crimes, Bah Ap?' Donald asked.

'Some of them have been arrested, Don. The cases against them are still pending in courts,' Raji replied.

'But many times,' I added, 'the police could do nothing since entire villages and localities came forward to court arrest and protect the few ring leaders. And this is why we cannot analyse the problem by blaming the beliefs of any one religion—'

'But we Christians cannot be blamed for such superstition!' Evening interrupted. 'We may believe in the existence of Satan and his demons, but we do not believe in these Khasi demons!'

'You see, Bah Kynsai, this is what I have been trying to say all along,' Bah Kit said. 'Whether you like it or not, ha, there's a tendency among people to blame believers of Niam Khasi of being Thlen-keepers or Taro-keepers and whatnot. And by killing them and burning their houses and properties, ha, they are trying to force many of us to convert—'

'Now, wait a minute, both of you!' I butted in. 'You are both wrong. In the first place, some of those accused of being nongshohnohs were innocent Christians, not merely believers of Niam Khasi. Besides, in many of these lynchings, entire villages and localities were involved. And the population in all these villages and localities is mixed—'

'But always more Christian than Khasi-Khasi, Ap,' Raji pointed out.

'You are quite right, Raji. And that fact, Ning, proves that everyone was involved in the crimes, and therefore, everyone, regardless of their religion, still believes in the so-called Khasi demons. As Bah Kynsai said, this is a very strange phenomenon, and not even Christianity has been able to do anything about it—'

'How can we Christians do anything about it, huh?' Raji asked. 'We also believe in these demons, no? As you said, Christians and non-Christians alike have been accused of being instant killers and Thlen-keepers, and Christians and non-Christians alike have been involved in the recent lynchings. But I also have additional proof that all of us are superstitious. Recently, when I was covering the assembly of a particular church in West Khasi Hills, okay, I suddenly heard the organisers announcing that the church recommends such-and-such shops as safe. That means that the church had verified the shop owners as people who did not keep demons like Bih and Lasam. And this fellow,' he pointed at Evening, 'dares say that we Christians do not believe in Khasi demons! If we do not believe, then why do we accuse others of being Thlen-keepers or Bih-keepers or whatever, ha, liah? The accuser is as guilty of superstition as the accused, Evening!'

'Are you people absolutely sure that all those lynchings were the result of superstition?' Donald asked.

'What else could they be?' Raji asked.

'Then what about the shamans, faith healers, diviners and sacrificers that you guys have been speaking of? You told us that people, even educated ones, go to them when they fall ill or before something important has to be done. Even politicians, you said, go to them when contesting elections, to defeat their opponents and—'

'Not to defeat their opponents, Don,' Bah Su interrupted. 'A shaman cannot cause anyone any trouble without cause, and if he is a true shaman, ha, he will not even try to harm his client's opponent, for that is not a just cause and God would frown upon it. Shamans only help people by pleading before God to strengthen their essence and thus enhance their luck. In the case of politicians, ha, Don, the circumstances are very much the same as at archery competitions. Shamans plead before God—so he can come to the aid of their clients—by reciting their merits and by vividly laying out the reasons why they, and not their opponents, should be granted victory.'

'But if the stories about Sangkhni and Thlen and the other demons are superstition, then how come going to shamans is not?'

'Not all followers of Niam Khasi go to shamans and not all Christians do not go, Don,' I said. 'Again, some shamans are really gifted, while some are mere pretenders. In talking about them earlier, we were referring to people known to us, people who could see things and treat certain ailments successfully. The existence of such gifted people cannot simply be dismissed as superstition—not every human experience can be explained rationally through science. The incident of the boiling pot of rice, for example, is something that I cannot understand even now. How is it that after hours of boiling on a blazing fire, the rice would simply not cook and the water not dry up at all? Of course, you could say that I was merely telling a story—a lie even. But then, too many things about heaven and earth could be said to be lies. And even if religion itself is dismissed as a big lie, I would still believe that there exist on earth people with special gifts and abilities.

'And that is very different from believing in the serpent stories we have heard. The Nongtrais believe in the existence of Sangkhni, who carries off bridges and drowns people, rather than seeing in the story a metaphor for destructive humanity, which violates all that is sacred and which exploits and sells everything to satisfy an insatiable greed. The effect of that destruction has already been felt on a massive scale in these western lands. And many of these exploiters represent the outsiders who bring their own labour force, their own workers, who settle down and multiply and eventually outnumber the locals. But it is not their fault, for the locals are content to sell their land to them for easy money, cheaply. This is the unheeded warning of Sangkhni—'

'Who are these outsiders?' Hamkom asked.

'Some are non-Khasis, some are Khasis, okay?' Raji said. 'But the cheaper labour is always brought from outside Ri Khasi.'

Donald could not believe what he was hearing. 'Bah Ap, are you serious about locals in these parts being outnumbered by the contractors' employees?'

'In certain segments, yes,' I replied, 'and not merely by the contractors and their employees. People have been coming from Garo Hills, Assam and other Indian states to make their living from the forest and the land.'

'Didn't I tell you that half of West Khasi Hills is completely gone, Donald?' Evening demanded.

'Not half, mə, liah, but a large segment, yes,' Bah Kynsai said. 'But we are also our own worst enemies, na? Our politicians are partly to blame for initially bringing settlers from outside to bolster their vote banks. They did the same thing in Shillong, remember, Bah Su? But now these settlers have become so numerous they have their own representatives.'

'We have got to see this for ourselves, ha, Don, Mag?' Hamkom said.

'That's very easy, Ham,' Bah Kynsai responded. 'All you have to do, na, is visit some of the biggest towns in western and southern West Khasi Hills.'

'It's really depressing, man!' Raji moaned. 'Our ancestors had foreseen all this, but we did not listen to their warnings.'

'That's because we failed miserably in decoding their warnings, Raji,' I said. 'The Thlen parable, for instance, shows that man will save even a man-devouring monster for personal profit. In Khasi teaching, greed is the mother of all evils. But more importantly, for us as a community, the parable is about the inherent evil in the Khasi psyche, an evil symbolised by the nature of Thlen, who would take nothing but Khasi blood, who would force Khasis to eat Khasis—'

I paused for a moment before continuing, 'From the time before our himas were formed, when we were organised only as provinces governed by provincial rulers, the Khasis have been fighting each other. When the himas were formed, the fighting did not stop. If anything, it became worse, as those who were subjugated were enslaved or sold to slavery.'

'But the Khasi himas did not always fight among themselves, Ap, we have already discussed that!' Bah Su protested. 'There was a free movement of people for trade and settlement. And the Khasis always came together against a non-Khasi hima—'

'I know, Bah Su, I know,' I agreed. 'The presence of external enemies was what saved us from wiping each other out. But the internal strife was very real. That was why the old Khasis invented the story of Thlen, the demon who would have nothing but Khasi blood, out of an actual incident—the killing of a gigantic python-like snake at Daiñthlen after it had swallowed a market-goer on the way to Rangjyrteh. They turned that incident into a living legend, a warning against our fratricidal tendencies. But instead of taking the message to heart, we misread it and chose to make Thlen a reality, an excuse to turn on each other.

'When the British came, many traditional Khasi states allied with them and even helped them when other himas, led by Tirot Sing, fought their first war of freedom. Many years after that, when the traditional rulers and prominent leaders were campaigning for the establishment of a distinct administrative system based on our traditional democratic form of governance, Khasis fought Khasis to defeat the campaign. That paved the way for the formation of the District Council, which Bah Kynsai earlier condemned as a useless duplication of power. When Meghalaya came into being, Khasis fought Khasis so they could install a non-Khasi as the first chief minister of the state. Whenever a Khasi becomes the chief minister, Khasis fight Khasis to make sure he does not rule for five years, but when a non-Khasi is holding that office, Khasis fight Khasis to make sure he does rule for five years. And, do you remember what happened when we were protesting against the anti-Khasi job reservation policy? Our MLAs did not even support us, because their political survival was more important to them—'

'Ap, isn't your analysis rather too politically loaded?' Hamkom asked.

'Ham, can you think of any aspect of life that is untouched by politics?' I responded.

'That's why na, Ham,' Bah Kynsai said, 'because our politicians would even go against their own people, na, many of us have been calling them Thlens.'

'There you are, Ham, the symbolism of Thlen,' I said. 'In everything we do, we turn against each other—'

Raji interrupted me to say, 'Hey, Bah Kynsai, when militants started bumping off Khasi leaders, people called them Thlens, remember?'

'And before that?' Donald asked pointedly.

'Before that, they were champions, liah!' Bah Kynsai said sarcastically.

'Unfortunately, that's what people are like, no?' Hamkom said. 'Unless and until things happen to them personally, they don't care what is done to others.'

'Khasis have a saying for that,' Raji said. 'They used to say, *Katba ym pat tyngkhuh ha la khohsiew ym don ba salia*. As long as it doesn't collide with their own knees, nobody cares.'

Unexpectedly, Dale spoke up. 'But there were reasons, no, Bah Kynsai, why they were called champions?' We all looked at him in surprise, and seeming a bit flustered, he said, 'You explained those reasons yourself, no?'

Bah Kynsai laughed. 'So I did, so I did … Hey, Ap, are you done with your Thlen?'

'Almost. Three things about us, you know, worry me the most. One of them is the fight between us relating to the matrilineal system, which resulted in the slanging match between Ning and Mag—'

'Are you for or against?' Evening demanded.

'Look, Ning, I don't hold any rigid views about any of our cultural institutions—'

'That's because you don't have the guts!' Evening declared.

'Is that what you think?' I asked calmly, looking fixedly at him.

Evening dropped his eyes and said placatingly, 'So what is your reason, then?'

'Because there is both good and bad in them. You cannot simply praise or denounce them—'

'But the matrilineal system is a broken system, no?' Evening protested.

'Then fix it, na, liah!' Bah Kynsai cursed him. 'Why should we discard it just because something in it is broken? If you break a leg, should we throw you into the jungle?'

Amidst the laughter that followed, Bah Kynsai signalled to me to go on. 'The other worry I have is the great Khasi–Jaiñtia divide, based on a gross misunderstanding, which causes tempers to flare and blows to fly, as you have seen in the fight between Ning and Ham—'

'Evening is everywhere,' Raji said, laughing.

'And the last is the Khasi–Christian divide, an ugly example of which you saw in the fight between Halolihim and Bah Kit—'

Bah Kit disagreed sharply. 'I fought with Halolihim not because of the religious issue, Ap, but because he slapped an elderly person like Bah Su.'

'Let's be honest, Kit,' Bah Kynsai intervened, 'whether he hit Bah Su or not, na, it would have come to blows. But the divide is not simply between Khasi-Khasis and Khasi-Christians, ha, Ap, it's also there among Christians—'

'That's right, Bah Kynsai,' Raji concurred. 'We have become more and more intolerant, leh, really! Do you remember the recent newspaper report from Ri Bhoi? A man from a particular church married a woman from another and went to live in her village, okay? But the village was completely dominated by his wife's church. Every day, he was harassed by the villagers because they wanted him to change his church. But instead of changing, okay, he complained about it to his own church in Nongpoh. Because of that, the women's organisations of both churches nearly came to blows—'

'I know all about the case, Raji,' Magdalene interrupted. 'But why do you say this church and that church? Why don't you spell it out, man? Why don't you admit that the tension was between Catholics and Presbyterians? There's no need to hide it, no? I think we have inherited this from Europe.'

'I was trying to be politically correct, Mag,' Raji admitted. 'As a pressman, I should have known better. There are quite a few incidents like that, okay? At Umtung, again in Ri Bhoi, sixteen Catholic graves were desecrated by miscreants last year. And then, do you remember all those graves desecrated in Shillong by a so-called satanic cult?'

'Don't forget what miscreants did to the altar at Lum Sohpet Bneng, the most sacred site of the Khasi religion, Raji,' Bah Kit added. 'They desecrated it completely. And do you remember what happened in the villages of Mawlong and Mylliem near Shillong? Mag also talked about them earlier. The villagers in these places even prevented Khasis from cremating their dead. The cases had to be settled in court. Inhuman, really inhuman!'

'There's no doubt that we have become more and more polarised on religious lines,' I said. 'Instead of thinking of ourselves as primarily the children of a particular religion, why don't we think more about our identity as Khasis?'

'And Indians!' Hamkom put in.

'And Indians,' I agreed. 'How can we divide ourselves into Khasis and Christians or Khasis and Jaiñtias when we are but a handful? How can we see ourselves as matrilineal or patrilineal when we are one people? When Nehru came to Shillong, he referred to us as a drop in the ocean of India. Think about that. If influx is a problem, how do we face it unitedly when we are so divided among ourselves?'

'But Ap, just now you agreed with me and said being Indian is important! So why are you also talking about influx?' Hamkom objected.

'Being Indian is important, but—'

'But we should not also become Red Indian, na, liah!' Bah Kynsai contended. 'And why shouldn't we talk about influx just because we are Indians, huh? What have the two got to do with each other? Are the people who keep flooding into these hills Indians?'

'I think Ham was also referring to the objection to the so-called influx from mainland India, Bah Kynsai,' Donald said.

'You see, we are even fighting about this!' Evening exclaimed. 'Why shouldn't we object to influx from mainland India, huh? How many of us are there? A little more than a million! How can we not agree on a problem that is staring us in the face? That's why we Khasis are called the Thlen-keeping community, no? We will be the cause of our own death, liah!'

'Look, Ham,' I said, 'there's no contradiction in saying "I'm a Khasi and an Indian", just as there is no contradiction in a person from Maharashtra saying, "I'm a Maharashtrian and an Indian". The influx from other Indian states is a complicated issue. Bah Kynsai thinks that it may not be as life-threatening as the influx of foreigners, for they at least have a home they can go back to whenever the situation demands. But I believe that we, who are only a drop in the ocean of India, deserve special consideration from both the state and central governments. Safeguards of some kind must be worked out, and quickly, for this issue is always linked with the other problem here—communal riots.'

'But we are straying away from Thlen, na, Ap?' Bah Kynsai said.

'It's good, it's good, Bah Kynsai,' Evening told him. 'This is one more case where Khasis fight Khasis, no? And as we bicker among ourselves, ha, the problem will open its mouth wide and swallow us whole like Thlen.'

'How can you condemn a healthy debate as a Khasi-eat-Khasi Thlen mentality?' Hamkom protested. 'That will destroy us as a strong, democratic and plural society, no?'

'I don't mean that at all! But influx is a matter of life and death, you idiot!'

'The way I see it,' I said, 'debate, criticism, even disagreements are part and parcel of any democratic society, but in matters of life and death, we should also face every issue unitedly. In considering the question of illegal migration—'

'We must also give thought to the genuine non-tribal citizens here,' Hamkom interrupted me.

'What thought?' Evening demanded.

'Ham, is right, Ning,' I broke in. 'Nobody can simply wish them away. They must be part of the solution, not just part of the problem.'

'Right, quite right,' Donald responded enthusiastically. 'But also, what I want to know is, if the Khasi–Christian and Khasi–Jaiñtia divide is so bad, then what's keeping Khasi society together now?'

'Nobody's saying the divide is so bad, na?' Bah Kynsai said.

'I'll tell you what's keeping our society together,' I responded, 'the very clan system that certain people, like Ning here, want to dismantle. In a clan like mine, for instance, you have members from all religious faiths, and in a family or clan gathering, everyone comes together; all other peripheral considerations are laid aside—'

'True, true,' Bah Kit chimed in, 'and like I said before, ha, the Nongkynrihs and the Lyngdoh Nongbris of East Khasi Hills, the Lyngdoh Kynshis of West Khasi Hills, the Shadaps of Ri Bhoi and the Passahs of Jaiñtia Hills are all related, okay? Such relationships can be found in almost every clan in Ri Hynñiew Trep ... So, what does that mean?'

'That the clan system is a unifying one,' I replied. 'It has been keeping us together all along. Anyone wanting to dismantle it must keep that in mind ... But to come back to the Thlen story, you see, Don, these are the things we should remember when we deliberate on it. And we should think of the words of Thlen himself: "My thirst is for Khasi blood alone." This is a powerful warning about the Khasi-eat-Khasi evil that is in every one of us. The two serpent stories represent the case of the metaphor gone wrong; the metaphor misread; the metaphor mistaken for the literal truth. We must reread the metaphor, set it right, and stamp out the evil of mob murder in the name of Thlen and witchcraft, for it makes us seem like creatures from the dark ages.'

'Spot on, Ap, spot on. We must remember the words of Thlen, always!' Bah Kynsai asserted. 'And we must say, my thirst is not for blood at all, my thirst is for the survival of the race. That's important, but my thirst is also for peace, for unity, for things that will take us up and build us all—'

'Arre, Bah Kynsai, I didn't know you were such an idealist, ya!' Raji said teasingly.

'Aren't we all idealists, Raji?' I said. 'Why are we here? Is it not because, as we move into the future, we would like to preserve a bit of the past too, or at least keep a record of it? As Bah Kynsai said, we should think positive thoughts and say with our bard:

Because of Ri Khasi Ri Pnar,
O Lord and Master of the earth,
We'll beat, we'll make and all we'll farm,
From our Huts upwards we'll climb.

'The Thlen legacy can be defeated only by this kind of patriotism: the firm determination to build the country from within, to make it flourish in every sphere of activity.'

Donald, for whom I had translated the lines, analysed it thus: 'While we plead with God for the all-round prosperity of our land and our people, we must also promise before him that we will try our best to help ourselves grow towards this goal. Beautiful lines.'

'Good, good … We had a good last session, na? What do you think?'

'As always, as always, Bah Kynsai,' Raji said.

But Evening was intent on dampening the mood. 'Tonight's session, like that of every other night, may be good, but I doubt this formula will work with our people, Bah Kynsai.'

Donald disagreed. 'It's not about the formula, Evening, it's about the thought, and more importantly, it's about the discovery, our nights have been journeys of discovery—'

'And many things can come out of it, na?' Bah Kynsai agreed. 'Understanding ourselves as a people, respect and love for our culture, pride in it, recognition of its shortcomings, and even inspiration for action—many, many things, in fact. As Don said, it's not about conclusions and formulas; it's about the discovery. Think about that and the possibilities, na, tdong!'

'Well, if you put it that way, I suppose you could be right,' Evening admitted.

'Of course I'm right! You might even become a pro-matriliny activist, who knows?'

We all laughed at that, but Donald raised his hand for silence and said, 'Jokes apart, Bah Kynsai, we have really learnt so much from this journey, ya. Of course something good will come of it! Whoever says that knowledge is useless? At the very least, knowledge is inspiration. Thank you, everyone. For me, the journey has been good.'

Many of the others agreed with Donald and said a whole new world had opened up for them in the last few nights. They added their thanks to his, and we all embraced each other with genuine pleasure. Then we trooped out into the night for a stretch and a whistle.

I only hope that you, too, whoever you may be, wherever you may be, will find some good in our stories and our conversations, even though you may not agree with everything you have heard. In my position, what else can I hope for?

As Raji left the hut to drink with the Lyngngams and the others prepared to sleep, I thought of this little place, Nongshyrkon, which we had come to love so much, and its beautiful people, who had housed and fed and treated us with such warmth and generosity. Their caring benefaction had made our stay in the jungle seem like a vacation in some tropical paradise. But there is poverty and hardship and suffering here. Disease stalks these jungles, and there is not even a health centre around, only churches and primary schools—treatment for the soul and the mind. Darkness engulfs the village, relieved only by the weak lights of flambeaus and kerosene lamps. Yet, when dawn pulls back the shades of night, the still surviving trees of Nongshyrkon are like protective giants, keeping this little sanctuary sheltered, always hidden, always safe from strangers with the evil eye.

Will the road that Chirag dreams of, one that will showcase the beauty of Nongshyrkon, ever come? And if it does, will it bless the village, its wonderful lake and magnificent waterfalls, with the fame and wealth that he hopes for? Or will it only give Nongshyrkon more houses, more migrants and denser clouds of dust? Will the jungle and all its blessings remain? Or will the road take away its trees and bushes, its fruits and flowers, its herbs and mushrooms, its animals and birds, and consign them to oblivion? Will it silence every creature other than the treacherous beasts that roar and honk all day long? The progress of the road must be fought for, Chirag, but like other such blessings, it must be hailed with a touch of caution. Remember, every blessing hides a sting.

Author's Note

The description of the Phor Sorat funeral ceremony is partly based on the cremation of Ka De Nongsiang, performed between 2 and 7 February 1992 in Nongshyrkon. This was also the last cremation in the village. The event was recorded by the Khasi filmmaker Raphael Warjri, whose documentary film on the subject is titled *Ka Phor Sorat*.

Other sources of information on the funeral rites of the Lyngngams and Nongtrais came from the little Khasi monograph *Sangkhni* by Lostin Lawrence Kharbani and the various people I met in the area while researching the novel, which was completed on 18 October 2016. Among them were Chandra Shyrkon, Werly Shyrkon, whom I have mentioned in the 'Acknowledgements', and other relatives of Ka De Nongsiang.

While conducting my research, I read a lot of books by Khasi and non-Khasi authors. The names of many books I eventually used are mentioned in the novel. Others I referred to include:

Shillong Centenary Celebration Souvenir, Ka Shad Suk Mynsiem Centenary Souvenir, Studies in the Literature of Assam by S.K. Bhuyan, *The Prayer of the Frog* by Anthony de Mello, *A Book Called Hiraeth* by Dora Polk, *Around the Hearth: Khasi Legends, Hiraeth and the Poetry of Soso Tham* and *Ka Pyrkhat Niam ki Khanatang* by Kynpham Sing Nongkynrih, *Ka Kitab Niam Kheiñ ki Khasi* and *Ka Kitab Jingphawar* by Rabon Singh, *Ka Pyrkhat U Khasi* by H. Onderson Mawrie, *Ka Riti Jong ka Ri Laiphew Syiem* by G. Costa, *Ban Pynïeng la ka Rasong* by R. Tokin Roy Rymbai, *Ka Matïong ki Khanatang* by Bevan L. Swer, *Ki Syiem Khasi bad Synteng* by Homiwell Lyngdoh, *Ki Umjer Ksiar* and *Ki Khanatang bad u Sier Lapalang* by Primrose Gatphoh,

Ki Dienjat jong ki Longshuwa by J. Bacchiarello, *Ka Tynrai ka Ksaw ka Kpong* by D. T. Laloo, *Ka Rympei Jingkynmaw: Ka Ïew Sohra* by K. Syiemlieh, *Ka Sengkur Dkhar Sawkpoh* by Ka Sengkur Dkhar Sawkpoh, *Ka Ïawbeikulong ki Kharakor* by Philomena Kharakor and *Ka Khanasmari: U Khun u Hajar ka Ri u Hynñiewtrep* by Sumar Sing Sawian.

I am deeply grateful to everyone.